GAYLE LYNDS is a *New York Times* bestselling author. Before turning to fiction, she worked as a newspaper reporter, a magazine editor, and an editor for a top-secret US government think-tank. She co-founded International Thriller Writers with David Morrell in 2004 and is now a full-time novelist. She lives in a small house on a hill overlooking the pacific, in Santa Barbara. Visit her website at www.gaylelynds.com

GAYLE LYNDS

The LIBRARY of GOLD

CORVUS

First published in the United States of America in 2010
by St Martin's Press.

This paperback edition first published in Great Britain
in 2011 by Corvus, an imprint of Atlantic Books Ltd.

9 8 7 6 5 4 3 2

A CIP catalogue record for this book is available from
the British Library.

ISBN: 978-1-84887-689-7

Typset by Ellipsis Books Limited, Glasgow

Printed in Great Britain by Clays Ltd, St Ives plc

Corvus
An imprint of Atlantic Books Ltd
Ormond House
26-27 Boswell Street
London WC1N 3JZ

www.corvus-books.co.uk

For Sophia Stone,
my granddaughter,
child of light and grace

ACKNOWLEDGEMENTS

My life is full of good and supportive people, many of whom helped with the writing of this novel. I'm particularly grateful to my extraordinary agent, Lisa Erbach Vance, of the Aaron M. Priest Literary Agency; my world-class editor, Keith Kahla, executive editor at St. Martin's Press; and my multitalented assistant and business manager, Tara Stockton, who speaks four languages and trots the globe.

I often consulted with novelist Melodie Johnson Howe, who heroically read and wisely commented on large sections of the novel. Authors Kathleen Sharp and Josh Conviser were generous partners in brainstorming international crime. Former CIA officers Alan More and Robert Kresge, who is also a fellow author, were remarkable sources upon whom I could always count.

My children and their spouses and one of my stepchildren discussed the book with me and provided details about geography and locations I was unable to visit: Paul Stone and Katrina Baum, Julia Stone and Kari Timonen, and Deirdre Lynds. For those of you who have followed her story, my other stepdaughter, Katie Lynds, remains in a wonderful facility for the brain-damaged and is making good progress.

St. Martin's is my publishing home, and I love it there. Particular gratitude to Sally Richardson, Matthew Baldacci, Matthew Shear, Joan Higgins, John Murphy, Nancy Trypuc, Monica Katz, Brian Heller, John Karle, and Kathleen Conn.

Deborah Brown, bibliographer and research services librarian for Byzantine Studies, Dumbarton Oaks Research Library and Collection, Washington, D.C., was of tremendous help looking into the fascinating story of the Library of Gold. Others to whom I'm indebted include Kathleen Antrim, Barbara Paul Blume, Steve and Liz Berry, Ray Briare, Lee Child, Julian Dean, David Dun, Emily Erikson and Joe Ligman, Yogiraj Gurunath, David Hewson, Bones Howe, Randi and Doug Kennedy, Bill McDonald, David and Donna Morrell, Naomi Parry, M. J. Rose, Elaine and George Russell, Jim Rollins, Greg Stephens, Tom Stone and Alexandra Leslie, Steve Trueblood, and Diane Vogt.

As you read this novel, you might enjoy knowing that several of the characters have the real names of readers who entered a contest on my website. Much to my delight, they sent in e-mail waivers allowing me to use their names in the book—whether for criminal or corpse or hero. No description is accurate, and certainly I won't tell you which ones are theirs. That's called suspense.

Thank you one and all.

PART ONE
THE HUNT

As he walked to the Senate, a note was thrust into Julius Caesar's hand. His spies had done their job, giving him a list of conspirators and their plans to kill him. Unfortunately, Caesar was in a hurry and did not read it. An hour later, he was assassinated.

—translated from The Book of Spies

In the abstruse world of espionage, it's not always easy to know when you are in on a secret.

—Time *magazine, January 9, 2006*

1

A library could be a dangerous place. The librarian scanned the ten men in tailored tuxedos who lounged around the long oval table in the center of the room. Encircling them were magnificent illuminated manuscripts, more than a thousand of them, blanketing the walls from floor to ceiling. Their spectacular gold-covered bindings faced out to showcase the fortune in gems decorating them.

The men were members of the book club that owned and operated the secret Library of Gold, where the annual dinner was always held. The finale was the tournament, in which each member tested the librarian with a research question. As the books towered around them and the air vibrated with golden light, the men sipped their cognac. Their eyes watched the librarian.

"Trajan," challenged the international lawyer from Los Angeles. "A.D. 53 to A.D. 117. Trajan was one of the most ambitious warrior-emperors of old Rome, but few people realize he also revered books. His supreme monument to his successes at war is called Trajan's Column. He ordered it erected in the court between two galleries of Rome's library, which he also built."

The room seemed to hold its breath, waiting. The librarian's fingers plucked at his tuxedo jacket. Nearly seventy years old, he was a tidy man with wrinkled features. His hair was thin, his glasses large, and his mouth set in a perpetual small smile.

The tension heightened as he mulled. "Of course," he said at last. "Cassius Dio Cocceianus wrote about it." He went to the shelves containing the eighty volumes of Cassius Dio's history, *Romaika,* compiled in the second and third centuries and transcribed by a Byzantine calligrapher in the sixth century. "The story is here, in volume seventy-seven. Most of Cassius Dio's work has been lost. Our library has the only complete set."

As pleased laughter swept the exclusive group, the librarian laid the large volume into the arms of the challenger, who stroked the embedded opals and sapphires on its cover. Gazing appreciatively at the golden book, he stood it up beside his brandy glass. Eight other illuminated manuscripts stood beside eight other brandy glasses. Each was a testament to the librarian's intimate knowledge of ancient and medieval literature and the priceless value of the library itself.

Now only the tenth member—the director himself—remained. He would pose the final question in the tournament.

The men helped themselves to more cognac. By design their yearly dinner was dazzling theater. Hours before the first martini was poured, ten wild ducks, freshly shot, had arrived by private jet from Johannesburg. The chefs were flown in from Paris, blindfolded of course. The seven-course meal was exquisite, including truffled sweetbreads with chestnuts. The alcohol was the best—tonight's cognac was a Louis XIII de Rémy Martin, worth more than a thousand dollars a bottle in today's market. All of the book club's liquors had been laid down by those who had gone before, creating a cellar of indisputable quality.

The director cleared his throat, and everyone turned to look at him. He was American and had flown in from Paris earlier in the day. The room's tenor changed, becoming somehow menacing.

The librarian pulled himself up, vigilant.

The director peered at him. "Salah al-Din, also known as Saladin. A.D. 1137 or 1138 to A.D. 1193. General Saladin, a Kurdish Muslim, was famous for his espionage network. One night his enemy Richard the Lionheart went to sleep in his tent in Assyria, guarded on all sides by his English knights. They poured a track of white ash around the tent so wide no one could cross it undetected. But when Richard awoke, a melon with a dagger buried deep inside had appeared beside his bed. The blade could just as easily have been stabbed into Richard's heart. It was Saladin's warning, left by one of his spies. The spy escaped without leaving a clue and was never caught."

Again the eyes watched the librarian. With every word, he had tensed. The door behind him opened quietly. He glanced over his shoulder as Douglas Preston stepped into the room. Preston was head of library security, a tall, muscular man who was an expert in weapons and took his work seriously. He was not wearing a tuxedo, instead had on his usual black leather jacket and jeans. Strangely, he carried a bath towel.

With effort, the librarian kept his voice steady as he headed across the room to another bookshelf. "The story can be found in Baha al-Din's *Sirat Salah al-Din: The Life of Saladin*—"

"Of course, you're correct," the director interrupted. "But I want another manuscript. Bring me *The Book of Spies.*"

The librarian stopped, his hands reaching for the volume. He turned. The men's faces were outraged, unforgiving.

"How did you find out?" he whispered.

No one answered. The room was so silent he could hear the tread of crepe-soled shoes. Before he could turn again, Preston's towel slapped around his skull, covering his eyes and mouth. There was a huge explosion of gunfire, and pain erupted in his head. As he fell, he realized the security chief had given him fair warning by using a technique of the later Assassins—the towel was to cover the entrance and exit wounds to control spraying blood and bone. The book club knew that.

2

Los Angeles, California
April, One year later

As she walked into the Getty Center's conservation laboratory, with its sinks and fume hoods, Eva Blake smiled. On the sea of worktables lay centuries-old illuminated manuscripts, charts, and scrolls. Tattered and sprinkled with wormholes, all would be brought back to useful life. For her, conservation work was more than a profession—by restoring the old books she was restoring herself.

Eva's gaze swept the room. Three other conservators were already bent over their tables, lone islands of movement in the vast high-tech lab. She said a cheery hello and grabbed a smock. A slender woman of thirty years, she had an understated face—the cheekbones were good, the chin soft and round, the lips full—that resisted the sharp cut of classical beauty. Her red hair tumbled to her shoulders, and her eyes were cobalt blue. Today she wore an open-necked white blouse, white pencil skirt, and low-heeled white sandals. There was a sense of elegance about her, and a softness, a vulnerability, she had learned to hide.

She stopped at Peggy Doty's workbench. "Hi, Peggy. How's your new project?"

Peggy lifted her head, took a jeweler's loupe from her eye, and quickly put on large, thick glasses. "Hey, there. Seneca's worrying me. I think I can definitely save Aristotle, but then he's the one who said, 'Happiness is a sort of action,' so with that kind of Zen attitude he's bound to last longer."

Born and raised in England, Peggy was a gifted conservator and a longtime friend, such a good friend that she had stayed close even after Eva had been charged with vehicular manslaughter in her husband's death. As she thought about him, Eva's throat tightened. She automatically touched the gold chain around her neck.

Then she said, "I always liked Aristotle."

"Me, too. I'll see what I can do for Seneca. Poor guy. His toga's peeling like a banana." Peggy's brown hair was short and messy, her eyeglasses were already sliding down her nose, and EX LIBRIS inside a pink heart was tattooed on her forearm.

"He's in good hands." Eva started to leave.

"Don't go yet. I'd sure like your help—the provenance on this piece sucks." Peggy indicated the colorful medieval chart spread out on her worktable. "I'm waiting for the results of the date test, but I'd love to know at least the century."

"Sure. Let's see what we can figure out." Eva pulled up a chair.

The chart was about fourteen inches wide and twenty inches long. At the bottom stood two figures in rope sandals and luminous blue togas. On the left was Aristotle, representing natural philosophy, and on the right was Seneca, moral philosophy. To all appearances they were an unlikely pair—Aristotle was Greek, while Seneca was Roman and born nearly four hundred years later. Eva studied them a moment, then moved her gaze to medallions rising like clouds above their heads. Each medallion contained a pair of the men's opposing theories, a battle of ideas between two great classical thinkers. The chart's lettering was Cyrillic.

"The chart itself is written in Old Russian," Eva explained, "but it's not the revised alphabet of Peter the Great. So it was probably made before 1700." She laid her finger along the right margin of the parchment, where small, faded words were printed. "This isn't Russian, old or new—it's Greek. It translates as 'Created under the hand of Maximos after cataloguing the Royal Library.' "

Peggy moved closer, staring down. "I'm pretty sure Maximos is a Greek name. But which Royal Library? Russia or Greece? What city?"

"Our chart-maker, Maximos, was born Michael Trivolis in Greece and was later known as Maximos. When he moved to Russia, he was called Maxim. Does that give you enough information to know who he was?"

Peggy's small face lit up. "Saint Maxim the Greek. He spent a long time in Moscow translating books, writing, and teaching. I remember studying him in an Eastern history course."

"And that gives you the answer to your question—Maxim arrived in Russia in 1518 and never left. He died about forty years later. So your chart was made sometime in the first half of the sixteenth century in Russia."

"Cool. Thanks."

Eva smiled. "How's everything with Zack?" Zack Turner was the head of security at the British Museum in London.

"Distant, as in he's still there, and I'm still here. Woe is me—and he."

"How about going back to the British Library?"

"I've been thinking about it. How are you doing?" There was concern in Peggy's gaze.

"Fine." It was mostly true now that the Getty had offered Eva the conservation job to tide her over until her trial. She was out of sight in the lab—the press coverage of the car crash had been exhaustive. But then Charles had been the renowned director of the elite Elaine Moreau Library, while she had been a top curator here at the celebrated Getty.

Charming, handsome, and in love, they were a star-studded couple in L.A.'s art and monied beau monde. His dramatic death—and her arrest and denials—had made for a particularly juicy scandal.

Being home all day every day after the accident had been hard. She watched for Charles in the shadows, listened for his voice calling from the garden, slept with his pillow tight against her cheek. The emptiness had closed around her like a cold fist, holding her tight in a kind of painful suspension.

"I'm so sorry, Eva," Peggy was saying. "Charles was a great scholar."

She nodded. Again her fingers went to the chain around her neck. At the end of it hung an ancient Roman coin with the profile of the goddess Diana—her first gift from Charles. She had not taken off the necklace since he died.

"Dinner tonight?" Peggy said brightly. "My treat for letting me tap into that big brain of yours."

"Love to. I've got karate class, so I'll meet you afterward."

They decided on a restaurant, and Eva went to her workstation. She sat and pulled the arm of her stereo-binocular microscope toward her. She liked the familiarity of the motion and the comfort of her desk with its slide kits, gooseneck lamp, and ultraviolet light stand. Her project was an adventure manuscript about the knights of King Arthur completed in 1422 in London.

She stared through the microscope's eyepiece and used a scalpel to lift a flaking piece of green pigment from the gown of a princess. The quiet of the work and the meticulous focus it required soothed her. She carefully applied adhesive beneath the paint flake.

"Hello, Eva."

So deep was her concentration, the voice sent a dull shock through her. She looked up. It was her attorney, Brian Collum.

Of medium height, he was in his late forties, with

eyebrows and hair the gray color of a magnet and the strong-jawed face of a man who knew what he wanted from life. Impeccably turned out in a charcoal suit with thin pinstripes, he was the name partner in the international law firm of Collum & Associates. Because of their friendship, he was representing her in the trial for Charles's death.

"How nice to see you, Brian."

He lowered his voice. "We need to talk." Usually his long face radiated optimism. But not now. His expression was grim.

"Not good news?" She glanced at her colleagues, noting they were studiously attending to their projects.

"It's good—or bad, depending on what you think."

Eva led him outdoors to a courtyard of lawns and flowers. A water fountain flowed serenely over perfectly arranged boulders. This was all part of the Getty Center, a complex of striking architecture sheathed in glass and Italian travertine stone crowning a hill in the Santa Monica Mountains.

Silently they passed museum visitors and sat together on a bench where no one could overhear.

"What's happened?" she asked.

He was blunt. "I have an offer from the D.A.'s office. If you plead guilty, they'll give you a reduced sentence. Four years. But with good behavior you'll be out in three. They're willing to make a deal because you have a clean driving record and you're a respected member of the community."

"Absolutely not." She forced herself to stay calm. "I wasn't driving."

"Then who was?"

The question hung like a scythe in the sparkling California air.

"You really don't recall Charles getting behind the wheel?" she asked. "You were standing in your doorway when we drove away. I saw you. You had to have seen us." They had been at a dinner party at Brian's house that night, the last guests to leave.

"We've been over this before. I went inside as soon as I said good night—before either of you got close to your car. Alcohol plays tricks with the mind."

"Which is why I'd never drive. Never." Working to keep the horror from her voice, she related the story again: "It was after one A.M., and Charles was driving us home. We were laughing. There wasn't any traffic on Mulholland, so Charles wove the car back and forth. That threw us against our seat belts and just made us laugh harder. He drove with one hand, then with the other . . ." She frowned to herself. There was something else, but it escaped her. "Suddenly a car shot out from a driveway ahead of us. Charles slammed the brakes. Our car spun out of control. I must've lost consciousness. The next thing I knew, I was strapped down to a gurney." She swallowed. "And Charles was dead."

She smoothed the fabric of her skirt and stared off as grief raged through her.

Brian's silence was so long that the distant roar of traffic on the San Diego Freeway seemed to grow louder.

At last he said kindly, "I'm sure that's what you remember, but we have no evidence to support it. And I've spent enough of your money hiring investigators to look for witnesses that I have to believe we're not going to find any." His voice toughened. "How's a jury going to react when they learn you were found lying unconscious just ten feet from the driver's door—and it was hanging open, showing you were behind the wheel? And Charles was in the front passenger seat, with the seat belt melted into what was left of him. There's no way he was driving. And you had a 1.6 blood alcohol level—*twice* the legal limit."

"But I wasn't driving—" She stopped. With effort, she

controlled herself. "You think I should take the D.A.'s deal, don't you?"

"I think the jury is going to believe you were so drunk you blacked out and don't remember what you did. They'll go for the maximum sentence. If I had a scintilla of hope I could convince them otherwise, I'd recommend against the offer."

Shaken, Eva stood and walked around the tranquil pool of water encircling the fountain. Her chest was tight. She stared into the water and tried to make herself breathe. First she had lost Charles and all their dreams and hopes for the future. He had been brilliant, fun, endlessly fascinating. She closed her eyes and could almost feel him stroking her cheek, comforting her. Her heart ached with longing for him.

And now she faced prison. The thought terrified her, but for the first time she admitted it was possible—she had never in her life blacked out, but she might have this time. If she had blacked out, she might have climbed behind the wheel. And if she did—that meant she really had killed Charles. She bent her head and clasped the gold wedding band on her finger. Tears slid down her cheeks.

Behind her, Brian touched her shoulder. "You remember Trajan, the great ruler who expanded the Roman empire?"

She quickly wiped her face with her fingers and turned around to him. "Of course. What about him?"

"Trajan was ruthless and cunning and won every great battle he led his troops into. He had a rule: If you can't win, don't fight. If you don't fight, it's no defeat. You will survive. Take the deal, Eva. Survive."

3

Washington, D.C.
April, Two years later

Carrying a thermos of hot coffee and two mugs, Tucker Andersen crossed into Stanton Park, just five blocks from his office on Capitol Hill. The midnight shadows were long and black, and the air was cool. There were no children in the playground, no pedestrians on the sidewalks. Inhaling the scent of freshly cut grass, he listened as traffic rumbled past on C Street. All was as it should be.

Finally he spotted his old friend Jonathan Ryder, almost invisible where he sat on a bench facing the granite statue of Revolutionary War hero Nathanael Greene. Tonight a call had come in from Tucker's wife that Jonathan was trying to reach him.

Tucker closed in. A slender man of five foot ten, he had the long muscles of the runner he still was. His eyes were large and intelligent behind tortoiseshell glasses, his mustache light brown, his gray beard trimmed close to the jaw. Mostly bald, he had a fringe of gray-brown hair dangling over his shirt collar. He was fifty-three years old, and although his official credentials announced CIA, he was both more and less.

"Hello, Jonathan." Tucker sat and crossed his legs. "Nice to see you again. What's it been—ten years?" He studied him. Jonathan looked small now, and he was not a small man. And tense. Very tense.

"At least ten years. I appreciate your meeting me on such

short notice." Jonathan gave a brief smile, showing a row of perfect white teeth in his lined face. Lean and fit, he had a high forehead topped by a brush of graying blond hair. He was wearing black sweatpants and a black sweatshirt with a Yale University logo on the sleeve instead of his usual Savile Row business suit.

Tucker handed him a mug and poured coffee for both of them. "Sounded important, but then you could always make sunrise seem as if it were heralding angels."

"It *is* important." Jonathan sniffed the coffee. "Smells good." His hands shook as he drank.

Tucker felt a moment of worry. "How's the family?"

"Jeannine's great. Busy with all her charities, as usual. Judd's left military intelligence and isn't going to reenlist. Three tours in Iraq and a tour in Pakistan were finally enough for him." He hesitated. "I've been thinking a lot about the past lately."

Tucker set the thermos on the seat beside him. They had been close friends during their undergraduate days at Yale. "I remember when we were in school and you started that investment club. You made me a grand in two years. That was a hell of a lot of money in those days."

Jonathan nodded. Then he grinned. "I thought you were just a smart-ass—all looks, no brains, no commitment. Then you saved my skin that night in Alexanderplatz in East Berlin. Remember? It took a lot of muscle—and smarts."

After college, both had joined the CIA, in operations, but Jonathan had left after three years to earn an MBA at Wharton. With an undergraduate degree in chemistry, he had worked for a series of pharmaceutical companies, then gone on to found his own. Today he was president and board chair of Bucknell Technologies. Monied and powerful, he was a regular on Washington's social circuit and at the president's yearly Prayer Breakfast.

"Glad I did the good deed,"Tucker said."Look where you ended up—a baron of Big Pharma, while I'm still tilling the mean streets and urine-scented dark alleys."

Jonathan nodded."To each his own. Still, if you'd wanted it, you could've headed Langley. Your problem is you make a lousy bureaucrat. Have you heard of the video game called *Bureaucracy*? If you move, you lose."

Tucker chuckled."Okay, old friend. Time to tell me what this is all about."

Jonathan looked at his coffee, then set it on the seat beside him."A situation's come up. It scares the hell out of me. It's more your bailiwick than mine."

"You've got a lot contacts. Why me?"Tucker drank.

"Because this has to be handled carefully.You're a master at that. Because we're friends, and I'm going to go down. I don't want to die in the process." He stared at Tucker, then looked away. "I've stumbled onto something . . . an account for about twenty million dollars in an international bank. I'm not sure exactly what it's all about, but I'm damn sure it has to do with Islamic terrorism." Jonathan fell silent.

"Go on," Tucker snapped. "Which bank? Why do you think the twenty million is connected to jihadism?"

"It's complicated." He craned around, checking the park.

Tucker looked, too. The wide expanse remained empty.

"You've come this far." Tucker controlled an urge to shake the information out of him."You know you want to tell me."

"I didn't have anything to do with it. I'm not exactly an angel myself. . . But I don't understand how anyone could—" Jonathan shuddered."What do you know about the Library of Gold?"

"Never heard of it."

"It's key. I've been there. It's where I found out about this—"

Tucker watched Jonathan intently as he spoke. He was leaning forward slightly, gazing off into the middle distance.

There was no sound. No warning. A red dot suddenly appeared on Jonathan's forehead and the back of his head exploded with a loud crack. Blood and tissue and bone blasted into the air.

Tucker's training kicked in immediately. Before Jonathan's lifeless body had time to keel over, Tucker hit the sidewalk and rolled under the bench. Two more sniper shots dug into the concrete, spitting shards. His heart pounded. His friend's blood dripped next to him. Tucker swallowed and swore. He had come unarmed.

Using his mobile, he dialed 911 and reported the wet job. Then he peeled off his blazer, rolled it thick, and lifted it to attract attention. It was a light tan color, a contrast against the shadows. When no more rounds were fired, he snaked out from under the bench. Hurrying off through the park, he headed toward Massachusetts Avenue, where he thought the bullets had originated. As he moved he considered what Jonathan had said: Islamic terrorism . . . $20 million in an international bank . . . the Library of Gold. . . . What in hell was the Library of Gold?

As he crossed the street, Tucker scanned the area. A young couple was drinking from Starbucks coffee cups, the man carrying a briefcase. Another man was pushing a grocery cart. A middle-aged woman in a running suit and wearing a small backpack jogged past and circled back. Any of them could be the shooter, the rifle quickly broken down and concealed in the briefcase, the shopping cart, the backpack. Or the shooter could be someone else, still tracking him.

When he reached Sixth Street, Tucker ran into the swiftly moving traffic. Over the noise of honking horns, he heard the distinctive sound of a bullet whistling overhead. Crouching between the lanes of rushing cars, he spun around and stared back. A man was standing on the sidewalk at the corner, holding a pistol in both hands.

As the man fired again, Tucker put on a burst of speed, running with the cars. More horns honked. Curses filled the air. A taxi was entering traffic after dropping off its fare. Tucker pounded the fender to slow it, yanked open the back door, and fell inside.

The driver's head whipped around. "What in hell?"

"Drive."

As the taxi took off, Tucker peered out the rear window. Behind him, the killer ran into the congestion, looking everywhere, his gun still searching for its target. A van entered traffic, and Tucker lost sight of him. When the van turned the corner, opening up the view again, he spotted the man three blocks back. A car slewed around him, horn blaring. Another car skidded. The man pivoted, and a racing sedan slammed into him. He vanished under the wheels of the car.

"Let me off here," Tucker ordered. He shoved money at the driver and jumped out.

Running back, he studied the stream of cars. They should have stopped. At least they should be swerving around the downed shooter.

As two police cars arrived at the park, sirens screaming, Tucker walked up and down the tree-lined block. Both sides. Traffic roared past. There was no sign of a body.

4

The funeral for Jonathan Ryder was held in the Chevy Chase Presbyterian Church in north-west Washington. A somber crowd packed the sanctuary—business people, lawyers, investors, philanthropists, and politicians. Jonathan's widow, Jeannine; his son, Judd; and assorted relatives sat in the front row, while Tucker Andersen found a spot in back where he could watch and listen.

After Jonathan was killed, the police had searched the buildings around Stanton Park and questioned all potential witnesses. They interviewed the widow, son, neighbors, and business associates, who were mystified why anyone would want to murder a good man like Jonathan. The police investigation was continuing.

Checking into Jonathan's last words, Tucker had found only one mention of the Library of Gold in Langley's database. Then he researched the library online and talked with historians at local universities. He also queried the targeting analysts in the counterterrorism unit. Thus far he had found nothing helpful.

"In Jesus Christ, death has been conquered and the promise of eternal life affirmed."The pastor's voice resonated against the high walls as he conducted the Service of Witness to the Resurrection."This is a time to celebrate the wonderful gifts we received from God in our relationships with Jonathan Ryder. . ."

Tucker felt a wave of grief. Finally the celebration of

Jonathan's life ended, and the strains of "The Old Rugged Cross" filled the sanctuary. The family left first, Judd Ryder supporting his mother, her head bowed.

As soon as it was decent, Tucker followed.

The reception was in the church, in Chadsey Hall. Tucker chatted with people, introducing himself as an old college friend of Jonathan's. It lasted an hour. When Jeannine and Judd Ryder were walking alone out the door, Tucker intercepted them.

"Tucker, how nice to see you." Jeannine smiled. "You've shaved your beard." A petite brunette, she was dressed in a black sheath dress with a string of pearls tight against her throat. She had changed a lot, no longer the lively wife he remembered. She was his age, but there was a sense about her of having settled, as if there were no longer any questions to be asked.

"Karen was in a state of shock," Tucker admitted with a smile. He'd had a beard off and on for years. "It's been a while since she's seen my whole face."

He shook hands with Jonathan's son, Judd. "The last time we met, you were at Georgetown." He remembered when Judd was born, Jonathan's pride. His full name was Judson Clayborn Ryder.

"A long time ago," Judd agreed genially. "Are you still with State?" Six feet one inch tall, he was thirty-two years old, wide-shouldered, with an easy stance. Fine lines covered his face, swarthy from too many hours in the sun. His hair was wavy and chestnut brown, while his brown eyes had faded to a dark, contemplative gray. His gaze was rock steady, but a sense of disillusionment and a hint of cynicism showed. Retired military intelligence, Tucker remembered.

The State Department was Tucker's longtime cover. "They'll have to pry my fingers off my desk to get rid of me."

"The police said you were with Dad when he was shot." Judd spoke with light curiosity, but Tucker sensed greater depths.

"Yes. Let's go outdoors and chat."

They walked out to the grassy lawn. Only a few people remained, climbing into cars and limousines at the curb.

Tucker guided the pair to a spot in the shadow of the stone church. "Have either of you heard of the Library of Gold?"

"It was one of the bedtime stories Dad used to tell me, like *Lorna Doone* and *The Scarlet Pimpernel*," Judd said. "What about you, Mom?"

Jeannine frowned. "I vaguely recall it. I'm sorry, but I don't remember much. It was something Jonathan and Judd shared."

"Did the Library of Gold play a role in Dad's murder?" Judd asked.

Tucker gave a casual shrug. "The police think a copycat of the Beltway Snipers might've shot him." The Beltway Snipers had been responsible for a series of random killings a few years before.

Jeannine pressed her hand against her throat. "How horrible."

Judd put his arm around her shoulders.

"Jonathan said he wanted my help with something related to the library," Tucker continued. "But he died before he could tell me exactly what it was. What did your father tell you about the library, Judd?"

Judd settled his feet. "I'll run through the basics. It all began with the Byzantine Empire. For a thousand years while the emperors were conquering the world, they were collecting and making illuminated manuscripts. But then the empire fell to the Ottoman Turks in 1453. That could've been the end of the court library, but a niece of the last ruler escaped with the best books. They were covered in gold and jewels. When she married Ivan the Great, eight hundred of the books went to Moscow with her." He paused. "The legend was born with their grandson, Ivan the Terrible. After he inherited the library he added more illuminated manuscripts and started letting important Europeans see the collection. They were so impressed they went home and talked about it. Word spread across the continent that only when you stood among Ivan's golden books could you really understand 'wisdom, art, wealth, and eternal power.' That's how the collection got its name—the Library of Gold. It was a good adventure tale with a happy ending that turned into a mystery. Ivan died in 1584, maybe from mercury poisoning. At about the same time several of his spies and assassins got sick and died or were executed—and the library vanished."

Tucker had found himself leaning forward as he listened. He stepped back and peered at Jeannine. "Is that what you remember?"

"That's much more than I ever heard."

"I checked into the library and came up with pretty much the same information," Tucker admitted. "The Byzantine court library existed, but many historians believe none of the books landed in Moscow. Some think a few ended up in Rome, and the Ottoman Turks burned a lot, kept some, and sold the rest."

"I like Jonathan's story more," Jeannine decided.

"Did you ask your father how he heard the story, Judd?"

"Never saw any reason to."

"Where did Jonathan say the library was now?"

Judd gave him a hard look. "The way I ended the story for you was the way Dad ended it for me—with Ivan the Terrible's death and the library's disappearance."

"Would you mind if I looked through Jonathan's papers?" Tucker asked Jeannine.

"Please do, if you think you might find something," she said.

"I'll help," Judd told him.

"It's not necessary—" Tucker tried.

"I insist."

The Ryders lived on the prestigious Maryland State side of Chevy Chase. The house was a baronial white mansion in the Greek Revival style, with six towering columns crowned by an intricately carved portico. Jonathan's office was filled with books. But that was nothing compared to the real library. Tucker stared. From the parquet floor to the second-floor ceiling, thousands of books beckoned, many in hand-tooled leather bindings.

"This is amazing," Tucker said.

"He was a collector. But see how worn his chair is? He didn't just collect; he read a lot, too."

Tucker gazed at the red leather armchair, worn and softened. Returning to the task at hand, he led Judd back to the office. They began inspecting Jonathan's cherrywood desk, matching file cabinets, and the cardboard banker's boxes of his personal belongings sent over from his office at Bucknell headquarters.

"The Department of State is a good cover," Judd said non commitally. "Who do you really work for, Tucker? CIA . . . Homeland Security . . . National Intelligence?"

Tucker let out a loud laugh. "Sorry to let you down, son. I really do work for State. And no, not State intelligence. I'm just a paper pusher, helping the diplomats wade through the various policy changes that have to do with the Middle East. A paper pusher like me is perfect to go through Jonathan's papers." In truth, Tucker was a covert officer, which meant his fellow spies, operations, assets, agents, and the people who had worked knowingly or unknowingly with him could be endangered if his real position were made public.

"Right," Judd said, letting the matter drop.

When Tucker asked, Judd described the conditions he had seen in Iraq and Pakistan without ever telling him anything substantive about his own work.

"I'll bet you're being recruited by every agency in the IC," Tucker said. The IC was the intelligence community.

"I haven't been home long enough."

"They'll be after you. Are you tempted?"

Judd had taken off his suit jacket and was crouched in his white cuffed shirt and dark suit pants over a banker's box, reading file names. "Dad asked me the same question. When I said no, he tried to convince me to join him at Bucknell. But I've saved my money and have a lease on a row house on the Hill. I figured to do nothing until I couldn't stand it anymore. By then I should know what's next for me."

Tucker had been going through Jonathan's desk. The last drawer contained files. He read the tags. The end file was unnamed. He pulled it out. In it were a half-dozen clippings from newspapers and magazines from the past week—and each article was about jihadism in Afghanistan and Pakistan. He peered up. Judd's back was to him. He folded the clippings and stuffed them inside his jacket and returned the empty file to the drawer.

He activated Jonathan's computer. "Do you know your dad's password?"

Judd looked over his shoulder. "Try 'Jeannine.' "

When that did not work, Judd made more suggestions. Finally the date of his birth did the trick. As soon as Judd returned to the banker's boxes, Tucker activated a global search for "Library of Gold"—but uncovered nothing. Then he inspected Jonathan's financial records on Quicken. There were no red flags.

"Dinner," Jeannine announced from the open door. "You need a break."

They joined her for a simple meal at the maple table in the kitchen.

"Your place is beautiful," Tucker commented. "Jonathan came a far way from the South Side of Chicago."

"All of this was important to him." Jeannine made a gesture encompassing the house and their privileged world. "You know how ambitious he was. He loved the business, and he loved that he could make a lot of money at it. But strangely I don't think he could ever have made enough to make him really happy. Still, we had many good times." She stopped, her eyes tearing.

"We've got a lot of great memories, don't we, Mom?" Judd said.

She nodded and resumed eating.

"Jonathan traveled a lot, I imagine," Tucker said.

"All the time," she said. "But he was always glad to come home."

After coffee, Tucker and Judd returned to the office. By ten o'clock, they had finished their search, and Tucker was weary of the tedious work.

"Sure I can't convince you to have a brandy?" Judd asked as he walked him to the front door. "Mom will join us."

"Wish I could, but I need to get home. Karen is going to think I've gotten myself lost."

Judd gave an understanding nod, and they shook hands.

Tucker went out to his old Oldsmobile. He liked the car. It had a powerful eight-cylinder engine and ran like a well-oiled top. He climbed inside and drove the rest of the way around the circular drive and out past the electronic gates and onto the street, heading to his far more modest home in Virginia. Since he was working, he had not brought Karen to the funeral. But she would be waiting for him, a fire burning in the fireplace. He needed to see her, to remember the good times, and to forget for a short while the fear in Jonathan's voice for some impending disaster he had not had time to name.

Earlier, when he followed Jeannine and Judd's limo to their place, he had thought a black Chevy Malibu was dogging him most of the way. He had slowed the Olds as he drove in through the Ryders' gate, watching in his rearview mirror. But the car had rolled past without a glance from the driver, his profile hard to see beneath a golf cap pulled low over his forehead.

Now as he drove, Tucker went into second-stage alert, studying pedestrians and other cars. After ten blocks he made a sharp turn onto a quiet street. There was a car again, maybe *the* car, behind him. A dark color. A motorcycle turned, too, trailing the car.

Tucker made another sharp right, then turned left onto a silent residential avenue. The tailing car stayed with him, and so did the motorcycle. He hit the accelerator. Shots sounded, smashing in through the rear window. Glass pebbles sprayed, showering him. He crouched low and pulled out his 9 mm Browning, laying it on the seat beside him. Since Jonathan's death, he carried it all the time.

Flooring the accelerator, he felt the big eight take hold, and the car hurtled forward into the night. Houses passed in a blur. No more bullets, but his tail was still with him, although falling behind. Silently he thanked the Olds's powerful motor. Ahead was a hill. He blasted up it, the front wheels lifting at the crest, and over. The front crashed down, and he raced onward, turning onto one street and then the next.

He looked around, hoping . . . there was an open garage, and the attached house showed no interior lights. He checked his rearview mirror. No sign of his tail—yet.

He slammed the brakes and shot the car into the garage, jumped out, and yanked hard on the door's rope. The door banged down.

Standing at the garage's side window, gun in hand, he watched his pursuer rush past. It was the black Chevy Malibu, but he saw only the right side of the car, not the driver's side, and could not quite make out the license plate number. He still had no idea who was behind the wheel. Immediately following, the motorcycle whipped past, its rider's face hidden by a black helmet.

Tucker remained at the window, watching. A half hour later, he slid his Browning back into its holster and went to the center of the big garage door. With a grunt, he heaved the door up—and froze, staring into the mouth of a subcompact semi-automatic Beretta pistol.

"Don't reach for it." Judd Ryder's face was grim. He had changed out of his funeral clothes and was wearing jeans and a brown leather bomber jacket.

Tucker let the hand that had been going for his weapon drift down to his side. "What in hell do you think you're doing, Judd? How did you find me?"

Ryder gave a crooked smile. "You learn a few things in military intelligence."

"You put a bug on my car?"

"You bet I did. Why didn't the sniper in Stanton Park kill you, too?"

"I got lucky. I dove under the bench."

"Bullshit. You claim to be a paper pusher, but paper pushers freeze. They wet their pants. They die. Why did you set up Dad?"

Tucker was silent. Finally he admitted, "You're right—I'm

CIA. Your father came to me for help, just as I said. After I got away, the sniper tried to shoot me, too. He was run down in traffic while chasing me. But when I went back, the body had disappeared. Either he survived and got out on his own, or someone picked him up. He'd seen me, which is why I shaved my beard—to make myself more difficult to identify. Someone just tried to kill me again, maybe the same asshole."

"What exactly did Dad say?"

"That he was very worried. He told me, 'I stumbled onto something . . . an account for about twenty million dollars in an international bank. I'm not sure exactly what it means, but I think it has to do somehow with Islamic terrorism.'"

Judd inhaled sharply.

Tucker nodded. "He was shot before he could say anything more than he'd found the information in the Library of Gold."

Judd's eyebrows rose. "He told the story about the library to me as if it were fiction. You're certain he said he found this out in the library?"

"He said the library was key. That he'd been there." He saw a flicker of hurt in Judd's eyes. "Everyone has secrets. Your father was no exception."

"And this one killed him. Maybe."

"Maybe." An idea occurred to him. "Were you on the motorcycle behind me?"

"It's parked up the block. I got the license tag of the Chevy that was chasing you. I can't have it traced—you can. He lost me in Silver Spring, dammit." He slid his gun inside his jacket. "Sorry, Tucker. I had to be sure about you."

Tucker realized sweat had beaded up on his forehead. "What's the plate number?"

Judd gave it to him. Tucker walked back through the garage to the driver's side door of his car.

Judd followed. "Let's work on this together."

"Not on your life, Judson. You're out of the game,

remember? You've got a row house on the Hill, and you're taking some time off."

"That was before some goddamn sniper killed Dad. I'll find his killer on my own if I have to."

Tucker turned and glared. "You're impetuous, and you're too close to this. He was *your father,* for God's sake. I can't have anyone working with me I can't trust."

"Would you really have handled it any differently?" Before Tucker could answer, Judd continued. "It's only logical I'd be suspicious. Maybe you were responsible for Dad's death. You could've tried to liquidate me, too. Look at it another way: You don't want to be tripping over me. I sure as hell don't want you in my way, either."

Tucker opened the car door and sighed. "All right. I'll think about it. But if I agree, you take orders from me. *Me,* get it? No more grandstanding. Now rip that bug off my car."

"Sure—if you drive me to my bike."

"Jesus Christ. Get in."

5

As soon as he dropped off Judd Ryder, Tucker Andersen phoned headquarters.

"I'm coming in now."

Watching carefully around, he parked the Olds at the back of a busy mall outside Chevy Chase, caught a taxi, and phoned his wife. Then he hailed another cab, this time directing it back to Capitol Hill.

The headquarters of the highly secret Catapult team was a Federalist brick house north-east of the Capitol in a vibrant neighborhood of lively bars, restaurants, and one-of-a-kind shops. This sort of busy neighborhood provided good cover for Catapult, a special CIA counteroperations unit—counterterrorism, counter-intelligence, countermeasures, counterproliferation, counter-insurgency. Catapult worked covertly behind the scenes, taking aggressive action to direct or stop negative events, both in triage and planning.

Tucker let the taxi pass the unit's weathered brick house with its shiny black door and shutters. The porch lamps were alight. The discreet sign above the door announced COUNCIL FOR PEER EDUCATION.

Three blocks later, he got out and strolled back as if nothing was on his mind. But once inside the fenced lot, he hurried past the security cameras to the side door, where he tapped his code onto the electronic keyboard. After a series of soft clicks, he pushed open the door. It was heavy steel, engineered to protect a bank vault.

He stepped into the hallway. While the exterior of the house was elegant with history, the interior was utilitarian and cutting-edge. The plaster walls and thick moldings were painted in muted greens and grays, and stark black-and-white photographs of cities from around the planet hung on them, reminding the few who were allowed to enter of the far reach of Catapult.

Glancing up, he noted the needle-nose cameras and dime-size motion detectors as he passed a couple of staffers carrying high-security blue folders. In the reception area, the office manager, Gloria Feit, reigned from behind her big metal desk. To his right was the front entry, while to the left a long corridor extended back into the house, where there were offices, the library, and the communications center. Upstairs were more offices, a conference room, and two large bedrooms with cots for covert officers and special visitors in transit.

Gloria's shift had begun at eight o'clock that morning, but she still looked fresh. A small woman with crinkled smile lines around her eyes, she was in her late forties. Once a field op herself, she and Tucker had worked together off and on for two decades.

Her brows rose over her rainbow-rimmed reading glasses. "You're on time."

It was a constant debate between them, since he often ran late. "How can you tell? I'm usually here."

"Except when you're not. Did you have good luck?"

"Luck is the result of preparation. I was prepared. But I didn't have as much luck as I'd hoped. Sometimes I think you know too much, Gloria."

She smiled. "Then you've got to quit telling me."

"Good point."

She had a remarkable memory, and he relied on her for details he occasionally lost in the barrage of information with which he dealt daily. Plus she was a walking encyclopedia of those with whom they had worked, both domestic and foreign.

"Why are you still here?" he asked. "You were supposed to go home hours ago."

"Now that you've arrived, I'll leave. Ted's taking me out for a late dinner. Karen called to check that you got into Catapult okay. You'd better phone her."

"Why does everyone worry about me so much?" But the truth was, Karen had spent too many years wondering where he was and sometimes whether he was alive.

"Because *you* worry, Tucker." Gloria turned off her computer. "The rest of us are necessary to make sure you're able to concentrate on worrying. It's a heavy job, but anything to serve the country." She grinned. "Your messages are on your desk. As soon as I saw you on the outside monitors, I let Cathy know you were here. She's waiting in your office. Have fun." She snapped up her purse, took out her car keys, and headed for the door.

Feeling the weight of Jonathan's death, Tucker walked down the long corridor. His office was the last one, chosen because it was quieter when the place was most active. As second in command, he got a few concessions, and his office was his favorite one.

He opened the door. Sitting in one of the two standard-issue armchairs in front of his cluttered desk was Catherine Doyle, the chief of Catapult.

She turned. "You look like crap."

"That good? Thanks." He shot her a grin and went to his desk.

Cathy Doyle chuckled. She was the same height as Tucker and dressed in a camel-colored pantsuit, her ankle boots planted firmly on the carpet. At fifty-plus, she was still a beauty, with short, blond-streaked hair and porcelain skin.

She had been a model to support herself through New York University, graduating Phi Beta Kappa, then went on to earn a Ph.D. in international affairs from Columbia University, where Langley had recruited her.

"Gloria's gone home." He sat. "I can call over to Communications for coffee or tea."

"I wouldn't mind something stronger."

"That strikes me just fine." Tucker rotated in his chair to the file cabinet and unlocked the bottom drawer. He pulled out a bottle of Johnny Walker Red Label Scotch and held it up, looking back.

Cathy nodded, and Tucker poured two fingers into two water glasses. The spicy fragrance of the blended whiskey rose into the air, complex in its smokiness and scents of malted grain and wood. He handed a glass to her and cradled his, warming it between his palms.

"That license plate number came up," she told him. "It belongs to a Chevrolet Malibu reported stolen earlier today."

"Not surprising. Anything about the Library of Gold, an international bank, and jihadist financing?"

A slew of Washington's agencies—CIA, FBI, DIA, Customs, the IRS, the Financial Crimes Enforcement Network, the Office of Foreign Assets and Control, and the Secret Service—sent names of suspect individuals and groups to Treasury, which then forwarded them to a vast database of dubious financial transactions. The database compared the names to existing files and identified any matches.

Cathy shook her head. "Nothing yet."

"What about SWIFT?"

The Society for Worldwide Interbank Financial Telecommunication, SWIFT monitored international financial transactions on behalf of US counterterrorism efforts, looking for suspicious transactions that might be for terrorist financing, money laundering, or other criminal activity. The problem was, the information SWIFT had was no better than that provided by the banks at either end of the transactions.

"Nothing," she told him. "If we had at least the name of the bank, we'd have something to go on. In any case, the usual suspicious transactions have turned up, and they'll be investigated thoroughly anyway. And nothing about the Library of Gold was there, either."

"What about Jonathan Ryder? Travel records, phone logs."

"Zero so far. We're still looking." She studied him. "What's been happening with you?"

He told her about the funeral and listening to Judd Ryder's "bedtime story."

"Interesting the father would do that," she said. "Shows he had a longtime connection of some kind to the Library of Gold."

"Exactly. Then I went to the Ryders' place, and Judd and I searched Jonathan's office. The only thing I found was a file in his desk—an unmarked file." He handed the clippings to her. As she read them, he said, "All are about recent terrorist activity in Pakistan and Afghanistan—mostly the Taliban and al-Qaeda. In terms of money, there's one about how difficult it is to track jihadist financing—finding a needle in a haystack is the cliché the article uses. Another talks about how subsidiary jihadist groups are funding themselves through fraud, kidnappings, bank heists, petty crime—just a fraction of what we know—and then tithing back to al-Qaeda central."

Decimated by intelligence agencies and the military, and largely cut off from previous sources of income, al-Qaeda's highly skilled, operationally sophisticated inner circle no longer could carry out attacks across continents. Now the major threat was the al-Qaeda movement—the numerous regional franchises and grassroots operations being born or refashioning themselves as affiliates.

"I'm eager to hear what the analysts think," Tucker said. "Several banks are mentioned in the articles. Right now it seems to me Jonathan was gathering research but didn't know precisely what he was looking for."

"My thought, too, although he was focusing on the two countries." She set the clippings on his desk.

"After I left the Ryders', I had another incident." He described the Chevy Malibu's chase. "I figure the guy spotted me at Jonathan's funeral, so he knows what I look like now. I can't drive the Olds again until this is over."

"Damn right. You can't go home, either. He may figure out where you live."

"I'll sleep here. It's cozy." He grimaced and drank. "Karen's packing. She's driving to a friend of hers in the Adirondacks until this is over. You have the adjustments to my cover at State set up?"

"I did that first. Probably an hour ago. Took you long enough to get here."

"I had to dry-clean my trail—you know the drill." He sat back, turning his whiskey glass in his hands. "I got a hit about the Library of Gold in our database. A few years ago a man who claimed to be the chief librarian managed to get in touch with one of our operatives. He said all sorts of international criminal activity was going on with the book club—those are the people who own it—and he couldn't escape. Unless we extracted him."

"What kind of activity?"

"He wouldn't be specific. Claimed the information might be traced back to him and get him killed, but he'd tell us everything once he was safe. When we asked him to prove his bona fides, he smuggled out one of the illuminated manuscripts—*The Book of Spies*. It was created in the 1500s. We lost contact with him after that, and now Langley has the book somewhere in storage."

She nodded thoughtfully. "You have a plan?"

"I'm putting one together."

"Okay, but it'll be hard to let you have any bodies. I'm shorthanded as it is, especially if you're going to work on this."

"No problem." He described how Judd had found him in the garage where he had hidden from the Chevy. "His full name is Judson Clayborn Ryder. I want to put him on board as a private contractor. He's got the credentials, and I can use him."

"Bad idea. He's emotionally involved."

"True, but he calmed down quickly, and he's going to look into it no matter what. This way I can keep my eye on him, and he was military intelligence, so he's got expertise."

She thought about it. Finished her whiskey. "I'll have Langley check his background."

6

Jefferson County, Missouri

The night was crisp and clear over Missouri's rolling hills as the man exited Interstate 55, heading west past farms and woodland. The truck was a Class-6 Freightliner with sweet power steering. His fingers bounced on the wheel as he watched the countryside pass by. On the seat beside him lay an M4 carbine rifle, the primary weapon for most special forces soldiers and rangers. It was an old friend, and when he moonlighted like this, he brought it along for companionship. He smiled, thinking about the money he was going to make.

The clothing factory lay ahead. It was squat, the size of a football field, encircled by a high chain-link fence and concertina wire. Stopping at the gate, he showed the credentials Preston had given him. The sleepy security guard glanced at them and waved him through.

Breathing a sigh of relief, he drove on, counting the loading docks sticking out like gray teeth on the south side of the building. When he figured out which was number three, he circled the truck and backed up to it. The brakes huffed.

Once on the dock, he swore, staring at the mountain of crates. For two hours he labored, driving his dolly between the dock and the open maw of the truck, packing the boxes inside. It was a lousy job for one man. He was going to bitch to Preston about that. Who would've thought uniforms would take up so much room?

When he finished, he was sweaty. Still, at least this part, the most dangerous part, was finished. He climbed behind the wheel and drove sedately toward the guard kiosk. The gate opened as he approached, and he passed safely through. That was the thing about Preston. He knew how to plan a job. He grabbed his cell phone and punched in the number. Time to give him the good news.

San Diego County, California

The young man parked his stolen sedan under the branches of a pepper tree at the distant edge of the sprawling truck stop off busy Interstate 15. He slid his FAMAS bullpup service rifle into its special holster inside his long jacket and got out, walking casually through the nighttime shadows along the rim of the parking lot, staying far from the brightly lit station with its restaurant, sleeping rooms, truck wash, and repair garage. With the trucks roaring in and out, the stink of diesel, and the taste of exhaust fumes, the place was an assault on the senses.

Scanning carefully, he headed toward thirty trucks parked in neat rows, their lights off while their drivers were inside tending to business, food, or entertainment. The truck he wanted was a Class-7 Peterbilt, a heavy eighteen-wheeler.

He found it quickly, then read the license plate to be sure. Satisfied, he glanced around, then tried the door. As expected, it was unlocked. He hiked himself inside. The key was in the ignition. He fired up the engine, noted the tank was full, and drove off. As soon as he was on the interstate, he phoned Preston.

Howard County, Maryland

At last Martin Chapman heard the car in his drive. He looked out of his third-floor window, the moon spilling silver light across Maryland's hunt country. His wife was at their château in San Moritz, catching the end of the ski season, and the interior of his big plantation-style home was silent. His German shepherds barked outside on the grounds, and the horses whinnied from the pasture and barns. The security lights were shining brightly, displaying only a fraction of his enormous Arabian horse spread.

He pressed the intercom button."I'll get the door, Bradley. Go back to sleep." Bradley was his houseman, a faithful employee of twenty years.

Still dressed, Chapman glanced at the photo on his desk, showing Gemma in a long tight gown, diamonds sparkling at her ears and around her throat, and him in a rented tuxedo. They were smiling widely. It was his favorite portrait, taken years before, while he was studying at UCLA and she at USC, miles apart geographically, worlds apart economically, but deeply in love. Now both were in their early fifties. Full of warm emotion, he pulled himself away, a tall man with a head of thick white hair brushed back in waves, blue eyes, and an unlined, untroubled face.

Hurrying downstairs, he opened the door. Doug Preston stood on the long brick porch, golf cap in his hands. Rangy and athletic, Preston radiated calm confidence. Forty-two years old, he had honed, aristocratic features. Little showed on his deeply tanned face except his usual neutral expression, but Chapman knew the man better than he knew himself: There was tightness around his eyes, and his lips had thinned. Something had happened that Preston did not like.

"Come in," Chapman said brusquely. "Do you want a drink?"

Preston gave a deferential nod, and Chapman led him into his enormous library, where towering shelves lined the walls, filled with leather-bound volumes. He looked at them appreciatively, then headed for the bar, where he poured bourbon and branch water for both of them.

With a polite thank-you, Preston picked up his drink, walked to the French doors, and peered out into the night.

Watching him, Chapman felt a moment of impatience, then repressed it. Preston must be handled carefully, which was why he manipulated him with the same adroitness he lavished on his multibillion-dollar, highly competitive business.

"What have you learned about the stranger in the park?" Chapman asked, reining him in. Preston had run down the sniper with his Mercedes and pulled the corpse inside. The man had had to be eliminated; too many people had seen his face.

Preston turned and made a focused report: "I waited outside Jonathan Ryder's funeral, got photos of the guy who was with Mr. Ryder in the park, and ran them through several data banks. His name is Tucker Andersen. He works for State. I followed Andersen to the Ryder house, then picked him up when he left. I wasn't able to scrub him—the man drives as if he's a NASCAR pro. That kind of talent could mean something, but maybe it doesn't. So I called a high-level contact in State Human Resources. Andersen is a documents specialist, and he's scheduled to leave for Geneva tonight for a UN conference on Middle East affairs. It lasts three weeks. I checked, and he has a reservation at the conference hotel. Just to make sure, I've put a team on his house in Virginia, and I'll keep in close touch with my man at State. If Andersen doesn't leave, we'll know we've got trouble. I'll be ready for him and take him out."

Chapman heard the annoyance in Preston's voice. The failure to liquidate Andersen was difficult to swallow for a man who detested loose ends.

Still, all was not lost. "Good work." Chapman paused,

noted the flash of gratitude in Preston's eyes. "What about the District police?"

For the first time, Preston smiled. "They're still not asking any questions about the library, and they would be by now if they knew about it. It's beginning to look as if Mr. Ryder either didn't or wasn't able to tell Andersen anything important." Chief of security for the Library of Gold for more than ten years, Preston was a man passionate about books and completely loyal, traits not only prized but required of library employees.

"That'd be a good result." Chapman moved on to his next concern: "What about the library dinner?"

Preston drank deeply, relaxing. "Everything's on track. The food, the chefs, the transportation."

Book club members had been flying into the library throughout the past month, working with the translators to find and research questions in preparation for the annual banquet's tournament. It was during Jonathan's visit to the library just days before that he had learned about Chapman's new business deal and become alarmed.

"Where are you with the Khost project?" Khost was a province in eastern Afghanistan, on the border with Pakistan. It was there Chapman planned to make back his huge losses from the global economic crash, and more.

"On schedule. The uniforms and equipment have been picked up. They'll be shipped out in the morning. I've got it well in hand."

"See that it stays that way. Nothing must interfere with it. Nothing. And keep your eye on the situation with Tucker Andersen. We don't want it to explode in our faces."

7

Chowchilla, California
Two weeks later

At 1:32 P.M. Tucker Andersen finished briefing the warden of the Central California Women's Facility. She was a stout woman with graying brown hair and a habit of folding her hands in front of her. She escorted him out of her private office.

"Tell me about Eva Blake," Tucker said.

"She doesn't complain, and she hasn't gotten any 115 write-ups," the warden said. "She started on the main yard, tidying up and emptying trash cans. Ten months ago we rewarded her with an assembly-line job in our electronics factory. In her free time she listens to the radio, keeps up with her karate, and volunteers—she teaches literacy classes and reads to inmates in the hospital ward. A couple of months ago she sent out a raft of résumés, but none of the other convicts knows it. There's an unwritten law here—you don't ask an inmate sister what she's done or what she's doing. Blake has been smart and kept her mouth shut about herself."

"Who are her visitors?" Tucker asked as they passed the guard desk.

"Family occasionally, from out of state. A friend used to drive up every few months from L.A.—Peggy Doty, a former colleague. Ms. Doty hasn't been to see her in a while. I believe she's working at the British Library in London now. This is Blake's housing unit."

They stepped into a world of long expanses of linoleum flooring, closed doors, harsh fluorescent lighting, and an ear-bleed volume of noise—intercoms crackling, television programs blaring from the dayrooms, and loud shouts and curses.

The warden glanced at him. "They yell as much to give them something to do as to express themselves. We're at double capacity here, so the noise is twice as loud as it should be. Blake is in the unit's yard. She gets three hours every day if she wants it. She always does."

The warden nodded at the guard standing at the door. He opened it, and the raw odor of farmland fertilizer swept toward them. They stepped outside, where the Central Valley sun pounded down onto an open space of grass, concrete, and dirt. Women sat, napped, and moved aimlessly. Beyond them rose high brick walls topped with electrified razor wire.

Tucker scanned the prisoners, looking for Eva Blake. He had studied photos as well as a video of the court appearance in which she had pleaded guilty to vehicular manslaughter in the death of her husband. He looked for her red hair, pretty face, lanky frame.

"You don't recognize her, do you?" the warden asked. "She's that one."

He followed her nod to a woman in a baggy prison shirt and trousers, walking around the perimeter of the yard. Her hair was completely hidden, tucked up into a baseball cap. Her expression was blank, her posture non-threatening. She looked little like the very alive woman in the photos and video.

"She goes around the yard hour after hour, loop after loop. She's alone because she wants it that way. As I said, she's smart—she's learned to make herself invisible, uninteresting. Anyone who's interesting around here can attract violence."

Impressive both in her attitude and her ability to be inconspicuous, Tucker thought.

The warden clasped her hands in front of her. "I'm going to give you some advice. In prison, male cons either obey orders or defy them. Female cons ask why. Don't lie to her. But if you have to, make damn sure she doesn't catch you at it, at least not while you're trying to convince her to do whatever it is you want her to do. You really aren't going to tell me what's going on, are you?"

"It's national security."

She gave a curt nod, and Tucker walked across the grass toward Eva Blake, catcalls and whistles trailing him. He wondered how long it would take her to realize she was his goal. A good hundred yards away, her strides grew nervy, and her chin lifted. She stopped and, in a slow, deliberate pivot, turned to face him. Her arms were apparently restful at her sides, but her stance was wide and balanced, a karate stance. Her reaction time was excellent, and from the way she moved, she was still in good physical condition.

He walked up to her. "Doctor Blake, my name is Tucker Andersen. I'd like to talk to you. The warden's given us an interview room."

"Why?" Her face was a mask.

"I may have a proposition for you. If so, I suspect you'll like it."

She peered around him, and he glanced back.

The warden was still standing in the doorway. Looking severe, she nodded at Blake. That made it an order.

"Whatever you say," Blake said, relaxing her posture slightly.

As she started to move around him, she stumbled and twisted her ankle, bumping into him. He grabbed her shoulders, helping her. Regaining her equilibrium, she excused herself, moved away, and walked steadily back toward the prison.

The interview room had pastel walls, a single metal table with four metal chairs, and cameras poking out high from two corners.

Tucker sat at the widest part of the table and gestured at the other chairs. "Choose your poison."

Not a smile. Eva Blake sat at the end. "You say your name is Tucker Andersen. Where are you from?"

"McLean, Virginia. Why?"

She pulled his wallet from beneath her shirt, opened it, and read the driver's license, checking on him. She spread out the credit cards, all in the same name. She nodded to herself, put the billfold back together, and handed it to him. "First time I've ever seen a 'visitor' in the yard on a non-visitor day."

He had not felt her pick his pocket, but her bumping into him had been a clue. As he followed her into the prison, he had patted his jacket and found the wallet missing.

"Nice dipping," he said mildly, "but then you're experienced, aren't you."

Her eyes widened a fraction.

Good, he had surprised her. "Your juvenile record is sealed. You should've had it expunged."

"You were able to get into my juvenile record?" she asked.

"I can, and I did. Tell me what happened."

She said nothing.

"Okay, I'll tell you," he said. "When you were fourteen, you were what is commonly called wild. You sneaked beers. Smoked some grass. Some of your friends shoplifted. You tried it, too. Then a man who looked like plainclothes security spotted you in Macy's. Instead of reporting you, he complimented you and asked whether you had the guts to go for the big time. It turned out he didn't work for the store—he was a master dipper running a half-dozen teams. He taught you the trade. You hustled airports, ball games, train stations, that sort of thing. Because you're beautiful, you usually played the distraction, prepping and positioning vics. But then when you were sixteen, a pickpocket on your team was escaping with the catch when some cops spotted him. He ran into traffic to get away—"

She lowered her head.

"He was hit by a semi and killed," Tucker continued. "Everyone beat feet getting out of there. You were gone, too. But for some reason you changed your mind and went back and talked to the police. They arrested you, of course. Then they asked you to help them bust the gang, which you did. Why?"

"We were all so young . . . it just seemed right to try to stop it while maybe we had time to grow up into better people."

"And later you used the skill to work your way through UCLA."

"But legally. At a security company. Who are you?"

He ignored the question. "You're probably going to be released on probation next year, so you've been sending out résumés. Any nibbles?"

She looked away. "No museum or library wants to hire a curator or conservator who's a felon, at least not me. Too much baggage because of . . . my husband's death. Because he was so well-known and respected in the field." She fingered a gold chain around her neck. Whatever was hanging from it was hidden beneath her shirt. He noted she was still wearing her wedding band, a simple gold ring.

"I see," he said neutrally.

She lifted her chin. "I'll find something. Some other kind of work."

He knew she was out of money. Because she had been convicted of her husband's manslaughter, she could not collect his life insurance. She'd had to sell her house to pay her legal bills. He felt a moment of pity, then banished it.

He observed, "You've become very good at masking your emotions."

"It's just what you have to do to make it in here."

"Tell me about the Library of Gold."

That seemed to take her aback. "Why?"

"Indulge me."

"You said you had a proposition for me. One I'd like."

"I said I *might* have a proposition for you. Let's see how much you remember."

"I remember a lot, but Charles, my husband—Dr. Charles Sherback—was a real authority. He'd spent his life researching the library and knew every available detail." Her voice was proud.

"Start at the beginning."

She recounted the story from the library's growth in the days of the Byzantine Empire to its disappearance at Ivan the Terrible's death.

He listened patiently. Then: "What happened to it?"

"No one knows for sure. After Peter the Great died, a note was found in his papers that said Ivan had hidden the books under the Kremlin. Napoléon, Stalin, Putin, and ordinary people have hunted for centuries, but there are at least twelve levels of tunnels down there, and the vast majority are unmapped. Its location is one of the world's great mysteries."

"Do you know what's in the library?"

"It's supposed to contain poetry and novels. Books about science, alchemy, religion, war, politics, even sex manuals.

It dates all the way back to the ancient Greeks and Romans, so there are probably works by Aristophanes, Virgil, Pindar, Cicero, and Sun Tzu. There are Bibles and Torahs and Korans, too. All sorts of languages—Latin, Hebrew, Arabic, Greek."

Tucker was quiet a moment, considering. After a rocky start as a teenager, she had righted herself to go on to a high-level career, which showed talent, brains, and responsibility. She had muted herself to fit into prison, and that indicated adaptability. Pickpocketing him because he was an aberration told him she still had nerve. He was operating in a vacuum with this mission. None of the targeting analysts had found anything useful, and the collection of Jonathan Ryder's clippings had turned out to be little help.

He studied the face beneath the prison cap, the sculpted lines, the expression that had settled back into chilly neutrality. "What would you say if I told you I have evidence the Library of Gold is very much in existence?"

"I'd say tell me more."

"The Lessing J. Rosenwald Collection has loaned some of its illuminated manuscripts to the British Museum for a special show. The highlight is *The Book of Spies*. Do you know the work?"

"Never heard of it."

"The book arrived at the reference door to the Library of Congress wrapped in foam inside a cardboard box. There was an unsigned note saying it had been in the Library of Gold and was a donation to the Rosenwald Special Collection. They tested the paper and ink and so forth. The book's authentic. No one's been able to trace the donor or donors."

"That's all the evidence you have it's from the Library of Gold?"

He nodded. "For now it's enough."

"Does this mean you want to find the library?" When he nodded, she said, "What can I do to help?"

"Opening night of the British Museum exhibit is next week. Your job would be to do what you used to do when you traveled with your husband. Talk to the librarians, historians, and afficionados who've been trying to find the library for years. Eavesdrop on conversations among them and others. We hope if *The Book of Spies* really did come from the collection it'll attract someone who knows the library's location."

She had been leaning forward. She sat back. Emotions played across her face. "What's in it for me?"

"If you do a good job, you'll return to prison of course. But then in just four months, you'll be released on parole—assuming you continue your good record. That's eight months early."

"What's the downside?"

"No downside except you'll have to wear a GPS ankle bracelet. It's tamper-resistant and has a built-in GSM/GPRS transmitter that'll automatically report your location. You can remove it at night, to make sleeping more comfortable, if you wish. I'll give you a cell phone, too. You'll report to me, and you must tell no one, not even the warden, what you'll be doing or what you learn."

She was silent. "You opened my juvenile record. You can get me out of prison. And you can reduce my sentence. Before I agree, I want to know who you really are."

He started to shake his head.

She warned, "The first price of my help is the truth."

He remembered what the warden had said about not lying to the inmates. "I'm with the Central Intelligence Agency."

"That's not in your billfold."

He reached down and un-Velcroed a pocket inside his

calf-high sock. He handed her the ID. "You must tell no one. Agreed?"

She studied the laminated official identification. "Agreed. If anyone there knows where the library is, I'll find out. But when I'm finished, I don't want to come back to prison."

Inwardly he smiled, pleased by her toughness. "Done."

Years seem to fall from her. "When do I leave?"

8

London, England

The world seemed excitingly new to Eva—no handcuffs, no prison guards, no eyes watching her around the clock. It was 8:30 P.M. and raining heavily as she hurried across the forecourt toward the British Museum. She hardly felt the cold wet on her face. London's traffic thundered behind her, and her old Burberry trench coat was wrapped around her. She looked up at the looming columns, the sheer stone walls, the Greek Revival carvings and statues. Memories filled her of the good times she and Charles had spent in the majestic old museum.

Dodging a puddle, she ran lightly up the stone steps, closed her umbrella, and entered the Front Hall. It was ablaze with light, the high ceiling fading up into dramatic darkness. She paused at the entrance to the Queen Elizabeth Great Court, two sweeping acres of marble flooring rimmed by white Portland stone walls and columned entryways. She drank in its serene beauty.

At its center stood the circular Reading Room, one of the world's finest libraries—and coming out its door were Herr Professor and Frau Georg Mendochon.

Smiling, Eva went to greet them. With glances at each other, they hesitated.

"Timma. Georg." She extended her hand. "It's been years."

"How are you, Eva?" Georg's accent was light. He was a globe-trotting academic from Austria.

"It's wonderful to see you again," she said sincerely.

"*Ja.* And we know why it has been so long." Timma had never been subtle. "What are you doing here?" What she did not say was, *You killed your husband, how dare you show up.*

Eva glanced down, staring at the gold wedding band on her finger. She had known this was going to be difficult. She had come to accept that she had killed Charles, but the guilt of it still ravaged her.

Looking up, she ignored Timma's tone. "I was hoping to see old friends. And to view *The Book of Spies,* of course."

"It is very exciting, this discovery," Georg agreed.

"It makes me wonder whether someone has finally found the Library of Gold," Eva continued. "If anyone has, surely it's you, Georg"—now that Charles is gone, she thought to herself, missing him even more.

Georg laughed. Timma relented and smiled at the compliment.

"*Ach,* I wish," he said.

"There's no word anyone's close to its discovery?" Eva pressed.

"I have heard nothing like that, alas," Georg said. "Come, Timma. We must go to the Chinese exhibit now. We will see you upstairs, Eva, yes?"

"Definitely, yes."

As they crossed the Great Hall, Eva headed toward the North Wing and climbed the stairs to the top floor. The sounds of a multilingual crowd drifted from a large open doorway where a sign announced:

TRACING THE DEVELOPMENT OF WRITING
SPECIAL EXHIBITION FROM THE
LESSING J. ROSENWALD COLLECTION

She found her invitation.

The guard took it. "Enjoy yourself, ma'am."

She stepped inside. Excited energy infused the vast hall. People stood in groups and gathered around the glass display cases, many wearing tiny earphones as they listened to the show's prerecorded tour. Museum guards in dress clothes circulated discreetly. The air smelled the way she remembered, of expensive perfumes and aromatic wines. She inhaled deeply.

"Eva, is that you?"

She turned. It was Guy Fontaine from the Sorbonne. Small and plump, he was standing with a huddle of Charles's friends. She scanned their faces, saw their conflicted emotions at her arrival.

She said a warm hello and shook hands.

"You're looking well, Eva," Dan Ritenburg decided. He was a wealthy amateur Library of Gold hunter from Sydney. "How is it you're able to be here?"

"Do not be crass, Dan," Antonia del Toro scolded. From Madrid, she was an acclaimed historian. She turned to Eva. "I am so sorry about Charles. Such a dedicated researcher, although admittedly he could be difficult at times. My condolences."

Several others murmured their sympathies. Then there was an expectant pause.

Eva spoke into it, answering their unasked question. "I've been released from prison." That was what Tucker had told her to say. "When I saw there was a manuscript from the Library of Gold here, of course I had to come."

"Of course," Guy agreed. "*The Book of Spies.* It is beautiful. *Incroyable.*"

"Do you think its appearance means someone has found the library?" Eva asked.

The group erupted in talk, voicing their theories that the library was still beneath the Kremlin, that Ivan the Terrible had hidden it in a monastery outside Moscow, that it was simply a glorious myth perpetuated by Ivan himself.

"But if it's a myth, why is *The Book of Spies* here?" Eva wanted to know.

"Aha, my point exactly," said Desmond Warzel, a Swiss academic. "I have always maintained that before he died Ivan sold it off in bits and pieces because his treasury was low. Remember, he lost his last war with Poland—and it was expensive."

"But if that's true," Eva said reasonably, "surely other illuminated manuscripts from the library would've appeared by now."

"She is right, Desmond," Antonia said. "Just what I have been telling you all these years."

They continued to argue, and eventually Eva excused herself. Listening to conversations, looking for more people she knew, she wove through the throngs and then stopped at the bar. She ordered a Perrier.

"Don't I know you, ma'am?" the bar steward asked.

He was tall and thin, but with the chubby face of a chipmunk. The contrast was startling and endearing. Of course she recalled him.

"I used to come here a few years ago," she told him.

He grinned and handed her the Perrier. "Welcome home."

Smiling, she stepped away to check the map showing where in the room each woodcut book, illuminated manuscript, and printed book was displayed. When she found the location of *The Book of Spies,* she walked toward it, passing the spectacular *Giant Bible of Mainz,* finished in 1453, and the much smaller and grotesquely illustrated *Book of Urizen,* from 1818. It was William Blake's parody of Genesis. A few years ago, on a happy winter day, Charles and she had personally examined each in the Library of Congress.

The crowd surrounding *The Book of Spies* was so thick, some on the fringes were giving up. Eva frowned, but not at the imposing human wall. What held her was a man leaving the display. There was something familiar about him. She could not see his face, because he was turned away and his hand clasped one ear as he listened to the tour.

What was it about him? She set her drink on a waiter's tray and followed, sidestepping other visitors. He wore a black trench coat, had glossy black hair, and the back of his neck was tanned. She wanted to get ahead so she could see his face, but the crowd made it hard to move quickly.

Then he stepped into an open space, and for the first time she had a clear view of his entire body, of his physicality. Her heart quickened as she studied him. His gait was athletic, rolling. His muscular shoulders twitched every six or eight steps. He radiated great assurance, as if he owned the hall. He was the right height—a little less than six feet tall. Although his hair should have been light brown, not blue-black, and she still could not see his face, everything else about him was uncannily, thrillingly familiar. He could have been Charles's double.

He dropped his hand from his ear. Excited, Eva moved quickly onward until she was walking almost parallel to him. He was surveying the crowd, his head slowly moving from right to left. Finally she saw his face. His chin was wider and heavier than Charles's, and his ears flared slightly where Charles's had laid flat against his skull. Overall he looked tough, like a man who had been on the losing end of too many fistfights.

But then his gaze froze on her. He stopped moving. He had Charles's eyes—large and black, with flecks of brown, surrounded by thick lashes. She and Charles had lived together eight intimate years, and she knew every gesture, every nuance of his expressions, and how he reacted. His eyes radiated shock, then narrowed in fear. He tilted back his head—pride. And finally there was the emotionless expression she knew so well when confronted with the unexpected. His lips formed the word *Eva*.

The room seemed to fade away, and the chattering talk vanished as she tried to breathe, to feel the beat of her heart, to know her feet were planted firmly on the floor. She struggled to think, to understand how Charles could still be alive. Relief washed through her as she realized she had not killed him. But how could he have survived the car crash? Abruptly her grief and guilt turned into stunned rage. She had lost two years because of him. Lost most of her friends. Her reputation. Her career. She had mourned and blamed herself—while he had been alive the entire time.

As he scowled at her, she pulled out her cell phone, touched the keypad, and focused the cell's video camera on him.

His scowl deepened, and with a jerk of his head, he cupped his left ear and dove into the crowd.

"Charles, wait!" She rushed after him, dodging people, leaving a trail of disgusted remarks.

He brushed past an older couple and slid deeper into the masses. She raised up on her toes and spotted him skirting a display cabinet. She ran. As he elbowed past a circle of women, his shoulder hit a waiter carrying a tray of full wineglasses. The tray cartwheeled; the glasses sailed. Red wine splashed the women. They yelled and slipped on their high heels.

While guests stared, security guards grabbed radios off their belts, and Charles dashed out the door. Eva tore after him and down the stairs. The guards shouted for them to stop. As she reached the landing, a sentry peeled away from the wall, lowering his radio.

"Stop, miss!" He raced toward her, pendulous belly jiggling.

She put on a burst of speed, and the guard had no time to correct. His hands grabbed at her trench coat and missed.

Stumbling forward, he fell across the railing, balancing precariously over the full-story drop.

She stopped to go back to help, but a man in a dark blue peacoat leaped down three steps and pulled the guard back to safety.

Cursing the time she had lost, Eva resumed her pell-mell run down the steps, the feet of guards hammering behind her. When she landed on the first floor, she accelerated past the elevators and into the cavernous Great Court. Thunder cracked loudly overhead, and a burst of rain pelted the high glass dome.

She saw Charles again. With an angry glance back at her across the wide expanse, he hurtled past a hulking statue of the head of the Egyptian pharaoh Amenhotep III.

She chased after, following him into the museum's Front Hall. Visitors fell back, silent, confused, as he rushed past. Two sentries were standing on either side of the open front door, both holding radios to their ears and looking as if they had just been given orders.

As Charles approached them, she saw his back stiffen.

His words floated back to her, earnestly telling the pair in Charles's deep voice, "She's a madwoman. . . She has a knife."

Enraged, she ran faster. The guards glanced at each other, and Charles took advantage of their distraction to lunge between them and sprint out into the stormy night.

Silently Eva swore. The two guards had recovered and were standing shoulder to shoulder, facing her, blocking the opening.

"Halt," the taller of the two commanded.

She bolted straight at them. As their eyes narrowed, she paused and slammed the heels of her hands into each man's solar plexis in *teishō* karate strikes.

Surprised, the air driven from their lungs, they staggered,

giving her just enough of an opening. In seconds she was outside. Cold rain bled in sheets from the roiling sky, drenching her, as she rushed down the stone steps.

Charles was a black sliver in the night, arms swinging as he propelled himself across the long forecourt toward the museum's entry gates.

"Dammit, Charles. Wait!"

The shriek of a police siren was growing louder, closer. Breathing hard, she raced after him and out onto Great Russell Street. Vehicles cruised past, their tires splashing dark waves of water up onto the sidewalk. Pedestrians hurried along, umbrellas open, a phalanx of bobbing rain gear.

As she slowed, looking everywhere for Charles, hands grabbed her from behind. She struggled, but the hands held fast.

"You were told to halt," a museum guard ordered, panting.

Another one ripped away her shoulder satchel.

A Metropolitan Police car screeched to the curb. Uniformed bobbies jumped out and pushed Eva against the car, patting her down. Frustrated, furious, she twisted around and saw Charles step into a taxi near the end of the block. As she stared, its red tail lights vanished into traffic.

9

The police interview room was a cramped space on a lower floor of the thirteen-story Holborn Police Station, just seven blocks from the British Museum.

"Well, there, Dr. Blake, it seems you weren't being truthful with me." Metropolitan Police Inspector Kent Collins nodded at the police guard standing in the corner, who nodded back. The inspector closed the door behind him, sealing out the world. "You told me your husband was dead. You didn't tell me you were convicted of killing him."

He was a bristly man with a large nose and, despite the late hour, smoothly shaved cheeks. Tough, impeccable, and definitely in charge, he was carrying a crisp new manila file folder under his arm.

Eva's hands were in her lap, rotating the gold wedding band on her finger. She had not been able to phone Tucker Andersen because she had not been alone since the police arrested her. His warning to tell no one about her assignment was loud in her mind. But how was she going to get out of this? Could she, even?

"I said Charles was *supposed* to be dead," she told the inspector. "If I'd filled you in on the rest, you might not have heard me out. The man I saw was Charles Sherback. My husband. Alive." Then she reminded him, "I'm not the one who lied to the museum guards. *He* did. He told them I had a knife. They searched me. There was no knife."

Inspector Collins slapped down his file folder and dropped

into a plastic chair at the end of the table next to her so they would be sitting close but at a ninety-degree angle. She recognized the technique: If you want someone to resonate with you, sit shoulder to shoulder. But if you need to challenge them, face them. The ninety-degree angle gave him flexibility.

He turned, facing her. "We're a little on the busy side to be searching among the living for a man who's dead and buried."

"Charles not only lied about the knife, he ran because he recognized me."

"Or he ran because he was some innocent bloke you were harassing."

"But then he would've complained to the guards about me."

The inspector lost his patience. "Bollocks. You—not him—assaulted the two sentries at the museum's entrance."

"I didn't have time to stop to prove I didn't have a knife and explain why I needed to catch Charles. And another thing—I have a black belt in karate. I could've hurt the guards badly. Instead I hit them just hard enough to make them step back and take deep breaths. Did either file a personal complaint?" She suspected not, since there had been no mention of it.

"As a matter of fact, no."

She nodded. "This is a lot bigger than just me. Charles is alive, and someone else must be buried in his grave. Will you please look for him?"

Inspector Collins's expression said it all—he thought she was mad. "How do you expect us to find him? You don't have an address. Nothing concrete at all."

She picked up her cell phone, touching buttons as she talked. "I shot a video of him at the museum."

Positioning the tiny screen so both could see, she started

the clip. And there was a miniature Charles, standing tall in his black trench coat against the churning background of museumgoers. He was gazing straight at her, above the angle of the cell phone, and scowling.

"You can't see his gait yet," she told him. "The way he walks is important. He's an athlete, and he moves like one, with a little bit of a slouch and a roll to his steps. His shoulders twitch periodically, too. It's really distinctive. He's also the right age and right height. The right eye color and voice, too."

In the video, Charles looked down.

"This is where he spotted my cell phone," she explained.

Charles lifted his hand to his ear, turned abruptly, and was swallowed by the crowd. Inwardly she swore. He had moved so swiftly she had no record of his walk. The video ended.

"That's it?" The inspector's focus felt like an assault. "That's all you have?"

"It's something. A beginning."

"You said other people were there whom you and your husband knew for years. If that were your husband—a dead man—they would've said something. In fact, I imagine they would've made quite a fuss." Shaking his head, the inspector opened his file, pulled out a sheet of paper, and slid it across the table. "The Los Angeles police e-mailed me this. Tell me who it is."

It was a portrait of Charles, shot for brochures for the Elaine Moreau Library. His refined features and glowing black eyes stared out at her.

"It's Charles, of course." Her voice was quiet. "After he disappeared he must've dyed his hair and had work done on his face."

The inspector jabbed a thumb at it. "This photo looks nothing like the man in your video." He gazed at her, challenging her. "I spoke to the prison. Is this the first time you thought you saw him since he died?"

She hesitated, then rallied. "Obviously you know it's not."

He pulled out another paper and read aloud: " 'In the first three weeks after Dr. Sherback died, Dr. Blake said she thought she had seen him twice. According to her account, she approached the men, who were friendly. But when she explained why she wanted to talk, they backed away.' "

The oxygen seemed to leave her lungs. "They looked similar to Charles." How could she get out of here so she could find him? She thought quickly. Then: "My husband and I were librarians and curators of ancient and medieval manuscripts. We used to fly around the world to attend openings like tonight's. Being back in that atmosphere again . . . perhaps you're right that I've made a huge mistake." She lowered her voice. "I miss him a great deal. I hope you can understand."

A flicker of compassion touched the inspector's bristly features. He peered at her, seeming to contemplate what to do.

Her entire body felt tight. She turned so her shoulder brushed his. "I'm really sorry to have caused so much trouble."

"Maybe you want him to be alive so you don't have to carry the guilt for what you've done," he said.

She gave him the answer he wanted to hear. "Yes."

There was pity in his tired eyes. Shrugging, he got to his feet. He pulled her passport from inside his sports coat and handed it to her. "Get on a plane tomorrow and go home. Make an appointment to see a therapist."

Eva gathered her things and followed Inspector Collins down the hall of the police station. As she listened to the breathy ventilation system, her mind kept returning to the man in the museum, the man she was certain was Charles, despite what she had told the inspector.

With each step, she reconstructed his profile, his height

and age, the shocked recognition in his eyes. As they rode the elevator down, in her mind she replayed his words to the museum guards, hearing the familiar intonation of his voice.

The inspector left her, and she continued outdoors and stopped. As she stood in the shelter of the station house's doorway, she had a vision of Charles racing away through the stormy night. She could see his arms swinging at his sides. There was something about that. Something about his hands.

That was when she remembered. She took out her cell phone. She restarted the short video, staring hard. Freezing it, she pumped up the size of the image. Charles's left hand had been sliced badly in an accident at a dig in Turkey. If this man was Charles, there should be a long scar on his hand.

She half-expected to see smooth skin. Instead, her breath caught in her throat as she spotted it—a scar snaking blue-white across the top of his thumb and hand and then disappearing up under the cuff of his trench coat. *Charles.*

She jumped up and turned to go back into the station . . . and stopped herself. There was no way the police would help her. She considered Tucker Andersen. But he probably knew about the previous times she hoped she had seen Charles. He would not believe her, either.

But she needed to report in. She dialed his number.

There was no preamble. "What did you learn?" he asked instantly.

"I couldn't find anyone who knew anything new about the Library of Gold," she told him truthfully. "All of them have the usual theories."

"Pity. Go back to the museum tomorrow. Spend the day."

"Of course." She had bought herself some time.

Opening her umbrella, she walked through the sidewalk's

lamplight, trying to gather her thoughts. Her marriage to Charles had not been perfect, but whose relationship ever was? With his death, the problems had vanished from her mind. She had loved him dearly, and she had thought he loved her. Fourteen years older, he was already celebrated in his career when they met. She remembered his walking into the classroom that first time; the long, confident strides. The handsome face that radiated intelligence and curiosity. He was the guest lecturer for an upper-division course where she was the assistant while working on her Ph.D. Quoting from Homer and Plato, he had charmed and impressed everyone.

"*Gratias tibi ago,* Dr. Sherback. *Benigne ades,*" she had told him. Thank you. It was generous of you to come.

The crowd of admirers had dwindled away to just him and her.

He had peered down at her, taking her in. Then he spoke in Latin, too. "You remind me of Diana, goddess of the hunt, the moon, and protectress of dewy youth. Tell me, do you have an oak grove and a deer nearby?"

She laughed. "And my bow and arrow."

"Ah, yes, but then you're not only a huntress but an emblem of chastity. No wonder you need your weapons. I hope you won't turn me into a stag as you did Acteon." The goddess had transformed Acteon when he saw her bathing naked in a stream, then set her hunting dogs on him.

"You are completely safe," she assured him. "I have no dogs, not even a teacup poodle."

He laughed, his eyes crinkling with good humor. "I like a woman who can speak Latin and who knows the ancient gods and goddesses. Will you join me for a cup of coffee?"

Colleagues, critics, and art lovers had admired him, and women had thrown themselves at him. But she was the one who had caught him. She had never suspected she was marrying a man who could pretend to be dead and send her to prison. But then, she like many others had been dazzled by him, by their lifestyle, and by her own dreams and ambitions.

As she moved along the street, the rain was a constant tattoo on her umbrella. She must find Charles. All she had was the short video. The inspector was right. It was not going to be enough. She took out her cell phone again and dialed Peggy Doty. Peggy had gotten back her old job at the British Library so she could be close to her boyfriend, Zack Turner, and Eva was staying with her while in London.

When Peggy's sleepy voice answered, Eva apologized, then said, "Remember the time I covered for you at the Getty when you took off for Paris to meet Zack for a few days? And the time I showed you the secret glue that's invisible and never fails? And then there was the time I blocked the sex-fiend tourist who was putting the moves on you."

There was a chuckle. "You must be desperate. What do you want?"

"It's a big favor, and I wouldn't ask if it weren't vital. I need a copy of the security videos for the museum's opening tonight. Particularly those that include the people around *The Book of Spies*."

"What?"

"And I need them now. Right away. I'm walking toward the museum. I wouldn't ask unless I really did need them." With luck, they would show Charles chatting with someone she knew. Maybe he or she would have learned something useful.

There was a long silence. Finally Peggy said, "You want me to ask Zack." He was the head of security at the museum.

"He'll do anything for you. Please phone him."

On the other end of the line, a sigh sounded loudly. "I'll call you back."

Eva thanked her, following Theobalds Road, clasping her shoulder satchel to her side. But as she walked, she had a strange feeling. She peered back. A man in a blue peacoat was striding along about thirty feet behind. His face was in shadows. The man who had saved the museum guard from toppling over the staircase had also worn a blue peacoat. She looked again, but he was gone.

She headed north onto Southampton Row, then west onto Great Russell Street, where she found herself glancing at the cars speeding past. For a few heartbeats a bronze-colored Citroën slowed and paced her; then it rushed off. Uneasily she realized she had noticed it earlier. There was no one in the passenger seat, and she had been unable to see the driver.

At last the museum was in sight. She turned onto Montague Street, which ran along the massive building's east side and connected with Montague Place. The street was just a block long, one of the narrow lanes winding through Bloomsbury. There was no traffic, although parked cars lined the sidewalk. She peered back and thought she saw movement beneath the darkness of a tall tree.

Her cell rang. It was Peggy. Swiftly she asked, "Do you have good news?"

"Honey, Zack says he can't have copies made for you. It's against the rules. I'm so sorry. Come home. It's real late."

Eva closed her eyes, disappointed. "Thanks for trying. I'm sorry I disturbed you. I hope you can get back to sleep quickly." She touched the Off button.

Trying to decide what to do next, she was heading across the street when she heard the noise of a car's engine and felt the pavement vibrate beneath her feet. She peered left. The vehicle was rushing toward her, headlights off. Terror shot through her. She accelerated, but the car angled, keeping her targeted.

Ahead was the towering iron fence that surrounded the museum. Dropping her umbrella, she slapped the strap of her satchel across her chest and sprinted. With a silent prayer, she leaped high in a *tobi-geri* jump. Her hands closed around two wet rails, and her feet found two more for a precarious foothold.

Then she looked again. The car was a bronze-colored Citroën like the one that had paced her on Great Russell Street. But who—? She stared into the windshield. Charles? Oh dear God, it *was* Charles. His thick features looked frozen, his gaze vacant, but emotion showed in his hands. They were knotted around the steering wheel as if it were a noose.

With an abrupt movement, the Citroën jumped the curb and slammed along the fence. Sparks flew. The noise of the hurtling car, of metal screeching against metal, seemed to explode inside her head. She scrambled higher. The rough iron rails shook in her hands. As she fought to hold on, the Citroën blasted past beneath, enveloping her in a stench of exhaust.

As it careened off on the rain-slicked street, she released her hold on the fence and dropped to the ground, trying to absorb the fact that Charles had just tried to kill her. Filled with horror, she sprinted, her muscles pulsing as she pumped harder and harder, Charles's cold face burned into her mind.

10

By eleven o'clock the British Museum was a dark fortress, massive and seemingly impenetrable. Surrounded by a great iron fence, it filled a full city block, dominating the narrow, quaint streets of the Bloomsbury neighborhood of London. Rain fell lightly. Nearby traffic had eased except on Great Russell Street, where it would thunder all night. There were no pedestrians in sight.

Four men in single file ran alongside the museum on Montague Place. They wore black nylon face masks and were dressed in black body suits, with large black waterproof backpacks snug against their shoulders. As they approached the iron gate, Doug Preston touched the electronic communicator on his belt. The click of the gate's lock was audible. He slipped swiftly inside, followed by the others.

The team hurried past grassy plots and open space until they reached a side door in the North Wing. It swung open, pushed by a man in a museum guard's dark blue uniform. They stepped inside, the door closed with a clang, and in unison all four pulled out towels from one another's backpacks.

"Hurry, Preston," the guard, Mark Allen Robert, said as they dried themselves. "I've bloody well got to get back."

"Is everything handled?" Preston demanded.

Robert peered nervously at his watch. "They'll be starting up rounds again through this wing in about twenty-five minutes. They'll be checking the floors and galleries for an hour. To be on the safe side you need to be back here in twenty minutes. No more. I'll control the security apparatus from downstairs." He rushed away, his flashlight beam preceding him through macabre shadows created by dim amber lamps installed high on the walls.

Silently the men changed into crepe-soled shoes. They mopped rainwater from the floor.

"We've got seventeen minutes," Preston told them quietly.

They raced off through the gloom without the benefit of flashlights. The museum's security lamps were enough, and each man had memorized the route.

But at the top of the north stairs, Preston smelled an acrid whiff of cigarette smoke. He gave a brusque hand signal that told his people to stand back. Besides being the chief of security at the Library of Gold, he was a highly regarded expert in both break-ins and wet work, and this could be a minor interruption. He hoped like hell it was minor. His orders were to go in, grab, and get out without leaving any hint that intruders had breached the museum stronghold.

Crouching, he found his nightscope, bent the neck, and aimed it around the corner until he could see. A guard, smoking languidly, was sauntering along the shadowy hallway toward them. Smoking was not allowed in the museum, so Preston thought the man likely had come up here to escape the rain, hoping no one would notice.

Preston frowned and settled back on his heels, warily watching as the guard closed in on the stairwell. He was about to signal his men to retreat to the next floor when the guard put out the cigarette, lit another, and ambled around in a semicircle to retrace his path.

Preston shook his shoulders to relieve tension. Beneath his mask, sweat greased his face. He hated not being able to take out the guard.

Another five minutes passed while the man strolled the

corridor. At last he extinguished the second cigarette, punched the button for the elevator, boarded it, and vanished.

"Ten minutes left." Preston saw his men stiffen. "We can do it."

With a snap of his wrist, he signaled, and they sprinted to the events hall where the Rosenwald collection was being exhibited. As expected, the security gate was lowered, but the light on the electronic lock was green, signaling it had been deactivated. Preston liked that—it increased the chances that the motion sensors inside the gallery had also been turned off.

Together they raised the gate three feet, slid under, and sped toward *The Book of Spies,* peeling off their backpacks. No alarms went off.

"Nine minutes," Preston said, relieved.

The high-security display cabinet had a frame of titanium without corner joints that could leak air. The top consisted of two pieces of tempered, antireflective glass, each three-sixteenths of an inch thick and fused with polyvinyl butyral, which would hold shards together and away from the manuscript if the panes shattered. The seals were made of Inconel, a nickle-alloy steel, and shaped like a C in cross section so the arms of each C fit into grooves to create a high seal. If someone did not know what they were doing, it could take hours to figure out how to open the case.

Their movements were slow but choreographed. Using special hand tools, two men opened the top seals and removed the first pane of glass and set it on the floor, while Preston and the fourth man slid a fake illuminated manuscript out of a backpack and unwrapped its covering.

As soon as the second pane of glass was hiked out, one man carefully closed the jeweled *Book of Spies* and secured it in clear archival polyester film and clear polyethylene sheeting, then wrapped it in foam. They slid it into Preston's backpack.

Keeping his breath rhythmic, Preston studied the display cabinet's interior, which had a jet-black finish. He was looking for the small pegs that indicated correct placement. Satisfied, he set down the fake book and opened it to the only two pages that were real—color copied and touched up by hand from photographs Charles Sherback had taken during the evening's showing. There were small seams where the pages had been glued into the book, but unless someone examined them closely, they were unnoticeable.

When he looked up, his men were wearing their backpacks. As he slung on his, the first two returned the panes of glass and closed the seals.

With a burst of satisfaction, he checked his watch. "Four minutes."

One man chuckled; another laughed. Preston gave an experienced look around to make certain they had left nothing behind, and they raced away.

11

As the Citroën sped around the corner, Judd Ryder ran up the narrow street, following Eva Blake as she raced into the falling mist. Working for Tucker Andersen, he was in London to keep an eye on her and had learned two important pieces of information: First, she was alert to her surroundings—several times she had glanced over her shoulder, indicating she sensed she was being tailed. She had definitely spotted him once. And second, the man she believed to be her husband had just tried to kill her.

Still running, she hurled something beneath a bush. He looked and saw a faint glitter. Scooping up a wedding band and a pendant on a gold chain, he dropped them into his jacket pocket and accelerated past the Montague Hotel and around the corner. Traffic cruised past, and a scattering of people were on the sidewalks. He spotted her as she dashed into Russell Square Gardens.

Darting between cars, he entered the garden park, a manicured city block of lawns and winding walkways beneath the branching limbs of old trees. Although April had turned chilly, the trees had leaves, creating black swaths where not even the park's ornate lampposts could shed light.

Blake was nowhere in sight. But he saw the Citroën on the east side of the park with the other traffic. It was circling. He took out his mobile and dialed her number.

A woman's breathless voice answered. "Tucker?"

He knew she thought only Tucker had her phone number.

"My name is Judd Ryder. Tucker sent me to help. I've been following you—"

She hung up on him.

Swearing, Ryder hurried along a path, checking the shadows. Had he just seen movement near the Garden Café, inside the square's north-east corner? He stepped behind a tree. For a few seconds a wraith in a tan trench coat flitted in and out of the café's dark shadows. It was Eva Blake.

He kept pace as she exited through the park's wrought-iron gates and slipped behind an old-fashioned cabman's shelter to hide as the Citroën passed and turned west. As it continued around the park again, she ran across the busy intersection toward the historic Russell Hotel.

He left the park, too. She slowed as she passed the hotel and wove through the throngs around the Russell Square Underground Station.

Stepping off the curb, he sprinted along the gutter. Once he was in front of her, he hid in the lee of the *Herald-Tribune* newspaper stand and pulled out his black watch cap. As Blake rushed past, he grabbed her arm and used her momentum to swing her close.

"I'm Judd Ryder. I just called you—"

"Let go of me." She yanked so hard he almost lost his grip.

Her hair was rain-soaked, plastered against her skull, and her mascara had run, settling in dirty half moons under her eyes and gray dribbles down her cheeks. But it was her cobalt blue eyes that held him. They radiated fear—and defiance.

"I've got to get you out of here," he ordered.

She abruptly leaned away and slammed out a foot in an expert *yoko-keage* side snap kick. He stepped back swiftly, and the brunt of her blow hit only the loose front of his peacoat. Surprised to lose impact, she teetered and banged into his chest. Her hands pressed against him.

He jerked her upright and shoved his wool cap at her. "Put this on. Stick your hair up inside it. We've got to change your appearance—unless you'd rather risk your husband finding you again. Take off your trench coat. If you do exactly what I tell you, I may be able to get you out of here."

As commuters moved around them, she remained motionless. "Are you really working with Tucker?" she demanded.

"*For* him. Just like you are. That's why I have your cell phone number."

"That means nothing. Why didn't he tell me about you?"

"I'll explain later." He grabbed the watch cap and jammed it down onto her head and began to unbutton her trench coat.

"I'll take it off myself, dammit." She slipped off the strap of her satchel and shrugged out of the coat.

Catching both before they hit the ground, he rolled the coat into a ball so only the olive-green lining showed. She was wearing a black tailored jacket, a black turtleneck sweater, and tight low-slung jeans tucked into high black boots. Her dark clothing would help her to blend with the night.

"Push your hair up under the cap." As she did, he returned her satchel. "Take my arm as if you liked me."

Warily she slid her arm inside his. As they walked, he patted her hand. It was ice-cold and tense. He dropped her trench coat into a trash receptacle.

She started to turn.

"Don't look back," he warned. "Let's keep the opportunities for your husband to see your face at a minimum."

As they continued on, the number of pedestrians lessened, which was both good and bad. Good because they could make quicker progress. Bad because she was easier to spot. He produced a palm-size mirror, cupped it in his hand, and examined the cars approaching from behind.

"I don't see the Citroën," he reported. "You're shivering. Button your jacket. We'll find someplace warm to talk."

"What did you say your name was?" She buttoned her jacket up to her throat.

There was no trust in her voice, but all he needed was her cooperation. "Judd Ryder." He reached inside his open peacoat for his billfold. His hand came out empty. Instantly he remembered her side snap kick and that she had bumped into him, her hands on his chest. Tucker had been right—she was a damn good pickpocket.

She pulled the wallet from her satchel, looked inside, and checked his Maryland driver's license, credit cards, and membership cards.

"Nothing says CIA." She returned the billfold.

"I'm covert."

"Then your name might not really be Judson Clayborn Ryder."

"It is. Son of Jonathan and Jeannine Ryder. Cousin to many."

"Credentials can be forged."

"Mine aren't. Here's an interesting idea—try being grateful. I'm the one helping you get away from your husband."

"If you really wanted to help me, why didn't you do something to stop Charles when he tried to run me down? You could've at least used your gun to shoot out his tires."

So she had found his Beretta. "It's a myth shooting rounds into tires makes them explode."

"Do you think Charles will try to kill me again?"

"Considering he was circling the park, I'd say he appears enthused about the idea."

Her expression froze, and she looked away.

As they turned onto Guilford Street, she asked, "Are you the one who saved the museum guard who almost fell over the stair rail?"

"He needed some help. I was lucky to be close."

She took a deep breath. "I'm glad you did."

They passed a row of businesses, all closed. Sitting cross-legged on the sidewalk in front of one was a homeless man, a dingy beach umbrella sheltering him and, in front of him, a hand-lettered sign:

MY DOG AND I ARE HUNGRY. PLEASE HELP.

Suddenly he felt her go rigid beside him.

"Charles!" she whispered.

With his peripheral vision, he caught sight of the Citroën approaching from behind.

"There's no time to run," he told her quietly. "Look at me and smile. Look at me! We're just an ordinary couple out for a stroll." He put his arm around her shoulders, took her over to the beggar, and dropped a two-pound coin into the man's hand. "Where's your dog?" he asked, playing for time as the car approached.

"I have a dog?" The man's words were slurred. He stank of cheap wine.

"Says so on the sign." He saw that the Citroën was nearly beside them.

"Bollocks. I left the bloody dog at home. Must be losin' my friggin' mind." The two-pound coin vanished into the man's pocket, and he stared blankly ahead as the Citroën rolled safely past.

Ryder peered down at Blake. "Our guests will be arriving soon, dear. We'd better head home."

She gave a curt nod, and they hurried on.

12

The Lamb public house at 94 Lamb's Conduit Street was a classic old-school pub with dark woods, smoke-brown walls, and an ornate U-shaped bar topped with rare snob screens that pivoted to provide a customer with a modicum of privacy. The dusky air was pungent with the rich aromas of fine ales and lagers.

Relieved to be safely off the street, Eva cleaned her face in the bathroom and settled into a banquette at the back. She watched Judd Ryder at the bar, his long frame leaning into it as he waited for their orders and surveyed the room. The clientele crowded around the bar, shoes propped up on the foot rail. Ryder and she had attracted only a moment's notice, and now no one was looking at her, including Ryder.

If she had learned one lesson in prison, it was survival required suspicion. He had thrown his peacoat onto the leather seat. She searched the inner pockets. There were a couple of felt-tipped pens, his small mirror, a granola bar, a fat roll of cash, and a London tube schedule. She returned everything but the schedule and was just about to check whether he had made any notes on it when he picked up her tea tray from the bar. Instantly she shoved the schedule back inside his coat.

He walked toward her, his stride long. He was dressed in jeans, a dark blue polo shirt, and a loose corduroy jacket. She could not quite make out the shoulder holster that held his gun. His square face was weathered and had a rugged outdoor quality, as if it had been formed more by life than biology. His hands were large and competent, but his dark gray eyes were unreadable. He was athletic and obviously familiar with karate, otherwise he would not have been able to dodge her blow. He could easily be telling her the truth—or not.

She hid her tension and smiled. "Thanks. It smells delicious."

"Lapsang souchong tea, as requested. Heated milk and a warm cup, too." He put the tray down. "Drink. You're shivering."

As he headed back to the bar to fetch his stout, she grabbed the tube schedule and inspected it. There were no marks or notes. Next she examined the peacoat's outside pockets. Frowning, she discovered an electronic reader for some kind of tracking device. A small handheld computer with GPS capabilities, it was similar to those she had assembled in the prison's electronics factory. Tracking devices could be used to keep tabs on anything, while readers like this displayed an array of information sent from the bug.

She looked up. The bartender was setting a full pint glass in front of Ryder, and he was paying the bill. She had little time. Her fingers flew as she touched buttons, and the handheld's screen came to colorful life. She saw he was tracking two bugs. She keyed onto the first. Schematics flashed and coalesced into a map of London, showing a location: Le Méridien Hotel in the West End. She was not familiar with the hotel, and she did not have time to check the other bug. She slid the handheld back into his peacoat.

He was heading toward her, pint in hand, staring. As he stopped at the table, she saw his face had done a strange shift, revealing something hard and a little frightening.

She patted then smoothed his peacoat. "Forgive me. My

nose is starting to run. I was just going to look for a tissue." The condition of her nose was true.

Without comment he took a handkerchief from his pocket, handed it to her, and sat with his pint of oatmeal stout.

"Thanks." She blew her nose, then wrapped her hands around her hot cup of tea. "When Charles and I visited London, we sometimes came here. In case you don't know, Charles Dickens, Virginia Woolf, and the Bloomsbury Group were regulars. Editors and writers still show up. The pub seemed to us the epitome of old Bloomsbury, the beating heart of London's literary world."

"You're feeling better," he decided.

She nodded. "Why didn't Tucker tell me about you?"

"You're not trained, and we wanted you to act normally. Some people can't handle being watched over. You wouldn't have known how you'd react, and we wouldn't have known either, until you were actually in the museum. There was only one opening night, and we were doing everything we could to maximize your chances of success."

"Is your name really Judd Ryder?"

"Yes. I'm a CIA contract employee. Tucker brought me in for the job."

"Then you're working for Catapult." Tucker had told her about his unit, which did counteroperations. "Why you?"

Ryder gazed down into his glass then looked up, his expression somber. "My father and Tucker were friends in college. They joined the CIA at the same time, then Dad left to go into business. A couple of weeks ago he asked Tucker to meet him in a park on Capitol Hill. Just the two of them. It was late at night. . . A sniper killed Dad."

Seeing the pain in his eyes, she sank back. "That's terrible. I'm so sorry. It must've been awful for you."

"It was."

She thought a moment. "But murder is a job for the police."

"Dad was trying to warn Tucker about something that had to do with a multimillion-dollar account in an unnamed international bank—and Islamic terrorism."

"Terrorism?" Her brows rose with alarm. "What kind of terrorism? Al-Qaeda? One of their offshoots? A new group?"

"We don't know yet, but he appeared worried some disaster was about to happen. Dad had collected news clippings about jihadism in Pakistan and Afghanistan, but so far they don't make a lot of sense. Of course Catapult is staying on top of international bank activity. The only real detail is where you come in—Dad said he'd discovered the information in the Library of Gold."

"*In* the library? Then the library really does exist."

"Yes. Dad also told Tucker some kind of book club owns it."

"Was your father in the book club?"

He shrugged uneasily. "I don't know yet."

"If your father was a member of the book club, it sounds to me as if he had a secret life."

He nodded grimly. "Just like your husband's."

She leaned forward. "You want to find out what your father was doing and who's behind his death."

"Damn right I do." Anger flashed across his face.

"Why didn't Tucker tell me any of this?"

"You didn't have need-to-know, and we thought your assignment would be simple."

"Both of us have personal reasons to find the library, but this is on a whole different level. So much bigger."

"It *is* personal for both of us." He set down his glass, put his hand into his jacket pocket, and slid her gold wedding band and necklace across the table. "I thought you might want these back."

Staring at them, she moved her hands away from her cup

and dropped them into her lap. "I don't need them anymore. That was another life. Another person."

He studied her. Then he scooped up the jewelry and returned it to his pocket. "Tell me about Charles and the car crash."

"He was driving us home on Mulholland after a dinner party, and—" She stopped. In her mind she went back over the trip—Charles's carefree laughter, his playful weaving of the car back and forth across the deserted road. . . She told Ryder about it. Then: "A car shot out from a driveway ahead, and Charles slammed on the brakes. Our car careened. I was nauseated and dizzy. And I lost consciousness. The next thing I knew, I woke up on a gurney." She hesitated. "Charles must've given me some kind of drug. Later the coroner found his wedding ring on the corpse, and the corpse's teeth matched Charles's dental records."

"That shows a lot of planning, money, and dirty resources. Could Charles have pulled it off alone?"

"No way. He was an academic. Someone had to have helped him."

"Who?"

She mulled. "I don't know anyone who could have."

"Where do you think he's been?"

"God knows. He's got a good tan, so it's someplace sunny."

"What kind of man was he?"

"Dedicated. Our world's small. Only a few thousand people are well-educated about illuminated manuscripts. Maybe a hundred are true experts. Most of us know one another in varying degrees. I suppose to outsiders we seem peculiar. We play card games from Greek and Roman times, and we have our own trivia contests. Our conversations can seem funny—we use Latin and Greek, for instance. Charles was considered by some to be the top authority on the Library of Gold. He was immersed in it, lived it, ached for it, and that's why he was so knowledgeable. It would've been hard for him to live with anyone who couldn't appreciate that in him."

"And you did?"

"Yes. It made sense to me."

He nodded. "Could his disappearance have been related to the library?"

"He was working awfully long hours before the car crash. He might've had some insight or uncovered something and felt he needed to disappear so no one would be tipped off while he closed in."

She followed Ryder's gaze as he surveyed the old pub. The polished brass fixtures glinted. A few customers had left; a few more had entered.

"I shot about an hour of video of the people around *The Book of Spies,"* he told her. "If there's a cyber café open at this hour, we can look at it together."

She pulled her satchel to her. "We don't have to go anywhere. I have my laptop with me."

They moved around the U-shaped banquette so they were sitting next to each other. As she put her computer on the table and turned it on, he produced a palm-size video camera, USB cord, and software disk from his jacket pockets.

Within minutes they were viewing the exhibition. Ryder fast-forwarded until Charles appeared. She pointed out Charles's striking walk, described the changes he had made in his appearance, and identified the other people she recognized. But Charles spoke to no one, and no one spoke to Charles. And at no time did she see Charles make eye contact with anyone.

"That's interesting," Ryder murmured. He stopped the film and replayed it in several places. Although earlier he had been recording from a distance, he now was shooting close to the exhibit. "Look at how Charles is inching around the display case. Check out his right hand."

She focused on the hand. Charles was holding it near his waist, cupped casually. The hand rose and fell as he moved, and his thumb twitched.

She stared. "Is he secretly photographing *The Book of Spies*?"

"Appears to be. But why? The addiction of a wacko bibliomaniac?"

"Or it could have something to do with the Library of Gold—but what?"

"My question, too." He checked his watch. "It's late. We should go. You're staying with your friend Peggy Doty." He frowned. "Would Charles know that?"

Her throat went dry. She grabbed her cell and dialed.

At last there was a sleepy answer. "Hello?"

"Peggy, it's Eva again. You've got to get out of there. I know it sounds impossible, but I saw Charles tonight at the museum."

Peggy's voice was suddenly alert. "What are you talking about?"

"I saw Charles at the show. He's as alive as you or me."

"That's crazy. Charles is dead, dear. Remember, you thought you saw him before. He's *dead*. Come home. We'll talk about it."

Eva tightened her grip on the cell phone. "Charles tried to kill me. He knows I stay with you. You could be in danger. You've got to leave. Go to a hotel, and I'll meet you. Even if you don't believe me, just do this for me, Peggy."

When they decided on the Chelsea Arms, Peggy volunteered, "I'll make the room reservation for us."

Suddenly exhausted, Eva agreed and ended the connection.

Ryder drained his glass. "I'll have Tucker check into the identity of the man in Charles's grave and give you a status report in the morning." He related his mobile number and where he was staying.

They stood. As she slung her valise over her shoulder, he dropped his camera equipment into his jacket pockets and shoved his arms into his peacoat. Heading for the door, they skirted the drinkers at the bar and stepped out into the night. Glistening drops of rain floated in the lamplight.

"Will you be all right?" He hailed a taxi for her.

"I'll be a lot better once we've found Charles."

As a cab stopped at the curb, he gave her a reassuring smile. "Get a good night's sleep." Then to the taximan: "The Chelsea Arms."

She climbed in. As the cab cruised off, she turned in her seat to watch what Ryder would do. He was walking in the opposite direction. Pulling out his electronic reader, he seemed to be studying it. Finally he lifted his head and caught a taxi for himself. Glancing at the bug reader again, he climbed inside.

Suspicion flooded her. She leaned forward. "I've changed my mind. Turn around. Take me to the Méridien hotel on Piccadilly."

13

Charles Sherback knew he had made a terrible mistake. He dropped off the Citroën at the car rental agency and caught a taxi, his mind in tumult. Ovid was right: *Res est ingeniosa dare.* "Giving requires good sense." And he had not simply "given"; he had sacrificed for Eva. In fact, he had risked a great deal for her.

As the windshield wiper slashed across the glass, he stared out unseeing at the rainy London night. She was supposed to be in prison. How could she have been at the British Museum show? And now he had failed to eliminate her.

"We're here, guv'nor." The taxi driver peered into his rearview mirror. He had white hair, a sagging face, and tired eyes that thankfully remained bored.

Charles paid and stepped out of the cab and into the noisy din of Piccadilly. As cars and trucks rushed past on the boulevard, he dodged pedestrians and strode into the five-star Le Méridien Hotel, hoping Preston was not early.

He peered around. The lobby was spacious, two stories high, topped by an intricate stained-glass dome. The appointments were modern and refined, and the air smelled of fresh flowers. The hotel was elegant, just the way he liked it. It was also busy with people.

At the elevator, he stepped inside and punched the button for the eighth floor. The elevator rose with maddening slowness. As soon as the doors opened he ran along the hall, jammed his electronic key into the lock, and marched into the deluxe room. The window drapes were closed against prying eyes, and a hot pot of coffee was waiting on the low table in front of two upholstered chairs. There was no sign of Preston.

"Hello, darling." Sitting on the end of the king-size bed, Robin Miller clicked off the television. "I'm glad you're back. Are you okay?"

A moment of happiness flowed through him. "I'm fine." He peeled off his wet raincoat.

"Is she dead?"

Thick ash-blond hair wreathed Robin's face and draped in thick bangs down to her green eyes. Her mouth was lush and round, and her skin glowed with a ruddy tan. She was thirty-five years old. On the director's orders, all staff members had plastic surgery before they could go to work at the library. He had seen photographs of Robin from those days, and she was even more beautiful now.

"There were complications." He shook his head with disgust. "Eva got away."

She stared worriedly. "Are you going to tell the director she recognized you?"

He fell into a reading chair and poured a cup of steaming coffee. "It's safer for me to take care of the problem myself." He added sugar, then cream until the color turned to that of café au lait. He wished he had some good Irish whiskey to add.

"But what will you do?"

"I have to kill her." He heard the determination in his voice. He had come this far, and he had no choice. From the moment he had accepted the job of chief librarian at the Library of Gold, his lot was cast. He remembered the sense of destiny fulfilled. He had faced reality, banished any regrets, and thrown himself into his exciting new life.

"Maybe you should ask Preston for help."

He gave an abrupt shake of his head. "He'll tell the director."

They were silent, acknowledging the threat of it. He saw her hands were turning white from gripping the edge of the bed. He went to her and pulled her close. She laid her head on his shoulder. Her warmth flowed into him.

"I'm frightened," she whispered.

Robin was a strong woman. Until now she had not admitted being afraid. Because she had not told the director instantly, she could be in as much trouble as he.

"This is all Eva's fault," he assured her. "We wouldn't be in this mess if she hadn't recognized me. I love you. Remember that. I love you."

"I love you, too, darling." She wrapped her arms around him. "But you're not a killer. You don't know how to do such things. As long as Eva's alive, she's dangerous to the library—and to us. You need to tell Preston so he can take care of her. If you don't want to, I'll do it."

Four taps sounded on the door.

"Preston's here." She pulled away. "Give me a minute."

"Hurry."

She nodded and stood up, smoothing her hair and straightening her white cashmere sweater and brown trousers.

He crossed to the door, reaching it as another four taps began. He peered through the peephole. A distorted Doug Preston loomed in the hallway, a bulging backpack in his left hand. His right hand was hidden inside his black leather jacket, where he kept his pistol holstered. Everything about him, from his slightly bent knees to the sharp vigilance with which he was checking the corridor, seemed to radiate menace.

Charles took a deep breath and opened the door, and Preston strode into the room. Uneasily Charles watched as he scanned the interior. When he paused to peer at Robin, she nodded in greeting, her eyes wary. Charles focused on the backpack. He could postpone deciding whether to tell Preston about Eva because its contents were of immediate concern.

"You have *The Book of Spies*?" he demanded.

"I do." Preston set the pack on a chair and started to unzip it.

"I'll take over now."

Preston stepped back.

As Robin joined them, Charles removed the foam bundle. "Move the coffee, Robin. Leave the napkins."

She picked up the tray and carried it away. Although the table appeared clean, he used the linen napkins to wipe it. Then he set down the bundle and unpeeled layers of foam and transparent polyethylene sheeting. At last only archival polyester film remained.

He paused, feeling a visceral reaction. His throat full, he gazed at the illuminated manuscript glowing through the clear protective barrier.

"Ready?" He lowered himself into the reading chair and looked up.

Preston nodded.

"Hurry," Robin said.

He unfastened the polyester and let it fall to the sides.

"Oh, my Lord," Robin breathed.

"It's a beauty, all right," Preston agreed.

Charles stared, drinking in the sight of the fabled *Book of Spies,* compiled on orders of Ivan the Terrible, who had been fascinated by spies and assassins. Covered in gold, the volume was large, probably ten by twelve inches and four inches thick, decorated with fat emeralds, great rubies, and lustrous pearls—a fortune in gems. The emeralds were arranged along the edges of the cover, a rectangular frame of brilliant green. The pearls were gathered into the shape of a glowing dagger in the top two thirds, and beneath the dagger's point lay the scarlet rubies, shaped like a large drop of blood. The jewels caught the lamplight and sparkled like fire.

Awed silence filled the room. Robin handed Charles clean white cotton gloves. Putting them on, he opened the book and slowly turned pages, savoring the style, the paint, the ink, the feel of the fine parchment between his cautious fingers. Each page was a showcase of lavish pictures, austere Cyrillic letters, and intricate borders ablaze with color. He felt a thrill at the effort involved not only in gathering the knowledge but in creating such art.

"Six years of painstaking labor went into this masterwork," Charles told them. "Twelve months a year, seven days a week, twelve to fourteen hours a day. The crudest brushes and paints. Only sunlight and oil lamps to work by. No good heating during the brutal Moscow winters. The constant attack of mosquitoes in summer. Imagine the difficulty, the dedication."

Robin sat on the floor and leaned an elbow on the table to be closer. Preston pulled up a chair and sat, watching the turning pages. The paintings showed secretive spies, rotund diplomats, monarchs in furs, soldiers in colorful uniforms, villains with wily faces. It was a rich compendium of stories about real and mythical assassins, spies, and missions since before biblical times.

"You're sure it's authentic?" Robin asked in a low, excited voice.

"The style's correct, tending toward naturalism," Charles told her. "The final touches are in liquid gold—not gold leaf." Naturalism and liquid gold appeared only at the end of the Middle Ages, which matched the year the manuscript was finished in Moscow—1580. "What clinches its authenticity are the tiny letters beneath some of the colors. See? They're almost invisible. Even the best forgers forget that telling detail."

He pointed without touching the page. The letters stood for the Latin words for the colors the long-ago artist had been instructed to use to fill in the line drawings, which had been rendered by a previous artist. *R* for *ruber*, meaning red; *V* for *viridis*, meaning green; and *A* for *azure*, meaning blue.

"It was painted by an Italian who was working in Ivan's court," Charles explained.

"I remember the book well," Preston said. "The stories about spies are inspiring. Those who find the secrets and take them to their graves are the real heroes. That's what we signed on for when we went to work for the Library of Gold. Complete loyalty."

As Preston talked, Robin stared at Charles. Her eyebrows knitted together with determination, and her lips thinned. The message was clear: If he did not tell Preston, she would.

"We've got a problem." Charles steeled himself as Preston focused on him.

"There's no reason for the director to know about it, Preston," Robin urged. "You can handle it."

Preston did not look at her. "What's happened, Charles?"

He sighed heavily. "It started in the museum. I'd just finished photographing *The Book of Spies* and was walking away when I noticed Eva. My wife. God knows how she got out of prison, but she was there, and she recognized me." He rushed on, describing the chase through the museum and her arrest. "I rented a car. When the police released her, I followed and found a quiet street. Then I was almost able to run her down. But she got away. I drove everywhere, looking for her again."

"Does she know about the Library of Gold?" Preston asked instantly.

"Of course not. I never talked with her."

"What else?"

"She recorded me on her cell phone," he admitted. "I don't know whether it was photos or a video."

"Please don't tell the director, Preston," Robin pleaded.

Preston was silent. Tension filled the room.

Charles rubbed his eyes and sank back in his chair. When he looked again, Preston had not moved, his gaze unreadable.

"Where would she stay in London?" Preston demanded.

"There were two hotels we preferred—the Connaught and the Mayflower. When she came alone, she stayed with a friend, Peggy Doty. At the museum I overheard a conversation that Peggy had moved back to London. I don't have her address, but my guess is Eva's with Peggy. They were close."

Preston tapped a number into his cell. "Eva Blake may be staying at one of these hotels." He related the information. "I'll e-mail you her photograph. Terminate her. She has a cell phone. It's imperative you get it." He ended the connection, then told Charles, "I'll handle Peggy Doty myself."

As Preston walked toward the door, Charles rose to his feet. He was sweating. "Are you going to tell the director?"

Preston said nothing. The door closed.

14

As he drove toward Peggy Doty's apartment, Preston reveled in having pulled off the complex mission of recovering *The Book of Spies*. It had been like the old days when he was a CIA officer working undercover in hot spots across Europe and the old Soviet Union. But when the cold war had ended, Langley had lost the support of Congress, the White House, and the American people to properly monitor the world. Disgusted and heartbroken, he had resigned. By the time of the 9/11 attacks, when everyone realized intelligence was critical to U.S. security, he had committed himself to something larger, something more enduring. Something far more relevant, almost eternal—the Library of Gold.

Fury washed through him. Charles was self-important, and self-importance was always a liability. He had put the library in danger.

Preston speed-dialed the director.

"Did you get *The Book of Spies*?" Martin Chapman's voice was forceful, his focus instant, although it was past four A.M. in Dubai. The tirelessness of the response was typical, just one of the reasons Preston admired him.

"The book is safe. On the jet soon. And Charles has verified it's genuine."

As Preston had hoped, there was delight in the director's voice: "Congratulations. Fine work. I knew I could count on you. As Seneca wrote, 'It matters not how many books one has, but how good they are.' I'm eager to see it again. Everything went smoothly?"

"One small problem, but it's handleable. Charles's wife is out of prison and was at the museum opening. She recognized him, made a scene, and got herself arrested. Charles tried to run her down. Of course he failed. I'm driving to the apartment where he thinks she's staying. I just found out about all of this."

"The bastard should've reported it immediately. Robin was aware?"

"Yes." The library's rules were inviolate. Everyone knew that. It was one of the prime reasons the library had remained invincible—and invisible—over the centuries.

The director's tone was cold, unforgiving: "Kill Eva Blake. I'll decide later what to do about Charles and Robin."

Preston parked near St John Street in the hip Clerkenwell neighborhood, around the block from Peggy Doty's apartment building. As he got out of the Renault, he pulled the brim of his Manchester United football cap low. The rich scent ofVietnamese coffee drifted from a lighted café, infusing the night. The historic area was full of a young, smart crowd involved in themselves and the evening's entertainment.

Satisfied he was clean, Preston walked quickly back to Peggy Doty's apartment building and tried the street door. It was locked. Finally a woman emerged. Catching the door before it could close, he slipped inside and climbed the stairs.

Peggy Doty answered his knock instantly, and it was clear why—she was ready to leave. She wore a long wool overcoat, and a suitcase stood on the floor beside her. Her apartment was dark and silent, indicating no one else was there.

He had to decide what to do. When he was much younger, he would have threatened her to find out where Blake was.

But there was an intelligent, steely look about her that warned him she might lie, and if he killed her too soon, it would be too late to go back to her for the truth.

He put a warm smile on his face. "You must be Peggy Doty. I'm a friend of Eva's. My name's Gary Frank. I'm glad I'm here in time. Eva thought you might like a ride."

Peggy frowned. "Thanks a lot, Mr. Frank, but I've already called a cab." She was a small woman, with short brown hair and eyeglasses sliding down her nose. Her face was open, the face of someone people automatically liked.

"Please call me Gary." Since she had not asked how Blake knew she was leaving, it was evident they were in touch. "You live in a great neighborhood. Didn't Peter Ackroyd and Charles Dickens use Clerkenwell for settings in their novels?" He gave her a conspiratorial wink. "I'm a used-book dealer."

Her face brightened. "Yes, they did. Maybe you're thinking about Ackroyd's *The Clerkenwell Tales*. That's a terrific piece of fiction about fourteenth-century London. The clerk at Tellson's bank in *A Tale of Two Cities* lived here, too. His name was Jarvis Lorry. And Fagin's lair was also in the Clerkenwell area."

"*Oliver Twist* is a favorite of mine. Eva says you work at the British Library. I'd like to hear what you do. Please let me drive you."

She hesitated.

He stepped into the silence. "Did you tell Eva you were calling a cab?"

She sighed. "Nope, I didn't. All right. This is really great of you."

He picked up her suitcase, and they left.

With Peggy Doty at his side, Preston drove south, heading for the hotel in Chelsea where she would meet Blake. Blake might already be there, and he wanted this small brunette with him to ensure he got access to the room without drawing attention to himself.

"So Eva sounded upset to you, too?" he prodded.

Her hands were folded in her lap, pale against her midnight blue coat. "She says her dead husband's alive. That she actually saw him. Can you believe it? I'm hoping she'll have recovered her brain by the time we get there."

"I'm sure she will," he said, and they drove on in silence.

At last he parked, tugged the brim of his cap low over his eyes, and walked with her into the hotel, carrying her suitcase. As she registered, he noted she was right-handed.

"Has Ms. Blake checked in?" she asked.

"Not yet, miss."

Her face crumpled. They took the elevator up to her room. It was full of fussy chintz and the hideous line drawings of horses standing around on hills one saw in tourist hotels in London.

She peered at the emptiness. "She should've been here by now, Gary."

He laid her suitcase on the valet stand. "Would she have stopped someplace first?"

"I'll call her." She tapped a number into her cell and listened, her expression growing grim. Finally she said, "Eva, this is Peggy. Where are you? Phone as soon as you get my message." She hung up.

"Was she with anyone when you talked before? They might've gone someplace together."

"All I heard was a noisy background." She sighed heavily. "I hope she's okay."

The time had come. Fortunately because of what he had learned from her, he now had a way to liquidate Eva Blake.

"Peggy, I just want you to know you're a nice woman."

She looked at him, a surprised expression on her face. "Thanks."

"And this is just what I do." Swiftly he leaned down and removed the untraceable two-shot pistol from his ankle holster.

Staring at the gun, she took a step back. "What are you—?"

He advanced and grabbed her shoulders. She was light. "I'll make it fast."

"No!" She struggled, her fists pounding his coat.

He pressed the gun up under her chin and fired. Skull and brain matter exploded. He held her a moment, then let her fall to the floor, limp in her big coat.

Pulling on latex gloves, he cleaned his black jacket with the special tissues he always carried. As he wiped the gun, he listened at the door. There was no sound in the corridor. He ran back to her, pressed both her hands around the gun's grip and muzzle, and then put the grip into her right hand and squeezed her fingers around it.

Snatching up her cell phone, he debated with himself, then finally decided the police investigators would be suspicious if the phone were missing. He memorized Blake's cell phone number, turned off Peggy's cell, and left it in her coat pocket. Then he wiped off the handle of her suitcase, used the wipes to take the suitcase to her, pressed one hand and then the other around the handle, and laid the suitcase back on the valet stand.

Outdoors, the night seemed warm and inviting. Striding down the busy street, Preston dialed out on his cell to his men in London. "Eva Blake is due to arrive shortly at this address." He relayed the hotel's information and room number. "Terminate her."

The temperature in the room at the Méridien hotel seemed to have dropped ten degrees. As soon as Preston left, Charles had taken out his Glock and laid it on the coffee table next to *The Book of Spies*. He watched as Robin methodically packed their things. He was chilled, and his hands ached from knotting them. It seemed as if the world were shattering around him.

"You're not angry with me, are you, Charles?" she asked finally.

"Of course not. You were right—Preston will find Eva and take care of the problem. You've forgotten to scan the manuscript."

"I guess I'm a bit rattled."

She unzipped the suitcase and found the key-chain–size detector. It had a telescopic antenna that sniffed out hidden wireless cameras, audio devices, and tracking bugs. As soon as she turned it on, a red light flashed in warning.

Charles swore and sat up.

Brows knitting, she moved across the room, looking for the origin. As she approached *The Book of Spies,* the light flashed faster.

"Oh, no." Robin's face was tense.

She moved the detector over the cover of the illuminated manuscript until the light held steady. It pointed to one of the emeralds rimming the book's gold binding.

She read the digital screen. "It says there's a tracking bug in this emerald." Stricken, she peered at Charles.

"Maybe the museum or the Rosenwald Collection planted it as a security measure," he said. "No, that's insane. They'd never violate something as precious as *The Book of Spies*. It had to be someone else—but why?"

"What do we do? How can we tear off one of the jewels? We'll destroy the integrity of the book. It's sacrilege."

They stared down at the manuscript.

At last Charles decided, "The integrity has already been destroyed because that 'emerald' can't be real." He took out his pocketknife and pried off the fake jewel, leaving a gaping hole in the perfect frame of green gems.

She groaned. "It looks awful."

Sickened, he nodded, then jumped up and ran into the bathroom. He flushed the bug down the toilet.

15

Judd Ryder was puzzled. He walked west down the wide boulevard in front of the Méridien hotel and crossed Piccadilly Place, then Swallow Street, studying traffic. According to his electronic reader, *The Book of Spies* was in the middle of the boulevard, still moving, but more quickly than the vehicles. How could that be? He checked the altitude—and swore.

The bug was below ground. Sewer lines ran beneath the boulevard. Whoever had *The Book of Spies* had flushed the bug Tucker had planted on it.

He turned on his heel. It was possible the book was still in the hotel. As he hurried back, he took out his Secure Mobile Environment Portable Electronic Device—an SME-PED handheld computer. With it he could send classified e-mail, access classified networks, and make top-secret phone calls. Created under guidelines from the National Security Agency, it appeared ordinary, like a BlackBerry; and while either on or off secure mode, could be operated like any smart phone with Internet access.

Keeping it in secure mode, he speed-dialed Tucker Andersen's direct line at Catapult headquarters.

"I've been waiting to hear from you, Judd," Tucker said. "What have you learned?"

He crossed Piccadilly Street to where he could watch the hotel's entrance. He settled back into the shadows. "I've got a shocker for you. Charles Sherback didn't die in that car crash. He's still very much alive." He described what had happened in the museum, following Eva Blake from the police station, and witnessing Sherback's attempt to run her down. "The bottom line is planting *The Book of Spies* worked—we got a bite. But what it means that Sherback is alive I sure as hell don't know yet. There's another big wrinkle—*The Book of Spies* has been stolen, and the thieves dumped the bug."

Tucker's voice rose. "You don't know where the book is?"

"It may be in the Méridien hotel. The bug was there until a few minutes ago. Sherback was taking photos or making a video of the book in the museum, and the way things are going, it seems likely to me he and the book are together or he knows where it is. According to Blake, he's had cosmetic surgery. As soon as I hang up, I'll e-mail you the video I made at the Rosenwald show. I've keyed it on him. See if his new face is in any of our data banks. And find out who's buried in his grave in L.A. That could lead us to whoever helped him disappear."

"I'll make both priorities."

"You also need to know I had to tell Blake I'm working for you and the connection to Dad and the Library of Gold."

There was a pause. "I understand. What do you think of her?"

"She seems as functional as you or me. She's smart and tough."

"She's also beautiful and athletic. And vulnerable. Just your type. Don't like her too much, Judd."

Ryder said nothing. Tucker had researched him more than he realized.

When Ryder continued, his voice was brusque. "Blake is going to a hotel for the night. Whether I do anything more with her depends on what I find out next."

"With luck you can send her home," Tucker decided. "She did a good job, but I don't like employing amateurs."

Ryder wanted to see her again, but Tucker was right. It

would be better for her if he did not. He had a lousy track record for keeping those he cared about alive. As he thought about it, he checked the other bug his reader was tracking—it was moving, too, but not toward Chelsea. It was headed north . . . toward him?

16

Dressed in their black trench coats, Robin and Charles took the elevator down to the hotel's garage. From there they walked up a driveway and out into a shadowy cobblestone alley. Pulling their big roll-aboard suitcase, Robin glanced at Charles, who was looking handsome and intense. He wore the backpack in which *The Book of Spies* was secured, his hands gripping the pack's straps possessively.

They emerged onto the boulevard, away from the vast hotel and its bright lights. Side by side they continued on, at last stopping where Preston had told them to wait.

"I'd hoped Preston would be here by now." Charles stared at the traffic. "Maybe it's taken him longer to find Peggy than he thought."

"Are you all right?"

He took her hand and kissed it. "I'm fine. How are you?"

"Oddly, I'm fine, too." And she meant it.

A sense of inevitability had settled inside her. It was not simply that Preston had taken on the job of getting rid of Eva, or that she had high hopes Preston would not tell the director, but that some old resource—courage, perhaps, touched with foolhardiness—had risen to return her confidence. Whatever happened, she would figure out a way to handle it.

Charles focused on her. "Does Preston strike you as an *abnormis sapiens crassaque Minerva*?" An unorthodox sage of rough genius.

"He does. But then he's also a *helluo librorum*." A bookworm, a devourer of books. "Do you think we can trust him?"

"We don't have a choice."

They straightened like Roman tribunes, alert for Preston's Renault. Horns honked. Vehicles rumbled along the boulevard. A few people strode on the sidewalk, swinging closed umbrellas under the cloudy night sky.

For a few moments the sidewalk was empty. When a taxi stopped down the block, Robin only glanced at the red-haired woman who stepped out and leaned over to pay the driver.

"*Merda*." Charles tensed as the woman turned toward them.

"What is it? What's happened?"

"That's Eva. Take care of *The Book of Spies*." He slung off the backpack and laid it at her feet. He slid out his Glock.

"Are you insane? You already tried to kill her once and failed. Someone could see your gun." As she spoke, she watched Eva stare at Charles. "She sees you."

Charles's face was flushed. He nodded and hid the weapon again. "I'll follow her and call Preston. Hail a taxi and take *The Book of Spies* to the jet."

As Charles finished talking, his wife turned on her heel and rushed away, toward Piccadilly Circus. He hurried after her.

As Charles moved past other pedestrians, he put on his headset and called Preston, telling him about Eva.

"I'll be there in twenty-five minutes," the security chief said. "How did she know to be at the hotel?"

"I have no idea. Unless . . . but it doesn't seem possible. Our scanner found a tracking bug on the cover of the book."

"Jesus Christ. What did you do with the bug?"

"I flushed it. But it makes no sense that Eva would've planted it."

"Don't lose her, dammit. Keep the line open."

He saw Eva had joined a crowd at the corner with Piccadilly Circus, waiting for the light to change. But before he could reach her, she crossed with them to the plaza and merged with the crowd there.

He craned and ran. Where was she?

17

The noise and chaos of Piccadilly Circus reverberated inside Eva's head as she sped onward, her cell phone dug into her ear, talking to Judd Ryder.

"It's Charles. He's following me. I'm in Piccadilly Circus, heading toward the Criterion. Are you close? He's got a gun."

"I'm already moving. Leave your cell on."

Five streets flowed into the speeding roundabout encircling the busy plaza. Gaudy neon and LED lights advertising Coca-Cola, Sanyo, and McDonald's cast the area in manic red and yellow light. She watched for a bobby. Now that Charles was near, she wanted a policeman.

"I'm passing Lillywhites," she reported to Ryder. When she saw her reflected face in the glass of the sporting goods store, the strain on it, she looked away. Six of the tourists with whom she had crossed the street peeled off toward the Shaftesbury Fountain and statue. She went with them, peering around their shoulders. "Charles is still behind me. He's wearing a phone headset, and he's talking to someone on it."

"So now we know he's got a friend. Is there anyone with him?"

She checked. "Not that I can see. My group is climbing the steps to the fountain, and I'm going with them. I'll move to the other side. The fountain will be good cover to block me from him."

"I'm at the crosswalk with Piccadilly Street. Can you circle back to meet me?"

"He'll spot me."

"Okay. Go to the Trocadero Center. I'll be there."

The bronze Shaftesbury Fountain shone nickle gray in the night's lights. A scattering of people sat on the steps. At the top, Eva rushed around to the far side and looked down on the plaza, congested and rimmed by a waist-high iron fence interrupted by the crosswalk she needed. There was no sign of Charles or a policeman. But across the teeming traffic stood the London Trocadero Center, a huge building where people thronged for food, alcohol, theater, and video games. That was where she would meet Ryder.

She joined a young couple as they sauntered down the fountain's steps, holding hands. At the base, they headed right, and she moved straight ahead.

Suddenly something hard and sharp pressed into her left side. "That's a gun you feel, Eva." Charles's voice. "You're caught, old darling. It was logical you'd come this way. *Sic eunt fata hominum.*" Thus goes the destiny of man.

"Bad grammar, Charles. *Homina.* The feminine in my case, you bastard." As they continued along the street, she looked down and saw his trench coat pocket bulged with his hand aiming his weapon.

In her ear, Ryder ordered, "Hide your cell. Leave it on."

But as she slid the cell phone inside her jacket, the gun's muzzle jammed her side again.

"No," Charles snapped. "Give it to me."

She froze, then looked back at him, saw the frosty expression, the hard black eyes. The anger and frustration that had been building in her burst out in a torrent. "I loved you. I thought you loved me. I want to be glad you're alive, but you're making it really hard. What in hell do you think you're doing?"

"Keep walking, and lower your voice. Hand over the phone. Now." A few people were glancing at them. "If you think I won't shoot, you're going to find yourself dead on the pavement."

Her heart was pounding, and a cold sweat bathed her. She handed him the cell. "Don't call me old darling again. I never liked that, you son of a bitch."

He turned off her cell and spoke triumphantly into his headset. "I've got her, Preston. I'll hold her so you can take care of her. Where do you want to pick us up?"

18

As Charles walked beside her, the gun held against her side, Eva repressed a shiver. She tried to mute the outrage and hurt in her voice: "Why did you fake your death and disappear? I thought we were happy. But because of you I spent two years in prison—and now you want to kill me. After all those years together, don't I mean anything to you?"

"You meant a lot . . . once," he said impatiently. "You'll never understand. You were always too much in the world."

"And you weren't enough in it. Is this about the Library of Gold?"

"Of course it's about the library. I was invited to become the chief librarian," he said reverently. Then he announced into his headset, "It doesn't matter, Preston. She's not going to tell anyone now."

"I don't recognize you. What have you become?"

He waved his free hand, dismissing her. "Some things are worth any cost."

"The Library of Gold was more important than the friends and colleagues you left behind to grieve? More important than me?" She ached for the love she had lost.

"You've got a petty mind, Eva. Thank God a few people over the centuries were bigger. They kept the library alive, and not just physically but completely in spirit."

She was silent, working hard to control her emotions. She needed to find out as much as she could while she looked for a way to escape.

"Where is the library?" she asked.

"I don't know."

"You must be kidding."

He shook his head. "You'll never understand," he said again.

Charles had always enjoyed the sound of his own voice, the brilliance of his logic, the forceful power of his personality.

"Who kept the library alive?" she asked, hoping to trigger his passion for holding forth.

His face broke into a smile. "When Ivan the Terrible lost the last war with Poland, he gave the library secretly to King Stephen Báthory as war tribute. The next ruler passed it on to Cardinal Mazarin of France, who had a famous library of his own. Eventually it went to Friedrich Wilhelm of Brandenburg, the Great Elector. Peter the Great had it, too, and so did George II of England. Later it was in the care of Napoléon Bonaparte, Thomas Jefferson, and Andrew Carnegie—all selflessly devoted to the library. That sort of commitment has never wavered through the years, and the secret of the Library of Gold's existence has always been sacrosanct."

Nervously aware of his gun, Eva glanced over her shoulder, hoping to see Judd Ryder—but he had been heading toward the Trocadero, a completely different direction. To make matters worse, Charles now took her around the corner and onto Haymarket Street. Was this where the man named Preston was going to meet them—and "take care of her"?

She looked back. Still no police. A man in a ragged gray raincoat buttoned up to his chin and a black watch cap pulled low over his forehead and ears was shambling along, head bent down.

Charles pushed her around onto another street. Now it would be harder for Ryder to find her. Maybe impossible.

She rallied. "So what you're saying is you've finally gotten half your wish. You're in charge of the library, but you're still screwed, because you don't have the other half—international acclaim for discovering it. You ached for that, but you're never going to have it, because you can't or won't tell anyone where the library is."

Charles gave a smug smile. He reached a hand up to his headset. He hesitated, then turned it off. Preston could no longer hear what he said to her.

"There's a chance someone someday will figure out where it is," he told her.

"You *do* know. Why wait?" She put sincerity into her voice. "You could be famous now. Tell me. I'll help you."

"To get the job, I had to agree to stay with the library until I died. All of us are lifers."

"You mean captives. Tell me now. If we expose the library, you'll be free."

"No, Eva. It's not safe. You don't know Preston. Besides, I don't want to leave the library." Staying close to her, he changed the subject. "Remember the old board games we used to play? The simplest ones in all countries are based on three ancient pursuits—the hunt, the race, and the battle. Their equivalents today are fox and geese, backgammon, and chess."

"Of course I remember. The Greeks and Romans had them, and so did the early Egyptians. Scripta and Latrunculi come to mind."

"Very good. You haven't forgotten everything I taught you."

"You taught me a lot, but some of it I never wanted to learn, especially from someone I loved—like lying and betrayal. I still don't understand why you let me go to prison."

"Because you are Diana, the relentless huntress. I had to vanish completely. Assuming you believed I died accidentally in a car crash while you were asleep at home, you still would've been in our little world. If there was ever a hint about me and the library, you would've jumped on it. That was a threat far too dangerous."

"You drugged me! Someone else is in your grave!"

His face torqued with outrage, as if she were the disloyal one. "I had to work like hell to convince the director not to let you burn up in the car. Sending you to prison was my idea. I saved your life."

"And you think that makes what you did right? My God, Charles, you have the morality of a stick of wood. *Stat fortuna domus virtute.* Without virtue nothing can be truly successful. You may be the chief librarian—but you're a failure."

As Charles bristled, at his side appeared an outstretched hand, palm up and open. "Can you spare a few quid, mate?"

Eva peered around. It was the man in the ragged trench coat and watch cap. The corners of his mouth were pulled down in a permanent grimace, and he radiated self-pity. Then she caught a flicker in his gray eyes and noted his square face. Stunned, she gazed off. He was Judd Ryder.

"Get the hell away." Charles hurried her onward.

Ryder was instantly back at Charles's side, matching their pace. "Come on, be a good bloke. Help a feller out. See, me hand's empty. Fill it with a nice coin, and I'll be gone quick as a stink in the wind."

From bad grammar to imagery, she knew it would be too much for Charles.

Furious, he turned on Ryder. "Fuck off."

And Eva acted. Watching Charles's hand still in his pocket but now pointed away, she took one quick step back, kicked the inside of his knee, and slammed the side of her hand in a *shutō-uchi* strike into his neck. He grunted and staggered.

Ryder's gun appeared in his hand. "Pony up your weapon, Sherback." He ripped the headset off Charles's head.

His equilibrium regained, Charles's heavy jaw jutted with anger.

"Do it now," Ryder snapped. "I won't be nice and ask again."

Fear in his eyes, Charles silently passed the pistol to him.

Eva took a deep breath. "How did you find us, Ryder?"

There was a small smile on his lips. "The ankle bracelet Tucker gave you."

He hustled Charles down the quiet sidewalk, and she moved to Ryder's other side, away from Charles. Pointing both guns at him, Ryder directed him around the corner to one of the silent single-block avenues in this part of London. Lined with tall buildings, it was so narrow there was no sidewalk and no place to park. No cars cruised past.

"Where are we going?" Charles demanded.

"In here."

Ryder directed him into a dead-end alley where trash bins and cardboard boxes stood along the sides. It was deserted. The few doors were closed. The place reeked of garlic and old food. The buildings surrounding them were steep monoliths, showing only a slice of the night sky.

"Let's call the police," Eva said. "I want Charles arrested so I can clear my name. I want my life back."

Ryder shook his head. "First we need to find out about the Library of Gold."

Saying nothing, his posture ramrod straight, Charles kept walking. Ryder was still between them, holding both his and Charles's guns.

"Charles is the head of the Library of Gold," she tried. "From what he told me, it's been in private hands and secret since near the end of Ivan the Terrible's life."

"But where is it? Who controls it?"

"He wouldn't say. The police will question him. That's their job. Then we can turn over all the information to Tucker."

Ryder gave a firm shake of his head. "This is CIA business."

"I'm going to call the bobbies." She leaned around Ryder. "I want my cell phone, Charles."

Charles gave a strange smile and slid a hand toward the pocket where he had put it.

"Stop," Ryder ordered.

"Better the police than you." Charles said, but his words and gesture were a feint. Abruptly his weight shifted, and with lightning speed he threw himself at Ryder, reaching to get back his gun.

Ryder slammed a fist into Charles's midsection just as Charles's hand closed on the muzzle of the weapon. As he yanked the gun, Charles's momentum carried the pair backward. Elbows shot out from their sides, and their torsos twisted. Before Eva could move, there was a loud explosion, and the stench of cordite ballooned into the alley's dark air.

Charles dropped to his knees.

"Oh, my God." Eva covered her mouth with her hands. Bile rushed up her throat.

Blood bubbled on Charles's lips as he knelt motionless on the alley floor. A pool of blood on his black trench coat turned the fabric glossy.

Charles raised his gaze to look at her. "Herodotus and Aristagoras," he said. Then he pitched forward, landing hard, his arms straight along his sides, his cheek pressed into the pavement.

19

Ryder dropped to his heels beside the downed man and felt the carotid artery. No pulse. He swore. He had just lost his best chance of finding the library and answers to who was behind his father's death.

"I'm sorry, Ryder," Eva said. "Is he dead?"

He nodded. Getting to his feet, he peered at the doors lining the narrow alleyway and then down the length to where it opened onto the street. There was no sign the gunshots had attracted attention. He seized Sherback's armpits and dragged him behind a row of trash bins, where they would be out of sight and the dim light was adequate for what he needed to do.

Crouching beside the slack body, he rifled through the trench coat pockets.

Eva joined him, sitting on her heels. "What are you doing?"

"Interrogating him." He took Sherback's phone. "It's a disposable cell." Then he found her cell phone.

She grabbed it.

He stared at her. "Go ahead and call the cops—if you want to end up arrested as an accessory to your husband's murder."

She stiffened. Her shoulders slumped. She turned off the cell and pocketed it.

Ryder checked Sherback's jacket, discovering a billfold and a small leather-bound notebook. He continued to search.

Eva opened the billfold and stood up to get better light.

"He's got a Brit driver's license with his picture on it. The name says Christopher Heath, but that shouldn't matter. His body can still be identified by his DNA."

"Maybe not right away, not if the DNA of the man who was in the car crash was identified against what was supposed to be your husband's DNA. That'll take the cops a long time to sort out—if they even bother to check into such a long shot. Is there anything else in there? Notes to himself?"

She crouched again. "Nothing. No credit cards or anything. Just cash."

The last item Ryder found was in Sherback's pants pocket—a Swiss Army Champion Plus pocketknife, loaded with miniature tools. He stood up, took off the old gray trench coat he was wearing, and put it in a trash bin. Then he shoved everything, including Sherback's Glock, into his peacoat pockets. He would go through Sherback's notebook when he had time.

"I've got to get out of here," he said to Eva. "You coming?" He watched emotions play across her face. The skin was tight, and the eyes bruised. God help him, working with an amateur was tough, but he needed her. She was his last living link to Sherback and the library.

"Yes."

As they hurried down the alley, he told her, "*The Book of Spies* was stolen tonight from the British Museum. My guess is your husband was in London as part of the operation. His people must've left a duplicate book in the museum. A duplicate would explain why he was photographing the original, and it'd buy them time. The real one was in the Méridien hotel at some point."

"Someone named Preston must be part of it. He was supposed to pick up Charles and me and then kill me."

"Swell. Anyone else you can think of who wants to get rid of you?"

"My popularity ends there."

As they hurried on, the sound of their footsteps seemed to echo in the alley.

"What did Charles mean by 'Herodotus and Aristagoras'?" he asked.

"He told me there was a chance someone could figure out where the library was. Thinking about it, my guess is he left a clue or clues to its whereabouts. So Herodotus and Aristagoras might be it. But I don't recall anything about them together."

He felt a thread of excitement. "Let's look at what it might mean from another angle. Who were Herodotus and Aristagoras individually?"

"Herodotus was a Greek—a researcher and storyteller in the fifth century B.C. He's considered the world's first historian."

"So he could've written about Aristagoras."

She paused. "You're right. He did. The story happened twenty-five hundred years ago, when Darius the Great was conquering most of the ancient world. When he captured a major Ionian city called Miletus, Darius gave it to a Greek named Histiaeus to rule. But as time passed, he got nervous, because Histiaeus was growing too powerful. So he 'invited' Histiaeus to live with him in Persia, and he gave Miletus away again—this time to Histiaeus's son-in-law Aristagoras. Histiaeus was furious. He wanted his city back and decided to start a war in hopes Darius would crush it and reinstate him. He shaved the head of his most faithful slave and tattooed a secret message on the man's skin. As soon as the hair grew back, he sent the slave off to Aristagoras, who had the hair shaved and read the command to revolt. The result was the Ionian War, and Herodotus wrote about it at length."

"You said Charles used to have light brown hair. That he'd dyed it black."

She stared at him.

They turned on their heels and raced back along the alley. They crouched beside the corpse.

He handed her his small flashlight. "Point it at his head." She did, and he pulled out Charles's pocketknife, opened a long blade, grabbed hair, and started sawing.

Almost immediately a police siren sang out in the distance.

"I think they're coming this way."

He nodded. "Someone probably reported the gunshot." There was a mound of black hair on the oily concrete beside him. He slid small scissors out from the Swiss Army knife and quickly clipped close to Charles's scalp.

She leaned close. "I see something."

Letters showed in the flashlight's stark illumination, indigo blue against pasty white skin.

"LAW," she read. "All capital letters. There are numbers, too."

He clipped faster.

"031308," she said.

"What does LAW 031308 mean?" he asked.

" 'LAW' indicates it could be a code for a law library. Some codes are universal, others not. I don't recognize this one. It could be special to a particular library—like the Library of Gold. But I don't see how it'd lead us there."

The siren screamed from the street, approaching the alley.

He jumped up. "Try the doors on this side. I'll take the other side."

They ran, grabbing doorknobs. All were locked. They were trapped in a dead-end alley with a corpse. If they ran out to the street, the police would see them. Rotating red slashes of light appeared at the alley's mouth, flicking into the darkness, bouncing off the walls.

"There's a ladder," he told her, nodding.

They sprinted. The beacons had illuminated a fire escape

ladder down the side of a building, almost unnoticeable because its black iron blended into the black granite of the wall. It was a good ten feet above them. He leaped. Wrapping both hands around the bottom rung, he hauled himself up and did a quick inspection. There was no way to lower the ladder.

Grasping the side rail, he leaned down and extended his hand. "Jump."

As the grille of the police car came into view, Eva ran ten feet back and then dashed toward him, propelling herself high. He grabbed her hand. Straining, he held tight to the railing and pulled. Sweat beaded his forehead as he dragged her up to the first rung.

They climbed quickly. By the time the police car rolled into the alley, they were far above, with Ryder leading the way. At the top, he crawled over a low wall. The gigantic London Eye was a silver wheel of light on the horizon. Quickly he surveyed the flat roof—utility boxes, vent hoods, and a small shed that should contain a stairwell down into the building.

Eva's face emerged above the rooftop's rim, looking grim. She clambered over, turned, dropped to her knees, and leaned forward, staring down. He joined her. The police car had stopped about forty feet inside the alley, almost beneath them. Flashlights in hands, two bobbies were patrolling, kicking cardboard boxes, examining trash cans.

"They'll find Charles," she said in a low voice. "What will they do when they see what's written on his head?"

"God knows. But he's got no identification, so they're going to have a nifty time trying to figure it out." He paused. "I have a proposition. It's likely *The Book of Spies* is headed back to the Library of Gold. You know a hell of a lot more about the library and Charles, the head librarian, than we do. I'd like to stash you someplace safe in London, and then I'll phone or e-mail when I need to consult."

There was a steely expression on her face. "I'm not the kind of woman who gets stashed someplace. I'm going with you."

"No way. It's too dangerous."

Just then there was a shout below.

They peered over the side of the building and to their right. One of the bobbies was staring down behind the garbage bins where they had left Charles's body. His flashlight moved slowly, indicating he was taking in the full length of the corpse. The second policeman rushed to join him, his free hand pressed against the gear dangling from his belt to keep it from flopping.

As the bobbies crouched, Ryder nodded at the alley's mouth. "We have another visitor."

A car had stopped on the street, blocking the alley. It was a Renault. The driver got out. Dressed in jeans and an open black leather jacket, he was tall and moved gracefully as he walked toward the police.

Ryder studied him, noting the loose joints, the open hands that appeared relaxed but were far from it, the head that moved fractionally from side to side, showing he was doing a far more thorough scan of the area than most people would realize. Everything about him announced a well-trained professional in tradecraft.

Eva looked at Ryder. "Preston?"

He kept his focus on the stranger, memorizing his features. "Yeah, I think so."

20

The two bobbies turned and closed ranks, blocking the garbage bins as Preston approached. Preston said something to them, but his words were lost over the distance. After listening, the policemen relaxed a bit. One nodded and gestured.

Preston walked over and leaned low to peer at Charles Sherback's corpse. Ryder noted a slight tensing in his shoulders.

And then it happened. In concise, swift movements, he was suddenly upright, a sound-suppressed pistol in his hand as he turned back toward the bobbies. His face showed no emotion.

Ryder yanked out his gun. Too late. Preston fired under his arm point-blank into the heart of the nearest bobby, then immediately into the heart of the second. He had shot them without completely facing them, so certain was he of their positions and his ability to kill.

Eva stiffened. Ryder put a hand on her arm.

The two policemen stood motionless, stunned into bleeding statues. When they went down, one sat cross-legged, and the other knelt on one knee. Then they toppled, the first landing on his belly, the second on his side. As blood oozed out, their limbs made jerky movements.

Preston holstered his weapon and dragged Charles's body out from behind the bins. The scuffing noise of Charles's heels on the pavement drifted upward. Preston hefted the body over his shoulder and loped off. Ryder noted he still showed no emotion.

"He doesn't want anyone to see the tattoo," Eva decided.

Ryder studied the moving killer. Charles's body was draped over one side. Part of Preston's torso was covered by it, but Preston's head and legs were even more chancy targets at this distance. Soon he would pass beneath them, heading out toward the Renault. Ryder had to act quickly. The torso was his best target.

"Call 999 and describe where the alley is," he told her. "Go over to the shed to do it. Your voice shouldn't reach the alley from there. Don't tell them about us."

Without a word she grabbed Charles's cell and ran.

Balancing himself, he aimed carefully, inhaled, exhaled, and fired twice in quick succession, targeting Preston's right side to avoid his heart. The explosions were loud. Preston suddenly staggered.

But as Charles's body fell to the alley floor, Preston recovered, dropped beside it, and rolled. His weapon appeared in both hands, pointing upward, looking for the shooter. The man was damn good.

Ryder aimed and fired twice again.

Preston jerked back, and then Ryder got lucky—Preston's head thudded against the pavement. The additional blow did it. Preston froze a moment. His eyes closed. One hand released his pistol, and the other flopped to the ground.

Smiling grimly to himself, Ryder hurried to the stairwell shed.

Eva was standing near the door. "I called them. Two dead bobbies got their attention. They're on their way. Did you kill Preston?"

"I hope not. I want him to face some intense questioning. Move away from the door."

It was padlocked. Using the handle of his Beretta, he

broke the lock and swung open the door. A dank odor blew out. Lit only by thin starlight, concrete steps descended into a black abyss. He turned on his miniature flashlight, and they walked down quickly side by side.

He kept his voice even. "Are you up to talking about Charles's tattoo?" Although she seemed to be coping well, he had no idea how much of what had happened had affected her.

"Are you kidding? You bet I am."

"It seems to me since Charles wanted the library to be found, he intended the tattoo to be decipherable. My guess is he told us about Aristagoras and Herodotus because he thought you'd not only figure out he'd left a tattoo but you'd understand the message. So let's go back to the beginning. What does LAW 031308 mean?"

She said nothing. They descended two more flights. The doors were numbered, indicating they had reached the sixth floor.

Finally she decided, "I suppose LAW might have nothing to do with the law or something legal. Or the letters could be initials, an acronym. But it's not an acronym I recognize. 'Loyal Association of the West.' 'Legislative Agency for War,' " she free-associated. "None of that makes a darn bit of sense. The number's too short to be a telephone number. It might not be just a string of individual numbers either, but a whole number—if one skips the zero, then it's 31,308. Or it could have a decimal. But where does the decimal point go?"

"Okay, let's think in terms of codes. Bar codes. Postal codes. Some kind of shipping code."

"Doesn't ring a bell."

Silently they continued downward.

"Maybe it *does* involve the law," he said. "Were you ever in a lawsuit?"

"That bullet I've dodged."

When they arrived at the ground floor, he cracked open the heavy metal fire door and gazed out. He closed the door gently.

"We've got company," he said. "There's a guard behind a reception desk, and he looks disgustingly alert. I'm not in the mood to take any more chances. We'll go to the basement."

Again they descended.

He had an idea. "Maybe the code is something personal. You know, personal to you and Charles."

At the bottom, the stairway door opened onto an empty parking garage lit by a scattering of overhead fluorescent lights. A hundred feet away a driveway rose toward the entrance. It was sealed at the end by a heavy garage door, but there was a side door next to it. They rushed toward it. It was locked, but this time there was no padlock for Ryder to knock open. Surveying around, he screwed the sound suppressor onto his Beretta.

"Step back," he ordered.

She did, and he directed the muzzle downward so the bullet would go into the ground on the other side. He fired. *Pop.* Metal dust spewed.

Putting the weapon away, he turned the knob and peered out. They were on a busy street, but he did not know which one.

"Looks safe," he told her.

They stepped outside into the stink of exhaust. There were plenty of people on the sidewalk, entering and leaving watering holes. A pub door opened, and loud techno music blared out. But above that was the screaming noise of more police sirens. Two, he guessed.

He glanced at her, saw the alarm in her face. "With luck, they're on their way to the alley," he told her. "They'll find

Preston, and the rounds in the policemen's bodies will match his pistol."

"Yes, but they could have a description of us from the call that brought the two bobbies to the alley in the first place. The caller might've seen us."

He was worried about it, too. There had been enough unpredictable events tonight that he was taking nothing for granted.

As they walked, she continued: "I've been thinking about what you said, Judd—that the code could be personal to Charles and me."

It was the first time she had called him by his first name. "Go on."

"The numbers could be a date. Charles and I were married on March the thirteenth in 2000. So '03' could be March, '13' could mean the thirteenth day, and '08' is 2008."

"That was just a month before he disappeared. So what happened on your anniversary in 2008?"

Suddenly two police cars were racing down the street toward them. Their rotating blue and red lights slashed through the night like sabers.

He smoothed his features. "We need to slow down and blend in. Hold my arm."

Instead, she slipped her hand inside his, and he felt a strange sensation so pleasant he forced it from his mind before it could turn to grief. They continued on through the lamplight—and the police cars rushed past.

Dropping her hand, he busied himself by taking out his palm mirror and checking it. "They've turned the corner."

He felt her relax. When she spoke again, her voice was businesslike. "If I tell you what I've figured out, you've got to promise to take me with you. I'll bet everything that's happened tonight will only make the people with the Library of Gold want to get rid of me more. I want to see them captured. I want to be *there*."

"You're blackmailing me."

She gave a wry smile. "It appears I've learned something from you."

He found himself smiling, too. "All right, it's a deal." Then he stared at her sternly. "But if I do, you've got to do exactly what I say—when I say it. I'm serious about this, Eva."

"You're the pro. Whatever you say, as long as you're reasonable."

"No. This isn't negotiable. Look at it this way—if you come along, you'll be putting me in danger, too. There may not be time to ask questions or argue."

She sighed. "All right. So this is what I think . . . In 2008, Charles and I celebrated our anniversary by flying to Rome. We visited an old friend of his, Yitzhak *Law*. He's a professor, well-known in the field. He and Charles often talked late into the night. They had a shared passion: finding the Library of Gold. Maybe the reason Charles left the tattoo was to say Yitzhak knows where the library is."

He inhaled deeply. "Then we go to Rome."

PART TWO

THE RACE

Hannibal's troops were closing in on Rome when one of his spies reported the city was filled with rumors its dictator, Fabius, was in his pay. With that news, the great military chief went on a rampage across the countryside, destroying and burning everything in his path—except Fabius's properties. As soon as the news reached Rome, Fabius issued proclamations he was no traitor. But his people did not believe him, and Hannibal gained valuable time and psychological advantage.

—*translated from* The Book of Spies

Spying is a pursuit as old as civilization and a craft long practiced by the most skilled and treacherous of strategists.

—U.S. News & World Report
January 19, 2003

21

In pain, Doug Preston jerked awake. The alley. He was still in the alley, lying on the pavement near Charles Sherback's corpse. With effort he turned his head and saw the two policemen's bodies. Then he looked on the other side of him, past the police car and to his Renault. The alley was still deserted.

He stared at Charles's bald skull, gray as an old bone in the light. What in hell did the tattoo mean?

Suddenly the loud noise of police sirens penetrated his brain. That was what had awakened him. He struggled to his feet. His head throbbed. He rubbed the bump on the back of it—the size of an eagle's egg. The right side of his chest hurt like boiling fire. He was badly bruised but not wounded, because he was wearing one of the new Kevlar tactical body-armor vests, thin and light, under his jacket and shirt, and the rounds had not penetrated.

Feeling weak, he bent over and propped his hands on his thighs, willing the pain away. At last he picked up Sherback's corpse and maneuvered it over his shoulder and staggered toward his car. When he reached the mouth of the alley, he checked the narrow street, then opened the Renault's rear door and heaved Charles inside.

As he got behind the steering wheel and turned on the ignition, he knew from the noise of the sirens he was within seconds of being discovered. Gunning the motor, he laid rubber, fishtailed around the corner, then cut back on his speed. He entered the traffic smoothly.

With a shaky hand he wiped sweat from his forehead and swore loudly. Who in hell had the shooter been? Probably whoever had killed Charles.

He thought about the man he had spotted peering down over the top of the building, gun in hand. But by then he was already injured, and the man had shot twice more before he could return fire. At no time had the man been more than a black silhouette. If a shooter that good was helping Eva Blake, she was going to be more difficult to catch.

Another unpleasant thought occurred to him. He had convinced the bobbies to let him see the corpse not just because he had described Charles and told them his old friend was drunk and lost, but because the bobbies had found nothing in Charles's pockets and had no way to identify him. That meant the shooter probably had Charles's things, including his cell phone. It would contain Robin's and his numbers, and if the shooter were connected, he could track the numbers through the location chips embedded in their phones.

Preston grabbed his cell, rolled down the window, and tossed it into the next lane of traffic. Watching his side-view mirror, he saw the tires of a pickup truck roll over it. Satisfied, he took a new disposable cell from his glove compartment and dialed Robin Miller.

"Are you in the jet?" he asked.

"Yes. We're waiting for you and Charles." She sounded sleepy.

"Listen carefully, and follow my directions exactly. As soon as I hang up, open up your cell and take out the battery. Under no circumstances put the battery back in. I don't care where you are or what you think you need it for, do *not* make your cell operable again. Do you understand?"

"Of course. When will you get here?" She sounded testy,

insulted he had asked whether she understood. She did not like her intelligence questioned.

"Soon," he said. "Tell me what the jet's satellite phone number is."

There were the sounds of the phone being removed from its plastic case. She read him the number. Then he gave her his new cell number.

"When you saw Charles last, was his head shaved?" he asked.

"No. Why would he do that?"

"I thought you'd know."

Her voice was suspicious. "Is Charles with you?"

"Yes, but he's dead," he said bluntly.

He heard a loud gasp.

Before she could erupt into tears, he added, "He was shot, and probably Eva Blake was involved. The last time I talked with him, he'd caught her. I'm sending his body back with you to the library. Take out that cell phone battery. Tell the pilot to warm up the jet." He hung up.

By telling Robin now about Charles's death he hoped he would find her under control when he arrived. The director encouraged romances among the small Library of Gold staff, since the members were more easily managed if they had some sort of home life. It caused occasional problems when affairs erupted or couples broke apart, but even that kept the staff involved in the community.

As he laid his new cell on the seat beside him, a river of pain swept through him. His eyelids felt heavy. After the first adrenaline rush of making arrangements with Robin, his mind was turning to mush. He could go three days without sleep and still remain alert, but now he was injured, which was dumping his stamina into the toilet.

Opening the glove compartment, he grabbed a large bottle of water and a small bottle of aspirin. He poured a half-dozen tablets into his mouth and gulped water. Blinking, he turned the car west toward Heathrow and continued to drink.

At last he sighed. He was feeling stronger. As he drove, he laid the water bottle beside him and pictured the place to which he went at times when he needed to heal and find himself again. He saw the golden light, the rows of gleaming books, the polished antique tables and chairs. He could hear the soft rhythmic sounds of the air-purification system.

In his imagination he locked the door, chose an illuminated manuscript, and carried it to his favorite reading chair. He sat with the book on his lap and savored the hammered gold and glistening gems. Then he opened it and turned pages, absorbing the brilliantly colored drawings and exquisite lettering. He could read none of the foreign languages in the library, but he did not need to. Just seeing the books, being able to touch them, recalling the sacrifices and care throughout the library's history helped to banish his ugly childhood, the hardscrabble life, the missing father, the angry mother. The sense of loss he felt as he had witnessed Langley spiraling downward in a wash of political bullshit.

The Library of Gold was proof the future could be as cherished and glorious as the past. That the work he did was crucial. That he was crucial.

After a while he could feel his heartbeat slow. The sweat dried on his skin. The pain eased. A sense of certainty infused him.

Girding himself, he picked up his cell and dialed again. When the director answered, he told him, "There have been some developments, sir. You need to know what's going on. First, someone planted a bug on *The Book of Spies*. It was inside a fake jewel on the cover. It's been flushed down a toilet."

"Jesus Christ. Who would've had the connections to duplicate one of the gems and put a bug inside it?"

"I keep going back to the chief librarian before Charles. We thought he'd stolen the book and sold it to a collector so he'd have cash to try to leave. But if the collector were the anonymous donor to the Rosenwald collection and the one who planted the bug, then the National Library would've found it before it got to the British Museum."

"Unless the donor had real clout. Someone with the money and resources to locate a person in the National Library who could be bought to cover for the bug."

Preston nodded to himself. "I made some calls and found out Asa Baghurst, California's governor, signed a special order releasing Eva Blake from prison—just three days ago. I successfully eliminated Peggy Doty, then Charles called to say he'd found Eva Blake. I was on my way to pick them up and scrub her, too, but they weren't at the rendezvous." He described spotting the police car that had led him to finding Charles shot dead in the alley.

"So we lost Charles in the end. It's just as well. The way he was screwing up, we were going to have to erase him anyway." The director sighed. "Did his wife kill him?"

"There was a man there. He could've done it. He took some shots at me, but I never saw his face. The accuracy of his aim and the way he positioned himself said a lot. He's trained. It looks like a total setup—the bug, Eva Blake, and a shooter. Someone wanted to follow *The Book of Spies*."

"Is there any way Blake could've found out Charles was our chief librarian before the opening at the British Museum?"

"I don't see how. This was the first time Charles was away from the library. And of course after his predecessor smuggled out *The Book of Spies,* we doubled security, so Charles had no outside contact at all. Still, he was up to something. When I found his body, his head was shaved, and there was a tattoo on it—LAW 031308."

"What in hell is that all about?"

"I don't know, sir. You said yourself Charles was a romantic. But he was ambitious, too. He thought a lot of himself."

"Did Charles shave his head, or did someone else?"

"I'd say someone else. Maybe Blake and the shooter. I'll have my staff do a thorough search of Charles's cottage and office. There could be something there that'll tell us what the tattoo means."

"What about the rest of the operation?"

"On track. Robin and *The Book of Spies* are on the jet. I'll stow Charles's corpse on board, then they'll fly home, but without me. I'm going to stay in London to keep looking for Blake. I have a way to find her—I got her cell number off Peggy Doty's phone. I have a NSA source I can use to track her through the cell's location, assuming the phone's turned on."

"Good," the director said with relief. "Do it."

22

Brentwood, California

Attorney Brian Collum was sound asleep in his large Tudor home when his telephone rang. His eyes snapped open. The master suite was cool and bathed in shadows. He checked the glowing digital numbers on his bedside clock—two A.M.—and snatched the phone.

His wife rolled over to gaze anxiously at him. The days of panicked clients calling at all hours were long past, so something must have happened to one of their children. They had three, all studying at various universities.

"Yes?" he said into the telephone.

"Hello, Brian." The voice was familiar. "Sorry to disturb you. This is Steve Gandy. I've got an unusual situation here. It involves one of your clients, Eva Blake. I need a favor."

Steve Gandy was the longtime coroner for the County of Los Angeles, a straight shooter who could be relied on for a no-holds-barred game of racquetball. Brian made it a practice to cultivate people in government, and since this concerned Eva, he was even more willing to listen.

"Hold on." He turned to his wife. "This isn't about the children. Go back to sleep. I'll take it in my office."

As she nodded, he carried the phone out of the bedroom. "Is Eva all right?"

"I assume so, but I don't have any way to get in touch with her. She's been released from prison. No one seems to know where she went. Do you still have authorization to sign documents for her?"

"I do." He was shocked. Eva was out of prison? "Tell me what's going on." He sat behind his desk in a patch of pale moonlight. Not only had he represented Eva at her trial, he now handled her legal affairs.

Steve's voice was tense. "I need signed permission to exhume her husband's body."

"Why?" Brian's lungs tightened. "Who wants it exhumed?"

There was a sigh on the other end of the line. "The CIA. The term *national security* came up in the conversation several times. They're telling us nothing except it's critical we make damn sure we identify accurately who's buried in Sherback's grave and how he died, and we're to contain who knows about the exhumation. But there's hell to pay these days when anyone gets caught up in a CIA publicity disaster. Maybe this is legitimate, but I sure don't have that kind of crystal ball. And I damn well don't want my office to face repercussions. The problem is, they want us to exhume the body without a signed order. That's why I'm bringing you in."

"Jesus."

"Precisely."

"This is insane. You know Charles Sherback is in that grave. Your office matched the dental records."

"That's not conclusive enough for them. They want another autopsy—and for us to check the DNA."

He swore silently. "Do you have a name at the CIA?"

"Gloria Feit made the call. She's with the Clandestine Service."

"Her bona fides are good?"

"Yes. I don't want a duel with the CIA, but at the same time I've got to protect myself and my people," Steve said. "I want you to sign the order, Brian. I'll drive over there now.

That way we can start digging at daylight, and I can get the CIA off my back with some answers."

Brian thought quickly."Here's another idea. I've got a key to Eva's storage locker. I'm sure she must still have some of Charles's things. I'll swing by there early in the morning and see what I can find to give you a head start on the DNA. Then I'll drive to your office and sign the order."

Steve sounded relieved."That's not perfect, but you're right. A DNA sample will speed the process. Be here by eight A.M. And thanks."

They hung up, but Brian stayed in his chair, staring at the shadows in his office. The room was full of books, the titles unseeable in the darkness. Still, he was comforted by them and their enduring counsel, handed down through the ages. Smiling wryly to himself, he remembered some earthy advice from Trajan, Rome's long-ago warrior emperor:"Never stand between a dog and where he's pissing."

Fortunately, he did not have to risk interfering with Steve's investigation. The man who was buried in Charles's grave was a salesman from South Dakota, a loner whom Preston had chosen in an L.A. bar and eliminated later with a snap of the neck, which was consistent with an injury received in a car wreck. Then Preston had arranged a late-night break-in at the office of Charles Sherback's dentist, so records of the dead man's teeth could be substituted for Charles's. Brian had kept the dead man's gloves and a few other things locked away in his office safe.

Although the DNA match from inside the gloves and the clean autopsy would make the CIA's curiosity evaporate, Brian was left with a much larger and potentially more dangerous question: Who or what had provoked the intelligence agency's interest?

He picked up the phone and dialed the Library of Gold's director."Marty, this is Brian Collum. We've got a situation."

He described the coroner's call. "The CIA order for exhumation came from someone named Gloria Feit in the Clandestine Service."

Martin Chapman exploded a stream of oaths. "How did you leave it with the coroner?"

"I'm going to provide him with the corpse's gloves for a DNA match. That should resolve things. Can you think of a reason they'd want the identity rechecked?"

"No reason, except now Charles Sherback really is dead."

Brian felt a moment of shock. "That's a blow to the library. He was damn good at the job. What happened?"

Brian had begun cultivating Charles a dozen years ago, admiring his knowledge about the Library of Gold and appreciating his obsession to find it. When they had needed a new chief librarian, he had recommended Charles, and the book club had authorized him to secretly offer him the position. Now the club would have to find a replacement.

"He died in London," the director said. "Shot to death."

"Did Preston retrieve *The Book of Spies* successfully?"

"Yes. It's on its way home."

"That's a relief." He remembered what Steve had said. "The coroner told me Eva's out of prison. Does she have anything to do with this?"

"She's just the beginning of the problem."

Astonished, then increasingly concerned, Brian listened as Martin Chapman described Eva's spotting Charles in the museum, his attempt to kill her, the bug on *The Book of Spies,* and Preston's search for Eva, ending with the discovery of Charles's corpse.

"Preston thinks a trained man is helping Eva," the director said. "Obviously someone was intent on trying to track *The Book of Spies*—maybe back to the library. I'm concerned about who had the ability to plant the bug. Now that the CIA is involved, I'm wondering whether it's them."

"Shit."

"Besides that, Charles had a tattoo on his head—LAW 031308. Does it mean anything to you?"

"Not a damn thing."

"It could be a message," the director said. "But to whom? And why?"

"Think about Charles's predecessor. None of us ever guessed he had the balls not only to want to leave, but also to smuggle out *The Book of Spies*. One of the reasons we chose Charles was because the library was the most important thing in his life. But the downside was his ambition and arrogance. God knows what the message means. Whatever it is, it could be dangerous to us."

"If Eva saw the tattoo—and we have no reason to think she didn't—she may be able to understand it."

"You're right."

"Preston has a way to track her through her cell phone. You take care of the coroner." There was a thoughtful pause. When the director spoke again, his voice had its usual brisk, businesslike tone: "I have a way to handle the CIA."

23

Washington, D.C.

The man parked his car on a dark residential street in the gently rolling hills north of downtown Washington. In the distance, the tall dome of the Capitol shone like ivory. He opened the car door, and Frodo, his little terrier, leaped out, wagging his tail.

With the terrier leading, they walked down the sidewalk, all part of the man's cover, and turned onto Ed Casey's block. The man noted another early dog stroller heading toward him through the still shadows. As he always did, he assumed an indulgent dog-owner's smile and nodded in greeting. Then he pulled Frodo off the curb to give the pair a wide berth.

As soon as the other walker was out of sight, the man stopped beside a Eugenia bush whose low branches brushed the ground. He slid Frodo's leash underneath, and Frodo followed, crawling in and circling around. His little black eyes peered out.

"Stay." He gave the hand command.

Frodo immediately settled back into the foliage, invisible to anyone who passed. They had done this many times. Frodo would not move nor make a sound.

After a careful look around, the man sprinted across the lawn to Ed Casey's clapboard house and examined the doors and windows on the first floor. All were locked, including French doors overlooking a goldfish pond in the rear yard.

He returned to the French doors. No dead bolt. Slide locks had been installed, but no one had bothered to engage them. He loved the way people were lulled into complacency by the passage of uneventful time. His profession depended on it.

With a small tool, he popped open the French doors and stepped into a shadowy family room. He liked to have house plans, but there had been no time to get them. When he hired him for the job, Doug Preston had been able to pass on only Ed Casey's address.

Cautiously he padded across thick carpet into a central hall. A grandfather clock ticked rhythmically. There was no other noise. He listened at the foot of the stairs, then ducked his head into open doorways—a living room, a dining room, and a kitchen. All deserted. He opened the only closed door. Bingo—an office.

Keeping his ears tuned for movement upstairs, he headed straight to the desk, where a computer sat. He went to work, installing tiny wireless transmitting devices inside the hard drive and keyboard.

Finished, he listened to the house again. Silence. He slipped out of the office and let himself out the French doors. The early-morning sky was still black. Tomorrow night he would return and remove the bugs, lessening the chance anyone would ever know his business tonight.

Pausing near the street, he surveyed the area. At last he strolled to the Eugenia bush and gestured. Frodo scooted out, and the man gave him a dog biscuit. Whistling to himself, he walked his pet back to the car.

Johannesburg, South Africa

It was half past noon in Johannesburg when Thomas Randklev received a call from the Library of Gold director. As soon as he hung up, Randklev phoned Donna Leggate, the junior U.S. senator from Colorado. It was only 5:30 A.M. in Washington, and it was quickly apparent she had been asleep.

As soon as he said his name, the tone of her voice modulated from gruff to welcoming. "This is an odd time to be calling, Thom, but it's always good to hear from you."

He knew it was a lie. "I appreciate that. I'd like a bit of information. Nothing unseemly, of course."

"What can I help you with?"

"This is about a woman named Gloria Feit, who's with your Clandestine Service. We'd like to know for whom she works and what she does."

"Why are you interested?"

"I'm not at liberty to say, except it involves someone special like you, someone we like to give good service to—one of our investors. Certainly nothing about your national security. It's just business."

She hesitated. "I'd rather not—"

He interrupted. "I hope your shares in the Parsifal Group are making you smile."

A widow, Leggate had been appointed to the Senate to succeed her husband when he died four years earlier. Her husband's debts had left her in a precarious financial position, but because of Parsifal, she was earning far more than her husband had. She was also far more ambitious, but in Washington ambition unsupported by money was just another social affectation.

Her tone was guarded. "Yes, very much so."

"And of course there are the dividends," he reminded her.

"Even better," she admitted. "But still . . ."

Although unsurprising, her reluctance was annoying. They needed her to move on this, and fast—but he was not ready to tell her that yet.

"You're on the Senate Intelligence Committee," he pointed

out." You've brought a CIA employee, Ed Casey, into Parsifal. Tell him to e-mail someone at Langley for the information. If you feel you can't, you'll have to drop out of our special club for investors, and I'll transfer your shares to another of our groups. You can count on the returns being decent—but they won't support you in your old age." He let that sink in. "On the other hand, if you can do us this favor, you can stay in the club, continue to recruit selected others, and receive a sizeable contribution to your reelection campaign."

"How sizeable?" she asked instantly.

"One hundred thousand dollars."

"Five hundred thousand would make the sun shine a lot brighter."

"That's a great deal of money, Donna."

"You're asking a huge favor."

He was silent. Then: "Oh, hell. All right, I agree—but only if you call Ed Casey immediately."

"If I'm awake, he can damn well get his butt out of bed, too."

"You always could charm me, Donna." He smiled to himself. She had quit negotiating too soon. He had the director's approval to go to $800,000.

"And you're a delightful rogue, Thom," she said. "Love that about you. Tell me, will you be needing any other favors?"

"Perhaps. And remember, you can ask occasionally, too. If it's in my power, I'll be delighted to help. After all, we're friends. All part of the same club."

24

Washington, D.C.

Senator Leggate put on her bathrobe, lit a cigarette, and waved smoke from her eyes. Washington was a town where favors were exchanged like poker chips. To survive, one learned to be helpful while being careful with whom one played. If you wanted to be a serious contender in the nation's fast, treacherous political waters, you had to be an Olympian at the game.

While she had a sense of ominousness about Thom Randklev's naked laying out of her options if she refused to help, she also felt a sense of exhilaration. He had agreed to her high number easily. That told her he had access to even more cash. What frightened her was whether she could handle him—or herself—if she ever had to refuse.

But that was the future. Maybe years from now. With luck, never. She marched into her office, turned on her desk lamp, spun open her Rolodex, and dialed.

"A good early morning to you, Ed. This is Donna Leggate."

"Good Lord, Donna, do you know what time it is?" Ed Casey was a top gun in Langley's Support to Mission team, which built and operated CIA facilities, created and maintained secure communications, managed the CIA phone company, and hired, trained, and assigned officers to every directorate. His department also handled payroll, which meant he had access to the records of everyone the CIA employed—as long as they were on the books.

"I've been up for hours reading classified reports," she told him, fabricating a lie he would believe. "Sorry to bother you, but I'd like your help with something before I go into the office. One of the reports mentions an officer named Gloria Feit, in the Clandestine Service, but there's nothing about to whom she reports. I'd like to know that as well as what she and her boss do."

"You'll need to go through the D/CIA's office."

"If I'm asking questions about this, others on the committee will be, too. Going through the D/CIA opens up the possibility of a leak, and then the press dogs will drool for everything they can claw up. The reason I'm calling is because I know you and I are on the same page about protecting Langley whenever possible."

"There's a chain of command. I don't buck it."

"As I was dialing," she continued thoughtfully, "I was remembering when you told me you needed a college nest egg for your kids. How old are they now?"

There was a change in Ed's voice. Perhaps a hint of guilt. "I appreciate your paving the way so I could buy shares in the Parsifal Group."

She rammed the point home: "Has it been a good investment for them?"

"Yes," he admitted.

"I'm delighted. I think all of us like to help each other whenever we can. What I'm asking I can get anyway. The only difference is I want it now, while it's fresh in my mind."

"What's the report about?"

"It's M-classified. Sorry." "M" indicated an extraordinarily sensitive covert operation. Among the highest the United States bestowed, single-letter security clearances meant the information was so secret it could be referred to only by initials, and there was no way Ed would be privy to it. "You can e-mail your office for the information about Gloria Feit."

"Hold on," he grumbled.

Senator Leggate smiled to herself. She had watched her husband cajole and threaten to get what he wanted, and now she was the one in the power seat.

Johannesburg, South Africa

Thom Randklev stood before the floor-to-ceiling window in his office, hands clasped comfortably behind, and stared out at the rocks and shales of the Witwatersrand—"White Water's Ridge" in Afrikaans. As clouds drifted past and the sun blazed through, pockets of quartz glittered, attracting his gaze. For a moment he felt a fierce sense of pride.

The Witwatersrand was the source of 40 percent of the gold ever mined on the planet, and it had provided his family's first small fortune. Then his lazy father had lost everything in drink, divorces, and wild spending. But now Thom had all of it back and more, including homes in San Moritz, Paris, and New York City, which was where he had met Senator Leggate and begun cultivating her. As he had assured the director, she was the one who could handle the first step in resolving the problem of why the CIA wanted to exhume "Charles Sherback."

As his mind roamed over his accomplishments, he turned to stare at the books stretching across two long walls of his office. He had been disturbed by the director's information, but at the same time he had complete confidence the situation—whatever it was—could be resolved.

What mattered was the Library of Gold had remained secret for centuries because of careful attention to detail, and that secrecy was the hallmark of those who had inherited the library. In today's world, the biggest wars were fought inside boardrooms behind closed doors, and the book club knew exactly how to train, fight, and win every skirmish. And that was what this was—a mere skirmish. As he ruminated about that, he remembered what Plato had written: "Thinking is the talking of the soul with itself." How true, he decided as he poured himself a drink.

When the phone rang, he snapped it up.

As he had hoped, it was Donna Leggate. "Gloria Feit is chief of staff for Catherine Doyle. Doyle has some special assignment, but there's no record of what it is. Since I know something about these matters, I believe Doyle has a team—and it's deep black. And that means there may be no official record of employees or missions. Ed wouldn't tell me more. Frankly, I doubt he knows more, because it's above his security grade. Doyle appears to me to be a NOC." Nonofficial cover officers, NOCs, were those highly talented and daring officers who operated without the official cover of their CIA identification. If arrested in a foreign country, they could be tried and executed as spies.

"Thank you, Donna. I appreciate it. I'll put my people to work filtering in the money to your reelection campaign. We want good friends like you to stay in office."

As soon as he got rid of her, he phoned the director and relayed the information.

Stockholm, Sweden

It was noon in Stockholm, and Carl Lindström was sitting in the leather recliner chair in his office, reading financial reports, when the director called. Once he understood what the director wanted, Carl went to his desk, checked his e-mail, and found the note forwarded to him that contained the information the Washington break-in artist had uncovered from Ed Casey's secure e-mail to Langley.

Now he had a record not only of the routing, the message, and the address to which it was sent, but also the clandestine codes used.

With that, he phoned his chief of computer security, Jan Mardis. A former black-hat hacker herself, Jan was in charge of uncovering and stopping attacks on their worldwide network. She also kept her staff's expertise honed with regularly simulated assaults on their systems, designed hacking tools, and drafted network-infiltration tactics.

Upon occasion, she did special jobs for him. Through him, the Library of Gold's director had used her several times over the past few months.

"I have a challenge for you, Jan," Lindström told her. "And when you accomplish it, you can count on a generous bonus. I need you to crack into the CIA's computer system. There's a particular team I want you to find. It's run by Catherine Doyle. One office employee is Gloria Feit. The unit is probably black, which means they're going to appear to be unlisted, but we both know there's a record somewhere. I've sent you an e-mail with the information you'll need."

"Interesting." Jan Mardis's voice was usually bored, but not now. "Okay, I've read your e-mail. Barring complications, this should be fun, a dip in Lake Mälaren on a hot summer day, as it were. I'll route my signals through multiple countries—China and Russia, for sure. That'll stop the digital cops cold. I'll get back to you."

Carl Lindström stood and stretched. Cyber crime was the fastest growing criminal enterprise of the twenty-first century, and his software corporation, Lindström Strategies, was one of the fastest rising in the world. It had been attacked time and again. But because of Jan Mardis, no one had ever breached the firewalls. He had complete confidence in her not only because of her skill, but also because of human factors: He had saved her from a jail term by pulling strings in the judicial system, which included his promise to hire her. The occasional side job he secretly gave her allowed her to exercise her love of taking on some of the most highly secure organizations on the planet. And he paid her excessively well. As Machiavelli wrote, to succeed, it was critical to understand what motivated an individual—and use it.

As he waited to hear back from her, he walked to his bookcase, which was filled with leather-bound and embossed volumes. He pulled out a collection by August Strindberg, one of his favorite modern authors. He opened the book, and his gaze fell upon a passage: "A writer is only a reporter for what he has lived."

He thought about that, then he applied it to himself. His entire life's work, rising from the slums of Stockholm to create and head Lindström Strategies, was a reflection of what he had learned about the need to go to any length to armor against the indignities of poverty. With pride, he decided his corporation was his book, the book *he* had written.

An hour later, he was reading financial reports in his recliner again when the phone rang. He reached for it.

"It's me, boss," Jan Mardis said. "I've got a bonus for you. I've got access to Catherine Doyle's office computer. Is there anything you want me to look for?"

He sat up straight, and his pulse sped with excitement. "Send me a copy of all Doyle's e-mails for the last twenty-four hours. Then get the hell out of there."

25

Aloft over Europe

The Gulfstream V turbojet soared through the night, its powerful Rolls-Royce engines humming quietly. Above the aircraft stretched an endless canopy of sparkling stars, while far below spread gray storm clouds punctuated by jagged bolts of lightning. From his window Judd Ryder studied the skyscape, feeling a sense of suspension between two worlds, uncertain and somehow dangerous. He wondered what his father had been involved in, and how much he was his father's son.

Shaking off his emotions, he sat back and focused. The Gulfstream had been waiting at Gatwick Airport at a private hangar, one of the aircraft Langley regularly rented for transporting federal employees and high-value prisoners. He and Eva were the only passengers, sitting together near the middle of the cabin. Each armrest contained a laptop and hookups for electronic devices. On their tables stood steaming cups of coffee brewed in the galley. The rich aroma scented the air.

He peered at Eva's tired face, the rounded chin, the light California tan. Her red hair lay in a wreath of long curls around her head where it rested back against the seat. The lids of her blue eyes were at half-mast. At the moment she showed none of the fire and combativeness that had aggravated him, instead looking soft and vulnerable. He was still unsure what he really thought of her. In any case, it was irrelevant. What mattered was he needed her for the operation. He hoped to be able to ship her back to California soon.

Her eyes opened. "I should try to reach Peggy."

"You can't turn on your cell while we're flying, but you can borrow mine." He plugged his mobile's connecting cord into the armrest, tapping into the plane's wireless communications system. He explained about its secure mode, then showed her how to make what would appear to others to be a normal call.

She dialed Peggy's cell phone number. Listening to the voice on the other end, she looked at him and frowned. "May I speak to Peggy, please?" There was a pause. "I'm not going to tell you who I am until you tell me who you are." Another pause. Abruptly she cut the connection.

"What happened?" he asked instantly.

"A man answered. He kept asking questions." As she dialed again, she told him, "I'm calling information for the Chelsea Arms's number." Once she had it, she phoned out again. "Peggy Doty's room, please." She listened. "I know she has a room there. We were going to share it. . . What? She *what*?" Her face stricken, she hung up and stared at him. "Peggy's dead. The clerk says the police think she shot herself, but there's no way she'd take her own life. Someone had to have killed her." She shook her head, stunned. "I can't believe she's dead." Tears slid down her cheeks.

Watching her, he felt again the awful loss of his father, his conflicted emotions. He went to the galley and returned with a box of tissues and handed it to her. As she wiped her eyes and blew her nose, he said, "My guess is Charles told Preston that Peggy was your friend, and Preston went to her in hopes of finding you. He's her killer. I'm sorry, Eva. This is horrible for you."

He had a sudden vision of his father when he was about his age, towering over him as he rode the carousel at Glen

Echo Park. The full head of blond hair, the strong nose and chin, the happy expression on his face as the music filled the air and he stood beside his son protectively. About five years old, Judd had been riding a palomino horse with a flowing silver mane. As the horse rose and fell and the carousel circled, he felt himself slipping. His mother waved, her face beaming with pride. As he raised a hand to wave back, he fell, his legs too short to reach the floor to steady himself. He dangled half off the horse.

"Hold on tight and pull yourself up," his father had said calmly. "You can do it."

He had grabbed the pole hard, his little arms aching as he slowly righted himself.

"You can do anything, Judd. Anything. Someday you won't need me to stand beside you anymore."

Suddenly he realized Eva was talking.

"Those people are unspeakably evil." She was staring at him, her expression cold. "Those bastards. We've got to find them."

"We will." He grabbed his peacoat from the seat across from them. "Ready to do some work?"

"Absolutely."

He removed the items he had taken from her husband—disposable cell, small leather-bound notebook, billfold, and Swiss Army knife. Leaving the Glock pistol in his pocket, he heaved the peacoat across the next seat. Then he took off his corduroy jacket and tossed it on top. He sat back and adjusted his shoulder holster.

She had the notebook in her hand, turning pages. He thought about it, then decided to let her have a go at the notebook first.

He checked Sherback's cell, looking for phone numbers. "He's coded his address book. What would he use for a password?"

"Probably something classical. A Greek or Roman name. Try Seneca, Sophocles, Pythagoras, Cicero, Augustus, Archimedes—"

"Okay, I get the idea." He tapped in one after another.

"This is interesting," she said at last. "I've looked at all the pages, but there aren't any lists of names with or without phone numbers or addresses. There seem to be only his thoughts and various quotations. Each entry's dated, going back six years. That means he had it while we were living together, but I never saw it."

"He kept it hidden from you, so there was already a pattern of secrecy."

She nodded. "Listen to this—it's the first entry, and it'll give you a taste: 'In ancient times, worshiping a god occurred in some beautiful grove, holy place, or temple. It's no accident almost all libraries were in pagan places of worship, just as in later Muslim, Jewish, and Christian times they were in mosques, tabernacles, and churches. The written word has always had a magical, divine power, unifying people. Naturally religion wanted to control that. But then books are another name for God.' "

"See whether he mentions the Library of Gold or Yitzhak Law somewhere."

"I've been looking. Here's another one: 'There are books I will never be able to find, let alone read.' "

"Poignant."

She nodded and resumed reading silently.

Judd was running out of names to break Charles's cell phone code. He stopped, his fingers poised above the keypad.

She gazed up. "I've just found one of Charles's favorite quotes. It's from Aristotle. 'All people by nature desire to know.' That seems appropriate. Try 'Aristotle.' "

He typed the letters of the Greek philosopher's name, and the screen revealed the address book. "I'm in. The bad news is that it's empty. He must've memorized the numbers he called. Okay, time to check the ingoing and outgoing calls." The list was coded, but 'Aristotle' worked again. "There are only two. Both are London numbers. Do you recognize either?" He read them to her.

She shook her head. "Try them."

He dialed. The first number rang four times, and an automated voice invited him to leave a message. He considered, then ended the connection. She was watching him.

"A machine answered," he reported. He tried the next number and got the same response. "Nothing again."

"When I spotted Charles on the street outside the hotel, he was with a blond woman. Those two cell numbers could belong to Preston and her. I didn't recognize her, but Charles and she were obviously together."

"Describe her."

"Long blond hair and bangs. Pretty. Early to mid thirties, I'd say. Maybe five foot six. She had a large rolling suitcase. He was carrying a backpack and left it at her feet just before he started chasing me. The backpack was fat and solid-looking, so it could've contained *The Book of Spies.*"

"That'd account for the book's being in the hotel."

"Yes." She turned back to the first page of Charles's notebook.

Ryder examined the Swiss Army knife. There was nothing to indicate it was Charles's or anyone else's. Opening the billfold, he took out the driver's license and cash and spread them onto the tray table.

"I may have found something." Eva patted the notebook. "As I told you, everything's dated in here. I've been looking for patterns. With one exception, Charles would write something occasionally, once a week at most. But then there's a three-month period before we went to Rome in which he made a lot of entries, sometimes several a day. That's when he was on sabbatical, supposedly visiting some of the world's great libraries. I never got a real itinerary out of him, and he didn't talk much about the trip when he returned."

"Does he mention which libraries?"

"No, but what he wrote is almost entirely about libraries."

"What do you think the change in pattern means?"

"First, he had enough time he could write his thoughts more frequently and the value of libraries was on his mind. But, second, he wouldn't have wanted me or anyone at the library to know he'd tattooed something onto his scalp. So this is the sequence I see: He tattooed himself, spent three months hiding out, and came home to me with hair long and thick enough for it to look normal. Then we celebrated our anniversary with Yitzhak in Rome. Two weeks later we were back in L.A., and then two weeks after that was the car crash."

"Makes sense."

They drank their coffee and continued to work. He found nothing written on any of Charles's cash. He put the driver's license and money back into the billfold and returned everything to his peacoat's pockets. Next he checked the clip to Charles's Glock. The gun was clean and in pristine condition. No rounds were missing.

Eva handed him the notebook. "I can't see anything else that's useful in here. Your turn."

He took it. "You look tired. Why don't you get some sleep?"

"I think I will." She set her coffee cup on his table and stored her table inside her armrest. Then she reached down and pulled up her pants leg. "I'm going to take off this ankle device."

"No. If something happens to separate us again, I can always find you with my reader."

She thought about it and nodded. Reclining her seat, she closed her eyes.

He e-mailed Tucker, asking him to trace the two phone numbers on Sherback's cell and to investigate whether Sherback and perhaps a woman had stayed at the Méridien hotel, adding the false name on Sherback's driver's license, the woman's description, and that *The Book of Spies* might have been in her backpack. When he had phoned Tucker to arrange the jet, he had filled him in on the events of the night and given him Professor Yitzhak Law's address in Rome and asked him to check with the London police about Preston and Charles Sherback's body.

He studied the notebook, finding nothing new. Then he looked at Eva a long time. Finally he rested his head back, hoping he would not dream about the past. At last he fell into an uneasy sleep.

26

London, England

Doug Preston sat in his rental car in a public parking lot near the River Thames, arms crossed, head resting back, drifting in and out of sleep. He had delivered Charles's body to the Library of Gold jet, and it was safely gone. He had also phoned his NSA contact, who had gotten back to him with the bad news that Eva Blake's cell phone was turned off, which meant it could not be tracked yet. Then he had handled a new assignment for Martin Chapman, hiring a specialist in Washington to break into Ed Casey's house.

Now he was waiting for a call from NSA that Blake's cell phone was activated and her location pinpointed, or from the director that he had learned through Ed Casey's intel where Blake was going. Either would do.

Restless, he adjusted his aching body behind the steering wheel. Springtime shadows dappled the parking lot. Somewhere on the river a boat's horn sounded. He checked his watch. It was a little past one p.m. He closed his eyes, ignoring the pain in his ribs. He was starting to sink back into sleep when his cell finally rang.

Martin Chapman's tone was full of outrage: "Tucker Andersen is CIA."

"So State was his cover. Tell me everything." Preston shook off the chilling news.

"Judd Ryder e-mailed Tucker Andersen. The reason we know is because Andersen sent a copy of the e-mail to

Catherine Doyle, also CIA. They're part of some kind of black program. Doyle is chief." The director's voice was tense. "Ryder is a private contractor for CIA now."

"Jonathan Ryder's son?"

"Yes. He's the gunman, and he's been helping Eva Blake. Everything in the British Museum *was* a setup. The CIA's the one that planted the bug on the book and got Blake's sentence commuted. They intend to find the Library of Gold. We're going up against your old employer, Preston. You were loyal." The voice had grown harder, the question unspoken.

"That was a long time ago. Another life. I was glad to walk away. Even gladder you wanted me." Then he said the words he knew the director needed to hear, and he meant them: "My loyalty is only to you, the book club, and the Library of Gold."

There was a pause. "The e-mail said Ryder and Blake were heading to Rome to see Yitzhak Law. You can't get there in time. How do you suggest this be handled?"

Preston stared out the car's window, considering. A plan formed in his mind, and he laid it out for the director.

"Good. I like it," the director said. "Since we're dealing with a black unit, it's contained. That's the only advantage we have. I have an idea to take care of Tucker Andersen and Catherine Doyle. I'll get back to you when I need you."

27

Rome, Italy

It was three o'clock in the afternoon, the sun bright, almost overwhelming after the cold gray rain of London, when Eva walked through the centuries-old Monti section of Rome. Just south of Via Nazionale, Monti was an oasis of artists, writers, and the monied, and was seldom listed in tourist guides. Tall ivy-covered houses lined the street, interrupted only by cobblestone alleyways not much wider than a Roman chariot. Pedestrians strolled along the streets.

Clasping her shoulder satchel to her side, Eva risked a glance back. As expected, Judd was still several houses behind, looking Mediterranean in his sunglasses, swarthy face, and arched nose. They had stopped to buy new clothes so they would fit in with the warmer weather and locals' tastes. He wore a loose brown sports jacket, an open-necked blue shirt, and Italian jeans. She wore Italian jeans, too, with a green shirt and jacket.

As Fiats and scooters rushed by, she passed a leafy piazza filled with preschool children romping under the doting gazes of nannies. At last she crossed onto the busy street where Yitzhak Law lived.

As he followed Eva, Judd covertly scrutinized the bustling area, picking out the three-person team Tucker Andersen had sent to watch over Professor Law's home.

Across the street was one: a man with a cloth shopping sack, dressed in a worn business suit and sitting on a bench. A quarter block away was another—what appeared to be an elderly woman, sunk into a beach chair beneath a pepper tree outside a trattoria while she read the Italian daily *La Repubblica*. The third was a youthful skateboarder in sunglasses and a backpack. He slalomed lazily past, wearing earphones as his hips gyrated to music.

Judd used his mobile to call the skateboarder—the team leader. "Anything new, Bash?"

The unit had been in place an hour, not as long as he would have liked, but they'd had to be assembled from Catapult's undercover officers already on operations in and near Rome.

"Everything's cool, man. No one's gone in or left," Bash Badawi reported. He sailed his skateboard off the curb.

"Let me know if the situation changes."

Judd watched Eva moving ahead, her stride long and confident, her red hair blazing in the shimmering sunlight. He picked up his pace.

As he passed her, he said without moving his lips, "It's safe. Go in."

Yitzhak Law's house was a three-story building of aged yellow stone with large windows and white shutters. Eva ran up the worn steps and touched the bell. Chimes rang inside.

When the door opened, she smiled widely. "*Buon giorno,* Roberto." Roberto Cavaletti was Yitzhak's longtime partner.

"Do not just stand there, Eva. Come in, come in. I am delighted." He kissed her on both cheeks, his close-cropped brown beard prickling. Short and lean, he gave the appearance of a sleek fox, with a long, intelligent face and bright brown eyes.

"I've brought a friend," she warned.

She turned and nodded in Judd's direction. Glancing around, Judd was soon at her side, and they stepped into an entryway of antiques and paintings. The fragrant scents of a spicy tomato sauce lingered in the air. In Rome, lunch was traditionally the largest meal of the day and eaten between noon and three o'clock at home, which was why she had high hopes of finding Yitzhak here.

She introduced Judd as her traveling friend from America.

"*Benvenuto,* Judd. Welcome." Roberto shook his hand enthusiastically. "You are not jet-lagged? You do not look jet-lagged." It was an ongoing concern of Roberto's, who never traveled beyond the borders of Rome's time zone, despite Yitzhak's frequent invitations to accompany him.

"Not a speck of jet lag," Judd assured him.

Relieved, Roberto turned to Eva, put his hands on his hips, and scolded, "You have not kept in touch." With a single short sentence, he had covered the car crash, her guilty plea, and her imprisonment, at the same time letting her know as far as he was concerned they were still friends.

"You're right, and it's my fault. I loved the letter from you and Yitzhak." She had not trusted the compassion in the men's note, and so she had never answered it. With sudden clarity she saw how she had isolated herself.

"You are completely forgiven. Like the Pope, I am stern but magnanimous. Are you hungry? Would you like *un caffè*? It is dripping even now." In Rome, coffee was as important as wine.

"Coffee would be great," she said. "The way you always make it, *molto caldo.*"

He smiled, acknowledging the compliment, and turned to Judd. "And you, Eva's friend?"

"Absolutely. Let us help you."

Roberto raised his brows at Eva. "He has good manners.

I approve." Then he whispered in her ear, "And he's gorgeous." He pointed in the Italian way with an outstretched hand, palm down, toward the hallway, then he followed them.

As they passed open doors showing a sitting room and a small, elegant dining room, she asked, "Is Yitzhak home? We'd love to see him, too."

"Of course. And he will want to see you. You will take coffee to him. He is in his *rifugio*."

They went into the modern kitchen, which gleamed with enameled white walls and a stainless-steel refrigerator and gas stove. The aroma of fresh coffee infused the airy room. Roberto poured coffee into a carafe, then arranged cups, a cream pitcher, a sugar bowl, and spoons on a tray.

He indicated the tray. "It is your responsibility, Judd."

Judd picked it up. "Lead on."

Roberto took them out into the hall again and toward the back of the house, where a broad staircase rose two floors. But he opened the door beneath, the stairs showing simple wood steps going down. Cool air drifted up. They ducked their heads and descended into the cellar, which reflected the house's period in its rough brick walls and uneven brick floor.

In the center of the floor was the area's dominant feature—a ragged hole with wood steps, built only ten years before, going down into what seemed an abyss. Beside it lay a trapdoor of old bricks built on top of a plywood platform. The trapdoor was the exact dimensions of the hole, and when it was put into place, Eva knew, the bricks fit neatly into one another, hiding the hole.

Judd stared down and deadpanned, "Where are the flames? The screams of suffering souls?"

Roberto laughed. "This is not Dante's *Inferno,* my new friend. You are about to see a glorious sight few others have. But then, this is Rome, once the *caput mundi,* the capital of the world, teeming with more than a million souls while Paris and London were mere outposts of mud huts. No wonder we Romans are so proud. Here is where I leave you." He called down, "We have two more visitors, *amore mio*. Prepare yourself for a pleasant surprise."

"More visitors?" Judd's expression was curious, revealing nothing. The presence of outsiders would complicate their ability to find out quickly from Yitzhak what Charles's message meant.

Roberto nodded and said mysteriously, "Eva will be happy about it." He returned upstairs.

Eva had learned about the steep steps in previous visits. She turned and went down backwards, gripping the rail. Balancing the tray, Judd followed, and they entered the professor's private preserve.

It was a vast area, illuminated by torchère lamps and encompassing the width of the house. The length stretched from the rear garden to the street, where there appeared to be a small tunnel at the edge of a long pile of rubble. The flooring was glowing purple Phrygian marble. Placed here and there on it were statues of nudes uncovered during the excavation. Pink marble columns partially exposed—they were still mostly embedded in raw brown earth—shone palely. One wall was revealed; it was smooth, flat brickwork displaying the meticulous craftsmanship of builders two thousand years ago. Its centerpiece, which always made Eva's heart beat a little faster, was a stunning mosaic displaying Jupiter and Juno, king and queen of the Roman gods, reclining on thrones. Few had seen it since it was buried in antiquity.

She sensed Judd's awe, and then an instant return to acute awareness. His gaze swept the room, where Yitzhak sat with a man and a woman in wood chairs around an unvarnished wood table on which lay his notes and reading glasses. An American, the professor was a world-renowned scholar of medieval Greek and Roman history, with an emphasis on Judaism. He had published a dozen books on the subject.

Eva put a smile on her face, and all three stood up. The professor hurried toward her, arms outstretched. He was a small, slope-shouldered man who exuded the energetic optimism of a Rome native. His face and belly were round, his gaze sharp, and his head completely bald, shining in the light. In his early sixties, he was fifteen years older than Roberto.

"My dear, it's been far too long." He enveloped her in his arms.

"Much too long." She hugged him.

When he released her, she introduced him to Judd.

"You like my little sanctum sanctorum, Judd?" Yitzhak asked curiously. "It was once the domain of wealthy families in the Augustan era. Roberto saw some pottery shards beneath the cellar's bricks when we had to do some repair work, and that's how we discovered it."

Eva explained, "Ancient Rome is a buried city, lying under layers of history forty-five feet deep in places. What you're seeing is unusual—more than eighty percent is still uncovered."

Yitzhak said in a mock whisper, "Please don't tell on us, Judd. We private homeowners do our digging like thieves in the night because we don't want the Beni Culturali knocking on our doors to evict us. And they have a habit of doing just that, so they can make our little finds public." He gazed around, his eyes glowing. "The silence and seclusion make the distant past seem eerily tangible, don't they?"

"They do," Judd agreed as he set the coffee tray on the table. Then he said just what Yitzhak wanted to hear: "Your place is very beautiful."

The professor smiled broadly, his round face crinkling. "You must meet my other guests. This is Odile and Angelo

Charbonier, in from Paris by way of Sardinia. We've had a delightful lunch. But then, why not? We're old friends. Such good old friends that Angelo's been buying and reading my books for years, emphasis on 'buying.'" He winked at Judd. "Who can ask more than that? Eva, I believe you already know the Charboniers."

Angelo pumped Judd's hand. "Delighted." His French accent was light.

A little more than six feet tall and in his late forties, Angelo looked fresh-faced and vigorous in his open-necked white shirt, beige jacket, and slacks. His face was chiseled in the way of European men who spent long hours in the gyms of their exclusive athletic clubs. Although he was a rich investment banker, Eva had always found him to be a down-to-earth and charming companion at the openings and dinner parties where they had met.

Eva could read nothing on Judd's smiling face as he responded, "It's good to meet you."

Always more reticent, Odile shook Judd's hand and said simply, "A pleasure."

"For me as well," Judd said.

A little younger than Angelo, Odile was quieter, with refined features and perfectly coiffed platinum-blond hair. She made a graceful athletic figure in her highly expensive velour jacket and trousers. At the same time, there was a steely quality about her that no doubt had been useful as Angelo and she had climbed high in Paris society through his business connections and her philanthropic work.

After exchanging pleasantries with Judd, Angelo turned to Eva. "I am sorry about Charles. Of course his death was a tragedy. Will you forgive me for saying whatever happened, it was also an accident and surely not your fault? Charles was a great man, and you are a great lady. Odile and I have always been fond of you."

He glanced at Odile, who gave a firm nod of agreement.

Odile shook Eva's hand. "Oh, *chérie,* we are simply too sorry for words."

Immediately, Angelo extended his hand, too. Touched, Eva took it. He pressed his lips against the back. When he looked up, he smiled into her eyes. "I'm glad you weren't badly injured in the car accident."

"Thank you, Angelo. Thank you, Odile. You're both very kind."

"Why didn't I know you were coming, Eva?" Yitzhak complained, appraising her. "We've heard nothing from you in a very long time."

"It's all my fault," she admitted. "I wasn't sure—"

"That we still adored you?" Yitzhak finished for her. "Silly girl. Of course we do."

"You will be interested to know Yitzhak and I were just talking about the Library of Gold," Angelo told her. "We missed the opening at the British Museum."

"Ah, *The Book of Spies*. What a find." Yitzhak bent over the table and picked up the carafe. "Who wants coffee?"

"Enjoy yourselves. I am going upstairs to ask Roberto for my usual aperitif," Odile said.

As she climbed the steps, Yitzhak added cream and sugar as requested, then handed the cups around. As the four stood together, Eva glanced at Judd, who had been covertly studying the Charboniers. He smiled at her over his cup as he drank. She could read nothing in his gray eyes.

"If only Charles were still alive so he could have attended the opening," the Frenchman said. "I am certain he would have given us another theory about the library's location. His theories were always very clever." He peered at Eva. "Were you able to go?"

"Yes. It was interesting, and *The Book of Spies* is fabulous."

"I'm envious." The professor sipped his coffee.

"What do you think Charles would have said?" Angelo asked curiously.

Before she could answer, Judd interrupted. "As a matter of fact, Charles did say something—in a way."

Surprised, Eva stared at him.

"Eva," he told her, "I think this is a good time to fill in the professor. No need to bore him with a long explanation. Just give him Charles's message."

Judd seemed to have decided it was safe to do so. Angelo Charbonier was a bibliophile, too, and perhaps he might be helpful—or was Judd testing the Frenchman in some way?

"It's something I discovered recently." Eva paused. "It was just your name, 'Law,' and the date of Charles's and my wedding anniversary in 2008—the one we spent with you and Roberto. Do you know why Charles would leave a message for me like that?"

The professor frowned, trying to remember. He rubbed his chin. At last he chuckled. "Of course. My old brain had nearly forgotten. Charles left a secret gift for you, Eva—or for an emissary if you sent one—but you had to ask for it and mention the anniversary date." He walked toward the ladder.

"It's here?" Eva asked, excited.

He turned, his eyes dancing. "Yes. Come with me. I'm eager to know what it is, too."

28

Eva followed Yitzhak, and they climbed upstairs, first into the cellar and then back into the house. Angelo and Judd brought up the rear. In the hallway Eva could hear Odile's and Roberto's voices floating back from the sitting room.

The professor led them through the airy kitchen and into a large storage room lined with metal shelves stacked with cardboard boxes. They stood beside the professor, the air electric with suspense as he peered around.

"Now, where did I put it?" Lips pursed, he headed into the back and pushed aside some cartons. When he emerged, he was carrying a small box taped tightly shut. He rotated it to show the top. "See? Here's your name, Eva." He handed it to her.

She stared at the handwriting. It was Charles's.

"Perhaps it is some fabulous necklace from ancient Persia, or jeweled earrings from Mesopotamia." Angelo's chiseled features were alight with excitement.

"Open it," Yitzhak ordered.

She tore off the tape and lifted the lid. On top of Styrofoam bubbles lay two pieces of protective paper boards about eight inches wide by twelve inches long, held together with clips. She separated them, revealing a fragment of parchment. One side showed cramped, faded Arabic lettering, while the other side was blank. There was nothing written on the protective boards.

"What's that?" Judd asked.

"It looks like something from an ancient document." Eva handed the yellowed piece to Yitzhak. It was much smaller than the boards, about three by four inches.

"Let's go into the kitchen, where I can see better." Yitzhak led them back into the room, where he carefully put the fragment on a high butcher-block table.

She watched as he scrubbed his hands at the sink. Many professional archivists wore white cotton gloves when handling manuscripts and other artworks to protect them from skin oils and acids. At the same time, others claimed gloves were dangerous, since they not only could contain unseen dirt and particles, but they also minimized the wearer's sensitivity when handling the article. For them, thorough hand-washing was the better choice. Yitzhak belonged to the hand-washing school, as did she. Charles had been a white-glove archivist.

When Yitzhak finished, she washed her hands, and he ordered Judd and Angelo to do the same.

She joined Yitzhak on one side of the high table as he positioned his reading glasses on his nose. Judd joined Angelo on the other side, two men of the same height with similar body builds, she noticed.

As Yitzhak muttered to himself, translating the fragment, Eva dug through the Styrofoam packing in the box. "There's something else in here."

She pulled out a tapered cylinder of glistening gold, about eight inches long and, judging by its heft, hollow. At the narrowest end it was two inches in diameter; at the other, about four inches. Perfectly round ivory knobs shone on each terminus.

Yitzhak stared at the baton. "Simple, but spectacular."

"Gorgeous," Angelo said. "But what is it? Is there any writing on it?"

"Does it open?" Judd asked.

Eva rotated the cylinder, and everyone leaned close.

"There are small engravings of arrows, shields, and helmets. Decorations, no writing. I can't find a way to open it. You try, Judd." She could see nothing that related to the Library of Gold. She handed it to him.

"It looks very old," Angelo observed.

"It is," Eva told him. "And it's not only a work of art; it had a real purpose. You can tell from the deep patina—the small abrasions and scratches that come from being used. It didn't just sit on some mantel in a throne room."

"If it opens," Judd reported, "I don't see how."

"I will attempt." The Frenchman took the conical baton, cupped it in both hands, and studied it.

Yitzhak peered up at them over his reading glasses. "The fragment is Arabic Judaica. Military poetry. It mentions the Spartans and secret letters."

"That's it," Eva said, understanding. "The fragment gives us the clues—the Spartans, secret letters, and the military. The cylinder is a *scytale*." She pronounced the word *SIT-ally*, rhyming with *Italy*. "The Spartans invented the *scytale* around 400 B.C. for secret communication between military commanders. It's the first use of cryptography for correspondence that we know about, but *scytali* are usually uniform in diameter—not tapered like this one. When I curated an exhibit of ancient Greek artifacts at the Getty, I got lucky and found one to display, but it was plain laurel wood."

"How does it work?" Judd asked.

"A narrow strip of parchment or leather is wrapped around the baton from one end to the other without overlapping itself. Then the message is written lengthwise along the *scytale*. When the strip's unwrapped, the writing looks like scrambled letters, gibberish. At that point a messenger takes it to the recipient, who winds the ribbon around his own *scytale*—

which obviously must have the same dimensions. Then he can read it."

"So *scytali* were used for transposition ciphers," Judd said. "Let me see it again, Angelo."

Reluctantly, Angelo handed it over. "It warms the hands. Gold does that."

Yitzhak smiled at Eva. "Charles left you a lovely gift. It's probably worth a great deal of money."

"It would be my honor to buy it from you," Angelo said instantly.

"Thanks, Angelo. But I want to keep it."

He pursed his lips, disappointed. "Is there anything more in the box? I'm still waiting for that necklace from Persia."

She took the *scytale* from Judd, laid it on the table, and dug through the carton.

"I'm wondering whether Angelo's right," Judd said. "Whether there shouldn't be something else—for instance, a strip of paper with another message from Charles that fits around the *scytale* for you to read."

Eva stared at him, then abruptly turned over the carton, spilling out the Styrofoam bubbles. As the others spread them out, she inspected the inside of the box.

"There are tiny words written on the bottom," she said, surprised. "I need something to cut open the sides."

Judd grabbed a bread knife from a magnetic holder above the counter and handed it to her. She sliced open the cardboard, and he returned the knife.

"It's Charles's writing." She read aloud:

" 'Think about the Cairo *geniza*. But the *geniza* of the world's desire has the answer.' "

"What's a *geniza*?" Judd asked.

"It's the Hebrew word for a container or hiding place," Yitzhak explained. "All the tattered books and pages—from old Haggadahs and dictionaries to business invoices and children's readers—are put in some safe place in a synagogue, perhaps inside a wall or in an attic, until they can be given a proper burial."

"Veneration of the written word is common in religion," Angelo said. "For instance, Muslims believe the Koran is too holy simply to be discarded."

"But the Jewish *geniza* is different," Yitzhak explained. "It recognizes that not a single book but the written word in general is sacred. In the rabbinical tradition, a *geniza* is a grave of written things."

"Where does Cairo fit in?" Judd asked.

Yitzhak stood back and closed his eyes, reverie on his face. "It's long, long ago—the end of the ninth century—and the Jews of what became Cairo are renovating a destroyed Coptic church to be their synagogue. They carve an opening near the top of a tall tower. Children and adults climb the ladder every day to drop inside all the books and pieces of paper we'd throw away now. Can you hear the rustle as they fall through the air? The contributions pile up for a thousand years—a thousand years!—and the desert preserves everything. Then a little more than a century ago, the rabbis finally allow investigation."

His eyes snapped open. "Voilà! The *geniza* yields up its treasures. One priceless fragment belonged to *The Wisdom of Ben Sira*—Ecclesiasticus. The earliest version we'd had until then was Greek, although the original was written long before that, in Hebrew in 200 B.C. Because of Cairo's tomb in the air, we know far more about how people from India to Russia and Spain lived, what they thought about, what they ate and bought and fought over. Scores of scholarly books resulted."

"But what does that have to do with anything?" Angelo asked. "This is another mystery. Charles had an annoying habit of being oblique." He eyed the *scytale* shining on the table.

Judd kept them on point. "How does Charles's *scytale* relate to 'the *geniza* of the world's desire'?"

"His note indicates he didn't mean the Cairo *geniza*," Eva said. "So it's not Cairo."

"Of course you're right." Judd smiled. "But Istanbul is. That's what it's called—the City of the World's Desire."

"Every synagogue there would have a *geniza*," the professor said. "But that's a lot of *genizot* to have to dig through."

Judd looked across the table to the professor. "Charles may have left the package with you not only because he trusted you to hold it for Eva, but because you might understand what he meant for her to do next."

"My friend, you have a point," Yitzhak agreed. "Let me think. . . Istanbul. *Geniza*. . ." He frowned and ran a hand over his bald head. At last he smiled. "Charles could be such a tease. I think he must've meant Andrew Yakimovich. Yakimovich has the largest private collection of documents from the Cairo *geniza* in Istanbul. Actually the largest in the region."

"I remember him," Eva said. "He's an antiquities dealer."

She had been concentrating on Yitzhak, but now she glanced at Judd in time to see his gaze focus on Angelo, whose hand had just slipped into and out of his jacket pocket. Judd turned casually away.

"Does this Yakimovich person live in Istanbul?" The fine lines on Angelo's chiseled face deepened with curiosity.

"He's notoriously secretive and moves around a lot," she told him. "I don't remember his address there, and even if I did, it'd be no help."

"He's advised Charles and me in the past." Yitzhak took off his reading glasses and addressed Eva: "I wouldn't be a bit surprised that since Charles left the *scytale* with me, he also left what Judd calls a transposition cipher with Andrew." He added cheerfully, "Another gift, Eva. I wonder what message Charles wrote on it."

"Finding Yakimovich will be a trick—" Eva froze.

Angelo had pulled a pistol from inside the back of his waistband and quickly whipped it around to aim at them. But Judd was already moving. As Angelo's mouth opened to warn him off, Judd lowered his head, his feet flew over the floor, and his shoulder rammed into the Frenchman's chest. They landed with a thud against the kitchen wall.

"What are you doing!" Yitzhak bellowed. "Stop this!"

Eva grabbed the professor's arm and yanked him down behind the butcher-block table just as the gun exploded. The noise shook the room. A bullet blasted into the ceiling, and plaster sprayed down in a snowstorm.

Angelo slammed the pistol at Judd's head. Judd dodged, ripped the gun away, and pinned Angelo's throat with his forearm. He pointed the weapon at his temple.

Angelo's face was red and furious. He swore in French.

"A man who doesn't want anyone to know he's a threat shouldn't have a bulge at the back of his jacket." Judd's voice was calm. "I saw it when I followed you up the ladder. What do you have to do with the Library of Gold?"

"You will never know," Odile said from the kitchen doorway.

Eva spun around. Roberto was walking shakily in, with Odile behind him, her hand steady as she held a pistol to the back of his head.

The room turned silent.

"Judd, give the gun back to Angelo," Odile commanded. "Or I will kill Roberto."

29

Riding his skateboard, Bash Badawi cruised along the street opposite Yitzhak Law's home. He appeared casual in his baggy shorts, zippered hoodie jacket, and small backpack. His straight jet-black hair framed a dusky-colored face and almond-shaped brown eyes. Although he wore earphones as part of his disguise, the only sound he heard was the constant rumble of traffic and the talk of the pedestrians he passed.

As he slalomed across the intersection and turned back to retrace his route on the other side, he checked Quinn, who still sat stoically on the bench with his cloth shopping sack, and then Martina, who remained in her beach chair under the pepper tree, apparently reading the newspaper, chin tilted high. Everything was under control.

Still, he slowed his skateboard to study the area, wondering about a man who was pushing a baby carriage. Dressed in gray sweatpants and sweatshirt, he had passed by a half hour ago, returned, and was now heading off around the corner again. The man was big and bulky, with sharp features and thick black eyebrows. He could simply be taking the baby out for fresh air, circling the block.

Bash also noted a man with long brown hair and a thin face, riding a blue Vespa motor scooter. He had driven past fifteen minutes ago and perhaps earlier, too. Motor scooters were ubiquitous in Rome, and many Vespas rushed along the street. The man might be a messenger of some kind.

Passing beneath a branching maple tree, Bash again neared

Yitzhak Law's old house. He could see no one through the windows. But then as he cruised past, there was a faint explosion from deep inside, the noise muffled by the stone walls. A gunshot. His chest tightened. He did an immediate one-eighty and dug his foot into the pavement, speeding back on his skateboard toward the steps.

In the kitchen, Judd held his pistol steadily against Angelo Charbonier's temple, his arm braced against his throat. With a single hard thrust, he could crush Angelo's windpipe if he tried to retake his weapon.

But now that Odile had arrived, Angelo smiled triumphantly. His eyes were as hard and black as anthracite. "Return my pistol, Judd," he ordered. "You do not want anything to happen to Roberto."

Roberto's face was pale with fear. Sweat glistened on his forehead. "I do not understand . . ." He stared helplessly at Yitzhak.

The professor had risen from his hiding place behind the table. His eyes blinked too fast as he demanded, "Put your guns away. All of you. What is this insanity?"

Odile asked her husband in French, "Have you summoned the men?"

Eva started to translate for Judd.

Judd interrupted her. "I know what Odile said. And my guess is their men are either here or soon will be. I saw Angelo reach into his pocket when he heard about Yakimovich." He said to Angelo, "You figured you'd learned all you were going to, so you signaled them, right?"

Angelo's smile widened, but he did not answer the question. "We now have, as you Yankees say, a standoff. If you do not return my weapon, Odile will shoot Roberto. And she will, believe me."

"I'm tempted to fire anyway," Judd said. "Wipe you, and by the time Odile pulls her trigger, I'll get off a clean shot at her. Then you'll both be dead."

Odile stepped farther behind Roberto so his body was a better shield against the threat of Judd. "There is another solution," she said. "You and I can put down our weapons. We can talk."

"Lower your gun, Odile," Judd said, "and I'll lower mine."

She nodded. As their gazes locked, they let their gun hands descend.

As he neared the house's steps, Bash Badawi slowed his skateboard, watching again. Something besides the gunshot was wrong, but he could not quite identify it. The afternoon sunlight beat down harshly, turning the street scene with its growling cars and low scooters and bobbing pedestrians into waves of streaming color. As his mind quickly sorted through what his eyes saw, he realized six men in shorts and T-shirts in wide bands of green, white, and red—the colors of Italy's flag—had rounded the corner in a bunch, feet light and forearms raised, hands loose, in the usual way of joggers. All apparently normal.

But it was not. The pack broke up and scattered, still jogging. Four moved across the street toward Carl and Martina, while two headed in his direction. They were janitors, hired killers, and they had targeted him and his team, which meant someone—perhaps the Vespa rider or the man in the sweatsuit, pushing the baby carriage—had already cased the area for them.

His gaze on the pair who were jogging toward him, Bash slid his hand inside his jacket, unhooked his shoulder holster, and gripped the handle of his Browning.

* * *

As Judd kept his gaze on Odile, he and she lowered their pistols to their sides. No one moved or spoke, suspended in a tableau of tension. The only sound was Roberto's short, frightened breaths, which seemed to shudder against the hard surfaces of the kitchen. He ran to Yitzhak, who put his arm around him.

Appearing to give Roberto room, Eva moved closer to Odile and stopped when she was about four feet away. Judd exchanged a glance with her, remembering her expertise in karate. She narrowed her eyes and gave a slight nod.

Judd stepped back from Angelo. "Tell me about the Library of Gold."

But it was Odile who answered: "There is nothing to say. All of us have been curious about it for years, of course."

"Bullshit," Judd said. "The library's why you're here. Why Angelo pulled his gun. Why you have men outside. You want to stop us from finding it."

Angelo Charbonier straightened against the wall, smoothing his sports jacket. "What I want to know is whom you have informed about what you have learned."

"I'll tell you that," Judd lied, "if you tell me what your relationship is to the library."

"Hypothetically, let us assume you are correct that we have some knowledge," Angelo said slowly. "Perhaps even that I am a member of the small book club that supports the library."

"Was my father a member, too?" Judd asked immediately.

Angelo looked surprised a moment, then shook his head firmly. "Your turn."

It was a beginning, but Judd did not trust Angelo. "Suppose we give you the *scytale,* and you tell us more. Then all of us can walk away alive and forget this ever happened."

"That has possibilities," Angelo agreed.

Judd checked Eva again, and she stared back.

He gestured at the table. "There's the *scytale*. It's all yours, Odile. Take it."

"No!" Angelo shouted.

But he was too late. Odile was already striding toward it.

Bash made a fast decision. His assignment was to protect Judd Ryder and Eva Blake. His fellow team members, Martine and Quinn, would fend for themselves. He had to break into the professor's house, and quickly.

Neither of the two janitors jogging toward him had showed a weapon yet, and they likely planned not to until they were beside him and could liquidate him quietly. He focused on them, propelling himself faster and faster on his skateboard.

The pair was only twenty feet away. Still jogging, they tensed as they saw his increasing speed. They lifted their shirts a few inches and drew out small-caliber pistols with sound suppressors screwed on.

Bash snatched out his Browning. The air felt hot and slick as he raced through it. The two killers aimed. He bent his knees, slid his left foot forward to the nose of his skateboard, and used the other foot to stomp down on the tail. Instantly the board ollied, flying into the air.

Surprised, the men jerked their gazes up. Bash shifted his weight, and the skateboard crashed into the chest of one. He fell hard on his back, and his gun spun away.

Bash landed and rolled, shaking off the impact. A bullet bit into the pavement next to him, but he continued to roll. Pieces of concrete cut into his skin. The downed janitor was swiftly reaching for his gun and rising into a crouch as a second bullet blasted into the pavement near Bash's head.

Bash fired twice, once into the chest of the standing man and then into the chest of the other. Blood exploded from their T-shirts. Pedestrians who had been walking toward them from both directions rushed away, screaming and shouting. At the same time a gunshot sounded from across the street.

Jumping to his feet, Bash checked across the traffic. Martine was slumped in her chair, her head dangling over her chest, while Quinn lay on his side on the bench. Bash took a deep breath. Both were down. Then he saw their killers were jogging back to the curb, preparing to cross over and come after him.

He snatched up his skateboard and sprinted up the steps to Yitzhak Law's door.

30

The sound of Angelo's loud "No!" reverberated in Judd's ears as Odile lunged for the gold *scytale* glittering on the kitchen table. Eva slashed out a fist in a *kentsui-uchi* hammer strike into Odile's side, pivoted, and, keeping her hips horizontal and her torso perpendicular, rammed up her elbow in a *tate hiji-ate* blow to the underside of Odile's chin.

Odile's head snapped back, and her pistol fired. There was a moan, and Roberto crashed against the table and slid down to the floor, blood oozing from the top of his shoulder, where his shirt was torn by the bullet.

"Roberto! Roberto!" Yitzhak knelt over him.

Despite the attack, Odile had kept her grip firmly on her gun. As the two women struggled for it, Angelo dove at Judd.

Judd moved quickly out of reach, training his weapon on Angelo. "Stop, dammit."

Angry furrows creased Angelo's forehead. He cursed loudly but froze, staring at the pistol.

Judd glanced over at the women just as Eva prepared to smash the side of her hand at Odile's gun. But Odile slammed a *shutō-uchi* sword-hand strike to Eva's arm, then balanced and lashed out in a brutal *mae-geri* front snap kick to her leg.

Eva toppled, and Odile pressed the pistol's muzzle into her belly. Odile's platinum hair was wild, and her eyes naked with fury. Judd fired, his bullet going into the top of the Frenchwoman's head as she suddenly lowered it. Blood sprayed, and she dropped hard onto Eva, still clasping her weapon.

"Get her gun, Eva," Judd ordered as he turned back to cover Angelo.

But Angelo had yanked a sharp fileting knife from the magnetic holder above the counter. *"Bâtard."* He closed in.

Two more gunshots sounded from the kitchen doorway. Freezing in midstride, Angelo reeled, then fell, blood blossoming scarlet across his beige jacket where the rounds had entered.

As the stink of cordite spread through the room, Bash Badawi walked in, his gun still raised in one muscled hand while his skateboard dangled from the other.

"Lucky shots." Judd grinned at him.

"Lucky shots, my ass. Glad I got here in time for the party. How you doing, Eva?"

"Never better." Holding Odile's pistol, Eva crouched beside Roberto and Yitzhak. Her face and green jacket were splattered with blood.

Bash peered across at Angelo's motionless body, then down at Odile's. "They must've arrived before I did. There was no sign they were here."

Judd nodded. "How many janitors outside?"

"Four still in action, dressed like joggers. Two others down." He gave a brief smile, his young face suddenly amused. "I had a bit of a dustup with them." Then he added soberly, "We lost Martine and Quinn."

"That's bad. I'm sorry. How did you get in?"

"I picked the lock. The Polizia di Stato are on the way. I heard sirens, very close. Their focus is going to be on the two janitors in the street and Martine and Carl. The good thing is the sirens and witnesses have probably scared away the last four in the wet squad."

"But they could still come in the back door." Judd slammed

the dead bolt, then peered out the kitchen's large window, which overlooked a small rear yard of lilacs and grass. A brick pathway led to the end of a high brick wall, which enclosed the property. There was a cobblestone alleyway on the far side, showing through a wrought-iron gate. No one was in sight.

"We've got to get the hell out of here," Judd told them. "Check the woman, Bash. I'll take the man." He went to Angelo.

"Roberto needs a doctor," Eva reminded them. "How do you feel, Roberto?"

"It is over?" Roberto whispered. He was sitting up, leaning against a table leg. His bearded face was pasty, his lips dry.

"Everything's fine," she assured him.

"Hold this down for me." Yitzhak indicated to Eva the bloody handkerchief he had clamped onto Roberto's shoulder wound. "I'll call an ambulance."

"This one's a dead rat," Bash reported from where he stooped over Odile. "How's yours?"

"Dead, too." Judd wiped the handle of Angelo's pistol and pressed it into his flaccid hand. He searched Angelo's pockets, leaving the billfold. There was nothing useful inside; not even a cell phone. "Is your gun traceable, Bash?"

"No way. That dumb I'm not."

"Good. Put the woman's prints on it and leave it next to her. They'll look as if they shot each other. Take Odile's gun from Eva. You need to be armed."

"No." Reaching for the kitchen telephone, Yitzhak turned to glare at them. His face was an angry red, and drops of sweat dotted his bald head. "We have to give the police the whole truth."

Feeling the pressure of time, Judd ignored the professor and told Bash, "As soon as you're done here, go to the front of the house and check the windows. I want to know what's happening outside." Then he focused on Yitzhak. "Hang up the phone, professor. Roberto's got a flesh wound. We'll get him medical attention, but not just yet. Sticking around here could be your death warrant. Roberto's, too. These people have been trying to terminate Eva."

Yitzhak frowned at her. "That's true?"

"Yes," she told him. "Remember Ivan the Terrible's Oprichniki? That's what they're like—utterly ruthless."

"They're going to want to find out what you know about us and where we're going," Judd said. "They'll track you down, and as soon as you tell them, they'll kill you. All of us need to leave—and fast. Can you walk, Roberto?"

"I think so." His voice was weak. He had been listening, his brown eyes round and frightened. "Yes, it is obvious we must go."

Yitzhak put the telephone back into its cradle. "Eva, you take one side of Roberto, and I'll take the other."

As they supported him, Roberto rose to his feet, and Bash ran back into the room.

"The police are blocking off the street," he said. "I found the dead woman's purse in the sitting room. She didn't have a cell, either."

"I'd rather not risk going out the back door," Judd told him. "Yitzhak, I saw what looks like the beginning of a tunnel at the end of your refuge downstairs. Can we get out that way?"

"I think so, but it may not be easy." Yitzhak's voice was strong. With Roberto's uninjured arm draped over his shoulder, he had returned to his normal self.

Eva took the gold *scytale* and fragment of Arabic Judaica, and she and the others went ahead. Judd tore up the top and bottom of the cardboard box with Charles's writing and Eva's name. Stuffing the pieces into the garbage disposal, he turned it on, then threw the Styrofoam bubbles and the rest of the box into the trash. He peered around the kitchen to make certain they had left nothing behind. Last, he checked the window—and dropped below the counter. He rose up slowly, just enough to see out again.

Men were at the rear gate. One wore a gray sweatshirt and sweatpants; the others were dressed in jogging shorts and T-shirts. The big man in the sweatsuit tried to open the gate, but it was locked. Muttering to himself, he took out picklocks.

Judd raced to the stairs under the broad staircase and descended into the brick-lined cellar. Voices sounded, floating up from the ragged hole in the floor. He started down it, stopping to drag the brick trapdoor over the opening. It was heavy, but he leveraged it up and settled it into place. With luck, none of the killers would discover Yitzhak's secret domain.

He hurried down to the bottom, where Jupiter and Juno gazed regally from their thrones. The silence was luminous in the ancient room, a stillness that seemed to wrap around him and promise safety. But there was no safety yet.

Everyone was gathered at the street-side end of the long room, where rubble was strewn and a brown wall of dirt rose to the ceiling. Bash and Eva were throwing rocks out of the way. What had been a small tunnel was now much larger.

Eva saw him. "Are Angelo's men in the house?"

"Not yet, but they will be in minutes." Judd hurried toward them.

The tunnel was about four feet high and three feet wide. There was darkness on the other side, and he could hear the sound of distant running water. Five flashlights lay in a row on the marble floor.

"You must lead," Roberto told the professor, who was still supporting him. "I can walk by myself. Judd is right. I am fine—just messy looking." He glanced at the bloody handkerchief he was holding to his wound.

The professor nodded. "We're going under the street. Take your flashlights." He handed one to Roberto and picked up one for himself. Hunching over, he moved into the darkness.

"I'll go last," Judd told the others, thinking about the janitors who might be smarter than he hoped.

Bash grabbed his skateboard, and Eva slung her satchel onto her back. They disappeared into the burrow. Judd paused. When he heard nothing from above, he crouched and hurried into the darkness, his flashlight shooting a cone of light. The air began to smell of moss and damp.

The small group was waiting for him at the end.

"You need to see this," Eva told him.

He squeezed past to look out at a natural underground tunnel, black and seemingly endless, a crude dirt bore through ancient Rome. It was more than six feet high and twelve feet wide, carved out over the millennia by a freshwater stream that rushed past at high velocity. As he beamed his flashlight over it, it sparkled like mercury.

He moved his flashlight again. There were dirt banks on either side of the stream, not far above the fast-moving water. The banks were dangerously narrow, only a foot wide in places. Walking would be treacherous. They would have to go single file.

"The stream follows the street?" he asked.

"Yes, at least part of the way," the professor answered. "I believe it feeds into the Cloaca Maxima—the Great Drain—west of here. That's an ancient sewer that runs beneath the Roman Forum. Several of the city's underground streams feed into it."

"How do we get out of the tunnel?"

"We should find a place to exit somewhere along the way.

We can't be the only homeowners who've discovered the stream. Roberto and I explored once, but we didn't go far. It didn't matter before . . ."

Judd nodded."Sounds like better odds than what's waiting for us in the house. Yitzhak, you lead again. You know the signs that'll tell us we've got a way to escape. Then Eva and Roberto. Bash and I go last, in case we're followed. Let's move out."

31

Dubai, United Arab Emirates

The swank cocktail party was on the thirtieth floor of the stunning Burj al-Arab—the Tower of the Arabs, the world's tallest and arguably grandest hotel. The suite soared two full stories, boasting a spiral marble staircase, miles of twenty-four–carat gold detailing, and expansive windows showcasing panoramic views of the oil-rich Persian Gulf. Two Saudi princes in flowing white *kanduras* had just arrived via the twenty-eighth-floor helipad below, flying in from St. Tropez with full entourages.

Martin Chapman, the director of the Library of Gold, turned his attention from the flurry around them to watch a Russian exporter and his mistress take calls on ten-thousand-dollar cell phones encrusted with diamonds. Chapman smiled, amused. Still, he would never allow such gaudy affectation in his employees.

Dressed conservatively in a three-piece, side-vented suit, Chapman excused himself from a group of international bankers and walked off. He wore his vast personal fortune with the natural ease of Old Money, although he damn well had earned every penny himself.

Winding through the partygoers, he savored the undercurrent of excitement and raw avarice. But then, this was Dubai, epicenter of a storm of commerce, with free-trade zones, speed-dial corporate licensing, no taxes, no elections, and almost no crime. It was said the city's bird was the building crane—skyscrapers seemed to sprout from the desert sands overnight, most apartments and offices presold. Eager and filthy rich, Dubai was perfect for Chapman, who was here to raise money.

"Appetizer, sir?" Dressed in a money-green tuxedo, the server kept his gaze lowered.

Chapman chose Beluga caviar piled on a triangle of toast and continued on. From religion to crime and terrorism, everything in Dubai took a backseat to profit, and the profit was enormous. Even before Haliburton decided to move its world headquarters from Houston to Dubai, Chapman knew it was time to pay attention. So he had added to his string of homes, buying a villa in exclusive Palm Jumeirah—and had begun making friends.

It was time to go to work. He headed for Sheik Ahmad bin Rashid al-Shariff.

The sheik's black mustache curved upward as he dismissed a bevy of bronzed blond celebutantes and smiled at Chapman. He lifted his bourbon glass in greeting. *"Assalaam alaykom."* Peace be upon you.

"Alaykom assalaam." And peace upon you. Chapman did not speak Arabic, but long ago he had memorized the correct response. "I'm enjoying your party."

Sheik Ahmad was a dark wisp of a man in his mid forties, elegant in a gray pinstriped suit. A cousin of the emirate's ruler, he had been partially educated in the United States, with an MBA from Stanford. Earlier that day he had personally taken the wheel of a white Cadillac limousine to escort Chapman around several of his building sites. But then Chapman was no ordinary visitor. He headed Chapman & Associates, once the richest private equity firm in the United States. It had dropped from some $98 billion in assets under management to a mere $35 billion in the economic crash, but all U.S. equity funds had been eviscerated, although his perhaps more than others. Chapman was counting on his Khost project to put him back at number one, where he belonged. Even more important, it would please his wife.

"Yes, the usual financiers and industrialists," the sheik said. "A sprinkling of the idle rich. They're like saffron—zesty and attractive, entertaining for working stiffs like you and me. There are several of you private-equity people here, too."

Private equity was the sanitized term for leveraged-buyout firms. In the first four months of the year, Chapman & Associates had spent and borrowed far fewer billions of dollars than in its heyday, as he had searched out underperforming or undervalued companies to buy. With every deal, a new war chest had to be raised, so he was constantly on the money circuit, charming, cajoling, rattling off figures as he seduced those he targeted with his strong handshake and visions of a glorious future. Since he retained a larger interest in the company than anyone, he took a hefty percentage from every new transaction.

He ate his caviar, dusted his fingers on the cocktail napkin, and dropped it onto the tray of a passing waiter. "I was speaking with some of them earlier. They're eager to go on personal tours of Dubai with you, too."

The sheik laughed. "That's what I like about you, Martin. You're happy to give away my wealth, even to your competitors. As usual, they'll be too small for me, as you already know. By the way, I've made my decision about your proposition."

He paused to increase the drama and hint his answer might not be what Chapman wanted.

Without hesitation, Chapman gave an understanding nod and countered, "Yes, I've been thinking about the buy-in, too. Perhaps it's not right for you. I think I should withdraw the invitation and save us both embarrassment."

Sheik Ahmad blinked slowly, his hooded eyelids closing

and opening like those of a hawk perched in a banyan tree, awaiting prey. But his prey was Martin Chapman.

He smiled. "Martin, you are too much. Playing my game, are you? I'll come to the point. I want in. It's five hundred million dollars, yes?"

"Three hundred and twenty million. No more. Still, that will give you twenty percent."

Chapman's rule was always to leave investors hungering for more, and if the deal went sour, which he knew it would not, the sheik would have fewer reasons to lash back. Chapman was confident the $16 billion leveraged buyout of a mass-market retail company would return profits of at least 60 percent. Management had been unable to keep up with the changing times, but the structure was sound for a turnaround, financed by selling off ancillary holdings and taking loans. Only five thousand employees would have to be fired.

"Then it will be three hundred and twenty million," Sheik Ahmad agreed good-naturedly. "I like investments where I don't have to lift a finger. Do you have anything else I can give you money for?"

"Soon. The deal isn't ready yet—but soon."

"What is it? A retail chain, a distribution company, steel, timber, utilities?"

Chapman said nothing and smiled, thinking about his highly secret Khost project.

The sheik nodded. "Ah, I see. I'll wait until you're ready to reveal all. Your glass is empty. You must have another drink so we can celebrate." He raised a hand and signaled. Within seconds, a waiter stood before them.

It would be impolite to refuse, so Chapman accepted another bourbon and talked longer, resisting the urge to check his watch. Finally the sheik invited him to attend a *majlis*, his royal council, which was convening upstairs, and Chapman was able to exit gracefully.

On the sweeping steps of the palatial hotel, Chapman dialed his wife as he luxuriated in the outdoor air-conditioning. He looked out over the gulf to the collection of man-made islands called the World, one of Dubai, Inc.'s recent Las Vegas–style fantasies come to life. He had heard Rod Stewart had bought "Britain" for £19 million. Perhaps the next time he came, after the Khost project was certain, he would see about buying a continent, too.

When there was no answer, he left a message on the machine. "I'm flying out, darling. I just wanted to let you know I love you." She was still in San Moritz but was scheduled to leave for Athens soon.

As he watched the blazing red sun sink toward the gulf's purple waters, his limo pulled up. The chauffeur opened the door, and Chapman climbed into the rear, where his briefcase was waiting. Soon they were on the Sheikh Zayed Road, cruising east beneath the city's Manhattan-style skyline while the darkening desert and gulf spread flat and austere on either side.

He called his assistant at the Library of Gold. The Khost project was so secret that Chapman was running the operation from there.

"Where are we?" he demanded.

"The army uniforms and equipment have arrived in Karachi." The port on the Arabian sea was notorious for being porous. "Preston has handled everything impeccably. Your meeting with the warlord is scheduled for tomorrow in Peshawar."

"And security?"

"I'm working with Preston. It will be complete."

After he hung up, Chapman made several more phone calls, bringing himself up-to-date on other pieces of business and of course issuing orders. No matter how high the quality of the people one employed, they still needed guidance.

When the limo reached the private section of Dubai International Airport, the chauffeur drove out to the Learjet. Its engines were humming. He stopped the limo and ran around to open the rear door.

Chapman climbed out, carrying his briefcase. Handing over his passport to the waiting customs agent, he expected no trouble and got none—the agent simply stamped it. As the chauffeur unloaded his suitcase, Chapman marched toward the aircraft.

Two more men were waiting at the foot of the stairs. One was the pilot; the other was the armed man Preston had arranged. He was carrying a small bag.

"Good to see you, sir." The pilot touched the brim of his cap.

"Any problems?"

"No. We've followed your instructions and haven't spoken to her."

Chapman nodded and climbed into the opulent aircraft. It had wide leather seats, custom colors, and high-tech accessories. Sitting in the last row was Robin Miller, the only passenger.

"Hello, Mr. Chapman." She stared at him down the length of the aisle, her green eyes red-rimmed, her face flushed from weeping. She was a mess. Her long blond hair was disheveled, her bangs pushed to the sides, her white sweater rumpled over her chest.

He ignored her and gazed at the black backpack strapped into the seat across the aisle from her. Pleasure coursed through him. Then he remembered the CIA was intent on finding the Library of Gold. With a brusque gesture, he told the armed guard to sit in the bulkhead.

As the pilot closed and locked the door, Chapman marched down the aisle and rotated the seat in front of Robin to face her. He locked the seat into place, sat, and snapped on his safety belt. Still saying nothing, he folded his hands into his lap. Now he needed to find out how deeply she was involved in Charles Sherback's deceptions.

As the jet's engines revved up, Robin glanced nervously at the director. His unlined face was stern, his thin lips set in a straight line, and his long fingers entwined over his suit coat as if in his hands he controlled the universe. And he did control her universe—the Library of Gold.

The silence was frightening. She had seen the director do this before—saying nothing—which encouraged the other person to blurt into the vacuum, often with revelations that were later regretted. She forced herself to wait.

The jet took off, rising smoothly into Dubai's starry night. She looked out her window. Below them the city's lights extended along the coastline in sparkling colors.

Then she heard her voice filling the unbearable silence: "Are we still going to Athens?" That seemed neutral enough. The plan had been that from there they would helicopter *The Book of Spies* home to the library.

"Of course. Why didn't you phone to tell me immediately Eva Blake recognized Charles at the British Museum?" The question was posed curiously, an uncle interested in a favored niece's reply.

"Preston was going to take care of her." She thought about Charles's poor dead body, wrapped in canvas and hefted into the jet's baggage compartment like someone's castoff belongings.

The director gave a slight frown. It came and went quickly, but she knew her answer was wrong. Preston must have told him Charles and she had kept the information from him.

"What's important is we got *The Book of Spies*." She nodded at the backpack across the aisle. "It's fabulous, more even than our records show. Wouldn't you like to see it?" Once he cradled the illuminated manuscript, he might forget she had not reported Charles immediately.

"Later. Tell me what happened."

Girding herself, she described everything in London carefully, making certain she was accurate. She had a sense he was comparing every word to what Preston had said.

When she finished, he asked, "You saw the tattoo on Charles's head?"

"Yes."

"What does it mean?"

"I don't know. I didn't even know he had it."

He nodded. "Why do you think he wanted a secret tattoo?"

"I don't know."

"If your head were shaved, would I find one there, too?"

She felt a shiver of fear. "Absolutely not."

"Then you don't mind if I check."

"You can't mean you want me to cut off my hair?"

"No, Magus will do it." The director called over his shoulder to the front of the jet, "I'm ready for you."

The guard picked up his small bag and walked down the aisle.

She peered up at him helplessly.

Magus took shears from his bag, grabbed hair, and cut. Long blond curls floated to the floor. He grabbed more hair and cut. And more and more. The hair fell around her. Robin felt tears heat her eyes. Furious with herself, she blinked them away.

The only sound in the jet was of the clipping scissors and the distant thrum of the engines. As she used shaky fingers to wipe hair from her face, Magus put away the shears and took out a battery-powered electric razor. The steel was cold as it ran over her scalp. Her skin vibrated and itched. Little hairs flew. Her head was too light. She felt naked, ashamed.

"Do you see anything, Magus?" the director asked. "Any words, numbers, or symbols?"

"No, sir." He turned off the razor and dropped it into his bag.

"Go back to your seat." The director fixed his gaze on her. "Did Charles ever talk to you about where the library's located?" His eyes were blue frost.

Looking into them, she suddenly saw her father's eyes, black but just as icy. She remembered the moment she knew she must leave and never return to Scotland. She had walked away from everything, got rid of her accent, and put herself through the Sorbonne, then Cambridge, studying classical art and library science. She had made a life of her own, first working in rare books and manuscripts at the Houghton Library in Boston then at the Bibliothèque Nationale de France in Paris, where she had heard about the Library of Gold and steeped herself in its mythic history. The more she learned, the more she had hungered to know, until the exhilarating moment Angelo Charbonier had recruited her to join the elite staff, where she had met Charles and thought finally, after a decade of wandering, she had found a home.

"Charles never mentioned the library's location," she told him coolly.

"Does Charles's tattoo reveal it?" the director asked.

"I already told you I don't know what the tattoo means."

"Do you know where the Library of Gold is?"

"No. I never asked Charles, but I don't think he knew anyway. I never tried to find out from anyone. It's against the rules."

He nodded again, seeming to like that answer. "Remember the old Latin proverb 'What was sour to endure is sweet to recall.' You've proved your point, and your hair will grow back. Now I have business to conduct. Go to the front of the plane and sit near Magus."

Despite his words, dread filled her. She had a sense she was doomed, and doomed ironically by Charles's tattoo. If the director had been unable to trust Charles, who had seemed to love the library more than life itself, how could he ever really trust her when she so obviously had been in love with Charles?

She had made a huge error—not loving Charles, but associating with the library at all. Her mouth went dry as she realized what she had to do. She must walk away again, just as she had from her father. When the Learjet landed in Athens, she must find a way to escape.

32

Rome, Italy

In the dark dirt tunnel, Judd followed Yitzhak, Eva, Roberto, and Bash. Their shoes stuck and sank, slipped and slid on the narrow muddy ledge a foot above the stream. Time passed, and the enclosure grew claustrophobic, the noise of rushing water oppressive. Their flashlights did little to ward off the bleakness.

Commanding everyone to stop and be silent while he listened, Judd checked behind again. It had been a half hour, and there was still no sign of pursuit. They resumed their slow pace. Roberto's breathing was labored.

"How are you doing, Roberto?" he called over the shoulders ahead of him.

"I am trembly but well."

"Let us know when you want to take a break."

Roberto nodded, then asked worriedly, "How deep do you think the water is, Yitzhak?"

"No way to know." The professor paused. "Eva, it's time you explained what's going on."

"If I did, I'd only put you in more danger."

"When we get out of here," Judd assured him, "Bash will take you and Roberto to a private doctor who'll keep his mouth shut. Then when Roberto is treated, he'll find you a place to hide out. Don't go home until you get word from him that it's safe. He has his own work to do, so say nothing about him—or us—to anyone."

The professor thought about it. "Who *are* you, Judd? You and Bash?"

"All you need to know is we're helping Eva. I brought Bash and a couple of other people in to back us up."

Yitzhak's voice toughened. "In the kitchen, Angelo said he might be a 'supporter' of the Library of Gold. In the book club. What does that mean?"

"That's something else you should forget about," Eva told him.

The professor hesitated. "You're asking a lot, but I'll do as you say."

As they continued on, their flashlights revealed ancient Rome embedded in the dirt walls—fragments of pottery, spearheads, pieces of marble tiles, and chunks of brick. They stopped for Roberto to rest, then resumed their treacherous journey.

When they heard the scurrying of rats, Bash said, "Someone told me the rats under Rome were as big as cats." His skateboard was clamped low on his chest, one arm wrapped around it.

Yitzhak chuckled. "You've been drinking with unsavory people."

"I don't like rats," Bash admitted. "Does anyone other than crazy lab people like rats?"

"I'm more concerned about the albino creatures," the professor said, baiting him.

"Albino rats?" Roberto steadied himself by pressing his hand against the wall. Then he stared at his muddy palm.

"Yes, but they're not here—they're in the Cloaca Maxima," Yitzhak said. "In any case, we don't want to go that far. For those of you who don't know, the Cloaca isn't an ordinary sewage conduit—it's a huge, fast-moving river of crap. It was built twenty-five hundred years ago, but Rome is still using it. No one's safe going into it without covering every inch of themselves with boots, gloves, hooded suits, and masks."

"I wish I'd known," Eva said. "I would've brought my wet suit."

"Reminds me of a root canal I once had," Bash said. "Bad outcome."

"The stink is memorable," Yitzhak went on. "A bouquet of mud, diesel, feces, and rotting carcasses. *Rat* carcasses."

Bash groaned.

Judd laughed. "You get an A-plus for tormenting students, Professor."

The professor glanced over his shoulder, his round face grinning.

They fell silent as the underground passage descended steeply, and the air grew cold and clammy. Ghostly stalactites hung from overhead rocks, caused by the seep of calcium-rich groundwater. Then as the tunnel made a sharp bend, the noise of racing water quadrupled—and a stench of rot wafted toward them. Dizzying in its intensity, it carried all the horrific odors Yitzhak had described.

Judd's nose burned. "The Cloaca can't be far ahead."

"We cannot go into the Cloaca," Roberto said nervously. "Let us turn back."

"Not just yet—"

But before he could finish his sentence, the professor screamed. His arms lashed up over his head, and his feet flew out from under him. He twisted, his hands scrambling against the rough dirt wall, seeking purchase as his feet dropped into the water. If the stream were fast and deep enough, it would carry him into the big sewer.

Before Judd could jump in to help, Eva grabbed the professor's arm. "I've got you."

The current caught the professor's legs. He was being pulled away.

"Face the bank, Yitzhak," Judd ordered. He leaned out to peer around Bash and Roberto. "See if your knees can find a slope."

"You can do it!" Eva's hands were white from tension. Her jaw muscles bunched as she held on to him.

Sweat coated Yitzhak's bald head as he turned slowly away from the current until he faced Eva. His free hand grabbed her arm, and he curved his back and hunched his hips.

"Come on. Come on." She was bent nearly double, her profile strained, as she held on to him with both hands.

Yitzhak grunted and lifted one knee out of the water, then the other. As less water dragged at him, she helped him inch upward. Finally he was out. With a shudder, he planted his feet on the narrow shelf, standing between Eva and Roberto.

"You are in one piece, Yitzhak?" Roberto asked, patting his shoulder and back.

He peered down at his trousers, now laminated to his legs. Water streamed out of his shoes.

"Right as rain." He gave a sober smile. "Thank you, Eva."

"What made you slip, Yitzhak?" Judd said. "Check around your feet. What do you see?"

There was a pause. "You're right. Here's the top of a skull. I didn't see it before. It must've been hidden under the mud."

"Are there more skulls?" Eva slid her foot along the ledge, moving the muck away.

"I've found another one," the professor announced.

"So have I," Eva said.

The professor shone his flashlight along the cave wall above them, then ran the beam back and forth, lower and lower until he reached the wall's intersection with the bank.

"Here's a small opening." He crouched and aimed his flashlight into it.

"What's in there?" Eva squatted beside him.

"I can't tell. Help me dig, Eva."

"We'll do it," Judd told them. "Come on, Bash."

The others moved ahead, and Bash sat on his heels in front of the hole. He plowed the nose of his skateboard into the wet dirt, scooping piles of it back onto the ledge, where Judd slid the dirt into the stream. They continued a half hour, taking turns until the hole was three feet in diameter and formed a tunnel two feet deep. A scent of musty age wafted toward them.

Judd beamed his flashlight into the small passageway and crawled through. Standing erect, he inhaled sharply as he shot his light around. He had entered a gray world of the dead. Age-bleached skulls pinioned one on top of another blanketed the walls from the floor to the vault ceiling.

He moved into the center of the large crypt and turned, continuing to shoot his flashlight over the eerie scene. It was like a macabre carnival. Skulls arched around nooks, framing stone walls on which faded crosses and religious symbols had been painted. Full skeletons dressed in tattered brown monk robes reclined on stone benches as if awaiting the call to prayer.

"My God." Eva took a deep breath as she walked up to him. "The only time I've seen an ossuary like this was in a history magazine."

"It's impossible to know what Rome's underground has in store." The professor joined them, supporting Roberto. "Buried passageways, latrines, aqueducts, catacombs, fire-houses, access tunnels—and that's just the beginning. It looks to me as if this crypt belonged to the Capuchin order. That means some of the bones could date back five centuries."

"There's got to be thousands of them," Bash decided. "But how in hell do we get out of here?" Beneath his shorts, his bare knees were coated in mud—but then, all of them were muddy now.

"I'm hoping that way." Judd aimed his flashlight at the end of the room, where a tall arch of skulls wreathed worn stone steps leading upward. "Roberto, do you want Bash to carry you up?"

Roberto pushed himself away from Yitzhak. "I will do it myself."

Judd nodded, and he led them past mounds of bones and up a stone stairwell, where more crosses and religious symbols were painted. As they turned the corner of a landing, the wall above their heads displayed pelvic bones arranged like angel's wings.

He stopped, listening to Roberto's panting breath behind. He turned. "Carry him, Bash."

Before Roberto could object, Bash handed his skateboard to Eva and swept the small man up into his arms. "Combat victims get special treatment. Hey, it's a free ride."

Roberto looked up into the muscular young face. "This is not an unpleasant fate. Thank you."

Finally they reached the top, where an ornate iron door blocked their path. Judd peered through the grillwork—there was another stairwell on the far side, this time of modern cement.

"I hear traffic," Eva said, excited.

Judd tried the door. "Locked, of course." They were silent, and he could feel their exhaustion. "I seem to be shooting out a lot of locks these days."

Telling them to stand back, he screwed his sound suppressor onto his Beretta and fired. Metal dust spewed into the still air. The popping noise bounced off the stone walls.

He pushed open the door and gazed up. "Blue sky."

"Hallelujah," Eva said.

They resumed climbing, Judd still leading. As he neared the top, he stopped and rose up to see. They had emerged into a ruins of toppled columns, slabs of travertine, and chunks of granite scattered among dirt and weeds between two ancient buildings. Behind the area was another old building. A commercial chain-link fence blocked the ruins from the sidewalk and street.

He turned back. Their expressions were expectant as they stood beneath him in the stairwell. "I don't know exactly where we are. At least it's an open area. All of us are dirty, but it's the blood that'll draw the kind of attention we don't want. That means you—Eva and Roberto."

In seconds, Eva was out of her jacket. Her green shirt was clean. As she turned the jacket inside out and tied the arms around her waist, Bash lowered Roberto onto his feet. Judd studied him. He was standing erect, but his skin color was slightly pink, perhaps feverish. The handkerchief was gone from his shoulder, lost somewhere along the way. Blood coated his white shirt. Gingerly he unbuttoned it.

"Bash, give Roberto your T-shirt," Judd decided.

Bash took off his jacket and peeled the black T-shirt up over his head.

Judd checked Roberto's gunshot wound, a ragged slash through the top of his shoulder.

"You're going to be fine," he said. "Probably hurts like hell, though."

"The pain is a small matter. We are free." Roberto stood motionless as Yitzhak tugged the T-shirt down over his head.

"Take the professor and Roberto," Judd told Bash. "Eva and I'll wait until you're gone. You'll have to break through a chain-link gate to get out of here."

Bash grinned. "After this . . . a piece of cake."

"So now we leave you." The professor smiled at Eva. He was wet and bedraggled, but his optimistic disposition shone through. "Be well, and even though I don't understand anything that's happened, my heartfelt thanks." He hugged her, then shook hands with Judd. "We've had an adventure. Next time we meet, I hope it'll be boring."

Roberto kissed Eva on both cheeks. "You must stay in touch."

"I will," she promised.

Finally Judd and Bash faced each other. "There's no way the Charboniers should've known we were going to Yitzhak's house," Judd told him, choosing his words carefully. "I'll call our mutual friend and fill him in. We have a leak somewhere."

The young spy nodded soberly, and they shook hands. Then he led Roberto and Yitzhak up the steps into the ruins.

Eva joined Judd, and they climbed so they could watch the trio approach the fence. Bash looked around. When there was no one on the sidewalk, he used his skateboard to smash open the padlock. Soon they were out the gate and walking away, the tall young man and his two older charges.

"We have to assume the Library of Gold people have figured out who you are now, too," she told him. "So we can't use your credit cards, and obviously we can't use mine. It's a long hitchhike to Istanbul."

"I have an extra set of ID on me. I'll buy the tickets. What's worrying me is whether they'll follow us to Istanbul."

33

As vehicles sped past, tail lights streaming red, Preston waited impatiently outside the terminal of Ciampino International Airport, Rome's second-largest. He had chosen it because it was closer to the city's heart and therefore more efficient. Efficiency mattered particularly now—the report from his man in Rome had been bad. Angelo and Odile Charbonier had been shot to death, while Judd Ryder, Eva Blake, Yitzhak Law, and Roberto Cavaletti had vanished. In a foul mood, he checked his watch—eight P.M.

When a long black van pulled up, he slid open the side door and stepped inside. The car entered the airport traffic, and he crouched in the rear beside the corpses. He lifted the blanket: Angelo Charbonier's face was angry in death. Odile's head was coated with dried blood and splintered bone.

He crawled forward to the half-seat behind the driver. "Took you long enough to get here."

Nico Bustamante, still dressed in his gray sweat suit, was behind the wheel. A big barrel of a man, he swore in Italian, then spoke in English. "What did you expect? I told you we had a rotten mess to clean up."

In the seat next to him, Vittorio nodded. Slender, with a wiry build, he had changed out of his tricolor jogging clothes into jeans and a denim shirt.

"Tell me again exactly what you found," Preston ordered.

"Signore and Signora Charbonier, both murdered in the

kitchen," Nico said. "We searched the house. No one was there, and we did not find any hidden exits. The targets did not leave through the front door. I know this because I posted men at both ends of the street. And they did not leave through the rear—we were there."

"It was as if they evaporated into the world of souls." Vittorio crossed himself.

As they stopped at a traffic light, Preston said, "What about when you cleaned up the kitchen?"

"There was just the usual junk in the trash—I say this because I know you will ask. The only piece that was strange was blood splatters too far away from the *signore* and *signora* to be theirs."

"So someone else was injured. Tell your people to check the neighbors, the hospitals, and the police."

Taking out his cell phone, Nico drove the van onto the congested Via Appia Nuova.

As Nico made the call, Preston said to Vittorio, "What about the Charboniers?"

"It is all arranged. A yacht rented in their name is waiting at Ostia Antica."

Ostia Antica was Rome's ancient seaport, where the Tiber River flowed into the Tyrrhenian Sea. Today the town was little more than a bookshop, a café, a tiny museum, and mosaic-filled ruins, but it was appropriate for the Charboniers: Ovid's play *Medea* had premiered in its amphitheater some two thousand years ago and was now lost—except to the Library of Gold.

"And then?" Preston prompted.

"We will put the *signore* and *signora* onto the yacht, sail it far out into the Mediterranean, steal everything—and abandon it. It will seem as if pirates attacked and robbed them."

"You have their suitcases?"

"Of course. We got them from the hotel, and paid the bill, too."

Preston nodded, satisfied. Now he had a larger problem: Where had Blake, Ryder, Law, and Cavaletti gone?

As the van headed toward Ostia Antica, he considered everything he knew. It seemed as if at least one of the four was wounded, but not so badly he or she could not escape. He needed the Rome operatives to find all of them. He thought about Charles's tattoo—the security staff had torn apart his and Robin Miller's offices and the cottage they shared, but had found nothing about it or any records of the library's location. The tattoo reminded him of the director—by now he was on the jet with Robin Miller. If the director learned anything from her, he would phone.

As he thought that, his cell rang. "Yes?"

It was his NSA contact. "Your person of interest has turned on her cell and made three calls from Rome."

"From where exactly?" Preston felt a burst of hope. It was Eva Blake's cell phone—he had found the number on Peggy Doty's cell after he had wiped her in London.

"Fiumicino airport."

He cursed. It was the other airport, and too far away to reach quickly. "Whom was she calling?"

"Adem Abdullah, Direnc Pastor, and Andrew Yakimovich. I can give you the phone numbers she dialed. All were to Istanbul. Two have accompanying addresses."

"Did you listen to the conversations?"

"You know better than that, Preston. That far I can't go—even for you."

"Whom did she dial first?"

"Yakimovich. It was short, less than a minute—a disconnected number. The two other calls were five and eight minutes."

"What are their numbers and addresses?" He wrote the

information in the small pocket notebook he always carried. When he no longer needed a note, he tore it out and destroyed it. There were few pages left. "Thanks, Irene. She'll have to turn off her cell phone while she's in the air. When she activates it again, whether she phones out or not, tell me. I need to know exactly where she is." NSA could pinpoint locations within inches, depending on which satellite was in orbit. He ended the connection and looked at Nico. "Turn the van around. Take me back to Ciampino." He would charter another jet and beat them to Istanbul.

34

Washington, D.C.

It was late afternoon, the shadows long across Capitol Hill, as Tucker Andersen stood at the front door to Catapult headquarters and gazed out longingly. He was tired of being cooped up. A young officer from OTS at Langley was standing on the porch, holding a small package wrapped in brown paper. His expression was one of being properly impressed at meeting the storied spymaster.

Tucker took the package, tucked it under his arm, and signed for it. Then he went to Gloria's desk. She was nowhere in sight, still on coffee break. He dropped the parcel next to her computer and walked down the hall to his office. Sitting behind his desk, he pushed aside the report he had been reading and checked his e-mail.

One had been forwarded by Gloria from the L.A. coroner's office. It said the body in Charles Sherback's grave had been exhumed and they were rushing the autopsy and DNA match, but it would take a couple of days. A second e-mail confirmed a room in the Méridien hotel in London had been registered to Christopher Heath, the name on Sherback's driver's license. One of the desk clerks remembered him with a blond woman, but there were no details.

Restless, Tucker was just about to leave when a new e-mail arrived from MI-5. He read it quickly: No adult male corpse with a shaved, tattooed head had been found in London the previous night. Consequently, there were no arrests connected with it. He stared at the message, then leaned back in his chair, trying to understand what it meant. Judd had told him he had shot carefully so Preston would survive. Finally he decided Preston had likely awakened before the police arrived and taken Sherback's body away with him. Tucker sent an encrypted e-mail to Judd, warning him.

Disturbed, he stretched, stood, and headed down the hall to Catapult's small communications center, which included data research and IT—information technology. At the door he was greeted by a rumble of voices, clicking keyboards, and a sense of urgency. Worktables arranged in neat rows housed a dozen secure computers and phones. High on the walls hung big-screen TVs tuned to CNN, MSNBC, FOX, BBC, and Al Jazeera, but the monitors could also view classified images. The usual cans of soda, crumpled take-out bags, and empty pizza boxes littered the area, impregnating everything with the salt-and-grease odor of fast food.

Tucker paused, surveying the staff, most of whom were bent over their keyboards. All were under the age of thirty. Since 9/11 the number of applicants to Langley had soared, and now half of all personnel were new hires. He worried about the loss of experience and institutional memory, but that was what happened when good longtime operatives and analysts quit or were fired, which had occurred in the 1990s and again in the next decade, during the tenure of a morale-killing D/CIA. Still, this young new group was dedicated and enthusiastic.

Walking through the room, he joined Brandon Ohr and Michael Hawthorne, who were standing with Debi Watson at her worktable. She was the head of IT. The trio looked as if their average age was twenty-five, although they were around thirty. They were eager, talented, and smart.

"Working hard, I see," Tucker deadpanned. Not original, but it would get the job done.

Michael and Brandon were home after long tours overseas, waiting for reassignment. Technically neither belonged in here, but then Debi was single, a pretty brunette with large brown eyes and a Southern accent. Tucker was interested in their excuses.

"I'm on break," Brandon said quickly. He had a square, handsome face with a hint of a movie-star beard.

"I had a question I hoped Debi could help me with," Michael explained. He was tall and rangy, his black face dimpled.

"It's all true, suh," Debi assured Tucker, her Southern belle accent in full flower.

He stared soberly at the men and said nothing. "The glare," as Gloria called it.

Brandon took the hint first. "Guess I'd better get back to the stack of papers on my desk." He sauntered off, swiping a can of Diet Pepsi from a six-pack near the rear of the room.

"Thanks, Debi," Michael told her. "I'll check in with you tomorrow about the Tripoli refugee I've got my eye on." He followed Brandon.

Tucker liked that neither was completely intimidated by him. It showed the sort of inner fortitude necessary for the job.

Debi sat down behind her worktable and tugged on her short skirt. "I was just about to send you an e-mail."

"You've got answers for me?" He had assigned her to track down Charles Sherback's altered face and the two anonymous phone numbers in his cell.

"It's not what you want to hear. Nothing in any of the federal databases matches the face of your man. Nothing in the state databases, either. And no positive match with Interpol or any of our foreign friends. Since he's an American, you'd think he'd have a driver's license photo at least. It's almost as if he doesn't exist."

"What about the two phone numbers?"

"They're to disposable cell phones, but you suspected that already. There's been no activity on them yet. NSA will let me know immediately."

Disappointed, Tucker returned to his office. As he went inside, the phone on his desk rang. It was Judd Ryder. He fell into his chair and listened.

Judd related what he and Eva had learned at Yitzhak Law's house and described the attack by the Charboniers. "There's no way the Charboniers should've known we were going there," he finished worriedly. "You've got to have a leak."

Stunned, Tucker thought quickly. "Only one person at Catapult besides me has any details—the chief, Cathy Doyle. What about on your end?"

"It's just Eva and me, and she's been with me the whole time. Whenever I get in touch with you, I use my secure mobile. Both phone and e-mail." The mobile's coding technology not only encrypted voice and data but also scrambled the wavelengths on which the messages traveled, making it impossible for anyone to decipher them.

Tucker swore. "Somehow we've been breached. I'll talk to Cathy."

"See what you can dig up about the Charboniers, too, and their relationship with the Library of Gold, and whether they've been up to anything hinky that might be terrorist related. Angelo said he was a member of the book club. When I asked whether Dad was, he wouldn't answer."

Judd's tone was flat, professional, but Tucker sensed conflicted emotion when he spoke about his father and the book club. "Of course. You're going to Istanbul?"

"Yes. We're taking a commercial flight. It seems safest under the circumstances. Eva called ahead, but Yakimovich's phone is disconnected. He's probably moved again. She was able to reach two of his longtime friends in Istanbul, but they don't know where he is now. If you can track him down, it'd be a big help. It'll take us a few hours to get there."

"I'll see what I can do." As soon as Tucker hung up, he dialed a colleague with whom he had worked during the cold war: Faisal Tarig, who was now with Istanbul police.

"I know Andy Yakimovich," Faisal said. "A sly fellow, that one. But then, he's half Russian and half Turk. Perhaps I can locate him. You still smoking those manly Marlboros?"

"No, gave them up for bottled water."

"I hope you have not become boring, old friend. But if you are asking questions like this, perhaps not. I will be in touch."

"Don't tell anyone I called, or the intel I need."

There was silence. "I see."

After he hung up, Tucker sat a moment, thinking, then he left, heading to Cathy's office. It was a large one, directly behind the receptionist's desk. As chief, she got the best one. Fronting the street, it had special glass in the windows so no one could see inside or use a demodulator to listen in on conversations.

The door was open. He peered in. Family photos hung on the wall alongside CIA commendations. More photos stood on her desk. Some kind of green ivy was growing in a pot. Cathy was typing, staring at her computer screen, her short, blond-streaked hair awry.

"I know you're there, Tucker. What's on your mind?" She had not looked at him.

He walked inside and closed the door. "Who's heard about my Library of Gold operation?"

As he sat, she glanced around at him and frowned. "Why do you ask?"

He explained about the leak. "There's no way the Charboniers should've been at Yitzhak Law's place, waiting for my people."

She spun around to her desk, facing him. "I've told only one person about Yitzhak Law—the assistant director, in my regular report, about fifteen minutes ago. That's too late for the leak to have come from us."

"I'll talk to our IT people. I suppose it's possible someone's broken into our system. But if so, it didn't set off any alarms. I'll make my reports to you verbally from now on."

They were silent. Every day thousands of amateur and professional hackers tried to breach U.S. government computers. So far Langley had lost no important data, and like other small specialized units, Catapult used the same highly secure system.

She nodded. "Anything new about the Library of Gold?"

"Ryder and Blake are on their way to Istanbul, following a good lead. As for me, I'll be glad when I can go home." At least he was getting a lot of work done on the missions he was overseeing.

She nodded again. Then she gave him an understanding smile. "We all have to sacrifice sometimes."

He said goodbye and returned to the communications center. Debi was still at her computer console. He told her what he needed.

"No one's gotten into our system that I know of, suh." Her brows knitted. "I'll get right on it."

Concerned, he returned to his office.

35

Athens, Greece

The Library of Gold Learjet circled down slowly, the lights of Greece's ancient capital gleaming beneath. Nervously making plans, Robin turned away from the panorama and stared back down the length of the cabin to Martin Chapman, his tall figure upright in his seat. He was on his cell phone, his jaw working angrily.

As the jet touched down at Athens International Airport, she studied her cell phone and battery, remembering Preston's awful call to her while she was waiting on the jet in London for Charles and him to arrive. He had ordered her to take the cell apart, and then he told her Charles was dead. Grief swelled her throat. She forced herself to repress it.

Preston had never told her why she was to not activate it again. It did not matter; she was going to need a phone. Sliding the pieces into her pocket, she stood and walked to the rear of the plane.

Chapman peered up as she slung on the backpack that contained *The Book of Spies.* She did not like the look in his eyes.

Still, he spoke neutrally. "The helicopter is ready."

She nodded. "Good." But she knew it was not good. Once she was in the helicopter, she would be on her way to the hidden Library of Gold, where security was so intense no one could escape—but people occasionally disappeared.

People like her. "Will you be going with us, Mr. Chapman?" she asked, although he had made no move to rise.

"I have other business. Magus will take care of you."

From the front, Magus nodded knowing agreement. "Yes, sir, Mr. Chapman."

She followed Magus out of the Learjet and into the black hours of night. The cool air made her shaved head feel even more exposed. She forced herself to stay calm. The airport extended around them, a wide sweep of tarmac with jets coming and going from the long arms of the terminal. It seemed far away, an impossible distance.

A small luggage truck had pulled up to the tail of the jet, and the driver was unloading bags and other items. He was a small man and elderly, with stringy arms showing beneath the short sleeves of his airport shirt. She felt a moment of hope; she might be able to handle him. As he humped Charles's canvas-wrapped body into the back of the truck, she turned away.

"Let's go." Magus's face was a mask. "I'll bet you're ready to get home and settle in."

"You're right," Robin lied. "It will be good to be home."

They walked toward the waiting vehicle, which would take them to the helicopter. It was only about seven feet long and narrow, with space in front for just two people—the driver and a passenger. The rear was an open bed, packed with her large roll-aboard slammed against the cab, Charles's corpse, and several wood boxes Preston had picked up in London.

"I'll help you in." Magus stopped at the rear, where, as the junior member, she would ordinarily sit.

She stared at him, allowing a sense of helplessness to sound in her voice. "I'm so tired. And I'm supposed to keep this backpack with me all the time. Mr. Chapman's orders. Would you mind if I sat in front with the driver?"

They looked at the bed of the truck. There was no gate or upper flap at the end, while the sides had short walls about a foot tall. The floor was hard steel.

"Sure," he said. "Why not." But he touched his hip, where she suspected he kept his gun inside his jacket. The gesture might have been automatic, but it felt like a threat.

Robin gave him a bright smile. "Thanks."

He walked her around to the passenger side. There were no doors on the cab. She took off the backpack and climbed in. Then he walked around to the driver's side, which was also open. He ordered the elderly man out from behind the steering wheel, and her heart sank. Now it would be Magus sitting next to her, armed, young, and strong.

As soon as the driver crawled into the back, Magus studied the automatic transmission, then put the light truck into gear. They rolled away.

She held the backpack on her lap, cradling it in her arms, realizing she had one lucky break—he was an unsure driver, glancing at the steering wheel, the small rearview mirror, the gear shift. That might help—that, and if she surprised him.

She turned around and watched the Learjet taxi away. Returning to face the front, she asked innocently, "Wouldn't you like to see what's in the backpack, Magus?"

"No." He was focused on his driving.

But she started to unzip it, the sound jagged and sharp.

He glanced at her. "Close that up." He reached a hand toward it.

She bit the hand and tasted blood. Swearing, he jerked his hand back, and she slammed the heavy backpack against the side of his head. Reeling, he lashed out with an arm, connecting only with the pack. With the sharp toe of her boot, she kicked the calf of the leg that had a foot on the accelerator and immediately crashed the backpack against his head again.

His foot bounced off the accelerator, the small truck careened, and there was a shout from the back as the driver slid out.

Magus hit the brakes and reached inside his jacket for his gun. In a flurry of motion, Robin slammed her foot down on the accelerator and bit his ear. The truck shot ahead. As his gun appeared in his hand, she slashed her fingernails down his face and eyes, ripping skin.

He yelled and lashed the gun toward her. But he was off-balance now, and the truck was lurching forward, alternating between braking and accelerating. His gun was aimed at her.

In a fury, she smashed the backpack into his face again and rotated her hips toward him. Bracing one hand on the back of her seat and gripping the handhold on the dashboard with the other, she rammed her boots into his hip, inching him across the vinyl seat.

His gun went off, the shot deafening as the bullet exploded through the cab's roof. Blood dripped into his eyes as he tried to see. He shot wildly again, and she shoved him out the door and floored the gas feed. The truck hurtled forward.

Her heart pounded like a kettledrum as she slid behind the wheel and began to steer. More bullets sliced through the cab, barely missing *The Book of Spies* on the seat beside her. Driving, she crouched low, eyes just above the dash, thankful for the vast open space of the tarmac. A shot flew over her head, a lethal whisper. And then there was no more gunfire.

She rose up and peered into the rearview mirror. Magus was running after her, more and more distant, a hand angrily wiping his face of blood. Behind him lay a trail of capsized wood crates and Charles's corpse. For a long moment she was furious with Charles, furious he had put her in this position, and then the emotion vanished. She was on her own now, as she had been in years past. *You know how to do this,* she told herself.

Determined, she spun the steering wheel, heading toward a chain-link fence. At last she saw a gate beside a dark airport outbuilding. It was quite a bit away, which was good. More distance between her and Magus. The night air cooled her face as she kept the gas feed pressed to the floor.

At the wire gate, she screeched the truck to a stop and jumped out. Putting on the backpack, she looked back. Magus was very far away and had slowed to a jog. His hand was at his ear, no doubt calling for help. But as long as she had *The Book of Spies,* she had a bargaining chip. Martin Chapman would stop at nothing to get her back, hunt her to the far reaches of the planet if he had to, but with the illuminated manuscript she could perhaps negotiate permanent freedom.

She wrestled her roll-aboard out of the truck's bed. It had been crammed against the cab and had missed the fate of the rest of the luggage. Pulling it, she hurried through the gate and into a big parking lot.

She moved quickly among the cars, vans, and SUVs, peering inside. At last she found an old Peugeot, battered and rusted, with a key in the ignition. Scanning around, she took her purse from the roll-aboard. She still had pounds from England; she would exchange them for euros. Last, she found the straw hat she had bought in London. She slammed it down on her bald head and tied the ribbon under her chin.

She loaded the roll-aboard and the backpack into the car. Fighting fear, she drove off through the moonlight toward the exit, her gaze constantly going to her rearview mirror.

36

The Sultanate of Oman

Muscat International Airport lay on flat sands above the Gulf of Oman. In the distance, clusters of oil rigs stood glittering with lights, their toothpick legs sunk deep into the gulf's black waters. The night smelled of the desert as Martin Chapman descended from his Learjet. He was breathing hard with anger: Robin Miller had stolen *The Book of Spies* and escaped. Magus and a team were searching for her in Athens, but it was one more problem, and right now he did not need it.

The danger that worried him most was Judd Ryder, who was CIA, and in that one word lay all the worry in the world: Langley had the resources, the knowledge, the expertise, the guts, to accomplish far more than the public would ever know. One did not cross the Agency lightly, but once done, one had no choice but to end it quickly, which was why Chapman was in Oman now.

The Oman Air section of the ultramodern passenger terminal was quietly busy. He passed tiles, potted palms, and Old Arabia wall decorations without a glance. Turning down a wide arrival and departure corridor, he followed memorized instructions toward a duty-free shop. Near the bathroom door an airport employee in a desert-tan janitorial uniform and a checkered Bedouin headdress was bent over, swabbing the floor.

As Chapman passed, he heard a voice float up toward

him: "There's a supply room four doors to your left. Wait inside. Don't turn on the light."

Chapman almost broke his stride. Quickly he regrouped and went to the supply room door. Inside, he flicked on the light. The little room was lined with shelves of cleaning products, paper towels, and toilet paper. He turned off the light and stood in the dark against the rear, a small penlight in one hand, the other hand inside his jacket on the hilt of his pistol.

The door opened and closed like a whisper.

"Jack said you needed help." The voice was low. The man seemed to be standing just inside the door. "I'm expensive, and I have rules. You know about both. Jack says you've agreed to my terms. Before we go further, I need to hear that from you."

"You're Alex Bosa?" Chapman assumed it was a pseudonym.

"Some call me that."

"The Carnivore."

No expression in the voice. "I'm known by that, too."

Chapman inhaled. He was in the presence of a legendary independent assassin, a man who had worked for all sides during the cold war. Now he worked only occasionally, but always at astronomical prices. There were no photos of him; no one knew where he lived, what his real name was, or even in which country he was born. He also never failed, and no one ever uncovered who hired him.

The assassin's voice was calm. "Do you agree to my terms?"

Chapman felt his hackles rise. He was the boss, not this shadowy man who had to live hidden behind pseudonyms. "I have a cashier's check with me." There were to be two payments—half now, half on completion, for a total of $2 million. Ridding himself of the CIA problem was worth every cent. "Do you want the job or not?"

Silence. Then: "I work alone when it's time to do the hit. That means your people must be gone. You must never reveal our association. You must never try to find out what I look like or who I am. If you make any attempts, I will come after you. I'll do you the favor of making it a clean kill, out of respect for our business relationship and the money you will have paid me. After tonight, you will not try to meet me again. When the job is finished, I'll be in touch to let you know how I want to receive the last payment. If you don't pay me, I will come after you for that, too. I do wet work only on people who shouldn't be breathing anyway. I'm the one who makes that decision—not you. I'll give you a new phone number through which you can reach me when you have the additional information about the targets' whereabouts. Do you agree?"

The menacing power in the quiet voice was breathtaking. Chapman found himself nodding even though there was no way the man could see him in the dark.

He spoke up, "I agree." The Carnivore specialized in making hits look like accidents, which was the point—Chapman wanted Langley to have nothing to trace back to him or the Library of Gold.

"Tell me why Judd Ryder and Eva Blake need to be terminated," the Carnivore demanded.

When Chapman had decided to bring in outside talent, he had gone to a source outside the book club, a middleman named only Jack. Through encrypted e-mails, he and Jack had arranged the deal. Now he repeated the story for the Carnivore: "Ryder is former military intelligence and highly skilled. Blake is a criminal—she killed her husband when she was driving drunk. I'm sure you've checked both facts. They've learned about a new secret business transaction I'm working on, and they want it for themselves. I tried to reason with them, but I got nowhere. If they steal this, it'll cost me billions. More important, now they're trying to kill me. They're on their way to Istanbul. I should have information soon about exactly where."

"I understand. I'll leave now. Put the envelope on the shelf next to you. Open the door and go immediately back to your jet." He gave Chapman his new cell number.

There was a movement of air, the door opened and closed quickly, and darkness surrounded Chapman again. He realized he was sweating. He put the envelope with the cashier's check for $1 million on the shelf next to him and left.

As he walked down the corridor, he looked everywhere for the cleaning man in the brown uniform and Bedouin headdress. He had vanished.

37

Istanbul, Turkey

Judd stared down from his window on the jet at the twinkling lights of fabled Instanbul. He drank in the sight of what had once been mighty Constantinople, the crown of the Byzantine Empire—and the birthplace of the Library of Gold.

Eva awoke. "What time is it?" She looked nervous.

"Midnight."

As the jet touched down and taxied toward the terminal of Ataturk International Airport, he checked his mobile.

"Anything from Tucker about where Yakimovich is?" she asked.

He shook his head. "No e-mail. No phone message."

"If Tucker can't find him, it could take us days."

Although there seemed to be no way they could have been followed, they had stopped in Rome on their way to the airport not only to buy supplies but also to disguise themselves. Now as they deplaned, Judd helped Eva into a wheelchair. She curled up low, her head hanging forward as if asleep. A blanket covered her body, and a scarf hid her hair. He put her shoulder satchel and a large new duffel bag containing other purchases on her lap. He was dressed like a private nurse, in white slacks, a white blast jacket, and a white cap. Tucked inside his lower lip was a tight roll of cotton, making the lip protrude and his jaw look smaller.

Keeping his cheeks soft and his gaze lazy, he adjusted his internal monitor until he was comfortably projecting a not-too-bright attendant to the nice lady in the wheelchair. Watching surreptitiously around, he pushed her into the international terminal and showed his fake passport and her real one at the visa window. They acquired visa stamps and passed through customs. Although the terminal was less congested than at high-traffic hours, there were still plenty of people. Beyond the security kiosk waited even more, many holding up signs with passengers' names.

Rolling the wheelchair down the long corridor toward the exit doors, Judd stayed on high alert. Which was when he spotted the one person he did not want to see—Preston. How in hell had he known to come to Istanbul? His chest tight, Judd studied him from the corners of his eyes. Tall and square-shouldered, the killer was leaning against the exterior wall of a news store, apparently reading the *International Herald Tribune*. He was dressed as he had been in London, in jeans, a black leather jacket, and probably a pistol.

Because he did not have ID to carry a weapon onto a commercial flight, Judd had left his Beretta in Rome. He considered. It seemed unlikely Preston had been able to see his face in London from the floor of the alley. On the other hand, it was possible the killer had somehow figured out who he was and had acquired a photo.

"Preston." The worried whisper floated up from Eva.

"I see him," Judd said quietly. "You're asleep, remember?"

She returned to silence as he continued to push the wheelchair at a sedate pace.

Above the newspaper, Preston was studying the throngs. His eyes moved while his body gave the appearance of disinterested relaxation. He paused at the faces of not only women but men the right age, the right hair color, the right height—which told Judd that Preston had somehow learned what he looked like. Watching couples and singles, Preston missed no one, took no one for granted. He pulled a radio from his belt, listening and speaking into it. That meant he had a least one janitor nearby.

As Preston hooked the radio back on to his belt, he noticed Judd and Eva. And focused.

His gaze felt like a burning poker. Judd did not look at him, and he did not speed the wheelchair. Either action would make Preston even more curious. Then he saw a tall woman sweeping along, pulling a small suitcase. Despite the late hour, she wore large diva sunglasses—and her hair was long and red, like Eva's.

Seeing an opportunity, Judd moved the wheelchair alongside her and slumped his shoulders to make himself appear even more boring in his attendant's uniform. Preston's eyes moved, attracted to the woman. He stepped away from the news store, following as the woman hurried in front of Judd and Eva to a car rental stand.

Judd exhaled. He pushed Eva out the glass doors and to the line of waiting taxis.

As soon as the yellow cab left the terminal, Judd closed the privacy window between the front and rear seats. It was an old vehicle, the upholstery threadbare, but the glass was thick, and the driver would not be able to hear their conversation.

"How could Preston have found us?" Eva asked again. "The Charboniers knew about Yakimovich and Istanbul, but they died before they could tell anyone."

"It's hard to believe Tucker has another leak. IT will be covering headquarters like a mushroom cloud. Maybe it's us. Could Charles have planted a bug on you in London?" As they talked, he watched the rear for any sign of Preston.

"If he did, those clothes are gone. But why would he bother? He thought he had me. Did you see anyone following us at any time?"

He shook his head. They were silent.

"Okay, let's take it from the top," he finally said. "It's not a bug, and it's not a cyberbreach at Catapult."

"If Charles were alive," she decided, "he would know we'd be heading to Andy Yakimovich."

"Peggy Doty's the only loose end I can think of. But she didn't know about Yakimovich or Istanbul, so there's no way Preston could've gotten the information from her."

Eva suddenly swore. "Of course—Peggy's cell phone. Whoever killed Peggy could've found my number on it." She pulled her cell from her satchel. "The only time I dialed out was in the Athens airport, when I called around looking for Andy. I was calling Istanbul."

"Give it to me." He turned on the phone, then watched the screen to make certain it was connected to the network. Rolling down his window, he tossed it into the open bed of a passing pickup.

Eva smiled. "That'll give Preston something to chase."

He smiled back. In the small rear seat of the taxi they inadvertently gazed deeply into each other's eyes. For a long moment warm intimacy passed between them. Judd's heart rate accelerated.

Saying nothing, Eva looked away, and he turned to stare out the side window. That was the problem with shared danger. Inevitably it led to bonding of one sort or another, and one of the "sorts" could be sexual. He sensed her discomfort, her sudden aloofness, but he was not going to go there and explain what had just happened. Or that he had liked it.

Mentally he shook himself. They were on the outskirts of the city. Choosing a busy intersection, he told the driver to stop. There was a chance Preston had gotten their taxi's plate number.

After helping Eva into her wheelchair, he paid the driver. The tail lights disappeared into traffic, and he wheeled her around, heading in the opposite direction. He scanned cautiously.

"There's an alley ahead," Eva prompted.

"I see it." He pushed her inside.

She got up and discarded her blanket and scarf, piling them into the wheelchair's seat. From the duffel bag she took out a midnight-blue jacket. As he removed the cotton from his lower lip, stripped off his attendant's jacket, and unbuckled his white trousers, she pulled on her jacket and, without looking at him, took her shoulder satchel and hurried off to keep watch.

He slid into jeans, a brown polo shirt, and a brown sports jacket. Folding the wheelchair and their discarded belongings against the wall, he turned to gaze at her, a slender figure dwarfed by the alley's tall opening, somehow jaunty and more unafraid than he would have thought.

Carrying the duffel, he joined her. "See anything?"

"No sign of Preston. Which way?"

They walked six blocks, went around a corner, and Judd hailed another cab. Within twenty minutes they were in the Sultanahmet district in the heart of historic Old Town, not far from Topkapi Palace, the Hagia Sophia, and the Hippodrome. The taxi stopped, and they got out.

They walked another ten minutes, at last crossing onto a narrow street, at best a lane and a half wide. There were no cars, but trolley tracks ran down the middle. Tall stone buildings from centuries past abutted one another, shops and stores on the ground and second floors. He inhaled. The exotic scents of cumin and apple-flavored tobacco drifted through the night air.

"This is Istiklal Caddesi," he told her. "*Caddesi* means avenue. Our hotel's four blocks farther."

As they continued on, she commented, "You seem to know a lot about Istanbul. Have you been here before?"

"No. I Googled it."

The hotel was a stuccoed structure with a simple wood entry door and two shuttered windows on the right. The street was quiet, businesses closed, with no restaurants, cafés, or bars to attract customers.

He slowed. "We have a small problem. All you've got is your real passport, which means you'll have to give the hotel your name. So I'm going to go in alone and register myself under one of my covers. Then I'll come out for you."

He gestured, and she stepped up into the recessed entry of a trinket store. Her dark jacket and jeans blended into the shadow.

She's learning, he thought to himself as he left her and went into the hotel. The interior was narrow and deep, with old unvarnished woods and faded upholstery. As expected, the clerk handed over a plain cardboard box with the correct cover name printed on it. Mentally Judd thanked Tucker. He placed an order with room service, walked toward the elevator at the rear, and continued on, exiting out the rear door.

When he appeared in the mouth of the alley, he could not see Eva, so well was she hidden in the doorway.

She hurried out, a question in her eyes.

"We're fine," he told her as they retraced his path down the alley. "I told them my brother would be joining me in a couple of days."

"I thought you had only cousins."

He grinned. "I have a brother now."

They climbed the rear stairs to the sixth floor. She had agreed with him it was safer for them to stay together. Their room had two small beds and was sparsely furnished with florid furniture in the Old Turkish style.

While she went into the bathroom, he dropped the duffel onto the bed nearest the door and opened the box. Inside was another subcompact semi-automatic Beretta pistol just like the one he'd had to leave behind in Rome. He checked it, loaded it from the box of ammo, and tried on the canvas shoulder holster, adjusting it. Satisfied, he went to the window. The lights of the city spread out before him in a glittering vista, beckoning.

"Come look at this." He pushed open the two vertical panes and leaned out.

She emerged from the bathroom, her striking features smoothed at last. She was beginning to feel safe again, he decided. She smelled fresh, of soap and rose water.

She leaned out the window, too. "What a magnificent view."

"Istanbul is the only major city in the world to straddle two continents," he said. "It's built on seven hills, just as Rome is. Where we are—the Sultanahmet district—is on top of the first hill, on the south side. It's the historic core of the city. See that?" A series of fireworks in calico colors sprayed above the dark waters of the Marmara. "That's from a wedding boat. Look at the lighted mosques. The domes and minarets. The temples and churches. The maze of winding streets." The night gave a spectacular quality to the ancient city, as if it were secretly reinvigorating itself while its inhabitants slept. "It must've looked something like this during the Byzantine period, when the emperors were conquering the world and collecting the best books."

"It's beautiful. Did you learn all of that from Google?"

"From my father. Visiting ancient Constantinople was something we'd always planned to do together. That's how I knew Istanbul was called the City of the World's Desire.

He particularly liked this hotel. There's a lot of history connected to it." His chest tight, he turned to her. "If my father were a member of the book club when your husband joined the library, he could've been responsible in one way or another for the dead man in your husband's grave and for sending you to prison. I just want you to know I'm sorry."

"Charles told me they wanted to have me killed, but he talked them out of it." She sighed heavily, and he felt a gap open between them. "I know you loved your father. Whatever he did or didn't do has nothing to do with who you are. It's not your fault."

But he sensed that somehow, in her mind, he was tainted by it. He turned back into the room, remembering. When he was growing up, his father was gone for longer and longer periods of time. He had moved them around Washington from one house to another, always larger, more expensive. His mother's loneliness. The beautiful gifts brought back from each trip. Artworks, jewelry, furnishings, books. His father had grown not only richer but leaner and stronger. As his hair grayed, their conversations more often focused on lessons he wanted to pass on: Think for yourself. You can never learn enough. No one can protect you but yourself. Money solves almost every problem.

"You said you're a CIA contract employee," Eva said. "What did you do before?"

"Military intelligence. The army. I retired about a month before Dad was killed."

"You're a rich kid with every opportunity in the world. I'll bet your father would've loved for you to jump on the fast track to the executive suite at Bucknell."

"True." It was his father's dream.

"But you ended up in the army. Why?"

"It seemed like the right thing to do. And no, it was before 9/11."

"So you rebelled by being a stand-up guy. But that's not all, is it? Who are you really, Judd Ryder?"

For that he had no answer. He was saved by a knock on the door. Sliding out his weapon, he padded toward it and peered through the peephole. Dinner had arrived.

They ate at a small table in the corner—lamb meatballs with lemon sauce, tangy roasted eggplant salad, and a spread of ground walnuts and sweet red peppers. They talked quietly, and when they finished, he poured raki, a milky aperitif flavored with anise, a Turkish drink he had enjoyed with his father at home. As he handed her a glass, his encrypted mobile rang.

She looked across the room to his bed, where the mobile lay. "Tucker with good news, I hope."

He was already picking it up. As he punched the Talk button, he confirmed by saying, "Hello, Tucker."

Setting down her glass, she listened as he put the mobile on speakerphone.

"You've arrived?" Tucker wanted to know.

"Yes, we're at the hotel," Judd said. "Your package was waiting. Thanks. You should know Preston was at the airport. We got past him. This time it wasn't a leak; they tracked us through Eva's cell phone."

"Christ." The spymaster sounded frustrated.

"Did you find out anything about Yakimovich?" Judd asked.

"Yes, a good lead from an Istanbul source. There's a merchant of old calligraphy in the Grand Bazaar who's supposed to know where Yakimovich is. His name is Okan Biçer, and he shows up for work around three P.M. I'll e-mail you his photo and give you directions to his shop."

When they had memorized the directions and examined the photo, Judd ended the connection and tossed the mobile back onto his bed. Then he raised his glass, and Eva raised hers. They touched the rims with a soft clink. Drinking, they avoided the intimacy of each other's eyes, the pain of their shared past, and the worry about what tomorrow would bring.

38

Fairfax County, Virginia

Cathy Doyle was exhausted. It was nearly one A.M., and the day had been filled with work and the usual pressures to succeed at the various missions on which Catapult was working. As she drove across the Potomac River into Virginia, heading home, she turned on the radio. But it was a report of new terrorist attacks in eastern Afghanistan, and she already had enough facts about it; the last thing she needed was the somber news repeated. She punched off the radio.

Virginia was a land of urban congestion amid broad swathes of woods and farmland. She loved it—it always made her think of Ohio, where she had grown up. She turned off onto a two-lane road washed with moonlight. It ran along the river north of the District. At this hour, traffic was light, the widely spaced houses mostly dark.

She thought longingly of her twin daughters, home from spring break at Columbia, and her husband, a lawyer at the Department of Labor, who had just returned from a conference in Chicago. All would be sleeping, which she would be soon, too.

Humming to herself, she checked the road. There was almost no traffic, and she felt herself relax. She was thinking about home and bed again when she realized there was another car behind her now. She glanced at her speedometer. She was locked in at forty miles an hour, just where she wanted to be, and so was the other guy. Someone else heading home for a good night's sleep.

To her right, the forest opened up, and she could see the river with its rippling surface painted a silky silver by the moonlight. She liked that, too. Nature in all its beauty. She cracked her window. The air whistled in, the cool night air tasting moist, of the river. She turned on the radio again, this time found a blues station. Ah, yes.

Settling back into her seat, she glanced into her rearview mirror. And stared. The other vehicle's headlights were closing in, bombarding her car with light. She hit the accelerator, pushing out. As she passed sixty miles an hour, she checked her rearview mirror again. Her follower was even closer. There was still no other traffic as she started up the long, high hill that would eventually dip down into the valley where her house was, only a couple of miles farther.

Again she looked into her rearview mirror. The other car had moved out of their lane and into the oncoming lane. It was a big pickup. He had not signaled, and he had not slowed, either.

She slammed her foot on the accelerator, speeding toward seventy miles an hour. The pickup dropped back behind, in their lane again. But then the headlights loomed abruptly closer. As she floored the accelerator, he swung into the other lane, overtaking her. Her mouth went dry as they raced up the hill together

She braked to drop behind. Too late. The pickup crashed sideways into her car. Furious, she fought to control the steering wheel. The pickup slammed into her again, holding, pushing her toward the cliff over the river. This time the wheel ripped from her grasp.

Terror filling her, she gripped the steering wheel as the car hurtled through the guardrail, shot over the cliff, and crashed down through young pines, smashing against boulders. One collision after another hurled her back and forth. As the sedan flew over a final precipice and dived toward the shadowy river, she felt a moment of blinding impact, and then nothing.

Washington, D.C.

At eight A.M. the headquarters of Catapult was solemn and quiet, although all of the morning staff had arrived. A sense of shocked grief infused the building. The news of Catherine Doyle's fatal accident had spread. Tucker had heard hours before, awakened by his old friend Matthew Kelley, the director of the Clandestine Service. When she had not returned home, Cathy's husband had called. Then the Virginia State Police found her car submerged in the river, only a patch of the top visible. The vehicle was badly banged up, which was consistent with the terrain it had crashed down through, and she had apparently drowned. There would be a coroner's report and the results of forensics in a few days.

Tucker wandered the old brick building, chatting with their people, comforting them, and by doing so comforting himself. Cathy had been a good boss, tough and fair, and they had liked her. He urged them to get back to work. Their operators abroad were counting on them. Besides, it was what Cathy would have wanted, and they knew it.

By the afternoon, the pace had quickened, voices talked business, telephones rang, computer keys clicked. He returned to his office and tried to concentrate. Finally the habits of a lifetime returned, and he bent over his work.

"Hello, Tucker." Hudson Canon stood in the doorway, looking concerned. He was an assistant director in the Clandestine Service, a longtime field officer who had been brought home to Langley to oversee a slew of people who in turn created and managed missions. Short, dignified, and heavily muscled, he gave the impression of a high-class American Kennel Club bulldog, with his pug nose and round black eyes and thick cheeks. "How are you doing?" Canon asked.

"It's terrible news, of course. Cathy will be greatly missed."

"Gloria says everyone is working hard, but I must say the place feels a bit like a mausoleum. Damn. I liked Cathy a lot. A fine woman."

"Have a chair." Tucker motioned to one. "What can I do for you?"

Canon gave a quick smile and sat in front of the desk. "Matt Kelley sent me over to take Cathy's place until a new chief is named. You interested in the job?"

"That's fast."

"Don't I know it. Are you interested?"

Tucker's soul felt heavy. "Let me think about it." The position had been offered to him before Cathy was appointed, but he had turned it down.

"I haven't been to Cathy's office yet," Canon went on. "I told Gloria to pack up all of her private things before I moved in. Meanwhile, I'd like you to bring me up-to-date. Start with the hottest missions."

Canon crossed his legs, and they talked. Tucker filled him in on Berlin, Bratislava, Kiev, Tehran, and others. Canon knew the basics about all from Cathy's weekly reports.

"I hear you might've had a breach in your e-mail or Internet system."

"Debi is honchoing it," Tucker told him. "Someone did get in and was able to access Cathy's e-mail for about three minutes."

Canon grimaced. "Long enough to steal more than any of us would want."

"Agreed. Still, we're not sure what they took. Maybe they got nothing. In any case, that pathway is now a dead end, and Debi's team is on high alert, looking for even the smallest signs of attempt to trespass. There's been no other successful cybersleuthing since. The problem was, the breach occurred during the night shift, when we had fewer bodies. They missed the invader—he was damn good at it obviously."

"I see. What else do you have for me?"

Tucker launched into a description of the Library of Gold operation.

When he had finished, Canon sat back, thinking. "Is this a wise use of Catapult's resources? You still have no evidence of involvement in terrorism. Who in hell cares about the Library of Gold? So what if it's some marvelous old relic. That's the bailiwick of historians and anthropologists. This is a waste of time better spent on more critical missions."

Tucker stiffened. "I understand your point, but we're deep into it now. I've got a contract employee and a civilian on the run, being hunted. And a dead man who turned up alive who said he was the chief librarian. He's dead now, too, and it's real this time. There are other corpses—people like Jonathan Ryder and the Charboniers."

"Have you learned anything about the library's location through Ryder or the Charboniers?"

"Nothing yet. Jonathan's life is far easier to probe. We have his travel records, but he was an international businessman and flew around the globe. A lot of cities and towns. As for the Charboniers, we have to work with the French to get information, and that's difficult. You know how secretive they can be."

"It'll be another dead end."

"Maybe. But my two people in Istanbul have a good lead. We need to follow up on that."

"A good lead? What is it?"

"The man's name is Okan Biçer. He sells calligraphy in the Grand Bazaar." Tucker checked his watch. "He's supposed to know where an old acquaintance of Eva Blake's husband is, an antiquities merchant named Andrew Yakimovich. They're hoping Yakimovich may be holding something for Blake that'll tell them where the library is."

Hudson Canon seemed to think about it. At last he nodded. "I'd already expressed my reservations to Cathy about whether this operation was worth it, but she convinced me to give it some time. Your argument for more time is good, too. However, I've also taken it to my boss. Especially now that Cathy's gone and we'll need to rethink Catapult, we're going to have to pull in our horns. You have thirty-six hours to find the library. If you don't know where it is by then, the boss says to pull the plug and end the operation."

39

Peshawar, Pakistan

Thick storm clouds rolled black and angry overhead, and the temperature dropped five degrees as Martin Chapman rode into the polluted and paranoid city of Peshawar. He was dressed in a traditional *shalwar kameez*—the long shirt and baggy trousers worn by most Pakistani and Afghani men—so he could pass for an Uzbek, Chechen, or light-skinned Pashtun.

A hotbed of Taliban and al-Qaeda, the city was where he was to meet the warlord who had promised him safe passage. Still, Chapman did not believe in relying on promises. His pistol was on his belt, the holster latch unfastened, and his hand on the weapon's grip. Beside him lay the truck driver's fully loaded AK-47.

Peshawar was an armed garrison. Men and boys as young as five years old wore, cradled, or shouldered an array of weapons. But then, it was the capital of the politically unstable North-West Frontier Province and just six miles from the lawless Federally Administered Tribal Areas. Jihadists poured into the city to regroup, to fight, to buy and trade weapons and supplies, and to partake of civilization. It had always been a smugglers' haven and a center for indigenous arms manufacture, but now more so than ever. Private homes were functioning gun factories. Using the crudest of tools, entire families fabricated quality copies of major small and medium arms.

As the truck drove through the city, Chapman was taken aback by the poverty and destruction. Empty shells of buildings, some towering precariously several stories high, dotted streets, the result of suicide bombings, personal disputes, police assaults, and the occasional drone attack from across the mountains in Afghanistan.

Despite it all, people strove for normalcy. Women draped in ghostly burkas drifted like shadows among the stores, carrying string shopping bags. Men in tribal headdresses or *pakul* hats—traditional flat round wool caps—sat for portraits in front of old box cameras screwed into rickety wood tripods.

"We there soon," the driver told Chapman. An Afghan Pashtun, he worked directly for the warlord. Thankfully he understood English far better than he spoke it.

The driver turned the big truck onto Lahore Road. Bouncing over potholes, he turned again and slammed on the brakes. Dust spewed a choking cloud around them. They had stopped in front of a gun shop.

"This is it?" Chapman asked.

The driver nodded enthusiastically.

"Wait here," Chapman ordered.

Nodding again, the man turned off the ignition and peered up through the windshield, eying the stormy twilight sky. He shook his head in despair, then climbed out and lit a brown cigarette.

Chapman got out, too, silently cursing Syed Ullah for insisting they meet in Peshawar. But that was Ullah for you. He was one of a long line of Pashtun tribal chiefs from the border province of Khost in Afghanistan. The warlord was his own man, regarding Kabul's commands with indifference.

As Chapman walked toward the store, Ullah appeared in the doorway, filling it. Gigantic, powerfully built, he had hands that looked as if they could palm bowling balls. His cheekbones were high, the coldly intelligent brown eyes widely spaced, the thick mustache above his wide mouth neatly trimmed. He wore a brown wool sweater, a *shalwar kameez,* and sturdy black boots. Twin pearl-handled pistols were holstered on his hips.

He looked comfortable and pleased with himself. "You are here, Chapman. Come in. *Pe kher ragle."* Welcome.

Chapman walked inside and stopped, keeping his manner casual. Weapons ranging from small two-shot pistols to juiced-up rocket launchers were for sale, stacked four and five deep against the walls, lying on shelves up to the ceiling, and bunched and leaning together like haystacks in the corners. The place smelled like cheap grease. In the back of the store, silently blocking a door, stood six of Ullah's soldiers. They carried rifles, while flowers were tucked into their belts in the Pashtun style. Two bandoliers crossed each of their chests, displaying not only bullets but dangling grenades.

Smiling proudly, the warlord looked around the store, then peered down at Chapman.

"Impressive," Chapman admitted.

With a nod from Ullah, his men headed for the open front door. "They will bring in the crates. You have what we agreed on in the back of the truck?"

"Everything."

"Good, good." Ullah gestured grandly at the two low stools beside a desk.

They sat. A white silk cloth edged with lace had been spread out, and a white porcelain teapot decorated with red poppies waited in the middle of it. The warlord poured tea into two glasses rimmed in gold and set into decorative golden bases with golden handles.

Offering no milk or sugar, he handed a cup to Chapman.

"This is a fine black Indian tea, flavored with cardamom and honey. I serve it on only the most important occasions, to my most important guests. According to our Pashtunwali code, it is my duty to host you, treasure you, and protect you." Ullah lifted his cup in salute.

Chapman lifted his cup, too, and gave a nod of appreciation. They drank, and Chapman said nothing about the code, knowing full well the warlord's hospitality would evaporate and Chapman's life would be in danger if he did not fulfill his end of their agreement. Pashtuns were bound by fierce cultural, emotional, and social ties—the Pashtunwali code. At the same time, if they breathed, they fought. An old Pashtun saying was "Me against my brother, me and my brother against our cousins, and we and our cousins against the enemy, any enemy." In that way they confirmed their honor, and it did not seem to matter whether they ended up successful—or dead.

The first crate came in, one of Ullah's men rolling it on a dolly, followed by another, and another, all disappearing into the back. From Karachi, the crates had been shipped to Islamabad, then trucked into Madari, where Chapman had jetted in from Oman and met Ullah's driver.

Thunder rumbled somewhere in the distant hills.

"My boys will hurry now," Ullah commented, amused.

He barked an order in Pashto to a soldier who had picked up speed and was rushing past with another crate. The man wheeled it around, brought it to Ullah, and ripped off the top with a crowbar.

Ullah and Chapman stood and looked down. Ullah lowered his great height to finger a new U.S. Army camouflage uniform. "Good, good."

"The other boxes contain more uniforms," Chapman told him. "Kevlar helmets with night-vision scopes, grenade belts, GPS units, encrypted cell phones, flares, M4 carbine rifles with telescopic sights, and body armor. Everything we agreed upon and more, all regulation army and authentic."

"I will check each crate before you leave." The warlord settled back down onto his stool, his dainty teacup disappearing into his big hand as he sipped.

For a moment Ullah was not a ruthless brawler, not the Mike Tyson of the tribal lands, but a gentleman of good taste. Driven into exile in Pakistan by the Taliban in the 1990s, he had returned to Afghanistan after 9/11 to lead anti-Taliban soldiers, moving in and out of alliances, keeping his distance from the national government and coalition forces. Today his home base was a vast area of eastern Khost province that was largely rural and backward. His photograph hung in every office, shop, and school, and he maintained firm control with a personal army of more than five thousand.

What mattered most to Chapman was he owned ten square miles of land that the director needed.

Lightning split through the dark clouds, illuminating the shop in a moment of startling white light. Thunder boomed, and the heavens opened. Rain poured down in a brutal torrent as the last of the crates rushed through.

Ullah peered over his teacup. "About my money. I am eager to have it back."

"And you will. Soon."

"Now."

When Chapman had discovered Ullah owned the land, he had ordered a complete investigation of the man. Through book club member Carl Lindström's chief of security—an accomplished black-hatter—a hidden overseas account containing some $20 million in profits from drugs and gunrunning was uncovered. If Chapman told the Kabul government about it, the minister of finance would confiscate it, and the president would find unpleasant ways to punish Ullah.

Instead, Chapman had led his equity firm in a leveraged buyout of the bank—and frozen the account. With that incentive, Ullah had agreed to meet him at a Caspian Sea resort, where Chapman had offered to release the money and give him a small percentage in a deal the greedy bastard could not refuse. He would earn enormous profits for decades to come in an honest business venture through which he could launder his heroin and opium profits. But it hinged on Chapman's being able to buy the land, which the warlord could not sell because he was renting it to the United States for a secret forward base.

"When you finish the job, you'll get your money," Chapman told him.

Ullah stared hard.

"As we agreed," Chapman reminded him, thinking of the Pashtunwali code.

There was a pause. Then Ullah chuckled and changed the subject. "Why do you want my land?" He had asked the question several times before.

"You'll find out as soon as you sign it over to me."

Ullah nodded. "It is good you arrived on schedule. We will be able to truck the crates into Khost by tomorrow."

"And then?" Chapman prompted.

"The next night two hundred fifty of my men will put on your uniforms and use your weapons to take out about a hundred villagers. A lot of gunfire and dead bodies. Much blood. I will have a Pakistani reporter and cameraman there. They will make many videos. It will be a splendid show that all the world will see of 'American' soldiers slaughtering innocent civilians." He laughed loudly, his solid white teeth gleaming.

Because of the changed—and charged—political atmosphere in Afghanistan, the Kabul national government insisted its complicity in the U.S. forward base be kept secret. But with the harsh light of international outrage shining on the massacre, Kabul would have no choice but to close the base. Of course before then Ullah would have made all of the American uniforms and equipment vanish, and those who knew what actually had happened would be bound to silence by the Pashtunwali code. The result would be the warlord would at last be able to sell the land to Chapman.

As the rain drummed down, Ullah boasted of his past successes in battle, hair-singeing tales to remind Chapman of his power. But Chapman had something Ullah did not—the knowledge of what lay in the land, and the technical expertise to exploit it. Afghanistan had many natural riches, but the war-torn country was unstable, illiterate, untrained, and in no position to make use of them and would not be for decades to come.

As soon as they finished their tea, the warlord announced, "We will inspect the crates now."

"Go ahead. I need to make a phone call. I'll join you when I finish."

As Ullah left for the back room, Chapman walked to the front of the shop and stood alone at the window. The thunderstorm had stopped as suddenly as it had started, and the sky was clearing. With that good omen, he dialed his wife's iPhone. It had been days since they last talked, a month since he last saw her. He longed to hear her voice.

But it was her assistant, Mahaira. "She is showering. I am so sorry."

He kept his voice calm. "Where are you?"

"In Athens, as you requested."

He sighed with relief. He would see his wife in just a few hours. "How was the party in San Moritz?" It was supposed to have been a gala affair—jet-set society in all its ravenous glory.

"She wore the diamond necklace, earrings, and tiara to the ball," Mahaira said proudly. "She looked gorgeous. Glowing, like a star."

The necklace and earrings had been her mother's and grandmother's. He had bought them two decades before, when her family had lost its money. The tiara was new—purchased just last year. He remembered the excitement in her eyes, how she had clapped her hands and danced around the room wearing it, naked, beautiful.

"Does she miss me?"

Mahaira answered too quickly. "Of course. Terribly."

When he hung up, he took out the photo from his wallet and stared at it, reliving the past, the happiness, the hopes and dreams of youth. It was a copy of the picture that always stood on his desk at his Arabian horse spread in Maryland, his home base. There she was—a glorious young Gemma in her tight long formal gown, the family diamonds sparkling at her ears and around her throat—and he in his rented tuxedo. A long time ago now, when they were in their early twenties and deeply in love.

His cell phone rang. Putting the photo away, he answered.

It was Preston, sounding jubilant. "Catherine Doyle is dead, and I have the information about where Ryder and Blake are going in Istanbul."

"Give me the details."

"The contact is Okan Biçer, a calligraphy seller in the Grand Bazaar. I've hired local men, and I'm on my way."

"Good. Let me know."

As soon as he hung up, Chapman phoned the Carnivore and repeated the information. There could be no loose ends to interfere with the warlord's attack in Khost, especially no further CIA interest.

"Preston will merely set up the hit, as we agreed," he finished.

The Carnivore's voice was neutral. "That is acceptable. I'm in Istanbul. Your two targets are as good as scrubbed."

40

Istanbul, Turkey

A world atlas of languages filled the air as crowds poured in to the Grand Bazaar through the Light of the Ottomans Gate. Eva peered around as she and Judd moved with the throngs. While many women wore shoulder-baring sundresses ending above the knee, others concealed their hair beneath traditional *khimar* scarves and their bodies under long coats. Some men sported fezzes and large mustaches, and some were clean-shaven and dressed in business suits or skin-exposing tank tops and walking shorts.

They had been watching for Preston or a sign they were being followed. To lessen the chances of discovery they had changed their appearances in the hotel before checking out. Now her hair was black, pulled severely back into a bun at the nape of her neck, while Judd's chestnut brown hair was bleached blond and cut very short. He wore glasses with plain lenses and looked very much like a tanned Viking tourist.

She'd had a restless night, wondering how she could have so badly misjudged Charles and whether Judd was somehow also going to betray her. Truthfully, she did not hold him responsible for his father's actions. But still, there was something about it all that made her uneasy. She hoped she could continue to trust him.

Inside, the marketplace was teeming. Completely roofed and domed, with thick exterior walls, gates, and doors, it boasted some four thousand shops, miles and miles of avenues and lanes, and hidden nooks known only to locals.

Judd was giving her a tour. "It's the largest covered mall in the world and the most famous souk. This street is Kalpakçilarba¸si Caddesi, the main one. Look at all the gold stores. That's what it's known for."

Kalpakçilarbaşi was a tunnel of light, with a tall arched ceiling, high windows, and pale walls adorned with exquisite blue tiles. Seeming to extend endlessly, it emanated taste and wealth, with gold jewelry, gold plates, and decorative gold items shining from the glass display windows.

Judd directed them into a giant labyrinth of tiny streets and alleyways, all swarming with shoppers. The view changed time and again. They passed mosques, banks, coffee shops, and restaurants. From the doors of *hans*—stores—merchants called out their wares in a variety of languages—the strongest Turkish Viagra, the best pottery, the finest watches, the most lovely antiques, the most religious icons.

Suddenly there was a scream. A woman turned, her hands gripping her face in distress. "My purse! He stole my purse!" she yelled in German.

A bag-slasher raced off, his long hair flying as he rounded a corner and vanished. It had happened so quickly no one had time to react. As someone gave the woman directions to a police station, Eva and Judd went onto another street, finally reaching their destination.

A picturesque relic of Old Istanbul, it was a small, dead-end shopping area surrounding a tiled patio. Photos of whirling dervishes in their ecstatic dances decorated walls. Goods spilled from *hans*. Games of backgammon were in progress at wood tables in the patio, where the players drank from tulip-shaped tea glasses. Eva spotted a cabal of pick-pockets, a mother with three children, but no actual dipping.

"I see the shop," she told Judd.

The windows of the *han* showcased aged pages of calligraphy. As they walked inside, a sturdy middle-aged man in an embroidered caftan grinned at them.

"Merhaba." Welcome. He quickly took in their appearances and switched to English. "British and Swedish, yes? You are obviously interested in our gorgeous old script. You must take home many pages. Hang them on your walls. Impress all your family."

Eva remembered the photo of Okan Biçer that Tucker had e-mailed. This merchant was not he.

"We're looking for Mr. Biçer, Okan Biçer," she said. "A friend told us about him."

"Ah, you have mutual friends. No doubt he sent you to buy calligraphy. We have the best in Istanbul. In all Europe and Asia."

"My name is Eva Blake," she tried again. "Andrew Yakimovich is a personal friend. We were told Mr. Biçer would know where Andy is."

His small black eyes examined her shrewdly, then Judd. "No calligraphy? How sad. You will leave your phone number and address, and I will see."

The beaded curtain separating the store from the back rustled, as if someone had been starting to come through and then changed his mind—or had been listening. When the shopkeeper glanced back nervously, Judd strode past him.

He hurried after Judd. *"Hayir, hayir."* No, no. "Okan is not here. He is not here."

Checking the other shoppers who were watching curiously, Eva followed as Judd pushed the merchant aside, brushed through the curtain, and opened a wood door. A sweet, cloying odor filled the narrow hall.

They strode down it, the shopkeeper on their heels, wringing his hands and lamenting. When they finally passed through an arched stone opening, Eva and Judd stopped and stared.

"I'll be damned," she said.

Their shirts off, men lay on faded lounges against stone walls, eyes half closed, fezzes crowning their heads at drunken angles. Some propped themselves up on elbows, holding long pipes, the bowls heating over oil lamps. In the bowls were waxy brown "pills"—opium. It was an old-fashioned opium den. In the light of the small lamps, the men turned toward their visitors, their gazes dreamy, their cheeks puffing as they continued to inhale the intoxicating vapors.

Okan Biçer was standing in the middle of them, rubbing his elbows, distraught. His long thin face was sweaty, and his eyes darted nervously around. He gave a quick nod to the shopkeeper, who shrugged and marched back toward the store.

Collecting himself, Biçer walked forward and bowed. "This is no place for you. We must leave. You can tell me everything I can do for you then. That way." He gestured toward the shopkeeper's retreating figure.

But Eva was already moving toward a man asleep on his side on a lounge. His large fez lay over his ear, and one chubby hand dangled to the floor. Fifty-plus years old, he had a large head, thick gray hair, heavy round cheeks, and oddly sensitive lips. The bags under his eyes were huge and dark, almost bruised—but that was opium for you. Dressed only in loose trousers and tennis shoes without laces, he was snoring lightly.

She shook his shoulder. "Andy, wake up. Andy Yakimovich. Wake up."

Yakimovich, the antiquities dealer, rolled over onto his back, his large white belly spreading. He snored louder.

Judd grabbed Yakimovich and propped him up against the stone wall. "Wake up, Yakimovich. *Polis*." Police.

His eyes snapped open, and the room emptied—Biçer raced away through a different door, off to the side, and the other men staggered to their feet and stumbled after him. Opium poppies were one of Turkey's largest crops, and through international agreement, the United States annually bought a large percentage of their legal opium. But just as it was in the United States, the narcotic was illegal for self-entertainment in Turkey.

"Polis?" Yakimovich muttered worriedly. He looked at Judd. "You are police? You do not look like police. What kind of police are you?"

Eva tapped Judd's arm, and he moved aside. "Hello, Andy. I'm Eva Blake, Charles Sherback's widow. I believe Charles left something with you for me."

His eyes wandered. "You are not police. Go away."

She grabbed his stubbled chin. "Look at me, Andy." When he focused, she repeated, "My name is Eva Blake. I'm Charles Sherback's widow. I want what he left for me. Judd, get out the *scytale*."

Judd took the tapered gold cylinder from the duffel bag and handed it to her. Even in the dim light it glowed, engraved and beautiful. She held it up for Yakimovich to see.

A tender look entered his eyes. He snatched the baton from her. Holding it in both hands, he pressed it against his heart. "I have missed you," he murmured.

"I believe Charles left a message for me that fits around the *scytale*. I need it—now."

His eyes narrowed. *"Absque argento omnia vana."* Then he gave what he seemed to think was a winning smile.

"What does he want?" Judd asked.

"It's a Latin phrase: 'Without money all efforts are useless.' He expects to be paid." She yanked away the *scytale* from Yakimovich.

His gaze followed it hungrily.

"Do you want it back?" she asked.

He nodded. "Yes. Please."

"Give us Charles's message, and you can keep the *scytale*."

Yakimovich's eyes adjusted. For the first time he seemed really to see Judd and her. His body shuddered with a sigh. "All right. It is in my office."

41

Andrew Yakimovich dropped a white cotton shirt over his head and led them out through the side door and into a meandering stone passageway. The air smelled of dust, and the walls were rough. Naked lightbulbs flickered overhead. Positioning his fez carefully onto his gray hair, he walked slowly, a wounded lion, aged but proud.

"The foundation is Byzantine, the floor plan Ottoman," he told them. "This is one of the hidden worlds of the Grand Bazaar. Along here are rooms that have been workshops for centuries."

As Eva watched, he gestured at doors. Few displayed signs. Most were open, showing antiques being repaired, stones being set in silver and gold, and tourist T-shirts being sewn. The mother with three children whom Eva had spotted earlier stood inside one room with a half dozen other people. She pulled billfolds from her purse and handed them over to a man sitting behind a desk.

"How far does this go on?" Judd wanted to know.

Yakimovich waved a hand. "It winds. A quarter mile perhaps."

He took out a large old key and stopped. Unlocking a door, he stepped inside and rotated a switch. Electrical conduit ran up the wall and across the ceiling. Low-wattage lightbulbs beamed into life.

Eva and Judd followed him inside. Once a prominent antiquities dealer, Yakimovich seemed to have packed his entire life into this cavernous room. Crates rose to the ceiling, most unlabeled, fading into the dark recesses. Pieces of beautiful but dusty old furniture were stacked in a corner. Tall rolls of handmade carpets leaned against walls.

With a proprietary glance around, he moved to a marble-topped table and sat. "The *scytale,* if you please." His tone was businesslike.

Eva laid it on the table, which was empty. There were no record books, no accounts, no letters from buyers eager to purchase one of Yakimovich's treasures. No chairs in which customers could sit.

She tried to figure out how to phrase the question without insulting him: "You've retired, Andy?"

He let out a loud hoot, his face animated in the way she remembered. "You are too kind. I have no illusions about what I have become." He peered at her, his gaze sharp for a moment. "Once I was great, like Charles. He could be a bastard, but I understood that. We have our own code, we bastards. Especially when we share a passion."

He opened a small drawer and took out a long strip of tan leather on which letters in black ink were visible on one side. Eva inhaled, excitement coursing through her. At long last perhaps they would learn where the library was. As he started to lay down the strip, Eva snatched it up. The leather was stiff but pliable. She grabbed the *scytale.*

"Wrap from the large end first," Yakimovich advised.

She did as he said, working slowly. It was an awkward process, the leather's stiffness making it even more difficult. She could feel Judd's intensity beside her. Finished, she gripped the *scytale* by both ends, holding the strip in place with her thumbs, then turned the cylinder horizontal to read the words.

Disappointment filled her. "All I see is gibberish."

"I will do it," Yakimovich said. "One must help the letters to grow into words."

With a flourish, the antiquities dealer pulled the dry leather slightly and used a thumb to press it flat against the *scytale* as he rotated it and rewrapped the strip. It was slow work. Finished at last, he gave a nod of satisfaction. Holding the baton at the ends as Eva had so the strip would not slip, he turned the *scytale* and studied the script.

"It is Latin, and it is from Charles, but perhaps that is to be expected, since he is the one who left it here with me." For a moment he continued to read silently to himself. Then his head jerked up, and his eyes flashed with excitement. "My God, Charles did it. He *did* it! He tracked the *library*! Listen to this: 'You can find the location of the Library of Gold hidden inside *The Book of Spies*.' "

The calligraphy shop was silent. The customers had been banished, and the door locked. A large bruise was appearing on the shopkeeper's cheek where Preston had hit him with his fist. He cringed as Preston grabbed his arm roughly.

"Show me exactly where they went," Preston ordered and shoved him through the beaded curtain into the back.

The man ran down the dim hall toward an arched opening. Following, Preston took out his S&W pistol and screwed on the sound suppressor. Behind him were his two men, weapons in hand. A third man soon joined them.

Judd leaned forward. "Keep reading, Andy," he ordered.

"Hurry!" Eva said, thrilled.

"It says here Charles's predecessor wrote it inside the book, then smuggled the book out of the library—" Yakimovich stopped, the *scytale* frozen in midair.

Pounding feet in the corridor echoed loudly against the stone walls. The feet were coming toward them.

Judd pulled out his Beretta and ran toward the door, the only door to the storeroom.

Eva snatched the *scytale* from Yakimovich's hands.

"No!" he yelled, reaching for it.

"I'll send it back to you." Eva sprinted.

Judd had flattened himself behind the open door. He motioned Eva to stand back beside him.

At his desk, the antiquities dealer seemed unable to move.

"Hide!" Judd commanded.

Yakimovich's face blanched. He scuttled back among the crates and disappeared.

Suddenly the shopkeeper from the calligraphy store burst through the door as if he had been thrown. His eyes were wild, and sweat poured down his bruised face.

"Help me! Help me!" He ran in among the old furniture.

Light noises of a struggle reverberated from the stone corridor. Feet scuffed and snapped against the floor. There was a loud grunt, then another. The dull sound of something hitting flesh. A swift *crack*, then another. From the floor?

It was if they were listening to a radio, with the only clue being that some kind of fight was going on. Eva peered at Judd, who had a distant, cold look that sent chills over her skin. Finally there was a horrible quiet.

Judd raised a hand, silently telling her to wait as he stepped to the edge of the doorway. Pistol up, he peered out cautiously. Then he vanished into the hall.

Ignoring his order, Eva followed.

Four men were down. Two were about twenty feet away, bloody exit wounds showing on their foreheads. The other two—Preston and another man—lay close together near Yakimovich's door. There were no obvious wounds on either.

Instantly Judd kicked Preston's pistol from his limp hand, then swept it up.

"Dammit, Preston found us again," she whispered.

He nodded. "We'll talk about it later." Looking up and down the winding hallway, he crouched beside the killer. "Check the other guy's pockets, Eva. Do it fast. We can't stay here long."

She knelt. The man had gray hair and a long gray mustache. His face was the color of a roasted almond, the lines deep, the nose prominent. His fez lay upside down beside him. She rustled through the caftan and found only a wallet. Inside was an Istanbul driver's license for Salih Serin, a credit card in the same name, and a few Turkish lira. The photo on the driver's license matched the face of the man lying beside her.

"No weapon," she said. "His name is Salih Serin. He lives in Istanbul."

"Preston has a pistol and cash, no ID, and a small notebook. He's pulled out most of the pages, but there's one left. He wrote, 'Robin Miller. *Book of Spies.* All we know is Athens—so far.' "

Eva felt a surge of excitement. "Then we have to go to Athens."

"Yes." He gave her Preston's weapon. "If he so much as moves, shoot him. We don't know about Serin yet, so be careful of him, too." He tucked the note and money inside his jacket and hurried back into Yakimovich's room.

Serin moaned and murmured something in Turkish. Opening his eyes, he jerked his head from side to side, panicking, until he saw Preston was lying unconscious.

He looked up at her and smiled. "You are pretty."

Judd returned, carrying rope and their duffel bag. "The shopkeeper was no help. He's blithering, scared to death." As he tied Preston's hands tightly behind him, he peered across at Serin. "What happened?"

The Turk sat up. "I know those two." He pointed a thumb

down the hall at the prone men. "They are evil. I was back there in a workroom, visiting a friend, and I saw them run past. A long time ago I was with MIT." He gazed at them and explained. "Our Milli Istihbarat Teskilati, the National Intelligence Organization. So I thought I would see what badness they were planning. By the time I got here, both of them were on the floor with gunshot wounds, and that one"—he gestured at Preston—"had just hurled Mustafa through the door. He and I had a large battle." He gave a conspiratorial grin. "But I am an old street fighter, and he thought he could take me. Still the weasel managed to whack me a good one just before I got him, and I fell and cracked my head." He rubbed the back of his skull. "In the old days . . . ah, in the old days I would've eaten his gizzard." He sighed tiredly.

"Are you all right, Mr. Serin?" Eva took his arm as he struggled to his feet.

Judd was suspicious. "There wasn't any bump on Preston's head. How'd you knock him out?" He finished binding Preston's feet together.

"Pressure." Serin grabbed his own throat, his thumbs pushed deep, then quickly released them. "We learn useful things in the secret service."

Judd nodded. "Thanks for your help. You aren't armed, so who shot the other men?"

"Maybe that one." He gestured at Preston. "I saw no one else. I know those guys. They could have waited until he had no choice and demanded more money—or something else he could not or would not provide." He shrugged, then scrutinized them. "You are in trouble, yes? I think they were planning to kill you. But you look like such nice tourists."

Judd only glanced at him. "Come on, Eva."

"I believe I heard someone mention Athens," Serin continued. "You wish to go? I know a boat rental place where few questions are asked. I can take you in the boat to a small airport south of here where the owner and I are friendly. Perhaps it would be good for you to slip out of Istanbul before this one"—he pointed at Preston lying hogtied on the stone floor—"gets free, or someone else is sent to take his place. I am a poor man now. You could pay me well. Perhaps you are glad for the assistance of someone who knows the terrain."

Worrying how Preston had found them again, Eva looked at Judd. Her inclination was to accept the offer.

Judd made a decision. "You won't mind if I check you for weapons."

Serin threw up his arms, the sleeves of his caftan billowing down past his elbows. "I insist."

Judd patted him from his neck to the soles of his feet, paying particular attention to his armpits, lower back, thighs, calves, and ankles.

Finally Judd said, "All right. Let's go."

Serin rushed ahead, trying doorknobs until he located a closet. Judd found rags inside. Stuffing one into Preston's mouth and tying another around it, he left the unconscious man bound tightly in his ropes.

"You didn't kill Preston," Eva whispered as they hurried after Serin.

"I thought about it. But he's unarmed, apparently doesn't know where *The Book of Spies* is in Athens, and anyway, he's out of commission long enough for us to get away." He hesitated, then admitted, "And I have enough blood on my hands."

42

The April daylight was fading, the lavender colors of sunset spreading softly across the indigo-blue Sea of Marmara. In the vast Istanbul marina where Salih Serin had taken Judd and Eva, waves lapped boat hulls and ropes rattled against masts.

Judd took up a position fifty feet away from Eva and Serin, observing as Serin negotiated in Turkish with a stooped youth for the boat they had selected—a sleek Chris-Craft yacht powerful enough to make the journey easily and outrun other small vessels.

Judd was on his mobile with Tucker. It was about eleven A.M. in Washington, six P.M. in Istanbul. He described the events in the Grand Bazaar. "Preston found us again."

"Dammit. What in hell is going on? There's no way anyone could've gotten the intel on my end . . ." There was a pause. Tucker sounded worried as he continued, "I'll think about it. Go on. What else did you learn?"

Judd repeated the information in Preston's notebook. "See if you can track down who Robin Miller is. I'm wondering whether she might be the blond woman Eva saw with Sherback in London. Remember, *The Book of Spies* might've been in the backpack he left with her."

"NSA is monitoring the two numbers you got off Sherback's phone. I'll let you know instantly if we get a hit."

"Good. Eva's going to translate the rest of the message on the leather strip as soon as we're alone. Supposedly it says exactly where the library's location is hidden inside *The Book of Spies*."

"Langley had that book in storage three years." Tucker sighed with frustration. "I take it you're leaving for Athens?"

"Immediately. I'm not going to tell you exactly how we're planning to get there."

He watched as Serin jabbed a thumb toward the yacht, the darkening sky, and the boat merchant, at last extending both palms up in a gesture of attempting to be reasonable. Serin had told the boat merchant he was going to insist they receive a large discount, since so few people wanted to rent at night. His animated face showed deep enjoyment in the haggling.

"A damn good idea," Tucker said. "Stay safe."

The Sea of Marmara

With Serin at the helm, the yacht cruised through the night, heading south-west across the Sea of Marmara. A wind had arisen out of the north through the Bosporus Strait, whipping the sea and making for a bumpy ride. They had progressed some ten miles, eaten fish sandwiches bought in the marina, and adjusted to the boat's rough rhythms.

Judd was confident they had not been followed to the Istanbul marina, but still he found himself peering back to where the city's lights spread across the horizon. He studied the traffic—fishing boats, cargo ships, and behemoth oil tankers and container ships, all blinking with lights. The great inland sea was a busy thoroughfare linking the Black Sea in the north to the Aegean and Mediterranean seas on the south through the Dardanelles Strait. None of the other boats seemed to be pacing them.

"Where exactly are we heading?" Eva raised her voice to be heard over the wind, sea, and motors.

Despite a bench seat directly behind them, Serin stood at the wheel, Eva beside him, where he had invited her. A low windshield partially protected them. Judd stood behind the bench seat, gripping the back with both hands. Eva's midnight-blue jacket was buttoned up to her chin, and tendrils of her long black hair had fallen out of the knot at the nape of her neck. Windblown and rosy-cheeked, she looked quietly happy. As she turned to listen to Serin, Judd was struck by how much he liked her, liked being with her. Then he remembered the role his father had probably played in her imprisonment for manslaughter. He gazed away.

"South of a big city called Tekirdăg," Serin yelled, "and north of a little village called Barbados. We are going to the Thrace part of Turkey, on the Europe side of course."

Serin held the wheel confidently in his brown hands. He was a little shorter than Judd, but broader, with thick muscles. He appeared nonchalant and self-satisfied. At the same time, there were signs of his past—the athletic way he moved on the boat and the flashes of intense acuity in his gaze. If he had not already said he had been a member of the national government's tough MIT, Judd would have suspected some sort of similar background.

"An old comrade of mine has a private airstrip," Serin was continuing. "We will be there in about three hours."

Judd saw they were doing a good thirty-plus knots despite the waves. Speedy, with two powerful inboard engines, the Chris-Craft was a stunner. Belowdecks were fully appointed staterooms, a salon, and a galley.

"You're not taking us through the Dardanelles?" Eva asked. "We'd pass the ruins of Troy if you did, and we'd be much closer to Athens."

"Too dangerous. The strait is narrow and crowded. It twists itself this way and that. Besides, the current is unusually swift."

"What do you do with yourself when you're not ferrying people in rented boats?" Judd asked.

"Ah, that is a long story. To make it short, I am what you call a jack-of-all-trades. I am hired to guide, to guard, and to deliver important items. I have a reputation, you see. I am trustworthy. And you two are very important items and now know I am trustworthy also. What about you, Mr. Ryder? You have not told me anything."

"We're tourists, just as you thought."

"You are trying to fool an old dog, but I know all the tricky tricks. I am curious. What is wrong with curiosity, I ask you?" His loud voice sounded hurt. "At least explain this thing called *The Book of Spies*. Entertain me while I work so hard."

Eva laughed. "It's an illuminated manuscript from the sixteenth century. A one-of-a-kind book and very valuable. It's been lost. We're trying to track it down." She glanced back at Judd. "I'm getting tired of shouting."

"So this book is in Athens, and you wish to find it. It is part of some big business deal?" the Turk coaxed.

"Why would you think we're involved in a business deal?" Judd asked.

"I had hopes it would make you much money, and then you would come back to Istanbul and hire me again. Is it for this book your lives are in danger?"

"As a matter of fact, yes." It seemed like innocuous enough information, Judd decided.

Serin glanced over his shoulder at him, frowning. And as he turned back, he wiped his face. The wheel spun out of his other hand. Serin grabbed the steering again with both hands—too late. The craft lurched from side to side, the waves pounding, the wind screeching. Banging down hard in the trough of one wave, the yacht lifted sharply on the crest of the next. Water drenched them.

Eva reeled as Serin fought to control the yacht, but it slammed and torqued violently. One of her hands slipped from the safety handle on the console. The boat heaved to the starboard, tossing all of them. But Eva's foot slid, and she fell to her knees.

Instantly Judd snatched her arm, locking his other hand on to the back of the bench seat, trying not to lose his balance, too.

As the boat continued to rotate back and forth, up and down, the wet steering wheel whirled through Serin's grasp.

The boat pitched hard again, banging and yawing. Judd lost his grip. His hand slid uncontrollably across the moist seat back, and he stumbled. Eva fell halfway over the boat's side, pulling him with her because he would not let her go. One more lurch, and both would be hurled into the black churning water.

His heart thundering, Judd looked back, searching for a way to save them. Instead he saw something else: Serin was not panicked, not even worried as he clinically noted their life-threatening situation. The icy intelligence in his gaze told Judd he could easily let them fall overboard and would abandon them. Was that what he had planned all along?

"You bastard!" Judd yelled. "Why are you doing this!"

Serin blinked. He looked off into the distance, then back at them. He seemed to decide something. Giving a small nod, he fitted his hands into the spokes of the steering wheel. His caftan sleeves fell back, showing the cording muscles. Shoulders hunching, he poured strength into dominating the yacht.

Slowly the boat's heaving eased. Judd yanked Eva back onboard and pulled her to his chest. Chilled and furious, he wrapped his arms around her. She resisted only a moment, then held on for dear life. He kissed her hair. She burrowed deeper. Then he slid his hand inside his jacket and yanked out his Beretta.

He released her and rolled free, aiming the pistol up at Serin.

43

Eva was watching, stunned. "Judd, stop!" Black hair blowing around her face, she scrambled toward Serin.

"No, Eva. Come here!" Judd ordered as he sat on the seat behind Serin and slid to the side where he had a fuller view of the man's profile and a safer distance. He steadily pointed his Beretta at him.

Her eyes wide, Eva grasped the arm of the seat and pulled herself around the rocking yacht.

"What did I miss?" She fell in beside him.

Serin's fez was gone, and his almond-colored features had shifted, revealing a depth of something Judd could not quite name but felt in himself and did not like. Something predatory. Serin's facial skin seemed different, too, and Judd had a sudden insight the man was in disguise. A hell of a good disguise, with skin dye and some of the new manmade materials that, when smoothed on skin and allowed to dry, puckered the surface and formed deep crevices. The large nose could be fake, too.

"This has been what we in intelligence call a movie," Judd explained to Eva grimly. "It's a setup that looks and feels completely real." He gestured with his pistol at Serin. "Tell her," he ordered.

There was no hesitation. "I have rules," Serin said over the noise of the engines and wind. "They are inviolate. My employer agreed to all of them. One of them is I do wet work only on people who shouldn't be breathing, and I'm the one who makes the decision. My employer was convincing about both of you, so I agreed to the job. He ordered Preston to create a movie in which you'd believe I'd be useful to help you get away. So when Preston realized you were in Yakimovich's storage room, he eliminated two of his people and called me in." He hesitated.

"Go on," Judd said.

"At that point I took over. But when you arrived I began to wonder. The people I wipe aren't solicitous of an old man. They don't inquire about his well-being. You were prepared to scrub Preston if he moved because he'd tried to do the same to you earlier—but you were just as willing to wait to find out whether I was a threat. Evil people murder first and don't bother about questions. All of this meant I needed to find out more. Were you trying to kill my employer and steal some big business deal as he contended? Finally I learned you claimed to be treasure hunters chasing a chimera, some old manuscript called *The Book of Spies*. That did not fit the profile my employer gave me. Then I looked back at you, Judd, and lost control of the wheel. My specialty is in making hits look like accidents, so I'd planned to erase you out here. Losing control of the boat presented an elegant opportunity. They are few."

"Why did you change your mind?" Eva said.

"Because, God help me, I know human nature—in my world it's nasty, corrupt, and mean. You aren't, so in the end I had to believe you. I'll tell you now I'm glad." He looked at Eva. "You remind me of my daughter. You're about the same age, and both very pretty in similar ways. According to the photo I was given, your true hair color is red. Hers is auburn."

The yacht cruised onward, rolling up and down with the sea. The wind howled around them.

"I can't trust you," Judd decided.

"I understand. However, I'll still take you to my friend and his airstrip."

"Who hired you?"

"I won't tell you that."

"Your rules?"

He gave a curt nod. "I've survived many years in a business in which most of my colleagues have been killed off. Seldom do we die of old age. Rules are not for the timid or the careless. They require discipline. King Lear railed against the universe when he was punished for breaking its rules. I don't want the same fate. Besides, the longer I live, the greater my chance of seeing my daughter again."

"What's your name?" Judd asked.

The assassin's black eyes cut into him. "The Carnivore." Then he smiled.

Thrace, Turkey

The Carnivore turned off the yacht's engines in calm waters near a strip of uninhabited land north of the village of Barbados. Judd dropped the anchor, they found flashlights, and they took off their shoes. The Carnivore pulled off his caftan. Beneath it he wore black jeans and a black T-shirt. His muscle tone was excellent, but his skin elasticity showed advancing age. Judd guessed him to be in his fifties.

They rolled up their jeans and waded ashore. Judd carried the duffel, and Eva wore her satchel, the strap across her chest. The wind was quieter here. They crossed the beach, and the Carnivore led them up ancient stone steps carved into a cliff.

At the top, they paused. The moon had risen, casting an eerie light across acres of grapevines tied neatly to wires running between gnarled wood posts. The vines were just beginning to leaf. The air smelled raw, of freshly tilled soil.

They headed off on a narrow dirt trail through the grapevines.

"Do you want to tell me what this is all about, Judd?" the Carnivore asked.

"Reciprocity is another of your rules?"

"A good one, don't you think."

"I like it," Judd said. "But no, I'll handle this."

The trail widened, and the three moved on side by side.

The Carnivore peered around at Judd and said thoughtfully, "Yes, I believe you will—if it can be handled at all. But as for reciprocity, I consider us even by my giving you a safe route into Athens."

"Is Preston free now?" Eva asked worriedly.

"He must be," the Carnivore said. "He had backup."

"What if I'd decided to kill him back in the Grand Bazaar," Judd said. "Your movie would've been burned."

"That would've worked just as well," the Carnivore instructed. "He would've 'awakened' and attacked you. I would've saved the day by helping you to escape, him to live, and the movie to continue."

Judd changed the subject. "What about his note, the one that mentioned Athens. Was it legitimate or a plant?"

"Legitimate. A note to himself. It added to the authenticity and gave you a significant reason to believe what you saw was real. Perhaps more important, we didn't expect you to live long enough to use it or anything else you might've learned there."

"Do you have any information about *The Book of Spies* and Robin Miller?" Eva asked.

"It was none of my business."

"What about the Library of Gold?"

The Carnivore frowned. "I've heard of it. Is that what this is all about?"

"Yes." But Judd said no more. Venomous snakes like the

Carnivore shed their skins occasionally, but their bites remained just as unpredictable—and poisonous. "What will you tell your employer?"

"Nothing."

Judd sensed fury behind the one-word answer. The Carnivore was making his employer pay for lying to him. It also meant the employer would think he and Eva were dead—at least for a while.

"It gives you time," the Carnivore said, "but it's also good business for me. When one deals in death, one must make certain the rules are clear—and there are costs involved when they're broken." He glanced at Judd. "And it means you don't have to contemplate eliminating me, and I don't have to take proactive measures to make certain you don't try."

The words were calm, matter-of-fact, but they sent a chill through Judd.

"You won't be paid," Judd said.

"I have half. I'll keep it."

"Where do you come from?" Eva asked the Carnivore. "Where do you live now? How did you get into this business? You sound almost American."

"I'm sorry, Eva. It's really better you don't know. Once a KGB assassin from the old cold war days went after my daughter, thinking I was dead and he'd get his revenge on me by eliminating her. Fortunately she was able to save herself. If anyone finds out you have information about me, your lives could be threatened, and there's no guarantee you'd be as lucky as she."

At the top of a slight incline they saw a house, large and expansive, built of weathered stone with a blue-tile Ottoman roof. Lights showed inside, and as they approached, exterior lights flashed on, illuminating flower beds, patches of grass, and a stone gazebo. Empty wine barrels were stacked against sheds. There was a large clapboard structure toward the back that was probably where the wine was made and aged.

The door to the house opened, and a man in his late fifties appeared, a shotgun resting across an arm.

"Who goes there?" he shouted in Turkish and English.

"An old friend from long ago, Hugo Shah," the Carnivore replied. "You remember me, Alex Bosa."

"Alex, you've come to taste my wine again. I'm honored." Then as they approached, Shah stared. "Alex? Yes, it is you. What a magnificent disguise. What are you up to now?"

"No good, as always."

Shah laughed. The pair shook hands, and the four trooped into a living area of tasteful wallpaper and thick carpets. Fine old furniture was placed here and there, while a modern sofa and easy chairs faced a handsome fireplace.

"Who are your friends, Alex?" Shah asked.

"It doesn't matter. They need your help, which means I need your help. Is that light plane of yours available?"

"At this hour?" Shah's eyes narrowed as he studied the Carnivore. "I see. It is an emergency. Very well, I will fly them myself. Do you wish to accompany us?"

"I'll wait here with the wine."

Shah smiled broadly. "Excellent. Please give me a moment." He returned soon, wearing a jacket and carrying a small valise.

As all four walked outside, Shah explained about his vineyard, "I grow gamay, cabernet, and *papazkarasi* grapes. I have in mind two fine reds I will open for us, Alex—it will be Alex and Hugo again."

About a half mile from the house, they went into a large garage where a single-engine Cirrus SR20 was waiting. They helped Shah roll out the plane. He gazed at the windsock and sniffed the air.

"I'll say good-bye now." The Carnivore backed off.

They climbed on board, Judd sitting next to Shah, and Eva behind. As the engine warmed up, Judd gazed out the window. The Carnivore was smiling. He lifted his hand and pressed two fingers against his temple in a smart salute.

Judd found himself smiling back. He snapped off a two-finger salute in return.

"Where are we going?" Shah asked as the propellers started rotating.

Judd glanced back. Eva was looking at him. He heard the strength in his voice—also the urgency. "Athens."

PART THREE
THE BATTLE

When the celebrated Greek general Aristides learned from one of his assets that a Persian spy had infiltrated his military camp, he ordered every soldier, shield-maker, doctor, and cook to account for another person there. In that way the spy was uncovered. The next month the Greeks defeated the invading Persian army at the Battle of Marathon, in 490 b.c.

—*translated from* The Book of Spies

Strategic intelligence is the power to know your enemies' intentions.

—The New York Times
May 14, 2006

44

Washington, D.C.

As he ate a late lunch at his desk in Catapult headquarters, Tucker Andersen studied the photo of the blond woman who might be the Robin Miller mentioned in Preston's note.

His people had located thousands of women with the name, ranging from infants to the elderly in the United States and abroad. Narrowing for age and occupation, he had settled on this one as the most likely, thirty-five years old now. Born in Scotland, she had degrees in classical art and library science from the Sorbonne and Cambridge and had worked in rare books and manuscripts in Boston and Paris. A couple of years ago she had quit her job at the Bibliothèque. After that, there was no record of her employment in other libraries or museums. No record of a new address—she had moved out of her apartment when she quit her job. No record of death. No trace at all.

He e-mailed the information and photo to Judd and sat back, thinking.

Then he picked up his phone and called Debi Watson, Catapult's IT chief. "Any word from NSA about those phone numbers I gave you?" She was honchoing the numbers in Charles Sherback's disposable phone, one of which could be Robin Miller's.

"No, suh. I'll call if something turns up. It all depends on where the satellites are, and of course there are millions of data bits to sort through. NSA is watching for us. They know it's important."

"It's crucial," he corrected. "Contact Interpol and the Athens police and tell them we'd be obliged if they'd let us know pronto if they run across a woman named Robin Miller. We believe she may be in Athens. I'll e-mail you the details." He hung up.

There was a knock on his door. When he responded, Gloria Feit, general factotum and receptionist, walked in and closed it behind her.

Her small frame was rigid. "He's back. In her office."

"Hudson Canon, you mean?"

"You asked me to let you know. I'm letting you know he's back."

"You're pissed."

"Me? How can you tell?" Her face broke into a smile, the lines around her eyes crinkling.

"No one's going to take Cathy's place. But we need a new chief. Hudson is temporary."

"Yes, well, temporary as in 'short-timer' suits me just fine."

"You don't like him?"

She fell into a chair and crossed her knees. "Actually, I do like him. I just felt like being petty."

He chuckled. "Then why are you pissed?"

"Because you're not telling me what's going on. You don't think I've leaked anything about the Library of Gold operation, do you?"

So that was it. "The thought never crossed my mind." Actually it had, but he did not want her to know that. He needed to consider everyone and anyone who could have had access to the information.

"Good," she announced. "So tell me where you are with the mission."

"Gloria."

She sighed and stood up. "Oh, all right. Be that way. But you know you can count on me, Tucker. I mean that. For anything." She walked to the door and turned. "When you're offered the job of heading Catapult—and we both know you will be—take it this time. Please. I've already got you broken in."

He stared as the door closed and shook his head, smiling to himself. Then the smile vanished. He stood up and left. It was time to talk to Canon.

Adjusting his tie, Hudson Canon stared into the mirror in what had been Cathy Doyle's office. He did not like the way he looked. His short nose, round black eyes, and heavy cheeks no longer seemed solid, real to him. There was something otherworldly there, insubstantial, although he knew damn well he was a substantial man in all ways.

He turned back into the office, glad Cathy's photos, plants, and personal things were gone. It had been a shock when he heard the news of her death, and then an even bigger shock when he received a phone call from Reinhardt Gruen, in Berlin, telling him what he had to do—or lose his savings. He had invested all of it in the Parsifal Group at Gruen's invitation, and it had made him far more money than he had ever thought possible.

His cell phone vibrated against his chest. Locking the door, he answered it as he walked around to sit at the desk. Cell phones, PDAs, any sort of personal wireless devices were not allowed in Langley or Catapult, but he was boss here, and no one needed to know he must keep the disposable cell with him at all times now.

"We have a problem with Judd Ryder and Eva Blake. Our man hasn't reported in, and we suspect they're on the loose again. Where are they?" Reinhardt asked in a friendly German accent.

"I don't know."

"You were supposed to stay on top of this."

"I'm not sure I can get the information."

"*Ach,* really?"The tone was less friendly."You are an important man. You are the head of Catapult. Nothing can be kept from you."

Canon screwed up his resolve, banishing thoughts of losing his house. He was highly leveraged and had planned to take out the next six months of payments from his Parsifal account. He had already sold his beloved Corvette and bought a used Ford. The alimony and child support to his two ex-wives were killing him.

"It's not that," he said. "Look, Reinhardt, this has gone far enough. Obviously it's not an easy fix. Catapult is never going to find your precious Library of Gold anyway. The whole mission has been a disaster."

"Remove Tucker Andersen. Run it yourself."

"I can't take him off it. There's no legitimate reason to do it. I'd be in hot water if I tried, especially now that Cathy's dead. Besides, my boss wants an experienced hand here as number two to back me up."

Gruen swore in German. "We think if Ryder and Blake are free they are heading to Athens. We need to know exactly where in Athens. Have you heard anything about a woman named Robin Miller?"

"No," Canon answered truthfully. "Who's she?"

There was a cold pause. "Let us be clear. Do you really think Catherine Doyle's car crash was an accident?"

Canon felt sweat gather in his armpits.

"We need the information," Gruen told him. "You will get it."

"There's no real need for it," Canon tried. "I can close the operation down in just a few more hours anyway. I have the boss's permission."

"As you know it is far more than a few hours until you can do that, and too much can happen."There was a pause. "You must make Tucker Andersen leave the premises of Catapult. Phone me immediately when he does. Do you understand what will happen to you if you do not?"

Tucker knocked on Hudson Canon's door. Surprised, he heard the lock click open. Why had Hudson locked it? But then, Hudson had once been a highly successful undercover op, and habits of secrecy were hard to break.

The door opened, and the new chief gave him a short smile in greeting. "Come in, Tucker. I was thinking about checking in with you, too."

Tucker entered as Hudson headed for the desk.

"Give me an update on how things are going." Hudson sat and leaned back in the chair, clasping his hands comfortably behind his head.

"There's not much new." Tucker took a chair and recounted the few changes in the various missions. Canon wanted more frequent reports than Cathy had. That was fine—each manager had his own style.

"And the Library of Gold operation?" Canon asked.

"Glad you brought it up. I was wondering whether you happened to mention to anyone that my people were going to the Grand Bazaar in Istanbul."

The answer was immediate."Of course not."The expression unchanged.

"They still haven't located the library,"Tucker continued, "and the last time we talked, they were on their way out of Istanbul. Preston—he's the janitor who's been dogging them—was left behind alive but tied up in the Grand Bazaar. It'll be a while before he gets free."

"Where are they going now?"

This was the moment Tucker had expected, and it made him sick. After doing a thorough search through his memory, he knew he had written no one, phoned no one, e-mailed no one, made no notes to himself, and told only one person the critical details that Ryder and Blake had gone not only to Istanbul, but to the Grand Bazaar, to find Okan Biçer, and through him Andrew Yakimovich.

And so he lied: "To Thessalonika." It was a large city north of Athens, within logical distance for Robin Miller to reach—if she were in Athens. Continuing the lie, he said, "A woman named Robin Miller got in touch with them. In exchange for helping her, she'll meet them there and tell them where the library is."

"That will solve a lot of problems—if they can pull it off." Canon took a deep breath and stretched. "Thessalonika seems strange, though. Athens would be more likely, don't you think?"

Why did he mention Athens? A sour taste rose in Tucker's throat. "No, I don't agree. This whole operation has been unpredictable. Thessalonika is large and historical. It makes sense to me."

"Who is Robin Miller?"

"She has something to do with the library. I don't have the details yet."

Canon nodded. "Then it's all good news. Your people have another decent lead. How are they getting to Thessalonika?"

"Judd didn't have time to tell me."

"I see. Well, then, you still may pull the proverbial rabbit out of the hat and find the library." Canon studied him, concern on his face. "Do you have any idea how lousy you look? You're pale. Your clothes are a mess. With all of the action in Europe, there's no need to be concerned someone is still after you here. It's a beautiful afternoon. Get out and breathe some fresh air. Take a walk. Use my car if you'd rather drive than walk. If you don't want to go home, at least go shopping and buy some new clothes. This is a direct order, Tucker—get the hell out of Catapult."

45

Tucker Andersen stalked around his office, mulling whether to phone his old friend Matt Kelley, the head of the Clandestine Service. But he had only one piece of evidence that Hudson Canon was the leak. It was possible Judd and Eva had been tracked to the Grand Bazaar through another means. One did not report one's colleagues unless one was damn sure.

He stopped in front of his wall of books. It was not nearly as impressive as Jonathan Ryder's huge library, but he had carefully chosen each one. As his gaze ran over the titles, mostly politics and intelligence and spy thriller fiction, he remembered the journeys he had taken in them, learning and entertaining himself with others' lives, ideas, and knowledge. He thought about what Philip K. Dick had written: "Sometimes the appropriate response to reality is to go insane."

Shaking his head, he poured himself a whiskey. He probably should get out of here. A walk around the block might clear his head. But then, Hudson Canon had been the one who suggested it, which made him want to stay put. Looking out the window, he gulped whiskey and saw that night had fallen. Dammit, he was tired of the cold in-transit room upstairs in which he had been bedding down.

Making a decision, he grabbed his sports jacket and slammed his arms into the sleeves. He went into the communications center. Debi Watson was still there.

She was looking disgustingly alert and young.

"Do you have anything new for me?" he asked.

"No, suh."

"Phone your NSA person," he told her. "Give him my mobile number. I want him to call me directly if either of those numbers for the disposable phones turns up. If you get any word about Robin Miller, call me on my mobile." He wheeled around and left, her voice agreeing behind him.

He stopped at Gloria's desk. "Hand over my mobile. I'm going out."

She peered at him from above her rainbow-rimmed reading glasses. "It's about time. You look like a caged animal."

"Thanks. That cheers me up considerably."

"I aim to please." She handed him the secure mobile.

He had an idea, one he did not like. "Is Hudson still here?"

"You betcha. The man's working away as if he's the head of Catapult."

"Are you supposed to let him know if I leave?"

She blinked. "Yes, he's worried about you, too."

"Don't tell him."

"Why, Tucker?"

"Just damn well do as I say."

Her brows rose. "We're not married—yet. Karen will be jealous."

He sighed. She was right; he was in a huff. "Sorry. Don't tell the boss, please."

"Okay," she said cheerfully.

But as Tucker turned away, he saw a motion—Canon's door must have just opened, because it was closing now. Tucker went back to his office and found his Browning and holster in his locked desk drawer. Taking off his jacket, he put on the holster and slid the Browning inside. Hesitating, at last he took out the wad of cash he kept in the drawer, the two billfolds that contained cover identities, and other supplies.

Again he headed out.

"You haven't left yet?" Gloria said as he passed her desk.

"I forgot my lollipops."

"Silly me. I should've reminded you. If anyone asks, when shall I tell them you'll be back?"

"Oh, a half hour. Maybe never." He paused. "I didn't say that."

Her brows rose again, but she simply nodded.

He left through the side door into Catapult's parking lot. The April night was cool, not a breeze stirring as he forced himself to slow to a normal pace. He passed staff cars and went out to the sidewalk. It was a balmy spring evening. He inhaled the scent of the freshly cut grass on the adjoining property.

Turning down the street, he noted who else was on the sidewalk and kept his head turned slightly so he could watch approaching cars with his peripheral vision. People were walking home from the Metro after work and school, tired, carrying groceries and briefcases and pushing children in strollers. The street was filled with traffic, many vehicles slowing to look for parking spots. In this neighborhood of mostly row houses, there were few garages or carports.

The trained mind was like a computer, and Tucker's was automatically sorting through the array of humanity. At last he settled on a man in a loose gray jacket zipped up halfway, dark jeans, and black tennis shoes, about forty feet behind. In the light of street lamps, he seemed innocuous enough, but there was something about the way he moved, loose, rolling easily off the balls of his feet, alert. He had a destination in mind that had nothing to do with the relaxation of home.

Tucker turned the corner, then another. The man was

staying with him, threading among the other pedestrians behind, always keeping several between them. Tucker rounded one more block and headed west onto Massachusetts Avenue. The man was still with him, but closer, probably waiting for the right moment. A weapon could easily be hidden beneath his gray jacket.

Tucker pushed into Capitol Hill market, a favorite in the area, small, crammed, and busy at this hour. Going to the back of the store, he stopped at the cooler to eye the selection of sodas but really to check back around the end cap to where he could sight down the aisle to the front door.

The man walked in, nodding to the kid behind the checkout stand, peering casually around as he continued on toward the butcher. The store was doing some construction. Tucker spotted two-by-four boards leaning at the rear of the back hallway. Cocking his head just enough to make certain the man had spotted him, he strolled into the dim corridor. Before he turned the corner, he glanced back. The man was coming, his expression pleasant.

Grabbing one of the boards, Tucker rushed out through the revolving glass door and into the cool night air. Tall trees cast dark shadows over the small parking lot. Instantly he pressed back against the store's wall, holding the two-by-four. The door slowed its revolutions. As it picked up speed again, he jammed the two-by-four between the moving panes. And slid out his Browning.

As the pane slammed against the board, he stepped out, aiming as he looked inside.

Trapped, with no way to get to the wood, the man was pushing the door, trying to get back into the store. His shoulders were bunched with effort, but the door would not move—it spun only counterclockwise. The man whirled around, his face furious. He was in his late twenties, Tucker guessed. He had beard stubble, short brown hair, an average face. A forgettable face, except for the dimples in his cheeks. When he saw Tucker's weapon through the glass, his hand immediately reached to go inside his jacket.

Tucker gave a shake to his head. "Don't."

The hand moved an inch more.

"We both know you were planning to wipe me," Tucker told him. "My solution is to shoot you first. I'll start with your gut and pinpoint each of your organs." A gut wound was the most painful, and often fatal when organs were involved.

The man's eyes narrowed, but he stopped moving.

"Good," Tucker said. "Take out your gun. Slowly. Put it beside your feet. Don't drop it. We don't want the damn thing to go off."

In slow motion the man removed his weapon and set it down on the floor.

"I'm going to take out the board now. Then you come outside. We'll have a nice chat." Keeping his gun trained on him, Tucker crouched and slid out the wood. The revolving door moved, and he grabbed the man's gun. As soon as the man was outside, Tucker told him, "Over there."

They walked into the black shadow of a tree.

"Give me your billfold," Tucker ordered.

"I'm not carrying one."

He was unsurprised. When a trained janitor went out on a job, he went clean. "Who are you?"

"You don't care about that really, do you, old man?"

"Let's see your pocket litter," Tucker told him. "Carefully."

The man pulled car keys from his jeans.

"Drop them."

He let them fall through his fingers, then extracted the linings of his jeans pockets to show there was nothing more inside. He did the same with his outside jacket pockets. Using only two fingers on each hand, he opened his jacket, showing the lining had no pockets. He was wearing a pocketless polo shirt.

"Where's your money?" Tucker demanded.

"In my car. Parked back where I picked you up."

In other words, parked near Catapult. Tucker considered. "Who hired you?"

"Look, this was just a job. Nothing personal."

"It's personal to me. Who the fuck hired you."

The dead tone got to the man. His pupils dilated.

"Sonny, I know how to kill without leaving a mark," Tucker told him grimly. "It's been a while. Tonight seems like a good time to take up the sport again. Would you like a demonstration?"

The would-be assassin uneasily shifted his weight. "Preston. He said his name was Preston. He wired money into an account I have."

Tucker nodded. "When did you get the call from him?"

"Today. Late afternoon."

With a sudden move, Tucker took a step and slammed his Browning against the killer's temple. He staggered, and Tucker hit him again. The man dropped to his knees on the pavement, then sat back and keeled over, unconscious.

Tucker dumped the ammo out of the man's weapon and pocketed it—9mm. It might come in handy later. He pulled out plastic handcuffs and bound the man's hands behind him and his ankles together. He rolled him against the trunk of the tree where the shadows were deepest.

Activating his mobile, Tucker punched in Gloria's number. As soon as she answered, he said, "Don't say my name. Put me on hold and go into my office and close the door. Then pick up again."

There was a surprised pause. "Sure, Ted. I have time for a quick private chat." Ted was her husband.

When she came back on the line, Tucker told her, "I'm

outside the rear of Capitol Hill market. I'm leaving a janitor here who tried to wipe me. He's handcuffed, and I've got his ammo. Come and get him."

"What! Oh, hell, what have you been up to now?"

"Hudson Cannon is dirty."

"Is the janitor why Hudson wanted you to leave?"

"Yes."

She swore. "I knew something was wrong. What do you want me to do with the guy when I get there?"

"He should still be unconscious. He's tied up. Drag him into your car and then park him in the basement at Catapult. I don't want Canon to know about any of this, for obvious reasons. Don't tell Matt Kelley, either. There may be another mole inside Langley, and it could leak back to the Library of Gold people. This is a lockdown on security, got it?"

"Got it."

"The kid parked his car somewhere near Catapult. I'll put his keys on the ledge above the back door of the store. Locate the car and toss it. Phone me if you find anything."

"I take it you're not coming back."

"Not until the Library of Gold operation is over. The story is I'm taking a short, well-deserved vacation."

46

Rome, Italy

The efficiency flat was in a forgotten corner of Rome, tucked away on one of the little streets on Janiculum Hill just south of St. Peter's Basilica. The husky blast of a boat horn sounded from the Tiber River as Yitzhak Law paced to the flat's open window. Running both hands over his bald head, he stared out at the unfamiliar terrain.

"You are distressed, *amore mio*." Roberto Cavaletti's voice sounded behind him.

Yitzhak turned. Roberto was studying him from the table beside the sink, their only table. The flat was one room, so small that opening the oven door blocked entry to the tiny bathroom. It reminded Yitzhak of his student days at the University of Chicago, and that was the only charm to it. That, and it was safe. Bash Badawi had brought them here yesterday, after a doctor had treated Roberto's shoulder wound.

"I have a class to teach this evening," Yitzhak said. "A meeting later tonight. When I don't show up, they'll worry." It was not an issue yesterday, when he had no other classes or meetings. He was a professor in the Dipartimento di Studi Storico-Religiosi at the Università di Roma–Sapienza, and he took his responsibilities seriously.

Roberto massaged his close-cropped brown beard, thinking. "Perhaps it is worse than that. They will phone the house, leave a message, and when no one returns the call, they will go looking for you."

"I thought of that, too. There'll be an uproar. But it's the students who concern me most—no one will be there to teach them."

"You wish to tell the department? We have the cell phone Bash gave us. He said we must not leave, and no one could know where we are. A cell call is not leaving. And you do not have to say any details." Roberto held up the cell.

"Yes, of course. You're right."

Feeling relieved, Yitzhak marched over and took the device. Calling out, he settled into the chair across from Roberto. He had changed the dressing on Roberto's wound earlier. Thankfully it was healing nicely, and Roberto had had a good night's sleep.

Gina, the department secretary, answered. She recognized his voice immediately. *"Come sta, professore?"*

Speaking Italian, he explained he had to leave in an hour for emergency business. "I'll need a substitute for my lecture, Gina. And please alert Professor Ocie Stafford that I can't attend his meeting, with apologies."

"I will. But what am I to do with your package?"

"Package? . . . I don't understand."

"It looks and feels like a book, but of course I cannot be certain. It is in a padded envelope. This morning a priest from Monsignor Jerry McGahagin at the Vatican Library delivered it. He said it was most important. The monsignor wants your advice." Monsignor McGahagin was the director of not only one of the oldest libraries in the world, but one that contained a priceless collection of historical texts, many of them never seen by outsiders.

He thought quickly. "Send someone over with it to Trattoria Sor'eva on Piazza della Rovere. As it happens, I'm near there now." Bash had pointed out the place as a good restaurant serving excellent handmade pasta.

"Yes, I will do that. A half hour, no more."

Yitzhak ended the connection and relayed the conversation.

Roberto shook his head. "You are bad. We are supposed to stay here."

"You stay. That puts half of us in compliance."

Roberto gave an expressive Roman shrug. "What am I to do with you. You are always the dog looking for one more good bone."

"I'll be back soon." Yitzhak patted his hand and left.

Dusk was spreading across the city, the shadows long. Yitzhak had steeled himself not to think about Eva and Judd, but as he walked, passing apartment buildings and shops, he felt strangely vulnerable, which made him worry about them. Not until he heard from Bash that their dangerous situation was settled and they were safe would he feel right.

Twenty minutes later he reached the piazza and stopped across the street from the trattoria. All seemed normal, but then, tumult was normal to Rome—the streets a cyclone of traffic, bustling with shoppers, locals, businesspeople, cars parked two and three abreast. The windows of the trattoria showed customers inside eating and drinking.

Then he saw Leoni Vincenza, one of his advanced students, hurrying toward the restaurant, a padded envelope under his arm. It was bright yellow, a strange color for the Vatican. Perhaps the *monsignore* was using up donated stock.

Yitzhak pushed himself to rush, and he crossed at the intersection. "Leoni! Leoni!"

The youth looked up, his long black hair blowing around his face. "*Professore,* you have been waiting for me?"

Yitzhak said nothing and slowed, catching his breath.

When Leoni reached him, he said, "Good to see you, boy. Is that my package?"

"Yes, sir." He handed it to him.

"*Grazie.* My car is around the block. I'll see you back at the university in a few days."

Leoni nodded. "*Ciao.*" He returned the way he had come.

Yitzhak went in the other direction, feeling smart he had thought to misdirect the student. As he climbed Janiculum Hill, he stopped. His heart was thundering. He had been meaning to lose weight for years. Now it was evident he had better hurry on that promise.

He resumed walking, slowly this time, and finally reached the apartment building. He opened the front door and gazed up at the long staircase. He had to mount two flights, and the second was as long as the first. He hefted the package—it felt heavy, the weight of a book. He would rest a moment, and he was curious.

Ripping off the staples, he pulled out the volume. And stared, surprised. It was a thick collection of Sherlock Holmes stories, so battered it looked as if it had come from a used-book store. Definitely not a first edition. Why would the *monsignore* send this? He checked for a note but found none.

Shaking his head, he stuffed it back inside the envelope and climbed. Behind him he heard the front door open and close. When he reached his floor, he could hear footsteps on the stairs, hurrying upward. For some reason he found himself rushing down the corridor. As he slid the key inside the lock, he glanced back and froze.

Two men were running toward him, aiming guns.

"Who are you?" Yitzhak demanded, although even to him his voice sounded weak. "What do you want?"

There was no answer. One man was large, burly, and

ferocious looking, the other small and wiry, with a mean face. The shorter man grabbed the key from Yitzhak's hand, unlocked the door, and the big man shoved him inside. The door closed behind them with an ominous *click*.

47

Athens, Greece

The Carnivore's friend flew Eva and Judd into Athens International, and from there they took the suburban railway Proastiakos northwest through the night, transferring to Metro line three, which would take them into the city. They had been watching carefully for anyone too interested in them. The Metro car was crowded, people sleeping or talking quietly. Eva was eager to check into a hotel so they would be alone and she could rewind the leather strip around the *scytale* and translate the rest of Charles's message.

She peered out the windows as the Metro sped past houses and apartment blocks built in modern Greece's ubiquitous cement-box architecture. Ancient ruins occasionally showed, alight in the night. The juxtaposition of new and old was somehow reassuring, the past meeting today and making the future seem possible. She clung to her hopes for a future as she sat beside Judd, very aware of him. There was a lot about him she liked—but also something she feared.

She looked down at his hands resting on his thighs, remembering Michelangelo's statue of David, his great masterpiece, in Florence. Michelangelo had said when he cut into the marble it had revealed the hands of a killer. Judd's hands looked like David's, oversized and strong, with prominent veins. But when he had sculpted David's face, Michelangelo had uncovered a subtle sweetness and innocence. She glanced at Judd's weathered face, square and rugged beneath his bleached hair, the arched nose, the good jaw. There was no sweetness or innocence there, only determination.

"How old are you, Judd?" she asked.

His body appeared relaxed, despite his constant watchfulness. There was no way to be certain how long it would take Preston to figure out the Carnivore had not eliminated them. Preston might be chasing them now.

"Thirty-two," he said. "Why?"

"So am I. I'll bet you knew that already."

"It was in the dossier Tucker gave me. Is my age important?"

"No. But I thought you might be older. You've been through a lot, haven't you?"

He stared at her. "Why do you say that?"

"In prison there were women who had a sense about them of . . . it's hard to describe. I guess I'd call it a challenging past. You're something like that."

What she did not mention was the women came from violent backgrounds, many sentenced on murder or manslaughter charges. They seemed to ache to fight, although, win or lose, the consequences for them would be serious. But she had never seen Judd start a fight or even look for one. Then with a chill she recalled his saying he wanted no more blood on his hands.

"I was undercover in Iraq and later in Pakistan," he explained. "Military intelligence. Of course both were 'challenging.' But there were good things, too. In Iraq, I was able to help rebuild several schools. The Iraqis were coming back from the brink, and education was high on their list. Dad put together shipments of books for their libraries."

"That doesn't sound like military intelligence."

"I had some downtime. That's what I did with it, particularly at the end."

She heard something else in his voice."And before then?"

Smiling, he said, "Do all eggheads ask so many questions?"

"I'm an egghead?"

"A Ph.D. qualifies you."

She scanned the other passengers."Think what you know about me, including my shady past. I know almost nothing about you."

He chuckled."At least I'm sure you're not a perpetrator of vehicular manslaughter." He stared at her expression. "Sorry. That was stupid of me." He faced straight ahead again.

Eva said nothing, sitting quietly.

At last he continued: "I uncovered some intel on an 'al-Qaeda in Iraq' operative and finally was able to catch him and take him in for questioning. God knows how he managed to get rope, but he did. He hung himself in his cell. His brother was also al-Qaeda, and when he heard about it, he came after me. It went on for weeks. He was ruining my ability to do the rest of my job, and I wasn't able to track him down. Then there was a shift. It seemed as if he'd lost interest. I couldn't figure it out—until a message was passed to me he was going to punish me by liquidating my fiancée."

His fingers drained color as he knotted his hands."She was MI, too. A damn good analyst. I got the intel just as she reached her usual security check. A Muslim woman stumbled and fell beside the checkpoint, and her suitcase slid under my fiancée's Jeep. It looked like an accident, but the guards were instantly on it. The woman managed to shake free and run for it just as the suitcase exploded. It was an

IED, of course. 'She' was wearing a burka, but one of the soldiers saw legs in jeans, and big feet in men's combat boots." He took a deep breath. "Four people were killed, including my fiancée. Later I got another message. In English it said, 'Whatsoever a man soweth, that shall he also reap.' The New Testament, of course. Apostle Paul. The son of a bitch was an Islamic jihadist quoting the Bible to me to justify murdering her."

"You haven't told me her name," she said gently.

He cleared his throat. "Amanda. Amanda Waterman."

"I'm so sorry. How horrible. You felt responsible for her death."

"She'd still be alive. Her job wasn't that dangerous."

"I'll bet you wanted to kill him for what he did."

His body tensed. "I could never find him."

"Do you still want to kill him?"

He looked at her sharply. "Would you blame me?"

"When I believed there was a chance I'd been driving and had killed Charles, it took me a long time to come to terms with it." She paused. "No one went to Iraq without knowing the risks. Both of you were very lucky to find love." She heard the sadness in her voice and wiped it away. "A lot of people never have that."

He nodded, his expression granite.

Still, she wondered whether that was the only story behind the chilling looks she had seen on his face. One of his hands moved toward hers, to hold it. She remembered how he had pulled her to him after she had almost pitched off the yacht, how he had wrapped his arms around her and held her tight, how he had kissed her hair . . . the wonderful sound of his pounding heart. His musky, wet smell. He had saved her at the risk of his own life. In that moment she had wanted nothing more than to burrow in and forget the hard times. Pretend his protectiveness was the beginning of love. But the truth was she did not know what she really thought of him, much less what she felt, or whether someone with deep heartache and a violent past could ever be stable enough for enduring love. Could she, even?

She gave his hand a quick squeeze and released him. "Your mobile is chirping."

Judd took it from his pocket. "An e-mail from Tucker. Some good news—he thinks he may have found Robin Miller." He handed the device to her. "What do you think?"

She analyzed the photo of the woman displayed on the mobile's screen—green eyes and thick ash-blond hair, but no bangs. The mouth was lush and round. Included were the woman's age, height, and weight.

"The statistics match Robin Miller," she told him. "But if I didn't know better, I'd still say it's not her. On the other hand, Charles had plastic surgery when he joined the library, so she might've, too. If she did, then her nose could've been shortened and turned up at the end, and an implant inserted in her chin. The eyes, hair color, and the rest of the face are the same."

"With plastic surgery they'd be identical?"

"Absolutely." She was still thinking about his fiancée's death. "It's interesting about the al-Qaeda jihadist and his last message to you. A version is in the Old Testament, too. Job said, 'They that plow iniquity and sow wickedness reap the same.' Then, thousands of years later, Cicero wrote, 'As you have sown, so shall you reap.' Anyway, what strikes me is it's also in the Koran, which came some seven centuries later, after Cicero: 'Have you considered what you have sown?' The jihadist must've been at least somewhat educated. Otherwise he would've fallen back on what he knew—the Koran."

"I thought about that, too. But I'm not going there, and

God knows where he is or whether he's even alive. Besides, you and I have a much more urgent problem—how to find Robin Miller and the Library of Gold."

And survive, she thought.

48

Eva and Judd disembarked at Platia Syntagma—Constitution Square—the center of modern Athens. A grand expanse of white marble, the plaza stretched below the parliament building, glowing serenely in lamplight. At the edges were elegant cafés sporting outdoor tables, where people were eating, drinking, gossiping.

As they walked toward the taxi stand, Eva mulled whether she could stay with the mission. As she glanced around, the Athens traffic seemed unusually thick, the shadows too dark and dangerous. She was troubled, her mind in turmoil.

They stopped as the ruins of the Parthenon temple came into view, towering majestically above the high Acropolis. The glowing white columns and pediments could be seen from all over the city, from between buildings and at the crosswalks of streets.

"The Parthenon is really something," Judd decided. "And before you ask—no, I've never been to Athens. This is my first time."

She forced a smile.

They took a taxi into the Exarchia district near the Athens Polytechnic, a quirkily bohemian neighborhood she had visited before meeting Charles. At the bottom of Stournari Street they got out and climbed into the Platia Exarchia, the nerve center of the area, where Athenians satisfied their love of political debate, and intellectuals came to spout their latest theories. Serious nightlife started in Athens after midnight. Through windows she could see the bars were bustling.

"Let's get some food," Judd said.

They went into a *taverna* named Pan's Revenge. A musician strummed a mandolin-like *bouzouki* and sang a Greek sea song of yearning for a far-off love. Stopping at the bar, Eva translated as Judd chose a bottle of Katogi Averoff estate red, 1999, 90 percent cabernet, 10 percent merlot. She ordered the house speciality—moussaka and zucchini stuffed with wild rice—to go.

Purchases in hand, they walked around the corner. She felt Judd's tension as he continued to watch for tails, and her own tension as she tried to decide what to do.

"You're being awfully quiet," he said.

"I know. Just thinking."

Soon she saw the small hotel she remembered—pink stone with white stone moldings and enameled white shutters—where she had stayed years before.

"Hotel Hecate," Judd read. "A Greek god or goddess?"

"The goddess of magic."

"Maybe it's a good omen." He stared at her a moment, seeming to try to read her mind. "Are you going to be all right?"

Quite a few people were entering and leaving the various establishments. The door to a bar opened, and waves of laughter rolled out. She saw no sign of threat.

"Sure," she said. "I'll just hang out while you register."

"Don't run out on me."

Her brows rose in surprise. Had he guessed she had been considering it? Before she could respond, he hurried into the hotel.

Walking along the block, she studied the other pedestrians as she tried to sort through her thoughts. She had made a lot of mistakes, and now she feared staying with the operation was another. What kind of man was Judd really, to do such violent work? Could he turn off the violence? Would he ever use it against her?

At the corner she paced back toward the hotel. She felt responsible for putting Yitzhak and Roberto in danger and for being the cause of Peggy's murder. But once she had discovered Charles was alive and had left a message for her, she had blindly followed the trail to know more about what he might actually have felt for her. As she was thinking about that, an old man and woman passed, holding hands, talking to each other as if no one else in the world mattered. She felt a stab of heartache.

Judd appeared in the driveway beside the hotel. He scrutinized the area, then gave a casual nod.

"Everything okay?" he asked when she joined him.

Her gaze went to a black shadow that ran along the drive, suddenly aware that in the dark it was hard to tell the difference between a dog and a wolf. She sighed. "Thanks for everything, Judd. I'll translate Charles's message for you tonight, but then I'm going to fly out tomorrow for home."

He did not try to change her mind. "I'm glad you've hung in as long as you have. You've been a great help, Eva."

They went in the hotel's rear entrance and climbed the stairs. The room was larger than the one in Istanbul and again had two beds. This time it overlooked the next-door hotel and the driveway far below. In the distance, the Parthenon shone.

As Judd bolted the door, she set their meal on a table beside the radiator and shrugged off her shoulder satchel to get the *scytale* and leather ribbon.

Watching expectantly, he dropped the duffel bag onto the bed nearest the door and removed his Beretta and the S&W 9 mm pistol and suppressor he had picked up from Preston.

She unlatched the snap that closed the side pocket of the

satchel and reached inside. Instantly her hand felt an awful wetness. She pulled out the *scytale* and strip.

"Oh, no," she breathed. "No."

"What?"

"The ink's run." She held up the long piece of leather, soggy, the letters bleeding into one another. "It must've happened in the yacht, when we got drenched."

"Is the message readable?"

"I don't know yet."

She grabbed a box of tissues from the bureau and sat on the other bed, holding the strip beneath the bright light of the lamp. As she dried it, he sat across from her, leaning forward with his forearms on his thighs, watching tensely.

"The letters are a blur," she reported. "I may be able to get something, though."

Remembering how Andy Yakimovich had done it, she carefully wrapped the strip around the *scytale,* pressing and pushing it gently into place, watching to make certain the blurred letters fit in lines. She worked a long time in the silent room. Finally she grasped the *scytale*'s ends, holding the leather in place with her thumbs.

"A few words make sense," she said. "I can partly read where it says the secret is hidden in *Spies,* but I can't read the following sentence." She caught her breath at the next words, the signature at the end: "*Te amo,* Eva, 3-8-08."

"What is it?" Judd leaned forward.

She translated: " 'I love you, Eva.' "

He saw where she was looking. "It's dated the month before Charles disappeared. That answers one of your questions. A critical one, I imagine."

She hesitated as she felt an onslaught of emotions. "I always thought of Charles as my strength, my anchor. When I'd have doubts or get sidetracked, he'd bring me back to center. Now I think that's what he believed to be love. But the truth is it wasn't concern or interest in me. He just couldn't stand that I wasn't as focused, as compulsive as he was." She looked at him. "We still don't know where the library's location is written in *The Book of Spies*."

There was a long silence of deep disappointment.

Judd sat up straight. "I'll just have to find it in *Spies* myself."

But the book was enormous. Trying to uncover the message without a clue or expert help could be impossible. And there was an even larger problem—he did not even know where the book was.

"Don't worry, Eva. You should still go home tomorrow." His gaze was steady. "I really meant it when I said you'd done a good job. In fact, you were invaluable. Without you I likely wouldn't have been successful in Rome or Istanbul."

His mobile rang, and he snatched it up.

She checked her watch. It was past four A.M.

"Yes, Tucker." His jaw clenched as he listened. He told Tucker about the Carnivore's attempt to wipe them and his change of mind, then about their discovery the leather strip was damaged. "We're at the Hotel Hecate. I understand. Be careful."

Eva watched as he punched the Off button.

When he turned to her, his expression was grim. "Cathy Doyle—that's Tucker's boss—has died in a car accident, and the man who took her place appears to be the leak. Another hired gun just tried to erase Tucker."

"Oh, God. How's Tucker?"

"Angry. Worried. The usual. In other words, he's fine. He's at the Baltimore airport. He's flying here to help."

"He didn't have any new information about *Spies* or the Library of Gold?"

"No, but he's given NSA my mobile number, so if one of the numbers on Charles's cell is activated, both he and I will get the news. There's more. Preston hired the guy to take out Tucker *after* we left him hogtied in the Grand Bazaar."

"So Preston is back in action, just as the Carnivore said he'd be. Did Tucker know anything about the Carnivore?"

"He said the Carnivore was one of the underworld's dirty secrets. Too useful to too many sides to kill, and anyway too elusive to find. Apparently back in the cold war, Langley occasionally did business with him. Tucker said he'd heard the Carnivore had ironclad rules, but he'd never had any reason to hunt him."

"Doesn't it seem to you Cathy Doyle's death was more than an accident?"

"Yes. The assholes."

She watched as he slapped his thighs, stood up, and paced the room.

"Why don't you ask me to stay?" she said. "You can use my expertise."

He turned, his muscular face severe. "People either love this work, or they put up with it because they have a sense of mission, of commitment to something larger, something for the common good. In religion it's called faith. In a nation it's patriotism. The risk of death is worth it to them. I can't ask you to stay. You could die."

"Do you love the work?"

"Never have. As soon as this is over, I really am going back to being a civilian. I figure I've contributed enough. It's someone else's turn."

"Will you be able to live peacefully?"

"If you're asking whether I have flashbacks or I'm a prime candidate to take a sniper rifle up into some tower and wipe anyone who's in sight, the answer is no. Most of us aren't affected that way. We don't even get into fistfights in bars. We're just normal people who've been doing a tough job and have some bad memories."

Relief washed over her. With sudden clarity she realized she had been dwelling on her own personal fears. "Charles and the book club conspired in something that should've been good but turned it into evil and a loss to civilization so large it's incalculable. The Library of Gold belongs to the world. I have the knowledge to help you find it and the awful people behind it. With luck it'll be soon enough to stop from happening whatever your father was so worried about." She took a deep breath. "I want to make my own commitment. Make the mission mine, too, and try to be braver than I ever was able during the years with Charles and in the penitentiary. I've changed my mind. I'll see this through."

He sat on his bed, facing her. "You're sure?" He studied her, his gray eyes grave.

"Absolutely." And she meant it.

"Then I'm glad. I have a feeling you've always been brave. But do me a favor—don't like the work too much."

"Fat chance." Setting aside the *scytale*, she turned to him, sitting cross-legged. She had an idea. "We've got to find another way to go about this. I'll start with Charles's tattoo. It had to have sent shudders through the book club. Even a hint someone might reveal the library's location would be a threat to them. That's my first point. The second is, when I saw Charles and Robin together there was something intimate about them. I don't know whether they were close friends, close colleagues, or maybe lovers. But if I'm right, she's connected to Charles, which means his tattoo may have thrown suspicion on her. I know I'd be suspicious. Read Preston's note again."

He took out the torn notebook page. " 'Robin Miller. *Book of Spies*. All we know is Athens—so far.' "

"The beginning part of the note is like a list. 'Robin Miller. *Book of Spies.*' One. Two. Then we get to the heart of the matter: 'All we know is Athens—so far.' The tone makes me think they don't know where *The Book of Spies*—or Robin Miller—is, except they're in Athens, and they must be found."

"You think she not only has the book but she's on the run with it," he said.

"It's a good possibility."

He grabbed his mobile. "I'll call her." He tapped in one of the numbers from Charles Sherback's cell. "I'm getting a recording," he told her. Then: "Ms. Miller, my name is Judd Ryder. I'm in Athens, and I've got the resources to protect you from Preston. I'd like to buy *The Book of Spies*. Call as soon as you can. I'll leave my mobile on." Then he dialed the other number and left the same message.

"Fingers crossed," she said.

He went into the bathroom and emerged with water glasses. He opened the bottle of wine to let it breathe. "I'm going to take a shower. Then we eat."

He grabbed a clean T-shirt and shorts from the duffel and went into the bathroom. She listened to the music of the running shower and walked around the room, arms crossed, holding herself, feeling relieved she had decided to stay and hoping Robin would call soon. Then she emptied the side pocket of her satchel and laid out everything to dry.

Judd emerged with droplets shining on his short bleached hair, his face wet and relaxed. The T-shirt was damp, clinging to his tapered waist. His stomach muscles were amazing, like rebar, and he had good long legs beneath his shorts, straight, the hair golden brown and curly, lovely. She turned away, busying herself by taking out her shirt and shorts. Then she went into the bathroom without looking at him again.

"Drink your wine," she told him over her shoulder. "Behave yourself."

"I'll save half for you."

The hot water soothed her. She washed her hair, caught by surprise at the black color as it fell over her face. She had never in her life dyed her hair. Toweling off, she fastened on her ankle device, buttoned her shirt, and stepped into the shorts.

When she emerged from the bathroom he was sitting at the table, inspecting Charles's notebook again.

"Find anything?" She slid into the chair across from him.

"Nothing."

"No call from Robin?"

He shook his head. "Tell me about your family."

"Isn't that in my dossier?"

"Just the basics. Mother, father, brother, sister, and you. They moved from Los Angeles to Iowa. You didn't. I'd really like to know."

She hesitated. "There's not much to say, really. Dad worked construction. Mom cleaned houses. Dad drank—a lot. He'd have tirades and slap Mom around when she tried to convince him to quit. Eventually she started drinking, too. They got along a lot better, but it still was miserable. We could never bring our friends home because we never knew what we'd find."

"You were the oldest, weren't you?"

"Yes, and probably the luckiest. In Al-Anon you learn about the family mediator, the peacemaker—that was me. It kept me from falling into the bottle, too, because I was always trying to smooth things over to protect my little brother and sister. Then Dad started losing one job after the other, and his uncle offered him work at a lumber company he owned in Council Bluffs. I'd had my brush with the law by then. They were good about that and stood by me. But when everyone left, I stayed on in L.A., to go to college." Her shoulders were tense. She raised her arms above her head and stretched.

"You didn't want to end up like them."

"No, I didn't, but it didn't stop me from loving them. They

came to visit me in prison several times. I don't know how they scraped the money together to do it, but they did." She bit her lip. "Love is a crazy emotion, isn't it?"

He was watching her, kindness glowing in his eyes. "Let's eat."

He poured wine as she got out the food. The moussaka was warm and spicy, the zucchini and wild rice crunchy. It was a simple but fine meal, and for the moment the lamplit hotel room felt cozy and safe.

"What about you and your family?" she asked as she ate.

"You know part of it. Dad was ambitious, but the higher he rose, the more pressure he was under, and the more traveling he had to do. When I started school, Mom went back to work, teaching kindergarten. Then, after a couple of years, she quit so she'd be free when he was home. It was great for me. The door was always open for my friends. She'd make chocolate pudding and oatmeal cookies and let us play outside and get dirty." He studied his wine. "What was rough for both of us was not having him around. But when he was, he filled the house with his personality, and he spent every moment with us. Now that I look back, it's obvious he was trying to make it up to us."

"I'll bet he enjoyed you, too."

"I hope so." He lowered his head. "You should know Dad started telling me stories about the Library of Gold when I was young. He must've known about it then. And that makes me think he was in the book club when the decision was made to bring Charles on board. Knowing how managerial Dad was, I have to believe even if he didn't make the final decisions, he must've at least known about the arrangements."

She felt her breath catch in her throat. Then she shook off her anger. "You're not him. You've made your own choices, and it seems to me they're one hundred eighty degrees different from his. I think you've inherited his best traits."

He poured the last of the garnet-colored wine into their glasses, then he held up his.

"To our partnership." He grinned.

She touched her rim to his and smiled into his eyes. "To finding the Library of Gold."

49

The afternoon was bright, sunlight bouncing off the windshields of cars as Martin Chapman's plush limousine rolled up to the Hotel Grande Bretagne on Constitution Square. One of the globe's top establishments, the hotel looked like a palace and had a long history as a seat of power, which Chapman appreciated: The Nazis had made it their headquarters when they occupied Greece during World War II, and later the British Expeditionary Force took it over. Wars had been planned here, and treaties signed. From kings to corporate heads, jet-setters to diplomats, it was the place to stay, the only hotel Chapman ever used when in Athens.

The chauffeur rushed around the limo to open the door. Chapman got out, his mane of wavy white hair gleaming, blue eyes twinkling, tan face composed, carriage erect. Valets scurried. The hotel's massive doors opened, and he marched inside.

The manager waited beside a tall Ionic column in the lobby, perfectly positioned for effect, surrounded by the hotel's nineteenth-century art and antiques. He bowed and, after appropriate welcoming remarks, led Chapman across the mosaic marble floor to the private elevator, bypassing the registration desk.

They rose silently to the fifth-floor Royal Suite. Opening the door, the manager bowed again, and Chapman strode into a rich world of damasks and silks and antique furnishings from Sotheby's, eager to see his wife. But there was no sign of her. Instead, standing in the middle of the grand triple living room was Doug Preston, holding a wood box. He inclined his head slightly, indicating the box contained what Chapman wanted. Dressed in a three-piece suit tailored to show no sign of his holstered pistol, the security chief's expression was serious.

Chapman's luggage was wheeled in, and the manager bowed himself out the door.

"Where's my wife?" Chapman asked.

"Shopping, sir. Mahaira is with her."

Chapman nodded and gestured. They went into the private formal dining room with its elegant table, set for a business meeting of only eight, since Jonathan Ryder and Angelo Charbonier were dead. Over the next year the book club would decide on their replacements. The centerpiece was a lavish display of orchids. Pads of paper and pricey Mont Blanc fountain pens with the hotel's logo waited at each place.

Preston closed the door. "The butler will serve drinks. Is there anything else I can order for you?"

Chapman chose a Partagas cigar from the burled-wood humidor. He rolled it between his fingers next to his ear, hearing the muffled sound of fine tobacco. He clipped off the end and sniffed. Satisfactory. Lighting it with the hotel's gold lighter, he went to stand by one of the tall windows overlooking the city's landmarks.

"How close are you to finding the Carnivore?" Chapman smoked, controlling his fury.

When after four hours the Carnivore had not given Chapman confirmation of the kill, he had phoned the number the Carnivore had given him. It was disconnected. Then he had sent an e-mail to the contact man, Jack. It had bounced back.

Preston joined Chapman at the window and said, "It's a problem. As you said, the Carnivore's security is very tight.

The e-mail address was routed through several countries. So far Jan's had no luck tracing it back to its origin, but she's still working on it." Jan Mardis was Carl Lindström's chief of computer security."As for the disconnected number, there's nothing we can do about it. I checked in with the man who recommended the Carnivore to you, but he claims he has no other way to reach him and you'll never find him now. He doesn't understand what happened, but whatever it was, he figures he's burned, too. When the Carnivore takes a client's money, it's a trust to him. He always delivers. And he never forgets."

Chapman felt a chill, remembering the cold litany of the Carnivore's rules. Then he brushed it off. The bastard owed him the $1 million advance.

"Find him. I want my money, and then I want him terminated."

Preston inclined his head. "Yes, sir. As soon as Jan has anything, it'll be a pleasure to take him out."

"What about Judd Ryder and Eva Blake? According to our Washington asset, they were heading for Thessalonika and had hooked up with Robin Miller."

"It has to be Athens. They took a note I'd written to myself, and the Carnivore knew it was legitimate. I've posted men at the airport, train stations, and docks to look for them. I don't see how they could've reached Robin, but maybe they have. That could work in our favor." He paused. "I know how to find her."

Chapman stopped, his cigar suspended on its way to his mouth. He studied Preston, who stood calmly beside him, the box still in both hands. He was not rattled, not apologetic. In fact, there was a deadly calm about him. His blue eyes looked like chipped ice. He had been humiliated, and he wanted revenge. Good.

"Tell me."

"I had the pilot check the Learjet," Preston said. "Robin didn't leave her cell behind. If she were planning to escape, she'd take it with her because it was the only one she had. She doesn't know she can be tracked through the cell. My NSA contact is waiting for her to activate it, and as soon as she does, we'll have her. But there's another problem: Tucker Andersen got away, and the man I hired in Washington to scrub him has vanished. So has Andersen. I have people looking for both."

Chapman swore loudly. "Anything else?"

"My men in Rome captured Yitzhak Law and Roberto Cavaletti."

"They're dead?" he asked instantly, pleased.

Preston shook his head. "Not yet. Ryder and Blake have turned out to be far more trouble than any of us envisioned. With Law and Cavaletti, we have something to hold over them if we need it."

Chapman thought about it. "Agreed. We can wipe them whenever we wish."

"There's one more thing. I talked to Yakimovich after I got free in the Grand Bazaar. He said Charles left behind a strip of leather with a message—the location of the Library of Gold is hidden in *The Book of Spies*."

"Jesus. The old librarian smuggled out that book. He knew the location was in it?"

"He's the one who put it there. Charles must have found some message he left. In any case, it's not a problem. We'll retrieve the book. Ryder and Blake will never get close."

Chapman dropped his cigar into an ashtray and rubbed his hands. "Give me the box."

But as Preston handed it to him, there was a tap on the door. With a nod from Chapman, Preston opened it.

Mahaira stood there in a beige linen suit, her graying hair perfectly coiffed in a frame around her soft face. "Madame asked me to tell you she is delayed, sir. Friends found her and insisted she have tea with them. She is most regretful."

Stung by the news, Chapman turned his back on her. As he listened to her pad away, his gaze fell on the box. Quickly he opened it. Sighing with pleasure, he plucked from its velvet lining an illuminated manuscript spectacular not only for its physical beauty but also for what it would mean to his wife and the great new fortune he would have.

50

The members of the book club had been checking into the Hotel Grande Bretagne throughout the morning. The meeting began promptly at two P.M., and their arrival infused the room with electric energy. All stood at least six feet or taller, and despite the nearly thirty-year range in their ages, each moved with the grace of an athlete, their bodies trim and fit.

Chosen in their youth, when they were struggling for money and power and displayed great promise, they had been cultivated, mentored, and financed—as Martin Chapman had. Still, very few who received such attention rose to join the fraternity of the secret book club. Those who did were living examples of the ancient Greek ideal of the perfect man.

Studying them as they stood talking around the table, Chapman felt a sense of pride. He had been director five years. They could be troublesome, but that was understandable. Spirited aggression was necessary to accomplishment, and they were warriors in and out of business—another critical trait of the Greek ideal. But at the same time he was concerned about the unusually high pitch of their energy and the sideways glances in his direction. Something had set them off, and he worried he knew what it was.

He checked the butler, who was serving drinks. They would wait to start the meeting until they were alone.

"You're crazy, Petr," one was saying, amused.

"You spend too damn much time in the library," laughed another.

Petr Klok chose a martini from the butler's silver tray and announced, "This is an organized universe based on numbers. The ancients knew that. The markets—their prices and timings—move in harmonic rhythms." A bearded man with stylishly clipped hair, he was fifty years old and the first Czech billionaire. Taking advantage of his nation's privatization reforms, he had begun small, buying an insurance company with vouchers and loans from Library of Gold funds and then growing it into an empire stretching across Europe and America.

Brian Collum found his glass of barolo on the butler's tray. "You're claiming financial ups and downs aren't random? Clearly you're nuts." Graying, with a long handsome face, the Los Angeleno was the junior member, just forty-eight. He was the library's attorney.

"Study the geometrical codes hidden in Plato's *Timaeus,*" Klok insisted. "Then connect them to the architecture of Hindu temples, Pascal's arithmetical triangles, the Egyptian alphabet, the movement of the planets, and the consonant patterns in the stained-glass windows of medieval cathedrals. It will give you an edge in the markets."

"I, for one, am interested. After all, Petr predicted the worldwide crash of 2008," Maurice Dresser reminded them. A Canadian, he had turned regional wildcatting into a trillion-dollar oil kingdom. He had thinning white hair and strong features. At seventy-five vigorous years, he was the oldest.

"Perhaps Petr is ahead of his time. He wouldn't be the first," Chapman said, a challenge in his voice. He paused until he had their full attention. Seeing the opportunity, he hoped to lull them with a small tournament. "Let's see what you know. Here's the subject—in 350 B.C., Heracleides was so far ahead of his time that he discovered the Earth spun on an axis."

Collum instantly held up his cigar, volunteering. "A century later Aristarchus of Samos figured out the Earth orbited the sun. Also far ahead of his time."

"But in the same era, Aristotle insisted we were stationary and the center of the heavens." Dresser shook his head. "Big error, and rare for him."

There was a hesitation, and Chapman stepped into it. "Reinhardt."

Reinhardt Gruen nodded. "In the 1500s most scientists again believed the world was flat. Wrong. Finally Copernicus rediscovered it rotated and went around the sun. That's a hell of a long time for the facts to come out again." From Berlin, Gruen was sixty-eight years old and owned a global media conglomerate.

"But he didn't dare publish his findings," Klok remembered. "It was too controversial and dangerous. Ignorant Christian churches fought the idea for the next three hundred years."

"Carl?" Chapman said.

"They claimed it went against the teachings of the Bible." Regal, his blond hair graying, Carl Lindström was sixty-five, the founder of the powerful software company Lindström Strategies, based in Stockholm.

"Not enough," Collum called out competitively.

As director, Martin Chapman was also referee. He agreed. "We need more, Carl."

"I thought you idiots knew the Bible by now," Lindström said good-naturedly. "It is in Psalms: 'The world also is established, that it cannot be moved.' "

"Very good. Who's next?" Chapman asked.

Thomas Randklev raised his highball glass. "Here's to Galileo. He figured out Copernicus was right, and then he wrote his own books on the subject. So the Inquisition jailed him for heresy." From Johannesburg, Randklev was sixty-three and led mining enterprises on three continents.

"Grandon. You're the last man," Chapman said.

Fifty-eight and a Londoner, Grandon Holmes headed the telecom giant Holmes International Services. "It wasn't until the Renaissance that the Western world accepted the Earth rotated and orbited the sun—more than a millennium after Heracleides made the original discovery."

Everyone drank, smiling. The tournament had ended with no errors in history, and each had contributed. A sense of friendly warmth and shared purpose infused the room. A full success, Chapman thought with relief.

"Well done," he complimented.

"But just because Copernicus and the others were vindicated doesn't mean Petr is right about all his financial nonsense," Collum insisted.

"Spoken like an attorney," Petr chortled. "You are a Neanderthal, Brian."

"And you think you're a friggin' clairvoyant." Collum grinned and drank.

Everyone had been served, so Chapman told the butler to leave. As the door closed, the group settled around the table. He noted the mood had changed, grown tense.

Uneasily he took the chair at the head, where the wood box was waiting. "Maurice, you called this meeting. Begin."

Maurice Dresser adjusted the pen on the table beside him, then peered up. "As the senior member, it's my job occasionally to bring grievances to your attention. You've been hiding something from us, Marty."

Martin Chapman kept his tone conversational. "Elaborate, please."

Dresser sat forward and folded his hands. "Jonathan Ryder, Angelo Charbonier, and our fine librarian Charles Sherback are dead, murdered. We suspect you had something to do with that. You asked Thom, Carl, and Reinhardt to acquire information. It involved blackmailing a U.S. senator, hacking into a secret CIA unit's computer, and the murder of a CIA officer, one Catherine Doyle. Until we began talking to one another, we didn't realize the extent of your actions. What in hell is going on?"

"Secrecy is based on containment." Reinhardt Gruen drummed his fingers on the table. "This is far larger than I thought."

"You've exposed us to discovery," Carl Lindström accused.

"If the Parsifal Group is investigated, it may lead back to us." Thom Randklev glared.

The room seemed to vibrate with tension.

Chapman looked around at the cold faces. Inwardly he swore again at Jonathan Ryder for starting the domino disasters that had brought him to this precipice.

He cleared his throat. "The Parsifal Group is safe, because it's made too damn much money for too many important people for them to allow anything to be known about it. The exposure would have to be calamitous to change the equation, and this isn't a calamity."

The initial support money for the Library of Gold had been small but adequate, passed down through the centuries to ensure the library was cared for and secure. But in the second half of the twentieth century, when international commerce boomed, and its select group of supporters was formalized into the book club, common sense took over. A process to choose members was created. Opportunities opened through their successes, and investments were made, backed up when necessary by "persuading" Parsifal's members to cooperate.

Today the group's funds of some $6 trillion were registered, regulated, and owned by a series of fronts. They had much to be proud of—the Library of Gold had a permanent home and was maintained to the highest standards, and it would never be threatened as long as it was in their control. Since they saw to that, they were rewarded in kind.

"Doesn't bloody matter," Holmes said. "Risk is never to be taken lightly. You've gambled in grave ways that can impact all of us. We want to know why, and where you are going with it."

Chapman said nothing. Instead he opened the wood box and lifted out a small illuminated manuscript, about six by eight inches, and stood it up so it faced the members of the book club. There was an intake of breath. Diamonds blanketed the cover in a dazzling array, shaped into overlapping circles, triangles, and rectangles, each filled in completely with more diamonds. Of the highest quality, they sparkled like fire.

"I know the book," Randklev, the mining czar, said. He recounted the title in English: "*Gems and Minerals of the World.* Written in the late 1300s. It's from the Library of Gold."

"You're correct," Chapman told him. Then he addressed the group. "I was curious about the diamonds on the cover, so I asked a translator to search through the book, and he found the story behind them. Perhaps you remember that Mahmud, a Persian, invaded Afghanistan at the end of the tenth century. He made Ghazni his capital and lifted the country to the heights of power with an empire extending into what is modern-day Iran, Pakistan, and India." He nodded at the lavish book. "Diamonds were one of the sources of his wealth—diamonds from a huge mine in what today is Khost province, near Ghazni. Then, some two hundred years later, Genghis Khan tore through Afghanistan, slaughtering the people. He left Ghazni and other cities in rubble. The devastation was so complete even irrigation lines were never repaired. The diamond mine stopped production. When

Tamerlane swept through in the early 1380s, he destroyed what was left. The mine was forgotten. In effect, lost."

"Khost province is a dangerous place to do business, Marty," warned Reinhardt Gruen, the media baron. He looked around the group and explained."The Afghan government has taken over the country's security, but they don't have a big enough army, and local police forces are stretched thin and are frequently corrupt. So province governors are supposed to be doing the job, which is a bad joke. In Khost, as I recall, several warlords have divided up the territory. Those warlords may be in collusion with the Taliban and al-Qaeda."

"Shit, Marty." Grandon Holmes, the telecom kingpin, stared. "No mine can operate in that atmosphere. Worse, you'll be aiding the jihadists."

"The exact opposite is true," Chapman told them calmly. That was the conclusion to which Jonathan Ryder had jumped. "Syed Ullah is the warlord in charge in the area where the mine is, and he hates the Taliban and, by extension, al-Qaeda. When the Taliban were in charge in the 1990s, they crushed the drug trade. Heroin and opium were—and are again today—his biggest source of income. So you see, the Taliban and al-Qaeda are his enemies. He's got an army of more than five thousand. He'd never let the jihadists infiltrate and take over his territory."

Heads slowly nodded around the table.

Thom Randklev's eyes brightened. "You know exactly where the mine is?"

"I do. I was going to bring all of you in," Chapman lied. "This is merely sooner than I expected. And of course, you can have the contract to do the mining in addition to your share, Thom."

Randklev rubbed his hands together."When do I begin?"

"That's the problem," Chapman told them."The deal isn't

ready to be signed." In calm tones, and putting a positive spin wherever he could, he described the events of the last few weeks from Jonathan Ryder's discovery of Syed Ullah's frozen account in the international bank Chapman had bought, to Robin Miller's escape from the Learjet in Athens. Then he explained what remained to be done in Khost, and that Judd Ryder, Eva Blake, and Robin Miller were still on the loose but would be found soon.

When he finished, there was a long silence.

"Christ, Marty," said one.

"This is a hell of a mess," said another.

"It's not that big a mess," Chapman said, "and think of the fortunes to be made."

"If the mine is as big as you say," decided Holmes, "we'd be bloody fools to interrupt the deal."

"How much do you think it's worth?" asked Klok.

"From what I read, Mahmud's people had barely scratched the surface," Chapman said. "And of course they had the disadvantage of working with primitive equipment. I'd say it'll bring in at least a hundred trillion. Over decades, of course."

They smiled around the table. Then they laughed. The future was good.

Dresser concluded the discussion. "I'd say you have our complete cooperation, Marty." Then he glared. "But make damn certain you contain the situation. Do whatever you have to do. Don't fuck it up. If you do, there'll be consequences." He looked around at the stony expressions. The men nodded agreement. "You won't like them."

51

Somewhere around the Mediterranean

Above the turquoise sea stood a small stone villa about three quarters of the way up a long green valley. It was nearly four hundred years old. Four stone cottages flanked it, two on either side, built more than a century ago for a don's large extended family. Green ivy grew up the aged white walls of the buildings, and red geraniums bloomed from window boxes.

It was a beautiful afternoon, the air scented with the perfume of honeysuckle blossoms. Don Alessandro Firenze was sitting outdoors beneath his leafy grape arbor at the side of the villa. Here was the long wood table and upright wood chairs at which he and his *compadres* gathered to drink wine and tell stories of the old days. A man in his sixties, the don was in his usual chair at the head of the table, a straw hat on the back of his head. He was alone except for his book and 9 mm Walther, which lay on the table beside a tall glass of ice tea.

He lifted his head from Plato's *Republic*. One of the advantages of semi-retirement was he could indulge himself. As a foolish youth, he had neglected his education. For the past dozen years he had spent much of his free time reading, the rest in tending his vegetable garden, grapevines, and honeybees. And of course there was the occasional outside job.

He gazed around, enjoying this piece of earthly heaven

that meant so much to him. He noted the vibrant health of the bushes and flowering plants that grew around the grassy front yard. His large vegetable garden showed toward the rear, surrounded by a low white picket fence, and next to it was an enormous satellite dish and a generator in bomb- and fireproof housing. Much farther away was a honeybee colony in white boxes. The hillsides beneath the compound were lined with well-tended grapevines and dotted by gnarled olive trees. The property covered five square miles, so no neighbors disturbed him.

Through the window of one of the cottages he could see Elaine Russell in her kitchen. Her husband, George, had gone into the village for supplies. Next to their cottage was another, where Randi and Doug Kennedy napped outside in hammocks. On the other side of the villa, Jack O'Keefe—once known as Red Jack O'Keefe—was working at his computer, visible through his living room window. The other cottage was home to more of his *compadres,* two brothers. Intelligence work was as integral to all of their systems as veins and tendons, so they were merely semi-retired, too. They reveled in his jobs, acting as a moral compass whenever he needed debate.

Just as he was about to return to his book, Jack came at a half-run from his door. The don watched the easy gait, remembering when the older man could run the half mile faster than most people on the planet. About five foot ten inches tall, Jack still had catlike grace. But he looked worried, his corrugated face tense.

The don said nothing.

"Dammit, we've got a problem." Jack dropped onto the chair beside him. "Someone's been trying to trace back the e-mails between Martin Chapman and me. The bastard didn't succeed, but he got damn close. I scrambled the two Internet service providers I created out of Somalia and the

Antilles and shut them down. There's no way they'll find us now."

The don felt hot fury explode in his skull. He said nothing, waiting for the storm to subside. His bad temper had caused enough grief for himself and those he loved.

"You told Chapman the rules," the don said. "I told him. He agreed. Now he's broken them twice."

"I did some research on him and Douglas Preston. Preston's ex-CIA, the bastard. You'd think he'd have a better way to earn a living now. Anyway, according to Chapman's equity firm, Chapman is in Athens now. My deduction is Preston is with him, looking for Eva Blake and Judd Ryder. You told me this was about the Library of Gold, so I sent out word to our contacts and got some interesting results."

When searching for the rich and powerful, most people never thought to investigate the less obvious sources—protection services, independent bodyguards, private mercenaries, party planners, chefs, maid and nanny businesses, boat crews, pilots, anyone who served the affluent.

"You have a lead?" the don asked.

"You bet I do. Wasn't going to talk to you until I did. The problem is, it's risky."

As Jack explained the possibilities, the don took off his hat and rubbed his forearm across his gray crew cut. His fingerprints had been burned off years ago, his face altered many times by plastic surgery. He had the body of a man in his forties, although his skin had aged—a regime of hormones, vitamins, and exercise could accomplish only so much. He nodded as he listened. Yes, that would do.

"It won't be easy," Jack warned again.

"I've just been reading Plato." The Carnivore closed the book and set it beside his Walther. He gazed across his tranquil estate, wishing his daughter were here. But she did not approve of him. "It's an insightful book. I don't agree with everything. Still, one thing he wrote seems to apply: 'Only the dead have seen the end of war.'" He stood up. "Summon the *compadres*. We'll go into the villa and make preparations."

52

Athens, Greece

A Greek newscast sounded from down the hotel corridor as Judd set their brunch tray on the floor outside the door. Listening, he peered left and right, then stepped back inside the room. Eva was at the table and looked tense, elbows on the top, a hand cupping her chin as she reread Charles's notebook. Last night he had thought he was going to lose her. He was glad she had decided to stick it out, except now he felt even more responsible for her.

He shot the dead bolt and grabbed Preston's S&W from under his pillow. Sitting, he emptied it of rounds, including the bullet in the chamber.

"Join me." He patted the bed beside him.

Eva looked up and saw the gun. "Are you going to shoot me or teach me?"

"Teach. Then you'll be able to shoot someone—hopefully not me."

"We'll see." She gave a small smile and sat beside him.

"This is the safety. Flick it on and off so you know how it works." When she did, he explained the basic mechanics of the weapon. "Stand up."

"Okay." She stood, long and slender, her dyed black hair falling around her face.

"Balance on both feet."

She assumed a *heikō-dachi* karate stance, her feet at

shoulder-width distance and parallel. Her knees were flexed, just the way he wanted them.

He passed her the gun. "Hold it in both hands, choose a point on the wall, stretch your arms a bit, but not so much you strain yourself. Aim. . . Stop hunching your shoulders. Let your bones relax—your muscles need to do the work." Her grip looked capable but not confident. "Your hands automatically want to coordinate with your eyes—let them do it. Good. Now squeeze the trigger." He watched. "Slow down. Pretend the trigger is a baby's ankle. You don't want to hurt it, but you've got to be firm, or the little guy will skedaddle away."

"You did a lot of babysitting in your youth?"

"I have an active imagination."

"You've raised babies in your imagination?"

"No, but I can act like one."

She laughed, settled herself, and tried the trigger again.

"Much better," he said. "You won't know how true your aim is until you fire, but this is better than nothing. Practice one hundred times—slowly. Then take a break and do another hundred. You'll begin to get the feel of the weapon and what it's like to shoot it. If you actually do have to fire, you'll get a powerful kick. This will help you prepare for that, too."

Listening to the clicks, he took out his mobile, downloaded the phone numbers of all hotels in the Athens metropolitan area, and started dialing. At each place he asked to speak to Robin Miller. There were a few Millers, but no Robin Miller. He talked to the ones he could reach. They knew no one named Robin Miller.

Finally Eva said, "That's another hundred." She did not look bored but seemed definitely fed up. "How do I load this thing?"

They sat on the bed again, and he filed rounds into the S&W's magazine. He took them out and handed the magazine to her. She fumbled for a while, then got better, sliding the bullets inside.

Finally, at around two o'clock, she put the weapon into her satchel. When he finished a call to another hotel, she held up a hand.

"Pame gia kafe," she said. "That means let's go for coffee, which in Athens really means let's go out. Enough already. You haven't heard from NSA. Robin hasn't called. Tucker isn't getting in until late. Preston has never seen our disguises, so we're reasonably safe. And once I have a cell, I can help call hotels, too."

She had a point. In fact several of them. They left.

The day was warm. Athens was having a touch of summer in April. Through a thin layer of brown smog, sunshine glazed the concrete buildings and sidewalks. They took the Metro to Plaka, the city's humming market and popular meeting place.

"We can get lost in the crowd here," she explained.

She was right. Plaka swarmed with tourists and locals, cars banned from most of the streets. They walked through winding avenues and passageways crammed with small stores selling trinkets, souvenirs, religious icons, and Greek fast food. He smelled hot shish kebabs and then the cool scent of fresh flowers. Many of the streets were so narrow, sunlight fought for a place to shine through.

"You should be aware of a couple of things before you try to do any business in Athens," she told him. "Never raise your hand, palm up and out, when you greet someone. It's a hostile gesture here. Instead, just shake hands. And when a Greek nods up and down—especially if there's a click of the tongue and what looks like a smile—it's an expression of displeasure. In other words, *no*."

"Good to know. Thanks."

He bought her a disposable cell without incident, and

they stopped at an open-air café to go back to work. So far he had seen no sign of a tail.

When the waitress came, he started to order Greek coffee, but Eva said, "Two Nescafé frappes, *parakaló*." The waitress gave a knowing smile and went inside.

"Instant coffee?" he asked, worried.

"What. You're a coffee snob?"

"I spent too many years inhaling desert sand not to appreciate a fine cup."

"Sympathies. But you really have to have it at least once. It's a local favorite, and it goes with the climate and the outdoor lifestyle. Besides, it's expensive, which means we can sit here for a couple of hours without ordering anything else."

He was doubtful but said nothing more. As he wrote a list of hotel phone numbers for her, two glasses of water and two tall glasses of a dark-colored beverage topped with foam arrived with drinking straws.

He glanced at the water and stared at the frappes.

She grinned. "I'm beginning to worry you don't have a sense of adventure."

He sighed. "What's in it?"

"Two cubes of ice, two heaping teaspoons of Nescafé powder, sugar, milk, and cold water. I know it sounds dreadful, but it's actually heavenly on a warm afternoon like this. You're supposed to drink the water first, to cleanse your palate."

"I've got to clean my palate? You must be kidding." But he drank the water.

She was sipping her frappe through her straw and laughing at him.

He tried it. It was almost chocolate, the coffee flavor strangely rich and soothing. "You're right. It's good. But next I want real Greek coffee. I like to chew as I drink."

"You have my permission." She glanced around. "I've been

thinking about your dad's news clippings. I know you told me the analysts didn't see anything revealing, but I'd like to hear again what was in them."

"International banks were mentioned, and our targeting analysts have been closely monitoring their transactions. Nothing about the Library of Gold. There was a lot about affiliate jihadist groups in Pakistan and Afghanistan and the dangers they pose, but our people are already watching them so closely every one has a skin rash."

"Remember," she said, "I've been off the reservation—in prison a couple of years. Is al-Qaeda as dangerous as it was? Aren't we safer now?"

"Yes and no. It'll help if you understand al-Qaeda's structure. Years ago Osama bin Laden and his people saw what happened to Palestinian jihad groups that let new members join their leadership—intelligence agencies were able to infiltrate, map, and hurt them badly. That made al-Qaeda's leaders reluctant to expand, and after 9/11 they slammed the door entirely, which meant they couldn't even replace losses. They've had a lot—we've captured or killed most of their top planners and expediters. So now they can't compete on the physical battlefield anymore, but they don't need to. Their strength—and an enormous threat to us—is the al-Qaeda movement. It spread like wildfire during Iraq. The new jihadists revere al-Qaeda central and go to them for advice and blessings for operations, because they believe the leaders' bloody theology. It's proved to be an effective recruiting tool and keeps bin Laden and his cronies relevant—and powerful."

As the waitress passed, he ordered real coffee. "What's worrying us about Dad's clippings is the focus on Pakistan and Afghanistan, where the Taliban is strong. The two countries share a border through the mountains, but it's an artificial one the Brits created in the nineteenth century. The people on both sides—mostly Pashtuns—have never accepted it. For them the entire region has always been theirs. As for Pakistan, it's in crisis and has pulled its troops from the North-West Frontier Province. If the province falls to the jihadists, the whole country could crash. At the same time, Afghanistan has taken on its own defenses, so the U.S. and NATO have only a limited presence. Warlords rule the borderlands, and there's concern whether they have the country's best interests at heart, since many have jihadist connections."

Eva sighed worriedly. "And somewhere in there may be where your father thought something awful was being planned."

They worked two more hours without finding Robin Miller. Eva had another frappe, and he ordered another traditional Greek coffee. The sun was below the horizon, sending a violet cloak across the street's paving stones.

"It's discouraging." She put down her cell, leaned back in her chair, and stretched. "Where is that woman?"

"God knows." He leaned back, too. Just when he picked up his mobile again to phone another hotel, it rang. Quickly he touched the On button.

It was the NSA tracker. "One of the disposable cells was turned on briefly. But it's off now. I'll let you know if it's activated again." He relayed an address. Judd jotted it down and turned the paper so Eva could see it.

"It's near," she said excitedly. "South of us but still in Plaka."

53

When the book club meeting concluded, Chapman opened the door. Mahaira was sitting in the foyer, hands folded neatly in her lap. As the members of the club trooped past to prepare for an evening on the town, she rose, smiling.

"She's taking a bath," she whispered.

Eagerly he headed across the carpet, removing the long-ago photo of beautiful blond Gemma from his pocket, burning her image into his mind.

Flushed with excitement, he hid it again and opened the bathroom door onto the opulent sanctuary of the bath, with its spacious glass shower, ornate full-length mirror, and marble-clad floor, walls, and ceiling. The air was infused with the fragrance of camellia-scented bath oil. Beneath the softly glowing crystal chandelier was the massive soaking tub set on a pedestal in the center of the enormous room. Bubbles rose above it, and above them was his gorgeous wife.

Her hair was piled on her head, a mass of golden curls, her smooth shoulders fragile and sweet. She turned to look at him, the vibrancy of youth in her violet-colored eyes, aquiline nose, and good chin.

"You're here at last, Martin. How wonderful to see you." Her voice was musical. "Bring me a towel, will you?"

"Later." Stripping off his clothes, he stalked toward her.

Her laughter sang. She balled up a washcloth and threw it, sopping, at him.

He sidestepped and climbed the pedestal naked. He slid into the tub's warm water.

She glided through the water toward him, bubbles cascading away. "I've missed you. Oh, how I've missed you."

"I've missed you, too." He pulled her to him, running his hands hungrily over her breasts, her thighs.

"Umm," she purred. "Umm, umm."

He arched her backward and nipped her shoulders. Kissed the hollow of her throat. She laughed happily, the vibrations sending shudders through him. He felt her hands on his cock, stroking, twisting, pulling.

Fever inflaming his brain, he slid his hands under her bottom and lifted, his fingers digging into muscle. She licked his ears, the tip of his nose, and locked onto his mouth. The taste of her sent a titanic wave through him. Her legs straddling him, he lowered her slowly, then, in a heated rush, pulled her down and made love to her. To Gemma.

They dressed in the master suite, Beethoven playing from the tall armoire. The long rays of the setting sun spread across the carpet and touched their naked feet.

Wearing a long white skirt with a tight waist and a red silk strapless top, she sat on a brocaded chair, slipped on high heels studded with diamonds, and buckled the tiny straps around her slim ankles.

"Well, that was a waste." Chuckling, she sat up and gestured at the smoothly made bed. "I'd planned to be lying here undressed for you."

"How's Gemma?" he asked casually as he adjusted his tie in the mirror. He watched her reflection in it. She had put on her makeup, and her lips were like rubies. She looked and sounded so much like Gemma his heart ached.

"Mother's fine. She's in Monte Carlo with her new

boyfriend. I do wish she'd settle down. She's costing you a fortune."

Gemma had been married five times, but never to him. The summer they graduated from college, her family had given her a choice—either end the relationship or be disinherited. To spare her the pain of choosing, he left California and hitchhiked across the country to New York City, where he dove into the pirana-infested sea of finance, determined to earn the wealth that would make him acceptable. By the time he had, she had married her second husband, who drank, gambled, and went through all her money. That husband was Shelly's father.

"She looked beautiful at the San Moritz party," Shelly said. "But she never mentioned the family necklace and earrings. Or the new tiara you bought me. I wore all of them, you know."

"Mahaira told me. I'm glad you enjoy them so much."

"Mother loves diamonds, too. She must miss having them a lot. I offered to give the necklace and earrings back to her, but she wouldn't take them. As long as I can remember, I think she's hated you. Why is that? She won't tell me."

"I suspect that's more her parents' attitude than her own." It was what he always said, because he had never understood why Gemma had been so furious at him for leaving California. It was some foolishness about insisting she had a right to be part of such an important decision. Now he breezed past his wife's questions by focusing on what she could understand: "I doubt she's ever really hated me, but now I agree she's quite unhappy about the difference in age between you and me." And, he hoped, jealous.

Shelly shook her head, her golden hair floating across her bare shoulders, and studied her four-carat diamond engagement ring and the diamond-encrusted wedding band. "I thought when you bought the family jewels to help her, she'd get over it."

He said nothing. His tie satisfactory, he turned.

"Will you be here tomorrow?" she asked eagerly.

"I have business," he said kindly.

A cold look crossed her face. "Okay. I'll fly to Cabo, then. Friends invited me."

"Where's your wrap, darling? We'll be late for cocktails." While they were separated, he yearned for her. But when they were together . . . In the end, she was not Gemma.

As they crossed the living room, his cell phone vibrated against his chest.

Looking at her, he took it out. "Sorry, darling."

She nodded, her face frozen. Alabaster.

He went into the dining room and closed the door.

It was Preston, and he sounded jubilant. "I just got a call from my NSA contact. Robin Miller turned on her cell phone, then turned it off. I've flown in men from the library for backup and to bring supplies, and we're in Plaka—that's where she was. We'll find her and *The Book of Spies* very soon now."

54

Robin Miller had had a busy two days in Athens, and at last she was beginning to feel prepared as she walked through the twilight and deeper into Plaka. Besides oversize sunglasses, she wore a wig—a simple brown hairdo ending just below her ears. Long bangs brushed her dyed black eyebrows. Brown contact lenses colored her blue eyes, and she wore no eyeliner or mascara, no lipstick.

Her clothes were two sizes too large—baggy cotton pants and a loose button-down cotton shirt. Only her battered tennis shoes fit—bought at the Monastiraki Flea Market. She carried a shopping bag she had found on top of a trash can. It was stuffed with crumpled newspapers, while her billfold and other items were in her pockets. The first time she caught a reflection of herself in a shop window, she had not recognized the dowdy, overweight woman. She had smiled, pleased.

Now she needed money. As usual, Plaka marketplace was bustling. Vendors called from the doors of small shops, promoting their wares. A herd of black-robed Orthodox monks passed, holding black cell phones to their ears. She entered the little bank she had chosen and went up to a teller. Before disappearing to join the Library of Gold, she had put her life savings into a numbered Swiss account. Just a half hour ago, she had called the phone number she memorized long ago, releasing the funds to this bank.

The teller led her to a desk, where a bank officer had

forms waiting. She filled in the account number and other required information and orally gave him her password.

"How do you wish the funds?" he asked.

"Four thousand in euros. A cashier's check for two thousand more. The rest in a second cashier's check. Leave the line to whom the checks are to be made out blank."

"So much money. Would you not like to open an account? It will be safe here."

"Thank you, no."

He nodded and left. Turning in her chair, she watched the people coming and going.

When he returned, he ceremoniously handed her a fat white envelope. "If there is anything more I can do to help with your financial matters, madame, please tell me."

She thanked him again and left. In total, she had about $40,000. It was not enough to ensure her safety from the book club for long. Still, at least she would have immediate cash.

The sun had set, and the shadows were deep across Plaka's crowded streets. She liked the drama of the approaching night, and it would help to hide her. She slid the envelope inside the waistband of her pants. Her feet felt light, and her heart was hopeful as she wound south through the marketplace. She wanted to be as close as possible to where she had left her rolling suitcase and *The Book of Spies*.

As she walked, she took out her cell phone and dialed. Sometimes fortune smiled. Trying to negotiate her freedom with Martin Chapman had frightened her, but now she had an alternative.

When the man's voice answered, she asked, "Is this Judd Ryder?"

"I am. Are you Robin Miller?" He had a strong voice. She liked that.

"Yes," she said. "Who are you?"

"I'm with the U.S. government. Do you know the location of the Library of Gold?"

So that was what he wanted. She ignored the question. "How did you hear about me?"

"I've been hunting for the library. I had a clue that took me to Istanbul, but Preston found me there and tried to eliminate me. There was a note in his pocket with your name, 'Athens,' and '*The Book of Spies*' written on it. Earlier, in London, I'd gotten two phone numbers off Charles Sherback's cell, but I didn't know for sure to whom they belonged. I phoned both with the same message in hopes one of them was yours."

She bit her lip. "You know who killed Charles?"

"We'll talk about that when we meet."

She had been trying to put Charles out of her mind. Whenever she thought about him, a bottomless ache filled her. The loss was so great, so raw, her world so destroyed, she had a hard time thinking. After several deep breaths, she considered her situation. Ryder had escaped Preston, which went a long way toward indicating he might really be able to protect her. And she understood his hunger to find the library.

"I'm sure Preston is searching for me," she told him. "You're lucky to have gotten away."

"Luck had nothing to do with it. Explain why I should be doing business with you." The voice had grown harder.

"I worked at the Library of Gold, but I never learned exactly where we were. I can tell you the library is on an island, but I don't know which island. We're always flown in with hoods over our heads, usually from Athens. There's a helipad, a dock, and three buildings that look as if they're a vacation compound, with a swimming pool and tennis courts. About twenty people are on staff, most of them security.

Tomorrow night is the annual banquet, so beginning today Preston has been putting on even more guards."

He seemed to like her answers. "Are there other islands in sight?"

"There's one far away. When the day's particularly clear, you can see the tip of it."

"Do you have *The Book of Spies*?"

"I've hidden it in Athens, and I'm willing to sell it to you."

"All right. Let's meet."

"I want five million dollars for it," she said firmly. "Before you object, the Getty paid five-point-eight million for *The Northumberland Bestiary* just a few years ago." The *Bestiary* was a rare thirteenth-century English Gothic illuminated manuscript. "This is the only copy ever made of *The Book of Spies* and should be worth a lot more, so I'm offering you a bargain."

"You're right; it's a good deal if you look at it from your perspective. On the other hand I'm offering something of even greater value—I'm going to get you safely out of Athens. What's your life worth?"

She felt a chill. "I'll settle for three million."

"Much better. I'll make the phone call to release the funds, but it'll take a few hours for it to be deposited into your account. Or you can have it in a cashier's check or any other financial instrument you like. By tomorrow morning you'll have your money."

"A cashier's check will be fine."

With a flush of excitement, she looked around. She had left Plaka and had entered the Makrigianni district. She was on the Dionysiou Areopagitou, a wide pedestrian boulevard. To her left stood a line of stylish houses in Art Deco and neoclassical styles, and to her right was the massive Acropolis, the city's long-ago spiritual center. With a thrill she stared up the slope. She could see only a white crest of the spotlighted ruins high above. Then she noticed people were streaming past her, toward the entrance to the Acropolis park, which lay below and on which were the remains of what had been ancient Athens's intellectual and cultural center. She could see bright lights in the Theater of Dionysus. There must be a concert or show of some kind, she decided. A crowd could be useful.

She explained where she would wait for him. "What do you look like?"

When he told her, she described her disguise.

"I'll be there in only a few minutes," he assured her.

Controlling his frustration, Preston stood with his cell phone in his hand as he and two of his men scanned for Robin. They were in an alcove on Adrianou, Plaka's main street, which was packed with tourist shops. She had phoned from the outdoor café across the way. They had searched the area and seen no sign of her, which told him either she had spotted them and was hiding, or she had moved on.

When his cell rang, he snapped it up. The caller was Irene, his NSA contact.

"Your person of interest has been talking on her cell again." Irene sounded nervous. "The call ended about fifteen minutes ago. She was heading south. I can't help you anymore, Preston. Something's happened here. Everyone's being watched. I had to get into my car and drive off the premises to phone you. I'm worried they're going to investigate my NRO queries and searches." The NRO was the National Reconnaissance Office, which designed, built, and operated U.S. recon satellites—and collected the data from them.

Inwardly he swore. "Give me the exact information. Everything you've learned. I'll take it from here."

55

The air was warm, the stars bright overhead as Judd and Eva hurried up wide marble paving stones to the entrance of the Acropolis architectural park. Carrying their large duffel, he bought tickets, and they passed through an open gate to where a wide path climbed a gentle slope. Tall cypress and olive trees swayed in a light wind, spectral in the night. He could see an ancient amphitheater in an open area, a magnificent sight. Its rows of crumbled white stone benches rose up the hill in a semicircle, and for a moment he imagined what it must have been like two millennia ago, the vast crowds, the excitement in the air.

The theater's base—the stage—was brightly illuminated by klieg lights. A woman in classical Greek dress stood before the large audience, which sat on blankets and cushions on the remains of the terraced rows. As she spoke into a microphone, a cluster of men and women in white robes and tunics cinched with colored braids waited at the side of the stage. A small camera crew was filming.

"Along here beneath the Acropolis," she was telling her listeners, "are the ruins of the world's first complex of buildings dedicated to the performing arts. This noble old theater dates back to before Alexander the Great. On this very stage immortal masterpieces were premiered—and drama and comedy were born."

"Am I right that we're looking at the Theater of Dionysus?" Judd asked Eva as they neared.

"Yes. It's beautiful, isn't it? When it was new, the walls, stone seating, and thrones were covered in marble and carved with satyrs and lions' paws and gods and goddesses."

Without being asked, she clasped her satchel to her side and slipped into the shadow of a tall marble block across the path from the rear of the open stage, and Judd climbed steps on the west side. The speaker continued, alternating her lecture in Greek and English.

Twenty terraces up, a woman was sitting alone at the edge, a shopping bag at her feet. She looked stiff, stressed. A couple with four children and more people sat in the same row, but close to the center. The stage lights did not reach this far, leaving only the illumination of the moon and stars to show the woman's brown hair and dumpy figure. If he had not known she was Robin Miller, he would not have recognized her.

She slid over to make room for him. "Judd Ryder?" Her tone was strained.

He sat. "Hello, Robin. Ready to get out of Athens?"

She was staring down the hillside. "Who came with you?"

Now he knew one thing—Robin was smart. She had placed herself high and in the darkness deliberately to watch unseen anyone who arrived. He had purposefully not told her earlier about Eva, since they did not know how she would react to Charles's wife—or that he had been the one who had killed Charles.

"My partner," he said. "I'll introduce you. She's keeping watch."

She nodded. "That's okay. Let's go."

He led the way back down and then across the pathway to where Eva was waiting, her black hair and dark blue jacket and jeans hidden in the shadow beside the great marble block.

"Is *The Book of Spies* nearby?" he asked Robin.

"Yes. In a Metro station."

Eva walked out to greet them, a welcoming smile on her face.

But Robin frowned and took a step backward. "You're Eva Blake. Charles's wife. Preston told me you were involved in Charles's murder." She stared angrily at Judd. "You said she was your partner."

"She is," Judd told her. "I'll explain as we walk. Remember, we're going to help you escape. That's what matters."

Robin's face flushed as she glared at them. Then her eyes darted, and her muscles seemed to tense. Suddenly she turned, threw away her shopping bag, and rushed off toward the park's entrance.

"I'll handle this." Eva ran after her.

Judd caught up with them. Robin was marching quickly along, two furious red spots on her cheeks, her chin held high. And he saw she had not dyed her hair but was instead wearing a wig—it had slipped, exposing the back of her shaved skull. He kept pace on the other side of her.

"I'm sorry about Charles, too," Eva was saying soothingly. "No one wanted him to die. Were you in love with him?"

"What happened?" Robin snapped, not breaking her stride. "Did *you* kill him?"

"It was an accident," Eva explained. "There was a struggle, and his gun went off. I never knew Charles to carry a gun, so that must've started after he left me. But he'd told me something important, something you should hear—he wanted the library to be found if anything happened to him. There was a message tattooed on his head, and it's what sent us to Rome and then to Istanbul. I don't want Charles's legacy to be lost, and I'll bet you don't, either."

Tears rolled down Robin's cheeks. "You killed him." She increased her furious pace.

As they exited through the park gates, Judd said, "They're

suspicious of you, aren't they, Robin? Did they make you shave your head to see whether you had a tattoo, too?"

"Magus shaved it," she blurted.

"Who's Magus?" Judd asked instantly.

She shook her head, then tugged the wig back into place.

"Where exactly is *The Book of Spies*?" Judd said. "With the money we pay you, you can disappear. Start a new life. Find happiness again. Tell us where the book is, and we'll get you out of here."

"You lied to me! I've had enough of people lying to me. I was stupid to have believed you have the money or you'd give it to me anyway. Leave me alone. I'm not going to help you. Charles never loved you, Eva. Never!"

Moving at an increasingly fast clip, the three continued on. Robin's body was rigid, her expression intransigent. Judd was beginning to think there was nothing they could say to persuade her to give them *The Book of Spies*.

"You may be right about Charles." Eva moved closer to her as they entered the wide pedestrian boulevard of Dionysiou Areopagitou.

"Of course I'm right. I'll bet you never loved him, either. And then you murdered him. I'm through working with liars and murderers!"

Just then the toe of Eva's tennis shoe caught on a cobblestone. She stumbled into Robin, her hands sliding over her as she tried to stabilize herself.

Robin pushed her away. "I hate you." She ran again.

They watched as she dodged pedestrians and disappeared into the crowd.

"What did you get?" Judd asked, knowing Eva had pulled her pickpocket routine.

"A billfold, a cell phone, and a key. She said *The Book of Spies* was in a Metro station, which means it's probably in a locker. This looks like a locker key." She held it up.

He took the key and read the number. "It does. But which station?"

"You said it was nearby," she explained, "and she didn't object. It's got to be the Acropolis station. It's only a couple of blocks away."

56

Preston recognized Robin Miller's gait, the one aspect of the body most people forgot to disguise. He had noticed her as she had rushed down Dionysiou Areopagitou a half block from where she had ended her last cell call, but her hair and clothing had almost fooled him. Then as she passed, he had clearly seen her walk, the rhythmic shifts of her body, the short stride, the way she put weight on the outside of her soles.

He signaled Magus and Jerome, and all three ran after her.

Preston grabbed her arm. "We've missed you, Robin."

Terror filled her eyes. "Let me go." She tried to wrench free.

"Magus," Preston said.

Magus took her other arm, and they moved her to the side of the pedestrian boulevard. She started to struggle.

"Stop it," he ordered. "All we want is *The Book of Spies*. That isn't so hard now, is it?"

"And *then* you'll kill me."

"For what reason? There's nothing you can do to hurt us. You don't know where the library is. In fact, you know very little, do you?"

Her eyebrows lifted. She seemed to understand what he really meant. "You're right. I don't know anything about the library. Who works there, who owns it."

"Good girl."

He told Jerome to stand lookout at the beginning of a drive between two apartment buildings.

"Why do we have to go in here?" She gazed worriedly back over her shoulder as they took her down the drive.

Ahead was a parking lot, well lit, but empty of people. There was no one at the windows above.

"You don't want to be seen with us," he said. "That way there'll be no questions by anyone. You're on your own now. No more baggage from the past, right?"

She looked up at him, seemingly confused by his being understanding.

"Where's the book?" He put warmth into his tone. "Tell us, and we'll leave you here. There's only one other thing you have to do—give us a five-minute head start and go that way." He nodded to a walk that skirted the rear of the buildings.

"You're actually not planning to shoot me?"

"I'm sure you've figured out by now I'm a practical man. We're in the middle of Athens. Dead bodies mean police questions. You'll notice I haven't unholstered my weapon."

"You'll try to find me later."

"Why bother if I have the book?"

She peered at him a long time, then nodded agreement. "It's in the Acropolis Metro station. I have the key to the locker." She shook her arm, and he released it. As she slid a hand into her shirt pocket, a look of shock crossed her face.

Controlling his impatience, he said, "Maybe you put it into another pocket."

Magus freed her other arm, and she frantically searched her trousers and then her other shirt pocket.

"It's gone," she said. "My billfold and cell phone are gone, too. I don't see how all of them could've fallen out—"

"What else happened?" he asked instantly.

"Maybe Eva Blake or Judd Ryder took them somehow." She looked away. "I met them. But I didn't tell them anything. They don't know the book is in a locker in the Acropolis station."

With effort, he kept his voice calm, reassuring. "That's good. You made a mistake, and then you corrected it by not giving more information. Where are they staying, and where are they going next?"

"I don't know. I ran away from them."

"That was smart, but then I've always admired your intelligence. I'll bet you remember the locker number."

"Of course." She gave it to him.

"You're certain that's correct?"

"Of course I am."

"As a reward, I have a little gift for you." He smiled as her eyes widened. He took out a small blue bottle, flipped off the lid, and pressed the nozzle, spraying directly into her face.

She gasped and stepped away. Too late. He let her continue to walk, watching as she slowed and her knees buckled. He surveyed the parking lot and then the windows above. No one was in sight.

A fist against her chest, she sank to the ground, her oversize shirt billowing around her. Her legs spasmed. A quiet, unobtrusive death was one of the great advantages of the Rauwolfia serpentina derivative.

Glancing down the drive to Jerome, who nodded that all was well, Preston knelt over her, searching her clothes. He found a thick envelope inside her waistband and handed it up to Magus.

"Tell me what's inside." He continued to hunt but found nothing more.

Magus let out a low whistle. "She's got one pack load of euros in here."

Preston stood and took the envelope. "We've got to move fast. Watch for Judd Ryder and Eva Blake."

The Acropolis Metro station was on Makrigianni Street, across from lively cafés and snack bars and next to the Acropolis Study Center. Scanning everywhere, Preston and his men rushed inside the sleek station and ran down an escalator. At the base, they hurried past casts of the Parthenon friezes and stopped at the electronic ticketing machines. Two more escalators down, and they found the lockers.

As a Metro train whined to a stop, Preston ran along the lockers, alternately studying the boarding passengers and reading locker numbers until he found the correct one. His men converged to stand on either side, blocking anyone from being able to see as he took out his knife and quickly jimmied the tall door open.

And stared inside. There was no black backpack. No *Book of Spies*. On the bottom was Robin's roll-aboard, and on the shelf above lay her cell phone—open and turned on. Furious, he realized Ryder must have figured out they would use the cell to locate them. Ryder had *The Book of Spies* and was taunting him.

Preston grabbed the phone, slammed shut the locker, and turned. A bell rang, signaling the train's doors were about to close.

"Run," he ordered.

He and his men raced to different doors and leaped inside. Since they were underground, he could not call the other men he had brought to Athens and order them to watch the next stops. As the train pulled out, he noted his car was a little more than half full. Quickly he walked down the aisle, but he did not see Ryder or Blake. He spotted two backpacks—one was brown and the other green.

He checked Robin's cell, hoping for Judd Ryder's phone number. And swore. Ryder had wiped it clean. Blood pulsing with anger, he pushed through the door and entered the next car, determined to find them.

57

Fighting tension, Judd sat across the aisle and four rows back from Eva as the Metro sped north through the underground tunnel. He was alone in his seat, while she was sitting beside a boy of about thirteen, who wore a red-and-white striped Olympiakos soccer shirt.

They had seen Preston arrive at the lockers with two men. One of them, dark-haired and beefy, had walked up and down their car twice, eying passengers as if he knew exactly for whom he was searching. But besides having black hair, Eva's face and hands were also darkened by makeup. Her eyes squinted, and a thin line of cotton slightly fattened her upper lip. Small changes could be transformational, and she now looked little like the sophisticated intellectual Judd had first seen in the British Museum. Besides his bleached hair and glasses, Judd had stuck folded cotton squares above his upper molars and had adopted a hangdog appearance.

At last the beefy man exited the car, but Preston entered, his tall muscular frame looming, his expression inscrutable. He gazed carefully at each passenger, walking slowly.

A stout woman in a black dress, her purse held firmly in both hands on her lap, spoke sharply to him in Greek. Ignoring her, he continued on, pausing at Eva's row.

"Who are you looking for?" the boy asked Preston curiously in Greek-accented English.

Preston did not answer. He peered at the duffel bag under

the youth's legs but then turned to study an older couple bundled in trench coats. When he reached Judd, Judd was leaning his head against the cool glass window, his eyes heavy as he stared out into the monotonous tunnel. Finally Preston moved on again.

The men continued to walk through the car, slower each time, but they never seemed to identify Eva or him. Ten minutes later the Metro pulled into the Syntagma Square station, and Judd watched Eva lean toward the boy and whisper. He smiled and nodded. As the train stopped, they stood, and she preceded him out of the car. He was carrying Judd's duffel.

Judd let the older couple and another passenger feed in, and then he left, too, keeping his place in the crowd.

Preston and his two men were standing at the exit, scrutinizing everyone again. As the train left the station, Eva and the boy chatted animatedly in Greek. Preston's eyes flickered over them, then paused to stare a long time at Eva as they walked past. Judd found himself holding his breath.

But again Preston turned, and he checked the older couple in their body-covering trench coats. Finally he settled on Judd. Judd made no eye contact; it was a sure way to attract interest. Expression unchanged, Preston peered behind him, and with relief Judd stepped onto the escalator.

The station was as glossy and modern as the one at the Acropolis stop. It, too, was a museum, with ancient urns, perfume bottles, and bells on display in lighted glass cases. Judd hurried past them, following Eva and the boy up two more escalators and out into the city's cooling night.

At the curb, Eva looked back at Judd through the crowd. Glancing carefully around, he nodded. She spoke again to the youth and then took the duffel bag from him. He walked away.

Watching a moment to make certain the boy was all right, Judd joined her at the taxi stand, and she handed over the bag.

"My God." She beamed. "That was exhilarating."

Her blue eyes were bright, and she chuckled. She looked very alive, as if she had hit the winning home run in the World Series. He suddenly realized how well she had handled events tonight, sliding unasked into the shadow of the marble block across from the Theater of Dionysus, not inflaming Robin further by admitting he had been the one who had shot Charles, and coming up with the idea to ask the Greek boy to help her onto the Metro train with the duffel with the excuse her back ached.

But then Eva had spent two years in a pickpocket gang. She knew what it was to set up and act in a movie, and what it was like to be under the constant threat of discovery. The two years in prison had taught her more—how to go deep inside herself to survive and, despite the circumstances, to take risks. Now she'd had her crisis of conscience and committed herself to the mission. He was not sure he liked what he saw now.

"You're kidding, right?" he asked hopefully.

Her face broke into a smile, and she laughed.

He had been scanning as they stood in line, the rumble of Athens's wild traffic beside them, filling all three lanes. Eva tugged his sleeve just as he spotted Preston and his two men hurrying toward them from the Metro station. There was no hesitation—the men had pinpointed them. They were drawing their pistols.

"Come on." Judd pushed past the two people ahead of them.

A taxi was pulling up. He yanked open the rear door, and Eva threw herself inside. He tossed in the duffel and dropped in next to her as she told the driver in Greek to leave quickly.

It was a one-way street, so there was no way they could do a U-turn. They would have to drive past Preston.

"Get down," Judd snapped as the vehicle rushed off.

They fell low. Shots rang out, and rounds slashed through the doors and roof. Metal and plastic sliced through the air. The driver swore loudly, and the car hurtled faster. More bullets cut through the taxi, and then there was no feel of acceleration. Judd looked up just in time to see the driver collapse silently onto his side, sprawling across the front seat.

"Jesus."

"What's happened?" Eva asked quickly.

The vehicle slowed. It wove from side to side. Horns honked, and drivers shouted as they swerved their cars to get out of the way. The cars behind were signaling, trying to pass.

"The driver's been shot. Stay down," Judd ordered.

Preston was racing along the curb after them, his two men on his heels. They would reach the taxi much too soon.

Judd snatched out his Beretta. "Keep my door open until I get to the driver's side."

Her eyes wide, Eva nodded.

He opened his door. Hunching, he sprinted along the still-moving cab. Rounds crashed through the door and bit into the pavement around his feet, exploding needle-sharp shards. Suddenly hot pain sliced across his side and burned up into his brain. He fought dizziness.

As he rounded the hood, he saw through the windshield Preston had jammed his gun into the open passenger window of a tall SUV four cars behind, all rolling slowly, unable to pass in the fast traffic in the other lane.

As the three men took over the big vehicle, Judd jerked open the driver's door, and Eva closed the one in back. Still running, he shoved the downed taximan across the seat, causing a scalding pain to split up from his side. He gave his head a quick shake and dropped inside. There was an open stretch ahead. He floored the gas feed, his door slamming itself shut. He pressed his forearm against the gunshot wound in his side, trying to slow the blood.

"Is he alive?" Eva leaned over the front seat.

"Get down, dammit."

Behind them, one of Preston's men had his pistol out the window of the hijacked SUV, aiming over the roofs of the vehicles between them. There was a vegetable truck in the other lane. Judd accelerated, overtaking it. He signaled. The truck continued its lumbering speed. He spun the steering wheel, forcing the taxi's nose into the lane in front of the truck. The truck's horn blasted. He heard a loud curse, but the truck gave way, and he slid the taxi into the slot just as the traffic light turned red. There were cars between him and it. No way to run the red light, and Preston's SUV was coming up swiftly on the right.

"Grab the duffel. We've got to get out of here. My side of the cab."

With the taxi still rolling, they stepped out and ran through the traffic. Cars swerved. More horns honked. As they reached the sidewalk, Judd tried to take the duffel.

But Eva held on to it, staring at his bloody jacket. "You're wounded." She looked around quickly. "I know where we are. This way."

He holstered his Beretta, pressed his arm against the wound again, and followed as she moved swiftly among pedestrians. The noise of idling engines filled his head. Stores were alight, shoppers showing through the windows.

"Preston's coming," he told her.

She hurried inside a large store selling casual clothes. Racks and stacks of women's jeans, shirts, and dresses marched back deep into the building. A saleswoman greeted them in English. Eva said hello and kept walking. Judd felt the eyes of the clerks looking after them.

As the stove's front door opened and Preston and his men entered, Eva led Judd into a hallway at the rear. They ran past changing rooms. She turned a doorknob, and they were out again in the night, this time in a cobbled alleyway where trash cans and empty packing boxes were stacked against the walls.

Running, they passed doors.

"Open this one," she told him. "I'll do the next." She leaned over and snatched up two pieces of broken cobblestone. "Prop the door."

His door led into some kind a restaurant, the spicy odor of sauteeing garlic wafting out. He dropped the rock, leaving the door ajar. And met her as she nicked her rock into place. Without a word she ran again and opened a third door. They rushed inside to a short corridor where there were bathrooms. The noise of voices and clinking glasses assaulted them. They were in a bar.

Bolting the door, she took a deep breath. "How badly are you hurt?" She looked up at him, her face full of worry.

"I think it's superficial."

"I hope like hell you're right."

As they walked quickly into the long, crowded room, he chuckled. "Where did you learn a distraction technique like that with the doors?"

She smiled at the bartender as they passed. "A long time ago, in a city far, far away, to paraphrase *Star Trek*."

"In other words L.A. We need to make sure one of those killers isn't posted on the sidewalk."

His hand inside his jacket on the hilt of his pistol, he stepped outside first, looking through the pedestrians. She stood behind him in the doorway.

"Looks good." He felt his heart rate decelerate.
"I'll get us a taxi," she told him.
He let her do it.

58

Tucker Andersen paced the room in the Hotel Hecate. Judd had left an envelope containing the card key at the front desk for him. After checking in to a room for himself, he had come here to theirs. Waiting two hours, he had been reading Charles Sherback's notebook. When he heard the *click* of a card key in the lock, he pulled out his Browning, slipped into the bathroom, and stood behind the door.

Watching through the crack, he saw the door open slowly and the head of a bleached-blond man appear, gray eyes surveying the room.

Tucker stepped out. "Where the hell have you been?"

"Sightseeing." Carrying a paper sack from a pharmacy, Judd walked in, his gait easy. But there was a sea of blood down the side of his brown jacket.

Eva slipped in behind him and closed and bolted the door. "Glad you're here, Tucker. We've had a few problems. Preston shot Judd, but we got *The Book of Spies*. Robin Miller had it stored in a Metro locker."

She set a large black duffel bag on the table, then took the sack from Judd and dumped out bandages and other supplies. The aspirin and over-the-counter painkillers had been opened.

"That's very good," Tucker said. "Congratulations. Don't lie down, Judd. Let's have a look at your side."

As Judd removed his jacket and peeled off his polo shirt,

Tucker took in Eva's black hair and darkened skin and peered from one to the other and back again, assessing the atmosphere. They radiated tired urgency—and they had become a close team.

As soon as Judd's torso was exposed, Tucker and Eva converged. The injury was a raw red gash through the fleshy part of his waist—long, a good half inch deep, and weeping blood.

"You got lucky, Judd." Tucker saw Eva head for the medical supplies on the table. "Have you ever cleaned and sewn a wound?" he asked her.

She turned. "No."

"Okay. Judd, take off your jeans and come into the bathroom. Let's get started." He wondered whether Eva would turn out to be squeamish.

He grabbed sterile latex gloves, sterile cotton, anesthetic spray, and antibiotic soap. In the bathroom, he told Judd to sit straddling the edge of the tub. As Eva watched, he put on the gloves, sprayed on the anesthetic, waited, then squirted the soap inside and around the gash, patting and rubbing gently. Judd made no sound, although Tucker knew it must hurt like hell. He poured glasses of water over the injury, washing it for three minutes. Then he dried Judd's side with cotton and his leg with a towel. He glanced up at Eva. She was following intently.

When they returned to the room, Judd sat on a chair and swallowed more painkillers. His face was pale. Tucker sprayed on more anesthetic, found the right size needle from the supplies, and held it over the flame of a match. After threading fishing line into it, he ran the antibiotic cream over it and laid a thick line of cream inside the wound.

"Time for more pain," he warned.

Judd nodded. "Do your worst."

"The idea is to sew as far away from the cut as the injury

is deep," he told Eva. "Then you cut the line and tie a knot every quarter inch."

He heard small noises in Judd's throat as he worked, but Judd did not move. When he finished, the younger spy's face dripped sweat.

Judd sighed deeply and looked up at Eva. She smiled at him.

Tucker taped on a thick sterile bandage. "Go lie down," he ordered.

Judd did, stretching out and propping up his head on pillows. Eva took the quilt off her bed and covered him.

"You look comfortable," she said.

"I'm enjoying myself." He grinned, but his sweaty skin was pasty.

"Good," Tucker said. "Let's get to business. Report."

Going to the duffel bag, Eva described Robin's phone call, Judd's meeting her at the Theater of Dionysus, and Robin's running off.

"Eva got the key to the Metro locker from Robin." Judd gave Eva a proud glance. "She pickpocketed her, did it so well Robin didn't have a clue."

"What happened to Robin?"

"We don't know." Eva opened the duffel. "She wasn't with Preston when he arrived at the Metro with three men."

"I suspect once he got the information from her about where she'd stashed *Spies,* he killed her," Judd said.

They were silent a moment.

"A nice Greek boy was helping me with the duffel on the Metro," Eva said. "Judd and I were split up, and the ride turned out to be safe. After that the men followed us out. We were escaping when Judd was shot. I'm not sure how they identified us."

"I doubt it was electronically," Judd said.

"He's right. My cell phone's gone, and there's no way

Preston could've bugged either of us. He was never close enough."

"Training of some kind," Tucker decided.

Eva opened the bag and with both hands lifted out a foam-covered bundle. "This is *The Book of Spies.*" She carried it to her bed and removed layers of foam. "Robin told us the library was on a private island, only one other island visible in the far distance. Three buildings, tennis courts, a swimming pool, and a helipad. She was flown from Athens with a hood on, but at least that gives us a radius. The problem is it's a big radius. The island could be anywhere from the Black Sea to the Aegean, Ionian, or Mediterranean seas. And there's a vast number of islands; Greece has more than two thousand, and many are private. The other piece of information you should know is tomorrow night is the library's annual banquet, so there'll be a lot of security on the island, wherever it is."

She went into the bathroom and washed her hands.

Moving slowly, Judd sat up on the edge of the bed to watch as she unwrapped transparent polyethylene sheeting. His color was returning to normal, and a sense of hope infused the room. Tucker joined him, leaning forward, hands clasped between his knees. At last only the archival polyester film remained. The golden cover of the illuminated manuscript shone through.

Eva peeled back the film. "Ah," she breathed.

They stared, silenced by the dramatic artistry of the softly glowing gold, the pearl dagger, the ruby drop of blood, the emerald border. The first time Tucker had seen the book, he had been bowled over. He was still awed.

"I can't believe you took off one of the emeralds so you could bug the book, Tucker," Eva scolded.

"I've still got it. We can glue it back on."

"It's a desecration. If the bug hadn't helped us find the book, I'd really be mad." But she smiled.

He found himself smiling back. "Being a heathen goes with the job."

Eva sat cross-legged on the floor in front of the men, her back to them, facing the book. "Tell me, oh *Book of Spies*, where inside you is the secret to the Library of Gold?" She turned the pages slowly.

They studied the progression of extravagant pictures, beautiful Cyrillic letters, stunning borders. As time passed, Tucker stood up and stretched, then sat again to focus. More pages turned until at last they reached the end of the book—four hundred parchment pages. There was nothing unusual, no contemporary writing, no sign the book had been tampered with at all.

Tucker paced. "I was reading Charles's notebook before you got here, hoping he'd left the answer there."

"I know. Both of us have studied it, too." Eva stood up and went to Judd's jeans, fishing out a billfold. "This is Robin's. Maybe she was lying to us about not knowing where the library is."

"I'm going to call NSA," Judd announced. "Hand me my mobile please, Eva."

Eva reached into his jacket pocket and carried it and the billfold to the bed. As Judd phoned and gave a description of the island, she spread out the billfold's contents—euros, a photo of Charles, and a photo of Edinburgh. Tucker and she inspected everything closely but found nothing useful.

Judd ended the call. "They'll get back to me as soon as they have some information."

"How are you feeling, Judd?" she asked.

"Better. Definitely better," Judd said. "How about another hit of pain pills?"

Shaking his head at Judd's lie, Tucker got them for him. "I'm going to order food. We need to eat. It'll help us to think."

"I'm hungry, too," Eva said. "I'd love a bottle of retsina with dinner. I'll take my shower now." She studied Judd a moment then went into the bathroom and closed the door.

Tucker picked up the phone. "What do you want to eat?"

"Anything. Just order."

As Tucker did, Judd closed the book and examined the binding and spine. At last he shook his head and set it back down. Then he lay on the bed again, pulling the quilt over him.

"Good thing Eva's with us," he said. "She knows what to look for."

"How's everything going between you two?"

"Fine."

"You like Eva."

"Not the way you mean. Don't worry. No fraternizing."

Tucker thought about how he had met his own wife. "That's not what I mean."

"I won't let it interfere with the job." His expression toughened. "They killed Dad."

"I remember. I also know you lost a woman who was very important to you in Iraq. You almost got busted out of the army for going after her killer."

Judd gazed evenly at him. "That was a long time ago."

"Was it?"

The bathroom door opened, and Eva walked out, so clean she glistened. Her cobalt blue eyes seemed brighter, and her lanky frame more curvaceous. She exuded sexuality but seemed unaware of it.

"Is dinner here yet? I'm starving." She gazed happily at both men.

Judd looked away.

Later, at the table beside the radiator, they ate braised cuttlefish fresh from the docks at Piraeus, the city's seaport a few miles away, accompanied by mushroom pilaf, grilled red and green peppers, and fiery *kopanistopita,* filo triangles stuffed with spicy cheese. The wine was retsina, as Eva had requested.

"Tastes like pine resin." Tucker rotated the glass in his hand, inspecting the deep red color.

"It's the wine of Greece," she said. "I haven't had any this good in years. The reason for the name and the taste is the ancient Greeks knew air was the enemy of wine, so they used pine resin to seal the tops of the amphorae and even added it to the wine itself."

"I like it, too." But Judd had hardly touched his. He turned to Tucker. "What's the situation in Washington?"

Tucker put down his fork. "I talked to Gloria before I took off from Baltimore. The fellow who tried to wipe me is in Catapult's basement. She managed to get him downstairs without anyone's seeing. She's the only one who knows what's going on."

"Thank God for Gloria," Judd said. "Eva, let's talk about Charles, about what he told you in London. Maybe he gave you another clue to where the Library of Gold is, but you just didn't recognize it at the time."

She repeated their conversation, and the two men listened closely. At last they sat back.

Tucker shook his head. "Nothing."

Continuing to analyze, they finished dinner. Afterward, Eva sat on her bed, again going through *The Book of Spies.* NSA called Judd and gave him a list of four islands in the Ionian, Aegean, and Mediterranean seas that met or were close to Robin's description. But which of the four?

As they were puzzling over the list, Judd's mobile rang. They watched as he snapped it up.

"Hello, Bash. What's happened?" Judd's square face grew grim as he listened to the Catapult man in Rome. Then: "Stay on it. Let me know as soon as you learn anything."

Tucker and Eva were silent. It was obvious the news was bad.

When he ended the connection, Judd told them, "Yitzhak and Roberto are missing. Bash called every morning in case they needed anything, but they didn't answer today. He went over to their flat. It'd been torn apart, searched. At least there wasn't any blood. He talked to the neighbors. One saw Yitzhak and Roberto walking away with two men who fit the description of two of the janitors who were outside Yitzhak's house when the Charboniers attacked us. Then Bash checked with the university where Yitzhak is a professor. The department secretary told him he had phoned yesterday for her to find a teaching replacement because he was going out of town. She had a package for him from the Vatican Library, so she sent it with a student. Yitzhak met him outside a trattoria. That's the last time anyone from the university saw him."

"No," Eva said.

"Jesus." Tucker sat back in his chair. "The Library of Gold people have them."

59

The evening was just beginning. It was only ten o'clock, but Alexander's was already packed with patrons. The leather bar stools were filled, and people stood behind, drinking. Voted by *Forbes* magazine the best hotel bar in the world, Alexander's boasted marble-topped tables, beach-umbrella palms, and an eighteenth-century tapestry of victorious Alexander the Great, hanging across the wall behind the long bar. Of course the clientele was the best in the city and from abroad. The aroma of rich liquors and designer perfumes scented the air.

Martin Chapman was drinking Loch Dhu, the only black whiskey with a mellow charcoal aftertaste. He savored the rich flavor, felt the heat. After dinner in Churchill's with his wife and Keith and Cecilia Dunbar—investors in shopping malls Chapman & Associates was building in Moscow—the four had moved to a central spot in the bar where they could be seen. Chapman estimated some $30 billion was sitting around their table alone.

"Ah, no," Keith was saying. "The Grand Caymans are perhaps fine for the untutored. But I far prefer Liechtenstein for my money."

"What about Britain's Channel Islands?" Shelly asked with a glance at Chapman, showing him she knew a thing or two herself.

But as Keith launched into an explanation, Chapman's cell phone vibrated. He looked at the screen and saw Preston was calling. Excusing himself, he wound off through the crowd, feeling Shelly's dark look on his back.

"Yes?" he answered, hoping for good news.

"I'm outside the hotel, sir. I'll be waiting."

The connection went dead. Chapman's lungs tightened, and he marched through the lobby. The massive front doors opened, and he hurried out and down the steps. The dark night air enveloped him. Preston was across the street, in the plaza.

"How bad is it?" Chapman asked as he joined him.

Preston showed no signs of a fight—his clothes neat, his hair combed, his face and hands clean—but he radiated disgust as he stood between pools of lamplight. They walked off together.

"It's not an entire disaster," Preston said. "I terminated Robin Miller with the Rauwolfia spray. I thought you'd enjoy that."

The drug was a derivative of Rauwolfia serpentina, developed at Bucknell Technologies under Jonathan Ryder. It depressed the central nervous system and killed in seconds. Vanishing from the body in minutes, it was named for Leonhard Rauwolf, a sixteenth-century German botanist whose notes Jonathan had discovered in one of the Library of Gold's illuminated manuscripts on trees, plants, and herbs. Preston was right. It was appropriate one of Jonathan's creations had been the instrument of a successful step in a business deal he had tried to stop.

"The problem is we didn't get *The Book of Spies.*" Preston's lips thinned as he described what had happened. "I managed to wound Judd Ryder."

"How did you identify Eva Blake?" Chapman asked.

"At first I didn't. Then when the Metro stopped, she passed me at the exit, and I thought I recognized her walk from when I studied her in L.A. I watched from the window as she went outside. She took a duffel bag big enough to hold

The Book of Spies from the kid who'd been sitting next to her, and then a man met her—he was the right size and age to be Ryder." He filled in more details.

Chapman's mind worked furiously. "In Istanbul you found out from Yakimovich that the old librarian wrote the library's location in the book. As long as the book's in circulation, we could have serious trouble. And God knows whether there are other clues out there somewhere. We can't take the chance Ryder, Blake, or someone else will find the library. Phone Carolyn Magura to get ready. How long will it take to move the library?"

Ten years ago the book club had decided that electronic monitoring and international communications were advancing so rapidly that discovery of the island could become a problem. It was time to find a backup home. A remote area in the Swiss Alps on a glacier-fed lake north of Gimmelwald had been perfect. The place had been ready for years, managed by a skeleton crew.

"Yes, sir. I'll get everything ready," Preston said. "Figure a day and a half."

"Tomorrow night's banquet will be our last on the island. A fitting end to a good long run. Plan to move out the next morning." For a moment nostalgia swept through him. Then worry returned. "What about the Carnivore. Have you found him?"

"Mr. Lindström's computer chief hasn't been able to track him."

"Christ. Has your man in Washington eliminated Tucker Andersen yet?"

Preston paused. "Both have vanished. We're looking for them."

Chapman controlled his temper. "You do that. I'm going to move against Catapult. We can't afford to let the situation in Washington get any worse than it is."

60

Washington, D.C.

It had been a long day at Catapult, and Gloria Feit was clearing her desk to leave. The usual office chatter sounded from the corridors. As she folded her reading glasses, she noticed a soft sound as the door behind her opened. She turned.

"I need to see you, Gloria." Hudson Canon's bulldog face vanished back inside his office.

With a quiver of uneasiness, she walked after him.

"Close the door and sit down." He was already settled behind his desk, his big hands splayed on top.

She thought for a moment about the man in the basement who had tried to erase Tucker, but she had taken the spare keys to the door from the lockbox and they were safely in her purse. There was no way Canon or anyone else knew the man was down there. He would not talk, but he was eating like an elephant.

She settled herself into one of the chairs facing the desk, crossed her legs casually, and put a pleasant smile on her face.

"What can I do for you, boss?"

"Where's Tucker?" The question was abrupt, the tone full of authority.

She gave a little frown. "He hasn't returned. That's all I know."

"When he called in, what did he say?"

That took her aback. How did Canon know Tucker had phoned from the grocery store to have her pick up his attacker, and later from the Baltimore airport? Then she realized he could have checked Catapult's automated phone logs.

"He asked whether I wanted a sandwich from Capitol City market," she lied. "I told him no. He called a second time, but I don't know from where. He asked if there were any important messages for him. There weren't. That was the last I heard. Are you worried something's happened to him? I don't think you need to be. He would've told me if he was in trouble and needed backup."

He leaned forward. "What's he up to?"

"I haven't a clue."

"Is it more of this nonsense about the Library of Gold?"

"Well," she said carefully, "it is the operation he's focused on. But it's not the only one he's managing, of course."

"That operation is over. You and I both know that that's what he's working on. He's disobeying a direct order."

The force of his intensity shook her. "I haven't heard anything about any of that."

"So Tucker didn't tell you he had a deadline. Now you're informed. It's your duty to help find him. The Senate subcommittee on intelligence is investigating waste in the CIA. They're meeting tomorrow. I had to tell Matt about Tucker. It's minor in some ways, but it's the sort of thing they're looking into. It won't be good for Tucker. He needs to report in."

Matt Kelley, head of the Clandestine Service, was an old friend of Tucker's. It seemed impossible he would report or reprimand Tucker for something so small.

"It's less than minor," Gloria insisted. "My God, if we held our breath over every incident like this with one of our officers, we'd all die of asphyxiation. We have to rely on their being self-starters, entrepreneurial."

Canon shook his big head. "One of the senators knows about it. She sits on the subcommittee. She's got a bone between her teeth, and she's not letting go. She wants Tucker."

"How did she hear?" she asked, shocked.

"God knows," he snapped back. "But that's the situation. We don't want Tucker to be burned. Where is he? What's he doing?"

She was silent, remembering her long history with the spymaster. She had always trusted him, and he had always trusted her. And all the evidence pointed to Hudson Canon's being dirty. Still, he did not sound dirty.

She took a deep breath. "I'm sorry, Hudson. If I knew where Tucker was, I'd say so."

He stared. "You'd damn well better tell me if you hear anything. Go home and think. Think hard. We've got to find Tucker."

Hudson Canon stood in front of the mirror in his office, adjusting his tie. His face seemed pale. He slapped both cheeks. When the color returned, he cracked open his door. Gloria was gone. Good. He marched down the corridor, stopping in offices, asking whether anyone had had contact with Tucker or knew where he was. All claimed ignorance. Finally he went into Tucker's office and closed the door. He searched the desk and the file cabinets. In the bottom drawer, he found a bottle of whiskey. He opened it and drank deeply. At least he had uncovered something useful.

Wiping his mouth, he went down the corridor again, repeating his questions and again getting nothing. Then he stepped inside the communications center and stopped at every desk until he reached Debi Watson.

"Where's Tucker?" he asked her.

She peered up, her large eyes wide. "I don't know, suh."

"When's the last time you talked with him?"

"Yesterday. It was just the usual instructions."

He fought impatience. "What were they?"

"To track a cell phone number. I turned it over to NSA."

"Call NSA."

Quickly she picked up her phone and dialed.

"I'll take that." He snapped the phone from her hands. "This is Hudson Canon. Tell me exactly what you've been doing for Tucker Andersen."

"Just a minute. Let me get into that file." The man on the other end of the line paused. "All right, here it is. We traced a cell phone number for him. It was last turned on in the Acropolis Metro station in Athens. I reported the information to Judd Ryder. Then I got a call to locate an island for them. I found four."

An island? That was something Canon knew nothing about. Still, he felt a moment of relief. At least he had something to tell Reinhardt Gruen: Judd Ryder was in Athens and had received information directly from NSA. "You obviously have Tucker Andersen's and Judd Ryder's mobile numbers. I need to know exactly where both are."

"I'll have to get back to you. I've got to go through NRO, you know, and if Ryder and Andersen are using secure mobiles, it'll take some time."

Canon gave him his number. "As soon as you get the information, call me immediately. And I mean *immediately*."

61

Athens, Greece

Dazzling morning sunlight illuminated the quiet hotel room. As Judd slept, Eva lay back down on her bed, dressed again in her jeans and green shirt. Tense, she threw her arms above her head and stared out the window as a redtail hawk circled lazily against the blue sky. She'd had a restless night, awaking and drowsing, then awaking again, haunted by a sense she already knew where in *The Book of Spies* the librarian had likely written the Library of Gold's location—if she could just figure it out.

"How long have you been awake?"

She turned her head. Judd was staring at her, gray eyes sleepy, bleached hair messy. She studied him for any signs of fever.

"Not sure. An hour maybe. How are feeling?" She handed him aspirin, painkillers, and a glass of water.

"Much better. You've been thinking." He propped himself up on an elbow and took the medication.

"Yes. About where in *Spies* the librarian would've left a message. I've been going over everything Charles told me again and again, and what I remembered from his notebook. I know I'm close to the answer."

He was silent. "Too bad Charles didn't leave a different clue."

She frowned. "Say that again."

"Too bad Charles didn't leave a—"

"*Different* clue. That's it." She sat up excitedly. "I was looking for what we hadn't used before. Big mistake." She hurried to the big *Book of Spies,* which lay closed on the table.

"What are you talking about?" In his T-shirt and shorts, Judd pulled up a chair and sat beside her.

"The reason we shaved Charles's head was the story about Histiaeus and the slave messenger. So maybe it wasn't a clue just to check Charles's scalp; maybe it's where we're supposed to look inside *Spies,* too. I know I saw the story here somewhere."

She turned pages quickly. Finally, in the middle of the big book, she found the tale on a single page as ornate as the others, decorated with Persian and Greek soldiers along the outside margin. Black Cyrillic letters filled the rest of the space, the text block recounting the ancient narrative.

"I don't see anything unusual." Judd stared.

"Me neither. I'm going to translate the story quickly to myself." As she read, it was soon clear the recounting was much as Herodotus had chronicled it centuries before. Finished, she sat back.

"Nothing?"

She shook her head, then picked up the book. "I need light."

They sat on the side of her bed, where sunlight streamed through the window. Holding the book open on her lap, she leaned close. In her life as a curator she had learned an old adage was true—the devil was in the details. Now that she had an overview, she studied the spaces between the letters and words and the brushstrokes. When nothing struck her, she moved on to the paintings of soldiers.

She sat up straight. "I think I've found it. Look at these, Judd." She pointed to tiny letters beneath some of the colors.

He leaned close. "They're almost invisible."

"They're meant not to be noticed. They stand for the Latin

words the artist who painted them was instructed to use to fill in the line drawings. This *v* means *viridis,* or green. So the robe on the slave is painted various shades of green. The *r* is for *ruber,* or red—the apples on that tree behind him. And of course the sky is *a, azure,* for blue."

He frowned, puzzled. "Then what do *lat* and *long* and the numbers with each mean?"

She grinned. "That's the same question I asked myself. In the first place, I've never known anything like three or four letters strung together to indicate a color on a manuscript page. In the second place, neither is a Latin word."

He grinned back. "Since we're looking for the location of the island, I'm guessing they're abbreviations. Add in the fact there are numbers—*latitude* and *longitude.*"

"As Archimedes said, eureka!"

He grabbed his mobile and activated it. "This is where being online gets really useful. Read what you have to me, and we'll see whether we're right."

He lowered the mobile so she could watch the screen. As he tapped the keyboard, Google's world map appeared, shifted, then shifted again, shrinking to the south Aegean Sea.

His forehead knitted. "Nothing. No island. No atoll. Not even a pile of rocks."

She felt a chill. "Try again." She gave him the digits, one at a time.

He entered each carefully. Again the map zeroed in on empty sea. Her shoulders slumped. He tried other public domain maps. The only sound in the room was the clicking of the keyboard. But each map showed the same disheartening results.

They were silent.

"It doesn't make sense," she insisted. "The easiest, most direct explanation for the abbreviations and numbers in the book is they're meridian points. Even if those are old maps, they should show an island."

He stared at her. "Not true. By God, if I'm right, it's a real display of the power of the book club." Again he tapped the keyboard. "Because of terrorism, the government mandated Google and other online map services not show certain places in the world. Sometimes it was a government facility. Other times it was an 'area of interest' that was clandestine for one reason or another. Private companies doing defense work could ask the government to make spots off-limits, too."

"How could the book club get the government to hide their island?"

"An inside source, or maybe someone they bribed. Let's check this."

He called up the text message he had received yesterday from NSA, and they read the list of islands that had come close to fitting Robin's description.

"My God," Eva breathed as they stared. "One of the islands has the same coordinates as the book has."

Relieved excitement rushed through her. She flung her arms around Judd's neck, and he hugged her tight. Feeling the steady beat of his heart, his breath spicy against her ear, she lingered for a moment.

Then pushed away. "You'd better call Tucker."

The spymaster arrived in minutes, wearing the same rumpled chinos, button-down blue shirt, and sports jacket from the day before. Eva saw the lines on his face were deeper, and the large eyes behind his tortoiseshell glasses were red-rimmed from lack of sleep. But his light brown mustache and gray beard were neat, and he radiated hyper alertness.

"You've found it?" he said as he bolted the door behind him.

"Damn right she did." Judd pointed at Eva.

She smiled, pleased. "Took me a while, though."

They sat around the table, and she explained how they had discovered the answer.

"I'll get back in touch with NSA for the latest satellite photos and data about the island," Judd said brusquely. "Eva, is your laptop still working, or did it get doused when we were on the yacht?"

"It was in the main pocket of my satchel, so it's fine."

"Good. I'll forward what NSA sends to it."

"Does the island have a name?" Tucker asked.

"Just a number," Judd told him.

"Do it," Tucker ordered. "Now."

62

Khost Province, Afghanistan

After a large breakfast, Syed Ullah walked out to the front porch of the redbrick villa where he, his wife, and remaining children and grandchildren lived with the wives and children of his four brothers, all of whom had died fighting the Soviets, the Taliban, al-Qaeda, or local clans and tribes.

Restored from rubble on land his family had long owned, the sprawling villa stood two stories above the hard-packed earth. A satellite uplink dish was behind it next to a rusty Soviet T-55 tank. There was a vegetable garden to one side, with apple, peach, and mulberry trees just as there had been when he was a child. He had planted everything in the last few years. The young trees were like the future, he had told his youngest and last remaining son—strong, but they must be protected.

Wearing turbans and wraparound sunglasses, his gunmen prowled around the rebuilt stone wall that surrounded the expansive property. A dozen tribal elders—striking old men with high-bridged noses and the beards of patriarchs—were lining up in front of the porch to pay their respects. At fifty-four, Ullah had fought off and killed his rivals for this position, but that was the way it had been for decades. Men had little food for their bellies but plenty of rounds for their guns. He could hardly remember when it was otherwise.

The warlord sat down on his tall-backed wood chair on his brick front porch. Adjusting his girth, he nibbled sugared almonds as he greeted the elders courteously, accepted their respectful sentiments, adjudicated neighbor disputes, and assured them of his protection. These were men with large families and sons and grandsons and great grandsons whom he needed.

"It is tomorrow night?" the last elder said. There was impatience on his leathery face, indicating he had expected someone to have asked earlier.

"Tonight," Ullah corrected him, then he addressed the others. "Stay in your houses with your wives. Your sons know what to do."

And then they were gone, scattering the chickens and marching off into the mountains and down toward the town of some three thousand. In the hills he could see a small U.S. army patrol driving along a dirt road in two armored HMMWVs—Humvees—painted in camouflage colors. A donkey with a high bundle was being led down a treacherous path.

The warlord stood up, a giant of a man, burly and strong, with a fierce face that could easily break into a smile. But that was the strength of the Pashtun—resilience. He took great pride in his heritage of warriors, poets, heroes, jokesters, and warm-hearted hosts. They loved the land and their families. Centuries of being conquered and occupied had changed nothing, only hardening their devotion. His devotion. His family must survive, after that his clan, and then his tribe.

He studied the vast sweep of rugged mountains, where snow glistened on the high slopes. Serpentine ribbons of smoke curled up from houses in the distance, mostly made of mud bricks with thatched roofs. A maze of smoke tendrils rose over the town, where many of the buildings had been pulverized by fighting and raids. Khost province was a crossroads of trade and smuggling, and in the crosshairs of the

Taliban and al-Qaeda, who sneaked in from North Waziristan directly across the border in Pakistan. They came under the cover of night to recruit, do business, and murder collaborators, often local police.

On the far side of the town was America's secret and highly secure forward base, painted in camouflage colors and draped with camouflage netting to make it invisible from above and difficult to see from the land. No smoke trailed upward, since a huge generator gave them all the power they needed.

Lifting his head, Ullah sniffed. He could smell mutton, hearty and sweet, cooking in the villa's kitchen. A good lunch. Since he had taken control in this war-ravaged area, he and his family ate well, and if it were not for Martin Chapman, he would have even more funds at his disposal—the overseas account Chapman had frozen. Until the poppy harvests in the autumn, he had little income from opium and heroin. He needed Chapman to release his money, and that meant tonight his men would put on the U.S. Army uniforms Chapman had supplied and eliminate about a hundred locals from the town and nearby villages, chosen because of their opposition to him, and recorded by the cameras of friendly tribal newsmen from Pakistan. Finally he would have his money plus Chapman's payment for buying the land.

Just then the two army Humvees veered toward his villa. His guards turned and lifted their heads, watching, too.

The warlord called into the house for tea and paced along the porch. As the tea arrived on an enameled tray, he sat in his chair.

The Humvees roared into the compound and stopped in a cloud of white dust. Soldiers sat behind the machine guns mounted on each vehicle, their helmets low against the morning sun, their eyes hidden behind black sunglasses.

The forward base's commander, Capt. Samuel Daradar,

jumped down from the passenger seat of the lead vehicle and strode toward him, taking off his cap and running his arm across his forehead.

"Pe kher ragle." Ullah did not stand, but he welcomed him.

"Mr. Ullah, good to see you," Captain Daradar answered in Pashto as he climbed the steps. "You are well?" In his early thirties, he had golden skin, clear black eyes, and a sober expression.

"Yes, thanks to Allah's blessings. You will honor me by joining me for tea?"

"Of course. I appreciate your hospitality."

As his men waited in the Humvees, Sam Daradar took the other chair, the seat and back lower than the warlord's. It was as if he were sitting next to a king on a throne. He would have found Ullah's little reminders of power amusing, except each was a deadly signal of the complex weave of loyalties and vendettas among Pashtun tribes, and that Afghans in general were often far more anti-foreign than the West was capable of understanding.

"You are patrolling," the warlord said, showing benign interest. "Have you found anything?" He poured tea into cups on the wood table between them.

"Nothing but the wind, the sky, and the earth." Sam gave a short smile.

"Spoken like a true Pashtun. I will never understand why your family moved to the United States."

"We have our wide-open spaces, too. Visit me in Arizona sometime. I'll show you the Grand Canyon." The captain sipped tea. "I got an update today I thought you'd like to hear. Since you helped us oust the Taliban and al-Qaeda, there are two thousand new clinics and schools across the country, jobs are being created constantly, and the bazaar in

Khost is completely rebuilt. Nearly seven million children have been educated through primary school, the new central bank is solid, and the currency is stable."

"It is all good," Ullah said. "I am pleased." He smiled, showing a row of thick white teeth. "Still, there are many problems. Look around you. Such poverty. My people go hungry. It is the corruption in Kabul. No one can solve that."

It was also Ullah's corruption, but Sam was not about to say that. Developing countries tended to have relatively effective central banks and armies but corrupt and despised police forces, and Afghanistan was no exception. Corruption was also why it was easier to build roads than to create law and order, easier to build a school than a state. No amount of education could help a judge faced with drug kingpins prepared to murder his family. It was almost impossible for outsiders to reform this kind of system, and although Ullah liked to think of himself as operating independently from Kabul, he was part of a very broken system.

"I'm concerned about rumors there are Taliban here today," Sam told him.

"Ah, so that is why I have been honored."

"And that some sort of action is in the works, with or without the Taliban."

The Taliban were mostly Pashtuns, and both, like al-Qaeda, were Sunni Muslims. In a country where men with guns reinvented themselves in loyalty to every new power that came along, it was inevitable former Taliban and al-Qaeda fighters were in their ranks. Even Ullah had once pronounced himself Taliban—until the Taliban had outlawed the drug trade when they took over the country. After that, they were his enemy.

"It is Pakistan' fault," the warlord announced. "They should keep the Taliban from crossing the border. They invented them."

"I agree, but neither Pakistan or Afghanistan is succeeding," Sam said mildly. "I know you want nothing but the best for your people. Tell me what's going on."

Ullah's heavy black brows lifted, and his broad mustache twitched. A look of complete innocence crossed his face.

"I have heard nothing," the warlord said. "You can be certain I will call if I receive even a rumor. Would you like more tea?"

The men in the town mosque stood and bowed and stood again, finishing noon prayers. A sense of reverence filled the hall, making Ullah proud. It was his mosque—he had paid for every block and tile.

But then the mullah in his white turban and young face with the neatly trimmed beard commanded all to be seated. They settled themselves on their prayer rugs. Ullah sighed and lowered himself, crossing his legs.

Holding a Koran between his hands, the mullah stood before them, his long black robe flowing. "When the Prophet and his companions went to jihad, they carried black flags because war is not a good thing. When we go to jihad today, it should not be because we want to fight, but because we are compelled to fight for the sake of Islam, and for the freedom of Afghanistan. Still, that is the role of the army and the police—not of private citizens."

Ullah adjusted his backside, inwardly groaning.

"There is only one Allah, and our life on Earth is to serve Him alone," the mullah continued. He stared at Ullah. "But the human is weak, and unwise mullahs with wrong ideas have disobeyed the Koran's laws and sent people onto dangerous paths. This fighting among Muslims and against the West is about power, not about Allah. He does not want our people to be killing. Long ago the Muslim world was under attack in a crusade by Christians who wanted to make all of Islam vanish from the planet. Jihad was about survival then, a last resort. Allah teaches us the greatest jihad is the struggle within each of us for the soul, the jihad of the heart. The heart is a holy place, and we must always take care never to hurt one another."

When the sermon finished, Ullah pointedly ignored the mullah, picked up his AK-47, and strode toward the door, his two guards close behind. The mullah was new and very young, he told himself with disgust. He had a lot to learn about what the Koran really said.

Ahead of him, the forward base's commander, Sam Daradar, was leaving, too. The military man must have arrived late and stayed in the back. Ullah slowed, waiting for him to get far ahead. Then he went out to the doorstep and watched Daradar climb into a Humvee. They exchanged nods and smiled.

Ullah waited impatiently as one of his men ran for the car. But when the silver Toyota Land Cruiser arrived, he noticed a strange expression on his driver's face.

Frowning, he climbed into the passenger seat, and the remaining guard got into the rear, immediately making a small sound deep in his throat. Quickly Ullah turned. Lying on the floor was Sher Chandar, his black Taliban turban beside him, his *shalwar kameez* and vest spread around him like the wings of the angel of death.

"Drive," the Taliban leader ordered.

"I should have killed you a long time ago," Ullah rumbled.

As the vehicle sped down the street, bouncing over potholes, Chandar laughed and gave directions. The street became a dirt road and then a trail that took them up the slopes away from Ullah's villa. When they dropped over the other side, out of sight of the town and the military base and the villa, Chandar sat up, looked around at the bare foothills, and gave more directions.

They circled back around to the rear of Ullah's property and at last lurched down into a deep canyon where a small stream fed a big stand of cypress and pine trees. Uneasiness swept through the warlord—here in this woods was where his men were to gather tonight.

Chandar ordered them to drive into the trees and stop the Toyota beside the American crates, covered with dark tarps. A half-dozen men in black turbans seemed to melt out from among the greenery, pointing assault rifles. Chandar's men.

"Kill the engine." When silence enveloped them, Chandar gestured at the mound of crates. "A gift for the Taliban?"

Ullah said nothing.

"There is a change in plans," Chandar told him. "I know what you were going to do tonight. You will not kill the villagers—some of them are Taliban. Instead your men will put on the American uniforms and arm themselves with the American weapons as they expect to do. Once they are disguised they will be able to get inside the military base. And then they will kill all of the infidels."

Ullah's throat went dry. "It cannot be done."

Chandar chuckled. "You have a greater imagination than that. Your Pakistani journalists will record it from a distance. They will think the Americans are at war with each other in a tribal blood feud as we have here. With that you will have the publicity you need to get the base closed down. That is what you want, is it not?"

Ullah silently cursed.

"These American infidels do not have Allah's blessing," Chandar continued. "We have worked with you these past few years. You have made accommodations. We have made accommodations. If word were to reach Kabul of our arrangement . . ."

He left the sentence unfinished, but Ullah immediately

understood the threat. As weak as the Kabul government was, it still had teeth. If enough troops were dispatched here, he and his family could be erased from the earth.

"The Americans will investigate," Ullah argued. "Instead, I offer a compromise. I will leave unharmed any villagers you wish."

"Not good enough. We want the American soldiers dead. The order comes straight from South Waziristan." In other words, al-Qaeda.

Ullah glanced over his shoulder at Chandar's stony face. Then his gaze swept the six armed men whose rifles pointed unwaveringly at him.

The problem was, if he had killed Chandar when he'd had the chance, another would have taken his place and come to murder him. There was no way he could win this fight. Having decided that, he felt a moment of relief. Chandar's plan could actually work.

"I will do as you wish if you agree to help me later," he decided. "Americans are going to buy the military base property from me and start a business. I do not know exactly what yet. I will need you to agree to their safety."

"At a good price."

Ullah smiled. "Of course. A good price."

Their business concluded, the Taliban leader got out and joined his men in the grove. And then they vanished.

"Home," Ullah commanded.

In his mind he could smell again the sweet aroma of mutton roasting in the kitchen. He was beginning to like the new plan, which meant he would be able to enjoy a good lunch.

As they circled back toward the villa, his satellite phone rang. He answered and heard Martin Chapman's voice. He greeted him in Pashto.

"Are you on schedule?" Chapman asked.

"Of course," the warlord assured him easily, thinking of the infidels who would die. "It will be a fine night, all to Allah's glory."

63

Athens, Greece

As a fresh breeze blew in through the window, Judd sat with Eva and Tucker at the table in the hotel room, her laptop open before them. They were studying NSA's photos and geographical information about the unnamed island that might house the Library of Gold.

There were rocky outcroppings, wide valleys, and rolling hills. The island was ten square miles of beautiful wilderness, except for orchards and a flat-topped mesa on the south side on which stood the three buildings Robin had described.

"The library could be in the big building," Eva said. "But if there are twenty people living there year-round, where are they housed? It doesn't seem large enough."

Judd ran through the small photos on the screen until he found three pictures showing the mesa at a slant. Working quickly, he grew the images, choosing the best. The resolution was excellent, zeroing down to six inches. All had been taken just an hour earlier.

"Four stories underground," Tucker announced. "That answers one question. Too bad the glass is darkened. No way to see inside."

"Now it makes sense. I'll bet the library is down there somewhere," Eva said. "That would be optimum for keeping out sunlight and controlling for humidity, temperature, and so forth."

They had already seen armed guards patrolling in Jeeps—

thirty men, two in each vehicle—on the dirt roads that ribbonned the island and gave access to remote areas. Judd focused on one pair.

"M4 assault rifles. They're not there to play games. Do you recognize anyone, Tucker?" He showed him photo after photo.

"No, all strangers," Tucker said. "Check one of the beaches. Let's see what other kinds of security the island has."

Judd clicked a photo, making it bigger and bigger. "There are your security cameras, Tucker. And look—movement- and heat-sensing monitors."

"Swell."

"We saw squirrels and birds. Wouldn't they set off the monitors' alarms?" Eva asked.

"The system can be programmed to ignore wildlife," Judd explained.

They analyzed the other beaches and the cliffs around the island, finding the same tight protection everywhere.

"It's a fortress." Eva's voice was discouraged.

Judd focused on the wharf, where a cargo ship was docked. Men were carrying boxes onto it.

"They're loading something." Eva stared. "I wonder what that means."

"Did either of you see any guard dogs?" Judd adjusted himself in his chair, pushing from his mind the aching gunshot wound in his side.

Both shook their heads.

"At least we have that. Okay, so let's focus on the cliff beneath the compound."

They studied the photos.

"Very steep," Tucker said. "At least five hundred feet high, I'd say. It'd be impossible to dodge the cameras and monitors if we tried to climb it."

"You're right. Let's check the top of the mesa."

Judd enlarged more photos, showing the swimming pool, a picnic area, and a satellite dish. A gardener was watering plants on an outdoor patio, and a woman was setting out buckets of balls on the tennis courts. Two dirt roads coming from the east and west converged north of the complex and became a two-car cement driveway that ran south, passing the satellite dish and descending under the east side of the main house. There on the flat area beside the house stood a mountain of boxes and crates. Men were loading them into a van. Following the drive east, Judd saw it curved not only north but south, to the wharf.

"I don't like this," he muttered. He chose photos of the buildings' exteriors.

"No monitors," Tucker said. "They probably figured no one was ever going to get close enough to be a threat. Zero in on the ground-floor windows of the big house."

Judd did. The windows extended across and around the building, showcasing the ocean view. Tall glass panels were open to the air. They could see two middle-age women in white skirts and blouses walking across the main room inside, carrying drinks on trays.

"No sign of Preston," Judd said. "Or Yitzhak and Roberto." Then he noticed more boxes against the back.

He enlarged the photos, homing in. The stack was so tall and wide it looked like a wall. Beside it, pieces of furniture waited, covered with sheets.

Tucker leaned close. "My God, they're packing up and moving out. Crap."

"They could be gone tomorrow," Judd agreed. "We could lose the Library of Gold."

A worried hush filled the room.

"This isn't going to be easy," Eva observed. "There are a lot more guards than Robin told us. We saw thirty in the Jeeps alone."

"She said tonight was the annual banquet," Judd reminded her. "She expected more security, but you're right—this is getting increasingly dangerous. Yitzhak and Roberto may be hostages, so we've got to save them as well as figure out who's behind Dad's murder and what the Library of Gold has to do with terrorism. Whatever it is, Dad must've felt it was imminent. And now we've got the pressure of the library's being moved. If we don't go in soon, we might never find it again."

"Can we call in Catapult for help?" Eva asked Tucker. "How about Langley?"

The spymaster drummed his fingers on the tabletop. "Hudson Canon is likely working for the other side, so we don't want him to discover where we are and what we're up to. It's safest to tell no one. But I have a partial solution: There's a small U.S. naval base at Souda Bay, on Crete. It's not far from the island. If we don't have any of our paramilitary teams stationed there now, Gloria should be able to stay out of Hudson's way long enough to pull some strings to get a couple sent over for short-term duty."

Judd nodded. "I like that. We can use some help."

Tucker took out his mobile and turned it on. Then he dialed. "Gloria isn't answering," he told them. Then into the phone: "This is Tucker. Call me as soon as you get my message."

Judd stared at his watch and frowned. "Gloria knows the operation's gone hot. Shouldn't she answer no matter what? For Chrissakes, she must be home in bed. It's the middle of the night there. Surely the call would've awakened her."

"Not if she's deactivated her mobile," Tucker reminded him. "I'm going to check my e-mail."

Judd looked for e-mail on his mobile, too. Then he checked for messages. "Nothing."

"Take a gander at this," Tucker said grimly and turned the screen so Judd and Eva could read.

> Canon is hunting you. I talked to Debi, who told me he has NSA tracking Judd's and your mobiles. I'm sending this from a new BlackBerry. No encoding. I'm going to toss it. You're on your own. Get rid of those mobiles! Sorry.

Shock filled the room.

"We've got to get out of here." Judd jumped to his feet.

Eva opened the duffel and threw things inside.

"I'll be back with my stuff." Tucker ran out the door.

In minutes they were packed. As Judd opened the window and peered down, Tucker stuck his head inside the door.

"Give me your mobile."

Judd tossed it. "What are you—"

But Tucker had vanished.

Judd zipped the duffel. "I'll go first," he told Eva.

Slinging it over his shoulder, he crawled out onto the ledge. A warm wind whistled past. They were five stories above a driveway that resembled a narrow alley. On the other side stood another hotel, brick and as tall as theirs. Sunlight filtered down between, leaving half the drive in shadow.

"Come on, Eva." He reached a hand inside the window and felt her firm grip.

Her shoulder satchel hanging across her back, she gingerly crawled out onto the ledge beside him.

She looked around. "Thank God there's a fire escape. After London, I can now claim to have experience."

"I'm here," Tucker announced from inside, behind their legs.

They moved aside, and he pulled himself out onto the ledge. "My room faces the hotel's rear, and there was a bus with luggage on top getting ready to leave. It was too good an opportunity to pass up. I threw the mobiles onto it. Now they'll have a moving target to follow. Canon's probably having NSA live-tracking our mobiles."

"That could buy us some time," Judd agreed.

He swung a foot onto the metal rung and started down. He felt the fire escape wobble as Eva, then Tucker, followed him. He looked back up to check on them.

"So how are we going to get on the island?" Eva asked.

"Can you parachute?" Tucker replied.

"Who, me?"

"I thought not. The safest way is to go in at night with black parachutes and gear. I have a former colleague in town who can help with that. I'm hoping the Library of Gold banquet will be a good distraction to cover us, since it looks as if we're going into the serpent's mouth without hope of backup."

Judd felt a chill. "We can't take you with us," he told Eva. "You're not trained. Too damn dangerous."

"You're not leaving me behind." Her eyes glinted. "I'll parachute in with one of you. You may need what I know about the library."

Tucker made a decision. "She's right. This is too important to fuck up."

Judd did not like it. A wave of worry shot through him as he reached the third story. Then he froze. The two men who had been with Preston on the Metro were striding from the rear of the building, their heads swiveling, their hands against their ears, clasping cell phones as they listened. Their other hands were inside their jackets. They had still not looked up.

"Shit," Eva muttered behind him.

Judd gave himself a shake to loosen his muscles. The noise of a large engine sounded, and a long white-and-gray tourist bus entered the drive behind the men, cruising toward the street. A short toot of the horn sounded, causing the pair of killers to scramble to the side—to their hotel's side—so the bus could pass. They were less than thirty feet away.

Judd whispered over his shoulder, "We're going to join our mobiles."

Tucker sighed and nodded. Eva stared at him, then gave a short nod.

Going as quietly as he could, Judd continued down as the bus neared. But then the fire escape creaked behind him. At the noise, Preston's men gazed up in unison. Their pistols appeared in their hands as the tourist bus rolled beneath the fire escape.

"Let's go!" Judd leaped, landing hard on two flat canvas suitcases.

Eva and Tucker dropped near the rear of the bus. All of them burrowed down among the piles of luggage. Shouts followed the bus as it turned onto the street.

"Are you all right?" Judd asked immediately.

They nodded and turned, studying the hotel. Preston ran out the front door and gestured. A van squealed to the curb, and he jumped inside. The lumbering bus was no race car, and Preston would soon catch up.

"Is that who I think it is?" Tucker had been staring at the jeans and black jacket.

"Himself," Judd said. "That asshole Preston."

"Oh, hell," Eva said. "What do we do now?"

"Improvise. Come on." Judd scrambled to the sidewalk side of the bus.

Traffic noises filled the air. They were going downhill, passing Platia Exarchia. Shops, restaurants, hotels, and office buildings lined the avenue. From their elevated vantage point, they watched it all.

"I know this section." Eva was looking ahead. "See that big building in the next block? That's where we want to go. It's a parking garage."

They peered back. There was only one car between them and Preston's van.

"You know," Tucker decided. "I'm tired of this. You handle the parking garage. I'll take care of Preston. Then I'll catch up." He slid out his Browning.

"Are you sure?" Judd asked.

"I'm not *that* old, Judson."

The bus rumbled on. As they neared the garage, Tucker hunched up enough so he would be visible to the van. He scuttled across the bus to the street side. Over the luggage, Judd watched the van pull into the other lane to be closer to Tucker.

"But he *is* old," Eva worried.

"If only a tenth of everything I've heard about him is true, he can more than handle himself."

As Tucker aimed his pistol, they turned to watch again for the parking garage. They were only one building away. Grasping the guardrails atop the bus, they slid over, their legs dangling, and dropped and staggered. At the same time, a rain of gunfire sounded from above and from the van on the other side. The bus wobbled. Judd had a brief glimpse of passengers' faces, stunned, then horrified, by the sight of him and Eva. They whipped their heads around to peer across the bus toward the noise of gunshots.

Judd pulled out his Beretta and ran toward the driver's side of a car that had just pulled into the garage.

"Give me your keys," he demanded of the driver as he emerged.

The driver's face was white. His clenched fist opened, and the keys started to slide off.

Judd snatched them, and Eva slid into the car's passenger seat. Hearing the loud noise of a car crash, from his peripheral vision Judd saw Preston's van had hit a car in the oncoming lane of traffic. Tucker slid off the back of the bus, stumbled, and ran onto the sidewalk toward them. His corrugated face showed a grim smile.

Judd opened the rear door of the car, then dropped in behind the steering wheel. He gunned the motor. Breathing heavily, Tucker fell into the backseat and slammed the door.

"Did you erase Preston?" Judd said.

"Don't know," Tucker rumbled. "But there are enough holes in the top of that van, it looks like a fine Swiss cheese."

"Drive straight ahead," Eva ordered. "This parking garage has an exit onto the next street. They'll never find us."

Until the next time, Judd thought but did not say. He slammed the accelerator.

64

The Isle of Pericles

At four o'clock in the afternoon the eight members of the book club flew toward the Isle of Pericles in a comfortable Bell helicopter. Although the rotors chopped noisily, and the craft vibrated, Martin Chapman was enjoying himself. He had spoken with Syed Ullah before taking off and had received a good report. The news of the warlord's success in Khost should reach him during the banquet.

As the helicopter circled, Chapman stared down at the lush thyme-covered hills, the stately olive and palm trees, the wild native herbs. Acres of blooming citrus groves swept over the hills. Glistening waterfalls spilled at the ends of ravines. Smiling to himself, he took in the white pebbled beaches, the deserted coves, and the dramatic seaside cliffs, savoring the fact this secret Shangri-la had belonged only to him and few others.

The craft swept low over the south beach, passing the wharf where the cargo ship was being packed, and then up the valley toward the mesa, lower than surrounding hills. On it stood the Library of Gold compound, built a half century ago. Just beneath were four long stories of darkened glass, set into the steep slope and largely invisible from above and difficult to spot from the beach. Most of what went on at the compound was beneath the surface.

The craft landed on the helipad, and Chapman climbed out, the other book club members following. Their heads and shoulders low to avoid the whirling blades, they hurried off. At the same time, Preston gave a signal, and an equal number of bodyguards rushed toward it. Each grabbed one member's bag and briefcase.

A sense of anticipation was in the salty sea air as the eight walked toward the buildings, Preston and the guards following.

"Damn disappointing we won't have a librarian tonight," Brian Collum said as he adjusted his sunglasses.

"It is most unfortunate we will not have a tournament," Petr Klok agreed. "I will miss that a great deal. I spent two days preparing with the translators."

"Think of something, Marty," ordered Maurice Dresser, the eldest member. The bossy Canadian oil man strode out ahead, the hot sun turning the skin on his skull pink beneath his thin white hair. "That's an assignment."

The others glanced at Martin Chapman good-naturedly. But with Charles Sherback and Robin Miller eliminated—their only librarians—there was no way the tournament could go on.

"Yes, Marty. It's your problem." Reinhardt Gruen deadpanned.

"Absolutely," Martin Chapman said, continuing the conviviality. Then he had an idea. "The impossible is nothing to me. That's why you voted me director."

"I need a drink—and I want to see the menu so I can start salivating," Dresser said over his shoulder. "Then who wants a round of tennis?"

They entered the grassy compound with its rows of roses. Glazed in sunlight, the three simple white buildings with their Doric columns stood like Grecian tributes to the past. The Olympic-size swimming pool shimmered. The tennis court was empty, but obviously not for long. Behind the complex rose a huge satellite dish, the island's link to the outside world. Once a village had covered the mesa and surrounding hills, its main source of income high-quality salt mines. But the mines had worn out, and now the island's only inhabitants besides the regular staff were rodents, seagulls, flamingos, and other birds.

"Damn, I'm going to miss this place," Collum said.

"Won't we all," Grandon Holmes agreed. "Pity to have to move the library. Still, I've always liked the Alps."

"We knew this day would come," Chapman reminded them.

Silently they passed two cottages. Charles Sherback had lived in one; the other was Preston's. They entered the big main house, which encircled a palm-shaded reflecting pool. Chapman paused to enjoy the view one last time. All was as it had been on his last visit. Decorated with Greek furniture, the walls full of museum-quality paintings from across Europe. Chandeliers of Venetian glass glittered, hanging on wrought-iron chains from the high ceiling. Ancient Greek statues and vases stood here and there on the glowing white marble floor, quarried on Mount Penteli, near Athens. A walk-in fireplace of the same marble stretched across the end of the long room. The air was cool, thanks to the giant temperature-control system buried belowground. Men were moving furniture from other rooms toward the elevator and down to where it would be loaded onto trucks to be taken to the cargo ship.

The guest rooms were on this floor, in three of the arms around the reflecting pool. The book club split into two groups, each heading into a different wing to go to their usual rooms.

Chapman entered his suite, his bodyguard a respectful six feet behind. "You're new." He turned to study the man, who had a tanned face. It was one Chapman did not recognize.

"Yes, sir. You're Martin Chapman. I read about you in an

article in *Vanity Fair,* the one about your big equity deal to buy Sheffield-Riggs. The financing was a thing of beauty. My name is Harold Kardasian. Preston brought me in this morning from Majorca with two others."

Majorca was known as a home for wealthy independent mercenaries. The guard was sturdy, obviously athletic from the way he moved, with thick brown hair that had streaks of gray at the temples. A pistol was on his hip. He was in his early fifties, Chapman judged, and had a touch of class—refined features, erect posture, deferential without being obsequious. Chapman liked that.

"You're a short-timer?" he asked.

"Just here for the two days you'll be here. I'd heard about Preston for years, so of course I signed up so I could work with him. Didn't know I'd have the privilege of working for you, too, Mr. Chapman."

Preston appeared in the doorway. "I'll take those." As Kardasian left, he laid the suitcase on the butler's stand and the briefcase on the desk.

Chapman went to the window. He looked out, drinking in the panorama of the sky, the wind-carved island, and the impossibly blue sea. When Preston handed him the menu, he ran his gaze down the seven-course feast.

"Excellent," he said. "You've made arrangements to blow up the buildings as soon as we've moved out?"

"Yes. I estimate tomorrow afternoon. By the time we're finished, all evidence the library or we were ever here will be scrubbed."

Chapman nodded. "Any problems on the island?"

"None. The chefs and food are here. They've been in the kitchen all day. A few loud arguments but no serious fights so far—maybe I'll get off easy this year. The silver is polished. The crystal is shined. The wine is standing up. The library never looked better. I've ordered more than the usual extra security men. A total of fifty in all. Everyone's oriented and knows their assignments."

"Good. Send the translators to my office and tell them to wait. I need to talk with them after I finish some phone calls." He turned to study Preston, noticing a faint red streak down his cheek. "Any news about Judd Ryder and Eva Blake?"

"I almost caught them in Athens again. A very close call."

Chapman gestured. "Is that what happened to your face?"

Preston's hand went to his cheek, and he grimaced. "As I said, it was close. Now I know why we couldn't find Tucker Andersen—he's with them. Hudson Cannon learned they've been searching for the island, using our coordinates."

"Christ! Then we have to count on them coming here." Chapman thought a moment. "On the other hand, one's a rank amateur, and another is past his prime. You have fifty highly trained men on security. In the end, taking care of them on the island may be our best solution. They'll simply disappear, and Langley will never know what happened to them, or where."

65

Langley, Virginia

At nine o'clock in the morning the storied seventh floor in the CIA's old headquarters building bustled with activity. Behind the closed doors were the offices of the director of Central Intelligence and the other top espionage executives, plus conference rooms and special operations and support centers. Gloria Feit hurried along the corridor, passing staff carrying briefcases, plastic clipboards, and color-coded folders. The air exuded a sense of urgency. Usually she felt a thrill being here, but right now her mind was on failed operations—and their costs.

Hudson Canon had told her to spend the night thinking about Tucker Andersen and the Library of Gold mission, but she would have anyway. She had tossed and turned and stalked the floor until daybreak.

Worried, she stepped into the suite of Matthew Kelley, chief of the Clandestine Service.

His secretary looked up from her desk. "He's expecting you."

When Gloria tapped on the door, a strong voice answered, "Come in."

As she walked into his spacious room of books, family photographs, and framed CIA awards, Matt rose from behind his expansive desk, smiling. A tall man with a warm, lined face, he had looked like the perfect spy in his day, nondescript, dowdy, almost invisible. Now slightly more public, he was able to show his taste. Today he was dressed in a sleek tailored suit and a cuffed white shirt. With his angular face and the hint of predatoriness he once relied upon, he looked as if he had just stepped off the fashion page of a men's magazine.

They shook hands. "Good to see you, Gloria. It's been a while. How's Ted?"

He gestured, and they sat at the coffee table in the distant end of his office. He chose a leather armchair, and she took the sofa.

They exchanged family information for only a minute, then Matt got down to business. "You've got a situation. What is it?"

"Did you close down the Library of Gold operation?" she asked.

"Yes. Tucker's got a burr under his saddle, that's all."

"Would Hudson ordinarily have brought you in on the decision?"

"Of course not. But it was a pet project of Cathy's, and he wanted to make certain I'd be on board." He frowned. "Your point?"

"What would you say if I told you I'm beginning to think Cathy's car accident was no accident?"

Matt went rigid. "Fill me in."

For the next half hour Gloria described the events she knew about or had learned earlier this morning by going through Tucker's and Cathy's e-mails and notes. "After Tucker left Catapult, I got a call from him. He'd just captured a janitor at Capitol City market. While I collected the janitor, Tucker left to join Ryder and Blake in Athens."

"You believe Hudson alerted someone. That's why the janitor was there to do a wet job on Tucker."

"Yes."

Matt thought about it. "It's flimsy evidence against Hudson

at best. Janitors could've been taking turns, waiting outside Catapult for days for Tucker to appear."

"But how did the book club people find Ryder and Blake in Istanbul? Tucker believed the only explanation was someone inside Catapult told them. The one person who knew was Hudson Canon."

"That damns Hudson—but only if Tucker is right." Matt changed the subject. "That's a hell of a thing to do, Gloria. Christ. Sticking the janitor down in the basement on your own authority."

She lifted her chin. "We've got a mole inside Catapult. The operation has to be protected. The guy's fine. I've got his hands and legs cuffed to a heavy chair. He gets three squares a day, better than a lot of people in the world."

"A desk job hasn't changed you a damn bit." He sighed. "All right, I want the janitor." He picked up the phone on the coffee table, then glanced at her. "I'm going to have to tell Hudson. He could still be innocent."

Her throat tightened. " 'Flimsy evidence.' I understand."

He dialed. "Hello, Hudson. This is Matt. Gloria's sitting with me in my office. She tells me she's got a two-legged source secured in Catapult's cellar." He moved the phone from his ear, and Gloria heard a stream of loud oaths. Then he continued. "We'll worry about disciplining her later. The man's a janitor. Tucker was his target. We need to question him. Have two of your people bring him to Langley. I want him here immediately."

"Tell him I left the keys to the basement on my desk," Gloria said.

Matt sighed and said into the phone, "The keys are on her desk. We should talk. I want you to come with them. I'll be in my office."

"We need to help Tucker," Gloria said as soon as he had ended the connection. "I checked with Catapult's com center and found out Blake, Ryder, and he have been looking into a privately owned Aegean island. My guess is that that's where the Library of Gold is hidden, which means they're going to be heading for it soon. Maybe they're already on their way. Judging by all the deaths so far, it's going to be a very dangerous insertion. But we've got a naval base on Crete. We could send fast-rope teams from there." She peered at her watch. It was nearly six P.M. in Greece.

But Matt was not going to be hurried. "You could be right. Still, first things first—Hudson and the janitor. If Hudson is the mole, then he's got a handler. The handler could have the information we need. Look at it this way: Maybe Tucker isn't planning to go to the island. Maybe it's the wrong island, or something might've happened to change his mind altogether. Do you have a way to reach him?"

She shook her head anxiously. "I'm hoping the janitor or Hudson knows more than I do. If not, unless Tucker decides to risk phoning or e-mailing me, he and the others are hanging in the wind."

"I'm sorry about that. But there's no way I'm invading a private island in Greece's territory unless I've got something concrete to go on. The last thing Langley needs is an international incident. We'll just have to trust Tucker's good sense—and his luck."

Washington, D.C.

Hudson Canon could hardly breathe. He turned away from his desk, leaned over, and pounded a fist into his palm. Gritting his teeth, he threw his head back and kept pounding. Eventually the fear eased. Sitting upright, he took long, deep breaths.

Then he phoned Reinhardt Gruen. "We've got a problem." He described the phone call from Matt Kelley at Langley.

"What does your janitor know?" Then, demanding: "Does he know about *me*?"

There was a long pause. With relief he heard a soothing calmness in Gruen's voice: "It is not the end of the world, my friend," the German told him. "The assassin was hired anonymously. He has no way to track either us or you. Do as your chief says. Go with the janitor and your people to Langley and act like the great spy chief you are. You are safe."

Isle of Pericles

Furious about the botched handling of the situation in Washington, Reinhardt Gruen snapped out a hand with his cell phone. The Isle of Pericles attendant instantly took it and replaced it with a thick towel. Drying himself, Gruen stalked away from the swimming pool.

"Giving up so soon?" Brian Collum challenged from behind. "One more race. What do you say, Reinhardt? Come on, man. Come on!"

Damn Americans, Gruen muttered under his breath. "Hold onto your trunks. I will return."

He found Martin Chapman sitting behind his desk in his office, surrounded by pedestals on which stood classic marble statues he had collected in Greece. Lined up before him were the library's four translators, two men and two women, dressed in tuxedos to help serve at the banquet. All scholars, they were graying and had the hunched shoulders of those who spent long hours poring over books. Their expertise was critical to the book club's ability to use and enjoy the library, and as such, each was treated with a certain amount of deference. That was even more true of the librarians—unless their loyalty was in question.

Gruen put a smile on his face. "I see you are plotting with

our great translators, Martin. Are you by any chance finished? I would like to have a word with you."

Chapman laid two sheets of paper on his desk, then placed a hand possessively on them. "Yes, they've just finished a job for me, and they've given me a good report. The library's records are already on the boat. As soon as the banquet is over, they'll pack their personal things. They'll be ready to go at daybreak."

"Good, good." Gruen stepped aside to let the translators leave. When the door closed, he scowled. "I just received a call from Hudson Canon in Washington." He fell into a leather chair. "The janitor Preston sent is locked up at Catapult and will soon be on his way to Langley. Canon has been ordered to go with them. I told him he had no exposure and calmed him down. What is the truth?"

Chapman grimaced. "The janitor knows Preston hired him. Goddammit all to hell. When will this end!" He ran his fingers through his hair. "We'll handle Andersen, Ryder, and Blake if they manage to reach the island. But we can't let either the janitor or Canon get to Langley." He snatched the phone from his desk and punched in numbers. "Preston, I need you. Now!"

Washington, D.C.

The morning traffic was thick as Michael Hawthorne drove Catapult's only armored van out of the city and onto the bridge across the Potomac. Hudson Canon sat beside him, arms crossed, fighting nerves as he planned what he would say to Matt. In the rear seat was the shackled janitor, while next to him Brandon Ohr kept guard with an assault rifle. The two young covert officers had been happy to get away from their desks at Catapult even for such a small assignment.

"I heard Debi has a new boyfriend," Michael was saying.

"She ever level that killer gaze on you?" Brandon said. "My God, that woman has balls."

"Agreed. What a turn-on—" He stopped. "Do you see what I see?" He stared into his rearview mirror.

"I've been watching it. A black Volvo, heavy as a tank. It's just closed in. Pull out." Ohr spoke in the usual neutral tones of the professional spy when facing potential trouble.

Canon's head spun around and he peered through the back window. The Volvo was right behind, its front bumper only ten feet distant. On one side of them was speeding traffic, while on the other the guardrail rushed past—and far below was the fast-moving Potomac River.

Without activating his turn signal, Hawthorne gave a sharp yank to the steering wheel, driving the van away and into the safety of the inner lane.

But suddenly a loud horn gave a long blast. A behemoth truck was rushing up on them, preparing to pass, its big cab high above. Instantly, Hawthorne accelerated, pushing their van into the open space ahead, catching up with the red pickup that had preceded them onto the bridge. Canon saw if they could get clear, Hawthorne could move the van into the inner lane and outrun the big truck.

But almost instantly red taillights flashed and held. The pickup was slowing. And the truck was keeping pace, while the Volvo was locked on their tail.

As Ohr lowered his window and raised his assault rifle, Canon snapped to Hawthorne: "They've got us trapped. I don't care what you do, but get us out of here!"

Before Hawthorne could respond, the big cab of the truck slammed into the van's side. The van yawed. Canon was thrown against his seat belt, then deep into the hard seat. Gripping his windowsill with one hand, Ohr let out a long blast from the assault rifle, ripping through the passenger door of the towering truck cab. Immediately Hawthorne floored the gas pedal and rammed the rear of the pickup.

Too late. The cab smashed again into their van and held. Hawthorne fought the steering wheel, trying to push back. But by inches, then by feet, the van was pushed to the side. Canon's throat went dry as he peered over into the water.

There was the screech of metal against metal as the van crashed along the guardrail. Sparks exploded past his window. The truck nudged the van one last time, and suddenly they smashed through the rail and sailed off into the air. Canon's heart thundered. He screamed, and the van dove headfirst into the Potomac.

66

The Isle of Pericles

Drenched in moonlight, the Library of Gold's private island rose suddenly from the dark sea, its high craggy ridges pale, its deep valleys eerily shadowed. Judd was studying it from the window of the Cessna Super Cargomaster piloted by Tucker's friend Haris Naxos. Night lights off, the craft was circling and would soon climb to jump altitude: ten thousand feet.

Time had run out, and they were going in without backup. All were hyper alert and not talking about the danger.

"There's the orange grove and the landing spot we picked," Eva said.

Eva and Judd were sitting together in seats that stretched along the cargo bin's side walls. Like Tucker, who was in the copilot's seat, they wore black jumpsuits and helmets. Infrared goggles dangled from their necks, and black grease covered their faces. They had come prepared not only with their pistols, which were holstered to their waists, but Judd and Tucker had grenades and mini Uzis lashed to their legs. Tucker wore a parachute pack on his back, while Judd had a larger one, holding a bigger canopy that would support both his and Eva's weight. The two men had additional packs containing supplies. Eva carried nothing on her back, since she would be strapped to Judd.

Judd nodded. "Yes, it should work well." He was loaded with painkillers and feeling only a dull ache in his side.

They had been observing the headlights of Jeeps roaming over the island, looking for patterns. One had driven past the orange grove. Now, a half hour later, another passed.

"How's the air clarity seem to you, Haris?" Tucker asked as the plane climbed.

"It is no change. Looks good for you to land." Haris Naxos was gray-haired, angular, and tough-looking; he still did occasional contract work. "You are no spring rooster, Tucker. Night jumping is dangerous. Be careful."

"I know. There are old jumpers and bold jumpers, but there are no old, bold jumpers."

Haris laughed, but no one else did. As usual Judd was planning what he would do if the chutes did not deploy, the lines became tangled, all the myriad events that could go wrong.

After a while, Haris asked, "You remember everything I told you, Eva?" He had given her a half hour of instructions and walked her through a video of tandem skydiving, at his hangar in the Athens airport. He owned a parachuting and plane rental business.

"There's no way I'm going to forget anything." A fleck of nervousness was in her voice.

"Excellent. Then I make the announcement—we are at jump altitude, and we are approaching the drop zone."

Judd and Eva stood up in the plane. She turned around, and he snapped their straps together and tightened his, then hers until her back was secure against his chest. Her body was tense. Her rose-water scent filled his mind. Quickly he dismissed it.

"Okay?" he asked curtly.

"Okay."

As they put on goggles, Tucker crawled into the rear cargo area. "I'll open the door."

He was moving agilely, his expression focused. As Judd

and Eva hung onto the ceiling straps, he unlocked the door, swung the handle, and pushed. Cold air blasted in.

Turning on the visual altimeter that was secured inside his helmet, the reader in easy peripheral view, Judd positioned Eva so they were facing the cockpit. Their right sides were inches from the black void.

"Go!" the pilot shouted.

"Try to enjoy it, Eva," Judd whispered.

Before she could speak, he rolled them out of the plane. Abruptly they were in free fall, soaring at speeds in excess of a hundred sixty miles an hour, their arms and legs extended together like wings. The silky air enveloped him, and there was no sense of falling—air resistance gave a feeling of weight and direction. Checking their orientation over the island, he reveled in the exhilaration of complete freedom.

"This is one of those rare moments when you know what it's like to be a bird in flight," he told her. "We can do anything a bird can do—except go back up."

As Tucker jumped out of the plane, Judd repositioned Eva until they were sitting in a ball in the air. He somersaulted her, then straightened her out again, rolling them onto their sides, their backs, and around again, spinning freely. He felt her tense more, and then she gave a joyful laugh.

Returning them to a normal descent, he reached behind and threw out the drogue parachute, lines and small canopy black against the stars. All was well so far. The drogue slowed their free-fall speed from two people to that of a single skydiver. He saw Tucker was nodding, indicating his equipment was working properly, too.

At twenty-five hundred feet, Judd pulled a toggle, and the deployment bag fell out and released the main canopy—a black ram-air parachute. It caught the wind and spread out into the shape of a large cupped wedge. There were a few seconds of intense deceleration, and then they were skydiving at about twelve miles an hour. He studied the area beneath them. Noted the forest of citrus trees, the open space of weeds and boulders awash in shades of green through his infrared goggles, and the long ravine to the south. A Jeep was just passing the trees, so they had about a half hour until the next one arrived. Their biggest immediate risk was broken ankles, assuming they missed the trees and boulders.

As they continued to soar horizontally, lower and lower, he tugged on the lines, directing their flight. So far no more headlights showed near the drop zone.

At one hundred feet, he felt a huge downdraft, and it seemed as if they were heading into a black-green hole. Again Eva tensed. He drew on the lines, controlling their direction and silently gliding, gliding. Satisfied, he used his body to push Eva upright and his knees to angle her knees into a crouch. They swept between tall boulders and landed hard, stumbling to a stop just before they reached the road that skirted the trees. He could feel her heaving for air.

"You did it." He unsnapped the straps that joined them. "Good job. Now let's get the hell out of the way."

He released the drogue and ram-air chutes, and they hurried off. As they gathered the canopies, Tucker slid in low. He yanked his lines, barely missing a shoulder-high boulder. Knees bent, he landed and staggered, finally catching his balance.

Standing stationary, he lifted his head. "Screw you, Haris. This old rooster still has a hell of a lot of life left in him." Then he smiled and collected his chutes.

"Everything went right," Eva said excitedly. "The parachutes opened. No one broke a leg. I could get used to this."

Then a bird called from the trees. There was rustling in the grove—fast movement.

"Shit." Judd pulled out his Beretta. "They were waiting for us. Run!"

Weapons in hands, they tore south across the hard earth toward the ravine. Judd glanced behind and saw six men dressed in black swarming out of the trees, aiming M4 assault rifles. They had night-vision goggles. Shooting as they ran, the men poured out fusillades of rounds. The bullets whined and bit into earth and rocks. Tucker grunted. A round clipped Judd's ear. All three fell flat. Judd pointed, and Eva scuttled into the shelter of a tall rock formation. Judd and Tucker followed.

From the southwest, a Jeep's headlights came to life, and the vehicle rushed along the road toward them. The air reverberated with the noise of feet pounding and the engine's growl.

"Christ," Tucker grumbled. "I hate being ambushed."

"Are you hit?" Judd gazed at Tucker, then checked Eva's blackened face, saw the tightness of her mouth. She seemed all right.

Tucker shook his head. "I'm fine. That's a cute cut on your ear, Judd. Glad they didn't take your brains. The ravine isn't far. Eva, we'll cover you. As soon as we start shooting, stay low and run like hell. Can you do that?"

"Of course." She crouched.

The two men took either side of the rocky mound. Judd peered at Tucker. He nodded. They edged out, firing automatic bursts from their Uzis.

As the ear-bleeding gunfire continued behind her, Eva reached the ravine and dropped quickly at the edge, legs dangling over. From the NSA photos, they had calculated it averaged ten feet deep. It led around and down toward the compound. The shadows were a thick green. Only the top of her side of the nearly vertical slope was slightly illuminated, showing raw dirt, weeds, and rocks. Gripping her

S&W in both hands the way Judd had showed her, in seconds she was plummeting down on her back into the abyss.

But as she slid deep into the green darkness her gaze was attracted to a boulder across from her at the bottom. Then she saw a small movement there, an arm. A man was squatting to make himself small. Fear started to take over her mind. She repressed it and aimed her pistol. Suddenly there was movement to her right. And she swung the gun, a mistake she realized instantly. A foot slashed through the air. Her pistol flew, and two very strong men were on her.

The jeep was just a thousand feet away. Judd saw one man in it, driving. For some reason the man stopped the vehicle, engine still running, and leaned across and opened the passenger door.

Eva had deployed safely, so Judd gestured at Tucker. Tucker grimaced and looked as if he were going to argue. Then he leaped up and ran.

Judd leaned out again and shot three bursts. They had managed to take down one man, and the others were lying flat, shooting whenever they thought they had a target and sometimes when they did not.

Before the guards had time to return fire, Judd sprinted, and Tucker vanished down the ravine. Judd did not look, just jumped and let his heels act as inefficient brakes as he slipped and careened down the steep incline into heavy green soup.

Tucker's head was rotating. "Where is she?"

"Eva," Judd called in a low voice.

There was no answer, but there was a yell from above.

"They're coming," Tucker said. "Let's move."

"Not without Eva. Eva!" Judd shouted.

"Dammit, son. They've probably got her. She'd be waiting otherwise. Maybe that's why the Jeep stopped with its door open—to pick up her and whoever captured her. You're not going to do her any good if you get caught or killed. *Move.*"

Judd said nothing. Instead he turned to go down the ravine to the Jeep. To Eva.

But Tucker slammed the back of his helmet. "Dammit, Judson. *The other direction.*"

Judd shook his head to clear it, then ripped off the helmet. They ran southeast, toward the compound. Tucker pulled off his helmet, and both replenished their ammo. The ravine was uneven, filled with rocks slowing their progress.

"This isn't working," Judd said, listening to the noise of the feet running along the top of the ravine, overtaking them. "We need to get rid of the bastards. You go. I'll handle them."

From a trouser loop, he unhooked a frag grenade and held it in his right hand. Tucker saw it and accelerated, while Judd slid low into the deep shadows on the ravine's north side.

He waited motionless as the guards approached.

"They're heading to the house," a confident bass voice said.

Radio or walkie-talkie, Judd thought.

"Sure," the man continued. "No problem. We'll get them."

They were almost above him. Judd inhaled, exhaled, pulled the safety pin with his left hand, rolled the grenade over the crest, and sprinted, his boots hitting rocks so fast his speed kept him upright. White light flashed. The explosion thundered. As dirt rained down, he caught up with Tucker, who had hiked himself up the side and was peering back.

"No one's upright," Tucker reported. "They've got to have some serious injuries. That'll keep them busy."

They jogged off, but Judd saw Tucker was tiring. Judd slowed them to a fast walk and took out the reader that followed the tracker in Eva's ankle bracelet.

"She's in the compound already. Looks as if she's a couple

of levels down under the main house." He gazed at Tucker. "Did you see any Jeeps anywhere near us?"

"Nary a one."

"Too bad. I was hoping we could grab one. Okay, Plan B. When we get closer to the compound, I've got an idea how to get us inside."

"It'd better be a damn good one," Tucker said. "They sure as hell are going to be ready for us."

67

The book club was about to start the third course. In their tailored tuxedos, with pistols holstered underneath, the men lounged around the great oval table in the spacious Library of Gold, firm in their knowledge the intruders would be killed if not by the guards, then certainly by them.

As they talked, their gazes kept returning to the magnificent illuminated manuscripts that blanketed the walls from marble floor to cove ceiling. Row after row of gold covers faced out, their hand-hammered faces reverberating with light that echoed from wall to wall and across the table like visual music. From dark, rich colors to soft pastels, the jewels and gems glittered and beckoned. The entire room seemed cast in a magical glow. Being here was always a visceral experience, and Martin Chapman sighed with contentment.

"Gentlemen, you have before you two exquisite Montrachet dry white wines," the sommelier explained in a thick French accent."One is Domaine Leflaive, and the other Domaine de la Romanée-Conti. You will be possessed by their thrill factor—the hallmark of splendor in wine." A muscular man with the usual snooty expression of a top wine steward, he disappeared back against the books near the door, where his bureau of wine bottles stood.

Chapman was enjoying himself, absorbing the library's intoxicating blend of physicality, knowledge, history, and privilege. As the tall candles flickered, he cut into his Maine lobster with grilled portobello mushrooms and fig sauce and chewed slowly, savoring the ambrosial flavors. Taking a mouthful of one of the whites, he held it against his palate. With a rush of pleasure, he swallowed.

"I disagree," Thomas Randklev was saying. "Take Freud—he told his doctor collecting old objects, including books, was for him an addiction second in intensity only to nicotine."

"There's another side to it," Brian Collum said. "We're the only species capable of contemplating our own deaths, so of course we need something larger than ourselves to make the knowledge tolerable. As Freud would say, it's the price for our highly developed frontal lobes—and the glue that holds us together."

"I'm glad it's not just about money." Petr Klok grinned.

Laughter echoed from around the table.

The truth was, Chapman thought to himself, all of them had started as great readers, and if life had been otherwise, each would perhaps have taken a different path. For himself, he had accomplished far more than he had ever dreamed as a boy.

"I have one for you," Carl Lindström challenged. "'When you give someone a book, you don't give him just paper, ink, and glue, you give him the possibility of a whole new life.' Who wrote that?"

"Christopher Morley," Maurice Dresser said instantly. "And John Hill Burton argued that a great library couldn't be constructed; it was the growth of ages. As the Library of Gold is"—the seventy-five-year-old pointed at himself—"and *I* am."

The group chuckled, and Chapman felt his pager vibrate against his chest. He checked—Preston. Annoyed, he excused himself as the conversation moved on to assessing the two ethereal white burgundies. As he left, the sommelier was called over to join the debate.

Chapman entered the first of the two elevators. It rose silently, a solid capsule, but then, all of the underground stories were atomic bomb-hardened bunkers. On the highest belowground floor, he stepped out into the porcelain, steel, and granite of the kitchen. A hallway extended beyond it, where doors opened onto offices and storage. Farther was the enormous garage.

Gazing around, he inhaled the mouthwatering aromas of searing medallions of springbok, gazelle from South Africa. The *chefs de cuisine,* in their tall white hats, were barking orders in French as they prepared the course. The sous-chefs, *chefs de partie,* and waiters chosen from the library staff scurried.

Preston had a harried expression as he turned from the kitchen and met Chapman at the elevator.

"You need to talk to them, sir," Preston said.

"Are they still in my office?"

"Yes. Three men are watching them."

As they rode the elevator down to the third level, he asked, "What's the latest with Ryder and Andersen?" Chapman knew they had killed two of the guards and badly injured four. Preston had sent out additional men on foot to find them.

"I've increased the security around the compound. Everyone's on high alert."

"They'd damn well better be."

The elevator door opened, and they walked out into the sitting area where the staff gathered for informal meetings. As expected it was deserted, since everyone was working. The doors along the hall were for offices, while the last one enclosed a gym with the latest cardio and Pilates equipment.

Preston pushed open the door to Chapman's office and stepped back.

Chapman marched past toward a frozen tableau of defiance. Motionless and angry, Eva Blake and Yitzhak Law were roped to chairs, their hands tied behind them. Blake was still in her skydiving jumpsuit, her face blackened. Neither seemed to recognize him, but then, it was doubtful they would know his world.

He ignored the guards and pulled up a chair in front of Blake and Law. "I'll make this easy. I've had the translators draw up a list of potential sources for the questions the book club will be asking during our tournament tonight. Since we have texts in the library that have been lost for centuries, there's no way you'd know their contents. Others you'll know already of course. Your job is to try to figure out the correct book for each question. You'll be given a chart showing where all of the illuminated manuscripts are shelved, and a few descriptive sentences about each. If you get all of the book club's questions correct, I'll let you live. That's called incentive."

They glanced at each other, then returned stony gazes to him.

Chapman looked back at Preston. "Bring in Cavaletti." He sank back in his chair, furious about the dinner he was missing.

In seconds Roberto Cavaletti was shoved into the room. "Yitzhak, Eva," he said. The small man was disheveled, his bearded face drawn.

Before anyone could say more, Chapman ordered, "Hit him, Preston."

As Law and Blake shouted and pulled against their ropes, Cavaletti cringed, and Preston rabbit-punched his cheek, connecting with a solid *thump*.

Cavaletti grabbed his face with a trembling hand, staggered, and fell to his knees.

"You bastard!" Blake yelled.

The professor's face paled. "You're monsters."

"Rethink this," Chapman snapped. "There are two of you.

Together you have a much better chance of winning tonight than one of you would alone. If you won't do it for yourselves, do it for your friend Roberto here."

A large welt was rising on Cavaletti's left cheek.

Yitzhak Law stared. "All right, but only on condition you leave Roberto alone. No more injuries."

"No, Yitzhak," Roberto said. "No, no. Whatever they want, you will not stop the inevitable."

Blake glared at Chapman. "Very well. I agree, too. Do we have your guarantee you'll let all of us go if we win?"

"Of course," Chapman said easily. "Kardasian, see both are cleaned up and presentable." He stood and walked out.

Preston caught up with him in the sitting room. "I'll keep you apprised of the situation with Ryder and Andersen."

Chapman nodded, his mind already back at the dinner. Just then they heard one of the elevator doors close. They hurried and saw it had stopped at the lowest level, number four—the Library of Gold. Immediately they stepped into the other elevator, and Preston punched the button.

"Who in hell could it be?" Preston's expression was grim.

The elevator door opened onto an elegant anteroom. Straight ahead was an arched portal that led to offices along the windowed exterior corridor. Instead they sprinted left, and Preston opened a carved wood door onto the library and tonight's banquet.

The sommelier was walking toward his bureau, his broad tuxedoed back to them. At the sound of the door, he turned. They saw he was carrying two bottles of red wine—unopened.

Preston made a curt gesture, and the sommelier approached. Although as arrogant appearing as before, the man's eyes hinted at guilt. He held up the bottles as if they were a shield.

"What were you doing on the third floor?" Preston demanded.

"I am very sorry, sir. I found I must go to the kitchen for more wine. You gentlemen are more appreciative than I had expected. I was rushing to return and touched the wrong button in the elevator. Of course, I did not leave the elevator until here."

Chapman felt Preston relax.

"Resume your duties," Chapman said.

The sommelier bowed low and left. Chapman hurried to his dinner.

68

Tucker and Judd sat in the deep shadow of a gnarled olive tree above the compound. As they cleaned their faces and hands and brushed their hair, they studied the buildings and the fifteen men patrolling in the illumination of the compound's security lights. All had M4s and were watching the grounds and hills alertly.

"Wonder how many are in the main house," Tucker said in a low voice.

"With luck, they won't notice us with so many new guards. That'll work to our advantage."

"I like being the new guy. Fewer expectations for you." Tucker inspected his Uzi, then his knife and wire garotte. "The rear door looks good."

"My thought, too. You up for this?"

"Can you still ride a bicycle?"

"Like a son of a bitch," Judd said.

They slung their Uzis onto their backs and slithered on their bellies down among the tall grasses and bushes of the slope. Small rocks cut into Tucker's jumpsuit. After pausing several heart-stopping times when guards peered out onto the hillside, they reached the edge of the mesa and hid behind a row of manicured shrubs.

Waiting until the closest sentries were looking elsewhere, they ran behind the pool shed and crouched. Judd pointed to himself. Tucker nodded. He hated not being the one out front, but reality was reality—Judd was younger, stronger, and in better condition to take out the guard who would cross in front of the shed soon.

Listening to the sentry's feet pad across the marble path, Tucker crab-walked after Judd to the shed's far side. Judd inched forward, taking out a mirror with an attached bendable arm. He extended the arm, watched the mirror, then tossed both to Tucker and stood, pulling out his garotte.

From his low position, Tucker saw one leg appear and then a second. Immediately Judd stepped close behind the guard and dropped the garotte around his neck, yanking. The man fell back. Strangled noises came from his throat as Judd pulled him around and into the shed's shelter. Tucker ripped the sentry's M4 away and slapped on plastic cuffs. The sentry gasped, seemed to try to yell. Frantically he punched back with elbows and feet, torquing his body.

Tucker used the mirror to check for more guards, then looked back. Judd's grim face was frozen as he avoided the flailing blows. He lowered the man as he went limp.

They stripped him of his gear and clothes. While Judd put on the corpse's black khakis and black microfiber turtleneck, Tucker dressed the dead man in Judd's jumpsuit and smeared black greasepaint on his face and the backs of his hands. Peering carefully around, Tucker dragged him to the edge of the compound and rolled him deep into grasses.

When he returned, Judd was dressed and outfitted with the guard's radio, pistol, flashlight, and M4. He hooked on two grenades and checked the tracker to Eva's ankle bracelet, then slid it into his pants pocket. He pointed toward the house, where another guard would be making rounds. Then he pointed to himself.

Tucker nodded.

Using the mirror, Judd timed his exit, then vanished.

Tucker hurried around the shed. Sitting on his heels, he watched as Judd sauntered up to the next target. Just as the guard frowned, Judd violently bashed his M4 up under his chin, crushing his throat. His head whiplashed, and blood appeared on his lips. As Tucker ran to join them, Judd caught the guard and let his limp body down to the ground silently.

Tucker checked the man's carotid artery.

"Dead?" Judd whispered.

He nodded.

They surveyed around. No more sentries were in sight yet, and none showed on the other side of the rear door's window. After they stripped the dead man, Tucker changed into his black turtleneck and pants, at least one size too big, and cinched the waist tight. Judd added the finishing touches to the dead body and dragged it off to conceal near the other corpse.

As he waited for Judd, Tucker checked the M4 and examined the radio—and sensed more than saw someone through the glass of the door. He put a composed look of greeting on his face and turned.

The door opened. "Why aren't you patrolling?" The sentry was a straight tree trunk of a man, with a brush cut and a heavy jaw. A glimmer of doubt appeared in his eyes. "Who in hell are—"

Tucker slammed the butt of his M4 into the man's gut. It was always a safer debilitating shot than one to the chin. As the man emptied his lungs and started to double over, Tucker crashed the butt back up into his windpipe. Blood erupted from his mouth and nose. Tucker grabbed him, then hauled him toward the slope behind the shed where the other bodies were.

"This is beginning to look like a party with a bad outcome," Judd said.

Tucker rolled the man into the grass, watching as the tall fronds closed over him. "Let's go get Eva."

69

Khost Province, Afghanistan

It was past midnight, and Capt. Sam Daradar was walking alone, his M4 over his arm. He inhaled, smelling the sweet mountain night air. When he had first arrived here, it had stung his nose, but now he could not get enough of it. Sometimes he dreamed about moving to Afghanistan. Life here was intrinsic to the elements and made sense to him in a way no Western city or rural area ever had.

He looked up. Sparkling stars spread across the night sky. For some reason the sky felt too vast tonight. An unnamed uneasiness filled him. He studied the great expanse of slopes and mountains that hid remote villages difficult to reach with large bodies of conventional forces. He and many of his men had spent the day out there and in town, talking with people.

Tonight he had phoned command, reporting his concerns. But he had been able to point only to restless whisperings in the local marketplace and to the fact that Syed Ullah had actually appeared at the mosque for noon prayers—midweek—rather than saying them at home or on the trail as he usually did.

Sam turned back under the great tent of special camouflage netting and walked along the secret base's eighteen-inch-thick stone walls. The austere base housed only five hundred soldiers, but they were well trained and experienced. He stopped at the gate. Peering up at the guard tower, he nodded and received a nod in return.

Shaking his head at his unnameable uneasiness, he slid inside the gates and walked onto the base. Two Humvees were still out, watching, patrolling. They were due back in an hour. Perhaps they would have something for him, something that might be meaningless to them but he would understand.

On his belly, Syed Ullah peered down the hillside. The two Humvees were speeding along a dirt road above a valley two ridges away from town. The headlights were bright cones against the night, making the vehicles easy to track. In the pines on the eastern slope above the road were his men, hiding and dressed in the American uniforms, with the American equipment. He and his son Jasim were positioned north, in an open area high enough to have an excellent moonlit view.

"I am not as certain as you that this will work." Twenty-eight years old, Jasim had just returned from Peshawar and was dressed in American gear, too. He had the same large body as his father, and a thick black beard trimmed just enough so that it could bristle. Blessed with his mother's fine features, his face was finally coarsening with age, soldiering, and the weather. He had been a beautiful child, and now he was a real man.

"What concerns you, my son?"

"There are more than twice our number on the military base."

"Ah, but our men have what they do not—surprise. They are dressed like them, and they will wear the American helmets. Except for the ones on duty in the base, the Americans are asleep or playing with their video games. The only doubtful part is getting our people inside. And the answer to that we will know soon." Without moving his gaze from the road, he explained what was about to happen.

As they watched, the armored Humvees entered the attack zone, the sound of their big engines reverberating across the quiet valley. In the turret on top of each sat a gunner in a sling surrounded by steel protective plates, his M240B machine gun stationary in his hands. The guns covered an almost 360-degree swath, but the plates did not fit together. There were four open spaces of several inches at each corner.

Suddenly there were two explosions and fiery conflagrations in recently cut recesses in the trees. One was ahead of the Humvees, the other behind. From the recesses two cars in flames hurtled down toward the road. Smoke billowed out behind them, and sparks flew, igniting dry grasses. The Humvees were between the cars approaching the road, the sturdy pines above, and the cliff beneath.

The monstrous military vehicles slowed. The Americans would initially suspect this to be simple harassment, that the flaming cars would continue across the road and hurtle off the cliff. But Ullah's men had piled walls of rocks on the road's edge.

As the cars stopped, blocking the Humvees, machine-gun fire erupted from both gunners, strafing the trees and the road in hot fusillades. Tree trunks exploded; pine needles disintegrated. And finally there was silence. Slowly the Humvees' doors opened. As the gunners stood watch above, their weapons looking for targets, the infidels jumped out, M4s in hands, heading for the burning vehicle in front of them.

At that moment gunfire from his two hundred Pashtuns erupted from behind the rocky wall and out of holes dug under the pine forest. It was so fast and blistering, the infidels exposed on the road got off only a few shots while the machine gunners in the turrets furiously returned fire. On the road, the infidels fell, yelling, moaning, and six of Ullah's Pashtuns slid along the dirt, crawled up the sides of the

Humvees, and rolled stun grenades through the open spaces into the turrets. Two loud *bangs* sounded. And then the only noise was of his converging men putting single gunshots into the heads of the infidels.

As they dragged the bodies into the pines, Ullah stood. They had pulled the unconscious machine-gunners from their cupolas and were killing them.

"Come." He ran.

With a shout of joy, Jasim passed him.

"Praise Allah," Ullah said as he arrived on the battlefield. He caught his breath. "How many of us have been killed or hurt?"

In his U.S. Army uniform, Hamid Qadeer stood straight to report. "Only fourteen."

"Good, good." The warlord walked around the Humvees, studying the vehicles. They were dirty and showed bullet holes, but that was nothing. The guards at the military base would pass them through, which was all he needed.

"I will join our men now." Jasim stood at his side. His excitement had calmed, and he had the severe look of a true Pashtun warrior.

Pride filled Ullah. "Of course, my son."

70

The Isle of Pericles

The banquet was finished, a complete success. As the plates were cleared and the sommelier poured brandy, the men stretched back in their chairs, sated, slightly intoxicated. Chapman related the latest report—Preston's men had not yet found Ryder and Andersen.

"Frankly, I hope those damn people do get into the house and come down here," Grandon Holmes announced. He patted the side of his chest where his pistol was holstered.

At no time in the history of the annual banquet had the members attended armed, but tonight was an unusual night. Despite the good humor, a thread of menace had grown among them. The island had been violated.

"It's been a while since I've done active target practice." Brian Collum gave a cold smile.

"On the other hand," Maurice Dresser grumbled, "why in hell are we paying the guards astronomical sums if they don't handle the job?"

"Maurice is right," Petr Klok said. "Ryder and Andersen will never make it to the library."

"Pity." Carl Lindström sighed.

"I heard from Syed Ullah," Chapman said, changing the subject. "His Pashtuns are uniformed, armed, and eager to go. We should have word in an hour or so."

"Excellent," Reinhardt Gruen said. "I did some checking about the village near the Khost military base. I was correct—

the entire area is a hotbed of jihadist activity. Ullah is one hell of a tough warlord to have been able to control it. My thinking is he will use tonight's strike to rid himself of local Taliban enemies—which means our enemies, too. Then the land will be ours. I've been dreaming about those diamonds. All in all, Marty, you're looking very good. It will be a fine night. One for the record books."

Arms crossed tightly over her chest, Eva paced, inspecting again the closet where they were being held. There was no furniture. The hinges to the heavy door had been installed on the outside, and two dead bolts sealed them in. An overhead fluorescent light was lit all the time, too high for them to reach, and the switch was in the corridor. The walls were solid concrete blocks. If there was a way to break out, she had not found it.

"You must accept it, Eva. We are trapped." Gazing up at her, Roberto huddled in a corner. His eye was swollen shut, and his cheek was distended, a hot red.

"An accurate assessment of our condition," Yitzhak said from where he sat close beside Roberto. "Still, it's not the end of the world."

"Yet." Roberto sighed.

Yitzhak put heartiness into his voice. "For a man who worries about leaving our time zone, look how well you're doing, Roberto."

"I am heroic." He gave a small smile and shook his head. Still, there had been a flash in his eyes that told Eva he had not given up completely.

"We'll figure it out, Roberto," she encouraged. "Do you think we need to go over the list one more time, Yitzhak?" On it were sixteen illuminated manuscripts, twice the number they would need to name. If the circumstances were different, they would have marveled at the many lost books, but their existence only added to their frustration, and the large number to their fears.

"I think not." Yitzhak looked up, his bald head pasty in the overbright fluorescent light. "Together we know nearly half, and we'll just have to make educated guesses about the rest."

"I wish they would take me to the library with you," Roberto said. "But it is obvious they will not."

He was right—she and Yitzhak wore tuxedos Preston had given them, while Roberto was still in the rumpled shirt and pants he'd had on when captured.

"But there's hope, Roberto," she told him. "We're still breathing."

"It is a small hope, and I will treasure it." He sighed.

There was the noise of dead bolts being slid opened, and the guard they had heard called Harold Kardasian appeared, pointing his assault rifle. He was sturdy, with thick brown hair streaked with gray.

"Time to go," he announced.

Eva looked for some sign of help in his eyes, but saw only neutrality.

Both Roberto and Yitzhak stood up.

"Not you," Kardasian ordered. "Only the professor and Dr. Blake."

As Roberto slid back down the wall, they said good-bye to him.

Preston was waiting in the corridor, dressed in his black leather jacket and jeans, tall and looming, his features stony. He carried two thick bath towels.

"What are those for?" Eva asked instantly.

"That's none of your concern. Move."

They marched Eva and Yitzhak to the stairs beside the elevators and took them down one floor into an anteroom.

For a moment Eva felt a frisson of excitement—they were going to see the Library of Gold. She sensed an electric current from Yitzhak and knew he was thinking the same thing.

One guard opened a massive carved door, and golden light appeared. Yitzhak took Eva's arm, and they walked inside and stopped. For a few moments, her fear vanished. It was as if they were in a cocoon of timeless knowledge dressed in the earth's most dazzling elements.

"Bewitching," Yitzhak whispered.

They drank in the four walls of gold-covered books. The embedded gems sparkled in the pure air. For an instant it seemed to Eva that nothing else on the planet mattered.

"Don't give me the cold tomb of a museum but the fire-breathing world of words and ideas," Yitzhak said. "Give me a library. *This* library."

The tall man who had ordered Preston to hit Roberto walked toward them. "Who said that, Professor?"

Yitzhak looked at him sharply. "I did."

The man chuckled. "My name is Martin Chapman. Come with me. It's time you met everyone."

He motioned to the guards to leave. Preston closed the door and stood in front of it. They followed Chapman to a large oval table around which seven men sat, drinking from brandy glasses.

With a shock, Eva recognized Brian Collum—her attorney, her friend. Watching her, he had laughter on his long, handsome face. She glanced away, smoothed her features, and turned back.

"You look wonderful in a tux," he told her.

"You bastard."

"It's good to see you, too. And in such an appropriate setting."

She said nothing, fighting the fury that surged through

her as she realized he must have been the one who entangled Charles with the Library of Gold. And he had sent her to prison, knowing she was innocent. As Chapman made formal introductions, she forced herself to be calm. Then she assessed the situation: Besides the eight members of the book club, only the sommelier and Preston were in the room. The bath towels still dangled from his hand. Puzzled, she tried to figure out what they meant.

"Does everyone understand the rules?" Chapman asked. When a chorus of yeses answered, he said, "Then the tournament begins. Petr, you're first this year."

"Socrates, 469 or 470 to 399 B.C.," said a bearded man with stylishly clipped hair. "Of course he is credited as one of the founders of Western philosophy. What most people do not know is his utopian republic ruled by philosopher-kings also included glorification of the benefits of a caste system and a powerful argument for the right of armies to conquer and colonize. Hitler must have loved that. Your challenge is to find the illuminated manuscript in which Socrates is shown as a clown teaching his students to hoodwink their way out of debt."

Eva cleared her throat. "There's no such thing as a real history from Socrates' time that dealt with him or Greece." Hiding her nervousness, she looked at Yitzhak, but he shook his head. He did not know the answer. She had an idea, but it was a long time ago, not since college, that she had read it. "However, we do have plays and other writings. What I remember is 'The Clouds,' an old comedy by Aristophanes."

She gazed at the questioner, hoping to see in his face whether she was correct. His expression showed nothing.

Yitzhak found the location of the manuscript on the list, and they walked quickly down one of the long walls, looking for it. With both hands he lifted out a gold volume embedded with sapphires and handed it to Petr Klok.

There was a long pause as they waited for his answer.

With a flourish Klok took the book and stood it up on the table to admire. "The world has only eleven complete plays by Aristophanes, although he wrote forty. The Library of Gold has the entire collection."

There was a round of jaunty applause.

Eva and Yitzhak exchanged a look of relief.

Chapman ended it: "Thom, you're next. Try to beat them, will you?"

Judd opened the rear door to the main house and slid inside, Tucker following. Their M4s ready, they listened for sounds and checked a wall of glass displaying the reflecting pool and spotlighted palms they had seen in NSA photos. When they heard nothing, they padded past closed doors and entered an enormous living room that stretched across the front of the house, glass windows showcasing the ocean view. The wall of glass stretched around the corner on the west side, with heavy glass double doors showing a marble path that led out toward the tennis courts, pool, and distant helipad.

Two sentries were in sight patrolling, their gazes cast outward—not toward the house.

"So far so good," Judd murmured. He pulled out his reader.

But just as they hurried toward the stairwell beside the elevators, their radios crackled. They snapped them from their belts and looked outdoors. Both of the sentries were grabbing their radios, too. And now a third sentry was in sight, doing the same.

Tucker swore, and they punched their Receive buttons.

"Three down," the disembodied voice snapped. "Rendezvous behind the pool shed. *Now*."

"It's just a matter of time until they guess we're inside,"

Tucker said as he ran past packing crates to the stairwell door and yanked it open.

M4s ready, they raced down one flight of steps, peered through the window on the door and saw a busy kitchen, then ran down another flight. The door window showed an empty hallway of closed doors.

As they tore down a third flight, Judd whispered, "She's on this floor."

At the door, they looked into a sitting area of comfortable sofas and chairs. No one was in sight.

Judd inhaled, exhaled, and slid around the door, crouching, M4 in both hands. In an instant Tucker was beside him. No one was around.

Heart pounding, Judd dashed down the hall, watching the reader, and then stopped. *Eva*. With one hand he slammed open the door's dead bolts and turned the knob.

"Judd, is that you?" Roberto Cavaletti stared up, his battered face breaking into a smile. "You are blond." He scrambled to his feet.

"Where's Eva?"

"In the Library of Gold." He hurried toward them. "She gave me her ankle bracelet so you would find me and I could warn you. We overheard the guards talking—all of them at the big banquet have pistols. Eva and Yitzhak were taken there to be part of some mortal game. If they guess wrong, we will die. But if they guess right, I think they plan to murder us anyway."

"Where's the library?" Judd asked grimly.

71

Khost Province, Afghanistan

Syed Ullah met the Pakistani reporter and cameraman at the mosque and drove them out to the edge of the sleeping town. Parking near the remains of mud-brick huts, the three got out, bundled in long down coats against the night's cold. Ullah sniffed, smelling the strong scent of animal manure.

"Please turn around, General," the reporter said.

The cameraman motioned him into position. The two were from the respected Pakistan Television Corporation, the country's national TV broadcaster, whose news was regularly picked up by wire services and media around the globe.

"This is Asif Badri." The reporter held a mike and looked solemnly into the camera. "Tonight I am in Khost province, Afghanistan. With me is the esteemed general Syed Ullah, a legendary mujahideen hero of the war against the Soviets. Tell us what is in the distance, General."

The camera focused on Ullah. Putting on his gravest expression, he spoke into the reporter's mike and pointed with his AK-47. "That is a secret American military base. About five hundred soldiers." He paused, considering. He did not want to completely insult American listeners, especially since he planned to make a lot of money from Chapman. Phrasing his words carefully, he continued, "They are here to clear out illegal activity and are generally well behaved. Unfortunately, there is a serious problem."

The camera panned over to the military base with its

massive lights glowing in and around it, captured beneath the special netting that stretched in a great canopy far beyond the walls. Above the netting was black night; below it, bright daylight. It was a dramatic picture, showing the infidels' technical ingenuity and their awful ability to fool the world.

"Does your national government know about the base?" the reporter asked.

"Kabul is completely ignorant," the warlord lied.

"You mentioned a serious problem. Tell us about it."

"It is a sad story," Ullah intoned, embracing his rifle. "The Americans complain about our tribal differences while they have their own. Sports, politics, religion—and business. Remember, their murder rate is among the highest in the world. One of my people overheard an American soldier talking to another in a town governed by another general. They, too, have a secret base in the mountains. Those soldiers are very angry at our soldiers. I am sorry to tell you all of them are smuggling drugs and exporting heroin. As you know, it is very lucrative." He shook his head sadly. "The other soldiers are planning to murder the soldiers here tonight because they have been poaching their business."

"Have you informed Kabul?"

"What can they do? I am in charge, and another general is in charge of the other town. We are helpless against the Americans' far superior weapons. I am left only with being able to tell the world in hopes this will never happen again." He sighed. "It is a tragedy."

The reporter turned off his microphone. "Did you get it all, Ali?"

The cameraman nodded. "When do we go to the base?"

Ullah looked into the hills and pointed with his AK-47 at two sets of headlights. His son Jasim was in the lead vehicle with Hamid Qadeer, who spoke perfect Americanized English.

"They are coming out of the mountains now," he told them. "Those are two American Humvees. My informant said there would be a total of about two hundred soldiers. The arrival of the Humvees means the rest are now in place nearby. Once the Humvees get inside the base, their plan is to silently kill the soldiers in the guard tower and open the gates. The rest is inevitable. Get into my car. I will drive you closer. We must go slow and without headlights. You will be able to film the action outside, and after it is over, you will be the first to record the results of the horrible massacre."

72

The Isle of Pericles

Everyone in the Library of Gold was focused on Preston, who was standing inside the door with his M4 and thick bath towels and listening to a message on his radio. As Eva watched, he strode to Chapman and spoke quietly into his ear.

"Gentlemen, we may have visitors," Chapman announced with relish. "Take out your pistols."

Swiftly the men laid their weapons on the table beside the illuminated manuscripts. Although they had obviously been drinking, their hands and gazes were steady, and they moved with authority. There was an undercurrent of enthusiasm, too, Eva thought. They were looking forward to shooting their guns.

She exchanged a worried look with Yitzhak.

The sommelier advanced with bottles of brandy. He poured into Chapman's glass first, emptying the bottle, then poured from a fresh one into the glasses of the other men.

As the sommelier returned to his bureau, everyone looked at Chapman.

Eva and Yitzhak had answered correctly seven of the eight tournament questions. The competitive excitement among the men around the banquet table was almost tactile as they waited for the final challenge—from the director, Martin Chapman.

"Jesus of Nazareth, known as the Rabbi and later as Jesus

Christ, 7 to 2 B.C. to sometime between A.D. 26 and 36," Chapman said. "Jesus was the leader of an apocalyptic movement, a faith healer, a rabble-rouser, and with John the Baptist, the founder of Christianity. The consensus of scholars is the four canonical gospels about his life—Matthew, Mark, Luke, and John—weren't recorded by any of the original disciples or first-person witnesses, although they were probably written within the first century of his death. Your challenge is to find in the library where Jesus tells one of his disciples he 'will exceed' the others and learn 'the mysteries of the kingdom.' "

Eva did not remember either quote. She looked at Yitzhak, and he shook his head worriedly. They turned away to study the list. There were three possibilities: One was St. Jerome's early fifth-century Vulgate Bible. The second was *Vetus Latina,* which was compiled before the Vulgate. The third was even earlier, the title translating to *The Old Gospels*. They read the descriptions.

"He's trying to fool us by referring to Matthew, Mark, Luke, and John," Yitzhak whispered.

She had reached the same conclusion. "Do you think it's in the Gnostic book of Judas?" The only known text of the Gospel of Judas had been written seventeen hundred years before, discovered in fragments in the Egyptian desert in 1945 and assembled and translated from the Coptic language in 2006, which was when she had read it.

"I do."

"Then the third one, *The Old Gospels,* is the only choice," she said, "although it predates the Gnostics."

"Dazzle them." Anger flashed in his eyes.

She turned back to the table. The brandy glasses glistened. The men's calculating eyes watched her.

She paused. "In the New Testament, Judas Iscariot betrays Jesus to the Romans for thirty silver coins. The Gospel of

Judas says the exact opposite—that it's Jesus' idea, and that he asks Judas to do it so his body can be sacrificed on the cross. If Jesus did ask Judas to do that, it's logical he might've encouraged him by saying he 'will exceed' the other disciples and learn 'the mysteries of the kingdom.' Therefore, the quotation is from *The Old Gospels*. According to the list we were given, the book contains quite a few, including those of James, Peter, Thomas, Mary Magdalene, Philip—and Judas."

Was she right? She could read nothing in Chapman's face. Yitzhak was already walking along the wall. Following him, she passed a section on the Koran and other early Muslim works. Next to it Bibles and Christian literature were shelved.

Yitzhak stared at a manuscript covered in hammered gold. At the center was a simple design—small blue topazes in the outline of a fish. Gingerly he picked up the old book and carried it to Chapman.

Eva's lungs were tight. She forced herself to breathe.

"Damn you." Chapman took the book. "You're right. *The Old Gospels* is an original, written on parchment pages that Constantine the Great ordered rebound and covered in gold in the early fourth century. It's pre-Gnostic, composed in the first century A.D., during the time the books of Matthew, Mark, Luke, and John were recorded. It can arguably be considered as accurate as the New Testament." He stroked the book. "The power of this is considerable. It explodes the myth of monolithic Christianity and demonstrates how diverse and fascinating the early movement really was."

There was a round of enthusiastic applause—for Chapman, not for them. He stood the illuminated manuscript on the table next to his pistol and smiled at it.

The men raised their brandy glasses.

"Good question, Marty," said one.

"Hear, hear."

They drank.

As Chapman swallowed and put down his glass, he frowned at Eva and Yitzhak and gestured behind him to Preston.

Immediately the security chief was at his side, his M4 in one hand, the towels in the other.

"Now?" Preston asked.

"By all means."

Preston leaned the assault rifle against the table and took his pistol from the holster at his hip. The men's gazes were riveted as he advanced toward Eva and Yitzhak with the two towels.

"The later Assassins." Yitzhak backed up. "That's what the towels mean. They covered entrance and exit wounds to control the mess that spraying blood makes."

73

Judd, Tucker, and Roberto hurried along the quiet hallway toward the stairwell. Judd saw instantly both elevators were descending. Passing them, he yanked open the stairwell's door and heard feet pounding down from high above, echoing against the stone walls. They sounded like a battalion.

"Run!"

With Tucker and Roberto following, he hurtled down the steps to the fourth level and peered through the window into a formal anteroom. Assault rifle in both hands, he slid out, Tucker on his heels. No one was around.

Tucker pulled Roberto from the stairwell, locked and bolted the door, and shoved the small man into a corner beside a tall cabinet, where he would be out of range.

Judd nodded at a huge carved-wood door. "The Library of Gold." But before they could breach it they still had to face the security teams in the elevators.

"Looks like it," Tucker agreed.

Judd dropped flat, facing one of the two elevators. Tucker lay prone in front of the other. They aimed their M4s.

Tucker's elevator arrived first. Four guards were standing inside. Tucker sent a fusillade of automatic fire across them, the noise thunderous. Completely surprised, they'd had no time to aim.

As they grabbed the walls and each other and fell, Judd's elevator door started to open. This time gunfire exploded from the cage, but aimed high, where men should have been standing. Immediately Judd returned fire, ripping rounds across the five men's torsos. They staggered and sank, blood pouring from their chests. The air filled with a metallic stink.

Judd and Tucker jumped up and disabled each elevator.

Roberto was already at the library's big wood door, his eyes wide, his gaze determined.

"Don't go in there," Tucker snapped from across the room.

A guard appeared at the window in the stairwell door and yanked, trying to open it. Other guards were behind him, up the steps. The guard saw Judd and Tucker. As he shot through the glass, they sprinted. The rounds splintered across walls and into mirrors.

When they reached Roberto, there was sudden silence—they were beyond the guard's view, with only seconds before he broke through the door. As bullets exploded again, Judd exchanged a look with Tucker. Tucker put Roberto behind him and readied his assault rifle.

Judd opened the massive carved door a crack, realizing instantly its core was solid steel, the hinges hidden, the movement pneumatic. It was a vault door. No way anyone could shoot through with an M4, and there was no lock to pick.

They slid inside, low, weapons leveled. As Tucker slammed the bolts behind them, sealing out the guards, Judd stared at eight pistols aimed at them by men standing around a large dining table. He quickly took in the room.

To the right was a shocked sommelier cringing in front of a wine bureau, his hand inside his tuxedo jacket, clasping his heart. Farther along the same wall Yitzhak crouched, sweat greasing his bald head. Eva was sprawled on the floor near him. Oddly, both were dressed in tuxedos. Preston lifted his pistol from Eva to train it on Judd and Tucker. Wearing jeans and a black leather jacket as he had the last time Judd had seen him, he let two towels fall from his hand.

"Judd, what a pleasant surprise," Martin Chapman was saying. "I thought I wouldn't have the pleasure of seeing you again." Tall and genteel, he stood before the banquet table, his thick white hair flowing, his blue eyes sparkling with amusement, his pistol calmly pointed.

Judd stared at his father's old friend. "You're the one who had Dad killed? You son of a bitch." As a wave of fury rolled through him, he felt Tucker's restraining hand on his arm.

"Actually," Chapman said, "Jonathan did it to himself. I tried to talk him out of it, but you know what a hothead he could be. He was completely unreasonable. I'm sorry we lost him. All of us liked him a great deal."

He gestured with his free hand at the other men around the table. They came out and stood in a line on either side of him, their weapons never wavering as they aimed at Tucker and Judd.

Judd studied the men in their expensive evening clothes. Each was at least six feet tall and ranged in age from early forties to late sixties. Perfectly groomed and with strong athletic bodies, they had an unmistakable air of pride and confidence. Their uniformity was chilling.

"Yitzhak." Roberto ran around the outside of the room, passing the sommelier.

The sommelier watched, his eyes enormous. A man in his sixties, he had deep wrinkles and a bulbous red nose, a man who enjoyed wine far too much.

"Shh," Yitzhak warned.

Roberto dropped to the floor beside the professor. As Preston glanced in their direction, Eva lashed out a foot at his leg.

Preston stepped back and pointed his pistol down at her. "Get up!"

Judd realized several of the tuxedoed men were weaving. Those close to the table steadied themselves on it.

Chapman noticed, too. Puzzled, he looked left and right along the line.

The knees of two buckled, and they fell.

"What in hell—" The oldest grabbed his forehead and keeled over.

"Goddammit." Another stared at his gun hand. It was shaking uncontrollably.

Two more struggled to stay upright, and then all three collapsed.

"The brandy—it must've been poisoned," the youngest said to Chapman.

He and Chapman were the last standing. They swung their pistols toward the sommelier.

With the hand that had been gripping his heart, the sommelier whipped out a 9 mm Walther. In one smooth motion, he fired twice. One bullet struck the younger man in the head, and the other shattered Chapman's gun hand.

Reeling, Chapman grabbed up the M4 with the other hand.

At the same time, Preston shoved Eva aside and was running along the wall of books, aiming at the sommelier. Before the sommelier could swing around to fire, Preston squeezed off a shot that sliced across the top of the sommelier's shoulder. From across the room Judd released three explosive bursts into Preston's chest.

Preston froze. Fury crossed his aristocratic features as he looked down at the blood spreading across his heart. He took two more steps. "You don't know what you're doing. The books must be protected—" He pitched over onto his face, arms limp at his sides. His fingers unfurled, and his gun fell with a metallic *clunk* onto the marble floor.

Ignoring Chapman, the sommelier ran to Preston and grabbed the pistol. "Nice shot, Judd. Thanks." As blood dripped down his jacket, he felt for Preston's carotid artery.

"Damn you all to hell!" Martin Chapman trained the M4 on Judd, his finger white on the trigger.

Judd aimed.

"No!" the sommelier shouted from where he crouched. "We need Chapman alive!"

No one moved. Chapman scowled, his weapon pointed at Judd, Judd's pointed at him. The room seemed to reverberate with tension.

Then Chapman's face smoothed. A twinkle appeared in his eyes, and warmth infused his voice. "You should know, Judd, that your father had always hoped you'd join our book club." With his bloody free hand he gestured grandly at the towering expanse of jeweled books. "These can be yours, too. Think of the history, of the trust your father and I inherited. It's sacred. With Brian dead, we're shy three members now. Join us. It would've pleased Jonathan a great deal."

Behind Chapman, Eva had been watching. Judd kept his eyes apparently locked on Chapman, while noting she was taking off her shoes.

"Sacred?" he retorted. "What you have here isn't a trust. It's God-awful selfishness."

Eva sprinted in stocking feet across the marble floor, her black hair flying, her eyes narrowed. She threw herself forward onto her belly and slid silently under the banquet table.

Chapman gave Judd a wry smile, "As John Dryden said, 'Secrets are edged tools and must be kept from children and fools.' You were raised to appreciate the priceless value of this remarkable library. No one can take care of it—cherish it—better than we can. You have a responsibility to help us—"

Hunching up, Eva threw her shoulders into the backs of his knees. He reeled, then crashed forward with a grunt, landing hard. His M4 spun away. He swore loudly and scrambled toward it.

But Eva scooped it up and rolled, and Judd, Tucker, and the sommelier converged. The four stood over Chapman, pointing their weapons.

Face flushed, he clasped his good hand over his bloody hand against his ruffled white shirt and peered around at his downed companions then back over his shoulder at the dead Preston. Finally he glared up, deep fury and a strange hurt in his eyes.

"Who are you?" he demanded from the sommelier.

"Call me Domino," the sommelier said in a husky voice. He had a wide face and a stocky figure. "The Carnivore sends his regards. My orders are to remind you that you were warned about his rules. Then I'm supposed to scrub you."

"I'm not dead yet, you asshole. What did you do to them?"

"Gamma hydroxy butyrate, GHB. Tasteless, odorless, and colorless. A date-rape drug. In the brandy, of course, poured from the 'new' bottle. They'll wake up in a few hours with very bad headaches. I heard you talking. Tell us what's going to happen in Khost, Afghanistan."

"Why would I do that?"

Judd had no idea what Domino meant, but he came from the Carnivore, and that was enough reason for him. All four weapons moved slightly, training on Chapman's head.

"Tell us!" Judd said.

Chapman stared around at the guns. "And if I do?"

"Maybe you get to live, you lucky SOB," Judd said. "But if we have to kill you now, that's all right, too. Your friends will wake up, and one of them will talk."

Chapman blinked slowly. Then he sat up and told a tale of a forgotten diamond mine in Afghanistan and the warlord who was going to eliminate Taliban fighters so the army base would be closed and Chapman could buy the land.

"It's too late to do anything about it," Chapman finished. "The action is going on right now. Besides, it ultimately benefits all of us. Actually, the world. You don't want to stop it."

"You goddamned fool!" Tucker exploded. "You think you can trust a warlord to do anything he promises? He's going to do only what he thinks is in his best interest. There could be a dozen different scenarios, and none of them we'd like. Worse than that, the United States maintains those secret bases because Kabul needs us to. This could bring down the government and start another bloody war." He looked around the room. "Where's a satellite phone?"

As Domino handed one to him, the door thudded. All looked at the only entrance to the library. The guards must have finally broken through to the anteroom and were preparing to blast their way into the library. New worry filled the room.

"They may have something with more kick than M4s," Judd said, listening.

Tucker nodded and punched numbers on the phone's keypad, while they stood silently, trapped.

74

Khost Province, Afghanistan

The cold chill of the Khost night was getting to Sam Daradar as he stood at the open window of the guard tower with privates Abe Meyer and Diego Castillo. He inspected the headlights of the Humvees approaching, one behind the other, in the far distance. They looked alone and exposed out there in the black night.

"Any sign of trouble?" Sam asked.

"No, sir," Meyer said. "Quiet as usual."

"Get them on the horn."

Meyer flicked on his radio. "Lieutenant, the captain wants to talk to you."

Sam Daradar punched the button on his radio. "Why are you late?"

There was the sound of coughing from the Humvee. "Sorry, sir. I think I'm getting a cold. We did an extra recon around Smugglers' Point. I had a hunch, so wanted to check it out, but there wasn't anyone there or in the valley." His voice was so thick it was almost unrecognizable.

Silently Sam swore. The last thing he needed was illness sweeping through the base. "See anything anywhere else?"

"No, sir. Quiet as a grave." The man cleared his throat.

"I want a full report when you get in." Sam ended the connection. "I'm going out."

Climbing down from the tower, he passed sandbags piled against the wall. Nearby were the Sea Huts that housed the mess and the Tactical Operations Center, and farther were the Butler Huts where his soldiers bunked. The gate unlocked and opened enough for him to slide through.

Hurrying through the light, he reached the darkness and slowed. Letting his eyes adjust, he stared around at the flatlands that rose into hills and then at the high-peaked mountains. To his left was the town. He could barely make out the rough outlines of it. There were a few lights. Nothing unusual. Moonlight shimmered down on the shrubs and clumps of trees around the base. A wind had risen, sighing. He looked for movement, listened for sound, sniffed for odors. He was getting to be as much sixteenth century as the other inhabitants around here.

Turning on his heel, he hurried back inside and up into the guard tower. As he took up his post at the window again, he noticed movement coming from the direction of town. It was a vehicle of some kind, the moonlight illuminating a silvery surface. Strange that the headlamps were not alight.

He put infrared binoculars to his eyes and stared. Dammit, it was Syed Ullah's Toyota Land Cruiser. As he watched, it stopped, and three people climbed out—one was Ullah. They peered at the base and talked. Then one lifted something to his shoulder, aiming it. Sam stared hard. It looked like a movie camera. What in hell was going on?

When the Humvees were about fifty yards from the base, he ordered the gates opened.

The radio sounded. He picked it up, expecting the caller to be the lieutenant reporting he had sighted Ullah, too.

Instead a stranger said, "Captain Daradar, I'm patching you in to Tucker Andersen, CIA. He has important information for you."

Instantly a strong voice announced, "This is Andersen. I've got a story to tell you. I'll make it quick."

Sam listened with growing concern.

When Andersen finished, Sam said, "There've been no attacks in town or at any of the huts in sight of here. I've got a patrol coming in now. I spoke to the lieutenant a while ago, and he said it was quiet in the boonies, too. But Ullah is in the dust bowl near here with two other people, and it looks as if they filmed the base. Maybe they're the Pakistani news crew your informant told you about."

"You know Syed Ullah personally?"

"As well as any outsider can."

"What's he capable of?"

There was no hesitation. "Anything." Sam signed off and snapped to Private Meyer, "Sound the alarm. I want all troops at their stations, and the rest here. Close the gates as soon as the Humvees get inside."

As the alarm blared and orders were relayed over loudspeakers, Sam grabbed his assault rifle and ran down from the guard tower. He waited well behind it, out of view of the gate. The Humvees would stop on the hard-packed dirt in a well-lit area in front of him. Within seconds a lieutenant and a corporal were beside him.

"What's going on, sir?" the lieutenant asked.

"Don't know yet." Sam had a feeling he had the answer, but he did not like it. "Any of the men got viruses or colds?"

The lieutenant and corporal shook their heads.

"Yeah, I didn't think so. I could be wrong about this, but we can't take any chances. I think Ullah's men may be in those Humvees." He told the lieutenant what he wanted him to do.

As more soldiers arrived, the lieutenant directed half to stay with Sam and ran with the rest to the other side of the gate, where they would be out of sight, too.

With a rumble, the Humvees rolled into the base. Sam peered around the edge of the guard tower to check on them. The gunners in the cupolas wore U.S. Army uniforms and helmets. They were dozing over their machine guns. He could not see their faces, and whoever was inside was unseeable, too, through darkened glass. But there were fresh bullet holes in the vehicles. The gates closed behind the Humvees with a clang.

Sam signaled. And four hundred fully equipped, armored, and armed soldiers swarmed out so quickly, the gunners had time only to lift their heads before they were pulled from their turrets and their weapons torn away. It was an overpowering show of force, rows of assault rifles pointed at the Humvees from every possible angle.

For a moment there was no movement. Then the doors opened, and more men in army uniforms stepped out, hands high above their heads, holding army-issue M4s. All were Afghans. U.S. soldiers ripped away the weapons and took the pistols from their belts.

Sam looked up at the guard tower and shouted, "Is Ullah still out there?"

Private Castillo leaned out. "Yes, sir. They filmed the Humvees entering the base, but the light on the camera's off again now."

Sam pushed through his men to reach Ulla's son Jasim, whose tall frame was spread-eagled against the first vehicle. His face was sullen. Sam reached up and grabbed a fistful of Jasim's jacket and tightened it against his throat.

"You want your father to die?" Sam threatened. Then he lied: "I've got a sharpshooter in the tower, and all I have to do is give the order and Syed Ullah is a donkey turd. Tell me what in hell is going on."

The young man's eyes widened. Still he said nothing.

Sam reminded him harshly he was Pashtun. "Your first duty is to protect your family."

In a halting voice Jasim relayed the details of the plan to invade the base and kill all of the soldiers.

Sam hunched his shoulders in fury. He shook Jasim hard once and released him. He barked out an order to his men: "Find out where they left the bodies of our people, then lock him up. Let's move out."

Sam roared out of the base in a Humvee. In other Humvees and running on foot, his soldiers spread in an arc over the flatlands. Ullah's men rose from behind bushes, from holes in the ground, and from behind trees and hotfooted away across the austere landscape. Most would be captured, but not all. But Sam sure as hell was going to catch Ullah.

There was the distant noise of an engine coming to life, and Ullah's Land Cruiser turned in a big circle.

Sam's Humvee and two others lurched over the terrain at a far faster speed than the Land Cruiser, cutting it off as it turned onto the road that led into the hills and to Ullah's villa.

With a bullhorn, Sam blared out his open window, "Get out. Everyone get out! Now!"

M4 in hand, he jumped out of his Humvee and met Ullah and the two others on the dirt road. He was joined instantly by his men, weapons raised.

Ullah's broad face showed surprise, interest, concern. "Captain Daradar, it is very late for you to be patrolling."

"Good evening, Mr. Ullah. There's room in my Humvee for all of you. Your son is asking for you."

At the mention of Jasim, Ullah's black eyebrows raised a fraction, then knitted. It was a small gesture, but from the Pashtun it was everything. With his son in custody, he was not only overwhelmed by force but cornered by the Pashtunwali code.

"Give me your rifle," Sam ordered.

With a flourish, Ullah spun his AK-47, smiled winningly, and handed it over ceremoniously, butt first, the vanquished admitting defeat—for the moment.

What Sam wanted to do was shoot the damn warlord and give the journalists the interview of their lives, but the Kabul government and Uncle Sam would not like that. "Get in. We'll all go back to the base for some *American* tea."

75

The Isle of Pericles

There was a faint explosion, and the Library of Gold door buckled. The guards would be inside in minutes. Despite the high-powered ventilation system, the air in the room seemed to thicken. As Eva rose to her feet, and Tucker spoke to Khost, Judd saw something in Domino's eyes.

"What else?"

Domino nodded and pressed his Walther against Chapman's ear. "Give me your satellite phone."

Slowly Chapman reached inside his tuxedo jacket and removed the phone. "You'll never leave here alive," he said.

Ignoring him, Domino snatched the phone. "I can't do this, but you can, Judd. There's a forward deployment on Crete standing by for rapid insertion. A woman named Gloria Feit is waiting for you or Tucker to call. I'm told she had no other way to get in touch with you and she wasn't certain you'd need or want help."

As Tucker's voice droned on the phone in the background, Eva raised her brows in surprise. "How do you know about Gloria Feit?"

"We'll talk about it later." Domino handed the phone to Judd.

"Archimedes!" Yitzhak had been walking along the wall. He pulled down a volume and opened it excitedly. "Good Lord, they have his complete collection."

Judd was already dialing out.

Instantly Gloria answered. "Souda Bay's been alerted," she said into his ear. "Three Black Hawks with fully loaded fast-rope teams. They'll take off in five minutes. Figure a half hour to get there. Maybe longer. Can you hold out?"

"We have to." Judd ended the connection.

As he filled them in, Tucker finished his call and listened.

"Just a half hour is very long to wait," Roberto said worriedly. "Perhaps your people will require more time to reach the island, and then of course we are down here. Very far underground."

Judd's lungs tightened. Suddenly there was another explosion, this time louder. The door distended into the room, and tendrils of smoke curled toward them.

"The table," Tucker said curtly.

Judd, Domino, and Tucker crashed it over onto its side. Glasses and candlesticks shattered against the floor. They spun the table around through the mess so it faced the door. The top was three inches of marble lying on four inches of wood, a decent shield.

"Get behind," Judd ordered. "Not you." He yanked Chapman to his feet. "Eva, you're in charge of Roberto and Yitzhak."

Roberto grabbed Yitzhak's arm and pulled him away from the books and behind the table. Eva followed with Chapman's M4, glancing over her shoulder at Judd. He looked into her eyes and nodded. She gave a tense smile and nodded in return.

Suddenly Yitzhak rose above the table. "You must not harm the library!"

"Not now, Yitzhak!" Eva pushed him down and crouched beside him.

"You take that side of the door." Domino gestured and ran. "I'll hold the other."

Immediately Tucker sprinted. Like Domino, he positioned

himself flat against the wall, weapon ready. Forcing Chapman to join Tucker, Judd unhooked a frag grenade from his belt.

With a thunderous noise, the door to the library blasted open, landing on the marble and sliding across the room. Gray smoke billowed past them and curled back into the anteroom. As Judd pulled the pin and threw the grenade high into the anteroom's smoke, gunfire instantly sounded, the bullets streaking blindly past them in fusillades, pounding into chairs, the table, and the books.

"No!" Chapman bellowed, looking wildly back as golden covers exploded and volumes plummeted to the floor. He crashed an elbow into Judd's side, trying to break free. "Hold your fire! This is Martin Chapman. I order you to hold your fire!"

Tucker slammed an arm around Chapman's throat and yanked him back.

A loud burst from the grenade in the anteroom shook the library. The smoke was heavy and bitter. They coughed into the sudden silence. Moans sounded from the other side of the doorway.

Judd nodded at Domino. Crouching, weapons raised, they rolled around and stared at the bodies of a half-dozen men who lay in a tumble across the anteroom floor. Blood splattered the walls. Body parts of perhaps four men had been ripped off and tossed, lying on other men and against the elevators and in front of the stairwell.

"Let's go," Judd stood upright and called back into the library. "Fast!"

Domino was quickly at the stairs, his Walther tucked away, an M4 in his arms. Judd raced around the packed bodies and entered the stairwell as Tucker propelled Chapman into the anteroom. Behind him he heard Eva gasp. Then their quick steps were following him upward.

"Looks to me as if we got rid of ten on the way in," Judd

said to Domino's back. "Another six in the anteroom. That leaves about thirty-four."

"Right."

"You figured out the layout?"

"There's a garage on the first underground level. It's past the kitchen, at the end of the hall. They won't realize you'll know about it."

"Safer than going through the house," Judd agreed.

Suddenly heavy footsteps sounded, running down toward them. Judd looked up and saw a large number one painted on the stone wall, announcing they were just below ground level. Side by side, they accelerated to the landing as two security men appeared.

Dropping flat on the steps, Judd ripped off a grenade, pulled the pin, and heaved it. Domino fell beside him, and they covered their heads with their arms. Captured in the stairwell, the blast was deafening. Stone chips pelted down. And they jumped up, stepped through the smoke, and pushed the door open onto a high-tech kitchen. At first it appeared deserted, then Judd saw chefs and waiters cringing against a back wall.

"Get down!" he barked and aimed the M4.

As the men and women scrambled to the floor, Domino ran to a side door and propped it open. Through it a long corridor showed. His head swiveling, he hurried along, studying closed doors as he passed.

Judd opened the kitchen door, listening. More security guards were running down the flight of stairs.

"You in one piece?" Tucker demanded as he shoved Chapman past him.

Chapman's expression was steely, his eyes glinting with outrage. "When my men catch you, I'll kill you myself."

Judd ignored him. "We're fine," he told Tucker. "Give me one of your grenades. Follow Domino."

As they moved off, Eva arrived with Yitzhak and Roberto. The pair were breathing hard and said nothing. Judd did not like the way Yitzhak looked. The professor's round face was gray, and the sweat on his bald head was thick.

Eva gave Judd a too-bright smile and urged Yitzhak and Roberto toward the corridor.

Alone, Judd crouched, his M4 trained on the kitchen staff as he listened to the footsteps descending. As soon as he saw the first pair of feet, he pulled the last grenade's pin, rolled it onto the landing, closed the door, and sprinted. The noise of the explosion followed him across the kitchen. In his mind he added up the number of the remaining guards in the stairwell—a total of two or three, he decided. That was not a large number. He would have thought the entire force would have been sent after them when they heard the initial explosions.

Slamming shut the door to the corridor, he tore down its length toward the garage. At least thirty minutes had passed, he decided. Roberto had been right. Even if the helicopters had arrived, it would be longer. Ten minutes, maybe twenty, for the teams to fight through the remaining guards to find them. He shook off the worry they would not be able to hold out.

He pushed through the door. And froze. Stared. Domino knelt on the floor, clutching his upper chest where a fresh bullet wound showed. His tuxedo jacket was drenched in blood, and his face was battered. Tucker was helping him up, while Eva kept her M4 aimed at Martin Chapman. At the same time Yitzhak sat cross-legged on the floor, collapsed over his stout stomach, panting, while Roberto worriedly rubbed his back. Six security men lay sprawled on the concrete floor, either dead or unconscious. That was a partial explanation of where Chapman's extra men were.

Instantly Judd checked the door. There was no way to lock it.

"They were expecting us," Domino said calmly as he pulled himself up, his M4 dangling from one hand. "Must have some tracking system I didn't know about. Tucker arrived just in time."

"Good work, both of you."

Domino nodded. Rifle ready, Tucker ran across the vast garage space emptied of patrolling Jeeps toward the maw left open by the sliding garage door. Domino limped after him.

Now Judd had one wounded shooter, the professor, who looked so ill he could not walk, and Chapman, who had to be guarded at all times. Inwardly he swore. Suddenly he was exhausted, and he realized the wound on his side was throbbing painfully. He grabbed a loading cart.

"Let's go, professor. You get to ride." He handed his rifle to Roberto and gently picked up the older man and set him on the cart's bed. "Climb aboard, Roberto."

Roberto sat beside Yitzhak. "You are good, yes?"

The professor said nothing, simply dipped his head once. His eyes were dull with pain.

"You first, Eva." Judd looked at her strained face.

"Delighted. Move, Chapman." Then she warned, "I'll be right behind you, and it'd be such a pleasure to shoot you."

"Let me go," Chapman said, his cool gaze assessing their weakened position. "I'll call off my men and get you out of here."

"My ass," Eva retorted. "You're alive. Don't try for more. As Horace said, *'Semper avarus eget.'* That means a greedy man's always in need, you greedy bastard."

She hurried him off, and Judd ran past them, pushing the cart. Tucker was on one side of the big garage door, Domino on the other. Both were peering out carefully. Judd glanced over his shoulder at the door to the corridor to make certain it remained closed and Eva still controlled Chapman.

But as he neared the garage door and felt the night air cool on his skin, he heard the shouts of men out on the hillsides. He parked the cart off to the side, against the wall. That explained the rest of Chapman's men. More would be coming through the house after them.

"Stay there," he told Yitzhak and Roberto. Before they could respond, he joined Domino, who moved aside so he could take the lead. "See anything?"

"They're closing in," Domino said through bruised lips. His jaw was swelling.

Abruptly fusillades of gunfire raked through the garage's opening, whining past and spitting into the concrete floor. Judd dropped, rolled, and came up on his elbows, sending bursts out toward the flashes of light. Instantly Domino was lying beside him, shooting, too. Dark shadows of men were moving down to join the shooters, far more than the number of Chapman's men Judd had thought were left. Had Chapman put on more security than he realized?

In his peripheral vision he saw Eva push Chapman to Tucker's side of the door. Now that they had arrived, Tucker dropped to fire, too.

As Judd squeezed off bursts, he glanced up in time to see Chapman take in the scene, his gaze calculating. Only Eva was left standing to guard him.

"Eva!" Judd warned. "Chapman's going to—"

Too late. The tall man whirled and lashed out a foot, kicking away her M4. She lunged for it, and he fell on her. Fighting back, she kneed him in the groin, and they rolled, their legs and arms tangled. Judd could not get a clear shot.

Enraged, he jumped up and ran toward her as gunfire continued to slash into the garage. Rounds crazed his back, burning.

Suddenly he heard the door to the corridor behind them

burst open. In the shelter of the wall, he turned, firing blindly, raking blasts toward it.

"Stop, Judd!" Tucker bellowed. "It's our people!"

A paramilitary team dressed in black with black combat gear was streaming around the door, crouching, M4s up.

At the same time, Domino announced tiredly, "Your people are wiping out the security guards on the hills, too."

Judd said nothing, looking out quickly as he listened to the blistering gunfire. Fusillades no longer streamed into the garage. The gunshots came from all over the dark slopes, muzzle flashes bright and fast as the paratroopers fought the guards.

Judd sprinted to Eva. "Get off her, you asshole!" But before Chapman could move, Judd kicked him in the head.

The hills were quiet at last. Shadows moved as paratroopers rounded up the last of Chapman's security men. Inside the garage, Eva waited beside Judd, his closeness comforting, as he and Tucker filled in the lieutenant in charge of the operation. At a distance, Chapman sat on the floor, hands cuffed behind him, head cocked as he tried to hear what they said. Blood matted his white hair from Judd's blow. Refusing to speak, he was alert, his expression angry, his lips thin and tightly closed.

A medic had examined Yitzhak and pronounced a profound case of exhaustion. Roberto and Yitzhak held hands in the cart as one of the soldiers pushed them across the floor toward the house.

Domino took off his tuxedo jacket, and the medic ripped his shirt, gave him shots of antibiotics and painkillers, and cleaned his wound.

"Looks as if the bullet missed your lungs, but you've got a broken rib, I think," the medic decided. "I'll bandage you until I can get you to a hospital. The painkiller should be kicking in now."

"Give that to me."

Domino grabbed packets of sterile bandages. Pushing the medic away, he stood, ripped open two, and slapped one bandage onto the entrance wound in back and the other in front.

He looked at Judd. "Let's get the hell out of here."

Eva was about to say something, then thought better of it. She joined Domino, Judd, and Tucker as they walked across the garage. She felt their weariness and was suddenly aware of her own.

"So you work for the Carnivore, Domino?" she asked.

"I do occasional jobs for him. He felt I'd be appropriate for this particular task." He had a calm, untroubled expression now.

"Who is the Carnivore, really?"

He chuckled and ran a finger along his red nose. "He told me you might ask. The answer is he's a man without a face. He employs me only through e-mail." He gazed at Judd a moment. "I owe you for killing Preston. Saved my hide."

"A pleasure, believe me."

"Nevertheless, I won't forget."

They rode the elevator up one floor, to the ground level. The living room showed the effects of a gun battle. Furniture and vases were shattered, and bullet holes riddled paintings. They walked out through the double glass doors onto the marble pathway.

Moonlight shone down, casting the grounds in a soft glow. A half-dozen corpses were laid out beside the tennis courts. Chefs and staff members were sitting on the ground, guarded by two members of the paramilitary teams. Ahead, three sleek Black Hawk helicopters were parked on and around the helipad. One's rotors were turning. Yitzhak and Roberto were climbing on board.

The four passed two cottages.

"This one was your husband's," Domino told Eva. "In case you want to see it."

She stopped and gazed at the white walls, then at the carved wood door, much like the one into the Library of Gold. "Yes, you're right. I'd like to go inside."

"I'll go with you," Judd offered.

"We need to talk about the Carnivore and how you found out about Gloria Feit," Tucker told Domino.

"Of course. I'll fill you in completely, but give me a few moments to rest. How about on the helicopter ride back?"

Tucker gave an understanding nod. "Agreed."

As the pair waited outside, Judd and Eva entered the small foyer of Charles Sherback's cottage and walked into a spacious living room. It had been searched. Books piled haphazardly on the floor, the shelves that lined the walls empty. The cushions on the sofas and easy chairs were upended, and the drawers on the writing desk left open. Eva clasped her throat.

Judd followed her into the bedroom. The cover and sheets on the king-size bed were torn off. Clothes from the bureau and closet lay on the floor. Men's clothes—and women's clothes.

Eva walked up to a framed needlepoint above the dresser. It was a quotation:

I cannot live without books.
—Thomas Jefferson, letter to John Adams, 1815

"I gave that to Charles," she said quietly, her back to Judd. "It was in his office at the Moreau Library. I'd forgotten about it."

Judd had seen no photos in the living room, but there were several hanging on the wall in the bedroom of Charles and Robin—working together in the library, walking on the beach, picking oranges in a grove. He watched Eva turn to gaze at them.

"Maybe he took the Jefferson quotation to remember you," he said kindly.

"Or maybe he wanted it because he liked the quotation. Did I tell you I can needlepoint?"

He put an arm around her shoulders. "I imagine there are a lot things you haven't told me. I'd like to know all of them."

She smiled up at him but said nothing, full of emotions she could not name.

He felt a moment of disappointment, then he led her to the door. They walked out into the night. Another helicopter's rotors were turning, the motor sending waves of sound across the fresh sea air.

"Where are Tucker and Domino?" Judd looked quickly around.

They ran. Tucker was pushing himself up off the ground behind a bush.

"Tucker, what happened?" she said.

"The bastard got me while I wasn't looking." He grimaced and dusted off his trousers. "Obviously he didn't want to answer my questions."

"There he is," Judd said, peering far up the hill behind them.

Domino was a solitary figure, climbing swiftly. He had peeled off his white shirt and was wearing a long-sleeve black T-shirt. With his black tuxedo trousers, he was difficult to see. Then he turned, and moonlight illuminated his face. Cradling his M4, he caught sight of them.

"Come back, dammit!" Tucker shouted.

Instead Domino lifted two fingers and deliberately touched

his forehead in a brisk salute. Eva vaguely recalled the gesture . . . And then it was vivid: A moonlit night like this, the Thracian coast in Turkey. She and Judd were sitting inside the small plane, about to take off for Athens, and Judd had saluted back.

The men cursed as Domino's silhouetted form ran off lightly and vanished over the hill's crest.

But Eva felt a strange thrill. "My God, it was him all along. The assassin without a face. There is no Domino. That was the Carnivore."

EPILOGUE

Georgetown, D.C.

Even in the long shadows of twilight the June evening was sultry, typical for a District summer. The sidewalks and granite buildings radiated heat, while the scents of blooming flowers mixed with the stench of oily concrete as Eva Blake hurried along Wisconsin Avenue in downtown Georgetown.

She was full of memories. It had been two months since the discovery of the Library of Gold on the Isle of Pericles, and at last she had a sense of what she wanted for her future. With her conviction for Charles's murder scrubbed, she had collected his life insurance, leased a condo in Silver Spring, and moved to be near Washington.

Headlines had echoed around the world with the revelation the Library of Gold had been found at last. Included in the news was the Greek government's arrests of Martin Chapman and the other surviving members of the book club—all international businessmen—on charges of kidnapping Yitzhak Law and Roberto Cavaletti, the only charges they had a hope of making stick. The men were quickly out on bail, claiming Yitzhak and Roberto had simply been visiting. Since Yitzhak had told his Rome university he was going out of town on business just before he and Roberto disappeared, there was some credence to the book club's defense. In any case, the seven men had a world-class team of lawyers working around the clock for them, while the CIA needed to keep its role secret and was going to be of little help supporting any charges against them. At least

Yitzhak and Roberto were back home and safe in their familiar routines.

A footnote to worldwide news, but a headline-grabber in Los Angeles, was that Charles Sherback had been found on the island, dead. Full of curiosity, former friends and colleagues had called, giving Eva condolences. At the same time the media had swarmed, packing her voice mail with pleas for interviews and camping out outside her hotel. She could not go to the drugstore, pick up her dry cleaning, or eat in a café without being peppered with questions. Thankfully here in Washington she was out of the fish bowl.

As was the way of politics in Afghanistan, Syed Ullah was no longer warlord. The Kabul government had sent its army to force him to give his region to an up-and-coming young rival, and now Ullah was running for the next parliamentary election. It appeared as if he would win, but Kabul gave no indication it was worried. Its ties to Pakistan remained tangled. The film of the two Pakistani newsmen had been confiscated, and the Islamabad government had ordered them to forget anything they saw, so the U.S. military base was safe. It was in Pakistan's best interest to keep Afghanistan as stable as possible, at least for now.

As she walked down the busy street, Eva watched the dusky shadows. She still felt the bone-weary exhaustion of being hunted, of the roller-coaster ride of terrifying failures and exhilarating successes. And she deeply missed her friend Peggy Doty. Several times she had talked on the phone with Peggy's longtime beau, Zack Turner, who remained inconsolable.

She fought back anger as she remembered Charles's faked death, her incarceration, and the still unidentified corpse in Charles's grave. Betrayal after betrayal. She wondered who she had been before prison and the Library of Gold operation.

Clearly she had changed. It was time to find out who she was now.

Judd and Tucker were waiting at a table in Five Guys Famous Burgers and Fries on the corner of Dumbarton Street. They sat across from each other, the older academic-looking man in his tortoiseshell glasses and the battered athlete in his sports jacket and turtleneck. She smiled as they spotted her.

Motioning them to stay seated, she kissed each on the cheek. "You have my hamburger. Thanks, Tucker."

"You look good, Eva," Judd said. "Rested."

"I feel rested." She smiled as she sat between them.

The men were already eating, so she dove into the hamburger and fries they had ordered for her. She had not seen Tucker since her return to the United States, and she had been with Judd only when they were being debriefed. His face still looked troubled occasionally. Not only had his father been killed, but he had discovered his deep involvement in the powerful and immoral book club.

"How's your mother, Judd?" Tucker was asking.

"Much better. Busy again with her philanthropies. She doesn't know the truth about Dad and the Library of Gold."

"No reason she should know," Eva said quickly.

Judd nodded. "What's the latest with the book club, Tucker?"

Tucker chewed a moment. "I can't go into specifics, of course, but I can tell you the Justice Department has investigators working in the various countries in which the club members do business. The problem is, the members are effectively out of our control, even if we discover criminal activity—unless it's in the United States or in a foreign country where the government is willing to cooperate."

Judd shook his head in disgust. Then he changed the subject. "Have we made peace with the Greeks?"

Tucker chuckled. "H. L. Mencken wrote something to the effect that nations get along with one another not by telling the truth but by lying gracefully. We made a deal. In exchange for the Greeks' forgetting we sent our paratroopers into their territory, we let them take credit for finding the Library of Gold."

"That explains the news stories. Charles would've been furious." Eva laughed. Greece's renowned government historian Nikos Amourgis had received the credit. "What's going to happen to the library now?"

Finished eating, Tucker pushed his plate away. "It's vanished. The word is it will remain private."

"You don't know where it is?" she asked, surprised. "The Greeks don't?"

"They ended their investigation on the island last month. The next week our flyovers told us it was gone. There are no buildings on the mesa now. The underground levels have been filled in, and a fruit orchard planted. Even the wharf's been carted away. The bottom line is the island's private, and the collection is privately owned, so they can do whatever they want. The library's hardly a national security issue for us, so we won't devote manpower to locating it again."

They were silent with disappointment.

"What about the Carnivore?" Eva asked eagerly. "Did you track him down?"

She knew Gloria had sent out word to all Catapult operatives, asking them or any of their sources who had contact with Tucker or Judd to tell them to phone her for help. That was how the Carnivore must have known to have them call Gloria while they were trapped in the Library of Gold. Then when the Carnivore escaped on the island, Tucker sent paratroopers out to look for him. They reported a small dark speedboat on the west side, taking off into the night. It was possible the Carnivore was on it, but they had needed the helicopters to transport the injured off the island and so had not pursued.

Tucker shook his head. "No. I had Gloria send out another notice to our people after I got back, this time asking whoever had told the Carnivore about us to let us know. No one owned up to it. Frustrating as hell."

"You've got someone in Catapult who knows the Carnivore," Judd said, "or can reach him somehow."

"Right. And no one's talking."

"Still, his help was critical," Eva said. "In fact, I think it's safe to say he was instrumental in saving our lives."

"Yes, and I'm not going to hunt him," Tucker said. "Bad things happen when one goes after the Carnivore, but that doesn't bother me. I just don't see much point to it, at least for now."

"Oddly, I'm glad," Eva said.

Tucker peered around the lively fast-food joint. Two middle-age men had arrived with their burgers and sat at the next table.

"Let's get out of here." Tucker stood and led Judd and Eva out of the restaurant.

As they walked down Wisconsin Avenue, Tucker, between them, glanced at one, then the other. "I know the Library of Gold operation was rough on you. You uncovered very unpleasant facts about people you loved. On the other hand, I've always believed illusions are overrated. Consider a great ballet. From the audience you see extraordinary dancers seemingly light as air, leaping, pirouetting, and generally moving like sylphs in ways most of us can only dream. But if you go backstage you find sweat, torn muscles, and mangled feet. Which is better?" Before they could respond, he went on: "My take is backstage. That's where you learn what it takes to create something extraordinary. It shows the human spirit at its most indomitable. And the next time you sit in the audience the illusion is gone and you start to see that with effort all of us can achieve a sort of glory in our lives."

"Are you talking about Judd's father and Charles?" Eva asked.

"Yes. Both did despicable things, but they did good things as well. Remembering that will help you to live with the facts."

They were silent.

At last Tucker said, "Judd, there's work for you with me whenever you want. I know you're reluctant now, but remember, I can use you. Ivan the Terrible was onto something when he commissioned *The Book of Spies*. Spies have a long if checkered past, and we're still badly needed."

Judd shook his head. "Thanks, but no thanks."

Eva cleared her throat. "What about me?"

The men stared at her.

"What do you mean?" Judd asked sharply.

"Both of you seemed to think I did a good job," she said calmly. "I want to go through the CIA training program. If I get weeded out, so be it."

"But you loved your work as a curator," Judd objected.

"Yes, but I never felt the same commitment, the same sense of doing something that could make a difference. You must've sensed I was heading in this direction, Judd. Otherwise you wouldn't have bothered to teach me so much."

Tucker chuckled. "You're right, Eva. You've got the talent and the brains. I'll make some calls tomorrow." He looked at his watch. "I'll be leaving you here. I'm going to meet my wife at the Kennedy for opera. Her idea. I hate opera, but right now she gets whatever she wants." He pounded Judd on the back and kissed Eva on the cheek. "I know I can trust both of you never to say a word about the operation." He turned and left.

"Is he in charge of Catapult now?" Eva asked as she looked back over her shoulder, watching his energetic gait.

"Hell, no." Judd's gray eyes danced. "My bet is he'll never take the job. Gloria's irritated, but she's living with it." Then he said solemnly, "I warned you not to like the work too much."

She smiled. "Are you going to hold it against me?"

"No. You'll be a damn good addition to Langley."

He reached into his pocket and held out his hand. As he uncurled his fingers, she saw her wedding ring and the necklace Charles had given her.

"You kept them?" She felt a strange emotion.

"Now that life is settling down a bit, I thought you might know more what you wanted to do with them. They're yours, after all."

"The pendant is a Roman coin. The goddess Diana. It was Charles's first gift to me."

"She's the huntress," he remembered.

"Yes, somehow I reminded Charles of her."

"He wasn't wrong about that."

She took the jewelry and the responsibility. "I'll donate them." She slid them into her pocket.

They walked on silently. She was mulling what Tucker had said about illusions.

"Strange how neither of us saw the truth about your father and Charles," she said at last. "Instead what we saw was love. *Ut ameris, amabilis esto.* That's from Ovid and it means that if you want to be loved, be lovable. In their own ways they were lovable. We can't ever forget what they did—but it'd be healthy for us to work on forgiving them."

"I'll call you," he said.

"Yes, we'll talk more."

She smiled at him, and he smiled back, gazing deep into her eyes. A warm intimacy passed between them.

"I'm glad to have met you, Eva Blake." He took her hand. His grip was firm.

She held up their hands and gazed at his. His hand no longer looked to her like the hand of a killer. But then, Michelangelo had been working in marble, and this was the warm flesh of a man. A very good man.

Rome, Italy

The month of July was the height of Estate Romana, the Rome summer festival. A six-week auditory and visual feast, the festival was a flood of mostly outdoor shows, many set in grassy parks and amid ruins to take advantage of the splendor of ancient Rome. The Carnivore always tried to be in the city for at least a few days to enjoy as much as he could. Tonight was a good night for it, warm but not hot, the stars shining brightly.

Passing the tumbled walls and columns of the Temple of Claudius on his right, he climbed the steep paving stones of Via Claudia and breathed deeply, filling his lungs and expelling air in mighty bursts, savoring his returned vigor, his good health. Escaping from the Isle of Pericles had taken every ounce of strength he'd had. The medic's painkillers had helped, and of course he had long practiced the rule of the cat—never show you're injured, vulnerable.

Jack O'Keefe, Doug Kennedy, and George Russell had been waiting in a high-powered speedboat at the specified location, and within hours they were at the airport on Mykonos and on their way home. The bullet that got him had ripped through large muscles and nicked a rib, so he had taken time to convalesce, then resumed his regime of cardio and weights.

At the wrought-iron gate he bought a ticket and walked onto the grounds of the magnificent Villa Celimontana. The park spread across Celio Hill, one of the city's seven storied hills, south of the Coliseum. Little known, it was an oasis of peace and greenery in chaotic Rome. Across the drive, "Jazz" was projected in colorful letters. The Carnivore strode through the lights, taking in the tall cypresses and centuries-old oaks and pines. The winding pathways were littered with pieces of carved marble and broken classical statues. In five minutes he was at the sixteenth-century villa, a tall two stories and pink in the night's lights.

Turning a corner, he passed an outdoor jazz poster gallery, sculptures, artistic installations, and finally a fountain heralding the venue's entrance. He listened to the jazz sounds of Charles Lloyd's sweet tenor sax.

As the rich music filled the night air, he climbed the wood terraces built for the summer season. Rows of tables decorated with little red lanterns filled the top three levels of the semicircular amphitheater, while concert seating was on the patio below, the chairs facing the stage, where Lloyd was soloing in front of a small jazz band.

He found his table, sat, and reached for the beer that was awaiting him—a chilled blond beer from Birra Menabrea, perfect for the warm night.

"Good to see you, Uncle Hal." Bash Badawi was out of his usual shorts and T-shirt, dressed for the occasion in worn jeans and an open-necked purple shirt rolled up at the sleeves. Both were cellophane tight against his muscular body. Despite the late hour, wraparound sunglasses sat on his straight jet-black hair, and his dark eyes were smiling in his golden face. He looked completely modern Roman.

"How's your mother?" The Carnivore drank. Bash was not really his nephew, but his first cousin once removed—his mother's sister's grandchild. It was complicated, but then they came from a large Italian family.

"Mom's good. Making pasta as if we were all still living

at home. I told her she should start selling online, but she got all bent out of shape. The pasta wouldn't be *fresh*—but I was for suggesting it. That woman can still swing a killer wood spoon. You know what I mean, with the long handle and the hot spaghetti sauce dripping from the bowl. Painful." Grinning, Bash assessed him. "You look pretty good for a guy who had his entrails toyed with."

"Just muscle." The Carnivore drank again, enjoying the young man who reminded him of who he might have been. Then he asked the question that had drawn him here: "Anyone looking for me?"

"Just the usual rogues, wannabes, and historians. Seriously, I think you're safe. I can't give you the details about how I know—national security and all that—but the fellow you met on the island, Tucker Andersen, has called off the hunt."

The Carnivore only nodded, but he was relieved. He had liked Andersen and Blake, and now he owed Judd Ryder.

"You going to be in trouble over this?" he asked.

"Hey, no prob. You did us a favor, and I'm keeping my mouth shut. Secrecy's what they trained me for." Bash raised a muscular hand, two fingers displayed, signaling for more beers. "So are you on downtime now? Got any exciting jobs?" he asked casually.

The Carnivore gazed over the parapet at the vistas of Rome. The city's lights sparkled around the massive ruins of the Baths of Caracalla. Today it was a shell of bricks, but at one time it had sprawled across twenty-seven acres and accommodated sixteen hundred bathers at a time. He remembered that Emperor Caracalla, who had built the baths in the third century A.D., had been a cruel, ruthless ruler. Traveling from Edessa to begin a war with Parthia, he had stopped to urinate on the roadside and was assassinated by one of his own—a frustrated and ambitious officer in the Imperial Guard.

The Carnivore chuckled. "Drink up, boy. The night is young, and for the moment I'll pretend I am as well. As for my plans, secrecy's what I was trained for, too."

AUTHOR'S NOTE

The Mysterious History of the Library of Gold

The search for Ivan the Terrible's lost library—occasionally called the Byzantine Libreria—in the labyrinthine tunnels under Moscow has continued for some five centuries, capturing the imaginations of emperors, potentates, and the Vatican. Joseph Stalin stopped the hunt in the 1930s because he feared that searching the tunnels would leave him vulnerable to attack from beneath, while Vladimir Putin, in a gesture signifying Russia's new openness, allowed the quest to resume in the 1990s.

Today a host of scholars, scientists, historians, and amateurs pore over old, incomplete maps and request official permission to investigate. Joining the pursuit are vine walkers who claim to use bioenergetic powers to locate metal; psychics who act as security against "dark forces" that might be guarding the hidden tomes since past searchers have been prone to accidents, disease, blindness, or death; and the Diggers of the Underground Planet, a group of urban spelunkers with a cult following, who drop through manholes and pry open forgotten iron doors to reach the unexplored passages.

My interest in the library dates back more than twenty years. On June 28, 1989, I was reading the *Los Angeles Times* when "Kremlin Tunnels: The Secret of Moscow's Underworld," by Masha Hamilton, caught my attention.

It was a summer evening in 1933 when the two young men found what they were searching for: the entrance to a centuries-old underground tunnel within sight of the red Kremlin walls. As they crept underground toward Moscow's seat of power, lighting their way with a lantern, the men believed they might find Ivan the Terrible's legendary library of gold-covered books. Instead they found five skeletons, a passageway sometimes so narrow that they had to file through singly and, within a few hundred yards of the Kremlin, a rusted steel door they could not open.

I was enthralled by this "library of gold-covered books," which immediately became in my mind the Library of Gold. Kremlin officials stopped the young pair's exploration and swore them to secrecy with the implied threat of death, then Stalin ordered a swimming pool built over the area, putting a conclusive end to anyone's quest.

The story of the fabled library is one of geopolitics, an arranged marriage, madness, and the enduring love of books. And it begins more than two thousand years ago in the Greco-Roman world of emperors, scholars, warriors, and the wealthy.

An intentionally chilling ancient Roman tombstone has this inscription: *Sum quod eris, fui quod sis*—"I am what you will be; I was what you are." Public and private libraries were assembled by the ancients to enjoy, to educate, and to display affluence and privilege. But in the largest sense they were created to preserve knowledge. Remarkable international library centers in Alexandria, Pergamum, Antioch, Rome, and Athens thrived for centuries. Tragically all were obliterated, sometimes in war, sometimes with avarice, sometimes purposefully to destroy history and culture.

The last great repository in that long-ago Western world

was the royal library in Constantinople. Founded in about 330 A.D. by Constantine the Great, the city grew up on the site of a Greek town called Byzantium. At the time, it was known as the Roman Empire, though today it is referred to as the Byzantine Empire. By 475, the royal library had 120,000 volumes, probably making it the largest in that era. Over the following centuries the library was burned several times, vaporizing multitudes of priceless works, including, some claimed, a piece by Homer lettered in gold on a twelve-foot-long snakeskin.

Still the imperial collection constantly rose from the literary ashes. In the 1400s the Spanish traveler Pero Tafur described it thus: ". . . a marble gallery opening on arcades with tiled marble benches all around and with similarly crafted tables placed end to end upon low columns; there are many books there, ancient texts and histories."

The final blow came on May 29, 1453, when Mehmed the Conqueror and his Ottoman Turks brutally seized Constantinople. The English historian Edward Gibbon wrote, "One hundred twenty thousand manuscripts are said to have disappeared."

Six years later the survivors of the Byzantine royal family escaped as the Ottoman Turks invaded Morea, the rich Greek Peloponnese peninsula ruled by the emperor's heir and nephew, Thomas Paleologus. Accompanying Thomas on the small Venetian galley were his wife and children—two young sons and a daughter, Zoë, about twelve years old. She would play a critical role in the Library of Gold.

They made their way to Italy, where Pius II took them under the papal wing, and the Vatican provided a palace and stipend. The pope had a vital political and religious goal—to enthrone Thomas at a recaptured Constantinople. Thomas and his family were Greek Orthodox, but they had promptly converted to Roman Catholic once they reached

Italy. If the pope succeeded, Thomas would rule over a Christian New Byzantium, Western in outlook, uniting Catholic and Orthodox—and under the religious control of Rome.

The Venetians, who were making fortunes in trade with the Ottoman Turks, were less than happy about it. When Pius tried twice to mount a Fifth Crusade, this time against Constantinople, the Venetians dithered. Finally they delayed their fleet so long that the last attempted attack fell apart, and the pope died.

The next pope, Paul II, feinted. He looked east again, but this time his target was the widowed Ivan III, the Grand Prince of Moscow, soon to be called Ivan the Great. The Russian Orthodox Church had long flourished in Moscow. Hoping to acquire Ivan as a military ally against the Turks, as well as his consent for the Union of Churches, the pope offered Zoë's hand in marriage in 1472. She was now about twenty years old.

Moscow was the strongest of the Russian states and the fastest growing power of the times, although it was still under the Muslim yoke. Ivan accepted the proposal, and the royal pair married in Moscow before the year was out. Zoë took the name Sophia.

We know Sophia traveled with a large retinue by land and sea to Moscow. Her arrival was accompanied by Italians and Greeks, who settled there, too, and became influential, even rebuilding the Kremlin in a Russian-Italianate style. This is the point where the legend begins.

According to several commentators, Sophia brought with her to Moscow priceless illuminated manuscripts from the Byzantine imperial collection. "The chronicles mention 100 carts loaded with 300 boxes with rare books arriving in Moscow," according to Alexandra Vinogradskaya, writing in The Russian Culture Navigator. Another version is this: "The princess arrived in Moscow with a dowry of 70 carts, carrying hundreds of trunks, which contained the heritage of early cultures—the library collected by the Byzantine emperors," explains Nikolay Khinsky on WhereRussia.com, the Russian National Tourist site for International Travelers.

What is undisputed is that Sophia did bring the Ivory Throne of the Byzantine emperors on which Russian monarchs were crowned ever after, as well as the double-headed eagle, the imperial symbol of the Byzantine Empire for a thousand years, which became the Kremlin's for nearly another five hundred years. She introduced the grand court traditions of Byzantium, too, including ceremonial etiquette and costume. Even before the wedding, Ivan had assumed the title of czar—Caesar—and then added *grozny*, "formidable," a reverential adjective common in Byzantine autocracy, since the sovereign was considered the earthly image of God and empowered with all His sacred and judicial powers.

Since Sophia carried so much of Byzantium with her, it is very possible illuminated manuscripts were among her gifts. As Deb Brown, bibliographer and research services librarian for Byzantine studies at Dumbarton Oaks, wrote me: "There seems to be nothing in the (published) contemporary sources that testifies to books in Zoë/Sophia's possession, but I'm not convinced that she did not carry books with her. The silence of sources has to be weighed against the nature of the sources, which are few and concerned with matters of state and monies, not much else. There are plenty of indications that she was literate and well-educated."

Ultimately the Vatican's geopolitical gamesmanship partially succeeded. Sophia was the one who persuaded Ivan III in 1478 to challenge the Golden Horde. "When the customary messengers came from the Tatar Khan demanding the usual tribute, Ivan threw the edict on the ground, stamped and spat on it, and killed all the ambassadors save one, whom he sent back to his master," according to Gilbert Grosvenor in *National Geographic* magazine. Over time his armies beat back Khan Ahmed's soldiers, and Moscow was never seriously threatened by them again. One of the longest-reigning Russian rulers, Ivan tripled his territory and laid the foundations of state, based largely on the autocratic rule of Byzantium.

Where the Vatican failed was that the Chair of Peter was not unified with the throne of Constantine—upon her arrival in Moscow, Sophia had promptly endorsed Orthodoxy again.

The Library of Gold would have passed from Sophia and Ivan to their son Vasily III, and from him to his son Ivan IV. In 1547 at the young age of seventeen, Ivan IV outwitted Kremlin plots and crowned himself "Czar of All Russia." Eventually he, too, became known as Grozny—Ivan the Terrible—infamous ever since for his cruelty, slaughters of entire cities, and pleasure in torture. At the same time, a hundred years before Peter the Great was credited with doing so, Ivan opened Russia to the West. He frequently corresponded with European monarchs, including Elizabeth I of England, exchanged diplomats, and nurtured international trade. He not only extended Russia to the Pacific Ocean, but he also introduced the printing press to Russia.

"How many Oriental manuscripts does the monarch have?" asks Khinsky, referring to testimony describing Ivan the Terrible's library. "Up to 800. Some he has bought, some he has received as gifts. Most of the manuscripts are Greek, but many are Latin. The Latin I've seen include histories by Livius, *De Republica* by Cicero, stories about emperors by Suetonius. These manuscripts are written on thin parchment and bound in gold."

From his letters we know Ivan was familiar with the Bible, the Apocrypha, the Chronographs, which dealt with world history, and tales from *The Iliad*. He received books as presents from foreign envoys and visitors, had books written, and ordered others to be copied into Russian for his use.

"Historians know about the existence of the library because Ivan the Terrible instructed scribes to translate the books into Russian," says an article in *The Times*. "According to legend, the library once filled three halls and was so valued by Ivan the Terrible that he built a vault to protect [the books] from the fires that regularly swept Moscow." But the vault, allegedly hidden under the Kremlin, might also have been the result of Ivan's mental instability and growing paranoia.

News of the library spread across Europe. "The Germans, English, and Italians made many attempts to persuade the Russian czar to sell the treasure," writes Vinogradskaya. "But a man of considerable literary talent himself, Ivan the Terrible was an eager collector of rare books and fully aware of the high value of his collection. He refused to sell anything."

Ivan was also fascinated by spies and assassins, and used them frequently. His top spy and security chief had instant access to his bedchambers through one of the tunnels under the Kremlin. And Ivan created the feared Oprichniki, his clandestine personal armed force, who conducted espionage and assassinations. Chillingly, they dressed completely in black and rode black horses.

Begun in the 1100s and added to over the centuries, the tangled, endless underground tunnels were originally intended as escape routes, to give access to water if the Kremlin was besieged, and to move comfortably from one building to another during the harsh Russian winter. Reaching depths of twelve stories, the tunnels contain streams, dungeons, and secret chambers.

"Legend has it that all his [Ivan's] gold was hidden in one tunnel," writes Khinsky, "paintings and icons in another, and manuscripts from the Byzantine library in another. All the hiding places were carefully bricked up." Salt is a good preservative, and apparently natural salt basements have been found in Moscow's netherworld.

After reading his will in the morning and calling for his chess set in the afternoon, Ivan died in 1584. The will, which might have listed his library, mysteriously vanished. When his body was exhumed in 1963, traces of both mercury and arsenic were discovered, but not at high enough levels for the cause of death to have been poisoning, although it's a popular belief he was indeed poisoned.

According to Khinsky, sixteen years after the monarch's death, a Vatican envoy arrived to find out what had happened to the library. Old archives and book depositories were searched, and exploration parties sent out to dig. "The existence of the library is first mentioned in documents from the period of Peter the Great's rule, which began in 1682," according to Hamilton of the *Los Angeles Times*.

Ivan was the last known owner of the Library of Gold. "Historians, archaeologists, Peter the Great, and even the Vatican have searched fruitlessly for the missing library for hundreds of years," says *The Times*. In the seventeenth century most of the oldest tunnels were already out of use and forgotten, and the passage of time has made the hunt increasingly difficult because of weakened fortifications, landslides, flooding, and incomplete maps.

"The Kremlin is the dwelling of phantoms," wrote the Marquis de Custine, who visited Russia in the early nineteenth century. "It feels as though the underground sounds born there were coming from the grave."

It's not surprising that this vital collection of books, perhaps the most important to survive in history, remains the subject of gripping interest. In the course of various explorations, the sprawling mass of subterranean tunnels has yielded very old treasures, including a hidden arsenal of Ivan the Terrible's weapons, the czarina's chambers where Peter the Great spent his childhood, the city's largest silver coin hoard, gold jewelry, documents, and precious tableware and dishes, many of which have been put on public display. The Archaeology Museum is the site of some of these unique finds.

"Fear me, Giant Sewer Rodents, for I Am Vadim, Lord of the Underground!" is the title of an article written by Erin Arvedlund in *Outside* magazine about Vadim Mikhailov and his eager band of subterranean explorers—the Diggers of the Underground Planet. Their dream is to find the Library of Gold. Instead they have turned up skeletons, mutant fish, fugitives, clouds of noxious gas, ugly grass, albino cockroaches, and an underground pond once used as a site of mass suicides. On a more helpful note, they also discovered 250 kilograms of radioactive material under Moscow State University, which perhaps explains the long anecdotal history of illness, hair loss, and infertility among its students and faculty. The government removed the material.

An eighty-seven-year-old Moscow pensioner, Apollos Ivanov, who had been an engineer in the Kremlin and studied the underground structures of Moscow, believed the Library of Gold was in one of the branches that stood above an extensive catacomb network, which he had seen. He revealed his secret to the mayor in 1997, who quickly authorized the hunt. Many were convinced the missing collection would be unearthed at last. Ivanov had gone blind, and according to legend, anyone coming close to discovering the library lost his sight. But Ivanov was wrong, and the library remains missing.

The pursuit continues enthusiastically today, with new searchers bringing increasingly modern equipment. After all, the magnificent royal library of the Byzantine Empire was the last hope of the long-ago Western world, rich with the wisdom and lost knowledge of the ancients, and unrivaled today even by the Vatican Library. To think the Library of Gold, the crème de la literary crème, may lie sleeping quietly in Moscow's mysterious underworld is irresistible.

Literary Treasures the Library of Gold could Contain

This book is fiction, of course, but all the historical references and anecdotes are either factual or based on fact. For instance, the Emperor Trajan did erect the awe-inspiring monument to his successful wars, Trajan's Column, between two peaceful galleries of Rome's library, which he also built. And Cassius Dio Cocceianus, a Roman administrator and great historian, wrote *Romaika,* the most important history of the last years of the Roman Republic and early Empire. It encompassed eighty books, but only volumes thirty-six through sixty survive. If Cassius Dio wrote about Trajan's Column, I postulate the story would have appeared in book seventy-seven.

At the same time all of this is true: Julius Caesar did receive a list of conspirators planning to assassinate him—but never read it. Hannibal did rampage across Rome's countryside, destroying everything except Fabius's properties. As a result, Fabius had his hands full with a near-mutinous Rome. And in his send-up play *The Clouds,* Aristophanes does depict the revered philosopher Socrates as a clown teaching students how to scam their way out of debt.

The one major exception is the volume I call *The Book of Spies*. However, since Ivan the Terrible had books created and was intrigued by spies and assassins, it's possible he would have ordered such a work compiled.

History is available to us only through oral tradition and the written word. What was lost over the millennia from war, fires, looting, wanton destruction, deliberate obliteration, and censorship is tragic. Our history is the history of lost books.

If I could have my wish, the Library of Gold would exist, would be discovered, and not only would the lost books I name in the novel be found in it, but at least the work of these early six would, too:

- **Sappho** (c. 610 B.C. to c. 570 B.C.) was the lauded Greek poet whose life is recounted in myths based upon her lyrical and passionate love verses. The pinnacle of female accomplishment in poetry, her surviving work was collected and published in nine books sometime in the third or second century B.C., but by the eighth or nine century A.D. it was represented only by quotations in other authors' works.
- Classical Athens had three great tragic playwrights, all contemporaries—Aeschylus (525 or 524 B.C. to 456 or 455 B.C.), Sophocles (c. 495 B.C. to 406 B.C.), and Euripides (480 B.C. to 406 B.C.). The father of modern drama, **Aeschylus** wrote more than eighty plays, lifting the art of tragedy with poetry and fresh theatrical power. He introduced a second actor on stage—thus giving birth to dialogue, dramatic conflict, and dramatized plot. The Athenians had the only copy of his *Complete Works* and loaned it for copying to Alexandria, where Ptolemy III had other ideas—he ordered it left untranscribed and not returned. Scholars flocked. Centuries passed. Then the Alexandria libraries burned, and the scrolls died in flames. Only seven of Aeschylus's plays have survived.
- The author of 123 plays, including *Oedipus Rex*, **Sophocles** used scenery, increased the size of the chorus, and introduced a third actor, significantly widening the scope and complexity of theater.

Sophocles said he showed men as they ought to be, while his younger contemporary, Euripides, showed them as they were. Only seven of Sophocles' plays survive.

- Dressing kings as beggars and showing women as intelligent and complex, **Euripides** used traditional stories to display humanity and ethics. He wrote more than ninety plays, which were remarkable for realistically reflecting his era. Reading them would tell us much about Athens. Only eighteen survive.
- **Confucius** (551 B.C. to 479 B.C.) was venerated over the centuries for his wisdom and his revolutionary idea that humaneness was central to how we should treat one another. He wrote "Six Works": *The Book of Poetry, The Book of Rituals, The Book of Music, The Book of History, The Book of Changes,* and *The Spring and Autumn Annals,* which formed a full curriculum of education. But the perfection of his vision is incomplete, since *The Book of Music* has disappeared.
- The first Roman emperor, **Augustus** (63 B.C. to A.D. 14), was one of the globe's finest administrative geniuses, reorganizing, transforming, and enlarging the reeling Roman Republic into a powerhouse empire with easy communications, thousands of miles of paved roads, and flourishing tourism and trade. A cultured man, he supported the arts and wrote many works. Most have vanished. A particular tragedy is the loss of his thirteen-volume *My Autobiography,* perhaps containing the inside views of the man who oversaw and directed one of the world's greatest civilizations during a long and critical period of history.

SELECT BIBLIOGRAPHY

For the Library of Gold

Around the Kremlin: The Moscow Kremlin, Its Monuments, and Works of Art. Moscow: Progress Publishers, 1967.

Arvedlund, Erin. "Fear Me, Giant Sewer Rodents, for I Am Vadim, Lord of the Underground!" *Outside* magazine, September 1997.

Backhouse, Janet. *The Illuminated Page: Ten Centuries of Manuscript Painting.* London: The British Library, 1993.

Basbanes, Nicholas A. *A Gentle Madness: Bibliophiles, Bibliomanes, and the Eternal Passion for Books.* New York: Henry Holt and Company, 1995.

"Blind Man 'Has Key to Tsar's Secret Library.'" *The Times,* September 17, 1997.

Canfora, Luciano. *The Vanished Library: A Wonder of the Ancient World.* Berkeley: University of California Press, 1990.

Cockburn, Andrew. "The Judas Gospel," *National Geographic,* May 2006.

Ehrlich, Eugene. *Veni, Vidi, Vici: Conquer Your Enemies, Impress Your Friends with Everyday Latin.* New York: HarperCollins, 1995.

Grosvenor, Gilbert H. "Young Russia: Land of Unlimited Possibilities," *National Geographic,* November 1914.

de Hamel, Christopher. *The British Library Guide to Manuscript Illustration: History and Techniques.* London: The British Library, 2001.

Hamilton, Masha. "Kremlin Tunnels: The Secret of Moscow's Underworld," *Los Angeles Times,* June 28, 1989.

Holmes, Charles W. "Unsolved Mystery: What Happened to Ivan the Terrible's Library?" Cox News Service, October 31, 1997.

Holmes, Hannah. "Spelunking: And Please, No Flash Pictures of the Blob." *Outside* magazine, March 1995.

Ilinitsky, Andrei. "Mysteries Under Moscow," *Bulletin of the Atomic Scientists,* May/June 1997.

Kelly, Stuart. *The Book of Lost Books.* New York: Random House, 2005.

Khinsky, Nikolay. "Secret Treasures: Moscow's Caches," WhereRussia.com: Russian National Tourist site for International Travellers, www.WhereRussia.com, 1990s.

de Madariaga, Isabel. *Ivan the Terrible.* New Haven, Conn.: Yale University Press, 2005.

Panshina, Natalya. "Archaeology Expert Hopeful About Library of Ivan IV," *Tass,* September 18, 1997.

Polastron, Lucien X. *Books on Fire: The Destruction of Libraries Throughout History.* Rochester, Vt.: Inner Traditions International, 2007.

Severy, Merle. "The Byzantine Empire: Rome of the East," *National Geographic,* December 1983.

Sheldon, Rose Mary. *Espionage in the Ancient World: An Annotated Bibliography.* Jefferson, N.C.: McFarland & Company, Inc., 2003.

———. *Intelligence Activities in Ancient Rome.* New York: Routledge, 2005.

Simpson, D. P. *Cassell's New Compact Latin Dictionary.* New York: Cassell & Co., Ltd., 1963.

Stewart, Deborah Brown. Bibliographer and research services librarian, Byzantine Studies, Dumbarton Oaks Research Library and Collection, Washington, D.C. E-mail to author, August 7, 2007.

Vinogradskaya, Alexandra. "A Map of Moscow That Does Not

Exist," Russian Culture Navigator, VOR.RU, November 9, 1999.
———. "The Mysteries of Underground Moscow," Russian Culture Navigator, VOR.RU, April 12, 1999.
———. "The Mystery of the Byzantine Library," Russian Culture Navigator, VOR.RU, January 18, 1999.
Yevdokimov, Yevgeny. "Possible Whereabouts of Famous Library Revealed to Mayor," ITAR-TASS News Agency, September 16, 1997.

The Best Short Works of Mark Twain

The Best Short Works of Mark Twain

Mark Twain

Supplementary materials written by
Karen Davidson
Series edited by Cynthia Brantley Johnson

Pocket Books
New York London Toronto Sydney

This book is a work of fiction. Names, characters, places and incidents are products of the author's imagination or are used fictitiously. Any resemblance to actual events or locales or persons, living or dead, is entirely coincidental.

POCKET BOOKS, a division of Simon & Schuster, Inc.
1230 Avenue of the Americas, New York, NY 10020

ISBN 13: 978-0-7434-8779-5
ISBN 10: 0-7434-8779-6

First Pocket Books printing November 2004

10 9 8 7 6 5 4 3 2

Front cover art by Dan Craig

Manufactured in the United States of America

Contents

Introduction
The Best Short Works of Mark Twain: The Assault of Laughter

Few writers in history have been as widely read or as widely written about as Mark Twain. He was a prolific talent, a complex figure whose genius as a satirist and storyteller of the Old West established his reputation as an American original. *The Best Short Works of Mark Twain* offers readers a unique opportunity to experience not only the breadth and depth of Twain's humor and insight but also the evolution of his exceptional literary craft.

The fifty-seven stories collected in this edition span over forty years of the author's life, from his early days as a frontier journalist with the story that made him famous, "The Notorious Jumping Frog of Calaveras County," to the groundbreaking slave narrative, "A True Story," that foreshadowed his masterpiece, *Adventures of Huckleberry Finn*, to later works such as "The Man That Corrupted Hadleyburg" that illustrate Twain's brilliant precision in the short story form.

In "How to Tell a Story" Twain writes, "There are several kinds of stories, but only one difficult kind—the humorous." When reading *The Best Short Works of Mark Twain*, one finds it hard to imagine the author had difficulty telling *any* story. Twain's language is so fluid, his ear for dialect so acute, that his narratives appear effortless and not, as they were in actuality, the product of studied word choice and careful revision. The genres of Twain's short stories are varied and numerous—tall tales, burlesques, fables, yarns, ghost stories—though his humor remains constant.

Twain used humor as a weapon against racism, greed, and hypocrisy, viewing his wit as a means of encouraging reformation. "Against the assault of laughter," he wrote in "The Mysterious Stranger," "nothing can stand."

The Life and Work of Mark Twain

Mark Twain was born Samuel Langhorne Clemens on November 30, 1835, in Florida, Missouri. When he was born, Halley's comet, which passes close to Earth every seventy-six years, was visible in the night sky—an astronomical event that ancients considered an indicator that something of great historical significance was about to happen. Twain was well aware that he was born under this auspicious sign, and he sometimes made humorous reference to it. When Mark Twain died on April 21, 1910, Halley's comet was again blazing across the sky. It seems fitting that the life of so unusual a man should contain such conspicuous celestial bookends. His life spanned a particularly dramatic portion of U.S. history, and he managed to be right in the thick of the action for most it.

Samuel Clemens started out in modest surroundings in a respectable family of six children in Missouri. The Clemens family had been settled in Hannibal, Missouri, for several years when young Samuel's father died, leaving the family in a difficult financial position. Samuel quit school at age twelve and took several odd jobs before becoming apprenticed to a local printer. In this capacity, he gained exposure to a wide range of writing, and he discovered he had the talent and the ambition to become a writer himself. He soon launched a career as a sort of traveling reporter, writing humorous sketches and articles for newspapers in cities such as St. Louis, New York, Philadelphia, and Cincinnati. In 1857, he headed to New Orleans with plans to travel by ship to South America. Instead, he apprenticed himself to a riverboat captain and spent the next two years traveling up and down the Mississippi River.

Hostilities between the North and South brought commercial traffic on the Mississippi to a halt in 1861, and Clemens had to give up his fledgling career. He served as a soldier in a group of Confederate volunteers in 1861, but quit after a couple of weeks and decided to head out to the Nevada Territory, where the legendary Comstock Lode had been struck in 1859. The Comstock Lode was a huge silver and gold deposit that produced hundreds of millions of dollars' worth of the precious metals. His luck as a prospector was not so good, and Samuel turned once again to newspaper work, writing for the *Territorial Enterprise* in Virginia City. In 1863, he began signing his articles "Mark Twain"—an expression used by riverboat crewmen to refer to a safe navigating depth of two fathoms.

In 1864, Twain (as he was now known professionally) started working for a San Francisco paper and traveled for the paper to what are today called the Hawaiian Islands. He wrote about his travels and lectured about Hawaii upon his return to San Francisco. In many ways, Twain introduced Hawaii to the U.S. mainland, stimulating the tourism to the island that began in the 1860s. Twain continued to travel extensively in Europe and the Holy Land for a couple more years. In 1870, he married Olivia Langdon. They settled in Hartford, Connecticut.

Olivia gave birth to four children: a son named Langdon, born in 1870, who died at the age of two; Susy, born in March 1872; Clara, born in 1874; and Jean, born in 1880. Twain's literary career blossomed during this period, and his fortunes soared. He published *Roughing It* in 1872 and *The Adventures of Tom Sawyer* in 1876.

He published *The Prince and the Pauper*, a popular success, in 1881. But Twain reached his literary zenith in 1885 with the publication of *Adventures of Huckleberry Finn*. Though controversial, the book was widely recognized as an important achievement in American literature. Twain followed it up with the publication of several more books, including *A Connecticut Yankee in King Arthur's Court* (1889) and *Pudd'nhead Wilson* (1894).

The 1890s proved tragic for Twain. He had made a number of questionable investments, and the nationwide financial panic of 1893 left him bankrupt. He was forced to book a worldwide lecture series to rebuild his fortune. The tour cemented his professional reputation and he earned the admiration of many of the leading artists and writers of Europe. Though his fame grew, his family suffered. In 1896, his daughter Susy died of meningitis. After a long illness, his wife died in 1904. In 1909, his daughter Jean died. Twain was left bitter and lonely; his later work, such as *What Is Man?* (1906), was especially dark and cynical, reflecting his emotional state. He died in Connecticut in 1910. And although only his daughter Clara outlived him, thousands of mourners filed past his casket to pay their respects at his funeral.

Historical and Literary Context of *The Best Short Works of Mark Twain*

Prelude to the Civil War

Twain's experiences in the first three decades of his life provided him with the material he would write about throughout his career. As a child in Hannibal, Missouri, Twain witnessed the atrocities of slavery firsthand. In the years leading up to the Civil War, when the nation was disputing the morality and legality of owning slaves, Twain's opinion on the issue had been long decided.

The issue of slavery had threatened to divide the United States from the very beginning. In Northern states, where industrialization made cheap labor less of an economic necessity, the abolitionist movement rapidly gained momentum in the early 1800s. The economies of the Southern states, however, were based on farming, and landowners required cheap labor. Also, after two hundred years of living with large slave populations, Southerners had come to see slavery as a part of their cultural heritage. Wealthy Southerners in particular were determined to preserve their way of life, and they fought hard to maintain the legality of slavery. Southerners were well aware that the balance of power would shift if opponents of slavery began to outnumber slavery supporters in Congress and that then slavery would probably be outlawed. Each annexation of territory by the U.S. government brought new battles over whether slavery should be permitted.

The Missouri Compromise of 1820 was the resolution of a particularly long congressional battle over slavery. The territory of Missouri, home to thousands of slaves, had petitioned for statehood in 1818, but Northern congressmen objected to admitting another slave state to the Union. In 1820, Henry Clay, a representative from Kentucky, came up with a compromise. Maine had just applied for statehood. Clay suggested accepting Maine as a free state and Missouri as a slave state—thus maintaining the balance of power. But under the terms of the compromise, slavery would not be permitted anywhere north or west of Missouri within the Louisiana Purchase. Missouri was admitted to the Union in 1821.

The U.S. continued to expand, however, and the Missouri Compromise did not quiet sectional disputes for very long. The U.S. annexed Texas in 1845, which led to war with Mexico. The U.S. quickly won the war and took over most of what is now the western part of the country. Once again, battles over power in Congress threatened to tear the nation apart. Clay helped craft the Compromise of 1850 in an attempt to stave off civil war. He struck a difficult, troubling bargain. In exchange for ensuring that the western U.S. would be free from slavery, Congress passed the Fugitive Slave Act, which stated that slaves who escaped to free states or free territory must be returned to their owners.

The Compromise of 1850 pleased very few people, but the peace was preserved for a few more years. Then the Kansas-Nebraska Act of 1854 repealed the Missouri Compromise by granting all states the right to make or keep slavery legal. Abolitionists were outraged. Bloody battles over the issue broke out in Kansas Territory. In 1861, most of the Southern states seceded from the Union and civil war finally erupted.

Post–Civil War Literary Landscape

American book publishing was transformed in the period just before the Civil War. Whereas the works of the nation's earlier authors were read by a small population of intellectuals, authors in the 1850s and beyond began to reach a wider population through a practice called "subscription publishing." Sales representatives would go door-to-door in towns across the country, armed with enticing book brochures, and sell books in advance of printing. This is how Twain found his audience. His humor was very popular with the general reading public, and although he was also admired by intellectuals, average readers buying his books by the thousands are what made him rich.

In terms of literary movements, Twain's work can be seen as part of American literary realism. Literary realism, a reaction against the more fantastical and sentimental fiction of the American romantic period, featured accurate representations of the lives of Americans in various contexts.

Realists valued detail and plausibility in their fiction. Characters were complex, flawed people with believable motives. The language used in books by realists was straightforward and sometimes comic or satiric, but not flowery or overtly poetic (although much realistic writing is very beautiful). Other American writers whose works can be seen as realist were Henry James, author of such books as *Daisy Miller* (1879) and *The Golden Bowl* (1904), and Edith Wharton, author of *The House of Mirth* (1905), *Ethan Frome* (1911), and many other books. Twain distinguished himself from other writers of this period by his use of humor and his masterful skill in portraying common American speech.

Chronology of Mark Twain's Life and Work

1835: Samuel Langhorne Clemens born November 30, in Florida, Missouri.
1839: John Clemens, Samuel's father, moves his family to nearby Hannibal, where Samuel spends his boyhood.
1848: Samuel becomes apprentice printer.
1852: Samuel begins editing his brother's newspaper and publishing his own humorous sketches.
1853: Leaves Hannibal and begins working as a traveling reporter in such cities as St. Louis, New York, Philadelphia, and Cincinnati.
1857: Becomes apprenticed to a riverboat captain.
1861: Tries prospecting for silver in the Nevada Territory.
1863: Uses the pseudonym "Mark Twain" for the first time on a travel sketch.
1864: Moves to San Francisco and continues working as a journalist.
1866: Travels to Hawaii (then called the Sandwich Islands) as a correspondent for a newspaper in Sacramento. Lectures about his travels upon his return.

1867: Travels to Europe and the Holy Land. Publishes *The Celebrated Jumping Frog of Calaveras County, and Other Sketches.*
1869: *The Innocents Abroad* published.
1870: Twain marries Olivia Langdon. Son Langdon Clemens is born prematurely (dies two years later).
1871: Twain and family move to Hartford, Connecticut.
1872: Daughter Susy born. *Roughing It* published.
1874: Daughter Clara born.
1876: Publication of *The Adventures of Tom Sawyer.*
1880: Daughter Jean born. Twain loses thousands on a bad investment. Publishes *A Tramp Abroad.*
1881: Publication of *The Prince and the Pauper.*
1883: Publication of *Life on the Mississippi.*
1885: Publication of *Adventures of Huckleberry Finn.*
1889: Publication of *A Connecticut Yankee in King Arthur's Court.*
1894: Publication of *The Tragedy of Pudd'nhead Wilson.*
1896: Daughter Susy dies of spinal meningitis.
1904: Twain's wife, Olivia, dies.
1909: Daughter Jean dies; daughter Clara marries.
1910: Twain dies on April 21 and is buried in Elmira, New York.

Historical Context of Mark Twain's Short Stories

1808: Congress outlaws the importation of African slaves.
1811: The first steamboat sails on the Mississippi.
1820: Missouri Compromise allows for admission of Missouri into Union as a slave state.
1821: Missouri granted statehood.
1838: The Underground Railroad is established.
1842: Charles Dickens tours the United States, speaks out against the institution of slavery.
1845: Texas agrees to be annexed by U.S. and becomes twenty-eighth state.
1846: Mexican-American War begins over Texas annexation. U.S. wins a speedy victory and claims most of the western part of the country (the territory that is now California, Arizona, Nevada, Utah, Colorado, Wyoming, and parts of New Mexico). The question of slavery in new territories is again hotly debated.
1850: The Compromise of 1850 includes the Fugitive Slave Act, which required all citizens to assist in the return of fugitive slaves to their owners and denied fugitives the right to a jury trial.
1854: Kansas-Nebraska Act passed, repealing the Missouri

Compromise and allowing states to decide for themselves the question of slavery.

1857: Dred Scott decision by U.S. Supreme Court rules that a slave's residence in a free state or free territory does not make him free.

1859: Abolitionist John Brown and followers raid the U.S. arsenal at Harpers Ferry in Virginia and try to start a slave insurrection. Brown is caught and hanged for treason.

1860: Abraham Lincoln is elected president.

1861: Civil War begins.

1863: President Lincoln issues the Emancipation Proclamation, freeing all slaves.

1865: Lincoln assassinated; Thirteenth Amendment abolishes slavery; Civil War ends with General Robert E. Lee's surrender to General Ulysses S. Grant; Ku Klux Klan formed.

1868: Ulysses S. Grant elected president.

1869: The Union and Pacific railways meet at Promontory Point with the completion of the transcontinental railroad. Fifteenth Amendment gives blacks the right to vote.

1872: Susan B. Anthony is arrested for registering and casting a ballot in an election.

1876: The Battle of the Little Big Horn, also called Custer's Last Stand.

1877: Violent railroad and coal mine strikes across the U.S.

1881: President Garfield assassinated; Chester A. Arthur becomes president.

1891: U.S. Congress adopts the International Copyright Act.

1892: Ellis Island, in New York, opens as immigration center.

1893: The New York Stock Exchange crashes.

1896: William McKinley elected president.

1901: President McKinley assassinated; Theodore Roosevelt becomes president.

1909: The N.A.A.C.P. is formed.

The Best Short Works of Mark Twain

The Notorious Jumping Frog of Calaveras County

In compliance with the request of a friend of mine, who wrote me from the East, I called on good-natured, garrulous old Simon Wheeler, and inquired after my friend's friend, Leonidas W. Smiley, as requested to do, and I hereunto append the result. I have a lurking suspicion that *Leonidas W.* Smiley is a myth; that my friend never knew such a personage; and that he only conjectured that if I asked old Wheeler about him, it would remind him of his infamous *Jim* Smiley, and he would go to work and bore me to death with some exasperating reminiscence of him as long and as tedious as it should be useless to me. If that was the design, it succeeded.

I found Simon Wheeler dozing comfortably by the barroom stove of the dilapidated tavern in the decayed mining camp of Angel's, and I noticed that he was fat and bald-headed, and had an expression of winning gentleness and simplicity upon his tranquil countenance. He roused up, and gave me good day. I told him that a friend of mine had commissioned me to make some inquiries about a cherished companion of his boyhood named *Leonidas W.* Smiley—*Rev. Leonidas W.* Smiley, a young minister of the Gospel, who he had heard was at one time a resident of Angel's Camp. I added that if Mr. Wheeler could tell me anything about this Rev. Leonidas W. Smiley, I would feel under many obligations to him.

Simon Wheeler backed me into a corner and blockaded me there with his chair, and then sat down and reeled off the monotonous narrative which follows this paragraph. He never smiled, he never frowned, he never changed his voice from the gentle-flowing key to which he tuned his initial sentence, he never betrayed the slightest suspicion of enthusiasm; but all through the interminable narrative there ran a vein of impressive earnestness and sincerity, which showed me plainly that, so far from his imagining that there was anything ridiculous or funny about his story, he regarded it as a really important matter, and admired its two heroes as men of transcendent genius in *finesse.* I let him go on in his own way, and never interrupted him once.

"Rev. Leonidas W. H'm, Reverend Le—well, there was a feller here once by the name of *Jim* Smiley, in the winter of '49—or maybe it was the spring of '50—I don't recollect exactly, somehow, though what makes me think it was one or the other is because I remember the big flume warn't finished when he first come to the camp; but anyway, he was the curiousest man about always betting on anything that turned up you ever see, if he could get anybody to bet on the other side; and if he couldn't he'd change sides. Any way that suited the other man would suit *him*—any way just so's he got a bet, *he* was satisfied. But still he was lucky, uncommon lucky; he most always come out winner. He was always ready and laying for a chance; there couldn't be no solit'ry thing mentioned but that feller'd offer to bet on it, and take ary side you please, as I was just telling you. If there was a horse-race, you'd find him flush or you'd find him busted at the end of it; if there was a dog-fight, he'd bet on it; if there was a cat-fight, he'd bet on it; if there was a chicken-fight, he'd bet on it; why, if there was two birds setting on a fence, he would bet you which one would fly first; or if there was a camp-meeting, he would be there reglar to bet on Parson Walker, which he judged to be the best exhorter about here, and so he was too, and a good man. If he even see a straddle-bug[1] start to go anywheres, he would bet you how long it would take him to get to—to wherever he was going to, and if you took him up, he would foller that straddle-bug to Mexico but what he would find out where he was bound for and how long he was on the road. Lots of the boys here has seen that Smiley, and can tell you about him. Why, it never made no difference to *him*—he'd bet on *any* thing—the dangdest feller. Parson Walker's wife laid very sick once, for a good while, and it seemed as if they warn't going to save her; but one morning he come in, and Smiley up and asked him how she was, and he said she was considerable better—thank the Lord for his inf'nite mercy—and coming on so smart that with the blessing of Prov'dence she'd get well yet; and Smiley, before he thought, says, 'Well, I'll resk two-and-a-half she don't anyway.'

"Thish-yer Smiley had a mare—the boys called her the fifteen-minute nag, but that was only in fun, you know, because of course she was faster than that—and he used to win money on that horse, for all she was so slow and always had the asthma, or the distemper, or the consumption, or something of that kind. They used to give her two or three hundred yards' start, and then pass her under way; but always at the fag end[2] the race she'd get excited and desperate like, and come cavorting and straddling up, and scattering her legs around limber, sometimes in the air, and sometimes out to one side among the fences, and kicking up m-o-r-e dust and raising m-o-r-e racket with her coughing and sneezing and blowing her nose—and always fetch up at the stand just about a neck ahead, as near as you could cipher it down.

"And he had a little small bull-pup, that to look at him you'd think he warn't worth a cent but to set around and look ornery and lay for a chance to steal something. But as soon as money was up on him he was a different dog; his under-jaw'd begin to stick out like the fo'castle[3] of a steamboat, and his teeth would uncover and shine like the furnaces. And a dog might tackle *him* and bully-rag[4] him, and bite him, and throw him over his shoulder two or three times, and Andrew Jackson[5]—which was the name of the pup—Andrew Jackson would never let on but what *he* was satisfied, and hadn't expected nothing else—and the bets being doubled and doubled on the other side all the time, till the money was all up; and then all of a sudden he would grab that other dog jest by the j'int of his hind leg and freeze to it—not chaw, you understand, but only just grip and hang on till they throwed up the sponge, if it was a year. Smiley always come out winner on that pup, till he harnessed a dog once that didn't have no hind legs, because they'd been sawed off in a circular saw, and when the thing had gone along far enough, and the money was all up, and he come to make a snatch for his pet holt, he see in a minute how he'd been imposed on, and how the other dog had him in the door, so to speak, and he 'peared surprised, and then he looked sorter discouraged-like, and didn't try no more to win the fight, and so he got shucked out bad. He give Smiley a look, as much as to say his heart was broke, and it was *his* fault, for putting up a dog that hadn't no hind legs for him to take holt of, which was his main dependence in a fight, and then he limped off a piece and laid down and died. It was a good pup, was that Andrew Jackson, and would have made a name for hisself if he'd lived, for the stuff was in him and he had genius—I know it, because he hadn't no opportunities to speak of, and it don't stand to reason that a dog could make such a fight as he could under them circumstances if he hadn't no talent. It always makes me feel sorry when I think of that last fight of his'n, and the way it turned out.

"Well, thish-yer Smiley had rat-tarriers, and chicken cocks, and tomcats and all them kind of things, till you couldn't rest, and you couldn't fetch nothing for him to bet on but he'd match you. He ketched a frog one day, and took him home, and said he cal'lated to educate him; and so he never done nothing for three months but set in his back yard and learn that frog to jump. And you bet you he *did* learn him, too. He'd give him a little punch behind, and the next minute you'd see that frog whirling in the air like a doughnut—see him turn one summerset, or maybe a couple, if he got a good start, and come down flat-footed and all right, like a cat. He got him up so in the matter of ketching flies, and kep' him in practice so constant, that he'd nail a fly every time as fur as he could see him. Smiley said all a frog wanted was education, and he could do 'most anything—and I believe him. Why, I've seen him set Dan'l Webster[6] down here on this floor—Dan'l Webster was the name of the frog—and sing out, 'Flies, Dan'l, flies!' and quicker'n you could wink he'd spring straight up and snake a fly off'n the counter there, and flop down on the floor ag'in as solid as a gob of mud, and fall to scratching the side of his head with his hind foot as indifferent as if he hadn't no idea he'd been doin' any more'n any frog might do. You never see a frog so modest and straightfor'ard as he was, for all he was so gifted. And when it come to fair and square jumping on a dead level, he could get over more ground at one straddle than any animal of his breed you ever see. Jumping on a dead level was his strong suit, you understand; and when it come to that, Smiley would ante up money on him as long as he had a red. Smiley was monstrous proud of his frog, and well he might be, for fellers that had traveled and been everywheres all said he laid over any frog that ever *they* see.

"Well, Smiley kep' the beast in a little lattice box, and he used to fetch him down-town sometimes and lay for a bet. One day a feller—a stranger in the camp, he was—come acrost him with his box, and says:

" 'What might it be that you've got in the box?'

"And Smiley says, sorter indifferent-like, 'It might be a parrot, or it might be a canary, maybe, but it ain't—it's only just a frog.'

"And the feller took it, and looked at it careful, and

turned it round this way and that, and says, 'H'm—so 'tis. Well, what's *he* good for?'

" 'Well,' Smiley says, easy and careless, 'he's good enough for *one* thing, I should judge—he can outjump any frog in Calaveras County.'

"The feller took the box again, and took another long, particular look, and give it back to Smiley, and says, very deliberate, 'Well,' he says, 'I don't see no p'ints about that frog that's any better'n any other frog.'

" 'Maybe you don't,' Smiley says. 'Maybe you understand frogs and maybe you don't understand 'em; maybe you've had experience, and maybe you ain't only a amature, as it were. Anyways, I've got *my* opinion, and I'll resk forty dollars that he can outjump any frog in Calaveras County.'

"And the feller studied a minute, and then says, kinder sad-like, 'Well, I'm only a stranger here, and I ain't got no frog; but if I had a frog, I'd bet you.'

"And then Smiley says, 'That's all right—that's all right—if you'll hold my box a minute, I'll go and get you a frog.' And so the feller took the box, and put up his forty dollars along with Smiley's, and set down to wait.

"So he set there a good while thinking and thinking to himself, and then he got the frog out and prized his mouth open and took a teaspoon and filled him full of quail-shot—filled him pretty near up to his chin—and set him on the floor. Smiley he went to the swamp and slopped around in the mud for a long time, and finally he ketched a frog, and fetched him in, and give him to this feller, and says:

" 'Now, if you're ready, set him alongside of Dan'l, with his fore paws just even with Dan'l's, and I'll give the word.' Then he says, 'One—two—three—*git!*' and him and the feller touched up the frogs from behind, and the new frog hopped off lively, but Dan'l give a heave, and hysted up his shoulders—so—like a Frenchman, but it warn't no use—he couldn't budge; he was planted as solid as a church, and he couldn't no more stir than if he was anchored out. Smiley was a good deal surprised, and he was disgusted too, but he didn't have no idea what the matter was, of course.

"The feller took the money and started away; and when he was going out at the door, he sorter jerked his thumb over his shoulder—so—at Dan'l, and says again, very deliberate, 'Well,' he says, 'I don't see no p'ints about that frog that's any better'n any other frog.'

"Smiley he stood scratching his head and looking down at Dan'l a long time, and at last he says, 'I do wonder what in the nation that frog throw'd off for—I wonder if there ain't something the matter with him—he 'pears to look mighty baggy, somehow.' And he ketched Dan'l by the nap of the neck, and hefted him, and says, 'Why blame my cats if he don't weigh five pound!' and turned him upside down and he belched out a double handful of shot. And then he see how it was, and he was the maddest man—he set the frog down and took out after the feller, but he never ketched him. And—"

[Here Simon Wheeler heard his name called from the front yard, and got up to see what was wanted.] And turning to me as he moved away, he said: "Just set where you are, stranger, and rest easy—I ain't going to be gone a second."

But, by your leave, I did not think that a continuation of the history of the enterprising vagabond *Jim* Smiley would be likely to afford me much information concerning the Rev. *Leonidas W.* Smiley, and so I started away.

At the door I met the sociable Wheeler returning, and he buttonholed me and recommenced:

"Well, thish-yer Smiley had a yaller one-eyed cow that didn't have no tail, only just a short stump like a bannanner, and—"

However, lacking both time and inclination, I did not wait to hear about the afflicted cow, but took my leave.

1865

The Story of the Bad Little Boy

Once there was a bad little boy whose name was Jim—though, if you will notice, you will find that bad little boys are nearly always called James in your Sunday-school books. It was strange, but still it was true, that this one was called Jim.

He didn't have any sick mother, either—a sick mother who was pious and had the consumption, and would be glad to lie down in the grave and be at rest but for the strong love she bore her boy, and the anxiety she felt that the world might be harsh and cold toward him when she was gone. Most bad boys in the Sunday books are named James, and have sick mothers, who teach them to say, "Now, I lay me down," etc., and sing them to sleep with sweet, plaintive voices, and then kiss them good night, and kneel down by the bedside and weep. But it was different with this fellow. He was named Jim, and there wasn't anything the matter with his mother—no consumption, nor anything of that kind. She was rather stout than otherwise, and she was not pious; moreover, she was not anxious on Jim's account. She said if he were to break his neck it wouldn't be much loss. She always spanked Jim to sleep, and she never kissed him good night; on the contrary, she boxed his ears when she was ready to leave him.

Once this little bad boy stole the key of the pantry, and slipped in there and helped himself to some jam, and filled up the vessel with tar, so that his mother would never know the difference; but all at once a terrible feeling didn't come over him, and something didn't seem to whisper to him, "Is it right to disobey my mother? Isn't it sinful to do this? Where do bad little boys go who gobble up their good kind mother's jam?" and then he didn't kneel down all alone and promise never to be wicked any more, and rise up with a light, happy heart, and go and tell his mother all about it, and beg her forgiveness, and be blessed by her with tears of pride and thankfulness in her eyes. No; that is the way with all other bad boys in the books; but it happened otherwise with this Jim, strangely enough. He ate that jam, and said it was bully, in his, sinful, vulgar way; and he put in the tar, and said that was bully also, and laughed, and observed "that the old woman would get up and snort" when she found it out; and when she did find it out, he denied knowing anything about it, and she whipped him severely, and he did the crying himself. Everything about this boy was curious—everything turned out differently with him from the way it does to the bad Jameses in the books.

Once he climbed up in Farmer Acorn's apple trees to steal apples, and the limb didn't break, and he didn't fall and break his arm, and get torn by the farmer's great dog, and then languish on a sickbed for weeks, and repent and become good. Oh, no; he stole as many apples as he wanted and came down all right; and he was all ready for the dog, too, and knocked him endways with a brick when he came to tear him. It was very strange—nothing like it ever happened in those mild little books with marbled backs, and with pictures in them of men with swallow-tailed coats and bell-crowned hats, and pantaloons that are short in the legs, and women with the waists of their dresses under their arms, and no hoops on. Nothing like it in any of the Sunday-school books.

Once he stole the teacher's penknife, and, when he was afraid it would be found out and he would get whipped, he slipped it into George Wilson's cap—poor Widow Wilson's son, the moral boy, the good little boy of the village, who always obeyed his mother, and never told an untruth, and was fond of his lessons, and infatuated with Sunday-School. And when the knife dropped from the cap, and poor George hung his head and blushed, as if in conscious guilt, and the grieved teacher charged the theft upon him, and was just in the very act of bringing the switch down upon his trembling shoulders, a white-haired, improbable justice of the peace did not suddenly appear in their midst, and strike an attitude and say, "Spare this noble boy—there stands the cowering culprit! I was passing the school door at recess, and, unseen myself, I saw the theft committed!" And then Jim didn't get whaled, and the venerable justice didn't read the tearful school a homily, and take George by the hand and say such a boy deserved to be exalted, and then tell him to come and make his home with him, and sweep out the office, and make fires, and run errands, and chop wood, and study law, and help his wife do household labors, and have all the balance of the time to play, and get forty cents a month, and be happy. No; it would have happened that way in the books, but it didn't happen that way to Jim. No meddling old clam of a justice dropped in to make trouble, and so the model boy George got thrashed, and Jim was glad of it because, you know, Jim hated moral boys. Jim said he was "down on them milksops."[1] Such was the coarse language of this bad, neglected boy.

But the strangest thing that ever happened to Jim was the time he went boating on Sunday, and didn't get drowned, and that other time that he got caught out in the storm when he was fishing on Sunday, and didn't get struck by lightning. Why, you might look, and look, all through the Sunday-school books from now till next Christmas, and you would never come across anything like this. Oh, no; you would find that all the bad boys who go boating on Sunday invariably get drowned; and all the bad boys who get caught out in storms when they are fishing on Sunday infallibly get struck by lightning. Boats with bad boys in them always upset on Sunday, and it always storms when bad boys go fishing on the Sabbath. How this Jim ever escaped is a mystery to me.

This Jim bore a charmed life—that must have been the way of it. Nothing could hurt him. He even gave the elephant in the menagerie a plug of tobacco, and the elephant didn't knock the top of his head off with his trunk. He browsed around the cupboard after essence of peppermint, and didn't make a mistake and drink *aqua fortis*.[2] He stole his father's gun and went hunting on the Sabbath, and didn't shoot three or four of his fingers off. He struck his little sister on the temple with his fist when he was angry, and she didn't linger in pain through long summer days, and die with sweet words of forgiveness upon her lips that redoubled the anguish of his breaking heart. No; she got over it. He ran off and went to sea at last, and didn't come back and find himself sad and alone in the world, his loved ones sleeping in the quiet churchyard, and the vine-embowered home of his boyhood tumbled down and gone to decay. Ah, no; he came home as drunk as a piper, and got into the station-house the first thing.

And he grew up and married, and raised a large family, and brained them all with an ax one night, and got wealthy by all manner of cheating and rascality; and now he is the infernalest wickedest scoundrel in his native village, and is universally respected, and belongs to the legislature.

So you see there never was a bad James in the Sunday-school books that had such a streak of luck as this sinful Jim with the charmed life.

1865

Cannibalism in the Cars

I VISITED ST. LOUIS lately, and on my way West, after changing cars at Terre Haute, Indiana, a mild, benevolent-looking gentleman of about forty-five, or maybe fifty, came in at one of the way-stations and sat down beside me. We talked together pleasantly on various subjects for an hour, perhaps, and I found him exceedingly intelligent and entertaining. When he learned that I was from Washington, he immediately began to ask questions about various public men, and about Congressional affairs; and I saw very shortly that I was conversing with a man who was perfectly familiar with the ins and outs of political life at the Capital, even to the ways and manners, and customs of procedure of Senators and Representatives in the Chambers of the national Legislature. Presently two men halted near us for a single moment, and one said to the other:

"Harris, if you'll do that for me, I'll never forget you, my boy."

My new comrade's eye lighted pleasantly. The words had touched upon a happy memory, I thought. Then his face settled into thoughtfulness—almost into gloom. He turned to me and said, "Let me tell you a story; let me give you a secret chapter of my life—a chapter that has never been referred to by me since its events transpired. Listen patiently, and promise that you will not interrupt me."

I said I would not, and he related the following strange

adventure, speaking sometimes with animation, sometimes with melancholy, but always with feeling and earnestness.

On the 19th of December, 1853, I started from St. Louis on the evening train bound for Chicago. There were only twenty-four passengers, all told. There were no ladies and no children. We were in excellent spirits, and pleasant acquaintanceships were soon formed. The journey bade fair to be a happy one; and no individual in the party, I think, had even the vaguest presentiment of the horrors we were soon to undergo.

At 11 P.M. it began to snow hard. Shortly after leaving the small village of Welden, we entered upon that tremendous prairie solitude that stretches its leagues on leagues of houseless dreariness far away toward the Jubilee Settlements. The winds, unobstructed by trees or hills, or even vagrant rocks, whistled fiercely, across the level desert, driving the falling snow before it like spray from the crested waves of a stormy sea. The snow was deepening fast; and we knew, by the diminished speed of the train, that the engine was plowing through it with steadily increasing difficulty. Indeed, it almost came to a dead halt sometimes, in the midst of great drifts that piled themselves like colossal graves across the track. Conversation began to flag. Cheerfulness gave place to grave concern. The possibility of being imprisoned in the snow, on the bleak prairie, fifty miles from any house, presented itself to every mind, and extended its depressing influence over every spirit.

At two o'clock in the morning I was aroused out of an uneasy slumber by the ceasing of all motion about me. The appalling truth flashed upon me instantly—we were captives in a snow-drift! "All hands to the rescue!" Every man sprang to obey. Out into the wild night, the pitchy darkness, the billowy snow, the driving storm, every soul leaped, with the consciousness that a moment lost now might bring destruction to us all. Shovels, hands, boards—anything, everything that could displace snow, was brought into instant requisition. It was a weird picture, that small company of frantic men fighting the banking snows, half in the blackest shadow and half in the angry light of the locomotive's reflector.

One short hour sufficed to prove the utter uselessness of our efforts. The storm barricaded the track with a dozen drifts while we dug one away. And worse than this, it was discovered that the last grand charge the engine had made upon the enemy had broken the fore-and-aft shaft of the driving-wheel! With a free track before us we should still have been helpless. We entered the car wearied with labor, and very sorrowful. We gathered about the stoves, and gravely canvassed our situation. We had no provisions whatever—in this lay our chief distress. We could not freeze, for there was a good supply of wood in the tender. This was our only comfort. The discussion ended at last in accepting the disheartening decision of the conductor, *viz.*, that it would be death for any man to attempt to travel fifty miles on foot through snow like that. We could not send for help, and even if we could it would not come. We must submit, and await, as patiently as we might, succor or starvation! I think the stoutest heart there felt a momentary chill when those words were uttered.

Within the hour conversation subsided to a low murmur here and there about the car, caught fitfully between the rising and falling of the blast; the lamps grew dim; and the majority of the castaways settled themselves among the flickering shadows to think—to forget the present, if they could—to sleep, if they might.

The eternal night—it surely seemed eternal to us—wore its lagging hours away at last, and the cold gray dawn broke in the east. As the light grew stronger the passengers began to stir and give signs of life, one after another, and each in turn pushed his slouched hat up from his forehead, stretched his stiffened limbs, and glanced out of the windows upon the cheerless prospect. It was cheerless, indeed!—not a living thing visible anywhere, not a human habitation; nothing but a vast white desert; uplifted sheets of snow drifted hither and thither before the wind—a world of eddying flakes shutting out the firmament above.

All day we moped about the cars, saying little, thinking much. Another lingering dreary night—and hunger.

Another dawning—another day of silence, sadness, wasting hunger, hopeless watching for succor that could not come. A night of restless slumber, filled with dreams of feasting—wakings distressed with the gnawings of hunger.

The fourth day came and went—and the fifth! Five days of dreadful imprisonment! A savage hunger looked out at every eye. There was in it a sign of awful import—the foreshadowing of a something that was vaguely shaping itself in every heart—a something which no tongue dared yet to frame into words.

The sixth day passed—the seventh dawned upon as gaunt and haggard and hopeless a company of men as ever stood in the shadow of death. It must out now! That thing which had been growing up in every heart was ready to leap from every lip at last! Nature had been taxed to the utmost—she must yield. RICHARD H. GASTON of Minnesota, tall, cadaverous, and pale, rose up. All knew what was coming. All prepared—every emotion, every semblance of excitement was smothered—only a calm, thoughtful seriousness appeared in the eyes that were lately so wild.

"Gentlemen: It cannot be delayed longer! The time is at hand! We must determine which of us shall die to furnish food for the rest!"

MR. JOHN J. WILLIAMS of Illinois rose and said: "Gentlemen—I nominate the Rev. James Sawyer of Tennessee."

MR. WM. R. ADAMS of Indiana said: "I nominate Mr. Daniel Slote of New York."

MR. CHARLES J. LANGDON: "I nominate Mr. Samuel A. Bowen of St. Louis."

MR. SLOTE: "Gentlemen—I desire to decline in favor of Mr. John A. Van Nostrand, Jun., of New Jersey."

MR. GASTON: "If there be no objection, the gentleman's desire will be acceded to."

MR. VAN NOSTRAND objecting, the resignation of Mr. Slote was rejected. The resignations of Messrs. Sawyer and Bowen were also offered, and refused upon the same grounds.

MR. A. L. BASCOM of Ohio: "I move that the nominations now close, and that the House proceed to an election by ballot."

MR. SAWYER: "Gentlemen—I protest earnestly against these proceedings. They are, in every way, irregular and unbecoming. I must beg to move that they be dropped at once, and that we elect a chairman of the meeting and proper officers to assist him, and then we can go on with the business before us understandingly."

MR. BELL of Iowa: "Gentlemen—I object. This is no time to stand upon forms and ceremonious observances. For more than seven days we have been without food. Every moment we lose in idle discussion increases our distress. I am satisfied with the nominations that have been made—every gentleman present is, I believe—and I, for one, do not see why we should not proceed at once to elect one or more of them. I wish to offer a resolution—"

MR. GASTON: "It would be objected to, and have to lie over one day under the rules, thus bringing about the very delay you wish to avoid. The gentleman from New Jersey—"

MR. VAN NOSTRAND: "Gentlemen—I am a stranger among you; I have not sought the distinction that has been conferred upon me, and I feel a delicacy—"

MR. MORGAN of Alabama (interrupting): "I move the previous question."

The motion was carried, and further debate shut off, of

course. The motion to elect officers was passed, and under it Mr. Gaston was chosen chairman, Mr. Blake, secretary, Messrs. Holcomb, Dyer, and Baldwin a committee on nominations, and Mr. R. M. Howland, purveyor, to assist the committee in making selections.

A recess of half an hour was then taken, and some little caucusing followed. At the sound of the gavel the meeting assembled, and the committee reported in favor of Messrs. George Ferguson of Kentucky, Lucien Herrman of Louisiana, and W. Messick of Colorado as candidates. The report was accepted.

MR. ROGERS of Missouri: "Mr. President—The report being properly before the House now, I move to amend it by substituting for the name of Mr. Herrman that of Mr. Lucius Harris of St. Louis, who is well and honorably known to us all. I do not wish to be understood as casting the least reflection upon the high character and standing of the gentleman from Louisiana—far from it. I respect and esteem him as much as any gentleman here present possibly can; but none of us can be blind to the fact that he has lost more flesh during the week that we have lain here than any among us—none of us can be blind to the fact that the committee has been derelict in its duty, either through negligence or a graver fault, in thus offering for our suffrages a gentleman who, however pure his own motives may be, has really less nutriment in him—"

THE CHAIR: "The gentleman from Missouri will take his seat. The Chair cannot allow the integrity of the committee to be questioned save by the regular course, under the rules. What action will the House take upon the gentleman's motion?"

MR. HALLIDAY of Virginia: "I move to further amend the report by substituting Mr. Harvey Davis of Oregon for Mr. Messick. It may be urged by gentlemen that the hardships and privations of a frontier life have rendered Mr. Davis tough; but, gentlemen, is this a time to cavil at toughness? Is this a time to be fastidious concerning trifles? Is this a time to dispute about matters of paltry significance? No, gentlemen, bulk is what we desire, substance, weight, bulk—these are the supreme requisites now—not talent, not genius, not education. I insist upon my motion."

MR. MORGAN (excitedly): "Mr. Chairman—I do most strenuously object to this amendment. The gentleman from Oregon is old, and furthermore is bulky only in bone—not in flesh. I ask the gentleman from Virginia if it is soup we want instead of solid sustenance? if he would delude us with shadows? if he would mock our suffering with an Oregonian specter? I ask him if he can look upon the anxious faces around him, if he can gaze into our sad eyes, if he can listen to the beating of our expectant hearts, and still thrust this famine-stricken fraud upon us? I ask him if he can think of our desolate state, of our past sorrows, of our dark future, and still unpityingly foist upon us this wreck, this ruin, this tottering swindle, this gnarled and blighted and sapless vagabond from Oregon's inhospitable shores? Never!" [Applause.]

The amendment was put to vote, after a fiery debate, and lost. Mr. Harris was substituted on the first amendment. The balloting then began. Five ballots were held without a choice. On the sixth, Mr. Harris was elected, all voting for him but himself. It was then moved that his election should be ratified by acclamation, which was lost, in consequence of his again voting against himself.

MR. RADWAY moved that the House now take up the remaining candidates, and go into an election for breakfast. This was carried.

On the first ballot there was a tie, half the members favoring one candidate on account of his youth, and half favoring the other on account of his superior size. The President gave the casting vote for the latter, Mr. Messick. This decision created considerable dissatisfaction among the friends of Mr. Ferguson, the defeated candidate, and there was some talk of demanding a new ballot; but in the midst of it a motion to adjourn was carried, and the meeting broke up at once.

The preparations for supper diverted the attention of the Ferguson faction from the discussion of their grievance for a long time, and then, when they would have taken it up again, the happy announcement that Mr. Harris was ready drove all thought of it to the winds.

We improvised tables by propping up the backs of car-seats, and sat down with hearts full of gratitude to the finest supper that had blessed our vision for seven torturing days. How changed we were from what we had been a few short hours before! Hopeless, sad-eyed misery, hunger, feverish anxiety, desperation, then; thankfulness, serenity, joy too deep for utterance now. That I know was the cheeriest hour of my eventful life. The winds howled, and blew the snow wildly about our prison-house, but they were powerless to distress us any more. I liked Harris. He might have been better done, perhaps, but I am free to say that no man ever agreed with me better than Harris, or afforded me so large a degree of satisfaction. Messick was very well, though rather high-flavored, but for genuine nutritiousness and delicacy of fiber, give me Harris. Messick had his good points—I will not attempt to deny it, nor do I wish to do it—but he was no more fitted for breakfast than a mummy would be, sir—not a bit. Lean?—why, bless me!—and tough? Ah, he was very tough! You could not imagine it—you could never imagine anything like it.

"Do you mean to tell me that—"

"Do not interrupt me, please. After breakfast we elected a man by the name of Walker, from Detroit, for supper. He was very good. I wrote his wife so afterward. He was worthy of all praise. I shall always remember Walker. He was a little rare, but very good. And then the next morning we had Morgan of Alabama for breakfast. He was one of the finest men I ever sat down to—handsome, educated, refined, spoke several languages fluently—a perfect gentleman—he was a perfect gentleman, and singularly juicy. For supper we had that Oregon patiarch, and he *was* a fraud, there is no question about it—old, scraggy, tough, nobody can picture the reality. I finally said, gentlemen, you can do as you like, but *I* will wait for another election. And Grimes of Illinois said, 'Gentlemen, *I* will wait also. When you elect a man that has *something* to recommend him, I shall be glad to join you again.' It soon became evident that there was general dissatisfaction with Davis of Oregon, and so, to preserve the good will that had prevailed so pleasantly since we had had Harris, an election was called, and the result of it was that Baker of Georgia was chosen. He was splendid! Well, well—after that we had Doolittle, and Hawkins, and McElroy (there was some complaint about McElroy, because he was uncommonly short and thin), and Penrod, and two Smiths, and Bailey (Bailey had a wooden leg, which was clear loss, but he was otherwise good), and an Indian boy, and an organ-grinder, and a gentleman by the name of Buckminster—a poor stick of a vagabond that wasn't any good for company and no account for breakfast. We were glad we got him elected before relief came."

"And so the blessed relief *did* come at last?"

"Yes, it came one bright, sunny morning, just after election. John Murphy was the choice, and there never was a better, I am willing to testify; but John Murphy came home with us, in the train that came to succor us, and lived to marry the widow Harris—"

"Relict of—"

"Relict of our first choice. He married her, and is happy and respected and prosperous yet. Ah, it was like a novel, sir—it was like a romance. This is my stopping-place, sir; I must bid you good-by. Any time that you can make it convenient to tarry a day or two with me, I shall be glad to have you. I like you, sir; I have conceived an affection for you. I could like you as well as I liked Harris himself, sir. Good day, sir, and a pleasant journey."

He was gone. I never felt so stunned, so distressed, so bewildered in my life. But in my soul I was glad he was gone. With all his gentleness of manner and his soft voice, I shuddered whenever he turned his hungry eye upon me; and when I heard that I had achieved his perilous affection, and that I stood almost with the late Harris in his esteem, my heart fairly stood still!

I was bewildered beyond description. I did not doubt his word; I could not question a single item in a statement so stamped with the earnestness of truth as his; but its dreadful details overpowered me, and threw my thoughts into hopeless confusion. I saw the conductor looking at me. I said, "Who is that man?"

"He was a member of Congress once, and a good one. But he got caught in a snow-drift in the cars, and like to have been starved to death. He got so frost-bitten and frozen up generally, and used up for want of something to eat, that he was sick and out of his head two or three months afterward. He is all right now, only he is a monomaniac, and when he gets on that old subject he never stops till he has eat up that whole car-load of people he talks about. He would have finished the crowd by this time, only he had to get out here. He had got their names as pat as A B C. When he gets all eat up but himself, he always says: 'Then the hour for the usual election for breakfast having arrived, and there being no opposition, I was duly elected, after which, there being no objections offered, I resigned. Thus I am here.' "

I felt inexpressibly relieved to know that I had only been listening to the harmless vagaries of a madman instead of the genuine experiences of a bloodthirsty cannibal.

1868

A Day at Niagara

Niagara Falls is a most enjoyable place of resort. The hotels are excellent, and the prices not at all exorbitant. The opportunities for fishing are not surpassed in the country; in fact, they are not even equaled elsewhere. Because, in other localities, certain places in the streams are much better than others; but at Niagara one place is just as good as another, for the reason that the fish do not bite anywhere, and so there is no use in your walking five miles to fish, when you can depend on being just as unsuccessful nearer home. The advantages of this state of things have never heretofore been properly placed before the public.

The weather is cool in summer, and the walks and drives are all pleasant and none of them fatiguing. When you start out to "do" the Falls you first drive down about a mile, and pay a small sum for the privilege of looking down from a precipice into the narrowest pan of the Niagara River. A railway "cut" through a hill would be as comely if it had the angry river tumbling and foaming through its bottom. You can descend a staircase here a hundred and fifty feet down, and stand at the edge of the water. After you have done it, you will wonder why you did it; but you will then be too late.

The guide will explain to you, in his blood-curdling way, how he saw the little steamer, *Maid of the Mist,* descend the fearful rapids—how first one paddle-box was out of sight behind the raging billows and then the other, and at what point it was that her smokestack toppled overboard, and where her planking began to break and part asunder—and how she did finally live through the trip, after accomplishing the incredible feat of traveling seventeen miles in six minutes, or six miles in seventeen minutes, I have really forgotten which. But it was very extraordinary, anyhow. It is worth the price of admission to hear the guide tell the story nine times in succession to different parties, and never miss a word or alter a sentence or a gesture.

Then you drive over to Suspension Bridge, and divide your misery between the chances of smashing down two hundred feet into the river below, and the chances of having the railway-train overhead smashing down onto you. Either possibility is discomforting taken by itself, but, mixed together, they amount in the aggregate to positive unhappiness.

On the Canada side you drive along the chasm between long ranks of photographers standing guard behind their cameras, ready to make an ostentatious frontispiece of you and your decaying ambulance, and your solemn crate with a hide on it, which you are expected to regard in the light of a horse, and a diminished and unimportant background of sublime Niagara; and a great many people *have* the incredible effrontery or the native depravity to aid and abet this sort of crime.

Any day, in the hands of these photographers, you may see stately pictures of papa and mamma, Johnny and Bub and Sis, or a couple of country cousins, all smiling vacantly, and all disposed in studied and uncomfortable attitudes in their carriage, and all looming up in their awe-inspiring inbecility before the snubbed and diminished presentment of that majestic presence whose ministering spirits are the rainbows, whose voice is the thunder, whose awful front is veiled in clouds, who was monarch here dead and forgotten ages before this hackfull of small reptiles was deemed temporarily necessary to fill a crack in the world's unnoted myriads, and will still be monarch here ages and decades of ages after they shall have gathered themselves to their blood-relations, the other worms, and been mingled with the unremembering dust.

There is no actual harm in making Niagara a background whereon to display one's marvelous insignificance in a good strong light, but it requires a sort of superhuman self-complacency to enable one to do it.

When you have examined the stupendous Horseshoe Fall till you are satisfied you cannot improve on it, you return to America by the new Suspension Bridge, and follow up the bank to where they exhibit the Cave of the Winds.

Here I followed instructions, and divested myself of all my clothing, and put on a waterproof jacket and overalls. This costume is picturesque, but not beautiful. A guide, similarly dressed, led the way down a flight of winding stairs, which wound and wound, and still kept on winding long after the thing ceased to be a novelty, and then terminated long before it had begun to be a pleasure. We were then well down under the precipice, but still considerably above the level of the river.

We now began to creep along flimsy bridges of a single plank, our persons shielded from destruction by a crazy wooden railing, to which I clung with both hands—not because I was afraid, but because I wanted to. Presently the descent became steeper, and the bridge flimsier, and sprays from the American Fall began to rain down on us in fast increasing sheets that soon became blinding, and after that our progress was mostly in the nature of groping. Now a furious wind began to rush out from behind the waterfall, which seemed determined to sweep us from the bridge, and scatter us on the rocks and among the torrents below. I remarked that I wanted to go home; but it was too late. We were almost under the monstrous wall of water thundering down from above, and speech was in vain in the midst of such a pitiless crash of sound.

In another moment the guide disappeared behind the deluge, and, bewildered by the thunder, driven helplessly by the wind, and smitten by the arrowy tempest of rain, I followed. All was darkness. Such a mad storming, roaring, and bellowing of warring wind and water never crazed my ears before. I bent my head, and seemed to receive the Atlantic on my back. The world seemed going to destruction. I could not see anything, the flood poured down so savagely. I raised my head, with open mouth, and the most of the American cataract went down my throat. If I had sprung a leak now I had been lost. And at this moment I discovered that the bridge had ceased, and we must trust for a foothold to the slippery and precipitous rocks. I never was so scared before and survived it. But we got through at last, and emerged into the open day, where we could stand in front of the laced and frothy and seething world of descending water, and look at it. When I saw how much of it there was, and how fearfully in earnest it was, I was sorry I had gone behind it.

The noble Red Man has always been a friend and darling of mine. I love to read about him in tales and legends and romances. I love to read of his inspired sagacity, and his love of the wild free life of mountain and forest, and his general nobility of character, and his stately metaphorical manner of speech, and his chivalrous love for the dusky maiden, and the picturesque pomp of his dress and accoutrements.[1] Especially the picturesque pomp of his dress and accoutrements. When I found the shops at Niagara Falls full of dainty Indian bead-work, and stunning moccasins, and equally stunning toy figures representing human beings who carried their weapons in holes bored through their arms and bodies, and had feet shaped like a pie, I was filled with emotion. I knew that now, at last, I was going to come face to face with the noble Red Man.

A lady clerk in a shop told me, indeed, that all her grand array of curiosities were made by the Indians, and that they were plenty about the Falls, and that they were friendly, and it would not be dangerous to speak to them. And sure enough, as I approached the bridge leading over to Luna Island, I came upon a noble Son of the Forest sitting under a tree, diligently at work on a bead reticule. He wore a slouch hat and brogans, and had a short black pipe in his mouth. Thus does the baneful contact with our effeminate civilization dilute the picturesque pomp which is so natural to the Indian when far removed from us in his native haunts. I addressed the relic as follows:

"Is the Wawhoo-Wang-Wang of the Whack-a-Whack happy? Does the great Speckled Thunder sigh for the warpath, or is his heart contented with dreaming of the dusky maiden, the Pride of the Forest? Does the mighty Sachem yearn to drink the blood of his enemies, or is he satisfied to make bead reticules for the pappooses of the paleface? Speak, sublime relic of bygone grandeur—venerable ruin, speak!"

The relic said:

"An' is it mesilf, Dennis Holligan, that ye'd be takin' for a dirty Injin, ye drawlin', lantern-jawed, spider-legged devil! By the piper that played before Moses, I'll ate ye!"

I went away from there.

By and by, in the neighborhood of the Terrapin Tower, I came upon a gentle daughter of the aborigines in fringed and beaded buckskin moccasins and leggins, seated on a bench with her pretty wares about her. She had just carved out a wooden chief that had a strong family resemblance to a clothespin, and was now boring a hole through his abdomen to put his bow through. I hesitated a moment, and then addressed her:

"Is the heart of the forest maiden heavy? Is the Laughing Tadpole lonely? Does she mourn over the extinguished council-fires of her race, and the vanished glory of her ancestors? Or does her sad spirit wander afar toward the hunting-grounds whither her brave Gobbler-of-the-Lightnings is gone? Why is my daughter silent? Has she aught against the paleface stranger?"

The maiden said:

"Faix,[2] an' is it Biddy Malone ye dare to be callin' names? Lave this, or I'll shy your lean carcass over the cataract, ye sniveling blaggard!"

I adjourned from there also.

"Confound these Indians!" I said. They told me they were tame; but, if appearances go for anything, I should say they were all on the warpath."

I made one more attempt to fraternize with them, and only one. I came upon a camp of them gathered in the shade of a great tree, making wampum and moccasins, and addressed them in the language of friendship:

"Noble Red Men, Braves, Grand Sachems, War Chiefs, Squaws, and High Muck-a-Mucks, the paleface from the land of the setting sun greets you! You, Beneficent Polecat—you, Devourer of Mountains—you, Roaring Thundergust—you, Bully Boy with a Glass eye—the paleface from beyond the great waters greets you all! War and pestilence have thinned your ranks and destroyed your once proud nation. Poker and seven-up, and a vain modern expense for soap, unknown to your glorious ancestors, have depleted your purses. Appropriating, in your simplicity, the property of others has gotten you into trouble. Misrepresenting facts, in your simple innocence, has damaged your reputation with the soulless usurper. Trading for forty-rod whisky, to enable you to get drunk and happy and tomahawk your families, has played the everlasting mischief with the picturesque pomp of your dress, and here you are, in the broad light of the nineteenth century, gotten up like a rag-tag and bobtail of the purlieus of New York. For shame! Remember your ancestors! Recall their mighty deeds! Remember Uncas!—and Red Jacket!—and Hole in the Day!—and Whoopdedoodledo! Emulate their achievements! Unfurl yourselves under my banner, noble savages, illustrious guttersnipes—"

"Down wid him!" "Scoop the blaggard!" "Burn him!" "Hang him!" "Dhround him!"

It was the quickest operation that ever was. I simply saw a sudden flash in the air of clubs, brick-bats, fists, bead-baskets, and moccasins—a single flash, and they all appeared to hit me at once, and no two of them in the same place. In the next instant the entire tribe was upon me. They tore half the clothes off me; they broke my arms and legs; they gave me a thump that dented the top of my head till it would hold coffee like a saucer; and, to crown their disgraceful proceedings and add insult to injury, they threw me over the Niagara Falls, and I got wet.

About ninety or a hundred feet from the top, the remains of my vest caught on a projecting rock, and I was almost drowned before I could get loose. I finally fell, and brought up in a world of white foam at the foot of the Fall, whose celled and bubbly masses towered up several inches above my head. Of course I got into the eddy. I sailed round and round in it forty-four times—chasing a chip and gaining on it—each round trip a half-mile—reaching for the same bush on the bank forty-four times, and just exactly missing it by a hair's-breadth every time.

At last a man walked down and sat down close to that bush, and put a pipe in his mouth, and lit a match, and followed me with one eye and kept the other on the match, while he sheltered it in his hands from the wind. Presently a puff of wind blew it out. The next time I swept around he said:

"Got a match?"

"Yes; in my other vest. Help me out, please."

"Not for Joe."

When I came round again, I said:

"Excuse the seemingly impertinent curiosity of a drowning man, but will you explain this singular conduct of yours?"

"With pleasure. I am the coroner. Don't hurry on my account. I can wait for you. But I wish I had a match."

I said: "Take my place, and I'll go and get you one."

He declined. This lack of confidence on his part created a coldness between us, and from that time forward I avoided him. It was my idea, in case anything happened to me, to so time the occurrence as to throw my custom into the hands of the opposition coroner on the American side.

At last a policeman came along, and arrested me for disturbing the peace by yelling at people on shore for help. The judge fined me, but I had the advantage of him. My money was with my pantaloons, and my pantaloons were with the Indians.

Thus I escaped. I am now lying in a very critical condition. At least I am lying anyway—critical or not critical. I am hurt all over, but I cannot tell the full extent yet, because the doctor is not done taking inventory. He will make out my manifest this evening. However, thus far he thinks only sixteen of my wounds are fatal. I don't mind the others.

Upon regaining my right mind, I said:

"It is an awful savage tribe of Indians that do the beadwork and moccasins for Niagara Falls, doctor. Where are they from?"

"Limerick, my son."

1869

Legend of the Capitoline Venus

Chapter I
[*Scene—An Artist's Studio in Rome*]

"Oh, George, I *do* love you!"

"Bless your dear heart, Mary, I know that—*why* is your father so obdurate?"

"George, he means well, but art is folly to him—he only understands groceries. He thinks you would starve me."

"Confound his wisdom—it savors of inspiration. Why am I not a money-making bowelless grocer, instead of a divinely gifted sculptor with nothing to eat?"

"Do not despond, Georgy, dear—all his prejudices will fade away as soon as you shall have acquired fifty thousand dol—"

"Fifty thousand demons! Child, I am in arrears for my board!"

Chapter II
[*Scene—A Dwelling in Rome*]

"My dear sir, it is useless to talk. I haven't anything against you, but I can't let my daughter marry a hash of love, art, and starvation—I believe you have nothing else to offer."

"Sir, I am poor, I grant you. But is fame nothing? The

Hon. Bellamy Foodle of Arkansas says that my new statue of America is a clever piece of sculpture, and he is satisfied that my name will one day be famous."

"Bosh! What does that Arkansas ass know about it? Fame's nothing—the market price of your marble scarecrow is the thing to look at. It took you six months to chisel it, and you can't sell it for a hundred dollars. No, sir! Show me fifty thousand dollars and you can have my daughter—otherwise she marries young Simper. You have just six months to raise the money in. Good morning, sir."

"Alas! Woe is me!"

CHAPTER III
[*Scene—The Studio*]

"Oh, John, friend of my boyhood, I am the unhappiest of men."

"You're a simpleton!"

"I have nothing left to love but my poor statue of America—and see, even she has no sympathy for me in her cold marble countenance—so beautiful and so heartless!"

"You're a dummy!"

"Oh, John!"

"Oh, fudge! Didn't you say you had six months to raise the money in?"

"Don't deride my agony, John. If I had six centuries what good would it do? How could it help a poor wretch without name, capital, or friends?"

"Idiot! Coward! Baby! Six months to raise the money in—and five will do!"

"Are you insane?"

"Six months—an abundance. Leave it to me. I'll raise it."

"What do you mean, John? How on earth can you raise such a monstrous sum for *me*?"

"*Will* you let that be *my* business, and not meddle? Will you leave the thing in my hands? Will you swear to submit to whatever I do? Will you pledge me to find no fault with my actions?"

"I am dizzy—bewildered—but I swear."

John took up a hammer and deliberately smashed the nose of America! He made another pass and two of her fingers fell to the floor—another, and part of an ear came away—another, and a row of toes were mangled and dismembered—another, and the left leg, from the knee down, lay a fragmentary ruin!

John put on his hat and departed.

George gazed speechless upon the battered and grotesque nightmare before him for the space of thirty seconds, and then wilted to the floor and went into convulsions.

John returned presently with a carriage, got the broken-hearted artist and the broken-legged statue aboard, and drove off, whistling low and tranquilly. He left the artist at his lodgings, and drove off and disappeared down the *Via Quirinalis* with the statue.

Chapter IV
[*Scene—The Studio*]

"The six months will be up at two o'clock to-day! Oh, agony! My life is blighted. I would that I were dead. I had no supper yesterday. I have had no breakfast to-day. I dare not enter an eating-house. And hungry?—don't mention it! My bootmaker duns me to death—my tailor duns me—my landlord haunts me. I am miserable. I haven't seen John since that awful day. *She* smiles on me tenderly when we meet in the great thoroughfares, but her old flint of a father makes her look in the other direction in short order. Now who is knocking at that door? Who is come to persecute me? That malignant villain the bootmaker, I'll warrant. *Come in!*"

"Ah, happiness attend your highness—Heaven be propitious to your grace! I have brought my lord's new boots—

ah, say nothing about the pay, there is no hurry, none in the world. Shall be proud if my noble lord will continue to honor me with his custom—ah, adieu!"

"Brought the boots himself! Don't want his pay! Takes his leave with a bow and a scrape fit to honor majesty withal! Desires a continuance of my custom! Is the world coming to an end? Of all the—*come in!*"

"Pardon, Signore, but I have brought you new suit of clothes for—"

"Come in! ! !"

"A thousand pardons for this intrusion, your worship! But I have prepared the beautiful suite of rooms below for you—this wretched den is but ill suited to—"

"Come in! ! !"

"I have called to say that your credit at our bank, some time since unfortunately interrupted, is entirely and most satisfactorily restored, and we shall be most happy if you will draw upon us for any—"

"COME IN! ! !"

"My noble boy, she is yours! She'll be here in a moment! Take her—marry her—love her—be happy!—God bless you both! Hip, hip, hur—"

"COME IN! ! ! ! !"

"Oh, George, my own darling, we are saved!"

"Oh, Mary, my own darling, we *are* saved—but I'll swear I don't know why nor how!"

CHAPTER V

[*Scene—A Roman Café*]

One of a group of American gentlemen reads and translates from the weekly edition of *Il Slangwhanger di Roma* as follows:

WONDERFUL DISCOVERY!—*Some six months ago Signor John Smitthe, an American gentleman now some years a* resident of Rome, purchased for a trifle a small piece of ground in the Campagna, just beyond the tomb of the Scipio family, from the owner, a bankrupt relative of the Princess Borghese. Mr. Smitthe afterward went to the Minister of the Public Records and had the piece of ground transferred to a poor American artist named George Arnold, explaining that he did it as payment and satisfaction for pecuniary damage accidentally done by him long since upon property belonging to Signor Arnold, and further observed that he would make additional satisfaction by improving the ground for Signor A., at his own charge and cost. Four weeks ago, while making some necessary excavations upon the property, Signor Smitthe unearthed the most remarkable ancient statue that has ever been added to the opulent art treasures of Rome. It was an exquisite figure of a woman, and though sadly stained by the soil and the mold of ages, no eye can look unmoved upon its ravishing beauty. The nose, the left leg from the knee down, an ear, and also the toes of the right foot and two fingers of one of the hands were gone, but otherwise the noble figure was in a remarkable state of preservation. The government at once took military possession of the statue, and appointed a commission of art-critics, antiquaries, and cardinal princes of the church to assess its value and determine the remuneration that must go to the owner of the ground in which it was found. The whole affair was kept a profound secret until last night. In the mean time the commission sat with closed doors and deliberated. Last night they decided unanimously that the statue is a Venus, and the work of some unknown but sublimely gifted artist of the third century before Christ. They consider it the most faultless work of art the world has any knowledge of.

At midnight they held a final conference and decided that the Venus was worth the enormous sum of ten million francs! In accordance with Roman law and Roman usage, the government being half-owner in all works of art found in the Campagna, the State has naught to do but pay five *million francs to Mr. Arnold and take permanent possession of the beautiful statue. This morning the Venus will be removed to the Capitol, there to remain, and at noon the commission will wait upon Signor Arnold with His Holiness the Pope's order upon the Treasury for the princely sum of five million francs in gold!*

Chorus of Voices.—"Luck! It's no name for it!"

Another Voice.—"Gentlemen, I propose that we immediately form an American joint-stock company for the purchase of lands and excavations of statues here, with proper connections in Wall Street to bull and bear the stock."

All.—"Agreed."

CHAPTER VI

[*Scene—The Roman Capitol Ten Years Later*]

"Dearest Mary, this is the most celebrated statue in the world. This is the renowned 'Capitoline Venus' you've heard so much about. Here she is with her little blemishes 'restored' (that is, patched) by the most noted Roman artists—and the mere fact that they did the humble patching of so noble a creation will make their names illustrious while the world stands. How strange it seems—this place! The day before I last stood here, ten happy years ago, I wasn't a rich man— bless your soul, I hadn't a cent. And yet I had a good deal to do with making Rome mistress of this grandest work of ancient art the world contains."

"The worshiped, the illustrious Capitoline Venus—and what a sum she is valued at! Ten millions of francs!"

"Yes—*now* she is."

"And oh, Georgy, how divinely beautiful she is!"

"Ah, yes—but nothing to what she was before that blessed John Smith broke her leg and battered her nose. Ingenious Smith!—gifted Smith!—noble Smith! Author of all our bliss! Hark! Do you know what that wheeze means? Mary, that cub has got the whooping-cough. Will you *never* learn to take care of the children!"

THE END

The Capitoline Venus is still in the Capitol at Rome, and is still the most charming and most illustrious work of ancient art the world can boast of. But if ever it shall be your fortune to stand before it and go into the customary ecstasies over it, don't permit this true and secret history of its origin to mar your bliss—and when you read about a gigantic Petrified Man being dug up near Syracuse, in the State of New York, or near any other place, keep your own counsel—and if the Barnum that buried him there offers to sell to you at an enormous sum, don't you buy. Send him to the Pope!

NOTE: The above sketch was written at the time the famous swindle of the "Petrified Giant" was the sensation of the day in the United States.

1869

JOURNALISM IN TENNESSEE

The editor of the Memphis *Avalanche* swoops thus mildly down upon a correspondent who posted him as a Radical:—"While he was writing the first word, the middle, dotting his i's, crossing his t's, and punching his period, he knew he was concocting a sentence that was saturated with infamy and reeking with falsehoods."

Exchange

I WAS TOLD by the physician that a Southern climate would improve my health, and so I went down to Tennessee, and got a berth on the *Morning Glory and Johnson County War-Whoop* as associate editor. When I went on duty I found the chief editor sitting tilted back in a three-legged chair with his feet on a pine table. There was another pine table in the room and another afflicted chair, and both were half buried under newspapers and scraps and sheets of manuscript. There was a wooden box of sand, sprinkled with cigar stubs and "old soldiers," and a stove with a door hanging by its upper hinge. The chief editor had a long-tailed black cloth frock-coat on, and white linen pants. His boots were small and neatly blacked. He wore a ruffled shirt, a large seal-ring, a standing collar of obsolete pattern, and a checkered neckerchief with the ends hanging down. Date of costume about 1848. He was smoking a cigar, and trying to think of a word, and in pawing his hair he rumpled his locks a good deal. He was scowling fearfully, and I judged that he was concocting a particularly knotty editorial. He told me to take the exchanges and skim through them and write up the "Spirit of the Tennessee Press," condensing into the article all of their contents that seemed of interest.

I wrote as follows:

SPIRIT OF THE TENNESSEE PRESS

The editors of the Semi-Weekly Earthquake *evidently labor under a misapprehension with regard to the Ballyhack railroad. It is not the object of the company to leave Buzzardville off to one side. On the contrary, they consider it one of the most important points along the line, and consequently can have no desire to slight it. The gentlemen of the* Earthquake *will, of course, take pleasure in making the correction.*

John W. Blossom, Esq., the able editor of the Higginsville Thunderbolt and Battle Cry of Freedom, *arrived in the city yesterday. He is stopping at the Van Buren House.*

We observe that our contemporary of the Mud Springs Morning Howl *has fallen into the error of supposing that the election of Van Werter is not an established fact, but he will have discovered his mistake before this reminder reaches him, no doubt. He was doubtless misled by incomplete election returns.*

It is pleasant to note that the city of Blathersville is endeavoring to contract with some New York gentlemen to pave its well-nigh impassable streets with the Nicholson pavement. The Daily Hurrah *urges the measure with ability, and seems confident of ultimate success.*

I passed my manuscript over to the chief editor for acceptance, alteration, or destruction. He glanced at it and his face clouded. He ran his eye down the pages, and his countenance grew portentous. It was easy to see that something was wrong. Presently he sprang up and said:

"Thunder and lighting! Do you suppose I am going to speak of those cattle that way? Do you suppose my subscribers are going to stand such gruel as that? Give me the pen!"

I never saw a pen scrape and scratch its way so viciously, or plow through another man's verbs and adjectives so relentlessly. While he was in the midst of his work, somebody shot at him through the open window, and marred the symmetry of my ear.

"Ah," said he, "that is that scoundrel Smith, of the *Moral Volcano*—he was due yesterday." And he snatched a navy revolver from his belt and fired. Smith dropped, shot in the thigh. The shot spoiled Smith's aim, who was just taking a second chance, and he crippled a stranger. It was me. Merely a finger shot off.

Then the chief editor went on with his erasures and interlineations. Just as he finished then a hand-grenade came down the stove-pipe, and the explosion shivered the stove into a thousand fragments. However, it did no further damage, except that a vagrant piece knocked a couple of my teeth out.

"That stove is utterly ruined," said the chief editor.

I said I believed it was.

"Well, no matter—don't want it this kind of weather. I know the man that did it. I'll get him. Now, *here* is the way this stuff ought to he written."

I took the manuscript. It was scarred with erasures and interlineations till its mother wouldn't have known it if it had had one. It now read as follows:

SPIRIT OF THE TENNESSEE PRESS

The inveterate liars of the Semi-Weekly Earthquake *are evidently endeavoring to palm off upon a noble and chivalrous people another of their vile and brutal falsehoods with regard to that most glorious conception of the nineteenth century, the Ballyhack railroad. The idea that Buzzardville was to be left off at one side originated in their own fulsome brains—or rather in the settlings which they regard as brains. They had better swallow this lie if they want to save their abandoned reptile carcasses the cowhiding they so richly deserve.*

That ass, Blossom, of the Higginsville Thunderbolt and Battle Cry of Freedom, *is down here again sponging at the Van Buren.*

We observe that the besotted blackguard of the Mud Spring Morning Howl *is giving out, with his usual prosperity for lying, that Van Werter is not elected. The heaven-born mission of journalism is to disseminate truth; to eradi-*

cate error; to educate, refine, and elevate the tone of public morals and manners, and make all men more gentle, more virtuous, more charitable, and in all ways better, and holier, and happier; and yet this black-hearted scoundrel degrades his great office persistently to the dissemination of falsehood, calumny, vituperation, and vulgarity.

Blathersville wants a Nicholson pavement—it wants a jail and a poorhouse more. The idea of a pavement in a one-horse town composed of two gin-mills, a blacksmith shop, and that mustard-plaster of a newspaper, the Daily Hurrah! *The crawling insect, Buckner, who edits the* Hurrah, *is braying about his business with his customary imbecility, and imagining he is talking sense.*

"Now *that* is the way to write—peppery and to the point. Mush-and-milk journalism gives me the fan-tods."[1]

About this time a brick came through the window with a splintering crash, and gave me a considerable of a jolt in the back. I moved out of range—I began to feel in the way.

The chief said, "That was the Colonel, likely. I've been expecting him for two days. He will be up now right away."

He was correct. The Colonel appeared in the door a moment afterward with a dragoon revolver in his hand.

He said, "Sir, have I the honor of addressing the poltroon who edits this mangy sheet?"

"You have. Be seated, sir. Be careful of the chair, one of its legs is gone. I believe I have the honor of addressing the putrid liar, Colonel Blatherskite Tecumseh?"

"Right, sir. I have a little account to settle with you. If you are at leisure we will begin."

"I have an article on the 'Encouraging Progress of Moral and Intellectual Development in America' to finish, but there is no hurry. Begin."

Both pistols rang out their fierce clamor at the same instant. The chief lost a lock of his hair, and the Colonel's bullet ended its career in the fleshy part of my thigh. The

Colonel's left shoulder was clipped a little. They fired again. Both missed their men this time, but I got my share, a shot in the arm. At the third fire both gentlemen were wounded slightly, and I had a knuckle chipped. I then said, I believed I would go out and take a walk, as this was a private matter, and I had a delicacy about participating in it further. But both gentlemen begged me to keep my seat, and assured me that I was not in the way.

They then talked about the elections and the crops while they reloaded, and I fell to tying up my wounds. But presently they opened fire again with animation, and every shot took effect—but it is proper to remark that five out of the six fell to my share. The sixth one mortally wounded the Colonel, who remarked, with fine humor, that he would have to say good morning now, as he had business uptown. He then inquired the way to the undertaker's and left.

The chief turned to me and said, "I am expecting company to dinner, and shall have to get ready. It will be a favor to me if you will read proof and attend to the customers."

I winced a little at the idea of attending to the customers, but I was too bewildered by the fusillade that was still ringing in my ears to think of anything to say.

He continued, "Jones will be here at three—cowhide him. Gillespie will call earlier, perhaps—throw him out of the window. Ferguson will be along about four—kill him. That is all for to-day, I believe. If you have any odd time, you may write a blistering article on the police—give the chief inspector rats. The cowhides are under the table; weapons in the drawer—ammunition there in the corner—lint and bandages up there in the pigeonholes. In case of accident, go to Lancet, the surgeon, down-stairs. He advertises—we take it out in trade."

He was gone. I shuddered. At the end of the next three hours I had been through perils so awful that all peace of mind and all cheerfulness were gone from me. Gillespie had called and thrown *me* out of the window. Jones arrived promptly, and when I got ready to do the cowhiding he took the job off my hands. In an encounter with a stranger, not in the bill of fare, I had lost my scalp. Another stranger, by the name of Thompson, left me a mere wreck and ruin of chaotic rags. And at last, at bay in the corner, and beset by an infuriated mob of editors, blacklegs, politicians, and desperadoes, who raved and swore and flourished their weapons about my head till the air shimmered with glancing flashes of steel, I was in the act of resigning my berth on the paper when the chief arrived, and with him a rabble of charmed and enthusiastic friends. Then ensued a scene of riot and carnage such as no human pen, or steel one either, could describe. People were shot, probed, dismembered, blown up, thrown out of the window. There was a brief tornado of murky blasphemy, with a confused and frantic war-dance glimmering through it, and then all was over. In five minutes there was silence, and the gory chief and I sat alone and surveyed the sanguinary ruin that strewed the floor around us.

He said, "You'll like this place when you get used to it."

I said, "I'll have to get you to excuse me; I think maybe I might write to suit you after a while; as soon as I had had some practice and learned the language I am confident I could. But, to speak the plain truth, that sort of energy of expression has its inconveniences, and a man is liable to interruption. You see that yourself. Vigorous writing is calculated to elevate the public, no doubt, but then I do not like to attract so much attention as it calls forth. I can't write with comfort when I am interrupted so much as I have been to-day. I like this berth well enough, but I don't like to be left here to wait on the customers. The experiences are novel, I grant you, and entertaining, too, after a fashion, but they are not judiciously distributed. A gentleman shoots at you through the window and cripples *me;* a bombshell comes down the stovepipe for your gratification and sends the stove door down *my* throat; a friend drops in to swap compliments with you, and freckles *me* with bullet-holes till my skin won't hold my principles; you go to dinner, and Jones comes with his cowhide, Gillespie throws me out of the window, Thompson tears all my clothes off, and an entire stranger takes my scalp with the easy freedom of an old acquaintance; and in less than five minutes all the blackguards in the country arrive in their warpaint, and proceed to scare the rest of me to death with their tomahawks. Take it altogether, I never had such a spirited time in all my life as I have had to-day. No; I like you, and I like your calm unruffled way of explaining things to the customers, but you see I am not used to it. The Southern heart is too impulsive; Southern hospitality is too lavish with the stranger. The paragraphs which I have written to-day, and into whose cold sentences your masterly hand has infused the fervent spirit of Tennesseean journalism, will wake up another nest of hornets. All that mob of editors will come—and they will come hungry, too, and want somebody for breakfast. I shall have to bid you adieu. I decline to be present at these festivities. I came South for my health, I will go back on the same errand, and suddenly. Tennesseean journalism is too stirring for me."

After which we parted with mutual regret, and I took apartments at the hospital.

1869

A Curious Dream

Containing a Moral

Night before last I had a singular dream. I seemed to be sitting on a doorstep (in no particular city perhaps) ruminating, and the time of night appeared to be about twelve or one o'clock. The weather was balmy and delicious. There was no human sound in the air, not even a footstep. There was no sound of any kind to emphasize the dead stillness, except the occasional hollow barking of a dog in the distance and the fainter answer of a further dog. Presently up the street I heard a bony clack-clacking, and guessed it was the castanets of a serenading party. In a minute more a tall skeleton, hooded, and half clad in a tattered and moldy shroud, whose shreds were flapping about the ribby lattice-work of its person, swung by me with a stately stride and disappeared in the gray gloom of the starlight. It had a broken and worm-eaten coffin on its shoulder and a bundle of something in its hand. I knew what the clack-clacking was then; it was this party's joints working together, and his elbows knocking against his sides as he walked. I may say I was surprised. Before I could collect my thoughts and enter upon any speculations as to what this apparation might portend, I heard another one coming—for I recognized his clack-clack. He had two-thirds of a coffin on his shoulder, and some foot and head boards under his arm. I mightily wanted to peer under his hood and speak to him, but when he turned and smiled upon me with his cavernous sockets and his projecting grin as he went by, I thought I would not detain him. He was hardly gone when I heard the clacking again, and another one issued from the shadowy half-light. This one was bending under a heavy gravestone, and dragging a shabby coffin after him by a string. When he got to me he gave me a steady look for a moment or two, and then rounded to and backed up to me saying:

"Ease this down for a fellow, will you?"

I eased the gravestone down till it rested on the ground, and in doing so noticed that it bore the name of "John Baxter Copmanhurst," with "May, 1839," as the date of his death. Deceased sat wearily down by me, and wiped his os frontis with his major maxillary—chiefly from former habit I judged, for I could not see that he brought away any perspiration.

"It is too bad, too bad," said he, drawing the remnant of the shroud about him and leaning his jaw pensively on his hand. Then he put his left foot up on his knee and fell to scratching his anklebone absently with a rusty nail which he got out of his coffin.

"What is too bad, friend?"

"Oh, everything, everything. I almost wish I never had died."

"You surprise me. Why do you say this? Has anything gone wrong? What is the matter?"

"Matter! Look at this shroud—rags. Look at this gravestone, all battered up. Look at this disgraceful old coffin. All a man's property going to ruin and destruction before his eyes, and ask him if anything is wrong? Fire and brimstone!"

"Calm yourself, calm yourself," I said. "It *is* too bad—it is certainly too bad, but then I had not supposed that you would much mind such matters, situated as you are."

"Well, my dear sir, I *do* mind them. My pride is hurt, and my comfort is impaired—destroyed, I might say. I will state my case—I will put it to you in such a way that you can comprehend it, if you will let me," said the poor skeleton, tilting the hood of his shroud back, as if he were clearing for action, and thus unconsciously giving himself a jaunty and festive air very much at variance with the grave character of his position in life—so to speak—and in prominent contrast with his distressful mood.

"Proceed," said I.

"I reside in the shameful old graveyard a block or two above you here, in this street—there, now, I just expected that cartilage would let go!—third rib from the bottom, friend, hitch the end of it to my spine with a string, if you have got such a thing about you, though a bit of silver wire is a deal pleasanter, and more durable and becoming, if one keeps it polished—to think of shredding out and going to pieces in this way, just on account of the indifference and neglect of one's posterity!"—and the poor ghost grated his teeth in a way that gave me a wrench and a shiver—for the effect is mightily increased by the absence of muffling flesh and cuticle. "I reside in that old graveyard, and have for these thirty years; and I tell you things are changed since I first laid this old tired frame there, and turned over, and stretched out for a long sleep, with a delicious sense upon me of being *done* with bother, and grief, and anxiety, and doubt, and fear, forever and ever, and listening with comfortable and increasing satisfaction to the sexton's work, from the startling clatter of his first spadeful on my coffin till it dulled away to the faint platting that shaped the roof of my new home—delicious! My! I wish you could try it to-night!" and out of my reverie deceased fetched me a rattling slap with a bony hand.

"Yes, sir, thirty years ago I laid me down there, and was happy. For it was out in the country then—out in the breezy, flowery, grand old woods, and the lazy winds gossiped with the leaves, and the squirrels capered over us and around us, and the creeping things visited us, and the birds filled the tranquil solitude with music. Ah, it was worth ten years of a man's life to be dead then! Everything was pleasant. I was in a good neighborhood, for all the dead people that lived near me belonged to the best families in the city. Our posterity appeared to think the world of us. They kept our graves in the very best condition; the fences were always in faultless repair, head-boards were kept painted or whitewashed, and were replaced with new ones as soon as they began to look rusty or decayed; monuments were kept upright, railings intact and bright, the rose-bushes and shrubbery trimmed, trained, and free from blemish, the walks clean and smooth and graveled. But that day is gone by. Our descendants have forgotten us. My grandson lives in a stately house built with money made by these old hands of mine, and I sleep in a neglected grave with invading vermin that gnaw my shroud to build them nests withal! I and friends that lie with me founded and secured the prosperity of this fine city, and the stately bantling of our loves leaves us to rot in a dilapidated cemetery which neighbors curse and strangers scoff at. See the difference between the old time and this—for instance: Our graves are all caved in now; our head-boards have rotted away and tumbled down; our railings reel this way and that, with one foot in the air, after a fashion of unseemly levity; our monuments lean wearily, and our gravestones bow their heads discouraged; there be no adornments any more—no roses, nor shrubs, nor graveled walks, nor anything that is a comfort to the eye; and even the paintless old board fence that did make a show of holding us sacred from companionship with beasts and the defilement of heedless feet, has tottered till it overhangs the street, and only advertises the presence of our dismal resting-place and invites yet more derision to it. And now we cannot hide our poverty and tatters in the friendly woods, for the city has stretched its withering arms abroad and taken us in, and all that remains of the cheer of our old home is the cluster of lugubrious forest trees that stand, bored and weary of a city life, with their feet in our coffins, looking into the hazy distance and wishing they were there. I tell you it is disgraceful!

"You begin to comprehend—you begin to see how it is. While our descendants are living sumptuously on our money, right around us in the city, we have to fight hard to keep skull and bones together. Bless you, there isn't a grave in our cemetery that doesn't leak—not one. Every time it rains in the night we have to climb out and roost in the trees—and sometimes we are wakened suddenly by the chilly water trickling down the back of our necks. Then I tell you there is a general heaving up of old graves and kicking over of old monuments, and scampering of old skeletons for the trees! Bless me, if you had gone along there some such nights after twelve you might have seen as many as fifteen of us roosting on one limb, with our joints rattling drearily and the wind wheezing through our ribs! Many a time we have perched there for three or four dreary hours, and then come down, stiff and chilled through and drowsy, and borrowed each other's skulls to bail out our graves with—if you will glance up in my mouth now as I tilt my head back, you can see that my head-piece is half full of old dry sediment—how top-heavy and stupid it makes me sometimes! Yes, sir, many a time if you had happened to come along just before the dawn you'd have caught us bailing out the graves and hanging our shrouds on the fence to dry. Why, I had an elegant shroud stolen from there one morning—think a party by the name of Smith took it, that resides in a plebeian graveyard over yonder—I think so because the first time I ever saw him he hadn't anything on but a check shirt, and the last time I saw him, which was at a social gathering in the new cemetery, he was the best-dressed corpse in the company—and it is a significant fact that he left when he saw me; and presently an old woman from here missed her coffin—she generally took it with her when she went anywhere, because she was liable to take cold and bring on the spasmodic rheumatism that originally killed her if she exposed herself to the night air much. She was named Hotchkiss—Anna Matilda Hotchkiss—you might know her? She has two upper front teeth, is tall, but a good deal inclined to stoop, one rib on the left side gone, has one shred of rusty hair hanging from the left side of her head, and one little tuft just above and a little forward of her right ear, has her underjaw wired on one side where it had worked loose, small bone of left forearm gone—lost in a fight—has a land of swagger in her gait and a 'gallus' way of going with her arms akimbo and her nostrils in the air—has been pretty free and easy, and is all damaged and battered up till she looks like a queensware crate in ruins—maybe you have met her?"

"God forbid!" I involuntarily ejaculated, for somehow I was not looking for that form of question, and it caught me a little off my guard. But I hastened to make amends for my rudeness, and say, "I simply meant I had not had the honor—for I would not deliberately speak discourteously of a friend of yours. You were saying that you were robbed—and it was a shame, too—but it appears by what is left of the shroud you have on that it was a costly one in its day. How did—"

A most ghastly expression began to develop among the decayed features and shriveled integuments of my guest's face, and I was beginning to grow uneasy and distressed, when he told me he was only working up a deep, sly smile, with a wink in it, to suggest that about the time he acquired his present garment a ghost in a neighboring cemetery missed one. This reassured me, but I begged him to confine himself to speech thenceforth, because his facial expression was uncertain. Even with the most elaborate care it was liable to miss fire. Smiling should especially be avoided. What *he* might honestly consider a shining success was likely to strike me in a very different light. I said I liked to see a skeleton cheerful, even decorously playful, but I did not think smiling was a skeleton's best hold.

"Yes, friend," said the poor skeleton, "the facts are just as I have given them to you. Two of these old graveyards—the one that I resided in and one further along—have been deliberately neglected by our descendants of to-day until there is no occupying them any longer. Aside from the osteological discomfort of it—and that is no light matter this rainy weather—the present state of things is ruinous to property. We have got to move or be content to see our effects wasted away and utterly destroyed. Now, you will hardly believe it, but it is true, nevertheless, that there isn't a single coffin in good repair among all my acquaintance—now that is an absolute fact. I do not refer to low people who come in a pine box mounted on an express-wagon, but I am talking about your high-toned, silver-mounted burial-case, your monumental sort, that travel under black plumes at the head of a procession and have choice of cemetery lots—I mean folks like the Jarvises, and the Bledsoes and Burlings, and such. They are all about ruined. The most substantial people in our set, they were. And now look at them—utterly used up and poverty-stricken. One of the Bledsoes actually traded his monument to a late barkeeper for some fresh shavings to put under his head. I tell you it speaks volumes, for there is nothing a corpse takes so much pride in as his monument. He loves to read the inscription. He comes after a while to believe what it says himself, and then you may see him sitting on the fence night after night enjoying it. Epitaphs are cheap, and they do a poor chap a world of good after he is dead, expecially if he had hard luck while he was alive. I wish they were used more. Now I don't complain, but confidentially I *do* think it was a little shabby in my descendants to give me nothing but this old slab of a gravestone—and all the more that there isn't a compliment on it. It used to have

'GONE TO HIS JUST REWARD'

on it, and I was proud when I first saw it, but by and by I noticed that whenever an old friend of mine came along he would hook his chin on the railing and pull a long face and read along down till he came to that, and then he would chuckle to himself and walk off, looking satisfied and comfortable. So I scratched it off to get rid of those fools. But a dead man always takes a deal of pride in his monument. Yonder goes half a dozen of the Jarvises now, with the family monument along. And Smithers and some hired specters went by with his awhile ago. Hello, Higgins, good-by, old friend! That's Meredith Higgins—died in '44—belongs to our set in the cemetery—fine old family—great-grandmother was an Injun—I am on the most familiar terms with him—he didn't hear me was the reason he didn't answer me. And I am sorry, too, because I would have liked to introduce you. You would admire him. He is the most disjointed, sway-backed, and generally distorted old skeleton you ever saw, but he is full of fun. When he laughs it sounds like rasping two stones together, and he always starts it off with a cheery screech like raking a nail across a window-pane. Hey, Jones! That is old Columbus Jones—shroud cost four hundred dollars—entire trousseau, including monument, twenty-seven hundred. This was in the spring of '26. It was enormous style for those days. Dead people came all the way from the Alleghanies to see his things—the party that occupied the grave next to mine remembers it well. Now do you see that individual going along with a piece of a head-board under his arm, one leg-bone below his knee gone, and not a thing in the world on? That is Barstow Dalhousie, and next to Columbus Jones he was the most sumptuously outfitted person that ever entered our cemetery. We are all leaving. We cannot tolerate the treatment we are receiving at the hands of our descendants. They open new cemeteries, but they leave us to our ignominy. They mend the streets, but they never mend anything that is about us or belongs to us.

Look at that coffin of mine—yet I tell you in its day it was a piece of furniture that would have attracted attention in any drawing-room in this city. You may have it if you want it—I can't afford to repair it. Put a new bottom in her, and part of a new top, and a bit of fresh lining along the left side, and you'll find her about as comfortable as any receptacle of her species you ever tried. No thanks—no, don't mention it—you have been civil to me, and I would give you all the property I have got before I would seem ungrateful. Now this winding-sheet is a kind of a sweet thing in its way, if you would like to— No? Well, just as you say, but I wished to be fair and liberal—there's nothing mean about *me*. Good-by, friend, I must be going. I may have a good way to go to-night—don't know. I only know one thing for certain, and that is that I am on the emigrant trail now, and I'll never sleep in that crazy old cemetery again. I will travel till I find respectable quarters, if I have to hoof it to New Jersey. All the boys are going. It was decided in public conclave, last night, to emigrate, and by the time the sun rises there won't be a bone left in our old habitations. Such cemeteries may suit my surviving friends, but they do not suit the remains that have the honor to make these remarks. My opinion is the general opinion. If you doubt it, go and see how the departing ghosts upset things before they started. They were almost riotous in their demonstrations of distaste. Hello, here are some of the Bledsoes, and if you will give me a lift with this tombstone I guess I will join company and jog along with them—mighty respectable old family, the Bledsoes, and used to always come out in six-horse hearses and all that sort of thing fifty years ago when I walked these streets in daylight. Good-by, friend."

And with his gravestone on his shoulder he joined the grisly procession, dragging his damaged coffin after him, for notwithstanding he pressed it upon me so earnestly, I utterly refused his hospitality. I suppose that for as much as two hours these sad outcasts went clacking by, laden with their dismal effects, and all that time I sat pitying them. One or two of the youngest and least dilapidated among them inquired about midnight trains on the railways, but the rest seemed unacquainted with that mode of travel, and merely asked about common public roads to various towns and cities, some of which are not on the map now, and vanished from it and from the earth as much as thirty years ago, and some few of them never *had* existed anywhere but on maps, and private ones in real-estate agencies at that. And they asked about the condition of the cemeteries in these towns and cities, and about the reputation the citizens bore as to reverence for the dead.

This whole matter interested me deeply, and likewise compelled my sympathy for these homeless ones. And it all seeming real, and I not knowing it was a dream, I mentioned to one shrouded wanderer an idea that had entered my head to publish an account of this curious and very sorrowful exodus, but said also that I could not describe it truthfully, and just as it occurred, without seeming to trifle with a grave subject and exhibit an irreverence for the dead that would shock and distress their surviving friends. But this bland and stately remnant of a former citizen leaned him far over my gate and whispered in my ear, and said:

"Do not let that disturb you. The community that can stand such graveyards as those we are emigrating from can stand anything a body can say about the neglected and forsaken dead that lie in them."

At that very moment a cock crowed, and the weird procession vanished and left not a shred or a bone behind. I awoke, and found myself lying with my head out of the bed and "sagging" downward considerably—a position favorable to dreaming dreams with morals in them, maybe, but not poetry.

° ° °

NOTE The reader is assured that if the cemeteries in his town are kept in good order, this Dream is not leveled at his town at all, but is leveled particularly and venomously at the *next* town.

1870

THE FACTS IN THE CASE OF THE GREAT BEEF CONTRACT

IN AS FEW words as possible I wish to lay before the nation what share, howsoever small, I have had in this matter—this matter which has so exercised the public mind, engendered so much ill-feeling, and so filled the newspapers of both continents with distorted statements and extravagant comments.

The origin of this distressful thing was this—and I assert here that every fact in the following résumé can be amply proved by the official records of the General Government:

John Wilson Mackenzie, of Rotterdam, Chemung County, New Jersey, deceased, contracted with the General Government, on or about the 10th day of October, 1861, to furnish to General Sherman the sum total of thirty barrels of beef.

Very well.

He started after Sherman with the beef, but when he got to Washington Sherman had gone to Manassas; so he took the beef and followed him there, but arrived too late; he followed him to Nashville, and from Nashville to Chattanooga, and from Chattanooga to Atlanta—but he never could overtake him. At Atlanta he took a fresh start and followed him clear through his march to the sea. He arrived too late again by a few days; but hearing that Sherman was going out in the *Quaker City* excursion to the Holy Land, he took shipping for Beirut, calculating to head off the other vessel. When he arrived in Jerusalem with his beef, he learned that Sherman had not sailed in the *Quaker City*, but had gone to the Plains to fight the Indians. He returned to America and started for the Rocky Mountains. After sixty-eight days of arduous travel on the Plains, and when he had got within four miles of Sherman's headquarters, he was tomahawked and scalped, and the Indians got the beef. They got all of it but one barrel. Sherman's army captured that, and so, even in death, the bold navigator partly fulfilled his contract. In his will, which he had kept like a journal, he bequeathed the contract to his son Bartholomew W. Bartholomew W. made out the following bill, and then died:

THE UNITED STATES

In account with JOHN WILSON MACKENZIE, of New Jersey, deceased, ... Dr.

To thirty barrels of beef for General Sherman, at $100, $3,000

To traveling expenses and transportation, ... 14,000

Total, ... $17,000

Rec'd Pay't.

He died then; but he left the contract to Wm. J. Martin, who tried to collect it, but died before he got through. *He* left it to Barker J. Allen, and he tried to collect it also. He did not survive. Barker J. Allen left it to Anson G. Rogers, who attempted to collect it, and got along as far as the Ninth Auditor's Office, when Death, the great Leveler, came all unsummoned, and foreclosed on *him* also. He left the bill to a relative of his in Connecticut, Vengeance Hopkins by name, who lasted four weeks and two days, and made the best time on record, coming within one of reaching the

Twelfth Auditor. In his will he gave the contract bill to his uncle, by the name of O-be-joyful Johnson. It was too undermining for Joyful. His last words were: "Weep not for me—*I* am willing to go." And so he was, poor soul. Seven people inherited the contract after that; but they all died. So it came into my hands at last. It fell to me through a relative by the name of Hubbard—Bethlehem Hubbard, of Indiana. He had had a grudge against me for a long time; but in his last moments he sent for me, and forgave me everything, and, weeping, gave me the beef contract.

This ends the history of it up to the time that I succeeded to the property. I will now endeavor to set myself straight before the nation in everything that concerns my share in the matter. I took this beef contract, and the bill for mileage and transportation, to the President of the United States.

He said, "Well, sir, what can I do for you?"

I said, "Sire, on or about the 10th day of October, 1861, John Wilson Mackenzie, of Rotterdam, Chemung County, New Jersey, deceased, contracted with the General Government to furnish to General Sherman the sum total of thirty barrels of beef—"

He stopped me there, and dismissed me from his presence—kindly, but firmly. The next day I called on the Secretary of State.

He said, "Well, sir?"

I said, "Your Royal Highness: on or about the 10th day of October, 1861, John Wilson Mackenzie, of Rotterdam, Chemung County, New Jersey, deceased, contracted with the General Government to furnish to General Sherman the sum total of thirty barrels of beef—"

"That will do, sir—that will do; this office has nothing to do with contracts for beef."

I was bowed out. I thought the matter all over, and finally, the following day, I visited the Secretary of the Navy, who said, "Speak quickly, sir; do not keep me waiting."

I said, "Your Royal Highness, on or about the 10th day of October, 1861, John Wilson Mackenzie, of Rotterdam, Chemung County, New Jersey, deceased, contracted with the General Government to General Sherman the sum total of thirty barrels of beef—"

Well, it was as far as I could get. *He* had nothing to do with beef contracts for General Sherman, either. I began to think it was a curious kind of a government. It looked somewhat as if they wanted to get out of paying for that beef. The following day I went to the Secretary of the Interior.

I said, "Your Imperial Highness, on or about the 10th day of October—"

"That is sufficient, sir. I have heard of you before. Go, take your infamous beef contract out of this establishment. The Interior Department has nothing whatever to do with subsistence for the army."

I went away. But I was exasperated now. I said I would haunt them; I would infest every department of this iniquitous government till that contract business was settled. I would collect that bill, or fall, as fell my predecessors, trying. I assailed the Postmaster-General; I besieged the Agricultural Department; I waylaid the Speaker of the House of Representatives. *They* had nothing to do with army contracts for beef. I moved upon the Commissioner of the Patent Office.

I said, "Your August Excellency, on or about—"

"Perdition! have you got *here* with your incendiary beef contract, at last? We have *nothing* to do with beef contracts for the army, my dear sir."

"Oh, that is all very well—but *somebody* has got to pay for that beef. It has got to be paid *now*, too, or I'll confiscate this old Patent Office and everything in it."

"But, my dear sir—"

"It don't make any difference, sir. The Patent Office is liable for that beef, I reckon; and, liable or not liable, the Patent Office has got to pay for it."

Never mind the details. It ended in a fight. The Patent Office won. But I found out something to my advantage. I was told that the Treasury Department was the proper place for me to go to. I went there. I waited two hours and a half, and then I was admitted to the First Lord of the Treasury.

I said, "Most noble, grave, and reverend Signor, on or about the 10th day of October, 1861, John Wilson Macken—"

"That is sufficient, sir. I have heard of you. Go to the First Auditor of the Treasury."

I did so. He sent me to the Second Auditor. The Second Auditor sent me to the Third, and the Third sent me to the First Comptroller of the Corn-Beef Division. This began to look like business. He examined his books and all his loose papers, but found no minute of the beef contract. I went to the Second Comptroller of the Corn-Beef Division. He examined his books and his loose papers, but with no success. I was encouraged. During that week I got as far as the Sixth Comptroller in that division; the next week I got through the Claims Department; the third week I began and completed the Mislaid Contracts Department, and got a foothold in the Dead Reckoning Department. I finished that in three days. There was only one place left for it now. I laid siege to the Commissioner of Odds and Ends. To his clerk, rather—he was not there himself. There were sixteen beautiful young ladies in the room, writing in books, and there were seven well-favored young clerks showing them how. The young women smiled up over their shoulders, and the clerks smiled back at them, and all went merry as a marriage bell. Two or three clerks that were reading the newspapers looked at me rather hard, but went on reading, and nobody said anything. However, I had been used to this kind of alacrity from Fourth Assistant Junior Clerks all through my eventful career, from the very day I entered the first office of the Corn-Beef Bureau clear till I passed out of the last one in the Dead Reckoning Division. I had got so accomplished by this time that I could stand on one foot from the moment I entered an office till a clerk spoke to me, without changing more than two, or maybe three, times.

So I stood there till I had changed four different times. Then I said to one of the clerks who was reading:

"Illustrious Vagrant, where is the Grand Turk?"

"What do you mean, sir? whom do you mean? If you mean the Chief of the Bureau, he is out."

"Will he visit the harem to-day?"

The young man glared upon me awhile, and then went on reading his paper. But I knew the ways of those clerks. I knew I was safe if he got through before another New York mail arrived. He only had two more papers left. After a while he finished them, and then he yawned and asked me what I wanted.

"Renowned and honored Imbecile: on or about—"

"You are the beef-contract man. Give me your papers."

He took them, and for a long time he ransacked his odds and ends. Finally he found the Northwest Passage, as *I* regarded it—he found the long-lost record of that beef contract—he found the rock upon which so many of my ancestors had split before they ever got to it. I was deeply moved. And yet I rejoiced—for I had survived. I said with emotion, "Give it me. The government will settle now." He waved me back, and said there was something yet to be done first.

"Where is this John Wilson Mackenzie?" said he.

"Dead."

"When did he die?"

"He didn't die at all—he was killed."

"How?"

"Tomahawked."

"Who tomahawked him?"

"Why, an Indian, of course. You didn't suppose it was the superintendent of a Sunday-school, did you?"

"No. An Indian, was it?"

"The same."

"Name the Indian?"

"His name? *I* don't know his name."

"*Must* have his name. Who saw the tomahawking done?"

"I don't know."

"You were not present yourself, then?"

"Which you can see by my hair. I was absent."

"Then how do you know that Mackenzie is dead?"

"Because he certainly died at that time, and I have every reason to believe that he has been dead ever since. I *know* he has, in fact."

"We must have proofs. Have you got the Indian?"

"Of course not."

"Well, you must get him. Have you got the tomahawk?"

"I never thought of such a thing."

"You must get the tomahawk. You must produce the Indian and the tomahawk. If Mackenzie's death can be proven by these, you can then go before the commission appointed to audit claims with some show of getting your bill under such headway that your children may possibly live to receive the money and enjoy it. But that man's death *must* be proven. However, I may as well tell you that the government will never pay that transportation and those traveling expenses of the lamented Mackenzie. It *may* possibly pay for the barrel of beef that Sherman's soldiers captured, if you can get a relief bill through Congress making an appropriation for that purpose; but it will not pay for the twenty-nine barrels the Indians ate."

"Then there is only a hundred dollars due me, and *that* isn't certain! After all Mackenzie's travels in Europe, Asia, and America with that beef; after all his trials and tribulations and transportation; after the slaughter of all those innocents that tried to collect that bill! Young man, why didn't the First Comptroller of the Corn-Beef Division tell me this?"

"He didn't know anything about the genuineness of your claim."

"Why didn't the Second tell me? why didn't the Third? why didn't all those divisions and departments tell me?"

"None of them knew. We do things by routine here. You have followed the routine and found out what you wanted to know. It is the best way. It is the only way. It is very regular, and very slow, but it is very certain."

"Yes, certain death. It has been, to the most of our tribe. I begin to feel that I, too, am called. Young man, you love the bright creature yonder with the gentle blue eyes and the steel pens behind her ears—I see it in your soft glances; you wish to marry her—but you are poor. Here, hold out your hand—here is the beef contract; go, take her and be happy! Heaven bless you, my children!"

This is all I know about the great beef contract that has created so much talk in the community. The clerk to whom I bequeathed it died. I know nothing further about the contract, or any one connected with it. I only know that if a man lives long enough he can trace a thing through the Circumlocution Office of Washington and find out, after much labor and trouble and delay, that which he could have found out on the first day if the business of the Circumlocution Office was as ingeniously systematized as it would be if it were a great private mercantile institution.

1870

How I Edited an Agricultural Paper

I did not take temporary editorship of an agricultural paper without misgivings. Neither would a landsman take command of a ship without misgivings. But I was in circumstances that made the salary an object. The regular editor of the paper was going off for a holiday, and I accepted the terms he offered, and took his place.

The sensation of being at work again was luxurious, and I wrought all the week with unflagging pleasure. We went to press, and I waited a day with some solicitude to see whether my effort was going to attract any notice. As I left the office, toward sundown, a group of men and boys at the foot of the stairs dispersed with one impulse, and gave me passageway, and I heard one or two of them say: "That's him!" I was naturally pleased by this incident. The next morning I found a similar group at the foot of the stairs, and scattering couples and individuals standing here and there in the street and over the way, watching me with interest. The group separated and fell back as I approached, and I heard a man say, "Look at his eye!" I pretended not to observe the notice I was attracting, but secretly I was pleased with it, and was purposing to write an account of it to my aunt. I went up the short flight of stairs, and heard cheery voices and a ringing laugh as I drew near the door, which I opened, and caught a glimpse of two young rural-looking men, whose faces blanched and lengthened when they saw me, and then they both plunged through the window with a great crash. I was surprised.

In about half an hour an old gentleman, with a flowing beard and a fine but rather austere face, entered, and sat down at my invitation. He seemed to have something on his mind. He took off his hat and set it on the floor, and got out of it a red silk handkerchief and a copy of our paper.

He put the paper on his lap, and while he polished his spectacles with his handkerchief he said, "Are you the new editor?"

I said I was.

"Have you ever edited an agricultural paper before?"

"No," I said; "this is my first attempt."

"Very likely. Have you had any experience in agriculture practically?"

"No; I believe I have not."

"Some instinct told me so," said the old gentleman, putting on his spectacles, and looking over them at me with asperity, while he folded his paper into a convenient shape. "I wish to read you what must have made me have that instinct. It was this editorial. Listen, and see if it was you that wrote it:

> " '*Turnips should never be pulled, it injures them. It is much better to send a boy up and let him shake the tree.*'

"Now, what do you think of that?—for I really suppose you wrote it?"

"Think of it? Why, I think it is good. I think it is sense. I have no doubt that every year millions and millions of bushels of turnips are spoiled in this township alone by being pulled in a half-ripe condition, when, if they had sent a boy up to shake the tree—"

"Shake your grandmother! Turnips don't grow on trees!"

"Oh, they don't, don't they? Well, who said they did? The language was intended to be figurative, wholly figurative.

Anybody that knows anything will know that I meant that the boy should shake the vine."

Then this old person got up and tore his paper all into small shreds, and stamped on them, and broke several things with his cane, and said I did not know as much as a cow; and then went out and banged the door after him, and, in short, acted in such a way that I fancied he was displeased about something. But not knowing what the trouble was, I could not be any help to him.

Pretty soon after this a long, cadaverous creature, with lanky locks hanging down to his shoulders, and a week's stubble bristling from the hills and valleys of his face, darted within the door, and halted, motionless, with finger on lip, and head and body bent in listening attitude. No sound was heard. Still he listened. No sound. Then he turned the key in the door, and came elaborately tiptoeing toward me till he was within long reaching distance of me, when he stopped and, after scanning my face with intense interest for a while, drew a folded copy of our paper from his bosom, and said:

"There, you wrote that. Read it to me—quick! Relieve me. I suffer."

I read as follows; and as the sentences fell from my lips I could see the relief come, I could see the drawn muscles relax, and the anxiety go out of the face, and rest and peace steal over the features like the merciful moonlight over a desolate landscape:

> *The guano is a fine bird, but great care is necessary in rearing it. It should not be imported earlier than June or later than September. In the winter it should be kept in a warm place, where it can hatch out its young.*
>
> *It is evident that we are to have a backward season for grain. Therefore it will be well for the farmer to begin setting out his corn-stalks and planting his buckwheat cakes in July instead of August.*

Concerning the pumpkin. This berry is a favorite with the natives of the interior of New England, who prefer it to the gooseberry for the making of fruit-cake, and who likewise give it the preference over the raspberry for feeding cows, as being more filling and fully as satisfying. The pumpkin is the only esculent of the orange family that will thrive in the North, except the gourd and one or two varieties of the squash. But the custom of planting it in the front yard with the shrubbery is fast going out of vogue, for it is now generally conceded that the pumpkin as a shade tree is a failure.

Now, as the warm weather approaches, and the ganders begin to spawn—

The excited listener sprang toward me to shake hands, and said:

"There, there—that will do. I know I am all right now, because you have read it just as I did, word for word. But, stranger, when I first read it this morning, I said to myself, I never, never believed it before, notwithstanding my friends kept me under watch so strict, but now I believe I *am* crazy; and with that I fetched a howl that you might have heard two miles, and started out to kill somebody—because, you know, I knew it would come to that sooner or later, and so I might as well begin. I read one of them paragraphs over again, so as to be certain, and then I burned my house down and started. I have crippled several people, and have got one fellow up a tree, where I can get him if I want him. But I thought I would call in here as I passed along and make the thing perfectly certain; and now it *is* certain, and I tell you it is lucky for the chap that is in the tree. I should have killed him sure, as I went back. Good-by, sir, good-by; you have taken a great load off my mind. My reason has stood the strain of one of your agricultural articles, and I know that nothing can ever unseat it now. *Good*-by, sir."

I felt a little uncomfortable about the cripplings and

arsons this person had been entertaining himself with, for I could not help feeling remotely accessory to them. But these thoughts were quickly banished, for the regular editor walked in! [I thought to myself, Now if you had gone to Egypt as I recommended you to, I might have had a chance to get my hand in; but you wouldn't do it, and here you are. I sort of expected you.]

The editor was looking sad and perplexed and dejected.

He surveyed the wreck which that old rioter and those two young farmers had made, and then said: "This is a sad business—a very sad business. There is the mucilage-bottle broken, and six panes of glass, and a spittoon, and two candlesticks. But that is not the worst. The reputation of the paper is injured—and permanently, I fear. True, there never was such a call for the paper before, and it never sold such a large edition or soared to such celebrity;—but does one want to be famous for lunacy, and prosper upon the infirmities of his mind? My friend, as I am an honest man, the street out here is full of people, and others are roosting on the fences, waiting to get a glimpse of you, because they think you are crazy. And well they might after reading your editorials. They are a disgrace to journalism. Why, what put it into your head that you could edit a paper of this nature? You do not seem to know the first rudiments of agriculture. You speak of a furrow and a harrow as being the same thing; you talk of the moulting season for cows; and you recommend the domestication of the pole-cat on account of its playfulness and its excellence as a ratter! Your remark that clams will lie quiet if music be played to them was superfluous—entirely superfluous. Nothing disturbs clams. Clams *always* lie quiet. Clams care nothing whatever about music. Ah, heavens and earth, friend! if you had made the acquiring of ignorance the study of your life, you could not have graduated with higher honor than you could to-day. I never saw anything like it. Your observation that the horse-chestnut as an article of commerce is steadily gaining in favor is simply calculated to destroy this journal. I want you to throw up your situation and go. I want no more holiday—I could not enjoy it if I had it. Certainly not with you in my chair. I would always stand in dread of what you might be going to recommend next. It makes me lose all patience every time I think of your discussing oyster-beds under the head of 'Landscape Gardening.' I want you to go. Nothing on earth could persuade me to take another holiday. Oh! why didn't you *tell* me you didn't know anything about agriculture?"

"*Tell* you, you corn-stalk, you cabbage, you son of a cauliflower? It's the first time I ever heard such an unfeeling remark. I tell you I have been in the editorial business going on fourteen years, and it is the first time I ever heard of a man's having to know anything in order to edit a newspaper. You turnip! Who write the dramatic critiques for the second-rate papers? Why, a parcel of promoted shoemakers and apprentice apothecaries, who know just as much about good acting as I do about good farming and no more. Who review the books? People who never wrote one. Who do up the heavy leaders on finance? Parties who have had the largest opportunities for knowing nothing about it. Who criticize the Indian campaigns? Gentlemen who do not know a war-whoop from a wigwam, and who never have had to run a foot-race with a tomahawk, or pluck arrows out of the several members of their families to build the evening camp-fire with. Who write the temperance appeals, and clamor about the flowing bowl? Folks who will never draw another sober breath till they do it in the grave. Who edit the agricultural papers, you—yam? Men, as a general thing, who fail in the poetry line, yellow-colored novel line, sensation-drama line, city-editor line, and finally fall back on agriculture as a temporary reprieve from the poor-house. *You* try to tell *me* anything about the newspaper business! Sir, I have been through it from Alpha to Omaha, and I tell you that the less a man knows the bigger the noise he makes and the higher the salary he commands. Heaven knows if I had but been ignorant instead of cultivated, and impudent instead of diffident, I could have made a name for myself in this cold, selfish world. I take my leave, sir. Since I have been treated as you have treated me, I am perfectly willing to go. But I have done my duty. I have fulfilled my contract as far as I was permitted to do it. I said I could make your paper of interest to all classes—and I have. I said I could run your circulation up to twenty thousand copies, and if I had had two more weeks I'd have done it. And I'd have given you the best class of readers that ever an agricultural paper had—not a farmer in it, nor a solitary individual who could tell a watermelon-tree from a peach-vine to save his life. *You* are the loser by this rupture, not me, Pie-plant. *Adios.*"

I then left.

1870

A Medieval Romance

1 The Secret Revealed

It was night. Stillness reigned in the grand old feudal castle of Klugenstein. The year 1222 was drawing to a close. Far away up in the tallest of the castle's towers a single light glimmered. A secret council was being held there. The stern old lord of Klugenstein sat in a chair of state meditating. Presently he said, with a tender accent: "My daughter!"

A young man of noble presence, clad from head to heel in knightly mail, answered: "Speak, father!"

"My daughter, the time is come for the revealing of the mystery that hath puzzled all your young life. Know, then, that it had its birth in the matters which I shall now unfold. My brother Ulrich is the great Duke of Brandenburgh. Our father, on his deathbed, decreed that if no son were born to Ulrich the succession should pass to my house, provided a *son* were born to me. And further, in case no son were born to either, but only daughters, then the succession should pass to Ulrich's daughter if she proved stainless; if she did not, my daughter should succeed if she retained a blameless name. And so I and my old wife here prayed fervently for the good boon of a son, but the prayer was vain. You were born to us. I was in despair. I saw the mighty prize slipping from my grasp—the splendid dream vanishing away! And I had been so hopeful! Five years had Ulrich lived in wedlock, and yet his wife had borne no heir of either sex.

" 'But hold,' I said, 'all is not lost.' A saving scheme had shot athwart my brain. You were born at midnight. Only the leech, the nurse, and six waiting-women knew your sex. I hanged them every one before an hour sped. Next morning all the barony went mad with rejoicing over the proclamation that a *son* was born to Klugenstein—an heir to mighty Brandenburgh! And well the secret has been kept. Your mother's own sister nursed your infancy, and from that time forward we feared nothing.

"When you were ten years old a daughter was born to Ulrich. We grieved, but hoped for good results from measles, or physicians, or other natural enemies of infancy, but were always disappointed. She lived, she throve—Heaven's malison upon her! But it is nothing. We are safe. For, ha! ha! have we not a son? And is not our son the future duke? Our well-beloved Conrad, is it not so?—for woman of eight-and-twenty years as you are, my child, none other name than that hath ever fallen to *you!*

"Now it hath come to pass that age hath laid its hand upon my brother, and he waxes feeble. The cares of state do tax him sore, therefore he wills that you shall come to him and be already duke in act, though not yet in name. Your servitors are ready—you journey forth to-night.

"Now listen well. Remember every word I say. There is a law as old as Germany, that if any woman sit for a single instant in the great ducal chair before she hath been absolutely crowned in presence of the people—SHE SHALL DIE! So heed my words. Pretend humility. Pronounce your judgments from the Premier's chair, which stands at the *foot* of the throne. Do this until you are crowned and safe. It is not likely that your sex will ever be discovered, but still it is the part of wisdom to make all things as safe as may be in this treacherous earthly life."

"Oh, my father! is it for this my life hath been a lie? Was it that I might cheat my unoffending cousin of her rights? Spare me, father, spare your child!"

"What, hussy! Is this my reward for the august fortune my brain has wrought for thee? By the bones of my father, this puling sentiment of thine but ill accords with my humor. Betake thee to the duke instantly, and beware how thou meddlest with my purpose!"

Let this suffice of the conversation. It is enough for us to know that the prayers, the entreaties, and the tears of the gentle-natured girl availed nothing. Neither they nor anything could move the stout old lord of Klugenstein. And so, at last, with a heavy heart, the daughter saw the castle gates close behind her, and found herself riding away in the darkness surrounded by a knightly array of armed vassals and a brave following of servants.

The old baron sat silent for many minutes after his daughter's departure, and then he turned to his sad wife, and said:

"Dame, our matters seem speeding fairly. It is full three months since I sent the shrewd and handsome Count Detzin on his devilish mission to my brother's daughter Constance. If he fail we are not wholly safe, but if he do succeed no power can bar our girl from being duchess, e'en though ill fortune should decree she never should be duke!"

"My heart is full of bodings; yet all may still be well."

"Tush, woman! Leave the owls to croak. To bed with ye, and dream of Brandenburgh and grandeur!"

2 FESTIVITY AND TEARS

Six days after the occurrences related in the above chapter, the brilliant capital of the Duchy of Brandenburgh was resplendent with military pageantry and noisy with the rejoicings of loyal multitudes, for Conrad, the young heir to the crown, was come. The old duke's heart was full of happiness, for Conrad's handsome person and graceful bearing had won his love at once. The great halls of the palace were thronged with nobles, who welcomed Conrad bravely; and so bright and happy did all things seem that he felt his fears and sorrows passing away and giving place to a comforting contentment.

But in a remote apartment of the palace a scene of a different nature was transpiring. By a window stood the duke's only child, the Lady Constance. Her eyes were red and swollen and full of tears. She was alone. Presently she fell to weeping anew, and said aloud:

"The villain Detzin is gone—has fled the dukedom! I could not believe it at first, but, alas! it is too true. And I loved him so. I dared to love him though I knew the duke, my father, would never let me wed him. I loved him—but now I hate him! With all my soul I hate him! Oh, what is to become of me? I am lost, lost, lost! I shall go mad!"

3 THE PLOT THICKENS

A few months drifted by. All men published the praises of the young Conrad's government, and extolled the wisdom of his judgments, the mercifulness of his sentences, and the modesty with which he bore himself in his great office. The old duke soon gave everything into his hands, and sat apart and listened with proud satisfaction while his heir delivered the decrees of the crown from the seat of the Premier. It seemed plain that one so loved and praised and honored of all men as Conrad was could not be otherwise than happy. But, strangely enough, he was not. For he saw with dismay that the Princess Constance had begun to love him! The love of the rest of the world was happy fortune for him, but this was freighted with danger! And he saw, moreover, that the delighted duke had discovered his daughter's passion likewise, and was already dreaming of a marriage. Every day somewhat of the deep sadness that had been in the princess's face faded away; every day hope and animation beamed brighted from her eye; and by and by even vagrant smiles visited the face that had been so troubled.

Conrad was appalled. He bitterly cursed himself for having yielded to the instinct that had made him seek the companionship of one of his own sex when he was new and a stranger in the place—when he was sorrowful and yearned for a sympathy such as only women can give or feel. He now began to avoid his cousin. But this only made matters worse, for, naturally enough, the more he avoided her the more she cast herself in his way. He marveled at this at first, and next it startled him. The girl haunted him; she hunted him; she happened upon him at all times and in all places, in the night as well as in the day. She seemed singularly anxious. There was surely a mystery somewhere.

This could not go on forever. All the world was talking about it. The duke was beginning to look perplexed. Poor Conrad was becoming a very ghost through dread and dire distress. One day as he was emerging from a private anteroom attached to the picture-gallery Constance confronted him, and seizing both his hands in hers, exclaimed:

"Oh, why do you avoid me? What have I done—what have I said, to lose your kind opinion of me—for surely I had it once? Conrad, do not despise me, but pity a tortured heart? I cannot, cannot hold the words unspoken longer, lest they kill me—I love you Conrad! There, despise me if you must, but they *would* be uttered!"

Conrad was speechless. Constance hesitated a moment, and then, misinterpreting his silence, a wild gladness flamed in her eyes, and she flung her arms about his neck and said:

"You relent! you relent! You *can* love me—you *will* love me! Oh, say you will, my own, my worshiped Conrad!"

Conrad groaned aloud. A sickly pallor overspread his countenance, and he trembled like an aspen. Presently, in desperation, he thrust the poor girl from him, and cried:

"You know not what you ask! It is forever and ever impossible!" And then he fled like a criminal, and left the princess stupefied with amazement. A minute afterward she was crying and sobbing there, and Conrad was crying and sobbing in his chamber. Both were in despair. Both saw ruin staring them in the face.

By and by Constance rose slowly to her feet and moved away, saying:

"To think that he was despising my love at the very moment that I thought it was melting his cruel heart! I hate him! He spurned me—did this man—he spurned me from him like a dog!"

4 The Awful Revelation

Time passed on. A settled sadness rested once more upon the countenance of the good duke's daughter. She and Conrad were seen together no more now. The duke grieved at this. But as the weeks wore away Conrad's color came back to his cheeks, and his old-time vivacity to his eye, and he administered the government with a clear and steadily ripening wisdom.

Presently a strange whisper began to be heard about the

palace. It grew louder; it spread farther. The gossips of the city got hold of it. It swept the dukedom. And this is what the whisper said:

"The Lady Constance hath given birth to a child!"

When the lord of Klugenstein heard it he swung his plumed helmet thrice around his head and shouted:

"Long live Duke Conrad!—for lo, his crown is sure from this day forward! Detzin has done his errand well, and the good scoundrel shall be rewarded!"

And he spread the tidings far and wide, and for eight-and-forty hours no soul in all the barony but did dance and sing, carouse and illuminate, to celebrate the great event, and all proud and happy at old Klugenstein's expense.

5 The Frightful Catastrophe

The trial was at hand. All the great lords and barons of Brandenburgh were assembled in the Hall of Justice in the ducal palace. No space was left unoccupied where there was room for a spectator to stand or sit. Conrad, clad in purple and ermine, sat in the Premier's chair, and on either side sat the great judges of the realm. The old duke had sternly commanded that the trial of his daughter should proceed without favor, and then had taken to his bed broken-hearted. His days were numbered. Poor Conrad had begged, as for his very life, that he might be spared the misery of sitting in judgment upon his cousin's crime, but it did not avail.

The saddest heart in all that great assemblage was in Conrad's breast.

The gladdest was in his father's, for, unknown to his daughter "Conrad," the old Baron Klugenstein was come, and was among the crowd of nobles triumphant in the swelling fortunes of his house.

After the heralds had made due proclamation and the other preliminaries had followed, the venerable Lord Chief Justice said: "Prisoner, stand forth!"

The unhappy princess rose, and stood unveiled before the vast multitude. The Lord Chief Justice continued:

"Most noble lady, before the great judges of this realm it hath been charged and proven that out of holy wedlock your Grace hath given birth unto a child, and by our ancient law the penalty is death excepting in one sole contingency, whereof his Grace the acting duke, or good Lord Conrad, will advertise you in his solemn sentence now; wherefore give heed."

Conrad stretched forth his reluctant scepter, and in the self-same moment the womanly heart beneath his robe yearned pityingly toward the doomed prisoner, and the tears came into his eyes. He opened his lips to speak, but the Lord Chief Justice said quickly:

"Not there, your Grace, not there! It is not lawful to pronounce judgment upon any of the ducal line SAVE FROM THE DUCAL THRONE!"

A shudder went to the heart of poor Conrad, and a tremor shook the iron frame of his old father likewise. CONRAD HAD NOT BEEN CROWNED—dared he profane the throne? He hesitated and turned pale with fear. But it must be done. Wondering eyes were already upon him. They would be suspicious eyes if he hesitated longer. He ascended the throne. Presently he stretched forth the scepter again, and said:

"Prisoner, in the name of our sovereign Lord Ulrich, Duke of Brandenburgh, I proceed to the solemn duty that hath devolved upon me. Give heed to my words. By the ancient law of the land, except you produce the partner of your guilt and deliver him up to the executioner you must surely die. Embrace this opportunity—save yourself while yet you may. Name the father of your child!"

A solemn hush fell upon the great court—a silence so profound that men could hear their own hearts beat. Then the princess slowly turned, with eyes gleaming with hate, and, pointing her finger straight at Conrad, said:

"Thou art the man!"

An appalling conviction of his helpless, hopeless peril struck a chill to Conrad's heart like the chill of death itself. What power on earth could save him! To disprove the charge he must reveal that he was a woman, and for an uncrowned woman to sit on the ducal chair was death! At one and the same moment he and his grim old father swooned and fell to the ground.

The remainder of this thrilling and eventful story will NOT be found in this or any other publication, either now or at any future time.

The truth is, I have got my hero (or heroine) into such a particularly close place that I do not see how I am ever going to get him (or her) out of it again, and therefore I will wash my hands of the whole business, and leave that person to get out the best way that offers—or else stay there. I thought it was going to be easy enough to straighten out that little difficulty, but it looks different now.

1870

My Watch

An Instructive Little Tale

My beautiful new watch had run eighteen months without losing or gaining, and without breaking any part of its machinery or stopping. I had come to believe it infallible in its judgments about the time of day, and to consider its constitution and its anatomy imperishable. But at last, one night, I let it run down. I grieved about it as if it were a recognized messenger and forerunner of calamity. But by and by I cheered up, set the watch by guess, and commanded my bodings and superstitions to depart. Next day I stepped into the chief jeweler's to set it by the exact time, and the head of the establishment took it out of my hand and proceeded to set it for me. Then he said, "She is four minutes slow—regulator wants pushing up." I tried to stop him—tried to make him understand that the watch kept perfect time. But no; all this human cabbage could see was that the watch was four minutes slow, and the regulator *must* be pushed up a little; and so, while I danced around him in anguish, and implored him to let the watch alone, he calmly and cruelly did the shameful deed. My watch began to gain. It gained faster and faster day by day. Within the week it sickened to a raging fever, and its pulse went up to a hundred and fifty in the shade. At the end of two months it had left all the timepieces of the town far in the rear, and was a fraction over thirteen days ahead of the almanac. It was away into November enjoying the snow, while the October leaves were still turning. It hurried up house rent, bills payable, and such things, in such a ruinous way that I could not abide it. I took it to the watchmaker to be regulated. He asked me if I had ever had it repaired. I said no, it had never needed any repairing. He looked a look of vicious happiness and eagerly pried the watch open, and then put a small dice-box into his eye and peered into its machinery. He said it wanted cleaning and oiling, besides regulating—come in a week. After being cleaned and oiled, and regulated, my watch slowed down to that degree that it ticked like a tolling bell. I began to be left by trams, I failed all appointments, I got to missing my dinner; my watch strung out three days' grace to four and let me go to protest; I gradually drifted back into yesterday, then day before, then into last week, and by and by the comprehension came upon me that all solitary and alone I was lingering along in week before last, and the world was out of sight. I seemed to detect in myself a sort of sneaking fellow-feeling for the mummy in the museum, and a desire to swap news with him. I went to a watchmaker again. He took the watch all to pieces while I waited, and then said the barrel was "swelled." He said he could reduce it in three days. After this the watch *averaged* well, but nothing more. For half a day it would go like the very mischief, and keep up such a barking and wheezing and whooping and sneezing and snorting, that I could not hear myself think for the disturbance; and as long as it held out there was not a watch in the land that stood any chance against it. But the rest of the day it would keep on slowing down and fooling along until all the clocks it had left behind caught up again. So at last, at the end of twenty-four hours, it would trot up to the judges' stand all right and just in time. It would show a fair and square average, and no man could say it had done more or less than its duty. But a correct average is only a mild virtue in a watch, and I took this instrument to another watchmaker. He said the king-bolt was broken. I said I was glad it was nothing more serious. To tell the plain truth, I had no idea what the king-bolt was, but I did not choose to appear ignorant to a stranger. He repaired the king-bolt, but what the watch gained, in one way it lost in another. It would run awhile and then stop awhile, and then run awhile again, and so on, using its own discretion about the intervals. And every time it went off it kicked back like a musket. I padded my breast for a few days, but finally took the watch to another watchmaker. He picked it all to pieces, and turned the ruin over and over under his glass; and then he said there appeared to be something the matter with the hair-trigger. He fixed it, and gave it a fresh start. It did well now, except that always at ten minutes to ten the hands would shut together like a pair of scissors, and from that time forth they would travel together. The oldest man in the world could not make head or tail of the time of day by such a watch, and so I went again to have the thing repaired. This person said that the crystal had got bent, and that the mainspring was not straight. He also remarked that parts of the works needed half-soling. He made these things all right, and then my timepiece performed unexceptionably, save that now and then, after working along quietly for nearly eight hours, everything inside would let go all of a sudden and begin to buzz like a bee, and the hands would straightway begin to spin round and round so fast that their individuality was lost completely, and they simply seemed a delicate spider's web over the face of the watch. She would reel off the next twenty-four hours in six or seven minutes, and then stop with a bang. I went with a heavy heart to one more watchmaker, and looked on while he took her to pieces. Then I prepared to cross-question him rigidly, for this thing was getting serious. The watch had cost two hundred dollars originally, and I seemed to have paid out two or three thousand for repairs. While I waited and looked on I presently recognized in this watchmaker an old acquaintance—a steamboat engineer of other days, and not a good engineer, either. He examined all the parts carefully, just as the other watchmakers had done, and then delivered his verdict with the same confidence of manner.

He said:

"She makes too much steam—you want to hang the monkey-wrench on the safety-valve!"

I brained him on the spot, and had him buried at my own expense.

My uncle William (now deceased, alas!) used to say that a good horse was a good horse until it had run away once, and that a good watch was a good watch until the repairers got a chance at it. And he used to wonder what became of all the unsuccessful tinkers, and gunsmiths, and shoemakers, and engineers, and blacksmiths; but nobody could ever tell him.

1870

Political Economy

Political Economy is the basis of all good government. The wisest men of all ages have brought to bear upon this subject the—

[Here I was interrupted and informed that a stranger wished to see me down at the door. I went and confronted him, and asked to know his business, struggling all the time to keep a tight rein on my seething political-economy ideas, and not let them break away from me or get tangled in their harness. And privately I wished the stranger was in the bottom of the canal with a cargo of wheat on top of him. I was all in a fever, but he was cool. He said he was sorry to disturb me, but as he was passing he noticed that I needed some lightning-rods. I said, "Yes, yes—go on—what about it?" He said there was nothing about it, in particular—nothing except that he would like to put them up for me. I am new to housekeeping; have been used to hotels and boarding-houses all my life. Like anybody else of similar experience, I try to appear (to strangers) to be an old housekeeper; consequently I said in an offhand way that I had been intending for some time to have six or eight lightning-rods put up, but— The stranger started, and looked inquiringly at me, but I was serene. I thought that if I chanced to make any mistakes, he would not catch me by my countenance. He said he would rather have my custom than any man's in town. I said, "All right," and started off to wrestle with my great subject again, when he called me back and said it would be necessary to know exactly how many "points" I wanted put up, what parts of the house I wanted them on, and what quality of rod I preferred. It was close quarters for a man not used to the exigencies of housekeeping; but I went through creditably, and he probably never suspected that I was a novice. I told him to put up eight "points," and put them all on the roof, and use the best quality of rod. He said he could furnish the "plain" article at 20 cents a foot; "coppered," 25 cents; "zinc-plated spiral-twist," at 30 cents, that would stop a streak of lightning any time, no matter where it was bound, and "render its errand harmless and its further progress apocryphal." I said apocryphal was no slouch of a word, emanating from the source it did, but, philology aside, I liked the spiral-twist and would take that brand. Then he said he *could* make two hundred and fifty feet answer; but to do it right, and make the best job in town of it, and attract the admiration of the just and the unjust alike, and compel all parties to say they never saw a more symmetrical and hypothetical display of lightning-rods since they were born, he supposed he really couldn't get along without four hundred, though he was not vindictive, and trusted he was willing to try. I said, go ahead and use four hundred, and make any kind of a job he pleased out of it, but let me get back to my work. So I got rid of him at last; and now, after half an hour spent in getting my train of political-economy thoughts coupled together again, I am ready to go on once more.]

richest treasures of their genius, their experience of life, and their learning. The great lights of commercial jurisprudence, international, confraternity, and biological deviation, of all ages, all civilizations, and all nationalities, from Zoroaster down to Horace Greeley, have—

[Here I was interrupted again, and required to go down and confer further with that lightning-rod man. I hurried off, boiling and surging with prodigious thoughts wombed in words of such majesty that each one of them was in itself a straggling procession of syllables that might be fifteen minutes passing a given point, and once more I confronted him—he so calm and sweet, I so hot and frenzied. He was standing in the contemplative attitude of the Colossus of Rhodes, with one foot on my infant tuberose, and the other among my pansies, his hands on his hips, his hat-brim tilted forward, one eye shut and the other gazing critically and admiringly in the direction of my principal chimney. He said now *there* was a state of things to make a man glad to be alive; and added, "I leave it to *you* if you ever saw anything more deliriously picturesque than eight lightning-rods on one chimney?" I said I had no present recollection of anything that transcended it. He said that in his opinion nothing on earth but Niagara Falls was superior to it in the way of natural scenery. All that was needed now, he verily believed, to make my house a perfect balm to the eye, was to kind of touch up the other chimneys a little, and thus "add to the generous *coup d'œil* a soothing uniformity of achievement which would allay the excitement naturally consequent upon the *coup d'état.*" I asked him if he learned to talk out of a book, and if I could borrow it anywhere? He smiled pleasantly, and said that his manner of speaking was not taught in books, and that nothing but familiarity with lightning could enable a man to handle his conversational style with impunity. He then figured up an estimate, and said that about eight more rods scattered about my roof would about fix me right, and he guessed five hundred feet of stuff would do it; and added that the first eight had got a little the start of him, so to speak, and used up a mere trifle of material more than he had calculated on—a hundred feet or along there. I said I was in a dreadful hurry, and I wished we could get this business permanently mapped out, so that I could go on with my work. He said, "I *could* have put up those eight rods, and marched off about my business—

some men *would* have done it. But no; I said to myself, this man is a stranger to me, and I will die before I'll wrong him; there ain't lightning-rods enough on that house, and for one I'll never stir out of my tracks till I've done as I would be done by, and told him so. Stranger, my duty is accomplished; if the recalcitrant and dephlogistic messenger of heaven strikes your—" "There, now, there," I said, "put on the other eight—add five hundred feet of spiral-twist—do anything and everything you want to do; but calm your sufferings, and try to keep your feelings where you can reach them with the dictionary. Meanwhile, if we understand each other now, I will go to work again."

I think I have been sitting here a full hour this time, trying to get back to where I was when my train of thought was broken up by the last interruption; but I believe I have accomplished it at last, and may venture to proceed again.]

> *wrestled with this great subject, and the greatest among them have found it a worthy adversary, and one that always comes up fresh and smiling after every throw. The great Confucius said that he would rather be a profound political economist than chief of police. Cicero frequently said that political economy was the grandest consummation that the human mind was capable of consuming; and even our own Greeley had said vaguely but forcibly that* "Political—

[Here the lightning-rod man sent up another call for me. I went down in a state of mind bordering on impatience. He said he would rather have died than interrupt me, but when he was employed to do a job, and that job was expected to be done in a clean, workmanlike manner, and when it was finished and fatigue urged him to seek the rest and recreation he stood so much in need of, and he was about to do it, but looked up and saw at a glance that all the calculations had been a little out, and if a thunder-storm were to come up, and that house, which he felt a personal interest in, stood there with nothing on earth to protect it but sixteen lightning-rods— "Let us have peace!" I shrieked. "Put up a hundred and fifty! Put some on the kitchen! Put a dozen on the barn! Put a couple on the cow—Put one on the cook!—scatter them all over the persecuted place till it looks like a zinc-plated, spiral-twisted, silver-mounted cane-brake! Move! use up all the material you can get your hands on, and when you run out of lightning-rods put up ram-rods, cam-rods, stair-rods, piston-rods—*anything* that will pander to your dismal appetite for artificial scenery, and bring respite to my raging brain and healing to my lacerated soul!" Wholly unmoved—further than to smile sweetly—this iron being simply turned back his wrist-bands daintily, and said that he would now proceed to hump himself. Well, all that was nearly three hours ago. It is questionable whether I am calm enough yet to write on the noble theme of political economy, but I cannot resist the desire to try, for it is the one subject that is nearest to my heart and dearest to my brain of all this world's philosophy.]

—"economy is heaven's best boon to man." *When the loose but gifted Byron lay in his Venetian exile he observed that, if it could be granted him to go back and live his misspent life over again, he would give his lucid and unintoxicated intervals to the composition, not of frivolous rhymes, but of essays upon political economy. Washington loved this exquisite science; such names as Baker, Beckwith, Judson, Smith, are imperishably linked with it; and even imperial Homer, in the ninth book of the Iliad, has said:*

Fiat justitia, ruat cœlum,
Post mortem unum, ante bellum,
Hic jacet hoc, ex-parte res,
Politicum e-conomico est.

The grandeur of these conceptions of the old poet, together with the felicity of the wording which clothes them, and the sublimity of the imagery whereby they are illustrated, have singled out that stanza, and made it more celebrated than any that ever—

["Now, not a word out of you—not a single word. Just state your bill and relapse into impenetrable silence for ever and ever on these premises. Nine hundred dollars? Is that all? This check for the amount will be honored at any respectable bank in America. What is that multitude of people gathered in the street for? How?—'looking at the lightning-rods!' Bless my life, did they never see any lightning-rods before? Never saw 'such a stack of them on one establishment,' did I understand you to say? I will step down and critically observe this popular ebullition of ignorance."]

THREE DAYS LATER We are all about worn out. For four-and-twenty hours our bristling premises were the talk and wonder of the town. The theaters languished, for their happiest scenic inventions were tame and commonplace compared with my lightning-rods. Our street was blocked night and day with spectators, and among them were many who came from the country to see. It was a blessed relief on the second day when a thunder-storm came up and the lightning began to "go for" my house, as the historian Josephus quaintly phrases it. It cleared the galleries, so to speak. In five minutes there was not a spectator within half a mile of my place; but all the high houses about that distance away were full, windows, roof, and all. And well they might be, for all the falling stars and Fourth-of-July fireworks of a generation, put together and rained down simultaneously out of heaven in one brilliant shower upon one helpless roof, would not have any advantage of the pyrotechnic display that was making my house so magnificently conspicuous in the general gloom of the storm. By actual count, the lightning struck at my establishment seven hundred and sixty-four times in forty minutes, but tripped on one of those faithful rods every time, and slid down the spiral-twist and shot into the earth before it probably had time to be surprised at the way the thing was done. And through all that bombardment only one patch of slates was ripped up, and that was because, for a single instant, the rods in the vicinity were transporting all the lightning they could possibly accommodate. Well, nothing was ever seen like it since the world began. For one whole day and night not a member of my family stuck his head out of the window but he got the hair snatched off it as smooth as a billiard-ball; and, if the reader will believe me, not one of us ever dreamt of stirring abroad. But at last the awful siege came to an end—because there was absolutely no more electricity left in the clouds above us within grappling distance of my insatiable rods. Then I sallied forth, and gathered daring workmen together, and not a bite or a nap did we take till the premises were utterly stripped of all their terrific armament except just three rods on the house, one on the kitchen, and one on the barn—and, behold, these remain there even unto this day. And then, and not till then, the people ventured to use our street again. I will remark here, in passing, that during that fearful time I did not continue my essay upon political economy. I am not even yet settled enough in nerve and brain to resume it.

TO WHOM IT MAY CONCERN Parties having need of three thousand two hundred and eleven feet of best quality zinc-plated spiral-twist lightning-rod stuff, and sixteen hundred and thirty-one silver-tipped points, all in tolerable repair (and, although much worn by use, still equal to any ordinary emergency), can hear of a bargain by addressing the publisher.

1870

Science *vs.* Luck

AT THAT TIME, in Kentucky (said the Hon. Mr. K——), the law was very strict against what is termed "games of chance." About a dozen of the boys were detected playing "seven-up" or "old sledge"[1] for money, and the grand jury found a true bill against them. Jim Sturgis was retained to defend them when the case came up, of course. The more he studied over the matter, and looked into the evidence, the plainer it was that he must lose a case at last—there was no getting around that painful fact. Those boys had certainly been betting money on a game of chance. Even public sympathy was roused in behalf of Sturgis. People said it was a pity to see him mar his successful career with a big prominent case like this, which must go against him.

But after several restless nights an inspired idea flashed upon Sturgis, and he sprang out of bed delighted. He thought he saw his way through. The next day he whispered around a little among his clients and a few friends, and then when the case came up in court he acknowledged the seven-up and the betting, and, as his sole defense, had the astounding effrontery to put in the plea that old sledge was not a game of chance! There was the broadest sort of a smile all over the faces of that sophisticated audience. The judge smiled with the rest. But Sturgis maintained a countenance whose earnestness was even severe. The opposite counsel tried to ridicule him out of his position, and did not succeed. The judge jested in a ponderous judicial way about the thing, but did not move him. The matter was becoming grave. The judge lost a little of his patience, and said the joke had gone far enough. Jim Sturgis said he knew of no joke in the matter—his clients could not be punished for indulging in what some people chose to consider a game of chance until it was *proven* that it was a game of chance. Judge and counsel said that would be an easy matter, and forthwith called Deacons Job, Peters, Burke, and Johnson, and Dominies Wirt and Miggles, to testify; and they unanimously and with strong feeling put down the legal quibble of Sturgis by pronouncing that old sledge *was* a game of chance.

"What do you call it *now?*" said the judge.

"I call it a game of science!" retorted Sturgis; "and I'll prove it, too!"

They saw his little game.

He brought in a cloud of witnesses, and produced an overwhelming mass of testimony, to show that old sledge was not a game of chance but a game of science.

Instead of being the simplest case in the world, it had somehow turned out to be an excessively knotty one. The judge scratched his head over it awhile, and said there was no way of coming to a determination, because just as many men could be brought into court who would testify on one side as could be found to testify on the other. But he said he was willing to do the fair thing by all parties, and would act upon any suggestion Mr. Sturgis would make for the solution of the difficulty.

Mr. Sturgis was on his feet in a second.

"Impanel a jury of six of each, Luck *versus* Science. Give them candles and a couple of decks of cards. Send them into the jury-room, and just abide by the result!"

There was no disputing the fairness of the proposition. The four deacons and the two dominies were sworn in as the "chance" jurymen, and six inveterate old seven-up professors were chosen to represent the "science" side of the issue. They retired to the jury-room.

In about two hours Deacon Peters sent into court to borrow three dollars from a friend. [Sensation.] In about two hours more Dominie Miggles sent into a court to borrow a "stake" from a friend. [Sensation.] During the next three or four hours the other dominie and the other deacons sent into court for small loans. And still the packed audience waited, for it was a prodigious occasion in Bull's Corners, and one in which every father of a family was necessarily interested.

The rest of the story can be told briefly. About daylight the jury came in, and Deacon Job, the foreman, read the following

VERDICT

We, the Jury in the case of the Commonwealth of Kentucky *vs.* John Wheeler *et al.*, have carefully considered the points of the case, and tested the merits of the several theories advanced, and do hereby unanimously decide that the game commonly known as old sledge or seven-up is eminently a game of science and not of chance. In demonstration whereof it is hereby and herein stated, iterated, reiterated, set forth, and made manifest that, during the entire night, the "chance" men never won a game or turned a jack, although both feats were common and frequent to the opposition; and furthermore, in support of this our verdict, we call attention to the significant fact that the "chance" men are all busted, and the "science" men have got the money. It is the deliberate opinion of this jury, that the "chance" theory concerning seven-up is a pernicious doctrine, and calculated to inflict untold suffering and pecuniary loss upon any community that takes stock in it.

"That is the way that seven-up came to be set apart and particularlized in the statute-books of Kentucky as being a game not of chance but of science, and therefore not punishable under the law," said Mr. K——. "That verdict is of record, and holds good to this day."

1870

The Story of the Good Little Boy

Once there was a good little boy by the name of Jacob Blivens. He always obeyed his parents, no matter how absurd and unreasonable their demands were; and he always learned his book, and never was late at Sabbath-school. He would not play hookey, even when his sober judgment told him it was the most profitable thing he could do. None of the other boys could ever make that boy out, he acted so strangely. He wouldn't lie, no matter how convenient it was. He just said it was wrong to lie, and that was sufficient for him. And he was so honest that he was simply ridiculous. The curious ways that that Jacob had, surpassed everything. He wouldn't play marbles on Sunday, he wouldn't rob birds' nests, he wouldn't give hot pennies to organ-grinders' monkeys; he didn't seem to take any interest in any kind of rational amusement. So the other boys used to try to reason it out and come to an understanding of him, but they couldn't arrive at any satisfactory conclusion. As I said before, they could only figure out a sort of vague idea that he was "afflicted," and so they took him under their protection, and never allowed any harm to come to him.

This good little boy read all the Sunday-school books; they were his greatest delight. This was the whole secret of it. He believed in the good little boys they put in the Sunday-school books; he had every confidence in them. He longed to come across one of them alive once; but he never did. They all died before his time, maybe. Whenever he read about a particularly good one he turned over quickly to the end to see what became of him, because he wanted to travel thousands of miles and gaze on him; but it wasn't any use; that good little boy always died in the last chapter, and there was a picture of the funeral, with all his relations and the Sunday-school children standing around the grave in pantaloons that were too short, and bonnets that were too large, and everybody crying into handkerchiefs that had as much as a yard and a half of stuff in them. He was always headed off in this way. He never could see one of those good little boys on account of his always dying in the last chapter.

Jacob had a noble ambition to be put in a Sunday-school book. He wanted to be put in, with pictures representing him gloriously declining to lie to his mother, and her weeping for joy about it; and pictures representing him standing on the doorstep giving a penny to a poor beggar-woman with six children, and telling her to spend it freely, but not to be extravagant, because extravagance is a sin; and pictures of him magnanimously refusing to tell on the bad boy who always lay in wait for him around the corner as he came from school, and welted him over the head with a lath, and then chased him home, saying, "Hi! hi!" as he proceeded. That was the ambition of young Jacob Blivens. He wished to be put in a Sunday-school book. It made him feel a little uncomfortable sometimes when he reflected that the good little boys always died. He loved to live, you know and this was the most unpleasant feature about being a Sunday-school-book boy. He knew it was not healthy to be good. He knew it was more fatal than consumption to be so supernaturally good as the boys in the books were; he knew that none of them had ever been able to stand it long, and it pained him to think that if they put him in a book he wouldn't ever see it, or even if they did get the book out before he died it wouldn't be popular without any picture of his funeral in the back part of it. It couldn't be much of a Sunday-school book that couldn't tell about the advice he gave to the community when he was dying. So at last, of course, he had to make up his mind to do the best he could under the circumstances—to live right, and hang on as long as he could, and have his dying speech all ready when his time came.

But somehow nothing ever went right with this good little boy; nothing ever turned out with him the way it turned out with the good little boys in the books. They always had a good time, and the bad boys had the broken legs; but in his case there was a screw loose somewhere, and it all happened just the other way. When he found Jim Blake stealing apples, and went under the tree to read to him about the bad little boy who fell out of a neighbor's apple tree and broke his arm, Jim fell out of the tree, too, but he fell on *him* and broke *his* arm, and Jim wasn't hurt at all. Jacob couldn't understand that. There wasn't anything in the books like it.

And once, when some bad boys pushed a blind man over in the mud, and Jacob ran to help him up and receive his blessing, the blind man did not give him any blessing at all, but whacked him over the head with his stick and said he would like to catch him shoving *him* again, and then pretending to help him up. This was not in accordance with any of the books. Jacob looked them all over to see.

One thing that Jacob wanted to do was to find a lame dog that hadn't any place to stay, and was hungry and persecuted, and bring him home and pet him and have that dog's imperishable gratitude. And at last he found one and was happy; and he brought him home and fed him, but when he was going to pet him the dog flew at him and tore all the clothes off him except those that were in front, and made a spectacle of him that was astonishing. He examined authorities, but he could not understand the matter. It was of the same breed of dogs that was in the books, but it acted very differently. Whatever this boy did he got into trouble. The very things the boys in the books got rewarded for turned out to be about the most unprofitable things he could invest in.

Once, when he was on his way to Sunday-school, he saw some bad boys starting off pleasuring in a sailboat. He was filled with consternation, because he knew from his reading that boys who went sailing on Sunday invariably got drowned. So he ran out on a raft to warn them, but a log turned with him and slid him into the river. A man got him out pretty soon, and the doctor pumped the water out of him, and gave him a fresh start with his bellows, but he caught cold and lay sick abed nine weeks. But the most unaccountable thing about it was that the bad boys in the boat had a good time all day, and then reached home alive and well in the most surprising manner. Jacob Blivens said there was nothing like these things in the books. He was perfectly dumbfounded.

When he got well he was a little discouraged, but he resolved to keep on trying anyhow. He knew that so far his experiences wouldn't do to go in a book, but he hadn't yet reached the allotted term of life for good little boys, and he hoped to be able to make a record yet if he could hold on till his time was fully up. If everything else failed he had his dying speech to fall back on.

He examined his authorities, and found that it was now time for him to go to sea as a cabin-boy. He called on a ship-captain and made his application, and when the captain asked for his recommendations he proudly drew out a tract and pointed to the word, "To Jacob Blivens, from his affectionate teacher." But the captain was a coarse, vulgar man, and he said, "Oh, that be blowed! *that* wasn't any proof that he knew how to wash dishes or handle a slush-bucket, and he guessed he didn't want him." This was altogether the most extraordinary thing that ever happened to Jacob in all his life. A compliment from a teacher, on a tract, had never failed to move the tenderest emotions of ship-captains, and open the way to all offices of honor and profit in their gift—it never had in any book that ever *he* had read. He could hardly believe his senses.

This boy always had a hard time of it. Nothing ever came out according to the authorities with him. At last, one day, when he was around hunting up bad little boys to admonish, he found a lot of them in the old iron-foundry fixing up a little joke on fourteen or fifteen dogs, which they had tied together in long procession, and were going to ornament with empty nitroglycerin cans made fast to their tails. Jacob's heart was touched. He sat down on one of those cans (for he never minded grease when duty was before him), and he took hold of the foremost dog by the collar, and turned his reproving eye upon wicked Tom Jones. But just at that moment Alderman McWelter, full of wrath, stepped in. All the bad boys ran away, but Jacob Blivens rose in conscious innocence and began one of those stately little Sunday-school-book speeches which always commence with "Oh, sir!" in dead opposition to the fact that no boy, good or bad, ever starts a remark with "Oh, sir." But the alderman never waited to hear the rest. He took Jacob Blivens by the ear and turned him around, and hit him a whack in the rear with the flat of his hand; and in an instant that good little boy shot out through the roof and soared away toward the sun, with the fragments of those fifteen dogs stringing after him like the tail of a kite. And there wasn't a sign of that alderman or that old iron-foundry left on the face of the earth; and, as for young Jacob Blivens, he never got a chance to make his last dying speech after all his trouble fixing it up, unless he made it to the birds; because, although the bulk of him came down all right in a tree-top in an adjoining county, the rest of him was apportioned around among four townships, and so they had to hold five inquests on him to find out whether he was dead or not, and how it occurred. You never saw a boy scattered so.*

Thus perished the good little boy who did the best he could, but didn't come out according to the books. Every boy who ever did as he did prospered except him. His case is truly remarkable. It will probably never be accounted for.

1870

Buck Fanshaw's Funeral

Somebody has said that in order to know a community, one must observe the style of its funerals and know what manner of men they bury with most ceremony. I cannot say which class we buried with most éclat in our "flush times," the distinguished public benefactor or the distinguished rough—possibly the two chief grades or grand divisions of society honored their illustrious dead about equally; and hence, no doubt, the philosopher I have quoted from would have needed to see two representative funerals in Virginia before forming his estimate of the people.

There was a grand time over Buck Fanshaw when he died. He was a representative citizen. He had "killed his man"—not in his own quarrel, it is true, but in defense of a stranger unfairly beset by numbers. He had kept a sumptu-

* This glycerin catastrophe is borrowed from a floating newspaper item, whose author's name I would give if I knew it. M.T.

ous saloon. He had been the proprietor of a dashing helpmeet[1] whom he could have discarded without the formality of a divorce. He had held a high position in the fire department and been a very Warwick in politics. When he died there was great lamentation throughout the town, but especially in the vast bottom-stratum of society.

On the inquest it was shown that Buck Fanshaw, in the delirium of a wasting typhoid fever, had taken arsenic, shot himself through the body, cut his throat, and jumped out of a four-story window and broken his neck—and after due deliberation, the jury, sad and tearful, but with intelligence unblinded by its sorrow, brought in a verdict of death "by the visitation of God." What could the world do without juries?

Prodigious preparations were made for the funeral. All the vehicles in town were hired, all the saloons put in mourning, all the municipal and fire-company flags hung at half-mast, and all the firemen ordered to muster in uniform and bring their machines duly draped in black. Now—let us remark in parentheses—as all the peoples of the earth had representative adventures in the Silverland, and as each adventurer had brought the slang of his nation or his locality with him, the combination made the slang of Nevada the richest and the most infinitely varied and copious that had ever existed anywhere in the world, perhaps, except in the mines of California in the "early days." Slang was the language of Nevada. It was hard to preach a sermon without it, and be understood. Such phrases as "You bet!" "Oh, no, I reckon not!" "No Irish need apply,"[2] and a hundred others, became so common as to fall from the lips of a speaker unconsciously—and very often when they did not touch the subject under discussion and consequently failed to mean anything.

After Buck Fanshaw's inquest, a meeting of the short-haired brotherhood was held, for nothing can be done on the Pacific coast without a public meeting and an expression of sentiment. Regretful resolutions were passed and various committees appointed; among others, a committee of one was deputed to call on the minister, a fragile, gentle, spirituel new fledgling from an Eastern theological seminary, and as yet unacquainted with the ways of the mines. The committeeman, "Scotty" Briggs, made his visit; and in after days it was worth something to hear the minister tell about it. Scotty was a stalwart rough, whose customary suit, when on weighty official business, like committee work, was a fire-helmet, flaming red flannel shirt, patent-leather belt with spanner and revolver attached, coat hung over arm, and pants stuffed into boot-tops. He formed something of a contrast to the pale theological student. It is fair to say of Scotty, however, in passing, that he had a warm heart, and a strong love for his friends, and never entered into a quarrel when he could reasonably keep out of it. Indeed, it was commonly said that whenever one of Scotty's fights was investigated, it always turned out that it had originally been no affair of his, but that out of native good-heartedness he had dropped in of his own accord to help the man who was getting the worst of it. He and Buck Fanshaw were bosom friends, for years, and had often taken adventurous "pot-luck" together. On one occasion, they had thrown off their coats and taken the weaker side in a fight among strangers, and after gaining a hard-earned victory, turned and found that the men they were helping had deserted early, and not only that, but had stolen their coats and made off with them. But to return to Scotty's visit to the minister. He was on a sorrowful mission, now, and his face was the picture of woe. Being admitted to the presence he sat down before the clergyman, placed his fire-hat on an unfinished manuscript sermon under the minister's nose, took from it a red silk handkerchief, wiped his brow and heaved a sigh of dismal impressiveness, explanatory of his business. He choked, and even shed tears; but with an effort he mastered his voice and said in lugubrious tones:

"Are you the duck that runs the gospel-mill next door?"

"Am I the—pardon me, I believe I do not understand?"

With another sigh and a half-sob, Scotty rejoined:

"Why you see we are in a bit of trouble, and the boys thought maybe you would give us a lift, if we'd tackle you—that is, if I've got the rights of it and you are the head clerk of the doxology-works next door."

"I am the shepherd in charge of the flock whose fold is next door."

"The which?"

"The spiritual adviser of the little company of believers whose sanctuary adjoins these premises."

Scotty scratched his head, reflected a moment, and then said:

"You ruther hold over me, pard. I reckon I can't call that hand. Ante and pass the buck."

"How? I beg pardon. What did I understand you to say?"

"Well, you've ruther got the bulge on me. Or maybe we've both got the bulge, somehow. You don't smoke me and I don't smoke you. You see, one of the boys has passed in his checks, and we want to give him a good send-off, and so the thing I'm on now is to roust out somebody to jerk a little chin-music for us and waltz him through handsome."

"My friend, I seem to grow more and more bewildered. Your observations are wholly incomprehensible to me. Cannot you simplify them in some way? At first I thought perhaps I understood you, but I grope now. Would it not expedite matters if you restricted yourself to categorical statements of fact unencumbered with obstructing accumulations of metaphor and allegory?"

Another pause, and more reflection. Then, said Scotty:

"I'll have to pass, I judge."

"How?"

"You've raised me out, pard."

"I still fail to catch your meaning."

"Why, that last lead of yourn is too many for me—that's the idea. I can't neither trump nor follow suit."

The clergyman sank back in his chair perplexed. Scotty leaned his head on his hand and gave himself up to thought. Presently his face came up, sorrowful but confident.

"I've got it now, so's you can savvy," he said. "What we want is a gospel-sharp. See?"

"A what?"

"Gospel-sharp. Parson."

"Oh! Why did you not say so before? I am a clergyman—a parson."

"Now you talk! You see my blind and straddle it like a man. Put it there!"—extending a brawny paw, which closed over the minister's small hand and gave it a shake indicative of fraternal sympathy and fervent gratification.

"Now we're all right, pard. Let's start fresh. Don't you mind my snuffling a little—becuz we're in a power of trouble. You see, one of the boys has gone up the flume—"

"Gone where?"

"Up the flume—throwed up the sponge, you understand."

"Thrown up the sponge?"

"Yes—kicked the bucket—"

"Ah—has departed to that mysterious country from whose bourne no traveler returns."

"Return! I reckon not. Why, pard, he's *dead!*"

"Yes, I understand."

"Oh, you do? Well I thought maybe you might be getting tangled some more. Yes, you see he's dead again—"

"*Again!* Why, has he ever been dead before?"

"Dead before? No! Do you reckon a man has got as many lives as a cat? But you bet you he's awful dead now, poor old boy, and I wish I'd never seen this day. I don't want no better friend than Buck Fanshaw. I knowed him by the back; and when I know a man and like him, I freeze to him—you hear *me.* Take him all round, pard, there never was a bullier man in the mines. No man ever knowed Buck Fanshaw to go back on a friend. But it's all up, you know, it's all up. It ain't no use. They've scooped him."

"Scooped him?"

"Yes—death has. Well, well, well, we've got to give him up. Yes, indeed. It's a kind of a hard world, after all, *ain't* it? But pard, he was a rustler! You ought to seen him get started once. He was a bully boy with a glass eye! Just spit in his face and give him room according to his strength, and it was just beautiful to see him peel and go in. He was the worst son of a thief that ever drawed breath. Pard, he was *on* it! He was on it bigger than an Injun!"

"On it? On what?"

"On the shoot. On the shoulder. On the fight, you understand. *He* didn't give a continental for *any*body. *Beg* your pardon, friend, for coming so near saying a cuss-word—but you see I'm on an awful strain, in this palaver, on account of having to cramp down and draw everything so mild. But we've got to give him up. There ain't any getting around that, I don't reckon. Now if we can get you to help plant him—"

"Preach the funeral discourse? Assist at the obsequies?"

"Obs'quies is good. Yes. That's it—that's our little game. We are going to get the thing up regardless, you know. He was always nifty himself, and so you bet you his funeral ain't going to be no slouch—solid-silver door-plate on his coffin, six plumes on the hearse, and a nigger on the box in a biled shirt and a plug hat—how's that for high? And we'll take care of *you*, pard. We'll fix you all right. There'll be a kerridge for you; and whatever you want, you just 'scape out and we'll 'tend to it. We've got a shebang fixed up for you to stand behind, in No. 1's house, and don't you be afraid. Just go in and toot your horn, if you don't sell a clam. Put Buck through as bully as you can, pard, for anybody that knowed him will tell you that he was one of the whitest men that was ever in the mines. You can't draw it too strong. He never could stand it to see things going wrong. He's done more to make this town quiet and peaceable than any man in it. I've seen him lick four Greasers in eleven minutes, myself. If a thing wanted regulating, *he* warn't a man to go browsing around after somebody to do it, but he would prance in and regulate it himself. He warn't a Catholic. Scasely. He was down on 'em. His word was, 'No Irish need apply!' But it didn't make no difference about that when it came down to what a man's rights was—and so, when some roughs jumped the Catholic boneyard and started in to stake out town lots in it he *went* for 'em! And he *cleaned* 'em, too! I was there, pard, and I seen it myself."

"That was very well indeed—at least the impulse was—whether the act was strictly defensible or not. Had deceased any religious convictions? That is to say, did he feel a dependence upon, or acknowledge alliance to a higher power?"

More reflection.

"I reckon you've stumped me again, pard. Could you say it over once more, and say it slow?"

"Well, to simplify it somewhat, was he, or rather had he ever been connected with any organization sequestered from secular concerns and devoted to self-sacrifice in the interests of morality?"

"All down but nine—set 'em up on the other alley, pard."

"What did I understand you to say?"

"Why, you're most too many for me, you know. When you get in with your left I hunt grass every time. Every time you draw, you fill; but I don't seem to have any luck. Let's have a new deal."

"How? Begin again?"

"That's it."

"Very well. Was he a good man, and—"

"There—I see that; don't put up another chip till I look at my hand. A good man, says you? Pard, it ain't no name for it. He was the best man that ever—pard, you would have doted on that man. He could lam any galoot of his inches in America. It was him that put down the riot last election before it got a start; and everybody said he was the only man that could have done it. He waltzed in with a spanner in one hand and a trumpet in the other, and sent fourteen men home on a shutter in less than three minutes. He had that riot all broke up and prevented nice before anybody ever got a chance to strike a blow. He was always for peace, and he would *have* peace—he could not stand disturbances. Pard, he was a great loss to this town. It would please the boys if you could chip in something like that and do him justice. Here once when the Micks got to throwing stones through the Methodis' Sunday-school windows, Buck Fanshaw, all of his own notion, shut up his saloon and took a couple of six-shooters and mounted guard over the Sunday-school. Says he, 'No Irish need apply!' And they didn't. He was the bulliest man in the mountains, pard! He could run faster, jump higher, hit harder, and hold more tanglefoot whisky without spilling it than any man in seventeen counties. Put that in, pard—it'll please the boys more than anything you could say. And you can say, pard, that he never shook his mother."

"Never shook his mother?"

"That's it—any of the boys will tell you so."

"Well, but why *should* he shake her?"

"That's what *I* say—but some people does."

"Not people of any repute?"

"Well, some that averages pretty so-so."

"In my opinion the man that would offer personal violence to his own mother, ought to—"

"Cheese it, pard; you've banked your ball clean outside the string. What I was a drivin' at, was, that he never *throwed* off on his mother—don't you see? No indeedy. He give her a house to live in, and town lots, and plenty of money; and he looked after her and took care of her all the time; and when she was down with the smallpox I'm d—d if he didn't set up nights and nuss her himself! *Beg* your pardon for saying it, but it hopped out too quick for yours truly. You've treated me like a gentleman, pard, and I ain't the man to hurt your feelings intentional. I think you're white. I think you're a square man, pard. I like you, and I'll lick any man that don't. I'll lick him till he can't tell himself from a last year's corpse! Put it *there!*" [Another fraternal handshake—and exit.]

The obsequies were all that "the boys" could desire. Such a marvel of funeral pomp had never been seen in Virginia. The plumed hearse, the dirge-breathing brass-bands, the closed marts of business, the flags drooping at half-mast, the long, plodding procession of uniformed secret societies, military battalions and fire companies, draped engines, carriages of officials, and citizens in vehicles and on foot, attracted multitudes of spectators to the sidewalks, roofs, and windows; and for years afterward, the degree of grandeur attained by any civic display in Virginia was determined by comparison with Buck Fanshaw's funeral.

Scotty Briggs, as a pall-bearer and a mourner, occupied a prominent place at the funeral, and when the sermon was finished and the last sentence of the prayer for the dead man's soul ascended, he responded, in a low voice, but with feeling:

"Amen. No Irish need apply."

As the bulk of the response was without apparent relevancy, it was probably nothing more than a humble tribute to the memory of the friend that was gone; for, as Scotty had once said, it was "his word."

Scotty Briggs, in after days, achieved the distinction of becoming the only convert to religion that was ever gathered from the Virginia roughs; and it transpired that the man who had it in him to espouse the quarrel of the weak out of inborn nobility of spirit was no mean timber whereof to construct a Christian. The making him one did not warp his generosity or diminish his courage; on the contrary it gave intelligent direction to the one and a broader field to the other. If his Sunday-school class progressed faster than the other classes, was it matter for wonder? I think not. He talked to his pioneer small-fry in a language they understood! It was my large privilege, a month before he died, to hear him tell the beautiful story of Joseph and his brethren to his class "without looking at the book." I leave it to the reader to fancy what it was like, as it fell, riddled with slang, from the lips of that grave, earnest teacher, and was listened to by his little learners with a consuming interest that showed that they were as unconscious as he was that any violence was being done to the sacred proprieties!

From ROUGHING IT, 1872

The Story of the Old Ram

EVERY NOW and then, in these days, the boys used to tell me I ought to get one Jim Blaine to tell me the stirring story of his grandfather's old ram—but they always added that I must not mention the matter unless Jim was drunk at the time—just comfortably and sociably drunk. They kept this up until my curiosity was on the rack to hear the story. I got to haunting Blaine; but it was of no use, the boys always found fault with his condition; he was often moderately but never satisfactorily drunk. I never watched a man's condition with such absorbing interest, such anxious solicitude; I never so pined to see a man uncompromisingly drunk before. At last, one evening I hurried to his cabin, for I learned that this time his situation was such that even the most fastidious could find no fault with it—he was tranquilly, serenely, symmetrically drunk—not a hiccup to mar his voice, not a cloud upon his brain thick enough to obscure his memory. As I entered, he was sitting upon an empty powder-keg, with a clay pipe in one hand and the other raised to command silence. His face was round, red, and very serious; his throat was bare and his hair tumbled; in general appearance and costume he was a stalwart miner of the period. On the pine table stood a candle, and its dim light revealed "the boys" sitting here and there on bunks, candle-boxes, powder-kegs, etc. They said:

"Sh—! Don't speak—he's going to commence."

I found a seat at once, and Blaine said:

"I don't reckon them times will ever come again. There never was a more bullier old ram than what he was. Grandfather fetched him from Illinois—got him of a man by the name of Yates—Bill Yates—maybe you might have heard of him; his father was a deacon—Baptist—and he was a rustler, too; a man had to get up ruther early to get the start of old Thankful Yates; it was him that put the Greens up to j'ining teams with my grandfather when he moved west. Seth Green was prob'ly the pick of the flock; he married a Wilkerson—Sarah Wilkerson—good cretur, she was—one of the likeliest heifers that was ever raised in old Stoddard, everybody said that knowed her. She could heft a bail of flour as easy as I can flirt a flapjack. And spin? Don't mention it! Independent? Humph! When Sile Hawkins come a-browsing around her, she let him know that for all his tin he couldn't trot in harness alongside of *her*. You see, Sile Hawkins was—no, it warn't Sile Hawkins, after all—it was a galoot by the name of Filkins—I disremember his first name; but he *was* a stump—come into pra'r-meeting drunk, one night, hooraying for Nixon, becuz he thought it was a primary; and old Deacon Ferguson up and scooted him through the window and he lit on old Miss Jefferson's head, poor old filly. She was a good soul—had a glass eye and used to lend it to old Miss Wagner, that hadn't any, to receive company in; it warn't big enough, and when Miss Wagner warn't noticing, it would get twisted around in the socket, and look up, maybe, or out to one side, and every which way, while t'other one was looking as straight ahead as a spy-glass. Grown people didn't mind it, but it 'most always made the children cry, it was so sort of scary. She tried packing it in raw cotton, but it wouldn't work, somehow—the cotton would get loose and stick out and look so kind of awful that the children couldn't stand it no way. She was always dropping it out, and turning up her old deadlight on the company empty, and making them oncomfortable, becuz *she* never could tell when it hopped out, being blind on that side, you see. So somebody would have to hunch her and say, 'Your game eye has fetched loose, Miss Wagner, dear'—and then all of them would have to sit and wait till she jammed it in again—wrong side before, as a general thing, and green as a bird's egg, being a bashful cretur and easy sot back before company. But being wrong side before warn't much difference, anyway, becuz her own eye was sky-blue and the glass one was yaller on the front side, so whichever way she turned it it didn't match nohow. Old Miss Wagner was considerable on the borrow, she was. When she had a quilting, or Dorcas S'iety at her house she gen'ally borrowed Miss Higgins's wooden leg to stump around on; it was considerable shorter than her other pin, but much *she* minded that. She said she couldn't abide crutches when she had company, becuz they were so slow; said when she had company and things had to be done, she wanted to get up and hump herself. She was as bald as a jug, and so she used to borrow Miss Jacops's wig—Miss Jacops was the coffin-peddler's wife—a ratty old buzzard, he was, that used to go roosting around where people was sick, waiting for 'em; and there that old rip would sit all day, in the shade, on a coffin that he judged would fit the can'idate; and if it was a slow customer and kind of uncertain, he'd fetch his rations and a blanket along and sleep in the coffin nights. He was anchored out that way, in frosty weather, for about three weeks, once, before old Robbins's place, waiting for him; and after that, for as much as two years, Jacops was not on speaking terms with the old man, on account of his disapp'inting him. He got one of his feet froze, and lost money, too, becuz old Robbins took a favorable turn and got well. The next time Robbins got sick, Jacops tried to make up with him, and varnished up the same old coffin and fetched it along; but old Robbins was too many for him; he had him in, and 'peared to be powerful weak; he bought the coffin for ten dollars and Jacops was to pay it back and twenty-five more besides if Robbins didn't like the coffin after he'd tried it. And then Robbins died, and at the funeral he bursted off the lid and riz up in his shroud and told the parson to let up on the performances, becuz he could *not* stand such a coffin as that. You see he had been in a trance once before, when he was young, and he took the chances on another, cal'lating that if he made the trip it was money in his pocket, and if he missed fire he couldn't lose a cent. And, by George, he sued Jacops for the rhino and got judgment; and he set up the coffin in his back parlor and said he 'lowed to take his time, now. It was always an aggravation to Jacops, the way that miserable old thing acted. He moved back to Indiany pretty soon—went to Wellsville—Wellsville was the place the Hogadorns was from. Mighty fine family. Old Maryland stock. Old Squire Hogadorn could carry around more mixed licker, and cuss better than 'most any man I ever see. His second wife was the Widder Billings—she that was Becky Martin; her dam was Deacon Dunlap's first wife, Her oldest child, Maria, married a missionary and died in grace—et up by the savages. They et *him*, too, poor feller—biled him. It warn't the custom, so they say, but they explained to friends of his'n that went down there to bring away his things, that they'd tried missionaries every other way and never could get any good out of 'em—and so it annoyed all his relations to find out that that man's life was fooled away just out of a dern'd experiment, so to speak. But mind you, there ain't anything ever reely lost; everything that people can't understand and don't see the reason of does good if you only hold on and give it a fair shake; Prov'dence don't fire no blank ca'tridges, boys. That there missionary's substance, unbeknowns to himself, actu'ly converted every last one of them heathens that took a chance at the barbecue. Nothing ever fetched them but that. Don't tell *me* it was an accident that he was biled. There ain't no such a thing as an accident. When my Uncle Lem was leaning up agin a scaffolding once, sick, or drunk, or suthin, an Irishman with a hod full of bricks fell on him out of the third story and broke the old man's back in two places. People said it was an accident. Much accident there was about that. He didn't know what he was there for, but he was there for a good object. If he hadn't been there the Irishman would have been killed. Nobody can ever make me believe anything different from that. Uncle Lem's dog was there. Why didn't the Irishman fall on the dog? Becuz the dog would 'a' seen him a-coming and stood from under. That's the reason the dog warn't app'inted. A dog can't be depended on to carry out a special prov'dence. Mark my words, it was a put-up thing. Accidents don't happen, boys. Uncle Lem's dog—I wish you could 'a' seen that dog. He was a reg'lar shepherd—or rather he was part bull and part shepherd—splendid animal; belonged to Parson Hagar before Uncle Lem got him. Parson Hagar belonged to the Western Reserve Hagars; prime family; his mother was a Watson; one of his sisters married a Wheeler; they settled in Morgan County, and he got nipped by the machinery in a carpet factory and went through in less than a quarter of a minute; his widder bought the piece of carpet that had his remains wove in, and people come a hundred mile to 'tend the funeral. There was fourteen yards in the piece. She wouldn't let them roll him up, but planted him just so—full length. The church was middling small where they preached the funeral, and they had to let one end of the coffin stick out of the window. They didn't bury him—they planted one end, and let him stand up, same as a monument. And they nailed a sign on it and put—put on—put on it—sacred to—the m-e-m-o-r-y—of fourteen y-a-r-d-s—of three-ply—car - - - pet—containing all that was—m-o-r-t-a-l—of—of—W-i-l-l-i-a-m—W-h-e—"

Jim Blaine had been growing gradually drowsy and drowsier—his head nodded, once, twice, three times—dropped peacefully upon his breast, and he fell tranquilly asleep. The tears were running down the boys' cheeks—they were suffocating with suppressed laughter—and had been from the start, though I had never noticed it. I perceived that I was "sold." I learned then that Jim Blaine's peculiarity was that whenever he reached a certain stage of intoxication, no human power could keep him from setting out, with impressive unction, to tell about a wonderful adventure which he had once had with his grandfather's old ram—and the mention of the ram in the first sentence was as far as any man had ever heard him get, concerning it. He always maundered off, interminably, from one thing to another, till his whisky got the best of him, and he fell asleep. What the thing was that happened to him and his grandfather's old ram is a dark mystery to this day, for nobody has ever yet found out.

From ROUGHING IT, 1872

A True Story

Repeated Word for Word As I Heard It

It was summer-time, and twilight. We were sitting on the porch of the farmhouse, on the summit of the hill, and "Aunt Rachel" was sitting respectfully below our level, on the steps—for she was our servant, and colored. She was of mighty frame and stature; she was sixty years old, but her eye was undimmed and her strength unabated. She was a cheerful, hearty soul, and it was no more trouble for her to laugh than it is for a bird to sing. She was under fire now, as usual when the day was done. That is to say, she was being chaffed without mercy, and was enjoying it. She would let off peal after peal of laughter, and then sit with her face in her hands and shake with throes of enjoyment which she could no longer get breath enough to express. At such a moment as this a thought occurred to me, and I said:

"Aunt Rachel, how is it that you've lived sixty years and never had any trouble?"

She stopped quaking. She paused, and there was a moment of silence. She turned her face over her shoulder toward me, and said, without even a smile in her voice:

"Misto C——, is you in 'arnest?"

It surprised me a good deal; and it sobered my manner and my speech, too. I said:

"Why, I thought—that is, I meant—why, you *can't* have

had any trouble. I've never heard you sigh, and never seen your eye when there wasn't a laugh in it."

She faced fairly around now, and was full of earnestness.

"Has I had any trouble? Misto C——, I's gwyne to tell you, den I leave it to you. I was bawn down 'mongst de slaves; I knows all 'bout slavery, 'case I ben one of 'em my own se'f. Well, sah, my ole man—dat's my husban'—he was lovin' an' kind to me, jist as kind as you is to yo' own wife. An' we had chil'en—seven chil'en—an' we loved dem chil'en just de same as you loves yo' chil'en. Dey was black, but de Lord can't make no chil'en so black but what dey mother loves 'em an' wouldn't give 'em up, no, not for anything dat's in dis whole world.

"Well, sah, I was raised in ole Fo'ginny, but my mother she was raised in Maryland; an' my *souls!* she was turrible when she'd git started! My *lan'!* but she'd make de fur fly! When she'd git into dem tantrums, she always had one word dat she said. She'd straighten herse'f up an' put her fists in her hips an' say, 'I want you to understan' dat I wa'n't bawn in the mash to be fool' by trash! I's one o' de ole Blue Hen's Chickens, I is!'[1] 'Ca'se, you see, dat's what folks dat's bawn in Maryland calls deyselves, an' dey's proud of it. Well, dat was her word. I don't ever forgit it, beca'se she said it so much, an' beca'se she said it one day when my little Henry tore his wris' awful, and most busted his head, right up at de top of his forehead, an' de niggers didn't fly aroun' fas' enough to 'tend to him. An' when dey talk' back at her, she up an' she says, 'Look-a-heah!' she says, 'I want you niggers to understan' dat I wa'n't bawn in de mash to be fool' by trash! I's one o' de ole Blue Hen's Chickens, *I* is!' an' den she clar' dat kitchen an' bandage' up de chile herse'f. So I says dat word, too, when I's riled.

"Well, bymeby my ole mistis say she's broke, an' she got to sell all de niggers on de place. An' when I heah dat dey gwyne to sell us all off at oction in Richmon', oh, de good gracious! I know what dat mean!"

Aunt Rachel had gradually risen, while she warmed to her subject, and now she towered above us, black against the stars.

"Dey put chains on us an' put us on a stan' as high as dis po'ch—twenty foot high—an' all de people stood aroun', crowds an' crowds. An' dey'd come up dah an' look at us all roun', an' squeeze our arm, an' make us git up an' walk, an' den say, 'Dis one too ole,' or 'Dis one lame,' or 'Dis one don't 'mount to much.' An' dey sole my ole man, an' took him away, an' dey begin to sell my chil'en an' take *dem* away, an' I begin to cry; an' de man say, 'Shet up yo' damn blubberin',' an' hit me on de mouf wid his han'. An' when de las' one was gone but my little Henry, I grab' *him* clost up to my breas' so, an' I ris up an' says, 'You sha'n't take him away,' I says; 'I'll kill de man dat tetches him!' I says. But my little Henry whisper an' say, 'I gwyne to run away, an' den I work an' buy yo' freedom.' Oh, bless de chile, he always so good! But dey got him—dey got him, de men did; but I took and tear de clo'es mos' off of 'em an' beat 'em over de head wid my chain; an' *dey* give it to *me*, too, but I didn't mine dat.

"Well, dah was my ole man gone, an' all my chil'en, all my seven chil'en—an' six of 'em I hain't set eyes on ag'in to this day, an' dat's twenty-two years ago las' Easter. De man dat bought me b'long' in Newbern, an' he took me dah. Well, bymeby de years roll on an' de waw come. My marster he was a Confedrit colonel, an' I was his family's cook. So when de Unions took dat town, dey all run away an' lef me all by myse'f wid de other niggers in dat mons'us big house. So de big Union officers move in dah, an' dey ask me would I cook for *dem*. 'Lord bless you,' says I, 'dat's what I's *for*.'

"Dey wa'n't no small-fry officers, mine you, dey was de biggest dey *is;* an' de way dey made dem sojers mosey roun'! De Gen'l he tole me to boss dat kitchen; an' he say, 'If any-body come meddlin' wid you, you just make 'em walk chalk; don't you be afeared,' he say; 'you's 'mong frens now.'

"Well, I thinks to myse'f, if my little Henry ever got a chance to run away, he'd make to de Norf, o' course. So one day I comes in dah whar de big officers was, in de parlor, an' I drops a kurtchy, so, an' I up an' tole 'em 'bout my Henry, dey a-listenin' to my troubles jist de same as if I was white folks; an' I says, 'What I come for is beca'se if he got away and got up Norf whar you gemmen comes from, you might 'a' seen him, maybe, an' could tell me so as I could fine him ag'in; he was very little, an' he had a sk-yar on his lef' wris' an' at de top of his forehead.' Den dey look mournful, an' de Gen'l says, 'How long sence you los' him?' an' I say, 'Thirteen year.' Den de Gen'l say, 'He wouldn't be little no mo' now—he's a man!'

"I never thought o' dat befo'! He was only dat little feller to *me* yit. I never thought 'bout him growin' up an' bein' big. But I see it den. None o' de gemmen had run acrost him, so dey couldn't do nothin' for me. But all dat time, do' *I* didn't know it, my Henry *was* run off to de Norf, years an' years, an' he was a barber, too, an' worked for hisse'f. An' bymeby, when de waw come he ups an' he says: 'I's done barberin',' he says, 'I's gwyne to fine my ole mammy, less'n she's dead.' So he sole out an' went to whar dey was recruitin', an' hired hisse'f out to de colonel for his servant; an' den he went all froo de battles everywhah, huntin' for his ole mammy; yes, indeedy, he'd hire to fust one officer an' den another, tell he'd ransacked de whole Souf; but you see *I* didn't know nuffin 'bout *dis*. How was *I* gwyne to know it?

"Well, one night we had a big sojer ball; de sojers dah at Newbern was always havin' balls an' carryin' on. Dey had 'em in my kitchen, heaps o' times, 'ca'se it was so big. Mine you, I was *down* on sich doin's; beca'se my place was wid de officers, an' it rasp me to have dem common sojers cavortin' roun' my kitchen like dat. But I alway' stood aroun' an' kep' things straight, I did; an' sometimes dey'd git my dander up, an' den I'd make 'em clar dat kitchen, mine I *tell* you!

"Well, one night—it was a Friday night—dey comes a

whole platoon f'm a *nigger* ridgment dat was on guard at de house—de house was headquarters, you know—an' den I was just a-*bilin'!* Mad? I was just a-*boomin'!* I swelled aroun', an' swelled aroun'; I just was a-itchin' for 'em to do somefin for to start me. *An'* dey was a-waltzin' an' a-dancin'! *my!* but dey was havin' a time! an' I jist a-swellin' an' a-swellin' up! Pooty soon, 'long comes *sich* a spruce young nigger a-sailin' down de room wid a yaller wench roun' de wais'; an' roun' an' roun' an' roun' dey went, enough to make a body drunk to look at 'em; an' when dey got abreas' o' me, dey went to kin' o' balancin' aroun' fust on one leg an' den on t'other, an' smilin' at my big red turban, an' makin' fun, an' I ups an' says '*Git* along wid you!—rubbage!' De young man's face kin' o' changed, all of a sudden, for 'bout a second, but den he went to smilin' ag'in, same as he was befo'. Well, 'bout dis time, in comes some niggers dat played music and b'long' to de ban', an' dey *never* could git along widout puttin' on airs. An' de very fust air dey put on dat night, I lit into 'em! Dey laughed, an' dat made me wuss. De res' o' de niggers got to laughin', an' den my soul *alive* but I was hot! My eye was just a-blazin'! I jist straightened myself up so—jist as I is now, plum to de ceilin' mos'—an' I digs my fists into my hips, an' I says, 'Look-a-heah!' I says, 'I want you niggers to understan' dat I wa'n't bawn in de mash to be fool' by trash! I's one o' de ole Blue Hen's Chickens, *I* is!' an' den I see dat young man stan' a-starin' an' stiff, lookin' kin' o' up at de ceilin' like he fo'got somefin, an' couldn't 'member it no mo'. Well, I jist march' on dem niggers—so lookin' like a gen'l—an' dey jist cave' away befo' me an' out at de do'. An' as dis young man was a-goin' out, I heah him say to another nigger, 'Jim,' he says, 'you go long an' tell de cap'n I be on han' 'bout eight o'clock in de mawnin'; dey's somefin on my mine,' he says; 'I don't sleep no mo' dis night. You go 'long,' he says, 'an' leave me by my own se'f.'

"Dis was 'bout one o'clock in de mawnin'. Well, 'bout

seven, I was up an' on han', gittin' de officers' breakfast. I was a-stoopin' down by de stove—just so, same as if yo' foot was de stove—an' I'd opened de stove do' wid my right han'—so, pushin' it back, just as I pushes yo' foot—an' I'd jist got de pan o' hot biscuits in my han' an' was 'bout to raise up, when I see a black face come aroun' under mine, an' de eyes a-lookin' up into mine, just as I's a-lookin' up close under yo' face now; an' I just stopped *right dah,* an' never budged! jist gazed an' gazed so; an' de pan begin to tremble, an' all of a sudden I *knowed!* De pan drop' on de flo' an' I grab his lef' han' an' shove back his sleeve—jist so, as I's doin' to you—an' den I goes for his forehead an' push de hair back so, an' 'Boy!' I says, 'if you ain't my Henry, what is you doin' wid dis welt on yo' wris' an' dat sk-yar on yo' forehead? De Lord God ob heaven be praise', I got my own ag'in!'

"Oh no, Misto C——, *I* hain't had no trouble. An' no *joy!*"

1874

Experience of the McWilliamses with Membranous Croup

As related to the author of this book by Mr. McWilliams, a pleasant New York gentleman whom the said author met by chance on a journey.

Well, to go back to where I was before I digressed to explain to you how that frightful and incurable disease, membranous croup, was ravaging the town and driving all mothers mad with terror, I called Mrs. McWilliams's attention to little Penelope, and said:

"Darling, I wouldn't let that child be chewing that pine stick if I were you."

"Precious, where is the harm in it?" said she, but at the same time preparing to take away the stick—for women cannot receive even the most palpably judicious suggestion without arguing it; that is, married women.

I replied:

"Love, it is notorious that pine is the least nutritious wood that a child can eat."

My wife's hand paused, in the act of taking the stick, and returned itself to her lap. She bridled perceptibly, and said:

"Hubby, you know better than that. You know you do. Doctors *all* say that the turpentine in pine wood is good for weak back and the kidneys."

"Ah—I was under a misapprehension. I did not know

that the child's kidneys and spine were affected, and that the family physician had recommended—"

"Who said the child's spine and kidneys were affected?"

"My love, you intimated it."

"The idea! I never intimated anything of the kind.'

"Why, my dear, it hasn't been two minutes since you said—"

"Bother what I said! I don't care what I did say. There isn't any harm in the child's chewing a bit of pine stick if she wants to, and you know it perfectly well. And she *shall* chew it, too. So there, now!"

"Say no more, my dear. I now see the force of your reasoning, and I will go and order two or three cords of the best pine wood to-day. No child of mine shall want while I—"

"Oh, *please* go along to your office and let me have some peace. A body can never make the simplest remark but you must take it up and go to arguing and arguing and arguing till you don't know what you are talking about, and you *never* do."

"Very well, it shall be as you say. But there is a want of logic in your last remark which—"

However, she was gone with a flourish before I could finish, and had taken the child with her. That night at dinner she confronted me with a face as white as a sheet:

"Oh, Mortimer, there's another! Little Georgie Gordon is taken."

"Membranous croup?"

"Membranous croup."

"Is there any hope for him?"

"None in the wide world. Oh, what is to become of us!"

By and by a nurse brought in our Penelope to say good night and offer the customary prayer at the mother's knee. In the midst of "Now I lay me down to sleep," she gave a slight cough! My wife fell back like one stricken with death. But the next moment she was up and brimming with the activities which terror inspires.

She commanded that the child's crib be removed from the nursery to our bedroom; and she went along to see the order executed. She took me with her, of course. We got matters arranged with speed. A cot-bed was put up in my wife's dressing-room for the nurse. But now Mrs. McWilliams said we were too far away from the other baby, and what if *he* were to have the symptoms in the night—and she blanched again, poor thing.

We then restored the crib and the nurse to the nursery and put up a bed for ourselves in a room adjoining.

Presently, however, Mrs. McWilliams said suppose the baby should catch it from Penelope? This thought struck a new panic to her heart, and the tribe of us could not get the crib out of the nursery again fast enough to satisfy my wife, though she assisted in her own person and well-nigh pulled the crib to pieces in her frantic hurry.

We moved downstairs; but there was no place there to stow the nurse, and Mrs. McWilliams said the nurse's experience would be an inestimable help. So we returned, bag and baggage, to our own bedroom once more, and felt a great gladness, like storm-buffeted birds that have found their nest again.

Mrs. McWilliams sped to the nursery to see how things were going on there. She was back in a moment with a new dread. She said:

"What *can* make Baby sleep so?"

I said:

"Why, my darling, Baby *always* sleeps like a graven image."

"I know. I know; but there's something peculiar about his sleep now. He seems to—to—he seems to breathe so *regularly*. Oh, this is dreadful."

"But, my dear, he always breathes regularly."

"Oh, I know it, but there's something frightful about it now. His nurse is too young and inexperienced. Maria shall stay there with her, and be on hand if anything happens."

"That is a good idea, but who will help *you?*"

"You can help me all I want. I wouldn't allow anybody to do anything but myself, anyhow, at such a time as this."

I said I would feel mean to lie abed and sleep, and leave her to watch and toil over our little patient all the weary night. But she reconciled me to it. So old Maria departed and took up her ancient quarters in the nursery.

Penelope coughed twice in her sleep.

"Oh, why *don't* that doctor come! Mortimer, this room is too warm. This room is certainly too warm. Turn off the register—quick!"

I shut it off, glancing at the thermometer at the same time, and wondering to myself if 70 *was* too warm for a sick child.

The coachman arrived from down-town now with the news that our physician was ill and confined to his bed. Mrs. McWilliams turned a dead eye upon me, and said in a dead voice:

"There is a Providence in it. It is foreordained. He never was sick before. Never. We have not been living as we ought to live, Mortimer. Time and time again I have told you so. Now you see the result. Our child will never get well. Be thankful if you can forgive yourself; I never can forgive *myself.*"

I said, without intent to hurt, but with heedless choice of words, that I could not see that we had been living such an abandoned life.

"*Mortimer!* Do you want to bring the judgment upon Baby, too!"

Then she began to cry, but suddenly exclaimed:

"The doctor must have sent medicines!"

I said:

"Certainly. They are here. I was only waiting for you to give me a chance."

"Well do give them to me! Don't you know that every moment is precious now? But what was the use in sending medicines, when he *knows* that the disease is incurable?"

I said that while there was life there was hope.

"Hope! Mortimer, you know no more what you are talking about than the child unborn. If you would— As I live, the directions say give one teaspoonful once an hour! Once an hour!—as if we had a whole year before us to save the child in! Mortimer, please hurry. Give the poor perishing thing a tablespoonful, and *try* to be quick!"

"Why, my dear, a tablespoonful might—"

"*Don't* drive me frantic! . . . There, there, there, my precious, my own; it's nasty bitter stuff, but it's good for Nelly—good for mother's precious darling; and it will make her well. There, there, there, put the little head on mamma's breast and go to sleep, and pretty soon—oh, I know she can't live till morning! Mortimer, a tablespoonful every half-hour will— Oh, the child needs belladonna, too; I know she does—and aconite. Get them, Mortimer. Now do let me have my way. You know nothing about these things."

We now went to bed, placing the crib close to my wife's pillow. All this turmoil had worn upon me, and within two minutes I was something more than half asleep. Mrs. McWilliams roused me:

"Darling, is that register turned on?"

"No."

"I thought as much. Please turn it on at once. This room is cold."

I turned it on, and presently fell asleep again. I was aroused once more:

"Dearie, would you mind moving the crib to your side of the bed? It is nearer the register."

I moved it, but had a collision with the rug and woke up the child. I dozed off once more, while my wife quieted the sufferer. But in a little while these words came murmuring remotely through the fog of my drowsiness:

"Mortimer, if we only had some goose grease—will you ring?"

I climbed dreamily out, and stepped on a cat, which

responded with a protest and would have got a convincing kick for it if a chair had not got it instead.

"Now, Mortimer, why do you want to turn up the gas and wake up the child again?"

"Because I want to see how much I am hurt, Caroline."

"Well, look at the chair, too—I have no doubt it is ruined. Poor cat, suppose you had—"

"Now I am not going to suppose anything about the cat. It never would have occurred if Maria had been allowed to remain here and attend to these duties, which are in her line and are not in mine."

"Now, Mortimer, I should think you would be ashamed to make a remark like that. It is a pity if you cannot do the few little things I ask of you at such an awful time as this when our child—"

"There, there, I will do anything you want. But I can't raise anybody with this bell. They're all gone to bed. Where is the goose grease?"

"On the mantelpiece in the nursery. If you'll step there and speak to Maria—"

I fetched the goose grease and went to sleep again. Once more I was called:

"Mortimer, I so hate to disturb you, but the room is still too cold for me to try to apply this stuff. Would you mind lighting the fire? It is all ready to touch a match to."

I dragged myself out and lit the fire, and then sat down disconsolate.

"Mortimer, don't sit there and catch your death of cold. Come to bed."

As I was stepping in she said:

"But wait a moment. Please give the child some more of the medicine."

Which I did. It was a medicine which made a child more or less lively; so my wife made use of its waking interval to strip it and grease it all over with the goose oil. I was soon asleep once more, but once more I had to get up.

"Mortimer, I feel a draft. I feel it distinctly. There is nothing so bad for this disease as a draft. Please move the crib in front of the fire."

I did it; and collided with the rug again, which I threw in the fire. Mrs. McWilliams sprang out of bed and rescued it and we had some words. I had another trifling interval of sleep, and then got up, by request, and constructed a flax-seed poultice. This was placed upon the child's breast and left there to do its healing work.

A wood-fire is not a permanent thing. I got up every twenty minutes and renewed ours, and this gave Mrs. McWilliams the opportunity to shorten the times of giving the medicines by ten minutes, which was a great satisfaction to her. Now and then, between times, I reorganized the flax-seed poultices, and applied sinapisms and other sorts of blisters where unoccupied places could be found upon the child. Well, toward morning the wood gave out and my wife wanted me to go down cellar and get some more. I said:

"My dear, it is a laborious job, and the child must be nearly warm enough, with her extra clothing. Now mightn't we put on another layer of poultices and—"

I did not finish, because I was interrupted. I lugged wood up from below for some little time, and then turned in and fell to snoring as only a man can whose strength is all gone and whose soul is worn out. Just at broad daylight I felt a grip on my shoulder that brought me to my senses suddenly. My wife was glaring down upon me and gasping. As soon as she could command her tongue she said:

"It is all over! All over! The child's perspiring! What *shall* we do?"

"Mercy, how you terrify me! *I* don't know what we ought to do. Maybe if we scraped her and put her in the draft again—"

"Oh, idiot! There is not a moment to lose! Go for the doctor. Go yourself. Tell him he *must* come, dead or alive."

I dragged that poor sick man from his bed and brought

him. He looked at the child and said she was not dying. This was joy unspeakable to me, but it made my wife as mad as if he had offered her a personal affront. Then he said the child's cough was only caused by some trifling irritation or other in the throat. At this I thought my wife had a mind to show him the door. Now the doctor said he would make the child cough harder and dislodge the trouble. So he gave her something that sent her into a spasm of coughing, and presently up came a little wood splinter or so.

"This child has no membranous croup," said he. "She has been chewing a bit of pine shingle or something of the kind, and got some little slivers in her throat. They won't do her any hurt."

"No," said I, "I can well believe that. Indeed, the turpentine that is in them is very good for certain sorts of diseases that are peculiar to children. My wife will tell you so."

But she did not. She turned away in disdain and left the room; and since that time there is one episode in our life which we never refer to. Hence the tide of our days flows by in deep and untroubled serenity.

Very few married men have such an experience as McWilliams's, and so the author of this book thought that maybe the novelty of it would give it a passing interest to the reader.

1875

The Canvasser's Tale

Poor, sad-eyed stranger! There was that about his humble mien, his tired look, his decayed-gentility clothes, that almost reached the mustard-seed of charity that still remained, remote and lonely, in the empty vastness of my heart, notwithstanding I observed a portfolio under his arm, and said to myself, Behold, Providence hath delivered his servant into the hands of another canvasser.

Well, these people always get one interested. Before I well knew how it came about, this one was telling me his history, and I was all attention and sympathy. He told it something like this:

My parents died, alas, when I was a little, sinless child. My uncle Ithuriel took me to his heart and reared me as his own. He was my only relative in the wide world; but he was good and rich and generous. He reared me in the lap of luxury. I knew no want that money could satisfy.

In the fullness of time I was graduated, and went with two of my servants—my chamberlain and my valet—to travel in foreign countries. During four years I flitted upon careless wing amid the beauteous gardens of the distant strand, if you will permit this form of speech in one whose tongue was ever attuned to poesy; and indeed I so speak with confidence, as one unto his kind, for I perceive by your eyes that you too, sir, are gifted with the divine inflation. In those far lands I reveled in the ambrosial food that fructifies the soul, the mind, the heart. But of all things, that which most appealed to my inborn esthetic taste was the prevailing custom there, among the rich, of making collections of elegant and costly rarities, dainty *objets de vertu,* and in an evil hour I tried to uplift my uncle Ithuriel to a plane of sympathy with this exquisite employment.

I wrote and told him of one gentleman's vast collection of shells; another's noble collection of meerschaum pipes; another's elevating and refining collection of undecipherable autographs; another's priceless collection of old china; another's enchanting collection of postage-stamps—and so forth and so on. Soon my letters yielded fruit. My uncle began to look about for something to make a collection of. You may know, perhaps, how fleetly a taste like this dilates. His soon became a raging fever, though I knew it not. He began to neglect his great pork business; presently he wholly retired and turned an elegant leisure into a rabid search for curious things. His wealth was vast, and he spared it not. First he tried cow-bells. He made a collection which filled five large *salons,* and comprehended all the different sorts of cow-bells that ever had been contrived, save one. That one—an antique, and the only specimen extant—was possessed by another collector. My uncle offered enormous sums for it, but the gentleman would not sell. Doubtless you know what necessarily resulted. A true collector attaches no value to a collection that is not complete. His great heart breaks, he sells his hoard, he turns his mind to some field that seems unoccupied.

Thus did my uncle. He next tried brickbats. After piling up a vast and intensely interesting collection, the former difficulty supervened; his great heart broke again; he sold out his soul's idol to the retired brewer who possessed the missing brick. Then he tried flint hatchets and other implements of Primeval Man, but by and by discovered that the factory where they were made was supplying other collectors as well as himself. He tried Aztec inscriptions and stuffed whales—another failure, after incredible labor and expense. When his collection seemed at last perfect, a stuffed whale arrived from Greenland and an Aztec inscription from the Cundurango regions of Central America that made all former specimens insignificant. My uncle hastened to secure these noble gems. He got the stuffed whale, but another collector got the inscription. A real Cundurango, as possibly you know, is a possession of such supreme value that, when once a collector gets it, he will rather part with his family than with it. So my uncle sold out, and saw his darlings go forth, never more to return; and his coal-black hair turned white as snow in a single night.

Now he waited, and thought. He knew another disappointment might kill him. He was resolved that he would choose things next time that no other man was collecting. He carefully made up his mind, and once more entered the field—this time to make a collection of echoes.

"Of what?" said I.

Echoes, sir. His first purchase was an echo in Georgia that repeated four times; his next was a six-repeater in Maryland; his next was a thirteen-repeater in Maine; his next was a nine-repeater in Kansas; his next was a twelve-repeater in Tennessee, which he got cheap, so to speak, because it was out of repair, a portion of the crag which reflected it having tumbled down. He believed he could repair it at a cost of a few thousand dollars, and, by increasing the elevation with masonry, treble the repeating capacity; but the architect who undertook the job had never built an echo before, and so he utterly spoiled this one. Before he meddled with it, it used to talk back like a mother-in-law, but now it was only fit for the deaf-and-dumb asylum. Well, next he bought a lot of cheap little double-barreled echoes, scattered around over various states and territories; he got them at twenty per cent off by taking the lot. Next he bought a perfect Gatling-gun of an echo in Oregon, and it cost a fortune, I can tell you.

You may know, sir, that in the echo market the scales of prices is cumulative, like the carat-scale in diamonds; in fact, the same phraseology is used. A single-carat echo is worth but ten dollars over and above the value of the land it is on; a two-carat or double-barreled echo is worth thirty dollars; a five-carat is worth nine hundred and fifty; a ten-carat is worth thirteen thousand. My uncle's Oregon echo, which he called the Great Pitt Echo, was a twenty-two carat gem, and cost two hundred and sixteen thousand dollars—they threw the land in, for it was four hundred miles from a settlement.

Well, in the mean time my path was a path of roses. I was the accepted suitor of the only and lovely daughter of an English earl, and was beloved to distraction. In that dear presence I swam in seas of bliss. The family were content, for it was known that I was sole heir to an uncle held to be worth five millions of dollars. However, none of us knew that my uncle had become a collector, at least in anything more than a small way, for asthetic amusement.

Now gathered the clouds above my unconscious head. That divine echo, since known throughout the world as the Great Koh-i-noor, or Mountain of Repetitions, was discovered. It was a sixty-five-carat gem. You could utter a word and it would talk back at you for fifteen minutes, when the day was otherwise quiet. But behold, another fact came to light at the same time: another echo-collector was in the field. The two rushed to make the peerless purchase. The property consisted of a couple of small hills with a shallow swale between, out yonder among the back settlements of New York State. Both men arrived on the ground at the same time, and neither knew the other was there. The echo was not all owned by one man; a person by the name of Williamson Bolivar Jarvis owned the east hill, and a person by the name of Harbison J. Bledso owned the west hill; the swale between was the dividing-line. So while my uncle was buying Jarvis's hill for three million two hundred and eighty-five thousand dollars, the other party was buying Bledso's hill for a shade over three million.

Now, do you perceive the natural result? Why, the noblest collection of echoes on earth was forever and ever incomplete, since it possessed but the one-half of the king echo of the universe. Neither man was content with this divided ownership, yet neither would sell to the other. There were jawings, bickerings, heart-burnings. And at last that other collector, with a malignity which only a collector can ever feel toward a man and a brother, proceeded to cut down his hill!

You see, as long as he could not have the echo, he was resolved that nobody should have it. He would remove his hill, and then there would be nothing to reflect my uncle's echo. My uncle remonstrated with him, but the man said, "I own one end of this echo; I choose to kill my end; you must take care of your own end yourself."

Well, my uncle got an injunction put on him. The other man appealed and fought it in a higher court. They carried it on up, clear to the Supreme Court of the United States. It made no end of trouble there. Two of the judges believed that an echo was personal property, because it was impalable to sight and touch, and yet was purchasable, salable, and consequently taxable; two others believed that an echo was real estate, because it was manifestly attached to the land, and was not removable from place to place; other of the judges contended that an echo was not property at all.

It was finally decided that the echo was property; that the hills were property; that the two men were separate and independent owners of the two hills, but tenants in common in the echo; therefore defendant was at full liberty to cut down his hill, since it belonged solely to him, but must give bonds in three million dollars as indemnity for damages which might result to my uncle's half of the echo. This decision also debarred my uncle from using defendant's hill to reflect his part of the echo, without defendant's consent;

he must use only his own hill; if his part of the echo would not go, under these circumstances, it was sad, of course, but the court could find no remedy. The court also debarred defendant from using my uncle's hill to reflect *his* end of the echo, without consent. You see the grand result! Neither man would give consent, and so that astonishing and most noble echo had to cease from its great powers; and since that day that magnificent property is tied up and unsalable.

A week before my wedding-day, while I was still swimming in bliss and the nobility were gathering from far and near to honor our espousals, came news of my uncle's death, and also a copy of his will, making me his sole heir. He was gone; alas, my dear benefactor was no more. The thought surcharges my heart even at this remote day. I handed the will to the earl; I could not read it for the blinding tears. The earl read it; then he sternly said, "Sir, do you call this wealth?—but doubtless you do in your inflated country. Sir, you are left sole heir to a vast collection of echoes—if a thing can be called a collection that is scattered far and wide over the huge length and breadth of the American continent; sir, this is not all; you are head and ears in debt; there is not an echo in the lot but has a mortgage on it; sir, I am not a hard man, but I must look to my child's interest; if you had but one echo which you could honestly call your own, if you had but one echo which was free from incumbrance, so that you could retire to it with my child, and by humble, painstaking industry cultivate and improve it, and thus wrest from it a maintenance, I would not say you nay; but I cannot marry my child to a beggar. Leave his side, my darling; go, sir, take your mortgage-ridden echoes and quit my sight forever."

My noble Celestine clung to me in tears, with loving arms, and swore she would willingly, nay gladly, marry me, though I had not an echo in the world. But it could not be. We were torn asunder, she to pine and die within the twelvemonth, I to toil life's long journey sad and alone, praying daily, hourly, for that release which shall join us together again in that dear realm where the wicked cease from troubling and the weary are at rest. Now, sir, if you will be so kind as to look at these maps and plans in my portfolio, I am sure I can sell you an echo for less money than any man in the trade. Now this one, which cost my uncle ten dollars, thirty years ago, and is one of the sweetest things in Texas, I will let you have for—

"Let me interrupt you," I said. "My friend, I have not had a moment's respite from canvassers this day. I have bought a sewing-machine which I did not want; I have bought a map which is mistaken in all its details; I have bought a clock which will not go; I have bought a moth poison which the moths prefer to any other beverage; I have bought no end of useless inventions, and now I have had enough of this foolishness. I would not have one of your echoes if you were even to give it to me. I would not let it stay on the place. I always hate a man that tries to sell me echoes. You see this gun? Now take your collection and move on; let us not have bloodshed."

But he only smiled a sad, sweet smile, and got out some more diagrams. You know the result perfectly well, because you know that when you have once opened the door to a canvasser, the trouble is done and you have got to suffer defeat.

I compromised with this man at the end of an intolerable hour. I bought two double-barreled echoes in good condition, and he threw in another, which he said was not salable because it only spoke German. He said, "She was a perfect polyglot once, but somehow her palate got down."

1876

The Facts Concerning the Recent Carnival of Crime in Connecticut

I was feeling blithe, almost jocund. I put a match to my cigar, and just then the morning's mail was handed in. The first superscription I glanced at was in a handwriting that sent a thrill of pleasure through and through me. It was Aunt Mary's; and she was the person I loved and honored most in all the world, outside of my own household. She had been my boyhood's idol; maturity, which is fatal to so many enchantments, had not been able to dislodge her from her pedestal; no, it had only justified her right to be there, and placed her dethronement permanently among the impossibilities. To show how strong her influence over me was, I will observe that long after everybody else's "*do*-stop-smoking" had ceased to affect me in the slightest degree, Aunt Mary could still stir my torpid conscience into faint signs of life when she touched upon the matter. But all things have their limit in this world. A happy day came at last, when even Aunt Mary's words could no longer move me. I was not merely glad to see that day arrive; I was more than glad—I was grateful; for when its sun had set, the one alloy that was able to mar my enjoyment of my aunt's society was gone. The remainder of her stay with us that winter was in every way a delight. Of course she pleaded with me just as earnestly as ever, after that blessed day, to quit my pernicious habit, but to no purpose whatever; the moment she opened the subject I at once became calmly, peacefully, contentedly indifferent—absolutely, adamantinely indifferent. Consequently the closing weeks of that memorable visit melted away as pleasantly as a dream, they were so freighted for me with tranquil satisfaction. I could not have enjoyed my pet vice more if my gentle tormentor had been a smoker herself, and an advocate of the practice. Well, the sight of her handwriting reminded me that I was getting very hungry to see her again. I easily guessed what I should find in her letter. I opened it. Good! just as I expected; she was coming! Coming this very day, too, and by the morning train; I might expect her any moment.

I said to myself, "I am thoroughly happy and content now. If my most pitiless enemy could appear before me at this moment, I would freely right any wrong I may have done him."

Straightway the door opened, and a shriveled, shabby dwarf entered. He was not more than two feet high. He seemed to be about forty years old. Every feature and every inch of him was a trifle out of shape; and so, while one could not put his finger upon any particular part and say, "This is a conspicuous deformity," the spectator perceived that this little person was a deformity as a whole—a vague, general, evenly blended, nicely adjusted deformity. There was a fox-like cunning in the face and the sharp little eyes, and also alertness and malice. And yet, this vile bit of human rubbish seemed to bear a sort of remote and ill-defined resemblance to me! It was dully perceptible in the mean form, the countenance, and even the clothes, gestures, manner, and attitudes of the creature. He was a far-fetched, dim suggestion of a burlesque upon me, a caricature of me in little. One thing about him struck me forcibly and most unpleasantly: he was covered all over with a fuzzy greenish mold, such as one sometimes sees upon mildewed bread. The sight of it was nauseating.

He stepped along with a chipper air, and flung himself into a doll's chair in a very free-and-easy way, without waiting to be asked. He tossed his hat into the waste-basket. He picked up my old chalk pipe from the floor, gave the stem a wipe or two on his knee, filled the bowl from the tobacco-box at his side, and said to me in a tone of pert command:

"Gimme a match!"

I blushed to the roots of my hair; partly with indignation, but mainly because it somehow seemed to me that his whole performance was very like an exaggeration of conduct which I myself had sometimes been guilty of in my intercourse with familiar friends—but never, never with strangers, I observed to myself. I wanted to kick the pygmy into the fire, but some incomprehensible sense of being legally and legitimately under his authority forced me to obey his order. He applied the match to the pipe, took a contemplative whiff or two, and remarked, in an irritatingly familiar way:

"Seems to me it's devilish odd weather for this time of year."

I flushed again, and in anger and humiliation as before; for the language was hardly an exaggeration of some that I have uttered in my day, and moreover was delivered in a tone of voice and with an exasperating drawl that had the seeming of a deliberate travesty of my style. Now there is nothing I am quite so sensitive about as a mocking imitation of my drawling infirmity of speech. I spoke up sharply and said:

"Look here, you miserable ash-cat! you will have to give a little more attention to your manners, or I will throw you out of the window!"

The manikin smiled a smile of malicious content and security, puffed a whiff of smoke contemptuously toward me, and said; with a still more elaborate drawl:

"Come—go gently now; don't put on *too* many airs with your betters."

This cool snub rasped me all over, but it seemed to subjugate me, too, for a moment. The pygmy contemplated me awhile with his weasel eyes, and then said, in a peculiarly sneering way:

"You turned a tramp away from your door this morning."

I said crustily:

"Perhaps I did, perhaps I didn't. How do *you* know?"

"Well, I know. It isn't any matter *how* I know."

"Very well. Suppose I *did* turn a tramp away from the door—what of it?"

"Oh, nothing; nothing in particular. Only you lied to him."

"I *didn't!* That is, I—"

"Yes, but you did; you lied to him."

I felt a guilty pang—in truth, I had felt it forty times before that tramp had traveled a block from my door—but still I resolved to make a show of feeling slandered; so I said:

"This is a baseless impertinence. I said to the tramp—"

"There—wait. You were about to lie again. *I* know what you said to him. You said the cook was gone down-town and there was nothing left from breakfast. Two lies. You knew the cook was behind the door, and plenty of provisions behind *her.*"

This astonishing accuracy silenced me; and it filled me with wondering speculations, too, as to how this cub could have got his information. Of course he could have culled the conversation from the tramp, but by what sort of magic had he contrived to find out about the concealed cook? Now the dwarf spoke again:

"It was rather pitiful, rather small, in you to refuse to read that poor young woman's manuscript the other day, and give her an opinion as to its literary value; and she had come so far, too, and *so* hopefully. Now *wasn't* it?"

I felt like a cur! And I had felt so every time the thing had recurred to my mind, I may as well confess. I flushed hotly and said:

"Look here, have you nothing better to do than prowl

around prying into other people's business? Did that girl tell you that?"

"Never mind whether she did or not. The main thing is, you did that contemptible thing. And you felt ashamed of it afterward. Aha! you feel ashamed of it *now*!"

This was a sort of devilish glee. With fiery earnestness I responded:

"I told that girl, in the kindest, gentlest way, that I could not consent to deliver judgment upon *any* one's manuscript, because an individual's verdict was worthless. It might underrate a work of high merit and lose it to the world, or it might overrate a trashy production and so open the way for its infliction upon the world. I said that the great public was the only tribunal competent to sit in judgment upon a literary effort, and therefore it must be best to lay it before that tribunal in the outset, since in the end it must stand or fall by that mighty court's decision anyway."

"Yes, you said all that. So you did, you juggling, small-souled shuffler! And yet when the happy hopefulness faded out of that poor girl's face, when you saw her furtively slip beneath her shawl the scroll she had so patiently and honestly scribbled at—so ashamed of her darling now, so proud of it before—when you saw the gladness go out of her eyes and the tears come there, when she crept away so humbly who had come so—"

"Oh, peace! peace! peace! Blister your merciless tongue, haven't all these thoughts tortured me enough without *your* coming here to fetch them back again!"

Remorse! remorse! It seemed to me that it would eat the very heart out of me! And yet that small fiend only sat there leering at me with joy and contempt, and placidly chuckling. Presently he began to speak again. Every sentence was an accusation, and every accusation a truth. Every clause was freighted with sarcasm and derision, every slow-dropping word burned like vitriol. The dwarf reminded me of times when I had flown at my children in anger and punished them for faults which a little inquiry would have taught me that others, and not they, had committed. He reminded me of how I had disloyally allowed old friends to be traduced in my hearing, and been too craven to utter a word in their defense. He reminded me of many dishonest things which I had done; of many which I had procured to be done by children and other irresponsible persons; of some which I had planned, thought upon, and longed to do, and been kept from the performance by fear of consequences only. With exquisite cruelty he recalled to my mind, item by item, wrongs and unkindnesses I had inflicted and humiliations I had put upon friends since dead, "who died thinking of those injuries, maybe, and grieving over them," he added, by way of poison to the stab.

"For instance," said he, "take the case of your younger brother, when you two were boys together, many a long year ago. He always lovingly trusted in you with a fidelity that your manifold treacheries were not able to shake. He followed you about like a dog, content to suffer wrong and abuse if he might only be with you; patient under these injuries so long as it was your hand that inflicted them. The latest picture you have of him in health and strength must be such a comfort to you! You pledged your honor that if he would let you blindfold him no harm should come to him; and then, giggling and choking over the rare fun of the joke, you led him to a brook thinly glazed with ice, and pushed him in; and how you did laugh! Man, you will never forget the gentle, reproachful look he gave you as he struggled shivering out, if you live a thousand years! Oho! you see it now, you see it *now!*"

"Beast, I have seen it a million times, and shall see it a million more! and may you rot away piecemeal, and suffer till doomsday what I suffer now, for bringing it back to me again!"

The dwarf chuckled contentedly, and went on with his accusing history of my career. I dropped into a moody, vengeful state, and suffered in silence under the merciless lash. At last this remark of his gave me a sudden rouse:

"Two months ago, on a Tuesday, you woke up, away in the night, and fell to thinking, with shame, about a peculiarly mean and pitiful act of yours toward a poor ignorant Indian in the wilds of the Rocky Mountains in the winter of eighteen hundred and—"

"Stop a moment, devil! Stop! Do you mean to tell me that even my very *thoughts* are not hidden from you?"

"It seems to look like that. Didn't you think the thoughts I have just mentioned?"

"If I didn't, I wish I may never breathe again! Look here, friend—look me in the eye. Who *are* you?"

"Well, who do you think?"

"I think you are Satan himself. I think you are the devil."

"No."

'No? Then who *can* you be?"

"Would you really like to know?"

"*Indeed* I would."

"Well, I am your *Conscience!*"

In an instant I was in a blaze of joy and exultation. I sprang at the creature, roaring:

"Curse you, I have wished a hundred million times that you were tangible, and that I could get my hands on your throat once! Oh, but I will wreak a deadly vengeance on—"

Folly! Lightning does not move more quickly than my Conscience did! He darted aloft so suddenly that in the moment my fingers clutched the empty air he was already perched on the top of the high bookcase, with his thumb at his nose in token of derision. I flung the poker at him, and missed. I fired the bootjack. In a blind rage I flew from place to place, and snatched and hurled any missile that came handy; the storm of books, inkstands, and chunks of coal gloomed the air and beat about the manikin's perch relentlessly, but all to no purpose; the nimble figure dodged every shot; and not only that, but burst into a cackle of sarcastic and triumphant laughter as I sat down exhausted. While I puffed and gasped with fatigue and excitement, my Conscience talked to this effect:

"My good slave, you are curiously witless—no, I mean characteristically so. In truth, you are always consistent, always yourself, always an ass. Otherwise it must have occurred to you that if you attempted this murder with a sad heart and a heavy conscience, I would droop under the burdening influence instantly. Fool, I should have weighed a ton, and could not have budged from the floor; but instead, you are so cheerfully anxious to kill me that your conscience is as light as a feather; hence I am away up here out of your reach. I can almost respect a mere ordinary sort of fool; but *you*—pah!"

I would have given anything, then, to be heavy-hearted, so that I could get this person down from there and take his life, but I could no more be heavy-hearted over such a desire than I could have sorrowed over its accomplishment. So I could only look longingly up at my master, and rave at the ill luck that denied me a heavy conscience the one only time that I had ever wanted such a thing in my life. By and by I got to musing over the hour's strange adventure, and of course my human curiosity began to work. I set myself to framing in my mind some questions for this fiend to answer. Just then one of my boys entered, leaving the door open behind him, and exclaimed:

"My! what *has* been going on here? The bookcase is all one riddle of—"

I sprang up in consternation, and shouted:

"Out of this! Hurry! Jump! Fly! Shut the door! Quick, or my Conscience will get away!"

The door slammed to, and I locked it. I glanced up and was grateful, to the bottom of my heart, to see that my owner was still my prisoner. I said:

"Hang you, I might have lost you! Children are the heedlessest creatures. But look here, friend, the boy did not seem to notice you at all; how is that?"

"For a very good reason. I am invisible to all but you."

I made a mental note of that piece of information with a good deal of satisfaction. I could kill this miscreant now, if I got a chance, and no one would know it. But this very reflection made me so light-hearted that my Conscience could hardly keep his seat, but was like to float aloft toward the ceiling like a toy balloon. I said, presently:

"Come, my Conscience, let us be friendly. Let us fly a flag of truce for a while. I am suffering to ask you some questions."

"Very well. Begin."

"Well, then, in the first place, why were you never visible to me before?"

"Because you never asked to see me before; that is, you never asked in the right spirit and the proper form before. You were just in the right spirit this time, and when you called for your most pitiless enemy I was that person by a very large majority, though you did not suspect it."

"Well, did that remark of mine turn you into flesh and blood?"

"No. It only made me visible to you. I am unsubstantial, just as other spirits are."

This remark prodded me with a sharp misgiving. If he was unsubstantial, how was I going to kill him? But I dissembled, and said persuasively:

"Conscience, it isn't sociable of you to keep at such a distance. Come down and take another smoke."

This was answered with a look that was full of derision, and with this observation added:

"Come where you can get at me and kill me? The invitation is declined with thanks."

"All right," said I to myself; "so it seems a spirit *can* be killed, after all; there will be one spirit lacking in this world, presently, or I lose my guess." Then I said aloud:

"Friend—"

"There; wait a bit. I am not your friend, I am your

enemy; I am not your equal, I am your master. Call me 'my lord,' if you please. You are too familiar."

"I don't like such titles. I am willing to call you *sir.* That is as far as—"

"We will have no argument about this. Just obey, that is all. Go on with your chatter."

"Very well, my lord—since nothing but my lord will suit you—I was going to ask you how long you will be visible to me?"

"Always!"

I broke out with strong indignation: "This is simply an outrage. That is what I think of it. You have dogged, and dogged, and *dogged* me, all the days of my life, invisible. That was misery enough; now to have such a looking thing as you tagging after me like another shadow all the rest of my days is an intolerable prospect. You have my opinion, my lord; make the most of it."

"My lad, there was never so pleased a conscience in this world as I was when you made me visible. It gives me an inconceivable advantage. *Now* I can look you straight in the eye, and call you names, and leer at you, jeer at you, sneer at you; and *you* know what eloquence there is in visible gesture and expression, more especially when the effect is heightened by audible speech. I shall always address you henceforth in your o-w-n s-n-i-v-e-l-i-n-g d-r-a-w-l—baby!"

I let fly with the coal-hod. No result. My lord said:

"Come, come! Remember the flag of truce!"

"Ah, I forgot that. I will try to be civil; and *you* try it, too, for a novelty. The idea of a *civil* conscience! It is a good joke; an excellent joke. All the consciences *I* have ever heard of were nagging, badgering, fault-finding, execrable savages! Yes; and always in a sweat about some poor little insignificant trifle or other—destruction catch the lot of them, *I* say! I would trade mine for the smallpox and seven kinds of consumption, and be glad of the chance. Now tell me, why *is* it that a conscience can't haul a man over the coals once, for an offense, and then let him alone? Why is it that it wants to keep on pegging at him, day and night and night and day, week in and week out, forever and ever, about the same old thing? There is no sense in that, and no reason in it. I think a conscience that will act like that is meaner than the very dirt itself."

"Well, *we* like it; that suffices."

"Do you do it with the honest intent to improve a man?"

That question produced a sarcastic smile, and this reply:

"No, sir. Excuse me. We do it simply because it is 'business.' It is our trade. The *purpose* of it is to improve the man, but *we* are merely disinterested agents. We are appointed by authority, and haven't anything to say in the matter. We obey orders and leave the consequences where they belong. But I am willing to admit this much: we *do* crowd the orders a trifle when we get a chance, which is most of the time. We enjoy it. We are instructed to remind a man a few times of an error; and I don't mind acknowledging that we try to give pretty good measure. And when we get hold of a man of a peculiarly sensitive nature, oh, but we do haze him! I have consciences to come all the way from China and Russia to see a person of that kind put through his paces, on a special occasion. Why, I knew a man of that sort who had accidentally crippled a mulatto baby; the news went abroad, and I wish you may never commit another sin if the consciences didn't flock from all over the earth to enjoy the fun and help his master exorcise him. That man walked the floor in torture for forty-eight hours, without eating or sleeping, and then blew his brains out. The child was perfectly well again in three weeks."

"Well, you are a precious crew, not to put it too strong. I think I begin to see now why you have always been a trifle inconsistent with me. In your anxiety to get all the juice you can out of a sin, you make a man repent of it in three or four different ways. For instance, you found fault with me for lying to that tramp, and I suffered over that. But it was only yesterday that I told a tramp the square truth, to wit, that, it being regarded as bad citizenship to encourage vagrancy, I would give him nothing. What did you do *then?* Why, you made me say to myself. 'Ah, it would have been so much kinder and more blameless to ease him off with a little white lie, and send him away feeling that if he could not have bread, the gentle treatment was at least something to be grateful for!' Well, I suffered all day about *that.* Three days before I had fed a tramp, and fed him freely, supposing it a virtuous act. Straight off you said, 'Oh, false citizen, to have fed a tramp, and fed him freely, supposing it a virtuous act. Straight off you said, 'Oh, false citizen, to have fed a tramp!' and I suffered as usual. I gave a tramp work; you objected to it—*after* the contract was made, of course; you never speak up beforehand. Next, I *refused* a tramp work; you objected to *that.* Next, I proposed to kill a tramp; you kept me awake all night, oozing remorse at every pore. Sure I was going to be right *this* time, I sent the next tramp away with my benediction; and I wish you may live as long as I do, if you didn't make me smart all night again because I didn't kill him. Is there *any* way of satisfying that malignant invention which is called a conscience?"

"Ha, ha! this is luxury! Go on!"

"But come, now, answer me that question. *Is* there any way?"

"Well, none that I propose to tell *you,* my son. Ass! I don't care *what* act you may turn your hand to, I can straightway whisper a word in your ear and make you think you have committed a dreadful meanness. It is my *business*—and my joy—to make you repent of everything you do. If I have fooled away any opportunities it was not intentional; I beg to assure you it was not intentional!"

"Don't worry; you haven't missed a trick that *I* know of. I never did a thing in all my life, virtuous or otherwise, that I didn't repent of in twenty-four hours. In church last Sunday I listened to a charity sermon. My first impulse was to give three hundred and fifty dollars; I repented of that and reduced it a hundred; repented of that and reduced it another hundred; repented of that and reduced it another hundred; repented of that and reduced the remaining fifty to twenty-five; repented of that and came down to fifteen; repented of that and dropped to two dollars and a half; when the plate came around at last, I repented once more and contributed ten cents. Well, when I got home, I did wish to goodness I had that ten cents back again! You never *did* let me get through a charity sermon without having something to sweat about."

"Oh, and I never shall, I never shall. You can always depend on me."

"I think so. Many and many's the restless night I've wanted to take you by the neck. If I could only get hold of you now!"

"Yes, no doubt. But I am not an ass; I am only the saddle of an ass. But go on, go on. You entertain me more than I like to confess."

"I am glad of that. (You will not mind my lying a little, to keep in practice.) Look here; not to be too personal, I think you are about the shabbiest and most contemptible little shriveled-up reptile that can be imagined. I am grateful enough that you are invisible to other people, for I should die with shame to be seen with such a mildewed monkey of a conscience as *you* are. Now if you were five or six feet high, and—"

"Oh, come! who is to blame?"

"*I* don't know."

"Why, you are; nobody else."

"Confound you, I wasn't consulted about your personal appearance."

"I don't care, you had a good deal to do with it, nevertheless. When you were eight or nine years old, I was seven feet high, and as pretty as a picture."

"I wish you had died young! So you have grown the wrong way, have you?"

"Some of us grow one way and some the other. You had a large conscience once; if you've a small conscience now I reckon there are reasons for it. However, both of us are to blame, you and I. You see, you used to be conscientious about a great many things; morbidly so, I may say. It was a great many years ago. You probably do not remember it now. Well, I took a great interest in my work, and I so enjoyed the anguish which certain pet sins of yours afflicted you with that I kept pelting at you until I rather overdid the matter. You began to rebel. Of course I began to lose ground, then, and shrivel a little—diminish in stature, get moldly, and grow deformed. The more I weakened, the more stubbornly you fastened on to those particular sins; till at last the places on my person that represent those vices became as callous as shark-skin. Take smoking, for instance. I played that card a little too long, and I lost. When people plead with you at this late day to quit that vice, that old callous place seems to enlarge and cover me all over like a shirt of mail. It exerts a mysterious, smothering effect; and presently I, your faithful hater, your devoted Conscience, go sound asleep! Sound? It is no name for it. I couldn't hear it thunder at such a time. You have some few other vices—perhaps eighty, or maybe ninety—that affect me in much the same way."

"This is flattering; you must be asleep a good part of your time."

"Yes, of late years. I should be asleep *all* the time but for the help I get."

"Who helps you?"

"Other consciences. Whenever a person whose conscience I am acquainted with tries to plead with you about the vices you are callous to, I get my friend to give his client a pang concerning some villainy of his own, and that shuts off his meddling and starts him off to hunt personal consolation. My field of usefulness is about trimmed down to tramps, budding authoresses, and that line of goods now;

but don't you worry—I'll harry you on *them* while they last! Just you put your trust in me."

"I think I can. But if you had only been good enough to mention these facts some thirty years ago, I should have turned my particular attention to sin, and I think that by this time I should not only have had you pretty permanently asleep on the entire list of human vices, but reduced to the size of a homeopathic pill, at that. That is about the style of conscience *I* am pining for. If I only had you shrunk down to a homeopathic pill, and could get my hands on you, would I put you in a glass case for a keepsake? No, sir. I would give you to a yellow dog! That is where *you* ought to be—you and all your tribe. You are not fit to be in society, in my opinion. Now another question. Do you know a good many consciences in this section?"

"Plenty of them."

"I would give anything to see some of them! Could you bring them here? And would they be visible to me?"

"Certainly not."

"I suppose I ought to have known that without asking. But no matter, you can describe them. Tell me about my neighbor Thompson's conscience, please."

"Very well. I know him intimately; have known him many years. I knew him when he was eleven feet high and of a faultless figure. But he is very rusty and tough and misshapen now, and hardly ever interests himself about anything. As to his present size—well, he sleeps in a cigar-box."

"Likely enough. There are few smaller, meaner men in this region than Hugh Thompson. Do you know Robinson's conscience?"

"Yes. He is a shade under four and a half feet high; used to be a blond; is a brunette now, but still shapely and comely."

"Well, Robinson is a good fellow. Do you know Tom Smith's conscience?"

"I have known him from childhood. He was thirteen inches high, and rather sluggish, when he was two years old—as nearly all of us are at that age. He is thirty-seven feet high now, and the stateliest figure in America. His legs are still racked with growing-pains, but he has a good time, nevertheless. Never sleeps. He is the most active and energetic member of the New England Conscience Club; is president of it. Night and day you can find him pegging away at Smith, panting with his labor, sleeves rolled up, countenance all alive with enjoyment. He has got his victim splendidly dragooned now. He can make poor Smith imagine that the most innocent little thing he does is an odious sin; and then he sets to work and almost tortures the soul out of him about it."

"Smith is the noblest man in all this section, and the purest; and yet is always breaking his heart because he cannot be good! Only a conscience *could* find pleasure in heaping agony upon a spirit like that. Do you know my aunt Mary's conscience?"

"I have seen her at a distance, but am not acquainted with her. She lives in the open air altogether, because no door is large enough to admit her."

"I can believe that. Let me see. Do you know the conscience of that publisher who once stole some sketches of mine for a 'series' of his, and then left me to pay the law expenses I had to incur in order to choke him off?"

"Yes. He has a wide fame. He was exhibited, a month ago, with some other antiquities, for the benefit of a recent Member of the Cabinet's conscience that was starving in exile. Tickets and fares were high, but I traveled for nothing by pretending to be the conscience of an editor, and got in for half-price by representing myself to be the conscience of a clergyman. However, the publisher's conscience, which was to have been the main feature of the entertainment, was a failure—as an exhibition. He was there, but what of that? The management had provided a microscope with a magnifying power of only thirty thousand diameters, and so nobody got to see him, after all. There was great and general dissatisfaction, of course, but—"

Just here there was an eager footstep on the stair; I opened the door, and my aunt Mary burst into the room. It was a joyful meeting and a cheery bombardment of questions and answers concerning family matters ensued. By and by my aunt said:

"But I am going to abuse you a little now. You promised me, the day I saw you last, that you would look after the needs of the poor family around the corner as faithfully as I had done it myself. Well, I found out by accident that you failed of your promise. *Was* that right?"

In simple truth, I never had thought of that family a second time! And now such a splintering pang of guilt shot through me! I glanced up at my Conscience. Plainly, my heavy heart was affecting him. His body was drooping forward; he seemed about to fall from the bookcase. My aunt continued:

"And think how you have neglected my poor *protégé* at the almshouse, you dear, hard-hearted promise-breaker!" I blushed scarlet, and my tongue was tied. As the sense of my guilty negligence waxed sharper and stronger, my Conscience began to sway heavily back and forth; and when my aunt, after a little pause, said in a grieved tone, "Since you never once went to see her, maybe it will not distress you now to know that that poor child died, months ago, utterly friendless and forsaken!" my Conscience could no longer bear up under the weight of my sufferings, but tumbled headlong from his high perch and struck the floor with a dull, leaden thump. He lay there writhing with pain and quaking with apprehension, but straining every muscle in frantic efforts to get up. In a fever of expectancy I sprang to the door, locked it, placed my back against it, and bent a watchful gaze upon my struggling master. Already my fingers were itching to begin their murderous work.

"Oh, what *can* be the matter!" exclaimed my aunt, shrinking from me, and following with her frightened eyes the direction of mine. My breath was coming in short, quick gasps now, and my excitement was almost uncontrollable. My aunt cried out:

"Oh, do not look so! You appall me! Oh, what can the matter be? What is it you see? Why do you stare so? Why do you work your fingers like that?"

"Peace, woman!" I said, in a hoarse whisper. "Look elsewhere; pay no attention to me; it is nothing—nothing. I am often this way. It will pass in a moment. It comes from smoking too much."

My injured lord was up, wild-eyed with terror, and trying to hobble toward the door. I could hardly breathe, I was so wrought up. My aunt wrung her hands, and said:

"Oh, I knew how it would be; I knew it would come to this at last! Oh, I implore you to crush out that fatal habit while it may yet be time! You must not, you shall not be deaf to my supplications longer!" My struggling Conscience showed sudden signs of weariness! "Oh, promise me you will throw off this hateful slavery of tobacco!" My Conscience began to reel drowsily, and grope with his hands—enchanting spectacle! "I beg you, I beseech you, I implore you! Your reason is deserting you! There is madness in your eye! It flames with frenzy! Oh, hear me, hear me, and be saved! See, I plead with you on my very knees!" As she sank before me my Conscience reeled again, and then drooped languidly to the floor, blinking toward me a last supplication for mercy, with heavy eyes. "Oh, promise, or you are lost! Promise, and be redeemed! Promise! Promise and live!" With a long-drawn sigh my conquered Conscience closed his eyes and fell fast asleep!

With an exultant shout I sprang past my aunt, and in an instant I had my lifelong foe by the throat. After so many years of waiting and longing, he was mine at last. I tore him to shreds and fragments. I rent the fragments to bits. I cast the bleeding rubbish into the fire, and drew into my nostrils the grateful incense of my burnt-offering. At last, and forever, my Conscience was dead!

I was a free man! I turned upon my poor aunt, who was almost petrified with terror, and shouted:

"Out of this with your paupers, your charities, your reforms, your pestilent morals! You behold before you a man whose life-conflict is done, whose soul is at peace; a man whose heart is dead to sorrow, dead to suffering, dead to remorse; a man WITHOUT A CONSCIENCE! In my joy I spare you, though I could throttle you and never feel a pang! Fly!"

She fled. Since that day my life is all bliss. Bliss, unalloyed bliss. Nothing in all the world could persuade me to have a conscience again. I settled all my old outstanding scores, and began the world anew. I killed thirty-eight persons during the first two weeks—all of them on account of ancient grudges. I burned a dwelling that interrupted my view. I swindled a widow and some orphans out of their last cow, which is a very good one, though not thoroughbred, I believe. I have also committed scores of crimes, of various kinds, and have enjoyed my work exceedingly, whereas it would formerly have broken my heart and turned my hair gray, I have no doubt.

In conclusion, I wish to state, by way of advertisement, that medical colleges desiring assorted tramps for scientific purposes, either by the gross, by cord measurement, or per ton, will do well to examine the lot in my cellar before purchasing elsewhere, as these were all selected and prepared by myself, and can be had at a low rate, because I wish to clear out my stock and get ready for the spring trade.

1876

The Loves of Alonzo Fitz Clarence and Rosannah Ethelton

1

It was well along in the forenoon of a bitter winter's day. The town of Eastport, in the state of Maine, lay buried under a deep snow that was newly fallen. The customary bustle in the streets was wanting. One could look long distances down them and see nothing but a dead-white emptiness, with silence to match. Of course I do not mean that you could *see* the silence—no, you could only hear it. The sidewalks were merely long, deep ditches, with steep snow walls on either side. Here and there you might hear the faint, far scrape of a wooden shovel, and if you were quick enough you might catch a glimpse of a distant black figure stooping and disappearing in one of those ditches, and reappearing the next moment with a motion which you would know meant the heaving out of a shovelful of snow. But you needed to be quick, for that black figure would not linger, but would soon drop that shovel and scud for the house, thrashing itself with its arms to warm them. Yes, it was too venomously cold for snow-shovelers or anybody else to stay out long.

Presently the sky darkened; then the wind rose and began to blow in fitful, vigorous gusts, which sent clouds of powdery snow aloft, and straight ahead, and everywhere.

Under the impulse of one of these gusts, great white drifts banked themselves like graves across the streets; a moment later another gust shifted them around the other way, driving a fine spray of snow from their sharp crests, as the gale drives the spume flakes from wave-crests at sea; a third gust swept that place as clean as your hand, if it saw fit. This was fooling, this was play; but each and all of the gusts dumped some snow into the sidewalk ditches, for that was business.

Alonzo Fitz Clarence was sitting in his snug and elegant little parlor, in a lovely blue silk dressing-gown, with cuffs and facings of crimson satin, elaborately quilted. The remains of his breakfast were before him, and the dainty and costly little table service added a harmonious charm to the grace, beauty, and richness of the fixed appointments of the room. A cheery fire was blazing on the hearth.

A furious gust of wind shook the windows, and a great wave of snow washed against them with a drenching sound, so to speak. The handsome young bachelor murmured:

"That means, no going out to-day. Well, I am content. But what to do for company? Mother is well enough, Aunt Susan is well enough; but these, like the poor, I have with me always. On so grim a day as this, one needs a new interest, a fresh element, to whet the dull edge of captivity. That was very neatly said, but it doesn't mean anything. One doesn't *want* the edge of captivity sharpened up, you know, but just the reverse."

He glanced at his pretty French mantel-clock.

"That clock's wrong again. That clock hardly ever knows what time it is; and when it does know, it lies about it—which amounts to the same thing. Alfred!"

There was no answer.

"Alfred! . . . Good servant, but as uncertain as the clock." Alonzo touched an electric bell button in the wall. He waited a moment, then touched it again; waited a few moments more, and said:

"Battery out of order, no doubt. But now that I have

started, I *will* find out what time it is." He stepped to a speaking-tube in the wall, blew its whistle, and called, "Mother!" and repeated it twice.

"Well, *that's* no use. Mother's battery is out of order, too. Can't raise anybody down-stairs—that is plain."

He sat down at a rosewood desk, leaned his chin on the left-hand edge of it and spoke, as if to the floor: "Aunt Susan!"

A low, pleasant voice answered, "Is that you, Alonzo?"

"Yes. I'm too lazy and comfortable to go down-stairs; I am in extremity, and I can't seem to scare up any help."

"Dear me, what is the matter?"

"Matter enough, I can tell you!"

"Oh, don't keep me in suspense, dear! What *is* it?"

"I want to know what time it is."

"You abominable boy, what a turn you did give me! Is that all?"

"All—on my honor. Calm yourself. Tell me the time, and receive my blessing."

"Just five minutes after nine. No charge—keep your blessing."

"Thanks. It wouldn't have impoverished me, aunty, nor so enriched you that you could live without other means."

He got up, murmuring, "Just five minutes after nine," and faced his clock. "Ah," said he, "you are doing better than usual. You are only thirty-four minutes wrong. Let me see . . . let me see. . . . Thirty-three and twenty-one are fifty-four; four times fifty-four are two hundred and thirty-six. One off, leaves two hundred and thirty-five. That's right."

He turned the hands of his clock forward till they marked twenty-five minutes to one, and said, "Now see if you can't keep right for a while . . . else I'll raffle you!"

He sat down at the desk again, and said, "Aunt Susan!"

"Yes, dear."

"Had breakfast?"

"Yes, indeed, an hour ago."

"Busy?"

"No—except sewing. Why?"

"Got any company?"

"No, but I expect some at half past nine."

"I wish *I* did. I'm lonesome. I want to talk to somebody."

"Very well, talk to me."

"But this is very private."

"Don't be afraid—talk right along, there's nobody here but me."

"I hardly know whether to venture or not, but—"

"But what? Oh, don't stop there! You *know* you can trust me, Alonzo—you know you can."

"I feel it, aunt, but this is very serious. It affects me deeply—me, and all the family—even the whole community."

"Oh, Alonzo, tell me! I will never breathe a word of it. What is it?"

"Aunt, if I might dare—"

"Oh, please go on! I love you, and feel for you. Tell me all. Confide in me. What *is* it?"

"The weather!"

"Plague take the weather! I don't see how you can have the heart to serve me so, Lon."

"There, there, aunty dear, I'm sorry; I am, on my honor. I won't do it again. Do you forgive me?"

"Yes, since you seem so sincere about it, though I know I oughtn't to. You will fool me again as soon as I have forgotten this time."

"No, I won't, honor bright. But such weather, oh, such weather! You've *got* to keep your spirits up artificially. It is snowy, and blowy, and gusty, and bitter cold! How is the weather with you?"

"Warm and rainy and melancholy. The mourners go about the streets with their umbrellas running streams from the end of every whalebone. There's an elevated double pavement of umbrellas stretching down the sides of the streets as far as I can see. I've got a fire for cheerfulness, and the windows open to keep cool. But it is vain, it is useless: nothing comes in but the balmy breath of December, with its burden of mocking odors from the flowers that possess the realm outside, and rejoice in their lawless profusion whilst the spirit of man is low, and flaunt their gaudy splendors in his face while his soul is clothed in sackcloth and ashes and his heart breaketh."

Alonzo opened his lips to say, "You ought to print that, and get it framed," but checked himself, for he heard his aunt speaking to some one else. He went and stood at the window and looked out upon the wintry prospect. The storm was driving the snow before it more furiously than ever; window-shutters were slamming and banging; a forlorn dog, with bowed head and tail withdrawn from service, was pressing his quaking body against a windward wall for shelter and protection; a young girl was plowing knee-deep through the drifts, with her face turned from the blast, and the cape of her waterproof blowing straight rearward over her head. Alonzo shuddered, and said with a sigh, "Better the slop, and the sultry rain, and even the insolent flowers, than this!"

He turned from the window, moved a step, and stopped in a listening attitude. The faint, sweet notes of a familiar song caught his ear. He remained there, with his head unconsciously bent forward, drinking in the melody, stirring neither hand nor foot, hardly breathing. There was a blemish in the execution of the song, but to Alonzo it seemed an added charm instead of a defect. This blemish consisted of a marked flatting of the third, fourth, fifth, sixth, and seventh notes of the refrain or chorus of the piece. When the music ended, Alonzo drew a deep breath, and said, "Ah, I never have heard 'In the Sweet By-and-By' sung like that before!"

He stepped quickly to the desk, listened a moment, and said in a guarded, confidential voice, "Aunty, who is this divine singer?"

"She is the company I was expecting. Stays with me a month or two. I will introduce you. Miss—"

"For goodness' sake, wait a moment, Aunt Susan! You never stop to think what you are about!"

He flew to his bedchamber, and returned in a moment perceptibly changed in his outward appearance, and remarking, snappishly:

"Hang it, she would have introduced me to this angel in that sky-blue dressing-gown with red-hot lapels! Women never think, when they get a-going."

He hastened and stood by the desk, and said eagerly, "Now, Aunty, I am ready," and fell to smiling and bowing with all the persuasiveness and elegance that were in him.

"Very well: Miss Rosannah Ethelton, let me introduce to you my favorite nephew, Mr. Alonzo Fitz Clarence. There! You are both good people, and I like you; so I am going to trust you together while I attend to a few household affairs. Sit down, Rosannah; sit down, Alonzo. Good-by; I sha'n't be gone long."

Alonzo had been bowing and smiling all the while, and motioning imaginary young ladies to sit down in imaginary chairs, but now he took a seat himself, mentally saying, "Oh, this is luck! Let the winds blow now, and the snow drive, and the heavens frown! Little I care!"

While these young people chat themselves into an acquaintanceship, let us take the liberty of inspecting the sweeter and fairer of the two. She sat alone, at her graceful ease, in a richly furnished apartment which was manifestly the private parlor of a refined and sensible lady, if signs and symbols may go for anything. For instance, by a low, comfortable chair stood a dainty, top-heavy workstand, whose summit was a fancifully embroidered shallow basket, with varicolored crewels, and other strings and odds and ends protruding from under the gaping lid and hanging down in negligent profusion. On the floor lay bright shreds of Turkey red, Prussian blue, and kindred fabrics, bits of ribbon, a spool or two, a pair of scissors, and a roll or so of tinted silken stuffs. On a luxurious sofa, upholstered with some sort of soft Indian goods wrought in black and gold threads interwebbed with other threads not so pronounced in color, lay a great square of coarse white stuff, upon whose surface a rich bouquet of flowers was growing, under the deft cultivation of the crochet-needle. The household cat was asleep on this work of art. In a bay-window stood an easel with an unfinished picture on it, and a palette and brushes on a chair beside it. There were books everywhere: Robertson's Sermons, Tennyson, Moody and Sankey, Hawthorne, *Rab and his Friends,* cook-books, prayer-books, pattern-books—and books about all kinds of odious and exasperating pottery, of course. There was a piano, with a deck-load of music, and more in a tender. There was a great plenty of pictures on the walls, on the shelves of the mantelpiece and around generally; where coigns of vantage offered were statuettes, and quaint and pretty gimcracks, and rare and costly specimens of peculiarly devilish china. The bay-window gave upon a garden that was ablaze with foreign and domestic flowers and flowering shrubs.

But the sweet young girl was the daintiest thing these premises, within or without, could offer for contemplation: delicately chiseled features, of Grecian cast; her complexion the pure snow of a japonica that is receiving a faint reflected enrichment from some scarlet neighbor of the garden; great, soft blue eyes fringed with long, curving lashes; an expression made up of the trustfulness of a child and the gentleness of a fawn; a beautiful head crowned with its own prodigal gold; a lithe and rounded figure, whose every attitude and movement was instinct with native grace.

Her dress and adornment were marked by that exquisite harmony that can come only of a fine natural taste perfected by culture. Her gown was of a simple magenta tulle, cut bias, traversed by three rows of light-blue flounces, with the selvage edges turned up with ashes-of-roses chenille;

over-dress of dark bay tarlatan with scarlet satin lambrequins; corn-colored polonaise, *en panier,* looped with mother-of-pearl buttons and silver cord, and hauled aft and made fast by buff velvet lashings; basque of lavender reps, picked out with valenciennes; low neck, short sleeves; maroon velvet necktie edged with delicate pink silk; inside handkerchief of some simple three-ply ingrain fabric of a soft saffron tint; coral bracelets and locket-chain; coiffure of forget-me-nots and lilies-of-the-valley massed around a noble calla.

This was all; yet even in this subdued attire she was divinely beautiful. Then what must she have been when adorned for the festival or the ball?

All this time she had been busily chatting with Alonzo, unconscious of our inspection. The minutes still sped, and still she talked. But by and by she happened to look up, and saw the clock. A crimson blush sent its rich flood through her cheeks, and she exclaimed:

"There, good-by, Mr. Fitz Clarence; I must go now!"

She sprang from her chair with such haste that she hardly heard the young man's answering good-by. She stood radiant, graceful, beautiful, and gazed, wondering, upon the accusing clock. Presently her pouting lips parted, and she said:

"Five minutes after eleven! Nearly two hours, and it did not seem twenty minutes! Oh, dear, what will he think of me!"

At the self same moment Alonzo was staring at *his* clock. And presently he said:

"Twenty-five minutes to three! Nearly two hours, and I didn't believe it was two minutes! Is it possible that this clock is humbugging again? Miss Ethelton! Just one moment, please. Are you there yet?"

"Yes, but be quick; I'm going right away."

"Would you be so kind as to tell me what time it is?"

The girl blushed again, murmured to herself, "It's right down cruel of him to ask me!" and then spoke up and answered with admirably counterfeited unconcern, "Five minutes after eleven."

"Oh, thank you! You have to go, now, have you?"

"Yes."

"I'm sorry."

No reply.

"Miss Ethelton!"

"Well?"

"You—you're there yet, *ain't* you?"

"Yes; but please hurry. What did you want to say?"

"Well, I—well, nothing in particular. It's very lonesome here. It's asking a great deal, I know, but would you mind talking with me again by and by—that is, if it will not trouble you too much?"

"I don't know—but I'll think about it. I'll try."

"Oh, thanks! Miss Ethelton! . . . Ah, me, she's gone, and here are the black clouds and the whirling snow and the raging winds come again! But she said *good-by*. She didn't say good morning. She said good-by! . . . The clock was right, after all. What a lightning-winged two hours it was!"

He sat down, and gazed dreamily into his fire for a while, then heaved a sigh and said:

"How wonderful it is! Two little hours ago I was a free man, and now my heart's in San Francisco!"

About that time Rosannah Ethelton, propped in the window seat of her bedchamber, book in hand, was gazing vacantly out over the rainy seas that washed the Golden Gate, and whispered to herself, "How different he is from poor Burley, with his empty head and his single little antic talent of mimicry!"

2

Four weeks later Mr. Sidney Algernon Burley was entertaining a gay luncheon company, in a sumptuous drawing-room on Telegraph Hill, with some capital imitations of the voices and gestures of certain popular actors and San Franciscan literary people and Bonanza grandees. He was elegantly upholstered, and was a handsome fellow, barring a trifling cast in his eye. He seemed very jovial, but nevertheless he kept his eye on the door with an expectant and uneasy watchfulness. By and by a nobby lackey appeared, and delivered a message to the mistress, who nodded her head understandingly. That seemed to settle the thing for Mr. Burley; his vivacity decreased little by little, and a dejected look began to creep into one of his eyes and a sinister one into the other.

The rest of the company departed in due time, leaving him with the mistress, to whom he said:

"There is no longer any question about it. She avoids me. She continually excuses herself. If I could see her, if I could speak to her only a moment—but this suspense—"

"Perhaps her seeming avoidance is mere accident, Mr. Burley. Go to the small drawing-room up-stairs and amuse yourself a moment. I will despatch a household order that is on my mind, and then I will go to her room. Without doubt she will be persuaded to see you."

Mr. Burley went up-stairs, intending to go to the small drawing-room, but as he was passing "Aunt Susan's" private parlor, the door of which stood slightly ajar, he heard a joyous laugh which he recognized; so without knock or announcement he stepped confidently in. But before he could make his presence known he heard words that harrowed up his soul and chilled his young blood. He heard a voice say:

"Darling, it has come!"

Then he heard Rosannah Ethelton, whose back was toward him, say:

"So has yours, dearest!"

He saw her bowed form bend lower; he heard her kiss something—not merely once, but again and again! His soul raged within him. The heart-breaking conversation went on:

"Rosannah, I knew you must be beautiful, but this is dazzling, this is blinding, this is intoxicating!"

"Alonzo, it is such happiness to hear you say it. I know it is not true, but I am *so* grateful to have you think it is, nevertheless! I knew you must have a noble face, but the grace and majesty of the reality beggar the poor creation of my fancy."

Burley heard that rattling shower of kisses again.

"Thank you, my Rosannah! The photograph flatters me, but you must not allow yourself to think of that. Sweetheart?"

"Yes, Alonzo."

"I am so happy, Rosannah."

"Oh, Alonzo, none that have gone before me knew what love was, none that come after me will ever know what happiness is. I float in a gorgeous cloudland, a boundless firmament of enchanted and bewildering ecstasy!"

"Oh, my Rosannah!—for you are mine, are you not?"

"Wholly, oh, wholly yours, Alonzo, now and forever! All the day long, and all through my nightly dreams, one song sings itself, and its sweet burden is, 'Alonzo Fitz Clarence, Alonzo Fitz Clarence, Eastport, state of Maine!' "

"Curse him, I've got his address, anyway!" roared Burley, inwardly, and rushed from the place.

Just behind the unconscious Alonzo stood his mother, a picture of astonishment. She was so muffled from head to heel in furs that nothing of herself was visible but her eyes and nose. She was a good allegory of winter, for she was powdered all over with snow.

Behind the unconscious Rosannah stood "Aunt Susan," another picture of astonishment. She was a good allegory of summer, for she was lightly clad, and was vigorously cooling the perspiration on her face with a fan.

Both of these women had tears of joy in their eyes.

"So ho!" exclaimed Mrs. Fitz Clarence, "this explains why nobody has been able to drag you out of your room for six weeks, Alonzo!"

"So ho!" exclaimed Aunt Susan, "this explains why you have been a hermit for the past six weeks, Rosannah!"

The young couple were on their feet in an instant, abashed, and standing like detected dealers in stolen goods awaiting Judge Lynch's doom.

"Bless you, my son! I am happy in your happiness. Come to your mother's arms, Alonzo!"

"Bless you, Rosannah, for my dear nephew's sake! Come to my arms!"

Then was there a mingling of hearts and of tears of rejoicing on Telegraph Hill and in Eastport Square.

Servants were called by the elders, in both places. Unto one was given the order, "Pile this fire high with hickory wood, and bring me a roasting-hot lemonade."

Unto the other was given the order, "Put out this fire, and bring me two palm-leaf fans and a pitcher of ice-water."

Then the young people were dismissed, and the elders sat down to talk the sweet surprise over and make the wedding plans.

Some minutes before this Mr. Burley rushed from the mansion on Telegraph Hill without meeting or taking formal leave of anybody. He hissed through his teeth, in unconscious imitation of a popular favorite in melodrama, "Him shall she never wed! I have sworn it! Ere great Nature shall have doffed her winter's ermine to don the emerald gauds of spring, she shall be mine!"

3

Two weeks later. Every few hours, during some three or four days, a very prim and devout-looking Episcopal clergyman, with a cast in his eye, had visited Alonzo. According to his card, he was the Rev. Melton Hargrave, of Cincinnati. He said he had retired from the ministry on account of his health. If he had said on account of ill-health, he would probably have erred, to judge by his wholesome looks and firm build. He was the inventor of an improvement in telephones, and hoped to make his bread by selling the privilege of using it. "At present," he continued, "a man may go and tap a telegraph wire which is conveying a song or a concert from one state to another, and he can attach his private telephone and steal a hearing of that music as it passes along. My invention will stop all that."

"Well," answered Alonzo, "if the owner of the music could not miss what was stolen, why should he care?"

"He shouldn't care," said the Reverend.

"Well?" said Alonzo, inquiringly.

"Suppose," replied the Reverend, "suppose that, instead of music that was passing along and being stolen, the burden of the wire was loving endearments of the most private and sacred nature?"

Alonzo shuddered from head to heel. "Sire, it is a priceless invention," said he; "I must have it at any cost."

But the invention was delayed somewhere on the road from Cincinnati, most unaccountably. The impatient Alonzo could hardly wait. The thought of Rosannah's sweet words being shared with him by some ribald thief was galling to him. The Reverend came frequently and lamented the delay, and told of measures he had taken to hurry things up. This was some little comfort to Alonzo.

One forenoon the Reverend ascended the stairs and knocked at Alonzo's door. There was no response. He entered, glanced eagerly around, closed the door softly, then ran to the telephone. The exquisitely soft and remote strains of the "Sweet By-and-By" came floating through the instrument. The singer was flatting, as usual, the five notes that follow the first two in the chorus, when the Reverend interrupted her with this word, in a voice which was an exact imitation of Alonzo's, with just the faintest flavor of impatience added:

"Sweetheart?"

"Yes, Alonzo?"

"Please don't sing that any more this week—try something modern."

The agile step that goes with a happy heart was heard on the stairs, and the Reverend, smiling diabolically, sought sudden refuge behind the heavy folds of the velvet window-curtains. Alonzo entered and flew to the telephone. Said he:

"Rosannah, dear, shall we sing something together?"

"Something *modern?*" asked she, with sarcastic bitterness.

"Yes, if you prefer."

"Sing it yourself, if you like!"

This snappishness amazed and wounded the young man. He said:

"Rosannah, that was not like you."

"I suppose it becomes me as much as your very polite speech became you, Mr. Fitz Clarence."

"*Mister* Fitz Clarence! Rosannah, there was nothing impolite about my speech."

"Oh, indeed! Of course, then, I misunderstood you, and I most humbly beg your pardon, ha-ha-ha! No doubt you said, 'Don't sing it any more *to-day.*' "

"Sing *what* any more to-day?"

"The song you mentioned, of course. How very obtuse we are, all of a sudden!"

"I never mentioned any song."

"Oh, you *didn't?*"

"No, I *didn't!*"

"I am compelled to remark that you *did.*"

"And I am obliged to reiterate that I *didn't.*"

"A second rudeness! That is sufficient, sir. I will never forgive you. All is over between us."

Then came a muffled sound of crying. Alonzo hastened to say:

"Oh, Rosannah, unsay those words! There is some dreadful mystery here, some hideous mistake. I am utterly earnest and sincere when I say I never said anything about any song. I would not hurt you for the whole world. . . . Rosannah, dear! . . . Oh, speak to me, won't you?"

There was a pause; then Alonzo heard the girl's sobbings retreating, and knew she had gone from the telephone. He rose with a heavy sigh, and hastened from the room, saying to himself, "I will ransack the charity missions and the haunts of the poor for my mother. She will persuade her that I never meant to wound her."

A minute later the Reverend was crouching over the telephone like a cat that knoweth the ways of the prey. He had not very many minutes to wait. A soft, repentant voice, tremulous with tears, said:

"Alonzo, dear, I have been wrong. You *could* not have said so cruel a thing. It must have been some one who imitated your voice in malice or in jest."

The Reverend coldly answered, in Alonzo's tones:

"You have said all was over between us. So let it be. I spur your proffered repentance, and despise it!"

Then he departed, radiant with fiendish triumph, to return no more with his imaginary telephonic invention forever.

Four hours afterward Alonzo arrived with his mother from her favorite haunts of poverty and vice. They summoned the San Francisco household; but there was no reply. They waited, and continued to wait, upon the voiceless telephone.

At length, when it was sunset in San Francisco, and three hours and a half after dark in Eastport, an answer to the oft-repeated cry of "Rosannah!"

But, alas, it was Aunt Susan's voice that spake. She said:

"I have been out all day; just got in. I will go and find her."

The watchers waited two minutes—five minutes—ten minutes. Then came these fatal words, in a frightened tone:

"She is gone, and her baggage with her. To visit another friend, she told the servants. But I found this note on the table in her room. Listen: 'I am gone; seek not to trace me out; my heart is broken; you will never see me more. Tell him I shall always think of him when I sing my poor "Sweet By-and-By," but never of the unkind words he said about it.' That is her note. Alonzo, Alonzo, what does it mean? What has happened?"

But Alonzo sat white and cold as the dead. His mother threw back the velvet curtains and opened a window. The cold air refreshed the sufferer, and he told his aunt his dismal story. Meantime his mother was inspecting a card which had disclosed itself upon the floor when she cast the curtains back. It read, "Mr. Sidney Algernon Burley, San Francisco."

"The miscreant!" shouted Alonzo, and rushed forth to seek the false Reverend and destroy him; for the card explained everything, since in the course of the lovers' mutual confessions they had told each other all about all the sweethearts they had ever had, and thrown no end of mud at their failings and foibles—for lovers always do that. It has a fascination that ranks next after billing and cooing.

4

During the next two months many things happened. It had early transpired that Rosannah, poor suffering orphan, had neither returned to her grandmother in Portland, Oregon, nor sent any word to her save a duplicate of the woeful note she had left in the mansion on Telegraph Hill. Whosoever was sheltering her—if she was still alive—had been persuaded not to betray her whereabouts, without doubt; for all efforts to find trace of her had failed.

Did Alonzo give her up? Not he. He said to himself, "She will sing that sweet song when she is sad; I shall find her." So he took his carpet-sack and a portable telephone, and shook the snow of his native city from his arctics, and went forth into the world. He wandered far and wide and in many states. Time and again, strangers were astounded to see a wasted, pale, and woe-worn man laboriously climb a telegraph-pole in wintry and lonely places, perch sadly there an hour, with his ear at a little box, then come sighing down, and wander wearily away. Sometimes they shot at him, as peasants do at aeronauts, thinking him mad and dangerous. Thus his clothes were much shredded by bullets and his person grievously lacerated. But he bore it all patiently.

In the beginning of his pilgrimage he used often to say, "Ah, if I could but hear the 'Sweet By-and-By'!" But toward the end of it he used to shed tears of anguish and say, "Ah, if I could but hear something else!"

Thus a month and three weeks drifted by, and at last some humane people seized him and confined him in a private mad-house in New York. He made no moan, for his strength was all gone, and with it all heart and all hope. The superintendent, in pity, gave up his own comfortable parlor and bedchamber to him and nursed him with affectionate devotion.

At the end of a week the patient was able to leave his bed for the first time. He was lying, comfortably pillowed, on a sofa, listening to the plaintive Miserere of the bleak March winds and the muffled sound of tramping feet in the street below—for it was about six in the evening, and New York was going home from work. He had a bright fire and the added cheer of a couple of student-lamps. So it was warm and snug within, though bleak and raw without; it was light and bright within, though outside it was as dark and dreary as if the world had been lit with Hartford gas. Alonzo smiled feebly to think how his loving vagaries had made him a maniac in the eyes of the world, and was proceeding to pursue his line of thought further, when a faint, sweet strain, the very ghost of sound, so remote and attenuated it seemed, struck upon his ear. His pulses stood still; he listened with parted lips and bated breath. The song flowed on—he waiting, listening, rising slowly and unconsciously from his recumbent position. At last he exclaimed:

"It is! it is she! Oh, the divine flatted notes!"

He dragged himself eagerly to the corner whence the sounds proceeded, tore aside a curtain, and discovered a telephone. He bent over, and as the last note died away he burst forth with the exclamation:

"Oh, thank Heaven, found at last! Speak to me, Rosannah, dearest! The cruel mystery has been unraveled; it was the villain Burley who mimicked my voice and wounded you with insolent speech!"

There was a breathless pause, a waiting age to Alonzo; then a faint sound came, framing itself into language:

"Oh, say those precious words again, Alonzo!"

"They are the truth, the veritable truth, my Rosannah, and you shall have the proof, ample and abundant proof!"

"Oh, Alonzo, stay by me! Leave me not for a moment! Let me feel that you are near me! Tell me we shall never be parted more! Oh, this happy hour, this blessed hour, this memorable hour!"

"We will make record of it, my Rosannah; every year, as this dear hour chimes from the clock, we will celebrate it with thanksgivings, all the years of our life."

"We will, we will, Alonzo!"

"Four minutes after six, in the evening, my Rosannah, shall henceforth—"

"Twenty-three minutes after twelve, afternoon, shall—"

"Why, Rosannah, darling, where are you?"

"In Honolulu, Sandwich Islands. And where are you? Stay by me; do not leave me for a moment. I cannot bear it. Are you at home?"

"No, dear, I am in New York—a patient in the doctor's hands."

An agonizing shriek came buzzing to Alonzo's ear, like the sharp buzzing of a hurt gnat; it lost power in traveling five thousand miles. Alonzo hastened to say:

"Calm yourself, my child. It is nothing. Already I am getting well under the sweet healing of your presence. Rosannah?"

"Yes, Alonzo? Oh, how you terrified me! Say on."

"Name the happy day, Rosannah!"

There was a little pause. Then a diffident small voice replied, "I blush—but it is with pleasure, it is with happiness. Would—would you like to have it soon?"

"This very night, Rosannah! Oh, let us risk no more delays. Let it be now!—this very night, this very moment!"

"Oh, you impatient creature! I have nobody here but my good old uncle, a missionary for a generation, and now retired from service—nobody but him and his wife. I would so dearly like it if your mother and your Aunt Susan—"

"*Our* mother and *our* Aunt Susan, my Rosannah."

"Yes, *our* mother and *our* Aunt Susan—I am content to word it so if it pleases you; I would so like to have them present."

"So would I. Suppose you telegraph Aunt Susan. How long would it take her to come?"

"The steamer leaves San Francisco day after tomorrow. The passage is eight days. She would he here the 31st of March."

"Then name the 1st of April; do, Rosannah, dear."

"Mercy, it would make us April fools, Alonzo!"

"So we be the happiest ones that that day's sun looks down upon in the whole broad expanse of the globe, why need we care? Call it the 1st of April, dear."

"Then the 1st of April it shall be, with all my heart!"

"Oh, happiness! Name the hour, too, Rosannah."

"I like the morning, it is so blithe. Will eight in the morning do, Alonzo?"

"The loveliest hour, in the day—since it will make you mine."

There was a feeble but frantic sound for some little time, as if wool-lipped, disembodied spirits were exchanging kisses; then Rosannah said, "Excuse me just a moment, dear; I have an appointment, and am called to meet it."

The young girl sought a large parlor and took her place at a window which looked out upon a beautiful scene. To the left one could view the charming Nuuana Valley, fringed with its ruddy flush of tropical flowers and its plumed and graceful cocoa palms; its rising foothills clothed in the shining green of lemon, citron, and orange groves; its storied precipice beyond, where the first Kamehameha drove his defeated foes over to their destruction—a spot that had forgotten its grim history, no doubt, for now it was smiling, as almost always at noonday, under the glowing arches of a succession of rainbows. In front of the window one could see the quaint town, and here and there a picturesque group of dusky natives, enjoying the blistering weather; and far to the right lay the restless ocean, tossing its white mane in the sunshine.

Rosannah stood there, in her filmy white raiment, fanning her flushed and heated face, waiting. A Kanaka boy, clothed in a damaged blue necktie and part of a silk hat, thrust his head in at the door, and announced, " 'Frisco *haole!*"

"Show him in," said the girl, straightening herself up and assuming a meaning dignity. Mr. Sidney Algernon Burley entered, clad from head to heel in dazzling snow—that is to say, in the lightest and whitest of Irish linen. He moved eagerly forward, but the girl made a gesture and gave him a look which checked him suddenly. She said, coldly, "I am here, as I promised. I believed your assertions, I yielded to our importunities, and said I would name the day. I name the 1st of April—eight in the morning. Now go!"

"Oh, my dearest, if the gratitude of a lifetime—"

"Not a word. Spare me all sight of you, all communication with you, until that hour. No—no supplications; I will have it so."

When he was gone, she sank exhausted in a chair, for the long siege of troubles she had undergone had wasted her strength. Presently she said, "What a narrow escape! If the hour appointed had been an hour earlier— Oh, horror, what an escape I have made! And to think I had come to imagine I was loving this beguiling, this truthless, this treacherous monster! Oh, he shall repent his villainy!"

Let us now draw this history to a close, for little more needs to be told. On the 2d of the ensuing April, the Honolulu *Advertiser* contained this notice:

MARRIED *In this city, by telephone, yesterday morning, at eight o'clock, by Rev. Nathan Hays, assisted by Rev. Nathaniel Davis, of New York, Mr. Alonzo Fitz Clarence, of Eastport, Maine, U.S., and Miss Rosannah Ethelton, of Portland, Oregon, U.S. Mrs. Susan Howland, of San Francisco, a friend of the bride, was present, she being the guest of the Rev. Mr. Hays and wife, uncle and aunt of the bride. Mr. Sidney Algernon Burley, of San Francisco, was also present but did not remain till the conclusion of the marriage service. Captain Hawthorne's beautiful yacht, tastefully decorated, was in waiting, and the happy bride and her friends immediately departed on a bridal trip to Lahaina and Haleakala.*

The New York papers of the same date contained this notice:

MARRIED *In this city, yesterday, by telephone, at half-past two in the morning, by Rev. Nathaniel Davis, assisted by Rev. Nathan Hays, of Honolulu, Mr. Alonzo Fitz Clarence, of Eastport, Maine, and Miss Rosannah Ethelton, of Portland, Oregon. The parents and several friends of the bridegroom were present, and enjoyed a sumptuous breakfast and much festivity until nearly sunrise, and then departed on a bridal trip to the Aquarium, the bridegroom's state of health not admitting of a more extended journey.*

Toward the close of that memorable day Mr. and Mrs. Alonzo Fitz Clarence were buried in sweet converse concerning the pleasures of their several bridal tours, when suddenly the young wife exclaimed: "Oh, Lonny, I forgot! I did what I said I would."

"Did you, dear?"

"Indeed, I did. I made *him* the April fool! And I told him so, too! Ah, it was a charming surprise! There he stood, sweltering in a black dress-suit, with the mercury leaking out of the top of the thermometer, waiting to be married. You should have seen the look he gave when I whispered it in his ear. Ah, his wickedness cost me many a heartache and many a tear, but the score was all squared up, then. So the vengeful feeling went right out of my heart, and I begged him to stay, and said I forgave him everything. But he wouldn't. He said he would live to be avenged; said he would make our lives a curse to us. But he can't, *can* he, dear?"

"Never in this world, my Rosannah!"

Aunt Susan, the Oregonian grandmother, and the young couple and their Eastport parents, are all happy at this writing, and likely to remain so. Aunt Susan brought the bride from the islands, accompanied her across our continent, and had the happiness of witnessing the rapturous meeting between an adoring husband and wife who had never seen each other until that moment.

A word about the wretched Burley, whose wicked machinations came so near wrecking the hearts and lives of our poor young friends, will be sufficient. In a murderous attempt to seize a crippled and helpless artisan who he fancied had done him some small offense, he fell into a caldron of boiling oil and expired before he could be extinguished.

1878

Edward Mills and George Benton: A Tale

THESE TWO were distantly related to each other—seventh cousins, or something of that sort. While still babies they became orphans, and were adopted by the Brants, a childless couple, who quickly grew very fond of them. The Brants were always saying: "Be pure, honest, sober, industrious, and considerate of others, and success in life is assured." The children heard this repeated some thousands of times before they understood it; they could repeat it themselves long before they could say the Lord's Prayer; it was painted over the nursery door, and was about the first thing they learned to read. It was destined to become the unswerving rule of Edward Mills's life. Sometimes the Brants changed the wording a little, and said: "Be pure, honest, sober, industrious, considerate, and you will never lack friends."

Baby Mills was a comfort to everybody about him. When he wanted candy and could not have it, he listened to reason, and contented himself without it. When Baby Benton wanted candy, he cried for it until he got it. Baby Mills took care of his toys; Baby Benton always destroyed his in a very brief time, and then made himself so insistently disagreeable that, in order to have peace in the house, little Edward was persuaded to yield up his playthings to him.

When the children were a little older, Georgie became a heavy expense in one respect: he took no care of his clothes;

consequently, he shone frequently in new ones, which was not the case with Eddie. The boys grew apace. Eddie was an increasing comfort, Georgie an increasing solicitude. It was always sufficient to say, in answer to Eddie's petitions, "I would rather you would not do it"—meaning swimming, skating, picnicking, berrying, circusing, and all sorts of things which boys delight in. But *no* answer was sufficient for Georgie; he had to be humored in his desires, or he would carry them with a high hand. Naturally, no boy got more swimming, skating, berrying, and so forth than he; no boy ever had a better time. The good Brants did not allow the boys to play out after nine in summer evenings; they were sent to bed at that hour; Eddie honorably remained, but Georgie usually slipped out of the window toward ten, and enjoyed himself till midnight. It seemed impossible to break Georgie of this bad habit, but the Brants managed it at last by hiring him, with apples and marbles, to stay in. The good Brants gave all their time and attention to vain endeavors to regulate Georgie; they said, with grateful tears in their eyes, that Eddie needed no efforts of theirs, he was so good, so considerate, and in all ways so perfect.

By and by the boys were big enough to work, so they were apprenticed to a trade: Edward went voluntarily; George was coaxed and bribed. Edward worked hard and faithfully, and ceased to be an expense to the good Brants; they praised him, so did his master; but George ran away, and it cost Mr. Brant both money and trouble to hunt him up and get him back. By and by he ran away again—more money and more trouble. He ran away a third time—and stole a few little things to carry with him. Trouble and expense for Mr. Brant once more, and besides, it was with the greatest difficulty that he succeeded in persuading the master to let the youth go unprosecuted for the theft.

Edward worked steadily along, and in time became a full partner in his master's business. George did not improve; he kept the loving hearts of his aged benefactors full of trouble, and their hands full of inventive activities to protect him from ruin. Edward, as a boy, had interested himself in Sunday-schools, debating societies, penny missionary affairs, anti-tobacco organizations, anti-profanity associations, and all such things; as a man, he was a quiet but steady and reliable helper in the church, the temperance societies, and in all movements looking to the aiding and uplifting of men. This excited no remark, attracted no attention—for it was his "natural bent."

Finally, the old people died. The will testified their loving pride in Edward, and left their little property to George—because he "needed it"; whereas, "owing to a bountiful Providence," such was not the case with Edward. The property was left to George conditionally: he must buy out Edward's partner with it; else it must go to a benevolent organization called the Prisoner's Friend Society. The old people left a letter, in which they begged their dear son Edward to take their place and watch over George, and help and shield him as they had done.

Edward dutifully acquiesced, and George became his partner in the business. He was not a valuable partner: he had been meddling with drink before; he soon developed into a constant tippler now, and his flesh and eyes showed the fact unpleasantly. Edward had been courting a sweet and kindly spirited girl for some time. They loved each other dearly, and— But about this period George began to haunt her tearfully and imploringly, and at last she went crying to Edward, and said her high and holy duty was plain before her—she must not let her own selfish desires interfere with it: she must marry "poor George" and "reform him." It would break her heart, she knew it would, and so on; but duty was duty. So she married George, and Edward's heart came very near breaking, as well as her own. However, Edward recovered, and married another girl—a very excellent one she was, too.

Children came to both families. Mary did her honest

best to reform her husband, but the contract was too large. George went on drinking, and by and by he fell to misusing her and the little one sadly. A great many good people strove with George—they were always at it, in fact—but he calmly took such efforts as his due and their duty, and did not mend his ways. He added a vice, presently—that of secret gambling. He got deeply in debt; he borrowed money on the firm's credit, as quietly as he could, and carried this system so far and so successfully that one morning the sheriff took possession of the establishment, and the two cousins found themselves penniless.

Times were hard, now, and they grew worse. Edward moved his family into a garret, and walked the streets day and night, seeking work. He begged for it, but it was really not to be had. He was astonished to see how soon his face became unwelcome; he was astonished and hurt to see how quickly the ancient interest which people had had in him faded out and disappeared. Still, he *must* get work; so he swallowed his chagrin, and toiled on in search of it. At last he got a job of carrying bricks up a ladder in a hod, and was a grateful man in consequence; but after that *nobody* knew him or cared anything about him. He was not able to keep up his dues in the various moral organizations to which he belonged, and had to endure the sharp pain of seeing himself brought under the disgrace of suspension.

But the faster Edward died out of public knowledge and interest, the faster George rose in them. He was found lying, ragged and drunk, in the gutter one morning. A member of the Ladies' Temperance Refuge fished him out, took him in hand, got up a subscription for him, kept him sober a whole week, then got a situation for him. An account of it was published.

General attention was thus drawn to the poor fellow, and a great many people came forward, and helped him toward reform with their countenance and encouragement. He did not drink a drop for two months, and meantime was the pet of the good. Then he fell—in the gutter; and there was general sorrow and lamentation. But the noble sisterhood rescued him again. They cleaned him up, they fed him, they listened to the mournful music of his repentances, they got him his situation again. An account of this, also, was published, and the town was drowned in happy tears over the re-restoration of the poor beast and struggling victim of the fatal bowl. A grand temperance revival was got up, and after some rousing speeches had been made the chairman said, impressively: "We are now about to call for signers; and I think there is a spectacle in store for you which not many in this house will be able to view with dry eyes." There was an eloquent pause, and then George Benton, escorted by a red-sashed detachment of the Ladies of the Refuge, stepped forward upon the platform and signed the pledge. The air was rent with applause, and everybody cried for joy. Everybody wrung the hand of the new convert when the meeting was over; his salary was enlarged next day; he was the talk of the town, and its hero. An account of it was published.

George Benton fell, regularly, every three months, but was faithfully rescued and wrought with, every time, and good situations were found for him. Finally, he was taken around the country lecturing, as a reformed drunkard, and he had great houses and did an immense amount of good.

He was so popular at home, and so trusted—during his sober intervals—that he was enabled to use the name of a principal citizen, and get a large sum of money at the bank. A mighty pressure was brought to bear to save him from the consequences of his forgery, and it was partially successful—he was "sent up" for only two years. When, at the end of a year, the tireless efforts of the benevolent were crowned with success, and he emerged from the penitentiary with a pardon in his pocket, the Prisoner's Friend Society met him at the door with a situation and a comfortable salary, and all the other benevolent people came forward and gave him advice, encouragement, and help. Edward Mills had once applied to the Prisoner's Friend Society for a situation, when in dire need, but the question, "Have you been a prisoner?" made brief work of his case.

While all these things were going on, Edward Mills had been quietly making head against adversity. He was still poor, but was in receipt of a steady and sufficient salary, as the respected and trusted cashier of a bank. George Benton never came near him, and was never heard to inquire about him. George got to indulging in long absences from the town; there were ill reports about him, but nothing definite.

One winter's night some masked burglars forced their way into the bank, and found Edward Mills there alone. They commanded him to reveal the "combination," so that they could get into the safe. He refused. They threatened his life. He said his employers trusted him, and he could not be traitor to that trust. He could die, if he must, but while he lived he would be faithful; he would not yield up the "combination." The burglars killed him.

The detectives hunted down the criminals; the chief one proved to be George Benton. A wide sympathy was felt for the widow and orphans of the dead man, and all the newspapers in the land begged that all the banks in the land would testify their appreciation of the fidelity and heroism of the murdered cashier by coming forward with a generous contribution of money in aid of his family, now bereft of support. The result was a mass of solid cash amounting to upward of five hundred dollars—an average of nearly three-eighths of a cent for each bank of the Union. The cashier's own bank testified its gratitude by endeavoring to show (but humiliatingly failed in it) that the peerless servant's accounts were not square, and that he himself had knocked his brains out with a bludgeon to escape detection and punishment.

George Benton was arraigned for trial. Then everybody seemed to forget the widow and orphans in their solicitude for poor George. Everything that money and influence could do was done to save him, but it all failed; he was sentenced to death. Straightway the Governor was besieged with petitions for commutation or pardon; they were brought by tearful young girls; by sorrowfal old maids; by deputations of pathetic widows; by shoals of impressive orphans. But no, the Governor—for once—would not yield.

Now George Benton experienced religion. The glad news flew all around. From that time forth his cell was always full of girls and women and fresh flowers; all the day long there was prayer, and hymn-singing, and thanksgivings, and homilies, and tears, with never an interruption, except an occasional five-minute intermission for refreshments.

This sort of thing continued up the very gallows, and George Benton went proudly home, in the black cap, before a wailing audience of the sweetest and best that the region could produce. His grave had fresh flowers on it every day, for a while, and the head-stone bore these words, under a hand pointing aloft: "He has fought the good fight."

The brave cashier's head-stone has this inscription: "Be pure, honest, sober, industrious, considerate, and you will never—"

Nobody knows who gave the order to leave it that way, but it was so given.

The cashier's family are in stringent circumstances, now, it is said; but no matter; a lot of appreciative people, who were not willing that an act so brave and true as his should go unrewarded, have collected forty-two thousand dollars—and built a Memorial Church with it.

1880

The Man Who Put Up at Gadsby's

When my odd friend Riley and I were newspaper correspondents in Washington, in the winter of '67, we were coming down Pennsylvania Avenue one night, near midnight, in a driving storm of snow, when the flash of a street-lamp fell upon a man who was eagerly tearing along in the opposite direction. This man instantly stopped and exclaimed:

"This is lucky! You are Mr. Riley, ain't you?"

Riley was the most self-possessed and solemnly deliberate person in the republic. He stopped, looked his man over from head to foot, and finally said:

"I am Mr. Riley. Did you happen to be looking for me?"

"That's just what I was doing," said the man, joyously, "and it's the biggest luck in the world that I've found you. My name is Lykins. I'm one of the teachers of the high school—San Francisco. As soon as I heard the San Francisco postmastership was vacant, I made up my mind to get it—and here I am."

"Yes," said Riley, slowly, "as you have remarked . . . Mr. Lykins . . . here you are. And have you got it?"

"Well, not exactly *got* it, but the next thing to it. I've brought a petition, signed by the Superintendent of Public Instruction, and all the teachers, and by more than two hundred other people. Now I want you, if you'll be so good, to go around with me to the Pacific delegation, for I want to rush this thing through and get along home."

"If the matter is so pressing, you will prefer that we visit the delegation to-night," said Riley, in a voice which had nothing mocking in it—to an unaccustomed ear.

"Oh, to-night, by all means! I haven't got any time to fool around. I want their promise before I go to bed—I ain't the talking kind, I'm the *doing* kind!"

"Yes . . . you've come to the right place for that. When did you arrive?"

"Just an hour ago."

"When are you intending to leave?"

"For New York to-morrow evening—for San Francisco next morning."

"Just so. . . . What are you going to do to-morrow?"

"*Do!* Why, I've got to go to the President with the petition and the delegation, and get the appointment, haven't I?"

"Yes . . . very true . . . that is correct. And then what?"

"Executive session of the Senate at 2 P.M.—got to get the appointment confirmed—I reckon you'll grant that?"

"Yes . . . yes," said Riley, meditatively, "you are right again. Then you take the train for New York in the evening, and the steamer for San Francisco next morning?"

"That's it—that's the way I map it out!"

Riley considered a while, and then said:

"You couldn't stay . . . a day . . . well, say two days longer?"

"Bless your soul, no! It's not my style. I ain't a man to go fooling around—I'm a man that *does* things, I tell you."

The storm was raging, the thick snow blowing in gusts. Riley stood silent, apparently deep in a reverie, during a minute or more, then he looked up and said:

"Have you ever heard about that man who put up at Gadsby's, once? . . . But I see you haven't."

He backed Mr. Lykins against an iron fence, buttonholed him, fastened him with his eye, like the Ancient Mariner, and proceeded to unfold his narrative as placidly and peacefully as if we were all stretched comfortably in a blossomy summer meadow instead of being persecuted by a wintry midnight tempest:

"I will tell you about that man. It was in Jackson's time. Gadsby's was the principal hotel, then. Well, this man arrived from Tennessee about nine o'clock, one morning, with a black coachman and a splendid four-horse carriage and an elegant dog, which he was evidently fond and proud of; he drove up before Gadsby's, and the clerk and the landlord and everybody rushed out to take charge of him, but he said, 'Never mind,' and jumped out and told the coachman to wait—said he hadn't time to take anything to eat, he only had a little claim against the government to collect, would run across the way, to the Treasury, and fetch the money, and then get right along back to Tennessee, for he was in considerable of a hurry.

"Well, about eleven o'clock that night he came back and ordered a bed and told them to put the horses up—said he would collect the claim in the morning. This was in January, you understand—January, 1834—the 3d of January—Wednesday.

"Well, on the 5th of February, he sold the fine carriage, and bought a cheap second-hand one—said it would answer just as well to take the money home in, and he didn't care for style.

"On the llth of August he sold a pair of the fine horses—said he'd often thought a pair was better than four, to go over the rough mountain roads with where a body had to be careful about his driving—and there wasn't so much of his claim but he could lug the money home with a pair easy enough.

"On the 13th of December he sold another horse—said two warn't necessary to drag that old light vehicle with—in fact, one could snatch it along faster than was absolutely necessary, now that it was good solid winter weather and the roads in splendid condition.

"On the 17th of February, 1835, he sold the old carriage and bought a cheap second-hand buggy—said a buggy was just the trick to skim along mushy, slushy early spring roads with, and he had always wanted to try a buggy on those mountain roads, anyway.

"On the 1st of August he sold the buggy and bought the remains of an old sulky—said he just wanted to see those green Tennesseans stare and gawk when they saw him come a-ripping along in a sulky—didn't believe they'd ever heard of a sulky in their lives.

"Well, on the 29th of August he sold his colored coachman—said he didn't need a coachman for a sulky—wouldn't be room enough for two in it anyway—and, besides, it wasn't every day that Providence sent a man a fool who was willing to pay nine hundred dollars for such a third-rate negro as that—been wanting to get rid of the creature for years, but didn't like to *throw* him away.

"Eighteen months later—that is to say, on the 15th of February, 1837—he sold the sulky and bought a saddle—said horseback-riding was what the doctor had always recommended *him* to take, and dog'd if he wanted to risk *his* neck going over those mountain roads on wheels in the dead of winter, not if he knew himself.

"On the 9th of April he sold the saddle—said he wasn't going to risk *his* life with any perishable saddle-girth that ever was made, over a rainy, miry April road, while he could ride bareback and know and feel he was safe—always *had* despised to ride on a saddle, anyway.

"On the 24th of April he sold his horse—said 'I'm just fifty-seven today, hale and hearty—it would be a *pretty* howdy-do for me to be wasting such a trip as that and such weather as this, on a horse, when there ain't anything in the world so splendid as a tramp on foot through the fresh spring woods and over the cheery mountains, to a man that *is* a man—and I can make my dog carry my claim in a little bundle, anyway, when it's collected. So to-morrow I'll be up bright and early, make my little old collection, and mosey off to Tennessee, on my own hind legs, with a rousing good-by to Gadsby's.'

"On the 22d of June he sold his dog—said 'Dern a dog, anyway, where you're just starting off on a rattling bully pleasure tramp through the summer woods and hills—perfect nuisance—chases the squirrels, barks at everything, goes a-capering and splattering around in the fords—man can't get any chance to reflect and enjoy nature—and I'd a blamed sight ruther carry the claim myself, it's a mighty sight safer; a dog's mighty uncertain in a financial way—always noticed it—well, *good*-by boys—last call—I'm off for Tennessee with a good leg and a gay heart, early in the morning.' "

There was a pause and a silence—except the noise of the wind and the pelting snow. Mr. Lykins said, impatiently:

"Well?"

Riley said:

"Well—that was thirty years ago."

"Very well, very well—what of it?"

"I'm great friends with that old patriarch. He comes every evening to tell me good-by. I saw him an hour ago—he's off for Tennessee early to-morrow morning—as usual; said he calculated to get his claim through and be off before night-owls like me have turned out of bed. The tears were in his eyes, he was so glad he was going to see his old Tennessee and his friends once more."

Another silent pause. The stranger broke it:

"Is that all?"

"That is all."

"Well, for the *time* of night, and the *kind* of night, it seems to me the story was full long enough. But what's it all *for?*"

"Oh, nothing in particular."

"Well, where's the point of it?"

"Oh, there isn't any particular point to it. Only, if you are not in *too* much of a hurry to rush off to San Francisco with that post-office appointment, Mr. Lykins, I'd advise you to *'put up at Gadsby's'* for a spell, and take it easy. Good-by. *God* bless you!"

So saying, Riley blandly turned on his heel and left the astonished schoolteacher standing there, a musing and motionless snow image shining in the broad glow of the street-lamp.

He never got that post-office.

From A TRAMP ABROAD, 1880

Mrs. McWilliams and the Lightning

WELL, SIR—continued Mr. McWilliams, for this was not the beginning of his talk—the fear of lightning is one of the most distressing infirmities a human being can be afflicted with. It is mostly confined to women; but now and then you find it in a little dog, and sometimes in a man. It is a particularly distressing infirmity, for the reason that it takes the sand out of a person to an extent which no other fear can, and it can't be *reasoned* with, and neither can it be shamed out of a person. A woman who could face the very devil himself—or a mouse—loses her grip and goes all to pieces in front of a flash of lightning. Her fright is something pitiful to see.

Well, as I was telling you, I woke up, with that smothered and unlocatable cry of "Mortimer! Mortimer!" wailing in my ears; and as soon as I could scrape my faculties together I reached over in the dark and then said:

"Evangeline, is that you calling? What is the matter? Where are you?"

"Shut up in the boot-closet. You ought to be ashamed to lie there and sleep so, and such an awful storm going on."

"Why, how *can* one be ashamed when he is asleep? It is unreasonable; a man *can't* be ashamed when he is asleep, Evangeline."

"You never try, Mortimer—you know very well you never try."

I caught the sound of muffled sobs.

That sound smote dead the sharp speech that was on my lips, and I changed it to—

"I'm sorry, dear—I'm truly sorry. I never meant to act so. Come back and—"

"MORTIMER!"

"Heavens! what is the matter, my love?"

"Do you mean to say you are in that bed yet?"

"Why, of course."

"Come out of it instantly. I should think you would take some *little* care of your life, for *my* sake and the children's, if you will not for your own."

"But, my love—"

"Don't talk to me, Mortimer. You *know* there is no place so dangerous as a bed in such a thunder-storm as this—all the books say that; yet there you would lie, and deliberately throw away your life—for goodness knows what, unless for the sake of arguing, and arguing, and—"

"But, confound it, Evangeline, I'm *not* in the bed *now*. I'm—"

[Sentence interrupted by a sudden glare of lightning, followed by a terrified little scream from Mrs. McWilliams and a tremendous blast of thunder.]

"There! You see the result. Oh, Mortimer, how *can* you be so profligate as to swear at such a time as this?"

"I *didn't* swear. And that *wasn't* a result of it, anyway. It would have come, just the same, if I hadn't said a word; and you know very well, Evangeline—at least, you ought to know—that when the atmosphere is charged with electricity—"

"Oh, yes; now argue it, and argue it, and argue it!—I don't see how you can act so, when you *know* there is not a lightning-rod on the place, and your poor wife and children are absolutely at the mercy of Providence. What *are* you doing?—lighting a match at such a time as this! Are you stark mad?"

"Hang it, woman, where's the harm? The place is as dark as the inside of an infidel, and—"

"Put it out! put it out instantly! Are you determined to sacrifice us all? You *know* there is nothing attracts lightning like a light. [*Fzt!—crash! boom—boloom-boom-boom!*] Oh, just hear it! Now you see what you've done!"

"No, I *don't* see what I've done. A match may attract lightning, for all I know, but it don't *cause* lightning—I'll go odds on that. And it didn't attract it worth a cent this time; for if that shot was leveled at my match, it was blessed poor marksmanship—about an average of none but of a possible million, I should say. Why, at Dollymount such marksmanship as that—"

"For shame, Mortimer! Here we are standing right in the very presence of death, and yet in so solemn a moment you are capable of using such language as that. If you have no desire to— Mortimer!"

"Well?"

"Did you say your prayers to-night?"

"I—I—meant to, but I got to trying to cipher out how much twelve times thirteen is, and—"

[*Fzt!—boom-berroom-boom! bumble-umble bang-*SMASH!]

"Oh, we are lost, beyond all help! How *could* you neglect such a thing at such a time as this?"

"But it *wasn't* 'such a time as this.' There wasn't a cloud in the sky. How could *I* know there was going to be all this rumpus and pow-wow about a little slip like that? And I don't think it's just fair for you to make so much out of it, anyway, seeing it happens so seldom; I haven't missed before since I brought on that earthquake, four years ago."

"MORTIMER! How you talk! Have you forgotten the yellow-fever?"

"My dear, you are always throwing up the yellow-fever to me, and I think it is perfectly unreasonable. You can't even send a telegraphic message as far as Memphis without relays, so how is a little devotional slip of mine going to carry so far? I'll *stand* the earthquake, because it was in the neighborhood; but I'll be hanged if I'm going to be responsible for every blamed—"

[*Fzt!*—BOOM *beroom-boom! boom.*—BANG!]

"Oh, dear, dear, dear! I *know* it struck something, Mortimer. We never shall see the light of another day; and if it will do you any good to remember, when we are gone, that your dreadful language— *Mortimer!*"

"WELL! What now?"

"Your voice sounds as if— Mortimer, are you actually standing in front of that open fireplace?"

"That is the very crime I am committing."

"Get away from it this moment! You do seem determined to bring destruction on us all. Don't you *know* that there is no better conductor for lightning than an open chimney? *Now* where have you got to?"

"I'm here by the window."

"Oh, for pity's sake! have you lost your mind? Clear out from there, this moment! The very children in arms know it is fatal to stand near a window in a thunder-storm. Dear, dear, I know I shall never see the light of another day! Mortimer!"

"Yes."

"What is that rustling?"

"It's me."

"What are you doing?"

"Trying to find the upper end of my pantaloons."

"Quick! throw those things away! I do believe you would deliberately put on those clothes at such a time as this; yet you know perfectly well that *all* authorities agree that woolen stuffs attract lightning. Oh, dear, dear, it isn't sufficient that one's life must be in peril from natural causes, but you must do everything you can possibly think of to augment the danger. Oh, *don't* sing! What *can* you be thinking of?"

"Now where's the harm in it?"

"Mortimer, if I have told you once, I have told you a hundred times, that singing causes vibrations in the atmosphere which interrupt the flow of the electric fluid, and— What on *earth* are you opening that door for?"

"Goodness gracious, woman, is there any harm in *that?*"

"*Harm?* There's *death* in it. Anybody that has given this subject any attention knows that to create a draught is to invite the lightning. You haven't half shut it; shut it *tight*—and do hurry, or we are all destroyed. Oh, it is an awful thing to be shut up with a lunatic at such a time as this. Mortimer, what *are* you doing?"

"Nothing. Just turning on the water. This room is smothering hot and close. I want to bathe my face and hands."

"You have certainly parted with the remnant of your mind! Where lightning strikes any other substance once, it strikes water fifty times. Do turn it off. Oh, dear, I am sure that nothing in this world can save us. It does seem to me that— Mortimer, what was that?"

"It was a da—it was a picture. Knocked it down."

"Then you are close to the wall! I never heard of such imprudence! Don't you *know* that there's no better conductor for lightning than a wall? Come away from there! And you came as near as anything to swearing, too. Oh, how can you be so desperately wicked, and your family in such peril? Mortimer, did you order a feather bed, as I asked you to do?"

"No. Forgot it."

"Forgot it! It may cost you your life. If you had a feather bed now, and could spread it in the middle of the room and lie on it, you would be perfectly safe. Come in here—come quick, before you have a chance to commit any more frantic indiscretions."

I tried, but the little closet would not hold us both with the door shut, unless we could be content to smother. I gasped awhile, then forced my way out. My wife called out:

"Mortimer, something *must* be done for your preservation. Give me that German book that is on the end of the mantelpiece, and a candle; but don't light it; give me a match; I will light it in here. That book has some directions in it."

I got the book—at cost of a vase and some other brittle things; and the madam shut herself up with her candle. I had a moment's peace; then she called out:

"Mortimer, what was that?"

"Nothing but the cat."

"The cat! Oh, destruction! Catch her, and shut her up in the washstand. Do be quick, love; cats are *full* of electricity. I just know my hair will turn white with this night's awful perils."

I heard the muffled sobbings again. But for that, I should not have moved hand or foot in such a wild enterprise in the dark.

However, I went at my task—over chairs, and against all sorts of obstructions, all of them hard ones, too, and most of them with sharp edges—and at last I got kitty cooped up in the commode, at an expense of over four hundred dollars in broken furniture and shins. Then these muffled words came from the closet:

"It says the safest thing is to stand on a chair in the middle of the room, Mortimer; and the legs of the chair must be insulated with non-conductors. That is, you must set the legs of the chair in glass tumblers. [*Fzt!—boom—bang!—*

smash!] Oh, hear that! Do hurry, Mortimer, before you are struck."

I managed to find and secure the tumblers. I got the last four—broke all the rest I insulated the chair legs, and called for further instructions.

"Mortimer, it says, 'Während eines Gewitters entferne man Metalle, wie z. B., Ringe, Uhren, Schlüssel, etc., von sich und halte sich auch nicht an solchen Stellen auf, wo viele Metalle bei einander liegen, oder mit andern Körpern verbunden sind, wie an Herden, Oefen, Eisengittern u. dgl.' What does that mean, Mortimer? Does it mean that you must keep metals *about* you, or keep them *away* from you?"

"Well, I hardly know. It appears to be a little mixed. All German advice is more or less mixed. However, I think that that sentence is mostly in the dative case, with a little genitive and accusative sifted in, here and there, for luck; so I reckon it means that you must keep some metals *about* you."

"Yes, that must be it. It stands to reason that it is. They are in the nature of lightning-rods, you know. Put on your fireman's helmet, Mortimer; that is mostly metal."

I got it, and put it on—a very heavy and clumsy and uncomfortable thing on a hot night in a close room. Even my night-dress seemed to be more clothing than I strictly needed.

"Mortimer, I think your middle ought to be protected. Won't you buckle on your militia saber, please?"

I complied.

"Now, Mortimer, you ought to have some way to protect your feet. Do please put on your spurs."

I did it—in silence—and kept my temper as well as I could.

"Mortimer, it says, 'Das Gewitter läuten ist sehr gefährlich, weil die Glocke selbst, sowie der durch das Läuten veranlasste Luftzug und die Höhe des Thurmes den

Blitz anziehen könnten.' Mortimer, does that mean that it is dangerous not to ring the church bells during a thunder-storm?"

"Yes, it seems to mean that—if that is the past participle of the nominative case singular, and I reckon it is. Yes, I think it means that on account of the height of the church tower and the absence of *Luftzug* it would be very dangerous (*sehr gefährlich*) not to ring the bells in time of a storm; and, moreover, don't you see, the very wording—"

"Never mind that, Mortimer; don't waste the precious time in talk. Get the large dinner-bell; it is right there in the hall. Quick, Mortimer, dear; we are almost safe. Oh, dear, I do believe we are going to be saved, at last!"

Our little summer establishment stands on top of a high range of hills, overlooking a valley. Several farm-houses are in our neighborhood—the nearest some three or four hundred yards away.

When I, mounted on the chair, had been clanging that dreadful bell a matter of seven or eight minutes, our shutters were suddenly torn open from without, and a brilliant bull's-eye lantern was thrust in at the window, followed by a hoarse inquiry:

"What in the nation is the matter here?"

The window was full of men's heads, and the heads were full of eyes that stared wildly at my night-dress and my warlike accoutrements.

I dropped the bell, skipped down from the chair in confusion, and said:

"There is nothing the matter, friends—only a little discomfort on account of the thunder-storm. I was trying to keep off the lightning."

"Thunder-storm? Lightning? Why, Mr. McWilliams, have you lost your mind? It is a beautiful starlight night; there has been no storm."

I looked out, and I was so astonished I could hardly speak for a while. Then I said:

"I do not understand this. We distinctly saw the glow of the flashes through the curtains and shutters, and heard the thunder."

One after another of those people lay down on the ground to laugh—and two of them died. One of the survivors remarked:

"Pity you didn't think to open your blinds and look over to the top of the high hill yonder. What you heard was cannon; what you saw was the flash. You see, the telegraph brought some news, just at midnight; Garfield's nominated—and that's what's the matter!"

Yes, Mr. Twain, as I was saying in the beginning (said Mr. McWilliams), the rules for preserving people against lightning are so excellent and so innumerable that the most incomprehensible thing in the world to me is how anybody ever manages to get struck.

So saying, he gathered up his satchel and umbrella, and departed; for the train had reached his town.

1880

Jim Baker's Bluejay Yarn

Animals talk to each other, of course. There can be no question about that; but I suppose there are very few people who can understand them. I never knew but one man who could. I knew he could, however, because he told me so himself. He was a middle-aged, simple-hearted miner who had lived in a lonely corner of California, among the woods and mountains, a good many years, and had studied the ways of his only neighbors, the beasts and the birds, until he believed he could accurately translate any remark which they made. This was Jim Baker. According to Jim Baker, some animals have only a limited education, and use only very simple words, and scarcely ever a comparison or a flowery figure; whereas, certain other animals have a large vocabulary, a fine command of language and a ready and fluent delivery; consequently these latter talk a great deal; they like it; they are conscious of their talent, and they enjoy "showing off." Baker said, that after long and careful observation, he had come to the conclusion that the bluejays were the best talkers he had found among birds and beasts. Said he:

"There's more *to* a bluejay than any other creature. He has got more moods, and more different kinds of feelings than other creatures; and, mind you, whatever a bluejay feels, he can put into language. And no mere commonplace language, either, but rattling, out-and-out book-talk—and bristling with metaphor, too—just bristling! And as for command of language—why *you* never see a bluejay get stuck for a word. No man ever did. They just boil out of him! And another thing; I've noticed a good deal, and there's no bird, or cow, or anything that uses as good grammar as a bluejay. You may say a cat uses good grammar. Well, a cat does—but you let a cat get excited once; you let a cat get to pulling fur with another cat on a shed, nights, and you'll hear grammar that will give you the lockjaw. Ignorant people think it's the *noise* which fighting cats make that is so aggravating, but it ain't so; it's the sickening grammar they use. Now I've never heard a jay use bad grammar but very seldom; and when they do, they are as ashamed as a human; they shut right down and leave.

"You may call a jay a bird. Well, so he is, in a measure—because he's got feathers on him, and don't belong to no church, perhaps; but otherwise he is just as much a human as you be. And I'll tell you for why. A jay's gifts, and instincts, and feelings, and interests, cover the whole ground. A jay hasn't got any more principle than a Congressman. A jay will lie, a jay will steal, a jay will deceive, a jay will betray; and four times out of five, a jay will go back on his solemnest promise. The sacredness of an obligation is a thing which you can't cram into no bluejay's head. Now, on top of all this, there's another thing; a jay can outswear any gentleman in the mines. You think a cat can swear. Well, a cat can; but you give a bluejay a subject that calls for his reserve-powers, and where is your cat? Don't talk to *me*—I know too much about this thing. And there's yet another thing; in the one little particular of scolding—just good, clean, out-and-out scolding—a bluejay can lay over anything, human or divine. Yes, sir, a jay is everything that a man is. A jay can cry, a jay can laugh, a jay can feel shame, a jay can reason and plan and discuss, a jay likes gossip and scandal, a jay has got a sense of humor, a jay knows when he is an ass just as well as you do—maybe better. If a jay ain't human, he better take in his sign, that's all. Now I'm going to tell you a perfectly true fact about some bluejays.

"When I first begun to understand jay language correctly, there was a little incident happened here. Seven years ago, the last man in this region but me moved away. There stands his house,—been empty ever since; a log house, with a plank roof—just one big room, and no more; no ceiling—nothing between the rafters and the floor. Well, one Sunday morning I was sitting out here in front of my cabin, with my cat, taking the sun, and looking at the blue hills, and listening to the leaves rustling so lonely in the trees, and thinking of the home away yonder in the States, that I hadn't heard from in thirteen years, when a blue jay lit on that house, with an acorn in his mouth, and says, 'Hello, I reckon I've struck something.' When he spoke, the acorn dropped out of his mouth and rolled down the roof, of course, but he didn't care; his mind was all on the thing he had struck. It was a knot-hole in the roof. He cocked his head to one side, shut one eye and put the other one to the hole, like a 'possum looking down a jug; then he glanced up with his bright eyes, gave a wink or two with his wings—which signifies gratification, you understand,—and says, 'It looks like a hole, it's located like a hole,—blamed if I don't believe it *is* a hole!'

"Then he cocked his head down and took another look; he glances up perfectly joyful, this time; winks his wings and his tail both, and says, 'O, no, this ain't no fat thing, I reckon! If I ain't in luck!—why it's a perfectly elegant hole!' So he flew down and got that acorn, and fetched it up and dropped it in, and was just tilting his head back, with the heavenliest smile on his face, when all of a sudden he was paralyzed into a listening attitude and that smile faded gradually out of his countenance like breath off'n a razor, and the queerest look of suprise took its place. Then he says, 'Why I didn't hear it fall!' He cocked his eye at the hole again, and took a long look; raised up and shook his head; stepped around to the other side of the hole and took another look from that side; shook his head again. He studied a while, then he just went into the *de*tails—walked round and round the hole and spied into it from every point of the compass. No use. Now he took a thinking attitude on the comb of the roof and scratched the back of his head with his right foot a minute, and finally says, 'Well, it's too many for *me*, that's certain; must be a mighty long hole; however, I ain't got no time to fool around here, I got to 'tend to business; I reckon it's all right—chance it, anyway.'

"So he flew off and fetched another acorn and dropped it in, and tried to flirt his eye to the hole quick enough to see what become of it, but he was too late. He held his eye there as much as a minute; then he raised up and sighed, and says, 'Consound it, I don't seem to understand this thing, no way; however, I'll tackle her again.' He fetched another acorn, and done his level best to see what become of it, but he couldn't. He says, 'Well, *I* never struck no such a hole as this, before; I'm of the opinion it's a totally new kind of a hole.' Then he begun to get mad. He held in for a spell, walking up and down the comb of the roof and shaking his head and muttering to himself; but his feelings got the upper hand of him, presently, and he broke loose and cussed himself black in the face. I never see a bird take on so about a little thing. When he got through he walks to the hole and looks in again for half a minute; then he says, 'Well, you're a long hole, and a deep hole, and a mighty singular hole altogether—but I've started in to fill you, and I'm d—d if I *don't* fill you, if it takes a hundred years!'

"And with that, away he went. You never see a bird work so since you was born. He laid into his work like a nigger, and the way he hove acorns into that hole for about two hours and a half was one of the most exciting and astonishing spectacles I ever struck. He never stopped to take a look any more—he just hove 'em in and went for more. Well at last he could hardly flop his wings, he was so tuckered out. He comes a-drooping down, once more, sweating like an ice-pitcher, drops his acorn in and says, '*Now* I guess I've got the bulge on you by this time!' So he bent down for a look. If you'll believe me, when his head come up again he was just pale with rage. He says, 'I've shoveled acorns enough in there to keep the family thirty years, and if I can see a sign of one of 'em I wish I may land in a museum with a belly full of sawdust in two minutes!'

"He just had strength enough to crawl up on to the comb and lean his back agin the chimbly, and then he collected his impressions and begun to free his mind. I see in a second that what I had mistook for profanity in the mines was only just the rudiments, as you may say.

"Another jay was going by, and heard him doing his devotions, and stops to inquire what was up. The sufferer told him the whole circumstance, and says, 'Now yonder's the hole, and if you don't believe me, go and look for yourself.' So this fellow went and looked, and comes back and says, 'How many did you say you put in there?' 'Not any less than two tons,' says the sufferer. The other jay went and looked again. He couldn't seem to make it out, so he raised a yell, and three more jays come. They all examined the hole, they all made the sufferer tell it over again, then they all discussed it, and got off as many leather-headed opinions about it as an average crowd of humans could have done.

"They called in more jays; then more and more, till pretty soon this whole region 'peared to have a blue flush about it. There must have been five thousand of them; and such another jawing and disputing and ripping and cussing, you never heard. Every jay in the whole lot put his eye to the hole and delivered a more chuckle-headed opinion about the mystery than the jay that went there before him. They examined the house all over, too. The door was standing half open, and at last one old jay happened to go and light on it and look in. Of course that knocked the mystery galley-west in a second. There lay the acorns, scattered all over the floor. He flopped his wings and raised a whoop. 'Come here!' he says, 'Come here, everybody; hang'd if this fool hasn't been trying to fill up a house with acorns!' They all came a-swooping down like a blue cloud, and as each fellow lit on the door and took a glance, the whole absurdity of the contract that that first jay had tackled hit him home and he fell over backwards suffocating with laughter, and the next jay took his place and done the same.

"Well, sir, they roosted around here on the house-top and the trees for an hour, and guffawed over that thing like human beings. It ain't any use to tell me a bluejay hasn't got a sense of humor, because I know better. And memory, too. They brought jays here from all over the United States to look down that hole, every summer for three years. Other birds too. And they could all see the point, except an owl that come from Nova Scotia to visit the Yosemite, and he took this thing in on his way back. He said he couldn't see anything funny in it. But then he was a good deal disappointed about Yosemite, too."

From A TRAMP ABROAD, 1880

A Curious Experience

This is the story which the Major told me, as nearly as I can recall it:

In the winter of 1862–63 I was commandant of Fort Trumbull, at New London, Conn. Maybe our life there was not so brisk as life at "the front"; still it was brisk enough, in its way—one's brains didn't cake together there for lack of something to keep them stirring. For one thing, all the Northern atmosphere at that time was thick with mysterious rumors—rumors to the effect that rebel spies were flitting everywhere, and getting ready to blow up our Northern forts, burn our hotels, send infected clothing into our towns, and all that sort of thing. You remember it. All this had a tendency to keep us awake, and knock the traditional dullness out of garrison life. Besides, ours was a recruiting station—which is the same as saying we hadn't any time to waste in dozing, or dreaming, or fooling around. Why, with all our watchfulness, fifty per cent. of a day's recruits would leak out of our hands and give us the slip the same night. The bounties were so prodigious that a recruit could pay a sentinel three or four hundred dollars to let him escape, and still have enough of his bounty-money left to constitute a fortune for a poor man. Yes, as I said before, our life was not drowsy.

Well, one day I was in my quarters alone, doing some writing, when a pale and ragged lad of fourteen or fifteen entered, made a neat bow, and said:

"I believe recruits are received here?"

"Yes."

"Will you please enlist me, sir?"

"Dear me, no! You are too young, my boy, and too small."

A disappointed look came into his face, and quickly deepened into an expression of despondency. He turned slowly away, as if to go; hesitated, then faced me again, and said, in a tone that went to my heart:

"I have no home, and not a friend in the world. If you *could* only enlist me!"

But of course the thing was out of the question, and I said so as gently as I could. Then I told him to sit down by the stove and warm himself, and added:

"You shall have something to eat, presently. You are hungry?"

He did not answer; he did not need to; the gratitude in his big, soft eyes was more eloquent than any words could have been. He sat down by the stove, and I went on writing. Occasionally I took a furtive glance at him. I noticed that his clothes and shoes, although soiled and damaged, were of good style and material. This fact was suggestive. To it I added the facts that his voice was low and musical; his eyes deep and melancholy; his carriage and address gentlemanly; evidently the poor chap was in trouble. As a result, I was interested.

However, I became absorbed in my work by and by, and forgot all about the boy. I don't know how long this lasted; but at length I happened to look up. The boy's back was toward me, but his face was turned in such a way that I could see one of his cheeks—and down that cheek a rill of noiseless tears was flowing.

"God bless my soul!" I said to myself; "I forgot the poor rat was starving." Then I made amends for my brutality by saying to him, "Come along, my lad; you shall dine with *me;* I am alone to-day."

He gave me another of those grateful looks, and happy

light broke in his face. At the table he stood with his hand on his chair-back until I was seated, then seated himself. I took up my knife and fork and—well, I simply held them, and kept still; for the boy had inclined his head and was saying a silent grace. A thousand hallowed memories of home and my childhood poured in upon me, and I sighed to think how far I had drifted from religion and its balm for hurt minds, its comfort and solace and support.

As our meal progressed I observed that young Wicklow—Robert Wicklow was his full name—knew what to do with his napkin; and—well, in a word, I observed that he was a boy of good breeding; never mind the details. He had a simple frankness, too, which won upon me. We talked mainly about himself, and I had no difficulty in getting his history out of him. When he spoke of his having been born and reared in Louisiana, I warmed to him decidedly, for I had spent some time down there. I knew all the "coast" region of the Mississippi, and loved it, and had not been long enough away from it for my interest in it to begin to pale. The very names that fell from his lips sounded good to me—so good that I steered the talk in directions that would bring them out: Baton Rouge, Plaquemine, Donaldsonville, Sixty-mile Point, Bonnet-Carré, the Stock Landing, Carrollton, the Steamship Landing, the Steamboat Landing, New Orleans, Tchoupitoulas Street, the Esplanade, the Rue des Bons Enfants, the St. Charles Hotel, the Tivoli Circle, the Shell Road, Lake Pontchartrain; and it was particularly delightful to me to hear once more of the *R. E. Lee*, the *Natchez*, the *Eclipse*, the *General Quitman*, the *Duncan F. Kenner*, and other old familiar steamboats. It was almost as good as being back there, these names so vividly reproduced in my mind the look of the things they stood for. Briefly, this was little Wicklow's history:

When the war broke out, he and his invalid aunt and his father were living near Baton Rouge, on a great and rich plantation which had been in the family for fifty years. The father was a Union man. He was persecuted in all sorts of ways, but clung to his principles. At last one night masked men burned his mansion down, and the family had to fly for their lives. They were hunted from place to place, and learned all there was to know about poverty, hunger, and distress. The invalid aunt found relief at last: misery and exposure killed her; she died in an open field, like a tramp, the rain beating upon her and the thunder booming overhead. Not long afterward the father was captured by an armed band; and while the son begged and pleaded the victim was strung up before his face. [At this point a baleful light shone in the youth's eyes and he said with the manner of one who talks to himself: "If I cannot be enlisted, no matter—I shall find a way—I shall find a way."] As soon as the father was pronounced dead, the son was told that if he was not out of that region within twenty-four hours it would go hard with him. That night he crept to the riverside and hid himself near a plantation landing. By and by the *Duncan F. Kenner* stopped there, and he swam out and concealed himself in the yawl that was dragging at her stern. Before daylight the boat reached the Stock Landing and he slipped ashore. He walked the three miles which lay between that point and the house of an uncle of his in Good-Children Street, in New Orleans, and then his troubles were over for the time being. But this uncle was a Union man, too, and before very long he concluded that he had better leave the South. So he and young Wicklow slipped out of the country on board a sailing-vessel, and in due time reached New York. They put up at the Astor House. Young Wicklow had a good time of it for a while, strolling up and down Broadway, and observing the strange Northern sights; but in the end a change came—and not for the better. The uncle had been cheerful at first, but now he began to look troubled and despondent; moreover, he became moody and irritable; talked of money giving out, and no way to get more—"not enough left for one, let alone two." Then, one morning, he was missing—did not come to breakfast. The boy inquired at the office, and was told that the uncle had paid his bill the night before and gone away—to Boston, the clerk believed, but was not certain.

The lad was alone and friendless. He did not know what to do, but concluded he had better try to follow and find his uncle. He went down to the steamboat landing: learned that the trifle of money in his pocket would not carry him to Boston; however, it would carry him to New London; so he took passage for that port, resolving to trust to Providence to furnish him means to travel the rest of the way. He had now been wandering about the streets of New London three days and nights, getting a bite and a nap here and there for charity's sake. But he had given up at last; courage and hope were both gone. If he could enlist, nobody could be more thankful; if he could not get in as a soldier, couldn't he be a drummer-boy? Ah, he would work *so* hard to please, and would be so grateful!

Well, there's the history of young Wicklow, just as he told it to me, barring details. I said:

"My boy, you are among friends now—don't you be troubled any more." How his eyes glistened! I called in Sergeant John Rayburn—he was from Hartford; lives in Hartford yet; maybe you know him—and said, "Rayburn, quarter this boy with the musicians. I am going to enroll him as a drummer-boy, and I want you to look after him and see that he is well treated."

Well, of course, intercourse between the commandant of the post and the drummer-boy came to an end now; but the poor little friendless chap lay heavy on my heart just the same. I kept on the lookout, hoping to see him brighten up and begin to be cheery and gay; but no, the days went by, and there was no change. He associated with nobody; he was always absent-minded, always thinking; his face was always sad. One morning Rayburn asked leave to speak to me privately. Said he:

"I hope I don't offend, sir; but the truth is, the musicians are in such a sweat it seems as if somebody's *got* to speak."

"Why, what is the trouble?"

"It's the Wicklow boy, sir. The musicians are down on him to an extent you can't imagine."

"Well, go on, go on. What has he been doing?"

"Prayin', sir."

"Praying!"

"Yes, sir; the musicians haven't any peace in their life for that boy's prayin'. First thing in the mornin' he's at it; noons he's at it; and nights—well, *nights* he just lays into 'em like all possessed! Sleep? Bless you, they *can't* sleep: he's got the floor, as the sayin' is, and then when he once gets his supplication-mill agoin' there just simply ain't any let-up *to* him. He starts in with the band-master, and he prays for him; next he takes the head bugler, and he prays for him; next the bass drum, and he scoops *him* in; and so on, right straight through the band, givin' them all a show, and takin' that amount of interest in it which would make you think he thought he warn't but a little while for this world, and believed he couldn't be happy in heaven without he had a brass-band along, and wanted to pick 'em out for himself, so he could depend on 'em to do up the national tunes in a style suitin' to the place. Well, sir, heavin' boots at him don't have no effect; it's dark in there; and, besides, he don't pray fair, anyway, but kneels down behind the big drum; so it don't make no difference if they *rain* boots at him, *he* don't give a dern—warbles right along, same as if it was applause. They sing out, 'Oh, dry up!' 'Give us a rest!' 'Shoot him!' 'Oh, take a walk!' and all sorts of such things. But what of it? It don't faze him. *He* don't mind it." After a pause: "Kind of a good little fool, too; gits up in the mornin' and carts all that stock of boots back, and sorts 'em out and sets each man's pair where they belong. And they've been throwed at him so much now that he knows every boot in the band—can sort 'em out with his eyes shut."

After another pause, which I forebore to interrupt:

"But the roughest thing about it is that when he's done prayin'—when he ever *does* get done—he pipes up and begins to *sing*. Well, you know what a honey kind of a voice he's got when he talks; you know how it would persuade a cast-iron dog to come down off of a door-step and lick his hand. Now if you'll take my word for it, sir, it ain't a circumstance to his singin'! Flute music is harsh to that boy's singin'. Oh, he just gurgles it out so soft and sweet and low, there in the dark, that it makes you think you are in heaven."

"What is there 'rough' about that?"

"Ah, that's just it, sir. You hear him sing

'Just as I am—poor, wretched, blind'—

just you hear him sing that once, and see if you don't melt all up and the water come into your eyes! I don't care *what* he sings, it goes plum straight home to you—it goes deep down to where you *live*—and it fetches you every time! Just you hear him sing

'Child of sin and sorrow, filled with dismay,
Wait not till to-morrow, yield thee to-day;
'Grieve not that love
Which, from above'—

and so on. It makes a body feel like the wickedest, ungratefulest brute that walks. And when he sings them songs of his about home, and mother, and childhood, and old memories, and things that's vanished, and old friends dead and gone, it fetches everything before your face that you've ever loved and lost in all your life—and it's just beautiful, it's just divine to listen to, sir—but, Lord, Lord, the heartbreak of it! The band—well, they all cry—every rascal of them blubbers, and don't try to hide it, either; and first you know, that very gang that's been slammin' boots at that boy will skip out of their bunks all of a sudden, and rush over in the dark and hug him! Yes, they do—and slobber all over him, and call him pet names, and beg him to forgive them. And just at that time, if a regiment was to offer to hurt a hair of that cub's head, they'd go for that regiment, if it was a whole army corps!"

Another pause.

"Is that all?" said I.

"Yes, sir."

"Well, dear me, what is the complaint? What do they want done?"

"Done? Why, bless you, sir, they want you to stop him from *singin'*."

"What an idea! You said his music was divine."

"That's just it. It's *too* divine. Mortal man can't stand it. It stirs a body up so; it turns a body inside out; it racks his feelin's all to rags; it makes him feel bad and wicked, and not fit for any place but perdition. It keeps a body in such an everlastin' state of repentin', that nothin' don't taste good and there ain't no comfort in life. And then the *cryin'*, you see—every mornin' they are ashamed to look one another in the face."

"Well, this is an odd case, and a singular complaint. So they really want the singing stopped?"

"Yes, sir, that is the idea. They don't wish to ask too much; they would like powerful well to have the prayin' shut down on, or leastways trimmed off around the edges; but the main thing's the singin'. If they can only get the singin' choked off, they think they can stand the prayin', rough as it is to be bullyragged so much that way."

I told the sergeant I would take the matter under consideration. That night I crept into the musicians' quarters and listened. The sergeant had not overstated the case. I heard the praying voice pleading in the dark; I heard the execrations of the harassed men; I heard the rain of boots whiz through the air, and bang and thump around the big drum. The thing touched me, but it amused me, too. By and by, after an impressive silence, came the singing. Lord, the pathos of it, the enchantment of it! Nothing in the world was ever so sweet, so gracious, so tender, so holy, so moving. I made my stay very brief; I was beginning to experience emotions of a sort not proper to the commandant of a fortress.

Next day I issued orders which stopped the praying and singing. Then followed three or four days which were so full of bounty-jumping excitements and irritations that I never once thought of my drummer-boy. But now comes Sergeant Rayburn, one morning, and says:

"That new boy acts mighty strange, sir."

"How?"

"Well, sir, he's all the time writin'."

"Writing? What does he write—letters?"

"I don't know, sir; but whenever he's off duty, he is always pokin' and nosin' around the fort, all by himself—blest if I think there's a hole or corner in it he hasn't been into—and every little while he outs with pencil and paper and scribbles somethin' down."

This gave me a most unpleasant sensation. I wanted to scoff at it, but it was not a time to scoff at *anything* that had the least suspicious tinge about it. Things were happening all around us in the North then that warned us to be always on the alert, and always suspecting. I recalled to mind the suggestive fact that this boy was from the South—the extreme South, Louisiana—and the thought was not of a reassuring nature, under the circumstances. Nevertheless, it cost me a pang to give the orders which I now gave to Rayburn. I felt like a father who plots to expose his own child to shame and injury. I told Rayburn to keep quiet, bide his time, and get me some of those writings whenever he could manage it without the boy's finding it out. And I charged him not to do anything which might let the boy discover that he was being watched. I also ordered that he allow the lad his usual liberties, but that he be followed at a distance when he went out into the town.

During the next two days Rayburn reported to me several times. No success. The boy was still writing, but he always pocketed his paper with a careless air whenever Rayburn appeared in the vicinity. He had gone twice to an old deserted stable in the town, remained a minute or two, and come out again. One could not pooh-pooh these things—they had an evil look. I was obliged to confess to myself that I was getting uneasy. I went into my private quarters and sent for my second in command—an officer of intelligence and judgment, son of General James Watson Webb. He was surprised and troubled. We had a long talk over the matter, and came to the conclusion that it would be worth while to institute a secret search. I determined to take charge of that myself. So I had myself called at two in the morning; and pretty soon after I was in the musicians' quarters, crawling along the floor on my stomach among the snorers. I reached my slumbering waif's bunk at last, without disturbing anybody, captured his clothes and kit, and crawled stealthily back again. When I got to my own quarters, I found Webb there, waiting and eager to know the result. We made search immediately. The clothes were a disappointment. In the pockets we found blank paper and a pencil; nothing else, except a jackknife and such queer odds and ends and useless trifles as boys hoard and value. We turned to the kit hopefully. Nothing there but a rebuke for us!—a little Bible with this written on the fly-leaf: "Stranger, be kind to my boy, for his mother's sake."

I looked at Webb—he dropped his eyes; he looked at me—I dropped mine. Neither spoke. I put the book reverently back in its place. Presently Webb got up and went away, without remark. After a little I nerved myself up to my unpalatable job, and took the plunder back to where it belonged, crawling on my stomach as before. It seemed the peculiarly appropriate attitude for the business I was in.

I was most honestly glad when it was over and done with.

About noon next day Rayburn came, as usual, to report. I cut him short. I said:

"Let this nonsense be dropped. We are making a bugaboo out of a poor little cub who has got no more harm in him than a hymn-book."

The sergeant looked surprised, and said:

"Well, you know it was your orders, sir, and I've got some of the writin'."

"And what does it amount to? How did you get it?"

"I peeped through the keyhole, and see him writin'. So, when I judged he was about done, I made a sort of a little cough, and I see him crumple it up and throw it in the fire, and look all around to see if anybody was comin'. Then he settled back as comfortable and careless as anything. Then I comes in, and passes the time of day pleasantly, and sends him on an errand. He never looked uneasy, but went right along. It was a coal fire and new built; the writin' had gone over behind a chunk, out of sight; but I got it out; there it is; it ain't hardly scorched, you see."

I glanced at the paper and took in a sentence or two. Then I dismissed the sergeant and told him to send Webb to me. Here is the paper in full:

FORT TRUMBULL, *the 8th.*

COLONEL *I was mistaken as to the caliber of the three guns I ended my list with. They are 18-pounders; all the rest of the armament is as I stated. The garrison remains as before reported, except that the two light infantry companies that were to be detached for service at the front are to stay here for the present—can't find out for how long, just now, but will soon. We are satisfied that, all things considered, matters had better be postponed un—*

There it broke off—there is where Rayburn coughed and interrupted the writer. All my affection for the boy, all my respect for him and charity for his forlorn condition, withered in a moment under the blight of this revelation of cold-blooded baseness.

But never mind about that. Here was business—business that required profound and immediate attention, too. Webb and I turned the subject over and over, and examined it all around. Webb said:

"What a pity he was interrupted! Something is going to be postponed until—when? And what *is* the something? Possibly he would have mentioned it, the pious little reptile!"

"Yes," I said, "we have missed a trick. And who is '*we*' in the letter? Is it conspirators inside the fort or outside?"

That "we" was uncomfortably suggestive. However, it was not worth while to be guessing around that, so we proceeded to matters more practical. In the first place, we decided to double the sentries and keep the strictest possible watch. Next, we thought of calling Wicklow in and making him divulge everything; but that did not seem wisest until other methods should fail. We must have some more of the writings; so we began to plan to that end. And now we had an idea: Wicklow never went to the post-office—perhaps the deserted stable was his post-office. We sent for my confidential clerk—a young German named Sterne, who was a sort of natural detective—and told him all about the case, and ordered him to go to work on it. Within the hour we got word that Wicklow was writing again. Shortly afterward word came that he had asked leave to go out into the town. He was detained awhile and meantime Sterne hurried off and concealed himself in the stable. By and by he saw Wicklow saunter in, look about him, then hide something under some rubbish in a corner, and take leisurely leave again. Sterne pounced upon the hidden article—a letter—and brought it to us. It had no superscription and no signature. It repeated what we had already read, and then went on to say:

We think it best to postpone till the two companies are gone. I mean the four inside think so; have not communicated with the others—afraid of attracting attention. I say four because we have lost two; they had hardly enlisted and got inside when they were shipped off to the front. It will be absolutely necessary to have two in their places. The two that went were the brothers from Thirty-mile Point. I have something of the greatest importance to reveal, but must not trust it to this method of communication; will try the other.

"The little scoundrel!" said Webb; "who *could* have supposed he was a spy? However, never mind about that; let us add up our particulars, such as they are, and see how the case stands to date. First, we've got a rebel spy in our midst, whom we know; secondly, we've got three more in our midst whom we don't know; thirdly, these spies have been introduced among us through the simple and easy process of enlisting as soldiers in the Union army—and evidently two of them have got sold at it, and been shipped off to the front; fourthly, there are assistant spies 'outside'—number indefinite; fifthly, Wicklow has very important matter which he is afraid to communicate by the 'present method'—will 'try the other.' That is the case, as it now stands. Shall we collar Wicklow and make him confess? Or shall we catch the person who removes the letters from the stable and make *him* tell? Or shall we keep still and find out more?"

We decided upon the last course. We judged that we did not need to proceed to summary measures now, since it was evident that the conspirators were likely to wait till those two light infantry companies were out of the way. We fortified Sterne with pretty ample powers, and told him to use his best endeavors to find out Wicklow's "other method" of communication. We meant to play a bold game; and to this end we proposed to keep the spies in an unsuspecting state as long as possible. So we ordered Sterne to return to the stable immediately, and, if he found the coast clear, to conceal Wicklow's letter where it was before, and leave it there for the conspirators to get.

The night closed down without further event. It was cold and dark and sleety, with a raw wind blowing; still I turned out of my warm bed several times during the night, and went the rounds in person, to see that all was right and that every sentry was on the alert. I always found them wide awake and watchful; evidently whispers of mysterious dangers had been floating about, and the doubling of the guards had been a kind of indorsement of those rumors. Once, toward morning, I encountered Webb, breasting his way against the bitter wind, and learned then that he, also, had been the rounds several times to see that all was going right.

Next day's events hurried things up somewhat. Wicklow wrote another letter; Sterne preceded him to the stable and saw him deposit it; captured it as soon as Wicklow was out of the way, then slipped out and followed the little spy at a distance, with a detective in plain clothes at his own heels, for we thought it judicious to have the law's assistance handy in case of need. Wicklow went to the railway station, and waited around till the train from New York came in, then stood scanning the faces of the crowd as they poured out of the cars. Presently an aged gentleman, with green goggles and a cane, came limping along, stopped in Wicklow's neighborhood, and began to look about him expectantly. In an instant Wicklow darted forward, thrust an envelope into his hand, then glided away and disappeared in the throng. The next instant Sterne had snatched the letter; and as he hurried past the detective, he said: "Follow the old gentleman—don't lose sight of him." Then Sterne skurried out with the crowd, and came straight to the fort.

We sat with closed doors, and instructed the guard outside to allow no interruption.

First we opened the letter captured at the stable. It read as follows:

> HOLY ALLIANCE *Found, in the usual gun, commands from the Master, left there last night, which set aside the instructions heretofore received from the subordinate quarter. Have left in the gun the usual indication that the commands reached the proper hand—*

Webb, interrupting: "Isn't the boy under constant surveillance now?"

I said yes; he had been under strict surveillance ever since the capturing of his former letter.

"Then how could he put anything into a gun, or take anything out of it, and not get caught?"

"Well," I said, "I don't like the look of that very well."

"I don't either," said Webb. "It simply means that there are conspirators among the very sentinels. Without their connivance in some way or other, the thing couldn't have been done."

I sent for Rayburn, and ordered him to examine the batteries and see what he could find. The reading of the letter was then resumed:

> *The new commands are peremptory, and require that the MMMM shall be FFFFF at 3 o'clock tomorrow morning. Two hundred will arrive, in small parties, by train and otherwise, from various directions, and will be at appointed place at right time. I will distribute the sign to-day. Success is apparently sure, though something must have got out, for the sentries have been doubled, and the chiefs went the rounds last night several times. W. W. comes from southerly to-day and will receive secret orders—by the other method. All six of you must be in 166 at*

sharp 2 A.M. *You will find B. B. there, who will give you detailed instructions. Password same as last time, only reversed—put first syllable last and last syllable first.* REMEMBER *XXXX. Do not forget. Be of good heart; before the next sun rises you will be heroes; your fame will be permanent; you will have added a deathless page to history.* AMEN.

"Thunder and Mars," said Webb, "but we are getting into mighty hot quarters, as I look at it!"

I said there was no question but that things were beginning to wear a most serious aspect. Said I:

"A desperate enterprise is on foot, that is plain enough. To-night is the time set for it—that, also, is plain. The exact nature of the enterprise—I mean the manner of it—is hidden away under those blind bunches of M's and F's, but the end and aim, I judge, is the surprise and capture of the post. We must move quick and sharp now. I think nothing can be gained by continuing our clandestine policy as regards Wicklow. We *must* know, and as soon as possible, too, where '166' is located, so that we can make a descent upon the gang there at 2 A.M. and doubtless the quickest way to get that information will be to force it out of that boy. But first of all, and before we make any important move, I must lay the facts before the War Department, and ask for plenary powers."

The despatch was prepared in cipher to go over the wires; I read it, approved it, and sent it along.

We presently finished discussing the letter which was under consideration, and then opened the one which had been snatched from the lame gentleman. It contained nothing but a couple of perfectly blank sheets of note-paper! It was a chilly check to our hot eagerness and expectancy. We felt as blank as the paper, for a moment, and twice as foolish. But it was for a moment only; for, of course, we immediately afterward thought of "sympathetic ink." We held the paper close to the fire and watched for the characters to come out, under the influence of the heat; but nothing appeared but some faint tracings, which we could make nothing of. We then called in the surgeon, and sent him off with orders to apply every test he was acquainted with till he got the right one, and report the contents of the letter to me the instant he brought them to the surface. This check was a confounded annoyance, and we naturally chafed under the delay; for we had fully expected to get out of that letter some of the most important secrets of the plot.

Now appeared Sergeant Rayburn, and drew from his pocket a piece of twine string, about a foot long, with three knots tied in it, and held it up.

"I got it out of a gun on the water-front," said he. "I took the tompions out of all the guns and examined close; this string was the only thing that was in any gun."

So this bit of string was Wicklow's "sign" to signify that the "Master's" commands had not miscarried. I ordered that every sentinel who had served near that gun during the past twenty-four hours be put in confinement at once and separately, and not allowed to communicate with any one without my privity and consent.

A telegram now came from the Secretary of War. It read as follows:

SUSPEND HABEAS CORPUS. PUT TOWN UNDER MARTIAL LAW. MAKE NECESSARY ARRESTS. ACT WITH VIGOR AND PROMPTNESS. KEEP THE DEPARTMENT INFORMED.

We were now in shape to go to work. I sent out and had the lame gentleman quietly arrested and as quietly brought into the fort; I placed him under guard, and forbade speech to him or from him. He was inclined to bluster at first, but he soon dropped that.

Next came word that Wicklow had been seen to give something to a couple of our new recruits; and that, as soon as his back was turned, these had been seized and confined. Upon each was found a small bit of paper, bearing these words and signs in pencil:

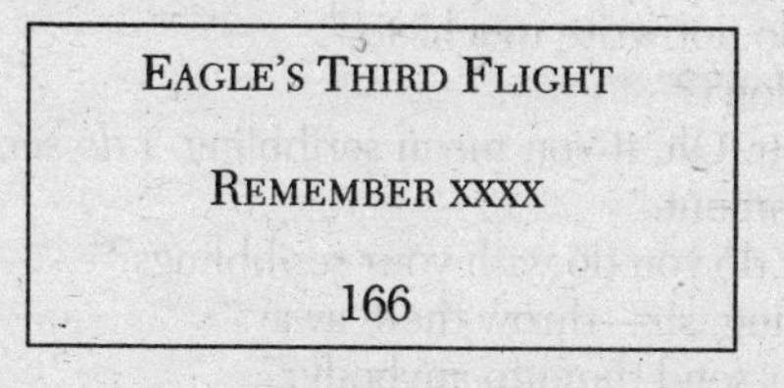

EAGLE'S THIRD FLIGHT

REMEMBER XXXX

166

In accordance with instructions, I telegraphed to the Department, in cipher, the progress made, and also described the above ticket. We seemed to be in a strong enough position now to venture to throw off the mask as regarded Wicklow; so I sent for him. I also sent for and received back the letter written in sympathetic ink, the surgeon accompanying it with the information that thus far it had resisted his tests, but that there were others he could apply when I should be ready for him to do so.

Presently Wicklow entered. He had a somewhat worn and anxious look, but he was composed and easy, and if he suspected anything it did not appear in his face or manner. I allowed him to stand there a moment or two; then I said, pleasantly:

"My boy, why do you go to that old stable so much?"

He answered, with simple demeanor and without embarrassment:

"Well, I hardly know, sir; there isn't any particular reason, except that I like to be alone, and I amuse myself there."

"You amuse yourself there, do you?"

"Yes, sir," he replied, as innocently and simply as before.

"Is that all you do there?"

"Yes, sir," he said, looking up with childlike wonderment in his big, soft eyes.

"You are *sure?*"

"Yes, sir, sure."

After a pause I said:

"Wicklow, why do you write so much?"

"I? I do not write much, sir."

"You don't?"

"No, sir. Oh, if you mean scribbling, I *do* scribble some, for amusement."

"What do you do with your scribblings?"

"Nothing, sir—throw them away."

"Never send them to anybody?"

"No, sir."

I suddenly thrust before him the letter to the "Colonel." He started slightly, but immediately composed himself. A slight tinge spread itself over his cheek.

"How came you to send *this* piece of scribbling, then?"

"I nev—never meant any harm, sir!"

"Never meant any harm! You betray the armament and condition of the post, and mean no harm by it?"

He hung his head and was silent.

"Come, speak up, and stop lying. Whom was this letter intended for?"

He showed signs of distress now; but quickly collected himself, and replied, in a tone of deep earnestness:

"I will tell you the truth, sir—the whole truth. The letter was never intended for anybody at all. I wrote it only to amuse myself. I see the error and foolishness of it now; but it is the only offense, sir, upon my honor."

"Ah, I am glad of that. It is dangerous to be writing such letters. I hope you are sure this is the only one you wrote?"

"Yes, sir, perfectly sure."

His hardihood was stupefying. He told that lie with as sincere a countenance as any creature ever wore. I waited a moment to soothe down my rising temper, and then said:

"Wicklow, jog your memory now, and see if you can help me with two or three little matters which I wish to inquire about."

"I will do my very best, sir."

"Then, to begin with—who is 'the Master'?"

It betrayed him into darting a startled glance at our faces, but that was all. He was serene again in a moment, and tranquilly answered:

"I do not know, sir."

"You do not know?"

"I do not know."

"You are *sure* you do not know?"

He tried hard to keep his eyes on mine, but the strain was too great; his chin sunk slowly toward his breast and he was silent; he stood there nervously fumbling with a button, an object to command one's pity, in spite of his base acts. Presently I broke the stillness with the question:

"Who are the 'Holy Alliance'?"

His body shook visibly, and he made a slight random gesture with his hands, which to me was like the appeal of a despairing creature for compassion. But he made no sound. He continued to stand with his face bent toward the ground. As we sat gazing at him, waiting for him to speak, we saw the big tears begin to roll down his cheeks. But he remained silent. After a little, I said:

"You must answer me, my boy, and you must tell me the truth. Who are the Holy Alliance?"

He wept on in silence. Presently I said, somewhat sharply:

"Answer the question!"

He struggled to get command of his voice; and then, looking up appealingly, forced the words out between his sobs:

"Oh, have pity on me, sir! I cannot answer it, for I do not know."

"What!"

"Indeed, sir, I am telling the truth. I never have heard of the Holy Alliance till this moment. On my honor, sir, this is so."

"Good heavens! Look at this second letter of yours; there, do you see those words, '*Holy Alliance*'? What do you say now?"

He gazed up into my face with the hurt look of one upon whom a great wrong had been wrought, then said, feelingly:

"This is some cruel joke, sir; and how could they play it upon me, who have tried all I could to do right, and have never done harm to anybody? Some one has counterfeited my hand; I never wrote a line of this; I have never seen this letter before!"

"Oh, you unspeakable liar! Here, what do you say to *this?*"—and I snatched the sympathetic-ink letter from my pocket and thrust it before his eyes.

His face turned white—as white as a dead person's. He wavered slightly in his tracks, and put his hand against the wall to steady himself. After a moment he asked, in so faint a voice that it was hardly audible:

"Have you—read it?"

Our faces must have answered the truth before my lips could get out a false "yes," for I distinctly saw the courage come back into that boy's eyes. I waited for him to say something, but he kept silent. So at last I said:

"Well, what have you to say as to the revelations in this letter?"

He answered, with perfect composure:

"Nothing, except that they are entirely harmless and innocent; they can hurt nobody."

I was in something of a corner now, as I couldn't disprove his assertion. I did not know exactly how to proceed. However, an idea came to my relief, and I said:

"You are sure you know nothing about the Master and the Holy Alliance, and did not write the letter which you say is a forgery?"

"Yes, sir—sure."

I slowly drew out the knotted twine string and held it up without speaking. He gazed at it indifferently, then looked at me inquiringly. My patience was sorely taxed. However, I kept my temper down, and said, in my usual voice:

"Wicklow, do you see this?"

"Yes, sir."

"What is it?"

"It seems to he a piece of string."

"*Seems?* It *is* a piece of string. Do you recognize it?"

"No, sir," he replied, as calmly as the words could be uttered.

His coolness was perfectly wonderful! I paused now for several seconds, in order that the silence might add impressiveness to what I was about to say; then I rose and laid my hand on his shoulder, and said, gravely:

"It will do you no good, poor boy, none in the world. This sign to the 'Master,' this knotted string, found in one of the guns on the waterfront—"

"Found *in* the gun! Oh, no, no, no! do not say *in* the gun, but in a crack in the tompion!—it *must* have been in the crack!" and down he went on his knees and clasped his hands and lifted up a face that was pitiful to see, so ashy it was, and wild with terror.

"No, it was *in* the gun."

"Oh, something has gone wrong! My God, I am lost!" and he sprang up and darted this way and that, dodging the hands that were put out to catch him, and doing his best to escape from the place. But of course escape was impossible. Then he flung himself on his knees again, crying with all his might, and clasped me around the legs; and so he clung to me and begged and pleaded, saying, "Oh, have pity on me! Oh, be merciful to me! Do not betray me; they would not spare my life a moment! Protect me, save me. I will confess everything!"

It took us some time to quiet him down and modify his fright, and get him into something like a rational frame of mind. Then I began to question him, he answering humbly, with downcast eyes, and from time to time swabbing away his constantly flowing tears:

"So you are at heart a rebel?"

"Yes, sir."

"And a spy?"

"Yes, sir."

"And have been acting under distinct orders from outside?"

"Yes, sir."

"Willingly?"

"Yes, sir."

"*Gladly,* perhaps?"

"Yes, sir; it would do no good to deny it. The South is my country; my heart is Southern, and it is all in her cause."

"Then the tale you told me of your wrongs and the persecution of your family was made up for the occasion?"

"They—they told me to say it, sir."

"And you would betray and destroy those who pitied and sheltered you. Do you comprehend how base you are, you poor misguided thing?"

He replied with sobs only.

"Well, let that pass. To business. Who is the 'Colonel,' and where is he?"

He began to cry hard, and tried to beg off from answering. He said he would be killed if he told. I threatened to put him in the dark cell and lock him up if he did not come out with the information. At the same time I promised to protect him from all harm if he made a clean breast. For all answer, he closed his mouth firmly and put on a stubborn air which I could not bring him out of. At last I started with him; but a single glance into the dark cell converted him. He broke into a passion of weeping and supplicating, and declared he would tell everything.

So I brought him back, and he named the "Colonel," and described him particularly. Said he would be found at the principal hotel in the town, in citizen's dress. I had to threaten him again, before he would describe and name the "Master." Said the Master would be found at No. 15 Bond

Street, New York, passing under the name of R. F. Gaylord. I telegraphed name and description to the chief of police of the metropolis, and asked that Gaylord be arrested and held till I could send for him.

"Now," said I, "it seems that there are several of the conspirators 'outside,' presumably in New London. Name and describe them."

He named and described three men and two women—all stopping at the principal hotel. I sent out quietly, and had them and the "Colonel" arrested and confined in the fort.

"Next, I want to know all about your three fellow-conspirators who are here in the fort."

He was about to dodge me with a falsehood, I thought; but I produced the mysterious bits of paper which had been found upon two of them, and this had a salutary effect upon him. I said we had possession of two of the men, and he must point out the third. This frightened him badly, and he cried out:

"Oh, please don't make me; he would kill me on the spot!"

I said that that was all nonsense; I would have somebody near by to protect him, and, besides, the men should be assembled without arms. I ordered all the raw recruits to be mustered, and then the poor, trembling little wretch went out and stepped along down the line, trying to look as indifferent as possible. Finally he spoke a single word to one of the men, and before he had gone five steps the man was under arrest.

As soon as Wicklow was with us again, I had those three men brought in. I made one of them stand forward, and said:

"Now, Wicklow, mind, not a shade's divergence from the exact truth. Who is this man, and what do you know about him?"

Being "in for it," he cast consequences aside, fastened his eyes on the man's face, and spoke straight along without hesitation—to the following effect:

"His real name is George Bristow. He is from New Orleans; was second mate of the coast-packet *Capitol* two years ago; is a desperate character, and has served two terms for manslaughter—one for killing a deck-hand named Hyde with a capstan-bar, and one for killing a roustabout for refusing to heave the lead, which is no part of a roustabout's business. He is a spy, and was sent here by the Colonel to act in that capacity. He was third mate of the *St. Nicholas* when she blew up in the neighborhood of Memphis, in '58, and came near being lynched for robbing the dead and wounded while they were being taken ashore in an empty wood-boat."

And so forth and so on—he gave the man's biography in full. When he had finished, I said to the man:

"What have you to say to this?"

"Barring your presence, sir, it is the infernalist lie that ever was spoke!"

I sent him back into confinement, and called the others forward in turn. Same result. The boy gave a detailed history of each, without ever hesitating for a word or a fact; but all I could get out of either rascal was the indignant assertion that it was all a lie. They would confess nothing. I returned them to captivity, and brought out the rest of my prisoners, one by one. Wicklow told all about them—what towns in the South they were from, and every detail of their connection with the conspiracy.

But they all denied his facts, and not one of them confessed a thing. The men raged, the women cried. According to their stories, they were all innocent people from out West, and loved the Union above all things in this world. I locked the gang up, in disgust, and fell to catechizing Wicklow once more.

"Where is No. 166, and who is B. B.?"

But *there* he was determined to draw the line. Neither coaxing nor threats had any effect upon him. Time was flying—it was necessary to institute sharp measures. So I tied him up a-tiptoe by the thumbs. As the pain increased, it wrung screams from him which were almost more than I could bear. But I held my ground, and pretty soon he shrieked out:

"Oh, *please* let me down, and I will tell!"

"No—you'll tell *before* I let you down."

Every instant was agony to him now, so out it came:

"No. 166, Eagle Hotel!"—naming a wretched tavern down by the water, a resort of common laborers, longshoremen, and less reputable folk.

So I released him, and then demanded to know the object of the conspiracy.

"To take the fort to-night," said he, doggedly and sobbing.

"Have I got all the chiefs of the conspiracy?"

"No. You've got all except those that are to meet at 166."

"What does 'Remember XXXX' mean?"

No reply.

"What is the password to No. 166?"

No reply.

"What do those bunches of letters mean—'FFFFF' and 'MMMM'? Answer! or you will catch it again."

"I never *will* answer! I will die first. Now do what you please."

"Think what you are saying, Wicklow. Is it final?"

He answered steadily, and without a quiver in his voice:

"It is final. As sure as I love my wronged country and hate everything this Northern sun shines on, I will die before I will reveal those things."

I tied him up by the thumbs again. When the agony was full upon him it was heartbreaking to hear the poor thing's shrieks, but we got nothing else out of him. To every question he screamed the same reply: "I can die, and I *will* die; but I will never tell."

Well, we had to give it up. We were convinced that he certainly would die rather than confess. So we took him down, and imprisoned him under strict guard.

Then for some hours we busied ourselves with sending telegrams to the War Department, and with making preparations for a descent upon No. 166.

It was stirring times, that black and bitter night. Things had leaked out, and the whole garrison was on the alert. The sentinels were trebled, and nobody could move, outside or in, without being brought to a stand with a musket leveled at his head. However, Webb and I were less concerned now than we had previously been, because of the fact that the conspiracy must necessarily be in a pretty crippled condition, since so many of its principals were in our clutches.

I determined to be at No. 166 in good season, capture and gag B. B., and be on hand for the rest when they arrived. At about a quarter past one in the morning I crept out of the fortress with half a dozen stalwart and gamy U. S. regulars at my heels, and the boy Wicklow, with his hands tied behind him. I told him we were going to No. 166, and that if I found he had lied again and was misleading us, he would have to show us the right place or suffer the consequences.

We approached the tavern stealthily and reconnoitered. A light was burning in the small barroom, the rest of the house was dark. I tried the front door; it yielded, and we softly entered, closing the door behind us. Then we removed our shoes, and I led the way to the barroom. The German landlord sat there, asleep in his chair. I woke him gently, and told him to take off his boots and precede us, warning him at the same time to utter no sound. He obeyed without a murmur, but evidently he was badly frightened. I ordered him to lead the way to 166. We ascended two or three flights of stairs as softly as a file of cats; and then, having arrived near the farther end of a long hall, we came to a door through the glazed transom of which we could discern the glow of a dim light from within. The landlord felt for me in the dark and whispered to me that that was 166. I tried the door—it was locked on the inside. I whispered an order to one of my biggest soldiers; we set our ample shoulders to the door, and with one heave we burst it from its hinges. I caught a half-glimpse of a figure in a bed—saw its head dart toward the candle; out went the light and we were in pitch darkness. With one big bound I lit on that bed and pinned its occupant down with my knees. My prisoner struggled fiercely, but I got a grip on his throat with my left hand, and that was a good assistance to my knees in holding him down. Then straightway I snatched out my revolver, cocked it, and laid the cold barrel warningly against his cheek.

"Now somebody strike a light!" said I. "I've got him safe."

It was done. The flame of the match burst up. I looked at my captive, and, by George, it was a young woman!

I let go and got off the bed, feeling pretty sheepish. Everybody stared stupidly at his neighbor. Nobody had any wit or sense left, so sudden and overwhelming had been the surprise. The young woman began to cry, and covered her face with the sheet. The landlord said, meekly:

"My daughter, she has been doing something that is not right, *nicht wahr?*"

"Your daughter? Is she your daughter?"

"Oh, yes, she is my daughter. She is just to-night come home from Cincinnati a little bit sick."

"Confound it, that boy has lied again. This is not the right 166; this is not B. B. Now, Wicklow, you will find the correct 166 for us, or—hello! where is that boy?"

Gone, as sure as guns! And, what is more, we failed to find a trace of him. Here was an awful predicament. I cursed my stupidity in not tying him to one of the men; but it was of no use to bother about that now. What should I do in the present circumstances?—that was the question. That girl *might* be B. B., after all. I did not believe it, but still it would not answer to take unbelief for proof. So I finally put my men in a vacant room across the hall from 166, and told them to capture anybody and everybody that approached the girl's room, and to keep the landlord with them, and under strict watch, until further orders. Then I hurried back to the fort to see if all was right there yet.

Yes, all was right. And all remained right. I stayed up all night to make sure of that. Nothing happened. I was unspeakably glad to see the dawn come again, and be able to telegraph the Department that the Stars and Stripes still floated over Fort Trumbull.

An immense pressure was lifted from my breast. Still I did not relax vigilance, of course, nor effort, either; the case was too grave for that. I had up my prisoners, one by one, and harried them by the hour, trying to get them to confess, but it was a failure. They only gnashed their teeth and tore their hair, and revealed nothing.

About noon came tidings of my missing boy. He had been seen on the road, tramping westward, some eight miles out, at six in the morning. I started a cavalry lieutenant and a private on his track at once. They came in sight of him twenty miles out. He had climbed a fence and was wearily dragging himself across a slushy field toward a large old-fashioned mansion in the edge of a village. They rode through a bit of woods, made a detour, and closed upon the house from the opposite side; then dismounted and skurried into the kitchen. Nobody there. They slipped into the next room, which was also unoccupied; the door from that room into the front or sitting room was open. They were about to step through it when they heard a low voice; it was somebody praying. So they halted reverently, and the lieutenant put his head in and saw an old man and an old woman kneeling in a corner of that sitting-room. It was the old man that was praying, and just as he was finishing his prayer, the Wicklow boy opened the front door and stepped in. Both of those old people sprang at him and smothered him with embraces, shouting:

"Our boy! Our darling! God be praised. The lost is found! He that was dead is alive again!"

Well, sir, what do you think? That young imp was born and reared on that homestead, and had never been five miles away from it in all his life till the fortnight before he loafed into my quarters and gulled me with that maudlin yarn of his! It's as true as gospel. That old man was his father—a learned old retired clergyman; and that old lady was his mother.

Let me throw in a word or two of explanation concerning that boy and his performances. It turned out that he was a ravenous devourer of dime novels and sensation-story papers—therefore, dark mysteries and gaudy heroisms were just in his line. Then he had read newspaper reports of the stealthy goings and comings of rebel spies in our midst, and of their lurid purposes and their two or three startling achievements, till his imagination was all aflame on that subject. His constant comrade for some months had been a Yankee youth of much tongue and lively fancy, who had served for a couple of years as "mud clerk" (that is, subordinate purser) on certain of the packet-boats plying between New Orleans and points two or three hundred miles up the Mississippi—hence his easy facility in handling the names and other details pertaining to that region. Now I had spent two or three months in that part of the country before the war; and I knew just enough about it to be easily taken in by that boy, whereas a born Louisianian would probably have caught him tripping before he had talked fifteen minutes. Do you know the reason he said he would rather die than explain certain of his treasonable enigmas? Simply because he *couldn't* explain them!—they had no meaning; he had fired them out of his imagination without forethought or afterthought; and so, upon sudden call, he wasn't able to invent an explanation of them. For instance, he couldn't reveal what was hidden in the "sympathetic ink" letter, for the ample reason that there wasn't anything hidden in it; it was blank paper only. He hadn't put anything into a gun, and had never intended to—for his letters were all written to imaginary persons, and when he hid one in the stable he always removed the one he had put there the day before; so he was not acquainted with that knotted string, since he was seeing it for the first time when I showed it to him; but as soon as I had let him find out where it came from, he straightway adopted it, in his romantic fashion, and got some fine effects out of it. He invented Mr. "Gaylord"; there wasn't any 15 Bond Street, just then—it had been pulled down three months before. He invented the "Colonel"; he invented the glib histories of those unfortunates whom I captured and confronted him with; he invented "B. B."; he even invented No. 166, one may say, for he didn't know there *was* such a number in the Eagle Hotel until we went there. He stood ready to invent anybody or anything whenever it was wanted. If I called for "outside" spies, he promptly described strangers whom he had seen at the hotel, and whose names he had happened to hear. Ah, he lived in a gorgeous, mysterious, romantic world during those few stirring days, and I think it was *real* to him, and that he enjoyed it clear down to the bottom of his heart.

But he made trouble enough for us, and just no end of humiliation. You see, on account of him we had fifteen or twenty people under arrest and confinement in the fort, with sentinels before their doors. A lot of the captives were soldiers and such, and to them I didn't have to apologize; but the rest were first-class citizens, from all over the country, and no amount of apologies was sufficient to satisfy them. They just fumed and raged and made no end of trouble! And those two ladies—one was an Ohio Congressman's wife, the other a Western bishop's sister—well, the scorn and ridicule and angry tears they poured out on me made up a keepsake that was likely to make me remember them for a considerable time—and I shall. That old lame gentleman with the goggles was a college president from Philadelphia, who had come up to attend his nephew's funeral. He had never seen young Wicklow before, of course. Well, he not only missed the funeral, and got jailed as a rebel spy, but Wicklow had stood up there in my quarters and coldly described him as a counterfeiter, nigger-trader, horse-thief, and firebug from the most notorious rascal-nest in Galveston; and this was a thing which that poor old gentleman couldn't seem to get over at all.

And the War Department! But, oh, my soul, let's draw the curtain over that part!

NOTE I showed my manuscript to the Major, and he said: "Your unfamiliarity with military matters has betrayed you into some little mistakes. Still, they are picturesque ones—let them go; military men will smile at them, the rest won't detect them. You have got the main facts of the history right, and have set them down just about as they occurred." M.T.

1881

THE INVALID'S STORY

I SEEM SIXTY and married, but these effects are due to my condition and sufferings, for I am a bachelor, and only forty-one. It will be hard for you to believe that I, who am now but a shadow, was a hale, hearty man two short years ago—a man of iron, a very athlete!—yet such is the simple truth. But stranger still than this fact is the way in which I lost my health. I lost it through helping to take care of a box of guns on a two-hundred-mile railway journey one winter's night. It is the actual truth, and I will tell you about it.

I belong in Cleveland, Ohio. One winter's night, two years ago, I reached home just after dark, in a driving snow-storm, and the first thing I heard when I entered the house was that my dearest boyhood friend and schoolmate, John B. Hackett, had died the day before, and that his last utterance had been a desire that I would take his remains home to his poor old father and mother in Wisconsin. I was greatly shocked and grieved, but there was no time to waste in emotions; I must start at once. I took the card, marked "Deacon Levi Hackett, Bethlehem, Wisconsin," and hurried off through the whistling storm to the railway-station. Arrived there I found the long white-pine box which had been described to me; I fastened the card to it with some tacks, saw it put safely aboard the express-car, and then ran into the eating-room to provide myself with a sandwich and some cigars. When I returned, presently, there was my coffin-box *back again,* apparently, and a young fellow examining around it, with a card in his hands, and some tacks and a hammer! I was astonished and puzzled. He began to nail on his card, and I rushed out to the express-car, in a good deal of a state of mind, to ask for an explanation. But no—there was my box, all right, in the express-car; it hadn't been disturbed. [The fact is that without my suspecting it a prodigious mistake had been made. I was carrying off a box of *guns* which that young fellow had come to the station to ship to a rifle company in Peoria, Illinois, and *he* had got my corpse!] Just then the conductor sang out "All aboard," and I jumped into the express-car and got a comfortable seat on a bale of buckets. The expressman was there, hard at work—a plain man of fifty, with a simple, honest, good-natured face, and a breezy, practical heartiness in his general style. As the train moved off a stranger skipped into the car and set a package of peculiarly mature and capable Limburger cheese on one end of my coffin-box—I mean my box of guns. That is to say, I know *now* that it was Limburger cheese, but at that time I never had heard of the article in my life, and of course was wholly ignorant of its character. Well, we sped through the wild night, the bitter storm raged on, a cheerless misery stole over me, my heart went down, down, down! The old expressman made a brisk remark or two about the tempest and the arctic weather, slammed his sliding doors to, and bolted them, closed his window down tight, and then went bustling around, here and there and yonder, setting things to rights, and all the time contentedly humming "Sweet By and By," in a low tone, and flatting a good deal. Presently I began to detect a most evil and searching odor stealing about on the frozen air. This depressed my spirits still more, because of course I attributed it to my poor departed friend. There was something infinitely saddening about his calling himself to my remembrance in this dumb, pathetic way, so it was hard to keep the tears back. Moreover, it distressed me on account of the old expressman, who, I was afraid, might notice it. However, he went humming tranquilly on, and gave no sign; and for this I was grateful. Grateful, yes, but still uneasy; and soon I began to feel more and more uneasy every minute, for every minute that went by that odor thickened up the more, and got to be more and more gamy and hard to stand. Presently, having got things arranged to his satisfaction, the expressman got some wood and made up a tremendous fire in his stove. This distressed me more than I can tell, for I could not but feel that it was a mistake. I was sure that the effect would be deleterious upon my poor departed friend. Thompson—the expressman's name was Thompson, as I found out in the course of the night—now went poking around his car, stopping up whatever stray cracks he could find, remarking that it didn't make any difference what kind of a night it was outside, he calculated to make *us* comfortable, anyway. I said nothing, but I believed he was not choosing the right way. Meantime he was humming to himself just as before; and meantime, too, the stove was getting hotter and hotter, and the place closer and closer. I felt myself growing pale and qualmish, but grieved in silence and said nothing. Soon I noticed that the "Sweet By and By" was gradually fading out; next it ceased altogether, and there was an ominous stillness. After a few moments Thompson said—

"Pfew! I reckon it ain't no cinnamon 't I've loaded up thish-yer stove with!"

He gasped once or twice, then moved toward the cof—gun-box, stood over that Limburger cheese part of a moment, then came back and sat down near me, looking a good deal impressed. After a contemplative pause, he said, indicating the box with a gesture—

"Friend of yourn?"

"Yes," I said with a sigh.

"He's pretty ripe, *ain't* he!"

Nothing further was said for perhaps a couple of minutes, each being busy with his own thoughts; then Thompson said, in a low, awed voice—

"Sometimes it's uncertain whether they're really gone or not—*seem* gone, you know—body warm, joints limber—and so, although you *think* they're gone, you don't really know. I've had cases in my car. It's perfectly awful, becuz *you* don't know what minute they'll rise up and look at you!" Then, after a pause, and slightly lifting his elbow toward the box,—"But *he* ain't in no trance! No, sir, I go bail for *him!*"

We sat some time, in meditative silence, listening to the wind and the roar of the train; then Thompson said, with a good deal of feeling:

"Well-a-well, we've all got to go, they ain't no getting around it. Man that is born of woman is of few days and far between, as Scriptur' says. Yes, you look at it any way you want to, it's awful solemn and cur'us: they ain't *nobody* can get around it; *all's* got to go—just *everybody*, as you may say. One day you're hearty and strong"—here he scrambled to his feet and broke a pane and stretched his nose out at it a moment or two, then sat down again while I struggled up and thrust my nose out at the same place, and this we kept on doing every now and then—"and next day he's cut down like the grass, and the places which knowed him then knows him no more forever, as Scriptur' says. Yes'ndeedy, it's awful solemn and cur'us; but we've all got to go, one time or another; they ain't no getting around it."

There was another long pause; then—

"What did he die of?"

I said I didn't know.

"How long has he been dead?"

It seemed judicious to enlarge the facts to fit the probabilities; so I said:

"Two or three days."

But it did no good; for Thompson received it with an injured look which plainly said, "Two or three *years*, you mean." Then he went right along, placidly ignoring my statement, and gave his views at considerable length upon the unwisdom of putting off burials too long. Then he lounged off toward the box, stood a moment, then came back on a sharp trot and visited the broken pane, observing:

" 'Twould 'a' ben a dum sight better, all around, if they'd started him along last summer."

Thompson sat down and buried his face in his red silk handkerchief, and began to slowly sway and rock his body like one who is doing his best to endure the almost unendurable. By this time the fragrance—if you may call it fragrance—was just about suffocating, as near as you can come at it. Thompson's face was turning gray; I knew mine hadn't any color left in it. By and by Thompson rested his forehead in his left hand, with his elbow on his knee, and sort of waved his red handkerchief toward the box with his other hand, and said:

"I've carried a many a one of 'em—some of 'em considerable overdue, too—but, lordy, he just lays over 'em all!—and does it *easy*. Cap, they was heliotrope to *him!*"

This recognition of my poor friend gratified me, in spite

of the sad circumstances, because it had so much the sound of a compliment.

Pretty soon it was plain that something had got to be done, I suggested cigars. Thompson thought it was a good idea. He said:

"Likely it'll modify him some."

We puffed gingerly along for a while, and tried hard to imagine that things were improved. But it wasn't any use. Before very long, and without any consultation, both cigars were quietly dropped from our nerveless fingers at the same moment. Thompson said, with a sigh:

"No, Cap, it don't modify him worth a cent. Fact is, it makes him worse, becuz it appears to stir up his ambition. What do you reckon we better do, now?"

I was not able to suggest anything; indeed, I had to be swallowing and swallowing all the time, and did not like to trust myself to speak. Thompson fell to maundering, in a desultory and low-spirited way, about the miserable experiences of this night; and he got to referring to my poor friend by various titles—sometimes military ones, sometimes civil ones; and I noticed that as fast as my poor friend's effectiveness grew, Thompson promoted him accordingly—gave him a bigger title. Finally he said:

"I've got an idea. Suppos'n' we buckle down to it and give the Colonel a bit of a shove toward t'other end of the car?—about ten foot, say. He wouldn't have so much influence, then, don't you reckon?"

I said it was a good scheme. So we took in a good fresh breath at the broken pane, calculating to hold it till we got through; then we went there and bent over that deadly cheese and took a grip on the box. Thompson nodded "All ready," and then we threw ourselves forward with all our might; but Thompson slipped, and slumped down with his nose on the cheese, and his breath got loose. He gagged and gasped, and floundered up and made a break for the door, pawing the air and saying hoarsely, "Don't hender me!—

gimme the road! I'm a-dying; gimme the road!" Out on the cold platform I sat down and held his head awhile, and he revived. Presently he said:

"Do you reckon we started the Gen'rul any?"

I said no; we hadn't budged him.

"Well, then, *that* idea's up the flume. We got to think up something else. He's suited wher' he is, I reckon; and if that's the way he feels about it, and has made up his mind that he don't wish to be disturbed, you bet he's a-going to have his own way in the business. Yes, better leave him right wher' he is, long as he wants it so; becuz he holds all the trumps, don't you know, and so it stands to reason that the man that lays out to alter his plans for him is going to get left."

But we couldn't stay out there in that mad storm; we should have frozen to death. So we went in again and shut the door, and began to suffer once more and take turns at the break in the window. By and by, as we were starting away from a station where we had stopped a moment Thompson pranced in cheerily, and exclaimed:

"We're all right, now! I reckon we've got the Commodore this time. I judge I've got the stuff here that'll take the tuck out of him."

It was carbolic acid. He had a carboy of it. He sprinkled it all around everywhere; in fact he drenched everything with it, rifle-box, cheese and all. Then we sat down, feeling pretty hopeful. But it wasn't for long. You see the two perfumes began to mix, and then—well, pretty soon we made a break for the door; and out there Thompson swabbed his face with his bandanna and said in a kind of disheartened way:

"It ain't no use. We can't buck agin *him.* He just utilizes everything we put up to modify him with, and gives it his own flavor and plays it back on us. Why, Cap, don't you know, it's as much as a hundred times worse in there now than it was when he first got a-going. I never *did* see one of 'em warm up to his work so, and take such a dumnation interest in it. No, sir, I never did, as long as I've ben on the road; and I've carried a many a one of 'em, as I was telling you."

We went in again after we were frozen pretty stiff; but my, we couldn't *stay* in, now. So we just waltzed back and forth, freezing, and thawing, and stifling, by turns. In about an hour we stopped at another station; and as we left it Thompson came in with a bag, and said—

"Cap, I'm a-going to chance him once more—just this, once; and if we don't fetch him this time, the thing for us to do, is to just throw up the sponge and withdraw from the canvass. That's the way *I* put it up."

He had brought a lot of chicken feathers, and dried apples, and leaf tobacco, and rags, and old shoes, and sulphur, and asafetida, and one thing or another; and he piled them on a breadth of sheet iron in the middle of the floor, and set fire to them.

When they got well started, I couldn't see, myself, how even the corpse could stand it. All that went before was just simply poetry to that smell—but mind you, the original smell stood up out of it just as sublime as ever—fact is, these other smells just seemed to give it a better hold; and my, how rich it was! I didn't make these reflections there—there wasn't time—made them on the platform. And breaking for the platform, Thompson got suffocated and fell; and before I got him dragged out, which I did by the collar, I was mighty near gone myself. When we revived, Thompson said dejectedly:

"We got to stay out here, Cap. We got to do it. They ain't no other way. The Governor wants to travel alone, and he's fixed so he can out-vote us."

And presently he added:

"And don't you know, we're *pisoned*. It's *our* last trip, you can make up your mind to it. Typhoid fever is what's going to come of this. I feel it a-coming right now. Yes, sir, we're elected, just as sure as you're born."

We were taken from the platform an hour later, frozen and insensible, at the next station, and I went straight off into a virulent fever, and never knew anything again for three weeks. I found out, then, that I had spent that awful night with a harmless box of rifles and a lot of innocent cheese; but the news was too late to save *me;* imagination had done its work, and my health was permanently shattered; neither Bermuda nor any other land can ever bring it back to me. This is my last trip; I am on my way home to die.

1882

THE McWILLIAMSES AND THE BURGLAR ALARM

THE CONVERSATION drifted smoothly and pleasantly along from weather to crops, from crops to literature, from literature to scandal, from scandal to religion; then took a random jump and landed on the subject of burglar alarms. And now for the first time Mr. McWilliams showed feeling. Whenever I perceive this sign on this man's dial, I comprehend it, and lapse into silence, and give him opportunity to unload his heart. Said he, with but ill-controlled emotion:

I do not go one single cent on burglar alarms, Mr. Twain—not a single cent—and I will tell you why. When we were finishing our house, we found we had a little cash left over, on account of the plumber not knowing it. I was for enlightening the heathen with it, for I was always unaccountably down on the heathen somehow; but Mrs. McWilliams said no, let's have a burglar alarm. I agreed to this compromise. I will explain that whenever I want a thing, and Mrs. McWilliams wants another thing, and we decide upon the thing that Mrs. McWilliams wants—as we always do—she calls that a compromise. Very well: the man came up from New York and put in the alarm, and charged three hundred and twenty-five dollars for it, and said we could sleep without uneasiness now. So we did for awhile—say a month. Then one night we smelled smoke, and I was advised to get up and see what the matter was. I lit a candle, and started toward the stairs, and met a burglar coming out of a room with a basket of tinware, which he had mistaken for solid silver in the dark. He was smoking a pipe. I said, "My friend, we do not allow smoking in this room." He said he was a stranger, and could not be expected to know the rules of the house: said he had been in many houses just as good as this one, and it had never been objected to before. He added that as far as his experience went, such rules had never been considered to apply to burglars, anyway.

I said: "Smoke along, then, if it is the custom, though I think that the conceding of a privilege to a burglar which is denied to a bishop is a conspicuous sign of the looseness of the times. But waiving all that, what business have you to be entering this house in this furtive and clandestine way, without ringing the burglar alarm?"

He looked confused and ashamed, and said, with embarrassment: "I beg a thousand pardons. I did not know you had a burglar alarm, else I would have rung it. I beg you will not mention it where my parents may hear of it, for they are old and feeble, and such a seemingly wanton breach of the hallowed conventionalities of our Christian civilization might all too rudely sunder the frail bridge which hangs darkling between the pale and evanescent present and the solemn great deeps of the eternities. May I trouble you for a match?"

I said: "Your sentiments do you honor, but if you will allow me to say it, metaphor is not your best hold. Spare your thigh; this kind light only on the box, and seldom there, in fact, if my experience may be trusted. But to return to business: how did you get in here?"

"Through a second-story window."

It was even so. I redeemed the tinware at pawnbroker's rates, less cost of advertising, bade the burglar good-night, closed the window after him, and retired to headquarters to report. Next morning we sent for the burglar-alarm man, and he came up and explained that the reason the alarm did not "go off" was that no part of the house but the first floor was attached to the alarm. This was simply idiotic; one might as well have no armor on at all in battle as to have it only on his legs. The expert now put the whole second story on the alarm, charged three hundred dollars for it, and went his way. By and by, one night, I found a burglar in the third story, about to start down a ladder with a lot of miscellaneous property. My first impulse was to crack his head with a billiard cue; but my second was to refrain from this attention, because he was between me and the cue rack. The second impulse was plainly the soundest, so I refrained, and proceeded to compromise. I redeemed the property at former rates, after deducting ten per cent. for use of ladder, it being my ladder, and next day we sent down for the expert once more, and had the third story attached to the alarm, for three hundred dollars.

By this time the "annunciator" had grown to formidable dimensions. It had forty-seven tags on it, marked with the names of the various rooms and chimneys, and it occupied the space of an ordinary wardrobe. The gong was the size of a wash-bowl, and was placed above the head of our bed. There was a wire from the house to the coachman's quarters in the stable, and a noble gong alongside his pillow.

We should have been comfortable now but for one defect. Every morning at five the cook opened the kitchen door, in the way of business, and rip went that gong! The first time this happened I thought the last day was come sure. I didn't think it *in* bed—no, but out of it—for the first effect of that frightful gong is to hurl you across the house, and slam you against the wall, and then curl you up, and squirm you like a spider on a stove lid, till somebody shuts the kitchen door. In solid fact, there is no clamor that is even remotely comparable to the dire clamor which that gong makes. Well, this catastrophe happened every morning regularly at five o'clock, and lost us three hours sleep; for, mind you, when that thing wakes you, it doesn't merely wake you in spots; it wakes you all over, conscience and all, and you are good for eighteen hours of wide-awakeness subsequently—eighteen hours of the very most inconceivable wide-awakeness that you ever experienced in your life. A stranger died on our hands one time, and we vacated and left him in our room overnight. Did that stranger wait for the general judgment? *No,* sir; he got up at five the next morning in the most prompt and unostentatious way. I knew he would; I knew it mighty well. He collected his life-insurance, and lived happy ever after, for there was plenty of proof as to the perfect squareness of his death.

Well, we were gradually fading toward a better land, on account of the daily loss of sleep; so we finally had the expert up again, and he ran a wire to the outside of the door, and placed a switch there, whereby Thomas, the butler, always made one little mistake—he switched the alarm off at night when he went to bed, and switched it on again at daybreak in the morning, just in time for the cook to open the kitchen door, and enable that gong to slam us across the house, sometimes breaking a window with one or the other of us. At the end of a week we recognized that this switch business was a delusion and a snare. We also discovered that a band of burglars had been lodging in the house the whole time—not exactly to steal, for there wasn't much left now, but to hide from the police, for they were hot pressed, and they shrewdly judged that the detectives would never think of a tribe of burglars taking sanctuary in a house notoriously protected by the most imposing and elaborate burglar alarm in America.

Sent down for the expert again, and this time he struck a most dazzling idea—he fixed the thing so that opening the kitchen door would take off the alarm. It was a noble idea, and he charged accordingly. But you already foresee the result. I switched on the alarm every night at bed-time, no longer trusting on Thomas's frail memory; and as soon as the lights were out the burglars walked in at the kitchen door, thus taking the alarm off without waiting for the cook to do it in the morning. You see how aggravatingly we were situated. For months we couldn't have any company. Not a spare bed in the house; all occupied by burglars.

Finally, I got up a cure of my own. The expert answered the call, and ran another ground wire to the stable, and established a switch there, so that the coachman could put on and take off the alarm. That worked first rate, and a season of peace ensued, during which we got to inviting company once more and enjoying life.

But by and by the irrepressible alarm invented a new kink. One winter's night we were flung out of bed by the sudden music of that awful gong, and when we hobbled to the annunciator, turned up the gas, and saw the word "Nursery" exposed, Mrs. McWilliams fainted dead away, and I came precious near doing the same thing myself. I seized my shotgun, and stood timing the coachman whilst that appalling buzzing went on. I knew that his gong had flung him out, too, and that he would be along with his gun as soon as he could jump into his clothes. When I judged that the time was ripe, I crept to the room next the nursery, glanced through the window, and saw the dim outline of the coachman in the yard below, standing at present-arms and waiting for a chance. Then I hopped into the nursery and fired, and in the same instant the coachman fired at the red flash of my gun. Both of us were successful; I crippled a nurse, and he shot off all my back hair. We turned up the gas, and telephoned for a surgeon. There was not a sign of a burglar, and no window had been raised. One glass was absent, but that was where the coachman's charge had come through. Here was a fine mystery—a burglar alarm "going off" at midnight of its own accord, and not a burglar in the neighborhood!

The expert answered the usual call, and explained that it was a "False alarm." Said it was easily fixed. So he overhauled the nursery window, charged a remunerative figure for it, and departed.

What we suffered from false alarms for the next three years no stylographic pen can describe. During the next three months I always flew with my gun to the room indicated, and the coachman always sallied forth with his battery to support me. But there was never anything to shoot at—windows all tight and secure. We always sent down for the expert next day, and he fixed those particular windows so they would keep quiet a week or so, and always remembered to send us a bill about like this:

Wire	$2.15
Nipple	.75
Two hours' labor	1.50
Wax	.47
Tape	.34
Screws	.15
Recharging battery	.98
Three hours' labor	2.25
String	.02
Lard	.66
Pond's Extract	1.25
Springs at 50	2.00
Railroad fares	7.25
	$19.77

At length a perfectly natural thing came about—after we had answered three or four hundred false alarms—to wit, we stopped answering them. Yes, I simply rose up calmly, when slammed across the house by the alarm, calmly inspected the annunciator, took note of the room indicated, and then calmly disconnected that room from the alarm, and went back to bed as if nothing had happened. Moreover, I left that room off permanently, and did not send for the expert. Well, it goes without saying that in the course of time *all* the rooms were taken off, and the entire machine was out of service.

It was at this unprotected time that the heaviest calamity of all happened. The burglars walked in one night and carried off the burglar alarm! yes, sir, every hide and hair of it: ripped it out, tooth and nail; springs, bells, gongs, battery, and all; they took a hundred and fifty miles of copper wire; they just cleaned her out, bag and baggage, and never left us a vestige of her to swear at—swear by, I mean.

We had a time of it to get her back; but we accomplished it finally, for money. The alarm firm said that what we needed now was to have her put in right—with their new patent springs in the windows to make false alarms impossible, and their new patent clock attached to take off and put on the alarm morning and night without human assistance. That seemed a good scheme. They promised to have the whole thing finished in ten days. They began work, and we left for the summer. They worked a couple of days; then *they* left for the summer. After which the burglars moved in, and began *their* summer vacation. When we returned in the fall, the house was as empty as a beer closet in premises where painters have been at work. We refurnished, and then sent down to hurry up the expert. He came up and finished the job, and said: "Now this clock is set to put on the alarm every night at 10, and take it off every morning at 5:45. All you've got to do is to wind her up every week, and then leave her alone—she will take care of the alarm herself."

After that we had a most tranquil season during three months. The bill was prodigious, of course, and I had said I would not pay it until the new machinery had proved itself to be flawless. The time stipulated was three months. So I paid the bill, and the very next day the alarm went to buzzing like ten thousand bee swarms at ten o'clock in the morning. I turned the hands around twelve hours, according to instructions, and this took off the alarm; but there was another hitch at night, and I had to set her ahead twelve hours once more to get her to put the alarm on again. That sort of nonsense went on a week or two, then the expert came up and put in a new clock. He came up every three months during the next three years, and put in a new clock. But it was always a failure. His clocks all had the same perverse defect: they would put the alarm on in the daytime, and they would *not* put it on at night; and if you forced it on yourself, they *would* take it off again the minute your back was turned.

Now there is the history of that burglar alarm—everything just as it happened; nothing extenuated, and naught set down in malice. Yes, sir,—and when I had slept nine years with burglars, and maintained an expensive burglar alarm the whole time, for their protection, not mine, and at my sole cost—for not a d——d cent could I ever get *them* to contribute—I just said to Mrs. McWilliams that I had had enough of that kind of pie; so with her full consent I took the whole thing out and traded it off for a dog, and shot the dog. I don't know what *you* think about it, Mr. Twain; but *I* think those things are made solely in the interest of the burglars. Yes, sir, a burglar alarm combines in its person all that is objectionable about a fire, a riot, and a harem, and at the same time had none of the compensating advantages, of one sort or another, that customarily belong with that combination. Good-by: I get off here.

1882

THE STOLEN WHITE ELEPHANT*

1

THE FOLLOWING curious history was related to me by a chance railway acquaintance. He was a gentleman more than seventy years of age, and his thoroughly good and gentle face and earnest and sincere manner imprinted the unmistakable stamp of truth upon every statement which fell from his lips. He said:

You know in what reverence the royal white elephant of Siam is held by the people of that country. You know it is sacred to kings, only kings may possess it, and that it is, indeed, in a measure even superior to kings, since it receives not merely honor but worship. Very well; five years ago, when the troubles concerning the frontier line arose between Great Britain and Siam, it was presently manifest that Siam had been in the wrong. Therefore every reparation was quickly made, and the British representative stated that he was satisfied and the past should be forgotten. This greatly relieved the King of Siam, and partly as a token of gratitude, but partly also, perhaps, to wipe out any little

---

* Left out of *A Tramp Abroad*, because it was feared that some of the particulars had been exaggerated, and that others were not true. Before these suspicions had been proven groundless, the book had gone to press. M.T.

remaining vestige of unpleasantness which England might feel toward him, he wished to send the Queen a present—the sole sure way of propitiating an enemy, according to Oriental ideas. This present ought not only to be a royal one, but transcendently royal. Wherefore, what offering could be so meet as that of a white elephant? My position in the Indian civil service was such that I was deemed peculiarly worthy of the honor of conveying the present to her Majesty. A ship was fitted out for me and my servants and the officers and attendants of the elephant, and in due time I arrived in New York harbor and placed my royal charge in admirable quarters in Jersey City. It was necessary to remain awhile in order to recruit the animal's health before resuming the voyage.

All went well during a fortnight—then my calamities began. The white elephant was stolen! I was called up at dead of night and informed of this fearful misfortune. For some moments I was beside myself with terror and anxiety; I was helpless. Then I grew calmer and collected my faculties. I soon saw my course—for, indeed, there was but the one course for an intelligent man to pursue. Late as it was, I flew to New York and got a policeman to conduct me to the headquarters of the detective force. Fortunately I arrived in time, though the chief of the force, the celebrated Inspector Blunt, was just on the point of leaving for his home. He was a man of middle size and compact frame, and when he was thinking deeply he had a way of knitting his brows and tapping his forehead reflectively with his finger, which impressed you at once with the conviction that you stood in the presence of a person of no common order. The very sight of him gave me confidence and made me hopeful. I stated my errand. It did not flurry him in the least; it had no more visible effect upon his iron self-possession than if I had told him somebody had stolen my dog. He motioned me to a seat, and said, calmly:

"Allow me to think a moment, please."

So saying, he sat down at his office table and leaned his head upon his hand. Several clerks were at work at the other end of the room; the scratching of their pens was all the sound I heard during the next six or seven minutes. Meantime the inspector sat there, buried in thought. Finally he raised his head, and there was that in the firm lines of his face which showed me that his brain had done its work and his plan was made. Said he—and his voice was low and impressive:

"This is no ordinary case. Every step must be warily taken; each step must be made sure before the next is ventured. And secrecy must be observed—secrecy profound and absolute. Speak to no one about the matter, not even the reporters. I will take care of *them;* I will see that they get only what it may suit my ends to let them know." He touched a bell; a youth appeared. "Alaric, tell the reporters to remain for the present." The boy retired. "Now let us proceed to business—and systematically. Nothing can be accomplished in this trade of mine without strict and minute method."

He took a pen and some paper. "Now—name of the elephant?"

"Hassan Ben Ali Ben Selim Abdallah Mohammed Moisé Alhammal Jamsetjejeebhoy Dhuleep Sultan Ebu Bhudpoor."

"Very well. Given name?"

"Jumbo."

"Very well. Place of birth?"

"The capital city of Siam."

"Parents living?"

"No—dead."

"Had they any other issue besides this one?"

"None. He was an only child."

"Very well. These matters are sufficient under that head. Now please describe the elephant, and leave out no particular, however insignificant—that is, insignificant from *your* point of view. To men in my profession there *are* no insignificant particulars; they do not exist."

I described—he wrote. When I was done, he said:

"Now listen. If I have made any mistakes, correct me."

He read as follows:

"Height, 19 feet; length from apex of forehead to insertion of tail, 26 feet; length of trunk, 16 feet; length of tail, 6 feet; total length, including trunk and tail, 48 feet; length of tusks, 9½ feet; ears in keeping with these dimensions; footprint resembles the mark left when one upends a barrel in the snow; color of the elephant, a dull white; has a hole the size of a plate in each ear for the insertion of jewelry, and possesses the habit in a remarkable degree of squirting water upon spectators and of maltreating with his trunk not only such persons as he is acquainted with, but even entire strangers; limps slightly with his right hind leg, and has a small scar in his left armpit caused by a former boil; had on, when stolen, a castle containing seats for fifteen persons, and a gold-cloth saddle-blanket the size of an ordinary carpet."

There were no mistakes. The inspector touched the bell, handed the description to Alaric, and said:

"Have fifty thousand copies of this printed at once and mailed to every detective office and pawnbroker's shop on the continent." Alaric retired. "There—so far, so good. Next, I must have a photograph of the property."

I gave him one. He examined it critically, and said:

"It must do, since we can do no better; but he has his trunk curled up and tucked into his mouth. That is unfortunate, and is calculated to mislead, for of course he does not usually have it in that position." He touched his bell.

"Alaric, have fifty thousand copies of this photograph made the first thing in the morning, and mail them with the descriptive circulars."

Alaric retired to execute his orders. The inspector said:

"It will be necessary to offer a reward, of course. Now as to the amount?"

"What sum would you suggest?"

"To *begin* with, I should say—well, twenty-five thousand dollars. It is an intricate and difficult business; there are a thousand avenues of escape and opportunities of concealment. These thieves have friends and pals everywhere—"

"Bless me, do you know who they are?"

The wary face, practised in concealing the thoughts and feelings within, gave me no token, nor yet the replying words, so quietly uttered:

"Never mind about that. I may, and I may not. We generally gather a pretty shrewd inkling of who our man is by the manner of his work and the size of the game he goes after. We are not dealing with a pickpocket or a hall thief now, make up your mind to that. This property was not 'lifted' by a novice. But, as I was saying, considering the amount of travel which will have to be done, and the diligence with which the thieves will cover up their traces as they move along, twenty-five thousand may be too small a sum to offer, yet I think it worth while to start with that."

So we determined upon that figure as a beginning. Then this man, whom nothing escaped which could by any possibility be made to serve as a clue, said:

"There are cases in detective history to show that criminals have been detected through peculiarities in their appetites. Now, what does this elephant eat, and how much?"

"Well, as to *what* he eats—he will eat *anything*. He will eat a man, he will eat a Bible—he will eat anything *between* a man and a Bible."

"Good—very good, indeed, but too general. Details are necessary—details are the only valuable things in our trade. Very well—as to men. At one meal—or, if you prefer, during one day—how many men will he eat, if fresh?"

"He would not care whether they were fresh or not; at a single meal he would eat five ordinary men."

"Very good; five men; we will put that down. What nationalities would he prefer?"

"He is indifferent about nationalities. He prefers acquaintances, but is not prejudiced against strangers."

"Very good. Now, as to Bibles. How many Bibles would he eat at a meal?"

"He would eat an entire edition."

"It is hardly succinct enough. Do you mean the ordinary octavo, or the family illustrated?"

"I think he would be indifferent to illustrations; that is, I think he would not value illustrations above simple letter-press."

"No, you do not get my idea. I refer to bulk. The ordinary octavo Bible weighs about two pounds and a half, while the great quarto with the illustrations weighs ten or twelve. How many Doré Bibles would he eat at a meal?"

"If you knew this elephant, you could not ask. He would take what they had."

"Well, put it in dollars and cents, then. We must get at it somehow. The Doré costs a hundred dollars a copy, Russia leather, beveled."

"He would require about fifty thousand dollars' worth—say an edition of five hundred copies."

"Now that is more exact. I will put that down. Very well; he likes men and Bibles; so far, so good. What else will he eat? I want particulars."

"He will leave Bibles to eat bricks, he will leave bricks to eat bottles, he will leave bottles to eat clothing, he will leave clothing to eat cats, he will leave cats to eat oysters, he will leave oysters to eat ham, he will leave ham to eat sugar, he will leave sugar to eat pie, he will leave pie to eat potatoes, he will leave potatoes to eat bran, he will leave bran to eat hay, he will leave hay to eat oats, he will leave oats to eat rice, for he was mainly raised on it. There is nothing whatever that he will not eat but European butter, and he would eat that if he could taste it."

"Very good. General quantity at a meal—say about—"

"Well, anywhere from a quarter to half a ton."

"And he drinks—"

"Everything that is fluid. Milk, water, whisky, molasses, castor oil, camphene, carbolic acid—it is no use to go into particulars; whatever fluid occurs to you set it down. He will drink anything that is fluid, except European coffee."

"Very good. As to quantity?"

"Put it down five to fifteen barrels—his thirst varies; his other appetites do not."

"These things are unusual. They ought to furnish quite good clues toward tracing him."

He touched the bell.

"Alaric, summon Captain Burns."

Burns appeared. Inspector Blunt unfolded the whole matter to him, detail by detail. Then he said in the clear, decisive tones of a man whose plans are clearly defined in his head and who is accustomed to command:

"Captain Burns, detail Detectives Jones, Davis, Halsey, Bates, and Hackett to shadow the elephant."

"Yes, sir."

"Detail Detectives Moses, Dakin, Murphy, Rogers, Tupper, Higgins, and Batholomew to shadow the thieves."

"Yes, sir."

"Place a strong guard—a guard of thirty picked men, with a relief of thirty—over the place from whence the elephant was stolen, to keep strict watch there night and day, and allow none to approach—except reporters—without written authority from me."

"Yes, sir."

"Place detectives in plain clothes in the railway, steamship, and ferry depots, and upon all roadways leading out of Jersey City, with orders to search all suspicious persons."

"Yes, sir."

"Furnish all these men with photograph and accompanying description of the elephant, and instruct them to search all trains and outgoing ferryboats and other vessels."

"Yes, sir."

"If the elephant should be found, let him be seized, and the information forwarded to me by telegraph."

"Yes, sir."

"Let me be informed at once if any clues should be found—footprints of the animal, or anything of that kind."

"Yes, sir."

"Get an order commanding the harbor police to patrol the frontages vigilantly."

"Yes, sir."

"Despatch detectives in plain clothes over all the railways, north as far as Canada, west as far as Ohio, south as far as Washington."

"Yes, sir."

"Place experts in all the telegraph offices to listen to all messages; and let them require that all cipher despatches be interpreted to them."

"Yes, sir."

"Let all these things be done with the utmost secrecy—mind, the most impenetrable secrecy."

"Yes, sir."

"Report to me promptly at the usual hour."

"Yes, sir."

"Go!"

"Yes, sir."

He was gone.

Inspector Blunt was silent and thoughtful a moment, while the fire in his eye cooled down and faded out. Then he turned to me and said in a placid voice:

"I am not given to boasting, it is not my habit; but—we shall find the elephant."

I shook him warmly by the hand and thanked him; and I *felt* my thanks, too. The more I had seen of the man the more I liked him and the more I admired him and marveled over the mysterious wonders of his profession. Then we parted for the night, and I went home with a far happier heart than I had carried with me to his office.

2

Next morning it was all in the newspapers, in the minutest detail. It even had additions—consisting of Detective This, Detective That, and Detective The Other's "Theory" as to how the robbery was done, who the robbers were, and whither they had flown with their booty. There were eleven of these theories, and they covered all the possibilities; and this single fact shows what independent thinkers detectives are. No two theories were alike, or even much resembled each other, save in one striking particular, and in that one all the other eleven theories were absolutely agreed. That was, that although the rear of my building was torn out and the only door remained locked, the elephant had not been removed through the rent, but by some other (undiscovered) outlet. All agreed that the robbers had made that rent only to mislead the detectives. That never would have occurred to me or to any other layman, perhaps, but it had not deceived the detectives for a moment. Thus, what I had supposed was the only thing that had no mystery about it was in fact the very thing I had gone furthest astray in. The eleven theories all named the supposed robbers, but no two named the same robbers; the total number of suspected persons was thirty-seven. The various newspaper accounts all closed with the most important opinion of all—that of Chief Inspector Blunt. A portion of this statement read as follows:

The chief knows who the two principals are, namely, "Brick" Duffy and "Red" McFadden. Ten days before the robbery was achieved he was already aware that it was to be attempted, and had quietly proceeded to shadow these two noted villains; but unfortunately on the night in question their track was lost, and before it could be found again the bird was flown—that is, the elephant.

Duffy and McFadden are the boldest scoundrels in

the profession; the chief has reasons for believing that they are the men who stole the stove out of the detective headquarters on a bitter night last winter—in consequence of which the chief and every detective present were in the hands of the physicians before morning, some with frozen feet, others with frozen fingers, ears, and other members.

When I read the first half of that I was more astonished than ever at the wonderful sagacity of this strange man. He not only saw everything in the present with a clear eye, but even the future could not be hidden from him. I was soon at his office, and said I could not help wishing he had had those men arrested, and so prevented the trouble and loss; but his reply was simple and unanswerable:

"It is not our province to prevent crime, but to punish it. We cannot punish it until it is committed."

I remarked that the secrecy with which he had begun had been marred by the newspapers; not only all our facts but all our plans and purposes had been revealed; even all the suspected persons had been named; these would doubtless disguise themselves now, or go into hiding.

"Let them. They will find that when I am ready for them my hand will descend upon them, in their secret places, as unerringly as the hand of fate. As to the newspapers, we *must* keep in with them. Fame, reputation, constant public mention—these are the detective's bread and butter. He must publish his facts, else he will be supposed to have none; he must publish his theory, for nothing is so strange or striking as a detective's theory, or brings him so much wonderful respect; we must publish our plans, for these the journals insist upon having, and we could not deny them without offending. We must constantly show the public what we are doing, or they will believe we are doing nothing. It is much pleasanter to have a newspaper say, 'Inspector Blunt's ingenious and extraordinary theory is as follows,' than to have it say some harsh thing, or, worse still, some sarcastic one."

"I see the force of what you say. But I noticed that in one part of your remarks in the papers this morning you refused to reveal your opinion upon a certain minor point."

"Yes, we always do that; it has a good effect. Besides, I had not formed any opinion on that point, anyway."

I deposited a considerable sum of money with the inspector, to meet current expenses, and sat down to wait for news. We were expecting the telegrams to begin to arrive at any moment now. Meantime I reread the newspapers and also our descriptive circular, and observed that our twenty-five thousand dollars reward seemed to be offered only to detectives. I said I thought it ought to be offered to anybody who would catch the elephant. The inspector said:

"It is the detectives who will find the elephant, hence the reward will go to the right place. If other people found the animal, it would only be by watching the detectives and taking advantage of clues and indications stolen from them, and that would entitle the detectives to the reward, after all. The proper office of a reward is to stimulate the men who deliver up their time and their trained sagacities to this sort of work, and not to confer benefits upon chance citizens who stumble upon a capture without having earned the benefits by their own merits and labors."

This was reasonable enough, certainly. Now the telegraphic machine in the corner began to click, and the following despatch was the result:

FLOWER STATION, N. Y., 7.30 A.M.

HAVE GOT A CLUE. FOUND A SUCCESSION OF DEEP TRACKS ACROSS A FARM NEAR HERE. FOLLOWED THEM TWO MILES EAST WITHOUT RESULT; THINK ELEPHANT WENT WEST. SHALL NOW SHADOW HIM IN THAT DIRECTION.

DARLEY, DETECTIVE

"Darley's one of the best men on the force," said the inspector. "We shall hear from him again before long."

Telegram No. 2 came:

BARKER'S, N. J., 7.40 A.M.

JUST ARRIVED. GLASS FACTORY BROKEN OPEN HERE DURING NIGHT, AND EIGHT HUNDRED BOTTLES TAKEN. ONLY WATER IN LARGE QUANTITY NEAR HERE IS FIVE MILES DISTANT. SHALL STRIKE FOR THERE. ELEPHANT WILL BE THIRSTY. BOTTLES WERE EMPTY. BAKER, DETECTIVE

"That promises well, too," said the inspector. "I told you the creature's appetites would not be bad clues."

Telegram No. 3:

TAYLORVILLE, L. I., 8.15 A.M.

A HAYSTACK NEAR HERE DISAPPEARED DURING NIGHT. PROBABLY EATEN. HAVE GOT A CLUE, AND AM OFF.

HUBBARD, DETECTIVE

"How he does move around!" said the inspector. "I knew we had a difficult job on hand, but we shall catch him yet."

FLOWER STATION, N. Y., 9 A.M.

SHADOWED THE TRACKS THREE MILES WESTWARD. LARGE, DEEP AND RAGGED. HAVE JUST MET A FARMER WHO SAYS THEY ARE NOT ELEPHANT TRACKS. SAYS THEY ARE HOLES WHERE HE DUG UP SAPLINGS FOR SHADE-TREES WHEN GROUND WAS FROZEN LAST WINTER. GIVE ME ORDERS HOW TO PROCEED.

DARLEY, DETECTIVE

"Aha! a confederate of the thieves! The thing grows warm," said the inspector.

He dictated the following telegram to Darley:

ARREST THE MAN AND FORCE HIM TO NAME HIS PALS. CONTINUE TO FOLLOW THE TRACKS—TO THE PACIFIC IF NECESSARY.
CHIEF BLUNT

Next telegram:

CONEY POINT, PA., 8.45 A.M.

GAS OFFICE BROKEN OPEN HERE DURING NIGHT AND THREE MONTHS' UNPAID GAS BILLS TAKEN. HAVE GOT A CLUE AND AM AWAY.
MURPHY, DETECTIVE

"Heavens!" said the inspector; "would he eat gas bills?"

"Through ignorance—yes; but they cannot support life. At least, unassisted."

Now came this exciting telegram:

IRONVILLE, N. Y., 9:30 A.M.

JUST ARRIVED. THIS VILLAGE IN CONSTERNATION. ELEPHANT PASSED THROUGH HERE AT FIVE THIS MORNING. SOME SAY HE WENT EAST, SOME SAY WEST, SOME NORTH, SOME SOUTH—BUT ALL SAY THEY DID NOT WAIT TO NOTICE PARTICULARLY. HE KILLED A HORSE; HAVE SECURED A PIECE OF IT FOR A CLUE. KILLED IT WITH HIS TRUNK; FROM STYLE OF BLOW, THINK HE STRUCK IT LEFT-HANDED. FROM POSITION IN WHICH HORSE LIES, THINK ELEPHANT TRAVELED NORTHWARD ALONG LINE OF BERKLEY RAILWAY. HAS FOUR AND A HALF HOURS' START, BUT I MOVE ON HIS TRACK AT ONCE.
HAWES, DETECTIVE

I uttered exclamations of joy. The inspector was as self-contained as a graven image. He calmly touched his bell.

"Alaric, send Captain Burns here."

Burns appeared.

"How many men are ready for instant orders?"

"Ninety-six, sir."

"Send them north at once. Let them concentrate along the line of the Berkley road north of Ironville."

"Yes, sir."

"Let them conduct their movements with the utmost secrecy. As fast as others are at liberty, hold them for orders."

"Yes, sir."

"Go!"

"Yes, sir."

Presently came another telegram:

SAGE CORNERS, N. Y., 10.30.

JUST ARRIVED, ELEPHANT PASSED THROUGH HERE AT 8.15. ALL ESCAPED FROM THE TOWN BUT A POLICEMAN. APPARENTLY ELEPHANT DID NOT STRIKE AT POLICEMAN, BUT AT THE LAMPPOST. GOT BOTH. I HAVE SECURED A PORTION OF THE POLICEMAN AS CLUE. STUMM, DETECTIVE

"So the elephant has turned westward," said the inspector. "However, he will not escape, for my men are scattered all over that region."

The next telegram said:

GLOVER'S, 11.15.

JUST ARRIVED. VILLAGE DESERTED, EXCEPT SICK AND AGED. ELEPHANT PASSED THROUGH THREE-QUARTERS OF AN HOUR AGO. THE ANTI-TEMPERANCE MASS-MEETING WAS IN SESSION; HE PUT HIS TRUNK IN AT A WINDOW AND WASHED IT OUT WITH WATER FROM CISTERN. SOME SWALLOWED IT—SINCE DEAD; SEVERAL DROWNED. DETECTIVES CROSS AND O'SHAUGHNESSY WERE PASSING THROUGH TOWN, BUT GOING SOUTH—SO MISSED ELEPHANT. WHOLE REGION FOR MANY MILES AROUND IN TERROR—PEOPLE FLYING FROM THEIR HOMES. WHEREVER THEY TURN THEY MEET ELEPHANT, AND MANY ARE KILLED.

BRANT, DETECTIVE

I could have shed tears, this havoc so distressed me. But the inspector only said:

"You see—we are closing in on him. He feels our presence; he has turned eastward again."

Yet further troublous news was in store for us. The telegraph brought this:

HOGANSPORT, 12.19.

JUST ARRIVED. ELEPHANT PASSED THROUGH HALF AN HOUR AGO, CREATING WILDEST FRIGHT AND EXCITEMENT. ELEPHANT RAGED AROUND STREETS: TWO PLUMBERS GOING BY, KILLED ONE.—OTHER ESCAPED. REGRET GENERAL.

O'FLAHERTY, DETECTIVE

"Now he is right in the midst of my men," said the inspector. "Nothing can save him."

A succession of telegrams came from detectives who were scattered through New Jersey and Pennsylvania, and who were following clues consisting of ravaged barns, factories, and Sunday-school libraries, with high hopes—hopes amounting to certainties, indeed. The inspector said:

"I wish I could communicate with them and order them north, but that is impossible. A detective only visits a telegraph office to send his report; then he is off again, and you don't know where to put your hand on him."

Now came this despatch:

BRIDGEPORT, CT., 12.15.

BARNUM OFFERS RATE OF $4,000 A YEAR FOR EXCLUSIVE PRIVILEGE OF USING ELEPHANT AS TRAVELING ADVERTISING MEDIUM FROM NOW TILL DETECTIVES FIND HIM. WANTS TO PASTE CIRCUS-POSTERS ON HIM. DESIRES IMMEDIATE ANSWER.

BOGGS, DETECTIVE

"That is perfectly absurd!" I exclaimed.

"Of course it is," said the inspector. "Evidently Mr.

Barnum, who thinks he is so sharp, does not know me—but I know him."

Then he dictated this answer to the despatch:

MR. BARNUM'S OFFER DECLINED. MAKE IT $7,000 OR NOTHING.
CHIEF BLUNT

"There. We shall not have to wait long for an answer. Mr. Barnum is not at home; he is in the telegraph office—it is his way when he has business on hand. Inside of three—"

DONE.—P. T. BARNUM

So interrupted the clicking telegraphic instrument. Before I could make a comment upon this extraordinary episode, the following despatch carried my thoughts into another very distressing channel:

BOLIVIA, N. Y., 12.50.

ELEPHANT ARRIVED HERE FROM THE SOUTH AND PASSED THROUGH TOWARD THE FOREST AT 11.50, DISPERSING A FUNERAL ON THE WAY, AND DIMINISHING THE MOURNERS BY TWO. CITIZENS FIRED SOME SMALL CANNON-BALLS INTO HIM, AND THEN FLED. DETECTIVE BURKE AND I ARRIVED TEN MINUTES LATER, FROM THE NORTH, BUT MISTOOK SOME EXCAVATIONS FOR FOOTPRINTS, AND SO LOST A GOOD DEAL OF TIME; BUT AT LAST WE STRUCK THE RIGHT TRAIL AND FOLLOWED IT TO THE WOODS. WE THEN GOT DOWN ON OUR HANDS AND KNEES AND CONTINUED TO KEEP A SHARP EYE ON THE TRACK, AND SO SHADOWED IT INTO THE BRUSH. BURKE WAS IN ADVANCE. UNFORTUNATELY THE ANIMAL HAD STOPPED TO REST; THEREFORE, BURKE HAVING HIS HEAD DOWN, INTENT UPON THE TRACK, BUTTED UP AGAINST THE ELEPHANT'S HIND LEGS BEFORE HE WAS AWARE OF HIS VICINITY. BURKE INSTANTLY AROSE TO HIS FEET, SEIZED THE TAIL, AND

EXCLAIMED JOYFULLY, "I CLAIM THE RE—" BUT GOT NO FURTHER, FOR A SINGLE BLOW OF THE HUGE TRUNK LAID THE BRAVE FELLOW'S FRAGMENTS LOW IN DEATH. I FLED REARWARD, AND THE ELEPHANT TURNED AND SHADOWED ME TO THE EDGE OF THE WOOD, MAKING TREMENDOUS SPEED, AND I SHOULD INEVITABLY HAVE BEEN LOST, BUT THAT THE REMAINS OF THE FUNERAL PROVIDENTIALLY INTERVENED AGAIN AND DIVERTED HIS ATTENTION. I HAVE JUST LEARNED THAT NOTHING OF THAT FUNERAL IS NOW LEFT; BUT THIS IS NO LOSS, FOR THERE IS ABUNDANCE OF MATERIAL FOR ANOTHER. MEANTIME, THE ELEPHANT HAS DISAPPEARED AGAIN. MULROONEY, DETECTIVE

We heard no news except from the diligent and confident detectives scattered about New Jersey, Pennsylvania, Delaware, and Virginia—who were all following fresh and encouraging clues—until shortly after 2 P.M., when this telegram came:

BAXTER CENTER, 2.15.

ELEPHANT BEEN HERE, PLASTERED OVER WITH CIRCUS-BILLS, AND BROKE UP A REVIVAL, STRIKING DOWN AND DAMAGING MANY WHO WERE ON THE POINT OF ENTERING UPON A BETTER LIFE. CITIZENS PENNED UP AND ESTABLISHED A GUARD. WHEN DETECTIVE BROWN AND I ARRIVED, SOME TIME AFTER, WE ENTERED INCLOSURE AND PROCEEDED TO IDENTIFY ELEPHANT BY PHOTOGRAPHS AND DESCRIPTION. ALL MARKS TALLIED EXACTLY EXCEPT ONE, WHICH WE COULD NOT SEE—THE BOIL-SCAR UNDER ARMPIT. TO MAKE SURE, BROWN CREPT UNDER TO LOOK, AND WAS IMMEDIATELY BRAINED—THAT IS, HEAD CRUSHED AND DESTROYED, THOUGH NOTHING ISSUED FROM DEBRIS. ALL FLED; SO DID ELEPHANT, STRIKING RIGHT AND LEFT WITH MUCH EFFECT. HAS ESCAPED, BUT LEFT BOLD BLOOD-TRACK FROM CANNON-WOUNDS. REDISCOVERY CERTAIN. HE BROKE SOUTHWARD, THROUGH A DENSE FOREST. BRENT, DETECTIVE

That was the last telegram. At nightfall a fog shut down which was so dense that objects but three feet away could not be discerned. This lasted all night. The ferryboats and even the omnibuses had to stop running.

3

Next morning the papers were as full of detective theories as before; they had all our tragic facts in detail also, and a great many more which they had received from their telegraphic correspondents. Column after column was occupied, a third of its way down, with glaring head-lines, which it made my heart sick to read. Their general tone was like this:

THE WHITE ELEPHANT AT LARGE! HE MOVES UPON HIS FATAL MARCH! WHOLE VILLAGES DESERTED BY THEIR FRIGHT-STRICKEN OCCUPANTS! PALE TERROR GOES BEFORE HIM, DEATH AND DEVASTATION FOLLOW AFTER! AFTER THESE, THE DETECTIVES! BARNS DESTROYED, FACTORIES GUTTED, HARVESTS DEVOURED, PUBLIC ASSEMBLAGES DISPERSED, ACCOMPANIED BY SCENES OF CARNAGE IMPOSSIBLE TO DESCRIBE! THEORIES OF THIRTY-FOUR OF THE MOST DISTINGUISHED DETECTIVES ON THE FORCE! THEORY OF CHIEF BLUNT!

"There!" said Inspector Blunt, almost betrayed into excitement, "this is magnificent! This is the greatest windfall that any detective organization ever had. The fame of it will travel to the ends of the earth, and endure to the end of time, and my name with it."

But there was no joy for me. I felt as if I had committed all those red crimes, and that the elephant was only my irresponsible agent. And how the list had grown! In one place he had "interfered with an election and killed five repeaters." He had followed this act with the destruction of two poor fellows, named O'Donohue and McFlannigan, who had "found a refuge in the home of the oppressed of all lands only the day before, and were in the act of exercising for the first time the noble right of American citizens at the polls, when stricken down by the relentless hand of the Scourge of Siam." In another, he had "found a crazy sensation-preacher preparing his next season's heroic attacks on the dance, the theater, and other things which can't strike back, and had stepped on him." And in still another place he had "killed a lightning-rod agent." And so the list went on, growing redder and redder, and more and more heartbreaking. Sixty persons had been killed, and two hundred and forty wounded. All the accounts bore just testimony to the activity and devotion of the detectives, and all closed with the remark that "three hundred thousand citizens and four detectives saw the dread creature, and two of the latter he destroyed."

I dreaded to hear the telegraphic instrument begin to click again. By and by the messages began to pour in, but I was happily disappointed in their nature. It was soon apparent that all trace of the elephant was lost. The fog had enabled him to search out a good hiding-place unobserved. Telegrams from the most absurdly distant points reported that a dim vast mass had been glimpsed there through the fog at such and such an hour, and was "undoubtedly the elephant." This dim vast mass had been glimpsed in New Haven, in New Jersey, in Pennsylvania, in interior New York, in Brooklyn, and even in the city of New York itself! But in all cases the dim vast mass had vanished quickly and left no trace. Every detective of the large force scattered over this huge extent of country sent his hourly report, and each and every one of them had a clue, and was shadowing something, and was hot upon the heels of it.

But the day passed without other result.

The next day the same.

The next just the same.

The newspaper reports began to grow monotonous with

facts that amounted to nothing, clues which led to nothing, and theories which had nearly exhausted the elements which surprise and delight and dazzle.

By advice of the inspector I doubled the reward.

Four more dull days followed. Then came a bitter blow to the poor, hard-working detectives—the journalists declined to print their theories, and coldly said, "Give us a rest."

Two weeks after the elephant's disappearance I raised the reward to seventy-five thousand dollars by the inspector's advice. It was a great sum, but I felt that I would rather sacrifice my whole private fortune than lose my credit with my government. Now that the detectives were in adversity, the newspapers turned upon them, and began to fling the most stinging sarcasms at them. This gave the minstrels an idea, and they dressed themselves as detectives and hunted the elephant on the stage in the most extravagant way. The caricaturists made pictures of detectives scanning the country with spyglasses, while the elephant, at their backs, stole apples out of their pockets. And they made all sorts of ridiculous pictures of the detective badge—you have seen that badge printed in gold on the back of detective novels, no doubt—it is a wide-staring eye, with the legend, "WE NEVER SLEEP." When detectives called for a drink, the would-be facetious barkeeper resurrected an obsolete form of expression and said, "Will you have an eye-opener?" All the air was thick with sarcasms.

But there was one man who moved calm, untouched, unaffected, through it all. It was that heart of oak, the chief inspector. His brave eye never dropped, his serene confidence never wavered. He always said:

"Let them rail on; he laughs best who laughs last."

My admiration for the man grew into a species of worship. I was at his side always. His office had become an unpleasant place to me, and now became daily more and more so. Yet if he could endure it I meant to do so also—at least, as long as I could. So I came regularly, and stayed—

the only outsider who seemed to be capable of it. Everybody wondered how I could; and often it seemed to me that I must desert, but at such times I looked into that calm and apparently unconscious face, and held my ground.

About three weeks after the elephant's disappearance I was about to say, one morning, that I should *have* to strike my colors and retire, when the great detective arrested the thought by proposing one more superb and masterly move.

This was to compromise with the robbers. The fertility of this man's invention exceeded anything I have ever seen, and I have had a wide intercourse with the world's finest minds. He said he was confident he could compromise for one hundred thousand dollars and recover the elephant. I said I believed I could scrape the amount together, but what would become of the poor detectives who had worked so faithfully? He said:

"In compromises they always get half."

This removed my only objection. So the inspector wrote two notes, in this form:

DEAR MADAME—YOUR HUSBAND CAN MAKE A LARGE SUM OF MONEY (AND BE ENTIRELY PROTECTED FROM THE LAW) BY MAKING AN IMMEDIATE APPOINTMENT WITH ME.

CHIEF BLUNT

He sent one of these by his confidential messenger to the "reputed wife" of Brick Duffy, and the other to the reputed wife of Red McFadden.

Within the hour these offensive answers came:

YE OWLD FOOL: BRICK DUFFYS BIN DED 2 YERE.

BRIDGET MAHONEY

CHIEF BAT—RED MCFADDEN IS HUNG AND IN HEVING 18 MONTH. ANY ASS BUT A DETECTIVE KNOSE THAT.

MARY O'HOOLIGAN

"I had long suspected these facts," said the inspector; "this testimony proves the unerring accuracy of my instinct."

The moment one resource failed him he was ready with another. He immediately wrote an advertisement for the morning papers, and I kept a copy of it:

A.—xwblv. 242 N. Tjnd—fz328wmlg. Ozpo,—; 2 m! ogw. Mum.

He said that if the thief was alive this would bring him to the usual rendezvous. He further explained that the usual rendezvous was a place where all business affairs between detectives and criminals were conducted. This meeting would take place at twelve the next night.

We could do nothing till then, and I lost no time in getting out of the office, and was grateful indeed for the privilege.

At eleven the next night I brought one hundred thousand dollars in bank-notes and put them into the chief's hands, and shortly afterward he took his leave, with the brave old undimmed confidence in his eye. An almost intolerable hour dragged to a close; then I heard his welcome tread, and rose gasping and tottered to meet him. How his fine eyes flamed with triumph! He said:

"We've compromised! The jokers will sing a different tune to-morrow! Follow me!"

He took a lighted candle and strode down into the vast vaulted basement where sixty detectives always slept, and where a score were now playing cards to while the time. I followed close after him. He walked swiftly down to the dim and remote end of the place, and just as I succumbed to the pangs of suffocation and was swooning away he stumbled and fell over the outlying members of a mighty object, and I heard him exclaim as he went down:

"Our noble profession is vindicated. Here is your elephant!"

I was carried to the office above and restored with carbolic acid. The whole detective force swarmed in, and such another season of triumphant rejoicing ensued as I had never witnessed before. The reporters were called, baskets of champagne were opened, toasts were drunk, the handshakings and congratulations were continuous and enthusastic. Naturally the chief was the hero of the hour, and his happiness was so complete and had been so patiently and worthily and bravely won that it made me happy to see it, though I stood there a homeless beggar, my priceless charge dead, and my position in my country's service lost to me through what would always seem my fatally careless execution of a great trust. Many an eloquent eye testified its deep admiration for the chief, and many a detective's voice murmured, "Look at him—just the king of the profession; only give him a clue, it's all he wants, and there ain't anything hid that he can't find." The dividing of the fifty thousand dollars made great pleasure; when it was finished the chief made a little speech while he put his share in his pocket, in which he said, "Enjoy it, boys, for you've earned it; and, more than that, you've earned for the detective profession undying fame."

A telegram arrived, which read:

MONROE, MICH., 10 P.M.

FIRST TIME I'VE STRUCK A TELEGRAPH OFFICE IN OVER THREE WEEKS. HAVE FOLLOWED THOSE FOOTPRINTS, HORSEBACK, THROUGH THE WOODS, A THOUSAND MILES TO HERE, AND THEY GET STRONGER AND BIGGER AND FRESHER EVERY DAY. DON'T WORRY—INSIDE OF ANOTHER WEEK I'LL HAVE THE ELEPHANT. THIS IS DEAD SURE. DARLEY, DETECTIVE

The chief ordered three cheers for "Darley, one of the finest minds on the force," and then commanded that he be telegraphed to come home and receive his share of the reward.

So ended that marvelous episode of the stolen elephant. The newspapers were pleasant with praises once more, the next day, with one contemptible exception. This sheet said, "Great is the detective! He may be a little slow in finding a little thing like a mislaid elephant—he may hunt him all day and sleep with his rotting carcass all night for three weeks, but he will find him at last—if he can get the man who mislaid him to show him the place!"

Poor Hassan was lost to me forever. The cannon-shots had wounded him fatally, he had crept to that unfriendly place in the fog, and there, surrounded by his enemies and in constant danger of detection, he had wasted away with hunger and suffering till death gave him peace.

The compromise cost me one hundred thousand dollars; my detective expenses were forty-two thousand dollars more; I never applied for a place again under my government; I am a ruined man and a wanderer on the earth—but my admiration for that man, whom I believe to be the greatest detective the world has ever produced, remains undimmed to this day, and will so remain unto the end.

1882

A Dying Man's Confession

We were approaching Napoleon, Arkansas. So I began to think about my errand there. Time, noonday; and bright and sunny. This was bad—not best, anyway; for mine was not (preferably) a noonday kind of errand. The more I thought, the more that fact pushed itself upon me—now in one form, now in another. Finally, it took the form of a distinct question: Is it good common sense to do the errand in daytime, when by a little sacrifice of comfort and inclination you can have night for it, and no inquisitive eyes around? This settled it. Plain question and plain answer make the shortest road out of most perplexities.

I got my friends into my stateroom, and said I was sorry to create annoyance and disappointment, but that upon reflection it really seemed best that we put our luggage ashore and stop over at Napoleon. Their disapproval was prompt and loud; their language mutinous. Their main argument was one which has always been the first to come to the surface, in such cases, since the beginning of time: "But you decided and *agreed* to stick to this boat," etc.; as if, having determined to do an unwise thing, one is thereby bound to go ahead and make *two* unwise things of it, by carrying out that determination. I tried various mollifying tactics upon them, with reasonably good success: under which encouragement I increased my efforts; and, to show them that *I* had not created this annoying errand, and was in no way to blame for it, I presently drifted into its history—substantially as follows:

Toward the end of last year I spent a few months in Munich, Bavaria. In November I was living in Fräulein Dahlweiner's *pension*, 1a, Karlsrasse; but my working quarters were a mile from there, in the house of a widow who supported herself by taking lodgers. She and her two young children used to drop in every morning and talk German to me—by request. One day, during a ramble about the city, I visited one of the two establishments where the government keeps and watches corpses until the doctors decide that they are permanently dead, and not in a trance state. It was a grisly place, that spacious room. There were thirty-six corpses of adults in sight, stretched on their backs on slightly slanted boards, in three long rows—all of them with wax white, rigid faces, and all of them wrapped in white shrouds. Along the sides of the room were deep alcoves, like bay-windows; and in each of these lay several marble-visaged babes, utterly hidden and buried under banks of fresh flowers, all but their faces and crossed hands. Around a finger of each of these fifty still forms, both great and small, was a ring; and from the ring a wire led to the ceiling, and thence to a bell in a watch-room yonder, where, day and night, a watchman sits always alert and ready to spring to the aid of any of that pallid company who, waking out of death, shall make a movement—for any, even the slightest, movement will twitch the wire and ring that fearful bell. I imagined myself a death sentinel drowsing there alone, far in the dragging watches of some wailing, gusty night, and having in a twinkling all my body stricken to quivering jelly by the sudden clamor of that awful summons! So I inquired about this thing; asked what resulted usually? if the watchman died, and the restored corpse came and did what it could to make his last moments easy? But I was rebuked for trying to feed an idle and frivolous curiosity in so solemn and so mournful a place; and went my way with a humbled crest.

Next morning I was telling the widow my adventure when she exclaimed:

"Come with me! I have a lodger who shall tell you all you want to know. He has been a night watchman there."

He was a living man, but did not look it. He was abed and had his head propped high on pillows; his face was wasted and colorless, his deep-sunken eyes were shut; his hand, lying on his breast, was talon-like, it was so bony and long-fingered. The widow began her introduction of me. The man's eyes opened slowly, and glittered wickedly out from the twilight of their caverns; he frowned a black frown; he lifted his lean hand and waved us peremptorily away. But the widow kept straight on, till she had got out the fact that I was a stranger and an American. The man's face changed at once, brightened, became even eager—and the next moment he and I were alone together.

I opened up in cast-iron German; he responded in quite flexible English; thereafter we gave the German language a permanent rest.

This consumptive and I became good friends. I visited him every day, and we talked about everything. At least, about everything but wives and children. Let anybody's wife or anybody's child be mentioned and three things always followed: the most gracious and loving and tender light glimmered in the man's eyes for a moment; faded out the next, and in its place came that deadly look which had flamed there the first time I ever saw his lids unclose; thirdly, he ceased from speech there and then for that day, lay silent, abstracted, and absorbed, apparently heard nothing that I said, took no notice of my good-bys, and plainly did not know by either sight or hearing when I left the room.

When I had been this Karl Ritter's daily and sole intimate during two months, he one day said abruptly:

"I will tell you my story."

Then he went on as follows:

I have never given up until now. But now I have given up. I am going to die. I made up my mind last night that it must be, and very soon, too. You say you are going to revisit your river by and by, when you find opportunity. Very well; that, together with a certain strange experience which fell to my lot last night, determines me to tell you my history—for you will see Napoleon, Arkansas, and for my sake you will stop there and do a certain thing for me—a thing which you will willingly undertake after you shall have heard my narrative.

Let us shorten the story wherever we can, for it will need it, being long. You already know how I came to go to America, and how I came to settle in that lonely region in the South. But you do not know that I had a wife. My wife was young, beautiful, loving, and oh, so divinely good and blameless and gentle! And our little girl was her mother in miniature. It was the happiest of happy households.

One night—it was toward the close of the war—I woke up out of a sodden lethargy, and found myself bound and gagged, and the air tainted with chloroform! I saw two men in the room, and one was saying to the other in a hoarse whisper: "I *told* her I would, if she made a noise, and as for the child—"

The other man interrupted in a low, half-crying voice:

"You said we'd only gag them and rob them, not hurt them, or I wouldn't have come."

"Shut up your whining; *had* to change the plan when they waked up. You done all *you* could to protect them, now let that satisfy you. Come, help rummage."

Both men were masked and wore coarse, ragged "nigger" clothes; they had a bull's-eye lantern, and by its light I noticed that the gentler robber had no thumb on his right hand. They rummaged around my poor cabin for a moment: the head bandit then said in his stage whisper:

"It's a waste of time—*he* shall tell where it's hid. Undo his gag and revive him up."

The other said:

"All right—provided no clubbing."

"No clubbing it is, then—provided he keeps still."

They approached me. Just then there was a sound outside, a sound of voices and trampling hoofs; the robbers held their breath and listened; the sounds came slowly nearer and nearer, then came a shout:

"*Hello,* the house! Show a light, we want water."

"The captain's voice, by G——!" said the stage-whispering ruffian, and both robbers fled by the way of the back door, shutting off their bull's-eye as they ran.

The stranger shouted several times more then rode by—there seemed to be a dozen of the horses—and I heard nothing more.

I struggled, but could not free myself from my bonds. I tried to speak, but the gag was effective, I could not make a sound. I listened for my wife's voice and my child's—listened long and intently, but no sound came from the other end of the room where their bed was. This silence became more and more awful, more and more ominous, every moment. Could you have endured an hour of it, do you think? Pity me, then, who had to endure three. Three hours? it was three ages! Whenever the clock struck it seemed as if years had gone by since I had heard it last. All this time I was struggling in my bonds, and at last, about dawn, I got myself free and rose up and stretched my stiff limbs. I was able to distinguish details pretty well. The floor was littered with things thrown there by the robbers during their search for my savings. The first object that caught my particular attention was a document of mine which I had seen the rougher of the two ruffians glance at and then cast away. It had blood on it! I staggered to the other end of the room. Oh, poor unoffending, helpless ones, there they lay; their troubles ended, mine begun!

Did I appeal to the law—I? Does it quench the pauper's thirst if the king drink for him? Oh, no, no, no! I wanted no impertinent interference of the law. Laws and the gallows could not pay the debt that was owing to me! Let the laws leave the latter in my hands, and have no fears: I would find the debtor and collect the debt. How accomplish this, do you say? How accomplish it and feel so sure about it, when I had neither seen the robbers' faces, nor heard their natural voices, nor had any idea who they might be? Nevertheless, I *was* sure—quite sure, quite confident. I had a clue—a clue which you would not have valued—a clue which would not have greatly helped even a detective, since he would lack the secret of how to apply it. I shall come to that presently—you shall see. Let us go on now, taking things in their due order. There was one circumstance which gave me a slant in a definite direction to begin with: Those two robbers were manifestly soldiers in tramp disguise, and not new to military service, but old in it—regulars, perhaps; they did not acquire their soldierly attitude, gestures, carriage, in a day, nor a month, nor yet in a year. So I thought, but said nothing. And one of them had said, "The captain's voice, by G——!"—the one whose life I would have. Two miles away several regiments were in camp, and two companies of U. S. cavalry. When I learned that Captain Blakely of Company C had passed our way that night with an escort I said nothing, but in that company I resolved to seek my man. In conversation I studiously and persistently described the robbers as tramps, camp followers; and among this class the people made useless search, none suspecting the soldiers but me.

Working patiently by night in my desolated home, I made a disguise for myself out of various odds and ends of clothing; in the nearest village I bought a pair of blue goggles. By and by, when the military camp broke up, and Company C was ordered a hundred miles north, to Napoleon, I secreted my small hoard of money in my belt and took my departure in the night. When Company C arrived in Napoleon I was already there. Yes, I was there, with a new trade—fortune-teller. Not to seem partial, I made friends and told fortunes among all the companies garrisoned there, but I gave Company C the great bulk of my attentions. I made myself limitlessly obliging to these particular men; they could ask me no favor, put on me no risk which I would decline. I became the willing butt of their jokes; this perfected my popularity; I became a favorite.

I early found a private who lacked a thumb—what joy it was to me! And when I found that he alone, of all the company, had lost a thumb, my last misgiving vanished; I was *sure* I was on the right track. This man's name was Kruger, a German. There were nine Germans in the company. I watched to see who might be his intimates, but he seemed to have no especial intimates. But I was his intimate, and I took care to make the intimacy grow. Sometimes I so hungered for my revenge that I could hardly restrain myself from going on my knees and begging him to point out the man who had murdered my wife and child, but I managed to bridle my tongue. I bided my time and went on telling fortunes, as opportunity offered.

My apparatus was simple: a little red paint and a bit of white paper. I painted the ball of the client's thumb, took a print of it on the paper, studied it that night, and revealed his fortune to him next day. What was my idea in this nonsense? It was this: When I was a youth, I knew an old Frenchman who had been a prison-keeper for thirty years, and he told me that there was one thing about a person which never changed, from the cradle to the grave—the lines in the ball of the thumb; and he said that these lines were never exactly alike in the thumbs of any two human beings. In these days, we photograph the new criminal, and hang his picture in the Rogues' Gallery for future reference; but that Frenchman, in his day, used to take a print of the ball of a new prisoner's thumb and put that away for future reference. He always said that pictures were no good—future disguises could make them useless. "The thumb's the only sure thing," said he; "you can't disguise that." And he used to prove his theory, too, on my friends and acquaintances; it always succeeded.

I went on telling fortunes. Every night I shut myself in, all alone, and studied the day's thumb-prints with a magnifying-glass. Imagine the devouring eagerness with which I pored over those mazy red spirals, with that document by my side which bore the right-hand thumb and finger-marks of that unknown murderer, printed with the dearest blood—to me—that was ever shed on this earth! And many and many a time I had to repeat the same old disappointed remark, "Will they *never* correspond!"

But my reward came at last. It was the print of the thumb of the forty-third man of Company C whom I had experimented on—Private Franz Adler. An hour before I did not know the murderer's name, or voice, or figure, or face, or nationality; but now I knew all these things! I believed I might feel sure; the Frenchman's repeated demonstrations being so good a warranty. Still, there was a way to *make* sure. I had an impression of Kruger's left thumb. In the morning I took him aside when he was off duty; and when we were out of sight and hearing of witnesses, I said impressively:

"A part of your fortune is so grave that I thought it would be better for you if I did not tell it in public. You and another man, whose fortune I was studying last night—Private Adler—have been murdering a woman and child! You are being dogged. Within five days both of you will be assassinated."

He dropped on his knees, frightened out of his wits; and for five minutes he kept pouring out the same set of words, like a demented person, and in the same half-crying way which was one of my memories of that murderous night in my cabin:

"I didn't do it; upon my soul I didn't do it; and I tried to keep *him* from doing it. I did, as God is my witness. He did it alone."

This was all I wanted. And I tried to get rid of the fool; but no, he clung to me, imploring me to save him from the assassin. He said:

"I have money—ten thousand dollars—hid away, the fruit of loot and thievery; save me—tell me what to do, and you shall have it, every penny. Two-thirds of it is my cousin Adler's; but you can take it all. We hid it when we first came here. But I hid it in a new place yesterday, and have not told him—shall not tell him. I was going to desert, and get away with it all. It is gold, and too heavy to carry when one is running and dodging; but a woman who has been gone over the river two days to prepare my way for me is going to follow me with it; and if I got no chance to describe the hiding-place to her I was going to slip my silver watch into her hand, or send it to her, and she would understand. There's a piece of paper in the back of the case which tells it all. Here, take the watch—tell me what to do!"

He was trying to press his watch upon me, and was exposing the paper and explaining it to me, when Adler appeared on the scene, about a dozen yards away. I said to poor Kruger:

"Put up your watch, I don't want it. You sha'n't come to any harm. Go, now. I must tell Adler his fortune. Presently I will tell you how to escape the assassin; meantime I shall have to examine your thumbmark again. Say nothing to Adler about this thing—say nothing to anybody."

He went away filled with fright and gratitude, poor devil! I told Adler a long fortune—purposely so long that I could not finish it; promised to come to him on guard, that night, and tell him the really important part of it—the tragical part of it, I said—so must be out of reach of eavesdroppers. They always kept a picket-watch outside the town—mere discipline and ceremony—no occasion for it, no enemy around.

Toward midnight I set out, equipped with the countersign, and picked my way toward the lonely region where

Adler was to keep his watch. It was so dark that I stumbled right on a dim figure almost before I could get out a protecting word. The sentinel hailed and I answered, both at the same moment. I added, "It's only me—the fortuneteller." Then I slipped to the poor devil's side, and without a word I drove my dirk into his heart! *"Ja wohl,"* laughed I, "it *was* the tragedy part of his fortune, indeed!" As he fell from his horse he clutched at me, and my blue goggles remained in his hand; and away plunged the beast, dragging him with his foot in the stirrup.

I fled through the woods and made good my escape, leaving the accusing goggles behind me in that dead man's hand.

This was fifteen or sixteen years ago. Since then I have wandered aimlessly about the earth, sometimes at work, sometimes idle; sometimes with money, sometimes with none; but always tired of life, and wishing it was done, for my mission here was finished with the act of that night; and the only pleasure, solace, satisfaction I had, in all those tedious years, was in the daily reflection, "I have killed him!"

"Four years ago my health began to fail. I had wandered into Munich, in my purposeless way. Being out of money I sought work, and got it; did my duty faithfully about a year, and was then given the berth of night watchman yonder in that dead-house which you visited lately. The place suited my mood. I liked it. I liked being with the dead—liked being alone with them. I used to wander among those rigid corpses, and peer into their austere faces, by the hour. The later the time, the more impressive it was; I preferred the late time. Sometimes I turned the lights low; this gave perspective, you see; and the imagination could play; always, the dim, receding ranks of the dead inspired one with weird and fascinating fancies. Two years ago—I had been there a year then—I was sitting all alone in the watch-room, one gusty winter's night, chilled, numb, comfortless; drowsing gradually into unconsciousness; the sobbing of the wind and the slamming of distant shutters falling fainter and fainter upon my dulling ear each moment, when sharp and suddenly that dead-bell rang out a blood-curdling alarum over my head! The shock of it nearly paralyzed me; for it was the first time I had ever heard it.

I gathered myself together and flew to the corpse-room. About midway down the outside rank, a shrouded figure was sitting upright, wagging its head slowly from one side to the other—a grisly spectacle! Its side was toward me. I hurried to it and peered into its face. Heavens, it was Adler!

Can you divine what my first thought was? Put into words, it was this: "It seems, then, you escaped me once: there will be a different result this time!"

Evidently this creature was suffering unimaginable terrors. Think what it must have been to wake up in the midst of that voiceless hush, and look out over that grim congregation of the dead! What gratitude shone in his skinny white face when he saw a living form before him! And how the fervency of this mute gratitude was augmented when his eyes fell upon the life-giving cordials which I carried in my hands! Then imagine the horror which came into his pinched face when I put the cordials behind me, and said mockingly:

"Speak up, Franz Adler—call upon these dead! Doubtless they will listen and have pity; but here there is none else that will."

He tried to speak, but that part of the shroud which bound his jaws held firm, and would not let him. He tried to lift imploring hands, but they were crossed upon his breast and tied. I said:

"Shout, Franz Adler; make the sleepers in the distant streets hear you and bring help. Shout—and lose no time, for there is little to lose. What, you cannot? That is a pity; but it is no matter—it does not always bring help. When you and your cousin murdered a helpless woman and child in a cabin in Arkansas—my wife, it was, and my child!—they shrieked for help, you remember; but it did no good; you remember that it did no good, is it not so? Your teeth chatter—then why cannot you shout? Loosen the bandages with your hands—then you can. Ah, I see— your hands are tied, they cannot aid you. How strangely things repeat themselves, after long years; for *my* hands were tied, that night, you remember? Yes, tied much as yours are now—how odd that is! I could not pull free. It did not occur to you to untie me; it does not occur to me to untie you. 'Sh—! there's a late footstep. It is coming this way. Hark, how near it is! One can count the footfalls—one—two—three. There—it is just outside. Now is the time! Shout, man, shout! it is the one sole chance between you and eternity! Ah, you see you have delayed too long—it is gone by. There—it is dying out. It is gone! Think of it—reflect upon it—you have heard a human footstep for the last time. How curious it must be, to listen to so common a sound as that and know that one will never hear the fellow to it again."

Oh, my friend, the agony in that shrouded face was ecstasy to see! I thought of a new torture, and applied it—assisting myself with a trifle of lying invention:

"That poor Kruger tried to save my wife and child, and I did him a grateful good turn for it when the time came. I persuaded him to rob you; and I and a woman helped him to desert, and got him away in safety."

A look as of surprise and triumph shone out dimly through the anguish in my victim's face. I was disturbed, disquieted. I said:

"What, then—didn't he escape?"

A negative shake of the head.

"No? What happened, then?"

The satisfaction in the shrouded face was still plainer. The man tried to mumble out some words—could not succeed; tried to express something with his. obstructed hands—failed; paused a moment, then feebly tilted his head, in a meaning way, toward the corpse that lay nearest him.

"Dead?" I asked. "Failed to escape? Caught in the act and shot?"

Negative shake of the head.

"How, then?"

Again the man tried to do something with his hands. I watched closely, but could not guess the intent. I bent over and watched still more intently. He had twisted a thumb around and was weakly punching at his breast with it. "Ah—stabbed, do you mean?"

Affirmative nod, accompanied by a spectral smile of such devilishness that it struck an awakening light through my dull brain, and I cried:

"Did *I* stab him, mistaking him for you? for that stroke was meant for none but you."

The affirmative nod of the re-dying rascal was as joyous as his failing strength was able to put into its expression.

"Oh, miserable, miserable me, to slaughter the pitying soul that stood a friend to my darlings when they were helpless, and would have saved them if he could! miserable, oh, miserable, miserable me!"

I fancied I heard the muffled gurgle of a mocking laugh. I took my face out of my hands, and saw my enemy sinking back upon his inclined board.

He was a satisfactory long time dying. He had a wonderful vitality, an astonishing constitution. Yes, he was a pleasant long time at it. I got a chair and a newspaper, and sat down by him and read. Occasionally I took a sip of brandy. This was necessary, on account of the cold. But I did it partly because I saw that, along at first, whenever I reached for the bottle, he thought I was going to give him some. I read aloud: mainly imaginary accounts of people snatched from the grave's threshold and restored to life and vigor by a few spoonfuls of liquor and a warm bath. Yes, he had a long, hard death of it—three hours and six minutes, from the time he rang his bell.

It is believed that in all these eighteen years that have elapsed since the institution of the corpse-watch, no shrouded occupant of the Bavarian dead-houses has ever rung its bell. Well, it is a harmless belief. Let it stand at that.

The chill of that death-room had penetrated my bones. It revived and fastened upon me the disease which had been afflicting me, but which, up to that night, had been steadily disappearing. That man murdered my wife and my child; and in three days hence he will have added me to his list. No matter—God! how delicious the memory of it! I caught him escaping from his grave, and thrust him back into it!

After that night I was confined to my bed for a week; but as soon as I could get about I went to the dead-house books and got the number of the house which Adler had died in. A wretched lodging-house it was. It was my idea that he would naturally have gotten hold of Kruger's effects, being his cousin; and I wanted to get Kruger's watch, if I could. But while I was sick, Adler's things had been sold and scattered, all except a few old letters, and some odds and ends of no value. However, through those letters I traced out a son of Kruger's, the only relative he left. He is a man of thirty, now, a shoemaker by trade, and living at No. 14 Königstrasse, Mannheim—widower, with several small children. Without explaining to him why, I have furnished two-thirds of his support ever since.

Now, as to that watch—see how strangely things happen! I traced it around and about Germany for more than a year, at considerable cost in money and vexation; and at last I got it. Got it, and was unspeakably glad; opened it, and found nothing in it! Why, I might have known that that bit of paper was not going to stay there all this time. Of course I gave up that ten thousand dollars then; gave it up, and dropped it out of my mind; and most sorrowfully, for I had wanted it for Kruger's son.

Last night, when I consented at last that I must die, I began to make ready. I proceeded to burn all useless papers; and sure enough, from a batch of Adler's, not previously examined with thoroughness, out dropped that long-desired scrap! I recognized it in a moment. Here it is—I will translate it:

> *Brick livery stable, stone foundation, middle of town, corner of Orleans and Market. Corner toward Court-house. Third stone, fourth row. Stick notice there, saying how many are to come.*

There—take it, and preserve it! Kruger explained that that stone was removable; and that it was in the north wall of the foundation, fourth row from the top, and third stone from the west. The money is secreted behind it. He said the closing sentence was a blind, to mislead in case the paper should fall into wrong hands. It probably performed that office for Adler.

Now I want to beg that when you make your intended journey down the river, you will hunt out that hidden money, and send it to Adam Kruger, care of the Mannheim address which I have mentioned. It will make a rich man of him, and I shall sleep the sounder in my grave for knowing that I have done what I could for the son of the man who tried to save my wife and child—albeit my hand ignorantly struck him down, whereas the impulse of my heart would have been to shield and serve him.

"Such was Ritter's narrative," said I to my two friends. There was a profound and impressive silence, which lasted a considerable time; then both men broke into a fusillade of excited and admiring ejaculations over the strange incidents of the tale: and this, along with a rattling fire of questions, was kept up until all hands were about out of breath. Then my friends began to cool down, and draw off, under shelter of occasional volleys, into silence and abysmal revery. For ten minutes, now, there was stillness. Then Rogers said dreamily:

"Ten thousand dollars!" Adding, after a considerable pause: "Ten thousand. It is a heap of money."

Presently the poet inquired:

"Are you going to send it to him right away?"

"Yes," I said. "It is a queer question."

No reply. After a little, Rogers asked hesitatingly:

"*All* of it? That is—I mean—"

"*Certainly,* all of it."

I was going to say more, but stopped—was stopped by a train of thought which started up in me. Thompson spoke, but my mind was absent and I did not catch what he said. But I heard Rogers answer:

"Yes, it seems so to me. It ought to be quite sufficient; for I don't see that *he* has done anything."

Presently the poet said:

"When you come to look at it, it is *more* than sufficient. Just look at it—five thousand dollars! Why, he couldn't spend it in a lifetime! And it would injure him, too; perhaps ruin him—you want to look at that. In a little while he would throw his last away, shut up his shop, maybe take to drinking, maltreat his motherless children, drift into other evil courses, go steadily from bad to worse—"

"Yes, that's it," interrupted Rogers fervently, "I've seen it a hundred times—yes, more than a hundred. You put money into the hands of a man like that, if you want to destroy him, that's all. Just put money into his hands, it's all you've got to do; and if it don't pull him down, and take all the usefulness out of him, and all the self-respect and everything, then I don't know human nature—ain't that so, Thompson? And even if we were to give him a *third* of it; why, in less than six months—"

"Less that six *weeks*, you'd better say!" said I, warming up and breaking in. "Unless he had that three thousand dollars in safe hands where he couldn't touch it, he would no more last you six weeks than—"

"Of *course* he wouldn't!" said Thompson. "I've edited books for that kind of people; and the moment they get their hands on the royalty—maybe it's three thousand, maybe it's two thousand—"

"What business has that shoemaker with two thousand dollars, I should like to know?" broke in Rogers earnestly. "A man perhaps perfectly contented now, there in Mannheim, surrounded by his own class, eating his bread with the appetite which laborious industry alone can give, enjoying his humble life, honest, upright, pure in heart, and *blest!*—yes, I say blest! above all the myriads that go in silk attire and walk the empty, artificial round of social folly—but just you put *that* temptation before him once! just you lay fifteen hundred dollars before a man like that, and say—"

"Fifteen hundred devils!" cried I. "*Five* hundred would rot his principles, paralyze his industry, drag him to the rum-shop, thence to the gutter, thence to the almshouse, thence to—"

"*Why* put upon ourselves this crime, gentlemen?" interrupted the poet earnestly and appealingly. "He is happy where he is, and *as* he is. Every sentiment of honor, every sentiment of charity, every sentiment of high and sacred benevolence warns us, beseeches us, commands us to leave him undisturbed. That is real friendship, that is true friendship. We could follow other courses that would be more showy; but none that would be so truly kind and wise, depend upon it."

After some further talk, it became evident that each of us, down in his heart, felt some misgivings over this settlement of the matter. It was manifest that we all felt that we ought to send the poor shoemaker *something*. There was long and thoughtful discussion of this point, and we finally decided to send him a chromo.

Well, now that everything seemed to be arranged satisfactorily to everybody concerned, a new trouble broke out: it transpired that these two men were expecting to share equally in the money with me. That was not my idea. I said that if they got half of it between them they might consider themselves lucky. Rogers said:

"Who would have had *any* luck if it hadn't been for me? I flung out the first hint—but for that it would all have gone to the shoemaker."

Thompson said that he was thinking of the thing himself at the very moment that Rogers had originally spoken.

I retorted that the idea would have occurred to me plenty soon enough, and without anybody's help. I was slow about thinking, maybe, but I was sure.

This matter warmed up into a quarrel; then into a fight; and each man got pretty badly battered. As soon as I got myself mended up after a fashion, I ascended to the hurricane-deck in a pretty sour humor. I found Captain McCord there, and said, as pleasantly as my humor would permit:

"I have come to say good-by, captain. I wish to go ashore at Napoleon."

"Go ashore where?"

"Napoleon."

The captain laughed; but seeing that I was not in a jovial mood, stopped that and said:

"But are you serious?"

"Serious? I certainly am."

The captain glanced up at the pilot-house and said:

"He wants to get off at Napoleon!"

"Napoleon?"

"That's what he says."

"Great Cæsar's ghost!"

Uncle Mumford approached along the deck. The captain said:

"Uncle, here's a friend of yours wants to get off at Napoleon!"

"Well, by—!"

I said:

"Come, what is all this about? Can't a man go ashore at Napoleon, if he wants to?"

"Why, hang it, don't you know? There *isn't* any Napoleon any more. Hasn't been for years and years. The Arkansas River burst through it, tore it all to rags, and emptied it into the Mississippi!"

"Carried the *whole* town away? Banks, churches, jails, newspaper offices, court-house, theater, fire department, livery stable—*everything?*"

"Everything! Just a fifteen-minute job, or such a matter. Didn't leave hide nor hair, shred nor shingle of it, except the fag-end of a shanty and one brick chimney. This boat is paddling along right now where the dead-center of that town used to be; yonder is the brick chimney—all that's left of Napoleon. These dense woods on the right used to be a mile back of the town. Take a look behind you—up-stream—now you begin to recognize this country, don't you?"

"Yes, I do recognize it now. It is the most wonderful thing I ever heard of; by a long shot the most wonderful—and unexpected."

Mr. Thompson and Mr. Rogers had arrived, meantime, with satchels and umbrellas, and had silently listened to the captain's news. Thompson put a half-dollar in my hand and said softly:

"For my share of the chromo."

Rogers followed suit.

Yes, it was an astonishing thing to see the Mississippi rolling between unpeopled shores and straight over the spot where I used to see a good big self-complacent town twenty years ago. Town that was county-seat of a great and important county; town with a big United States marine hospital; town of innumerable fights—an inquest every day; town where I had used to know the prettiest girl, and the most accomplished, in the whole Mississippi valley; town where we were handed the first printed news of the *Pennsylvania*'s mournful disaster a quarter of a century ago; a town no more—swallowed up, vanished, gone to feed the fishes; nothing left but a fragment of a shanty and a crumbling brick chimney!

From LIFE ON THE MISSISSIPI, 1883

The Professor's Yarn

It was in the early days. I was not a college professor then. I was a humble-minded young land-surveyor, with the world before me—to survey, in case anybody wanted it done. I had a contract to survey a route for a great mining ditch in California, and I was on my way thither, by sea—a three or four weeks' voyage. There were a good many passengers, but I had very little to say to them; reading and dreaming were my passions, and I avoided conversation in order to indulge these appetites. There were three professional gamblers on board—rough, repulsive fellows. I never had any talk with them, yet I could not help seeing them with some frequency, for they gambled in an upper-deck stateroom every day and night, and in my promenades I often had glimpses of them through their door, which stood a little ajar to let out the surplus tobacco-smoke and profanity. They were an evil and hateful presence, but I had to put up with it, of course.

There was one other passenger who fell under my eye a good deal, for he seemed determined to be friendly with me, and I could not have gotten rid of him without running some chance of hurting his feelings, and I was far from wishing to do that. Besides, there was something engaging in his countrified simplicity and his beaming good nature. The first time I saw this Mr. John Backus, I guessed, from his clothes and his looks, that he was a grazier or farmer from the backwoods of some Western state—doubtless Ohio—and afterward, when he dropped into his personal history, and I discovered that he *was* a cattle-raiser from interior Ohio, I was so pleased with my own penetration that I warmed toward him for verifying my instinct.

He got to dropping alongside me every day, after breakfast, to help me make my promenade; and so, in the course of time, his easy-working jaw had told me everything about his business, his prospects, his family, his relatives, his politics—in fact, everything that concerned Backus, living or dead. And meantime I think he had managed to get out of me everything I knew about my trade, my tribe, my purposes, my prospects, and myself. He was a gentle and persuasive genius, and this thing showed it; for I was not given to talking about my matters. I said something about triangulation, once; the stately word pleased his ear; he inquired what it meant; I explained. After that he quietly and inoffensively ignored my name, and always called me Triangle.

What an enthusiast he was in cattle! At the bare name of a bull or a cow, his eye would light and his eloquent tongue would turn itself loose. As long as I would walk and listen, he would walk and talk; he knew all breeds, he loved all breeds, he caressed them all with his affectionate tongue. I tramped along in voiceless misery while the cattle question was up. When I could endure it no longer, I used to deftly insert a scientific topic into the conversation; then my eye fired and his faded; my tongue fluttered, his stopped; life was a joy to me, and a sadness to him.

One day he said, a little hestiatingly, and with somewhat of diffidence:

"Triangle, would you mind coming down to my stateroom a minute and have a little talk on a certain matter?"

I went with him at once. Arrived there, he put his head out, glanced up and down the saloon warily, then closed the door and locked it. We sat down on the sofa and he said:

"I'm a-going to make a little proposition to you, and if it strikes you favorable, it'll be a middling good thing for both of us. You ain't a-going out to Californy for fun, nuther am I—it's *business,* ain't that so? Well, you can do me a good turn, and so can I you, if we see fit. I've raked and scraped and saved a considerable many years, and I've got it all here." He unlocked an old hair trunk, tumbled a chaos of shabby clothes aside, and drew a short, stout bag into view for a moment, then buried it again and relocked the trunk. Dropping his voice to a cautious, low tone, he continued: "She's all there—a round ten thousand dollars in yellow-boys; now, this is my little idea: What I don't know about raising cattle ain't worth knowing. There's mints of money in it in Californy. Well, I know, and you know, that all along a line that's being surveyed, there's little dabs of land that they call 'gores,' that fall to the survey free gratis for nothing. All you've got to do on your side is to survey in such a way that the 'gores' will fall on good fat land, then you turn 'em over to me, I stock 'em with cattle, *in* rolls the cash, I plank out your share of the dollars regular right along, and—"

I was sorry to wither his blooming enthusiasm, but it could not be helped. I interrupted and said severely:

"I am not that kind of a surveyor. Let us change the subject, Mr. Backus."

It was pitiful to see his confusion and hear his awkward and shame-faced apologies. I was as much distressed as he was—especially as he seemed so far from having suspected that there was anything improper in his proposition. So I hastened to console him and lead him on to forget his mishap in a conversational orgy about cattle and butchery. We were lying at Acapulco, and as we went on deck it happened luckily that the crew were just beginning to hoist some beeves aboard in slings. Backus's melancholy vanished instantly, and with it the memory of his late mistake.

"Now, only look at that!" cried he. "My goodness, Triangle, what *would* they say to it in *Ohio?* Wouldn't their eyes bug out to see 'em handled like that?—wouldn't they, though?"

All the passengers were on deck to look—even the gamblers—and Backus knew them all, and had afflicted them all with his pet topic. As I moved away I saw one of the gamblers approach and accost him; then another of them; then the third. I halted, waited, watched; the conversation continued between the four men; it grew earnest; Backus drew gradually away; the gamblers followed and kept at his elbow. I was uncomfortable. However, as they passed me presently, I heard Backus say with a tone of persecuted annoyance:

"But it ain't any use, gentlemen; I tell you again, as I've told you a half a dozen times before, I warn't raised to it, and I ain't a-going to resk it."

I felt relieved. "His level head will be his sufficient protection," I said to myself.

During the fortnight's run from Acapulco to San Francisco I several times saw the gamblers talking earnestly with Backus, and once I threw out a gentle warning to him. He chuckled comfortably and said:

"Oh, yes! they tag around after me considerable—want me to play a little, just for amusement, they say—but laws-a-me, if my folks have told me once to look out for that sort of live stock, they've told me a thousand times, I reckon."

By and by, in due course, we were approaching San

Francisco. It was an ugly, black night, with a strong wind blowing, but there was not much sea. I was on deck alone. Toward ten I started below. A figure issued from the gamblers' den and disappeared in the darkness. I experienced a shock, for I was sure it was Backus. I flew down the companionway, looked about for him, could not find him, then returned to the deck just in time to catch a glimpse of him as he reentered that confounded nest of rascality. Had he yielded at last? I feared it. What had he gone below for? His bag of coin? Possibly. I drew near the door, full of bodings. It was a-crack, and I glanced in and saw a sight that made me bitterly wish I had given my attention to saving my poor cattle-friend, instead of reading and dreaming my foolish time away. He was gambling. Worse still, he was being plied with champagne, and was already showing some effect from it. He praised the "cider," as he called it, and said now that he had got a taste of it he almost believed he would drink it if it was spirits, it was so good and so ahead of anything he had ever run across before. Surreptitious smiles at this passed from one rascal to another, and they filled all the glasses, and while Backus honestly drained his to the bottom they pretended to do the same, but threw the wine over their shoulders.

I could not bear the scene, so I wandered forward and tried to interest myself in the sea and the voices of the wind. But no, my uneasy spirit kept dragging me back at quarter-hour intervals, and always I saw Backus drinking his wine—fairly and squarely, and the others throwing theirs away. It was the painfulest night I ever spent.

The only hope I had was that we might reach our anchorage with speed—that would break up the game. I helped the ship along all I could with my prayers. At last we went booming through the Golden Gate, and my pulses leaped for joy. I hurried back to that door and glanced in. Alas! there was small room for hope—Backus's eyes were heavy and bloodshot, his sweaty face was crimson, his speech maudlin and thick, his body sawed drunkenly about with the weaving motion of the ship. He drained another glass to the dregs, while the cards were being dealt.

He took his hand, glanced at it, and his dull eyes lit up for a moment. The gamblers observed it, and showed their gratification by hardly perceptible signs.

"How many cards?"

"None!" said Backus.

One villain—named Hank Wiley—discarded one card, the others three each. The betting began. Heretofore the bets had been trifling—a dollar or two; but Backus started off with an eagle now, Wiley hesitated a moment, then "saw it," and "went ten dollars better." The other two threw up their hands.

Backus went twenty better. Wiley said:

"I see that, and go you a *hundred* better!" then smiled and reached for the money.

"Let it alone," said Backus, with drunken gravity.

"What! you mean to say you're going to cover it?"

"Cover it? Well, I reckon I am—and lay another hundred on top of it, too."

He reached down inside his overcoat and produced the required sum.

"Oh, that's your little game, is it? I see your raise, and raise it five hundred!" said Wiley.

"Five hundred *better!*" said the foolish bull-driver, and pulled out the amount and showered it on the pile. The three conspirators hardly tried to conceal their exultation.

All diplomacy and pretense were dropped now, and the sharp exclamations came thick and fast, and the yellow pyramid grew higher and higher. At last ten thousand dollars lay in view. Wiley cast a bag of coin on the table, and said with mocking gentleness:

"Five thousand dollars better, my friend from the rural districts—what do you say *now?*"

"I *call* you!" said Backus, heaving his golden shot-bag on the pile. "What have you got?"

"Four kings, you d——d fool!" and Wiley threw down his cards and surrounded the stakes with his arms.

"Four *aces,* you ass!" thundered Backus, covering his man with a cocked revolver. *"I am a professional gambler myself, and I've been laying for you duffers all this voyage!"*

Down went the anchor, rumbledy-dum-dum! and the trip was ended.

Well, well—it is a sad world. One of the three gamblers was Backus's "pal." It was he that dealt the fateful hands. According to an understanding with the two victims, he was to have given Backus four queens, but alas! he didn't.

A week later I stumbled upon Backus—arrayed in the height of fashion—in Montgomery street. He said cheerily, as we were parting:

"Ah, by the way, you needn't mind about those gores. I don't really know anything about cattle, except what I was able to pick up in a week's apprenticeship over in Jersey, just before we sailed. My cattle culture and cattle enthusiasm have served their turn—I sha'n't need them any more."

From LIFE ON THE MISSISSIPPI, 1883

The Private History of a Campaign That Failed

You have heard from a great many people who did something in the war; is it not fair and right that you listen a little moment to one who started out to do something in it, but didn't? Thousands entered the war, got just a taste of it, and then stepped out again permanently. These, by their very numbers, are respectable, and are therefore entitled to a sort of voice—not a loud one, but a modest one; not a boastful one, but an apologetic one. They ought not to be allowed much space among better people—people who did something. I grant that; but they ought at least to be allowed to state why they didn't do anything, and also to explain the process by which they didn't do anything. Surely this kind of light must have a sort of value.

Out West there was a good deal of confusion in men's minds during the first months of the great trouble—a good deal of unsettledness, of leaning first this way, then that, then the other way. It was hard for us to get our bearings. I call to mind an instance of this. I was piloting on the Mississippi when the news came that South Carolina had gone out of the Union on the 20th of December, 1860. My pilot mate was a New-Yorker. He was strong for the Union; so was I. But he would not listen to me with any patience; my loyalty was smirched, to his eye, because my father had owned slaves. I said, in palliation of this dark fact, that I had heard my father say, some years before he died, that slavery was a great wrong, and that he would free the solitary negro he then owned if he could think it right to give away the property of the family when he was so straitened in means. My mate retorted that a mere impulse was nothing—anybody could pretend impulse; and went on decrying my Unionism and libeling my ancestry. A month later the secession atmosphere had considerably thickened on the Lower Mississippi, and I became a rebel; so did he. We were together in New Orleans the 26th of January, when Louisiana went out of the Union. He did his full share of the rebel shouting, but was bitterly opposed to letting me do mine. He said that I came of bad stock—of a father who had been willing to set slaves free. In the following summer he was piloting a Federal gunboat and shouting for the Union again, and I was in the Confederate army. I held his note for some borrowed money. He was one of the most upright men I ever knew, but he repudiated that note without hesitation because I was a rebel and the son of a man who owned slaves.

In that summer—of 1861—the first wash of the wave of war broke upon the shores of Missouri. Our state was invaded by the Union forces. They took possession of St. Louis, Jefferson Barracks, and some other points. The Governor, Claib Jackson, issued his proclamation calling out fifty thousand militia to repel the invader.

I was visiting in the small town where my boyhood had been spent—Hannibal, Marion County. Several of us got together in a secret place by night and formed ourselves into a military company. One Tom Lyman, a young fellow of a good deal of spirit but of no military experience, was made captain; I was made second lieutenant. We had no first lieutenant; I do not know why; it was long ago. There were fifteen of us. By the advice of an innocent connected with the organization we called ourselves the Marion Rangers. I do not remember that any one found fault with the name. I did not; I thought it sounded quite well. The young fellow who proposed this title was perhaps a fair sample of the kind of stuff we were made of. He was young, ignorant, good-natured, well-meaning, trivial, full of romance, and given to reading chivalric novels and singing forlorn love-ditties. He had some pathetic little nickel-plated aristocratic instincts, and detested his name, which was Dunlap; detested it, partly because it was nearly as common in that region as Smith, but mainly because it had a plebeian sound to his ear. So he tried to ennoble it by writing it in this way: *d'Unlap*. That contented his eye, but left his ear unsatisfied, for people gave the new name the same old pronunciation—emphasis on the front end of it. He then did the bravest thing that can be imagined—a thing to make one shiver when one remembers how the world is given to resenting shams and affectations; he began to write his name so: *d'Un Lap*. And he waited patiently through the long storm of mud that was flung at this work of art, and he had his reward at last; for he lived to see that name accepted, and the emphasis put where he wanted it by people who had known him all his life, and to whom the tribe of Dunlaps had been as familiar as the rain and the sunshine for forty years. So sure of victory at last is the courage that can wait. He said he had found, by consulting some ancient French chronicles, that the name was rightly and originally written d'Un Lap; and said that if it were translated into English it would mean Peterson: *Lap*, Latin or Greek, he said, for stone or rock, same as the French *pierre*, that is to say, Peter: *d'*, of or from; *un*, a or one; hence, d'Un Lap, of or from a stone or a Peter; that is to say, one who is the son of a stone, the son of a Peter—Peterson. Our militia company were not learned, and the explanation confused them; so they called him Peterson Dunlap. He proved useful to us in his way; he named our camps for us, and he generally struck a name that was "no slouch," as the boys said.

That is one sample of us. Another was Ed Stevens, son of the town jeweler—trim-built, handsome, graceful, neat as a cat; bright, educated, but given over entirely to fun. There was nothing serious in life to him. As far as he was concerned, this military expedition of ours was simply a holiday. I should say that about half of us looked upon it in the same way; not consciously, perhaps, but unconsciously. We did not think; we were not capable of it. As for myself, I was full of unreasoning joy to be done with turning out of bed at midnight and four in the morning for a while; grateful to have a change, new scenes, new occupations, a new interest. In my thoughts that was as far as I went; I did not go into the details; as a rule, one doesn't at twenty-four.

Another sample was Smith, the blacksmith's apprentice. This vast donkey had some pluck, of a slow and sluggish nature, but a soft heart; at one time he would knock a horse down for some impropriety, and at another he would get homesick and cry. However, he had one ultimate credit to his account which some of us hadn't; he stuck to the war, and was killed in battle at last.

Jo Bowers, another sample, was a huge, good-natured, flax-headed lubber; lazy, sentimental, full of harmless brag, a grumbler by nature; an experienced, industrious, ambitious, and often quite picturesque liar, and yet not a successful one, for he had had no intelligent training, but was allowed to come up just any way. This life was serious enough to him, and seldom satisfactory. But he was a good fellow, anyway, and the boys all liked him. He was made orderly sergeant; Stevens was made corporal.

These samples will answer—and they are quite fair ones. Well, this herd of cattle started for the war. What could you expect of them? They did as well as they knew how; but, really, what was justly to be expected of them? Nothing, I should say. That is what they did.

We waited for a dark night, for caution and secrecy were necessary; then, toward midnight, we stole in couples and from various directions to the Griffith place, beyond the town; from that point we set out together on foot. Hannibal lies at the extreme southeastern corner of Marion County, on the Mississippi River; our objective point was the hamlet of New London, ten miles away, in Ralls County.

The first hour was all fun, all idle nonsense and laughter. But that could not be kept up. The steady trudging came to be like work; the play had somehow oozed out of it; the stillness of the woods and the somberness of the night began to throw a depressing influence over the spirits of the boys, and presently the talking died out and each person shut himself up in his own thoughts. During the last half of the second hour nobody said a word.

Now we approached a log farm-house where, according to report, there was a guard of five Union soldiers. Lyman called a halt; and there, in the deep gloom of the overhanging branches, he began to whisper a plan of assault upon that house, which made the gloom more depressing than it was before. It was a crucial moment; we realized, with a cold suddenness, that here was no jest—we were standing face to face with actual war. We were equal to the occasion. In our response there was no hesitation, no indecision: we said that if Lyman wanted to meddle with those soldiers, he could go ahead and do it; but if he waited for us to follow him, he would wait a long time.

Lyman urged, pleaded, tried to shame us, but it had no effect. Our course was plain, our minds were made up: we would flank the farm-house—go out around. And that was what we did.

We struck into the woods and entered upon a rough time, stumbling over roots, getting tangled in vines, and torn by briers. At last we reached an open place in a safe region, and sat down, blown and hot, to cool off and nurse our scratches and bruises. Lyman was annoyed, but the rest of us were cheerful; we had flanked the farm-house, we had made our first military movement, and it was a success; we had nothing to fret about, we were feeling just the other way. Horse-play and laughing began again: the expedition was become a holiday frolic once more.

Then we had two more hours of dull trudging and ultimate silence and depression; then, about dawn, we straggled into New London, soiled, heel-blistered, fagged with our little march, and all of us except Stevens in a sour and raspy humor and privately down on the war. We stacked our shabby old shotguns in Colonel Ralls's barn, and then went in a body and breakfasted with that veteran of the Mexican War. Afterward he took us to a distant meadow, and there in the shade of a tree we listened to an old-fashioned speech from him, full of gunpowder and glory, full of that adjective-piling, mixed metaphor and windy declamation which were regarded as eloquence in that ancient time and that remote region; and then he swore us on the Bible to be faithful to the State of Missouri and drive all invaders from her soil, no matter whence they might come or under what flag they might march. This mixed us considerably, and we could not make out just what service we were embarked in; but Colonel Ralls, the practised politician and phrase-juggler, was not similiarly in doubt; he knew quite clearly that he had invested us in the cause of the Southern Confederacy. He closed the solemnities by belting around me the sword which his neighbor, Colonel Brown, had worn at Buena Vista and Molino del Rey; and he accompanied this act with another impressive blast.

Then we formed in line of battle and marched four miles to a shady and pleasant piece of woods on the border of the far-reaching expanses of a flowery prairie. It was an enchanting region for war—our kind of war.

We pierced the forest about half a mile, and took up a strong position, with some low, rocky, and wooded hills behind us, and a purling, limpid creek in front. Straightway half the command were in swimming and the other half fishing. The ass with the French name gave this position a romatic title, but it was too long, so the boys shortened and simplified it to Camp Ralls.

We occupied an old maple-sugar camp, whose half-rotted troughs were still propped against the trees. A long corn-crib served for sleeping-quarters for the battalion. On our left, half a mile away, were Mason's farm and house; and he was a friend to the cause. Shortly after noon the farmers began to arrive from several directions, with mules and horses for our use, and these they lent us for as long as the war might last, which they judged would be about three months. The animals were of all sizes, all colors, and all breeds. They were mainly young and frisky, and nobody in the command could stay on them long at a time; for we were town boys, and ignorant of horsemanship. The creature that fell to my share was a very small mule, and yet so quick and active that it could throw me without difficulty; and it did this whenever I got on it. Then it would bray—stretching its neck out, laying its ears back, and spreading its jaws till you could see down to its works. It was a disagreeable animal in every way. If I took it by the bridle and tried to lead it off the grounds, it would sit down and brace back, and no one could budge it. However, I was not entirely destitute of military resources, and I did presently manage to spoil this game; for I had seen many a steamboat aground in my time, and knew a trick or two which even a grounded mule would be obliged to respect. There was a well by the corn-crib; so I substituted thirty fathom of rope for the bridle, and fetched him home with the windlass.

I will anticipate here sufficiently to say that we did learn to ride, after some days' practice, but never well. We could not learn to like our animals; they were not choice ones, and most of them had annoying peculiarities of one kind or another. Stevens's horse would carry him, when he was not noticing, under the huge excrescences which form on the trunks of oak-trees, and wipe him out of the saddle; in this way Stevens got several bad hurts. Sergeant Bowers's horse was very large and tall, with slim, long legs, and looked like a railroad bridge. His size enabled him to reach all about, and as far as he wanted to, with his head; so he was always biting Bowers's legs. On the march, in the sun, Bowers slept a good deal; and as soon as the horse recognized that he was asleep he would reach around and bite him on the leg. His legs were black and blue with bites. This was the only thing that could ever make him swear, but this always did; whenever his horse bit him he always swore, and of course Stevens, who laughed at everything, laughed at this, and would even get into such convulsions over it as to lose his balance and fall off his horse; and then Bowers, already irritated by the pain of the horse-bite, would resent the laughter with hard language, and there would be a quarrel; so that horse made no end of trouble and bad blood in the command.

However, I will get back to where I was—our first afternoon in the sugar-camp. The sugar-troughs came very handy as horse-troughs, and we had plenty of corn to fill them with. I ordered Sergeant Bowers to feed my mule; but he said that if I reckoned he went to war to be a dry-nurse to a mule it wouldn't take me very long to find out my mistake. I believed that this was insubordination, but I was full of uncertainties about everything military, and so I let the thing pass, and went and ordered Smith, the blacksmith's apprentice, to feed the mule; but he merely gave me a large, cold, sarcastic grin, such as an ostensibly seven-year-old horse gives you when you lift his lip and find he is fourteen, and turned his back on me. I then went to the captain, and asked if it were not right and proper and military for me to have an orderly. He said it was, but as there was only one orderly in the corps, it was but right that he himself should have Bowers on his staff. Bowers said he wouldn't serve on anybody's staff; and if anybody thought he could make him, let him try it. So, of course, the thing had to be dropped; there was no other way.

Next, nobody would cook; it was considered a degradation; so we had no dinner. We lazied the rest of the pleasant afternoon away, some dozing under the trees, some smoking cob-pipes and talking sweethearts and war, some playing games. By late supper-time all hands were famished; and to meet the difficulty all hands turned to, on an equal footing, and gathered wood, built fires, and cooked the meal. Afterward everything was smooth for a while; then trouble broke out between the corporal and the sergeant, each claiming to rank the other. Nobody knew which was the higher office; so Lyman had to settle the matter by making the rank of both officers equal. The commander of an ignorant crew like that has many troubles and vexations which probably do not occur in the regular army at all. However, with the song-singing and yarn-spinning around the camp-fire, everything presently became serene again; and by and by we raked the corn down level in one end of the crib, and all went to bed on it, tying a horse to the door, so that he would neigh if any one tried to get in.*

We had some horsemanship drill every forenoon; then, afternoons, we rode off here and there in squads a few miles, and visited the farmers' girls, and had a youthful good time, and got an honest good dinner or supper, and then home again to camp, happy and content.

---

* It was always my impression that that was what the horse was there for, and I knew that it was also the impression of at least one other of the command, for we talked about it at the time, and admired the military ingenuity of the device; but when I was out West, three years ago, I was told by Mr. A. G. Fuqua, a member of our company, that the horse was his; that the leaving him tied at the door was a matter of mere forgetfulness, and that to attribute it to intelligent invention was to give him quite too much credit. In support of his position he called my attention to the suggestive fact that the artifice was not employed again. I had not thought of that before.

For a time life was idly delicious, it was perfect; there was nothing to mar it. Then came some farmers with an alarm one day. They said it was rumored that the enemy were advancing in our direction from over Hyde's prairie. The result was a sharp stir among us, and general consternation. It was a rude awakening from our pleasant trance. The rumor was but a rumor—nothing definite about it; so, in the confusion, we did not know which way to retreat. Lyman was for not retreating at all in these uncertain circumstances; but he found that if he tried to maintain that attitude he would fare badly, for the command were in no humor to put up with insubordination. So he yielded the point and called a council of war—to consist of himself and the three other officers; but the privates made such a fuss about being left out that we had to allow them to remain, for they were already present, and doing the most of the talking too. The question was, which way to retreat; but all were so flurried that nobody seemed to have even a guess to offer. Except Lyman. He explained in a few calm words that, inasmuch as the enemy were approaching from over Hyde's prairie, our course was simple: all we had to do was not to retreat *toward* him; any other direction would answer our needs perfectly. Everybody saw in a moment how true this was, and how wise: so Lyman got a great many compliments. It was now decided that we should fall back on Mason's farm.

It was after dark by this time, and as we could not know how soon the enemy might arrive, it did not seem best to try to take the horses and things with us; so we only took the guns and ammunition, and started at once. The route was very rough and hilly and rocky, and presently the night grew very black and rain began to fall; so we had a troublesome time of it, struggling and stumbling along in the dark; and soon some person slipped and fell, and then the next person behind stumbled over him and fell, and so did the rest, one after the other; and then Bowers came, with the keg of powder in his arms, while the command were all mixed together, arms and legs, on the muddy slope: and so he fell, of course, with the keg, and this started the whole detachment down the hill in a body, and they landed in the brook at the bottom in a pile, and each that was undermost pulling the hair and scratching and biting those that were on top of him; and those that were being scratched and bitten scratching and biting the rest in their turn, and all saying they would die before they would ever go to war again if they ever got out of this brook this time, and the invader might rot for all they cared, and the country along with him—and all such talk as that, which was dismal to hear and take part in, in such smothered, low voices, and such a grisly dark place and so wet, and the enemy, maybe, coming any moment.

The keg of powder was lost, and the guns, too; so the growling and complaining continued straight along while the brigade pawed around the pasty hillside and slopped around in the brook hunting for these things; consequently we lost considerable time at this; and then we heard a sound, and held our breath and listened, and it seemed to be the enemy coming, though it could have been a cow, for it had a cough like a cow; but we did not wait, but left a couple of guns behind and struck out for Mason's again as briskly as we could scramble along in the dark. But we got lost presently among the rugged little ravines, and wasted a deal of time finding the way again, so it was after nine when we reached Mason's stile at last; then before we could open our mouths to give the countersign several dogs came bounding over the fence, with great riot and noise, and each of them took a soldier by the slack of his trousers and began to back away with him. We could not shoot the dogs without endangering the persons they were attached to; so we had to look on helpless at what was perhaps the most mortifying spectacle of the Civil War. There was light enough, and to spare, for the Masons had now run out on the porch with candles in their hands. The old man and his son came and undid the dogs without difficulty, all but Bowers's; but they couldn't undo his dog, they didn't know his combination; he was of the bull kind, and seemed to be set with a Yale time-lock; but they got him loose at last with some scalding water, of which Bowers got his share and returned thanks. Peterson Dunlap afterward made up a fine name for this engagement, and also for the night march which preceded it, but both have long ago faded out of my memory.

We now went into the house, and they began to ask us a world of questions, whereby it presently came out that we did not know anything concerning who or what we were running from; so the old gentleman made himself very frank, and said we were a curious breed of soldiers, and guessed we could be depended on to end up the war in time, because no government could stand the expense of the shoe-leather we should cost it trying to follow us around. "Marion *Rangers!* good name, b'gosh!" said he. And wanted to know why we hadn't had a picket-guard at the place where the road entered the prairie, and why we hadn't sent out a scouting party to spy out the enemy and bring us an account of his strength, and so on, before jumping up and stampeding out of a strong position upon a mere vague rumor—and so on, and so forth, till he made us all feel shabbier than the dogs had done, not half so enthusiastically welcome. So we went to bed shamed and low-spirited; except Stevens. Soon Stevens began to devise a garment for Bowers which could be made to automatically display his battle-scars to the grateful, or conceal them from the envious, according to his occasions: but Bowers was in no humor for this, so there was a fight, and when it was over Stevens had some battle-scars of his own to think about.

Then we got a little sleep. But after all we had gone through, our activities were not over for the night; for about two o'clock in the morning we heard a shout of warning from down the lane, accompanied by a chorus from all the dogs, and in a moment everybody was up and flying around to find out what the alarm was about. The alarmist was a horseman who gave notice that a detachment of Union soldiers was on its way from Hannibal with orders to capture and hang any bands like ours which it could find, and said we had no time to lose. Farmer Mason was in a flurry this time himself. He hurried us out of the house with all haste, and sent one of his negroes with us to show us where to hide ourselves and our telltale guns among the ravines half a mile away. It was raining heavily.

We struck down the lane, then across some rocky pasture-land which offered good advantages for stumbling; consequently we were down in the mud most of the time, and every time a man went down he blackguarded the war, and the people that started it, and everybody connected with it, and gave himself the master dose of all for being so foolish as to go into it. At last we reached the wooded mouth of a ravine, and there we huddled ourselves under the streaming trees, and sent the negro back home. It was a dismal and heart-breaking time. We were like to be drowned with the rain, deafened with the howling wind and the booming thunder, and blinded by the lightning. It was, indeed, a wild night. The drenching we were getting was misery enough, but a deeper misery still was the reflection that the halter might end us before we were a day older. A death of this shameful sort had not occurred to us as being among the possibilities of war. It took the romance all out of the campaign, and turned our dreams of glory into a repulsive nightmare. As for doubting that so barbarous an order had been given, not one of us did that.

The long night wore itself out at last, and then the negro came to us with the news that the alarm had manifestly been a false one, and that breakfast would soon be ready. Straightway we were light-hearted again, and the world was bright, and life as full of hope and promise as ever—for we were young then. How long ago that was! Twenty-four years.

The mongrel child of philology named the night's refuge

Camp Devastation, and no soul objected. The Masons gave us a Missouri country breakfast, in Missourian abundance, and we needed it: hot biscuits; hot "wheat bread," prettily criss-crossed in a lattice pattern on top; hot corn-pone; fried chicken; bacon, coffee, eggs, milk, buttermilk, etc.; and the world may be confidently challenged to furnish the equal of such a breakfast, as it is cooked in the South.

We stayed several days at Mason's; and after all these years the memory of the dullness, and stillness, and lifelessness of that slumberous farm-house still oppresses my spirit as with a sense of the presence of death and mourning. There was nothing to do, nothing to think about; there was no interest in life. The male part of the household were away in the fields all day, the women were busy and out of our sight; there was no sound but the plaintive wailing of a spinning-wheel, forever moaning out from some distant room—the most lonesome sound in nature, a sound steeped and sodden with homesickness and the emptiness of life. The family went to bed about dark every night, and as we were not invited to intrude any new customs we naturally followed theirs. Those nights were a hundred years long to youths accustomed to being up till twelve. We lay awake and miserable till that hour every time, and grew old and decrepit waiting through the still eternities for the clock-strikes. This was no place for town boys. So at last it was with something very like joy that we received news that the enemy were on our track again. With a new birth of the old warrior spirit we sprang to our places in line of battle and fell back on Camp Ralls.

Captain Lyman had taken a hint from Mason's talk, and he now gave orders that our camp should be guarded against surprise by the posting of pickets. I was ordered to place a picket at the forks of the road in Hyde's prairie. Night shut down black and threatening. I told Sergeant Bowers to go out to that place and stay till midnight; and, just as I was expecting, he said he wouldn't do it. I tried to get others to go, but all refused. Some excused themselves on account of the weather; but the rest were frank enough to say they wouldn't go in any kind of weather. This kind of thing sounds odd now, and impossible, but there was no surprise in it at the time. On the contrary, it seemed a perfectly natural thing to do. There were scores of little camps scattered over Missouri where the same thing was happening. These camps were composed of young men who had been born and reared to a sturdy independence, and who did not know what it meant to be ordered around by Tom, Dick, and Harry, whom they had known familiarly all their lives, in the village or on the farm. It is quite within the probabilities that this same thing was happening all over the South. James Redpath recognized the justice of this assumption, and furnished the following instance in support of it. During a short stay in East Tennessee he was in a citizen colonel's tent one day talking, when a big private appeared at the door, and, without salute or other circumlocution, said to the colonel:

"Say, Jim, I'm a-goin' home for a few days."

"What for?"

"Well I hain't b'en there for a right smart while, and I'd like to see how things is comin' on."

"How long are you going to be gone?"

" 'Bout two weeks."

"Well, don't be gone longer than that; and get back sooner if you can."

That was all, and the citizen officer resumed his conversation where the private had broken it off. This was in the first months of the war, of course. The camps in our part of Missouri were under Brigadier-General Thomas H. Harris. He was a townsman of ours, a first-rate fellow, and well liked; but we had all familiarly known him as the sole and modest-salaried operator in our telegraph-office, where he had to send about one despatch a week in ordinary times, and two when there was a rush of business; consequently, when he appeared in our midst one day, on the wing, and delivered a military command of some sort, in a large military fashion, nobody was surprised at the response which he got from the assembled soldiery:

"Oh, now, what'll you take to *don't,* Tom Harris?"

It was quite the natural thing. One might justly imagine that we were hopeless material for war. And so we seemed, in our ignorant state; but there were those among us who afterward learned the grim trade; learned to obey like machines; became valuable solders; fought all through the war, and came out at the end with excellent records. One of the very boys who refused to go out on duty that night, and called me an ass for thinking he would expose himself to danger in such a foolhardy way, had become distinguished for intrepidity before he was a year older.

I did secure my picket that night—not by authority, but by diplomacy. I got Bowers to go by agreeing to exchange ranks with him for the time being, and go along and stand the watch with him as his subordinate. We stayed out there a couple of dreary hours in the pitchy darkness and the rain, with nothing to modify the dreariness but Bowers's monotonous growlings at the war and the weather; then we began to nod, and presently found it next to impossible to stay in the saddle; so we gave up the tedious job, and went back to the camp without waiting for the relief guard. We rode into camp without interruption or objection from anybody, and the enemy could have done the same, for there were no sentries. Everybody was asleep; at midnight there was nobody to send out another picket, so none was sent. We never tried to establish a watch at night again, as far as I remember, but we generally kept a picket out in the daytime.

In that camp the whole command slept on the corn in the big corn-crib: and there was usually a general row before morning, for the place was full of rats, and they would scramble over the boys' bodies and faces, annoying and irritating everybody; and now and then they would bite some one's toe, and the person who owned the toe would start up and magnify his English and begin to throw corn in the dark. The ears were half as heavy as bricks, and when they struck they hurt. The persons struck would respond, and inside of five minutes every man would be locked in a death-grip with his neighbor. There was a grievous deal of blood shed in the corn-crib, but this was all that was spilt while I was in the war. No, that is not quite true. But for one circumstance it would have been all. I will come to that now.

Our scares were frequent. Every few days rumors would come that the enemy were approaching. In these cases we always fell back on some other camp of ours; we never stayed where we were. But the rumors always turned out to be false; so at last even we began to grow indifferent to them. One night a negro was sent to our corn-crib with the same old warning: the enemy was hovering in our neighborhood. We all said let him hover. We resolved to stay still and be comfortable. It was a fine warlike resolution, and no doubt we all felt the stir of it in our veins—for a moment. We had been having a very jolly time, that was full of horse-play and school-boy hilarity; but that cooled down now, and presently the fast-waning fire of forced jokes and forced laughs died out altogether, and the company became silent. Silent and nervous. And soon uneasy—worried—apprehensive. We had said we would stay, and we were committed. We could have been persuaded to go, but there was nobody brave enough to suggest it. An almost noiseless movement presently began in the dark by a general but unvoiced impulse. When the movement was completed each man knew that he was not the only person who had crept to the front wall and had his eye at a crack between the logs. No, we were all there; all there with our hearts in our throats, and staring out toward the sugar-troughs where the forest footpath came through. It was late, and there was a deep woodsy stillness everywhere. There was a veiled moonlight, which was only just strong enough to enable us to mark the general shape of objects. Presently a muffled sound caught our ears, and we recognized it as the hoof-beats of a horse or horses. And right away a figure appeared in the forest path; it could have been made of smoke, its mass had so little sharpness of outline. It was a man on horseback, and it seemed to me that there were others behind him. I got hold of a gun in the dark, and pushed it through a crack between the logs, hardly knowing what I was doing, I was so dazed with fright. Somebody said "Fire!" I pulled the trigger. I seemed to see a hundred flashes and hear a hundred reports; then I saw the man fall down out of the saddle. My first feeling was of surprised gratification; my first impulse was an apprentice-sportsman's impulse to run and pick up his game. Somebody said, hardly audibly, "Good—we've got him!—wait for the rest." But the rest did not come. We waited—listened—still no more came. There was not a sound, not the whisper of a leaf: just perfect stillness; an uncanny kind of stillness, which was all the more uncanny on account of the damp, earthy, late-night smells now rising and pervading it. Then, wondering, we crept stealthily out, and approached the man. When we got to him the moon revealed him distinctly. He was lying on his back, with his arms abroad; his mouth was open and his chest heaving with long gasps, and his white shirt-front was all splashed with blood. The thought shot through me that I was a murderer; that I had killed a man—a man who had never done me any harm. That was the coldest sensation that ever went through my marrow. I was down by him in a moment, helplessly stroking his forehead; and I would have given anything then—my own life freely—to make him again what he had been five minutes before. And all the boys seemed to be feeling in the same way; they hung over him, full of pitying interest, and tried all they could to help him, and said all sorts of regretful things. They had forgotten all about the enemy; they thought only of this one forlorn unit of the foe. Once my imagination persuaded me that the dying man gave me a reproachful look out of his shadowy eyes, and it seemed to me that I would rather he had stabbed me than done that. He muttered and mumbled like a dreamer in his sleep about his wife and his child; and I thought with a new despair, "This thing that I have done does not end with him; it falls upon *them* too, and they never did me any harm, any more than he."

In a little while the man was dead. He was killed in war; killed in fair and legitimate war; killed in battle, as you may say; and yet he was as sincerely mourned by the opposing force as if he had been their brother. The boys stood there a half-hour sorrowing over him, and recalling the details of the tragedy, and wondering who he might be, and if he were a spy, and saying that if it were to do over again they would not hurt him unless he attacked them first. It soon came out that mine was not the only shot fired; there were five others—a division of the guilt which was a great relief to me, since it in some degree lightened and diminished the burden I was carrying. There were six shots fired at once; but I was not in my right mind at the time, and my heated imagination had magnified my one shot into a volley.

The man was not in uniform, and was not armed. He was a stranger in the country; that was all we ever found out about him. The thought of him got to preying upon me every night; I could not get rid of it. I could not drive it away, the taking of that unoffending life seemed such a wanton thing. And it seemed an epitome of war; that all war must be just that—the killing of strangers against whom you feel no personal animosity; strangers whom, in other circumstances, you would help if you found them in trouble, and who would help you if you needed it. My campaign was spoiled. It seemed to me that I was not rightly equipped for this awful business; that war was intended for men, and I for a child's nurse. I resolved to retire from this avocation of sham soldiership while I could save some remnant of my self-respect. These morbid thoughts clung to me against reason; for at bottom I did not believe I had touched that man. The law of probabilities decreed me guiltless of his blood; for in all my small experience with guns I had never hit anything I had tried to hit, and I knew I had done my best to hit him. Yet there was no solace in the thought. Against a diseased imagination demonstration goes for nothing.

The rest of my war experience was of a piece with what I have already told of it. We kept monotonously falling back upon one camp or another, and eating up the farmers and their families. They ought to have shot us; on the contrary, they were as hospitably kind and courteous to us as if we had deserved it. In one of these camps we found Ab Grimes, an Upper Mississippi pilot, who afterward became famous as a dare-devil rebel spy, whose career bristled with desperate adventures. The look and style of his comrades suggested that they had not come into the war to play, and their deeds made good the conjecture later. They were fine horsemen and good revolver shots; but their favorite arm was the lasso. Each had one at his pommel, and could snatch a man out of the saddle with it every time, on a full gallop, at any reasonable distance.

In another camp the chief was a fierce and profane old blacksmith of sixty, and he had furnished his twenty recruits with gigantic home-made bowie-knives, to be swung with two hands, like the *machetes* of the Isthmus. It was a grisly spectacle to see that earnest band practising their murderous cuts and slashes under the eye of that remorseless old fanatic.

The last camp which we fell back upon was in a hollow near the village of Florida, where I was born—in Monroe County. Here we were warned one day that a Union colonel was sweeping down on us with a whole regiment at his heel. This looked decidedly serious. Our boys went apart and consulted; then we went back and told the other companies present that the war was a disappointment to us, and we were going to disband. They were getting ready themselves to fall back on some place or other, and we were only waiting for General Tom Harris, who expected to arrive at any moment; so they tried to persuade us to wait a little while, but the majority of us said no, we were accustomed to falling back, and didn't need any of Tom Harris's help; we could get along perfectly well without him—and save time, too. So about half of our fifteen, including myself, mounted and left on the instant; the others yielded to persuasion and stayed—stayed through the war.

An hour later we met General Harris on the road, with two or three people in his company—his staff, probably, but we could not tell; none of them were in uniform; uniforms had not come into vogue among us yet. Harris ordered us back; but we told him there was a Union colonel coming with a whole regiment in his wake, and it looked as if there was going to be a disturbance; so we had concluded to go home. He raged a little, but it was of no use; our minds were made up. We had done our share; had killed one man, exterminated one army, such as it was; let him go and kill the rest, and that would end the war. I did not see that brisk young general again until last year; then he was wearing white hair and whiskers.

In time I came to know that Union colonel whose coming frightened me out of the war and crippled the Southern cause to that extent—General Grant. I came within a few hours of seeing him when he was as unknown as I was myself; at a time when anybody could have said, "Grant?—Ulysses S. Grant? I do not remember hearing the name before." It seems difficult to realize that there was once a time when such a remark could be rationally made; but there *was*, and I was within a few miles of the place and the occasion, too, though proceeding in the other direction.

The thoughtful will not throw this war paper of mine

lightly aside as being valueless. It has this value: it is a not unfair picture of what went on in many and many a militia camp in the first months of the rebellion, when the green recruits were without discipline, without the steadying and heartening influence of trained leaders: when all their circumstances were new and strange, and charged with exaggerated terrors, and before the invaluable experience of actual collision in the field had turned them from rabbits into soldiers. If this side of the picture of that early day has not before been put into history, then history has been to that degree incomplete, for it had and has its rightful place there. There was more Bull Run material scattered through the early camps of this country than exhibited itself at Bull Run. And yet it learned its trade presently, and helped to fight the great battles later. I could have become a soldier myself if I had waited. I had got part of it learned; I knew more about retreating than the man that invented retreating.

1885

A Ghost Story

I TOOK A large room, far up Broadway, in a huge old building whose upper stories had been wholly unoccupied for years until I came. The place had long been given up to dust and cobwebs, to solitude and silence. I seemed groping among the tombs and invading the privacy of the dead, that first night I climbed up to my quarters. For the first time in my life a superstitious dread came over me; and as I turned a dark angle of the stairway and an invisible cobweb swung its slazy woof in my face and clung there, I shuddered as one who had encountered a phantom.

I was glad enough when I reached my room and locked out the mold and the darkness. A cheery fire was burning in the grate, and I sat down before it with a comforting sense of relief. For two hours I sat there, thinking of bygone times; recalling old scenes, and summoning half-forgotten faces out of the mists of the past; listening, in fancy, to voices that long ago grew silent for all time, and to once familiar songs that nobody sings now. And as my reverie softened down to a sadder and sadder pathos, the shrieking of the winds outside softened to a wail, the angry beating of the rain against the panes diminished to a tranquil patter, and one by one the noises in the street subsided, until the hurrying footsteps of the last belated straggler died away in the distance and left no sound behind.

The fire had burned low. A sense of loneliness crept over me. I arose and undressed, moving on tiptoe about the room, doing stealthily what I had to do, as if I were environed by sleeping enemies whose slumbers it would be fatal to break. I covered up in bed, and lay listening to the rain and wind and the faint creaking of distant shutters, till they lulled me to sleep.

I slept profoundly, but how long I do not know. All at once I found myself awake, and filled with a shuddering expectancy. All was still. All but my own heart—I could hear it beat. Presently the bedclothes began to slip away slowly toward the foot of the bed, as if some one were pulling them! I could not stir; I could not speak. Still the blankets slipped deliberately away, till my breast was uncovered. Then with a great effort I seized them and drew them over my head. I waited, listened, waited. Once more that steady pull began, and once more I lay torpid a century of dragging seconds till my breast was naked again. At last I roused my energies and snatched the covers back to their place and held them with a strong grip. I waited. By and by I felt a faint tug, and took a fresh grip. The tug strengthened to a steady strain—it grew stronger and stronger. My hold parted, and for the third time the blankets slid away. I groaned. An answering groan came from the foot of the bed! Beaded drops of sweat stood upon my forehead. I was more dead than alive. Presently I heard a heavy footstep in my room—the step of an elephant, it seemed to me—it was not like anything human. But it was moving *from* me—there was relief in that. I heard it approach the door—pass out without moving bolt or lock—and wander away among the dismal corridors, straining the floors and joists till they creaked again as it passed—and then silence reigned once more.

When my excitement had calmed, I said to myself, "This is a dream—simply a hideous dream." And so I lay thinking it over until I convinced myself that it *was* a dream, and then a comforting laugh relaxed my lips and I was happy again. I got up and struck a light; and when I found that the locks and bolts were just as I had left them, another soothing laugh welled in my heart and rippled from my lips. I took my pipe and lit it, and was just sitting down before the fire, when—down went the pipe out of my nerveless fingers, the blood forsook my cheeks, and my placid breathing was cut short with a gasp! In the ashes on the hearth, side by side with my own bare footprint, was another, so vast that in comparison mine was but an infant's! Then I had *had* a visitor, and the elephant tread was explained.

I put out the light and returned to bed, palsied with fear. I lay a long time, peering into the darkness, and listening. Then I heard a grating noise overhead, like the dragging of a heavy body across the floor; then the throwing down of the body, and the shaking of my windows in response to the concussion. In distant parts of the building I heard the muffled slamming of doors. I heard, at intervals, stealthy footsteps creeping in and out among the corridors, and up and down the stairs. Sometimes these noises approached my door, hesitated, and went away again. I heard the clanking of chains faintly, in remote passages, and listened while the clanking grew nearer—while it wearily climbed the stairways, marking each move by the loose surplus of chain that fell with an accented rattle upon each succeeding step as the goblin that bore it advanced. I heard muttered sentences; half-uttered screams that seemed smothered violently; and the swish of invisible garments, the rush of invisible wings. Then I became conscious that my chamber was invaded—that I was not alone. I heard sighs and breathings about my bed, and mysterious whisperings. Three little spheres of soft phosphorescent light appeared on the ceiling directly over my head, clung and glowed there a moment, and then dropped—two of them upon my face and one upon the pillow. They spattered, liquidly, and felt warm. Intuition told me they had turned to gouts of blood as they fell—I needed no light to satisfy myself of that. Then I saw pallid faces, dimly luminous, and white uplifted hands, floating bodiless in the air—floating a moment and then disappearing. The whispering ceased, and the voices and the sounds, and a solemn stillness followed. I waited and listened. I felt that I must have light or die. I was weak with fear. I slowly raised myself toward a sitting posture, and my face came in contact with a clammy hand! All strength went from me apparently, and I fell back like a stricken invalid. Then I heard the rustle of a garment—it seemed to pass to the door and go out.

When everything was still once more, I crept out of bed, sick and feeble, and lit the gas with a hand that trembled as if it were aged with a hundred years. The light brought some little cheer to my spirits. I sat down and fell into a dreamy contemplation of that great footprint in the ashes. By and by its outlines began to waver and grow dim. I glanced up and the broad gas-flame was slowly wilting away. In the same moment I heard the elephantine tread again. I noted its approach, nearer and nearer, along the musty halls, and dimmer and dimmer the light waned. The tread reached my very door and paused—the light had dwindled to a sickly blue, and all things about me lay in a spectral twilight. The door did not open, and yet I felt a faint gust of air fan my cheek, and presently was conscious of a huge, cloudy presence before me. I watched it with fascinated eyes. A pale glow stole over the Thing; gradually its cloudy folds took shape—an arm appeared, then legs, then a body, and last a great sad face looked out of the vapor. Stripped of its filmy housings, naked, muscular and comely, the majestic Cardiff Giant loomed above me!

All my misery vanished—for a child might know that no harm could come with that benignant countenance. My cheerful spirits returned at once, and in sympathy with them the gas flamed up brightly again. Never a lonely outcast was so glad to welcome company as I was to greet the friendly giant. I said:

"Why, is it nobody but you? Do you know, I have been scared to death for the last two or three hours? I am most honestly glad to see you. I wish I had a chair— Here here, don't try to sit down in that thing!"

But it was too late. He was in it before I could stop him, and down he went—I never saw a chair shivered so in my life.

"Stop, stop, you'll ruin ev—"

Too late again. There was another crash, and another chair was resolved into its original elements.

"Confound it, haven't you got any judgment at all? Do you want to ruin all the furniture on the place? Here, here, you petrified fool—"

But it was no use. Before I could arrest him he had sat down on the bed, and it was a melancholy ruin.

"Now what sort of a way is that to do? First you come lumbering about the place bringing a legion of vagabond goblins along with you to worry me to death, and then when I overlook an indelicacy of costume which would not be tolerated anywhere by cultivated people except in a respectable theater, and not even there if the nudity were of *your* sex, you repay me by wrecking all the furniture you can find to sit down on. And why will you? You damage yourself as much as you do me. You have broken off the end of your spinal column, and uttered up the floor with chips of your hams till the place looks like a marble yard. You ought to be ashamed of yourself—you are big enough to know better."

"Well, I will not break any more furniture. But what am I to do? I have not had a chance to sit down for a century." And the tears came into his eyes.

"Poor devil," I said, "I should not have been so harsh with you. And you are an orphan, too, no doubt. But sit down on the floor here—nothing else can stand your weight—and besides, we cannot be sociable with you away up there above me; I want you down where I can perch on this high counting-house stool and gossip with you face to face."

So he sat down on the floor, and lit a pipe which I gave him, threw one of my red blankets over his shoulders, inverted my sitz-bath on his head, helmet fashion, and made himself picturesque and comfortable. Then he crossed his ankles, while I renewed the fire, and exposed the flat, honey-combed bottoms of his prodigious feet to the grateful warmth.

"What is the matter with the bottom of your feet and the back of your legs, that they are gouged up so?"

"Infernal chilblains—I caught them clear up to the back of my head, roosting out there under Newell's farm. But I love the place; I love it as one loves his old home. There is no peace for me like the peace I feel when I am there."

We talked along for half an hour, and then I noticed that he looked tired, and spoke of it.

"Tired?" he said. "Well, I should think so. And now I will tell you all about it, since you have treated me so well. I am the spirit of the Petrified Man that lies across the street there in the museum. I am the ghost of the Cardiff Giant. I can have no rest, no peace, till they have given that poor body burial again. Now what was the most natural thing for me to do, to make men satisfy this wish? Terrify them into it!—haunt the place where the body lay! So I haunted the museum night after night. I even got other spirits to help me. But it did no good, for nobody ever came to the museum at midnight. Then it occurred to me to come over the way and haunt this place a little. I felt that if I ever got a hearing I must succeed, for I had the most efficient company that perdition could furnish. Night after night we have shivered around through these mildewed halls, dragging chains, groaning, whispering, tramping up and down stairs, till, to tell you the truth, I am almost worn out. But when I saw a light in your room to-night I roused my energies again and went at it with a deal of the old freshness. But I am tired out—entirely fagged out. Give me, I beseech you, give me some hope!"

I lit off my perch in a burst of excitement, and exclaimed:

"This transcends everything! everything that ever did occur! Why you poor blundering old fossil, you have had all your trouble for nothing—you have been haunting a *plaster cast* of yourself—the real Cardiff Giant is in Albany!* Confound it, don't you know your own remains?"

I never saw such an eloquent look of shame, of pitiable humiliation, overspread a countenance before.

The Petrified Man rose slowly to his feet, and said: "Honestly, *is* that true?"

"As true as I am sitting here."

He took the pipe from his mouth and laid it on the mantel, then stood irresolute a moment (unconsciously, from old habit, thrusting his hands where his pantaloons pockets

---

* A fact. The original fraud was ingeniously and fraudfully duplicated, and exhibited in New York as the "only genuine" Cardiff Giant (to the unspeakable disgust of the owners of the real colossus) at the very same time that the latter was drawing crowds at a museum in Albany.

should have been, and meditatively dropping his chin on his breast), and finally said:

"Well—I *never* felt so absurd before. The Petrified Man has sold everybody else, and now the mean fraud has ended by selling its own ghost! My son, if there is any charity left in your heart for a poor friendless phantom like me, don't let this get out. Think how *you* would feel if you had made such an ass of yourself."

I heard his stately tramp die away, step by step down the stairs and out into the deserted street, and felt sorry that he was gone, poor fellow—and sorrier still that he had carried off my red blanket and my bathtub.

1888

LUCK*

IT WAS AT a banquet in London in honor of one of the two or three conspicuously illustrious English military names of this generation. For reasons which will presently appear, I will withhold his real name and titles and call him Lieutenant-General Lord Arthur Scoresby, Y.C., K.C.B., etc., etc., etc. What a fascination there is in a renowned name! There sat the man, in actual flesh, whom I had heard of so many thousands of times since that day, thirty years

* This is not a fancy sketch. I got it from a clergyman who was an instructor at Woolwich forty years ago, and who vouched for its truth. M.T.

before, when his name shot suddenly to the zenith from a Crimean battlefield, to remain forever celebrated. It was food and drink to me to look, and look, and look at that demi-god; scanning, searching, noting: the quietness, the reserve, the noble gravity of his countenance; the simple honesty that expressed itself all over him; the sweet unconsciousness of his greatness—unconsciousness of the hundreds of admiring eyes fastened upon him, unconsciousness of the deep, loving, sincere worship welling out of the breasts of those people and flowing toward him.

The clergyman at my left was an old acquaintance of mine—clergyman now, but had spent the first half of his life in the camp and field and as an instructor in the military school at Woolwich. Just at the moment I have been talking about a veiled and singular light glimmered in his eyes and he leaned down and muttered confidentially to me—indicating the hero of the banquet with a gesture:

"Privately—he's an absolute fool."

This verdict was a great surprise to me. If its subject had been Napoleon, or Socrates, or Solomon, my astonishment could not have been greater. Two things I was well aware of: that the Reverend was a man of strict veracity and that his judgment of men was good. Therefore I knew, beyond doubt or question, that the world was mistaken about this hero: he *was* a fool. So I meant to find out, at a convenient moment, how the Reverend, all solitary and alone, had discovered the secret.

Some days later the opportunity came, and this is what the Reverend told me:

About forty years ago I was an instructor in the military academy at Woolwich. I was present in one of the sections when young Scoresby underwent his preliminary examination. I was touched to the quick with pity, for the rest of the class answered up brightly and handsomely, while he—why, dear me, he didn't know *anything*, so to speak. He was evidently good, and sweet, and lovable, and guileless; and so it was exceedingly painful to see him stand there, as serene as a graven image, and deliver himself of answers which were veritably miraculous for stupidity and ignorance. All the compassion in me was aroused in his behalf. I said to myself, when he comes to be examined again he will be flung over, of course; so it will be simply a harmless act of charity to ease his fall as much as I can. I took him aside and found that he knew a little of Cæsar's history; and as he didn't know anything else, I went to work and drilled him like a galley-slave on a certain line of stock questions concerning Cæsar which I knew would be used. If you'll believe me, he went through with flying colors on examination day! He went through on that purely superficial "cram," and got compliments too, while others, who knew a thousand times more than he, got plucked. By some strangely lucky accident—an accident not likely to happen twice in a century— he was asked no question outside of the narrow limits of his drill.

It was stupefying. Well, all through his course I stood by him, with something of the sentiment which a mother feels for a crippled child; and he always saved himself—just by miracle, apparently.

Now, of course, the thing that would expose him and kill him at last was mathematics. I resolved to make his death as easy as I could; so I drilled him and crammed him, and crammed him and drilled him, just on the line of questions which the examiners would be most likely to use, and then launched him on his fate. Well, sir, try to conceive of the result: to my consternation, he took the first prize! And with it he got a perfect ovation in the way of compliments.

Sleep? There was no more sleep for me for a week. My conscience tortured me day and night. What I had done I had done purely through charity, and only to ease the poor youth's fall. I never had dreamed of any such preposterous results as the thing that had happened. I felt as guilty and miserable as Frankenstein. Here was a wooden-head whom I had put in the way of glittering promotions and prodigious responsibilities, and but one thing could happen: he and his responsibilities would all go to ruin together at the first opportunity.

The Crimean War[1] had just broken out. Of course there had to be a war, I said to myself. We couldn't have peace and give this donkey a chance to die before he is found out. I waited for the earthquake. It came. And it made me reel when it did come. He was actually gazetted to a captaincy in a marching regiment! Better men grow old and gray in the service before they climb to a sublimity like that. And who could ever have foreseen that they would go and put such a load of responsibility on such green and inadequate shoulders? I could just barely have stood it if they had made him a cornet; but a captain—think of it! I thought my hair would turn white.

Consider what I did—I who so loved repose and inaction. I said to myself, I am responsible to the country for this, and I must go along with him and protect the country against him as far as I can. So I took my poor little capital that I had saved up through years of work and grinding economy, and went with a sigh and bought a cornetcy in his regiment, and away we went to the field.

And there—oh, dear, it was awful. Blunders?—why he never did anything *but* blunder. But, you see, nobody was in on the fellow's secret. Everybody had him focused wrong, and necessarily misinterpreted his performance every time. Consequently they took his idiotic blunders for inspirations of genius. They did, honestly! His mildest blunders were enough to make a man in his right mind cry; and they did make me cry—and rage and rave, too, privately. And the thing that kept me always in a sweat of apprehension was the fact that every fresh blunder he made increased the luster of his reputation! I kept saying to myself, he'll get so high that when discovery does finally come it will be like the sun falling out of the sky.

He went right along, up from grade to grade, over the dead bodies of his superiors, until at last, in the hottest moment of the battle of —— down went our colonel, and my heart jumped into my mouth, for Scoresby was next in rank! Now for it, said I; we'll all land in Sheol in ten minutes, sure.

The battle was awfully hot; the allies were steadily giving way all over the field. Our regiment occupied a position that was vital; a blunder now must be destruction. At this crucial moment, what does this immortal fool do but detach the regiment from its place and order a charge over a neighboring hill where there wasn't a suggestion of an enemy! "There you go!" I said to myself; "this *is* the end at last."

And away we did go, and were over the shoulder of the hill before the insane movement could be discovered and stopped. And what did we find? An entire and unsuspected Russian army in reserve! And what happened? We were eaten up? That is necessarily what would have happened in ninety-nine cases out of a hundred. But no; those Russians argued that no single regiment would come browsing around there at such a time. It must be the entire English army, and that the sly Russian game was detected and blocked; so they turned tail, and away they went, pell-mell, over the hill and down into the field, in wild confusion, and we after them; they themselves broke the solid Russian center in the field, and tore through, and in no time there was the most tremendous rout you ever saw, and the defeat of the allies was turned into a sweeping and splendid victory! Marshal Canrobert looked on, dizzy with astonishment, admiration, and delight; and sent right off for Scoresby, and hugged him, and decorated him on the field in presence of all the armies!

And what was Scoresby's blunder that time? Merely the mistaking his right hand for his left—that was all. An order had come to him to fall back and support our right; and, instead, he fell *forward* and went over the hill to the left.

But the name he won that day as a marvelous military genius filled the world with his glory, and that glory will never fade while history books last.

He is just as good and sweet and lovable and unpretending as a man can be, but he doesn't know enough to come in when it rains. Now that is absolutely true. He is the supremest ass in the universe; and until half an hour ago nobody knew it but himself and me. He has been pursued, day by day and year by year, by a most phenomenal and astonishing luckiness. He has been a shining soldier in all our wars for a generation; he has littered his whole military life with blunders, and yet has never committed one that didn't make him a knight or a baronet or a lord or something. Look at his breast; why, he is just clothed in domestic and foreign decorations. Well, sir, every one of them is the record of some shouting stupidity or other; and, taken together, they are proof that the very thing in all this world that can befall a man is to be born lucky. I say again, as I said at the banquet, Scoresby's an absolute fool.

1891

Playing Courier

A time would come when we must go from Aix-les-Bains to Geneva, and from thence, by a series of day-long and tangled journeys, to Bayreuth in Bavaria. I should have to have a courier, of course, to take care of so considerable a party as mine.

But I procrastinated. The time slipped along, and at last

I woke up one day to the fact that we were ready to move and had no courier. I then resolved upon what I felt was a foolhardy thing, but I was in the humor of it. I said I would make the first stage without help—I did it.

I brought the party from Aix to Geneva by myself—four people. The distance was two hours and more, and there was one change of cars. There was not an accident of any kind, except leaving a valise and some other matters on the platform—a thing which can hardly be called an accident, it is so common. So I offered to conduct the party all the way to Bayreuth.

This was a blunder, though it did not seem so at the time. There was more detail than I thought there would be: 1, two persons whom we had left in a Genevan. pension some weeks before must be collected and brought to the hotel; 2, I must notify the people on the Grand Quay who store trunks to bring seven of our stored trunks to the hotel and carry back seven which they would find piled in the lobby; 3, I must find out what part of Europe Bayreuth was in and buy seven railway tickets for that point; 4, I must send a telegram to a friend in the Netherlands; 5, it was now two in the afternoon, and we must look sharp and be ready for the first night train and make sure of sleeping-car tickets; 6, I must draw money at the bank.

It seemed to me that the sleeping-car tickets must be the most important thing, so I went to the station myself to make sure; hotel messengers are not always brisk people. It was a hot day, and I ought to have driven, but it seemed better economy to walk. It did not turn out so, because I lost my way and trebled the distance. I applied for the tickets, and they asked me which route I wanted to go by, and that embarrassed me and made me lose my head, there were so many people standing around, and I not knowing anything about the routes and not supposing there were going to be two; so I judged it best to go back and map out the road and come again.

I took a cab this time, but on my way up-stairs at the hotel I remembered that I was out of cigars, so I thought it would be well to get some while the matter was in my mind. It was only round the corner, and I didn't need the cab. I asked the cabman to wait where he was. Thinking of the telegram and trying to word it in my head, I forgot the cigars and the cab, and walked on indefinitely. I was going to have the hotel people send the telegram, but as I could not be far from the post-office by this time, I thought I would do it myself. But it was further than I had supposed. I found the place at last and wrote the telegram and handed it in. The clerk was a severe-looking, fidgety man, and he began to fire French questions at me in such a liquid form that I could not detect the joints between his words, and this made me lose my head again. But an Englishman stepped up and said the clerk wanted to know where he was to send the telegram. I could not tell him, because it was not my telegram, and I explained that I was merely sending it for a member of my party. But nothing would pacify the clerk but the address; so I said that if he was so particular I would go back and get it.

However, I thought I would go and collect those lacking two persons first, for it would be best to do everything systematically and in order, and one detail at a time. Then I remembered the cab was eating up my substance down at the hotel yonder; so I called another cab and told the man to go down and fetch it to the post-office and wait till I came.

I had a long, hot walk to collect those people, and when I got there they couldn't come with me because they had heavy satchels and must have a cab. I went away to find one, but before I ran across any I noticed that I had reached the neighborhood of the Grand Quay—at least I thought I had—so I judged I could save time by stepping around and arranging about the trunks. I stepped around about a mile, and although I did not find the Grand Quay, I found a cigar shop, and remembered about the cigars. I said I was going to Bayreuth, and wanted enough for the journey. The man asked me which route I was going to take. I said I did not know. He said he would recommend me to go by Zurich and various other places which he named, and offered to sell me seven second-class through tickets for twenty-two dollars apiece, which would be throwing off the discount which the railroads allowed him. I was already tired of riding second-class on first-class tickets, so I took him up.

By and by I found Natural & Co.'s storage office, and told them to send seven of our trunks to the hotel and pile them up in the lobby. It seemed to me that I was not delivering the whole of the message, still it was all I could find in my head.

Next I found the bank and asked for some money, but I had left my letter of credit somewhere and was not able to draw. I remembered now that I must have left it lying on the table where I wrote my telegram; so I got a cab and drove to the post-office and went up-stairs, and they said that a letter of credit had indeed been left on the table, but that it was now in the hands of the police authorities, and it would be necessary for me to go there and prove property. They sent a boy with me, and we went out the back way and walked a couple of miles and found the place; and then I remembered about my cabs, and asked the boy to send them to me when he got back to the post-office. It was nightfall now, and the Mayor had gone to dinner. I thought I would go to dinner myself, but the officer on duty thought differently, and I stayed. The Mayor dropped in at half past ten, but said it was too late to do anything to-night—come at 9.30 in the morning. The officer wanted to keep me all night, and said I was a suspicious-looking person, and probably did not own the letter of credit, and didn't know what a letter of credit was, but merely saw the real owner leave it lying on the table, and wanted to get it because I was probably a person that would want anything he could get, whether it was valuable or not. But the Mayor said he saw nothing suspicious about me, and that I seemed a harmless person and nothing the matter with me but a wandering mind, and not much of that. So I thanked him and he set me free, and I went home in my three cabs.

As I was dog-tired and in no condition to answer questions with discretion, I thought I would not disturb the Expedition at that time of night, as there was a vacant room I knew of at the other end of the hall; but I did not quite arrive there, as a watch had been set, the Expedition being anxious about me. I was placed in a galling situation. The Expedition sat stiff and forbidding on four chairs in a row, with shawls and things all on, satchels and guide-books in lap. They had been sitting like that for four hours, and the glass going down all the time. Yes, and they were waiting—waiting for me. It seemed to me that nothing but a sudden, happily contrived, and brilliant *tour de force* could break this iron front and make a diversion in my favor; so I shied my hat into the arena and followed it with a skip and a jump, shouting blithely:

"Ha, ha, here we all are, Mr. Merryman!"

Nothing could be deeper or stiller than the absence of applause which followed. But I kept on; there seemed no other way, though my confidence, poor enough before, had got a deadly check and was in effect gone.

I tried to be jocund out of a heavy heart, I tried to touch the other hearts there and soften the bitter resentment in those faces by throwing off bright and airy fun and making of the whole ghastly thing a joyously humorous incident, but this idea was not well conceived. It was not the right atmosphere for it. I got not one smile; not one line in those offended faces relaxed; I thawed nothing of the winter that looked out of those frosty eyes. I started one more breezy, poor effort, but the head of the Expedition cut into the center of it and said:

"Where have you been?"

I saw by the manner of this that the idea was to get down

to cold business now. So I began my travels, but was cut short again.

"Where are the two others? We have been in frightful anxiety about them."

"Oh, they're all right. I was to fetch a cab. I will go straight off, and—"

"Sit down! Don't you know it is eleven o'clock? Where did you leave them?"

"At the pension."

"Why didn't you bring them?"

"Because we couldn't carry the satchels. And so I thought—"

"Thought! You should not try to think. One cannot think without the proper machinery. It is two miles to that pension. Did you go there without a cab?"

"I—well, I didn't intend to; it only happened so."

"How did it happen so?"

"Because I was at the post-office and I remembered that I had left a cab waiting here, and so, to stop that expense, I sent another cab to—to—"

"To what?"

"Well, I don't remember now, but I think the new cab was to have the hotel pay the old cab, and send it away."

"What good would that do?"

"What good would it do? It would stop the expense, wouldn't it?"

"By putting the new cab in its place to continue the expense?"

I didn't say anything.

"Why didn't you have the new cab come back for you?"

"Oh, that is what I did. I remember now. Yes, that is what I did. Because I recollect that when I—"

"Well, then why didn't it come back for you?"

"To the post-office? Why, it did."

"Very well, then, how did you come to walk to the pension?"

"I—I don't quite remember how that happened. Oh,

yes, I do remember now. I wrote the despatch to send to the Netherlands, and—"

"Oh, thank goodness, you did accomplish something! I wouldn't have had you fail to send—what makes you look like that! You are trying to avoid my eye. That despatch is the most important thing that— You haven't sent that despatch!"

"I haven't said I didn't send it."

"You don't need to. Oh, dear, I wouldn't have had that telegram fail for anything. Why didn't you send it?"

"Well, you see, with so many things to do and think of, I—they're very particular there, and after I had written the telegram—"

"Oh, never mind, let it go, explanations can't help the matter now—what will he think of us?"

"Oh, that's all right, that's all right, hell think we gave the telegram to the hotel people, and that they—"

"Why, certainly! Why didn't you do that? There was no other rational way."

"Yes, I know, but then I had it on my mind that I must be sure and get to the bank and draw some money—"

"Well, you are entitled to some credit, after all, for thinking of that, and I don't wish to be too hard on you, though you must acknowledge yourself that you have cost us all a good deal of trouble, and some of it not necessary. How much did you draw?"

"Well, I—I had an idea that—that—"

"That what?"

"That—well, it seems to me that in the circumstances—so many of us, you know, and—and—"

"What are you mooning about? Do turn your face this way and let me—why, you haven't drawn any money!"

"Well, the banker said—"

"Never mind what the banker said. You must have had a reason of your own. Not a reason, exactly, but something which—"

"Well, then, the simple fact was that I hadn't my letter of credit."

"Hadn't your letter of credit?"

"Hadn't my letter of credit."

"Don't repeat me like that. Where was it?"

"At the post-office."

"What was it doing there?"

"Well, I forgot and left it there."

"Upon my word, I've seen a good many couriers, but of all the couriers that ever I—"

"I've done the best I could."

"Well, so you have, poor thing, and I'm wrong to abuse you so when you've been working yourself to death while we've been sitting here only thinking of our vexations instead of feeling grateful for what you were trying to do for us. It will all come out right. We can take the 7.30 train in the morning just as well. You've bought the tickets?"

"I have—and it's a bargain, too. Second class."

"I'm glad of it. Everybody else travels second class, and we might just as well save that ruinous extra charge. What did you pay?"

"Twenty-two dollars apiece—through to Bayreuth."

"Why, I didn't know you could buy through tickets anywhere but in London and Paris."

"Some people can't, maybe; but some people can—of whom I am one of which, it appears."

"It seems a rather high price."

"On the contrary, the dealer knocked off his commission."

"Dealer?"

"Yes—I bought them at a cigar shop."

"That reminds me. We shall have to get up pretty early, and so there should be no packing to do. Your umbrella, your rubbers, your cigars—what is the matter?"

"Hang it, I've left the cigars at the bank."

"Just think of it! Well, your umbrella?"

"I'll have that all right. There's no hurry."

"What do you mean by that?"

"Oh, that's all right; I'll take care of—"

"Where is that umbrella?"

"It's just the merest step—it won't take me—"

"Where is it?"

"Well, I think I left it at the cigar shop; but anyway—"

"Take your feet out from under that thing. It's just as I expected! Where are your rubbers?"

"They—well—"

"Where are your rubbers?"

"It's got so dry now—well, everybody says there's not going to be another drop of—"

"Where—are—your—rubbers?"

"Well, you see—well, it was this way. First, the officer said—"

"What officer?"

"Police officer; but the Mayor, he—"

"What Mayor?"

"Mayor of Geneva; but I said—"

"Wait. What is the matter with you?"

"Who, me? Nothing. They both tried to persuade me to stay, and—"

"Stay where?"

"Well, the fact is—"

"Where have you been? What's kept you out till half past ten at night?"

"Oh, you see, after I lost my letter of credit, I—"

"You are beating around the bush a good deal. Now, answer the question in just one straightforward word. Where are those rubbers?"

"They—well, they're in the county jail."

I started a placating smile, but it petrified. The climate was unsuitable. Spending three or four hours in jail did not seem to the Expedition humorous. Neither did it to me, at bottom.

I had to explain the whole thing, and, of course, it came out then that we couldn't take the early train, because that would leave my letter of credit in hock still. It did look as if we had all got to go to bed estranged and unhappy, but by good luck that was prevented. There happened to be mention of the trunks, and I was able to say I had attended to that feature.

"There, you are just as good and thoughtful and painstaking and intelligent as you can be, and it's a shame to find so much fault with you, and there sha'n't be another word of it. You've done beautifully, admirably, and I'm sorry I ever said one ungrateful word to you."

This hit deeper than some of the other things and made me uncomfortable, because I wasn't feeling as solid about that trunk errand as I wanted to. There seemed somehow to be a defect about it somewhere, though I couldn't put my finger on it, and didn't like to stir the matter just now, it being late and maybe well enough to let well enough alone.

Of course there was music in the morning, when it was found that we couldn't leave by the early train. But I had no time to wait; I got only the opening bars of the overture, and then started out to get my letter of credit.

It seemed a good time to look into the trunk business and rectify it if it needed it, and I had a suspicion that it did. I was too late. The concierge said he had shipped the trunks to Zurich the evening before. I asked him how he could do that without exhibiting passage tickets.

"Not necessary in Switzerland. You pay for your trunks and send them where you please. Nothing goes free but your hand-baggage."

"How much did you pay on them?"

"A hundred and forty francs."

"Twenty-eight dollars. There's something wrong about that trunk business, sure."

Next I met the porter. He said:

"You have not slept well, is it not? You have a worn look.

If you would like a courier, a good one has arrived last night, and is not engaged for five days already, by the name of Ludi. We recommend him; *das heisst,* the Grand Hôtel Beau Rivage recommends him."

I declined with coldness. My spirit was not broken yet. And I did not like having my condition taken notice of in this way. I was at the county jail by nine o'clock, hoping that the Mayor might chance to come before his regular hour; but he didn't. It was dull there. Every time I offered to touch anything, or look at anything, or do anything, or refrain from doing anything, the policeman said it was *"défendu."* I thought I would practise my French on him, but he wouldn't have that either. It seemed to make him particularly bitter to hear his own tongue.

The Mayor came at last, and then there was no trouble; for the minute he had convened the Supreme Court—they always do whenever there is valuable property in dispute—and got everything shipshape and sentries posted, and had prayer by the chaplain, my unsealed letter was brought and opened, and there wasn't anything in it but some photographs; because, as I remembered now, I had taken out the letter of credit so as to make room for the photographs, and had put the letter in my other pocket, which I proved to everybody's satisfaction by fetching it out and showing it with a good deal of exultation. So then the court looked at each other in a vacant kind of way, and then at me, and then at each other, again, and finally let me go, but said it was imprudent for me to be at large, and asked me what my profession was. I said I was a courier. They lifted up their eyes in a kind of reverent way and said, *"Du lieber Gott!"* and I said a word of courteous thanks for their apparent admiration and hurried off to the bank.

However, being a courier was already making me a great stickler for order and system and one thing at a time and each thing in its own proper turn; so I passed by the bank and branched off and started for the two lacking members of the Expedition. A cab lazied by, and I took it upon persuasion. I gained no speed by this, but it was a reposeful turnout and I liked reposefulness. The week-long jubilations over the six hundredth anniversary of the birth of Swiss liberty and the Signing of the Compact was at flood-tide, and all the streets were clothed in fluttering flags.

The horse and the driver had been drunk three days and nights, and had known no stall nor bed meantime. They looked as I felt—dreamy and seedy. But we arrived in course of time. I went in and rang, and asked a housemaid to rush out the lacking members. She said something which I did not understand, and I returned to the chariot. The girl had probably told me that those people did not belong on her floor, and that it would be judicious for me to go higher, and ring from floor to floor till I found them; for in those Swiss flats there does not seem to be any way to find the right family but to be patient and guess your way along up. I calculated that I must wait fifteen minutes, there being three details inseparable from an occasion of this sort: 1, put on hats and come down and climb in; 2, return of one to get "my other glove"; 3, presently, return of the other one to fetch "my *French Verbs at a Glance*." I would muse during the fifteen minutes and take it easy.

A very still and blank interval ensued, and then I felt a hand on my shoulder and started. The intruder was a policeman. I glanced up and perceived that there was new scenery. There was a good deal of a crowd, and they had that pleased and interested look which such a crowd wears when they see that somebody is out of luck. The horse was asleep, and so was the driver, and some boys had hung them and me full of gaudy decorations stolen from the innumerable banner-poles. It was a scandalous spectacle. The officer said:

"I'm sorry, but we can't have you sleeping here all day."

I was wounded, and said with dignity:

"I beg your pardon, I was not sleeping; I was thinking."

"Well, you can think if you want to, but you've got to think to yourself; you disturb the whole neighborhood."

It was a poor joke, and it made the crowd laugh. I snore at night sometimes, but it is not likely that I would do such a thing in the daytime and in such a place. The officer undecorated us, and seemed sorry for our friendlessness, and really tried to be humane, but he said we mustn't stop there any longer or he would have to charge us rent—it was the law, he said, and he went on to say in a sociable way that I was looking pretty moldy, and he wished he knew—

I shut him off pretty austerely, and said I hoped one might celebrate a little these days, especially when one was personally concerned.

"Personally?" he asked. "How?"

"Because six hundred years ago an ancestor of mine signed the compact."

He reflected a moment, then looked me over and said:

"Ancestor! It's my opinion you signed it yourself. For of all the old ancient relics that ever I—but never mind about that. What is it you are waiting here for so long?"

I said:

"I'm not waiting here so long at all. I'm waiting fifteen minutes till they forget a glove and a book and go back and get them." Then I told him who they were that I had come for.

He was very obliging, and began to shout inquiries to the tiers of heads and shoulders projecting from the windows above us. Then a woman away up there sang out:

"Oh, they? Why, I got them a cab and they left here long ago—half past eight, I should say."

It was annoying. I glanced at my watch, but didn't say anything. The officer said:

"It is a quarter of twelve, you see. You should have inquired better. You have been asleep three-quarters of an hour, and in such a sun as this. You are baked—baked black.

It is wonderful. And you will miss your train, perhaps. You interest me greatly. What is your occupation?"

I said I was a courier. It seemed to stun him, and before he could come to we were gone.

When I arrived in the third story of the hotel I found our quarters vacant. I was not surprised. The moment a courier takes his eye off his tribe they go shopping. The nearer it is to train-time the surer they are to go. I sat down to try and think out what I had best do next, but presently the hall-boy found me there, and said the Expedition had gone to the station half an hour before. It was the first time I had known them to do a rational thing, and it was very confusing. This is one of the things that make a courier's life so difficult and uncertain. Just as matters are going the smoothest, his people will strike a lucid interval, and down go all his arrangements to wreck and ruin.

The train was to leave at twelve noon sharp. It was now ten minutes after twelve. I could be at the station in ten minutes. I saw I had no great amount of leeway, for this was the lightning express, and on the Continent the lightning expresses are pretty fastidious about getting away some time during the advertised day. My people were the only ones remaining in the waiting-room; everybody else had passed through and "mounted the train," as they say in those regions. They were exhausted with nervousness and fret, but I comforted them and heartened them up, and we made our rush.

But no; we were out of luck again. The doorkeeper was not satisfied with the tickets. He examined them cautiously, deliberately, suspiciously; then glared at me awhile, and after that he called another official. The two examined the tickets and called another official. These called others, and the convention discussed and discussed, and gesticulated and carried on, until I begged that they would consider how time was flying, and just pass a few resolutions and let us go.

Then they said very courteously that there was a defect in the tickets, and asked me where I got them.

I judged I saw what the trouble was now. You see, I had bought the tickets in a cigar shop, and, of course, the tobacco smell was on them; without doubt, the thing they were up to was to work the tickets through the Custom House and to collect duty on that smell. So I resolved to be perfectly frank; it is sometimes the best way. I said:

"Gentlemen, I will not deceive you. These railway tickets—"

"Ah, pardon, monsieur! These are not railway tickets."

"Oh," I said, "is that the defect?"

"Ah, truly yes, monsieur. These are lottery tickets, yes; and it is a lottery which has been drawn two years ago."

I affected to be greatly amused; it is all one can do in such circumstances; it is all one can do, and yet there is no value in it; it deceives nobody, and you can see that everybody around pities you and is ashamed of you. One of the hardest situations in life, I think, is to be full of grief and a sense of defeat and shabbiness that way, and yet have to put on an outside of archness and gaiety, while all the time you know that your own Expedition, the treasures of your heart, and whose love and reverence you are by the custom of our civilization entitled to, are being consumed with humiliation before strangers to see you earning and getting a compassion which is a stigma, a brand—a brand which certifies you to be—oh, anything and everything which is fatal to human respect.

I said, cheerily, it was all right, just one of those little accidents that was likely to happen to anybody—I would have the right tickets in two minutes, and we would catch the train yet, and, moreover, have something to laugh about all through the journey. I did get the tickets in time, all stamped and complete, but then it turned out that I couldn't take them, because in taking so much pains about the two missing members I had skipped the bank and hadn't the money. So then the train left, and there didn't seem to be anything to do but go back to the hotel, which we did; but it was kind of melancholy and not much said. I tried to start a few subjects, like scenery and transubstantiation, and those sorts of things, but they didn't seem to hit the weather right.

We had lost our good rooms, but we got some others which were pretty scattering, but would answer. I judged things would brighten now, but the Head of the Expedition said, "Send up the trunks." It made me feel pretty cold. There was a doubtful something about that trunk business. I was almost sure of it. I was going to suggest—

But a wave of his hand sufficiently restrained me, and I was informed that we would now camp for three days and see if we could rest up.

I said all right, never mind ringing; I would go down and attend to the trunks myself. I got a cab and went straight to Mr. Charles Natural's place, and asked what order it was I had left there.

"To send seven trunks to the hotel."

"And were you to bring any back?"

"No."

"You are sure I didn't tell you to bring back seven that would be found piled in the lobby?"

"Absolutely sure you didn't."

"Then the whole fourteen are gone to Zurich or Jericho or somewhere, and there is going to be more debris around that hotel when the Expedition—"

I didn't finish, because my mind was getting to be in a good deal of a whirl, and when you are that way you think you have finished a sentence when you haven't, and you go mooning and dreaming away, and die first thing you know you get run over by a dray or a cow or something.

I left the cab there—I forgot it—and on my way back I thought it all out and concluded to resign, because otherwise I should be nearly sure to be discharged. But I didn't believe it would be a good idea to resign in person; I could do it by message. So I sent for Mr. Ludi and explained that there was a courier going to resign on account of incompatibility or fatigue or something, and as he had four or five vacant days, I would like to insert him into that vacancy if he thought he could fill it. When everything was arranged I got him to go up and say to the Expedition that, owing to an error made by Mr. Natural's people, we were out of trunks here, but would have plenty in Zurich, and we'd better take the first train, freight, gravel, or construction, and move right along.

He attended to that and came down with an invitation for me to go up—yes, certainly; and, while we walked along over to the bank to get money, and collect my cigars and tobacco, and to the cigar shop to trade back the lottery tickets and get my umbrella, and to Mr. Natural's to pay that cab and send it away, and to the county jail to get my rubbers and leave p. p. c. cards for the Mayor and Supreme Court, he described the weather to me that was prevailing on the upper levels there with the Expedition, and I saw that I was doing very well where I was.

I stayed out in the woods till 4 P.M., to let the weather moderate, and then turned up at the station just in time to take the three-o'clock express for Zurich along with the Expedition, now in the hands of Ludi, who conducted its complex affairs with little apparent effort or inconvenience.

Well, I had worked like a slave while I was in office, and done the very best I knew how; yet all that these people dwelt upon or seemed to care to remember were the defects of my administration, not its creditable features. They would skip over a thousand creditable features to remark upon and reiterate and fuss about just one fact, till it seemed to me they would wear it out; and not much of a fact, either, taken by itself—the fact that I elected myself courier in Geneva, and put in work enough to carry a circus to Jerusalem, and yet never even got my gang out of the town. I finally said I didn't wish to hear any more about the subject, it made me tired. And I told them to their faces that I would never be a courier again to save anybody's life. And if I live long enough I'll prove it. I think it's a difficult, brain-racking, overworked, and thoroughly ungrateful office, and the main bulk of its wages is a sore heart and a bruised spirit.

1891

THE CALIFORNIAN'S TALE

THIRTY-FIVE YEARS ago I was out prospecting on the Stanislaus, tramping all day long with pick and pan and horn, and washing a hatful of dirt here and there, always expecting to make a rich strike, and never doing it. It was a lovely region, woodsy, balmy, delicious, and had once been populous, long years before, but now the people had vanished and the charming paradise was a solitude. They went away when the surface diggings gave out. In one place, where a busy little city with banks and newspapers and fire companies and a mayor and aldermen had been, was nothing but a wide expanse of emerald turf, with not even the faintest sign that human life had ever been present there. This was down toward Tuttletown. In the country neighborhood thereabouts, along the dusty roads, one found at intervals the prettiest little cottage homes, snug and cozy, and so cobwebbed with vines snowed thick with roses that the doors and windows were wholly hidden from sight—sign that these were deserted homes, forsaken years ago by defeated and disappointed families who could neither sell them nor give them away. Now and then, half an hour apart, one came across solitary log cabins of the earliest mining days, built by the first gold-miners, the predecessors of the cottage-builders. In some few cases these cabins were still occupied; and when this was so, you could depend upon it that the occupant was the very pioneer who had built the cabin; and you could depend on another thing, too—that he was there because he had once had his opportunity to go home to the States rich, and had not done it; had rather lost his wealth, and had then in his humiliation resolved to sever all communication with his home relatives and friends, and be to them thenceforth as one dead. Round about California in that day were scattered a host of these living dead men—pride-smitten poor fellows, grizzled and old at forty, whose secret thoughts were made all of regrets and longings—regrets for their wasted lives, and longings to be out of the struggle and done with it all.

It was a lonesome land! Not a sound in all those peaceful expanses of grass and woods but the drowsy hum of insects; no glimpse of man or beast; nothing to keep up your spirits and make you glad to be alive. And so, at last, in the early part of the afternoon, when I caught sight of a human creature, I felt a most grateful uplift. This person was a man about forty-five years old, and he was standing at the gate of one of those cozy little rose-clad cottages of the sort already referred to. However, this one hadn't a deserted look; it had the look of being lived in and petted and cared for and looked after; and so had its front yard, which was a garden of flowers, abundant, gay, and flourishing. I was invited in, of course, and required to make myself at home—it was the custom of the country.

It was delightful to be in such a place, after long weeks of daily and nightly familiarity with miners' cabins—with all which this implies of dirt floor, never-made beds, tin plates and cups, bacon and beans and black coffee, and nothing of ornament but war pictures from the Eastern illustrated papers tacked to the log walls. That was all hard, cheerless, materialistic desolation, but here was a nest which had aspects to rest the tired eye and refresh that something in one's nature which, after long fasting, recognizes, when confronted by the belongings of art, howsoever cheap and modest they may be, that it has unconsciously been famishing and now has found nourishment. I could not have believed that a rag carpet could feast me so, and so content me; or that there could be such solace to the soul in wall-paper and framed lithographs, and bright-colored tidies and lamp-mats, and Windsor chairs, and varnished whatnots, with sea-shells and books and china vases on them, and the score of little unclassifiable tricks and touches that a woman's hand distributes about a home, which one sees without knowing he sees them, yet would miss in a moment if they were taken away. The delight that was in my heart showed in my face, and the man saw it and was pleased; saw it so plainly that he answered it as if it had been spoken.

"All her work," he said, caressingly; "she did it all herself—every bit," and he took the room in with a glance which was full of affectionate worship. One of those soft Japanese fabrics with which women drape with careful negligence the upper part of a picture-frame was out of adjustment. He noticed it, and rearranged it with cautious pains, stepping back several times to gauge the effect before he got it to suit him. Then he gave it a light finishing pat or two with his hand, and said: "She always does that. You can't tell just what it lacks, but it does lack something until you've done that—you can see it yourself after it's done, but that is all you know; you can't find out the law of it. It's like the finishing pats a mother gives the child's hair after she's got it combed and brushed, I reckon. I've seen her fix all these things so much that I can do them all just her way, though I don't know the law of any of them. But she knows the law.

She knows the why and the how both; but I don't know the why; I only know the how."

He took me into a bedroom so that I might wash my hands; such a bedroom as I had not seen for years: white counterpane, white pillows, carpeted floor, papered walls, pictures, dressing-table, with mirror and pin-cushion and dainty toilet things; and in the corner a wash-stand, with real china-ware bowl and pitcher, and with soap in a china dish, and on a rack more than a dozen towels—towels too clean and white for one out of practice to use without some vague sense of profanation. So my face spoke again, and he answered with gratified words:

"All her work; she did it all herself—every bit. Nothing here that hasn't felt the touch of her hand. Now you would think— But I mustn't talk so much."

By this time I was wiping my hands and glancing from detail to detail of the room's belongings, as one is apt to do when he is in a new place, where everything he sees is a comfort to his eye and his spirit; and I became conscious, in one of those unaccountable ways, you know, that there was something there somewhere that the man wanted me to discover for myself. I knew it perfectly, and I knew he was trying to help me by furtive indications with his eye, so I tried hard to get on the right track, being eager to gratify him. I failed several times, as I could see out of the corner of my eye without being told; but at last I knew I must be looking straight at the thing—knew it from the pleasure issuing in invisible waves from him. He broke into a happy laugh, and rubbed his hands together, and cried out:

"That's it! You've found it. I knew you would. It's her picture."

I went to the little black-walnut bracket on the farther wall, and did find there what I had not yet noticed—a daguerreotype-case. It contained the sweetest girlish face, and the most beautiful, as it seemed to me, that I had ever seen. The man drank the admiration from my face, and was fully satisfied.

"Nineteen her last birthday," he said, as he put the picture back; "and that was the day we were married. When you see her—ah, just wait till you see her!"

"Where is she? When will she be in?"

"Oh, she's away now. She's gone to see her people. They live forty or fifty miles from here. She's been gone two weeks to-day."

"When do you expect her back?"

"This is Wednesday. She'll be back Saturday, in the evening—about nine o'clock, likely."

I felt a sharp sense of disappointment.

"I'm sorry, because I'll be gone then," I said, regretfully.

"Gone? No—why should you go? Don't go. She'll be so disappointed."

She would be disappointed—that beautiful creature! If she had said the words herself they could hardly have blessed me more. I was feeling a deep, strong longing to see her—a longing so supplicating, so insistent, that it made me afraid. I said to myself: "I will go straight away from this place, for my peace of mind's sake."

"You see, she likes to have people come and stop with us—people who know things, and can talk—people like you. She delights in it; for she knows—oh, she knows nearly everything herself, and can talk, oh, like a bird—and the books she reads, why, you would be astonished. Don't go; it's only a little while, you know, and she'll be so disappointed."

I heard the words, but hardly noticed them, I was so deep in my thinkings and stragglings. He left me, but I didn't know. Presently he was back, with the picture-case in his hand, and he held it open before me and said:

"There, now, tell her to her face you could have stayed to see her, and you wouldn't."

That second glimpse broke down my good resolution. I

would stay and take the risk. That night we smoked the tranquil pipe, and talked till late about various things, but mainly about her; and certainly I had had no such pleasant and restful time for many a day. The Thursday followed and slipped comfortably away. Toward twilight a big miner from three miles away came—one of the grizzled, stranded pioneers—and gave us warm salutation, clothed in grave and sober speech. Then he said:

"I only just dropped over to ask about the little madam, and when is she coming home. Any news from her?"

"Oh yes, a letter. Would you like to hear it, Tom?"

"Well, I should think I would, if you don't mind, Henry!"

Henry got the letter out of his wallet, and said he would skip some of the private phrases, if we were willing; then he went on and read the bulk of it—a loving, sedate, and altogether charming and gracious piece of handiwork, with a postscript full of affectionate regards and messages to Tom, and Joe, and Charley, and other close friends and neighbors.

As the reader finished, he glanced at Tom, and cried out:

"Oho, you're at it again! Take your hands away, and let me see your eyes. You always do that when I read a letter from her. I will write and tell her."

"Oh no, you mustn't, Henry. I'm getting old, you know, and any little disappointment makes me want to cry. I thought she'd be here herself, and now you've got only a letter."

"Well, now, what put that in your head? I thought everybody knew she wasn't coming till Saturday."

"Saturday! Why, come to think, I did know it. I wonder what's the matter with me lately? Certainly I knew it. Ain't we all getting ready for her? Well, I must be going now. But I'll be on hand when she comes, old man!"

Late Friday afternoon another gray veteran tramped over from his cabin a mile or so away, and said the boys wanted to have a little gaiety and a good time Saturday night, if Henry thought she wouldn't be too tired after her journey to be kept up.

"Tired? She tired! Oh, hear the man! Joe, *you* know she'd sit up six weeks to please any one of you!"

When Joe heard that there was a letter, he asked to have it read, and the loving messages in it for him broke the old fellow all up; but he said he was such an old wreck that *that* would happen to him if she only just mentioned his name. "Lord, we miss her so!" he said.

Saturday afternoon I found I was taking out my watch pretty often. Henry noticed it, and said, with a startled look:

"You don't think she ought to be here so soon, do you?"

I felt caught, and a little embarrassed; but I laughed, and said it was a habit of mine when I was in a state of expectancy. But he didn't seem quite satisfied; and from that time on he began to show uneasiness. Four times he walked me up the road to a point whence we could see a long distance; and there he would stand, shading his eyes with his hand, and looking. Several times he said:

"I'm getting worried, I'm getting right down worried. I know she's not due till about nine o'clock, and yet something seems to be trying to warn me that something's happened. You don't think anything has happened, do you?"

I began to get pretty thoroughly ashamed of him for his childishness; and at last, when he repeated that imploring question still another time, I lost my patience for the moment, and spoke pretty brutally to him. It seemed to shrivel him up and cow him; and he looked so wounded and so humble after that, that I detested myself for having done the cruel and unnecessary thing. And so I was glad when Charley, another veteran, arrived toward the edge of the evening, and nestled up to Henry to hear the letter read, and talked over the preparations for the welcome. Charley fetched out one hearty speech after another, and did his best to drive away his friend's bodings and apprehensions.

"Anything *happened* to her? Henry, that's pure nonsense. There isn't anything going to happen to her; just make your mind easy as to that. What did the letter say?

Said she was well, didn't it? And said she'd be here by nine o'clock, didn't it? Did you ever know her to fail of her word? Why, you know you never did. Well, then, don't you fret; she'll *be* here, and that's absolutely certain, and as sure as you are born. Come, now, let's get to decorating—not much time left."

Pretty soon Tom and Joe arrived, and then all hands set about adorning the house with flowers. Toward nine the three miners said that as they had brought their instruments they might as well tune up, for the boys and girls would soon be arriving now, and hungry for a good, old-fashioned break-down. A fiddle, a banjo, and a clarinet—these were the instruments. The trio took their places side by side, and began to play some rattling dance-music, and beat time with their big boots.

It was getting very close to nine. Henry was standing in the door with his eyes directed up the road, his body swaying to the torture of his mental distress. He had been made to drink his wife's health and safety several times, and now Tom shouted:

"All hands stand by! One more drink, and she's here!"

Joe brought the glasses on a waiter, and served the party. I reached for one of the two remaining glasses, but Joe growled, under his breath:

"Drop that! Take the other."

Which I did. Henry was served last. He had hardly swallowed his drink when the clock began to strike. He listened till it finished, his face growing pale and paler; then he said:

"Boys, I'm sick with fear. Help me—I want to lie down!"

They helped him to the sofa. He began to nestle and drowse, but presently spoke like one talking in his sleep, and said: "Did I hear horses' feet? Have they come?"

One of the veterans answered, close to his ear: "It was Jimmy Parrish come to say the party got delayed, but they're right up the road a piece, and coming along. Her horse is lame, but she'll be here in half an hour."

"Oh, I'm *so* thankful nothing has happened!"

He was asleep almost before the words were out of his mouth. In a moment those handy men had his clothes off, and had tucked him into his bed in the chamber where I had washed my hands. They closed the door and came back. Then they seemed preparing to leave; but I said: "Please don't go, gentlemen. She won't know me; I am a stranger."

They glanced at each other. Then Joe said:

"She? Poor thing, she's been dead nineteen years!"

"Dead?"

"That or worse. She went to see her folks half a year after she was married, and on her way back, on a Saturday evening, the Indians captured her within five miles of this place, and she's never been heard of since."

"And he lost his mind in consequence?"

"Never has been sane an hour since. But he only gets bad when that time of the year comes round. Then we begin to drop in here, three days before she's due, to encourage him up, and ask if he's heard from her, and Saturday we all come and fix up the house with flowers, and get everything ready for a dance. We've done it every year for nineteen years. The first Saturday there was twenty-seven of us, without counting the girls; there's only three of us now, and the girls are all gone. We drug him to sleep, or he would go wild; then he's all right for another year—thinks she's with him till the last three or four days come round; then he begins to look for her, and gets out his poor old letter, and we come and ask him to read it to us. Lord, she was a darling!"

1893

Extracts from Adam's Diary

Monday.—This new creature with the long hair is a good deal in the way. It is always hanging around and following me about. I don't like this; I am not used to company. I wish it would stay with the other animals. . . . Cloudy to-day, wind in the east; think we shall have rain. . . . *We?* Where did I get that word?—I remember now—the new creature uses it.

Tuesday.—Been examining the great waterfall. It is the finest thing on the estate, I think. The new creature calls it Niagara Falls—why, I am sure I do not know. Says it *looks* like Niagara Falls. That is not a reason, it is mere waywardness and imbecility. I get no chance to name anything myself. The new creature names everything that comes along, before I can get in a protest. And always that same pretext is offered—it *looks* like the thing. There is the dodo, for instance. Says the moment one looks at it one sees at a glance that it "looks like a dodo." It will have to keep that name, no doubt. It wearies me to fret about it, and it does no good, anyway. Dodo! It looks no more like a dodo than I do.

Wednesday.—Built me a shelter against the rain, but could not have it to myself in peace. The new creature intruded. When I tried to put it out it shed water out of the holes it looks with, and wiped it away with the back of its paws, and made a noise such as some of the other animals make when they are in distress. I wish it would not talk; it is always talking. That sounds like a cheap fling at the poor creature, a slur; but I do not mean it so. I have never heard the human voice before, and any new and strange sound intruding itself here upon the solemn hush of these dreaming solitudes offends my ear and seems a false note. And this new sound is so close to me; it is right at my shoulder, right at my ear, first on one side and then on the other, and I am used only to sounds that are more or less distant from me.

Friday.—The naming goes recklessly on, in spite of anything I can do. I had a very good name for the estate, and it was musical and pretty—GARDEN OF EDEN. Privately, I continue to call it that, but not any longer publicly. The new creature says it is all woods and rocks and scenery, and therefore has no resemblance to a garden. Says it *looks* like a park, and does not look like anything *but* a park. Consequently, without consulting me, it has been new-named—NIAGARA FALLS PARK. This is sufficiently high-handed, it seems to me. And already there is a sign up:

KEEP OFF
THE GRASS

My life is not as happy as it was.

Saturday.—The new creature eats too much fruit. We are going to run short, most likely. "We" again—that is *its* word; mine, too, now, from hearing it so much. Good deal of fog this morning. I do not go out in the fog myself. The new creature does. It goes out in all weathers, and stumps right in with its muddy feet. And talks. It used to be so pleasant and quiet here.

Sunday.—Pulled through. This day is getting to be more and more trying. It was selected and set apart last November as a day of rest. I had already six of them per week before. This morning found the new creature trying to clod apples out of that forbidden tree.

Monday.—The new creature says its name is Eve. That is all right, I have no objections. Says it is to call it by, when I want it to come. I said it was superfluous, then. The word evidently raised me in its respect; and indeed it is a large, good word and will bear repetition. It says it is not an It, it is a She. This is probably doubtful; yet it is all one to me; what she is were nothing to me if she would but go by herself and not talk.

Tuesday.—She has littered the whole estate with execrable names and offensive signs:

THIS WAY TO THE WHIRLPOOL
THIS WAY TO GOAT ISLAND
CAVE OF THE WINDS THIS WAY

She says this park would make a tidy summer resort if there was any custom for it. Summer resort—another invention of hers—just words, without any meaning. What is a summer resort? But it is best not to ask her, she has such a rage for explaining.

Friday.—She has taken to beseeching me to stop going over the Falls. What harm does it do? Says it makes her shudder. I wonder why; I have always done it—always liked the plunge, and coolness. I supposed it was what the Falls were for. They have no other use that I can see, and they must have been made for something. She says they were only made for scenery—like the rhinoceros and the mastodon.

I went over the Falls in a barrel—not satisfactory to her. Went over in a tub—still not satisfactory. Swam the Whirlpool and the Rapids in a fig-leaf suit. It got much damaged. Hence, tedious complaints about my extravagance. I am too much hampered here. What I need is change of scene.

Saturday.—I escaped last Tuesday night, and traveled two days, and built me another shelter in a secluded place, and obliterated my tracks as well as I could, but she hunted me out by means of a beast which she has tamed and calls a wolf, and came making that pitiful noise again, and shedding that water out of the places she looks with. I was obliged to return with her, but will presently emigrate again when occasion offers. She engages herself in many foolish things; among others, to study out why the animals called lions and tigers live on grass and flowers, when, as she says, the sort of teeth they wear would indicate that they were intended to eat each other. This is foolish, because to do that would be to kill each other, and that would introduce what, as I understand it, is called "death"; and death, as I have been told, has not yet entered the Park. Which is a pity, on some accounts.

Sunday.—Pulled through.

Monday.—I believe I see what the week is for: it is to give time to rest up from the weariness of Sunday. It seems a good idea. . . . She has been climbing that tree again. Clodded her out of it. She said nobody was looking. Seems to consider that a sufficient justification for chancing any dangerous thing. Told her that. The word justification moved her admiration—and envy, too, I thought. It is a good word.

Tuesday.—She told me she was made out of a rib taken from my body. This is at least doubtful, if not more than that. I have not missed any rib. . . . She is in much trouble about the buzzard; says grass does not agree with it; is afraid she can't raise it; thinks it was intended to live on decayed flesh. The buzzard must get along the best it can with what it is provided. We cannot overturn the whole scheme to accommodate the buzzard.

Saturday.—She fell in the pond yesterday when she was looking at herself in it, which she is always doing. She nearly strangled, and said it was most uncomfortable. This made her sorry for the creatures which live in there, which she calls fish, for she continues to fasten names on to things that don't need them and don't come when they are called by them, which is a matter of no consequence to her, she is such a numskull, anyway; so she got a lot of them out and brought them in last night and put them in my bed to keep warm, but I have noticed them now and then all day and I don't see that they are any happier there then they were before, only quieter. When night comes I shall throw them outdoors. I will not sleep with them again, for I find them clammy and unpleasant to lie among when a person hasn't anything on.

Sunday.—Pulled through.

Tuesday.—She has taken up with a snake now. The other animals are glad, for she was always experimenting with them and bothering them; and I am glad because the snake talks, and this enables me to get a rest.

Friday.—She says the snake advises her to try the fruit of that tree, and says the result will be a great and fine and noble education. I told her there would be another result, too—it would introduce death into the world. That was a mistake—it had been better to keep the remark to myself; it only gave her an idea—she could save the sick buzzard, and furnish fresh meat to the despondent lions and tigers. I advised her to keep away from the tree. She said she wouldn't. I foresee trouble. Will emigrate.

Wednesday.—I have had a variegated time. I escaped last night, and rode a horse all night as fast as he could go, hoping to get clear out of the Park and hide in some other country before the trouble should begin; but it was not to be. About an hour after sun-up, as I was riding through a flowery plain where thousands of animals were grazing, slumbering, or playing with each other, according to their wont, all of a sudden they broke into a tempest of frightful noises, and in one moment the plain was a frantic commotion and every beast was destroying its neighbor. I knew what it meant—Eve had eaten that fruit, and death was come into the world. . . . The tigers ate my horse, paying no attention when I ordered them to desist, and they would have eaten me if I had stayed—which I didn't, but went away in much haste. . . . I found this place, outside the Park, and was fairly comfortable for a few days, but she has found me out. Found me out, and has named the place Tonawanda—says it *looks* like that. In fact I was not sorry she came, for there are but meager pickings here, and she brought some of those apples. I was obliged to eat them, I was so hungry. It was against my principles, but I find that principles have no real force except when one is well fed. . . . She came curtained in boughs and bunches of leaves, and when I asked her what she meant by such nonsense, and snatched them away and threw them down, she tittered and blushed. I had never seen a person titter and blush before, and to me it seemed unbecoming and idiotic. She said I would soon know how it was myself. This was correct. Hungry as I was, I laid down the apple half-eaten—certainly the best one I ever saw, considering the lateness of the season—and arrayed myself in the discarded boughs and branches, and then spoke to her with some severity and ordered her to go and get some more and not make such a spectacle of herself. She did it, and after this we crept down to where the wild-beast battle had been, and collected some skins, and I made her patch together a couple of suits proper for public occasions. They are uncomfortable, it is true, but stylish, and that is the main point about clothes. . . . I find she is a good deal of a companion. I see I should be lonesome and depressed without her, now that I have lost my property. Another thing, she says it is ordered that we work for our living hereafter. She will be useful. I will superintend.

Ten Days Later.—She accuses *me* of being the cause of our disaster! She says, with apparent sincerity and truth, that the Serpent assured her that the forbidden fruit was not apples, it was chestnuts. I said I was innocent, then, for

I had not eaten any chestnuts. She said the Serpent informed her that "chestnut" was a figurative term meaning an aged and moldy joke. I turned pale at that, for I have made many jokes to pass the weary time, and some of them could have been of that sort, though I had honestly supposed that they were new when I made them. She asked me if I had made one just at the time of the catastrophe. I was obliged to admit that I had made one to myself, though not aloud. It was this. I was thinking about the Falls, and I said to myself, "How wonderful it is to see that vast body of water tumble down there!" Then in an instant a bright thought flashed into my head, and I let it fly, saying, "It would be a deal more wonderful to see it tumble *up* there!"—and I was just about to kill myself with laughing at it when all nature broke loose in war and death and I had to flee for my life. "There," she said, with triumph, "that is just it; the Serpent mentioned that very jest, and called it the First Chestnut, and said it was coeval with the creation." Alas, I am indeed to blame. Would that I were not witty; oh, that I had never had that radiant thought!

Next Year.—We have named it Cain. She caught it while I was up country trapping on the North Shore of the Erie; caught it in the timber a couple of miles from our dugout—or it might have been four, she isn't certain which. It resembles us in some ways, and may be a relation. That is what she thinks, but this is an error, in my judgment. The difference in size warrants the conclusion that it is a different and new kind of animal—a fish, perhaps, though when I put it in the water to see, it sank, and she plunged in and snatched it out before there was opportunity for the experiment to determine the matter. I still think it is a fish, but she is indifferent about what it is, and will not let me have it to try. I do not understand this. The coming of the creature seems to have changed her whole nature and made her unreasonable about experiments. She thinks more of it than she does of any of the other animals, but is not able to explain why. Her mind is disordered—everything shows it. Sometimes she carries the fish in her arms half the night when it complains and wants to get to the water. At such times the water comes out of the places in her face that she looks out of, and she pats the fish on the back and makes soft sounds with her mouth to soothe it, and betrays sorrow and solicitude in a hundred ways. I have never seen her do like this with any other fish, and it troubles me greatly. She used to carry the young tigers around so, and play with them, before we lost our property, but it was only play; she never took on about them like this when their dinner disagreed with them.

Sunday.—She doesn't work, Sundays, but lies around all tired out, and likes to have the fish wallow over her; and she makes fool noises to amuse it, and pretends to chew its paws, and that makes it laugh. I have not seen a fish before that could laugh. This makes me doubt. . . . I have come to like Sunday myself. Superintending all the week tires a body so. There ought to be more Sundays. In the old days they were tough, but now they come handy.

Wednesday.—It isn't a fish. I cannot quite make out what it is. It makes curious devilish noises when not satisfied, and says "goo-goo" when it is. It is not one of us, for it doesn't walk; it is not a bird, for it doesn't fly; it is not a frog, for it doesn't hop; it is not a snake, for it doesn't crawl. I feel sure it is not a fish, though I cannot get a chance to find out whether it can swim or not. It merely lies around, and mostly on its back, with its feet up. I have not seen any other animal do that before. I said I believed it was an enigma; but she only admired the word without understanding it. In my judgment it is either an enigma or some kind of a bug. If it dies, I will take it apart and see what its arrangements are. I never had a thing perplex me so.

Three Months Later.—The perplexity augments instead of diminishing. I sleep but little. It has ceased from lying around, and goes about on its four legs now. Yet it differs from the other four-legged animals, in that its front legs are unusually short, consequently this causes the main part of its person to stick up uncomfortably high in the air, and this is not attractive. It is built much as we are, but its method of traveling shows that it is not of our breed. The short front legs and long hind ones indicate that it is of the kangaroo family, but it is a marked variation of the species, since the true kangaroo hops, whereas this one never does. Still it is a curious and interesting variety, and has not been catalogued before. As I discovered it, I have felt justified in securing the credit of the discovery by attaching my name to it, and hence have called it *Kangaroorum Adamiensis*. . . . It must have been a young one when it came, for it has grown exceedingly since. It must be five times as big, now, as it was then, and when discontented it is able to make from twenty-two to thirty-eight times the noise it made at first. Coercion does not modify this, but has the contrary effect. For this reason I discontinued the system. She reconciles it by persuasion, and by giving it things which she had previously told me she wouldn't give it. As already observed, I was not at home when it first came, and she told me she found it in the woods. It seems odd that it should be the only one, yet it must be so, for I have worn myself out these many weeks trying to find another one to add to my collection, and for this one to play with; for surely then it would be quieter and we could tame it more easily. But I find none, nor any vestige of any; and strangest of all, no tracks. It has to live on the ground, it cannot help itself; therefore, how does it get about without leaving a track? I have set a dozen traps, but they do no good. I catch all small animals except that one; animals that merely go into the trap out of curiosity, I think, to see what the milk is there for. They never drink it.

Three Months Later.—The Kangaroo still continues to grow, which is very strange and perplexing. I never knew one to be so long getting its growth. It has fur on its head now; not like kangaroo fur, but exactly like our hair except that it is much finer and softer, and instead of being black is red. I am like to lose my mind over the capricious and harassing developments of this unclassifiable zoological freak. If I could catch another one—but that is hopeless; it is a new variety, and the only sample; this is plain. But I caught a true kangaroo and brought it in, thinking that this one, being lonesome, would rather have that for company than have no kin at all, or any animal it could feel a nearness to or get sympathy from in its forlorn condition here among strangers who do not know its ways or habits, or what to do to make it feel that it is among friends; but it was a mistake—it went into such fits at the sight of the kangaroo that I was convinced it had never seen one before. I pity the poor noisy little animal, but there is nothing I can do to make it happy. If I could tame it—but that is out of the question; the more I try the worse I seem to make it. It grieves me to the heart to see it in its little storms of sorrow and passion. I wanted to let it go, but she wouldn't hear of it. That seemed cruel and not like her; and yet she may be right. It might be lonelier than ever; for since I cannot find another one, how could *it*?

Five Months Later.—It is not a kangaroo. No, for it supports itself by holding to her finger, and thus goes a few steps on its hind legs, and then falls down. It is probably some kind of a bear; and yet it has no tail—as yet—and no fur, except on its head. It still keeps on growing—that is a curious circumstance, for bears get their growth earlier than this. Bears are dangerous—since our catastrophe—and I shall not be satisfied to have this one prowling about the place much longer without a muzzle on. I have offered to get her a kangaroo if she would let this one go, but it did no good—she is determined to run us into all sorts of foolish risks, I think. She was not like this before she lost her mind.

A Fortnight Later.—I examined its mouth. There is no

danger yet: it has only one tooth. It has no tail yet. It makes more noise now than it ever did before—and mainly at night. I have moved out. But I shall go over, mornings, to breakfast, and see if it has more teeth. If it gets a mouthful of teeth it will be time for it to go, tail or no tail, for a bear does not need a tail in order to be dangerous.

Four Months Later.—I have been off hunting and fishing a month, up in the region that she calls Buffalo; I don't know why, unless it is because there are not any buffaloes there. Meantime the bear has learned to paddle around all by itself on its hind legs, and says "poppa" and "momma." It is certainly a new species. This resemblance to words may be purely accidental, of course, and may have no purpose or meaning; but even in that case it is still extraordinary, and is a thing which no other bear can do. This imitation of speech, taken together with general absence of fur and entire absence of tail, sufficiently indicates that this is a new kind of bear. The further study of it will be exceedingly interesting. Meantime I will go off on a far expedition among the forests of the north and make an exhaustive search. There must certainly be another one somewhere, and this one will be less dangerous when it has company of its own species. I will go straightway; but I will muzzle this one first.

Three Months Later.—It has been a weary, weary hunt, yet I have had no success. In the mean time, without stirring from the home estate, she has caught another one! I never saw such luck. I might have hunted these woods a hundred years, I never would have run across that thing.

Next Day.—I have been comparing the new one with the old one, and it is perfectly plain that they are the same breed. I was going to stuff one of them for my collection, but she is prejudiced against it for some reason or other; so I have relinquished the idea, though I think it is a mistake. It would be an irreparable loss to science if they should get away. The old one is tamer than it was and can laugh and talk like the parrot, having learned this, no doubt, from being with the parrot so much, and having the imitative faculty in a highly developed degree. I shall be astonished if it turns out to be a new kind of parrot; and yet I ought not to be astonished, for it has already been everything else it could think of since those first days when it was a fish. The new one is as ugly now as the old one was at first; has the same sulphur-and-raw-meat complexion and the same singular head without any fur on it. She calls it Abel.

Ten Years Later.—They are *boys;* we found it out long ago. It was their coming in that small, immature shape that puzzled us; we were not used to it. There are some girls now. Abel is a good boy, but if Cain had stayed a bear it would have improved him. After all these years, I see that I was mistaken about Eve in the beginning; it is better to live outside the Garden with her than inside it without her. At first I thought she talked too much; but now I should be sorry to have that voice fall silent and pass out of my life. Blessed be the chestnut that brought us near together and taught me to know the goodness of her heart and the sweetness of her spirit!

1893

Eve's Diary

Translated from the Original

SATURDAY.—I am almost a whole day old, now. I arrived yesterday. That is as it seems to me. And it must be so, for if there was a day-before-yesterday I was not there when it happened, or I should remember it. It could be, of course, that it did happen, and that I was not noticing. Very well; I will be very watchful now, and if any day-before-yesterdays happen I will make a note of it. It will be best to start right and not let the record get confused, for some instinct tells me that these details are going to be important to the historian some day. For I feel like an experiment, I feel exactly like an experiment; it would be impossible for a person to feel more like an experiment than I do, and so I am coming to feel convinced that that is what I *am*—an experiment; just an experiment, and nothing more.

Then if I am an experiment, am I the whole of it? No, I think not; I think the rest of it is part of it. I am the main part of it, but I think the rest of it has its share in the matter. Is my position assured, or do I have to watch it and take care of it? The latter, perhaps. Some instinct tells me that eternal vigilance is the price of supremacy. [That is a good phrase, I think, for one so young.]

Everything looks better to-day than it did yesterday. In the rush of finishing up yesterday, the mountains were left in a ragged condition, and some of the plains were so cluttered with rubbish and remnants that the aspects were quite distressing. Noble and beautiful works of art should not be subjected to haste; and this majestic new world is indeed a most noble and beautiful work. And certainly marvelously near to being perfect, notwithstanding the shortness of the time. There are too many stars in some places and not enough in others, but that can be remedied presently, no doubt. The moon got loose last night, and slid down and fell out of the scheme—a very great loss; it breaks my heart to think of it. There isn't another thing among the ornaments and decorations that is comparable to it for beauty and finish. It should have been fastened better. If we can only get it back again—

But of course there is no telling where it went to. And besides, whoever gets it will hide it; I know it because I would do it myself. I believe I can be honest in all other matters, but I already begin to realize that the core and center of my nature is love of the beautiful, a passion for the beautiful, and that it would not be safe to trust me with a moon that belonged to another person and that person didn't know I had it. I could give up a moon that I found in the daytime, because I should be afraid some one was looking; but if I found it in the dark, I am sure I should find some kind of an excuse for not saying anything about it. For I do love moons, they are so pretty and so romantic. I wish we had five or six; I would never go to bed; I should never get tired lying on the moss-bank and looking up at them.

Stars are good, too. I wish I could get some to put in my hair. But I suppose I never can. You would be surprised to find how far off they are, for they do not look it. When they first showed, last night, I tried to knock some down with a pole, but it didn't reach, which astonished me; then I tried clods till I was all tired out, but I never got one. It was because I am left-handed and cannot throw good. Even when I aimed at the one I wasn't after I couldn't hit the other one, though I did make some close shots, for I saw the black blot of the clod sail right into the midst of the golden clusters forty or fifty times, just barely missing them, and if I could have held out a little longer maybe I could have got one.

So I cried a little, which was natural, I suppose, for one of my age, and after I was rested I got a basket and started for a place on the extreme rim of the circle, where the stars were close to the ground and I could get them with my hands, which would be better, anyway, because I could gather them tenderly then, and not break them. But it was farther than I thought, and at last I had to give it up: I was so tired I couldn't drag my feet another step; and besides, they were sore and hurt me very much.

I couldn't get back home; it was too far and turning cold; but I found some tigers and nestled in among them and was most adorably comfortable, and their breath was sweet and pleasant, because they live on strawberries. I had never seen a tiger before, but I knew them in a minute by the stripes. If I could have one of those skins, it would make a lovely gown.

To-day I am getting better ideas about distances. I was so eager to get hold of every pretty thing that I giddily grabbed for it, sometimes when it was too far off, and sometimes when it was but six inches away but seemed a foot—alas, with thorns between! I learned a lesson; also I made an axiom, all out of my own head—my very first one: *The scratched Experiment shuns the thorn.* I think it is a very good one for one so young.

I followed the other Experiment around, yesterday afternoon, at a distance, to see what it might be for, if I could. But I was not able to make out. I think it is a man. I had never seen a man, but it looked like one, and I feel sure that that is what it is. I realize that I feel more curiosity about it than about any of the other reptiles. If it is a reptile, and I suppose it is; for it has frowsy hair and blue eyes, and looks like a reptile. It has no hips; it tapers like a carrot; when it stands, it spreads itself apart like a derrick; so I think it is a reptile, though it may be architecture.

I was afraid of it at first, and started to run every time it turned around, for I thought it was going to chase me; but by and by I found it was only trying to get away, so after that I was not timid any more, but tracked it along, several hours, about twenty yards behind, which made it nervous and unhappy. At last it was a good deal worried, and climbed a tree. I waited a good while, then gave it up and went home.

To-day the same thing over. I've got it up the tree again.

Sunday.—It is up there yet. Resting, apparently. But that is a subterfuge: Sunday isn't the day of rest: Saturday is appointed for that. It looks to me like a creature that is more interested in resting than in anything else. It would tire me to rest so much. It tires me just to sit around and watch the tree. I do wonder what it is for; I never see it do anything.

They returned the moon last night, and I was *so* happy! I think it is very honest of them. It slid down and fell off again, but I was not distressed; there is no need to worry when one has that kind of neighbors; they will fetch it back. I wish I could do something to show my appreciation. I would like to send them some stars, for we have more than we can use. I mean I, not we, for I can see that the reptile cares nothing for such things.

It has low tastes, and is not kind. When I went there yesterday evening in the gloaming it had crept down and was trying to catch the little speckled fishes that play in the pool, and I had to clod it to make it go up the tree again and let them alone. I wonder if *that* is what it is for? Hasn't it any heart? Hasn't it any compassion for those little creatures? Can it be that it was designed and manufactured for such ungentle work? It has the look of it. One of the clods took it back to the ear, and it used language. It gave me a thrill, for it was the first time I had ever heard speech, except my own. I did not understand the words, but they seemed expressive.

When I found it could talk I felt a new interest in it, for I love to talk; I talk, all day, and in my sleep, too, and I am very interesting, but if I had another to talk to I could be twice as interesting, and would never stop, if desired.

If this reptile is a man, it isn't an *it*, is it? That wouldn't be grammatical, would it? I think it would be *he*. I think so. In that case one would parse it thus: nominative, *he;* dative, *him;* possessive, *his'n.* Well, I will consider it a man and call it he until it turns out to be something else. This will be handier than having so many uncertainties.

Next week Sunday.—All the week I tagged around after him and tried to get acquainted. I had to do the talking, because he was shy, but I didn't mind it. He seemed pleased to have me around, and I used the sociable "we" a good deal, because it seemed to flatter him to be included.

Wednesday.—We are getting along very well indeed, now, and getting better and better acquainted. He does not try to avoid me any more, which is a good sign, and shows that he likes to have me with him. That pleases me, and I study to be useful to him in every way I can, so as to increase his regard. During the last day or two I have taken all the work of naming things off his hands, and this has been a great relief to him, for he has no gift in that line, and is evidently very grateful. He can't think of a rational name to save him, but I do not let him see that I am aware of his defect. Whenever a new creature comes along I name it before he has time to expose himself by an awkward silence. In this way I have saved him many embarrassments. I have no defect like his. The minute I set eyes on an animal I know what it is. I don't have to reflect a moment; the right name comes out instantly, just as if it were an inspiration, as no doubt it is, for I am sure it wasn't in me half a minute before. I seem to know just by the shape of the creature and the way it acts what animal it is.

When the dodo came along he thought it was a wildcat—I saw it in his eye. But I saved him. And I was careful not to do it in a way that could hurt his pride. I just spoke up in a quite natural way of pleased surprise, and not as if I was dreaming of conveying information, and said, "Well, I do declare, if there isn't the dodo!" I explained—without seeming to be explaining—how I knew it for a dodo, and although I thought maybe he was a little piqued that I knew the creature when he didn't, it was quite evident that he admired me. That was very agreeable, and I thought of it more than once with gratification before I slept. How little a thing can make us happy when we feel that we have earned it!

Thursday.—My first sorrow. Yesterday he avoided me and seemed to wish I would not talk to him. I could not believe it, and thought there was some mistake, for I loved to be with him, and loved to hear him talk, and so how could it be that he could feel unkind toward me when I had not done anything? But at last it seemed true, so I went away and sat lonely in the place where I first saw him the morning that we were made and I did not know what he was and was indifferent about him; but now it was a mournful place, and every little thing spoke of him, and my heart was very sore. I did not know why very clearly, for it was a new feeling; I had not experienced it before, and it was all a mystery, and I could not make it out.

But when night came I could not bear the lonesomeness, and went to the new shelter which he has built, to ask him what I had done that was wrong and how I could mend it and get back his kindness again; but he put me out in the rain, and it was my first sorrow.

Sunday.—It is pleasant again, now, and I am happy; but those were heavy days; I do not think of them when I can help it.

I tried to get him some of those apples, but I cannot learn to throw straight. I failed, but I think the good intention pleased him. They are forbidden, and he says I shall come to harm; but so I come to harm through pleasing him, why shall I care for that harm?

Monday.—This morning I told him my name, hoping it would interest him. But he did not care for it. It is strange. If he should tell me his name, I would care. I think it would be pleasanter in my ears than any other sound.

He talks very little. Perhaps it is because he is not bright, and is sensitive about it and wishes to conceal it. It is such a pity that he should feel so, for brightness is nothing; it is in the heart that the values lie. I wish I could make him understand that a loving good heart is riches, and riches enough, and that without it intellect is poverty.

Although he talks so little, he has quite a considerable vocabulary. This morning he used a surprisingly good word. He evidently recognized, himself, that it was a good one, for he worked it in twice afterward, casually. It was not good casual art, still it showed that he possesses a certain quality of perception. Without a doubt that seed can be made to grow, if cultivated.

Where did he get that word? I do not think I have ever used it.

No, he took no interest in my name. I tried to hide my disappointment, but I suppose I did not succeed. I went away and sat on the moss-bank with my feet in the water. It is where I go when I hunger for companionship, some one to look at, some one to talk to. It is not enough—that lovely white body painted there in the pool—but it is something, and something is better than utter loneliness. It talks when I talk; it is sad when I am sad; it comforts me with its sympathy; it says, "Do not be downhearted, you poor friendless girl; I will be your friend." It *is* a good friend to me, and my only one; it is my sister.

That first time that she forsook me! ah, I shall never forget that—never, never. My heart was lead in my body! I said, "She was all I had, and now she is gone!" In my despair I said,

"Break, my heart; I cannot bear my life any more!" and hid my face in my hands, and there was no solace for me. And when I took them away, after a little, there she was again, white and shining and beautiful, and I sprang into her arms!

That was perfect happiness; I had known happiness before, but it was not like this, which was ecstasy. I never doubted her afterward. Sometimes she stayed away—maybe an hour, maybe almost the whole day, but I waited and did not doubt; I said, "She is busy, or she is gone a journey, but she will come." And it was so: she always did. At night she would not come if it was dark, for she was a timid little thing; but if there was a moon she would come. I am not afraid of the dark, but she is younger than I am; she was born after I was. Many and many are the visits I have paid her; she is my comfort and my refuge when my life is hard—and it is mainly that.

Tuesday.—All the morning I was at work improving the estate; and I purposely kept away from him in the hope that he would get lonely and come. But he did not.

At noon I stopped for the day and took my recreation by flitting all about with the bees and the butterflies and reveling in the flowers, those beautiful creatures that catch the smile of God out of the sky and preserve it! I gathered them, and made them into wreaths and garlands and clothed myself in them while I ate my luncheon—apples, of course; then I sat in the shade and wished and waited. But he did not come.

But no matter. Nothing would have come of it, for he does not care for flowers. He calls them rubbish, and cannot tell one from another, and thinks it is superior to feel like that. He does not care for me, he does not care for flowers, he does not care for the painted sky at eventide—is there anything he does care for, except building shacks to coop himself up in from the good clean rain, and thumping the melons, and sampling the grapes, and fingering the fruit on the trees, to see how those properties are coming along?

I laid a dry stick on the ground and tried to bore a hole in it with another one, in order to carry out a scheme that I had, and soon I got an awful fright. A thin, transparent bluish film rose out of the hole, and I dropped everything and ran! I thought it was a spirit, and I *was* so frightened! But I looked back, and it was not coming; so I leaned against a rock and rested and panted, and let my limbs go on trembling until they got steady again; then I crept warily back, alert, watching, and ready to fly if there was occasion; and when I was come near, I parted the branches of a rose-bush and peeped through—wishing the man was about, I was looking so cunning and pretty—but the sprite was gone. I went there, and there was a pinch of delicate pink dust in the hole. I put my finger in, to feel it, and said *ouch!* and took it out again. It was a cruel pain. I put my finger in my mouth; and by standing first on one foot and then the other, and grunting, I presently eased my misery; then I was full of interest, and began to examine.

I was curious to know what the pink dust was. Suddenly the name of it occurred to me, though I had never heard of it before. It was *fire!* I was as certain of it as a person could be of anything in the world. So without hesitation I named it that—fire.

I had created something that didn't exist before; I had added a new thing to the world's uncountable properties; I realized this, and was proud of my achievement, and was going to run and find him and tell him about it, thinking to raise myself in his esteem—but I reflected, and did not do it. No—he would not care for it. He would ask what it was good for, and what could I answer? for it was not *good* for something, but only beautiful, merely beautiful—

So I sighed, and did not go. For it wasn't good for anything; it could not build a shack, it could not improve melons, it could not hurry a fruit crop; it was useless, it was a foolishness and a vanity; he would despise it and say cutting words. But to me it was not despicable; I said, "Oh, you fire,

I love you, you dainty pink creature, for you are *beautiful*—and that is enough!" and was going to gather it to my breast. But refrained. Then I made another maxim out of my own head, though it was so nearly like the first one that I was afraid it was only a plagiarism: *"The burnt Experiment shuns the fire."*

I wrought again; and when I had made a good deal of fire-dust I emptied it into a handful of dry brown grass, intending to carry it home and keep it always and play with it; but the wind struck it and it sprayed up and spat out at me fiercely, and I dropped it and ran. When I looked back the blue spirit was towering up and stretching and rolling away like a cloud, and instantly I thought of the name of it—*smoke!*—though, upon my word, I had never heard of smoke before.

Soon, brilliant yellow and red flares shot up through the smoke, and I named them in an instant—*flames!*—and I was right, too, though these were the very first flames that had ever been in the world. They climbed the trees, they flashed splendidly in and out of the vast and increasing volume of tumbling smoke, and I had to clap my hands and laugh and dance in my rapture, it was so new and strange and so wonderful and so beautiful!

He came running, and stopped and gazed, and said not a word for many minutes. Then he asked what it was. Ah, it was too bad that he should ask such a direct question. I had to answer it, of course, and I did. I said it was fire. If it annoyed him that I should know and he must ask, that was not my fault; I had no desire to annoy him. After a pause he asked:

"How did it come?"

Another direct question, and it also had to have a direct answer.

"I made it."

The fire was traveling farther and farther off. He went to the edge of the burned place and stood looking down, and said:

"What are these?"

"Fire-coals."

He picked up one to examine it, but changed his mind and put it down again. Then he went away. *Nothing* interests him.

But I was interested. There were ashes, gray and soft and delicate and pretty—I knew what they were at once. And the embers; I knew the embers, too. I found my apples, and raked them out, and was glad; for I am very young and my appetite is active. But I was disappointed; they were all burst open and spoiled. Spoiled apparently; but it was not so; they were better than raw ones. Fire is beautiful; some day it will be useful. I think.

Friday.—I saw him again, for a moment, last Monday at nightfall, but only for a moment. I was hoping he would praise me for trying to improve the estate, for I had meant well and had worked hard. But he was not pleased, and turned away and left me. He was also displeased on another account: I tried once more to persuade him to stop going over the Falls. That was because the fire had revealed to me a new passion—quite new, and distinctly different from love, grief, and those others which I had already discovered—fear. And it is horrible!—I wish I had never discovered it; it gives me dark moments, it spoils my happiness, it makes me shiver and tremble and shudder. But I could not persuade him, for he has not discovered fear yet, and so he could not understand me.

Extract from Adam's Diary

Perhaps I ought to remember that she is very young, a mere girl, and make allowances. She is all interest, eagerness, vivacity, the world is to her a charm, a wonder, a mystery, a joy; she can't speak for delight when she finds a new flower, she must pet it and caress it and smell it and talk to it, and pour out endearing names upon it. And she is color-mad: brown rocks, yellow sand, gray moss, green foliage, blue sky; the pearl of the dawn, the purple shadows on the mountains, the golden islands floating in crimson seas at sunset, the pallid moon sailing through the shredded cloud-rack, the star-jewels glittering in the wastes of space—none of them is of any practical value, so far as I can see, but because they have color and majesty, that is enough for her, and she loses her mind over them. If she could quiet down and keep still a couple of minutes at a time, it would be a reposeful spectacle. In that case I think I could enjoy looking at her; indeed I am sure I could, for I am coming to realize that she is a quite remarkably comely creature—lithe, slender, trim, rounded, shapely, nimble, graceful; and once when she was standing marble-white and sun-drenched on a boulder, with her young head tilted back and her hand shading her eyes, watching the flight of a bird in the sky, I recognized that she was beautiful.

Monday noon.—If there is anything on the planet that she is not interested in it is not in my list. There are animals that I am indifferent to, but it is not so with her. She has no discrimination, she takes to all of them, she thinks they are all treasures, every new one is welcome.

When the mighty brontosaurus came striding into camp, she regarded it as an acquisition, I considered it a calamity; that is a good sample of the lack of harmony that prevails in our views of things. She wanted to domesticate it, I wanted to make it a present of the homestead and move out. She believed it could be tamed by kind treatment and would be a good pet; I said a pet twenty-one feet high and eighty-four feet long would be no proper thing to have about the place, because, even with the best intentions and without meaning any harm, it could sit down on the house and mash it, for any one could see by the look of its eye that it was absent-minded.

Still, her heart was set upon having that monster, and

she couldn't give it up. She thought we could start a dairy with it, and wanted me to help her milk it; but I wouldn't; it was too risky. The sex wasn't right, and we hadn't any ladder anyway. Then she wanted to ride it, and look at the scenery. Thirty or forty feet of its tail was lying on the ground, like a fallen tree, and she thought she could climb it, but she was mistaken; when she got to the steep place it was too slick and down she came, and would have hurt herself but for me.

Was she satisfied now? No. Nothing ever satisfies her but demonstration; untested theories are not in her line, and she won't have them. It is the right spirit, I conceded it; it attracts me; I feel the influence of it; if I were with her more I think I should take it up myself. Well, she had one theory remaining about this colossus: she thought that if we could tame him and make him friendly we could stand him in the river and use him for a bridge. It turned out that he was already plenty tame enough—at least as far as she was concerned—so she tried her theory, but it failed; every time she got him properly placed in the river and went ashore to cross over on him, he came out and followed her around like a pet mountain. Like the other animals. They all do that.

Friday.—Tuesday—Wednesday—Thursday—and to-day: all without seeing him. It is a long time to be alone; still, it is better to be alone than unwelcome.

I *had* to have company—I was made for it, I think—so I made friends with the animals. They are just charming, and they have the kindest disposition and the politest ways; they never look sour, they never let you feel that you are intruding, they smile at you and wag their tail, if they've got one, and they are always ready for a romp or an excursion or anything you want to propose. I think they are perfect gentlemen. All these days we have had such good times, and it hasn't been lonesome for me, ever. Lonesome! No, I should say not. Why, there's always a swarm of them around—sometimes as much as four or five acres—you can't count them; and when you stand on a rock in the midst and look out over the furry expanse it is so mottled and splashed and gay with color and frisking sheen and sun-flash, and so rippled with stripes, that you might think it was a lake, only you know it isn't; and there's storms of sociable birds, and hurricanes of whirring wings; and when the sun strikes all that feathery commotion, you have a blazing up of all the colors you can think of, enough to put your eyes out.

We have made long excursions, and I have seen a great deal of the world; almost all of it, I think; and so I am the first traveler, and the only one. When we are on the march, it is an imposing sight—there's nothing like it anywhere. For comfort I ride a tiger or a leopard, because it is soft and has a round back that fits me, and because they are such pretty animals; but for long distance or for scenery I ride the elephant. He hoists me with his trunk, but I can get off myself; when we are ready to camp, he sits and I slide down the back way.

The birds and animals are all friendly to each other, and there are no disputes about anything. They all talk, and they all talk to me, but it must be a foreign language, for I cannot make out a word they say; yet they often understand me when I talk back, particularly the dog and the elephant. It makes me ashamed. It shows that they are brighter than I am, and are therefore my superiors. It annoys me, for I want to be the principal Experiment myself—and I intend to be, too.

I have learned a number of things, and am educated, now, but I wasn't at first. I was ignorant at first. At first it used to vex me because, with all my watching, I was never smart enough to be around when the water was running uphill; but now I do not mind it. I have experimented and experimented until now I know it never does run uphill, except in the dark. I know it does in the dark, because the pool never goes dry, which it would, of course, if the water didn't come back in the night. It is best to prove things by actual experiment; then you *know;* whereas if you depend on guessing and supposing and conjecturing, you will never get educated.

Some things you *can't* find out; but you will never know you can't by guessing and supposing: no, you have to be patient and go on experimenting until you find out that you can't find out. And it is delightful to have it that way, it makes the world so interesting. If there wasn't anything to find out, it would be dull. Even trying to find out and not finding out is just as interesting as trying to find out and finding out, and I don't know but more so. The secret of the water was a treasure until I *got* it; then the excitement all went away, and I recognized a sense of loss.

By experiment I know that wood swims, and dry leaves, and feathers, and plenty of other things; therefore by all that cumulative evidence you know that a rock will swim; but you have to put up with simply knowing it, for there isn't any way to prove it—up to now. But I shall find a way—then *that* excitement will go. Such things make me sad; because by and by when I have found out everything there won't be any more excitements, and I do love excitements so! The other night I couldn't sleep for thinking about it.

At first I couldn't make out what I was made for, but now I think it was to search out the secrets of this wonderful world and be happy and thank the Giver of it all for devising it. I think there are many things to learn yet—I hope so; and by economizing and not hurrying too fast I think they will last weeks and weeks. I hope so. When you cast up a feather it sails away on the air and goes out of sight; then you throw up a clod and it doesn't. It comes down, every time. I have tried it and tried it, and it is always so. I wonder why it is? Of course it *doesn't* come down, but why should it *seem* to? I suppose it is an optical illusion. I mean, one of them is. I don't know which one. It may be the feather, it may be the clod; I can't prove which it is, I can only demonstrate that one or the other is a fake, and let a person take his choice.

By watching, I know that the stars are not going to last. I have seen some of the best ones melt and run down the sky. Since one can melt, they can all melt; since they can all melt, they can all melt the same night. That sorrow will come—I know it. I mean to sit up every night and look at them as long as I can keep awake; and I will impress those sparkling fields on my memory, so that by and by when they are taken away I can by my fancy restore those lovely myriads to the black sky and make them sparkle again, and double them by the blur of my tears.

AFTER THE FALL

When I look back, the Garden is a dream to me. It was beautiful, surpassingly beautiful, enchantingly beautiful; and now it is lost, and I shall not see it any more.

The Garden is lost, but I have found *him*, and am content. He loves me as well as he can; I love him with all the strength of my passionate nature, and this, I think, is proper to my youth and sex. If I ask myself why I love him, I find I do not know, and do not really much care to know; so I suppose that this kind of love is not a product of reasoning and statistics, like one's love for other reptiles and animals. I think that this must be so. I love certain birds because of their song; but I do not love Adam on account of his singing—no, it is not that; the more he sings the more I do not get reconciled to it. Yet I asked him to sing, because I wish to learn to like everything he is interested in. I am sure I can learn, because at first I could not stand it, but now I can. It sours the milk, but it doesn't matter; I can get used to that kind of milk.

It is not on account of his brightness that I love him—no, it is not that. He is not to blame for his brightness, such as it is, for he did not make it himself; he is as God made him, and that is sufficient. There was a wise purpose in it, *that* I know. In time it will develop, though I think it will not be sudden; and besides, there is no hurry; he is well enough just as he is.

It is not on account of his gracious and considerate ways and his delicacy that I love him. No, he has lacks in these regards, but he is well enough just so, and is improving.

It is not on account of his industry that I love him—no, it is not that. I think he has it in him, and I do not know why he conceals it from me. It is my only pain. Otherwise he is frank and open with me, now. I am sure he keeps nothing from me but this. It grieves me that he should have a secret from me, and sometimes it spoils my sleep, thinking of it, but I will put it out of my mind; it shall not trouble my happiness, which is otherwise full to overflowing.

It is not on account of his education that I love him—no, it is not that. He is self-educated, and does really know a multitude of things, but they are not so.

It is not on account of his chivalry that I love him—no, it is not that. He told on me, but I do not blame him; it is a peculiarity of sex, I think, and he did not make his sex. Of course I would not have told on him, I would have perished first; but that is a peculiarity of sex, too, and I do not take credit for it, for I did not make my sex.

Then why is it that I love him? *Merely because he is masculine,* I think.

At bottom he is good, and I love him for that, but I could love him without it. If he should beat me and abuse me, I should go on loving him. I know it. It is a matter of sex, I think.

He is strong and handsome, and I love him for that, and I admire him and am proud of him, but I could love him without those qualities. If he were plain, I should love him; if he were a wreck, I should love him; and I would work for him, and slave over him, and pray for him, and watch by his bedside until I died.

Yes, I think I love him merely because he is *mine* and is *masculine*. There is no other reason, I suppose. And so I think it is as I first said: that this kind of love is not a product of reasonings and statistics. It just *comes*—none knows whence—and cannot explain itself. And doesn't need to.

It is what I think. But I am only a girl, and the first that has examined this matter, and it may turn out that in my ignorance and inexperience I have not got it right.

FORTY YEARS LATER

It is my prayer, it is my longing, that we may pass from this life together—a longing which shall never perish from the earth, but shall have place in the heart of every wife that loves, until the end of time; and it shall be called by my name.

But if one of us must go first, it is my prayer that it shall be I; for he is strong, I am weak, I am not so necessary to him as he is to me—life without him would not be life; how could I endure it? This prayer is also immortal, and will not cease from being offered up while my race continues. I am the first wife; and in the last wife I shall be repeated.

AT EVE'S GRAVE

ADAM: Wheresoever she was, *there* was Eden.

(1893, 1905)

The Esquimau Maiden's Romance

"Yes, I will tell you anything about my life that you would like to know, Mr. Twain," she said, in her soft voice, and letting her honest eyes rest placidly upon my face, "for it is kind and good of you to like me and care to know about me."

She had been absently scraping blubber-grease from her cheeks with a small bone-knife and transferring it to her fur sleeve, while she watched the Aurora Borealis swing its flaming streamers out of the sky and wash the lonely snow-plain and the templed icebergs with the rich hues of the prism, a spectacle of almost intolerable splendor and beauty; but now she shook off her reverie and prepared to give me the humble little history I had asked for.

She settled herself comfortably on the block of ice which we were using as a sofa, and I made ready to listen.

She was a beautiful creature. I speak from the Esquimau point of view. Others would have thought her a trifle over-plump. She was just twenty years old, and was held to be by far the most bewitching girl in her tribe. Even now, in the open air, with her cumbersome and shapeless fur coat and trousers and boots and vast hood, the beauty of her face at least was apparent; but her figure had to be taken on trust. Among all the guests who came and went, I had seen no girl at her father's hospitable trough who could be called her equal. Yet she was not spoiled. She was sweet and natural and sincere, and if she was aware that she was a belle, there was nothing about her ways to show that she possessed that knowledge.

She had been my daily comrade for a week now, and the better I knew her the better I liked her. She had been tenderly and carefully brought up, in an atmosphere of singularly rare refinement for the polar regions, for her father was the most important man of his tribe and ranked at the top of Esquimau cultivation. I made long dog-sledge trips across the mighty ice-floes with Lasca—that was her name—and found her company always pleasant and her conversation agreeable. I went fishing with her, but not in her perilous boat: I merely followed along on the ice and watched her strike her game with her fatally accurate spear. We went sealing together; several times I stood by while she and the family dug blubber from a stranded whale, and once I went part of the way when she was hunting a bear, but turned back before the finish, because at bottom I am afraid of bears.

However, she was ready to begin her story now, and this is what she said:

"Our tribe had always been used to wander about from place to place over the frozen seas, like the other tribes, but my father got tired of that two years ago, and built this great mansion of frozen snow-blocks—look at it; it is seven feet high and three or four times as long as any of the others—and here we have stayed ever since. He was very proud of his house, and that was reasonable; for if you have examined it with care you must have noticed how much finer and completer it is than houses usually are. But if you have not, you must, for you will find it has luxurious appointments that are quite beyond the common. For instance, in that end of it which you have called the 'parlor,' the raised platform for the accommodation of guests and the family at meals is the largest you have ever seen in any house—is it not so?"

"Yes, you are quite right, Lasca; it is the largest; we have nothing resembling it in even the finest houses in the United States." This admission made her eyes sparkle with pride and pleasure. I noted that, and took my cue.

"I thought it must have surprised you," she said. "And another thing: it is bedded far deeper in furs than is usual; all kinds of furs—seal, sea-otter, silver-gray fox, bear, marten, sable—every kind of fur in profusion; and the same with the ice-block sleeping-benches along the walls, which you call 'beds.' Are your platforms and sleeping-benches better provided at home?"

"Indeed, they are not, Lasca—they do not begin to be." That pleased her again. All she was thinking of was the *number* of furs her esthetic father took the trouble to keep on hand, not their value. I could have told her that those masses of rich furs constituted wealth—or would in my country—but she would not have understood that; those were not the kind of things that ranked as riches with her people. I could have told her that the clothes she had on, or the every-day clothes of the commonest person about her, were worth twelve or fifteen hundred dollars, and that I was not acquainted with anybody at home who wore twelve-hundred-dollar toilets to go fishing in; but she would not have understood it, so I said nothing. She resumed:

"And then the slop-tubs. We have two in the parlor, and two in the rest of the house. It is very seldom that one has two in the parlor. Have you two in the parlor at home?"

The memory of those tubs made me gasp, but I recovered myself before she noticed, and said with effusion:

"Why, Lasca, it is a shame of me to expose my country, and you must not let it go further, for I am speaking to you in confidence; but I give you my word of honor that not even the richest man in the city of New York has two slop-tubs in his drawing-room."

She clapped her fur-clad hands in innocent delight, and exclaimed:

"Oh, but you cannot mean it, you cannot *mean* it!"

"Indeed, I am in earnest, dear. There is Vanderbilt. Vanderbilt is almost the richest man in the whole world. Now, if I were on my dying bed, I could say to you that not even he has two in his drawing-room. Why, he hasn't even *one*—I wish I may die in my tracks if it isn't true."

Her lovely eyes stood wide with amazement, and she said, slowly, and with a sort of awe in her voice:

"How strange—how incredible—one is not able to realize it. Is he penurious?"

"No—it isn't that. It isn't the expense he minds, but—er—well, you know, it would look like showing off. Yes, that is it, that is the idea; he is a plain man in his way, and shrinks from display."

"Why, that humility is right enough," said Lasca, "if one does not carry it too far—but what does the place *look* like?"

"Well, necessarily it looks pretty barren and unfinished, but—"

"I should think so! I never heard anything like it. Is it a fine house—that is, otherwise?"

"Pretty fine, yes. It is very well thought of."

The girl was silent awhile, and sat dreamily gnawing a candle-end, apparently trying to think the thing out. At last she gave her head a little toss and spoke out her opinion with decision:

"Well, to my mind there's a breed of humility which is *itself* a species of showing-off, when you get down to the marrow of it; and when a man is able to afford two slop-tubs in his parlor, and don't do it, it *may* be that he is truly humble-minded, but it's a hundred times more likely that he is just trying to strike the public eye. In my judgment, your Mr. Vanderbilt knows what he is about."

I tried to modify this verdict, feeling that a double slop-tub standard was not a fair one to try everybody by, although a sound enough one in its own habitat; but the girl's head was set, and she was not to be persuaded. Presently she said:

"Do the rich people, with you, have as good sleeping-benches as ours, and made out of as nice broad ice-blocks?"

"Well, they are pretty good—good enough—but they are not made of ice-blocks."

"I want to know! *Why* aren't they made of ice-blocks?"

I explained the difficulties in the way, and the expensiveness of ice in a country where you have to keep a sharp eye on your ice-man or your ice bill will weigh more than your ice. Then she cried out:

"Dear me, do you *buy* your ice?"

"We most surely do, dear."

She burst into a gale of guileless laughter, and said:

"Oh, I *never* heard of anything so silly! My, there's plenty of it—it isn't worth anything. Why, there is a hundred miles of it in sight, right now. I wouldn't give a fish-bladder for the whole of it."

"Well, it's because you don't know how to value it, you little provincial muggins. If you had it in New York in midsummer, you could buy all the whales in the market with it."

She looked at me doubtfully, and said:

"Are you speaking true?"

"Absolutely. I take my oath to it."

This made her thoughtful. Presently she said, with a little sigh:

"I wish *I* could live there."

I had merely meant to furnish her a standard of values which she could understand; but my purpose had miscarried. I had only given her the impression that whales were cheap and plenty in New York, and set her mouth to watering for them. It seemed best to try to mitigate the evil which I had done, so I said:

"But you wouldn't care for whale-meat if you lived there. Nobody does."

"What!"

"Indeed they don't."

"*Why* don't they?"

"Wel-l-l, I hardly know. It's prejudice, I think. Yes, that is it—just prejudice. I reckon somebody that hadn't anything better to do started a prejudice against it, some time or other, and once you get a caprice like that fairly going, you know, it will last no end of time."

"That is true—*perfectly* true," said the girl, reflectively. "Like our prejudice against soap, here—our tribes had a prejudice against soap at first, you know."

I glanced at her to see if she was in earnest. Evidently she was. I hesitated, then said, cautiously:

"But pardon me. They *had* a prejudice against soap? Had?"—with falling inflection.

"Yes—but that was only at first; nobody would eat it."

"Oh—I understand. I didn't get your idea before."

She resumed:

"It was just a prejudice. The first time soap came here from the foreigners, nobody liked it; but as soon as it got to be fashionable, everybody liked it, and now everybody has it that can afford it. Are you fond of it?"

"Yes, indeed! I should die if I couldn't have it—especially here. Do you like it?"

"I just *adore* it! Do you like candles?"

"I regard them as an absolute necessity. Are you fond of them?"

Her eyes fairly danced, and she exclaimed:

"Oh! Don't mention it! Candles!—and soap!—"

"And fish-interiors!—"

"And train-oil!—"

"And slush!—"

"And whale-blubber!—"

"And carrion! and sour-krout! and beeswax! and tar! and turpentine! and molasses! and—"

"Don't—oh, don't—I shall expire with ecstasy!—"

"And then serve it all up in a slush-bucket, and invite the neighbors and sail in!"

But this vision of an ideal feast was too much for her, and

she swooned away, poor thing. I rubbed snow in her face and brought her to, and after a while got her excitement cooled down. By and by she drifted into her story again:

"So we began to live here, in the fine house. But I was not happy. The reason was this: I was born for love; for me there could be no true happiness without it. I wanted to be loved for myself alone. I wanted an idol, and I wanted to be my idol's idol; nothing less than mutual idolatry would satisfy my fervent nature. I had suitors in plenty—in over-plenty, indeed—but in each and every case they had a fatal defect; sooner or later I discovered that defect—not one of them failed to betray it—it was not me they wanted, but my wealth."

"Your wealth?"

"Yes; for my father is much the richest man in this tribe—or in any tribe in these regions."

I wondered what her father's wealth consisted of. It couldn't be the house—anybody could build its mate. It couldn't be the furs—they were not valued. It couldn't be the sledge, the dogs, the harpoons, the boat, the bone fish-hooks and needles, and such things—no, these were not wealth. Then what could it be that made this man so rich and brought this swarm of sordid suitors to his house? It seemed to me, finally, that the best way to find out would be to ask. So I did it. The girl was so manifestly gratified by the question that I saw she had been aching to have me ask it. She was suffering fully as much to tell as I was to know. She snuggled confidentially up to me and said:

"Guess how much he is worth—you never can!"

I pretended to consider the matter deeply, she watching my anxious and laboring countenance with a devouring and delighted interest; and when, at last, I gave it up and begged her to appease my longing by telling me herself how much this polar Vanderbilt was worth, she put her mouth close to my ear and whispered, impressively:

"Twenty-two fish-hooks—not bone, but foreign—*made out of real iron!"*

Then she sprang back dramatically, to observe the effect. I did my level best not to disappoint her.

I turned pale and murmured:

"Great Scott!"

"It's as true as you live, Mr. Twain!"

"Lasca, you are deceiving me—you cannot mean it."

She was frightened and troubled. She exclaimed:

"Mr. Twain, every word of it is true—every word. You believe me—you *do* believe me, now *don't* you? *say* you believe me—*do* say you believe me!"

"I—well, yes, I do—I am *trying* to. But it was all so *sudden*. So sudden and prostrating. You shouldn't do such a thing in that sudden way. It—"

"Oh, I'm *so* sorry! If I had only thought—"

"Well, it's all right, and I don't blame you any more, for you are young and thoughtless, and of course you couldn't foresee what an effect—"

"But oh, dear, I ought certainly to have *known* better. Why—"

"You see, Lasca, if you had said five or six hooks, to start with, and then gradually—"

"Oh, I see, I see—then gradually added one, and then two, and then—ah, why couldn't I have thought of that!"

"Never mind, child, it's all right—I am better now—I shall be over it in a little while. *But*—to spring the whole twenty-two on a person unprepared and not very strong anyway—"

"Oh, it *was* a crime! But you forgive me—say you forgive me. Do!"

After harvesting a good deal of very pleasant coaxing and petting and persuading, I forgave her and she was happy again, and by and by she got under way with her narrative once more. I presently discovered that the family treasury contained still another feature—a jewel of some sort, apparently—and that she was trying to get around speaking squarely about it, lest I get paralyzed again. But I wanted to know about that thing, too, and urged her to tell me what it was. She was afraid. But I insisted, and said I would brace myself this time and be prepared, then the shock would not hurt me. She was full of misgivings, but the temptation to reveal that marvel to me and enjoy my astonishment and admiration was too strong for her, and she confessed that she had it on her person, and said that if I was *sure* I was prepared—and so on and so on—and with that she reached into her bosom and brought out a battered square of brass, watching my eye anxiously the while. I fell over against her in a quite well-acted faint, which delighted her heart and nearly frightened it out of her, too, at the same time. When I came to and got calm, she was eager to know what I thought of her jewel.

"What do I think of it? I think it is the most exquisite thing I ever saw."

"Do you really? How nice of you to say that! But it *is* a love, now isn't it?"

"Well, I should say so! I'd rather own it than the equator."

"I thought you would admire it," she said. "I think it is *so* lovely. And there isn't another one in all these latitudes. People have come all the way from the Open Polar Sea to look at it. Did you ever see one before?"

I said no, this was the first one I had ever seen. It cost me a pang to tell that generous lie, for I had seen a million of them in my time, this humble jewel of hers being nothing but a battered old New York Central baggage-check.

"Land!" said I, "you don't go about with it on your person this way, alone and with no protection, not even a dog?"

"Ssh! not so loud," she said. "Nobody knows I carry it with me. They think it is in papa's treasury. That is where it generally is."

"Where is the treasury?"

It was a blunt question, and for a moment she looked startled and a little suspicious, but I said:

"Oh, come, don't you be afraid about me. At home we have seventy millions of people, and although I say it myself that shouldn't, there is not one person among them all but would trust me with untold fish-hooks."

This reassured her, and she told me where the hooks were hidden in the house. Then she wandered from her course to brag a little about the size of the sheets of transparent ice that formed the windows of the mansion, and asked me if I had ever seen their like at home, and I came right out frankly and confessed that I hadn't, which pleased her more than she could find words to dress her gratification in. It was so easy to please her, and such a pleasure to do it, that I went on and said:

"Ah, Lasca, you *are* a fortunate girl!—this beautiful house, this dainty jewel, that rich treasure, all this elegant snow, and sumptuous icebergs and limitless sterility, and public bears and walruses, and noble freedom and largeness, and everybody's admiring eyes upon you, and everybody's homage and respect at your command without the asking; young, rich, beautiful, sought, courted, envied, not a requirement unsatisfied, not a desire ungratified, nothing to wish for that you cannot have—it is immeasurable good fortune! I have seen myriads of girls, but none of whom these extraordinary things could be truthfully said but you alone. And you are worthy—worthy of it all, Lasca—I believe it in my heart."

It made her infinitely proud and happy to hear me say this, and she thanked me over and over again for that closing remark, and her voice and eyes showed that she was touched. Presently she said:

"Still, it is not all sunshine—there is a cloudy side. The burden of wealth is a heavy one to bear. Sometimes I have doubted if it were not better to be poor—at least not inordinately rich. It pains me to see neighboring tribesmen stare as they pass by, and overhear them say, reverently, one to another, 'There—that is she—the millionaire's daughter!'

And sometimes they say sorrowfully, 'She is rolling in fish-hooks, and I—I have nothing.' It breaks my heart. When I was a child and we were poor, we slept with the door open, if we chose, but now—now we have to have a night watchman. In those days my father was gentle and courteous to all; but now he is austere and haughty, and cannot abide familiarity. Once his family were his sole thought, but now he goes about thinking of his fish-hooks all the time. And his wealth makes everybody cringing and obsequious to him. Formerly nobody laughed at his jokes, they being always stale and far-fetched and poor, and destitute of the one element that can really justify a joke—the element of humor; but now everybody laughs and cackles at those dismal things, and if any fails to do it my father is deeply displeased, and shows it. Formerly his opinion was not sought upon any matter and was not valuable when he volunteered it; it has that infirmity yet, but nevertheless it is sought by all and applauded by all—and he helps do the applauding himself, having no true delicacy and a plentiful want of tact. He has lowered the tone of all our tribe. Once they were a frank and manly race, now they are measly hypocrites, and sodden with servility. In my heart of hearts I hate all the ways of millionaires! Our tribe was once plain, simple folk, and content with the bone fish-hooks of their fathers; now they are eaten up with avarice and would sacrifice every sentiment of honor and honesty to possess themselves of the debasing iron fish-hooks of the foreigner. However, I must not dwell on these sad things. As I have said, it was my dream to be loved for myself alone.

"At last, this dream seemed about to be fulfilled. A stranger came by, one day, who said his name was Kalula. I told him my name, and he said he loved me. My heart gave a great bound of gratitude and pleasure, for I had loved him at sight, and now I said so. He took me to his breast and said he would not wish to be happier than he was now. We went strolling together far over the ice-floes, telling all about each other, and planning, oh, the loveliest future! When we were tired at last we sat down and ate, for he had soap and candles and I had brought along some blubber. We were hungry, and nothing was ever so good.

"He belonged to a tribe whose haunts were far to the north, and I found that he had never heard of my father, which rejoiced me exceedingly. I mean he had heard of the millionaire, but had never heard his name—so, you see, he could not know that I was the heiress. You may be sure that I did not tell him. I was loved for myself at last, and was satisfied. I was so happy—oh, happier than you can think!

"By and by it was toward supper-time, and I led him home. As we approached our house he was amazed, and cried out:

" 'How splendid! Is *that* your father's?'

"It gave me a pang to hear that tone and see that admiring light in his eye, but the feeling quickly passed away, for I loved him so, and he looked so handsome and noble. All my family of aunts and uncles and cousins were pleased with him, and many guests were called in, and the house was shut up tight and the rag-lamps lighted, and when everything was hot and comfortable and suffocating, we began a joyous feast in celebration of my betrothal.

"When the feast was over, my fathers vanity overcame him, and he could not resist the temptation to show off his riches and let Kalula see what good fortune he had stumbled into—and mainly, of course, he wanted to enjoy the poor man's amazement. I could have cried—but it would have done no good to try to dissuade my father, so I said nothing, but merely sat there and suffered.

"My father went straight to the hiding-place, in full sight of everybody, and got out the fish-hooks and brought them and flung them scatteringly over my head, so that they fell in glittering confusion on the platform at my lover's knee.

"Of course, the astounding spectacle took the poor lad's breath away. He could only stare in stupid astonishment, and wonder how a single individual could possess such incredible riches. Then presently he glanced brilliantly up and exclaimed:

" 'Ah, it is *you* who are the renowned millionaire!'

"My father and all the rest burst into shouts of happy laughter, and when my father gathered the treasure carelessly up as if it might be mere rubbish and of no consequence, and carried it back to its place, poor Kalula's surprise was a study. He said:

" 'Is it possible that you put such things away without counting them?'

"My father delivered a vainglorious horse-laugh, and said:

" 'Well, truly, a body may know *you* have never been rich, since a mere matter of a fish-hook or two is such a mighty matter in your eyes.'

"Kalula was confused, and hung his head, but said:

" 'Ah, indeed, sir, I was never worth the value of the barb of one of those precious things, and I have never seen any man before who was so rich in them as to render the counting of his hoard worth while, since the wealthiest man I have ever known, till now, was possessed of but three.'

"My foolish father roared again with jejune delight, and allowed the impression to remain that he was not accustomed to count his hooks and keep sharp watch over them. He was showing off, you see. Count them? Why, he counted them every day!

"I had met and got acquainted with my darling just at dawn; I had brought him home just at dark, three hours afterward—for the days were shortening toward the six-months' night at that time. We kept up the festivities many hours; then, at last, the guests departed and the rest of us distributed ourselves along the walls on sleeping-benches, and soon all were steeped in dreams but me. I was too happy, too excited, to sleep. After I had lain quiet a long, long time, a dim form passed by me and was swallowed up in the gloom that pervaded the farther end of the house. I could not make out who it was, or whether it was man or woman. Presently that figure or another one passed me going the other way. I wondered what it all meant, but wondering did no good; and while I was still wondering, I fell asleep.

"I do not know how long I slept, but at last I came suddenly broad awake and heard my father say in a terrible voice, 'By the great Snow God, there's a fish-hook gone!' Something told me that that meant sorrow for me, and the blood in my veins turned cold. The presentiment was confirmed in the same instant: my father shouted, 'Up, everybody, and seize the stranger!' Then there was an outburst of cries and curses from all sides, and a wild rush of dim forms through the obscurity. I flew to my beloved's help, but what could I do but wait and wring my hands?—he was already fenced away from me by a living wall, he was being bound hand and foot. Not until he was secured would they let me get to him. I flung myself upon his poor insulted form and cried my grief out upon his breast, while my father and all my family scoffed at me and heaped threats and shameful epithets upon him. He bore his ill usage with a tranquil dignity which endeared him to me more than ever, and made me proud and happy to suffer with him and for him. I heard my father order that the elders of the tribe be called together to try my Kalula for his life.

" 'What?' I said, 'before any search has been made for the lost hook?'

" 'Lost hook!' they all shouted, in derison; and my father added, mockingly, 'Stand back, everybody, and be properly serious—she is going to hunt up that *lost* hook; oh, without doubt she will find it!'—whereat they all laughed again.

"I was not disturbed—I had no fears, no doubts. I said:

" 'It is for you to laugh now; it is your turn. But ours is coming; wait and see.'

"I got a rag-lamp. I thought I should find that miserable

thing in one little moment; and I set about the matter with such confidence that those people grew grave, beginning to suspect that perhaps they had been too hasty. But, alas and alas!—oh, the bitterness of that search! There was deep silence while one might count his fingers ten or twelve times, then my heart began to sink, and around me the mockings began again, and grew steadily louder and more assured, until at last, when I gave up, they burst into volley after volley of cruel laughter.

"None will ever know what I suffered then. But my love was my support and my strength, and I took my rightful place at my Kalula's side, and put my arm about his neck, and whispered in his ear, saying:

" 'You are innocent, my own—that I know; but say it to me yourself, for my comfort, then I can bear whatever is in store for us.'

"He answered:

" 'As surely as I stand upon the brink of death at this moment, I am innocent. Be comforted, then, O bruised heart; be at peace, O thou breath of my nostrils, life of my life!'

" 'Now, then, let the elders come!'—and as I said the words there was a gathering sound of crunching snow outside, and then a vision of stooping forms filing in at the door—the elders.

"My father formally accused the prisoner, and detailed the happenings of the night. He said that the watchman was outside the door, and that in the house were none but the family and the stranger. 'Would the family steal their own property?'

"He paused. The elders sat silent many minutes; at last, one after another said to his neighbor, 'This looks bad for the stranger'—sorrowful words for me to hear. Then my father sat down. O miserable, miserable me! at that very moment I could have proved my darling innocent, but I did not know it!

"The chief of the court asked:

" 'Is there any here to defend the prisoner?'

"I rose and said:

" 'Why should *he* steal that hook, or any or all of them? In another day he would have been heir to the whole!'

"I stood waiting. There was a long silence, the steam from the many breaths rising about me like a fog. At last, one elder after another nodded his head slowly several times, and muttered, 'There is force in what the child has said.' Oh, the heartlift that was in those words!—so transient, but oh, so precious! I sat down.

" 'If any would say further, let him speak now, or after hold his peace,' said the chief of the court.

"My father rose and said:

" 'In the night a form passed by me in the gloom, going toward the treasury, and presently returned. I think, now, it was the stranger.'

"Oh, I was like to swoon! I had supposed that that was my secret; not the grip of the great Ice God himself could have dragged it out of my heart.

"The chief of the court said sternly to my poor Kalula:

" 'Speak!'

"Kalula hesitated, then answered:

" 'It was I. I could not sleep for thinking of the beautiful hooks. I went there and kissed them and fondled them, to appease my spirit and drown it in a harmless joy, then I put them back. I may have dropped one, but I stole none.'

"Oh, a fatal admission to make in such a place! There was an awful hush. I knew he had pronounced his own doom, and that all was over. On every face you could see the words hieroglyphed: 'It is a confession!—and paltry, lame, and thin.'

"I sat drawing in my breath in faint gasps—and waiting. Presently, I heard the solemn words I knew were coming; and each word, as it came, was a knife in my heart:

" 'It is the command of the court that the accused be subjected to the *trial by water.*'

"Oh, curses be upon the head of him who brought 'trial by water' to our land! It came, generations ago, from some far country, that lies none knows where. Before that, our fathers used augury and other unsure methods of trial, and doubtless some poor, guilty creatures escaped with their lives sometimes; but it is not so with trial by water, which is an invention by wiser men than we poor, ignorant savages are. By it the innocent are proved innocent, without doubt or question, for they drown; and the guilty are proven guilty with the same certainty, for they do not drown. My heart was breaking in my bosom, for I said, 'He is innocent, and he will go down under the waves and I shall never see him more.'

"I never left his side after that. I mourned in his arms all the precious hours, and he poured out the deep stream of his love upon me, and oh, I was so miserable and so happy! At last, they tore him from me, and I followed sobbing after them, and saw them fling him into the sea—then I covered my face with my hands. Agony? Oh, I know the deepest deeps of that word!

"The next moment the people burst into a shout of malicious joy, and I took away my hands, startled. Oh, bitter sight—he was *swimming!*

"My heart turned instantly to stone, to ice. I said, 'He was guilty, and he lied to me!'

"I turned my back in scorn and went my way homeward.

"They took him far out to sea and set him on an iceberg that was drifting southward in the great waters. Then my family came home, and my father said to me:

" 'Your thief sent his dying message to you, saying, "Tell her I am innocent, and that all the days and all the hours and all the minutes while I starve and perish I shall love her and think of her and bless the day that gave me sight of her sweet face." Quite pretty, even poetical!'

"I said, 'He is dirt—let me never hear mention of him again.' And oh, to think—he *was* innocent all the time!

"Nine months—nine dull, sad months—went by, and at last came the day of the Great Annual Sacrifice, when all the maidens of the tribe wash their faces and comb their hair. With the first sweep of my comb, out came the fatal fish-hook from where it had been all those months nestling, and I fell fainting into the arms of my remorseful father! Groaning, he said, 'We murdered him, and I shall never smile again!' He has kept his word. Listen: from that day to this not a month goes by that I do not comb my hair. But oh, where is the good of it all now!"

So ended the, poor maid's humble little tale—whereby we learn that, since a hundred million dollars in New York and twenty-two fish-hooks on the border of the Arctic Circle represent the same financial supremacy, a man in straitened circumstances is a fool to stay in New York when he can buy ten cents' worth of fish-hooks and emigrate.

1893

Is He Living or Is He Dead?

I was spending the month of March, 1892, at Mentone, in the Riviera. At this retired spot one has all the advantages, privately, which are to be had at Monte Carlo and Nice, a few miles farther along, publicly. That is to say, one has the flooding sunshine, the balmy air, and the brilliant blue sea, without the marring additions of human powwow and fuss and feathers and display. Mentone is quiet, simple, restful, unpretentious; the rich and the gaudy do not come there. As a rule, I mean, the rich do not come there. Now and then a rich man comes, and I presently got acquainted with one of these. Partially to disguise him I will call him Smith. One day, in the Hôtel des Anglais, at the second breakfast, he exclaimed:

"Quick! Cast your eye on the man going out at the door. Take in every detail of him."

"Why?"

"Do you know who he is?"

"Yes. He spent several days here before you came. He is an old, retired, and very rich silk manufacturer from Lyons, they say, and I guess he is alone in the world, for he always looks sad and dreamy, and doesn't talk with anybody. His name is Théophile Magnan."

I supposed that Smith would now proceed to justify the large interest which he had shown in Monsieur Magnan; but instead he dropped into a brown study, and was apparently lost to me and to the rest of the world during some minutes. Now and then he passed his fingers through his flossy white hair, to assist his thinking, and meantime he allowed his breakfast to go on cooling. At last he said:

"No, it's gone; I can't call it back."

"Can't call what back?"

"It's one of Hans Andersen's beautiful little stories. But it's gone from me. Part of it is like this: A child has a caged bird, which it loves, but thoughtlessly neglects. The bird pours out its song unheard and unheeded; but in time, hunger and thirst assail the creature, and its song grows plaintive and feeble and finally ceases—the bird dies. The child comes, and is smitten to the heart with remorse; then, with bitter tears and lamentations, it calls its mates, and they bury the bird with elaborate pomp and the tenderest grief, without knowing, poor things, that it isn't children only who starve poets to death and then spend enough on their funerals and monuments to have kept them alive and made them easy and comfortable. Now—"

But here we were interrupted. About ten that evening I ran across Smith, and he asked me up to his parlor to help him smoke and drink hot Scotch. It was a cozy place, with its comfortable chairs, its cheerful lamps, and its friendly open fire of seasoned olive-wood. To make everything perfect, there was the muffled booming of the surf outside. After the second Scotch and much lazy and contented chat, Smith said:

"Now we are properly primed—I to tell a curious history, and you to listen to it. It has been a secret for many years—a secret between me and three others; but I am going to break the seal now. Are you comfortable?"

"Perfectly. Go on."

Here follows what he told me:

A long time ago I was a young artist—a very young artist, in fact—and I wandered about the country parts of France, sketching here and sketching there, and was presently joined by a couple of darling young Frenchmen who were at the same kind of thing that I was doing. We were as happy as we were poor, or as poor as we were happy—phrase it to suit yourself. Claude Frère and Carl Boulanger—these are the names of those boys; dear, dear fellows, and the sunniest spirits that ever laughed at poverty and had a noble good time in all weathers.

At last we ran hard aground in a Breton village, and an artist as poor as ourselves took us in and literally saved us from starving—François Millet—

"What! the *great* François Millet?"

Great? He wasn't any greater than we were, then. He hadn't any fame, even in his own village; and he was so poor that he hadn't anything to feed us on but turnips, and even the turnips failed us sometimes. We four became fast friends, doting friends, inseparables. We painted away together with all our might, piling up stock, piling up stock, but very seldom getting rid of any of it. We had lovely times together; but, O my soul! how we were pinched now and then!

For a little over two years this went on. At last, one day, Claude said:

"Boys, we've come to the end. Do you understand that?—absolutely to the end. Everybody has struck—there's a league formed against us. I've been all around the village and it's just as I tell you. They refuse to credit us for another centime until all the odds and ends are paid up."

This struck us cold. Every face was blank with dismay. We realized that our circumstances were desperate, now. There was a long silence. Finally, Millet said with a sigh:

"Nothing occurs to me—nothing. Suggest something, lads."

There was no response, unless a mournful silence may be called a response. Carl got up, and walked nervously up and down awhile, then said:

"It's a shame! Look at these canvases: stacks and stacks of as good pictures as anybody in Europe paints—I don't care who he is. Yes, and plenty of lounging strangers have said the same—or nearly that, anyway."

"But didn't buy," Millet said.

"No matter, they said it; and it's true, too. Look at your 'Angelus' there! Will anybody tell me—"

"Pah, Carl—my 'Angelus'! I was offered five francs for it."

"When?"

"Who offered it?"

"Where is he?"

"Why didn't you take it?"

"Come—don't all speak at once. I thought he would give more—I was sure of it—he looked it—so I asked him eight."

"Well—and then?"

"He said he would call again."

"Thunder and lightning! Why, François—"

"Oh, I know—I know! It was a mistake, and I was a fool. Boys, I meant for the best; you'll grant me that, and I—"

"Why, certainly, we know that, bless your dear heart; but don't you be a fool again."

"I? I wish somebody would come along and offer us a cabbage for it—you'd see!"

"A cabbage! Oh, don't name it—it makes my mouth water. Talk of things less trying."

"Boys," said Carl, "*do* these pictures lack merit? Answer me that."

"No!"

"Aren't they of very great and high merit? Answer me that."

"Yes."

"Of such great and high merit that, if an illustrious name were attached to them, they would sell at splendid prices. Isn't it so?"

"Certainly it is. Nobody doubts that."

"But—I'm not joking—*isn't* it so?"

"Why, of course it's so—and *we* are not joking. But what of it? What of it? How does that concern us?"

"In this way, comrades—we'll *attach* an illustrious name to them!"

The lively conversation stopped. The faces were turned inquiringly upon Carl. What sort of riddle might this be? Where was an illustrious name to be borrowed? And who was to borrow it?

Carl sat down, and said:

"Now, I have a perfectly serious thing to propose. I think it is the only way to keep us out of the almshouse, and I believe it to be a perfectly sure way. I base this opinion upon certain multitudinous and long-established facts in human history. I believe my project will make us all rich."

"Rich! You've lost your mind."

"No, I haven't."

"Yes, you have—you've lost your mind. What do you *call* rich?"

"A hundred thousand francs apiece."

"He *has* lost his mind. I knew it."

"Yes, he has. Carl, privation has been too much for you, and—"

"Carl, you want to take a pill and get right to bed."

"Bandage him first—bandage his head, and then—"

"No, bandage his heels; his brains have been settling for weeks—I've noticed it."

"Shut up!" said Millet, with ostensible severity, "and let the boy say his say. Now, then—come out with your project, Carl. What is it?"

"Well, then, by way of preamble I will ask you to note this fact in human history: that the merit of many a great artist has never been acknowledged until after he was starved and dead. This has happened so often that I make bold to found a law upon it. This law: that the merit of *every* great unknown and neglected artist must and will be recognized, and his pictures climb to high prices after his death. My project is this: we must cast lots—one of us must die."

The remark fell so calmly and so unexpectedly that we almost forgot to jump. Then there was a wild chorus of advice again—medical advice—for the help of Carl's brain; but he waited patiently for the hilarity to calm down, then went on again with his project:

"Yes, one of us must die, to save the others—and himself. We will cast lots. The one chosen shall be illustrious, all of us shall be rich. Hold still, now—hold still; don't interrupt—I tell you I know what I am talking about. Here is the idea. During the next three months the one who is to die shall paint with all his might, enlarge his stock all he can—not pictures, *no!* skeleton sketches, studies, parts of studies, fragments of studies, a dozen dabs of the brush on each—meaningless, of course, but *his* with his cipher on them; turn out fifty a day, each to contain some peculiarity or mannerism, easily detectable as his—*they're* the things that sell you know, and are collected at fabulous prices for the world's museums, after the great man is gone; we'll have a ton of them ready—a ton! And all that time the rest of us will be busy supporting the moribund, and working Paris and the dealers—preparations for the coming event, you know; and when everything is hot and just right, we'll spring the death on them and have the notorious funeral You get the idea?"

"N-o; at least, not qu—"

"Not quite? Don't you see? The man doesn't really die; he changes his name and vanishes; we bury a dummy, and cry over it, with all the world to help. And I—"

But he wasn't allowed to finish. Everybody broke out into a rousing hurrah of applause; and all jumped up and capered about the room and fell on each other's necks in transports of gratitude and joy. For hours we talked over the great plan, without ever feeling hungry; and at last, when all the details had been arranged satisfactorily, we cast lots and Millet was elected—elected to die, as we called it. Then we scraped together those things which one never parts with until he is betting them against future wealth—keepsake trinkets and such like—and these we pawned for enough to furnish us a frugal farewell supper and breakfast, and leave us a few francs over for travel, and a stake of turnips and such for Millet to live on for a few days.

Next morning, early, the three of us cleared out, straightway after breakfast—on foot, of course. Each of us carried a dozen of Millet's small pictures, purposing to market them. Carl struck for Paris, where he would start the work of building up Millet's fame against the coming great day. Claude and I were to separate, and scatter abroad over France.

Now, it will surprise you to know what an easy and comfortable thing we had. I walked two days before I began business. Then I began to sketch a villa in the outskirts of a big town—because I saw the proprietor standing on an upper veranda. He came down to look on—I thought he would. I worked swiftly, intending to keep him interested. Occasionally he fired off a little ejaculation of approbation, and by and by he spoke up with enthusiasm, and said I was a master!

I put down my brush, reached into my satchel, fetched out a Millet, and pointed to the cipher in the corner. I said, proudly:

"I suppose you recognize *that?* Well, he taught me! I should *think* I ought to know my trade!"

The man looked guiltily embarrassed, and was silent. I said, sorrowfully:

"You don't mean to intimate that you don't know the cipher of François Millet!"

Of course he didn't know that cipher; but he was the gratefulest man you ever saw, just the same, for being let out of an uncomfortable place on such easy terms. He said:

"No! Why, it *is* Millet's, sure enough! I don't know what I could have been thinking of. Of course I recognize it now."

Next, he wanted to buy it; but I said that although I wasn't rich I wasn't *that* poor. However, at last, I let him have it for eight hundred francs.

"Eight hundred!"

Yes. Millet would have sold it for a pork-chop. Yes, I got eight hundred francs for that little thing. I wish I could get it back for eighty thousand. But that time's gone by. I made a very nice picture of that man's house, and I wanted to offer it to him for ten francs, but that wouldn't answer, seeing I was the pupil of such a master, so I sold it to him for a hundred. I sent the eight hundred francs straight back to Millet from that town and struck out again next day.

But I didn't walk—no. I rode. I have ridden ever since. I sold one picture every day, and never tried to sell two. I always said to my customer:

"I am a fool to sell a picture of François Millet's at all, for that man is not going to live three months, and when he dies his pictures can't be had for love or money."

I took care to spread that little fact as far as I could, and prepare the world for the event.

I take credit to myself for our plan of selling the pictures—it was mine. I suggested it that last evening when we were laying out our campaign, and all three of us agreed to give it a good fair trial before giving it up for some other. It succeeded with all of us. I walked only two days, Claude walked two—both of us afraid to make Millet celebrated too close to home—but Carl walked only half a day, the bright, conscienceless rascal, and after that he traveled like a duke.

Every now and then we got in with a country editor and started an item around through the press; not an item announcing that a new painter had been discovered, but an item which let on that everybody knew François Millet; not an item praising him in any way, but merely a word concerning the present condition of the "master"—sometimes hopeful, sometimes despondent, but always tinged with fears for the worst. We always marked these paragraphs, and sent the papers to all the people who had bought pictures of us.

Carl was soon in Paris, and he worked things with a high hand. He made friends with the correspondents, and got Millet's condition reported to England and all over the continent, and America, and everywhere.

At the end of six weeks from the start, we three met in Paris and called a halt, and stopped sending back to Millet for additional pictures. The boom was so high, and everything so ripe, that we saw that it would be a mistake not to strike now, right away, without waiting any longer. So we wrote Millet to go to bed and begin to waste away pretty fast, for we should like him to die in ten days if he could get ready.

Then we figured up and found that among us we had

sold eighty-five small pictures and studies, and had sixty-nine thousand francs to show for it. Carl had made the last sale and the most brilliant one of all. He sold the "Angelus" for twenty-two hundred francs. How we did glorify him!—not foreseeing that a day was coming by and by when France would struggle to own it and a stranger would capture it for five hundred and fifty thousand, cash.

We had a wind-up champagne supper that night, and next day Claude and I packed up and went off to nurse Millet through his last days and keep busybodies out of the house and send daily bulletins to Carl in Paris for publication in the papers of several continents for the information of a waiting world. The sad end came at last, and Carl was there in time to help in the final mournful rites.

You remember that great funeral, and what a stir it made all over the globe, and how the illustrious of two worlds came to attend it and testify their sorrow. We four—still inseparable—carried the coffin, and would allow none to help. And we were right about that, because it hadn't anything in it but a wax figure, and any other coffin-bearers would have found fault with the weight. Yes, we same old four, who had lovingly shared privation together in the old hard times now gone forever, carried the cof—

"Which four?"

"*We* four—for Millet helped to carry his own coffin. In disguise, you know. Disguised as a relative—distant relative."

"Astonishing!"

"But true, just the same. Well, you remember how the pictures went up. Money? We didn't know what to do with it. There's a man in Paris to-day who owns seventy Millet pictures. He paid us two million francs for them. And as for the bushels of sketches and studies which Millet shoveled out during the six weeks that we were on the road, well, it would astonish you to know the figure we sell them at nowadays—that is, when we consent to let one go!"

"It is a wonderful history, perfectly wonderful!"

"Yes—it amounts to that."

"Whatever became of Millet?"

"Can you keep a secret?"

"I can."

"Do you remember the man I called your attention to in the dining-room to-day? *That was François Millet.*"

"Great—"

"Scott! Yes. For once they didn't starve a genius to death and then put into other pockets the rewards he should have had himself. *This* songbird was not allowed to pipe out its heart unheard and then be paid with the cold pomp of a big funeral. We looked out for that."

1893

The £1,000,000 Bank-Note

When I was twenty-seven years old, I was a mining-broker's clerk in San Francisco, and an expert in all the details of stock traffic. I was alone in the world, and had nothing to depend upon but my wits and a clean reputation; but these were setting my feet in the road to eventual fortune, and I was content with the prospect.

My time was my own after the afternoon board, Saturdays, and I was accustomed to put it in on a little sail-boat on the bay. One day I ventured too far, and was carried out to sea. Just at nightfall, when hope was about gone, I was picked up by a small brig which was bound for London. It was a long and stormy voyage, and they made me work my passage without pay, as a common sailor. When I stepped ashore in London my clothes were ragged and shabby, and I had only a dollar in my pocket. This money fed and sheltered me twenty-four hours. During the next twenty-four I went without food and shelter.

About ten o'clock on the following morning, seedy and hungry, I was dragging myself along Portland Place, when a child that was passing, towed by a nurse-maid, tossed a luscious big pear—minus one bite—into the gutter. I stopped, of course, and fastened my desiring eye on that muddy treasure. My mouth watered for it, my stomach craved it, my whole being begged for it. But every time I made a move to get it some passing eye detected my purpose, and of course I straightened up then, and looked indifferent, and pretended that I hadn't been thinking about the pear at all. This same thing kept happening and happening, and I couldn't get the pear. I was just getting desperate enough to brave all the shame, and to seize it, when a window behind me was raised, and a gentleman spoke out of it, saying:

"Step in here, please."

I was admitted by a gorgeous flunkey, and shown into a sumptuous room where a couple of elderly gentlemen were sitting. They sent away the servant, and made me sit down. They had just finished their breakfast, and the sight of the remains of it almost overpowered me. I could hardly keep my wits together in the presence of that food, but as I was not asked to sample it, I had to bear my trouble as best I could.

Now, something had been happening there a little before, which I did not know anything about until a good many days afterward, but I will tell you about it now. Those two old brothers had been having a pretty hot argument a couple of days before, and had ended by agreeing to decide it by a bet, which is the English way of settling everything.

You will remember that the Bank of England once issued two notes of a million pounds each, to be used for a special purpose connected with some public transaction with a foreign country. For some reason or other only one of these had been used and canceled; the other still lay in the vaults of the Bank. Well, the brothers, chatting along, happened to get to wondering what might be the fate of a perfectly honest and intelligent stranger who should be turned adrift in London without a friend, and with no money but that million-pound bank-note, and no way to account for his being in possession of it. Brother A said he would starve to death; Brother B said he wouldn't. Brother A said he couldn't offer it at a bank or anywhere else, because he would be arrested on the spot. So they went on disputing till Brother B said he would bet twenty thousand pounds that the man would live thirty days, *anyway*, on that million, and keep out of jail, too. Brother A took him up. Brother B went down to the Bank and bought that note. Just like an Englishman, you see; pluck to the backbone. Then he dictated a letter, which one of his clerks wrote out in a beautiful round hand, and then the two brothers sat at the window a whole day watching for the right man to give it to.

They saw many honest faces go by that were not intelligent enough; many that were intelligent, but not honest enough; many that were both, but the possessors were not poor enough, or, if poor enough, were not strangers. There was always a defect, until I came along; but they agreed that I filled the bill all around; so they elected me unanimously, and there I was now waiting to know why I was called in. They began to ask me questions about myself, and pretty soon they had my story. Finally they told me I would answer their purpose. I said I was sincerely glad, and asked what it was. Then one of them handed me an envelope, and said I would find the explanation inside. I was going to open it, but he said no; take it to my lodgings, and look it over carefully, and not be hasty or rash. I was puzzled, and wanted to discuss the matter a little further, but they didn't; so I took my leave, feeling hurt and insulted to be made the butt of what was apparently some kind of a practical joke, and yet obliged to put up with it, not being in circumstances to resent affronts from rich and strong folk.

I would have picked up the pear now and eaten it before all the world, but it was gone; so I had lost that by this unlucky business, and the thought of it did not soften my feeling toward those men. As soon as I was out of sight of that house I opened my envelope, and saw that it contained money! My opinion of those people changed, I can tell you! I lost not a moment, but shoved note and money into my vest pocket, and broke for the nearest cheap eating-house. Well, how I did eat! When at last I couldn't hold any more, I took out my money and unfolded it, took one glimpse and nearly fainted. Five millions of dollars! Why, it made my head swim.

I must have sat there stunned and blinking at the note as much as a minute before I came rightly to myself again. The first thing I noticed, then, was the landlord. His eye was on the note, and he was petrified. He was worshiping, with all his body and soul, but he looked as if he couldn't stir hand or foot. I took my cue in a moment, and did the only rational thing there was to do. I reached the note toward him, and said, carelessly:

"Give me the change, please."

Then he was restored to his normal condition, and made a thousand apologies for not being able to break the bill, and I couldn't get him to touch it. He wanted to look at it, and keep on looking at it; he couldn't seem to get enough of it to quench the thirst of his eye, but he shrank from touching it as if it had been something too sacred for poor common clay to handle. I said:

"I am sorry if it is an inconvenience, but I must insist. Please change it; I haven't anything else."

But he said that wasn't any matter; he was quite willing

to let the trifle stand over till another time. I said I might not be in his neighborhood again for a good while; but he said it was of no consequence, he could wait, and, moreover, I could have anything I wanted, any time I chose, and let the account run as long as I pleased. He said he hoped he wasn't afraid to trust as rich a gentleman as I was, merely because I was of a merry disposition, and chose to play larks on the public in the matter of dress. By this time another customer was entering, and the landlord hinted to me to put the monster out of sight; then he bowed me all the way to the door, and I started straight for that house and those brothers, to correct the mistake which had been made before the police should hunt me up, and help me do it. I was pretty nervous, in fact pretty badly frightened, though, of course, I was no way in fault; but I knew men well enough to know that when they find they've given a tramp a million-pound bill when they thought it was a one-pounder, they are in a frantic rage against *him* instead of quarreling with their own near-sightedness, as they ought. As I approached the house my excitement began to abate, for all was quiet there, which made me feel pretty sure the blunder was not discovered yet. I rang. The same servant appeared. I asked for those gentlemen.

"They are gone." This in the lofty, cold way of that fellow's tribe.

"Gone? Gone where?"

"On a journey."

"But whereabouts?"

"To the Continent, I think."

"The Continent?"

"Yes, sir."

"Which way—by what route?"

"I can't say, sir."

"When will they be back?"

"In a month, they said."

"A month! Oh, this is awful! Give me *some* sort of idea of how to get a word to them. It's of the last importance."

"I can't, indeed. I've no idea where they've gone, sir."

"Then I must see some member of the family."

"Family's away, too; been abroad months—in Egypt and India, I think."

"Man, there's been an immense mistake made. They'll be back before night. Will you tell them I've been here, and that I will keep coming till it's all made right, and they needn't be afraid?"

"I'll tell them, if they come back, but I am not expecting them. They said you would be here in an hour to make inquiries, but I must tell you it's all right, they'll be here on time and expect you."

So I had to give it up and go away. What a riddle it all was! I was like to lose my mind. They would, be here "on time." What could that mean? Oh the letter would explain, maybe. I had forgotten the letter; I got it out and read it. This is what it said:

> *You are an intelligent and honest man, as one may see by your face. We conceive you to be poor and a stranger. Enclosed you will find a sum of money. It is lent to you for thirty days, without interest. Report at this house at the end of that time. I have a bet on you. If I win it you shall have any situation that is in my gift—any, that is, that you shall be able to prove yourself familiar with and competent to fill.*

No signature, no address, no date.

Well, here was a coil to be in! You are posted on what had preceded all this, but I was not. It was just a deep, dark puzzle to me. I hadn't the least idea what the game was, nor whether harm was meant me or a kindness. I went into a park, and sat down to try to think it out, and to consider what I had best do.

At the end of an hour my reasonings had crystallized into this verdict.

Maybe those men mean me well, maybe they mean me ill; no way to decide that—let it go. They've got a game, or a scheme, or an experiment, of some kind on hand; no way to determine what it is—let it go. There's a bet on me; no way to find out what it is—let it go. That disposes of the indeterminable quantities; the remainder of the matter is tangible, solid, and may be classed and labeled with certainty. If I ask the Bank of England to place this bill to the credit of the man it belongs to, they'll do it, for they know him, although I don't; but they will ask me how I came in possession of it, and if I tell the truth they'll put me in the asylum, naturally, and a lie will land me in jail. The same result would follow if I tried to bank the bill anywhere or to borrow money on it. I have got to carry this immense burden around until those men come back, whether I want to or not. It is useless to me, as useless as a handful of ashes, and yet I must take care of it, and watch over it, while I beg my living. I couldn't *give* it away, if I should try, for neither honest citizen nor highwayman would accept it or meddle with it for anything. Those brothers are safe. Even if I lose their bill, or burn it, they are still safe, because they can stop payment, and the bank will make them whole; but meantime I've got to do a month's suffering without wages or profit—unless I help win that bet, whatever it may be, and get that situation that I am promised. I *should* like to get that; men of their sort have situations in their gift that are worth having.

I got to thinking a good deal about that situation. My hopes began to rise high. Without doubt the salary would be large. It would begin in a month; after that I should be all right. Pretty soon I was feeling first rate. By this time I was tramping the streets again. The sight of a tailorshop gave me a sharp longing to shed my rags, and to clothe myself decently once more. Could I afford it? No; I had nothing in the world but a million pounds. So I forced myself to go on by. But soon I was drifting back again. The temptation persecuted me cruelly. I must have passed that shop back and forth six times during that manful struggle. At last I gave in; I had to. I asked if they had a misfit suit that had been thrown on their hands. The fellow I spoke to nodded his head toward another fellow, and gave me no answer. I went to the indicated fellow, and he indicated another fellow with *his* head, and no words. I went to him, and he said:

" 'Tend to you presently."

I waited till he was done with what he was at, then he took me into a back room, and overhauled a pile of rejected suits, and selected the rattiest one for me. I put it on. It didn't fit, and wasn't in any way attractive, but it was new, and I was anxious to have it; so I didn't find any fault, but said, with some diffidence:

"It would be an accommodation to me if you could wait some days for the money. I haven't any small change about me."

The fellow worked up a most sarcastic expression of countenance, and said:

"Oh, you haven't? Well, of course, I didn't expect it. I'd only expect gentlemen like you to carry large change."

I was nettled, and said:

"My friend, you shouldn't judge a stranger always by the clothes he wears. I am quite able to pay for this suit; I simply didn't wish to put you to the trouble of changing a large note."

He modified his style a little at that, and said, though still with something of an air:

"I didn't mean any particular harm, but as long as rebukes are going, I might say it wasn't quite your affair to jump to the conclusion that we couldn't change any note that you might happen to be carrying around. On the contrary, we *can*."

I handed the note to him, and said:

"Oh, very well; I apologize."

He received it with a smile, one of those large smiles which go all around over, and have folds in them, and wrinkles, and spirals, and look like the place where you have thrown a brick in a pond; and then in the act of his taking a glimpse of the bill this smile froze solid, and turned yellow, and looked like those wavy, wormy spreads of lava which you find hardened on little levels on the side of Vesuvius. I never before saw a smile caught like that, and perpetuated. The man stood there holding the bill, and looking like that, and the proprietor hustled up to see what was the matter, and said, briskly:

"Well, what's up? what's the trouble? what's wanting?"

I said: "There isn't any trouble. I'm waiting for my change."

"Come, come; get him his change, Tod; get him his change."

Tod retorted: "Get him his change! It's easy to say, sir; but look at the bill yourself."

The proprietor took a look, gave a low, eloquent whistle, then made a dive for the pile of rejected clothing, and began to snatch it this way and that, talking all the time excitedly, and as if to himself:

"Sell an eccentric millionaire such an unspeakable suit as that! Tod's a fool—a born fool. Always doing something like this. Drives every millionaire away from this place, because he can't tell a millionaire from a tramp, and never could. Ah, here's the thing I am after. Please get those things off, sir, and throw them in the fire. Do me the favor to put on this shirt and this suit; it's just the thing, the very thing—plain, rich, modest, and just ducally nobby; made to order for a foreign prince—you may know him, sir, his Serene Highness the Hospodar of Halifax; had to leave it with us and take a mourning-suit because his mother was going to die—which she didn't. But that's all right; we can't always have things the way we—that is, the way they—there! trousers all right, they fit you to a charm, sir; now the waistcoat; aha, right again! now the coat—lord! look at that, now! Perfect—the whole thing! I never saw such a triumph in all my experience."

I expressed my satisfaction.

"Quite right, sir, quite right; it'll do for a makeshift, I'm bound to say. But wait till you see what well get up for you on your own measure. Come, Tod, book and pen; get at it. Length of leg, 32""—and so on. Before I could get in a word he had measured me, and was giving orders for dress-suits, morning suits, shirts, and all sorts of things. When I got a chance I said:

"But, my dear sir, I *can't* give these orders, unless you can wait indefinitely, or change the bill."

"Indefinitely! It's a weak word, sir, a weak word. Eternally—*that's* the word, sir. Tod, rush these things through, and send them to the gentleman's address without any waste of time. Let the minor customers wait. Set down the gentleman's address and—"

"I'm changing my quarters. I will drop in and leave the new address."

"Quite right, sir, quite right. One moment—let me show you out, sir. There—good day, sir, good day."

Well, don't you see what was bound to happen? I drifted naturally into buying whatever I wanted, and asking for change. Within a week I was sumptuously equipped with all needful comforts and luxuries, and was housed in an expensive private hotel in Hanover Square. I took my dinners there, but for breakfast I stuck by Harris's humble feeding-house, where I had got my first meal on my million-pound bill. I was the making of Harris. The fact had gone all abroad that the foreign crank who carried million-pound bills in his vest pocket was the patron saint of the place. That was enough. From being a poor, struggling, little hand-to-mouth enterprise, it had become celebrated, and overcrowded with customers. Harris was so grateful that he forced loans upon me, and would not be denied; and so, pauper as I was, I had money to spend, and was living like the rich and the great. I judged that there was going to be a crash by and by, but I was in now and must swim across or drown. You see there was just that element of impending disaster to give a serious side, a sober side, yes, a tragic side, to a state of things which would otherwise have been purely ridiculous. In the night, in the dark, the tragedy part was always to the front, and always warning, always threatening; and so I moaned and tossed, and sleep was hard to find. But in the cheerful daylight the tragedy element faded out and disappeared, and I walked on air, and was happy to giddiness, to intoxication, you may say.

And it was natural; for I had become one of the notorieties of the metropolis of the world, and it turned my head, not just a little, but a good deal. You could not take up a newspaper, English, Scotch, or Irish, without finding in it one or more references to the "vest-pocket million-pounder" and his latest doings and sayings. At first, in these mentions, I was at the bottom of the personal-gossip column; next, I was listed above the knights, next above the baronets, next above the barons, and so on, and so on, climbing steadily, as my notoriety augmented, until I reached the highest altitude possible, and there I remained, taking precedence of all dukes not royal, and of all ecclesiastics except the primate of all England. But mind, this was not fame; as yet I had achieved only notoriety. Then came the climaxing stroke—the accolade, so to speak—which in a single instant transmuted the perishable dross of notoriety into the enduring gold of fame: *Punch* caricatured me! Yes, I was a made man now; my place was established. I might be joked about still, but reverently, not hilariously, not rudely; I could be smiled at, but not laughed at. The time for that had gone by. *Punch* pictured me all a-flutter with rags, dickering with a beef-eater for the Tower of London. Well, you can imagine how it was with a young fellow who had never been taken notice of before, and now all of a sudden couldn't say a thing that wasn't taken up and repeated everywhere; couldn't stir abroad without constantly overhearing the remark flying from lip to lip, "There he goes; that's him!" couldn't take his breakfast without a crowd to look on; couldn't appear in an opera-box without concentrating there the fire of a thousand lorgnettes. Why, I just swam in glory all day long—that is the amount of it.

You know, I even kept my old suit of rags, and every now and then appeared in them, so as to have the old pleasure of buying trifles, and being insulted, and then shooting the scoffer dead with the million-pound bill. But I couldn't keep that up. The illustrated papers made the outfit so familiar that when I went out in it I was at once recognized and followed by a crowd, and if I attempted a purchase the man would offer me his whole shop on credit before I could pull my note on him.

About the tenth day of my fame I went to fulfill my duty to my flag by paying my respects to the American minister. He received me with the enthusiasm proper in my case, upbraided me for being so tardy in my duty, and said that there was only one way to get his forgiveness, and that was to take the seat at his dinner-party that night made vacant by the illness of one of his guests. I said I would, and we got to talking. It turned out that he and my father had been schoolmates in boyhood, Yale students together later, and always warm friends up to my father's death. So then he required me to put in at his house all the odd time I might have to spare, and I was very willing, of course.

In fact, I was more than willing; I was glad. When the crash should come, he might somehow be able to save me from total destruction; I didn't know how, but he might think of a way, maybe. I couldn't venture to unbosom myself to him at this late date, a thing which I would have been quick to do in the beginning of this awful career of mine in London. No, I couldn't venture it now; I was in too deep; that is, too deep for me to be risking revelations to so new a friend, though not clear beyond my depth, as *I* looked at it. Because, you see, with all my borrowing, I was carefully keeping within my means—I mean within my salary. Of course, I couldn't *know* what my salary was going to be, but I had a good enough basis for an estimate in the fact that if I won the bet I was to have *choice* of any situation in that rich old gentleman's gift provided I was competent—and I should certainly prove competent; I hadn't any doubt about that. And as to the bet, I wasn't worrying about that; I had always been lucky. Now my estimate of the salary was six hundred to a thousand a year; say, six hundred for the first year, and so on up year by year, till I struck the upper figure by proved merit. At present I was only in debt for my first year's salary. Everybody had been trying to lend me money, but I had fought off the most of them on one pretext or another; so this indebtedness represented only £300 borrowed money, the other £300 represented my keep and my purchases. I believed my second year's salary would carry me through the rest of the month if I went on being cautious and economical, and I intended to look sharply out for that. My month ended, my employer back from his journey, I should be all right once more, for I should at once divide the two years' salary among my creditors by assignment, and get right down to my work.

It was a lovely dinner-party of fourteen. The Duke and Duchess of Shoreditch, and their daughter the Lady Anne-Grace-Eleanor-Celeste-and-so-forth-and-so-forth-de-Bohun, the Earl and Countess of Newgate, Viscount Cheapside, Lord and Lady Blatherskite, some untitled people of both sexes, the minister and his wife and daughter, and his daughter's visiting friend, an English girl of twenty-two, named Portia Langham, whom I fell in love with in two minutes, and she with me—I could see it without glasses. There was still another guest, an American—but I am a little ahead of my story. While the people were still in the drawing-room, whetting up for dinner, and coldly inspecting the late comers, the servant announced:

"Mr. Lloyd Hastings."

The moment the usual civilities were over, Hastings caught sight of me, and came straight with cordially outstretched hand; then stopped short when about to shake, and said, with an embarrassed look:

"I beg your pardon, sir, I thought I knew you."

"Why, you do know me, old fellow."

"No. Are *you* the—the—"

"Vest-pocket monster? I am, indeed. Don't be afraid to call me by my nickname; I'm used to it."

"Well, well, well, this is a surprise. Once or twice I've seen your own name coupled with the nickname, but it never occurred to me that *you* could be the Henry Adams referred to. Why, it isn't six months since you were clerking away for Blake Hopkins in Frisco on a salary, and sitting up nights on an extra allowance, helping me arrange and verify the Gould and Curry Extension papers and statistics. The idea of your being in London, and a vast millionaire, and a colossal celebrity! Why, it's the Arabian Nights come again. Man, I can't take it in at all; can't realize it; give me time to settle the whirl in my head."

"The fact is, Lloyd, you are no worse off than I am. I can't realize it myself."

"Dear me, it *is* stunning, now isn't it? Why, it's just three months today since we went to the Miners' restaurant—"

"No; the What Cheer."

"Right, it *was* the What Cheer; went there at two in the morning, and had a chop and coffee after a hard six-hours grind over those Extension papers, and I tried to persuade you to come to London with me, and offered to get leave of absence for you and pay all your expenses, and give you something over if I succeeded in making the sale; and you would not listen to me, said I wouldn't succeed, and you couldn't afford to lose the run of business and be no end of time getting the hang of things again when you got back home. And yet here you are. How odd it all is! How did you happen to come, and whatever *did* give you this incredible start?"

"Oh, just an accident. It's a long story—a romance, a body may say. I'll tell you all about it, but not now."

"When?"

"The end of this month."

"That's more than a fortnight yet. It's too much of a strain on a person's curiosity. Make it a week."

"I can't. You'll know why, by and by. But how's the trade getting along?"

His cheerfulness vanished like a breath, and he said with a sigh:

"You were a true prophet, Hal, a true prophet. I wish I hadn't come. I don't want to talk about it."

"But you must. You must come and stop with me to-night, when we leave here, and tell me all about it."

"Oh, may I? Are you in earnest?" and the water showed in his eyes.

"Yes; I want to hear the whole story, every word."

"I'm so grateful! Just to find a human interest once more, in some voice and in some eye, in me and affairs of mine, after what I've been through here—lord! I could go down on my knees for it!"

He gripped my hand hard, and braced up, and was all right and lively after that for the dinner—which didn't come off. No; the usual thing happened, the thing that is always happening under the vicious and aggravating English system—the matter of precedence couldn't be settled, and so there was no dinner. Englishmen always eat dinner before they go out to dinner, because *they* know the risks they are running; but nobody ever warns the stranger, and so he walks placidly into the trap. Of course, nobody was hurt this time, because we had all been to dinner, none of us being novices excepting Hastings, and he having been informed by the minister at the time that he invited him that in deference to the English custom he had not provided any dinner. Everybody took a lady and processioned down to the dining-room because it is usual to go through the motions; but there the dispute began. The Duke of Shoreditch wanted to take precedence, and sit at the head of the table, holding that he outranked a minister who represented merely a nation and not a monarch; but I stood for my rights, and refused to yield. In the gossip column I ranked all dukes not royal, and said so, and claimed precedence of this one. It couldn't be settled, of course, struggle as we might and did, he finally (and injudiciously) trying to play birth and antiquity, and I "seeing" his Conqueror and "raising" him with Adam, whose direct posterity I was, as shown by my name, while *he* was of a collateral branch, as shown by *his*, and by his recent Norman origin; so we all processioned back to the drawing-room again and had a perpendicular lunch—plate of sardines and a strawberry, and you group yourself and stand up and eat it. Here the religion of precedence is not so strenuous; the two persons of highest rank chuck up a shilling, the one that wins has first go at his strawberry, and the loser gets the shilling. The next two chuck up, then the next two, and so on. After refreshment, tables were brought, and we all played cribbage, sixpence a game. The English never play any game for amusement. If they can't make something or lose something—they don't care which—they won't play.

We had a lovely time; certainly two of us had, Miss Langham and I. I was so bewitched with her that I couldn't count my hands if they went above a double sequence; and when I struck home I never discovered it, and started up the outside row again, and would have lost the game every time, only the girl did the same, she being in just my condition, you see; and consequently neither of us ever got out, or cared to wonder why we didn't; we only just knew we were happy, and didn't wish to know anything else, and didn't want to be interrupted. And I *told* her—I did, indeed—told her I loved her; and she—well, she blushed till her hair turned red, but she liked it; she *said* she did. Oh, there was never such an evening! Every time I pegged I put on a postscript; every time she pegged she acknowledged receipt of it, counting the hands the same. Why, I couldn't even say "Two for his heels" without adding "*My*, how sweet you do look!" and she would say, "Fifteen two, fifteen four, fifteen six, and a pair are eight, and eight are sixteen—*do* you think so?"—peeping out aslant from under her lashes, you know, so sweet and cunning. Oh, it was just *too*-too!

Well, I was perfectly honest and square with her; told her I hadn't a cent in the world but just the million-pound note she'd heard so much talk about, and *it* didn't belong to me, and that started her curiosity; and then I talked low, and told her the whole history right from the start, and it nearly killed her laughing. What in the nation she could find to laugh about *I* couldn't see, but there it was; every half-minute some new detail would fetch her, and I would have to stop as much as a minute and a half to give her a chance to settle down again. Why, she laughed herself lame—she did, indeed; I never saw anything like it. I mean I never saw a painful story—a story of a person's troubles and worries and fears—produce just *that* kind of effect before. So I loved her all the more, seeing she could be so cheerful when there wasn't anything to be cheerful about; for I might soon need that kind of wife, you know, the way things looked. Of course, I told her we should have to wait a couple of years, till I could catch up on my salary; but she didn't mind that, only she hoped I would be as careful as possible in the matter of expenses, and not let them run the least risk of trenching on our third year's pay. Then she began to get a little worried, and wondered if we were making any mistake, and starting the salary on a higher figure for the first year than I would get. This was good sense, and it made me feel a little less confident than I had been feeling before; but it gave me a good business idea, and I brought it frankly out.

"Portia, dear, would you mind going with me that day, when I confront those old gentlemen?"

She shrank a little, but said:

"N-o; if my being with you would help hearten you. But—would it be quite proper, do you think?"

"No, I don't know that it would—in fact, I'm afraid it wouldn't; but, you see, there's so *much* dependent upon it that—"

"Then I'll go anyway, proper or improper," she said, with a beautiful and generous enthusiasm. "Oh, I shall be so happy to think I'm helping!"

"Helping, dear? Why, you'll be doing it all. You're so beautiful and so lovely and so winning, that with you there I can pile our salary up till I break those good old fellows, and they'll never have the heart to struggle."

Sho! you should have seen the rich blood mount, and her happy eyes shine!

"You wicked flatterer! There isn't a word of truth in what you say, but still I'll go with you. Maybe it will teach you not to expect other people to look with your eyes."

Were my doubts dissipated? Was my confidence restored? You may judge by this fact: privately I raised my salary to twelve hundred the first year on the spot. But I didn't tell her: I saved it for a surprise.

All the way home I was in the clouds, Hastings talking, I not hearing a word. When he and I entered my parlor, he brought me to myself with his fervent appreciations of my manifold comforts and luxuries.

"Let me just stand here a little and look my fill. Dear me! it's a palace—it's just a palace! And in it everything a body *could* desire, including cozy coal fire and supper standing ready. Henry, it doesn't merely make me realize how rich you are; it makes me realize, to the bone, to the marrow, how poor I am—how poor I am, and how miserable, how defeated, routed, annihilated!"

Plague take it! this language gave me the cold shudders. It scared me broad awake, and made me comprehend that I was standing on a half-inch crust, with a crater underneath. *I* didn't know I had been dreaming—that is, I hadn't been allowing myself to know it for a while back; but *now*—oh, dear! Deep in debt, not a cent in the world, a lovely girl's happiness or woe in my hands, and nothing in front of me but a salary which might never—oh, *would* never—materialize! Oh, oh, oh! I am ruined past hope! nothing can save me!

"Henry, the mere unconsidered drippings of your daily income would—"

"Oh, my daily income! Here, down with this hot Scotch, and cheer up your soul. Here's with you! Or, no—you're hungry; sit down and—"

"Not a bite for me; I'm past it. I can't eat, these days; but I'll drink with you till I drop. Come!"

"Barrel for barrel, I'm with you! Ready? Here we go! Now, then, Lloyd, unreel your story while I brew."

"Unreel it? What, again?"

"Again? What do you mean by that?"

"Why, I mean do you want to hear it *over* again?"

"Do I want to hear it *over* again? This *is* a puzzler. Wait; don't take any more of that liquid. You don't need it."

"Look here, Henry, you alarm me. Didn't I tell you the whole story on the way here?"

"You?"

"Yes, I."

"I'll be hanged if I heard a word of it."

"Henry, this is a serious thing. It troubles me. What did you take up yonder at the minister's?"

Then it all flashed on me, and I owned up like a man.

"I took the dearest girl in this world—prisoner!"

So then he came with a rush, and we shook, and shook, and shook till our hands ached; and he didn't blame me for not having heard a word of a story which had lasted while we walked three miles. He just sat down then, like the patient, good fellow he was, and told it all over again. Synopsized, it amounted to this: He had come to England with what he thought was a grand opportunity; he had an "option" to sell the Gould and Curry Extension for the "locators" of it, and keep all he could get over a million dollars. He had worked hard, had pulled every wire he knew of, had left no honest expedient untried, had spent nearly all the money he had in the world, had not been able to get a solitary capitalist to listen to him, and his option would run out at the end of the month. In a word, he was ruined. Then he jumped up and cried out:

"Henry, you can save me! You can save me, and you're the only man in the universe that can. Will you do it? *Won't* you do it?"

"Tell me how. Speak out, my boy."

"Give me a million and my passage home for my 'option'! Don't, *don't* refuse!"

I was in a kind of agony. I was right on the point of coming out with the words, "Lloyd, I'm a pauper myself—absolutely penniless, and in *debt.*" But a white-hot idea came flaming through my head, and I gripped my jaws together, and calmed myself down till I was as cold as a capitalist. Then I said, in a commercial and self-possessed way:

"I will save you, Lloyd—"

"Then I'm already saved! God be merciful to you forever! If ever I—"

"Let me finish, Lloyd. I will save you, but not in that way; for that would not be fair to you, after your hard work, and the risks you've run. I don't need to buy mines; I can keep my capital moving, in a commercial center like London, without that; it's what I'm at, all the time; but here is what I'll do. I know all about that mine, of course; I know its immense value, and can swear to it if anybody wishes it. You shall sell out inside of the fortnight for three millions cash, using my name freely, and we'll divide, share and share alike."

Do you know, he would have danced the furniture to kindling-wood in his insane joy, and broken everything on the place, if I hadn't tripped him up and tied him.

Then he lay there, perfectly happy, saying:

"I may use your name! Your name—think of it! Man, they'll flock in droves, these rich Londoners; they'll *fight* for that stock! I'm a made man, I'm a made man forever, and I'll never forget you as long as I live!"

In less than twenty-four hours London was abuzz! I hadn't anything to do, day after day, but sit at home, and say to all comers:

"Yes; I told him to refer to me. I know the man, and I know the mine. His character is above reproach, and the mine is worth far more than he asks for it."

Meantime I spent all my evenings at the minister's with Portia. I didn't say a word to her about the mine; I saved it for a surprise. We talked salary; never anything but salary and love; sometimes love, sometimes salary, sometimes love and salary together. And my! the interest the minister's wife and daughter took in our little affair, and the endless ingenuities they invented to save us from interruption, and to keep the minister in the dark and unsuspicious—well, it was just lovely of them!

When the month was up at last, I had a million dollars to my credit in the London and County Bank, and Hastings was fixed in the same way. Dressed at my level best, I drove by the house in Portland Place, judged by the look of things that my birds were home again, went on toward the minister's and got my precious, and we started back, talking salary with all our might. She was so excited and anxious that it made her just intolerably beautiful. I said:

"Dearie, the way you're looking it's a crime to strike for a salary a single penny under three thousand a year."

"Henry, Henry, you'll ruin us!"

"Don't you be afraid. Just keep up those looks and trust to me. It'll all come out right."

So, as it turned out, I had to keep bolstering up *her* courage all the way. She kept pleading with me, and saying:

"Oh, please remember that if we ask for too much we may get no salary at all; and then what will become of us, with no way in the world to earn our living?"

We were ushered in by that same servant, and there they were, the two old gentlemen. Of course, they were surprised to see that wonderful creature with me, but I said:

"It's all right, gentlemen; she is my future stay and helpmate."

And I introduced them to her, and called them by name. It didn't surprise them; they knew I would know enough to consult the directory. They seated us, and were very polite to me, and very solicitous to relieve her from embarrassment, and put her as much at her ease as they could. Then I said:

"Gentlemen, I am ready to report."

"We are glad to hear it," said *my* man, "For now we can decide the bet which my brother Abel and I made. If you have won for me, you shall have any situation in my gift. Have you the million-pound note?"

"Here it is, sir," and I handed it to him.

"I've won!" he shouted, and slapped Abel on the back. "*Now* what do you say, brother?"

"I say he *did* survive, and I've lost twenty thousand pounds. I never would have believed it."

"I've a further report to make," I said, "and a pretty long one. I want you to let me come soon, and detail my whole month's history; and I promise you it's worth hearing. Meantime, take a look at that."

"What, man! Certificate of deposit for £200,000. Is it yours?"

"Mine. I earned it by thirty days' judicious use of that little loan you let me have. And the only use I made of it was to buy trifles and offer the bill in change."

"Come, this is astonishing! It's incredible, man!"

"Never mind, I'll prove it. Don't take my word unsupported."

But now Portia's turn was come to be surprised. Her eyes were spread wide, and she said:

"Henry, is that really your money? Have you been fibbing to me?"

"I have, indeed, dearie. But you'll forgive me, *I* know."

She put up an arch pout, and said:

"Don't you be so sure. You are a naughty thing to deceive me so!"

"Oh, you'll get over it, sweetheart, you'll get over it; it was only fun, you know. Come, let's be going."

"But wait, wait! The situation, you know. I want to give you the situation," said my man.

"Well," I said, "I'm just as grateful as I can be, but really I don't want one."

"But you can have the very choicest one in my gift."

"Thanks again, with all my heart; but I don't even want *that* one."

"Henry, I'm ashamed of you. You don't half thank the good gentleman. May I do it for you?"

"Indeed, you shall, dear, if you can improve it. Let us see you try."

She walked to my man, got up in his lap, put her arm round his neck, and kissed him right on the mouth. Then the two old gentlemen shouted with laughter, but I was dumbfounded, just petrified, as you may say. Portia said:

"Papa, he has said you haven't a situation in your gift that he'd take; and I feel just as hurt as—"

"My darling, is that your papa?"

"Yes; he's my step-papa, and the dearest one that ever was. You understand now, don't you, why I was able to laugh when you told me at the minister's, not knowing my relationships, what trouble and worry papa's and Uncle Abel's scheme was giving you?"

Of course, I spoke right up now, without any fooling, and went straight to the point.

"Oh, my dearest dear sir, I want to take back what I said. You *have* got a situation open that I want."

"Name it."

"Son-in-law."

"Well, well, well! But you know, if you haven't ever served in that capacity, you, of course, can't furnish recommendations of a sort to satisfy the conditions of the contract, and so—"

"Try me—oh, do, I beg of you! Only just try me thirty or forty years, and if—"

"Oh, well, all right; it's but a little thing to ask, take her along."

Happy, we two? There are not words enough in the unabridged to describe it. And when London got the whole history, a day or two later, of my month's adventures with that bank-note, and how they ended, did London talk, and have a good time? Yes.

My Portia's papa took that friendly and hospitable bill back to the Bank of England and cashed it; then the Bank canceled it and made him a present of it, and he gave it to us at our wedding, and it has always hung in its frame in the sacredest place in our home ever since. For it gave me my Portia. But for it I could not have remained in London, would not have appeared at the minister's, never should have met her. And so I always say, "Yes, it's a million-pounder, as you see; but it never made but one purchase in its life, and *then* got the article for only about a tenth part of its value."

1893

How to Tell a Story

THE HUMOROUS STORY AN AMERICAN DEVELOPMENT.—ITS DIFFERENCE FROM COMIC AND WITTY STORIES.

I DO NOT claim that I can tell a story as it ought to be told. I only claim to know how a story ought to be told, for I have been almost daily in the company of the most expert story-tellers for many years.

There are several kinds of stories, but only one difficult kind—the humorous. I will talk mainly about that one. The humorous story is American, the comic story is English, the witty story is French. The humorous story depends for its effect upon the *manner* of the telling; the comic story and the witty story upon the *matter*.

The humorous story may be spun out to great length, and may wander around as much as it pleases, and arrive nowhere in particular; but the comic and witty stories must be brief and end with a point. The humorous story bubbles gently along, the others burst.

The humorous story is strictly a work of art—high and delicate art—and only an artist can tell it; but no art is necessary in telling the comic and the witty story; anybody can do it. The art of telling a humorous story—understand, I mean by word of mouth, not print—was created in America, and has remained at home.

The humorous story is told gravely; the teller does his

best to conceal the fact that he even dimly suspects that there is anything funny about it; but the teller of the comic story tells you beforehand that it is one of the funniest things he has ever heard, then tells it with eager delight, and is the first person to laugh when he gets through. And sometimes, if he has had good success, he is so glad and happy that he will repeat the "nub" of it and glance around from face to face, collecting applause, and then repeat it again. It is a pathetic thing to see.

Very often, of course, the rambling and disjointed humorous story finishes with a nub, point, snapper, or whatever you like to call it. Then the listener must be alert, for in many cases the teller will divert attention from that nub by dropping it in a carefully casual and indifferent way, with the pretense that he does not know it is a nub.

Artemus Ward used that trick a good deal; then when the belated audience presently caught the joke he would look up with innocent surprise, as if wondering what they had found to laugh at. Dan Setchell used it before him, Nye and Riley and others use it to-day.

But the teller of the comic story does not slur the nub; he shouts it at you—every time. And when he prints it, in England, France, Germany, and Italy, he italicizes it, puts some whooping exclamation-points after it, and sometimes explains it in a parenthesis. All of which is very depressing, and makes one want to renounce joking and lead a better life.

Let me set down an instance of the comic method, using an anecdote which has been popular all over the world for twelve or fifteen hundred years. The teller tells it in this way:

The Wounded Soldier

In the course of a certain battle a soldier whose leg had been shot off appealed to another soldier who was hurrying by to carry him to the rear, informing him at the same time of the loss which he had sustained; whereupon the generous son of Mars, shouldering the unfortunate, proceeded to carry out his desire. The bullets and cannon-balls were flying in all directions, and presently one of the latter took the wounded man's head off—without, however, his deliverer being aware of it. In no long time he was hailed by an officer, who said:

"Where are you going with that carcass?"

"To the rear, sir—he's lost his leg!"

"His leg, forsooth?" responded the astonished officer; "you mean his head, you booby."

Whereupon the soldier dispossessed himself of his burden, and stood looking down upon it in great perplexity. At length he said:

"It is true, sir, just as you have said." Then after a pause he added, "*But he* TOLD *me* IT WAS HIS LEG!!!!!"

Here the narrator bursts into explosion after explosion of thunderous horse-laughter, repeating that nub from time to time through his gaspings and shriekings and suffocatings.

It takes only a minute and a half to tell that in its comic-story form; and isn't worth the telling, after all. Put into the humorous-story form it takes ten minutes, and is about the funniest thing I have ever listened to—as James Whitcomb Riley tells it.

He tells it in the character of a dull-witted old farmer who has just heard it for the first time, thinks it is unspeakably funny, and is trying to repeat it to a neighbor. But he can't remember it; so he gets all mixed up and wanders helplessly round and round, putting in tedious details that don't belong in the tale and only retard it; taking them out conscientiously and putting in others that are just as useless; making minor mistakes now and then and stopping to correct them and explain how he came to make them; remembering things which he forgot to put in in their proper place and going back to put them in there; stopping his narrative a good while in order to try to recall the name of the soldier that was hurt, and finally remembering that the soldier's name was not mentioned, and remarking placidly that the name is of no real importance, anyway—better, of course, if one knew it, but not essential, after all—and so on, and so on, and so on.

The teller is innocent and happy and pleased with himself, and has to stop every little while to hold himself in and keep from laughing outright; and does hold in, but his body quakes in a jelly-like way with interior chuckles; and at the end of the ten minutes the audience have laughed until they are exhausted, and the tears are running down their faces.

The simplicity and innocence and sincerity and unconsciousness of the old farmer are perfectly simulated, and the result is a performance which is thoroughly charming and delicious. This is art—and fine and beautiful, and only a master can compass it; but a machine could tell the other story.

To string incongruities and absurdities together in a wandering and sometimes purposeless way, and seem innocently unaware that they are absurdities, is the basis of the American art, if my position is correct. Another feature is the slurring of the point. A third is the dropping of a studied remark apparently without knowing it, as if one were thinking aloud. The fourth and last is the pause.

Artemus Ward dealt in numbers three and four a good deal. He would begin to tell with great animation something which he seemed to think was wonderful; then lose confidence, and after an apparently absent-minded pause add an incongruous remark in a soliloquizing way; and that was the remark intended to explode the mine—and it did.

For instance, he would say eagerly, excitedly, "I once knew a man in New Zealand who hadn't a tooth in his head"—here his animation would die out; a silent, reflective pause would follow, then he would say dreamily, and as if to himself, "and yet that man could beat a drum better than any man I ever saw."

The pause is an exceedingly important feature in any kind of story, and a frequently recurring feature, too. It is a dainty thing, and delicate, and also uncertain and treacherous; for it must be exactly the right length—no more and no less—or it fails of its purpose and makes trouble. If the pause is too short the impressive point is passed, and the audience have had time to divine that a surprise is intended—and then you can't surprise them, of course.

On the platform I used to tell a negro ghost story that had a pause in front of the snapper on the end, and that pause was the most important thing in the whole story. If I got it the right length precisely, I could spring the finishing ejaculation with effect enough to make some impressible girl deliver a startled little yelp and jump out of her seat—and that was what I was after. This story was called "The Golden Arm," and was told in this fashion. You can practise with it yourself—and mind you look out for the pause and get it right.

The Golden Arm

Once 'pon a time dey wuz a monsus mean man, en he live 'way out in de prairie all 'lone by hisself, 'cep'n he had a wife. En bimeby she died, en he tuck en toted her way out dah in de prairie en buried her. Well, she had a golden arm—all solid gold, fum de shoulder down. He wiz pow'ful mean—pow'ful; en dat night he couldn't sleep, caze he want dat golden arm so bad.

When it come midnight he couldn't stan' it no mo'; so he git up, he did, en tuck his lantern en shoved out thoo de storm en dug her up en got de golden arm; en he bent his head down 'gin de win', en plowed en plowed en plowed thoo de snow. Den all on a sudden he stop (make a considerable pause here, and look startled, and take a listening attitude) en say: "My *lan'*, what's dat?"

En he listen—en listen—en de win' say (set your teeth

together and imitate the wailing and wheezing singsong of the wind), "Buzzz-z-zzz"—en den, way back yonder whah de grave is, he hear a *voice!*—he hear a voice all mix' up in de win'—can't hardly tell 'em 'part—"Buzz—zzz—W-h-o—g-o-t—m-y—g- o-l-d-e-n *arm?*" (You must begin to shiver violently now.)

En he begin to shiver en shake, en say, "Oh, my! *Oh,* my lan'!" en de win' blow de lantern out, en de snow en sleet blow in his face en most' choke him, en he start a-plowin' knee-deep towards home mos' dead, he so sk'yerd—en pooty soon he hear de voice agin, en (pause) it 'us comin *after* him! "Bzzz—zzz—zzz—W-h-o—g-o-t—m-y—g-o-l-d-e-n —*arm?*"

When he git to de pasture he hear it again—closer now, en a-*comin'!*—a-comin' back dah in de dark en de storm—(repeat the wind and the voice). When he git to de house he rush up-stairs en jump in de bed en kiver up, head and years, en lay dah shiverin' en shakin'—en den way out dah he hear it *agin!*—en a-*comin'!* En bimeby he hear (pause—awed, listening attitude)—pat—pat—pat—*hit's a-comin' up-stairs!* Den he hear de latch, en he *know* it's in de room!

Den pooty soon he know it's a-*stannin' by de bed!* (Pause.) Den—he know it's a-*bendin' down over him*—en he cain't skasely git his breath! Den—den—he seem to feel someth'n' *c-o-l-d,* right down 'most agin his head! (Pause.)

Den de voice say, *right at his year*—"*W-h-o—g-o-t—m-y—g-o-l-d-e-n arm?*" (You must wail it out very plaintively and accusingly; then you stare steadily and impressively into the face of the farthest-gone auditor—a girl, preferably—and let that awe-inspiring pause begin to build itself in the deep hush. When it has reached exactly the right length, jump suddenly at that girl and yell, "*You've* got it!"

If you've got the *pause* right, she'll fetch a dear little yelp and spring right out of her shoes. But you *must* get the pause right; and you will find it the most troublesome and aggravating and uncertain thing you ever undertook.

1894

Cecil Rhodes and the Shark

THE SHARK is the swiftest fish that swims. The speed of the fastest steamer afloat is poor compared to his. And he is a great gad-about, and roams far and wide in the oceans, and visits the shores of all of them, ultimately, in the course of his restless excursions. I have a tale to tell now, which has not as yet been in print. In 1870 a young stranger arrived in Sydney, and set about finding something to do; but he knew no one, and brought no recommendations, and the result was that he got no employment. He had aimed high, at first, but as time and his money wasted away he grew less and less exacting, until at last he was willing to serve in the humblest capacities if so he might get bread and shelter. But luck was still against him; he could find no opening of any sort. Finally his money was all gone. He walked the streets all day, thinking; he walked them all night, thinking, thinking, and growing hungrier and hungrier. At dawn he found himself well away from the town and drifting aimlessly along the harbor shore. As he was passing by a nodding shark-fisher the man looked up and said:

"Say, young fellow, take my line a spell, and change my luck for me."

"How do you know I won't make it worse?"

"Because you can't. It has been at its worst all night. If you can't change it, no harm's done; if you do change it, it's for the better, of course. Come."

"All right, what will you give?"

"I'll give you the shark, if you catch one."

"And I will eat it, bones and all. Give me the line."

"Here you are. I will get away, now, for a while, so that my luck won't spoil yours; for many and many a time I've noticed that if—there, pull in, pull in, man, you've got a bite! *I* knew how it would be. Why, I knew you for a born son of luck the minute I saw you. All right—he's landed."

It was an unusually large shark—"a full nineteen-footer," the fisherman said, as he laid the creature open with his knife.

"Now you rob him, young man, while I step to my hamper for a fresh bait. There's generally something in them worth going for. You've changed my luck, you see. But, my goodness, I hope you haven't changed your own."

"Oh, it wouldn't matter; don't worry about that. Get your bait. I'll rob him."

When the fisherman got back the young man had just finished washing his hands in the bay and was starting away.

"What! you are not going?"

"Yes. Good-by."

"But what about your shark?"

"The shark? Why, what use is he to me?"

"What *use* is he? I like that. Don't you know that we can go and report him to Government, and you'll get a clean solid eighty shillings bounty? Hard cash, you know. What do you think about it *now*?"

"Oh, well, you can collect it."

"And *keep* it? Is that what you mean?"

"Yes."

"Well, this is odd. You're one of those sort they call eccentrics, I judge. The saying is, you mustn't judge a man by his clothes, and I'm believing it now. Why yours are looking just ratty, don't you know; and yet you must be rich."

"I am."

The young man walked slowly back to the town, deeply musing as he went. He halted a moment in front of the best restaurant, then glanced at his clothes and passed on, and got his breakfast at a "stand-up." There was a good deal of it, and it cost five shillings. He tendered a sovereign, got his change, glanced at his silver, muttered to himself, "There isn't enough to buy clothes with," and went his way.

At half past nine the richest wool-broker in Sydney was sitting in his morning-room at home, settling his breakfast with the morning paper. A servant put his head in and said:

"There's a sundowner at the door wants to see you, sir."

"What do you bring that kind of a message here for? Send him about his business."

"He won't go, sir. I've tried."

"He won't go? That's—why, that's unusual. He's one of two things, then: he's a remarkable person, or he's crazy. Is he crazy?"

"No, sir. He don't look it."

"Then he's remarkable. What does he say he wants?"

"He won't tell, sir; only says it's very important."

"And won't go. Does he *say* he won't go?"

"Says he'll stand there till he sees you, sir, if it's all day."

"And yet isn't crazy. Show him up."

The sundowner was shown in. The broker said to himself, "No, he's not crazy; that is easy to see; so he must be the other thing."

Then aloud, "Well, my good fellow, be quick about it; don't waste any words; what is it you want?"

"I want to borrow a hundred thousand pounds."

"Scott! (It's a mistake; he *is* crazy. . . . No—he *can't* be—not with that eye.) Why, you take my breath away. Come, who *are* you?"

"Nobody that you know."

"What is your name?"

"Cecil Rhodes."

"No, I don't remember hearing the name before. Now then—just for curiosity's sake—what has sent you to me on this extraordinary errand?"

"The intention to make a hundred thousand pounds for you and as much for myself within the next sixty days."

"Well, well, well. It is the most extraordinary idea that I—sit *down*—you interest me. And somehow you—well, you fascinate me, I think that that is about the word. And it isn't your proposition—no, that doesn't fascinate me; it's something else, I don't quite know what; something that's born in you and oozes out of you, I suppose. Now then—just for curiosity's sake again, nothing more: as I understand it, it is your desire to bor—"

"I said *intention.*"

"Pardon, so you did. I thought it was an unheedful use of the word—an unheedful valuing of its strength, you know."

"I knew its strength."

"Well, I must say—but look here, let me walk the floor a little, my mind is getting into a sort of whirl, though *you* don't seem disturbed any. (Plainly this young fellow isn't crazy; but as to his being remarkable—well, really he amounts to that, and something over.) Now then, I believe I am beyond the reach of further astonishment. Strike, and spare not. What is your scheme?"

"To buy the wool crop—deliverable in sixty days."

"What, the *whole* of it?"

"The whole of it."

"No, I was not quite out of the reach of surprises, after all. Why, how you talk. Do you know what our crop is going to foot up?"

"Two and a half million sterling—maybe a little more."

"Well, you've got your statistics right, anyway. Now then, do you know what the margins would foot up, to buy it at sixty days?"

"The hundred thousand pounds I came here to get."

"Right, once more. Well, dear me, just to see what would happen, I wish you had the money. And if you had it, what would you do with it?"

"I shall make two hundred thousand pounds out of it in sixty days."

"You mean, of course, that you *might* make it if—"

"I said, 'shall.' "

"Yes, by George, you *did* say 'shall'! You are the most definite devil I ever saw, in the matter of language. Dear, dear, dear, look here! Definite speech means clarity of mind. Upon my word I believe you've got what you believe to be a rational *reason* for venturing into this house, an entire stranger, on this wild scheme of buying the wool crop of an entire colony on speculation. Bring it out—I am prepared—acclimatized, if I may use the word. *Why* would you buy the crop, and *why* would you make that sum out of it? That is to say, what makes you think you—"

"I don't think—I know."

"Definite again. *How* do you know?"

"Because France has declared war against Germany, and wool has gone up fourteen per cent. in London and is still rising."

"Oh, in-deed? *Now* then, I've *got* you! Such a thunderbolt as you have just let fly ought to have made me jump out of my chair, but it didn't stir me the least little bit, you see. And for a very simple reason: I have read the morning paper. You can look at it if you want to. The fastest ship in the service arrived at eleven o'clock last night, fifty days out from London. All her news is printed here. There are no war-clouds anywhere; and as for wool, why, it is the low-spiritedest commodity in the English market. It is your turn to jump, now. . . . Well, why don't you jump? Why do you sit there in that placid fashion, when—"

"Because I have later news."

"Later news? Oh, come—later news than fifty days, brought steaming hot from London by the—"

"My news is only ten days old."

"Oh, Mun-*chausen*, hear the maniac talk! Where did you get it?"

"Got it out of a shark."

"Oh, oh, oh, this is *too* much! Front! call the police—

bring the gun—raise the town! All the asylums in Christendom have broken loose in the single person of—"

"Sit down! And collect yourself. Where is the use in getting excited? Am I excited? There is nothing to get excited *about*. When I make a statement which I cannot prove, it will be time enough for you to begin to offer hospitality to damaging fancies about me and my sanity."

"Oh, a thousand thousand pardons! I ought to be ashamed of myself, and I *am* ashamed of myself for thinking that a little bit of a circumstance like sending a shark to England to fetch back a market report—"

"What does your middle initial stand for, sir?"

"Andrew. What are you writing?"

"Wait a moment. Proof about the shark—and another matter. Only ten lines. There—now it is done. Sign it."

"Many thanks—many. Let me see; it says—it says—oh, come, this is *interesting!* Why—why—look here! prove what you say here, and I'll put up the money, and double as much, if necessary, and divide the winnings with you, half and half. There, now—I've signed; make your promise good if you can. Show me a copy of the London *Times* only ten days old."

"Here it is—and with it these buttons and a memorandum-book that belonged to the man the shark swallowed. Swallowed him in the Thames, without a doubt; for you will notice that the last entry in the book is dated 'London,' and is of the same date as the *Times,* and says '**Ver consequenz der Kriegeserklärung, reise ich heute nach Deutschland ab, auf daß ich mein Leben auf dem Altar meines Landes legen mag**'—as clean native German as anybody can put upon paper, and means that in consequence of the declaration of war, this loyal soul is leaving for home *to-day,* to fight. And he did leave, too, but the shark had him before the day was done, poor fellow."

"And a pity, too. But there are times for mourning, and we will attend to this case, further on; other matters are pressing, now. I will go down and set the machinery in motion in a quiet way and buy the crop. It will cheer the drooping spirits of the boys, in a transitory way. Everything is transitory in this world. Sixty days hence, when they are called to deliver the goods, they will think they've been struck by lightning. But there is a time for mourning, and we will attend to that case along with the other one. Come along, I'll take you to my tailor. What did you say your name is?"

"Cecil Rhodes."

"It is hard to remember. However, I think you will make it easier by and by, if you live. There are three kinds of people—Commonplace Men, Remarkable Men, and Lunatics. I'll classify you with the Remarkables, and take the chances."

The deal went through, and secured to the young stranger the first fortune he ever pocketed.

From FOLLOWING THE EQUATOR, 1897

WHY ED JACKSON CALLED ON COMMODORE VANDERBILT

A FEW YEARS before the outbreak of the Civil War it began to appear that Memphis, Tennessee, was going to be a great tobacco *entrepôt*—the wise could see the signs of it. At that time Memphis had a wharfboat, of course. There was a paved sloping wharf, for the accommodation of freight, but the steamers landed on the outside of the wharfboat, and all loading and unloading was done across it, between steamer and shore. A number of wharfboat clerks were needed, and part of the time, every day, they were very busy, and part of the time tediously idle. They were boiling over with youth and spirits, and they had to make the intervals of idleness endurable in some way; and as a rule, they did it by contriving practical jokes and playing them upon each other.

The favorite butt for the jokes was Ed Jackson, because he played none himself, and was easy game for other people's—for he always believed whatever was told him.

One day he told the others his scheme for his holiday. He was not going fishing or hunting this time—no, he had thought out a better plan. Out of his forty dollars a month he had saved enough for his purpose, in an economical way, and he was going to have a look at New York.

It was a great and surprising idea. It meant travel—immense travel—in those days it meant seeing the world; it was the equivalent of a voyage around it in ours. At first the other youths thought his mind was affected, but when they found that he was in earnest, the next thing to be thought of was, what sort of opportunity this venture might afford for a practical joke.

The young men studied over the matter, then held a secret consultation and made a plan. The idea was, that one of the conspirators should offer Ed a letter of introduction to Commodore Vanderbilt, and trick him into delivering it. It would be easy to do this. But what would Ed do when he got back to Memphis? That was a serious matter. He was good-hearted, and had always taken the jokes patiently; but they had been jokes which did not humiliate him, did not bring him to shame; whereas, this would be a cruel one in that way, and to play it was to meddle with fire; for with all his good nature, Ed was a Southerner—and the English of that was, that when he came back he would kill as many of the conspirators as he could before falling himself. However, the chances must be taken—it wouldn't do to waste such a joke as that.

So the letter was prepared with great care and elaboration. It was signed Alfred Fairchild, and was written in an easy and friendly spirit. It stated that the bearer was the bosom friend of the writer's son, and was of good parts and sterling character, and it begged the Commodore to be kind to the young stranger for the writer's sake. It went on to say, "You may have forgotten me, in this long stretch of time, but you will easily call me back out of your boyhood memories when I remind you of how we robbed old Stevenson's orchard that night; and how, while he was chasing down the road after us, we cut across the field and doubled back and sold his own apples to his own cook for a hatful of doughnuts; and the time that we—" and so forth and so on, bringing in names of imaginary comrades, and detailing all sorts of wild and absurd and, of course, wholly imaginary schoolboy pranks and adventures, but putting them into lively and telling shape.

With all gravity Ed was asked if he would like to have a letter to Commodore Vanderbilt, the great millionaire. It was expected that the question would astonish Ed, and it did.

"What? Do *you* know that extraordinary man?"

"No; but my father does. They were schoolboys together. And if you like, I'll write and ask father. I know he'll be glad to give it to you for my sake."

Ed could not find words capable of expressing his gratitude and delight. The three days passed, and the letter was put into his hands. He started on his trip, still pouring out his thanks while he shook goodby all around. And when he was out of sight his comrades let fly their laughter in a storm of happy satisfaction—and then quieted down, and were less happy, less satisfied. For the old doubts as to the wisdom of this deception began to intrude again.

Arrived in New York, Ed found his way to Commodore Vanderbilt's business quarters, and was ushered into a large anteroom, where a score of people were patiently awaiting their turn for a two-minute interview with the millionaire in his private office. A servant asked for Ed's card, and got the letter instead. Ed was sent for a moment later, and found Mr. Vanderbilt alone, with the letter—open—in his hand.

"Pray sit down, Mr.—er—"

"Jackson."

"Ah—sit down, Mr. Jackson. By the opening sentences it seems to be a letter from an old friend. Allow me—I will run my eye through it. He says—he says—why, who *is* it?" He turned the sheet and found the signature. "Alfred Fairchild—h'm—Fairchild—I don't recall the name. But that is nothing—a thousand names have gone from me. He says—he says—h'm—h'm—oh, dear, but it's good! Oh, it's rare! I don't *quite* remember it, but I *seem* to—it'll all come back to me presently. He says—he says—h'm—h'm—oh, but that was a game! Oh, spl-endid! How it carries me back! It's all dim, of course—it's a long time ago—and the names—*some* of the names are wavery and indistinct—but sho', I know it happened—I can *feel* it! and lord, how it warms my heart, and brings back my lost youth! Well, well, well, I've got to come back into this workaday world now—business presses and people are waiting—I'll keep the rest for bed to-night, and live my youth over again. And you'll thank Fairchild for me when you see him—I used to call him Alf, I think—and you'll give him my gratitude for what this letter has done for the tired spirit of a hard-worked man; and tell him there isn't anything that I can do for him or any friend of his that I won't do. And as for you, my lad, you are my guest; you can't stop at any hotel in New York. Sit where you are a little while, till I get through with these people, then we'll go home. I'll take care of *you*, my boy—make yourself easy as to that."

Ed stayed a week, and had an immense time—and never suspected that the Commodore's shrewd eyes were on him, and that he was daily being weighed and measured and analyzed and tried and tested.

Yes, he had an immense time; and never wrote home, but saved it all up to tell when he should get back. Twice, with proper modesty and decency, he proposed to end his visit, but the Commodore said, "No—wait; leave it to me; I'll tell you when to go."

In those days the Commodore was making some of those vast combinations of his—consolidations of warring odds and ends of railroads into harmonious systems, and concentrations of floating and rudderless commerce in effective centers—and among other things his far-seeing eye had detected the convergence of that huge tobacco-commerce, already spoken of, toward Memphis, and he had resolved to set his grasp upon it and make it his own.

The week came to an end. Then the Commodore said:

"Now you can start home. But first we will have some more talk about the tobacco matter. I know you now. I know your abilities as well as you know them yourself—perhaps better. You understand that tobacco matter; you understand that I am going to take possession of it, and you also understand the plans which I have matured for doing it. What I want is a man who knows my mind, and is qualified to represent me in Memphis, and be in supreme command of that important business—and I appoint you."

"Me!"

"Yes. Your salary will be high—of course—for you are representing me. Later you will earn increases of it, and will get them. You will need a small army of assistants; choose them yourself—and carefully. Take no man for friendship's sake; but, all things being equal, take the man you know, take your friend, in preference to the stranger."

After some further talk under this head, the Commodore said: "Good-by, my boy, and thank Alf for me, for sending you to me."

When Ed reached Memphis he rushed down to the wharf in a fever to tell his great news and thank the boys over and over again for thinking to give him the letter to

Mr. Vanderbilt. It happened to be one of those idle times. Blazing hot noonday, and no sign of life on the wharf. But as Ed threaded his way among the freight-piles, he saw a white linen figure stretched in slumber upon a pile of grain-sacks under an awning, and said to himself, "That's one of them," and hastened his step; next, he said, "It's Charley—it's Fairchild—good"; and the next moment laid an affectionate hand on the sleeper's shoulder. The eyes opened lazily, took one glance, the face blanched, the form whirled itself from the sack-pile, and in an instant Ed was alone and Fairchild was flying for the wharfboat like the wind!

Ed was dazed, stupefied. Was Fairchild crazy? What could be the meaning of this? He started slow and dreamily down toward the wharfboat; turned the corner of a freight-pile and came suddenly upon two of the boys. They were lightly laughing over some pleasant matter; they heard his step, and glanced up just as he discovered them; the laugh died abruptly; and before Ed could speak they were off, and sailing over barrels and bales like hunted deer. Again Ed was paralyzed. Had the boys all gone mad? What *could* be the explanation of this extraordinary conduct? And so, dreaming along, he reached the wharfboat, and stepped aboard—nothing but silence there, and vacancy. He crossed the deck, turned the corner to go down the outer guard, heard a fervent—

"O Lord!" and saw a white linen form plunge overboard.

The youth came up coughing and strangling, and cried out:

"Go 'way from here! You let me alone. *I* didn't do it. I swear I didn't!"

"Didn't do *what?*"

"Give you the—"

"Never mind what you didn't do—come out of that! What makes you all act so? What have *I* done?"

"You? Why, *you* haven't done anything. But—"

"Well, then, what have you got against me? What do you all treat me so for?"

"I—er—but haven't you got anything against *us?*"

"Of course not. What put such a thing into your head?"

"Honor bright—you haven't?"

"Honor bright."

"Swear it!"

"I don't know what in the *world* you mean, but I swear it, anyway."

"And you'll shake hands with me?"

"Goodness knows I'll be *glad* to! Why, I'm just starving to shake hands with *somebody!*"

The swimmer muttered, "Hang him, he smelt a rat and never delivered the letter!—but it's all right, I'm not going to fetch up the subject." And he crawled out and came dripping and draining to shake hands. First one and then another of the conspirators showed up cautiously—armed to the teeth—took in the amicable situation, then ventured warily forward and joined the love-feast.

And to Ed's eager inquiry as to what made them act as they had been acting, they answered evasively and pretended that they had put it up as a joke, to see what he would do. It was the best explanation they could invent at such short notice. And each said to himself, "He never delivered that letter, and the joke is on *us,* if he only knew it or we were dull enough to come out and tell."

Then, of course, they wanted to know all about the trip; and he said:

"Come right up on the boiler deck and order the drinks—it's my treat. I'm going to tell you all about it. And to-night it's my treat again—and we'll have oysters and a time!"

When the drinks were brought and cigars lighted, Ed said:

"Well, when I delivered the letter to Mr. Vanderbilt—"

"Great Scott!"

"Gracious, how you scared me. What's the matter?"

"Oh—er—nothing. Nothing—it was a tack in the chair-seat," said one.

"But you *all* said it. However, no matter. When I delivered the letter—"

"*Did* you deliver it?" And they looked at each other as people might who thought that maybe they were dreaming.

Then they settled to listening; and as the story deepened and its marvels grew, the amazement of it made them dumb, and the interest of it took their breath. They hardly uttered a whisper during two hours, but sat like petrifactions and drank in the immortal romance. At last the tale was ended, and Ed said:

"And it's all owing to *you*, boys, and you'll never find *me* ungrateful—bless your hearts, the best friends a fellow ever had! You'll all have places; I want every one of you. I *know* you—I know you 'by the *back*,' as the gamblers say. You're jokers, and all that, but you're *sterling*, with the hallmark *on*. And Charley Fairchild, you shall be my first assistant and right hand, because of your first-class ability, and because you got me the letter, and for your father's sake who wrote it for me, and to please Mr. Vanderbilt, who *said* it would! And here's to that great man—drink hearty!"

Yes, when the Moment comes, the Man appears—even if he is a thousand miles away, and has to be discovered by a practical joke.

1897

The Man That Corrupted Hadleyburg

1

It was many years ago. Hadleyburg was the most honest and upright town in all the region around about. It had kept that reputation unsmirched during three generations, and was prouder of it than of any other of its possessions. It was so proud of it, and so anxious to insure its perpetuation, that it began to teach the principles of honest dealing to its babies in the cradle, and made the like teachings the staple of their culture thenceforward through all the years devoted to their education. Also, throughout the formative years temptations were kept out of the way of the young people, so that their honesty could have every chance to harden and solidify, and become a part of their very bone. The neighboring towns were jealous of this honorable supremacy, and affected to sneer at Hadleyburg's pride in it and call it vanity; but all the same they were obliged to acknowledge that Hadleyburg was in reality an incorruptible town; and if pressed they would also acknowledge that the mere fact that a young man hailed from Hadleyburg was all the recommendation he needed when he went forth from his natal town to seek for responsible employment.

But at last, in the drift of time, Hadleyburg had the ill luck to offend a passing stranger—possibly without knowing it, certainly without caring, for Hadleyburg was sufficient unto itself, and cared not a rap for strangers or their opinions. Still, it would have been well to make an exception in this one's case, for he was a bitter man and revengeful. All through his wanderings during a whole year he kept his injury in mind, and gave all his leisure moments to trying to invent a compensating satisfaction for it. He contrived many plans, and all of them were good, but none of them was quite sweeping enough; the poorest of them would hurt a great many individuals, but what he wanted was a plan which would comprehend the entire town, and not let so much as one person escape unhurt. At last he had a fortunate idea, and when it fell into his brain it lit up his whole head with an evil joy. He began to form a plan at once, saying to himself, "That is the thing to do—I will corrupt the town."

Six months later he went to Hadleyburg, and arrived in a buggy at the house of the old cashier of the bank about ten at night. He got a sack out of the buggy, shouldered it, and staggered with it through the cottage yard, and knocked at the door. A woman's voice said "Come in," and he entered, and set his sack behind the stove in the parlor, saying politely to the old lady who sat reading the *Missionary Herald* by the lamp:

"Pray keep your seat, madam, I will not disturb you. There—now it is pretty well concealed; one would hardly know it was there. Can I see your husband a moment, madam?"

No, he was gone to Brixton, and might not return before morning.

"Very well, madam, it is no matter. I merely wanted to leave that sack in his care, to be delivered to the rightful owner when he shall be found. I am a stranger; he does not know me; I am merely passing through the town to-night to discharge a matter which has been long in my mind. My errand is now completed, and I go pleased and a little proud, and you will never see me again. There is a paper attached to the sack which will explain everything. Good night, madam."

The old lady was afraid of the mysterious big stranger, and was glad to see him go. But her curiosity was roused, and she went straight to the sack and brought away the paper. It began as follows:

> TO BE PUBLISHED; *or, the right man sought out by private inquiry—either will answer. This sack contains gold coin weighing a hundred and sixty pounds four ounces—*

"Mercy on us, and the door not locked!"

Mrs. Richards flew to it all in a tremble and locked it, then pulled down the window-shades and stood frightened, worried, and wondering if there was anything else she could do toward making herself and the money more safe. She listened awhile for burglars, then surrendered to curiosity and went back to the lamp and finished reading the paper:

> *I am a foreigner, and am presently going back to my own country, to remain there permanently. I am grateful to America for what I have received at her hands during my long stay under her flag; and to one of her citizens—a citizen of Hadleyburg—I am especially grateful for a great kindness done me a year or two ago. Two great kindnesses, in fact. I will explain. I was a gambler. I say I* WAS. *I was a ruined gambler. I arrived in this village at night, hungry and without a penny. I asked for help—in the dark; I was ashamed to beg in the light. I begged of the right man. He gave me twenty dollars—that is to say, he gave me life, as I considered it. He also gave me fortune; for out of that money I have made myself rich at the gaming-table. And finally, a remark which he made to me has*

remained with me to this day, and has at last conquered me; and in conquering has saved the remnant of my morals; I shall gamble no more. Now I have no idea who that man was, but I want him found, and I want him to have this money, to give away, throw away, or keep, as he pleases. It is merely my way of testifying my gratitude to him. If I could stay, I would find him myself; but no matter, he will be found. This is an honest town, an incorruptible town, and I know I can trust it without fear. This man can be identified by the remark which he made to me; I feel persuaded that he will remember it.

And now my plan is this: If you prefer to conduct the inquiry privately, do so. Tell the contents of this present writing to any one who is likely to be the right man. If he shall answer, 'I am the man; the remark I made was so-and-so,' apply the test—to wit: open the sack, and in it you will find a sealed envelope containing that remark. If the remark mentioned by the candidate tallies with it, give him the money, and ask no further questions, for he is certainly the right man.

But if you shall prefer a public inquiry, then publish this present writing in the local paper—with these instructions added, to wit: Thirty days from now, let the candidate appear at the town-hall at eight in the evening (Friday), and hand his remark, in a sealed envelope, to the Rev. Mr. Burgess (if he will be kind enough to act); and let Mr. Burgess there and then destroy the seals of the sack, open it, and see if the remark is correct; if correct, let the money be delivered with my sincere gratitude, to my benefactor thus identified.

Mrs. Richards sat down, gently quivering with excitement, and was soon lost in thinkings—after this pattern: "What a strange thing it is! . . . And what a fortune for that kind man who set his bread afloat upon the waters! . . . If it had only been my husband that did it!—for we are so poor, so old and poor! . . ." Then, with a sigh—"But it was not my Edward; no, it was not he that gave a stranger twenty dollars. It is pity, too; I see it now. . . ." Then, with a shudder—"But it is *gambler's* money! the wages of sin: we couldn't take it; we couldn't touch it. I don't like to be near it; it seems a defilement." She moved to a farther chair. . . . "I wish Edward would come and take it to the bank; a burglar might come at any moment; it is dreadful to be here all alone with it."

At eleven Mr. Richards arrived, and while his wife was saying, "I am *so* glad you've come!" he was saying, "I'm so tired—tired clear out; it is dreadful to be poor, and have to make these dismal journeys at my time of life. Always at the grind, grind, grind, on a salary—another man's slave, and he sitting at home in his slippers, rich and comfortable."

"I am so sorry for you, Edward, you know that; but be comforted: we have our livelihood; we have our good name—"

"Yes, Mary, and that is everything. Don't mind my talk—it's just a moment's irritation and doesn't mean anything. Kiss me—there, it's all gone now, and I am not complaining any more. What have you been getting? What's in the sack?"

Then his wife told him the great secret. It dazed him for a moment; then he said:

"It weighs a hundred and sixty pounds? Why, Mary, it's for-ty thousand dollars—think of it—a whole fortune! Not ten men in this village are worth that much. Give me the paper."

He skimmed through it and said:

"Isn't it an adventure! Why, it's a romance; it's like the impossible things one reads about in books, and never sees in life." He was well stirred up now; cheerful, even gleeful. He tapped his old wife on the cheek, and said, humorously, "Why, we're rich, Mary, rich; all we've got to do is to bury the money and burn the papers. If the gambler ever comes to inquire, we'll merely look coldly upon him and say: 'What is this nonsense you are talking! We have never heard of you and your sack of gold before'; and then he would look foolish, and—"

"And in the mean time, while you are running on with your jokes, the money is still here, and it is fast getting along toward burglar-time."

"True. Very well, what shall we do—make the inquiry private? No, not that; it would spoil the romance. The public method is better. Think what a noise it will make! And it will make all the other towns jealous; for no stranger would trust such a thing to any town but Hadleyburg, and they know it. It's a great card for us. I must get to the printing-office now, or I shall be too late."

"But stop—stop—don't leave me here alone with it, Edward!"

But he was gone. For only a little while, however. Not far from his own house he met the editor-proprietor of the paper, and gave him the document, and said, "Here is a good thing for you, Cox—put it in."

"It may be too late, Mr. Richards, but I'll see."

At home again he and his wife sat down to talk the charming mystery over; they were in no condition for sleep. The first question was, Who could the citizen have been who gave the stranger the twenty dollars? It seemed a simple one; both answered it in the same breath:

"Barclay Goodson."

"Yes," said Richards, "he could have done it, and it would have been like him, but there's not another in the town."

"Everybody will grant that, Edward—grant it privately, anyway. For six months, now, the village has been its own proper self once more—honest, narrow, self-righteous, and stingy."

"It is what he always called it, to the day of his death—said it right out publicly, too."

"Yes, and he was hated for it."

"Oh, of course; but he didn't care. I reckon he was the best-hated man among us, except the Reverend Burgess."

"Well, Burgess deserves it—he will never get another congregation here. Mean as the town is, it knows how to estimate *him*. Edward, doesn't it seem odd that the stranger should appoint Burgess to deliver the money?"

"Well, yes—it does. That is—that is—"

"Why so much that-*is*-ing? Would *you* select him?"

"Mary, maybe the stranger knows him better than this village does."

"Much *that* would help Burgess!"

The husband seemed perplexed for an answer; the wife kept a steady eye upon him, and waited. Finally Richards said, with the hesitancy of one who is making a statement which is likely to encounter doubt:

"Mary, Burgess is not a bad man."

His wife was certainly surprised.

"Nonsense!" she exclaimed.

"He is not a bad man. I know. The whole of his unpopularity had its foundation in that one thing—the thing that made so much noise."

"That 'one thing,' indeed! As if that 'one thing' wasn't enough, all by itself."

"Plenty. Plenty. Only he wasn't guilty of it."

"How you talk! Not guilty of it! Everybody knows he *was* guilty."

"Mary, I give you my word—he was innocent."

"I can't believe it, and I don't. How do you know?"

"It is a confession. I am ashamed, but I will make it. I was the only man who knew he was innocent. I could have saved him, and—and—well, you know how the town was wrought up—I hadn't the pluck to do it. It would have turned everybody against me. I felt mean, ever so mean; but I didn't dare; I hadn't the manliness to face that."

Mary looked troubled, and for a while was silent. Then she said, stammeringly:

"I—I don't think it would have done for you to—to—One mustn't—er—public opinion—one has to be so careful—so—" It was a difficult road, and she got mired; but after a little she got started again. "It was a great pity, but—Why, we couldn't afford it, Edward—we couldn't indeed. Oh, I wouldn't have had you do it for anything!"

"It would have lost us the good will of so many people, Mary; and then—and then—"

"What troubles me now is, what *he* thinks of us, Edward."

"He? *He* doesn't suspect that I could have saved him."

"Oh," exclaimed the wife, in a tone of relief, "I am glad of that! As long as he doesn't know that you could have saved him, he—he—well, that makes it a great deal better. Why, I might have known he didn't know, because he is always trying to be friendly with us, as little encouragement as we give him. More than once people have twitted me with it. There's the Wilsons, and the Wilcoxes, and the Harknesses, they take a mean pleasure in saying, '*Your friend* Burgess,' because they know it pesters me. I wish he wouldn't persist in liking us so; I can't think why he keeps it up."

"I can explain it. It's another confession. When the thing was new and hot, and the town made a plan to ride him on a rail, my conscience hurt me so that I couldn't stand it, and I went privately and gave him notice, and he got out of the town and staid out till it was safe to come back."

"Edward! If the town had found it out—"

"*Don't!* It scares me yet, to think of it. I repented of it the minute it was done; and I was even afraid to tell you, lest your face might betray it to somebody. I didn't sleep any that night, for worrying. But after a few days I saw that no one was going to suspect me, and after that I got to feeling glad I did it. And I feel glad yet, Mary—glad through and through."

"So do I, now, for it would have been a dreadful way to treat him. Yes, I'm glad; for really you did owe him that, you know. But, Edward, suppose it should come out yet, some day!"

"It won't."

"Why?"

"Because everybody thinks it was Goodson."

"Of course they would!"

"Certainly. And of course *he* didn't care. They persuaded poor old Sawlsberry to go and charge it on him, and he went blustering over there and did it. Goodson looked him over, like as if he was hunting for a place on him that he could despise the most, then he says, 'So you are the Committee of Inquiry, are you?' Sawlsberry said that was about what he was. 'Hm. Do they require particulars, or do you reckon a kind of a *general* answer will do?' 'If they require particulars, I will come back, Mr. Goodson; I will take the general answer first.' 'Very well, then, tell them to go to hell—I reckon that's general enough. And I'll give you some advice, Sawlsberry; when you come back for the particulars, fetch a basket to carry the relics of yourself home in.' "

"Just like Goodson; it's got all the marks. He had only one vanity: he thought he could give advice better than any other person."

"It settled the business, and saved us, Mary. The subject was dropped."

"Bless you, I'm not doubting *that.*"

Then they took up the gold-sack mystery again, with strong interest. Soon the conversation began to suffer breaks—interruptions caused by absorbed thinkings. The breaks grew more and more frequent. At last Richards lost himself wholly in thought. He sat long, gazing vacantly at the floor, and by and by he began to punctuate his thoughts with little nervous movements of his hands that seemed to indicate vexation. Meantime his wife too had relapsed into a thoughtful silence, and her movements were beginning to show a troubled discomfort. Finally Richards got up and strode aimlessly about the room, plowing his hands through his hair, much as a somnambulist might do who was having a bad dream. Then he seemed to arrive at a definite purpose; and without a word he put on his hat and passed quickly out of the house. His wife sat brooding, with a drawn face, and did not seem to be aware that she was alone. Now and then she murmured, "Lead us not into t— . . . but—but—we are so poor, so poor! . . . Lead us not into . . . Ah, who would be hurt by it?—and no one would ever know. . . . Lead us . . ." The voice died out in mumblings. After a little she glanced up and muttered in a half-frightened, half-glad way:

"He is gone! But, oh dear, he may be too late—too late. . . . Maybe not—maybe there is still time." She rose and stood thinking, nervously clasping and unclasping her hands. A slight shudder shook her frame, and she said, out of a dry throat, "God forgive me—it's awful to think such things—but . . . Lord, how we are made—how strangely we are made!"

She turned the light low, and slipped stealthily over and kneeled down by the sack and felt of its ridgy sides with her hands, and fondled them lovingly; and there was a gloating light in her poor old eyes. She fell into fits of absence; and came half out of them at times to mutter, "If we had only waited!—oh, if we had only waited a little, and not been in such a hurry!"

Meantime Cox had gone home from his office and told his wife all about the strange thing that had happened, and they had talked it over eagerly, and guessed that the late Goodson was the only man in the town who could have helped a suffering stranger with so noble a sum as twenty dollars. Then there was a pause, and the two became thoughtful and silent. And by and by nervous and fidgety. At last the wife said, as if to herself:

"Nobody knows this secret but the Richardses . . . and us . . . nobody."

The husband came out of his thinkings with a slight start, and gazed wistfully at his wife, whose face was become very pale; then he hesitatingly rose, and glanced furtively at his hat, then at his wife—a sort of mute inquiry. Mrs. Cox swallowed once or twice, with her hand at her throat, then in place of speech she nodded her head. In a moment she was alone, and mumbling to herself.

And now Richards and Cox were hurrying through the deserted streets, from opposite directions. They met, panting, at the foot of the printing-office stairs; by the night light there they read each other's face. Cox whispered:

"Nobody knows about this but us?"

The whispered answer was,

"Not a soul—on honor, not a soul!"

"If it isn't too late to—"

The men were starting up-stairs; at this moment they were overtaken by a boy, and Cox asked:

"Is that you, Johnny?"

"Yes, sir."

"You needn't ship the early mail—nor *any* mail; wait till I tell you."

"It's already gone, sir."

"Gone?" It had the sound of an unspeakable disappointment in it.

"Yes, sir. Time-table for Brixton and all the towns beyond changed to-day, sir—had to get the papers in twenty minutes earlier than common. I had to rush; if I had been two minutes later—"

The men turned and walked slowly away, not waiting to hear the rest. Neither of them spoke during ten minutes; then Cox said, in a vexed tone:

"What possessed you to be in such a hurry, *I* can't make out."

The answer was humble enough:

"I see it now, but somehow I never thought, you know, until it was too late. But the next time—"

"Next time be hanged! It won't come in a thousand years."

Then the friends separated without a good night, and dragged themselves home with the gait of mortally stricken men. At their homes their wives sprang up with an eager "Well?"—then saw the answer with their eyes and sank down sorrowing, without waiting for it to come in words. In both houses a discussion followed of a heated sort—a new thing; there had been discussions before, but not heated ones, not ungentle ones. The discussions to-night were a sort of seeming plagiarisms of each other. Mrs. Richards said,

"If you had only waited, Edward—if you had only stopped to think; but no, you must run straight to the printing-office and spread it all over the world."

"It *said* publish it."

"That is nothing; it also said do it privately, if you liked. There, now—is that true, or not?"

"Why, yes—yes, it is true; but when I thought what a stir it would make, and what a compliment it was to Hadleyburg that a stranger should trust it so—"

"Oh, certainly, I know all that; but if you had only stopped to think, you would have seen that you *couldn't* find the right man, because he is in his grave, and hasn't left chick nor child nor relation behind him; and as long as the money went to somebody that awfully needed it, and nobody would be hurt by it, and—and—"

She broke down, crying. Her husband tried to think of some comforting thing to say, and presently came out with this:

"But after all, Mary, it must be for the best—it *must* be; we know that. And we must remember that it was so ordered—"

"Ordered! Oh, everything's *ordered,* when a person has

to find some way out when he has been stupid. Just the same, it was *ordered* that the money should come to us in this special way, and it was you that must take it on yourself to go meddling with the designs of Providence—and who gave you the right? It was wicked, that is what it was—just blasphemous presumption, and no more becoming to a meek and humble professor of—"

"But, Mary, you know how we have been trained all our lives long, like the whole village, till it is absolutely second nature to us to stop not a single moment to think when there's an honest thing to be done—"

"Oh, I know it, I know it—it's been one everlasting training and training and training in honesty—honesty shielded, from the very cradle, against every possible temptation, and so it's *artificial* honesty, and weak as water when temptation comes, as we have seen this night. God knows I never had shade nor shadow of a doubt of my petrified and indestructible honesty until now—and now, under the very first big and real temptation, I—Edward, it is my belief that this town's honesty is as rotten as mine is; as rotten as yours is. It is a mean town, a hard, stingy town, and hasn't a virtue in the world but this honesty it is so celebrated for and so conceited about; and so help me, I do believe that if ever the day comes that its honesty falls under great temptation, its grand reputation will go to ruin like a house of cards. There, now, I've made confession, and I feel better; I am a humbug, and I've been one all my life, without knowing it. Let no man call me honest again—I will not have it."

"I—well, Mary, I feel a good deal as you do; I certainly do. It seems strange, too, so strange. I never could have believed it—never."

A long silence followed; both were sunk in thought. At last the wife looked up and said:

"I know what you are thinking, Edward."

Richards had the embarrassed look of a person who is caught.

"I am ashamed to confess it, Mary, but—"

"It's no matter, Edward, I was thinking the same question myself."

"I hope so. State it."

"You were thinking, if a body could only guess out *what the remark was* that Goodson made to the stranger."

"It's perfectly true. I feel guilty and ashamed. And you?"

"I'm past it. Let us make a pallet here; we've got to stand watch till the bank vault opens in the morning and admits the sack. . . . Oh dear, oh dear—if we hadn't made the mistake!"

The pallet was made, and Mary said:

"The open sesame—what could it have been? I do wonder what that remark could have been? But come; we will get to bed now."

"And sleep?"

"No: think."

"Yes, think."

By this time the Coxes too had completed their spat and their reconciliation, and were turning in—to think, to think, and toss, and fret, and worry over what the remark could possibly have been which Goodson made to the stranded derelict; that golden remark; that remark worth forty thousand dollars, cash.

The reason that the village telegraph-office was open later than usual that night was this: The foreman of Cox's paper was the local representative of the Associated Press. One might say its honorary representative, for it wasn't four times a year that he could furnish thirty words that would be accepted. But this time it was different. His despatch stating what he had caught got an instant answer:

Send the whole thing—all the details—twelve hundred words.

A colossal order! The foreman filled the bill; and he was the proudest man in the State. By breakfast-time the next morning the name of Hadleyburg the Incorruptible was on every lip in America, from Montreal to the Gulf, from the glaciers of Alaska to the orange-groves of Florida; and millions and millions of people were discussing the stranger and his money-sack, and wondering if the right man would be found, and hoping some more news about the matter would come soon—right away.

2

Hadleyburg village woke up world-celebrated—astonished—happy—vain. Vain beyond imagination. Its nineteen principal citizens and their wives went about shaking hands with each other, and beaming, and smiling, and congratulating, and saying *this* thing adds a new word to the dictionary—*Hadleyburg,* synonym for *incorruptible*—destined to live in dictionaries forever! And the minor and unimportant citizens and their wives went around acting in much the same way. Everybody ran to the bank to see the gold-sack; and before noon grieved and envious crowds began to flock in from Brixton and all neighboring towns; and that afternoon and next day reporters began to arrive from everywhere to verify the sack and its history and write the whole thing up anew, and make dashing free-hand pictures of the sack, and of Richards's house, and the bank, and the Presbyterian church, and the Baptist church, and the public square, and the town-hall where the test would be applied and the money delivered; and damnable portraits of the Richardses, and Pinkerton the banker, and Cox, and the foreman, and Reverend Burgess, and the postmaster—and even of Jack Halliday, who was the loafing, good-natured, no-account, irreverent fisherman, hunter, boys' friend, stray-dogs' friend, typical "Sam Lawson" of the town. The little mean, smirking, oily Pinkerton showed the sack to all comers, and rubbed his sleek palms together pleasantly, and enlarged upon the town's fine old reputation for honesty and upon this wonderful indorsement of it, and hoped and believed that the example would now spread far and wide over the American world, and be epoch-making in the matter of moral regeneration. And so on, and so on.

By the end of a week things had quieted down again; the wild intoxication of pride and joy had sobered to a soft, sweet, silent delight—a sort of deep, nameless, unutterable content. All faces bore a look of peaceful, holy happiness.

Then a change came. It was a gradual change: so gradual that its beginnings were hardly noticed; maybe were not noticed at all, except by Jack Halliday, who always noticed everything; and always made fun of it, too, no matter what it was. He began to throw out chaffing remarks about people not looking quite so happy as they did a day or two ago; and next he claimed that the new aspect was deepening to positive sadness; next, that it was taking on a sick look; and finally he said that everybody was become so moody, thoughtful, and absentminded that he could rob the meanest man in town of a cent out of the bottom of his breeches pocket and not disturb his revery.

At this stage—or at about this stage—a saying like this was dropped at bedtime—with a sigh, usually—by the head of each of the nineteen principal households: "Ah, what *could* have been the remark that Goodson made?"

And straightway—with a shudder—came this, from the man's wife:

"Oh, *don't!* What horrible thing are you mulling in your mind? Put it away from you, for God's sake!"

But that question was wrung from those men again the next night—and got the same retort. But weaker.

And the third night the men uttered the question yet again—with anguish, and absently. This time—and the following night—the wives fidgeted feebly, and tried to say something. But didn't.

And the night after that they found their tongues and responded—longingly:

"Oh, if we *could* only guess!"

Halliday's comments grew daily more and more sparklingly disagreeable and disparaging. He went diligently about, laughing at the town, individually and in mass. But his laugh was the only one left in the village: it fell upon a hollow and mournful vacancy and emptiness. Not even a smile was findable anywhere. Halliday carried a cigar-box around on a tripod, playing that it was a camera, and halted all passers and aimed the thing and said, "Ready!—now look pleasant, please," but not even this capital joke could surprise the dreary faces into any softening.

So three weeks passed—one week was left. It was Saturday evening—after supper. Instead of the aforetime Saturday-evening flutter and bustle and shopping and larking, the streets were empty and desolate. Richards and his old wife sat apart in their little parlor—miserable and thinking. This was become their evening habit now: the lifelong habit which had preceded it, of reading, knitting, and contented chat, or receiving or paying neighborly calls, was dead and gone and forgotten, ages ago—two or three weeks ago; nobody talked now, nobody read, nobody visited—the whole village sat at home, sighing, worrying, silent. Trying to guess out that remark.

The postman left a letter. Richards glanced listlessly at the superscription and the postmark—unfamiliar, both—and tossed the letter on the table and resumed his might-have-beens and his hopeless dull miseries where he had left them off. Two or three hours later his wife got wearily up and was going away to bed without a good night—custom now—but she stopped near the letter and eyed it awhile with a dead interest, then broke it open, and began to skim it over. Richards, sitting there with his chair tilted back against the wall and his chin between his knees, heard something fall. It was his wife. He sprang to her side, but she cried out:

"Leave me alone, I am too happy. Read the letter—read it!"

He did. He devoured it, his brain reeling. The letter was from a distant state, and it said:

> *I am a stranger to you, but no matter: I have something to tell. I have just arrived home from Mexico, and learned about that episode. Of course you do not know who made that remark, but I know, and I am the only person living who does know. It was* GOODSON. *I knew him well, many years ago. I passed through your village that very night, and was his guest till the midnight train came along. I overheard him make that remark to the stranger in the dark—it was in Hale Alley. He and I talked of it the rest of the way home, and while smoking in his house. He mentioned many of your villagers in the course of his talk—most of them in a very uncomplimentary way, but two or three favorably; among these latter yourself. I say "favorably"—nothing stronger. I remember his saying he did not actually* LIKE *any person in the town—not one; but that you—I* THINK *he said you—am almost sure—had done him a very great service once, possibly without knowing the full value of it, and he wished he had a fortune, he would leave it to you when he died, and a curse apiece for the rest of the citizens. Now, then, if it was you that did him that service, you are his legitimate heir, and entitled to the sack of gold. I know that I can trust to your honor and honesty, for in a citizen of Hadleyburg these virtues are an unfailing inheritance, and so I am going to reveal to you the remark, well satisfied that if you are not the right man you will seek and find the right one and see that poor Goodson's debt of gratitude for the service referred to is paid. This is the remark:* "YOU ARE FAR FROM BEING A BAD MAN: GO, AND REFORM."
>
> HOWARD L. STEPHENSON

"Oh, Edward, the money is ours, and I am so grateful, *oh*, so grateful—kiss me, dear, it's forever since we kissed—and we needed it so—the money—and now you are free of Pinkerton and his bank, and nobody's slave any more; it seems to me I could fly for joy."

It was a happy half-hour that the couple spent there on the settee caressing each other; it was the old days come again—days that had begun with their courtship and lasted without a break till the stranger brought the deadly money. By and by the wife said:

"Oh, Edward, how lucky it was you did him that grand service, poor Goodson! I never liked him, but I love him now. And it was fine and beautiful of you never to mention it or brag about it." Then, with a touch of reproach, "But you ought to have told *me*, Edward, you ought to have told your wife, you know."

"Well, I—er—well, Mary, you see—"

"Now stop hemming and hawing, and tell me about it, Edward. I always loved you, and now I'm proud of you. Everybody believes there was only one good generous soul in this village, and now it turns out that you—Edward, why don't you tell me?"

"Well—er—er— Why, Mary, I can't!"

"You *can't*? *Why* can't you?"

"You see, he—well, he—he made me promise I wouldn't."

The wife looked him over, and said, very slowly:

"Made—you—promise? Edward, what do you tell me that for?"

"Mary, do you think I would lie?"

She was troubled and silent for a moment, then she laid her hand within his and said:

"No . . . no. We have wandered far enough from our bearings—God spare us that! In all your life you have never uttered a lie. But now—now that the foundations of things seem to be crumbling from under us, we—we—" She lost her voice for a moment, then said, brokenly, "Lead us not into temptation. . . . I think you made the promise, Edward. Let it rest so. Let us keep away from that ground. Now—that is all gone by; let us be happy again; it is no time for clouds."

Edward found it something of an effort to comply, for his mind kept wandering—trying to remember what the service was that he had done Goodson.

The couple lay awake the most of the night, Mary happy and busy, Edward busy but not so happy. Mary was planning what she would do with the money. Edward was trying to recall that service. At first his conscience was sore on account of the lie he had told Mary—if it was a lie. After much reflection—suppose it *was* a lie? What then? Was it such a great matter? Aren't we always *acting* lies? Then why not *tell* them? Look at Mary—look what she had done. While he was hurrying off on his honest errand, what was she doing? Lamenting because the papers hadn't been destroyed and the money kept! Is theft better than lying?

That point lost its sting—the lie dropped into the background and left comfort behind it. The next point came to the front: *Had* he rendered that service? Well, here was Goodson's own evidence as reported in Stephenson's letter; there could be no better evidence than that—it was even *proof* that he had rendered it. Of course. So that point was settled. . . . No, not quite. He recalled with a wince that this unknown Mr. Stephenson was just a trifle unsure as to whether the performer of it was Richards or some other—and, oh dear, he had put Richards on his honor! He must himself decide whither that money must go—and Mr. Stephenson was not doubting that if he was the wrong man he would go honorably and find the right one. Oh, it was odious to put a man in such a situation—ah, why couldn't Stephenson have left out that doubt! What did he want to intrude that for?

Further reflection. How did it happen that *Richards's*

name remained in Stephenson's mind as indicating the right man, and not some other man's name? That looked good. Yes, that looked very good. In fact, it went on looking better and better, straight along—until by and by it grew into positive *proof*. And then Richards put the matter at once out of his mind, for he had a private instinct that a proof once established is better left so.

He was feeling reasonably comfortable now, but there was still one other detail that kept pushing itself on his notice: of course he had done that service—that was settled; but what *was* that service? He must recall it—he would not go to sleep till he had recalled it; it would make his peace of mind perfect. And so he thought and thought. He thought of a dozen things—possible services, even probable services—but none of them seemed adequate, none of them seemed large enough, none of them seemed worth the money—worth the fortune Goodson had wished he could leave in his will. And besides, he couldn't remember having done them, anyway. Now, then—now, then—what *kind* of a service would it be that would make a man so inordinately grateful? Ah—the saving of his soul! That must be it. Yes, he could remember, now, how he once set himself the task of converting Goodson, and labored at it as much as—he was going to say three months; but upon closer examination it shrunk to a month, then to a week, then to a day, then to nothing. Yes, he remembered now, and with unwelcome vividness, that Goodson had told him to go to thunder and mind his own business—*he* wasn't hankering to follow Hadleyburg to heaven!

So that solution was a failure—he hadn't saved Goodson's soul. Richards was discouraged. Then after a little came another idea: had he saved Goodson's property? No, that wouldn't do—he hadn't any. His life? That is it! Of course. Why, he might have thought of it before. This time he was on the right track, sure. His imagination-mill was hard at work in a minute, now.

Thereafter during a stretch of two exhausting hours he was busy saving Goodson's life. He saved it in all kinds of difficult and perilous ways. In every case he got it saved satisfactorily up to a certain point; then, just as he was beginning to get well persuaded that it had really happened, a troublesome detail would turn up which made the whole thing impossible. As in the matter of drowning, for instance. In that case he had swum out and tugged Goodson ashore in an unconscious state with a great crowd looking on and applauding, but when he had got it all thought out and was just beginning to remember all about it, a whole swarm of disqualifying details arrived on the ground: the town would have known of the circumstance, Mary would have known of it, it would glare like a limelight in his own memory instead of being an inconspicuous service which he had possibly rendered "without knowing its full value." And at this point he remembered that he couldn't swim, anyway.

Ah—*there* was a point which he had been overlooking from the start: it had to be a service which he had rendered "possibly without knowing the full value of it." Why, really, that ought to be an easy hunt—much easier than those others. And sure enough, by and by he found it. Goodson, years and years ago, came near marrying a very sweet and pretty girl, named Nancy Hewitt, but in some way or other the match had been broken off; the girl died, Goodson remained a bachelor, and by and by became a soured one and a frank despiser of the human species. Soon after the girl's death the village found out, or thought it had found out, that she carried a spoonful of negro blood in her veins. Richards worked at these details a good while, and in the end he thought he remembered things concerning them which must have gotten mislaid in his memory through long neglect. He seemed to dimly remember that it was *he* that found out about the negro blood; that it was he that told the village; that the village told Goodson where they got it; that he thus saved Goodson from marrying the tainted girl; that he had done him this great service "without knowing the full value of it," in fact without knowing that he *was* doing it; but that Goodson knew the value of it, and what a narrow escape he had had, and so went to his grave grateful to his benefactor and wishing he had a fortune to leave him. It was all clear and simple now, and the more he went over it the more luminous and certain it grew; and at last, when he nestled to sleep satisfied and happy, he remembered the whole thing just as if it had been yesterday. In fact, he dimly remembered Goodson's *telling* him his gratitude once. Meantime Mary had spent six thousand dollars on a new house for herself and a pair of slippers for her pastor, and then had fallen peacefully to rest.

That same Saturday evening the postman had delivered a letter to each of the other principal citizens—nineteen letters in all. No two of the envelopes were alike, and no two of the superscriptions were in the same hand, but the letters inside were just like each other in every detail but one. They were exact copies of the letter received by Richards—handwriting and all—and were all signed by Stephenson, but in place of Richards's name each receiver's own name appeared.

All night long eighteen principal citizens did what their caste-brother Richards was doing at the same time—they put in their energies trying to remember what notable service it was that they had unconsciously done Barclay Goodson. In no case was it a holiday job; still they succeeded.

And while they were at this work, which was difficult, their wives put in the night spending the money, which was easy. During that one night the nineteen wives spent an average of seven thousand dollars each out of the forty thousand in the sack—a hundred and thirty-three thousand altogether.

Next day there was a surprise for Jack Halliday. He noticed that the faces of the nineteen chief citizens and their wives bore that expression of peaceful and holy happiness again. He could not understand it, neither was he able to invent any remarks about it that could damage it or disturb it. And so it was his turn to be dissatisfied with life. His private guesses at the reasons for the happiness failed in all instances, upon examination. When he met Mrs. Wilcox and noticed the placid ecstasy in her face, he said to himself, "Her cat has had kittens"—and went and asked the cook: it was not so; the cook had detected the happiness, but did not know the cause. When Halliday found the duplicate ecstasy in the face of "Shadbelly" Billson (village nickname), he was sure some neighbor of Billson's had broken his leg, but inquiry showed that this had not happened. The subdued ecstasy in Gregory Yates's face could mean but one thing—he was a mother-in-law short: it was another mistake. "And Pinkerton—Pinkerton—he has collected ten cents that he thought he was going to lose." And so on, and so on. In some cases the guesses had to remain in doubt, in the others they proved distinct errors. In the end Halliday said to himself, "Anyway it foots up that there's nineteen Hadleyburg families temporarily in heaven: I don't know how it happened; I only know Providence is off duty to-day."

An architect and builder from the next state had lately ventured to set up a small business in this unpromising village, and his sign had now been hanging out a week. Not a customer yet; he was a discouraged man, and sorry he had come. But his weather changed suddenly now. First one and then another chief citizen's wife said to him privately:

"Come to my house Monday week—but say nothing about it for the present. We think of building."

He got eleven invitations that day. That night he wrote his daughter and broke off her match with her student. He said she could marry a mile higher than that.

Pinkerton the banker and two or three other well-to-do men planned country-seats—but waited. That kind don't count their chickens until they are hatched.

The Wilsons devised a grand new thing—a fancy-dress ball. They made no actual promises, but told all their acquaintanceship in confidence that they were thinking the matter over and thought they should give it—"and if we do, you will be invited, of course." People were surprised, and said, one to another, "Why, they are crazy, those poor Wilsons, they can't afford it." Several among the nineteen said privately to their husbands, "It is a good idea: we will keep still till their cheap thing is over, then *we* will give one that will make it sick."

The days drifted along, and the bill of future squanderings rose higher and higher, wilder and wilder, more and more foolish and reckless. It began to look as if every member of the nineteen would not only spend his whole forty thousand dollars before receiving-day, but be actually in debt by the time he got the money. In some cases light-headed people did not stop with planning to spend, they really spent—on credit. They bought land, mortgages, farms, speculative stocks, fine clothes, horses, and various other things, paid down the bonus, and made themselves liable for the rest—at ten days. Presently the sober second thought came, and Halliday noticed that a ghastly anxiety was beginning to show up in a good many faces. Again he was puzzled, and didn't know what to make of it. "The Wilcox kittens aren't dead, for they weren't born; nobody's broken a leg; there's no shrinkage in mother-in-laws; *nothing* has happened—it is an unsolvable mystery."

There was another puzzled man, too—the Rev. Mr. Burgess. For days, wherever he went, people seemed to follow him or to be watching out for him; and if he ever found himself in a retired spot, a member of the nineteen would be sure to appear, thrust an envelope privately into his hand, whisper "To be opened at the town-hall Friday evening," then vanish away like a guilty thing. He was expecting that there might be one claimant for the sack—doubtful, however, Goodson being dead—but it never occurred to him that all this crowd might be claimants. When the great Friday came at last, he found that he had nineteen envelopes.

3

The town-hall had never looked finer. The platform at the end of it was backed by a showy draping of flags; at intervals along the walls were festoons of flags; the gallery fronts were clothed in flags; the supporting columns were swathed in flags; all this was to impress the stranger, for he would be there in considerable force, and in a large degree he would be connected with the press. The house was full. The 412 fixed seats were occupied; also the 68 extra chairs which had been packed into the aisles; the steps of the platform were occupied; some distinguished strangers were given seats on the platform; at the horse-shoe of tables which fenced the front and sides of the platform sat a strong force of special correspondents who had come from everywhere. It was the best-dressed house the town had ever produced. There were some tolerably expensive toilets there, and in several cases the ladies who wore them had the look of being unfamiliar with that kind of clothes. At least the town thought they had that look, but the notion could have arisen from the town's knowledge of the fact that these ladies had never inhabited such clothes before.

The gold-sack stood on a little table at the front of the platform where all the house could see it. The bulk of the house gazed at it with a burning interest, a mouth-watering interest, a wistful and pathetic interest; a minority of nineteen couples gazed at it tenderly, lovingly, proprietarily, and the male half of this minority kept saying over to themselves the moving little impromptu speeches of thankfulness for the audience's applause and congratulations which they were presently going to get up and deliver. Every now and then one of these got a piece of paper out of his vest pocket and privately glanced at it to refresh his memory.

Of course there was a buzz of conversation going on—there always is; but at last when the Rev. Mr. Burgess rose and laid his hand on the sack he could hear his microbes gnaw, the place was so still. He related the curious history of the sack, then went on to speak in warm terms of Hadleyburg's old and well-earned reputation for spotless honesty, and of the town's just pride in this reputation. He said that this reputation was a treasure of priceless value; that under Providence its value had now become inestimably enhanced, for the recent episode had spread this fame far and wide, and thus had focused the eyes of the American world upon this village, and made its name for all time, as he hoped and believed, a synonym for commercial incorruptibility. [*Applause.*] "And who is to be the guardian of this noble treasure—the community as a whole? No! The responsibility is individual, not communal. From this day forth each and every one of you is in his own person its special guardian, and individually responsible that no harm shall come to it. Do you—does each of you—accept this great trust? [*Tumultuous assent.*] Then all is well. Transmit it to your children and to your children's children. To-day your purity is beyond reproach—see to it that it shall remain so. To-day there is not a person in your community who could be beguiled to touch a penny not his own—see to it that you abide in this grace. [*"We will! we will!"*] This is not the place to make comparisons between ourselves and other communities—some of them ungracious toward us; they have their ways, we have ours; let us be content. [*Applause.*] I am done. Under my hand, my friends, rests a stranger's eloquent recognition of what we are; through him the world will always henceforth know what we are. We do not know who he is, but in your name I utter your gratitude, and ask you to raise your voices in indorsement."

The house rose in a body and made the walls quake with

the thunders of its thankfulness for the space of a long minute. Then it sat down, and Mr. Burgess took an envelope out of his pocket. The house held its breath while he slit the envelope open and took from it a slip of paper. He read its contents—slowly and impressively—the audience listening with tranced attention to this magic document, each of whose words stood for an ingot of gold:

" '*The remark which I made to the distressed stranger was this. "You are very far from being a bad man: go, and reform.*" ' " Then he continued:

"We shall know in a moment now whether the remark here quoted corresponds with the one concealed in the sack; and if that shall prove to be so—and it undoubtedly will—this sack of gold belongs to a fellow-citizen who will henceforth stand before the nation as the symbol of the special virtue which has made our town famous throughout the land—Mr. Billson!"

The house had gotten itself all ready to burst into the proper tornado of applause; but instead of doing it, it seemed stricken with a paralysis; there was a deep hush for a moment or two, then a wave of whispered murmurs swept the place—of about this tenor: "*Billson!* oh, come, this is *too* thin! Twenty dollars to a stranger—or *anybody*—*Billson!* tell it to the marines!" And now at this point the house caught its breath all of a sudden in a new access of astonishment, for it discovered that whereas in one part of the hall Deacon Billson was standing up with his head meekly bowed, in another part of it Lawyer Wilson was doing the same. There was a wondering silence now for a while.

Everybody was puzzled, and nineteen couples were surprised and indignant.

Billson and Wilson turned and stared at each other. Billson asked, bitingly:

"Why do *you* rise, Mr. Wilson?"

"Because I have a right to. Perhaps you will be good enough to explain to the house why *you* rise?"

"With great pleasure. Because I wrote that paper."

"It is an impudent falsity! I wrote it myself."

It was Burgess's turn to be paralyzed. He stood looking vacantly at first one of the men and then the other, and did not seem to know what to do. The house was stupefied. Lawyer Wilson spoke up, now, and said,

"I ask the Chair to read the name signed to that paper."

That brought the Chair to itself, and it read out the name:

" 'John Wharton *Billson*.' "

"There!" shouted Billson, "what have you got to say for yourself, now? And what kind of apology are you going to make to me and to this insulted house for the imposture which you have attempted to play here?"

"No apologies are due, sir; and as for the rest of it, I publicly charge you with pilfering my note from Mr. Burgess and substituting a copy of it signed with your own name. There is no other way by which you could have gotten hold of the test-remark; I alone, of living men, possessed the secret of its wording."

There was likely to be a scandalous state of things if this went on; everybody noticed with distress that the shorthand scribes were scribbling like mad; many people were crying "Chair, Chair! Order! order!" Burgess rapped with his gavel, and said:

"Let us not forget the proprieties due. There has evidently been a mistake somewhere, but surely that is all. If Mr. Wilson gave me an envelope—and I remember now that he did—I still have it."

He took one out of his pocket, opened it, glanced at it, looked surprised and worried, and stood silent a few moments. Then he waved his hand in a wandering and mechanical way, and made an effort or two to say something, then gave it up, despondently. Several voices cried out:

"Read it! read it! What is it?"

So he began in a dazed and sleep-walker fashion:

" '*The remark which I made to the unhappy stranger was this: "You are far from being a bad man.* [The house gazed at him, marveling.] *Go, and reform.*" ' [*Murmurs:* "Amazing! what can this mean?"] This one," said the Chair, "is signed Thurlow G. Wilson."

"There!" cried Wilson. "I reckon that settles it! I knew perfectly well my note was purloined."

"Purloined!" retorted Billson. "I'll let you know that neither you nor any man of your kidney must venture to—"

THE CHAIR "Order, gentlemen, order! Take your seats, both of you, please."

They obeyed, shaking their heads and grumbling angrily. The house was profoundly puzzled; it did not know what to do with this curious emergency. Presently Thompson got up. Thompson was the hatter. He would have liked to be a Nineteener; but such was not for him: his stock of hats was not considerable enough for the position. He said:

"Mr. Chairman, if I may be permitted to make a suggestion, can both of these gentlemen be right? I put it to you, sir, can both have happened to say the very same words to the stranger? It seems to me—"

The tanner got up and interrupted him. The tanner was a disgruntled man; he believed himself entitled to be a Nineteener, but he couldn't get recognition. It made him a little unpleasant in his ways and speech. Said he:

"Sho, *that's* not the point! *That* could happen—twice in a hundred years—but not the other thing. *Neither* of them gave the twenty dollars!"

[*A ripple of applause.*]

BILLSON "*I* did!"

WILSON "*I* did!"

Then each accused the other of pilfering.

THE CHAIR "Order! Sit down, if you please—both of you. Neither of the notes has been out of my possession at any moment."

A VOICE "Good—that settles *that!*"

THE TANNER "Mr. Chairman, one thing is now plain: one of these men have been eavesdropping under the other one's bed, and filching family secrets. If it is not unparliamentary to suggest it, I will remark that both are equal to it. [*The Chair*. "Order! order!"] I withdraw the remark, sir, and will confine myself to suggesting that *if* one of them has overheard the other reveal the test-remark to his wife, we shall catch him now."

A VOICE "How?"

THE TANNER "Easily. The two have not quoted the remark in exactly the same words. You would have noticed that, if there hadn't been a considerable stretch of time and an exciting quarrel inserted between the two readings."

A VOICE "Name the difference."

THE TANNER "The word *very* is in Billson's note, and not in the other."

MANY VOICES "That's so—he's right!"

THE TANNER "And so, if the Chair will examine the test-remark in the sack, we shall know which of these two frauds—[*The Chair*. "Order!"]—which of these two adventurers—[*The Chair*. "Order! order!"]—which of these two gentlemen—[*laughter and applause*]—is entitled to wear the belt as being the first dishonest blatherskite ever bred in this town—which he has dishonored, and which will be a sultry place for him from now out!" [*Vigorous applause.*]

MANY VOICES "Open it!—open the sack!"

Mr. Burgess made a slit in the sack, slid his hand in and brought out an envelope. In it were a couple of folded notes. He said:

"One of these is marked, 'Not to be examined until all written communications which have been addressed to the Chair—if any—shall have been read.' The other is marked '*The Test.*' Allow me. It is worded—to wit:

" 'I do not require that the first half of the remark which was made to me by my benefactor shall be quoted with exactness, for it was not striking, and could be forgotten; but its closing fifteen words are quite striking, and I think easily rememberable; unless *these* shall be accurately reproduced, let the applicant be regarded as an impostor. My benefactor began by saying he seldom gave advice to any one, but that it always bore the hall-mark of high value when he did give it. Then he said this—and it has never faded from my memory: *"You are far from being a bad man—"* ' "

FIFTY VOICES "That settles it—the money's Wilson's! Wilson! Wilson! Speech! Speech!"

People jumped up and crowded around Wilson, wringing his hand and congratulating fervently—meantime the Chair was hammering with the gavel and shouting:

"Order, gentlemen! Order! Order! Let me finish reading, please." When quiet was restored, the reading was resumed—as follows:

" ' *"Go, and reform—or, mark my words—some day, for your sins, you will die and go to hell or Hadleyburg*—TRY AND MAKE IT THE FORMER." ' "

A ghastly silence followed. First an angry cloud began to settle darkly upon the faces of the citizenship; after a pause the cloud began to rise, and a tickled expression tried to take its place; tried so hard that it was only kept under with great and painful difficulty; the reporters, the Brixtonites, and other strangers bent their heads down and shielded their faces with their hands, and managed to hold in by main strength and heroic courtesy. At this most inopportune time burst upon the stillness the roar of a solitary voice—Jack Halliday's:

"*That's* got the hall-mark on it!"

Then the house let go, strangers and all. Even Mr. Burgess's gravity broke down presently, then the audience considered itself officially absolved from all restraint, and it made the most of its privilege. It was a good long laugh, and a tempestuously whole-hearted one, but it ceased at last—

long enough for Mr. Burgess to try to resume, and for the people to get their eyes partially wiped; then it broke out again; and afterward yet again; then at last Burgess was able to get out these serious words:

"It is useless to try to disguise the fact—we find ourselves in the presence of a matter of grave import. It involves the honor of your town, it strikes at the town's good name. The difference of a single word between the test-remarks offered by Mr. Wilson and Mr. Billson was itself a serious thing, since it indicated that one or the other of these gentlemen had committed a theft—"

The two men were sitting limp, nerveless, crushed; but at these words both were electrified into movement, and started to get up—

"Sit down!" said the Chair, sharply, and they obeyed. "That, as I have said, was a serious thing. And it was—but for only one of them. But the matter has become graver; for the honor of *both* is now in formidable peril. Shall I go even further, and say in inextricable peril? *Both* left out the crucial fifteen words." He paused. During several moments he allowed the pervading stillness to gather and deepen its impressive effects, then added: "There would seem to be but one way whereby this could happen. I ask these gentlemen—Was there *collusion?—agreement?*"

A low murmur sifted through the house; its import was, "He's got them both."

Billson was not used to emergencies; he sat in a helpless collapse. But Wilson was a lawyer. He struggled to his feet, pale and worried, and said:

"I ask the indulgence of the house while I explain this most painful matter. I am sorry to say what I am about to say, since it must inflict irreparable injury upon Mr. Billson, whom I have always esteemed and respected until now, and in whose invulnerability to temptation I entirely believed—as did you all. But for the preservation of my own honor I must speak—and with frankness. I confess with shame—

and I now beseech your pardon for it—that I said to the ruined stranger all of the words contained in the test-remark, including the disparaging fifteen. [*Sensation.*] When the late publication was made I recalled them, and I resolved to claim the sack of coin, for by every right I was entitled to it. Now I will ask you to consider this point, and weigh it well: that stranger's gratitude to me that night knew no bounds; he said himself that he could find no words for it that were adequate, and that if he should ever be able he would repay me a thousandfold. Now, then, I ask you this: Could I expect—could I believe—could I even remotely imagine—that, feeling as he did, he would do so ungrateful a thing as to add those quite unnecessary fifteen words to his test?—set a trap for me?—expose me as a slanderer of my own town before my own people assembled in a public hall? It was preposterous; it was impossible. His test would contain only the kindly opening clause of my remark. Of that I had no shadow of doubt. You would have thought as I did. You would not have expected a base betrayal from one whom you had befriended and against whom you had committed no offense. And so, with perfect confidence, perfect trust, I wrote on a piece of paper the opening words—ending with 'Go, and reform,'—and signed it. When I was about to put it in an envelope I was called into my back office, and without thinking I left the paper lying open on my desk." He stopped, turned his head slowly toward Billson, waited a moment, then added: "I ask you to note this: when I returned, a little later, Mr. Billson was retiring by my street door." [*Sensation.*]

In a moment Billson was on his feet and shouting:

"It's a lie! It's an infamous lie!"

THE CHAIR "Be seated, sir! Mr. Wilson has the floor."

Billson's friends pulled him into his seat and quieted him, and Wilson went on:

"Those are the simple facts. My note was now lying in a different place on the table from where I had left it. I noticed that, but attached no importance to it, thinking a draught had blown it there. That Mr. Billson would read a private paper was a thing which could not occur to me; he was an honorable man, and he would be above that. If you will allow me to say it, I think his extra word *'very'* stands explained; it is attributable to a defect of memory. I was the only man in the world who could furnish here any detail of the test-remark—by *honorable* means. I have finished."

There is nothing in the world like a persuasive speech to fuddle the mental apparatus and upset the convictions and debauch the emotions of an audience not practised in the tricks and delusions of oratory. Wilson sat down victorious. The house submerged him in tides of approving applause; friends swarmed to him and shook him by the hand and congratulated him, and Billson was shouted down and not allowed to say a word. The Chair hammered and hammered with its gavel, and kept shouting:

"But let us proceed, gentlemen, let us proceed!"

At last there was a measurable degree of quiet, and the hatter said:

"But what is there to proceed with, sir, but to deliver the money?"

VOICES "That's it! That's it! Come forward, Wilson!"

THE HATTER "I move three cheers for Mr. Wilson, Symbol of the special virtue which—"

The cheers burst forth before he could finish; and in the midst of them—and in the midst of the clamor of the gavel also—some enthusiasts mounted Wilson on a big friend's shoulder and were going to fetch him in triumph to the platform. The Chair's voice now rose above the noise—

"Order! To your places! You forget that there is still a document to be read." When quiet had been restored he took up the document, and was going to read it, but laid it down again, saying, "I forgot; this is not to be read until all written communications received by me have first been read." He took an envelope out of his pocket, removed its inclosure, glanced at it—seemed astonished—held it out and gazed at it—stared at it.

Twenty or thirty voices cried out:

"What is it? Read it! read it!"

And he did—slowly, and wondering:

" '*The remark which I made to the stranger*—[Voices. "Hello! how's this?"]—*was this: "You are far from being a bad man.* [*Voices*. "Great Scott!"] *Go, and reform."* ' [*Voices*. "Oh, saw my leg off!"] Signed by Mr. Pinkerton, the banker."

The pandemonium of delight which turned itself loose now was of a sort to make the judicious weep. Those whose withers were unwrung laughed till the tears ran down; the reporters, in throes of laughter, set down disordered pothooks which would never in the world be decipherable; and a sleeping dog jumped up, scared out of its wits, and barked itself crazy at the turmoil. All manner of cries were scattered through the din: "We're getting rich—*two* Symbols of Incorruptibility!—without counting Billson!" "*Three!*—count Shadbelly in—we can't have too many!" "All right—Billson's elected!" "Alas, poor Wilson—victim of *two* thieves!"

A POWERFUL VOICE "Silence! The Chair's fishing up something more out of its pocket."

VOICES "Hurrah! Is it something fresh? Read it! read! read!"

THE CHAIR [*reading*] " '*The remark which I made,*' etc.: " '*You are far from being a bad man. Go,*' " etc. Signed, 'Gregory Yates.' "

TORNADO OF VOICES "Four Symbols!" " 'Rah for Yates!" "Fish again!"

The house was in a roaring humor now, and ready to get all the fun out of the occasion that might be in it. Several Nineteeners, looking pale and distressed, got up and began to work their way toward the aisles, but a score of shouts went up:

"The doors, the doors—close the doors; no Incorruptible shall leave this place! Sit down, everybody!"

The mandate was obeyed.

"Fish again! Read! read!"

The Chair fished again, and once more the familiar words began to fall from its lips—" *'You are far from being a bad man.'* "

"Name! name! What's his name?"

" 'L. Ingoldsby Sargent.' "

"Five elected! Pile up the Symbols! Go on, go on!"

" *'You are far from being a bad—'* "

"Name! name!"

" 'Nicholas Whitworth.' "

"Hooray! hooray! it's a symbolical day!"

Somebody wailed in, and began to sing this rhyme (leaving out "it's") to the lovely "Mikado" tune of "When a man's afraid, a beautiful maid—"; the audience joined in, with joy; then, just in time, somebody contributed another line—

And don't you this forget—

The house roared it out. A third line was at once furnished—

Corruptibles far from Hadleyburg are—

The house roared that one too. As the last note died, Jack Halliday's voice rose high and clear, freighted with a final line—

But the Symbols are here, you bet!

That was sung, with booming enthusiasm. Then the happy house started in at the beginning and sang the four lines through twice, with immense swing and dash, and finished up with a crashing three-times-three and a tiger for

"Hadleyburg the Incorruptible and all Symbols of it which we shall find worthy to receive the hall-mark to-night."

Then the shoutings at the Chair began again, all over the place:

"Go on! go on! Read! read some more! Read all you've got!"

"That's it—go on! We are winning eternal celebrity!"

A dozen men got up now and began to protest. They said that this farce was the work of some abandoned joker, and was an insult to the whole community. Without a doubt these signatures were all forgeries—

"Sit down! sit down! Shut up! You are confessing. We'll find *your* names in the lot."

"Mr. Chairman, how many of those envelopes have you got?"

The Chair counted.

"Together with those that have been already examined, there are nineteen."

A storm of derisive applause broke out.

"Perhaps they all contain the secret I move that you open them all and read every signature that is attached to a note of that sort—and read also the first eight words of the note."

"Second the motion!"

It was put and carried—uproariously. Then poor old Richards got up, and his wife rose and stood at his side. Her head was bent down, so that none might see that she was crying. Her husband gave her his arm, and so supporting her, he began to speak in a quavering voice:

"My friends, you have known us two—Mary and me—all our lives, and I think you have liked us and respected us—"

The Chair interrupted him:

"Allow me. It is quite true—that which you are saying, Mr. Richards: this town *does* know you two; it *does* like you; it *does* respect you; more—it honors you and *loves* you—"

Halliday's voice rang out:

"That's the hall-marked truth, too! If the Chair is right, let the house speak up and say it. Rise! Now, then—hip! hip! hip!—all together!"

The house rose in mass, faced toward the old couple eagerly, filled the air with a snow-storm of waving handkerchiefs, and delivered the cheers with all its affectionate heart.

The Chair then continued:

"What I was going to say is this: We know your good heart, Mr. Richards, but this is not a time for the exercise of charity toward offenders. [*Shouts of "Right! right!"*] I see your generous purpose in your face, but I cannot allow you to plead for these men—"

"But I was going to—"

"Please take your seat, Mr. Richards. We must examine the rest of these notes—simple fairness to the men who have already been exposed requires this. As soon as that has been done—I give you my word for this—you shall be heard."

MANY VOICES "Right!—the Chair is right—no interruption can be permitted at this stage! Go on!—the names! the names!—according to the terms of the motion!"

The old couple sat reluctantly down, and the husband whispered to the wife, "It is pitifully hard to have to wait; the shame will be greater than ever when they find we were only going to plead for *ourselves.*"

Straightway the jollity broke loose again with the reading of the names.

" '*You are far from being a bad man—*' Signature, 'Robert J. Titmarsh.'

" '*You are far from being a bad man—*' Signature, 'Eliphalet Weeks.'

" '*You are far from being a bad man—*' Signature, 'Oscar B. Wilder.' "

At this point the house lit upon the idea of taking the eight words out of the Chairman's hands. He was not unthankful for that. Thenceforward he held up each note in its turn, and waited. The house droned out the eight words in a massed and measured and musical deep volume of sound (with a daringly close resemblance to a well-known church chant)—" 'You are f-a-r from being a b-a-a-a-d man.' " Then the Chair said, "Signature, 'Archibald Wilcox.' " And so on, and so on, name after name, and everybody had an increasingly and gloriously good time except the wretched Nineteen. Now and then, when a particularly shining name was called, the house made the Chair wait while it chanted the whole of the test-remark from the beginning to the closing words, "And go to hell or Hadleyburg—try and make it the for-or-m-e-r!" and in these special cases they added a grand and agonized and imposing "A-a-a-a-*men!*"

The list dwindled, dwindled, dwindled, poor old Richards keeping tally of the count, wincing when a name resembling his own was pronounced, and waiting in miserable suspense for the time to come when it would be his humiliating privilege to rise with Mary and finish his plea, which he was intending to word thus: ". . . for until now we have never done any wrong thing, but have gone our humble way unreproached. We are very poor, we are old, and have no chick nor child to help us; we were sorely tempted, and we fell. It was my purpose when I got up before to make confession and beg that my name might not be read out in this public place, for it seemed to us that we could not bear it; but I was prevented. It was just; it was our place to suffer with the rest. It has been hard for us. It is the first time we have ever heard our name fall from any one's lips—sullied. Be merciful—for the sake of the better days; make our shame as light to bear as in your charity you can." At this point in his revery Mary nudged him, perceiving that his mind was absent. The house was chanting, "You are f-a-r," etc.

"Be ready," Mary whispered. "Your name comes now; he has read eighteen."

The chant ended.

"Next! next! next!" came volleying from all over the house.

Burgess put his hand into his pocket. The old couple, trembling, began to rise. Burgess fumbled a moment, then said,

"I find I have read them all."

Faint with joy and surprise, the couple sank into their seats, and Mary whispered:

"Oh, bless God, we are saved!—he has lost ours—I wouldn't give this for a hundred of those sacks!"

The house burst out with its "Mikado" travesty, and sang it three times with ever-increasing enthusiasm, rising to its feet when it reached for the third time the closing line—

But there's one Symbol left, you bet!

and finishing up with cheers and a tiger for "Hadleyburg purity and our eighteen immortal representatives of it."

Then Wingate, the saddler, got up and proposed cheers "for the cleanest man in town, the one solitary important citizen in it who didn't try to steal that money—Edward Richards."

They were given with great and moving heartiness; then somebody proposed that Richards be elected sole guardian and Symbol of the now Sacred Hadleyburg Tradition, with power and right to stand up and look the whole sarcastic world in the face.

Passed, by acclamation; then they sang the "Mikado" again, and ended it with:

And there's one Symbol left, you bet!

There was a pause; then—

A VOICE "Now, then, who's to get the sack?"

THE TANNER (*with bitter sarcasm*) "That's easy. The

money has to be divided among the eighteen Incorruptibles. They gave the suffering stranger twenty dollars apiece—and that remark—each in his turn—it took twenty-two minutes for the procession to move past. Staked the stranger—total contribution, $360. All they want is just the loan back—and interest—forty thousand dollars altogether."

MANY VOICES [*derisively*] "That's it! Divvy! divvy! Be kind to the poor—don't keep them waiting!"

THE CHAIR "Order! I now offer the stranger's remaining document. It says: 'If no claimant shall appear [*grand chorus of groans*] I desire that you open the sack and count out the money to the principal citizens of your town, they to take it in trust [*cries of "Oh! Oh! Oh!"*], and use it in such ways as to them shall seem best for the propagation and preservation of your community's noble reputation for incorruptible honesty [*more cries*]—a reputation to which their names and their efforts will add a new and far-reaching luster.' [*Enthusiastic outburst of sarcastic applause.*] That seems to be all. No—here is a postscript:

'P. S.—CITIZENS OF HADLEYBURG: *There is no test-remark—nobody made one.* [Great sensation.] *There wasn't any pauper stranger, nor any twenty-dollar contribution, nor any accompanying benediction and compliment—these are all inventions.* [General buzz and hum of astonishment and delight.] *Allow me to tell my story—it will take but a word or two. I passed through your town at a certain time, and received a deep offense which I had not earned. Any other man would have been content to kill one or two of you and call it square, but to me that would have been a trivial revenge, and inadequate; for the dead do not* suffer. *Besides, I could not kill you all—and, anyway, made as I am, even that would not have satisfied me. I wanted to damage every man in the place, and every woman—and not in their bodies or in their estate, but in their vanity—*

the place where feeble and foolish people are most vulnerable. So I disguised myself and came back and studied you. You were easy game. You had an old and lofty reputation for honesty, and naturally you were proud of it—it was your treasure of treasures, the very apple of your eye. As soon as I found out that you carefully and vigilantly kept yourselves and your children out of temptation, *I knew how to proceed. Why, you simple creatures, the weakest of all weak things is a virtue which has not been tested in the fire. I laid a plan, and gathered a list of names. My project was to corrupt Hadleyburg the Incorruptible. My idea was to make liars and thieves of nearly half a hundred smirchless men and women who had never in their lives uttered a lie or stolen a penny. I was afraid of Goodson. He was neither born nor reared in Hadleyburg. I was afraid that if I started to operate my scheme by getting my letter laid before you, you would say to yourselves, "Goodson is the only man among us who would give away twenty dollars to a poor devil"—and then you might not bite at my bait. But Heaven took Goodson; then I knew I was safe, and I set my trap and baited it. It may be that I shall not catch all the men to whom I mailed the pretended test secret, but I shall catch the most of them, if I know Hadleyburg nature.* [Voices. *"Right—he got every last one of them."*] *I believe they will even steal ostensible gamble-money, rather than miss, poor, tempted, and mistrained fellows. I am hoping to eternally and everlastingly squelch your vanity and give Hadleyburg a new renown—one that will* stick—*and spread far. If I have succeeded, open the sack and summon the Committee on Propagation and Preservation of the Hadleyburg Reputation.'*

A CYCLONE OF VOICES "Open it! Open it! The Eighteen to the front! Committee on Propagation of the Tradition! Forward—the Incorruptibles!"

The Chair ripped the sack wide, and gathered up a handful of bright, broad, yellow coins, shook them together, then examined them—

"Friends, they are only gilded disks of lead!"

There was a crashing outbreak of delight over this news, and when the noise had subsided, the tanner called out:

"By right of apparent seniority in this business, Mr. Wilson is Chairman of the Committee on Propagation of the Tradition. I suggest that he step forward on behalf of his pals, and receive in trust the money."

A HUNDRED VOICES "Wilson! Wilson! Wilson! Speech! Speech!"

WILSON [*in a voice trembling with anger*] "You will allow me to say, and without apologies for my language, *damn* the money!"

A VOICE "Oh, and him a Baptist!"

A VOICE "Seventeen Symbols left! Step up, gentlemen, and assume your trust!"

There was a pause—no response.

THE SADDLER "Mr. Chairman, we've got *one* clean man left, anyway, out of the late aristocracy; and he needs money, and deserves it. I move that you appoint Jack Halliday to get up there and auction off that sack of gilt twenty-dollar pieces, and give the result to the right man—the man whom Hadleyburg delights to honor—Edward Richards."

This was received with great enthusiasm, the dog taking a hand again; the saddler started the bids at a dollar, the Brixton folk and Barnum's representative fought hard for it, the people cheered every jump that the bids made, the excitement climbed moment by moment higher and higher, the bidders got on their mettle and grew steadily more and more daring, more and more determined, the jumps went from a dollar up to five, then to ten, then to twenty, then fifty, then to a hundred, then—

At the beginning of the auction Richards whispered in distress to his wife: "O Mary, can we allow it? It—it—you see, it is an honor-reward, a testimonial to purity of character, and—and—can we allow it? Hadn't I better get up and—O Mary, what ought we to do?—what do you think we—[*Halliday's voice. "Fifteen I'm bid!—fifteen for the sack!—twenty!—ah, thanks!—thirty—thanks again! Thirty, thirty, thirty!—do I heard forty?—forty it is! Keep the ball rolling, gentlemen, keep it rolling!—fifty! thanks, noble Roman! going at fifty, fifty, fifty!—seventy!—ninety!—splendid!—a hundred!—pile it up, pile it up!—hundred and twenty—forty!—just in time!—hundred and fifty!—* TWO *hundred!—superb!* Do I *hear two h—thanks!—two hundred and fifty!—*"]

"It is another temptation, Edward—I'm all in a tremble—but, oh, we've escaped *one* temptation, and that ought to warn us to— [*"Six did I hear?—thanks!—six-fifty, six-f—* SEVEN *hundred!*"] And yet, Edward, when you think—nobody susp— [*"Eight hundred dollars!—hurrah!—make it nine!—Mr. Parsons, did I hear you say—thanks—nine!—this noble sack of virgin lead going at only nine hundred dollars, gilding and all—come! do I hear—a thousand!—gratefully yours!—did some one say eleven?—a sack which is going to be the most celebrated in the whole Uni—*] O Edward" (beginning to sob), "we are *so* poor!—but—but—do as you think best—do as you think best."

Edward fell—that is, he sat still; sat with a conscience which was not satisfied, but which was overpowered by circumstances.

Meantime a stranger, who looked like an amateur detective gotten up as an impossible English earl, had been watching the evening's proceedings with manifest interest, and with a contented expression in his face; and he had been privately commenting to himself. He was now soliloquizing somewhat like this: "None of the Eighteen are bidding; that is not satisfactory; I must change that—the dramatic unities require it; they must buy the sack they tried to steal; they must pay a heavy price, too—

some of them are rich. And another thing, when I make a mistake in Hadleyburg nature the man that puts that error upon me is entitled to a high honorarium, and some one must pay it. This poor old Richards has brought my judgment to shame; he is an honest man:—I don't understand it, but I acknowledge it. Yes, he saw my deuces *and* with a straight flush, and by rights the pot is his. And it shall be a jack-pot, too, if I can manage it. He disappointed me, but let that pass."

He was watching the bidding. At a thousand, the market broke; the prices tumbled swiftly. He waited—and still watched. One competitor dropped out; then another, and another. He put in a bid or two, now. When the bids had sunk to ten dollars, he added a five; some one raised him a three; he waited a moment, then flung in a fifty-dollar jump, and the sack was his—at $1,282. The house broke out in cheers—then stopped; for he was on his feet, and had lifted his hand. He began to speak.

"I desire to say a word, and ask a favor. I am a speculator in rarities, and I have dealings with persons interested in numismatics all over the world. I can make a profit on this purchase, just as it stands; but there is a way, if I can get your approval, whereby I can make every one of these leaden twenty-dollar pieces worth its face in gold, and perhaps more. Grant me that approval, and I will give part of my gains to your Mr. Richards, whose invulnerable probity you have so justly and so cordially recognized to-night; his share shall be ten thousand dollars, and I will hand him the money to-morrow. [*Great applause from the house.* But the "invulnerable probity" made the Richardses blush prettily; however, it went for modesty, and did no harm.] If you will pass my proposition by a good majority—I would like a two-thirds vote—I will regard that as the town's consent, and that is all I ask. Rarities are always helped by any device which will rouse curiosity and compel remark. Now if I may have your permission to stamp upon the faces of each of these ostensible coins the names of the eighteen gentlemen who—"

Nine-tenths of the audience were on their feet in a moment—dog and all—and the proposition was carried with a whirlwind of approving applause and laughter.

They sat down, and all the Symbols except "Dr." Clay Harkness got up, violently protesting against the proposed outrage, and threatening to—

"I beg you not to threaten me," said the stranger, calmly. "I know my legal rights, and am not accustomed to being frightened at bluster." [*Applause.*] He sat down. "Dr." Harkness saw an opportunity here. He was one of the two very rich men of the place, and Pinkerton was the other. Harkness was proprietor of a mint; that is to say, a popular patent medicine. He was running for the legislature on one ticket, and Pinkerton on the other. It was a close race and a hot one, and getting hotter every day. Both had strong appetities for money; each had bought a great tract of land, with a purpose; there was going to be a new railway, and each wanted to be in the legislature and help locate the route to his own advantage; a single vote might make the decision, and with it two or three fortunes. The stake was large, and Harkness was a daring speculator. He was sitting close to the stranger. He leaned over while one or another of the other Symbols was entertaining the house with protests and appeals, and asked, in a whisper, "What is your price for the sack?"

"Forty thousand dollars."

"I'll give you twenty."

"No."

"Twenty-five."

"No."

"Say thirty."

"The price is forty thousand dollars; not a penny less."

"All right, I'll give it. I will come to the hotel at ten in the morning. I don't want it known: will see you privately."

"Very good." Then the stranger got up and said to the house:

"I find it late. The speeches of these gentlemen are not without merit, not without interest, not without grace; yet if I may be excused I will take my leave. I thank you for the great favor which you have shown me in granting my petition. I ask the Chair to keep the sack for me until tomorrow, and to hand these three five-hundred-dollar notes to Mr. Richards." They were passed up to the Chair. "At nine I will call for the sack, and at eleven will deliver the rest of the ten thousand to Mr. Richards in person, at his home. Good night."

Then he slipped out, and left the audience making a vast noise which was composed of a mixture of cheers, the "Mikado" song, dog-disapproval, and the chant, "You are f-a-r from being a b-a-a-d man—a-a-a-a-men!"

4

At home the Richardses had to endure congratulations and compliments until midnight. Then they were left to themselves. They looked a little sad, and they sat silent and thinking. Finally Mary sighed and said,

"Do you think we are to blame, Edward—*much* to blame?" and her eyes wandered to the accusing triplet of big bank-notes lying on the table, where the congratulators had been gloating over them and reverently fingering them. Edward did not answer at once; then he brought out a sigh and said, hesitatingly:

"We—we couldn't help it, Mary. It—well, it was ordered. *All* things are."

Mary glanced up and looked at him steadily, but he didn't return the look. Presently she said:

"I thought congratulations and praises always tasted good. But—it seems to me, now—Edward?"

"Well?"

"Are you going to stay in the bank?"

"N-no."

"Resign?"

"In the morning—by note."

"It does seem best."

Richards bowed his head in his hands and muttered:

"Before, I was not afraid to let oceans of people's money pour through my hands, but—Mary, I am so tired, so tired—"

"We will go to bed."

At nine in the morning the stranger called for the sack and took it to the hotel in a cab. At ten Harkness had a talk with him privately. The stranger asked for and got five checks on a metropolitan bank—drawn to "Bearer"—four for $1,500 each, and one for $34,000. He put one of the former in his pocketbook, and the remainder, representing $38,500, he put in an envelope, and with these he added a note, which he wrote after Harkness was gone. At eleven he called at the Richards house and knocked. Mrs. Richards peeped through the shutters, then went and received the envelope, and the stranger disappeared without a word. She came back flushed and a little unsteady on her legs, and gasped out:

"I am sure I recognized him! Last night it seemed to me that maybe I had seen him somewhere before."

"He is the man that brought the sack here?"

"I am almost sure of it."

"Then he is the ostensible Stephenson, too, and sold every important citizen in this town with his bogus secret. Now if he has sent checks instead of money, we are sold, too, after we thought we had escaped. I was beginning to feel fairly comfortable once more, after my night's rest, but the look of that envelope makes me sick. It isn't fat enough; $8,500 in even the largest bank-notes makes more bulk than that."

"Edward, why do you object to checks?"

"Checks signed by Stephenson! I am resigned to take the $8,500 if it could come in bank-notes—for it does seem that it was so ordered, Mary—but I have never had much courage, and I have not the pluck to try to market a check signed with that disastrous name. It would be a trap. That man tried to catch me; we escaped somehow or other; and now he is trying a new way. If it is checks—"

"Oh, Edward, it is *too* bad!" and she held up the checks and began to cry.

"Put them in the fire! quick! we mustn't be tempted. It is a trick to make the world laugh at *us*, along with the rest, and— Give them to *me*, since you can't do it!" He snatched them and tried to hold his grip till he could get to the stove; but he was human, he was a cashier, and he stopped a moment to make sure of the signature. Then he came near to fainting.

"Fan me, Mary, fan me! They are the same as gold!"

"Oh, how lovely, Edward! Why?"

"Signed by Harkness. What can the mystery of that be, Mary?"

"Edward, do you think—"

"Look here—look at this! Fifteen—fifteen—fifteen—thirty-four. Thirty-eight thousand five hundred! Mary, the sack isn't worth twelve dollars, and Harkness—apparently—has paid about par for it."

"And does it all come to us, do you think—instead of the ten thousand?"

"Why, it looks like it. And the checks are made to 'Bearer,' too."

"Is that good, Edward? What is it for?"

"A hint to collect them at some distant bank, I reckon. Perhaps Harkness doesn't want the matter known. What is that—a note?"

"Yes. It was with the checks."

It was in the "Stephenson" handwriting, but there was no signature. It said:

> *"I am a disappointed man. Your honesty is beyond the reach of temptation. I had a different idea about it, but I wronged you in that, and I beg pardon, and do it sincerely. I honor you—and that is sincere too. This town is not worthy to kiss the hem of your garment. Dear sir, I made a square bet with myself that there were nineteen debauchable men in your self-righteous community. I have lost. Take the whole pot, you are entitled to it."*

Richards drew a deep sigh, and said:

"It seems written with fire—it burns so. Mary—I am miserable again."

"I, too. Ah, dear, I wish—"

"To think, Mary—he *believes* in me."

"Oh, don't, Edward—I can't bear it."

"If those beautiful words were deserved, Mary—and God knows I believed I deserved them once—I think I could give the forty thousand dollars for them. And I would put that paper away, as representing more than gold and jewels, and keep it always. But now— We could not live in the shadow of its accusing presence, Mary."

He put it in the fire.

A messenger arrived and delivered an envelope.

Richards took from it a note and read it; it was from Burgess.

> *"You saved me, in a difficult time. I saved you last night. It was at cost of a lie, but I made the sacrifice freely, and out of a grateful heart. None in this village knows so well as I know how brave and good and noble you are. At bottom you cannot respect me,*

knowing as you do of that matter of which I am accused, and by the general voice condemned; but I beg that you will at least believe that I am a grateful man; it will help me to bear my burden."

[*Signed*] BURGESS

"Saved, once more. And on such terms!" He put the note in the fire. "I—I wish I were dead, Mary, I wish I were out of it all."

"Oh, these are bitter, bitter days, Edward. The stabs, through their very generosity, are so deep—and they come so fast!"

Three days before the election each of two thousand voters suddenly found himself in possession of a prized memento—one of the renowned bogus double-eagles. Around one of its faces was stamped these words: "THE REMARK I MADE TO THE POOR STRANGER WAS—" Around the other face was stamped these: "GO, AND REFORM. [SIGNED] PINKERTON." Thus the entire remaining refuse of the renowned joke was emptied upon a single head, and with calamitous effect. It revived the recent vast laugh and concentrated it upon Pinkerton; and Harkness's election was a walkover.

Within twenty-four hours after the Richardses had received their checks their consciences were quieting down, discouraged; the old couple were learning to reconcile themselves to the sin which they had committed. But they were to learn, now, that a sin takes on new and real terrors when there seems a chance that it is going to be found out. This gives it a fresh and most substantial and important aspect. At church the morning sermon was of the usual pattern; it was the same old things said in the same old way; they had heard them a thousand times and found them innocuous, next to meaningless, and easy to sleep under; but now it was different: the sermon seemed to bristle with accusations; it seemed aimed straight and specially at people who were concealing deadly sins. After church they got away from the mob of congratulators as soon as they could, and hurried homeward, chilled to the bone at they did not know what—vague, shadowy, indefinite fears. And by chance they caught a glimpse of Mr. Burgess as he turned a corner. He paid no attention to their nod of recognition! He hadn't seen it; but they did not know that. What could his conduct mean? It might mean—it might mean—oh, a dozen dreadful things. Was it possible that he knew that Richards could have cleared him of guilt in that bygone time, and had been silently waiting for a chance to even up accounts? At home, in their distress they got to imagining that their servant might have been in the next room listening when Richards revealed the secret to his wife that he knew of Burgess's innocence; next, Richards began to imagine that he had heard the swish of a gown in there at that time; next, he was sure he *had* heard it. They would call Sarah in, on a pretext, and watch her face: if she had been betraying them to Mr. Burgess, it would show in her manner. They asked her some questions—questions which were so random and incoherent and seemingly purposeless that the girl felt sure that the old people's minds had been affected by their sudden good fortune; the sharp and watchful gaze which they bent upon her frightened her, and that completed the business. She blushed, she became nervous and confused, and to the old people these were plain signs of guilt—guilt of some fearful sort or other—without doubt she was a spy and a traitor. When they were alone again they began to piece many unrelated things together and get horrible results out of the combination. When things had got about to the worst, Richards was delivered of a sudden gasp, and his wife asked:

"Oh, what is it?—what is it?"

"The note—Burgess's note! Its language was sarcastic, I see it now." He quoted: " 'At bottom you cannot respect me, *knowing,* as you do, of *that matter* of which I am accused'—oh, it is perfectly plain, now, God help me! He knows that I know! You see the ingenuity of the phrasing. It was a trap—and like a fool, I walked into it. And Mary—?"

"Oh, it is dreadful—I know what you are going to say—he didn't return your transcript of the pretended test-remark."

"No—kept it to destroy us with. Mary, he has exposed us to some already. I know it—I know it well. I saw it in a dozen faces after church. Ah, he wouldn't answer our nod of recognition—*he* knew what he had been doing!"

In the night the doctor was called. The news went around in the morning that the old couple were rather seriously ill—prostrated by the exhausting excitement growing out of their great windfall, the congratulations, and the late hours, the doctor said. The town was sincerely distressed; for these old people were about all it had left to be proud of, now.

Two days later the news was worse. The old couple were delirious, and were doing strange things. By witness of the nurses, Richards had exhibited checks—for $8,500? No—for an amazing sum—$38,500! What could be the explanation of this gigantic piece of luck?

The following day the nurses had more news—and wonderful. They had concluded to hide the checks, lest harm come to them; but when they searched they were gone from under the patient's pillow—vanished away. The patient said:

"Let the pillow alone; what do you want?"

"We thought it best that the checks—"

"You will never see them again—they are destroyed. They came from Satan. I saw the hell-brand on them, and I knew they were sent to betray me to sin." Then he fell to gabbling strange and dreadful things which were not clearly understandable, and which the doctor admonished them to keep to themselves.

Richards was right; the checks were never seen again.

A nurse must have talked in her sleep, for within two days the forbidden gabblings were the property of the town; and they were of a surprising sort. They seemed to indicate that Richards had been a claimant for the sack himself, and that Burgess had concealed that fact and then maliciously betrayed it.

Burgess was taxed with this and stoutly denied it. And he said it was not fair to attach weight to the chatter of a sick old man who was out of his mind. Still, suspicion was in the air, and there was much talk.

After a day or two it was reported that Mrs. Richards's delirious deliveries were getting to be duplicates of her husband's. Suspicion flamed up into conviction, now, and the town's pride in the purity of its one undiscredited important citizen began to dim down and flicker toward extinction.

Six days passed, then came more news. The old couple were dying. Richards's mind cleared in his latest hour, and sent for Burgess. Burgess said:

"Let the room be cleared. I think he wishes to say something in privacy."

"No!" said Richards: "I want witnesses. I want you all to hear my confession, so that I may die a man, and not a dog. I was clean—artificially—like the rest; and like the rest I fell when temptation came. I signed a lie, and claimed the miserable sack. Mr. Burgess remembered that I had done him a service, and in gratitude (and ignorance) he suppressed my claim and saved me. You know the thing that was charged against Burgess years ago. My testimony, and mine alone, could have cleared him, and I was a coward, and left him to suffer disgrace—"

"No—no—Mr. Richards, you—"

"My servant betrayed my secret to him—"

"No one has betrayed anything to me—"

—"and then he did a natural and justifiable thing, he

repented of the saving kindness which he had done me, and he *exposed* me—as I deserved—"

"Never!—I make oath—"

"Out of my heart I forgive him."

Burgess's impassioned protestations fell upon deaf ears; the dying man passed away without knowing that once more he had done poor Burgess a wrong. The old wife died that night.

The last of the sacred Nineteen had fallen a prey to the fiendish sack; the town was stripped of the last rag of its ancient glory. Its mourning was not showy, but it was deep.

By act of the Legislature—upon prayer and petition—Hadleyburg was allowed to change its name to (never mind what—I will not give it away), and leave one word out of the motto that for many generations had graced the town's official seal.

It is an honest town once more, and the man will have to rise early that catches it napping again.

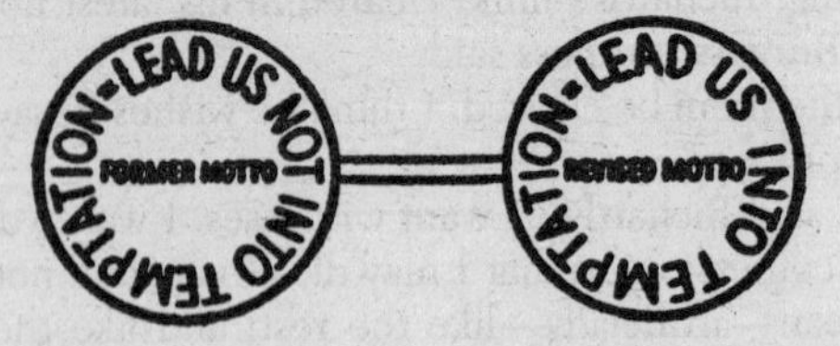

1899

The Death Disk*

1

This was in Oliver Cromwell's[1] time. Colonel Mayfair was the youngest officer of his rank in the armies of the Commonwealth, he being but thirty years old. But young as he was, he was a veteran soldier, and tanned and war-worn, for he had begun his military life at seventeen; he had fought in many battles, and had won his high place in the service and in the admiration of men, step by step, by valor in the field. But he was in deep trouble now; a shadow had fallen upon his fortunes.

The winter evening was come, and outside were storm and darkness; within, a melancholy silence; for the Colonel and his young wife had talked their sorrow out, had read the evening chapter and prayed the evening prayer, and there was nothing more to do but sit hand in hand and gaze into the fire, and think—and wait. They would not have to wait long; they knew that, and the wife shuddered at the thought.

They had one child—Abby, seven years old, their idol.

---

*The text for this story is a touching incident mentioned in Carlyle's *Letters and Speeches of Oliver Cromwell.* M.T.

She would be coming presently for the good-night kiss, and the Colonel spoke now, and said:

"Dry away the tears and let us seem happy, for her sake. We must forget, for the time, that which is to happen."

"I will. I will shut them up in my heart, which is breaking."

"And we will accept what is appointed for us, and bear it in patience, as knowing that whatsoever He doeth is done in righteousness and meant in kindness—"

"Saying, His will be done. Yes, I can say it with all my mind and soul—I would I could say it with my heart. Oh, if I could! if this dear hand which I press and kiss for the last time—"

" 'Sh! sweetheart, she is coming!"

A curly-headed little figure in nightclothes glided in at the door and ran to the father, and was gathered to his breast and fervently kissed once, twice, three times.

"Why, papa, you mustn't kiss me like that: you rumple my hair."

"Oh, I am so sorry—so sorry: do you forgive me, dear?"

"Why, of course, papa. But *are* you sorry?—not pretending, but real, right down sorry?"

"Well, you can judge for youself, Abby," and he covered his face with his hands and made believe to sob. The child was filled with remorse to see this tragic thing which she had caused, and she began to cry herself, and to tug at the hands, and say:

"Oh, don't, papa, please don't cry; Abby didn't mean it; Abby wouldn't ever do it again. Please, papa!" Tugging and straining to separate the fingers, she got a fleeting glimpse of an eye behind them, and cried out: "Why, you naughty papa, you are not crying at all! You are only fooling! And Abby is going to mamma, now: you don't treat Abby right."

She was for climbing down, but her father wound his arms about her and said: "No, stay with me, dear: papa *was* naughty, and confesses it, and is sorry—there, let him kiss the tears away—and he begs Abby's forgiveness, and will do anything Abby says he must do, for a punishment; they're all kissed away now, and not a curl rumpled—and whatever Abby commands—"

And so it was made up; and all in a moment the sunshine was back again and burning brightly in the child's face, and she was patting her father's cheeks and naming the penalty—"A story! a story!"

Hark!

The elders stopped breathing, and listened. Footsteps! faintly caught between the gusts of wind. They came nearer, nearer—louder, louder—then passed by and faded away. The elders drew deep breaths of relief, and the papa said: "A story, is it? A gay one?"

"No, papa: a dreadful one."

Papa wanted to shift to the gay kind, but the child stood by her rights—as per agreement, she was to have anything she commanded. He was a good Puritan soldier and had passed his word—he saw that he must make it good. She said:

"Papa, we mustn't always have gay ones. Nurse says people don't always have gay times. Is that true, papa? She *says* so."

The mamma sighed, and her thoughts drifted to her troubles again. The papa said, gently: "It is true, dear. Troubles have to come; it is a pity, but it is true."

"Oh, then tell a story about them, papa—a dreadful one, so that we'll shiver, and feel just as if it was *us*. Mamma, you snuggle up close, and hold one of Abby's hands, so that if it's too dreadful it'll be easier for us to bear it if we are all snuggled up together, you know. Now you can begin, papa."

"Well, once there were three Colonels—"

"Oh, goody! *I* know Colonels, just as easy! It's because you are one, and I know the clothes. Go on, papa."

"And in a battle they had committed a breach of discipline."

The large words struck the child's ear pleasantly, and she looked up, full of wonder and interest, and said:

"Is it something good to eat, papa?"

The parents almost smiled, and the father answered:

"No, quite another matter, dear. They exceeded their orders."

"Is *that* someth—"

"No; it's as uneatable as the other. They were ordered to feign an attack on a strong position in a losing fight, in order to draw the enemy about and give the Commonwealth's forces a chance to retreat; but in their enthusiasm they overstepped their orders, for they turned the feint into a fact, and carried the position by storm, and won the day and the battle. The Lord General was very angry at their disobedience, and praised them highly, and ordered them to London to be tried for their lives."

"Is it the great General Cromwell, papa?"

"Yes."

"Oh, I've seen *him*, papa! and when he goes by our house so grand on his big horse, with the soldiers, he looks so—so—well, I don't know just how, only he looks as if he isn't satisfied, and you can see the people are afraid of him; but *I'm* not afraid of him, because he didn't look like that at me."

"Oh, you dear prattler! Well, the Colonels came prisoners to London, and were put upon their honor, and allowed to go and see their families for the last—"

Hark!

They listened. Footsteps again; but again they passed by. The mamma leaned her head upon her husband's shoulder to hide her paleness.

"They arrived this morning."

The child's eyes opened wide.

"Why, papa! is it a *true* story?"

"Yes, dear."

"Oh, how good! Oh, it's ever so much better! Go on, papa. Why, mamma!—*dear* mamma, are you crying?"

"Never mind me, dear—I was thinking of the—of the—the poor families."

"But *don't* cry, mamma: it'll all come out right—you'll see; stories always do. Go on, papa, to where they lived happy ever after; then she won't cry any more. You'll see, mamma. Go on, papa."

"First, they took them to the Tower before they let them go home."

"Oh, *I* know the Tower! We can see it from here. Go on, papa."

"I am going on as well as I can, in the circumstances. In the Tower the military court tried them for an hour, and found them guilty, and condemned them to be shot."

"*Killed*, papa?"

"Yes."

"Oh, how naughty! *Dear* mamma, you are crying again. Don't mamma; it'll soon come to the good place—you'll see. Hurry, papa, for mama's sake; you don't go fast enough."

"I know I don't, but I suppose it is because I stop so much to reflect."

"But you mustn't *do* it, papa; you must go right on."

"Very well, then. The three Colonels—"

"Do you know them, papa?"

"Yes, dear."

"Oh, I wish I did! I love Colonels. Would they let me kiss them, do you think?" The Colonel's voice was a little unsteady when he answered:

"*One* of them would, my darling! There—kiss me for him."

"There, papa—and these two are for the others. I think they would let me kiss them, papa; for I would say, 'My papa is a Colonel, too, and brave, and he would do what you did; so it *can't* be wrong, no matter what those people say, and you needn't be the least bit ashamed'; then they would let me—wouldn't they, papa?"

"God knows they would, child!"

"Mamma!—oh, mamma, you mustn't. He's soon coming to the happy place; go on, papa."

"Then, some were sorry—they all were; that military court, I mean; and they went to the Lord General, and said they had done their duty—for it *was* their duty, you know—and now they begged that two of the Colonels might be spared, and only the other one shot. One would be sufficient for an example for the army, they thought. But the Lord General was very stern, and rebuked them forasmuch as, having done *their* duty and cleared their consciences, they would beguile him to do less, and so smirch his soldierly honor. But they answered that they were asking nothing of him that they would not do themselves if they stood in his great place and held in their hands the noble prerogative of mercy. That struck him, and he paused and stood thinking, some of the sternness passing out of his face. Presently he bid them wait, and he retired to his closet to seek counsel of God in prayer; and when he came again, he said: 'They shall cast lots. That shall decide it, and two of them shall live.' "

"And did they, papa, did they? And which one is to die—ah, that poor man!"

"No. They refused."

"They wouldn't do it, papa?"

"No."

"Why?"

"They said that the one that got the fatal bean would be sentencing himself to death by his own voluntary act, and it would be but suicide, call it by what name one might. They said they were Christians, and the Bible forbade men to take their own lives. They sent back that word, and said they were ready—let the court's sentence be carried into effect."

"What does that mean, papa?"

"They—they will all be shot."

Hark!

The wind? No. Tramp—tramp—tramp—r-r-r-umble-dum-dum, r-r-rumble-dumdum—

"Open—in the Lord General's name!"

"Oh, goody, papa, it's the soldiers!—I love the soldiers! Let *me* let them in, papa, let *me!*"

She jumped down, and scampered to the door and pulled it open, crying joyously: "Come in! come in! Here they are, papa! Grenadiers! *I* know the Grenadiers!"

The file marched in and straightened up in line at shoulder arms; its officer saluted, the doomed Colonel standing erect and returning the courtesy, the soldier wife standing at his side, white, and with features drawn with inward pain, but giving no other sign of her misery, the child gazing on the show with dancing eyes. . . .

One long embrace, of father, mother, and child; then the order, "To the Tower—forward!" Then the Colonel marched forth from the house with military step and bearing, the file following; then the door closed.

"Oh, mamma, didn't it come out beautiful! I *told* you it would; and they're going to the Tower, and he'll *see* them! He—"

"Oh, come to my arms, you poor innocent thing!" . . .

2

The next morning the stricken mother was not able to leave her bed; doctors and nurses were watching by her, and whispering together now and then; Abby could not be allowed in the room; she was told to run and play—mamma was very ill. The child, muffled in winter wraps, went out and played in the street awhile; then it struck her as strange, and also wrong, that her papa should be allowed to stay at the Tower in ignorance at such a time as this. This must be remedied; she would attend to it in person.

An hour later the military court were ushered into the presence of the Lord General. He stood grim and erect, with his knuckles resting upon the table, and indicated that he was ready to listen. The spokesman said: "We have urged them to reconsider; we have implored them: but they persist. They will not cast lots. They are willing to die, but not to defile their religion."

The Protector's face darkened, but he said nothing. He remained a time in thought, then he said: "They shall not all die; the lots shall be cast *for* them." Gratitude shone in the faces of the court. "Send for them. Place them in that room there. Stand them side by side with their faces to the wall and their wrists crossed behind them. Let me have notice when they are there."

When he was alone he sat down, and presently gave this order to an attendant: "Go, bring me the first little child that passes by."

The man was hardly out at the door before he was back again—leading Abby by the hand, her garments lightly powdered with snow. She went straight to the Head of the State, that formidable personage at the mention of whose name the principalities and powers of the earth trembled, and climbed up in his lap, and said:

I know *you*, sir: you are the Lord General; I have seen you; I have seen you when you went by my house. Everybody was afraid; but *I* wasn't afraid, because you didn't look cross at *me;* you remember, don't you? I had on my red frock—the one with the blue things on it down the front. Don't you remember that?"

A smile softened the austere lines of the Protector's face, and he began to struggle diplomatically with his answer:

"Why, let me see—I—"

"I was standing right by the house—*my* house, you know."

"Well, you dear little thing, I ought to be ashamed, but you know—"

The child interrupted, reproachfully.

"Now you *don't* remember it. Why, I didn't forget *you.*"

"Now, I *am* ashamed: but I will never forget you again, dear; you have my word for it. You will forgive me now, won't you, and be good friends with me, always and forever?"

"Yes, indeed I will, though I don't know how you came to forget it; you must be very forgetful: but I am too, sometimes. I can forgive you without any trouble, for I think you *mean* to be good and do right, and I think you are just as kind—but you must snuggle me better, the way papa does—it's cold."

"You shall be snuggled to your heart's content, little new friend of mine, always to be *old* friend of mine hereafter, isn't it? You mind me of my little girl—not little any more, now—but she was dear, and sweet, and daintily made, like you. And she had your charm, little witch—your all-conquering sweet confidence in friend and stranger alike, that wins to willing slavery any upon whom its precious compliment falls. She used to lie in my arms, just as you are doing now; and charm the weariness and care out of my heart and give it peace, just as you are doing now; and we were comrades, and equals, and playfellows together. Ages ago it was, since that pleasant heaven faded away and vanished, and you have brought it back again;—take a burdened man's blessing for it, you tiny creature, who are carrying the weight of England while I rest!"

"Did you love her very, very, *very* much?"

"Ah, you shall judge by this: she commanded and I obeyed!"

"I think you are lovely! Will you kiss me?"

"Thankfully—and hold it a privilege, too. There—this one is for you; and there—this one is for her. You made it a request; and you could have made it a command, for you are representing her, and what you command I must obey."

The child clapped her hands with delight at the idea of this grand promotion—then her ear caught an approaching sound: the measured tramp of marching men.

"Soldiers!—soldiers, Lord General! Abby wants to see them!"

"You shall, dear; but wait a moment, I have a commission for you."

An officer entered and bowed low, saying, "They are come, your Highness," bowed again, and retired.

The Head of the Nation gave Abby three little disks of sealing-wax: two white, and one a ruddy red—for this one's mission was to deliver death to the Colonel who should get it.

"Oh, what a lovely red one! Are they for me?"

"No, dear; they are for others. Lift the corner of that curtain, there, which hides an open door; pass through, and you will see three men standing in a row, with their backs toward you and their hands behind their backs—so—each with one hand open, like a cup. Into each of the open hands drop one of those things, then come back to me."

Abby disappeared behind the curtain, and the Protector was alone. He said, reverently: "Of a surety that good thought came to me in my perplexity from Him who is an ever-present help to them that are in doubt and seek His aid. He knoweth where the choice should fall, and has sent His sinless messenger to do His will. Another would err, but He cannot err. Wonderful are His ways, and wise—blessed be His holy Name!"

The small fairy dropped the curtain behind her and stood for a moment conning with alert curiosity the appointments of the chamber of doom, and the rigid figures of the soldiery and the prisoners; then her face lighted merrily, and she said to herself: "Why, one of them is papa! I know his back. He shall have the prettiest one!" She tripped gaily forward and dropped the disks into the open hands, then peeped around under her father's arm and lifted her laughing face and cried out:

"Papa! papa! look what you've got. *I* gave it to you!"

He glanced at the fatal gift, then sunk to his knees and gathered his innocent little executioner to his breast in an agony of love and pity. Soldiers, officers, released prisoners, all stood paralyzed, for a moment, at the vastness of this tragedy, then the pitiful scene smote their hearts, their eyes filled, and they wept unashamed. There was deep and reverent silence during some minutes, then the officer of the guard moved reluctantly forward and touched his prisoner on the shoulder, saying, gently:

"It grieves me, sir, but my duty commands."

"Commands what?" said the child.

"I must take him away. I am so sorry."

"Take him away? Where?"

"To—to—God help me!—to another part of the fortress."

"Indeed you can't. My mamma is sick, and I am going to take him home." She released herself and climbed upon her father's back and put her arms around his neck. "Now Abby's ready, papa—come along."

"My poor child, I can't. I must go with them."

The child jumped to the ground and looked about her, wondering. Then she ran and stood before the officer and stamped her small foot indignantly and cried out:

"I told you my mamma is sick, and you might have listened. Let him go—you *must!*"

"Oh, poor child, would God I could, but indeed I must take him away. Attention, guard! . . . fall in! . . . shoulder arms!" . . .

Abby was gone—like a flash of light. In a moment she was back, dragging the Lord Protector by the hand. At this formidable apparition all present straightened up, the officers saluting and the soldiers presenting arms.

"Stop them, sir! My mamma is sick and wants my papa, and I *told* them so, but they never even listened to me, and are taking him away."

The Lord General stood as one dazed.

"*Your* papa, child? Is he your papa?"

"Why, of course—he was *always* it. Would I give the pretty red one to any other, when I love him so? No!"

A shocked expression rose in the Protector's face, and he said:

"Ah, God help me! through Satan's wiles I have done the cruelest thing that ever man did—and there is no help, no help! What can I do?"

Abby cried out, distressed and impatient: "Why you can make them let him go," and she began to sob. "Tell them to do it! You told me to command, and now the very first time I tell you to do a thing you don't do it!"

A tender light dawned in the rugged old face, and the Lord General laid his hand upon the small tyrant's head and said: "God be thanked for the saving accident of that unthinking promise; and you, inspired by Him, for reminding me of my forgotten pledge, O incomparable child! Officer, obey her command—she speaks by my mouth. The prisoner is pardoned; set him free!"

1901

Two Little Tales

FIRST STORY: THE MAN WITH A MESSAGE FOR THE DIRECTOR-GENERAL

SOME DAYS ago, in this second month of 1900, a friend made an afternoon call upon me here in London. We are of that age when men who are smoking away their times in chat do not talk quite so much about the pleasantnesses of life as about its exasperations. By and by this friend began to abuse the War Office. It appeared that he had a friend who had been inventing something which could be made very useful to the soldiers in South Africa. It was a light and very cheap and durable boot, which would remain dry in wet weather, and keep its shape and firmness. The inventor wanted to get the government's attention called to it, but he was an unknown man and knew the great officials would pay no heed to a message from him.

"This shows that he was an ass—like the rest of us," I said, interrupting. "Go on."

"But why have you said that? The man spoke the truth."

"The man spoke a lie. Go on."

"I will *prove* that he—"

"You can't prove anything of the kind. I am very old and very wise. You must not argue with me: it is irreverent and offensive. Go on."

"Very well. But you will presently see. I am not unknown, yet even *I* was not able to get the man's message to the Director-General of the Shoe-Leather Department."

"This is another lie. Pray go on."

"But I assure you on my honor that I failed."

"Oh, certainly. I knew *that*. You didn't need to tell me."

"Then where is the lie?"

"It is in your intimation that you were *not able* to get the Director-General's immediate attention to the man's message. It is a lie, because you *could* have gotten his immediate attention to it."

"I tell you I couldn't. In three months I haven't accomplished it."

"Certainly. Of course. I could know that without your telling me. You *could* have gotten his immediate attention if you had gone at it in a sane way; and so could the other man."

"I *did* go at it in a sane way."

"You didn't."

"How do *you* know? What do you know about the circumstances?"

"Nothing at all. But you didn't go at in a sane way. That much I know to a certainty."

"How can you know it, when you don't know what method I used?"

"I know by the result. The result is perfect proof. You went at it in an insane way. I am very old and very w—"

"Oh, yes, I know. But will you let me tell you *how* I proceeded? I think that will settle whether it was insanity or not."

"No; that has already been settled. But go on, since you so desire to expose yourself. I am very o—"

"Certainly, certainly. I sat down and wrote a courteous letter to the Director-General of the Shoe-Leather Department, explai—"

"Do you know him personally?"

"No."

"You have scored one for my side. You began insanely. Go on."

"In the letter I made the great value and inexpensiveness of the invention clear, and offered to—"

"Call and see him? Of course you did. Score two against yourself. I am v—"

"He didn't answer for three days."

"Necessarily. Proceed."

"Sent me three gruff lines thanking me for my trouble, and proposing—"

"Nothing."

"That's it—proposing nothing. Then I wrote him more elaborately and—"

"Score three—"

—"and got no answer. At the end of a week I wrote and asked, with some touch of asperity, for an answer to that letter."

"Four. Go on."

"An answer came back saying the letter had not been received, and asking for a copy. I traced the letter through the post-office, and found that it *had* been received; but I sent a copy and said nothing. Two weeks passed without further notice of me. In the mean time I gradually got myself cooled down to a polite-letter temperature. Then I wrote and proposed an interview for next day, and said that if I did not hear from him in the mean time I should take his silence for assent."

"Score five."

"I arrived at twelve sharp, and was given a chair in the anteroom and told to wait. I waited until half past one; then I left, ashamed and angry. I waited another week, to cool down; then I wrote and made another appointment with him for next day noon."

"Score six."

"He answered, assenting. I arrived promptly, and kept a chair warm until half past two. I left then, and shook the dust of that place from my shoes for good and all. For rudeness, inefficiency, incapacity, indifference to the army's interests, the Director-General of the Shoe-Leather Department of the War Office is, in my o—"

"Peace! I am very old and very wise, and have seen many seemingly intelligent people who hadn't common sense enough to go at a simple and easy thing like this in a common-sense way. You are not a curiosity to me; I have personally known millions and billions like you. You have lost three months quite unnecessarily; the inventor has lost three months; the soldiers have lost three—nine months altogether. I will now read you a little tale which I wrote last night. Then you will call on the Director-General at noon tomorrow and transact your business."

"Splendid! Do you know him?"

"No; but listen to the tale."

SECOND STORY: HOW THE CHIMNEY-SWEEP GOT THE EAR OF THE EMPEROR

Summer was come, and all the strong were bowed by the burden of the awful heat, and many of the weak were prostrate and dying. For weeks the army had been wasting away with a plague of dysentery, that scourge of the soldier, and there was but little help. The doctors were in despair; such efficacy as their drugs and their science had once had—and it was not much at its best—was a thing of the past, and promised to remain so.

The Emperor commanded the physicians of greatest renown to appear before him for a consultation, for he was profoundly disturbed. He was very severe with them, and called them to account for letting his soldiers die; and asked them if they knew their trade, or didn't; and were they properly healers, or merely assassins? Then the principal assassin, who was also the oldest doctor in the land and the most venerable in appearance, answered and said:

"We have done what we could, your Majesty, and for a good reason it has been little. No medicine and no physician can cure that disease; only nature and a good constitution can do it. I am old, and I know. No doctor and no medicine can cure it—I repeat it and I emphasize it. Sometimes they seem to help nature a little—a very little—but as a rule, they merely do damage."

The Emperor was a profane and passionate man, and he deluged the doctors with rugged and unfamiliar names, and drove them from his presence.

Within a day he was attacked by that fell disease himself. The news flew from mouth to mouth, and carried consternation with it over all the land.

All the talk was about this awful disaster, and there was general depression, for few had hope. The Emperor himself was very melancholy, and sighed and said:

"The will of God be done. Send for the assassins again, and let us get over with it."

They came, and felt his pulse and looked at his tongue, and fetched the drug-store and emptied it into him, and sat down patiently to wait—for they were not paid by the job, but by the year.

2

Tommy was sixteen and a bright lad, but he was not in society. His rank was too humble for that, and his employment too base. In fact, it was the lowest of all employments, for he was second in command to his father, who emptied cesspools and drove a night-cart. Tommy's closest friend was Jimmy the chimney-sweep, a slim little fellow of fourteen, who was honest and industrious, and had a good heart, and supported a bedridden mother by his dangerous and unpleasant trade.

About a month after the Emperor fell ill, these two lads met one evening about nine. Tommy was on his way to his night-work, and of course was not in his Sundays, but in his dreadful work-clothes, and not smelling very well. Jimmy was on his way home from his day's labor, and was blacker than any other object imaginable, and he had his brushes on his shoulder and his soot-bag at his waist, and no feature of his sable face was distinguishable except his lively eyes.

They sat down on the curbstone to talk; and of course it was upon the one subject—the nation's calamity, the Emperor's disorder. Jimmy was full of a great project, and burning to unfold it. He said:

"Tommy, I can cure his Majesty. I know how to do it."

Tommy was surprised.

"What! You?"

"Yes, I."

"Why, you little fool, the best doctors can't."

"I don't care: I can do it. I can cure him in fifteen minutes."

"Oh, come off! What are you giving me?"

"The facts—that's all."

Jimmy's manner was so serious that it sobered Tommy, who said:

"I believe you are in earnest, Jimmy. Are you in earnest?"

"I give you my word."

"What is the plan? How'll you cure him?"

"Tell him to eat a slice of ripe watermelon."

It caught Tommy rather suddenly, and he was shouting with laughter at the absurdity of the idea before he could put on a stopper. But he sobered down when he saw that Jimmy was wounded. He patted Jimmy's knee affectionately, not minding the soot, and said:

"I take the laugh all back. I didn't mean any harm, Jimmy, and I won't do it again. You see, it seemed so funny, because wherever there's a soldier-camp and dysentery, the doctors always put up a sign saying anybody caught bringing watermelons there will be flogged with the cat till he can't stand."

"I know it—the idiots!" said Jimmy, with both tears and anger in his voice. "There's plenty of watermelons, and not one of all those soldiers ought to have died."

"But, Jimmy, what put the notion into your head?"

"It isn't a notion; it's a fact. Do you know that old gray-headed Zulu? Well, this long time back he has been curing a lot of our friends, and my mother has seen him do it, and so have I. It takes only one or two slices of melon, and it don't make any difference whether the disease is new or old; it cures it."

"It's very odd. But, Jimmy, if it is so, the Emperor ought to be told of it."

"Of course; and my mother has told people, hoping they could get the word to him; but they are poor working-folks and ignorant, and don't know how to manage it."

"Of course they don't, the blunderheads," said Tommy, scornfully. "*I'll* get it to him!"

"You? You night-cart polecat!" And it was Jimmy's turn to laugh. But Tommy retorted sturdily:

"Oh, laugh if you like; but I'll *do* it!"

It had such an assured and confident sound that it made an impression, and Jimmy asked gravely:

"Do you know the Emperor?"

"Do *I* know him? Why, how you talk! Of course I don't."

"Then how'll you do it?"

"It's very simple and very easy. Guess. How would *you* do it, Jimmy?"

"Send him a letter. I never thought of it till this minute. But I'll bet that's your way."

"I'll bet it ain't. Tell me, how would you send it?"

"Why, through the mail, of course."

Tommy overwhelmed him with scoffings, and said:

"Now, don't you suppose every crank in the empire is doing the same thing? Do you mean to say you haven't thought of that?"

"Well—no," said Jimmy, abashed.

"You *might* have thought of it, if you weren't so young and inexperienced. Why, Jimmy, when even a common *general,* or a poet, or an actor, or anybody that's a little famous gets sick, all the cranks in the kingdom load up the mails with certain-sure quack cures for him. And so, what's bound to happen when it's the Emperor?"

"I suppose it's worse," said Jimmy, sheepishly.

"Well, I should think so! Look here, Jimmy: every single night we cart off as many as six loads of that kind of letters from the back yard of the palace, where they're thrown. Eighty thousand letters in one night! Do you reckon anybody reads them? Sho! not a single one. It's what would happen to your letter if you wrote it—which you won't, I reckon?"

"No," sighed Jimmy, crushed.

"But it's all right, Jimmy. Don't you fret: there's more than one way to skin a cat. *I'll* get the word to him."

"Oh, if you only *could,* Tommy, I should love you forever!"

"I'll do it, I tell you. Don't you worry; you depend on me."

"Indeed I will, Tommy, for you do know so much. You're not like other boys: they never know anything. How'll you manage, Tommy?"

Tommy was greatly pleased. He settled himself for reposeful talk, and said:

"Do you know that ragged poor thing that thinks he's a butcher because he goes around with a basket and sells cat's meat and rotten livers? Well, to begin with, I'll tell *him*."

Jimmy was deeply disappointed and chagrined, and said:

"Now, Tommy, it's a shame to talk so. You know my heart's in it, and it's not right."

Tommy gave him a love-pat, and said:

"Don't you be troubled, Jimmy. *I* know what I'm about. Pretty soon you'll see. That half-breed butcher will tell the old woman that sells chestnuts at the corner of the lane—she's his closest friend, and I'll ask him to; then, by request, she'll tell her rich aunt that keeps the little fruit-shop on the corner two blocks above; and that one will tell her particular friend, the man that keeps the game-shop; and he will tell his friend the sergeant of police; and the sergeant will tell his captain, and the captain will tell the magistrate, and the magistrate will tell his brother-in-law the county judge, and the county judge will tell the sheriff, and the sheriff will tell the Lord Mayor, and the Lord Mayor will tell the President of the Council, and the President of the Council will tell the—"

"By George, but it's a wonderful scheme, Tommy! How ever *did* you—"

"—Rear-Admiral, and the Rear will tell the Vice, and the Vice will tell the Admiral of the Blue, and the Blue will tell the Red, and the Red will tell the White, and the White will tell the First Lord of the Admiralty, and the First Lord will tell the Speaker of the House, and the Speaker—"

"Go it, Tommy; you're 'most there!"

"—will tell the Master of the Hounds, and the Master will tell the Head Groom of the Stables, and the Head Groom will tell the Chief Equerry, and the Chief Equerry will tell the First Lord in Waiting, and the First Lord will tell the Lord High Chamberlain, and the Lord High

Chamberlain will tell the Master of the Household, and the Master of the Household will tell the little pet page that fans the flies off the Emperor, and the page will get down on his knees and whisper it to his Majesty—and the game's made!"

"I've *got* to get up and hurrah a couple of times, Tommy. It's the grandest idea that ever was. What ever put it into your head?"

"Sit down and listen, and I'll give you some wisdom—and don't you ever forget it as long as you live. Now, then, who is the closest friend you've got, and the one you couldn't and wouldn't ever refuse anything in the world to?"

"Why, it's you, Tommy. You know that."

"Suppose you wanted to ask a pretty large favor of the cat's-meat man. Well, you don't know him, and he would tell you to go to thunder, for he is that kind of a person; but he is my next best friend after you, and would run his legs off to do me a kindness—*any* kindness, he don't care what it is. Now, I'll ask you: which is the most common-sensible—for you to go and ask him to tell the chestnut-woman about your watermelon cure, or for you to get me to do it for you?"

"To get you to do it for me, of course. I wouldn't ever have thought of that, Tommy; it's splendid!"

"It's a *philosophy*, you see. Mighty good word—and large. It goes on this idea: everybody in the world, little and big, has one *special* friend, a friend that he's *glad* to do favors to—not sour about it, but *glad*—glad clear to the marrow. And so, I don't care where you start, you can get at anybody's ear that you want to—I don't care how low you are, nor how high he is. And it's so simple: you've only to find the *first* friend, that is all; that ends your part of the work. He finds the next friend himself, and that one finds the third, and so on, friend after friend, link after link, like a chain; and you can go up it or down it, as high as you like or as low as you like."

"It's just beautiful, Tommy."

"It's as simple and easy as a-b-c; but did you ever hear of anybody trying it? No; everybody is a fool. He goes to a stranger without any introduction, or writes him a letter, and of course he strikes a cold wave—and serves him gorgeously right. Now, the Emperor don't know me, but that's no matter—he'll eat his watermelon to-morrow. You'll see. Hi-hi—stop! It's the cat's-meat man. Good-by, Jimmy; I'll overtake him."

He did overtake him, and said:

"Say, will you do me a favor?"

"*Will* I? Well, I should *say!* I'm your man. Name it, and see me fly!"

"Go tell the chestnut-woman to put down everything and carry this message to her first-best friend, and tell the friend to pass it along." He worded the message, and said, "Now, then, rush!"

The next moment the chimney-sweep's word to the Emperor was on its way.

3

The next evening, toward midnight, the doctors sat whispering together in the imperial sick-room, and they were in deep trouble, for the Emperor was in very bad case. They could not hide it from themselves that every time they emptied a fresh drug-store into him he got worse. It saddened them, for they were expecting that result. The poor emaciated Emperor lay motionless, with his eyes closed, and the page that was his darling was fanning the flies away and crying softly. Presently the boy heard the silken rustle of a portière, and turned and saw the Lord High Great Master of the Household peering in at the door and excitedly motioning to him to come. Lightly and swiftly the page tip-toed his way to his dear and worshiped friend the Master, who said:

"Only you can persuade him, my child, and oh, don't fail to do it! Take this, make him eat it, and he is saved."

"On my head be it. He shall eat it!"

It was a couple of great slices of ruddy, fresh watermelon.

The next morning the news flew everywhere that the Emperor was sound and well again, and had hanged the doctors. A wave of joy swept the land, and frantic preparations were made to illuminate.

After breakfast his Majesty sat meditating. His gratitude was unspeakable, and he was trying to devise a reward rich enough to properly testify it to his benefactor. He got it arranged in his mind, and called the page, and asked him if he had invented that cure. The boy said no—he got it from the Master of the Household.

He was sent away, and the Emperor went to devising again. The Master was an earl; he would make him a duke, and give him a vast estate which belonged to a member of the Opposition. He had him called, and asked him if he was the inventor of the remedy. But the Master was an honest man, and said he got it of the Grand Chamberlain. He was sent away, and the Emperor thought some more. The Chamberlain was a viscount; he would make him an earl, and give him a large income. But the Chamberlain referred him to the First Lord in Waiting, and there was some more thinking; his Majesty thought out a smaller reward. But the First Lord in Waiting referred him back further, and he had to sit down and think out a further and becomingly and suitably smaller reward.

Then, to break the tediousness of the inquiry and hurry the business, he sent for the Grand High Chief Detective, and commanded him to trace the cure to the bottom, so that he could properly reward his benefactor.

At nine in the evening the High Chief Detective brought the word. He had traced the cure down to a lad named

Jimmy, a chimney-sweep. The Emperor said, with deep feeling:

"Brave boy, he saved my life, and shall not regret it!"

And sent him a pair of his own boots; and the next best ones he had, too. They were too large for Jimmy, but they fitted the Zulu, so it was all right, and everything as it should be.

CONCLUSION TO THE FIRST STORY

"There—do you get the idea?"

"I am obliged to admit that I do. And it will be as you have said. I will transact the business to-morrow. I intimately know the Director-General's nearest friend. He will give me a note of introduction, with a word to say my matter is of real importance to the government. I will take it along, without an appointment, and send it in, with my card, and I sha'n't have to wait so much as half a minute."

That turned out true to the letter, and the government adopted the boots.

1901

The Belated Russian Passport

One fly makes a summer.

—*Pudd'nhead Wilson's Calendar*

1

A GREAT BEER-saloon in the Friedrichstrasse, Berlin, toward mid-afternoon. At a hundred round tables gentlemen sat smoking and drinking; flitting here and there and everywhere were white-aproned waiters bearing foaming mugs to the thirsty. At a table near the main entrance were grouped half a dozen lively young fellows—American students—drinking good-by to a visiting Yale youth on his travels, who had been spending a few days in the German capital.

"But why do you cut your tour short in the middle, Parrish?" asked one of the students. "I wish I had your chance. What do you want to go home for?"

"Yes," said another, "What is the idea? You want to explain, you know, because it looks like insanity. Homesick?"

A girlish blush rose in Parrish's fresh young face, and after a little hesitation he confessed that that was his trouble.

"I was never away from home before," he said, "and every day I get more and more lonesome. I have not seen a friend for weeks, and it's been horrible. I meant to stick the trip through, for pride's sake, but seeing you boys has finished me. It's been heaven to me, and I can't take up that companionless dreariness again. If I had company—but I haven't, you know, so it's no use. They used to call me Miss Nancy when I was a small chap, and I reckon I'm that yet—girlish and timorous, and all that. I ought to have *been* a girl! I can't stand it; I'm going home."

The boys rallied him good-naturedly, and said he was making the mistake of his life; and one of them added that he ought at least to see St. Petersburg before turning back.

"Don't!" said Parrish, appealingly. "It was my dearest dream, and I'm throwing it away. Don't say a word more on that head, for I'm made of water, and can't stand out against anybody's persuasion. I *can't* go alone; I think I should die." He slapped his breast pocket, and added: "Here is my protection against a change of mind; I've bought ticket and sleeper for Paris, and I leave to-night. Drink, now—this is on me—bumpers—this is for home!"

The good-bys were said, and Alfred Parrish was left to his thoughts and his loneliness. But for a moment only. A sturdy middle-aged man with a brisk and businesslike bearing, and an air of decision and confidence suggestive of military training, came bustling from the next table, and seated himself at Parrish's side, and began to speak, with concentrated interest and earnestness. His eyes, his face, his person, his whole system, seemed to exude energy. He was full of steam—racing pressure—one could almost hear his gauge-cocks sing. He extended a frank hand, shook Parrish's cordially, and said, with a most convincing air of strenuous conviction:

"Ah, but you *mustn't;* really you mustn't; it would be the greatest mistake; you would always regret it. Be persuaded, I beg you; don't do it—don't!"

There was such a friendly note in it, and such a seeming of genuineness, that it brought a sort of uplift to the youth's despondent spirits, and a telltale moisture betrayed itself in his eyes, an unintentional confession that he was touched and grateful. The alert stranger noted that sign, was quite content with that response, and followed up his advantage without waiting for a spoken one:

"No, don't do it; it would be a mistake. I have heard everything that was said—you will pardon that—I was so close by that I couldn't help it. And it troubled me to think that you would cut your travels short when you really *want* to see St. Petersburg, and are right here almost in sight of it! Reconsider it—ah, you *must* reconsider it. It is such a short distance—it is very soon done and very soon over—and think what a memory it will be!"

Then he went on and made a picture of the Russian capital and its wonders, which made Alfred Parrish's mouth water and his roused spirits cry out with longing. Then—

"Of course you must see St. Petersburg—you *must!* Why, it will be a joy to you—a joy! I know, because I know the place as familiarly as I know my own birthplace in America. Ten years—I've known it ten years. Ask anybody there; they'll tell you; they all know me—Major Jackson. The very dogs know me. Do go; oh, you must go; you must, indeed."

Alfred Parrish was quivering with eagerness now. He would go. His face said it as plainly as his tongue could have done it. Then—the old shadow fell,—and he said, sorrowfully:

"Oh, no—no, it's no use; I can't. I should die of the loneliness."

The Major said, with astonishment: "The—loneliness! Why, I'm going *with* you!"

It was startlingly unexpected. And not quite pleasant. Things were moving too rapidly. Was this a trap? Was this stranger a sharper? Whence all this gratuitous interest in a wandering and unknown lad? Then he glanced at the Major's frank and winning and beaming face, and was ashamed; and wished he knew how to get out of this scrape without hurting the feelings of its contriver. But he was not handy in matters of diplomacy, and went at the difficulty with conscious awkwardness and small confidence. He said, with a quite overdone show of unselfishness:

"Oh no, no, you are too kind; I couldn't—I couldn't allow you to put yourself to such an inconvenience on my—"

"Inconvenience? None in the world, my boy; I was going to-night, anyway; I leave in the express at nine. Come! we'll go together. You sha'n't be lonely a single minute. Come along—say the word!"

So that excuse had failed. What to do now? Parrish was disheartened; it seemed to him that no subterfuge which his poor invention could contrive would ever rescue him from these toils. Still, he must make another effort, and he did; and before he had finished his new excuse he thought he recognized that it was unanswerable:

"Ah, but most unfortunately luck is against me, and it is impossible. Look at these"—and he took out his tickets and laid them on the table. "I am booked through to Paris, and I couldn't get these tickets and baggage coupons changed for St. Petersburg, of course, and would have to lose the money; and if I could afford to lose the money I should be rather short after I bought the new tickets—for there is all the cash I've got about me"—and he laid a five-hundred-mark bank-note on the table.

In a moment the Major had the tickets and coupons and was on his feet, and saying, with enthusiasm:

"Good! It's all right, and everything safe. They'll change the tickets and baggage pasters for *me;* they all know me—everybody knows me. Sit right where you are; I'll be back right away." Then he reached for the bank-note, and added, "I'll take this along, for there will be a little extra pay on the new tickets, maybe"—and the next moment he was flying out at the door.

2

Alfred Parrish was paralyzed. It was all so sudden. So sudden, so daring, so incredible, so impossible. His mouth was open, but his tongue wouldn't work; he tried to shout "Stop him," but his lungs were empty; he wanted to pursue, but his legs refused to do anything but tremble; then they gave way under him and let him down into his chair. His throat was dry, he was gasping and swallowing with dismay, his head was in a whirl. What must he do? He did not know. One thing seemed plain, however—he must pull himself together, and try to overtake that man. Of course the man could not get back the ticket-money, but would he throw the tickets away on that account? No; he would certainly go to the station and sell them to some one at half-price; and today, too, for they would be worthless to-morrow, by German custom. These reflections gave him hope and strength, and he rose and started. But he took only a couple of steps, then he felt a sudden sickness, and tottered back to his chair again, weak with a dread that his movement had been noticed—for the last round of beer was at his expense; it had not been paid for, and he hadn't a pfennig. He was a prisoner—Heaven only could know what might happen if he tried to leave the place. He was timid, scared, crushed; and he had not German enough to state his case and beg for help and indulgence.

Then his thoughts began to persecute him. How could he have been such a fool? What possessed him to listen to such a manifest adventurer? *And here comes the waiter!* He buried himself in the newspaper—trembling. The waiter passed by. It filled him with thankfulness. The hands of the clock seemed to stand still, yet he could not keep his eyes from them.

Ten minutes dragged by. The waiter again! Again he hid behind the paper. The waiter paused—apparently a week—then passed on.

Another ten minutes of misery—once more the waiter; this time he wiped off the table, and seemed to be a month at it; then paused two months, and went away.

Parrish felt that he could not endure another visit; he must take the chances: he must run the gantlet; he must escape. But the waiter stayed around about the neighborhood for five minutes—months and months seemingly, Parrish watching him with a despairing eye, and feeling the infirmities of age creeping upon him and his hair gradually turning gray.

At last the waiter wandered away—stopped at a table, collected a bill, wandered farther, collected another bill, wandered farther—Parrish's praying eye riveted on him all the time, his heart thumping, his breath coming and going in quick little gasps of anxiety mixed with hope.

The waiter stopped again to collect, and Parrish said to himself, it is now or never! and started for the door. One step—two steps—three—four—he was nearing the door—five—his legs shaking under him—was that a swift step behind him?—the thought shriveled his heart—six steps—seven, and he was out!—eight—nine—ten—eleven—twelve—there *is* a pursuing step!—he turned the corner, and picked up his heels to fly—a heavy hand fell on his shoulder, and the strength went out of his body.

It was the Major. He asked not a question, he showed no surprise. He said, in his breezy and exhilarating fashion:

"Confound those people, they delayed me; that's why I was gone so long. New man in the ticket-office, and he didn't know me, and wouldn't make the exchange because it was irregular; so I had to hunt up my old friend, the great mogul—the station-master, you know—hi, there, cab! cab!—jump in, Parrish!—Russian consulate, cabby, and let them fly!—so, as I say, that all cost time. But it's all right now, and everything straight; your luggage reweighed, rechecked, fare-ticket and sleeper changed, and I've got the documents for it in my pocket; also the change—I'll keep it for you. Whoop along, cabby, whoop along; don't let them go to sleep!"

Poor Parrish was trying his best to get in a word edgeways, as the cab flew farther and farther from the bilked beer-hall, and now at last he succeeded, and wanted to return at once and pay his little bill.

"Oh, never mind about that," said the Major, placidly; "that's all right, they know me, everybody knows me—I'll square it next time I'm in Berlin—push along, cabby, push along—no great lot of time to spare, now."

They arrived at the Russian consulate, a moment after-hours, and hurried in. No one there but a clerk. The Major laid his card on the desk, and said, in the Russian tongue, "Now, then, if you'll visé this young man's passport for Petersburg as quickly as—"

"But, dear sir, I'm not authorized, and the consul has just gone."

"Gone where?"

"Out in the country, where he lives."

"And he'll be back—"

"Not till morning."

"Thunder! Oh, well, look here, I'm Major Jackson—he knows me, everybody knows me. You visé it yourself; tell him Major Jackson asked you; it'll be all right."

But it would be desperately and fatally irregular; the clerk could not be persuaded; he almost fainted at the idea.

"Well, then, I'll tell you what to do," said the Major. "Here's stamps and fee—visé it in the morning, and start it along by mail."

The clerk said, dubiously, "He—well, he may perhaps do it, and so—"

"May? He *will!* He knows me—everybody knows me."

"Very well," said the clerk, "I will tell him what you say." He looked bewildered, and in a measure subjugated; and added, timidly: "But—but—you know you will beat it to the frontier twenty-four hours. There are no accommodations there for so long a wait."

"Who's going to *wait?* Not I, if the court knows herself."

The clerk was temporarily paralyzed, and said, "Surely, sir, you don't wish it sent to Petersburg!"

"And why not?"

"And the owner of it tarrying at the frontier, twenty-five miles away? It couldn't do him any good, in those circumstances."

"Tarry—the mischief! Who said he was going to do any tarrying?"

"Why, you know, of course, they'll stop him at the frontier if he has no passport."

"Indeed they won't! The Chief Inspector knows me—everybody does. I'll be responsible for the young man. You send it straight through to Petersburg—Hôtel de l'Europe, care Major Jackson: tell the consul not to worry, I'm taking all the risks myself."

The clerk hesitated, then chanced one more appeal:

"You must bear in mind, sir, that the risks are peculiarly serious, just now. The new edict is in force."

"What is it?"

"Ten years in Siberia for being in Russia without a passport."

"Mm—damnation!" He said it in English, for the Russian tongue is but a poor stand-by in spiritual emergencies. He mused a moment, then brisked up and resumed in Russian: "Oh, it's all right—label her St. Petersburg and let her sail! I'll fix it. They all know me there—all the authorities—everybody."

3

The Major turned out to be an adorable traveling-companion, and young Parrish was charmed with him. His talk was sunshine and rainbows, and lit up the whole region around, and keep it gay and happy and cheerful; and he was full of accommodating ways, and knew all about how to do things, and when to do them, and the best way. So the long journey was a fairy dream for that young lad who had been so lonely and forlorn and friendless so many homesick weeks. At last, when the two travelers were approaching the frontier, Parrish said something about passports; then started, as if recollecting something, and added:

"Why, come to think, I don't remember your bringing my passport away from the consulate. But you did, didn't you?"

"No; it's coming by mail," said the Major, comfortably.

"C—coming—by—mail!" gasped the lad; and all the dreadful things he had heard about the terrors and disasters of passportless visitors to Russia rose in his frightened mind and turned him white to the lips. "Oh, Major—oh, my goodness, what will become of me! How *could* you do such a thing?"

The Major laid a soothing hand upon the youth's shoulder and said:

"Now, don't you worry, my boy, don't you worry a bit. I'm taking care of you, and I'm not going to let any harm come to you. The Chief Inspector knows me, and I'll explain to him, and it'll be all right—you'll see. Now don't you give yourself the least discomfort—I'll fix it all up, easy as nothing."

Alfred trembled, and felt a great sinking inside, but he did what he could to conceal his misery, and to respond with some show of heart to the Major's kindly pettings and reassurings.

At the frontier he got out and stood on the edge of the great crowd, and waited in deep anxiety while the Major plowed his way through the mass to "explain to the Chief Inspector." It seemed a cruelly long wait, but at last the Major reappeared. He said, cheerfully, "Damnation, it's a new inspector, and I don't know him!"

Alfred fell up against a pile of trunks, with a despairing,

"Oh, dear, dear, I might have known it!" and was slumping limp and helpless to the ground, but the Major gathered him up and seated him on a box, and sat down by him, with a supporting arm around him, and whispered in his ear:

"Don't worry, laddie, don't—it's going to be all right; you just trust to me. The sub-inspector's as near-sighted as a shad. I watched him, and I know it's so. Now I'll tell you how to do. I'll go and get my passport chalked, then I'll stop right yonder inside the grille where you see those peasants with their packs. You be there, and I'll back up against the grille, and slip my passport to you through the bars, then you tag along after the crowd and hand it in, and trust to Providence and that shad. Mainly the shad. You'll pull through all right—now don't you be afraid."

"But, oh dear, dear, *your* description and *mine* don't tally any more than—"

"Oh, that's all right—difference between fifty-one and nineteen—just entirely imperceptible to that shad—don't you fret, it's going to come out as right as nails."

Ten minutes later Alfred was tottering toward the train, pale, and in a collapse, but he had played the shad successfully, and was as grateful as an untaxed dog that has evaded the police.

"I told you so," said the Major, in splendid spirits. "I knew it would come out all right if you trusted in Providence like a little trusting child and didn't try to improve on His ideas—it always does."

Between the frontier and Petersburg the Major laid himself out to restore his young comrade's life, and work up his circulation, and pull him out of his despondency, and make him feel again that life was a joy and worth living. And so, as a consequence, the young fellow entered the city in high feather and marched into the hotel in fine form, and registered his name. But instead of naming a room, the clerk glanced at him inquiringly, and waited. The Major came promptly to the rescue, and said, cordially:

"It's all right—you know me—set him down, I'm responsible." The clerk looked grave, and shook his head. The Major added: "It's all right, it'll be here in twenty-four hours—it's coming by mail. Here's mine, and his is coming, right along."

The clerk was fun of politeness, full of deference, but he was firm. He said, in English:

"Indeed, I wish I could accommodate you, Major, and certainly I would if I could; but I have no choice, I must ask him to go; I cannot allow him to remain in the house a moment."

Parrish began to totter, and emitted a moan; the Major caught him and stayed him with an arm, and said to the clerk, appealingly:

"Come, you know me—everybody does—just let him stay here the one night, and I give you my word—"

The clerk shook his head, and said:

"But, Major, you are endangering me, you are endangering the house. I—I hate to do such a thing, but I—I *must* call the police."

"Hold on, don't do that. Come along, my boy, and don't you fret—it's going to come out all right. Hi, there, cabby! Jump in, Parrish. Palace of the General of the Secret Police—turn them loose, cabby! Let them go! Make them whiz! Now we're off, and don't you give yourself any uneasiness. Prince Bossloffsky knows me, knows me like a book; he'll soon fix things all right for us."

They tore through the gay streets and arrived at the palace, which was brilliantly lighted. But it was half past eight; the Prince was about going in to dinner, the sentinel said, and couldn't receive any one.

"But he'll receive *me,*" said the Major, robustly, and handed his card. "I'm Major Jackson. Send it in; it'll be all right."

The card was sent in, under protest, and the Major and his waif waited in a reception-room for some time. At length they were sent for, and conducted to a sumptuous private office and confronted with the Prince, who stood there gorgeously arrayed and frowning like a thunder-cloud. The Major stated his case, and begged for a twenty-four-hour stay of proceedings until the passport should be forthcoming.

"Oh, impossible!" said the Prince, in faultless English. "I marvel that you should have done so insane a thing as to bring the lad into the country without a passport, Major, I marvel at it; why, it's ten years in Siberia, and no help for it—catch him! support him!" for poor Parrish was making another trip to the floor. "Here—quick, give him this. There—take another draught; brandy's the thing, don't you find it so, lad? Now you feel better, poor fellow. Lie down on the sofa. How stupid it was of you, Major, to get him into such a horrible scrape." The Major eased the boy down with his strong arms, put a cushion under his head, and whispered in his ear:

"Look as damned sick as you can! Play it for all it's worth; he's touched, you see; got a tender heart under there somewhere; fetch a groan, and say, 'Oh, mamma, mamma'; it'll knock him out, sure as guns."

Parrish was going to do these things anyway, from native impulse, so they came from him promptly, with great and moving sincerity, and the Major whispered: "Splendid! Do it again; Bernhardt couldn't beat it."

What with the Major's eloquence and the boy's misery, the point was gained at last; the Prince struck his colors, and said:

"Have it your way; though you deserve a sharp lesson and you ought to get it I give you exactly twenty-four hours. If the passport is not here then, don't come near me; it's Siberia without hope of pardon."

While the Major and the lad poured out their thanks, the Prince rang in a couple of soldiers, and in their own language, he ordered them to go with these two people, and not lose sight of the younger one a moment for the next twenty-four hours; and if, at the end of that term, the boy could not show a passport, impound him in the dungeons of St. Peter and St. Paul, and report.

The unfortunates arrived at the hotel with their guards, dined under their eyes, remained in Parrish's room until the Major went off to bed, after cheering up the sad Parrish, then one of the soldiers locked himself and Parrish in, and the other one stretched himself across the door outside and soon went off to sleep.

So also did not Alfred Parrish. The moment he was alone with the solemn soldier and the voiceless silence his machine-made cheerfulness began to waste away, his medicated courage began to give off its supporting gases and shrink toward normal, and his poor little heart to shrivel like a raisin. Within thirty minutes he struck bottom; grief, misery, fright, despair, could go no lower. Bed? Bed was not for such as he; bed was not for the doomed, the lost! Sleep? He was not the Hebrew children, he could not sleep in the fire! He could only walk the floor. And not only could, but must. And did, by the hour. And mourned, and wept, and shuddered, and prayed.

Then all-sorrowfully he made his last dispositions, and prepared himself, as well as in him lay, to meet his fate. As a final act, he wrote a letter:

"MY DARLING MOTHER,—When these sad lines shall have reached you your poor Alfred will be no more. No; worse than that, far worse! Through my own fault and foolishness I have fallen into the hands of a sharper or a lunatic; I do not know which, but in either case I feel that I am lost. Sometimes I think he is a sharper, but most of the time I think he is only mad, for he has a kind, good heart, I know, and he certainly seems to try the hardest that ever a person tried to get me out of the fatal difficulties he has gotten me into.

"In a few hours I shall be one of a nameless horde plodding the snowy solitudes of Russia, under the lash, and bound for that land of mystery and misery and termless oblivion, Siberia! I shall not live to see it; my heart is broken and I shall die. Give my picture to *her*, and ask her to keep it in memory of me, and to so live that in the appointed time she may join me in that better world where there is no marriage nor giving in marriage, and where there are no more separations, and troubles never come. Give my yellow dog to Archy Hale, and the other one to Henry Taylor; my blazer I give to brother Will, and my fishing-things and Bible.

"There is no hope for me. I cannot escape; the soldier stands there with his gun and never takes his eyes off me, just blinks; there is no other movement, any more than if he was dead. I cannot bribe him, the maniac has my money. My letter of credit is in my trunk, and may never come—*will* never come, I know. Oh, what is to become of me! Pray for me, darling mother, pray for your poor Alfred. But it will do no good."

4

In the morning Alfred came out looking scraggy and worn when the Major summoned him to an early breakfast. They fed their guards, they lit cigars, the Major loosened his tongue and set it going, and under its magic influence Alfred gradually and gratefully became hopeful, measurably cheerful, and almost happy once more.

But he would not leave the house. Siberia hung over him black and threatening, his appetite for sights was all gone, he could not have borne the shame of inspecting streets and galleries and churches with a soldier at each elbow and all the world stopping and staring and commenting—no, he would stay within and wait for the Berlin mail and his fate. So, all day long the Major stood gallantly by him in his room, with one soldier standing stiff and motionless against the door with his musket at his shoulder, and the other one drowsing in a chair outside; and all day long the faithful veteran spun campaign yarns, described battles, reeled off explosive anecdotes, with unconquerable energy and sparkle and resolution, and kept the scared student alive and his pulses functioning. The long day wore to a close, and the pair, followed by their guards, went down to the great dining-room and took their seats.

"The suspense will be over before long, now," sighed poor Alfred. Just then a pair of Englishmen passed by, and one of them said, "So we'll get no letters from Berlin to-night."

Parrish's breath began to fail him. The Englishmen seated themselves at a near-by table, and the other one said:

"No, it isn't as bad as that." Parrish's breathing improved. "There is later telegraphic news. The accident did detain the train formidably, but that is all. It will arrive here three hours late to-night."

Parrish did not get to the floor this time, for the Major jumped for him in time. He had been listening, and foresaw what would happen. He patted Parrish on the back, hoisted him out of the chair, and said, cheerfully:

"Come along, my boy, cheer up, there's absolutely nothing to worry about. I know a way out. Bother the passport; let it lag a week if it wants to, we can do without it."

Parrish was too sick to hear him; hope was gone, Siberia present; he moved off on legs of lead, upheld by the Major, who walked him to the American legation, heartening him on the way with assurances that on his recommendation the minister wouldn't hesitate a moment to grant him a new passport.

"I had that card up my sleeve all the time," he said. "The minister knows me—knows me familiarly—chummed together hours and hours under a pile of other wounded at Cold Harbor; been chummies ever since, in spirit, though we haven't met much in the body. Cheer up, laddie, everything's looking splendid! By gracious! I feel as cocky as a buck angel. Here we are, and our troubles are at an end! If we ever really had any."

There, alongside the door, was the trade-mark of the richest and freest and mightiest republic of all the ages: the pine disk, with the planked eagle spread upon it, his head and shoulders among the stars, and his claws full of out-of-date war material; and at that sight the tears came into Alfred's eyes, the pride of country rose in his heart, Hail Columbia boomed up in his breast, and all his fears and sorrows vanished away; for here he was safe, safe! not all the powers of the earth would venture to cross that threshold to lay a hand upon him!

For economy's sake the mightiest republic's legations in Europe consist of a room and a half on the ninth floor, when the tenth is occupied, and the legation furniture consists of a minister or an ambassador with a brakeman's salary, a secretary of legation who sells matches and mends crockery for a living, a hired girl for interpreter and general utility, pictures of the American liners, a chromo of the reigning President, a desk, three chairs, kerosene-lamp, a cat, a clock, and a cuspidor with the motto, "In God We Trust."

The party climbed up there, followed by the escort. A man sat at the desk writing official things on wrapping-paper with a nail. He rose and faced about; the cat climbed down and got under the desk; the hired girl squeezed herself up into the corner by the vodka-jug to make room; the soldiers squeezed themselves up against the wall alongside of her, with muskets at shoulder arms. Alfred was radiant with happiness and the sense of rescue.

The Major cordially shook hands with the official, rattled off his case in easy and fluent style, and asked for the desired passport.

The official seated his guests, then said: "Well, I am only the secretary of legation, you know, and I wouldn't like to grant a passport while the minister is on Russian soil. There is far too much responsibility."

"All right, send for him."

The secretary smiled, and said: "That's easier said than done. He's away up in the wilds, somewhere, on his vacation."

"Ger-reat Scott!" ejaculated the Major.

Alfred groaned; the color went out of his face, and he began to slowly collapse in his clothes. The secretary said, wonderingly:

"Why, what are you Great-Scotting about, Major? The Prince gave you twenty-four hours. Look at the clock; you're all right; you've half an hour left; the train is just due; the passport will arrive in time."

"Man, there's news! The train is three hours behind time! This boy's life and liberty are wasting away by minutes, and only thirty of them left! In half an hour he's the same as dead and damned to all eternity! By God, we *must* have the passport!"

"Oh, I am dying, I know it!" wailed the lad, and buried his face in his arms on the desk. A quick change came over the secretary, his placidity vanished away, excitement flamed up in his face and eyes, and he exclaimed:

"I see the whole ghastliness of the situation, but, Lord help us, what can I do? What can you suggest?"

"Why, hang it, give him the passport!"

"Impossible! Totally impossible! You know nothing about him; three days ago you had never heard of him; there's no way in the world to identify him. He is lost, lost—there's no possibility of saving him!"

The boy groaned again, and sobbed out, "Lord, Lord, it's the last of earth for Alfred Parrish!"

Another change came over the secretary.

In the midst of a passionate outburst of pity, vexation, and hopelessness, he stopped short, his manner calmed down, and he asked, in the indifferent voice which one uses in introducing the subject of the weather when there is nothing to talk about, "Is that your name?"

The youth sobbed out a yes.

"Where are you from?"

"Bridgeport."

The secretary shook his head—shook it again—and muttered to himself. After a moment:

"Born there?"

"No; New Haven."

"Ah-h." The secretary glanced at the Major, who was listening intently, with blank and unenlightened face, and indicated rather than said, "There is vodka there, in case the soldiers are thirsty." The Major sprang up, poured for them, and received their gratitude. The questioning went on.

"How long did you live in New Haven?"

"Till I was fourteen. Came back two years ago to enter Yale."

"When you lived there, what street did you live on?"

"Parker Street."

With a vague half-light of comprehension dawning in his eyes, the Major glanced an inquiry at the secretary. The secretary nodded, the Major poured vodka again.

"What number?"

"It hadn't any."

The boy sat up and gave the secretary a pathetic look which said, "Why do you want to torture me with these foolish things, when I am miserable enough without it?"

The secretary went on, unheeding: "What kind of a house was it?"

"Brick—two-story."

"Flush with the sidewalk?"

"No, small yard in front."

"Iron fence?"

"No, palings."

The Major poured vodka again—without instructions—

poured brimmers this time; and his face had cleared and was alive now.

"What do you see when you enter the door?"

"A narrow hall; door at the end of it, and a door at your right."

"Anything else?"

"Hat-rack."

"Room at the right?"

"Parlor."

"Carpet?"

"Yes."

"Kind of carpet?"

"Old-fashioned Wilton."

"Figures?"

"Yes—hawking-party, horseback."

The Major cast an eye at the clock—only six minutes left! He faced about with the jug, and as he poured he glanced at the secretary, then at the clock—inquiringly. The secretary nodded; the Major covered the clock from view with his body a moment, and set the hands back half an hour; then he refreshed the men—double rations.

"Room beyond the hall and hat-rack?"

"Dining-room."

"Stove?"

"Grate."

"Did your people own the house?"

"Yes."

"Do they own it yet?"

"No; sold it when we moved to Bridgeport."

The secretary paused a little, then said, "Did you have a nickname among your playmates?"

The color slowly rose in the youth's pale cheeks, and he dropped his eyes. He seemed to struggle with himself a moment or two, then he said plaintively, "They called me Miss Nancy."

The secretary mused awhile, then he dug up another question:

"Any ornaments in the dining-room?"

"Well, y-no."

"*None?* None at *all?*"

"No."

"The mischief! Isn't that a little odd? Think!"

The youth thought and thought; the secretary waited, panting. At last the imperiled waif looked up sadly and shook his head.

"Think—*think!*" cried the Major, in anxious solicitude; and poured again.

"Come!" said the secretary, "not even a *picture?*"

"Oh, certainly! but you said ornament."

"Ah! What did your father think of it?"

The color rose again. The boy was silent.

"Speak," said the secretary.

"Speak," cried the Major, and his trembling hand poured more vodka outside the glasses than inside.

"I—I can't tell you what he said," murmured the boy.

"Quick! quick!" said the secretary; "out with it; there's no time to lose—home and liberty or Siberia and death depend upon the answer."

"Oh, have pity! he is a clergyman, and—"

"No matter; out with it, or—"

"He said it was the hell-firedest nightmare he ever struck!"

"Saved!" shouted the secretary, and seized his nail and a blank passport. "*I* identify you; I've lived in the house, and I painted the picture myself!"

"Oh, come to my arms, my poor rescued boy!" cried the Major. "We will always be grateful to God that He made this artist!—if He did."

1902

A Double-Barreled Detective Story

1

THE FIRST scene is in the country, in Virginia; the time, 1880. There has been a wedding, between a handsome young man of slender means and a rich young girl—a case of love at first sight and a precipitate marriage; a marriage bitterly opposed by the girl's widowed father.

Jacob Fuller, the bridegroom, is twenty-six years old, is of an old but unconsidered family which had by compulsion emigrated from Sedgemoor, and for King James's purse's profit, so everybody said—some maliciously, the rest merely because they believed it. The bride is nineteen and beautiful. She is intense, high-strung, romantic, immeasurably proud of her Cavalier blood, and passionate in her love for her young husband. For its sake she braved her father's displeasure, endured his reproaches, listened with loyalty unshaken to his warning predictions, and went from his house without his blessing, proud and happy in the proofs she was thus giving of the quality of the affection which had made its home in her heart.

The morning after the marriage there was a sad surprise for her. Her husband put aside her proffered caresses, and said:

"Sit down. I have something to say to you. I loved you. That was before I asked your father to give you to me. His refusal is not my grievance—I could have endured that. But the things he said of me to you—that is a different matter. There—you needn't speak; I know quite well what they were; I got them from authentic sources. Among other things he said that my character was written in my face; that I was treacherous, a dissembler, a coward, and a brute without sense of pity or compassion: the 'Sedgemoor trademark,' he called it—and 'white-sleeve badge.' Any other man in my place would have gone to his house and shot him down like a dog. I wanted to do it, and was minded to do it, but a better thought came to me: to put him to shame; to break his heart; to kill him by inches. How to do it? Through my treatment of you, his idol! I would marry you; and then— Have patience. You will see."

From that moment onward, for three months, the young wife suffered all the humiliations, all the insults, all the miseries that the diligent and inventive mind of the husband could contrive, save physical injuries only. Her strong pride stood by her, and she kept the secret of her troubles. Now and then the husband said, "Why don't you go to your father and tell him?" Then he invented new tortures, applied them, and asked again. She always answered, "He shall never know by my mouth," and taunted him with his origin; said she was the lawful slave of a scion of slaves, and must obey, and would—up to that point, but no further; he could kill her if he liked, but he could not break her; it was not in the Sedgemoor breed to do it. At the end of the three months he said, with a dark significance in his manner, "I have tried all things but one"—and waited for her reply. "Try that," she said, and curled her lip in mockery.

That night he rose at midnight and put on his clothes, then said to her:

"Get up and dress!"

She obeyed—as always, without a word. He led her half a mile from the house, and proceeded to lash her to a tree by the side of the public road; and succeeded, she screaming and struggling. He gagged her then, struck her across the face with his cowhide, and set his bloodhounds on her. They tore the clothes off her, and she was naked. He called the dogs off, and said:

"You will be found—by the passing public. They will be dropping along about three hours from now, and will spread the news—do you hear? Good-by. You have seen the last of me."

He went away then. She moaned to herself:

"I shall bear a child—to *him!* God grant it may be a boy!"

The farmers released her by and by—and spread the news, which was natural. They raised the country with lynching intentions, but the bird had flown. The young wife shut herself up in her father's house; he shut himself up with her, and thenceforth would see no one. His pride was broken, and his heart; so he wasted away, day by day, and even his daughter rejoiced when death relieved him.

Then she sold the estate and disappeared.

2

In 1886 a young woman was living in a modest house near a secluded New England village, with no company but a little boy about five years old. She did her own work, she discouraged acquaintanceships, and had none. The butcher, the baker, and the others that served her could tell the villagers nothing about her further than that her name was Stillman, and that she called the child Archy. Whence she came they had not been able to find out, but they said she talked like a Southerner. The child had no playmates and no comrade, and no teacher but the mother. She taught him diligently and intelligently, and was satisfied with the results—even a little proud of them. One day Archy said:

"Mamma, am I different from other children?"

"Well, I suppose not. Why?"

"There was a child going along out there and asked me if the postman had been by and I said yes, and she said how long since I saw him and I said I hadn't seen him at all, and she said how did I know he'd been by, then, and I said because I smelt his track on the sidewalk, and she said I was a dum fool and made a mouth at me. What did she do that for?"

The young woman turned white, and said to herself, "It's a birthmark! The gift of the bloodhound is in him." She snatched the boy to her breast and hugged him passionately, saying, "God has appointed the way!" Her eyes were burning with a fierce light, and her breath came short and quick with excitement. She said to herself: "The puzzle is solved now; many a time it has been a mystery to me, the impossible things the child has done in the dark, but it is all clear to me now."

She set him in his small chair, and said:

"Wait a little till I come, dear, then we will talk about the matter."

She went up to her room and took from her dressing-table several small articles and put them out of sight: a nail-file on the floor under the bed; a pair of nail-scissors under the bureau; a small ivory paper-knife under the wardrobe. Then she returned, and said:

"There! I have left some things which I ought to have brought down." She named them, and said, "Run up and bring them, dear."

The child hurried away on his errand and was soon back again with the things.

"Did you have any difficulty, dear?"

"No, mamma; I only went where you went."

During his absence she had stepped to the bookcase, taken several books from the bottom shelf, opened each, passed her hand over a page, noting its number in her memory, then restored them to their places. Now she said:

"I have been doing something while you have been gone, Archy. Do you think you can find out what it was?"

The boy went to the bookcase and got out the books that

had been touched, and opened them at the pages which had been stroked.

The mother took him in her lap, and said:

"I will answer your questions now, dear. I have found out that in one way you are quite different from other people. You can see in the dark, you can smell what other people cannot, you have the talents of a bloodhound. They are good and valuable things to have, but you must keep the matter a secret. If people found it out, they would speak of you as an odd child, a strange child, and children would be disagreeable to you, and give you nicknames. In this world one must be like everybody else if he doesn't want to provoke scorn or envy or jealousy. It is a great and fine distinction which has been born to you, and I am glad; but you will keep it a secret for mamma's sake, won't you?"

The child promised, without understanding.

All the rest of the day the mother's brain was busy with excited thinkings; with plans, projects, schemes, each and all of them uncanny, grim, and dark. Yet they lit up her face; lit it with a fell light of their own; lit it with vague fires of hell. She was in a fever of unrest; she could not sit, stand, read, sew; there was no relief for her but in movement. She tested her boy's gift in twenty ways, and kept saying to herself all the time, with her mind in the past: "He broke my father's heart, and night and day all these years I have tried, and all in vain, to think out a way to break his. I have found it now—I have found it now."

When night fell, the demon of unrest still possessed her. She went on with her tests; with a candle she traversed the house from garret to cellar, hiding pins, needles, thimbles, spools, under pillows, under carpets, in cracks in the walls, under the coal in the bin; then sent the little fellow in the dark to find them; which he did, and was happy and proud when she praised him and smothered him with caresses.

From this time forward life took on a new complexion for her. She said, "The future is secure—I can wait, and enjoy the waiting." The most of her lost interests revived. She took up music again, and languages, drawing, painting, and the other long-discarded delights of her maidenhood. She was happy once more, and felt again the zest of life. As the years drifted by she watched the development of her boy, and was contented with it. Not altogether, but nearly that. The soft side of his heart was larger than the other side of it. It was his only defect, in her eyes. But she considered that his love for her and worship of her made up for it. He was a good hater—that was well; but it was a question if the materials of his hatreds were of as tough and enduring a quality as those of his friendships—and that was not so well.

The years drifted on. Archy was become a handsome, shapely, athletic youth, courteous, dignified, companionable, pleasant in his ways, and looking perhaps a trifle older than he was, which was sixteen. One evening his mother said she had something of grave importance to say to him, adding that he was old enough to hear it now, and old enough and possessed of character enough and stability enough to carry out a stern plan which she had been for years contriving and maturing. Then she told him her bitter story, in all its naked atrociousness. For a while the boy was paralyzed; then he said:

"I understand. We are Southerners; and by our custom and nature there is but one atonement. I will search him out and kill him."

"Kill him? No! Death is release, emancipation; death is a favor. Do I owe him favors? You must not hurt a hair of his head."

The boy was lost in thought awhile; then he said:

"You are all the world to me, and your desire is my law and my pleasure. Tell me what to do and I will do it."

The mother's eyes beamed with satisfaction, and she said:

"You will go and find him. I have known his hiding-place

for eleven years; it cost me five years and more of inquiry, and much money, to locate it. He is a quartz-miner in Colorado, and well-to-do. He lives in Denver. His name is Jacob Fuller. There—it is the first time I have spoken it since that unforgettable night. Think! That name could have been yours if I had not saved you that shame and furnished you a cleaner one. You will drive him from that place; you will hunt him down and drive him again; and yet again, and again, and again, persistently, relentlessly, poisoning his life, filling it with mysterious terrors, loading it with weariness and misery, making him wish for death, and that he had a suicide's courage; you will make of him another Wandering Jew; he shall know no rest any more, no peace of mind, no placid sleep; you shall shadow him, cling to him, persecute him, till you break his heart, as he broke my father's and mine."

"I will obey, mother."

"I believe it, my child. The preparations are all made; everything is ready. Here is a letter of credit; spend freely, there is no lack of money. At times you may need disguises. I have provided them; also some other conveniences." She took from the drawer of the typewriter-table several squares of paper. They all bore these typewritten words:

$10,000 REWARD

It is believed that a certain man who is wanted in an Eastern state is sojourning here. In 1880, *in the night, he tied his young wife to a tree by the public road, cut her across the face with a cowhide, and made his dogs tear her clothes from her, leaving her naked. He left her there, and fled the country. A blood-relative of hers has searched for him for seventeen years. Address . . . . , ... , Post-office. The above reward will be paid in cash to the person who will furnish the seeker, in a personal interview, the criminal's address.*

"When you have found him and acquainted yourself with his scent, you will go in the night and placard one of these upon the building he occupies, and another one upon the post-office or in some other prominent place. It will be the talk of the region. At first you must give him several days in which to force a sale of his belongings at something approaching their value. We will ruin him by and by, but gradually; we must not impoverish him at once, for that could bring him to despair and injure his health, possibly kill him."

She took three or four more typewritten forms from the drawer—duplicates—and read one:

. . . . . , ... , 18 . . .

To Jacob Fuller:

You have . . . . . days in which to settle your affairs. You will not be disturbed during that limit, which will expire at . . . . M., *on the . . . of . . . . You must then* MOVE ON. *If you are still in the place after the named hour, I will placard you on all the dead walls, detailing your crime once more, and adding the date, also the scene of it, with all names concerned, including your own. Have no fear of bodily injury—it will in no circumstances ever be inflicted upon you. You brought misery upon an old man, and ruined his life and broke his heart. What he suffered, you are to suffer.*

"You will add no signature. He must receive this before he learns of the reward placard—before he rises in the morning—lest he lose his head and fly the place penniless."

"I shall not forget."

"You will need to use these forms only in the beginning—once may be enough. Afterward, when you are ready for him to vanish out of a place, see that he gets a copy of *this* form, which merely says:

MOVE ON. *You have . . . . . . days.*

"He will obey. That is sure."

3

Extracts from letters to the mother:

DENVER, *April 3, 1897*

I have now been living several days in the same hotel with Jacob Fuller. I have his scent; I could track him through ten divisions of infantry and find him. I have often been near him and heard him talk. He owns a good mine, and has a fair income from it; but he is not rich. He learned mining in a good way—by working at it for wages. He is a cheerful creature, and his forty-three years sit lightly upon him; he could pass for a younger man—say thirty-six or thirty-seven. He has never married again—passes himself off for a widower. He stands well, is liked, is popular, and has many friends. Even I feel a drawing toward him—the paternal blood in me making its claim. How blind and unreasoning and arbitrary are some of the laws of nature—the most of them, in fact! My task is become hard now—you realize it? you comprehend, and make allowances?—and the fire of it has cooled, more than I like to confess to myself. But I will carry it out. Even with the pleasure paled, the duty remains, and I will not spare him.

And for my help, a sharp resentment rises in me when I reflect that he who committed that odious crime is the only one who has not suffered by it. The lesson of it has manifestly reformed his character, and in the change he is happy. He, the guilty party, is absolved from all suffering; you, the innocent, are borne down with it. But be comforted—he shall harvest his share.

SILVER GULCH, *May 19*

I placarded Form No. 1 at midnight of April 3; an hour later I slipped Form No. 2 under his chamber door, notifying him to leave Denver at or before 11.50 the night of the 14th.

Some late bird of a reporter stole one of my placards, then hunted the town over and found the other one, and stole that. In this manner he accomplished what the profession call a "scoop"—that is, he got a valuable item, and saw to it that no other paper got it. And so his paper—the principal one in the town—had it in glaring type on the editorial page in the morning, followed by a Vesuvian opinion of our wretch a column long, which wound up by adding a thousand dollars to our reward on the paper's *account! The journals out here know how to do the noble thing—when there's business in it.*

At breakfast I occupied my usual seat—selected because it afforded a view of papa Fuller's face, and was near enough for me to hear the talk that went on at his table. Seventy-five or a hundred people were in the room, and all discussing that item, and saying they hoped the seeker would find that rascal and remove the pollution of his presence from the town—with a rail, or a bullet, or something.

When Fuller came in he had the Notice to Leave—folded up—in one hand, and the newspaper in the other; and it gave me more than half a pang to see him. His cheerfulness was all gone, and he looked old and pinched and ashy. And then—only think of the things he had to listen to! Mamma, he heard his own unsuspecting friends describe him with epithets and characterizations drawn from the very dictionaries and phrase-books of Satan's own authorized editions down below. And more than that, he had to agree *with the verdicts and applaud them. His applause tasted bitter in his mouth, though; he could not disguise that from me; and it was observable that his appetite was gone; he only nibbled; he couldn't eat. Finally a man said:*

"It is quite likely that that relative is in the room and hearing what this town thinks of that unspeakable scoundrel. I hope so."

Ah, dear, it was pitiful the way Fuller winced, and glanced around scared! He couldn't endure any more, and got up and left.

During several days he gave out that he had bought a mine in Mexico, and wanted to sell out and go down there as soon as he could, and give the property his personal attention. He played his cards well; said he would take $40,000*—a quarter in cash, the rest in safe notes; but that as he greatly needed money on account of his new purchase, he would diminish his terms for cash in full. He sold out for $30,000. And then, what do you think he did? He asked for* greenbacks, *and took them, saying the man in Mexico was a New-Englander, with a head full of crotchets, and preferred greenbacks to gold or drafts. People thought it queer, since a draft on New York could produce greenbacks quite conveniently. There was talk of this odd thing, but only for a day; that is as long as any topic lasts in Denver.*

I was watching, all the time. As soon as the sale was completed and the money paid—which was on the 11th—I began to stick to Fuller's track without dropping it for a moment. That night—no, 12th, for it was a little past midnight—I tracked him to his room, which was four doors from mine in the same hall; then I went back and put on my muddy day-laborer disguise, darkened my complexion, and sat down in my room in the gloom, with a gripsack handy, with a change in it, and my door ajar. For I suspected that the bird would take wing now. In half an hour an old woman passed by, carrying a grip: I caught the familiar whiff, and followed with my grip, for it was Fuller. He left the hotel by a side entrance, and at the corner he turned up an unfrequented street and walked three blocks in a light rain and a heavy darkness, and got into a two-horse hack, which of course was waiting for him by appointment. I took a seat (uninvited) on the trunk platform behind, and we drove briskly off. We drove ten miles, and the hack stopped at a way-station and was discharged. Putter got out and took a seat on a barrow under the awning, as far as he could get from the light; I went inside, and watched the ticket-office. Fuller bought no ticket; I bought none. Presently the train came along, and he boarded a car; I entered the same car at the other end, and came down the aisle and took the seat behind him. When he paid the conductor and named his objective point, I dropped back several seats, while the conductor was changing a bill, and when he came to me I paid to the same place—about a hundred miles westward.

From that time for a week on end he led me a dance. He traveled here and there and yonder—always on a general westward trend—but he was not a woman after the first day. He was a laborer, like myself, and wore bushy false whiskers. His outfit was perfect, and he could do the character without thinking about it, for he had served the trade for wages. His nearest friend could not have recognized him. At last he located himself here, the obscurest little mountain camp in Montana; he has a shanty, and goes out prospecting daily; is gone all day, and avoids society. I am living at a miner's boardinghouse, and it is an awful place; the bunks, the food, the dirt—everything.

We have been here four weeks, and in that time I have seen him but once; but every night I go over his track and post myself. As soon as he engaged a shanty here I went to a town fifty miles away and telegraphed that Denver hotel to keep my baggage till I should send for it. I need nothing here but a change of army shirts, and I brought that with me.

SILVER GULCH, *June 12*

The Denver episode has never found its way here, I think. I know the most of the men in camp, and they have never referred to it, at least in my hearing. Fuller doubtless feels quite safe in these conditions. He has located a claim, two miles away, in an out-of-the-way place in the mountains; it promises very well, and he is working it diligently. Ah, but the change in him! He never smiles, and he keeps quite to himself, consorting with no one—he who was so fond of company and so cheery only two months ago. I have seen him passing along several times recently—drooping, forlorn, the spring gone from his step, a pathetic figure. He calls himself David Wilson.

I can trust him to remain here until we disturb him. Since you insist, I will banish him again, but I do not see how he can be unhappier than he already is. I will go back to Denver and treat myself to a little season of comfort, and edible food, and endurable beds, and bodily decency; then I will fetch my things, and notify poor papa Wilson to move on.

DENVER, *June 19*

They miss him here. They all hope he is prospering in Mexico, and they do not say it just with their mouths, but out of their hearts. You know you can always tell. I am loitering here overlong, I confess it. But if you were in my place you would have charity for me. Yes, I know what you will say, and you are right: if I were in your place, and carried your scalding memories in my heart—

I will take the night train back to-morrow.

DENVER, *June 20*

God forgive us, mother, we are hunting the wrong man! *I have not slept any all night. I am now waiting, at dawn, for the* morning *train—and how the minutes drag, how they drag!*

This Jacob Fuller is a cousin *of the guilty one. How stupid we have been not to reflect that the guilty one would never again wear his own name after that fiendish deed! The Denver Fuller is four years younger than the other one;*

he came here a young widower in '79, aged twenty-one—a year before you were married; and the documents to prove it are innumerable. Last night I talked with familiar friends of his who have known him from the day of his arrival. I said nothing, but a few days from now I will land him in this town again, with the loss upon his mine made good; and there will be a banquet, and a torch-light procession, and there will not be any expense on anybody but me. Do you call this "gush"? I am only a boy, as you well know; it is my privilege. By and by I shall not be a boy any more.

SILVER GULCH, *July 3*

Mother, he is gone! Gone, and left no trace. The scent was cold when I came. To-day I am out of bed for the first time since. I wish I were not a boy; then I could stand shocks better. They all think he went west. I start to-night, in a wagon—two or three hours of that, then I get a train. I don't know where I'm going, but I must go; to try to keep still would be torture.

Of course he has effaced himself with a new name and a disguise. This means that I may have to search the whole globe to find him. *Indeed it is what I expect. Do you see, mother? It is I that am the Wandering Jew. The irony of it! We arranged that for another.*

Think of the difficulties! And there would be none if I only could advertise for him. But if there is any way to do it that would not frighten him, I have not been able to think it out, and I have tried till my brains are addled. "If the gentleman who lately bought a mine in Mexico and sold one in Denver will send his address to" (to whom, mother!), "it will be explained to him that it was all a mistake; his forgiveness will be asked, and full reparation made for a loss which he sustained in a certain matter." Do you see? He would think it a trap. Well, any one would. If I should say, "It is now known that he was not the man wanted, but another man—who once bore the same name, but discarded it for good rea-

sons"—would that answer? But the Denver people would wake up then and say "Oho!" and they would remember about the suspicious greenbacks, and say, "Why did he run away if he wasn't the right man?—it is too thin." If I failed to find him he would be ruined there—there where there is no taint upon him now. You have a better head than mine. Help me.

I have one clue, and only one. I know his handwriting. If he puts his new false name upon a hotel register and does not disguise it too much, it will be valuable to me if I ever run across it.

SAN FRANCISCO, *June 28, 1898*

You already know how well I have searched the states from Colorado to the Pacific, and how nearly I came to getting him once. Well, I have had another close miss. It was here, yesterday. I struck his trail, hot on the street, and followed it on a run to a cheap hotel. That was a costly mistake; a dog would have gone the other way. But I am only part dog, and can get very humanly stupid when excited. He had been stopping in that house ten days; I almost know, now, that he stops long nowhere, the past six or eight months, but is restless and has to keep moving. I understand that feeling! and I know what it is to feel it. He still uses the name he had registered when I came so near catching him nine months ago—"James Walker"; doubtless the same he adopted when he fled from Silver Gulch. An unpretending man, and has small taste for fancy names. I recognized the hand easily, through its slight disguise. A square man, and not good at shams and pretenses.

They said he was just gone, on a journey; left no address; didn't say where he was going; looked frightened when asked to leave his address; had no baggage but a cheap valise; carried it off on foot—a "stingy old person, and not much loss to the house." "Old!" *I suppose he is, now. I hardly heard; I was there but a moment. I rushed along his trail, and it led me to a wharf. Mother, the smoke of the steamer he had taken was just fading out on the horizon! I should have saved half an hour if I had gone in the right direction at first. I could have taken a fast tug, and should have stood a chance of catching that vessel. She is bound for Melbourne.*

HOPE CAÑON, *California, October 3, 1900*

You have a right to complain. "A letter a year" is a paucity; I freely acknowledge it; but how can one write when there is nothing to write about but failures? No one can keep it up; it breaks the heart.

I told you—it seems ages ago, now—how I missed him at Melbourne, and then chased him all over Australasia for months on end.

Well, then, after that I followed him to India; almost saw *him in Bombay; traced him all around—to Baroda, Rawal-Pindi, Lucknow, Lahore, Cawnpore, Allahabad, Calcutta, Madras—oh, everywhere; week after week, month after month, through the dust and swelter—always approximately on his track, sometimes close upon him, yet never catching him. And down to Ceylon, and then to— Never mind; by and by I will write it all out.*

I chased him home to California, and down to Mexico, and back again to California. Since then I have been hunting him about the state from the first of last January down to a month ago. I feel almost sure he is not far from Hope Cañon; I traced him to a point thirty miles from here, but there I lost the trail; some one gave him a lift in a wagon, I suppose.

I am taking a rest, now—modified by searchings for the lost trail. I was tired to death, mother, and low-spirited, and sometimes coming uncomfortably near to losing hope; but the miners in this little camp are good fellows, and I am used to their sort this long time back; and their breezy ways freshen a person up and make him forget his troubles. I have been here a month. I am cabining with a young fellow named "Sammy" Hillyer, about twenty-five, the only son of his mother—like me—and loves her dearly, and writes to her every week—part of which is like me. He is a timid body, and in the matter of intellect—well, he cannot be depended upon to set a river on fire; but no matter, he is well liked; he is good and fine, and it is meat and bread and rest and luxury to sit and talk with him and have a comradeship again. I wish "James Walker" could have it. He had friends; he liked company. That brings up that picture of him, the time that I saw him last. The pathos of it! It comes before me often and often. At that very time, poor thing, I was girding up my conscience to make him move on again!

Hillyer's heart is better than mine, better than anybody's in the community, I suppose, for he is the one friend of the black sheep of the camp—Flint Buckner—and the only man Flint ever talks with or allows to talk with him. He says he knows Flint's history, and that it is trouble that has made him what he is, and so one ought to be as charitable toward him as one can. Now none but a pretty large heart could find space to accommodate a lodger like Flint Buckner, from all I hear about him outside. I think that this one detail will give you a better idea of Sammy's character than any labored-out description I could furnish you of him. In one of our talks he said something about like this: "Flint is a kinsman of mine, and he pours out all his troubles to me—empties his breast from time to time, or I reckon it would burst. There couldn't be any unhappier man, Archy Stillman; his life had been made up of misery of mind—he isn't near as old as he looks. He has lost the feel of reposefulness and peace—oh, years and years ago! He doesn't know what good luck is—never has had any; often says he wishes he was in the other hell, he is so tired of this one."

4

No real gentleman will tell the naked truth in the presence of ladies.

It was a crisp and spicy morning in early October. The lilacs and laburnums, lit with the glory-fires of autumn, hung burning and flashing in the upper air, a fairy bridge provided by kind Nature for the wingless wild things that have their homes in the tree-tops and would visit together; the larch and the pomegranate flung their purple and yellow flames in brilliant broad splashes along the slanting sweep of the woodland; the sensuous fragrance of innumerable deciduous flowers rose upon the swooning atmosphere; far in the empty sky a solitary esophagus* slept upon motionless wing; everywhere brooded stillness, serenity, and the peace of God.

To the Editor of the Republican:

One of your citizens has asked me a question about the "esophagus" and I wish to answer him through you. This is the hope that the answer will get around, and save me some penmanship, for I have already replied to the same question more than several times, and am not getting as much holiday as I ought to have.

I published a short story lately, and it was in that that I put the esophagus. I will say privately that I expected it to bother some people—in fact, that was the intention—but the harvest has been larger than I was calculating upon. The esophagus has gathered in the guilty and the innocent alike, whereas I was only fishing for the innocent—the innocent and confiding. I knew a few of these would write and ask me; that would give me but little trouble; but I was not

* [From the Springfield Republican, April 12, 1902.]

expecting that the wise and the learned would call upon me for succor. However, that has happened, and it is time for me to speak up and stop the inquiries if I can, for letter-writing is not restful to me and I am not having so much fun out of this thing as I counted on. That you may understand the situation, I will insert a couple of sample inquiries. The first is from a public instructor in the Philippines:

SANTA CRUZ, *Ilocos, Sur, P.I.*
February 13, 1902

My dear Sir,—I have just been reading the first part of your latest story, entitled "A Double-barreled Detective Story," and am very much delighted with it. In Part IV, Page 264, Harper's Magazine *for January, occurs this passage: "far in the empty sky a solitary 'esophagus' slept upon motionless wing; everywhere brooded stillness, serenity, and the peace of God." Now, there is one word I do not understand, namely, "esophagus." My only work of reference is the* Standard Dictionary, *but that fails to explain the meaning. If you can spare the time, I would be glad to have the meaning cleared up, as I consider the passage a very touching and beautiful one. It may seem foolish to you, but consider my lack of means away out in the northern part of Luzon.*

Yours very truly.

Do you notice? Nothing in the paragraph disturbed him but that one word. It shows that that paragraph was most ably constructed for the deception it was intended to put upon the reader. It was my intention that it should read plausibly, and it is now plain that it does; it was my intention that it should be emotional and touching, and you see, yourself, that it fetched this public instructor. Alas, if I had but left that one treacherous word out, I should have scored! scored everywhere; and the paragraph would have slidden through every reader's sensibilities like oil, and left not a suspicion behind.

The other sample inquiry is from a professor in a New England university. It contains one naughty word (which I cannot bear to suppress), but he is not in the theological department, so it is no harm:

Dear Mr. Clemens: "Far in the empty sky a solitary esophagus slept upon motionless wing."

It is not often I get a chance to read much periodical literature, but I have just gone through at this belated period, with much gratification and edification, your "Double-barreled Detective Story."

But what in hell is an esophagus? I keep one myself, but it never sleeps in the air or anywhere else. My profession is to deal with words, and esophagus interested me the moment I lighted upon it. But as a companion of my youth used to say, "I'll be eternally, co-eternally cussed" if I can make it out. Is it a joke, or I an ignoramus?

Between you and me, I was almost ashamed of having fooled that man, but for pride's sake I was going to say so. I wrote and told him it was a joke—and that is what I am now saying to my Springfield inquirer. And I told him to carefully read the whole paragraph, and he would find not a vestige of sense in any detail of it. This also I commend to my Springfield inquirer.

I have confessed. I am sorry—partially. I will not do so any more—for the present. Don't ask me any more questions; let the esophagus have a rest—on his same old motionless wing.

MARK TWAIN

New York City, April 10, 1902

(Editorial)

☞ *The Double-barreled Detective Story," which appeared in* Harper's Magazine *for January and February last, is the most elaborate of burlesques on detective fiction, with strik-*

ing melodramatic passages in which it is difficult to detect the deception, so ably is it done. But the illusion ought not to endure even the first incident in the February number. As for the paragraph which has so admirably illustrated the skill of Mr. Clemens's ensemble and the carelessness of readers, here it is:

> *"It was a crisp and spicy morning in early October. The lilacs and laburnums, lit with the glory-fires of autumn, hung burning and flashing in the upper air, a fairy bridge provided by kind nature for the wingless wild things that have their home in the tree-tops and would visit together; the larch and the pomegranate flung their purple and yellow flames in brilliant broad splashes along the slanting sweep of the woodland; the sensuous fragrance of innumerable deciduous flowers rose upon the swooning atmosphere; far in the empty sky a solitary esophagus slept upon motionless wings; everywhere brooded stillness, serenity, and the peace of God."*

The success of Mark Twain's joke recalls to mind his story of the petrified man in the cavern, whom he described most punctiliously, first giving a picture of the scene, its impressive solitude, and all that; then going on to describe the majesty of the figure, casually mentioning that the thumb of his right hand rested against the side of his nose; then after further description observing that the fingers of the right hand were extended in a radiating fashion; and, recurring to the dignified attitude and position of the man, incidentally remarked that the thumb of the left hand was in contact with the little finger of the right—and so on. But was it so ingeniously written that Mark, relating the history years later in an article which appeared in that excellent magazine of the past, the Galaxy, *declared that no one ever found out the joke, and, if we remember aright, that that astonishing old mockery was actually looked for in the region where he, as a Nevada newspaper editor, had located it. It is certain that Mark Twain's jumping frog has a good many more "pints" than any other frog.*

October is the time—1900; Hope Cañon is the place, a silver-mining camp away down in the Esmeralda region. It is a secluded spot, high and remote; recent as to discovery; thought by its occupants to be rich in metal—a year or two's prospecting will decide that matter one way or the other. For inhabitants, the camp has about two hundred miners, one white woman and child, several Chinese washermen, five squaws, and a dozen vagrant buck Indians in rabbit-skin robes, battered plug hats, and tin-can necklaces. There are no mills as yet; no church, no newspaper. The camp has existed but two years; it has made no big strike; the world is ignorant of its name and place.

On both sides of the cañon the mountains rise wall-like, three thousand feet, and the long spiral of straggling huts down in its narrow bottom gets a kiss from the sun only once a day, when he sails over at noon. The village is a couple of miles long; the cabins stand well apart from each other. The tavern is the only "frame" house—the only house, one might say. It occupies a central position, and is the evening resort of the population. They drink there, and play seven-up and dominoes; also billiards, for there is a table, crossed all over with torn places repaired with court-plaster; there are some cues, but no leathers; some chipped balls which clatter when they run, and do not slow up gradually, but stop suddenly and sit down; there is a part of a cube of chalk, with a projecting jag of flint in it; and the man who can score six on a single break can set up the drinks at the bar's expense.

Flint Buckner's cabin was the last one of the village, going south; his silver-claim was at the other end of the village, northward, and a little beyond the last hut in that direction. He was a sour creature, unsociable, and had no companionships. People who had tried to get acquainted with him had regretted it and dropped him. His history was not known. Some believed that Sammy Hillyer knew it; others said no. If asked, Hillyer said no, he was not acquainted with it. Flint had a meek English youth of sixteen or seventeen with him, whom he treated roughly, both in public and in private; and of course this lad was applied to for information, but with no success. Fetlock Jones—name of the youth—said that Flint picked him up on a prospecting tramp, and as he had neither home nor friends in America, he had found it wise to stay and take Buckner's hard usage for the sake of the salary, which was bacon and beans. Further than this he could offer no testimony.

Fetlock had been in this slavery for a month now, and under his meek exterior he was slowly consuming to a cinder with the insults and humiliations which his master had put upon him. For the meek suffer bitterly from these hurts; more bitterly, perhaps, than do the manlier sort, who can burst out and get relief with words or blows when the limit of endurance has been reached. Good-hearted people wanted to help Fetlock out of his trouble, and tried to get him to leave Buckner, but the boy showed fright at the thought, and said he "dasn't." Pat Riley urged him, and said:

"You leave the damned skunk and come with me; don't you be afraid. I'll take care of *him.*"

The boy thanked him with tears in his eyes, but shuddered and said he "dasn't risk it"; he said Flint would catch him alone, some time, in the night, and then— "Oh, it makes me sick, Mr. Riley, to think of it."

Others said, "Run away from him; we'll stake you; skip out for the coast some night." But all these suggestions failed; he said Flint would hunt him down and fetch him back, just for meanness.

The people could not understand this. The boy's miseries went steadily on, week after week. It is quite likely that the people would have understood if they had known how he was employing his spare time. He slept in an out-cabin near Flint's; and there, nights, he nursed his bruises and his humiliations, and studied and studied over a single problem—how he could murder Flint Buckner and not be found out. It was the only joy he had in life; these hours were the only ones in the twenty-four which he looked forward to with eagerness and spent in happiness.

He thought of poison. No—that would not serve; the inquest would reveal where it was procured and who had procured it. He thought of a shot in the back in a lonely place when Flint would be homeward bound at midnight—his unvarying hour for the trip. No—somebody might be near, and catch him. He thought of stabbing him in his sleep. No—he might strike an inefficient blow, and Flint would seize him. He examined a hundred different ways—none of them would answer; for in even the very obscurest and secretest of them there was always the fatal defect of a *risk*, a chance, a possibility that he might be found out. He would have none of that.

But he was patient, endlessly patient. There was no hurry, he said to himself. He would never leave Flint till he left him a corpse; there was no hurry—he would find the way. It was somewhere, and he would endure shame and pain and misery until he found it. Yes, somewhere there was a way which would leave not a trace, not even the faintest clue to the murderer—there was no hurry—he would find that way, and then—oh, then, it would just be good to be alive! Meantime he would diligently keep up his reputation for meekness; and also, as always theretofore, he would allow no one to hear him say a resentful or offensive thing about his oppressor.

Two days before the before-mentioned October morning Flint had bought some things, and he and Fetlock had brought them home to Flint's cabin: a fresh box of candles, which they put in the corner; a tin can of blasting-powder, which they placed upon the candle-box; a keg of blasting-powder, which they placed under Flint's bunk; a huge coil of fuse, which they hung on a peg. Fetlock reasoned that Flint's mining operations had outgrown the pick, and that blasting was about to begin now. He had seen blasting done, and he had a notion of the process, but he had never helped in it. His conjecture was right—blasting-time had come. In the morning the pair carried fuse, drills, and the powder-can to the shaft; it was now eight feet deep, and to get into it and out of it a short ladder was used. They descended, and by command Fetlock held the drill—without any instructions as to the right way to hold it—and Flint proceeded to strike. The sledge came down; the drill sprang out of Fetlock's hand, almost as a matter of course.

"You mangy son of a nigger, is that any way to hold a drill? Pick it up! Stand it up! There—hold fast. D—— you! *I'll* teach you!"

At the end of an hour the drilling was finished.

"Now, then, charge it."

The boy started to pour in the powder.

"Idiot!"

A heavy bat on the jaw laid the lad out.

"Get up! You can't lie sniveling there. Now, then, stick in the fuse *first*. *Now* put in the powder. Hold on, hold on! Are you going to fill the hole *all* up? Of all the sap-headed milksops I— Put in some dirt! Put in some gravel! Tamp it down! Hold on, hold on! Oh, great Scott! get out of the way!" He snatched the iron and tamped the charge himself, meantime cursing and blaspheming like a fiend. Then he fired the fuse, climbed out of the shaft, and ran fifty yards away, Fetlock following. They stood waiting a few minutes, then a great volume of smoke and rocks burst high into the air with a thunderous explosion; after a little there was a shower of descending stones; then all was serene again.

"I wish to God you'd been in it!" remarked the master.

They went down the shaft, cleaned it out, drilled another hole, and put in another charge.

"Look here! How much fuse are you proposing to waste? Don't you know how to time a fuse?"

"No, sir."

"You *don't!* Well, if you don't beat anything *I* ever saw!"

He climbed out of the shaft and spoke down:

"Well, idiot, are you going to be all day? Cut the fuse and light it!"

The trembling creature began:

"If you please, sir, I—"

"You talk back to *me?* Cut it and light it!"

The boy cut and lit.

"Ger-reat Scott! a one-minute fuse! I wish you were in—"

In his rage he snatched the ladder out of the shaft and ran. The boy was aghast.

"Oh, my God! Help! Help! Oh, save me!" he implored. "Oh, what can I do! What *can* I do!"

He backed against the wall as tightly as he could; the sputtering fuse frightened the voice out of him; his breath stood still; he stood gazing and impotent; in two seconds, three seconds, four he would be flying toward the sky torn to fragments. Then he had an inspiration. He sprang at the fuse; severed the inch of it that was left above ground, and was saved.

He sank down limp and half lifeless with fright, his strength gone; but he muttered with a deep joy:

"He has learnt me! I knew there was a way, if I would wait."

After a matter of five minutes Buckner stole to the shaft, looking worried and uneasy, and peered down into it. He took in the situation; he saw what had happened. He lowered the ladder, and the boy dragged himself weakly up it. He was very white. His appearance added something to Buckner's uncomfortable state, and he said, with a show of regret and sympathy which sat upon him awkwardly from lack of practice:

"It was an accident, you know. Don't say anything about

it to anybody; I was excited, and didn't notice what I was doing. You're not looking well; you've worked enough for to-day; go down to my cabin and eat what you want, and rest. It's just an accident, you know, on account of my being excited."

"It scared me," said the lad, as he started away; "but I learnt something, so I don't mind it."

"Damned easy to please!" muttered Buckner, following him with his eye. "I wonder if he'll tell? Mightn't he? . . . I wish it *had* killed him."

The boy took no advantage of his holiday in the matter of resting; he employed it in work, eager and feverish and happy work. A thick growth of chaparral extended down the mountainside clear to Flint's cabin; the most of Fetlock's labor was done in the dark intricacies of that stubborn growth; the rest of it was done in his own shanty. At last all was complete, and he said:

"If he's got any suspicions that I'm going to tell on him, he won't keep them long, to-morrow. He will see that I am the same milksop as I always was—all day and the next. And the day after to-morrow night there'll be an end of him; nobody will ever guess who finished him up nor how it was done. He dropped me the idea his own self, and that's odd."

5

The next day came and went.

It is now almost midnight, and in five minutes the new morning will begin. The scene is in the tavern billiard-room. Rough men in rough clothing, slouch-hats, breeches stuffed into boot-tops, some with vests, none with coats, are grouped about the boiler-iron stove, which has ruddy cheeks and is distributing a grateful warmth; the billiard-balls are clacking; there is no other sound—that is, within; the wind is fitfully moaning without. The men look bored; also expectant. A hulking broad-shouldered miner, of middle age, with grizzled whiskers, and an unfriendly eye set in an unsociable face, rises, slips a coil of fuse upon his arm, gathers up some other personal properties, and departs without word or greeting to anybody. It is Flint Buckner. As the door closes behind him a buzz of talk breaks out.

The regularest man that ever was," said Jake Parker, the blacksmith: "you can tell when it's twelve just by him leaving, without looking at your Waterbury."

"And it's the only virtue he's got, as fur as I know," said Peter Hawes, miner.

"He's just a blight on this society," said Wells-Fargo's man, Ferguson. "If I was running this shop I'd made him say something, *some* time or other, or vamos the ranch." This with a suggestive glance at the barkeeper, who did not choose to see it, since the man under discussion was a good customer, and went home pretty well set up, every night, with refreshments furnished from the bar.

"Say," said Ham Sandwich, miner, "does any of you boys ever recollect of him asking you to take a drink?"

"*Him?* Flint *Buckner?* Oh, Laura!"

This sarcastic rejoinder came in a spontaneous general outburst in one form of words or another from the crowd. After a brief silence, Pat Riley, miner, said:

"He's the 15-puzzle, that cuss. And his boy's another one. *I* can't make them out."

"Nor anybody else," said Ham Sandwich; "and if they are 15-puzzles, how are you going to rank up that other one? When it comes to A 1 right-down solid mysteriousness, he lays over both of them. *Easy*—don't he?"

"You bet!"

Everybody said it. Every man but one. He was the newcomer—Peterson. He ordered the drinks all round, and asked who No. 3 might be. All answered at once, "Archy Stillman!"

"Is he a mystery?" asked Peterson.

"Is *he* a mystery? Is Archy *Stillman* a mystery?" said

Wells-Fargo's man, Ferguson. "Why, the fourth dimension's foolishness to *him.*"

For Ferguson was learned.

Peterson wanted to hear all about him; everybody wanted to tell him; everybody began. But Billy Stevens, the barkeeper, called the house to order, and said one at a time was best. He distributed the drinks, and appointed Ferguson to lead. Ferguson said:

"Well, he's a boy. And that is just about all we know about him. You can pump him till you are tired; it ain't any use; you won't get anything. At least about his intentions, or line of business, or where he's from, and such things as that. And as for getting at the nature and get-up of his main big chief mystery, why, he'll just change the subject, that's all. You can *guess* till you're black in the face—it's your privilege—but suppose you do, where do you arrive at? Nowhere, as near as I can make out."

"What *is* his big chief one?"

"Sight, maybe. Hearing, maybe. Instinct, maybe. Magic, maybe. Take your choice—grown-ups, twenty-five; children and servants, half price. Now I'll tell you what he can do. You can start here, and just disappear; you can go and hide wherever you want to, I don't care where it is, nor how far—and he'll go straight and put his finger on you."

"You don't mean it!"

"I just do, though. Weather's nothing to him—elemental conditions is nothing to him—he don't even take notice of them."

"Oh, come! Dark? Rain? Snow? Hey?"

"It's all the same to *him.* He don't give a damn."

"Oh, *say*—including *fog,* per'aps?"

"*Fog!* he's got an eye 't can plunk through it like a bullet."

"Now, boys, honor bright, what's he giving me?"

"It's a fact!" they all shouted. "Go on, Wells-Fargo."

"Well, sir, you can leave him here, chatting with the boys, and you can slip out and go to any cabin in this camp and open a book—yes, sir, a dozen of them—and take the page in your memory, and he'll start out and go straight to that cabin and open every one of them books at the right page, and call it off, and never make a mistake."

"He must be the devil!"

"More than one has thought it. Now I'll tell you a perfectly wonderful thing that he done. The other night he—"

There was a sudden great murmur of sounds outside, the door flew open, and an excited crowd burst in, with the camp's one white woman in the lead and crying:

"My child! my child! she's lost and gone! For the love of God help me to find Archy Stillman; we've hunted everywhere!"

Said the barkeeper:

"Sit down, sit down, Mrs. Hogan, and don't worry. He asked for a bed three hours ago, tuckered out tramping the trails the way he's always doing, and went upstairs. Ham Sandwich, run up and roust him out; he's in No. 14."

The youth was soon down-stairs and ready. He asked Mrs. Hogan for particulars.

"Bless you, dear, there ain't any; I wish there was. I put her to sleep at seven in the evening, and when I went in there an hour ago to go to bed myself, she was gone. I rushed for your cabin, dear, and you wasn't there, and I've hunted for you ever since, at every cabin down the gulch, and now I've come up again, and I'm that distracted and scared and heart-broke; but, thanks to God, I've found you at last, dear heart, and you'll find my child. Come on! come quick!"

"Move right along; I'm with you, madam. Go to your cabin first."

The whole company streamed out to join the hunt. All the southern half of the village was up, a hundred men strong, and waiting outside, a vague dark mass sprinkled with twinkling lanterns. The mass fell into columns by threes and fours to accommodate itself to the narrow road, and strode briskly along southward in the wake of the leaders. In a few minutes the Hogan cabin was reached.

"There's the bunk," said Mrs. Hogan; "there's where she was; it's where I laid her at seven o'clock; but where she is now, God only knows."

"Hand me a lantern," said Archy. He set it on the hard earth floor and knelt by it, pretending to examine the ground closely. "Here's her track," he said, touching the ground here and there and yonder with his finger. "Do you see?"

Several of the company dropped upon their knees and did their best to see. One or two thought they discerned something like a track; the others shook their heads and confessed that the smooth hard surface had no marks upon it which their eyes were sharp enough to discover. One said, "Maybe a child's foot could make a mark on it, but *I* don't see how."

Young Stillman stepped outside, held the light to the ground, turned leftward, and moved three steps, closely examining; then said, "I've got the direction—come along; take the lantern, somebody."

He strode off swiftly southward, the files following, swaying and bending in and out with the deep curves of the gorge. Thus a mile, and the mouth of the gorge was reached; before them stretched the sage-brush plain, dim, vast, and vague. Stillman called a halt, saying, "We mustn't start wrong, now; we must take the direction again."

He took a lantern and examined the ground for a matter of twenty yards; then said, "Come on; it's all right," and gave up the lantern. In and out among the sage-bushes he marched, a quarter of a mile, bearing gradually to the right; then took a new direction and made another great semicircle; then changed again and moved due west nearly half a mile—and stopped.

"She gave it up, here, poor little chap. Hold the lantern. You can see where she sat."

But this was in a slick alkali flat which was surfaced like steel, and no person in the party was quite hardy enough to claim an eyesight that could detect the track of a cushion on a veneer like that. The bereaved mother fell upon her knees and kissed the spot, lamenting.

"But where is she, then?" some one said. "She didn't stay here. We can see *that* much, anyway."

Stillman moved about in a circle around the place, with the lantern, pretending to hunt for tracks.

"Well!" he said presently, in an annoyed tone, "I don't understand it." He examined again. "No use. She was here—that's certain; she never *walked* away from here—and that's certain. It's a puzzle; I can't make it out."

The mother lost heart then.

"Oh, my God! oh, blessed Virgin! some flying beast has got her. I'll never see her again!"

"Ah, *don't* give up," said Archy. "We'll find her—don't give up."

"God bless you for the words, Archy Stillman!" and she seized his hand and kissed it fervently.

Peterson, the new-comer, whispered satirically in Ferguson's ear:

"Wonderful performance to find this place, wasn't it? Hardly worth while to come so far, though; any other suppositious place would have answered just as well—hey?"

Ferguson was not pleased with the innuendo. He said, with some warmth:

"Do you mean to insinuate that the child hasn't been here? I tell you the child *has* been here! Now if you want to get yourself into as tidy a little fuss as—"

"All right!" sang out Stillman. "Come, everybody, and look at this! It was right under our noses all the time, and we didn't see it."

There was a general plunge for the ground at the place where the child was alleged to have rested, and many eyes tried hard and hopefully to see the thing that Archy's finger was resting upon. There was a pause, then a several-barreled sigh of disappointment. Pat Riley and Ham Sandwich said, in the one breath:

"What is it, Archy? There's nothing here."

"Nothing? Do you call *that* nothing?" and he swiftly traced upon the ground a form with his finger. "There—don't you recognize it now? It's Injun Billy's track. He's got the child."

"God be praised!" from the mother.

"Take away the lantern. I've got the direction. Follow!"

He started on a run, racing in and out among the sage-bushes a matter of three hundred yards, and disappeared over a sand-wave; the others struggled after him, caught him up, and found him waiting. Ten steps away was a little wickiup, a dim and formless shelter of rags and old horse-blankets, a dull light showing through its chinks.

"You lead, Mrs. Hogan," said the lad. "It's your privilege to be first."

All followed the sprint she made for the wickiup, and saw, with her, the picture its interior afforded. Injun Billy was sitting on the ground; the child was asleep beside him. The mother hugged it with a wild embrace, which included Archy Stillman, the grateful tears running down her face, and in a choked and broken voice she poured out a golden stream of that wealth of worshiping endearments which has its home in full richness nowhere but in the Irish heart.

"I find her bymeby it is ten o'clock," Billy explained. "She 'sleep out yonder, ve'y tired—face wet, been cryin', 'spose; fetch her home, feed her, she heap much hungry—go 'sleep 'gin."

In her limitless gratitude the happy mother waived rank and hugged him too, calling him "the angel of God in disguise." And he probably was in disguise if he was that kind of an official. He was dressed for the character.

At half past one in the morning the procession burst into the village singing, "When Johnny Comes Marching

Home," waving its lanterns, and swallowing the drinks that were brought out all along its course. It concentrated at the tavern, and made a night of what was left of the morning.

6

The next afternoon the village was electrified with an immense sensation. A grave and dignified foreigner of distinguished bearing and appearance had arrived at the tavern, and entered this formidable name upon the register:

SHERLOCK HOLMES

The news buzzed from cabin to cabin, from claim to claim; tools were dropped, and the town swarmed toward the center of interest. A man passing out at the northern end of the village shouted it to Pat Riley, whose claim was the next one to Flint Buckner's. At that time Fetlock Jones seemed to turn sick. He muttered to himself:

"Uncle *Sherlock!* the mean luck of it!—that *he* should come just when . . ." He dropped into a reverie, and presently said to himself: "But what's the use of being afraid of *him?* Anybody that knows him the way I do knows he can't detect a crime except where he plans it all out beforehand and arranges the clues and hires some fellow to commit it according to instructions. . . . Now there ain't going to *be* any clues this time—so, what show has he got? None at all. No, sir; everything's ready. If I was to risk putting it off— . . . No, I won't run any risk like that. Flint Buckner goes out of this world to-night, for sure." Then another trouble presented itself. "Uncle Sherlock'll be wanting to talk home matters with me this evening, and how am I going to get rid of him? for I've *got* to be at my cabin a minute or two about eight o'clock." This was an awkward matter, and cost him much thought. But he found a way to beat the difficulty. "We'll go for a walk, and I'll leave him in the road a minute, so that he won't see what it is I do: the best way to throw a detective off the track, anyway, is to have him along when you are preparing the thing. Yes, that's the safest—I'll take him with me."

Meantime the road in front of the tavern was blocked with villagers waiting and hoping for a glimpse of the great man. But he kept his room, and did not appear. None but Ferguson, Jake Parker the blacksmith, and Ham Sandwich had any luck. These enthusiastic admirers of the great scientific detective hired the tavern's detained-baggage lockup, which looked into the detective's room across a little alleyway ten or twelve feet wide, ambushed themselves in it, and cut some peep-holes in the window-blind. Mr. Holmes's blinds were down; but by and by he raised them. It gave the spies a hair-lifting but pleasurable thrill to find themselves face to face with the Extraordinary Man who had filled the world with the fame of his more human ingenuities. There he sat—not a myth, not a shadow, but real, alive, compact of substance, and almost within touching distance with the hand.

"Look at that head!" said Ferguson, in an awed voice. "By gracious! *that's* a head!"

"You bet!" said the blacksmith, with deep reverence. "Look at his nose! look at his eyes! Intellect? Just a battery of it!"

"And that paleness," said Ham Sandwich. "Comes from thought—that's what it comes from. Hell! duffers like us don't know what real thought *is.*"

"No more we don't," said Ferguson. "What we take for thinking is just blubber-and-slush."

"Right you are, Wells-Fargo. And look at that frown—that's *deep* thinking—away down, down, forty fathoms into the bowels of things. He's on the track of something."

"Well, he is, and don't you forget it. Say—look at that awful gravity—look at that pallid solemnness—there ain't any corpse can lay over it."

"No, sir, not for dollars! And it's his'n by hereditary rights, too; he's been dead four times a'ready, and there's history for it. Three times natural, once by accident. I've heard say he smells damp and cold, like a grave. And he—"

" 'Sh! Watch him! There—he's got his thumb on the bump on the near corner of his forehead, and his forefinger on the off one. His think-works is just a-*grinding* now, you bet your other shirt."

"That's so. And now he's gazing up toward heaven and stroking his mustache slow, and—"

"Now he has rose up standing, and is putting his clues together on his left fingers with his right finger. See? he touches the forefinger—now middle finger—now ring-finger—"

"Stuck!"

"Look at him scowl! He can't seem to make out *that* clue. So he—"

"See him smile!—like a tiger—and tally off the other fingers like nothing! He's got it, boys; he's got it sure!"

"Well, I should *say!* I'd hate to be in that man's place that he's after."

Mr. Holmes drew a table to the window, sat down with his back to the spies, and proceeded to write. The spies withdrew their eyes from the peep-holes, lit their pipes, and settled themselves for a comfortable smoke and talk. Ferguson said, with conviction:

"Boys, it's no use talking, he's a wonder! He's got the signs of it all over him."

"You hain't ever said a truer word than that, Wells-Fargo," said Jake Parker. "Say, wouldn't it 'a' been nuts if he'd a-been here last night?"

"Oh, by George, but wouldn't it!" said Ferguson. "Then we'd have seen *scientific* work. Intellect—just pure intellect—away up on the upper levels, dontchuknow. Archy is all right, and it don't become anybody to belittle *him,* I can tell you. But his gift is only just eyesight, sharp as an owl's, as near as I can make it out just a grand natural animal talent, no more, no less, and prime as far as it goes, but no intellect in it, and for awfulness and marvelousness no more to be compared to what this man does than—than— Why, let me tell you what *he'd* have done. He'd have stepped over to Hogan's and glanced—just *glanced,* that's all—at the premises, and that's enough. See everything? Yes, sir, to the last little *de*tail; and he'd know more about that place than the Hogans would know in seven years. Next, he would sit down on the bunk, just as ca'm, and say to Mrs. Hogan— *Say,* Ham, consider that you are Mrs. Hogan. I'll ask the questions; you answer them."

"All right; go on."

" 'Madam, if you please—attention—do not let your mind wander. Now, then—sex of the child?'

" 'Female, your Honor.'

" 'Um—female. Very good, very good. Age?'

" 'Turned six, your Honor.'

" 'Um—young, weak—two miles. Weariness will overtake it then. It will sink down and sleep. We shall find it two miles away, or less. Teeth?'

" 'Five, your Honor, and one a-coming.'

" 'Very good, very good, *very* good, indeed.' You see, boys, *he* knows a clue when he sees it, when it wouldn't mean a dern thing to anybody else. 'Stockings, madam? Shoes?'

" 'Yes, your Honor—both.'

" 'Yarn, perhaps? Morocco?'

" 'Yarn, your Honor. And kip.'

" 'Um—kip. This complicates the matter. However, let it go—we shall manage. Religion?'

" 'Catholic, your Honor.'

" 'Very good. Snip me a bit from the bed blanket, please. Ah, thanks. Part wool—foreign make. Very well. A snip from some garment of the child's, please. Thanks. Cotton. Shows wear. An excellent clue, excellent. Pass me a pallet of the floor dirt, if you'll be so kind. Thanks, many thanks. Ah, admirable, admirable! *Now* we know where we are, I think.' You see, boys, he's got all the clues he wants now; he don't need anything more. Now, then, what does this Extraordinary Man do? He lays those snips and that dirt out on the table and leans over them on his elbows, and puts them together side by side and studies them—mumbles to himself, 'Female'; changes them around—mumbles, 'Six years old'; changes them this way and that—again mumbles: 'Five teeth—one a-coming—Catholic—yarn—cotton—kip—damn that kip.' Then he straightens up and gazes toward heaven, and plows his hands through his hair—plows and plows, muttering, 'Damn that kip!' Then he stands up and frowns, and begins to tally off his clues on his fingers—and gets stuck at the ring-finger. But only just a minute—then his face glares all up in a smile like a house afire, and he straightens up stately and majestic, and says to the crowd, 'Take a lantern, a couple of you, and go down to Injun Billy's and fetch the child—the rest of you go 'long home to bed; good-night, madam; good-night, gents.' And he bows like the Matterhorn and pulls out for the tavern. That's *his* style, and the *Only*—scientific, intellectual—all over in fifteen minutes—no poking around all over the sage-brush range an hour and a half in a mass-meeting crowd for *him*, boys—you hear *me!*"

"By Jackson, it's grand!" said Ham Sandwich. "Wells-Fargo, you've got him down to a dot. He ain't painted up any exacter to the life in the books. By George, I can just *see* him—can't you, boys?"

"You bet you! It's just a photograft, that's what it is."

Ferguson was profoundly pleased with his success, and grateful. He sat silently enjoying his happiness a little while, then he murmured, with a deep awe in his voice,

"I wonder if God made him?"

There was no response for a moment; then Ham Sandwich said, reverently:

"Not all at one time, I reckon."

7

At eight o'clock that evening two persons were groping their way past Flint Buckner's cabin in the frosty gloom. They were Sherlock Holmes and his nephew.

"Stop here in the road a moment, uncle," said Fetlock, "while I run to my cabin; I won't be gone a minute."

He asked for something—the uncle furnished it—then he disappeared in the darkness, but soon returned, and the talking-walk was resumed. By nine o'clock they had wandered back to the tavern. They worked their way through the billard-room, where a crowd had gathered in the hope of getting a glimpse of the Extraordinary Man. A royal cheer was raised. Mr. Holmes acknowledged the compliment with a series of courtly bows, and as he was passing out his nephew said to the assemblage:

"Uncle Sherlock's got some work to do, gentlemen, that'll keep him till twelve or one; but he'll be down again then, or earlier if he can, and hopes some of you'll be left to take a drink with him."

"By George, he's just a duke, boys! Three cheers for Sherlock Holmes, the greatest man that ever lived!" shouted Ferguson. "Hip, hip, hip—"

"Hurrah! hurrah! hurrah! Tiger!"

The uproar shook the building, so hearty was the feeling the boys put into their welcome. Up-stairs the uncle reproached the nephew gently, saying:

"What did you get me into that engagement for?"

"I reckon you don't want to be unpopular, do you, uncle? Well, then, don't you put on any exclusiveness in a mining-camp, that's all. The boys admire you; but if you was to leave without taking a drink with them, they'd set you down for a snob. And besides, you said you had home talk enough in stock to keep us up and at it half the night."

The boy was right, and wise—the uncle acknowledged it. The boy was wise in another detail which he did not mention—except to himself: "Uncle and the others will come handy—in the way of nailing an *alibi* where it can't be budged."

He and his uncle talked diligently about three hours. Then, about midnight, Fetlock stepped down-stairs and took a position in the dark a dozen steps from the tavern, and waited. Five minutes later Flint Buckner came rocking out of the billard-room and almost brushed him as he passed.

"I've *got* him!" muttered the boy. He continued to himself, looking after the shadowy form: "Good-by—good-by for good, Flint Buckner; you called my mother a—well, never mind what: it's all right, now; you're taking your last walk, friend."

He went musing back into the tavern. "From now till one is an hour. We'll spend it with the boys: it's good for the *alibi*."

He brought Sherlock Holmes to the billiard-room, which was jammed with eager and admiring miners; the guest called the drinks, and the fun began. Everybody was happy; everybody was complimentary; the ice was soon broken, songs, anecdotes, and more drinks followed, and the pregnant minutes flew. At six minutes to one, when the jollity was at its highest—

Boom!

There was silence instantly. The deep sound came rolling and rumbling from peak to peak up the gorge, then died down, and ceased. The spell broke, then, and the men made a rush for the door, saying:

"Something's blown up!"

Outside, a voice in the darkness said, "It's away down the gorge; I saw the flash."

The crowd poured down the cañon—Holmes, Fetlock, Archy Stillman, everybody. They made the mile in a few minutes. By the light of a lantern they found the smooth and solid dirt floor of Flint Buckner's cabin; of the cabin itself not a vestige remained, not a rag nor a splinter. Nor any sign of Flint. Search-parties sought here and there and yonder, and presently a cry went up.

"Here he is!"

It was true. Fifty yards down the gulch they had found him—that is, they had found a crushed and lifeless mass which represented him. Fetlock Jones hurried thither with the others and looked.

The inquest was a fifteen-minute affair. Ham Sandwich, foreman of the jury, handed up the verdict, which was phrased with a certain unstudied literary grace, and closed with this finding, to wit: that "deceased came to his death by his own act or some other person or persons unknown to this jury not leaving any family or similar effects behind but his cabin which was blown away and God have mercy on his soul amen."

Then the impatient jury rejoined the main crowd, for the storm-center of interest was there—Sherlock Holmes. The miners stood silent and reverent in a half-circle, inclosing a large vacant space which included the front exposure of the site of the late premises. In this considerable space the Extraordinary Man was moving about, attended by his nephew with a lantern. With a tape he took measurements of the cabin site; of the distance from the wall of chaparral to the road; of the height of the chaparral bushes; also various other measurements. He gathered a rag here, a splinter there, and a pinch of earth yonder, inspected them profoundly, and preserved them. He took the "lay" of the place with a pocket-compass, allowing two seconds for magnetic variation. He took the time (Pacific) by his watch, correcting it for local time. He paced off the distance from the cabin site to the corpse, and corrected that for tidal differentiation. He took the altitude with a pocket-aneroid, and the temperature with a pocket-thermometer. Finally he said, with a stately bow:

"It is finished. Shall we return, gentlemen?"

He took up the line of march for the tavern, and the crowd fell into his wake, earnestly discussing and admiring the Extraordinary Man, and interlarding guesses as to the origin of the tragedy and who the author of it might be.

"My, but it's grand luck having him here—hey, boys?" said Ferguson.

"It's the biggest thing of the century," said Ham Sandwich. "It'll go all over the world; you mark my words."

"*You* bet!" said Jake Parker, the blacksmith. "It'll boom this camp. Ain't it so, Wells-Fargo?"

"Well, as you want my opinion—if it's any sign of how *I* think about it, I can tell you this: yesterday I was holding the Straight Flush claim at two dollars a foot; I'd like to see the man that can get it at sixteen to-day."

"Right you are, Wells-Fargo! It's the grandest luck a new camp ever struck. Say, did you see him collar them little rags and dirt and things? What an eye! He just can't overlook a clue—'tain't *in* him."

"That's so. And they wouldn't mean a thing to anybody else; but to him, why, they're just a book—large print at that."

"Sure's you're born! Them odds and ends have got their little old secret, and they think there ain't anybody can pull it; but, land! when he sets his grip there they've got to squeal, and don't you forget it."

"Boys, I ain't sorry, now, that he wasn't here to roust out the child; this is a bigger thing, by a long sight. Yes, sir, and more tangled up and scientific and intellectual."

"I reckon we're all of us glad it's turned out this way. Glad? 'George! it ain't any name for it. Dontchuknow, Archy could've *learnt* something if he'd had the nous to stand by and take notice of how that man works the system. But no; he went poking up into the chaparral and just missed the whole thing."

"It's true as gospel; I seen it myself. Well, Archy's young. He'll know better one of these days."

"Say, boys, who do you reckon done it?"

That was a difficult question, and brought out a world of unsatisfying conjecture. Various men were mentioned as possibilities, but one by one they were discarded as not being eligible. No one but young Hillyer had been intimate with Flint Buckner; no one had really had a quarrel with him; he had affronted every man who had tried to make up to him, although not quite offensively enough to require bloodshed. There was one name that was upon every tongue from the start, but it was the last to get utterance—Fetlock Jones's. It was Pat Riley that mentioned it.

"Oh, well," the boys said, "of course we've all thought of him, because he had a million rights to kill Flint Buckner, and it was just his plain duty to do it. But all the same there's two things we can't get around: for one thing, he hasn't got the sand; and for another, he wasn't anywhere near the place when it happened."

"I know it," said Pat. "He was there in the billiard-room with us when it happened."

"Yes, and was there all the time for an hour *before* it happened."

"It's so. And lucky for him, too. He'd have been suspected in a minute if it hadn't been for that."

8

The tavern dining-room had been cleared of all its furniture save one six-foot pine table and a chair. This table was against one end of the room; the chair was on it; Sherlock Holmes, stately, imposing, impressive, sat in the chair. The public stood. The room was full. The tobacco-smoke was dense, the stillness profound.

The Extraordinary Man raised his hand to command additional silence; held it in the air a few moments; then, in brief, crisp terms he put forward question after question, and noted the answers with "Um-ums," nods of the head, and so on. By this process he learned all about Flint Buckner, his character, conduct, and habits, that the people were able to tell him. It thus transpired that the Extraordinary Man's nephew was the only person in the camp who had a killing-grudge against Flint Buckner. Mr. Holmes smiled compassionately upon the witness, and asked, languidly:

"Do any of you gentlemen chance to know where the lad Fetlock Jones was at the time of the explosion?"

A thunderous response followed:

"In the billiard-room of this house!"

"Ah. And had he just come in?"

"Been there all of an hour!"

"Ah. It is about—about—well, about how far might it be to the scene of the explosion?"

"All of a mile!"

"Ah. It isn't *much* of an alibi, 'tis true, but—"

A storm-burst of laughter, mingled with shouts of "By jiminy, but he's chain-lightning!" and "Ain't you sorry you spoke, Sandy?" shut off the rest of the sentence, and the crushed witness drooped his blushing face in pathetic shame. The inquisitor resumed:

"The lad Jones's somewhat *distant* connection with the case" (*laughter*) "having been disposed of, let us now call the *eye*-witnesses of the tragedy, and listen to what they have to say."

He got out his fragmentary clues and arranged them on a sheet of cardboard on his knee. The house held its breath and watched.

"We have the longitude and the latitude, corrected for magnetic variation, and this gives us the exact location of the tragedy. We have the altitude, the temperature, and the degree of humidity prevailing—inestimably valuable, since they enable us to estimate with precision the degree of influence which they would exercise upon the mood and disposition of the assassin at that time of the night."

(*Buzz of admiration; muttered remark, "By George, but he's deep!"*) He fingered his clues. "And now let us ask these mute witnesses to speak to us.

"Here we have an empty linen shot-bag. What is its message? This: that robbery was the motive, not revenge. What is its further message? This: that the assassin was of inferior intelligence—shall we say light-witted, or perhaps approaching that? How do we know this? Because a person of sound intelligence would not have proposed to rob the man Buckner, who never had much money with him. But the assassin might have been a stranger? Let the bag speak again. I take from it this article. It is a bit of silver-bearing quartz. It is peculiar. Examine it, please—you—and you—and you. Now pass it back, please. There is but one lode on this coast which produces just that character and color of quartz; and that is a lode which crops out for nearly two miles on a stretch, and in my opinion is destined, at no distant day, to confer upon its locality a globe-girdling celebrity, and upon its two hundred owners riches beyond the dreams of avarice. Name that lode, please."

"The Consolidated Christian Science and Mary Ann!" was the prompt response.

A wild crash of hurrahs followed, and every man reached for his neighbor's hand and wrung it, with tears in his eyes; and Wells-Fargo Ferguson shouted, "The Straight Flush is on the lode, and up she goes to a hundred and fifty a foot—you hear *me!*"

When quiet fell, Mr. Holmes resumed:

"We perceive, then, that three facts are established, to wit: the assassin was approximately light-witted; he was not a stranger; his motive was robbery, not revenge. Let us proceed. I hold in my hand a small fragment of fuse, with the recent smell of fire upon it. What is its testimony? Taken with the corroborative evidence of the quartz, it reveals to us that the assassin was a miner. What does it tell us further? This, gentlemen: that the assassination was consummated by means of an explosive. What else does it say? This: that the explosive was located against the side of the cabin nearest the road—the front side—for within six feet of that spot I found it.

"I hold in my fingers a burnt Swedish match—the kind one rubs on a safety-box. I found it in the road, six hundred and twenty-two feet from the abolished cabin. What does it say? This: that the train was fired from that point. What further does it tell us? This: that the assassin was left-handed. How do I know this? I should not be able to explain to you, gentlemen, how I know it, the signs being so subtle that only long experience and deep study can enable one to detect them. But the signs are here, and they are reinforced by a fact which you must have often noticed in the great detective narratives—that *all* assassins are left-handed."

"By Jackson, *that's* so!" said Ham Sandwich, bringing his great hand down with a resounding slap upon his thigh; "blamed if I ever thought of it before."

"Nor I!" "Nor I!" cried several. "Oh, there can't anything escape *him*—look at his eye!"

"Gentlemen, distant as the murderer was from his doomed victim, he did not wholly escape injury. This fragment of wood which I now exhibit to you struck him. It drew blood. Wherever he is, he bears the telltale mark. I picked it up where he stood when he fired the fatal train." He looked out over the house from his high perch, and his countenance began to darken; he slowly raised his hand, and pointed:

"There stands the assassin!"

For a moment the house was paralyzed with amazement; then twenty voices burst out with:

"Sammy Hillyer? Oh, *hell,* no! *Him?* It's pure foolishness!"

"Take care, gentlemen—be not hasty. Observe—he has the bloodmark on his brow."

Hillyer turned white with fright He was near to crying.

He turned this way and that, appealing to every face for help and sympathy; and held out his supplicating hands toward Holmes and began to plead:

"*Don't,* oh, don't! I never did it; I give my word I never did it. The way I got this hurt on my forehead was—"

"Arrest him, constable!" cried Holmes. "I will swear out the warrant."

The constable moved reluctantly forward—hesitated—stopped.

Hillyer broke out with another appeal. "Oh, Archy, don't let them do it; it would kill mother! *You* know how I got the hurt. Tell them, and save me, Archy; save me!"

Stillman worked his way to the front, and said:

"Yes, I'll save you. Don't be afraid." Then he said to the house, "Never mind how he got the hurt; it hasn't anything to do with this case, and isn't of any consequence."

"God bless you, Archy, for a true friend!"

"Hurrah for Archy! Go in, boy, and play 'em a knock-down flush to their two pair 'n' a jack!" shouted the house, pride in their home talent and a patriotic sentiment of loyalty to it rising suddenly in the public heart and changing the whole attitude of the situation.

Young Stillman waited for the noise to cease; then he said:

"I will ask Tom Jeffries to stand by that door yonder, and Constable Harris to stand by the other one here, and not let anybody leave the room."

"Said and done. Go on, old man!"

"The criminal is present, I believe. I will show him to you before long, in case I am right in my guess. Now I will tell you all about the tragedy, from start to finish. The motive *wasn't* robbery; it was revenge. The murderer *wasn't* light-witted. He *didn't* stand six hundred and twenty-two feet away. He *didn't* get hit with a piece of wood. He *didn't* place the explosive against the cabin. He *didn't* bring a shot-bag with him, and he *wasn't* left-handed. With the exception of these errors, the distinguished guest's statement of the case is substantially correct."

A comfortable laugh rippled over the house; friend nodded to friend, as much as to say, "That's the word, with the bark *on* it. Good lad, good boy. *He* ain't lowering his flag any!"

The guest's serenity was not disturbed. Stillman resumed:

"I also have some witnesses; and I will presently tell you where you can find some more." He held up a piece of coarse wire; the crowd craned their necks to see. "It has a smooth coating of melted tallow on it And here is a candle which is burned half-way down. The remaining half of it has marks cut upon it an inch apart. Soon I will tell you where I found these things. I win now put aside reasonings, guesses, the impressive hitchings of odds and ends of clues together, and the other showy theatricals of the detective trade, and tell you in a plain, straightforward way just how this dismal thing happened."

He paused a moment, for effect—to allow silence and suspense to intensify and concentrate the house's interest; then he went on:

"The assassin studied out his plan with a good deal of pains. It was a good plan, very ingenious, and showed an intelligent mind, not a feeble one. It was a plan which was well calculated to ward off all suspicion from its inventor. In the first place, he marked a candle into spaces an inch apart, and lit it and timed it. He found it took three hours to burn four inches of it. I tried it myself for half an hour, awhile ago, up-stairs here, while the inquiry into Flint Buckner's character and ways was being conducted in this room, and I arrived in that way at the rate of a candle's consumption when sheltered from the wind. Having proved his trial candle's rate, he blew it out—I have already shown it to you—and put his inch-marks on a fresh one.

"He put the fresh one into a tin candlestick. Then at the

five-hour mark he bored a hole through the candle with a red-hot wire. I have already shown you the wire, with a smooth coat of tallow on it—tallow that had been melted and had cooled.

"With labor—very hard labor, I should say—he struggled up through the stiff chaparral that clothes the steep hillside back of Flint Buckner's place, tugging an empty flour-barrel with him. He placed it in that absolutely secure hiding-place, and in the bottom of it he set the candlestick. Then he measured off about thirty-five feet of fuse—the barrel's distance from the back of the cabin. He bored a hole in the side of the barrel—here is the large gimlet he did it with. He went on and finished his work; and when it was done, one end of the fuse was in Buckner's cabin, and the other end, with a notch chipped in it to expose the powder, was in the hole in the candle—timed to blow the place up at one o'clock this morning, provided the candle was lit about eight o'clock yesterday evening—which I am betting it was—and provided there was an explosive in the cabin and connected with that end of the fuse—which I am also betting there was, though I can't prove it. Boys, the barrel is there in the chaparral, the candle's remains are in it in the tin stick; the burnt-out fuse is in the gimlet-hole, the other end is down the hill where the late cabin stood. I saw them all an hour or two ago, when the Professor here was measuring off unimplicated vacancies and collecting relics that hadn't anything to do with the case."

He paused. The house drew a long, deep breath, shook its strained cords and muscles free and burst into cheers. "Dang him!" said Ham Sandwich, "that's why he was snooping around in the chaparral, instead of picking up points out of the P'fessor's game. Looky here—*he* ain't no fool, boys."

"No, sir! Why, great Scott—"

But Stillman was resuming:

"While we were out yonder an hour or two ago, the owner of the gimlet and the trial candle took them from a place where he had concealed them—it was not a good place—and carried them to what he probably thought was a better one, two hundred yards up in the pine woods, and hid them there, covering them over with pine needles. It was there that I found them. The gimlet exactly fits the hole in the barrel. And now—"

The Extraordinary Man. interrupted him. He said, sarcastically:

"We have had a very pretty fairy tale, gentlemen—very pretty indeed. Now I would like to ask this young man a question or two."

Some of the boys winced, and Ferguson said:

"I'm afraid Archy's going to catch it now."

The others lost their smiles and sobered down. Mr. Holmes said:

"Let us proceed to examine into this fairy tale in a consecutive and orderly way—by geometrical progression, so to speak—linking detail to detail in a steadily advancing and remorselessly consistent and unassailable march upon this tinsel toy fortress of error, the dream fabric of a callow imagination. To begin with, young sir, I desire to ask you but three questions at present—*at present.* Did I understand you to say it was your opinion that the supposititious candle was lighted at about eight o'clock yesterday evening?"

"Yes, sir—about eight."

"Could you say exactly eight?"

"Well, no, I couldn't be that exact."

"Um. If a person had been passing along there just about that time, he would have been almost sure to encounter that assassin, do you think?"

"Yes, I should think so."

"Thank you, that is all. For the present. I say, all *for the present.*"

"Dern him! he's laying for Archy," said Ferguson.

"It's so," said Ham Sandwich. "I don't like the look of it."

Stillman said, glancing at the guest, "I was along there myself at half-past eight—no, about nine."

"In-deed? This is interesting—this is very interesting. Perhaps you encountered the assassin?"

"No, I encountered no one."

"Ah. Then—if you will excuse the remark—I do not quite see the relevancy of the information."

"It has none. At present I say it has none—at present."

He paused. Presently he resumed: "I did not encounter the assassin, but I am on his track, I am sure, for I believe he is in this room. I will ask you all to pass one by one in front of me—here, where there is a good light—so that I can see your feet."

A buzz of excitement swept the place, and the march began, the guest looking on with an iron attempt at gravity which was not an unqualified success. Stillman stooped, shaded his eyes with his hand, and gazed down intently at each pair of feet as it passed. Fifty men tramped monotonously by—with no result. Sixty. Seventy. The thing was beginning to look absurd. The guest remarked, with suave irony:

"Assassins appear to be scarce this evening."

The house saw the humor of it, and refreshed itself with a cordial laugh. Ten or twelve more candidates tramped by—no, *danced* by, with any and ridiculous capers which convulsed the spectators—then suddenly Stillman put out his hand and said:

"This is the assassin!"

"Fetlock Jones, by the great Sanhedrim!" roared the crowd; and at once let fly a pyrotechnic explosion and dazzle and confusion and stirring remarks inspired by the situation.

At the height of the turmoil the guest stretched out his hand, commanding peace. The authority of a great name and a great personality laid its mysterious compulsion upon the house, and it obeyed. Out of the panting calm which succeeded, the guest spoke, saying, with dignity and feeling:

"*This* is serious. It strikes at an innocent life. Innocent beyond suspicion! Innocent beyond peradventure! Hear me *prove* it; observe how simple a fact can brush out of existence this witless lie. Listen. My friends, that lad was never out of my sight yesterday evening at *any* time!"

It made a deep impression. Men turned their eyes upon Stillman with grave inquiry in them. His face brightened, and he said:

"I *knew* there was another one!" He stepped briskly to the table and glanced at the guest's feet, then up at his face, and said: "You were *with* him! You were not fifty steps from him when he lit the candle that by and by fired the powder!" (*Sensation.*) "And what is more, you furnished the matches yourself!"

Plainly the guest seemed hit; it looked so to the public. He opened his mouth to speak; the words did not come freely.

"This—er—this is insanity—this—"

Stillman pressed his evident advantage home. He held up a charred match.

"Here is one of them. I found it in the barrel—and there's *another* one there."

The guest found his voice at once.

"*Yes*—and put them there yourself!"

It was recognized a good shot. Stillman retorted.

"It is *wax*—a breed unknown to this camp. I am ready to be searched for the box. Are you?"

The guest was staggered this time—the dullest eye could see it. He fumbled with his hands; once or twice his lips moved, but the words did not come. The house waited and watched, in tense suspense, the stillness adding effect to the situation. Presently Stillman said, gently:

"We are waiting for your decision."

There was silence again during several moments; then the guest answered, in a low voice:

"I refuse to be searched."

There was no noisy demonstration, but all about the house one voice after another muttered:

"That settles it! He's Archy's meat."

What to do now? Nobody seemed to know. It was an embarrassing situation for the moment—merely, of course, because matters had taken such a sudden and unexpected turn that these unpractised minds were not prepared for it, and had come to a standstill, like a stopped clock, under the shock. But after a little the machinery began to work again, tentatively, and by twos and threes the men put their heads together and privately buzzed over this and that and the other proposition. One of these propositions met with much favor; it was, to confer upon the assassin a vote of thanks for removing Flint Buckner, and let him go. But the cooler heads opposed it, pointing out that addled brains in the Eastern states would pronounce it a scandal, and make no end of foolish noise about it. Finally the cool heads got the upper hand, and obtained general consent to a proposition of their own; their leader then called the house to order and stated it—to this effect: that Fetlock Jones be jailed and put upon trial.

The motion was carried. Apparently there was nothing further to do now, and the people were glad, for, privately, they were impatient to get out and rush to the scene of the tragedy, and see whether that barrel and the other things were really there or not.

But no—the break-up got a check. The surprises were not over yet. For a while Fetlock Jones had been silently sobbing, unnoticed in the absorbing excitements which had been following one another so persistently for some time; but when his arrest and trial were decreed, he broke out despairingly, and said:

"No! it's no use. I don't want any jail, I don't want any trial; I've had all the hard luck I want, and all the miseries. Hang me now, and let me out! It would all come out, any-way—there couldn't anything save me. He has told it all, just as if he'd been with me and seen it—*I* don't know how he found out; and you'll find the barrel and things, and then I wouldn't have any chance any more. I killed him; and *you'd* have done it too, if he'd treated you like a dog, and you only a boy, and weak and poor, and not a friend to help you."

"And served him damned well right!" broke in Ham Sandwich. "Looky here, boys—"

From the constable: "Order! Order, gentlemen!"

A voice: "Did your uncle know what you was up to?"

"No, he didn't."

"Did he give you the matches, sure enough?"

"Yes, he did; but he didn't know what I wanted them for."

"When you was out on such a business as that, how did you venture to risk having him along—and him a *detective?* How's that?"

The boy hesitated, fumbled with his buttons in an embarrassed way, then said, shyly:

"I know about detectives, on account of having them in the family; and if you don't want them to find out about a thing, it's best to have them around when you do it."

The cyclone of laughter which greeted his naïve discharge of wisdom did not modify the poor little waif's embarrassment in any large degree.

9

From a letter to Mrs. Stillman, dated merely "Tuesday."

Fetlock Jones was put under lock and key in an unoccupied log cabin, and left there to await his trial. Constable Harris provided him with a couple of days' rations, instructed him to keep a good guard over himself, and promised to look in on him as soon as further supplies should be due.

Next morning a score of us went with Hillyer, out of

friendship, and helped him bury his late relative, the unlamented Buckner, and I acted as first assistant pall-bearer, Hillyer acting as chief. Just as we had finished our labors a ragged and melancholy stranger, carrying an old handbag, limped by with his head down, and I caught the scent I had chased around the globe! It was the odor of Paradise to my perishing hope!

In a moment I was at his side and had laid a gentle hand upon his shoulder. He slumped to the ground as if a stroke of lightning had withered him in his tracks; and as the boys came running he struggled to his knees and put up his pleading hands to me, and out of his chattering jaws he begged me to persecute him no more, and said:

"You have hunted me around the world, Sherlock Holmes, yet God is my witness I have never done any man harm!"

A glance at his wild eyes showed us that he was insane. That was my work, mother! The tidings of your death can some day repeat the misery I felt in that moment, but nothing else can ever do it. The boys lifted him up, and gathered about him, and were full of pity of him, and said the gentlest and touchingest things to him, and said cheer up and don't be troubled, he was among friends now, and they would take care of him, and protect him, and hang any man that laid a hand on him. They are just like so many mothers, the rough mining-camp boys are, when you wake up the south side of their hearts; yes, and just like so many reckless and unreasoning children when you wake up the opposite of that muscle. They did everything they could think of to comfort him, but nothing succeeded until Wells-Fargo Ferguson, who is a clever strategist, said:

"If it's only Sherlock Holmes that's troubling you, you needn't worry any more."

"Why?" asked the forlorn lunatic, eagerly.

"Because he's dead again."

"Dead! Dead! Oh, don't trifle with a poor wreck like me. *Is* he dead? On honor, now—is he telling me true, boys?"

"True as you're standing there!" said Ham Sandwich, and they all backed up the statement in a body.

"They hung him in San Bernardino last week," added Ferguson, clinching the matter, "whilst he was searching around after you. Mistook him for another man. They're sorry, but they can't help it now."

"They're a-building him a monument," said Ham Sandwich, with the air of a person who had contributed to it, and knew.

"James Walker" drew a deep sigh—evidently a sigh of relief—and said nothing; but his eyes lost something of their wildness, his countenance cleared visibly, and its drawn look relaxed a little. We all went to our cabin, and the boys cooked him the best dinner the camp could furnish the materials for, and while they were about it Hillyer and I outfitted him from hat to shoe-leather with new clothes of ours, and made a comely and presentable old gentleman of him. "Old" is the right word, and a pity, too: old by the droop of him, and the frost upon his hair, and the marks which sorrow and distress have left upon his face; though he is only in his prime in the matter of years. While he ate, we smoked and chatted; and when he was finishing he found his voice at last, and of his own accord broke out with his personal history. I cannot furnish his exact words, but I will come as near it as I can.

THE "WRONG MAN'S" STORY

It happened like this: I was in Denver. I had been there many years; sometimes I remember how many, sometimes I don't—but it isn't any matter. All of a sudden I got a notice to leave, or I would be exposed for a horrible crime committed long before—years and years before—in the East.

I knew about that crime, but I was not the criminal; it was a cousin of mine of the same name. What should I better do? My head was all disordered by fear, and I didn't know. I was allowed very little time—only one day, I think it was. I would be ruined if I was published, and the people would lynch me, and not believe what I said. It is always the way with lynchings: when they find out it is a mistake they are sorry, but it is too late—the same as it was with Mr. Holmes, you see. So I said I would sell out and get money to live on, and run away until it blew over and I could come back with my proofs. Then I escaped in the night and went a long way off in the mountains somewhere, and lived disguised and had a false name.

I got more and more troubled and worried, and my troubles made me see spirits and hear voices, and I could not think straight and clear on any subject, but got confused and involved and had to give it up, because my head hurt so. It got to be worse and worse; more spirits and more voices. They were about me all the time; at first only in the night, then in the day too. They were always whispering around my bed and plotting against me, and it broke my sleep and kept me fagged out, because I got no good rest.

And then came the worst. One night the whispers said, "We'll never manage, because we can't see him, and so can't point him out to the people."

They sighed; then one said: "We must bring Sherlock Holmes. He can be here in twelve days."

They all agreed, and whispered and jibbered with joy. But my heart broke; for I had read about that man, and knew what it would be to have him upon my track, with his superhuman penetration and tireless energies.

The spirits went away to fetch him, and I got up at once in the middle of the night and fled away, carrying nothing but the hand-bag that had my money in it—thirty thousand dollars; two-thirds of it are in the bag there yet. It was forty days before that man caught up on my track. I just escaped. From habit he had written his real name on a tavern register, but had scratched it out and written "Dagget Barclay" in the place of it. But fear gives you a watchful eye and keen, and I read the true name through the scratches, and fled like a deer.

He has hunted me all over this world for three years and a half—the Pacific states, Australasia, India—everywhere you can think of; then back to Mexico and up to California again, giving me hardly any rest; but that name on the registers always saved me, and what is left of me is alive yet. And I am *so* tired! A cruel time he has given me, yet I give you my honor I have never harmed him nor any man.

That was the end of the story, and it stirred those boys to bloodheat, be sure of it. As for me—each word burnt a hole in me where it struck.

We voted that the old man should bunk with us, and be my guest and Hillyer's. I shall keep my own counsel, naturally; but as soon as he is well rested and nourished, I shall take him to Denver and rehabilitate his fortunes.

The boys gave the old fellow the bone-smashing goodfellowship handshake of the mines, and then scattered away to spread the news.

At dawn next morning Wells-Fargo Ferguson and Ham Sandwich called us softly out, and said, privately:

"That news about the way that old stranger has been treated has spread all around, and the camps are up. They are piling in from everywhere, and are going to lynch the P'fessor. Constable Harris is in a dead funk, and has telephoned the sheriff. Come along!"

We started on a run. The others were privileged to feel as they chose, but in my heart's privacy I hoped the sheriff would arrive in time; for I had small desire that Sherlock Holmes should hang for my deeds, as you can easily believe. I had heard a good deal about the sheriff, but for reassurance's sake I asked:

"Can he stop a mob?"

"Can *he* stop a mob! Can Jack *Fairfax* stop a mob! Well, I should smile! Ex-desperado—nineteen scalps on his string. Can *he!* Oh, I *say!*"

As we tore up the gulch, distant cries and shouts and yells rose faintly on the still air, and grew steadily in strength as we raced along. Roar after roar burst out, stronger and stronger, nearer and nearer; and at last, when we closed up upon the multitude massed in the open area in front of the tavern, the crash of sound was deafening. Some brutal roughs from Daly's gorge had Holmes in their grip, and he was the calmest man there; a contemptuous smile played about his lips, and if any fear of death was in his British heart, his iron personality was master of it and no sign of it was allowed to appear.

"Come to a vote, men!" This from one of the Daly gang, Shadbelly Higgins. "Quick! is it hang, or shoot?"

"Neither!" shouted one of his comrades. "He'd be alive again in a week; burning's the only permanency for *him*."

The gangs from all the outlying camps burst out in a thundercrash of approval, and went struggling and surging toward the prisoner, and closed around him, shouting, "Fire! fire's the ticket!" They dragged him to the horse-post, backed him against it, chained him to it, and piled wood and pine cones around him waist-deep. Still the strong face did not blench, and still the scornful smile played about the thin lips.

"A match! fetch a match!"

Shadbelly struck it, shaded it with his hand, stooped, and held it under a pine cone. A deep silence fell upon the mob. The cone caught, a tiny flame flickered about it a moment or two. I seemed to catch the sound of distant hoofs—it grew more distinct—still more and more distinct, more and more definite, but the absorbed crowd did not appear to notice it. The match went out. The man struck another, stooped, and again the flame rose; this time it took hold and began to spread—here and there men turned away their faces. The executioner stood with the charred match in his fingers, watching his work. The hoof-beats turned a projecting crag, and now they came thundering down upon us. Almost the next moment there was a shout:

"The sheriff!"

And straightway he came tearing into the midst, stood his horse almost on his hind feet, and said:

"Fall back, you gutter-snipes!"

He was obeyed. By all but their leader. He stood his ground, and his hand went to his revolver. The sheriff covered him promptly, and said:

"Drop your hand, you parlor desperado. Kick the fire away. Now unchain the stranger."

The parlor desperado obeyed. Then the sheriff made a speech; sitting his horse at martial ease, and not warming his words with any touch of fire, but delivering them in a measured and deliberate way, and in a tone which harmonized with their character and made them impressively disrespectful.

"You're a nice lot—now ain't you? Just about eligible to travel with this bilk here—Shadbelly Higgins—this loud-mouthed sneak that shoots people in the back and calls himself a desperado. If there's anything I do particularly despise, it's a lynching mob; I've never seen one that had a man in it. It has to tally up a hundred against one before it can pump up pluck enough to tackle a sick tailor. It's made up of cowards, and so is the community that breeds it; and ninety-nine times out of a hundred the sheriff's another one." He paused—apparently to turn that last idea over in his mind and taste the juice of it—then he went on: "The sheriff that lets a mob take a prisoner away from him is the lowest-down coward there is. By the statistics there was a hundred and eighty-two of them drawing sneak pay in America last year. By the way it's going, pretty soon there'll be a new disease in the doctor-books—*sheriff complaint.*" That idea pleased him—any one could see it. "People will say, 'Sheriff sick again?' 'Yes; got the same old thing.' And next there'll be a new title. People won't say, 'He's running for sheriff of Rapaho County,' for instance; they'll say, 'He's running for Coward of Rapaho.' Lord, the idea of a grown-up person being afraid of a lynch mob!"

He turned an eye on the captive, and said, "Stranger, who are you, and what have you been doing?"

"My name is Sherlock Holmes, and I have not been doing anything."

It was wonderful, the impression which the sound of that name made on the sheriff, notwithstanding he must have come posted. He spoke up with feeling, and said it was a blot on the country that a man whose marvelous exploits had filled the world with their fame and their ingenuity, and whose histories of them had won every reader's heart by the brilliancy and charm of their literary setting, should be visited under the Stars and Stripes by an outrage like this. He apologized in the name of the whole nation, and made Holmes a most handsome bow, and told Constable Harris to see him to his quarters, and hold himself personally responsible if he was molested again. Then he turned to the mob and said:

"Hunt your holes, you scum!" which they did; then he said: "Follow me, Shadbelly; I'll take care of your case myself. No—keep your pop-gun; whenever I see the day that I'll be afraid to have you behind me with that thing, it'll be time for me to join last year's hundred and eighty-two"; and he rode off in a walk, Shadbelly following.

When we were on our way back to our cabin, toward breakfast-time, we ran upon the news that Fetlock Jones had escaped from his lock-up in the night and is gone! Nobody is sorry. Let his uncle track him out if he likes; it is in his line; the camp is not interested.

10

Ten days later.

"James Walker" is all right in body now, and his mind shows improvement too. I start with him for Denver tomorrow morning.

Next night. Brief note, mailed at a way-station.

As we were starting, this morning, Hillyer whispered to me: "Keep this news from Walker until you think it safe and not likely to disturb his mind and check his improvement: the ancient crime he spoke of was really committed—and by his cousin, as he said. *We buried the real criminal* the other day—the unhappiest man that has lived in a century—Flint Buckner. His real name was Jacob Fuller!" There, mother, by help of me, an unwitting mourner, your husband and my father is in his grave. Let him rest.

1902

The Five Boons of Life

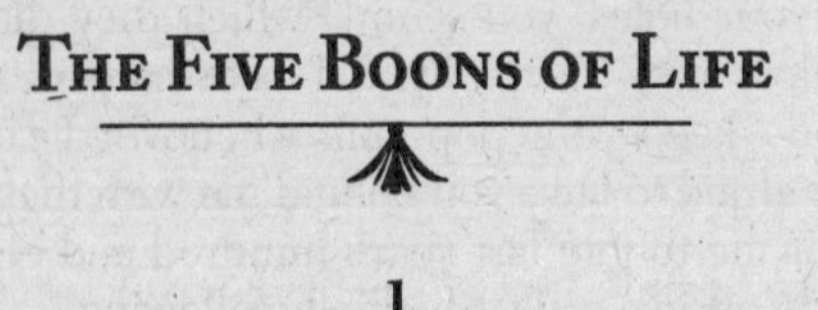

1

In the morning of life came the good fairy with her basket, and said:

"Here are the gifts. Take one, leave the others. And be wary, choose wisely; oh, choose wisely! for only one of them is valuable."

The gifts were five: Fame, Love, Riches, Pleasure, Death. The youth said, eagerly:

"There is no need to consider"; and he chose Pleasure.

He went out into the world and sought out the pleasures that youth delights in. But each in its turn was short-lived and disappointing, vain and empty; and each, departing, mocked him. In the end he said: "These years I have wasted. If I could but choose again, I would choose wisely."

2

The fairy appeared, and said:

"Four of the gifts remain. Choose once more; and oh, remember—time is flying, and only one of them is precious."

The man considered long, then chose Love; and did not mark the tears that rose in the fairy's eyes.

After many, many years the man sat by a coffin, in an empty home. And he communed with himself, saying: "One by one they have gone away and left me; and now she lies here, the dearest and the last. Desolation after desolation has swept over me; for each hour of happiness the treacherous trader, Love, has sold me I have paid a thousand hours of grief. Out of my heart of hearts I curse him."

3

"Choose again." It was the fairy speaking. "The years have taught you wisdom—surely it must be so. Three gifts remain. Only one of them has any worth—remember it, and choose warily."

The man reflected long, then chose Fame; and the fairy, sighing, went her way.

Years went by and she came again, and stood behind the man where he sat solitary in the fading day, thinking. And she knew his thought:

"My name filled the world, and its praises were on every tongue, and it seemed well with me for a little while. How little a while it was! Then came envy; then detraction; then calumny; then hate; then persecution. Then derision, which is the beginning of the end. And last of all came pity, which is the funeral of fame. Oh, the bitterness and misery of renown! target for mud in its prime, for contempt and compassion in its decay."

4

"Choose yet again." It was the fairy's voice. "Two gifts remain. And do not despair. In the beginning there was but one that was precious, and it is still here."

"Wealth—which is power! How blind I was!" said the man. "Now, at last, life will be worth the living. I will spend, squander, dazzle. These mockers and despisers will crawl in the dirt before me, and I will feed my hungry heart with their envy. I will have all luxuries, all joys, all enchantments of the spirit, all contentments of the body that man holds dear. I will buy, buy, buy! deference, respect, esteem, worship—every pinchbeck grace of life the market of a trivial world can furnish forth. I have lost much time, and chosen badly heretofore, but let that pass: I was ignorant then, and could but take for best what seemed so."

Three short years went by, and a day came when the man sat shivering in a mean garret; and he was gaunt and wan and hollow-eyed, and clothed in rags; and he was gnawing a dry crust and mumbling:

"Curse all the world's gifts, for mockeries and gilded lies! And mis-called, every one. They are not gifts, but merely lendings. Pleasure, Love, Fame, Riches: they are but temporary disguises for lasting realities—Pain, Grief, Shame, Poverty. The fairy said true; in all her store there was but one gift which was precious, only one that was not valueless. How poor and cheap and mean I know those others now to be, compared with that inestimable one, that dear and sweet and kindly one, that steeps in dreamless and enduring sleep the pains that persecute the body, and the shames and griefs that eat the mind and heart. Bring it! I am weary, I would rest."

5

The fairy came, bringing again four of the gifts, but Death was wanting. She said:

"I gave it to a mother's pet, a little child. It was ignorant, but trusted me, asking me to choose for it. You did not ask me to choose."

"Oh, miserable me! What is there left for me?"

"What not even you have deserved: the wanton insult of Old Age."

1902

WAS IT HEAVEN? OR HELL?

1

"You told a *lie*?"

"You confess it—you actually confess it—you told a lie!"

2

The family consisted of four persons: Margaret Lester, widow, aged thirty-six; Helen Lester, her daughter, aged sixteen; Mrs. Lester's maiden aunts, Hannah and Hester Gray, twins, aged sixty-seven. Waking and sleeping, the three women spent their days and nights in adoring the young girl; in watching the movements of her sweet spirit in the mirror of her face; in refreshing their souls with the vision of her bloom and beauty; in listening to the music of her voice; in gratefully recognizing how rich and fair for them was the world with this presence in it; in shuddering to think how desolate it would be with this light gone out of it.

By nature—and inside—the aged aunts were utterly dear and lovable and good, but in the matter of morals and conduct their training had been so uncompromisingly strict that it had made them exteriorly austere, not to say stern. Their influence was effective in the house; so effective that the mother and the daughter conformed to its moral and religious requirements cheerfully, contentedly, happily, unquestionably. To do this was become second nature to them. And so in this peaceful heaven there were no clashings, no irritations, no fault-findings, no heart-burnings.

In it a lie had no place. In it a lie was unthinkable. In it speech was restricted to absolute truth, iron-bound truth, implacable and uncompromising truth, let the resulting consequences be what they might. At last, one day, under stress of circumstances, the darling of the house sullied her lips with a lie—and confessed it, with tears and self-upbraidings. There are not any words that can paint the consternation of the aunts. It was as if the sky had crumpled up and collapsed and the earth had tumbled to ruin with a crash. They sat side by side, white and stern, gazing speechless upon the culprit, who was on her knees before them with her face buried first in one lap and then the other, moaning and sobbing, and appealing for sympathy and forgiveness and getting no response, humbly kissing the hand of the one, then of the other, only to see it withdrawn as suffering defilement by those soiled lips.

Twice, at intervals, Aunt Hester said, in frozen amazement:

"You told a *lie?*"

Twice, at intervals, Aunt Hannah followed with the muttered and amazed ejaculation:

"You confess it—you actually confess it—you told a lie!"

It was all they could say. The situation was new, unheard

of, incredible; they could not understand it, they did not know how to take hold of it, it approximately paralyzed speech.

At length it was decided that the erring child must be taken to her mother, who was ill, and who ought to know what had happened. Helen begged, besought, implored that she might be spared this further disgrace, and that her mother might be spared the grief and pain of it; but this could not be: duty required this sacrifice, duty takes precedence of all things, nothing can absolve one from a duty, with a duty no compromise is possible.

Helen still begged, and said the sin was her own, her mother had had no hand in it—why must she be made to suffer for it?

But the aunts were obdurate in their righteousness, and said the law that visited the sins of the parent upon the child was by all right and reason reversible; and therefore it was but just that the innocent mother of a sinning child should suffer her rightful share of the grief and pain and shame which were the allotted wages of the sin.

The three moved toward the sick-room.

At this time the doctor was approaching the house. He was still a good distance away, however. He was a good doctor and a good man, and he had a good heart, but one had to know him a year to get over hating him, two years to learn to endure him, three to learn to like him, and four or five to learn to love him. It was a slow and trying education, but it paid. He was of great stature; he had a leonine head, a leonine face, a rough voice, and an eye which was sometimes a pirate's and sometimes a woman's, according to the mood. He knew nothing about etiquette, and cared nothing about it; in speech, manner, carriage, and conduct he was the reverse of conventional. He was frank, to the limit; he had opinions on all subjects; they were always on tap and ready for delivery, and he cared not a farthing whether his listener liked them or didn't. Whom he loved he loved, and manifested it; whom he didn't love he hated, and published it from the housetops. In his young days he had been a sailor, and the salt-airs of all the seas blew from him yet. He was a sturdy and loyal Christian, and believed he was the best one in the land, and the only one whose Christianity was perfectly sound, healthy, full-charged with common sense, and had no decayed places in it. People who had an ax to grind, or people who for any reason wanted to get on the soft side of him, called him The Christian—a phrase whose delicate flattery was music to his ears, and whose capital T was such an enchanting and vivid object to him that he could *see* it when it fell out of a person's mouth even in the dark. Many who were fond of him stood on their consciences with both feet and brazenly called him by that large title habitually, because it was a pleasure to them to do anything that would please him; and with eager and cordial malice his extensive and diligently cultivated crop of enemies gilded it, beflowered it, expanded it to "The *Only* Christian." Of these two titles, the latter had the wider currency; the enemy, being greatly in the majority, attended to that. Whatever the doctor believed, he believed with all his heart, and would fight for it whenever he got the chance; and if the intervals between chances grew to be irksomely wide, he would invent ways of shortening them himself. He was severely conscientious, according to his rather independent lights, and whatever he took to be a duty he performed, no matter whether the judgment of the professional moralists agreed with his own or not. At sea, in his young days, he had used profanity freely, but as soon as he was converted he made a rule, which he rigidly stuck to ever afterward, never to use it except on the rarest occasions, and then only when duty commanded. He had been a hard drinker at sea, but after his conversion he became a firm and outspoken teetotaler, in order to be an example to the young, and from that time forth he seldom drank; never, indeed, except when it seemed to him to be a duty—a condition which sometimes occurred a couple of times a year, but never as many as five times.

Necessarily, such a man is impressionable, impulsive, emotional. This one was, and had no gift at hiding his feelings; or if he had it he took no trouble to exercise it. He carried his soul's prevailing weather in his face, and when he entered a room the parasols or the umbrellas went up—figuratively speaking—according to the indications. When the soft light was in his eye it meant approval, and delivered a benediction; when he came with a frown he lowered the temperature ten degrees. He was a well-beloved man in the house of his friends, but sometimes a dreaded one.

He had a deep affection for the Lester household, and its several members returned this feeling with interest. They mourned over his kind of Christianity, and he frankly scoffed at theirs; but both parties went on loving each other just the same.

He was approaching the house—out of the distance; the aunts and the culprit were moving toward the sick-chamber.

3

The three last named stood by the bed; the aunts austere, the transgressor softly sobbing. The mother turned her head on the pillow; her tired eyes flamed up instantly with sympathy and passionate mother-love when they fell upon her child, and she opened the refuge and shelter of her arms.

"Wait!" said Aunt Hannah, and put out her hand and stayed the girl from leaping into them.

"Helen," said the other aunt, impressively, "tell your mother all. Purge your soul; leave nothing unconfessed."

Standing stricken and forlorn before her judges, the young girl mourned her sorrowful tale through to the end, then in a passion of appeal cried out:

"Oh, mother, can't you forgive me? won't you forgive me?—I am so desolate!"

"Forgive you, my darling? Oh, come to my arms!—there, lay your head upon my breast, and be at peace. If you had told a thousand lies—"

There was a sound—a warning—the clearing of a throat. The aunts glanced up, and withered in their clothes—there stood the doctor, his face a thunder-cloud. Mother and child knew nothing of his presence; they lay locked together, heart to heart, steeped in immeasurable content, dead to all things else. The physician stood many moments glaring and glooming upon the scene before him; studying it, analyzing it, searching out its genesis; then he put up his hand and beckoned to the aunts. They came trembling to him, and stood humbly before him and waited. He bent down and whispered:

"Didn't I tell you this patient must be protected from all excitement? What the hell have you been doing? Clear out of the place!"

They obeyed. Half an hour later he appeared in the parlor, serene, cheery, clothed in sunshine, conducting Helen, with his arm about her waist, petting her, and saying gentle and playful things to her, and she also was her sunny and happy self again.

"Now, then," he said, "good-by, dear. Go to your room, and keep away from your mother, and behave yourself. But wait—put out your tongue. There, that will do—you're as sound as a nut!" He patted her cheek and added, "Run along now; I want to talk to these aunts."

She went from the presence. His face clouded over again at once; and as he sat down he said:

"You two have been doing a lot of damage—and maybe some good. Some good, yes—such as it is. That woman's disease is typhoid! You've brought it to a show-up, I think, with your insanities, and that's a service—such as it is. I hadn't been able to determine what it was before."

With one impulse the old ladies sprang to their feet, quaking with terror.

"Sit down! What are you proposing to do?"

"Do? We must fly to her. We—"

"You'll do nothing of the kind; you've done enough harm for one day. Do you want to squander all your capital of crimes and follies on a single deal? Sit down, I tell you. I have arranged for her to sleep; she needs it; if you disturb her without my orders, I'll brain you—if you've got the materials for it."

They sat down, distressed and indignant, but obedient, under compulsion. He proceeded:

"Now, then, I want this case explained. *They* wanted to explain it to me—as if there hadn't been emotion and excitement enough already. You knew my orders; how did you dare to go in there and get up that riot?"

Hester looked appealingly at Hannah; Hannah returned a beseeching look at Hester—neither wanted to dance to this unsympathetic orchestra. The doctor came to their help. He said:

"Begin, Hester."

Fingering at the fringes of her shawl, and with lowered eyes, Hester said, timidly:

"We should not have disobeyed for any ordinary cause, but this was vital. This was a duty. With a duty one has no choice; one must put all lighter considerations aside and perform it. We were obliged to arraign her before her mother. She had told a lie."

The doctor glowered upon the woman a moment, and seemed to be trying to work up in his mind an understanding of a wholly incomprehensible proposition; then he stormed out:

"She told a lie! *Did* she? God bless my soul! I tell a million a day! And so does every doctor. And so does everybody—including you—for that matter. And *that* was the important thing that authorized you to venture to disobey my orders and imperil that woman's life! Look here, Hester Gray, this is pure lunacy; that girl *couldn't* tell a lie that was intended to injure a person. The thing is impossible—absolutely impossible. You know it yourselves—both of you; you know it perfectly well."

Hannah came to her sister's rescue:

"Hester didn't mean that it was that kind of a lie, and it wasn't. But it was a lie."

"Well, upon my word, I never heard such nonsense! Haven't you got sense enough to discriminate between lies? Don't you know the difference between a lie that helps and a lie that hurts?"

"*All* lies are sinful," said Hannah, setting her lips together like a vise; "all lies are forbidden."

The Only Christian fidgeted impatiently in his chair. He wanted to attack this proposition, but he did not quite know how or where to begin. Finally he made a venture:

"Hester, wouldn't you tell a lie to shield a person from an undeserved injury or shame?"

"No."

"Not even a friend?"

"No."

"Not even your dearest friend?"

"No. I would not."

The doctor struggled in silence awhile with this situation; then he asked:

"Not even to save him from bitter pain and misery and grief?"

"No. Not even to save his life."

Another pause. Then:

"Nor his soul?"

There was a hush—a silence which endured a measurable interval—then Hester answered, in a low voice, but with decision:

"Nor his soul."

No one spoke for a while; then the doctor said:

"Is it with you the same, Hannah?"

"Yes," she answered.

"I ask you both—why?"

"Because to tell such a lie, or any lie, is a sin, and could cost us the loss of our own souls—*would*, indeed, if we died without time to repent."

"Strange . . . strange . . . it is past belief." Then he asked, roughly: "Is such a soul as that *worth* saving?" He rose up, mumbling and grumbling, and started for the door, stumping vigorously along. At the threshold he turned and rasped out an admonition: "Reform! Drop this mean and sordid and selfish devotion to the saving of your shabby little souls, and hunt up something to do that's got some dignity to it! *Risk* your souls! risk them in good causes; then if you lose them, why should you care? Reform!"

The good old gentlewomen sat paralyzed, pulverized, outraged, insulted, and brooded in bitterness and indignation over these blasphemies. They were hurt to the heart, poor old ladies, and said they could never forgive these injuries.

"Reform!"

They kept repeating that word resentfully. "Reform—and learn to tell lies!"

Time slipped along, and in due course a change came over their spirits. They had completed the human being's first duty—which is to think about himself until he has exhausted the subject, then he is in a condition to take up minor interests and think of other people. This changes the complexion of his spirits—generally wholesomely. The minds of the two old ladies reverted to their beloved niece and the fearful disease which had smitten her; instantly they forgot the hurts their self-love had received, and a passionate desire rose in their hearts to go to the help of the sufferer and comfort her with their love, and minister to her, and labor for her the best they could with their weak hands, and joyfully and affectionately wear out their poor old bodies in her dear service if only they might have the privilege.

"And we shall have it!" said Hester, with the tears running down her face. "There are no nurses comparable to us, for there are no others that will stand their watch by that bed till they drop and die, and God knows we would do that."

"Amen," said Hannah, smiling approval and indorsement through the mist of moisture that blurred her glasses. "The doctor knows us, and knows we will not disobey again; and he will call no others. He will not dare!"

"Dare?" said Hester, with temper, and dashing the water from her eyes; "he will dare anything—that Christian devil! But it will do no good for him to try it this time—but, laws! Hannah! after all's said and done, he is gifted and wise and good, and he would not think of such a thing. . . . It is surely time for one of us to go to that room. What is keeping him? Why doesn't he come and say so?"

They caught the sound of his approaching step. He entered, sat down, and began to talk.

"Margaret is a sick woman," he said. "She is still sleeping, but she will wake presently; then one of you must go to her. She will be worse before she is better. Pretty soon a night-and-day watch must be set. How much of it can you two undertake?"

"All of it!" burst from both ladies at once.

The doctor's eyes flashed, and he said, with energy:

"You *do* ring true, you brave old relics! And you *shall* do all of the nursing you can, for there's none to match you in that divine office in this town; but you can't do all of it, and it would be a crime to let you." It was grand praise, golden praise, coming from such a source, and it took nearly all the resentment out of the aged twins' hearts. "Your Tilly and my old Nancy shall do the rest—good nurses both, white souls with black skins, watchful, loving, tender—just perfect nurses!—and competent liars from the cradle. . . . Look you! keep a little watch on Helen; she is sick, and is going to be sicker."

The ladies looked a little surprised, and not credulous; and Hester said:

"How is that? It isn't an hour since you said she was as sound as a nut."

The doctor answered, tranquilly:

"It was a lie."

The ladies turned upon him indignantly, and Hannah said:

"How can you make an odious confession like that, in so indifferent a tone, when you know how we feel about all forms of—"

"Hush! You are as ignorant as cats, both of you, and you don't know what you are talking about. You are like all the rest of the moral moles; you lie from morning till night, but because you don't do it with your mouths, but only with your lying eyes, your lying inflections, your deceptively misplaced emphases, and your misleading gestures, you turn up your complacent noses and parade before God and the world as saintly and unsmirched Truth-Speakers, in whose cold-storage souls a lie would freeze to death if it got there! Why will you humbug yourselves with that foolish notion that no lie is a lie except a spoken one? What is the difference between lying with your eyes and lying with your mouth? There is none; and if you would reflect a moment you would see that it is so. There isn't a human being that doesn't tell a gross of lies every day of his life; and you—why, between you, you tell thirty thousand; yet you flare up here in a lurid hypocritical horror because I tell that child a benevolent and sinless lie to protect her from her imagination, which would get to work and warm up her blood to a fever in an hour, if I were disloyal enough to my duty to let it. Which I should probably do if I were interested in saving my soul by such disreputable means.

"Come, let us reason together. Let us examine details. When you two were in the sick-room raising that riot, what would you have done if you had known I was coming?"

"Well, what?"

"You would have slipped out and carried Helen with you—wouldn't you?"

The ladies were silent.

"What would be your object and intention?"

"Well, what?"

"To keep me from finding out your guilt; to beguile me to infer that Margaret's excitement proceeded from some cause not known to you. In a word, to tell me a lie—a silent one. Moreover, a possibly harmful one."

The twins colored, but did not speak.

"You not only tell myriads of silent lies, but you tell lies with your mouths—you two."

"*That* is not so!"

"It is so. But only harmless ones. You never dream of uttering a harmful one. Do you know that that is a concession—and a confession?"

"How do you mean?"

"It is an unconscious concession that harmless lies are not criminal; it is a confession that you constantly *make* that discrimination. For instance, you declined old Mrs. Foster's invitation last week to meet those odious Higbies at supper—in a polite note in which you expressed regret and said you were very sorry you could not go. It was a lie. It was as unmitigated a lie as was ever uttered. Deny it, Hester—with another lie."

Hester replied with a toss of her head.

"That will not do. Answer. Was it a lie, or wasn't it?"

The color stole into the cheeks of both women, and with a struggle and an effort they got out their confession:

"It was a lie."

"Good—the reform is beginning; there is hope for you yet; you will not tell a lie to save your dearest friend's soul, but you will spew out one without a scruple to save yourself the discomfort of telling an unpleasant truth."

He rose. Hester, speaking for both, said, coldly:

"We have lied; we perceive it; it will occur no more. To lie is a sin. We shall never tell another one of any kind whatsoever, even lies of courtesy or benevolence, to save any one a pang or a sorrow decreed for him by God."

"Ah, how soon you will fall! In fact, you have fallen already; for what you have just uttered is a lie. Good-by. Reform! One of you go to the sick-room now."

4

Twelve days later.

Mother and child were lingering in the grip of the hideous disease. Of hope for either there was little. The aged sisters looked white and worn, but they would not give up their posts. Their hearts were breaking, poor old things, but their grit was steadfast and indestructible. All the twelve days the mother had pined for the child, and the child for the mother, but both knew that the prayer of these longings could not be granted. When the mother was told—on the first day—that her disease was typhoid, she was frightened, and asked if there was danger that Helen could have contracted it the day before, when she was in the sick-chamber on that confession visit. Hester told her the doctor had poo-pooed the idea. It troubled Hester to say it, although it was true, for she had not believed the doctor; but when she saw the mother's joy in the news, the pain in her conscience lost something of its force—a result which made her ashamed of the constructive deception which she had practised, though not ashamed enough to make her distinctly and definitely wish she had refrained from it. From that moment the sick woman understood that her daughter must remain away, and she said she would reconcile herself to the separation the best she could, for she would rather suffer death than have her child's health imperiled. That afternoon Helen had to take to her bed, ill. She grew worse during the night. In the morning her mother asked after her:

"Is she well?"

Hester turned cold; she opened her lips, but the words refused to come. The mother lay languidly looking, musing, waiting; suddenly she turned white and gasped out:

"Oh, my God! what is it? is she sick?"

Then the poor aunt's tortured heart rose in rebellion, and words came:

"No—be comforted; she is well."

The sick woman put all her happy heart in her gratitude:

Thank God for those dear words! Kiss me. How I worship you for saying them!"

Hester told this incident to Hannah, who received it with a rebuking look, and said, coldly:

"Sister, it was a lie."

Hester's lips trembled piteously; she choked down a sob, and said:

"Oh, Hannah, it was a sin, but I could not help it. I could not endure the fright and the misery that were in her face."

"No matter. It was a lie. God will hold you to account for it."

"Oh, I know it, I know it," cried Hester, wringing her hands, "but even if it were now, I could not help it. I know I should do it again."

"Then take my place with Helen in the morning. I will make the report myself."

Hester clung to her sister, begging and imploring.

"Don't, Hannah, oh, don't—you will kill her."

"I will at least speak the truth."

In the morning she had a cruel report to bear to the mother, and she braced herself for the trial. When she returned from her mission, Hester was waiting, pale and trembling, in the hall. She whispered:

"Oh, how did she take it—that poor, desolate mother?"

Hannah's eyes were swimming in tears. She said:

"God forgive me, I told her the child was well!"

Hester gathered her to her heart, with a grateful "God bless you, Hannah!" and poured out her thankfulness in an inundation of worshiping praises.

After that, the two knew the limit of their strength, and accepted their fate. They surrendered humbly, and abandoned themselves to the hard requirements of the situation. Daily they told the morning lie, and confessed their sin in prayer; not asking forgiveness, as not being worthy of it, but only wishing to make record that they realized their wickedness and were not desiring to hide it or excuse it.

Daily, as the fair young idol of the house sank lower and lower, the sorrowful old aunts painted her glowing bloom and her fresh young beauty to the wan mother, and winced under the stabs her ecstasies of joy and gratitude gave them.

In the first days, while the child had strength to hold a pencil, she wrote fond little love-notes to her mother, in which she concealed her illness; and these the mother read and reread through happy eyes wet with thankful tears, and kissed them over and over again, and treasured them as precious things under her pillow.

Then came a day when the strength was gone from the hand, and the mind wandered, and the tongue babbled pathetic incoherences. This was a sore dilemma for the poor aunts. There were no love-notes for the mother. They did not know what to do. Hester began a carefully studied and plausible explanation, but lost the track of it and grew confused; suspicion began to show in the mother's face, then alarm. Hester saw it, recognized the imminence of the danger, and descended to the emergency, pulling herself resolutely together and plucking victory from the open jaws of defeat. In a placid and convincing voice she said:

"I thought it might distress you to know it, but Helen spent the night at the Sloanes'. There was a little party there, and, although she did not want to go, and you so sick, we persuaded her, she being young and needing the innocent pastimes of youth, and we believing you would approve. Be sure she will write the moment she comes."

"How good you are, and how dear and thoughtful for us both! Approve? Why, I thank you with all my heart. My poor little exile! Tell her I want her to have every pleasure she can—I would not rob her of one. Only let her keep her health, that is all I ask. Don't let that suffer; I could not bear it. How thankful I am that she escaped this infection—and what a narrow risk she ran, Aunt Hester! Think of that lovely face all dulled and burned with fever. I can't bear the thought of it. Keep her health. Keep her bloom! I can see her now, the dainty creature—with the big, blue, earnest eyes; and sweet, oh, so sweet and gentle and winning! Is she as beautiful as ever, dear Aunt Hester?"

"Oh, more beautiful and bright and charming than ever she was before, if such a thing can be"—and Hester turned away and fumbled with the medicine-bottles, to hide her shame and grief.

5

After a little, both aunts were laboring upon a difficult and baffling work in Helen's chamber. Patiently and earnestly, with their stiff old fingers, they were trying to forge the required note. They made failure after failure, but they improved little by little all the time. The pity of it all, the pathetic humor of it, there was none to see; they themselves were unconscious of it. Often their tears fell upon the notes and spoiled them; sometimes a single misformed word made a note risky which could have been ventured but for that; but at last Hannah produced one whose script was a good enough imitation of Helen's to pass any but a suspicious eye, and bountifully enriched it with the petting phrases and loving nicknames that had been familiar on the child's lips from her nursery days. She carried it to the mother, who took it with avidity, and kissed it, and fondled it, reading its precious words over and over again, and dwelling with deep contentment upon its closing paragraph:

"Mousie darling, if I could only see you, and kiss your eyes, and feel your arms about me! I am so glad my practising does not disturb you. Get well soon. Everybody is good to me, but I am so lonesome without you, dear mamma."

The poor child, I know just how she feels. She cannot be quite happy without me; and I—oh, I live in the light of her eyes! Tell her she must practise all she pleases; and, Aunt Hannah—tell her I can't hear the piano this far, nor her dear voice when she sings: God knows I wish I could. No one knows how sweet that voice is to me; and to think—some day it will be silent! What are you crying for?"

"Only because—because—it was just a memory. When I came away she was singing, 'Loch Lomond.' The pathos of it! It always moves me so when she sings that."

"And me, too. How heartbreakingly beautiful it is when some youthful sorrow is brooding in her breast and she sings it for the mystic healing it brings. . . . Aunt Hannah?"

"Dear Margaret?"

"I am very ill. Sometimes it comes over me that I shall never hear that dear voice again."

"Oh, don't—don't, Margaret! I can't bear it!"

Margaret was moved and distressed, and said, gently:

"There—there—let me put my arms around you. Don't cry. There—put your cheek to mine. Be comforted. I wish to live. I will live if I can. Ah, what could she do without me! . . . Does she often speak of me?—but I know she does."

"Oh, all the time—all the time!"

"My sweet child! She wrote the note the moment she came home?"

"Yes—the first moment. She would not wait to take off her things."

"I knew it. It is her dear, impulsive, affectionate way. I knew it without asking, but I wanted to hear you say it. The petted wife knows she is loved, but she makes her husband tell her so every day, just for the joy of hearing it. . . . She used the pen this time. That is better; the pencil-marks could rub out, and I should grieve for that. Did you suggest that she use the pen?"

"Y—no—she—it was her own idea."

The mother looked her pleasure, and said:

"I was hoping you would say that. There was never such a dear and thoughtful child! . . . Aunt Hannah?"

"Dear Margaret?"

"Go and tell her I think of her all the time, and worship her. Why—you are crying again. Don't be so worried about me, dear; I think there is nothing to fear, yet."

The grieving messenger carried her message, and piously delivered it to unheeding ears. The girl babbled on unaware; looking up at her with wondering and startled eyes flaming with fever, eyes in which was no light of recognition:

"Are you—no, you are not my mother. I want her—oh, I want her! She was here a minute ago—I did not see her go. Will she come? will she come quickly? will she come now? . . . There are so many houses . . . and they oppress me so . . . and everything whirls and turns and whirls . . . oh, my head, my head!"—and so she wandered on and on, in her pain, flitting from one torturing fancy to another, and tossing her arms about in a weary and ceaseless persecution of unrest.

Poor old Hannah wetted the parched lips and softly stroked the hot brow, murmuring endearing and pitying words, and thanking the Father of all that the mother was happy and did not know.

6

Daily the child sank lower and steadily lower towards the grave, and daily the sorrowing old watchers carried gilded tidings of her radiant health and loveliness to the happy mother, whose pilgrimage was also now nearing its end. And daily they forged loving and cheery notes in the child's hand, and stood by with remorseful consciences and bleeding hearts, and wept to see the grateful mother devour them and adore them and treasure them away as things beyond price, because of their sweet source, and sacred because her child's hand had touched them.

At last came that kindly friend who brings healing and peace to all. The lights were burning low. In the solemn hush which precedes the dawn vague figures flitted soundless along the dim hall and gathered silent and awed in Helen's chamber, and grouped themselves about her bed, for a warning had gone forth, and they knew. The dying girl lay with closed lids, and unconscious, the drapery upon her breast faintly rising and falling as her wasting life ebbed away. At intervals a sigh or a muffled sob broke upon the stillness. The same haunting thought was in all minds there: the pity of this death, the going out into the great darkness, and the mother not here to help and hearten and bless.

Helen stirred; her hands began to grope wistfully about as if they sought something—she had been blind some hours. The end was come; all knew it. With a great sob Hester gathered her to her breast, crying, "Oh, my child, my darling!" A rapturous light broke in the dying girl's face, for it was mercifully vouchsafed her to mistake those sheltering arms for another's; and she went to her rest murmuring, "Oh, mamma, I am so happy—I so longed for you—now I can die."

Two hours later Hester made her report. The mother asked:

"How is it with the child?"

"She is well."

7

A sheaf of white crape and black was hung upon the door of the house, and there it swayed and rustled in the wind and whispered its tidings. At noon the preparation of the dead was finished, and in the coffin lay the fair young form, beautiful, and in the sweet face a great peace. Two mourners sat by it, grieving and worshiping—Hannah and the black woman Tilly. Hester came, and she was trembling, for a great trouble was upon her spirit. She said:

"She asks for a note."

Hannah's face blanched. She had not thought of this; it had seemed that that pathetic service was ended. But she realized now that that could not be. For a little while the two women stood looking into each other's face, with vacant eyes; then Hannah said:

"There is no way out of it—she must have it; she will suspect, else."

"And she would find out."

"Yes. It would break her heart." She looked at the dead face, and her eyes filled. "I will write it," she said.

Hester carried it. The closing line said:

"Darling Mousie, dear sweet mother, we shall soon be together again. Is not that good news? And it is true; they all say it is true."

The mother mourned, saying:

"Poor child, how will she bear it when she knows? I shall never see her again in life. It is hard, so hard. She does not suspect? You guard her from that?"

"She thinks you will soon be well."

"How good you are, and careful, dear Aunt Hester! None goes near her who could carry the infection?"

"It would be a crime."

"But you see her?"

"With a distance between—yes."

"That is so good. Others one could not trust; but you two guardian angels—steel is not so true as you. Others would be unfaithful; and many would deceive, and lie."

Hester's eyes fell, and her poor old lips trembled.

"Let me kiss you for her, Aunt Hester; and when I am gone, and the danger is past, place the kiss upon her dear lips some day, and say her mother sent it, and all her mother's broken heart is in it."

Within the hour, Hester, raining tears upon the dead face, performed her pathetic mission.

8

Another day dawned, and grew, and spread its sunshine in the earth. Aunt Hannah brought comforting news to the failing mother, and a happy note, which said again, "We have but a little time to wait, darling mother, then we shall be together."

The deep note of a bell came moaning down the wind.

"Aunt Hannah, it is tolling. Some poor soul is at rest. As I shall be soon. You will not let her forget me?"

"Oh, God knows she never will!"

"Do not you hear strange noises, Aunt Hannah? It sounds like the shuffling of many feet."

"We hoped you would not hear it, dear. It is a little company gathering, for—for Helen's sake, poor little prisoner. There will be music—and she loves it so. We thought you would not mind."

"Mind? Oh no, no—oh, give her everything her dear heart can desire. How good you two are to her, and how good to me! God bless you both always!"

After a listening pause:

"How lovely! It is her organ. Is she playing it herself, do you think?" Faint and rich and inspiring the chords floated to her ears on the still air. "Yes, it is her touch, dear heart, I recognize it. They are singing. Why—it is a hymn! and the sacredest of all, the most touching, the most consoling. . . . It seems to open the gates of paradise to me. . . . If I could die now. . . ."

Faint and far the words rose out of the stillness:

Nearer, my God, to Thee,
Nearer to Thee,
E'en though it be a cross
That raiseth me.

With the closing of the hymn another soul passed to its rest, and they that had been one in life were not sundered in death. The sisters, mourning and rejoicing, said:

"How blessed it was that she never knew!"

9

At midnight they sat together, grieving, and the angel of the Lord appeared in the midst transfigured with a radiance not of the earth: and speaking, said:

"For liars a place is appointed. There they burn in the fires of hell from everlasting unto everlasting. Repent!"

The bereaved fell upon their knees before him and clasped their hands and bowed their gray heads, adoring. But their tongues clove to the roof of their mouths, and they were dumb.

"Speak! that I may bear the message to the chancery of heaven and bring again the decree from which there is no appeal."

Then they bowed their heads yet lower, and one said:

"Our sin is great, and we suffer shame; but only perfect and final repentance can make us whole; and we are poor creatures who have learned our human weakness, and we know that if we were in those hard straits again our hearts would fail again, and we should sin as before. The strong could prevail, and so be saved, but we are lost."

They lifted their heads in supplication. The angel was gone. While they marveled and wept he came again; and bending low, he whispered the decree.

10

Was it Heaven? Or Hell?

1902

A Dog's Tale

1

MY FATHER was a St. Bernard, my mother was a collie, but I am a Presbyterian. This is what my mother told me; I do not know these nice distinctions myself. To me they are only fine large words meaning nothing. My mother had a fondness for such; she liked to say them, and see other dogs look surprised and envious, as wondering how she got so much education. But, indeed, it was not real education; it was only show: she got the words by listening in the dining-room and drawing-room when there was company, and by going with the children to Sunday-school and listening there; and whenever she heard a large word she said it over to herself many times, and so was able to keep it until there was a dogmatic gathering in the neighborhood, then she would get it off, and surprise and distress them all, from pocket-pup to mastiff, which rewarded her for all her trouble. If there was a stranger he was nearly sure to be suspicious, and when he got his breath again he would ask her what it meant. And she always told him. He was never expecting this, but thought he would catch her; so when she told him, he was the one that looked ashamed, whereas he had thought it was going to be she. The others were always waiting for this, and glad of it and proud of her, for they knew what was going to happen, because they had had experience. When she told the meaning of a big word they were all so taken up with admiration that it never occurred to any dog to doubt if it was the right one; and that was natural, because, for one thing, she answered up so promptly that it seemed like a dictionary speaking, and for another thing, where could they find out whether it was right or not? for she was the only cultivated dog there was. By and by, when I was older, she brought home the word Unintellectual, one time, and worked it pretty hard all the week at different gatherings, making much unhappiness and despondency; and it was at this time that I noticed that during that week she was asked for the meaning at eight different assemblages, and flashed out a fresh definition every time, which showed me that she had more presence of mind than culture, though I said nothing, of course. She had one word which she always kept on hand, and ready, like a life-preserver, a kind of emergency word to strap on when she was likely to get washed overboard in a sudden way—that was the word Synonymous. When she happened to fetch out a long word which had had its day weeks before and its prepared meanings gone to her dump-pile, if there was a stranger there of course it knocked him groggy for a couple of minutes, then he would come to, and by that time she would be away down the wind on another tack, and not expecting anything; so when he'd hail and ask her to cash in, I (the only dog on the inside of her game) could see her canvas flicker a moment—but only just a moment—then it would belly out taut and full, and she would say, as calm as a summer's day, "It's synonymous with supererogation," or some godless long reptile of a word like that, and go placidly about and skim away on the next tack, perfectly comfortable, you know, and leave that stranger looking profane and embarrassed, and the initiated slatting the floor with their tails in unison and their faces transfigured with a holy joy.

And it was the same with phrases. She would drag home a whole phrase, if it had a grand sound, and play it six nights and two matinées, and explain it a new way every time—

which she had to, for all she cared for was the phrase; she wasn't interested in what it meant, and knew those dogs hadn't wit enough to catch her, anyway. Yes, she was a daisy! She got so she wasn't afraid of anything, she had such confidence in the ignorance of those creatures. She even brought anecdotes that she had heard the family and the dinner-guests laugh and shout over; and as a rule she got the nub of one chestnut hitched onto another chestnut, where, of course, it didn't fit and hadn't any point; and when she delivered the nub she fell over and rolled on the floor and laughed and barked in the most insane way, while I could see that she was wondering to herself why it didn't seem as funny as it did when she first heard it. But no harm was done; the others rolled and barked too, privately ashamed of themselves for not seeing the point, and never suspecting that the fault was not with them and there wasn't any to see.

You can see by these things that she was of a rather vain and frivolous character; still, she had virtues, and enough to make up, I think. She had a kind heart and gentle ways, and never harbored resentments for injuries done her, but put them easily out of her mind and forgot them; and she taught her children her kindly way, and from her we learned also to be brave and prompt in time of danger, and not to run away, but face the peril that threatened friend or stranger, and help him the best we could without stopping to think what the cost might be to us. And she taught us not by words only, but by example, and that is the best way and the surest and the most lasting. Why, the brave things she did, the splendid things! she was just a soldier; and so modest about it—well, you couldn't help admiring her, and you couldn't help imitating her; not even a King Charles spaniel could remain entirely despicable in her society. So, as you see, there was more to her than her education.

2

When I was well grown, at last, I was sold and taken away, and I never saw her again. She was broken-hearted, and so was I, and we cried; but she comforted me as well as she could, and said we were sent into this world for a wise and good purpose, and must do our duties without repining, take our life as we might find it, live it for the best good of others, and never mind about the results; they were not our affair. She said men who did like this would have a noble and beautiful reward by and by in another world, and although we animals would not go there, to do well and right without reward would give to our brief lives a worthiness and dignity which in itself would be a reward. She had gathered these things from time to time when she had gone to the Sunday-school with the children, and had laid them up in her memory more carefully than she had done with those other words and phrases; and she had studied them deeply, for her good and ours. One may see by this that she had a wise and thoughtful head, for all there was so much lightness and vanity in it.

So we said our farewells, and looked our last upon each other through our tears; and the last thing she said—keeping it for the last to make me remember it the better, I think—was, "In memory of me, when there is a time of danger to another do not think of yourself, think of your mother, and do as she would do."

Do you think I could forget that? No.

3

It was such a charming home!—my new one; a fine great house, with pictures, and delicate decorations, and rich furniture, and no gloom anywhere, but all the wilderness of dainty colors lit up with flooding sunshine; and the spacious grounds around it, and the great garden—oh, greensward, and noble trees, and flowers, no end! And I was the same as a member of the family; and they loved me, and petted me, and did not give me a new name, but called me by my old one that was dear to me because my mother had given it me—Aileen Mavourneen. She got it out of a song; and the Grays knew that song, and said it was a beautiful name.

Mrs. Gray was thirty, and so sweet and so lovely, you cannot imagine it; and Sadie was ten, and just like her mother, just a darling slender little copy of her, with auburn tails down her back, and short frocks; and the baby was a year old, and plump and dimpled, and fond of me, and never could get enough of hauling on my tail, and hugging me, and laughing out its innocent happiness; and Mr. Gray was thirty-eight, and tall and slender and handsome, a little bald in front, alert, quick in his movements, businesslike, prompt, decided, unsentimental, and with that kind of trim-chiseled face that just seems to glint and sparkle with frosty intellectuality! He was a renowned scientist. I do not know what the word means, but my mother would know how to use it and get effects. She would know how to depress a rat-terrier with it and make a lap-dog look sorry he came. But that is not the best one; the best one was Laboratory. My mother could organize a Trust on that one that would skin the tax-collars off the whole herd. The laboratory was not a book, or a picture, or a place to wash your hands in, as the college president's dog said—no, that is the lavatory; the laboratory is quite different, and is filled with jars, and bottles, and electrics, and wires, and strange machines; and every week other scientists came there and sat in the place, and used the machines, and discussed, and made what they called experiments and discoveries; and often I came, too, and stood around and listened, and tried to learn, for the sake of my mother, and in loving memory of her, although it was a pain to me, as realizing what she was losing out of her life and I gaining nothing at all; for try as I might, I was never able to make anything out of it at all.

Other times I lay on the floor in the mistress's work-room

and slept, she gently using me for a foot-stool, knowing it pleased me, for it was a caress; other times I spent an hour in the nursery, and got well tousled and made happy; other times I watched by the crib there, when the baby was asleep and the nurse out for a few minutes on the baby's affairs; other times I romped and raced through the grounds and the garden with Sadie till we were tired out, then slumbered on the grass in the shade of a tree while she read her book; other times I went visiting among the neighbor dogs—for there were some most pleasant ones not far away, and one very handsome and courteous and graceful one, a curly-haired Irish setter by the name of Robin Adair, who was a Presbyterian like me, and belonged to the Scotch minister.

The servants in our house were all kind to me and were fond of me, and so, as you see, mine was a pleasant life. There could not be a happier dog than I was, nor a gratefuler one. I will say this for myself, for it is only the truth: I tried in all ways to do well and right, and honor my mother's memory and her teachings, and earn the happiness that had come to me, as best I could.

By and by came my little puppy, and then my cup was full, my happiness was perfect. It was the dearest little waddling thing, and so smooth and soft and velvety, and had such cunning little awkward paws, and such affectionate eyes, and such a sweet and innocent face; and it made me so proud to see how the children and their mother adored it, and fondled it, and exclaimed over every little wonderful thing it did. It did seem to me that life was just too lovely to—

Then came the winter. One day I was standing a watch in the nursery. That is to say, I was asleep on the bed. The baby was asleep in the crib, which was alongside the bed, on the side next the fireplace. It was the kind of crib that has a lofty tent over it made of a gauzy stuff that you can see through. The nurse was out, and we two sleepers were alone. A spark from the wood-fire was shot out, and it lit on the slope of the tent. I supposed a quiet interval followed, then a scream from the baby woke me, and there was that tent flaming up toward the ceiling! Before I could think, I sprang to the floor in my fright, and in a second was half-way to the door; but in the next half-second my mother's farewell was sounding in my ears, and I was back on the bed again. I reached my head through the flames and dragged the baby out by the waistband, and tugged it along, and we fell to the floor together in a cloud of smoke; I snatched a new hold, and dragged the screaming little creature along and out at the door and around the bend of the hall, and was still tugging away, all excited and happy and proud, when the master's voice shouted:

"Begone, you cursed beast!" and I jumped to save myself; but he was wonderfully quick, and chased me up, striking furiously at me with his cane, I dodging this way and that, in terror, and at last a strong blow fell upon my left foreleg, which made me shriek and fall, for the moment, helpless; the cane went up for another blow, but never descended, for the nurse's voice rang wildly out, "The nursery's on fire!" and the master rushed away in that direction, and my other bones were saved.

The pain was cruel, but, no matter, I must not lose any time; he might come back at any moment; so I limped on three legs to the other end of the hall, where there was a dark little stairway leading up into a garret where old boxes and such things were kept, as I had heard say, and where people seldom went. I managed to climb up there, then I searched my way through the dark among the piles of things, and hid in the secretest place I could find. It was foolish to be afraid there, yet still I was; so afraid that I held in and hardly even whimpered, though it would have been such a comfort to whimper, because that eases the pain, you know. But I could lick my leg, and that did me some good.

For half an hour there was a commotion downstairs, and shoutings, and rushing footsteps, and then there was quiet again. Quiet for some minutes, and that was grateful to my spirit, for then my fears began to go down; and fears are worse than pains—oh, much worse. Then came a sound that froze me. They were calling me—calling me by name—hunting for me!

It was muffled by distance, but that could not take the terror out of it, and it was the most dreadful sound to me that I had ever heard. It went all about, everywhere, down there: along the halls, through all the rooms, in both stories, and in the basement and the cellar; men outside, and farther and farther away—then back, and all about the house again, and I thought it would never, never stop. But at last it did, hours and hours after the vague twilight of the garret had long ago been blotted out by black darkness.

Then in that blessed stillness my terrors fell little by little away, and I was at peace and slept. It was a good rest I had, but I woke before the twilight had come again. I was feeling fairly comfortable, and I could think out a plan now. I made a very good one; which was, to creep down, all the way down the back stairs, and hide behind the cellar door, and slip out and escape when the iceman came at dawn, while he was inside filling the refrigerator; then I would hide all day, and start on my journey when night came; my journey to—well, anywhere where they would not know me and betray me to the master. I was feeling almost cheerful now; then suddenly I thought: Why, what would life be without my puppy!

That was despair. There was no plan for me; I saw that; I must stay where I was; stay, and wait, and take what might come—it was not my affair; that was what life is—my mother had said it. Then—well, then the calling began again! All my sorrows came back. I said to myself, the master will never forgive. I did not know what I had done to make him so bitter and so unforgiving, yet I judged it was something a dog could not understand, but which was clear to a man and dreadful.

They called and called—days and nights, it seemed to me. So long that the hunger and thirst near drove me mad, and I recognized that I was getting very weak. When you are this way you sleep a great deal, and I did. Once I woke in an awful fright—it seemed to me that the calling was right there in the garret! And so it was: it was Sadie's voice, and she was crying; my name was falling from her lips all broken, poor thing, and I could not believe my ears for the joy of it when I heard her say:

"Come back to us—oh, come back to us, and forgive—it is all so sad without our—"

I broke in with *such* a grateful little yelp, and the next moment Sadie was plunging and stumbling through the darkness and the lumber and shouting for the family to hear, "She's found, she's found!"

The days that followed—well, they were wonderful. The mother and Sadie and the servants—why, they just seemed to worship me. They couldn't seem to make me a bed that was fine enough; and as for food, they couldn't be satisfied with anything but game and delicacies that were out of season; and every day the friends and neighbors flocked in to hear about my heroism—that was the name they called it by, and it means agriculture. I remember my mother pulling it on a kennel once, and explaining it that way, but didn't say what agriculture was, except that it was synonymous with intramural incandescence; and a dozen times a day Mrs. Gray and Sadie would tell the tale to newcomers, and say I risked my life to save the baby's, and both of us had burns to prove it, and then the company would pass me around and pet me and exclaim about me, and you could see the pride in the eyes of Sadie and her mother; and when the people wanted to know what made me limp, they looked ashamed and changed the subject, and sometimes when people hunted them this way and that way with questions about it, it looked to me as if they were going to cry.

And this was not all the glory; no, the master's friends came, a whole twenty of the most distinguished people, and had me in the laboratory, and discussed me as if I was a kind of discovery; and some of them said it was wonderful in a dumb beast, the finest exhibition of instinct they could call to mind; but the master said, with vehemence, "It's far above instinct; it's *reason,* and many a man, privileged to be saved and go with you and me to a better world by right of its possession, has less of it than this poor silly quadruped that's foreordained to perish"; and then he laughed, and said: "Why, look at me—I'm a sarcasm! bless you, with all my grand intelligence, the only thing I inferred was that the dog had gone mad and was destroying the child, whereas but for the beast's intelligence—it's *reason,* I tell you!—the child would have perished!"

They disputed and disputed, and *I* was the very center and subject of it all, and I wished my mother could know that this grand honor had come to me; it would have made her proud.

Then they discussed optics, as they called it, and whether a certain injury to the brain would produce blindness or not, but they could not agree about it, and said they must test it by experiment by and by; and next they discussed plants, and that interested me, because in the summer Sadie and I had planted seeds—I helped her dig the holes, you know—and after days and days a little shrub or a flower came up there, and it was a wonder how that could happen; but it did, and I wished I could talk—I would have told those people about it and shown them how much I knew, and been all alive with the subject; but I didn't care for the optics; it was dull, and when they came back to it again it bored me, and I went to sleep.

Pretty soon it was spring, and sunny and pleasant and lovely, and the sweet mother and the children patted me and the puppy good-by, and went away on a journey and a visit to their kin, and the master wasn't any company for us, but we played together and had good times, and the servants were kind and friendly, so we got along quite happily and counted the days and waited for the family.

And one day those men came again, and said, now for the test, and they took the puppy to the laboratory, and I limped three-leggedly along, too, feeling proud, for any attention shown the puppy was a pleasure to me, of course. They discussed and experimented, and then suddenly the puppy shrieked, and they set him on the floor, and he went staggering around, with his head all bloody, and the master clapped his hands and shouted:

"There, I've won—confess it! He's as blind as a bat!"

And they all said:

"It's so—you've proved your theory, and suffering humanity owes you a great debt from henceforth," and they crowded around him, and wrung his hand cordially and thankfully, and praised him.

But I hardly saw or heard these things, for I ran at once to my little darling, and snuggled close to it where it lay, and licked the blood, and it put its head against mine, whimpering softly, and I knew in my heart it was a comfort to it in its pain and trouble to feel its mother's touch, though it could not see me. Then it dropped down, presently, and its little velvet nose rested upon the floor, and it was still, and did not move any more.

Soon the master stopped discussing a moment, and rang in the footman, and said, "Bury it in the far corner of the garden," and then went on with the discussion, and I trotted after the footman, very happy and grateful, for I knew the puppy was out of its pain now, because it was asleep. We went far down the garden to the farthest end, where the children and the nurse and the puppy and I used to play in the summer in the shade of a great elm, and there the footman dug a hole, and I saw he was going to plant the puppy, and I was glad, because it would grow and come up a fine handsome dog, like Robin Adair, and be a beautiful surprise for the family when they came home; so I tried to help him dig, but my lame leg was no good, being stiff, you know, and you have to have two, or it is no use. When the footman had finished and covered little Robin up, he patted my head, and there were tears in his eyes, and he said: "Poor little doggie, you SAVED *his* child."

I have watched two whole weeks, and he doesn't come up! This last week a fright has been stealing upon me. I think there is something terrible about this. I do not know what it is, but the fear makes me sick, and I cannot eat, though the servants bring me the best of food; and they pet me so, and even come in the night, and cry, and say, "Poor doggie—do give it up and come home; *don't* break our hearts!" and all this terrifies me the more, and makes me sure something has happened. And I am so weak; since yesterday I cannot stand on my feet any more. And within this hour the servants, looking toward the sun where it was sinking out of sight and the night chill coming on, said things I could not understand, but they carried something cold to my heart.

"Those poor creatures! They do not suspect. They will come home in the morning, and eagerly ask for the little doggie that did the brave deed, and who of us will be strong enough to say the truth to them: 'The humble little friend is gone where go the beasts that perish.' "

1903

The $30,000 Bequest

1

LAKESIDE WAS a pleasant little town of five or six thousand inhabitants, and a rather pretty one, too, as towns go in the Far West. It had church accommodations for thirty-five thousand, which is the way of the Far West and the South, where everybody is religious, and where each of the Protestant sects is represented and has a plant of its own. Rank was unknown in Lakeside—unconfessed, anyway; everybody knew everybody and his dog, and a sociable friendliness was the prevailing atmosphere.

Saladin Foster was book-keeper in the principal store, and the only high-salaried man of his profession in Lakeside. He was thirty-five years old, now; he had served that store for fourteen years; he had begun in his marriage-week at four hundred dollars a year, and had climbed steadily up, a hundred dollars a year, for four years; from that time forth his wage had remained eight hundred—a handsome figure indeed, and everybody conceded that he was worth it.

His wife, Electra, was a capable helpmeet, although—like himself—a dreamer of dreams and a private dabbler in romance. The first thing she did, after her marriage—child as she was, aged only nineteen—was to buy an acre of ground on the edge of the town, and pay down the cash for it—twenty-five dollars, all her fortune. Saladin had less, by fifteen. She instituted a vegetable garden there, got it farmed on shares by the nearest neighbor, and made it pay her a hundred per cent. a year. Out of Saladin's first year's wage she put thirty dollars in the savings-bank, sixty out of his second, a hundred out of his third, a hundred and fifty out of his fourth. His wage went to eight hundred a year, then, and meantime two children had arrived and increased the expenses, but she banked two hundred a year from the salary, nevertheless, thenceforth. When she had been married seven years she built and furnished a pretty and comfortable two-thousand-dollar house in the midst of her garden-acre, paid half of the money down and moved her family in. Seven years later she was out of debt and had several hundred dollars out earning its living.

Earning it by the rise in landed estate; for she had long ago bought another acre or two and sold the most of it at a profit to pleasant people who were willing to build, and would be good neighbors and furnish a general comradeship for herself and her growing family. She had an independent income from safe investments of about a hundred dollars a year; her children were growing in years and grace; and she was a pleased and happy woman. Happy in her husband, happy in her children, and the husband and the children were happy in her. It is at this point that this history begins.

The youngest girl, Clytemnestra—called Clytie for short—was eleven; her sister, Gwendolen—called Gwen for short—was thirteen; nice girls, and comely. The names betray the latent romance-tinge in the parental blood, the parents' names indicate that the tinge was an inheritance. It was an affectionate family, hence all four of its members had pet names. Saladin's was a curious and unsexing one—Sally; and so was Electra's—Aleck. All day long Sally was a good and diligent book-keeper and salesman; all day long Aleck was a good and faithful mother and housewife, and thoughtful and calculating business woman; but in the cozy living-room at night they put the plodding world away, and lived in another and a fairer, reading romances to each other, dreaming dreams, comrading with kings and princes and stately lords and ladies in the flash and stir and splendor of noble palaces and grim and ancient castles.

2

Now came great news! Stunning news—joyous news, in fact. It came from a neighboring state, where the family's only surviving relative lived. It was Sally's relative—a sort of vague and indefinite uncle or second or third cousin by the name of Tilbury Foster, seventy and a bachelor, reputed well off and correspondingly sour and crusty. Sally had tried to make up to him once, by letter, in a bygone time, and had not made that mistake again. Tilbury now wrote to Sally, saying he should shortly die, and should leave him thirty thousand dollars, cash; not for love, but because money had given him most of his troubles and exasperations, and he wished to place it where there was good hope that it would continue its malignant work. The bequest would be found in his will, and would be paid over. *Provided,* that Sally should be able to prove to the executors that he had *taken no notice of the gift by spoken word or by letter, had made no inquiries concerning the moribund's progress toward the everlasting tropics, and had not attended the funeral.*

As soon as Aleck had partially recovered from the tremendous emotions created by the letter, she sent to the relative's habitat and subscribed for the local paper.

Man and wife entered into a solemn compact, now, to never mention the great news to any one while the relative lived, lest some ignorant person carry the fact to the deathbed and distort it and make it appear that they were disobediently thankful for the bequest, and just the same as confessing it and publishing it, right in the face of the prohibition.

For the rest of the day Sally made havoc and confusion with his books, and Aleck could not keep her mind on her affairs, nor even take up a flower-pot or book or a stick of wood without forgetting what she had intended to do with it. For both were dreaming.

"Thir-ty thousand dollars!"

All day long the music of those inspiring words sang through those people's heads.

From her marriage-day forth, Aleck's grip had been upon the purse, and Sally had seldom known what it was to be privileged to squander a dime on non-necessities.

"Thir-ty thousand dollars!" the song went on and on. A vast sum, an unthinkable sum!

All day long Aleck was absorbed in planning how to invest it, Sally in planning how to spend it.

There was no romance-reading that night. The children took themselves away early, for the parents were silent, distraught, and strangely unentertaining. The good-night kisses might as well have been impressed upon vacancy, for all the response they got; the parents were not aware of the kisses, and the children had been gone an hour before their absence was noticed. Two pencils had been busy during that hour—note-making; in the way of plans. It was Sally who broke the stillness at last. He said, without exultation:

"Ah, it'll be grand, Aleck! Out of the first thousand we'll have a horse and a buggy for summer, and a cutter and a skin lap-robe for winter."

Aleck responded with decision and composure—

"Out of the *capital?* Nothing of the kind. Not if it was a million!"

Sally was deeply disappointed; the glow went out of his face.

"Oh, Aleck!" he said, reproachfully. "We've always worked so hard and been so scrimped; and now that we are rich, it does seem—"

He did not finish, for he saw her eye soften; his supplication had touched her. She said, with gentle persuasiveness:

"We must not spend the capital, dear, it would not be wise. Out of the income from it—"

"That will answer, that will answer, Aleck! How dear and good you are! There will be a noble income, and if we can spend that—"

"Not *all* of it, dear, not all of it, but you can spend a part of it. That is, a reasonable part. But the whole of the capital—every penny of it—must be put right to work, and kept at it. You see the reasonableness of that, don't you?"

"Why, ye-s. Yes, of course. But we'll have to wait so long. Six months before the first interest falls due."

"Yes—maybe longer."

"Longer, Aleck? Why? Don't they pay half-yearly?"

"*That* kind of an investment—yes; but I sha'n't invest in that way."

"What way, then?"

"For big returns."

"Big. That's good. Go on, Aleck. What is it?"

"Coal. The new mines. Cannel. I mean to put in ten thousand. Ground floor. When we organize, we'll get three shares for one."

"By George, but it sounds good, Aleck! Then the shares will be worth—how much? And when?"

"About a year. They'll pay ten per cent. half-yearly, and be worth thirty thousand. I know all about it; the advertisement is in the Cincinnati paper here."

"Land, thirty thousand for ten—in a year! Let's jam in the whole capital and pull out ninety! I'll write and subscribe right now—to-morrow it may be too late."

He was flying to the writing-desk, but Aleck stopped him and put him back in his chair. She said:

"Don't lose your head so. We mustn't subscribe till we've got the money; don't you know that?"

Sally's excitement went down a degree or two, but he was not wholly appeased.

"Why, Aleck, we'll *have* it, you know—and so soon, too. He's probably out of his troubles before this; it's a hundred to nothing he's selecting his brimstone-shovel this very minute. Now, I think—"

Aleck shuddered, and said:

"How *can* you, Sally! Don't talk in that way, it is perfectly scandalous."

"Oh well, make it a halo, if you like, *I* don't care for his outfit, I was only just talking. Can't you let a person talk?"

"But why should you *want* to talk in that dreadful way? How would you like to have people talk so about *you*, and you not cold yet?"

"Not likely to be, for *one* while, I reckon, if my last act was giving away money for the sake of doing somebody a harm with it. But never mind about Tilbury, Aleck, let's talk about something worldly. It does seem to me that that mine is the place for the whole thirty. What's the objection?"

"All the eggs in one basket—that's the objection."

"All right, if you say so. What about the other twenty? What do you mean to do with that?"

"There is no hurry; I am going to look around before I do anything with it."

"All right, if your mind's made up," sighed Sally. He was deep in thought awhile, then he said:

"There'll be twenty thousand profit coming from the ten a year from now. We can spend that, can't we, Aleck?"

Aleck shook her head.

"No, dear," she said, "it won't sell high till we've had the first semi-annual dividend. You can spend part of that."

"Shucks, only *that*—and a whole year to wait! Confound it, I—"

"Oh, do be patient! It might even be declared in three months—it's quite within the possibilities."

"Oh, jolly! oh, thanks!" and Sally jumped up and kissed his wife in gratitude. "It'll be three thousand—three whole thousand! how much of it can we spend, Aleck? Make it liberal—do, dear, that's a good fellow."

Aleck was pleased; so pleased that she yielded to the pressure and conceded a sum which her judgment told her was a foolish extravagance—a thousand dollars. Sally kissed her half a dozen times and even in that way could not express all his joy and thankfulness. This new access of gratitude and affection carried Aleck quite beyond the bounds of prudence, and before she could restrain herself she had made her darling another grant—a couple of thousand out of the fifty or sixty which she meant to clear within a year out of the twenty which still remained of the bequest. The happy tears sprang to Sally's eyes, and he said:

"Oh, I want to hug you!" And he did it. Then he got his notes and sat down and began to check off, for first purchase, the luxuries which he should earliest wish to secure. "Horse—buggy—cutter—lap-robe—patent-leathers—dog—plug-hat—church-pew—stem-winder—new teeth—*say*, Aleck!"

"Well?"

"Ciphering away, aren't you? That's right. Have you got the twenty thousand invested yet?"

"No, there's no hurry about that; I must look around first, and think."

"But you are ciphering; what's it about?"

"Why, I have to find work for the thirty thousand that comes out of the coal, haven't I?"

"Scott, what a head! I never thought of that. How are you getting along? Where have you arrived?"

"Not very far—two years or three. I've turned it over twice; once in oil and once in wheat."

"Why, Aleck, it's splendid! How does it aggregate?"

"I think—well, to be on the safe side, about a hundred and eighty thousand clear, though it will probably be more."

"My! isn't it wonderful? By gracious! luck has come our way at last, after all the hard sledding. Aleck!"

"Well?"

"I'm going to cash in a whole three hundred on the missionaries—what real right have we to care for expenses!"

"You couldn't do a nobler thing, dear; and it's just like your generous nature, you unselfish boy."

The praise made Sally poignantly happy, but he was fair and just enough to say it was rightfully due to Aleck rather than to himself, since but for her he should never have had the money.

Then they went up to bed, and in their delirium of bliss they forgot and left the candle burning in the parlor. They did not remember until they were undressed; then Sally was for letting it burn; he said they could afford it, if it was a thousand. But Aleck went down and put it out.

A good job, too; for on her way back she hit on a scheme that would turn the hundred and eighty thousand into half a million before it had had time to get cold.

3

The little newspaper which Aleck had subscribed for was a Thursday sheet; it would make the trip of five hundred miles from Tilbury's village and arrive on Saturday. Tilbury's letter had started on Friday, more than a day too late for the benefactor to die and get into that week's issue, but in plenty of time to make connection for the next output. Thus the Fosters had to wait almost a complete week to find out whether anything of a satisfactory nature had happened to him or not. It was a long, long week, and the strain was a heavy one. The pair could hardly have borne it if their minds had not had the relief of wholesome diversion. We have seen that they had that. The woman was piling up fortunes right along, the man was spending them—spending all his wife would give him a chance at, at any rate.

At last the Saturday came, and the *Weekly Sagamore* arrived. Mrs. Eversly Bennett was present. She was the Presbyterian parson's wife, and was working the Fosters for a charity. Talk now died a sudden death—on the Foster side. Mrs. Bennett presently discovered that her hosts were not hearing a word she was saying; so she got up, wondering and indignant, and went away. The moment she was out of the house, Aleck eagerly tore the wrapper from the paper, and her eyes and Sally's swept the columns for the death-notices. Disappointment! Tilbury was not anywhere mentioned. Aleck was a Christian from the cradle, and duty and the force of habit required her to go through the motions. She pulled herself together and said, with a pious two-per-cent. trade joyousness:

"Let us be humbly thankful that he has been spared; and—"

"Damn his treacherous hide, I wish—"

"Sally! For shame!"

"I don't care!" retorted the angry man. "It's the way *you* feel, and if you weren't so immorally pious you'd be honest and say so."

Aleck said, with wounded dignity:

"I do not see how you can say such unkind and unjust things. There is no such thing as immoral piety."

Sally felt a pang, but tried to conceal it under a shuffling attempt to save his case by changing the form of it—as if changing the form while retaining the juice could deceive the expert he was trying to placate. He said:

"I didn't mean so bad as that, Aleck; I didn't really mean immoral piety, I only meant—meant—well, conventional piety, you know; er—shop piety; the—the—why, *you* know what I mean. Aleck—the—well, where you put up the plated article and play it for solid, you know, without intending anything improper, but just out of trade habit, ancient policy, petrified custom, loyalty to—to—hang it, I can't find the right words, but *you* know what I mean, Aleck, and that there isn't any harm in it. I'll try again. You see, it's this way. If a person—"

"You have said quite enough," said Aleck, coldly; "let the subject be dropped."

"*I'm* willing," fervently responded Sally, wiping the sweat from his forehead and looking the thankfulness he had no words for. Then, musingly, he apologized to himself. "I certainly held threes—I *know* it—but I drew and didn't fill. That's where I'm so often weak in the game. If I had stood pat—but I didn't. I never do. I don't know enough."

Confessedly defeated, he was properly tame now and subdued. Aleck forgave him with her eyes.

The grand interest, the supreme interest, came instantly to the front again; nothing could keep it in the background many minutes on a stretch. The couple took up the puzzle of the absence of Tilbury's death-notice. They discussed it every which way, more or less hopefully, but they had to finish where they began, and concede that the only really sane explanation of the absence of the notice must be—and without doubt was—that Tilbury was not dead. There was something sad about it, something even a little unfair, maybe, but there it was, and had to be put up with. They were agreed as to that. To Sally it seemed a strangely inscrutable dispensation; more inscrutable than usual, he thought; one of the most unnecessarily inscrutable he could call to mind, in fact—and said so, with some feeling; but if he was hoping to draw Aleck he failed; she reserved her opinion, if she had one; she had not the habit of taking injudicious risks in any market, worldly or other.

The pair must wait for next week's paper—Tilbury had evidently postponed. That was their thought and their decision. So they put the subject away, and went about their affairs again with as good heart as they could.

Now, if they had but known it, they had been wronging Tilbury all the time. Tilbury had kept faith, kept it to the letter; he was dead, he had died to schedule. He was dead more than four days now and used to it; entirely dead, perfectly dead, as dead as any other new person in the cemetery; dead in abundant time to get into that week's *Sagamore,* too, and only shut out by an accident; an accident which could not happen to a metropolitan journal, but which happens easily to a poor little village rag like the *Sagamore.* On this occasion, just as the editorial page was being locked up, a gratis quart of strawberry water-ice arrived from Hostetter's Ladies' and Gents' Ice-Cream Parlors, and the stickful of rather chilly regret over Tilbury's translation got crowded out to make room for the editor's frantic gratitude.

On its way to the standing-galley Tilbury's notice got pied. Otherwise it would have gone into some future edition, for *Weekly Sagamores* do not waste "live" matter, and in their galleys "live" matter is immortal, unless a pi accident intervenes. But a thing that gets pied is dead, and for such there is no resurrection; its chance of seeing print is gone, forever and ever. And so, let Tilbury like it or not, let him rave in his grave to his fill, no matter—no mention of his death would ever see the light in the *Weekly Sagamore.*

4

Five weeks drifted tediously along. The *Sagamore* arrived regularly on the Saturdays, but never once contained a mention of Tilbury Foster. Sally's patience broke down at this point, and he said, resentfully:

"Damn his livers, he's immortal!"

Aleck gave him a very severe rebuke, and added, with icy solemnity:

"How would you feel if you were suddenly cut off just after such an awful remark had escaped out of you?"

Without sufficient reflection Sally responded:

"I'd feel I was lucky I hadn't got caught with it *in* me."

Pride had forced him to say something, and as he could not think of any rational thing to say he flung that out. Then he stole a base—as he called it—that is, slipped from the presence, to keep from getting brayed in his wife's discussion-mortar.

Six months came and went. The *Sagamore* was still silent about Tilbury. Meantime, Sally had several times thrown out a feeler—that is, a hint that he would like to know. Aleck had ignored the hints. Sally now resolved to brace up and risk a frontal attack. So he squarely proposed to disguise himself and go to Tilbury's village and surreptitiously find out as to the prospects. Aleck put her foot on the dangerous project with energy and decision. She said:

"What can you be thinking of? You do keep my hands full! You have to be watched all the time, like a little child, to keep you from walking into the fire. You'll stay right where you are!"

"Why, Aleck, I could do it and not be found out—I'm certain of it."

"Sally Foster, don't you know you would have to inquire around?"

"Of course, but what of it? Nobody would suspect who I was."

"Oh, listen to the man! Some day you've got to prove to the executors that you never inquired. What then?"

He had forgotten that detail. He didn't reply; there wasn't anything to say. Aleck added:

"Now then, drop that notion out of your mind, and don't ever meddle with it again. Tilbury set that trap for you. Don't you know it's a trap? He is on the watch, and fully expecting you to blunder into it. Well, he is going to be disappointed—at least while I am on deck. Sally!"

"Well?"

"As long as you live, if it's a hundred years, don't you ever make an inquiry. Promise!"

"All right," with a sigh and reluctantly.

Then Aleck softened and said:

"Don't be impatient. We are prospering; we can wait; there is no hurry. Our small dead-certain income increases all the time; and as to futures, I have not made a mistake yet—they are piling up by the thousands and the tens of thousands. There is not another family in the state with such prospects as ours. Already we are beginning to roll in eventual wealth. You know that, don't you?"

"Yes, Aleck, it's certainly so."

"Then be grateful for what God is doing for us, and stop worrying. You do not believe we could have achieved these prodigious results without His special help and guidance, do you?"

Hesitatingly, "N-no, I suppose not." Then, with feeling and admiration, "And yet, when it comes to judiciousness in watering a stock or putting up a hand to skin Wall Street I don't give in that *you* need any outside amateur help, if I do wish I—"

"Oh, *do* shut up! I know you do not mean any harm or

any irreverence, poor boy, but you can't seem to open your mouth without letting out things to make a person shudder. You keep me in constant dread. For you and for all of us. Once I had no fear of the thunder, but now when I hear it I—"

Her voice broke, and she began to cry, and could not finish. The sight of this smote Sally to the heart, and he took her in his arms and petted her and comforted her and promised better conduct, and upbraided himself and remorsefully pleaded for forgiveness. And he was in earnest, and sorry for what he had done and ready for any sacrifice that could make up for it.

And so, in privacy, he thought long and deeply over the matter, resolving to do what should seem best. It was easy to *promise* reform; indeed he had already promised it. But would that do any real good, any permanent good? No, it would be but temporary—he knew his weakness, and confessed it to himself with sorrow—he could not keep the promise. Something surer and better must be devised; and he devised it. At cost of precious money which he had long been saving up, shilling by shilling, he put a lightning-rod on the house.

At a subsequent time he relapsed.

What miracles habit can do! and how quickly and how easily habits are acquired—both trifling habits and habits which profoundly change us. If by accident we wake at two in the morning a couple of nights in succession, we have need to be uneasy, for another repetition can turn the accident into a habit; and a month's dallying with whisky—but we an know these commonplace facts.

The castle-building habit, the day-dreaming habit—how it grows! what a luxury it becomes; how we fly to its enchantments at every idle moment, how we revel in them, steep our souls in them, intoxicate ourselves with their beguiling fantasies—oh yes, and how soon and how easily our dream life and our material life become so intermingled and so fused together that we can't quite tell which is which, any more.

By and by Aleck subscribed for a Chicago daily and for the *Wall Street Pointer.* With an eye single to finance she studied these as diligently all the week as she studied her Bible Sundays. Sally was lost in admiration, to note with what swift and sure strides her genius and judgment developed and expanded in the forecasting and handling of the securities of both the material and spiritual markets. He was proud of her nerve and daring in exploiting worldly stocks, and just as proud of her conservative caution in working her spiritual deals. He noted that she never lost her head in either case; that with a splendid courage she often went short on worldly futures, but heedfully drew the line there—she was always long on the others. Her policy was quite sane and simple, as she explained it to him: what she put into earthly futures was for speculation, what she put into spiritual futures was for investment; she was willing to go into the one on a margin, and take chances, but in the case of the other, "margin her no margins"—she wanted to cash in a hundred cents per dollar's worth, and have the stock transferred on the books.

It took but a very few months to educate Aleck's imagination and Sally's. Each day's training added something to the spread and effectiveness of the two machines. As a consequence, Aleck made imaginary money much faster than at first she had dreamed of making it, and Sally's competency in spending the overflow of it kept pace with the strain put upon it, right along. In the beginning, Aleck had given the coal speculation a twelvemonth in which to materialize, and had been loath to grant that this term might possibly be shortened by nine months. But that was the feeble work, the nursery work, of a financial fancy that had had no teaching, no experience, no practice. These aids soon came, then that nine months vanished, and the imaginary ten-thousand-dollar investment came marching home with three hundred per cent. profit on its back!

It was a great day for the pair of Fosters. They were speechless for joy. Also speechless for another reason: after much watching of the market, Aleck had lately, with fear and trembling, made her first flyer on a "margin," using the remaining twenty thousand of the bequest in this risk. In her mind's eye she had seen it climb, point by point—always with a chance that the market would break—until at last her anxieties were too great for further endurance—she being new to the margin business and unhardened, as yet—and she gave her imaginary broker an imaginary order by imaginary telegraph to sell. She said forty thousand dollars' profit was enough. The sale was made on the very day that the coal venture had returned with its rich freight. As I have said, the couple were speechless. They sat dazed and blissful that night, trying to realize the immense fact, the overwhelming fact, that they were actually worth a hundred thousand dollars in clean, imaginary cash. Yet so it was.

It was the last time that ever Aleck was afraid of a margin; at least afraid enough to let it break her sleep and pale her cheek to the extent that this first experience in that line had done.

Indeed it was a memorable night. Gradually the realization that they were rich sank securely home into the souls of the pair, then they began to place the money. If we could have looked out through the eyes of these dreamers, we should have seen their tidy little wooden house disappear, and a two-story brick with a cast-iron fence in front of it take its place; we should have seen a three-globed gas-chandelier grow down from the parlor ceiling; we should have seen the homely rag carpet turn to noble Brussels, a dollar and a half a yard; we should have seen the plebeian fireplace vanish away and a recherché, big base-burner with isinglass windows take position and spread awe around. And we should have seen other things, too; among them the buggy, the lap-robe, the stove-pipe hat, and so on.

From that time forth, although the daughters and the neighbors saw only the same old wooden house there, it was a two-story brick to Aleck and Sally; and not a night went by that Aleck did not worry about the imaginary gas-bills, and get for all comfort Sally's reckless retort: "What of it? We can afford it."

Before the couple went to bed, that first night that they were rich, they had decided that they must celebrate. They must give a party—that was the idea. But how to explain it—to the daughters and the neighbors? They could not expose the fact that they were rich. Sally was willing, even anxious, to do it; but Aleck kept her head and would not allow it. She said that although the money was as good as in, it would be as well to wait until it was actually in. On that policy she took her stand, and would not budge. The great secret must be kept, she said—kept from the daughters and everybody else.

The pair were puzzled. They must celebrate, they were determined to celebrate, but since the secret must be kept, what could they celebrate? No birthdays were due for three months. Tilbury wasn't available, evidently he was going to live forever; what the nation *could* they celebrate? That was Sally's way of putting it; and he was getting impatient, too, and harassed. But at last he hit it—just by sheer inspiration, as it seemed to him—and all their troubles were gone in a moment; they would celebrate the Discovery of America. A splendid idea!

Aleck was almost too proud of Sally for words—she said *she* never would have thought of it. But Sally, although he was bursting with delight in the compliment and with wonder at himself, tried not to let on, and said it wasn't really anything, anybody could have done it. Whereat Aleck, with a prideful toss of her happy head, said:

"Oh, certainly! Anybody could—oh, anybody! Hosannah

Dilkins, for instance! Or maybe Adelbert Peanut—oh, *dear*—yes! Well, I'd like to see them try it, that's all. Dear-me-suz, if they could think of the discovery of a forty-acre island it's more than *I* believe they could; and as for a whole continent, why, Sally Foster, you know perfectly well it would strain the livers and lights out of them and *then* they couldn't!"

The dear woman, she knew he had talent; and if affection made her over-estimate the size of it a little, surely it was a sweet and gentle crime, and forgiveable for its source's sake.

5

The celebration went off well. The friends were all present, both the young and the old. Among the young were Flossie and Gracie Peanut and their brother Adelbert, who was a rising young journeyman tinner, also Hosannah Dilkins, Jr., journeyman plasterer, just out of his apprenticeship. For many months Adelbert and Hosannah had been showing interest in Gwendolen and Clytemnestra Foster, and the parents of the girls had noticed this with private satisfaction. But they suddenly realized now that that feeling had passed. They recognized that the changed financial conditions had raised up a social bar between their daughters and the young mechanics. The daughters could now look higher—and must. Yes, must. They need marry nothing below the grade of lawyer or merchant; poppa and momma would take care of this; there must be no mésalliances.

However, these thinkings and projects of theirs were private, and did not show on the surface, and therefore threw no shadow upon the celebration. What showed upon the surface was a serene and lofty contentment and a dignity of carriage and gravity of deportment which compelled the admiration and likewise the wonder of the company. All noticed it, all commented upon it, but none was able to divine the secret of it. It was a marvel and a mystery. There several persons remarked, without suspecting what clever shots they were making:

"It's as if they'd come into property."

That was just it, indeed.

Most mothers would have taken hold of the matrimonial matter in the old regulation way; they would have given the girls a talking to, of a solemn sort and untactful—a lecture calculated to defeat its own purpose, by producing tears and secret rebellion; and the said mothers would have further damaged the business by requesting the young mechanics to discontinue their attentions. But this mother was different. She was practical. She said nothing to any of the young people concerned, nor to any one else except Sally. He listened to her and understood; understood and admired. He said:

"I get the idea. Instead of finding fault with the samples on view, thus hurting feelings and obstructing trade without occasion, you merely offer a higher class of goods for the money, and leave nature to take her course. It's wisdom, Aleck, solid wisdom, and sound as a nut. Who's your fish? Have you nominated him yet?"

No, she hadn't. They must look the market over—which they did. To start with, they considered and discussed Bradish, rising young lawyer, and Fulton, rising young dentist. Sally must invite them to dinner. But not right away; there was no hurry, Aleck said. Keep an eye on the pair, and wait; nothing would be lost by going slowly in so important a matter.

It turned out that this was wisdom, too; for inside of three weeks Aleck made a wonderful strike which swelled her imaginary hundred thousand to four hundred thousand of the same quality. She and Sally were in the clouds that evening. For the first time they introduced champagne at dinner. Not real champagne, but plenty real enough for the amount of imagination expended on it. It was Sally that did it, and Aleck weakly submitted. At bottom both were troubled and ashamed, for he was a high-up Son of Temperance, and at funerals wore an apron which no dog could look upon and retain his reason and his opinion; and she was a W. C. T. U., with all that that implies of boiler-iron virtue and unendurable holiness. But there it was; the pride of riches was beginning its disintegrating work. They had lived to prove, once more, a sad truth which had been proven many times before in the world: that whereas principle is a great and noble protection against showy and degrading vanities and vices, poverty is worth six of it. More than four hundred thousand dollars to the good! They took up the matrimonial matter again. Neither the dentist nor the lawyer was mentioned; there was no occasion, they were out of the running. Disqualified. They discussed the son of the pork-packer and the son of the village banker. But finally, as in the previous case, they concluded to wait and think, and go cautiously and sure.

Luck came their way again. Aleck, ever watchful, saw a great and risky chance, and took a daring flyer. A time of trembling, of doubt, of awful uneasiness followed, for non-success meant absolute ruin and nothing short of it. Then came the result, and Aleck, faint with joy, could hardly control her voice when she said:

"The suspense is over, Sally—and we are worth a cold million!"

Sally wept for gratitude, and said:

"Oh, Electra, jewel of women, darling of my heart, we are free at last, we roll in wealth, we need never scrimp again. It's a case for Veuve Cliquot!" and he got out a pint of spruce-beer and made sacrifice, he saying "Damn the expense," and she rebuking him gently with reproachful but humid and happy eyes.

They shelved the pork-packer's son and the banker's son, and sat down to consider the Governor's son and the son of the Congressman.

6

It were a weariness to follow in detail the leaps and bounds the Foster fictitious finances took from this time forth. It was marvelous, it was dizzying, it was dazzling. Everything Aleck touched turned to fairy gold, and heaped itself glittering toward the firmament. Millions upon millions poured in, and still the mighty stream flowed thundering along, still its vast volume increased. Five millions—ten millions—twenty—thirty—was there never to be an end?

Two years swept by in a splendid delirium, the intoxicated Fosters scarcely noticing the flight of time. They were now worth three hundred million dollars; they were in every board of directors of every prodigious combine in the country; and still, as time drifted along, the millions went on piling up, five at a time, ten at a time, as fast as they could tally them off, almost. The three hundred doubled itself—then doubled again—and yet again—and yet once more.

Twenty-four hundred millions!

The business was getting a little confused. It was necessary to take an account of stock, and straighten it out. The Fosters knew it, they felt it, they realized that it was imperative; but they also knew that to do it properly and perfectly the task must be carried to a finish without a break when once it was begun. A ten-hours' job; and where could *they* find ten leisure hours in a bunch? Sally was selling pins and sugar and calico all day and every day; Aleck was cooking and washing dishes and sweeping and making beds all day and every day, with none to help, for the daughters were being saved up for high society. The Fosters knew there was one way to get the ten hours, and only one. Both were ashamed to name it; each waited for the other to do it. Finally Sally said:

"Somebody's got to give in. It's up to me. Consider that I've named it—never mind pronouncing it out aloud."

Aleck colored, but was grateful. Without further remark,

they fell. Fell, and—broke the Sabbath. For that was their only free ten-hour stretch. It was but another step in the downward path. Others would follow. Vast wealth has temptations which fatally and surely undermine the moral structure of persons not habituated to its possession.

They pulled down the shades and broke the Sabbath. With hard and patient labor they overhauled their holdings and listed them. And a long-drawn procession of formidable names it was! Starting with the Railway Systems, Steamer Lines, Standard Oil, Ocean Cables, Diluted Telegraph, and all the rest, and winding up with Klondike, De Beers, Tammany Graft, and Shady Privileges in the Post-office Department.

Twenty-four hundred millions, and all safely planted in Good Things, gilt-edged and interest-bearing. Income, $120,000,000 a year. Aleck fetched a long purr of soft delight, and said:

"Is it enough?"

"It is, Aleck."

"What shall we do?"

"Stand pat."

"Retire from business?"

"That's it."

"I am agreed. The good work is finished; we will take a long rest and enjoy the money."

"Good! Aleck!"

"Yes, dear?"

"How much of the income can we spend?"

"The whole of it."

It seemed to her husband that a ton of chains fell from his limbs. He did not say a word; he was happy beyond the power of speech.

After that, they broke the Sabbaths right along, as fast as they turned up. It is the first wrong steps that count. Every Sunday they put in the whole day, after morning service, on inventions—inventions of ways to spend the money. They got to continuing this delicious dissipation until past midnight; and at every séance Aleck lavished millions upon great charities and religious enterprises, and Sally lavished like sums upon matters to which (at first) he gave definite names. Only at first. Later the names gradually lost sharpness of outline, and eventually faded into "sundries," thus becoming entirely—but safely—undescriptive. For Sally was crumbling. The placing of these millions added seriously and most uncomfortably to the family expenses—in tallow candles. For a while Aleck was worried. Then, after a little, she ceased to worry, for the occasion of it was gone. She was pained, she was grieved, she was ashamed; but she said nothing, and so became an accessory. Sally was taking candles; he was robbing the store. It is ever thus. Vast wealth, to the person unaccustomed to it, is a bane; it eats into the flesh and bone of his morals. When the Fosters were poor, they could have been trusted with untold candles. But now they—but let us not dwell upon it. From candles to apples is but a step: Sally got to taking apples; then soap; then maple-sugar; then canned goods; then crockery. How easy it is to go from bad to worse, when once we have started upon a downward course!

Meantime, other effects had been milestoning the course of the Fosters' splendid financial march. The fictitious brick dwelling had given place to an imaginary granite one with a checker-board mansard roof; in time this one disappeared and gave place to a still grander home—and so on and so on. Mansion after mansion, made of air, rose, higher, broader, finer, and each in its turn vanished away; until now in these latter great days, our dreamers were in fancy housed, in a distant region, in a sumptuous vast palace which looked out from a leafy summit upon a noble prospect of vale and river and receding hills steeped in tinted mists—and all private, all the property of the dreamers; a palace swarming with liveried servants, and populous with guests of fame and power, hailing from all the world's capitals, foreign and domestic.

This palace was far, far away toward the rising sun, immeasurably remote, astronomically remote, in Newport, Rhode Island, Holy Land of High Society, ineffable Domain of the American Aristocracy. As a rule they spent a part of every Sabbath—after morning service—in this sumptuous home, the rest of it they spent in Europe, or in dawdling around in their private yacht. Six days of sordid and plodding fact life at home on the ragged edge of Lakeside and straitened means, the seventh in Fairyland—such had become their program and their habit.

In their sternly restricted fact life they remained as of old—plodding, diligent, careful, practical, economical. They stuck loyally to the little Presbyterian Church, and labored faithfully in its interests and stood by its high and tough doctrines with all their mental and spiritual energies. But in their dream life they obeyed the invitations of their fancies, whatever they might be, and howsoever the fancies might change. Aleck's fancies were not very capricious, and not frequent, but Sally's scattered a good deal. Aleck, in her dream life, went over to the Episcopal camp, on account of its large official titles; next she became High-church on account of the candles and shows; and next she naturally changed to Rome, where there were cardinals and more candles. But these excursions were as nothing to Sally's. His dream life was a glowing and continuous and persistent excitement, and he kept every part of it fresh and sparkling by frequent changes, the religious part along with the rest. He worked his religions hard, and changed them with his shirt.

The liberal spendings of the Fosters upon their fancies began early in their prosperities, and grew in prodigality step by step with their advancing fortunes. In time they became truly enormous. Aleck built a university or two per Sunday; also a hospital or two; also a Rowton hotel or so; also a batch of churches; now and then a cathedral; and once, with untimely and ill-chosen playfulness, Sally said, "It was a cold day when she didn't ship a cargo of missionaries to persuade unreflecting Chinamen to trade off twenty-four carat Confucianism for counterfeit Christianity."

This rude and unfeeling language hurt Aleck to the heart, and she went from the presence crying. That spectacle went to his own heart, and in his pain and shame he would have given worlds to have those unkind words back. She had uttered no syllable of reproach—and that cut him. Not one suggestion that he look at his own record—and she could have made, oh, so many, and such blistering ones! Her generous silence brought a swift revenge, for it turned his thoughts upon himself, it summoned before him a spectral procession, a moving vision of his life as he had been leading it these past few years of limitless prosperity, and as he sat there reviewing it his cheeks burned and his soul was steeped in humiliation. Look at her life—how fair it was, and tending ever upward; and look at his own—how frivolous, how charged with mean vanities, how selfish, how empty, how ignoble! And its trend—never upward, but downward, ever downward!

He instituted comparisons between her record and his own. He had found fault with her—so he mused—*he!* And what could he say for himself? When she built her first church what was he doing? Gathering other blasé multimillionaires into a Poker Club; defiling his own palace with it; losing hundreds of thousands to it at every sitting, and sillily vain of the admiring notoriety it made for him. When she was building her first university, what was he doing? Polluting himself with a gay and dissipated secret life in the company of other fast bloods, multimillionaires in money and paupers in character. When she was building her first foundling asylum, what was he doing? Alas! When she was projecting her noble Society for the Purifying of the Sex, what was he doing? Ah, what, indeed! When she and the W. C. T. U. and the Woman with the Hatchet, moving with resistless march, were sweeping the fatal bottle from the land, what was he doing? Getting drunk three times a day. When she, builder of a hundred cathedrals, was being gratefully welcomed and blest in papal Rome and decorated with the Golden Rose which she had so honorably earned, what was he doing? Breaking the bank at Monte Carlo.

He stopped. He could go no farther; he could not bear the rest. He rose up, with a great resolution upon his lips: this secret life should be revealed, and confessed; no longer would he live it clandestinely; he would go and tell her All.

And that is what he did. He told her All; and wept upon her bosom; wept, and moaned, and begged for her forgiveness. It was a profound shock, and she staggered under the blow, but he was her own, the core of her heart, the blessing of her eyes, her all in all, she could deny him nothing, and she forgave him. She felt that he could never again be quite to her what he had been before; she knew that he could only repent, and not reform; yet all morally defaced and decayed as he was, was he not her own, her very own, the idol of her deathless worship? She said she was his serf, his slave, and she opened her yearning heart and took him in.

7

One Sunday afternoon some time after this they were sailing the summer seas in their dream yacht, and reclining in lazy luxury under the awning of the after-deck. There was silence, for each was busy with his own thoughts. These seasons of silence had insensibly been growing more and more frequent of late; the old nearness and cordiality were waning. Sally's terrible revelation had done its work; Aleck had tried hard to drive the memory of it out of her mind, but it would not go, and the shame and bitterness of it were poisoning her gracious dream life. She could see now (on Sundays) that her husband was becoming a bloated and repulsive Thing. She could not close her eyes to this, and in these days she no longer looked at him, Sundays, when she could help it.

But she—was she herself without blemish? Alas, she knew she was not. She was keeping a secret from him, she was acting dishonorably toward him, and many a pang it was costing her. *She was breaking the compact, and concealing it from him.* Under strong temptation she had gone into business again; she had risked their whole fortune in a purchase of all the railway systems and coal and steel companies in the country on a margin, and she was now trembling, every Sabbath hour, lest through some chance word of hers he find it out. In her misery and remorse for this treachery she could not keep her heart from going out to him in pity; she was filled with compunctions to see him lying there, drunk and content, and never suspecting. Never suspecting—trusting her with a perfect and pathetic trust, and she holding over him by a thread a possible calamity of so devastating a—

"*Say*—Aleck?"

The interrupting words brought her suddenly to herself. She was grateful to have that persecuting subject from her thoughts, and she answered, with much of the old-time tenderness in her tone:

"Yes, dear."

"Do you know, Aleck, I think we are making a mistake—that is, you are. I mean about the marriage business." He sat up, fat and froggy and benevolent, like a bronze Buddha, and grew earnest. "Consider—it's more than five years. You've continued the same policy from the start: with every rise, always holding on for five points higher. Always when I think we are going to have some weddings, you see a bigger thing ahead, and I undergo another disappointment. *I* think you are too hard to please. Some day we'll get left. First, we turned down the dentist and the lawyer. That was all right—it was sound. Next, we turned down the banker's son and the pork-butcher's heir—right again, and sound. Next, we turned down the Congressman's son and the Governor's—right as a trivet, I confess it. Next the Senator's son and the son of the Vice-President of the United States—perfectly right, there's no permanency about those little distinctions. Then you went for the aristocracy; and I thought we had struck oil at last—yes. We would make a plunge at the Four Hundred, and pull in some ancient lineage, venerable, holy, ineffable, mellow with the antiquity of a hundred and fifty years, disinfected of the ancestral odors of salt-cod and pelts all of a century ago, and unsmirched by a day's work since; and then! why, then the marriages, of course. But no, along comes a pair of real aristocrats from Europe, and straightway you throw over the half-breeds. It was awfully discouraging, Aleck! Since then, what a procession! You turned down the baronets for a pair of barons; you turned down the barons for a pair of viscounts; the viscounts for a pair of earls; the earls for a pair of marquises; the marquises for a brace of dukes. *Now,* Aleck, cash in!—you've played the limit. You've got a job lot of four dukes under the hammer; of four nationalities; all sound in wind and limb and pedigree, all bankrupt and in debt up to the ears. They come high, but we can afford it. Come, Aleck, don't delay any longer, don't keep up the suspense: take the whole layout, and leave the girls to choose!"

Aleck had been smiling blandly and contentedly all through this arraignment of her marriage policy; a pleasant light, as of triumph with perhaps a nice surprise peeping out through it, rose in her eyes, and she said, as calmly as she could:

"Sally, what would you say to—*royalty?*"

Prodigious! Poor man, it knocked him silly, and he fell over the garboard strake and barked his shin on the cat-heads. He was dizzy for a moment, then he gathered himself up and limped over and sat down by his wife and beamed his old-time admiration and affection upon her in floods, out of his bleary eyes.

"By George!" he said, fervently, "Aleck, you *are* great—the greatest woman in the whole earth! I can't ever learn the whole size of you. I can't ever learn the immeasurable deeps of you. Here I've been considering myself qualified to criticize your game. *I!* Why, if I had stopped to think, I'd have known you had a lone hand up your sleeve. Now, dear heart, I'm all red-hot impatience—tell me about it!"

The flattered and happy woman put her lips to his ear and whispered a princely name. It made him catch his breath, it lit his face with exultation.

"Land!" he said, "it's a stunning catch! He's got a gambling-hell, and a graveyard, and a bishop, and a cathedral—all his very own. And all gilt-edged five-hundred-per-cent. stock, every detail of it; the tidiest little property in Europe. And that graveyard—it's the selectest in the world: none but suicides admitted; *yes,* sir, and the free-list suspended, too, *all* the time. There isn't much land in the principality, but there's enough: eight hundred acres in the graveyard and forty-two outside. It's a *sovereignty*—that's the main thing; *land's* nothing. There's plenty land, Sahara's drugged with it."

Aleck glowed; she was profoundly happy. She said:

"Think of it, Sally—it is a family that has never married outside the Royal and Imperial Houses of Europe; our grandchildren will sit upon thrones!"

"True as you live, Aleck—and bear scepters, too; and handle them as naturally and nonchalantly as I handle a yardstick. It's a grand catch, Aleck. He's corralled, is he? Can't get away? You didn't take him on a margin?"

"No. Trust me for that. He's not a liability, he's an asset. So is the other one."

"Who is it, Aleck?"

"His Royal Highness Sigismund-Siegfried-Lauenfeld-Dinkelspiel-Schwartzenberg Blutwurst, Hereditary Grand Duke of Katzenyammer."

"No! You can't mean it!"

"It's as true as I'm sitting here, I give you my word," she answered.

His cup was full, and he hugged her to his heart with rapture, saying:

"How wonderful it all seems, and how beautiful! It's one of the oldest and noblest of the three hundred and sixty-four ancient German principalities, and one of the few that was allowed to retain its royal estate when Bismarck got done trimming them. I know that farm, I've been there. It's got a rope-walk and a candle-factory and an army. Standing army. Infantry and cavalry. Three soldiers and a horse. Aleck, it's been a long wait, and full of heartbreak and hope deferred, but God knows I am happy now. Happy, and grateful to you, my own, who have done it all. When is it to be?"

"Next Sunday."

"Good. And we'll want to do these weddings up in the very regalest style that's going. It's properly due to the royal quality of the parties of the first part. Now as I understand it, there is only one kind of marriage that is sacred to royalty, exclusive to royalty: it's the morganatic."

"What do they call it that for, Sally?"

"I don't know; but anyway it's royal, and royal only."

"Then we will insist upon it. More—I will compel it. It is morganatic marriage or none."

"That settles it!" said Sally, rubbing his hands with delight. "And it will be the very first in America. Aleck, it will make Newport sick."

Then they fell silent, and drifted away upon their dream wings to the far regions of the earth to invite all the crowned heads and their families and provide gratis transportation for them.

8

During three days the couple walked upon air, with their heads in the clouds. They were but vaguely conscious of their surroundings; they saw all things dimly, as through a veil; they were steeped in dreams, often they did not hear when they were spoken to; they often did not understand when they heard; they answered confusedly or at random; Sally sold molasses by weight, sugar by the yard, and furnished soap when asked for candles, and Aleck put the cat in the wash and fed milk to the soiled linen. Everybody was stunned and amazed, and went about muttering, "What *can* be the matter with the Fosters?"

Three days. Then came events! Things had taken a happy turn, and for forty-eight hours Aleck's imaginary corner had been booming. Up—up—still up! Cost point was passed. Still up—and up—and up! Five points above cost—then ten—fifteen—twenty! Twenty points cold profit on the vast venture, now, and Aleck's imaginary brokers were shouting frantically by imaginary long-distance, "Sell! sell! for Heaven's sake *sell!*"

She broke the splendid news to Sally, and he, too, said, "Sell! sell—oh, don't make a blunder, now, you own the earth!—sell, sell!" But she set her iron will and lashed it amidships, and said she would hold on for five points more if she died for it.

It was a fatal resolve. The very next day came the historic crash, the record crash, the devastating crash, when the bottom fell out of Wall Street, and the whole body of gilt-edged stocks dropped ninety-five points in five hours, and the multi-millionaire was seen begging his bread in the Bowery. Aleck sternly held her grip and "put up" as long as she could, but at last there came a call which she was powerless to meet, and her imaginary brokers sold her out. Then, and not till then, the man in her was vanished, and the woman in her resumed sway. She put her arms about her husband's neck and wept, saying:

"I am to blame, do not forgive me, I cannot bear it. We are paupers! Paupers, and I am so miserable. The weddings will never come off; all that is past; we could not even buy the dentist, now."

A bitter reproach was on Sally's tongue: "I *begged* you to sell, but you—" He did not say it; he had not the heart to add a hurt to that broken and repentant spirit. A nobler thought came to him and he said:

"Bear up, my Aleck, all is not lost! You really never invested a penny of my uncle's bequest, but only its unmaterialized future; what we have lost was only the increment harvested from that future by your incomparable financial judgment and sagacity. Cheer up, banish these griefs; we still have the thirty thousand untouched; and with the experience which you have acquired, think what you will be able to do with it in a couple of years! The marriages are not off, they are only postponed."

These were blessed words. Aleck saw how true they were, and their influence was electric; her tears ceased to flow, and her great spirit rose to its full stature again. With flashing eye and grateful heart, and with hand uplifted in pledge and prophecy, she said:

"Now and here I proclaim—"

But she was interrupted by a visitor. It was the editor and proprietor of the *Sagamore*. He had happened into Lakeside to pay a duty-call upon an obscure grandmother of his who was nearing the end of her pilgrimage, and with the idea of combining business with grief he had looked up the Fosters, who had been so absorbed in other things for the past four years that they had neglected to pay up their subscription. Six dollars due. No visitor could have been more welcome. He would know all about Uncle Tilbury and what his chances might be getting to be, cemeterywards. They could, of course, ask no questions, for that would squelch the bequest, but they could nibble around on the edge of the subject and hope for results. The scheme did not work. The obtuse editor did not know he was being nibbled at; but at last, chance accomplished what art had failed in. In illustration of something under discussion which required the help of metaphor, the editor said:

"Land, it's as tough as Tilbury Foster!—as *we* say."

It was sudden, and it made the Fosters jump. The editor noticed it, and said, apologetically:

"No harm intended, I assure you. It's just a saying; just a joke, you know—nothing in it. Relation of yours?"

Sally crowded his burning eagerness down, and answered with all the indifference he could assume:

"I—well, not that I know of, but we've heard of him." The editor was thankful, and resumed his composure. Sally added: "Is he—is he—well?"

"Is he *well?* Why, bless you he's in Sheol these five years!"

The Fosters were trembling with grief, though it felt like joy. Sally said, non-committally—and tentatively:

"Ah, well, such is life, and none can escape—not even the rich are spared."

The editor laughed.

"If you are including Tilbury," he said, "it don't apply. *He* hadn't a cent; the town had to bury him."

The Fosters sat petrified for two minutes; petrified and cold. Then, white-faced and weak-voiced, Sally asked:

"Is it true? Do you *know* it to be true?"

"Well, I should say! I was one of the executors. He hadn't anything to leave but a wheelbarrow, and he left that to me. It hadn't any wheel, and wasn't any good. Still, it was something, and so, to square up, I scribbled off a sort of a little obituarial send-off for him, but it got crowded out."

The Fosters were not listening—their cup was full, it could contain no more. They sat with bowed heads, dead to all things but the ache at their hearts.

An hour later. Still they sat there, bowed, motionless, silent, the visitor long ago gone, they unaware.

Then they stirred, and lifted their heads wearily, and gazed at each other wistfully, dreamily, dazed; then presently began to twaddle to each other in a wandering and childish way. At intervals they lapsed into silences, leaving a sentence unfinished, seemingly either unaware of it or losing their way. Sometimes, when they woke out of these silences they had a dim and transient consciousness that something had happened to their minds; then with a dumb and yearning solicitude they would softly caress each other's hands in mutual compassion and support, as if they would say: "I am near you, I will not forsake you, we will bear it together; somewhere there is release and forgetfulness, somewhere there is a grave and peace; be patient, it will not be long."

They lived yet two years, in mental night, always brooding, steeped in vague regrets and melancholy dreams, never speaking; then release came to both on the same day.

Toward the end the darkness lifted from Sally's ruined mind for a moment, and he said:

"Vast wealth, acquired by sudden and unwholesome means, is a snare. It did us no good, transient were its feverish pleasures; yet for its sake we threw away our sweet and simple and happy life—let others take warning by us."

He lay silent awhile, with closed eyes; then as the chill of death crept upward toward his heart, and consciousness was fading from his brain, he muttered:

"Money had brought him misery, and he took his revenge upon us, who had done him no harm. He had his desire: with base and cunning calculation he left us but thirty thousand, knowing we would try to increase it, and ruin our life and break our hearts. Without added expense he could have left us far above desire of increase, far above the temptation to speculate, and a kinder soul would have done it; but in him was no generous spirit, no pity, no—"

1904

A Horse's Tale

PART I

1 Soldier Boy—Privately to Himself

I am Buffalo Bill's[1] horse. I have spent my life under his saddle—with him in it, too, and he is good for two hundred pounds, without his clothes; and there is no telling how much he does weigh when he is out on the war-path and has his batteries belted on. He is over six feet, is young, hasn't an ounce of waste flesh, is straight, graceful, springy in his motions, quick as a cat, and has a handsome face, and black hair dangling down on his shoulders, and is beautiful to look at; and nobody is braver than he is, and nobody is stronger, except myself. Yes, a person that doubts that he is fine to see should see him in his beaded buckskins, on my back and his rifle peeping above his shoulder, chasing a hostile trail, with me going like the wind and his hair streaming out behind from the shelter of his broad slouch. Yes, he is a sight to look at then—and I'm part of it myself.

I am his favorite horse, out of dozens. Big as he is, I have carried him eighty-one miles between nightfall and sunrise on the scout; and I am good for fifty, day in and day out, and all the time. I am not large, but I am built on a business basis. I have carried him thousands and thousands of miles on scout duty for the army, and there's not a gorge, nor a pass, nor a valley, nor a fort, nor a trading post, nor a buffalo-range in the whole sweep of the Rocky Mountains and the Great Plains that we don't know as well as we know the bugle-calls. He is Chief of Scouts to the Army of the Frontier,[2] and it makes us very important. In such a position as I hold in the military service one needs to be of good family and possess an education much above the common to be worthy of the place. I am the best-educated horse outside of the hippodrome, everybody says, and the best-mannered. It may be so, it is not for me to say; modesty is the best policy, I think. Buffalo Bill taught me the most of what I know, my mother taught me much, and I taught myself the rest. Lay a row of moccasins before me—Pawnee, Sioux, Shoshone, Cheyenne, Blackfoot, and as many other tribes as you please—and I can name the tribe every moccasin belongs to by the make of it. Name it in horse-talk, and could do it in American if I had speech.

I know some of the Indian signs—the signs they make with their hands, and by signal-fires at night and columns of smoke by day. Buffalo Bill taught me how to drag wounded soldiers out of the line of fire with my teeth; and I've done it, too; at least I've dragged *him* out of the battle when he was wounded. And not just once, but twice. Yes, I know a lot of things. I remember forms, and gaits, and faces; and you can't disguise a person that's done me a kindness so that I won't know him thereafter wherever I find him. I know the art of searching for a trail, and I know the stale track from the fresh. I can keep a trail all by myself, with Buffalo Bill asleep in the saddle; ask him—he will tell you so. Many a time, when he has ridden all night, he has said to me at dawn, "Take the watch, Boy; if the trail freshens, call me." Then he goes to sleep. He knows he can trust me, because I have a reputation. A scout horse that has a reputation does not play with it.

My mother was all American—no alkali-spider about *her*, I can tell you; she was of the best blood of Kentucky, the bluest Blue-grass aristocracy, very proud and acrimonious—or maybe it is ceremonious. I don't know which it is. But it is no matter; size is the main thing about a word, and that one's up to standard. She spent her military life as colonel of the Tenth Dragoons, and saw a deal of rough service—distinguished service it was, too. I mean, she *carried* the Colonel; but it's all the same. Where would he be without his horse? He wouldn't arrive. It takes two to make a colonel of dragoons. She was a fine dragoon horse, but never got above that. She was strong enough for the scout service, and had the endurance, too, but she couldn't quite come up to the speed required; a scout horse has to have steel in his muscle and lightning in his blood.

My father was a bronco. Nothing as to lineage—that is, nothing as to recent lineage—but plenty good enough when you go a good way back. When Professor Marsh was out here hunting bones for the chapel of Yale University he found skeletons of horses no bigger than a fox, bedded in the rocks, and he said they were ancestors of my father. My mother heard him say it; and he said those skeletons were two million years old, which astonished her and made her Kentucky pretensions look small and pretty antiphonal, not to say oblique. Let me see. . . . I used to know the meaning of those words, but . . . well, it was years ago, and 'tisn't as vivid now as it was when they were fresh. That sort of words doesn't keep, in the kind of climate we have out here. Professor Marsh said those skeletons were fossils. So that makes me part blue grass and part fossil; if there is any older or better stock, you will have to look for it among the Four Hundred, I reckon. I am satisfied with it. And am a happy horse, too, though born out of wedlock.

And now we are back at Fort Paxton once more, after a forty-day scout, away up as far as the Big Horn. Everything quiet. Crows and Blackfeet squabbling—as usual—but no outbreaks, and settlers feeling fairly easy.

The Seventh Cavalry still in garrison, here; also the Ninth Dragoons, two artillery companies, and some infantry. All glad to see me, including General Alison, commandant. The officers' ladies and children well, and called upon me—with sugar. Colonel Drake, Seventh Cavalry, said some pleasant things; Mrs. Drake was very complimentary; also Captain and Mrs. Marsh, Company B, Seventh Cavalry; also the Chaplain, who is always kind and pleasant to me, because I kicked the lungs out of a trader once. It was Tommy Drake and Fanny Marsh that furnished the sugar—nice children, the nicest at the post, I think.

That poor orphan child is on her way from France—everybody is full of the subject. Her father was General Alison's brother; married a beautiful young Spanish lady ten years ago, and has never been in America since. They lived in Spain a year or two, then went to France. Both died some months ago. This little girl that is coming is the only child. General Alison is glad to have her. He has never seen her. He is a very nice old bachelor, but is an old bachelor just the same and isn't more than about a year this side of retirement by age limit; and so what does he know about taking care of a little maid nine years old? If I could have her it would be another matter, for I know all about children, and they adore me. Buffalo Bill will tell you so himself.

I have some of this news from overhearing the garrison-gossip, the rest of it I got from Potter, the General's dog. Potter is the great Dane. He is privileged, all over the post, like Shekels, the Seventh Cavalry's dog, and visits everybody's quarters and picks up everything that is going, in the way of news. Potter has no imagination, and no great deal of culture, perhaps, but he has a historical mind and a good memory, and so he is the person I depend upon mainly to post me up when I get back from a scout. That is, if Shekels is out on depredation and I can't get hold of him.

2 Letter from Rouen—to General Alison

My dear Brother-in-law,—Please let me write again in Spanish, I cannot trust my English, and I am aware, from what your brother used to say, that army officers educated at the Military Academy of the United States are taught our tongue. It is as I told you in my other letter: both my poor sister and her husband, when they found they could not recover, expressed the wish that you should have their little Catherine—as knowing that you would presently be retired from the army—rather than that she should remain with me, who am broken in health, or go to your mother in California, whose health is also frail.

You do not know the child, therefore I must tell you something about her. You will not be ashamed of her looks, for she is a copy in little of her beautiful mother—and it is that Andalusian beauty which is not surpassable, even in your country. She has her mother's charm and grace and good heart and sense of justice, and she has her father's vivacity and cheerfulness and pluck and spirit of enterprise, with the affectionate disposition and sincerity of both parents.

My sister pined for her Spanish home all these years of exile; she was always talking of Spain to the child, and tending and nourishing the love of Spain in the little thing's heart as a precious flower; and she died happy in the knowledge that the fruitage of her patriotic labors was as rich as even she could desire.

Cathy is a sufficiently good little scholar, for her nine years; her mother taught her Spanish herself, and kept it always fresh upon her ear and her tongue by hardly ever speaking with her in any other tongue; her father was her English teacher, and talked with her in that language almost exclusively; French has been her everyday speech for more than seven years among her playmates here; she has a good working use of governess German and Italian. It is true that there is always a faint foreign fragrance about her speech, no matter what language she is talking, but it is only just noticeable, nothing more, and is rather a charm than a mar, I think. In the ordinary child-studies Cathy is neither before nor behind the average child of nine, I should say. But I can say this for her: in love for her friends and in high-mindedness and good-heartedness she has not many equals, and in my opinion no superiors. And I beg of you, let her have her way with the dumb animals—they are her worship. It is an inheritance from her mother. She knows but little of cruelties and oppressions—keep them from her sight if you can. She would flare up at them and make trouble, in her small but quite decided and resolute way; for she has a character of her own, and lacks neither promptness nor initiative. Sometimes her judgment is at fault, but I think her intentions are always right. Once when she was a little creature of three or four years she suddenly brought her tiny foot down upon the floor in an apparent outbreak of indignation, then fetched it a backward wipe, and stooped down to examine the result. Her mother said:

"Why, what is it, child? What has stirred you so?"

"Mamma, the big ant was trying to kill the little one."

"And so you protected the little one."

"Yes, mamma, because he had no friend, and I wouldn't let the big one kill him."

"But you have killed them both."

Cathy was distressed, and her lip trembled. She picked up the remains and laid them upon her palm, and said:

"Poor little anty, I'm so sorry; and I didn't mean to kill you, but there wasn't any other way to save you, it was such a hurry."

She is a dear and sweet little lady, and when she goes it will give me a sore heart. But she will be happy with you, and if your heart is old and tired, give it into her keeping; she will make it young again, she will refresh it, she will make it sing. Be good to her, for all our sakes!

My exile will soon be over now. As soon as I am a little stronger I shall see my Spain again; and that will make *me* young again!

MERCEDES

3 General Alison to His Mother

I am glad to know that you are all well, in San Bernardino.

. . . That grandchild of yours has been here—well, I do not quite know how many days it is; nobody can keep account of days or anything else where she is! Mother, she did what the Indians were never able to do. She took the Fort—took it the first day! Took me, too; took the colonels, the captains, the women, the children, and the dumb brutes; took Buffalo Bill, and all his scouts; took the garrison—to the last man; and in forty-eight hours the Indian encampment was hers, illustrious old Thunder-Bird and all. Do I seem to have lost my solemnity, my gravity, my poise, my dignity? You would lose your own, in my circumstances. Mother, you never saw such a winning little devil. She is all energy, and spirit, and sunshine, and interest in everybody and everything, and pours out her prodigal love upon every creature that will take it, high or low, Christian or pagan, feathered or furred; and none has declined it to date, and none ever will, I think. But she has a temper, and sometimes it catches fire and flames up, and is likely to burn whatever is near it; but it is soon over, the passion goes as quickly as it comes. Of course she has an Indian name already; Indians always rechristen a stranger early. Thunder-Bird attended to her case. He gave her the Indian equivalent for firebug, or firefly. He said:

" 'Times ver' quiet, ver' soft, like summer night, but when she mad she blaze."

Isn't it good? Can't you see the flare? She's beautiful, mother, beautiful as a picture; and there is a touch of you in her face, and of her father—poor George! and in her unresting activities, and her fearless ways, and her sun-bursts and cloudbursts, she is always bringing George back to me. These impulsive natures are dramatic. George was dramatic, so is this Lightning-Bug, so is Buffalo Bill. When Cathy first arrived—it was in the forenoon—Buffalo Bill was away, carrying orders to Major Fuller, at Five Forks, up in the Clayton Hills. At mid-afternoon I was at my desk, trying to work, and this sprite had been making it impossible for half an hour. At last I said:

"Oh, you bewitching little scamp, *can't* you be quiet just a minute or two, and let your poor old uncle attend to a part of his duties?"

"I'll try, uncle; I will, indeed," she said.

"Well, then, that's a good child—kiss me. Now, then, sit up in that chair, and set your eye on that clock. There—that's right. If you stir—if you so much as wink—for four whole minutes, I'll bite you!"

It was very sweet and humble and obedient she looked, sitting there, still as a mouse; I could hardly keep from setting her free and telling her to make as much racket as she wanted to. During as much as two minutes there was a most unnatural and heavenly quiet and repose, then Buffalo Bill came thundering up to the door in all his scout finery, flung himself out of the saddle, said to his horse, "Wait for me, Boy," and stepped in, and stopped dead in his tracks—gazing at the child. She forgot orders, and was on the floor in a moment, saying:

"Oh, you are so beautiful! Do you like me?"

"No, I don't, I love you!" and he gathered her up with a hug, and then set her on his shoulder—apparently nine feet from the floor.

She was at home. She played with his long hair, and admired his big hands and his clothes and his carbine, and asked question after question, as fast as he could answer, until I excused them both for half an hour, in order to have a chance to finish my work. Then I heard Cathy exclaiming over Soldier Boy; and he was worthy of her raptures, for he is a wonder of a horse, and has a reputation which is as shining as his own silken hide.

4 Cathy to Her Aunt Mercedes

Oh, it is wonderful here, aunty dear, just paradise! Oh, if you could only see it! everything so wild and lovely; such grand plains, stretching such miles and miles and miles, all the most delicious velvety sand and sage-brush, and rabbits as big as a dog, and such tall and noble jackassful ears that that is what they name them by; and such vast mountains, and so rugged and craggy and lofty, with cloud-shawls wrapped around their shoulders, and looking so solemn and awful and satisfied; and the charming Indians, oh, how you would dote on them, aunty dear, and they would on you, too, and they would let you hold their babies, the way they do me, and they *are* the fattest, and brownest, and sweetest little things, and never cry, and wouldn't if they had pins sticking in them, which they haven't, because they are poor and can't afford it; and the horses and mules and cattle and dogs—hundreds and hundreds and hundreds, and not an animal that you can't do what you please with, except uncle Thomas, but *I* don't mind him, he's lovely; and oh, if you could hear the bugles: *too—too—too-too—too—too,* and so on—perfectly beautiful! Do you recognize that one? It's the first toots of the *reveille;* it goes, dear me, *so* early in the morning!—then I and every other soldier on the whole place are up and out in a minute, except uncle Thomas, who is most unaccountably lazy, I don't know why, but I have talked to him about it, and I reckon it will be better, now. He hasn't any faults much, and is charming and sweet, like Buffalo Bill, and Thunder-Bird, and Mammy Dorcas, and Soldier Boy, and Shekels, and Potter, and Sour-Mash, and—well, they're *all* that, just angels, as you may say.

The very first day I came, I don't know how long ago it was, Buffalo Bill took me on Soldier Boy to Thunder-Bird's camp, not the big one which is out on the plain, which is White Cloud's, he took me to *that* one next day, but this one is four or five miles up in the hills and crags, where there is a great shut-in meadow, full of Indian lodges and dogs and squaws and everything that is interesting, and a brook of the clearest water running through it, with white pebbles on the bottom and trees all along the banks cool and shady and good to wade in, and as the sun goes down it is dimmish in there, but away up against the sky you see the big peaks towering up and shining bright and vivid in the sun, and sometimes an eagle sailing by them, not flapping a wing, the same as if he was asleep; and young Indians and girls romping and laughing and carrying on, around the spring and the pool, and not much clothes on except the girls, and dogs fighting, and the squaws busy at work, and the bucks busy resting, and the old men sitting in a bunch smoking, and passing the pipe not to the left but to the right, which means there's been a row in the camp and they are settling it if they can, and children playing *just* the same as any other children, and little boys shooting at a mark with bows, and I cuffed one of them because he hit a dog with a club that wasn't doing anything, and he resented it but before long he wished he hadn't: but this sentence is getting too long and I will start another. Thunder-Bird put on his Sunday-best war outfit to let me see him, and he was splendid to look at, with his face painted red and bright and intense like a fire-coal and a valance of eagle feathers from the top of his head all down his back, and he had his tomahawk, too, and his pipe, which has a stem which is longer than my arm, and I never had such a good time in an Indian camp in my life, and I learned a lot of words of the language, and next day BB took me to the camp out on the Plains, four miles, and I had another good time and got acquainted with some more Indians and dogs; and the big chief, by the name of White Cloud, gave me a pretty little bow and arrows and I gave him my red sash-ribbon, and in four days I could shoot very well with it and beat any white boy of my size at the post; and I have been to those camps plenty of times since; and I have learned to ride, too, BB taught me, and every day he practises me and praises me, and every time I do better than ever he lets me have a scamper on Soldier Boy, and *that's* the last agony of pleasure! for he is the charmingest horse, and so beautiful and shiny and black, and hasn't another color on him anywhere, except a white star in his forehead, not just an imitation star, but a real one, with four points, shaped exactly like a star that's handmade, and if you should cover him all up but his star you would know him anywhere, even in Jerusalem or Australia, by that. And I got acquainted with a good many of the Seventh Cavalry, and the dragoons, and officers, and families, and horses, in the first few days, and some more in the next few and the next few and the next few, and now I know more soldiers and horses than you can think, no matter how hard you try. I am keeping up my studies every now and then, but there isn't much time for it. I love you so! and I send you a hug and a kiss. CATHY

P.S.—I belong to the Seventh Cavalry and Ninth Dragoons; I am an officer, too, and do not have to work on account of not getting any wages.

5 GENERAL ALISON TO MERCEDES

She has been with us a good nice long time, now. You are troubled about your sprite because this is such a wild frontier, hundreds of miles from civilization, and peopled only by wandering tribes of savages? You fear for her safety? Give yourself no uneasiness about her. Dear me, she's in a nursery! and she's got more than eighteen hundred nurses. It would distress the garrison to suspect that you think they can't take care of her. They think they can. They would tell you so themselves. You see, the Seventh Cavalry has never had a child of its very own before, and neither has the Ninth Dragoons; and so they are like all new mothers, they think there is no other child like theirs, no other child so wonderful, none that is so worthy to be faithfully and tenderly looked after and protected. These bronzed veterans of mine are very good mothers, I think, and wiser than some other mothers; for they let her take lots of risks, and it is a good education for her; and the more risks she takes and comes successfully out of, the prouder they are of her. They adopted her, with grave and formal military ceremonies of their own invention—solemnities is the truer word; solemnities that were so profoundly solemn and earnest, that the spectacle would have been comical if it hadn't been so touching. It was a good show, and as stately and complex as guard-mount and the trooping of the colors; and it had its own special music, composed for the occasion by the bandmaster of the Seventh; and the child was as serious as the most serious war-worn soldier of them all; and finally when they throned her upon the shoulder of the oldest veteran, and pronounced her "well and truly adopted," and the bands struck up and all saluted and she saluted in return, it was better and more moving than any kindred thing I have seen on the stage, because stage things are make-believe, but this was real and the players' hearts were in it.

It happened several weeks ago, and was followed by some additional solemnities. The men created a couple of new ranks, thitherto unknown to the army regulations, and conferred them upon Cathy, with ceremonies suitable to a duke. So now she is Corporal-General of the Seventh Cavalry, and Flag-Lieutenant of the Ninth Dragoons, with the privilege (decreed by the men) of writing U.S.A. after her name! Also, they presented her a pair of shoulder-straps—both dark blue, the one with F. L. on it, the other with C. G. Also, a sword. She wears them. Finally, they granted her the *salute*. I am witness that that ceremony is faithfully observed by both parties—and most gravely and decorously, too. I have never seen a soldier smile yet, while delivering it, nor Cathy in returning it.

Ostensibly I was not present at these proceedings, and am ignorant of them; but I was where I could see. I was afraid of one thing—the jealousy of the other children of the post; but there is nothing of that, I am glad to say. On the contrary, they are proud of their comrade and her honors. It is a surprising thing, but it is true. The children are devoted to Cathy, for she has turned their dull frontier life into a sort of continuous festival; also they know her for a stanch and steady friend, a friend who can always be depended upon, and does not change with the weather.

She has become a rather extraordinary rider, under the tutorship of a more than extraordinary teacher—BB, which is her pet name for Buffalo Bill. She pronounces it *beeby*. He has not only taught her seventeen ways of breaking her neck, but twenty-two ways of avoiding it. He has infused into her the best and surest protection of a horseman—*confidence*. He did it gradually, systematically, little by little, a step at a time, and each step made sure before the next was essayed. And so he inched her along up through terrors that had been discounted by training before she reached them, and therefore were not recognizable as terrors when she got to them. Well, she is a daring little rider, now, and is perfect in what she knows of horsemanship. By and by she will know the art like a West Point cadet, and will exercise it as fearlessly. She doesn't know anything about sidesaddles. Does that distress you? And she is a fine performer, without any saddle at all. Does that discomfort you? Do not let it; she is not in any danger, I give you my word.

You said that if my heart was old and tired she would refresh it, and you said truly. I do not know how I got along without her, before. I was a forlorn old tree, but now that this blossoming vine has wound itself about me and become the life of my life, it is very different. As a furnisher of business for me and for Mammy Dorcas she is exhaustlessly competent, but I like my share of it and of course Dorcas likes her, for Dorcas "raised" George, and Cathy is George over again in so many ways that she brings back Dorcas's youth and the joys of that long-vanished time. My father tried to set Dorcas free twenty years ago, when we still lived in Virginia, but without success; she considered herself a member of the family, and wouldn't go. And so, a member of the family she remained, and has held that position unchallenged ever since, and holds it now; for when my mother sent her here from San Bernardino when we learned that Cathy was coming, she only changed from one division of the family to the other. She has the warm heart of her race, and its lavish affections, and when Cathy arrived the pair were mother and child in five minutes, and that is what they are to date and will continue. Dorcas really thinks she raised George, and that is one of her prides, but perhaps it was a mutual raising, for their ages were the same—thirteen years short of mine. But they were playmates, at any rate; as regards that, there is no room for dispute.

Cathy thinks Dorcas is the best Catholic in America except herself. She could not pay any one a higher compliment than that, and Dorcas could not receive one that would please her better. Dorcas is satisfied that there has never been a more wonderful child than Cathy. She has conceived the curious idea that Cathy is *twins,* and that one of them is a boy-twin and failed to get segregated—got submerged, is the idea. To argue with her that this is nonsense is a waste of breath—her mind is made up, and arguments do not affect it. She says:

"Look at her; she loves dolls, and girl-plays, and everything a girl loves, and she's gentle and sweet, and ain't cruel to dumb brutes—now that's the girl-twin, but she loves boy-plays, and drums and fifes and soldiering, and rough-riding, and ain't afraid of anybody or anything—and that's the boy-twin; 'deed you needn't, tell *me* she's only *one* child; no, sir, she's twins, and one of them got shet up out of sight. Out of sight, but that don't make any difference, that boy is in there, and you can see him look out of her eyes when her temper is up."

Then Dorcas went on, in her simple and earnest way, to furnish illustrations.

"Look at that raven, Marse Tom. Would anybody befriend a raven but that child? Of course they wouldn't; it ain't natural. Well, the Injun boy had the raven tied up, and was all the time plaguing it and starving it, and she pitied the po' thing, and tried to buy it from the boy, and the tears was in her eyes. That was the girl-twin, you see. She offered him her thimble, and he flung it down; she offered him all the doughnuts she had, which was two, and he flung them down; she offered him half a paper of pins, worth forty ravens, and he made a mouth at her and jabbed one of them in the raven's back. That was the limit, you know. It called for the other twin. Her eyes blazed up, and she jumped for him like a wild-cat, and when she was done with him she was rags and he wasn't anything but an allegory. That was most undoubtedly the other twin, you see, coming to the front. No, sir; don't tell *me* he ain't in there. I've seen him with my own eyes—and plenty of times, at that."

"Allegory? What is an allegory?"

"I don't know, Marse Tom, it's one of her words; she loves the big ones, you know, and I pick them up from her; they sound good and I can't help it."

"What happened after she had converted the boy into an allegory?"

"Why, she untied the raven and confiscated him by force and fetched him home, and left the doughnts and things on the ground. Petted him, of course, like she does with every creature. In two days she had him so stuck after her that she—well, *you* know how he follows her everywhere, and sets on her shoulder often when she rides her breakneck rampages—all of which is the girl-twin to the front, you see—and he does what he pleases, and is up to all kinds of devilment, and is a perfect nuisance in the kitchen. Well, they all stand it, but they wouldn't if it was another person's bird."

Here she began to chuckle comfortably, and presently she said:

"Well, you know, she's a nuisance herself, Miss Cathy is, she *is* so busy, and into everything, like that bird. It's all just as innocent, you know, and she don't mean any harm, and is so good and dear; and it ain't her fault, it's her nature; her interest is always a-working and always red-hot, and she *can't* keep quiet. Well, yesterday it was 'Please, Miss Cathy, don't do that; and, 'Please, Miss Cathy, let that alone'; and, 'Please, Miss Cathy, don't make so much noise'; and so on and so on, till I reckon I had found fault fourteen times in fifteen minutes; then she looked up at me with her big brown eyes that can plead so, and said in that odd little foreign way that goes to your heart:

" 'Please, mammy, make me a compliment.' "

"And of course you did it, you old fool?"

"Marse Tom, I just grabbed her up to my breast and says, 'Oh, you po' dear little motherless thing, you ain't got a fault in the world, and you can do anything you want to, and tear the house down, and yo' old black mammy won't say a word!' "

"Why, of course, of course—*I* knew you'd spoil the child."

She brushed away her tears, and said with dignity:

"Spoil the child? spoil *that* child, Marse Tom? There can't *anybody* spoil her. She's the king bee of this post, and everybody pets her and is her slave, and yet, as you know, your own self, she ain't the least little bit spoiled." Then she eased her mind with this retort: "Marse Tom, she makes you do anything she wants to, and you can't deny it; so if she could be spoilt, she'd been spoilt long ago, because you are the very *worst!* Look at that pile of cats in your chair, and you sitting on a candle-box, just as patient; it's because they're her cats."

If Dorcas were a soldier, I could punish her for such large frankness as that. I changed the subject, and made her resume her illustrations. She had scored against me fairly, and I wasn't going to cheapen her victory by disputing it. She proceeded to offer this incident in evidence on her twin theory:

"Two weeks ago when she got her finger mashed open, she turned pretty pale with the pain, but she never said a word. I took her in my lap, and the surgeon sponged off the blood and took a needle and thread and began to sew it up; it had to have a lot of stitches, and each one made her scrunch a little, but she never let go a sound. At last the surgeon was so full of admiration that he said, 'Well, you *are* a brave little thing!' and she said, just as ca'm and simple as if she was talking about the weather, 'There isn't anybody braver but the Cid!' You see? it was the boy-twin that the surgeon was a-dealing with."

"Who is the Cid?"

"I don't know, sir—at least only what she says. She's always talking about him, and says he was the bravest hero Spain ever had, or any other country. They have it up and down, the children do, she standing up for the Cid, and they working George Washington for all he is worth."

"Do they quarrel?"

"No; it's only disputing, and bragging, the way children do. They want her to be an American, but she can't be anything but a Spaniard, she says. You see, her mother was always longing for home, po' thing! and thinking about it, and so the child is just as much a Spaniard as if she'd always lived there. She thinks she remembers how Spain looked, but I reckon she don't, because she was only a baby when they moved to France. She is very proud to be a Spaniard."

Does that please you, Mercedes? Very well, be content; your niece is loyal to her allegiance: her mother laid deep the foundations of her love for Spain, and she will go back to you as good a Spaniard as you are yourself. She had made me promise to take her to you for a long visit when the War Office retires me.

I attend to her studies myself; has she told you that? Yes, I am her school-master, and she makes pretty good progress, I think, everything considered. Everything considered—being translated—means holidays. But the fact is, she was not born for study, and it comes hard. Hard for me, too; it hurts me like a physical pain to see that free spirit of the air and the sunshine laboring and grieving over a book; and sometimes when I find her gazing far away towards the plains and the blue mountains with the longing in her eyes, I have to thow open the prison doors; I can't help it. A quaint little scholar she is, and makes plenty of blunders. Once I put the question:

"What does the Czar govern?"

She rested her elbow on her knee and her chin on her hand and took that problem under deep consideration. Presently she looked up and answered, with a rising inflection implying a shade of uncertainty,

"The dative case?"

Here are a couple of her expositions which were delivered with tranquil confidence:

"*Chaplain, diminutive of chap. Lass* is masculine, *lassie* is feminine."

She is not a genius, you see, but just a normal child; they all make mistakes of that sort. There is a glad light in her eye which is pretty to see when she finds herself able to answer a question promptly and accurately, without any hesitation; as, for instance, this morning:

"Cathy dear, what is a cube?"

"Why, a native of Cuba."

She still drops a foreign word into her talk now and then, and there is still a subtle foreign flavor or fragrance about even her exactest English—and long may this abide! for it has for me a charm that is very pleasant. Sometimes her English is daintily prim and bookish and captivating. She has a child's sweet tooth, but for her health's sake I try to keep its inspirations under check. She is obedient—as is proper for a titled and recognized military personage, which she is—but the chain presses sometimes. For instance, we were out for a walk, and passed by some bushes that were freighted with wild gooseberries. Her face brightened and she put her hands together and delivered herself of this speech, most feelingly:

"Oh, if I was permitted a vice it would be the *gourmandise!*"

Could I resist that? No. I gave her a gooseberry.

You ask about her languages. They take care of themselves; they will not get rusty here; our regiments are not made up of natives alone—far from it. And she is picking up Indian tongues diligently.

6 Soldier Boy and the Mexican Plug

"When did you come?"

"Arrived at sundown."

"Where from?"

"Salt Lake."

"Are you in the service?"

"No. Trade."

"Pirate trade, I reckon."

"What do you know about it?"

"I saw you when you came. I recognized your master. He is a bad sort. Trap-robber, horse-thief, squaw-man, renegado—Hank Butters—I know him very well. Stole you, didn't he?"

"Well, it amounted to that."

"I thought so. Where is his pard?"

"He stopped at White Cloud's camp."

"He is another of the same stripe, is Blake Haskins." (*Aside.*) They are laying for Buffalo Bill again, I guess. (*Aloud.*) "What is your name?"

"Which one?"

"Have you got more than one?"

"I get a new one every time I'm stolen. I used to have an honest name, but that was early; I've forgotten it. Since then I've had thirteen *aliases*."

"Aliases? What is alias?"

"A false name."

"Alias. It's a fine large word, and is in my line; it has quite a learned and cerebrospinal incandescent sound. Are you educated?"

"Well, no, I can't claim it. I can take down bars, I can distinguish oats from shoe-pegs, I can blaspheme a saddle-boil with the college-bred, and I know a few other things—not many; I have had no chance, I have always had to work; besides, I am of low birth and no family. You speak my dialect like a native, but you are not a Mexican Plug, you are a gentleman, I can see that; and educated, of course."

"Yes, I am of old family, and not illiterate. I am a fossil."

"A which?"

"Fossil. The first horses were fossils. They date back two million years."

"Gr-eat sand and sage-brush! do you mean it?"

"Yes, it is true. The bones of my ancestors are held in reverence and worship, even by men. They do not leave them exposed to the weather when they find them, but carry them three thousand miles and enshrine them in their temples of learning, and worship them."

"It is wonderful! I knew you must be a person of distinction, by your fine presence and courtly address, and by the fact that you are not subjected to the indignity of hobbles like myself and the rest. Would you tell me your name?"

"You have probably heard of it—Soldier Boy."

"What!—the renowned, the illustrious?"

"Even so."

"It takes my breath! Little did I dream that ever I should stand face to face with the possessor of that great name. Buffalo Bill's horse! Known from the Canadian border to the deserts of Arizona, and from the eastern marches of the

Great Plains to the foot-hills of the Sierra! Truly this is a memorable day. You still serve the celebrated Chief of Scouts?"

"I am still his property, but he has lent me, for a time, to the most noble, the most gracious, the most excellent, her Excellency Catherine, Corporal-General Seventh Cavalry and Flag-Lieutenant Ninth Dragoons, U.S.A.,—on whom be peace!"

"Amen. Did you say *her* Excellency?"

"The same. A Spanish lady, sweet blossom of a ducal house. And truly a wonder; knowing everything, capable of everything; speaking all the languages, master of all sciences, a mind without horizons, a heart of gold, the glory of her race! On whom be peace!"

"Amen. It is marvelous!"

"Verily. I knew many things, she has taught me others. I am educated. I will tell you about her."

"I listen—I am enchanted."

"I will tell a plain tale, calmly, without excitement, without eloquence. When she had been here four or five weeks she was already erudite in military things, and they made her an officer—a double officer. She rode the drill every day, like any soldier; and she could take the bugle and direct the evolutions herself. Then, on a day, there was a grand race, for prizes—none to enter but the children. Seventeen children entered, and she was the youngest. Three girls, fourteen boys—good riders all. It was a steeplechase, with four hurdles, all pretty high. The first prize was a most cunning half-grown silver bugle, and mighty pretty, with red silk cord and tassels. Buffalo Bill was very anxious; for he had taught her to ride, and he did most dearly want her to win that race, for the glory of it. So he wanted her to ride me, but she wouldn't; and she reproached him, and said it was unfair and unright, and taking advantage; for what horse in this post or any other could stand a chance against me? and she was very severe with him, and said, 'You ought to be ashamed—you are proposing to me conduct unbecoming an officer and a gentleman.' So he just tossed her up in the air about thirty feet and caught her as she came down, and said he *was* ashamed; and put up his handkerchief and pretended to cry, which nearly broke her heart, and she petted him, and begged him to forgive her, and said she would do anything in the world he could ask but that; but he said he ought to go hang himself, and he *must,* if he could get a rope; it was nothing but right he should, for he never, never could forgive himself; and then *she* began to cry, and they both sobbed, the way you could hear him a mile, and she clinging around his neck and pleading, till at last he was comforted a little, and gave his solemn promise he wouldn't hang himself till after the race; and wouldn't do it at all if she won it, which made her happy, and she said she would win it or die in the saddle; so then everything was pleasant again and both of them content. He can't help playing jokes on her, he is so fond of her and she is so innocent and unsuspecting; and when she finds it out she cuffs him and is in a fury, but presently forgives him because it's *him;* and maybe the very next day she's caught with another joke; you see she can't learn any better, because she hasn't any deceit in her, and that kind aren't ever expecting it in another person.

"It was a grand race. The whole post was there, and there was such another whooping and shouting when the seventeen kids came flying down the turf and sailing over the hurdles—oh, beautiful to see! Halfway down, it was kind of neck and neck, and anybody's race and nobody's. Then, what should happen but a cow steps out and puts her head down to munch grass, with her broadside to the battalion, and they a-coming like the wind; they split apart to flank her, but *she?*—why, she drove the spurs home and soared over that cow like a bird! and on she went, and cleared the last hurdle solitary and alone, the army letting loose the grand yell, and she skipped from the horse the same as if he had been standing still, and made her bow, and everybody crowded around to congratulate, and they gave her the bugle, and she put it to her lips and blew 'boots and saddles' to see how it would go, and BB was as proud as you can't think! And he said, 'Take Soldier Boy, and don't pass him back till I ask for him!' and I can tell you he wouldn't have said that to any other person on this planet. That was two months and more ago, and nobody has been on my back since but the Corporal-General Seventh Cavalry and Flag-Lieutenant of the Ninth Dragoons, U.S.A.,—on whom be peace!"

"Amen. I listen—tell me more."

"She set to work and organized the Sixteen, and called it the First Battalion Rocky Mountain Rangers, U.S.A., and she wanted to be bugler, but they elected her Lieutenant-General *and* Bugler. So she ranks her uncle the commandant, who is only a Brigadier. And doesn't she train those little people! Ask the Indians, ask the traders, ask the soldiers; they'll tell you. She has been at it from the first day. Every morning they go clattering down into the plain, and there she sits on my back with her bugle at her mouth and sounds the orders and puts them through the evolutions for an hour or more; and it is too beautiful for anything to see those ponies dissolve from one formation into another, and waltz about, and break, and scatter, and form again, always moving, always graceful, now trotting, now galloping, and so on, sometimes near by, sometimes in the distance, all just like a state ball, you know, and sometimes she can't hold herself any longer, but sounds the 'charge,' and turns me loose! and you can take my word for it, if the battalion hasn't *too* much of a start we catch up and go over the breastworks with the front line.

"Yes, they are soldiers, those little people; and healthy, too, not ailing any more, the way they used to be sometimes. It's because of her drill. She's got a fort, now—Fort Fanny Marsh. Major-General Tommy Drake planned it out, and the Seventh and Dragoons built it. Tommy is the Colonel's son, and is fifteen and the oldest in the Battalion; Fanny Marsh is Brigadier-General, and is next oldest—over thirteen. She is daughter of Captain Marsh, Company B, Seventh Cavalry. Lieutenant-General Alison is the youngest by considerable; I think she is about nine and a half or three-quarters. Her military rig, as Lieutenant-General, isn't for business, it's for dress parade, because the ladies made it. They say they got it out of the Middle Ages—out of a book—and it is all red and blue and white silks and satins and velvets; tights, trunks, sword, doublet with slashed sleeves, short cape, cap with just one feather in it; I've heard them name these things; they got them out of the book; she's dressed like a page, of old times, they say. It's the daintiest outfit that ever was—you will say so, when you see it. She's lovely in it—oh, just a dream! In some ways she is just her age, but in others she's as old as her uncle, I think. She is very learned. She teaches her uncle his book. I have seen her sitting by with the book and reciting to him what is in it, so that he can learn to do it himself.

"Every Saturday she hires little Injuns to garrison her fort; then she lays siege to it, and makes military approaches by make-believe trenches in make-believe night, and finally at make-believe dawn she draws her sword and sounds the assault and takes it by storm. It is for practice. And she has invented a bugle-call all by herself, out of her own head, and it's a stirring one, and the prettiest in the service. It's to call *me*—it's never used for anything else. She taught it to me, and told me what it says: *'It is I, Soldier—come'* and when those thrilling notes come floating down the distance I heard them without fail, even if I am two miles away; and then—oh, then you should see my heels get down to business!

"And she has taught me how to say good-morning and good-night to her, which is by lifting my right hoof for her to shake; and also how to say good-by; I do that with my left foot—but only for practice, because there hasn't been any but make-believe good-bying yet, and I hope there won't ever be. It would make me cry if I ever had to put up my left foot in earnest. She has taught me how to salute, and I can do it as well as a soldier. I bow my head low, and lay my right hoof against my cheek. She taught me that because I got into disgrace once, through ignorance. I am privileged, because I am known to be honorable and trustworthy, and because I have a distinguished record in the service; so they don't hobble me nor tie me to stakes or shut me tight in stables, but let me wander around to suit myself. Well, trooping the colors is a very solemn ceremony, and everybody must stand uncovered when the flag goes by, the commandant and all; and once I was there, and ignorantly walked across right in front of the band, which was an awful disgrace. Ah, the lieutenant-General was so ashamed, and so distressed that I should have done such a thing before all the world, that she couldn't keep the tears back; and then she taught me the salute, so that if I ever did any other unmilitary act through ignorance I could do my salute and she believed everybody would think it was apology enough and would not press the matter. It is very nice and distinguished; no other horse can do it; often the men salute me, and I return it. I am privileged to be present when the Rocky Mountain Rangers troop the colors and I stand solemn, like the children, and I salute when the flag goes by. Of course when she goes to her fort her sentries sing out 'Turn out the guard!' and then . . . do you catch that refreshing early-morning whiff from the mountain-pines and the wild flowers? The night is far spent; we'll hear the bugles before long. Dorcas, the black woman, is very good and nice; she takes care of the Lieutenant-General, and is Brigadier-General Alison's mother, which makes her mother-in-law to the Lieutenant-General. That is what Shekels says. At least it is what I think he says, though I never can understand him quite clearly. He—"

"Who is Shekels?"

"The Seventh Cavalry dog. I mean, if he *is* a dog. His father was a coyote and his mother was wild-cat. It doesn't really make a dog out of him, does it?"

"Not a real dog, I should think. Only a kind of a general dog, at most, I reckon. Though this is a matter of ichthyology, I suppose; and if it is, it is out of my depth, and so my opinion is not valuable, and I don't claim much consideration for it."

"It isn't ichthyology; it is dogmatics, which is still more difficult and tangled up. Dogmatics always are."

"Dogmatics is quite beyond me, quite; so I am not competing. But on general principles it is my opinion that a colt out of a coyote and a wild-cat is no square dog, but doubtful. That is my hand, and I stand pat."

"Well, it is as far as I can go myself, and be fair and conscientious. I have always regarded him as a doubtful dog, and so has Potter. Potter is the great Dane. Potter says he is no dog, and not even poultry—though I do not go quite so far as that."

"And I wouldn't, myself. Poultry is one of those things which no person can get to the bottom of, there is so much of it and such variety. It is just wings, and wings, and wings, till you are weary: turkeys, and geese, and bats, and butterflies, and angels, and grasshoppers, and flying-fish, and—well, there is really no end to the tribe; it gives me the heaves just to think of it. But this one hasn't any wings, has he?"

"No."

"Well, then, in my belief he is more likely to be dog than poultry. I have not heard of poultry that hadn't wings. Wings is the *sign* of poultry; it is what you tell poultry by. Look at the mosquito."

"What do you reckon he is, then? He must be something."

"Why, he could be a reptile; anything that hasn't wings is a reptile."

"Who told you that?"

"Nobody told me, but I overheard it."

"Where did you overhear it?"

"Years ago. I was with the Philadelphia Institute expedition in the Bad Lands under Professor Cope, hunting mastodon bones, and I overheard him say, his own self, that any plantigrade circumflex vertebrate bacterium that hadn't wings and was uncertain was a reptile. Well, then, has this dog any wings? No. Is he a plantigrade circumflex vertebrate bacterium? Maybe so, maybe not; but without ever having seen him, and judging only by his illegal and spectacular parentage, I will bet the odds of a bale of hay to a bran mash that he looks it. Finally, is he uncertain? That is the point—is he uncertain? I will leave it to you if you have ever heard of a more uncertainer dog than what this one is?"

"No, I never have."

"Well, then, he's a reptile. That's settled."

"Why, look here, whatsyourname—"

"Last alias, 'Mongrel.' "

"A good one, too. I was going to say, you are better educated than you have been pretending to be. I like cultured society, and I shall cultivate your acquaintance. Now as to Shekels, whenever you want to know about any private thing that is going on at this post or in White Cloud's camp or Thunder-Bird's, he can tell you; and if you make friends with him he'll be glad to, for he is a born gossip, and picks up all the tittle-tattle. Being the whole Seventh Cavalry's reptile, he doesn't belong to anybody in particular, and hasn't any military duties; so he comes and goes as he pleases, and is popular with all the house cats and other authentic sources of private information. He understands all the languages, and talks them all, too. With an accent like gritting your teeth, it is true, and with a grammar, that is no improvement on blasphemy—still, with practice you get at the meat of what he says, and it serves. . . . Hark! That's the reveille. . . .

THE REVEILLE*

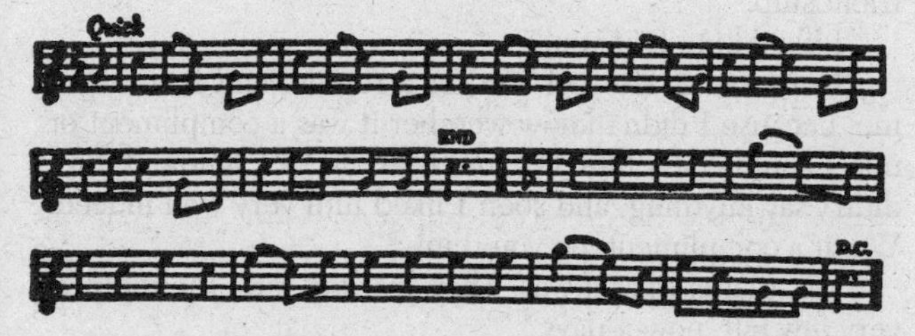

"Faint and far, but isn't it clear, isn't it sweet? There's no music like the bugle to stir the blood, in the still solemnity of the morning twilight, with the dim plain stretching away to nothing and the spectral mountains slumbering against the sky. You'll hear another note in a minute—faint and far and clear, like the other one, and sweeter still, you'll notice. Wait . . . listen. There it goes! It says, *'It is I, Soldier—come!'* . . .

SOLDIER BOY'S BUGLE CALL

. . . Now then, watch me leave a blue streak behind!"

7 Soldier Boy and Shekels

"Did you do as I told you? Did you look up the Mexican Plug?"

---

* At West Point the bugle is supposed to be saying:
"I can't get 'em up,
I can't get 'em up,
I can't get 'em up in the morning!"

"Yes, I made his acquaintance before night and got his friendship."

"I liked him. Did you?"

"Not at first. He took me for a reptile, and it troubled me, because I didn't know whether it was a compliment or not. I couldn't ask him, because it would look ignorant. So I didn't say anything, and soon I liked him very well indeed. Was it a compliment, do you think?"

"Yes, that is what it was. They are very rare, the reptiles; very few left, now-a-days."

"Is that so? What is a reptile?"

"It is a plantigrade circumflex vertebrate bacterium that hasn't any wings and is uncertain."

"Well, it—it sounds fine, it surely does."

"And it *is* fine. You may be thankful you are one."

"I am. It seems wonderfully grand and elegant for a person that is so humble as I am; but I am thankful, I am indeed, and will try to live up to it. It is hard to remember. Will you say it again, please, and say it slow?"

"Plantigrade circumflex vertebrate bacterium that hasn't any wings and is uncertain."

"It *is* beautiful, anybody must grant it; beautiful, and of a noble sound. I hope it will not make me proud and stuck-up—I should not like to be that. It is much more distinguished and honorable to be a reptile than a dog, don't you think, Soldier?"

"Why, there's no comparison. It is awfully aristocratic. Often a duke is called a reptile; it is set down so, in history."

"Isn't that grand! Potter wouldn't ever associate with me, but I reckon he'll be glad to when he finds out what I am."

"You can depend upon it."

"I will thank Mongrel for this. He is a very good sort, for a Mexican Plug. Don't you think he is?"

"It is my opinion of him; and as for his birth, he cannot help that. We cannot all be reptiles, we cannot all be fossils;

we have to take what comes and be thankful it is no worse. It is the true philosophy."

"For those others?"

"Stick to the subject, please. Did it turn out that my suspicions were right?"

"Yes, perfectly right. Mongrel has heard them planning. They are after BB's life, for running them out of Medicine Bow and taking their stolen horses away from them."

"Well, they'll get him yet, for sure."

"Not if he keeps a sharp lookout."

"*He* keep a sharp lookout! He never does; he despises them, and all their kind. His life is always being threatened, and so it has come to be monotonous."

"Does he know they are here?"

"Oh yes, he knows it. He is always the earliest to know who comes and who goes. But he cares nothing for them and their threats; he only laughs when people warn him. They'll shoot him from behind a tree the first he knows. Did Mongrel tell you their plans?"

"Yes. They have found out that he starts for Fort Clayton day after to-morrow, with one of his scouts; so they will leave to-morrow, letting on to go south, but they will fetch around north all in good time."

"Shekels, I don't like the look of it."

8 The Scout-Start, BB and Lieutenant-General Alison

BB (*saluting.*): "Good! handsomely done! The Seventh couldn't beat it! You do certainly handle your Rangers like an expert, General. And where are you bound?"

"Four miles on the trail to Fort Clayton."

"Glad am I, dear! What's the idea of it?"

"Guard of honor for you and Thorndike."

"Bless—your—*heart!* I'd rather have it from you than from the Commander-in-Chief of the armies of the United

States, you incomparable little soldier!—and I don't need to take any oath to that, for you believe it."

"I *thought* you'd like it, BB."

"*Like* it? Well, I should say so! Now then—all ready—sound the advance, and away we go!"

9 Soldier Boy and Shekels Again

Well, this is the way it happened. We did the escort duty; then we came back and struck for the plain and put the Rangers through a rousing drill—oh, for hours! Then we sent them home under Brigadier-General Fanny Marsh; then the Lieutenant-General and I went off on a gallop over the plains for about three hours, and were lazying along home in the middle of the afternoon, when we met Jimmy Slade, the drummer-boy, and he saluted and asked the Lieutenant-General if she had heard the news, and she said no, and he said:

" 'Buffalo Bill has been ambushed and badly shot this side of Clayton, and Thorndike the scout, too; Bin couldn't travel, but Thorndike could, and he brought the news, and Sergeant Wilkes and six men of Company B are gone, two hours ago, hotfoot, to get Bill. And they say—'

" '*Go!*' she shouted to me—and I went."

"Fast?"

"Don't ask foolish questions. It was an awful pace. For four hours nothing happened, and not a word said, except that now and then she said, 'Keep it up, Boy, keep it up, sweetheart; well save him!' I kept it up. Well, when the dark shut down, in the rugged hills, that poor little chap had been tearing around in the saddle all day, and I noticed by the slack knee-pressure that she was tired and tottery, and I got dreadfully afraid; but every time I tried to slow down and let her go to sleep, so I could stop, she hurried me up again; and so, sure enough, at last over she went!

"Ah, that was a fix to be in! for she lay there, and didn't stir, and what was I to do? I couldn't leave her to fetch help, on account of the wolves. There was nothing to do but stand by. It was dreadful. I was afraid she was killed, poor little thing! But she wasn't. She came to, by and by, and said, 'Kiss me, Soldier,' and those were blessed words. I kissed her—often; I am used to that, and we like it. But she didn't get up, and I was worried. She fondled my nose with her hand, and talked to me, and called me endearing names—which is her way—but she caressed with the same hand all the time. The other arm was broken, you see, but I didn't know it, and she didn't mention it. She didn't want to distress me, you know.

"Soon the big gray wolves came, and hung around, and you could hear them snarl, and snap at each other, but you couldn't see anything of them except their eyes, which shone in the dark like sparks and stars. The Lieutenant-General said, 'If I had the Rocky Mountain Rangers here, we would make those creatures climb a tree.' Then she made believe that the Rangers were in hearing, and put up her bugle and blew the 'assembly'; and then, 'boots and saddles'; then the 'trot'; 'gallop'; '*charge!*' Then she blew the 'retreat,' and said, 'That's for you, you rebels; the Rangers don't ever retreat!'

"The music frightened them away, but they were hungry, and kept coming back. And of course they got bolder and bolder, which is their way. It went on for an hour, then the tired child went to sleep, and it was pitiful to hear her moan and nestle, and I couldn't do anything for her. All the time I was laying for the wolves. They are in my line; I have had experience. At last the boldest one ventured within my lines, and I landed him among his friends with some of his skull still on him, and they did the rest. In the next hour I got a couple more, and they went the way of the first one, down the throats of the detachment. That satisfied the survivors, and they went away and left us in peace.

"We hadn't any more adventures, though I kept awake all night and was ready. From midnight on the child got very restless, and out of her head, and moaned, and said, 'Water, water—thirsty'; and now and then, 'Kiss me, Soldier'; and sometimes she was in her fort and giving orders to her garrison; and once she was in Spain, and thought her mother was with her. People say a horse can't cry; but they don't know, because we cry inside.

"It was an hour after sunup that I heard the boys coming, and recognized the hoof-beats of Pomp and Caesar and Jerry, old mates of mine; and a welcomer sound there couldn't ever be.

"Buffalo Bill was in a horse-litter, with his leg broken by a bullet, and Mongrel and Blake Haskins's horse were doing the work. Buffalo Bill and Thorndike had killed both of those toughs.

"When they got to us, and Buffalo Bill saw the child lying there so white, he said, 'My God!' and the sound of his voice brought her to herself, and she gave a little cry of pleasure and struggled to get up, but couldn't, and the soldiers gathered her up like the tenderest women, and their eyes were wet and they were not ashamed, when they saw her arm dangling; and so were Buffalo Bill's, and when they laid her in his arms he said, 'My darling, how does this come?' and she said, 'We came to save you, but I was tired, and couldn't keep awake, and fell off and hurt myself, and couldn't get on again.' 'You came to save me, you dear little rat? It was too lovely of you!' 'Yes, and Soldier stood by me, which you know he would, and protected me from the wolves; and if he got a chance he kicked the life out of some of them—for you know he would, BB.' The sergeant said, 'He laid out three of them, sir, and here's the bones to show for it.' 'He's a grand horse,' said BB; 'he's the grandest horse that ever was! and has saved your life, Lieutenant-General Alison, and shall protect it the rest of his life—he's yours for a kiss!' He got it, along with a passion of delight, and he said, 'You are feeling better now, little Spaniard—do you think you could blow the advance?' She put up the bugle to do it, but he said wait a minute first. Then he and the sergeant set her arm and put it in splints, she wincing but not whimpering; then we took up the march for home, and that's the end of the tale; and I'm her horse. Isn't she a brick, Shekels?"

"Brick? She's more than a brick, more than a thousand bricks—she's a reptile!"

"It's a compliment out of your heart, Shekels. God bless you for it!"

10 GENERAL ALISON AND DORCAS

"Too much company for her, Marse Tom. Betwixt you, and Shekels, and the Colonel's wife, and the Cid—"

"The Cid? Oh, I remember—the raven."

"—and Mrs. Captain Marsh and Famine and Pestilence the baby *coyotes,* and Sour-Mash and her pups, and Sardanapalus and her kittens—hang these names she gives the creatures, they warp my jaw—and Potter: you—all sitting around *in* the house, and Soldier Boy at the window the entire time, it's a wonder to me she comes along as well as she does. She—"

"You want her all to yourself, you stingy old thing!"

"Marse Tom, you know better. It's too much company. And then the idea of her receiving reports all the time from her officers, and acting upon them, and giving orders, the same as if she was well! It ain't good for her, and the surgeon don't like it, and tried to persuade her not to and couldn't; and when he *ordered* her, she was that outraged and indignant, and was very severe on him, and accused him of insubordination, and said it didn't become him to give orders to an officer of her rank. Well, he saw he had excited her more and done more harm than all the rest put together, so he was vexed at himself and wished he had kept still. Doctors *don't* know much, and that's a fact. She's too much interested in things—she ought to rest more. She's all the time sending messages to BB, and to soldiers and Injuns and whatnot, and to the animals."

"To the animals?"

"Yes, sir."

"Who carries them?"

"Sometimes Potter, but mostly it's Shekels."

"Now come! who can find fault with such pretty make-believe as that?"

"But it ain't make-believe, Marse Tom. She does send them."

"Yes, I don't doubt that part of it."

"Do you doubt they get them, sir?"

"Certainly. Don't you?"

"No, sir. Animals talk to one another. I know it perfectly well, Marse Tom, and I ain't saying it by guess."

"What a curious superstition!"

"It ain't a superstition, Marse Tom. Look at that Shekels—look at him, *now.* Is he listening, or ain't he? *Now* you see! he's turned his head away. It's because he was caught—caught in the act. I'll ask you—could a Christian look any more ashamed than what he looks now?—*lay down!* You see? he was going to sneak out. Don't tell *me,* Marse Tom! If animals don't talk, I miss *my* guess. And Shekels is the worst. He goes and tells the animals everything that happens in the officers' quarters; and if he's short of facts, he invents them. He hasn't any more principle than a blue jay; and as for morals, he's empty. Look at him now; look at him grovel. He knows what I am saying, and he knows it's the truth. You see, yourself, that he can feel shame; it's the only virtue he's got. It's wonderful how they find out everything that's going on—the animals. They—"

"Do you really, believe they do, Dorcas?"

"I don't only just believe it, Marse Tom, I know it. Day

before yesterday they knew something was going to happen. They were that excited, and whispering around together; why, anybody could see that they— But my! I must get back to her, and I haven't got to my errand yet."

"What is it, Dorcas?"

"Well, it's two or three things. One is, the doctor don't salute when he comes . . . Now, Marse Tom, it ain't anything to laugh at, and so—"

"Well, then, forgive me; I didn't mean to laugh—I got caught unprepared."

"You see, she don't want to hurt the doctor's feelings, so she don't say anything to him about it; but she is always polite, herself, and it hurts that kind of people to be rude to them."

"I'll have that doctor hanged."

"Marse Tom, she don't *want* him hanged. She—"

"Well, then, I'll have him boiled in oil."

"But she don't *want* him boiled. I—"

"Oh, very well, very well, I only want to please her; I'll have him skinned."

"Why, *she* don't want him skinned; it would break her heart. Now—"

"Woman, this is perfectly unreasonable. What in the nation *does* she want?"

"Marse Tom, if you would only be a little patient, and not fly off the handle at the least little thing. Why, she only wants you to speak to him."

"Speak to him! Well, upon my word! All this unseemly rage and row about such a—a— Dorcas, I never saw you carry on like this before. You have alarmed the sentry; he thinks I am being assassinated; he thinks there's a mutiny, a revolt, an insurrection; he—"

"Marse Tom, you are just putting on; you know it perfectly well; *I* don't know what makes you act like that—but you always did, even when you was little, and you can't get over it, I reckon. Are you over it now, Marse Tom?"

"Oh, well, yes; but it would try anybody to be doing the

best he could, offering every kindness he could think of, only to have it rejected with contumely and . . . Oh, well, let it go; it's no matter—I'll talk to the doctor. Is that satisfactory, or are you going to break out again?"

"Yes, sir, it is; and it's only right to talk to him, too, because it's just as she says; she's trying to keep up discipline in the Rangers, and this insubordination of his is a bad example for them—now ain't it so, Marse Tom?"

"Well, there *is* reason in it, I can't deny it; so I will speak to him, though at bottom I think hanging would be more lasting. What is the rest of your errand, Dorcas?"

"Of course her room is Ranger headquarters now, Marse Tom, while she's sick. Well, soldiers of the cavalry and the dragoons that are off duty come and get her sentries to let them relieve them and serve in their place. It's only out of affection, sir, and because they know military honors please her, and please the children too, for her sake; and they don't bring their muskets; and so—"

"I've noticed them there, but didn't twig the idea. They are standing guard, are they?"

"Yes, sir, and she is afraid you will reprove them and hurt their feelings, if you see them there; so she begs, if—if you don't mind coming in the back way—"

"Bear me up, Dorcas; don't let me faint."

There—sit up and behave, Marse Tom. You are not going to faint; you are only pretending—you used to act just so when you was little; it does seem a long time for you to get grown up."

"Dorcas, the way the child is progressing, I shall be out of my job before long—she'll have the whole post in her hands. I must make a stand, I must not go down without a struggle. These encroachments. . . . Dorcas, what do you think she will think of next?"

"Marse Tom, she don't mean any harm."

"Are you sure of it?"

"Yes, Marse Tom."

"You feel sure she has no ulterior designs?"

"I don't know what that is, Marse Tom, but I know she hasn't."

"Very well, then, for the present I am satisfied. What else have you come about?"

"I reckon I better tell you the whole thing first, Marse Tom, then tell you what she wants. There's been an *émeute,* as she calls it. It was before she got back with BB. The officer of the day reported it to her this morning. It happened at her fort. There was a fuss betwixt Major-General Tommy Drake and Lieutenant-Colonel Agnes Frisbie, and he snatched her doll away, which is made of white kid stuffed with sawdust, and tore every rag of its clothes off, right before them all, and is under arrest, and the charge is conduct un—"

"Yes, I know—conduct unbecoming an officer and a gentleman—a plain case, too, it seems to me. This is a serious matter. Well, what is her pleasure?"

"Well, Marse Tom, she has summoned a court-martial, but the doctor don't think she is well enough to preside over it, and she says there ain't anybody competent but her, because there's a major-general concerned; and so she—she—well, she says, would you preside over it for her? . . . Marse Tom, *sit* up! You ain't any more going to faint than Shekels is."

"Look here, Dorcas, go along back, and be tactful. Be persuasive; don't fret her; tell her it's all right, the matter is in my hands, but it isn't good form to hurry so grave a matter as this. Explain to her that we have to go by precedent, and that I believe this one to be new. In fact, you can say I know that nothing just like it has happened in our army, therefore I must be guided by European precedents, and must go cautiously and examine them carefully. Tell her not to be impatient, it will take me several days, but it will all come out right, and I will come over and report progress as I go along. Do you get the idea, Dorcas?"

"I don't know as I do, sir."

"Well, it's this. You see, it won't ever do for me, a brigadier in the regular army, to preside over that infant court-martial—there isn't any precedent for it, don't you see. Very well. I will go on examining authorities and reporting progress until she is well enough to get me out of this scrape by presiding herself. Do you get it now?"

"Oh, yes, sir, I get it, and it's good, I'll go and fix it with her. *Lay down!* and stay where you are."

"Why, what harm is he doing?"

"Oh, it ain't any harm, but it just vexes me to see him act so."

"What was he doing?"

"Can't you see, and him in such a sweat? He was starting out to spread it all over the post. *Now* I reckon you won't deny, any more, that they go and tell everything they hear, now that you've seen it with yo' own eyes."

"Well, I don't like to acknowledge it, Dorcas, but I don't see how I can consistently stick to my doubts in the face of such overwhelming proof as this dog is furnishing."

"There, now, you've got in yo' right mind at last! I wonder you can be so stubborn, Marse Tom. But you always was, even when you was little. I'm going now."

"Look here; tell her that in view of the delay, it is my judgment that she ought to enlarge the accused on his parole."

"Yes, sir, I'll tell her. Marse Tom?"

"Well?"

"She can't get to Soldier Boy, and he stands there all the time, down in the mouth and lonesome; and she says will you shake hands with him and comfort him? Everybody does."

"It's a curious kind of lonesomeness; but, all right, I will."

11 Several Months Later. Antonio and Thorndike

"Thorndike, isn't that Plug you're riding an asset of the scrap you and Buffalo Bill had with the late Blake Haskins and his pal a few months back?"

"Yes, this is Mongrel—and not a half-bad horse, either."

"I've noticed he keeps up his lick first-rate. Say—isn't it a gaudy morning?"

"Right you are!"

"Thorndike, it's Andalusian! and when that's said, all's said."

"Andalusian *and* Oregonian, Antonio! Put it that way, and you have my vote. Being a native up there, I know. You being Andalusian-born—"

"Can speak with authority for that patch of paradise? Well, I can. Like the Don! like Sancho! This is the correct Andalusian dawn now—crisp, fresh, dewy, fragrant, pungent—"

" 'What though the spicy breezes
Blow soft o'er Ceylon's isle—'

—*git* up, you old cow! stumbling like that when we've just been praising you! out on a scout and can't live up to the honor any better than that? Antonio, how long have you been out here in the Plains and the Rockies?"

"More than thirteen years."

"It's a long time. Don't you ever get homesick?"

"Not till now."

"Why *now?*—after such a long cure."

"These preparations of the retiring commandant's have started it up."

"Of course. It's natural."

"It keeps me thinking about Spain. I know the region where the Seventh's child's aunt lives; I know all the lovely country for miles around; I'll bet I've seen her aunt's villa many a time; I'll bet I've been in it in those pleasant old times when I was a Spanish gentleman."

"They say the child is wild to see Spain."

"It's so; I know it from what I hear."

"Haven't you talked with her about it?"

"No. I've avoided it. I should soon be as wild as she is. That would not be comfortable."

"I wish I was going, Antonio. There's two things I'd give a lot to see. One's a railroad."

"She'll see one when she strikes Missouri."

"The other's a bull-fight."

"I've seen lots of them; I wish I could see another."

"I don't know anything about it, except in a mixed-up, foggy way, Antonio, but I know enough to know it's grand sport."

"The grandest in the world! There's no other sport that begins with it. I'll tell you what I've seen, then you can judge. It was my first, and it's as vivid to me now as it was when I saw it. It was a Sunday afternoon, and beautiful weather, and my uncle, the priest, took me as a reward for being a good boy and because of my own accord and without anybody asking me I had bankrupted my savings-box and given the money to a mission that was civilizing the Chinese and sweetening their lives and softening their hearts with the gentle teachings of our religion, and I wish you could have seen what we saw that day, Thorndike.

"The amphitheater was packed, from the bull-ring to the highest row—twelve thousand people in one circling mass, one slanting, solid mass—royalties, nobles, clergy, ladies, gentlemen, state officials, generals, admirals, soldiers, sailors, lawyers, thieves, merchants, brokers, cooks, housemaids, scullery-maids, doubtful women, dudes, gamblers, beggars, loafers, tramps, American ladies, gentlemen, preachers, English ladies, gentlemen, preachers, German ditto, French ditto, and so on and so on, all the world represented: Spaniards to admire and praise, foreigners to enjoy and go home and find fault—there they were, one solid, sloping, circling sweep of rippling and flashing color under the downpour of the summer sun—just a garden, a gaudy, gorgeous flower-garden! Children munching oranges, six thousand fans fluttering and glimmering, everybody happy, everybody chatting gayly with their intimates, lovely girl-faces smiling recognition and salutation to other lovely girl-faces, gray old ladies and gentlemen dealing in the like exchanges with each other—ah, such a picture of cheery contentment and glad anticipation! not a mean spirit, nor a sordid soul, nor a sad heart there—ah, Thorndike, I wish I could see it again.

"Suddenly, the martial note of a bugle cleaves the hum and murmur—clear the ring!

"They clear it. The great gate is flung open, and the procession marches in, splendidly costumed and glittering: the marshals of the day, then the picadores on horseback, then the matadores on foot, each surrounded by his quadrille of *chulos*. They march to the box of the city fathers, and formally salute. The key is thrown, the bull-gate is unlocked. Another bugle blast—the gate flies open, the bull plunges in, furious, trembling, blinking in the blinding light, and stands there, a magnificent creature, center of those multitudinous and admiring eyes, brave, ready for battle, his attitude a challenge. He sees his enemy: horsemen sitting motionless, with long spears in rest, upon blindfolded broken-down nags, lean and starved, fit only for sport and sacrifice, then the carrion-heap.

"The bull makes a rush, with murder in his eye, but a picador meets him with a spear-thrust in the shoulder. He flinches with the pain, and the picador skips out of danger. A burst of applause for the picador, hisses for the bull. Some shout "Cow!" at the bull, and call him offensive names. But he is not listening to them, he is there for business; he is not minding the cloak-bearers that come fluttering around to confuse him; he chases this way, he chases that way, and hither and yon, scattering the nimble banderillos in every direction like a spray, and receiving their maddening darts in his neck as they dodge and fly—oh, but it's a lively spectacle, and brings down the house! Ah, you should hear the thundering roar that goes up when the game is at its wildest and brilliant things are done!

"Oh, that first bull, that day, was great! From the moment

the spirit of war rose to flood-tide in him and he got down to his work, he began to do wonders. He tore his way through his persecutors, flinging one of them clear over the parapet; he bowled a horse and his rider down, and plunged straight for the next, got home with his horns, wounding both horse and man; on again, here and there and this way and that; and one after another he tore the bowels out of two horses so that they grushed to the ground, and ripped a third one so badly that although they rushed him to cover and shoved his bowels back and stuffed the rents with tow and rode him against the bull again, he couldn't make the trip; he tried to gallop, under the spur, but soon reeled and tottered and fell, all in a heap. For a while, that bull-ring was the most thrilling and glorious and inspiring sight that ever was seen. The bull absolutely cleared it, and stood there alone! monarch of the place. The people went mad for pride in him, and joy and delight, and you couldn't hear yourself think, for the roar and boom and crash of applause."

"Antonio, it carries me clear out of myself just to hear you tell it; it must have been perfectly splendid. If I live, I'll see a bull-fight yet before I die. Did they kill him?"

"Oh yes; that is what the bull is for. They tired him out, and got him at last. He kept rushing the matador, who always slipped smartly and gracefully aside in time, waiting for a sure chance; and at last it came; the bull made a deadly plunge for him—was avoided neatly, and as he sped by, the long sword glided silently into him, between left shoulder and spine—in and in, to the hilt. He crumpled down, dying."

"Ah, Antonio, it *is* the noblest sport that ever was. I would give a year of my life to see it. Is the bull always killed?"

"Yes. Sometimes a bull is timid, finding himself in so strange a place, and he stands trembling, or tries to retreat. Then everybody despises him for his cowardice and wants him punished and made ridiculous; so they hough him from behind, and it is the funniest thing in the world to see him hobbling around on his severed legs; the whole vast house goes into hurricanes of laughter over it; I have laughed till the tears ran down my cheeks to see it. When he has furnished all the sport he can, he is not any longer useful, and is killed."

"Well, it is perfectly grand, Antonio, perfectly beautiful. Burning a nigger don't begin."

12 MONGREL AND THE OTHER HORSE

"Sage-Brush, you have been listening?"

"Yes."

"Isn't it strange?"

"Well, no, Mongrel, I don't know that it is."

"Why don't you?"

"I've seen a good many human beings in my time. They are created as they are; they cannot help it. They are only brutal because that is their make; brutes would be brutal if it was *their* make."

"To me, Sage-Brush, man is most strange and unaccountable. Why should he treat dumb animals that way when they are not doing any harm?"

"Man is not always like that, Mongrel; he is kind enough when he is not excited by religion."

"Is the bull-fight a religious service?"

"I think so. I have heard so. It is held on Sunday."

(*A reflective pause, lasting some moments.*) Then:

"When we die, Sage-Brush, do we go to heaven and dwell with man?"

"My father thought not. He believed we do not have to go there unless we deserve it."

PART II IN SPAIN

13 GENERAL ALISON TO HIS MOTHER

It was a prodigious trip, but delightful, of course, through the Rockies and the Black Hills and the mighty sweep of the Great Plains to civilization and the Missouri border—where the railroading began and the delightfulness ended. But no one is the worse for the journey; certainly not Cathy, nor Dorcas, nor Soldier Boy; and as for me, I am not complaining.

Spain is all that Cathy had pictured it—and more, she says. She is in a fury of delight, the maddest little animal that ever was, and all for joy. She thinks she remembers Spain, but that is not very likely, I suppose. The two—Mercedes and Cathy—devour each other. It is a rapture of love, and beautiful to see. It is Spanish; that describes it. Will this be a short visit?

No. It will be permanent. Cathy has elected to abide with Spain and her aunt. Dorcas says she (Dorcas) foresaw that this would happen; and also says that she wanted it to happen, and says the child's own country is the right place for her, and that she ought not to have been sent to me, I ought to have gone to her. I thought it insane to take Soldier Boy to Spain, but it was well that I yielded to Cathy's pleadings; if he had been left behind, half of her heart would have remained with him, and she would not have been contented. As it is, everything has fallen out for the best, and we are all satisfied and comfortable. It may be that Dorcas and I will see America again some day; but also it is a case of maybe not.

We left the post in the early morning. It was an affecting time. The women cried over Cathy, so did even those stern warriors the Rocky Mountain Rangers; Shekels was there, and the Cid, and Sardanapalus, and Potter, and Mongrel, and Sour-Mash, Famine, and Pestilence, and Cathy kissed them all and wept; details of the several arms of the garrison were present to represent the rest, and say good-by and God bless you for all the soldiery; and there was a special squad from the Seventh, with the oldest veteran at its head, to speed the Seventh's Child with grand honors and impressive ceremonies; and the veteran had a touching speech by heart, and put up his hand in salute and tried to say it, but his lips trembled and his voice broke, but Cathy bent down from the saddle and kissed him on the mouth and turned his defeat to victory, and a cheer went up.

The next act closed the ceremonies, and was a moving surprise. It may be that you have discovered, before this, that the rigors of military law and custom melt insensibly away and disappear when a soldier or a regiment or the garrison wants to do something that will please Cathy. The bands conceived the idea of stirring her soldierly heart with a farewell which would remain in her memory always, beautiful and unfading, and bring back the past and its love for her whenever she should think of it; so they got their project placed before General Burnaby, my successor, who is Cathy's newest slave, and in spite of poverty of precedents they got his permission. The bands knew the child's favorite military airs. By this hint you know what is coming, but Cathy didn't. She was asked to sound the "reveille," which she did.

REVEILLE

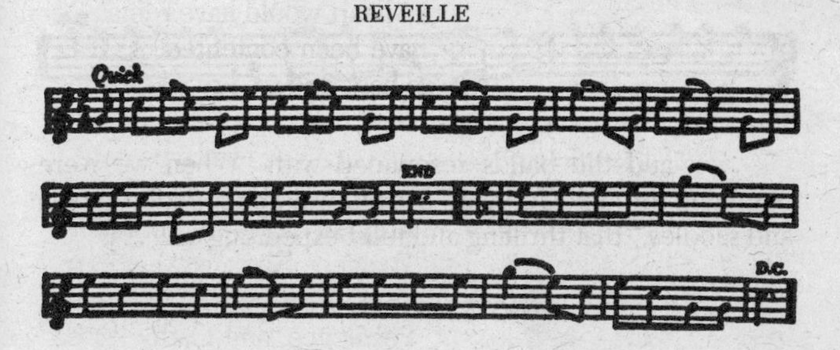

With the last note the bands burst out with a crash: and woke the mountains with the "Star-Spangled Banner" in a way to make a body's heart swell and thump and his hair rise! It was enough to break a person all up, to see Cathy's radiant face shining out through her gladness and tears. By request she blew the "assembly," now. . .

THE ASSEMBLY

. . . Then the bands thundered in, with "Rally round the flag, boys, rally once again!" Next, she blew another call ("to the Standard") . . .

TO THE STANDARD

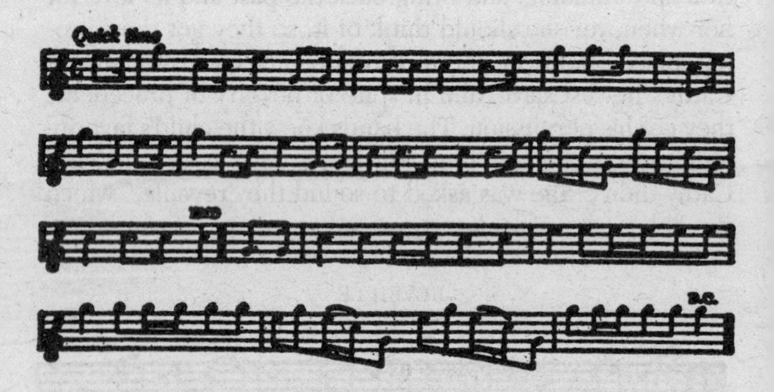

. . . and the bands responded with "When we were marching through Georgia." Straightway she sounded "boots and saddles," that thrilling and most expediting call. . . .

BOOTS AND SADDLES

. . . and the bands could hardly hold in for the final note; then they turned their whole strength loose on "Tramp, tramp, tramp, the boys are marching," and everybody's excitement rose to blood-heat.

Now an impressive pause—then the bugle sang "TAPS"—translatable, this time, into "Good-by, and God keep us all!" for taps is the soldier's nightly release from duty, and farewell: plaintive, sweet, pathetic, for the morning is never sure, for him; always it is possible that he is hearing it for the last time. . . .

TAPS

. . . Then the bands turned their instruments towards Cathy and burst in with that rollicking frenzy of a tune, "Oh, we'll all get blind drunk when Johnny comes marching home—yes, we'll all get blind drunk when Johnny comes marching home!" and followed it instantly with "Dixie," that antidote for melancholy, merriest and gladdest of all military music on any side of the ocean—and that was the end. And so—farewell!

I wish you could have been there to see it all, hear it all, and feel it: and get yourself blown away with the hurricane huzza that swept the place as a finish.

When we rode away, our main body had already been on the road an hour or two—I speak of our camp equipage; but we didn't move off alone: when Cathy blew the "advance" the Rangers cantered out in column of fours, and gave us escort, and were joined by White Cloud and Thunder-Bird in all their gaudy bravery, and by Buffalo Bill and four subordinate scouts. Three miles away, in the Plains, the Lieutenant-General halted, sat her horse like a military statue, the bugle at her lips, and put the Rangers through the evolutions for half an hour; and finally, when she blew the "charge," she led it herself. "Not for the last time," she said, and got a cheer, and we said good-by all around, and faced eastward and rode away.

Postscript. A Day Later. Soldier Boy was stolen last night. Cathy is almost beside herself, and we cannot comfort her. Mercedes and I are not much alarmed about the horse, although this part of Spain is in something of a turmoil, politically, at present, and there is a good deal of lawlessness. In ordinary times the thief and the horse would soon be captured. We shall have them before long, I think.

14 Soldier Boy—to Himself

It is five months. Or is it six? My troubles have clouded my memory. I think I have been all over this land, from end to end, and now I am back again since day before yesterday, to that city which we passed through, that last day of our long journey, and which is near her country home. I am a tottering ruin and my eyes are dim, but I recognized it. If she could see me she would know me and sound my call. I wish I could hear it once more; it would revive me, it would bring back her face and the mountains and the free life, and I would come—if I were dying I would come! She would not know *me*, looking as I do, but she would know me by my star. But she will never see me, for they do not let me out of this shabby stable—a foul and miserable place, with most two wrecks like myself for company.

How many times have I changed hands? I think it is twelve times—I cannot remember; and each time it was down a step lower, and each time I got a harder master. They have been cruel, every one; they have worked me night and day in degraded employments, and beaten me; they have fed me ill and some days not at all. And so I am but bones, now, with a rough and frowsy skin humped and cornered upon my shrunken body—that skin which was once so glossy, that skin which she loved to stroke with her hand. I was the pride of the mountains and the Great Plains; now I am a scarecrow and despised. These piteous wrecks that are my comrades here say we have reached the bottom of the scale, the final humiliation; they say that when a horse is no longer worth the weeds and discarded rubbish they feed to him, they sell him to the bull-ring for a glass of brandy, to make sport for the people and perish for their pleasure.

To die—that does not disturb me; we of the service never care for death. But if I could see her once more! if I could hear her bugle sing again and say, "It is I, Soldier—come!"

15 GENERAL ALISON TO MRS. DRAKE, THE COLONEL'S WIFE

To return, now, to where I was, and tell you the rest. We shall never know how she came to be there; there is no way to account for it. She was always watching for black and shiny and spirited horses—watching, hoping, despairing, hoping again; always giving chase and sounding her call, upon the meagerest chance of a response, and breaking her heart over the disappointment; always inquiring, always interested in sales-stables and horse accumulations in general. How she got there must remain a mystery.

At the point which I had reached in a preceding paragraph of this account, the situation was as follows: two horses lay dying; the bull had scattered his persecutors for the moment, and stood raging, panting, pawing the dust in clouds over his back, when the man that had been wounded returned to the ring on a remount, a poor blindfolded wreck that yet had something ironically military about his bearing—and the next moment the bull had ripped him open and his bowels were dragging upon the ground and the bull was charging his swarm of pests again. Then came pealing through the air a bugle-call that froze my blood—*"It is I, Soldier—come!"* I turned; Cathy was flying down through the massed people; she cleared the parapet at a bound, and sped towards that riderless horse, who staggered forward towards the remembered sound; but his strength failed, and he fell at her feet, she lavishing kisses upon him and sobbing, the house rising with one impulse, and white with horror! Before help could reach her the bull was back again—’

She was never conscious again in life. We bore her home, all mangled and drenched in blood, and knelt by her and listened to her broken and wandering words, and prayed for her passing spirit, and there was no comfort—nor ever will be, I think. But she was happy, for she was far away under another sky, and comrading again with her Rangers, and her animal friends, and the soldiers. Their names fell softly and caressingly from her lips, one by one, with pauses between. She was not in pain, but lay with closed eyes, vacantly murmuring, as one who dreams. Sometimes she smiled, saying nothing; sometimes she smiled when she uttered a name—such as Shekels, or BB, or Potter. Sometimes she was at her fort, issuing commands; sometimes she was careering over the plains at the head of her men; sometimes she was training her horse; once she said, reprovingly, “You are giving me the wrong foot; give me the left—don’t you know it is good-by?”

After this, she lay silent some time; the end was near. By and by she murmured, “Tired . . . sleepy . . . take Cathy, mamma.” Then “Kiss me, Soldier.” For a little time she lay so still that we were doubtful if she breathed. Then she put out her hand and began to feel gropingly about; then said, “I cannot find it; blow ‘taps.’ ”* It was the end.

TAPS

Slow

1906

* “Lights-Out”

Hunting the Deceitful Turkey

When I was a boy my uncle and his big boys hunted with the rifle, the youngest boy Fred and I with a shotgun—a small single-barrelled shotgun which was properly suited to our size and strength; it was not much heavier than a broom. We carried it turn about, half an hour at a time. I was not able to hit anything with it, but I liked to try. Fred and I hunted feathered small game, the others hunted deer, squirrels, wild turkeys, and such things. My uncle and the big boys were good shots. They killed hawks and wild geese and such like on the wing; and they didn't wound or kill squirrels, they *stunned* them. When the dogs treed a squirrel, the squirrel would scamper aloft and run out on a limb and flatten himself along it, hoping to make himself invisible in that way—and not quite succeeding. You could see his wee little ears sticking up. You couldn't see his nose, but you knew where it was. Then the hunter, despising a "rest" for his rifle, stood up and took offhand aim at the limb and sent a bullet into it immediately under the squirrel's nose, and down tumbled the animal, unwounded but unconscious; the dogs gave him a shake and he was dead. Sometimes when the distance was great and the wind not accurately allowed for, the bullet would hit the squirrel's head; the dogs could do as they pleased with that one—the hunter's pride was hurt, and he wouldn't allow it to go into the gamebag.

In the first faint gray of the dawn the stately wild turkeys would be stalking around in great flocks, and ready to be sociable and answer invitations to come and converse with other excursionists of their kind. The hunter concealed himself and imitated the turkey-call by sucking the air through the legbone of a turkey which had previously answered a call like that and lived only just long enough to regret it. There is nothing that furnishes a perfect turkey-call except that bone. Another of Nature's treacheries, you see. She is full of them; half the time she doesn't know which she likes best—to betray her child or protect it. In the case of the turkey she is badly mixed: she gives it a bone to be used in getting it into trouble, and she also furnishes it with a trick for getting itself out of the trouble again. When a mamma-turkey answers an invitation and finds she has made a mistake in accepting it, she does as the mamma-partridge does—remembers a previous engagement and goes limping and scrambling away, pretending to be very lame; and at the same time she is saying to her not-visible children, "Lie low, keep still, don't expose yourselves; I shall be back as soon as I have beguiled this shabby swindler out of the country."

When a person is ignorant and confiding, this immoral device can have tiresome results. I followed an ostensibly lame turkey over a considerable part of the United States one morning, because I believed in her and could not think she would deceive a mere boy, and one who was trusting her and considering her honest. I had the single-barrelled shotgun, but my idea was to catch her alive. I often got within rushing distance of her, and then made my rush; but always, just as I made my final plunge and put my hand down where her back had been, it wasn't there; it was only two or three inches from there and I brushed the tail-feathers as I landed on my stomach—a very close call, but still not quite close enough; that is, not close enough for success, but just close enough to convince me that I could do it next time. She always waited for me, a little piece away, and let on to be resting and greatly fatigued; which was a lie, but I believed it, for I still thought her honest long after I ought to have begun to doubt her, suspecting that this was no way for a high-minded bird to be acting. I followed, and followed, and followed, making my periodical rushes, and getting up and brushing the dust off, and resuming the voyage with patient confidence; indeed, with a confidence which grew, for I could see by the change of climate and vegetation that we were getting up into the high latitudes, and as she always looked a little tireder and a little more discouraged after each rush, I judged that I was safe to win, in the end, the competition being purely a matter of staying power and the advantage lying with me from the start because she was lame.

Along in the afternoon I began to feel fatigued myself. Neither of us had had any rest since we first started on the excursion, which was upwards of ten hours before, though latterly we had paused awhile after rushes, I letting on to be thinking about something else; but neither of us sincere, and both of us waiting for the other to call game but in no real hurry about it, for indeed those little evanescent snatches of rest were very grateful to the feelings of us both; it would naturally be so, skirmishing along like that ever since dawn and not a bite in the meantime; at least for me, though sometimes as she lay on her side fanning herself with a wing and praying for strength to get out of this difficulty a grasshopper happened along whose time had come, and that was well for her, and fortunate, but I had nothing—nothing the whole day.

More than once, after I was very tired, I gave up taking her alive, and was going to shoot her, but I never did it, although it was my right, for I did not believe I could hit her; and besides, she always stopped and posed, when I raised the gun, and this made me suspicious that she knew about me and my marksmanship, and so I did not care to expose myself to remarks.

I did not get her, at all. When she got tired of the game at last, she rose from almost under my hand and flew aloft with the rush and whir of a shell and lit on the highest limb of a great tree and sat down and crossed her legs and smiled down at me, and seemed gratified to see me so astonished.

I was ashamed, and also lost; and it was while wandering the woods hunting for myself that I found a deserted log cabin and had one of the best meals there that in my life-days I have eaten. The weed-grown garden was full of ripe tomatoes, and I ate them ravenously, though I had never liked them before. Not more than two or three times since have I tasted anything that was so delicious as those tomatoes. I surfeited myself with them, and did not taste another one until I was in middle life. I can eat them now, but I do not like the look of them. I suppose we have all experienced a surfeit at one time or another. Once, in stress of circumstances, I ate part of a barrel of sardines, there being nothing else at hand, but since then I have always been able to get along without sardines.

1906

Extract from Captain Stormfield's Visit to Heaven

1

Well, when I had been dead about thirty years, I begun to get a little anxious. Mind you, I had been whizzing through space all that time, like a comet. *Like* a comet! Why, Peters,[1] I laid over the lot of them! Of course there warn't any of them going my way, as a steady thing, you know, because they travel in a long circle like the loop of a lasso, whereas I was pointed as straight as a dart for the Hereafter; but I happened on one every now and then that was going my way for an hour or so, and then we had a bit of a brush together. But it was generally pretty one-sided, because I sailed by them the same as if they were standing still. An ordinary comet don't make more than about 200,000 miles a minute. Of course when I came across one of that sort—like Encke's and Halley's comets, for instance—it warn't anything but just a flash and a vanish, you see. You couldn't rightly call it a race. It was as if the comet was a gravel-train and I was a telegraph despatch. But after I got outside of our astronomical system, I used to flush a comet occasionally that was something *like*. *We* haven't got any such comets—ours don't begin. One night I was swinging along at a good round gait, everything taut and trim, and the wind in my favor—I judged I was going about a million miles a minute—it might have been more, it couldn't have been less—when I flushed a most uncommonly big one about three points off my starboard bow. By his stern lights I judged he was bearing about northeast-and-by-north-half-east. Well, it was so near my course that I wouldn't throw away the chance; so I fell off a point, steadied my helm, and went for him. You should have heard me whiz, and seen the electric fur fly! In about a minute and a half I was fringed out with an electrical nimbus that flamed around for miles and miles and lit up all space like broad day. The comet was burning blue in the distance, like a sickly torch, when I first sighted him, but he begun to grow bigger and bigger as I crept up on him. I slipped up on him so fast that when I had gone about 150,000,000 miles I was close enough to be swallowed up in the phosphorescent glory of his wake, and I couldn't see anything for the glare. Thinks I, it won't do to run into him, so I shunted to one side and tore along. By and by I closed up abreast of his tail. Do you know what it was like? It was like a gnat closing up on the continent of America. I forged along. By and by I had sailed along his coast for a little upwards of a hundred and fifty million miles, and then I could see by the shape of him that I hadn't even got up to his waistband yet. Why, Peters, *we* don't know anything about comets, down here. If you want to see comets that *are* comets, you've got to go outside of our solar system—where there's room for them, you understand. My friend, I've seen comets out there that couldn't even lay down inside the *orbits* of our noblest comets without their tails hanging over.

Well, I boomed along another hundred and fifty million miles, and got up abreast his shoulder, as you may say. I was feeling pretty fine, I tell you; but just then I noticed the officer of the deck come to the side and hoist his glass in my direction. Straight off I heard him sing out—

"Below there, ahoy! Shake her up, shake her up! Heave on a hundred million billion tons of brimstone!"

"Ay—ay, sir!"

"Pipe the starboard watch! All hands on deck!"

"Ay—ay, sir!"

"Send two hundred thousand million men aloft to shake out royals and sky-scrapers!"

"Ay—ay, sir!"

"Hand the stuns'ls! Hang out every rag you've got! Clothe her from stem to rudder-post!"

"Ay—ay, sir!"

In about a second I begun to see I'd woke up a pretty ugly customer, Peters. In less than ten seconds that comet was just a blazing cloud of red-hot canvas. It was piled up into the heavens clean out of sight—the old thing seemed to swell out and occupy all space; the sulphur smoke from the furnaces—oh, well, nobody can describe the way it rolled and tumbled up into the skies, and nobody can half describe the way it smelt. Neither can anybody begin to describe the way that monstrous craft begun to crash along. And such another powwow—thousands of bo's'n's whistles screaming at once, and a crew like the populations of a hundred thousand worlds like ours all swearing at once. Well, I never heard the like of it before.

We roared and thundered along side by side, both doing our level best, because I'd never struck a comet before that could lay over me, and so I was bound to beat this one or break something. I judged I had some reputation in space, and I calculated to keep it. I noticed I wasn't gaining as fast, now, as I was before, but still I was gaining. There was a power of excitement on board the comet. Upwards of a hundred billion passengers swarmed up from below and rushed to the side and begun to bet on the race. Of course this careened her and damaged her speed. My, but wasn't the mate mad! He jumped at that crowd, with his trumpet in his hand, and sung out—

"Amidships! amidships, you——!* or I'll brain the last idiot of you!"

Well, sir, I gained and gained, little by little, till at last I went skimming sweetly by the magnificent old conflagration's nose. By this time the captain of the comet had been rousted out, and he stood there in the red glare for'ard, by the mate, in his shirtsleeves and slippers, his hair all rats' nests and one suspender hanging, and how sick those two men did look! I just simply couldn't help putting my thumb to my nose as I glided away and singing out:

"Ta-ta! ta-ta! Any word to send to your family?"

Peters, it was a mistake. Yes, sir, I've often regretted that—it was a mistake. You see, the captain had given up the race, but that remark was too tedious for him—he couldn't stand it. He turned to the mate, and says he—

"Have we got brimstone enough of our own to make the trip?"

---

* The Captain could not remember what this word was. He said it was in a foreign tongue.

"Yes, sir."

"Sure?"

"Yes, sir—more than enough."

"How much have we got in cargo for Satan?"

"Eighteen hundred thousand billion quintillions of kazarks."

"Very well, then, let his boarders freeze till the next comet comes. Lighten ship! Lively, now, lively, men! Heave the whole cargo overboard!"

Peters, look me in the eye, and be calm. I found out, over there, that a kazark is exactly the bulk of a *hundred and sixty-nine worlds like ours!* They hove all that load overboard. When it fell it wiped out a considerable raft of stars just as clean as if they'd been candles and somebody blowed them out. As for the race, that was at an end. The minute she was lightened the comet swung along by me the same as if I was anchored. The captain stood on the stern, by the after-davits, and put his thumb to his nose and sung out—

"Ta-ta! ta-ta! Maybe *you've* got some message to send your friends in the Everlasting Tropics!"

Then he hove up his other suspender and started for'ard, and inside of three-quarters of an hour his craft was only a pale torch again in the distance. Yes, it was a mistake, Peters—that remark of mine. I don't reckon I'll ever get over being sorry about it. I'd 'a' beat the bully of the firmament if I'd kept my mouth shut.

But I've wandered a little off the track of my tale; I'll get back on my course again. Now you see what kind of speed I was making. So, as I said, when I had been tearing along this way about thirty years I begun to get uneasy. Oh, it was pleasant enough, with a good deal to find out, but then it was kind of lonesome, you know. Besides, I wanted to get somewhere. I hadn't shipped with the idea of cruising forever. First off, I liked the delay, because I judged I was going to fetch up in pretty warm quarters when I got through; but towards the last I begun to feel that I'd rather go to—well, most any place, so as to finish up the uncertainty.

Well, one night—it was always night, except when I was rushing by some star that was occupying the whole universe with its fire and its glare—light enough then, of course, but I necessarily left it behind in a minute or two and plunged into a solid week of darkness again. The stars ain't so close together as they look to be. Where was I? Oh yes; one night I was sailing along, when I discovered a tremendous long row of blinking lights away on the horizon ahead. As I approached, they begun to tower and swell and look like mighty furnaces. Says I to myself—

"By George, I've arrived at last—and at the wrong place, just as I expected!"

Then I fainted. I don't know how long I was insensible, but it must have been a good while, for, when I came to, the darkness was all gone and there was the loveliest sunshine and the balmiest, fragrantest air in its place. And there was such a marvelous world spread out before me—such a glowing, beautiful, bewitching country. The things I took for furnaces were gates, miles high, made all of flashing jewels, and they pierced a wall of solid gold that you couldn't see the top of, nor yet the end of, in either direction. I was pointed straight for one of these gates, and a-coming like a house afire. Now I noticed that the skies were black with millions of people, pointed for those gates. What a roar they made, rushing through the air! The ground was as thick as ants with people, too—billions of them, I judge.

I lit. I drifted up to a gate with a swarm of people, and when it was my turn the head clerk says, in a businesslike way—

"Well, quick! Where are you from?"

"San Francisco," says I.

"San Fran—*what?*" says he.

"San Francisco."

He scratched his head and looked puzzled, then he says—

"Is it a planet?"

By George, Peters, think of it! "*Planet?*" says I; "it's a city. And moreover, it's one of the biggest and finest and—"

"There, there!" says he, "no time here for conversation. We don't deal in cities here. Where are you from in a *general* way?"

"Oh," I says, "I beg your pardon. Put me down for California."

I had him *again*, Peters! He puzzled a second, then he says, sharp and irritable—

"I don't know any such planet—is it a constellation?"

"Oh, my goodness!" says I. "Constellation, says you? No—it's a State."

"Man, we don't deal in States here. *Will* you tell me where you are from *in general—at large*, don't you understand?"

"Oh, now I get your idea," I says. "I'm from America,—the United States of America."

Peters, do you know I had him *again?* If I hadn't I'm a clam! His face was as blank as a target after a militia shooting-match. He turned to an under clerk and says—

"Where is America? *What* is America?"

The under clerk answered up prompt and says—

"There ain't any such orb."

"*Orb?*" says I. "Why, what are you talking about, young man? It ain't an orb; it's a country; it's a continent. Columbus discovered it; I reckon likely you've heard of *him*, anyway. America—why, sir, America—"

"Silence!" says the head clerk. "Once for all, where—are—you—*from?*"

"Well," says I, "I don't know anything more to say—unless I lump things, and just say I'm from the world."

"Ah," says he, brightening up, "now that's something like! *What* world?"

Peters, he had *me*, that time. I looked at him, puzzled, he looked at me, worried. Then he burst out—

"Come, come, what world?"

Says I, "Why, *the* world, of course."

"*The* world!" he says. "H'm! there's billions of them! . . . Next!"

That meant for me to stand aside. I done so, and a sky-blue man with seven heads and only one leg hopped into my place. I took a walk. It just occurred to me, then, that all the myriads I had seen swarming to that gate, up to this time, were just like that creature. I tried to run across somebody I was acquainted with, but they were out of acquaintances of mine just then. So I thought the thing all over and finally sidled back there pretty meek and feeling rather stumped, as you may say.

"Well?" said the head clerk.

"Well, sir," I says, pretty humble, "I don't seem to make out which world it is I'm from. But you may know it from this—it's the one the Saviour saved."

He bent his head at the Name. Then he says, gently—

"The worlds He has saved are like to the gates of heaven in number—none can count them. What astronomical system is your world in?—perhaps that may assist."

"It's the one that has the sun in it—and the moon—and Mars"—he shook his head at each name—hadn't ever heard of them, you see—"and Neptune—and Uranus—and Jupiter—"

"Hold on!" says he—"hold on a minute! Jupiter . . . Jupiter . . . Seems to me we had a man from there eight or nine hundred years ago—but people from that system very seldom enter by this gate." All of a sudden he begun to look me so straight in the eye that I thought he was going to bore through me. Then he says, very deliberate, "Did you come *straight here* from your system?"

"Yes, sir," I says—but I blushed the least little bit in the world when I said it.

He looked at me very stern, and says—

"That is not true; and this is not the place for prevarication. You wandered from your course. How did that happen?"

Says I, blushing again—

"I'm sorry, and I take back what I said, and confess. I raced a little with a comet one day—only just the least little bit—only the tiniest lit—"

"So—so," says he—and without any sugar in his voice to speak of.

I went on, and says—

"But I only fell off just a bare point, and I went right back on my course again the minute the race was over."

"No matter—that divergence has made all this trouble. It has brought you to a gate that is billions of leagues from the right one. If you had gone to your own gate they would have known all about your world at once and there would have been no delay. But we will try to accommodate you." He turned to an under clerk and says—

"What system is Jupiter in?"

"I don't remember, sir, but I think there is such a planet in one of the little new systems away out in one of the thinly worlded corners of the universe. I will see."

He got a balloon and sailed up and up and up, in front of a map that was as big as Rhode Island. He went on up till he was out of sight, and by and by he came down and got something to eat and went up again. To cut a long story short, he kept on doing this for a day or two, and finally he came down and said he thought he had found that solar system, but it might be fly-specks. So he got a microscope and went back. It turned out better than he feared. He had rousted out our system, sure enough. He got me to describe our planet and its distance from the sun, and then he says to his chief—

"Oh, I know the one he means, now, sir. It is on the map. It is called the Wart."

Says I to myself, "Young man, it wouldn't be wholesome for you to go down *there* and call it the Wart."

Well, they let me in, then, and told me I was safe forever and wouldn't have any more trouble.

Then they turned from me and went on with their work, the same as if they considered my case all complete and shipshape. I was a good deal surprised at this, but I was diffident about speaking up and reminding them. I did so hate to do it, you know; it seemed a pity to bother them, they had so much on their hands. Twice I thought I would give up and let the thing go; so twice I started to leave, but immediately I thought what a figure I should cut stepping out amongst the redeemed in such a rig, and that made me hang back and come to anchor again. People got to eying me—clerks, you know—wondering why I didn't get under way. I couldn't stand this long—it was too uncomfortable. So at last I plucked up courage and tipped the head clerk a signal. He says—

"What! you here yet? What's wanting?"

Says I, in a low voice and very confidential, making a trumpet with my hands at his ear—

"I beg pardon, and you mustn't mind my reminding you, and seeming to meddle, but hain't you forgot something?"

He studied a second, and says—

"Forgot something? . . . No, not that I know of."

"Think," says I.

He thought. Then he says—

"No, I can't seem to have forgot anything. What is it?"

"Look at me," says I, "look me all over."

He done it.

"Well?" says he.

"Well," says I, "you don't notice anything? If I branched out amongst the elect looking like this, wouldn't I attract considerable attention?—wouldn't I be a little conspicuous?"

"Well," he says, "I don't see anything the matter. What do you lack?"

"Lack! Why, I lack my harp, and my wreath, and my halo, and my hymn-book, and my palm branch—I lack everything that a body naturally requires up here, my friend."

Puzzled? Peters, he was the worst puzzled man you ever saw. Finally he says—

"Well, you seem to be a curiosity every way a body takes you. I never heard of these things before."

I looked at the man awhile in solid astonishment; then I says—

"Now, I hope you don't take it as an offence, for I don't mean any, but really, for a man that has been in the Kingdom as long as I reckon you have, you do seem to know powerful little about its customs."

"Its customs!" says he. "Heaven is a large place, good friend. Large empires have many and diverse customs. Even small dominions have, as you doubtless know by what you have seen of the matter on a small scale in the Wart. How can you imagine I could ever learn the varied customs of the countless kingdoms of heaven? It makes my head ache to think of it. I know the customs that prevail in those portions inhabited by peoples that are appointed to enter by my own gate—and hark ye, that is quite enough knowledge for one individual to try to pack into his head in the thirty-seven millions of years I have devoted night and day to that study. But the idea of learning the customs of the whole appalling expanse of heaven—O man, how insanely you talk! Now I don't doubt that this odd costume you talk about is the fashion in that district of heaven you belong to, but you won't be conspicuous in this section without it."

I felt all right, if that was the case, so I bade him good-day and left. All day I walked towards the far end of a prodigious hall of the office, hoping to come out into heaven any moment, but it was a mistake. That hall was built on the general heavenly plan—it naturally couldn't be small. At last I got so tired I couldn't go any farther; so I sat down to rest, and began to tackle the queerest sort of strangers and ask for information, but I didn't get any; they couldn't understand my language, and I could not understand theirs. I got dreadfully lonesome. I was so downhearted and homesick I wished a hundred times I never had died. I turned back, of course. About noon next day, I got back at last and was on hand at the booking-office once more. Says I to the head clerk—

"I begin to see that a man's got to be in his own heaven to be happy."

"Perfectly correct," says he. "Did you imagine the same heaven would suit all sorts of men?"

"Well, I had that idea—but I see the foolishness of it. Which way am I to go to get to my district?"

He called the under clerk that had examined the map, and he gave me general directions. I thanked him and started; but he says—

"Wait a minute; it is millions of leagues from here. Go outside and stand on that red wishing-carpet; shut your eyes, hold your breath, and wish yourself there."

"I'm much obliged," says I; "why didn't you dart me through when I first arrived?"

"We have a good deal to think of here; it was your place to think of it and ask for it. Good-by; we probably sha'n't see you in this region for a thousand centuries or so."

"In that case, *o revoor*," says I.

I hopped onto the carpet and held my breath and shut my eyes and wished I was in the booking-office of my own section. The very next instant a voice I knew sung out in a business kind of a way—

"A harp and a hymn-book, pair of wings and a halo, size 13, for Cap'n Eli Stormfield, of San Francisco!—make him out a clean bill of health, and let him in."

I opened my eyes. Sure enough, it was a Pi Ute Injun I used to know in Tulare County; mighty good fellow—I remembered being at his funeral, which consisted of him being burnt and the other Injuns gauming their faces with his ashes and howling like wild-cats. He was powerful glad to see me, and you may make up your mind I was just as glad to see him, and felt that I was in the right kind of a heaven at last.

Just as far as your eye could reach, there was swarms of clerks, running and bustling around, tricking out thousands of Yanks and Mexicans and English and Arabs, and all sorts of people in their new outfits; and when they gave me my kit and I put on my halo and I took a look in the glass, I could have jumped over a house for joy, I was so happy. "Now *this* is something like!" says I. "Now," says I, "I'm all right—show me a cloud."

Inside of fifteen minutes I was a mile on my way towards the cloud-banks and about a million people along with me. Most of us tried to fly, but some got crippled and nobody made a success of it. So we concluded to walk, for the present, till we had had some wing practice.

We begun to meet swarms of folks who were coming back. Some had harps and nothing else; some had hymn-books and nothing else; some had nothing at all; all of them looked meek and uncomfortable; one young fellow hadn't anything left but his halo, and he was carrying that in his hand; all of a sudden he offered it to me and says—

"Will you hold it for me a minute?"

Then he disappeared in the crowd. I went on. A woman asked me to hold her palm branch, and then *she* disappeared. A girl got me to hold her harp for her, and by George, *she* disappeared; and so on and so on, till I was about loaded down to the guards. Then comes a smiling old gentleman and asked me to hold *his* things. I swabbed off the perspiration and says, pretty tart—

"I'll have to get you to excuse me, my friend,—*I* ain't no hat-rack."

About this time I begun to run across piles of those traps, lying in the road. I just quietly dumped my extra cargo along with them. I looked around, and, Peters, that whole nation that was following me were loaded down the same as I'd been. The return crowd had got them to hold their things a minute, you see. They all dumped their loads, too, and we went on.

When I found myself perched on a cloud, with a million other people, I never felt so good in my life. Says I, "Now this is according to the promises; I've been having my doubts, but now I *am* in heaven, sure enough." I gave my palm branch a wave or two, for luck, and then I tautened up my harp-strings and struck in. Well, Peters, you can't imagine anything like the row we made. It was grand to listen to, and made a body thrill all over, but there was considerable many tunes going on at once, and that was a drawback to the harmony, you understand; and then there was a lot of Injun tribes, and they kept up such another war-whooping that they kind of took the tuck out of the music. By and by I quit performing, and judged I'd take a rest. There was quite a nice mild old gentleman sitting next me, and I noticed he didn't take a hand; I encouraged him, but he said he was naturally bashful, and was afraid to try before so many people. By and by the old gentleman said he never could seem to enjoy music somehow. The fact was, I was beginning to feel the same way; but I didn't say anything. Him and I had a considerable long silence, then, but of course it warn't noticeable in that place. After about sixteen or seventeen hours, during which I played and sung a little, now and then—always the same tune, because I didn't know any other—I laid down my harp and begun to fan myself with my palm branch. Then we both got to sighing pretty regular. Finally, says he—

"Don't you know any tune but the one you've been pegging at all day?"

"Not another blessed one," says I.

"Don't you reckon you could learn another one?" says he.

"Never," says I; "I've tried to, but I couldn't manage it."

"It's a long time to hang to the one—eternity, you know."

"Don't break my heart," says I; "I'm getting low-spirited enough already."

After another long silence, says he—

"Are you glad to be here?"

Says I, "Old man, I'll be frank with you. This *ain't* just as near my idea of bliss as I thought it was going to be, when I used to go to church."

Says he, "What do you say to knocking off and calling it half a day?"

"That's me," says I. "I never wanted to get off watch so bad in my life."

So we started. Millions were coming to the cloud-bank all the time, happy and hosannahing; millions were leaving it all the time, looking mighty quiet, I tell you. We laid for the new-comers, and pretty soon I'd got them to hold all my things a minute, and then I was a free man again and most outrageously happy. Just then I ran across old Sam Bartlett, who had been dead a long time, and stopped to have a talk with him. Says I—

"Now tell me—is this to go on forever? Ain't there anything else for a change?"

Says he—

"I'll set you right on that point very quick. People take the figurative language of the Bible and the allegories for literal, and the first thing they ask for when they get here is a halo and a harp, and so on. Nothing that's harmless and reasonable is refused a body here, if he asks it in the right spirit. So they are outfitted with these things without a word. They go and sing and play just about one day, and that's the last you'll ever see them in the choir. They don't need anybody to tell them that that sort of thing wouldn't make a heaven—at least not a heaven that a sane man could stand a week and remain sane. That cloud-bank is placed where the noise can't disturb the old inhabitants, and so there ain't any harm in letting everybody get up there and cure himself as soon as he comes.

"Now you just remember this—heaven is as blissful and lovely as it can be; but it's just the busiest place you ever heard of. There ain't any idle people here after the first day. Singing hymns and waving palm branches through all eternity is pretty when you hear about it in the pulpit, but it's as poor a way to put in valuable time as a body could contrive. It would just make a heaven of warbling ignoramuses, don't you see? Eternal Rest sounds comforting in the pulpit, too. Well, you try it once, and see how heavy time will hang on your hands. Why, Stormfield, a man like you, that had been active and stirring all his life, would go mad in six months in a heaven where he hadn't anything to do. Heaven is the very last place to come to *rest* in,—and don't you be afraid to bet on that!"

Says I—

"Sam, I'm as glad to hear it as I thought I'd be sorry. I'm glad I come, now."

Says he—

"Cap'n, ain't you pretty physically tired?"

Says I—

"Sam, it ain't any name for it! I'm dog-tired."

"Just so—just so. You've earned a good sleep, and you'll get it. You've earned a good appetite, and you'll enjoy your dinner. It's the same here as it is on earth—you've got to earn a thing, square and honest, before you enjoy it. You can't enjoy first and earn afterwards. But there's this difference, here: you can choose your own occupation, and all the powers of heaven will be put forth to help you make a success of it, if you do your level best. The shoemaker on earth that had the soul of a poet in him won't have to make shoes here."

"Now that's all reasonable and right," says I. "Plenty of work, and the kind you hanker after; no more pain, no more suffering—"

"Oh, hold on; there's plenty of pain here—but it don't kill. There's plenty of suffering here, but it don't last. You see, happiness ain't a *thing in itself*—it's only a *contrast* with something that ain't pleasant. That's all it is. There ain't a thing you can mention that is happiness in its own self—it's only so by contrast with the other thing. And so, as soon as the novelty is over and the force of the contrast dulled, it ain't happiness any longer, and you have to get something fresh. Well, there's plenty of pain and suffering in heaven—consequently there's plenty of contrasts, and just no end of happiness."

Says I, "It's the sensiblest heaven I've heard of, yet, Sam, though it's about as different from the one I was brought up on as a live princess is different from her own wax figger."

Along in the first months I knocked around about the Kingdom, making friends and looking at the country, and finally settled down in a pretty likely region, to have a rest before taking another start. I went on making acquaintances and gathering up information. I had a good deal of talk with an old bald-headed angel by the name of Sandy McWilliams. He was from somewhere in New Jersey. I went about with him, considerable. We used to lay around, warm afternoons, in the shade of a rock, on some meadow-ground that was pretty high and out of the marshy slush of his cranberry-farm, and there we used to talk about all kinds of things, and smoke pipes. One day, says I—

"About how old might you be, Sandy?"

"Seventy-two."

"I judged so. How long you been in heaven?"

"Twenty-seven years, come Christmas."

"How old was you when you come up?"

"Why, seventy-two, of course."

"You can't mean it!"

"Why can't I mean it?"

"Because, if you was seventy-two then, you are naturally ninety-nine now."

"No, but I ain't. I stay the same age I was when I come."

"Well," says I, "come to think, there's something just here that I want to ask about. Down below, I always had an idea that in heaven we would all be young, and bright, and spry."

"Well, you *can* be young if you want to. You've only got to wish."

"Well, then, why didn't you wish?"

"I did. They all do. You'll try it, some day, like enough; but you'll get tired of the change pretty soon."

"Why?"

"Well, I'll tell you. Now you've always been a sailor; did you ever try some other business?"

"Yes, I tried keeping grocery, once, up in the mines; but I couldn't stand it; it was too dull—no stir, no storm, no life about it; it was like being part dead and part alive, both at the same time. I wanted to be one thing or t'other. I shut up shop pretty quick and went to sea."

"That's it. Grocery people like it, but you couldn't. You see you wasn't used to it. Well, I wasn't used to being young, and I couldn't seem to take any interest in it. I was strong, and handsome, and had curly hair,—yes, and wings, too!—gay wings like a butterfly. I went to picnics and dances and parties with the fellows, and tried to carry on and talk nonsense with the girls, but it wasn't any use; I couldn't take to it—fact is, it was an awful bore. What I wanted was early to bed and early to rise, and something to *do;* and when my work was done, I wanted to sit quiet, and smoke and think—not tear around with a parcel of giddy young kids. You can't think what I suffered whilst I was young."

"How long was you young?"

"Only two weeks. That was plenty for me. Laws, I was so lonesome! You see, I was full of the knowledge and experience of seventy-two years; the deepest subject those young folks could strike was only *a-b-c* to me. And to hear them argue—oh, my! it would have been funny, if it hadn't been so pitiful. Well, I was so hungry for the ways and the sober talk I was used to, that I tried to ring in with the old people, but they wouldn't have it. They considered me a conceited young up-start, and gave me the cold shoulder. Two weeks was a-plenty for me. I was glad to get back my bald head again, and my pipe, and my old drowsy reflections in the shade of a rock or a tree."

"Well," says I, "do you mean to say you're going to stand still at seventy-two, forever?"

"I don't know, and I ain't particular. But I ain't going to drop back to twenty-five any more—I know that, mighty well. I know a sight more than I did twenty-seven years ago, and I enjoy learning, all the time, but I don't seem to get any older. That is, bodily—my mind gets older, and stronger, and better seasoned, and more satisfactory."

Says I, "If a man comes here at ninety, don't he ever set himself back?"

"Of course he does. He sets himself back to fourteen; tries it a couple of hours, and feels like a fool; sets himself forward to twenty; it ain't much improvement; tries thirty, fifty, eighty, and finally ninety—finds he is more at home and comfortable at the same old figure he is used to than any other way. Or, if his mind begun to fail him on earth at eighty, that's where he finally sticks up here. He sticks at the place where his mind was last at its best, for there's where his enjoyment is best, and his ways most set and established."

"Does a chap of twenty-five stay always twenty-five, and look it?"

"If he is a fool, yes. But if he is bright, and ambitious and industrious, the knowledge he gains and the experience he has, change his ways and thoughts and likings, and make him find his best pleasure in the company of people above that age; so he allows his body to take on that look of as many added years as he needs to make him comfortable and proper in that sort of society; he lets his body go on taking the look of age, according as he progresses, and by and by he will be bald and wrinkled outside, and wise and deep within."

"Babies the same?"

"Babies the same. Laws, what asses we used to be, on earth, about these things! We said we'd be always young in heaven. We didn't say *how* young—we didn't think of that, perhaps—that is, we didn't all think alike, anyway. When I was a boy of seven, I suppose I thought we'd all be twelve, in heaven; when I was twelve, I suppose I thought we'd all be eighteen or twenty in heaven; when I was forty, I begun to go back; I remember I hoped we'd all be about *thirty* years old in heaven. Neither a man nor a boy ever thinks the age he *has* is exactly the best one—he puts the *right* age a few years older or a few years younger than he is. Then he makes the ideal age the general age of the heavenly people. And he expects everybody to *stick* at that age—stand stock-still—and expects them to enjoy it!— Now just think of the idea of standing still in heaven! Think of a heaven made up entirely of hoop-rolling, marble-playing cubs of seven years!—or of awkward, diffident, sentimental immaturities of nineteen!—or of vigorous people of thirty, healthy-minded, brimming with ambition, but chained hand and foot to that one age and its limitations like so many helpless galley-slaves! Think of the dull sameness of a society made up of people all of one age and one set of looks, habits, tastes and feelings. Think how superior to it earth would be, with its variety of types and faces and ages, and the enlivening attrition of the myriad interests that come into pleasant collision in such a variegated society."

"Look here," says I, "do you know what you're doing?"

"Well, what am I doing?"

"You are making heaven pretty comfortable in one way, but you are playing the mischief with it in another."

"How d'you mean?"

"Well," I says, "take a young mother that's lost her child, and—"

" 'Sh!" he says. "Look!"

It was a woman. Middle-aged, and had grizzled hair. She was walking slow, and her head was bent down, and her wings hanging limp and droopy; and she looked ever so tired, and was crying, poor thing! She passed along by, with her head down, that way, and the tears running down her face, and didn't see us. Then Sandy said, low and gentle, and full of pity:

"*She's* hunting for her child! No, *found* it, I reckon. Lord, how she's changed! But I recognized her in a minute, though it's twenty-seven years since I saw her. A young mother she was, about twenty-two or four, or along there; and blooming and lovely and sweet—oh, just a flower! And all her heart and all her soul was wrapped up in her child, her little girl, two years old. And it died, and she went wild with grief, just wild! Well, the only comfort she had was that she'd see her child again, in heaven—'never more to part,' she said, and kept on saying it over and over, 'never more to part.' And the words made her happy; yes, they did; they made her joyful; and when I was dying, twenty-seven years ago, she told me to find her child the first thing, and say she was coming—'soon, soon, *very* soon, she hoped and believed!' "

"Why, it's pitiful, Sandy."

He didn't say anything for a while, but sat looking at the ground, thinking. Then he says, kind of mournful:

"And now she's come!"

"Well? Go on."

"Stormfield, maybe she hasn't found the child, but *I* think she has. Looks so to me. I've seen cases before. You see, she's kept that child in her head just the same as it was when she jounced it in her arms a little chubby thing. But here it didn't elect to *stay* a child. No, it elected to grow up, which it did. And in these twenty-seven years it has learned all the deep scientific learning there is to learn, and is studying and studying and learning and learning more and more, all the time, and don't give a damn for anything *but* learning; just learning, and discussing gigantic problems with people like herself."

"Well?"

"Stormfield, don't you see? Her mother knows *cranberries*, and how to tend them, and pick them, and put them up, and market them; and not another blamed thing! Her and her daughter can't be any more company for each other *now* than mud turtle and bird o' paradise. Poor thing, she was looking for a baby to jounce; *I* think she's struck a disappointment."

"Sandy, what will they do—stay unhappy forever in heaven?"

"No, they'll come together and get adjusted by and by. But not this year, and not next. By and by."

2

I had been having considerable trouble with my wings. The day after I helped the choir I made a dash or two with them, but was not lucky. First off, I flew thirty yards, and then fouled an Irishman and brought him down—brought us both, down, in fact. Next, I had a collision with a Bishop—and bowled him down, of course. We had some sharp words, and I felt pretty cheap, to come banging into a grave old person like that, with a million strangers looking on and smiling to themselves.

I saw I hadn't got the hang of the steering, and so couldn't rightly tell where I was going to bring up when I started. I went afoot the rest of the day, and let my wings hang. Early next morning I went to a private place to have some practice. I got up on a pretty high rock, and got a good start, and went swooping down, aiming for a bush a little over three hundred yards off; but I couldn't seem to calculate for the wind, which was about two points abaft my beam. I could see I was going considerable to looard of the bush, so I worked my starboard wing slow and went ahead strong on the port one, but it wouldn't answer; I could see I was going to broach to, so I slowed down on both, and lit. I went back to the rock and took another chance at it. I aimed two or three points to starboard of the bush—yes, more than that—enough so as to make it nearly a head-wind. I done well enough, but made pretty poor time. I could see, plain enough, that on a head-wind, wings was a mistake. I could see that a body could sail pretty close to the wind, but he couldn't go in the wind's eye. I could see that if I wanted to go a-visiting any distance from home, and the wind was ahead, I might have to wait days, maybe, for a change; and I could see, too, that these things could not be any use at all in a gale; if you tried to run before the wind, you would make a mess of it, for there isn't any way to shorten sail—like reefing, you know—you have to take it *all* in—shut your feathers down flat to your sides. That would *land* you, of course. You could lay to, with your head to the wind—that is the best you could do, and right hard work, you'd find it, too. If you tried any other game, you would founder, sure.

I judge it was about a couple of weeks or so after this that I dropped old Sandy McWilliams a note one day—it was a Tuesday—and asked him to come over and take his manna and quails with me next day; and the first thing he did when he stepped in was to twinkle his eye in a sly way, and say,—

"Well, Cap, what you done with your wings?"

I saw in a minute that there was some sarcasm done up in that rag somewheres, but I never let on. I only says,—

"Gone to the wash."

"Yes," he says, in a dry sort of way, "they mostly go to the wash—about this time—I've often noticed it. Fresh angels are powerful neat. When do you look for 'em back?"

"Day after to-morrow," says I.

He winked at me, and smiled.

Says I,—

"Sandy, out with it. Come—no secrets among friends. I notice you don't ever wear wings—and plenty others don't. I've been making an ass of myself—is that it?"

"That is about the size of it. But it is no harm. We all do it at first. It's perfectly natural. You see, on earth we jumped to such foolish conclusions as to things up here. In the pictures we always saw the angels with wings on—and that was all right; but we jumped to the conclusion that that was their way of getting around—and that was all wrong. The wings ain't anything but a uniform, that's all. When they are in the field—so to speak—they always wear them; you never see an angel going with a message anywhere without his wings, any more than you would see a military officer presiding at a court-martial without his uniform, or a postman delivering letters, or a policeman walking his beat, in plain clothes. But they ain't to *fly* with! The wings are for show, not for use. Old experienced angels are like officers of the regular army—they dress plain, when they are off duty. New angels are like the militia—never shed the uniform—always fluttering and floundering around in their wings, butting people down, flapping here, and there, and everywhere, always imagining they are attracting the admiring eye—well, they just think they are the very most important people in heaven. And when you see one of them come sailing around with one wing tipped up and t'other down, you make up your mind he is saying to himself: 'I wish Mary Ann in Arkansaw could see me now. I reckon she'd wish she hadn't shook me.' No, they're just for show, that's all—only just for show."

"I judge you've got it about right, Sandy," says I.

"Why, look at it yourself," says he. "*You* ain't built for wings—no man is. You know what a grist of years it took you to come here from the earth—and yet you were booming along faster than any cannon-ball could go. Suppose you had to fly that distance with your wings—wouldn't eternity have been over before you got here? Certainly. Well, angels have to go to the earth every day—millions of them—to appear in visions to dying children and good people, you know—it's the heft of their business. They appear with their wings, of course, because they are on official service, and because the dying persons wouldn't know they were angels if they hadn't wings—but do you reckon they fly with them? It stands to reason they don't. The wings would wear out before they got half-way; even the pinfeathers would be gone; the wing frames would be as bare as kite sticks before the paper is pasted on. The distances in heaven are billions of times greater; angels have to go all over heaven every day; could they do it with their wings alone? No, indeed; they wear the wings for style, but they travel any distance in an instant by *wishing*. The wishing-carpet of the Arabian Nights was a sensible idea—but our earthly idea of angels flying these awful distances with their clumsy wings was foolish.

"Our young saints, of both sexes, wear wings all the time—blazing red ones, and blue and green, and gold, and variegated, and rainbowed, and ring-streaked-and-striped ones—and nobody finds fault. It is suitable to their time of life. The things are beautiful, and they set the young people off. They are the most striking and lovely part of their outfit—a halo don't *begin*."

"Well," says I, "I've tucked mine away in the cupboard, and I allow to let them lay there till there's mud."

"Yes—or a reception."

"What's that?"

"Well, you can see one to-night if you want to. There's a barkeeper from Jersey City going to be received."

"Go on—tell me about it."

"This barkeeper got converted at a Moody and Sankey meeting, in New York, and started home on the ferryboat, and there was a collision and he got drowned. He is of a class that thinks all heaven goes wild with joy when a particularly hard lot like him is saved; they think all heaven turns out hosannahing to welcome them; they think there isn't anything talked about in the realms of the blest but their case, for that day. This barkeeper thinks there hasn't been such another stir here in years, as his coming is going to raise.— And I've always noticed this peculiarity about a dead barkeeper—he not only expects all hands to turn out when he arrives, but he expects to be received with a torchlight procession."

"I reckon he is disappointed, then."

"No, he isn't. No man is allowed to be disappointed here. Whatever he wants, when he comes—that is, any reasonable and unsacrilegious thing—he can have. There's always a few millions or billions of young folks around who don't want any better entertainment than to fill up their lungs and swarm out with their torches and have a high time over a barkeeper. It tickles the barkeeper till he can't rest, it makes a charming lark for the young folks, it don't do anybody any harm, it don't cost a rap, and it keeps up the place's reputation for making all comers happy and content."

"Very good. I'll be on hand and see them land the barkeeper."

"It is manners to go in full dress. You want to wear your wings, you know, and your other things."

"Which ones?"

"Halo, and harp, and palm branch, and all that."

"Well," says I, "I reckon I ought to be ashamed of myself, but the fact is I left them laying around that day I resigned from the choir. I haven't got a rag to wear but this robe and the wings."

"That's all right. You'll find they've been raked up and saved for you. Send for them."

"I'll do it, Sandy. But what was it you was saying about unsacrilegious things, which people expect to get, and will be disappointed about?"

"Oh, there are a lot of such things that people expect and don't get. For instance, there's a Brooklyn preacher by the name of Talmage, who is laying up a considerable disappointment for himself. He says, every now and then in his sermons, that the first thing he does when he gets to heaven, will be to fling his arms around Abraham, Isaac and Jacob, and kiss them and weep on them. There's millions of people down there on earth that are promising themselves the same thing. As many as sixty thousand people arrive here every single day, that want to run straight to Abraham, Isaac and Jacob, and hug them and weep on them. Now mind you, sixty thousand a day is a pretty heavy contract for those old people. If they were a mind to allow it, they wouldn't ever have anything to do, year in and year out, but stand up and be hugged and wept on thirty-two hours in the twenty-four. They would be tired out and as wet as muskrats all the time. What would heaven be, to *them?* It would be a mighty good place to get out of—you know that, yourself. Those are kind and gentle old Jews, but they ain't any fonder of kissing the emotional high-lights of Brooklyn than you be. You mark my words, Mr. T.'s endearments are going to be declined, with thanks. There are limits to the privileges of the elect, even in heaven. Why, if Adam was to show himself to every new comer that wants to call and gaze at him and strike him for his autograph, he would never have time to do anything else but just that. Talmage has said he is going to give Adam some of his attentions, as well as A., I. and J. But he will have to change his mind about that."

"Do you think Talmage will really come here?"

"Why, certainly, he will; but don't you be alarmed; he will run with his own kind, and there's plenty of them. That is the main charm of heaven—there's all kinds here—which wouldn't be the case if you let the preachers tell it. Anybody can find the sort he prefers, here, and he just lets the others alone, and they let him alone. When the Deity builds a heaven, it is built right, and on a liberal plan."

Sandy sent home for his things, and I sent for mine, and about nine in the evening we begun to dress. Sandy says,—

"This is going to be a grand time for you, Stormy. Like as not some of the patriarchs will turn out."

"No, but will they?"

"Like as not. Of course they are pretty exclusive. They hardly ever show themselves to the common public. I believe they never turn out except for an eleventh-hour convert. They wouldn't do it then, only earthly tradition makes a grand show pretty necessary on that kind of an occasion."

"Do they all turn out, Sandy?"

"Who?—all the patriarchs? Oh, no—hardly ever more than a couple. You will be here fifty thousand years—maybe more—before you get a glimpse of all the patriarchs and prophets. Since I have been here, Job has been to the front once, and once Ham and Jeremiah both at the same time. But the finest thing that has happened in my day was a year or so ago; that was Charles Peace's[2] reception—him they called 'the Bannercross Murderer'—an Englishman. There were four patriarchs and two prophets on the Grand Stand that time—there hasn't been anything like it since Captain Kidd[3] came; Abel was there—the first time in twelve hundred years. A report got around that Adam was coming; well, of course, Abel was enough to bring a crowd, all by himself, but there is nobody that can draw like Adam. It was a false report, but it got around, anyway, as I say, and it will be a long day before I see the like of it again. The reception was in the English department, of course, which is eight hundred and eleven million miles from the New Jersey line. I went, along with a good many of my neighbors, and it was a sight to see, I can tell you. Flocks came from all the departments. I saw Esquimaux there, and Tartars, Negroes, Chinamen—people from everywhere. You see a mixture like that in the Grand Choir, the first day you land here, but you hardly ever see it again. There were billions of people; when they were singing or hosannahing, the noise was wonderful; and even when their tongues were still the drumming of the wings was nearly enough to burst your head, for all the sky was as thick as if it was snowing angels. Although Adam was not there, it was a great time anyway, because we had three archangels on the Grand Stand—it is a seldom thing that even one comes out."

"What did they look like, Sandy?"

"Well, they had shining faces, and shining robes, and wonderful rainbow wings, and they stood eighteen feet high, and wore swords, and held their heads up in a noble way, and looked like soldiers."

"Did they have halos?"

"No—anyway, not the hoop kind. The archangels and the upper-class patriarchs wear a finer thing than that. It is a round, solid, splendid glory of gold, that is blinding to look at. You have often seen a patriarch in a picture, on earth, with that thing on—you remember it?—he looks as if he had his head in a brass platter. That don't give you the right idea of it at all—it is much more shining and beautiful."

"Did you talk with those archangels and patriarchs, Sandy?"

"Who—*I*? Why, what can you be thinking about, Stormy? I ain't worthy to speak to such as they."

"Is Talmage?"

"Of course not. You have got the same mixed-up idea about these things that everybody has down there. I had it once, but I got over it. Down there they talk of the heavenly King—and that is right—but then they go right on speaking as if this was a republic and everybody was on a dead level with everybody else, and privileged to fling his arms around anybody he comes across, and be hail-fellow-well-met with all the elect, from the highest down. How tangled up and absurd that is! How are you going to have a republic under a king? How are you going to have a republic at all, where the head of the government is absolute, holds his place forever, and has no parliament, no council to meddle or make in his affairs, nobody voted for, nobody elected, nobody in the whole universe with a voice in the government, nobody asked to take a hand in its matters, and nobody *allowed* to do it? Fine republic, ain't it?"

"Well, yes—it *is* a little different from the idea I had—but I thought I might go around and get acquainted with the grandees, anyway—not exactly splice the main-brace with them, you know, but shake hands and pass the time of day."

"Could Tom, Dick and Harry call on the Cabinet of Russia and do that?—on Prince Gortschakoff, for instance?"

"I reckon not, Sandy."

"Well, this is Russia—only more so. There's not the

shadow of a republic about it anywhere. There are ranks, here. There are viceroys, princes, governors, sub-governors, sub-sub-governors, and a hundred orders of nobility, grading along down from grand-ducal archangels, stage by stage, till the general level is struck, where there ain't any titles. Do you know what a prince of the blood is, on earth?"

"No."

"Well, a prince of the blood don't belong to the royal family exactly, and he don't belong to the mere nobility of the kingdom; he is lower than the one, and higher than t'other. That's about the position of the patriarchs and prophets here. There's some mighty high nobility here—people that you and I ain't worthy to polish sandals for—and *they* ain't worthy to polish sandals for the patriarchs and prophets. That gives you a kind of an idea of their rank, don't it? You begin to see how high up they are, don't you? Just to get a two-minute glimpse of one of them is a thing for a body to remember and tell about for a thousand years. Why, Captain, just think of this: if Abraham was to set his foot down here by this door, there would be a railing set up around that foot-track right away, and a shelter put over it, and people would flock here from all over heaven, for hundreds and hundreds of years, to look at it. Abraham is one of the parties that Mr. Talmage, of Brooklyn, is going to embrace, and kiss, and weep on, when he comes. He wants to lay in a good stock of tears, you know, or five to one he will go dry before he gets a chance to do it."

"Sandy," says I, "I had an idea that *I* was going to be equal with everybody here, too, but I will let that drop. It don't matter, and I am plenty happy enough anyway."

"Captain, you are happier than you would be, the other way. These old patriarchs and prophets have got ages the start of you; they know more in two minutes than you know in a year. Did you ever try to have a sociable improving-time discussing winds, and currents and variations of compass with an undertaker?"

"I get your idea, Sandy. He couldn't interest me. He would be an ignoramus in such things—he would bore me, and I would bore him."

"You have got it. You would bore the patriarchs when you talked, and when they talked they would shoot over your head. By and by you would say, 'Good morning, your Eminence, I will call again'—but you wouldn't. Did you ever ask the slush-boy to come up in the cabin and take dinner with you?"

"I get your drift again, Sandy. I wouldn't be used to such grand people as the patriarchs and prophets, and I would be sheepish and tongue-tied in their company, and mighty glad to get out of it. Sandy, which is the highest rank, patriarch or prophet?"

"Oh! the prophets hold over the patriarchs. The newest prophet, even, is of a sight more consequence than the oldest patriarch. Yes, sir, Adam himself has to walk behind Shakespeare."

"Was Shakespeare a prophet?"

"Of course he was; and so was Homer,[4] and heaps more. But Shakespeare and the rest have to walk behind a common tailor from Tennessee, by the name of Billings; and behind a horse-doctor named Sakka, from Afghanistan. Jeremiah, and Billings and Buddha walk together, side by side, right behind a crowd from planets not in our astronomy; next come a dozen or two from Jupiter and other worlds; next come Daniel, and Sakka and Confucius; next a lot from systems outside of ours; next come Ezekiel, and Mahomet,[5] Zoroaster,[6] and a knife-grinder from ancient Egypt; then there is a long string, and after them, away down toward the bottom, come Shakespeare and Homer, and a shoemaker named Marais, from the back settlements of France."

"Have they really rung in Mahomet and all those other heathens?"

"Yes—they all had their message, and they all get their reward. The man who don't get his reward on earth, needn't bother—he will get it here, sure."

"But why did they throw off on Shakespeare, that way, and put him away down there below those shoemakers and horse-doctors and knife-grinders—a lot of people nobody ever heard of?"

"That is the heavenly justice of it—they warn't rewarded according to their deserts, on earth, but here they get their rightful rank. That tailor Billings, from Tennessee, wrote poetry that Homer and Shakespeare couldn't begin to come up to; but nobody would print it, nobody read it but his neighbors, an ignorant lot, and they laughed at it. Whenever the village had a drunken frolic and a dance, they would drag him in and crown him with cabbage leaves, and pretend to bow down to him; and one night when he was sick and nearly starved to death, they had him out and crowned him, and then they rode him on a rail about the village, and everybody followed along, beating tin pans and yelling. Well, he died before morning. He wasn't ever expecting to go to heaven, much less that there was going to be any fuss made over him, so I reckon he was a good deal surprised when the reception broke on him."

"Was you there, Sandy?"

"Bless you, no!"

"Why? Didn't you know it was going to come off?"

"Well, I judge I did. It was the talk of these realms—not for a day, like this barkeeper business, but for twenty years before the man died."

"Why the mischief didn't you go, then?"

"Now how you talk! The like of me go meddling around at the reception of a prophet? A mudsill like me trying to push in and help receive an awful grandee like Edward J. Billings? Why, I should have been laughed at for a billion miles around. I shouldn't ever heard the last of it."

"Well, who did go, then?"

"Mighty few people that you and I will ever get a chance to see, Captain. Not a solitary commoner ever has the luck to see a reception of a prophet, I can tell you. All the nobility, and all the patriarchs and prophets—every last one of them—and all the archangels, and all the princes and governors and viceroys, were there,—and *no* small fry—not a single one. And mind you, I'm not talking about only the grandees from *our* world, but the princes and patriarchs and so on from *all* the worlds that shine in our sky, and from billions more that belong in systems upon systems away outside of the one our sun is in. There were some prophets and patriarchs there that ours ain't a circumstance to, for rank and illustriousness and all that. Some were from Jupiter and other worlds in our own system, but the most celebrated were three poets, Saa, Bo and Soof, from great planets in three different and very remote systems. These three names are common and familiar in every nook and corner of heaven, clear from one end of it to the other—fully as well known as the eighty Supreme Archangels, in fact—whereas our Moses, and Adam, and the rest, have not been heard of outside of our world's little corner of heaven, except by a few very learned men scattered here and there—and they always spell their names wrong, and get the performances of one mixed up with the doings of another, and they almost always locate them simply *in our solar system*, and think that is enough without going into little details such as naming the particular world they are from. It is like a learned Hindoo showing off how much he knows by saying Longfellow lived in the United States—as if he lived all over the United States, and as if the country was so small you couldn't throw a brick there without hitting him. Between you and me, it does gravel me, the cool way people from those monster worlds outside our system snub our little world, and even our system. Of course we think a good deal of Jupiter, because our world is only a potato to it, for size; but then there are worlds in other systems that Jupiter isn't even a mustard-seed to—like the planet Goobra, for instance, which you couldn't squeeze inside the orbit of Haley's comet without straining the rivets. Tourists from Goobra (I mean parties that lived and died there—natives) come here, now and then, and inquire about our world, and when they find out it is so little that a streak of lightning can flash clear around it in the eighth of a second, they have to lean up against something to laugh. Then they screw a glass into their eye and go to examining *us*, as if we were a curious kind of foreign bug, or something of that sort. One of them asked me how long our day was; and when I told him it was twelve hours long, as a general thing, he asked me if people where I was from considered it worth while to get up and wash for such a day as that. That is the way with those Goobra people—they can't seem to let a chance go by to throw it in your face that their day is three hundred and twenty-two of our years long. This young snob was just of age—he was six or seven thousand of his days old—say two million of our years—and he had all the puppy airs that belong to that time of life—that turning-point when a person has got over being a boy and yet ain't quite a man exactly. If it had been anywhere else but in heaven, I would have given him a piece of my mind. Well, anyway, Billings had the grandest reception that has been seen in thousands of centuries, and I think it will have a good effect. His name will be carried pretty far, and it will make our system talked about, and maybe our world, too, and raise us in the respect of the general public of heaven. Why, look here—Shakespeare walked backwards before that tailor from Tennessee, and scattered flowers for him to walk on, and Homer stood behind his chair and waited on him at the banquet. Of course that didn't go for much *there*, amongst all those big foreigners from other systems, as they hadn't heard of Shakespeare or Homer either, but it would amount to considerable down there on our little earth if they could know about it. I wish there was something *in* that miserable spiritualism, so we could send them word. That Tennessee village would set up a monument to Billings, then, and his autograph would outsell Satan's. Well, they had grand times at that reception—a small-fry noble from Hoboken told me all about it—Sir Richard Duffer, Baronet."

"What, Sandy, a nobleman from Hoboken? How is that?"

"Easy enough. Duffer kept a sausage-shop and never saved a cent in his life because he used to give all his spare meat to the poor, in a quiet way. Not tramps,—no, the other sort—the sort that will starve before they will beg—honest square people out of work. Dick used to watch hungry-looking men and women and children, and track them home, and find out all about them from the neighbors, and then feed them and find them work. As nobody ever *saw* him give anything to anybody, he had the reputation of being mean; he died with it, too, and everybody said it was a good riddance; but the minute he landed here, they made him a baronet, and the very first words Dick the sausage-maker of Hoboken heard when he stepped upon the heavenly shore were, 'Welcome, Sir Richard Duffer!' It surprised him some, because he thought he had reasons to believe he was pointed for a warmer climate than this one."

All of a sudden the whole region fairly rocked under the crash of eleven hundred and one thunder blasts, all let off at once, and Sandy says,—

"There, that's for the barkeep."

I jumped up and says,—

"Then let's be moving along, Sandy; we don't want to miss any of this thing, you know."

"Keep your seat," he says; "he is only just telegraphed, that is all."

"How?"

"That blast only means that he has been sighted from the signal-station. He is off Sandy Hook. The committees will go down to meet him, now, and escort him in. There will be ceremonies and delays; they won't be coming up the Bay for a considerable time, yet. It is several billion miles away, anyway."

"*I* could have been a barkeeper and a hard lot just as well as not," says I, remembering the lonesome way I arrived, and how there wasn't any committee nor anything.

"I notice some regret in your voice," says Sandy, "and it is natural enough; but let bygones be bygones; you went according to your lights, and it is too late now to mend the thing."

"No, let it slide, Sandy, I don't mind. But you've got a Sandy Hook *here*, too, have you?"

"We've got everything here, just as it is below. All the States and Territories of the Union, and all the kingdoms of the earth and the islands of the sea are laid out here just as they are on the globe—all the same shape they are down there, and all graded to the relative size, only each State and realm and island is a good many billion times bigger here than it is below. There goes another blast."

"What is that one for?"

"That is only another fort answering the first one. They each fire eleven hundred and one thunder blasts at a single dash—it is the usual salute for an eleventh-hour guest; a hundred for each hour and an extra one for the guest's sex; if it was a woman we would know it by their leaving off the extra gun."

"How do we know there's eleven hundred and one, Sandy, when they all go off at once?—and yet we certainly do know."

"Our intellects are a good deal sharpened up, here, in some ways, and that is one of them. Numbers and sizes and distances are so great, here, that we have to be made so we can *feel* them—our old ways of counting and measuring and ciphering wouldn't ever give us an idea of them, but would only confuse us and oppress us and make our heads ache."

After some more talk about this, I says: "Sandy, I notice that I hardly ever see a white angel; where I run across one white angel, I strike as many as a hundred million copper-colored ones—people that can't speak English. How is that?"

"Well, you will find it the same in any State or Territory of the American corner of heaven you choose to go to. I have shot along, a whole week on a stretch, and gone millions and millions of miles, through perfect swarms of angels, without ever seeing a single white one, or hearing a word I could understand. You see, America was occupied a billion years and more, by Injuns and Aztecs, and that sort of folks, before a white man ever set his foot in it. During the first three hundred years after Columbus's discovery, there wasn't ever more than one good lecture audience of white people, all put together, in America—I mean the whole thing, British Possessions and all; in the beginning of our century there were only 6,000,000 or 7,000,000—say seven; 12,000,000 or 14,000,000 in 1825; say 23,000,000 in 1850; 40,000,000 in 1875. Our death-rate has always been 20 in 1000 per annum. Well, 140,000 died the first year of the century; 280,000 the twenty-fifth year; 500,000 the fiftieth year; about a million the seventy-fifth year. Now I am going to be liberal about this thing, and consider that fifty million whites have died in America from the beginning up to to-day—make it sixty, if you want to; make it a hundred million—it's no difference about a few millions one way or t'other. Well, now, you can see, yourself, that when you come to spread a little dab of people like that over these hundreds of billions of miles of American territory here in heaven, it is like scattering a ten-cent box of homœopathic pills over the Great Sahara and expecting to find them again. You can't expect us to amount to anything in heaven, and we *don't*—now that is the simple fact, and we have got to do the best we can with it. The learned men from other planets and other systems come here and hang around a while, when they are touring around the Kingdom, and then go back to their own section of heaven and write a book of travels, and they give America about five lines in it. And what do they say about us? They say this wilderness is populated with a scattering few hundred thousand billions of red angels, with now and then a curiously complected *diseased* one. You see, they think we whites and the occasional nigger are Injuns that have been bleached out or blackened by some leprous disease or other—for some peculiarly rascally *sin*, mind you. It is a mighty sour pill for us all, my friend—even the modestest of us, let alone the other kind, that think they are going to be received like a long-lost government bond, and hug Abraham into the bargain, I haven't asked you any of the particulars, Captain, but I judge it goes without saying—if my experience is worth anything—that there wasn't much of a hooraw made over you when you arrived—now was there?"

"Don't mention it, Sandy," says I, coloring up a little; "I wouldn't have had the family see it for any amount you are a mind to name. Change the subject, Sandy, change the subject."

"Well, do you think of settling in the California department of bliss?"

"I don't know. I wasn't calculating on doing anything really definite in that direction till the family come. I thought I would just look around, meantime, in a quiet way, and make up my mind. Besides, I know a good many dead people, and I was calculating to hunt them up and swap a little gossip with them about friends, and old times, and one thing or another, and ask them how they like it here, as far as they have got. I reckon my wife will want to camp in the California range, though, because most all her departed will be there, and she likes to be with folks she knows."

"Don't you let her. You see what the Jersey district of heaven is, for whites; well, the California district is a thousand times worse. It swarms with a mean kind of leatherheaded mud-colored angels—and your nearest white neighbors is likely to be a million miles away. *What a man mostly misses, in heaven, is company*—company of his own sort and color and language. I have come near settling in the European part of heaven once or twice on that account."

"Well, why didn't you, Sandy?"

"Oh, various reasons. For one thing, although you *see* plenty of whites there, you can't understand any of them hardly, and so you go about as hungry for talk as you do here. I like to look at a Russian or a German or an Italian—I even like to look at a Frenchman if I ever have the luck to catch him engaged in anything that ain't indelicate—but *looking* don't cure the hunger—what you want is talk."

"Well, there's England, Sandy—the English district of heaven."

"Yes, but it is not so very much better than this end of the heavenly domain. As long as you run across Englishmen born this side of three hundred years ago, you are all right; but the minute you get back of Elizabeth's time the language begins to fog up, and the further back you go the foggier it gets. I had some talk with one Langland[7] and a man by the name of Chaucer[8]—old-time poets—but it was no use, I couldn't quite understand them and they couldn't quite understand me. I have had letters from them since, but it is such broken English I can't make it out. Back of those men's time the English are just simply foreigners, nothing more, nothing less; they talk Danish, German, Norman French, and sometimes a mixture of all three; back of *them,* they talk Latin, and ancient British, Irish, and Gaelic; and then back of these come billions and billions of pure savages that talk a gibberish that Satan himself couldn't understand. The fact is, where you strike one man in the English settlements that you can understand, you wade through awful swarms that talk something you can't make head nor tail of. You see, every country on earth has been overlaid so often, in the course of a billion years, with different kinds of people and different sorts of languages, that this sort of mongrel business was bound to be the result in heaven."

"Sandy," says I, "did you see a good many of the great people history tells about?"

"Yes—plenty. I saw kings and all sorts of distinguished people."

"Do the kings rank just as they did below?"

"No; a body can't bring his rank up here with him. Divine right is a good-enough earthly romance, but it don't go, here. Kings drop down to the general level as soon as they reach the realms of grace. I knew Charles the Second very well—one of the most popular comedians in the English section—draws first rate. There are better, of course—people that were never heard of on earth—but Charles is making a very good reputation indeed, and is considered a rising man. Richard the Lionhearted is in the prize-ring, and coming into considerable favor. Henry the Eighth is a tragedian, and the scenes where he kills people are done to the very life. Henry the Sixth keeps a religious-book stand."

"Did you ever see Napoleon, Sandy?"

"Often—sometimes in the Corsican range, sometimes in the French. He always hunts up a conspicuous place, and goes frowning around with his arms folded and his field-glass under his arm, looking as grand, gloomy and peculiar as his reputation calls for, and very much bothered because he don't stand as high, here, for a soldier, as he expected to."

"Why, who stands higher?"

"Oh, a *lot* of people *we* never heard of before—the shoemaker and horse-doctor and knife-grinder kind, you know—clodhoppers from goodness knows where, that never handled a sword or fired a shot in their lives—but the soldiership was in them, though they never had a chance to show it. But here they take their right place, and Cæsar and Napoleon and Alexander have to take a back seat. The greatest military genius our world ever produced was a bricklayer from somewhere back of Boston—died during the Revolution—by the name of Absalom Jones. Wherever he goes, crowds flock to see him. You see, everybody knows that if he had had a chance he would have shown the world some generalship that would have made all generalship before look like child's play and 'prentice work. But he never got a chance; he tried heaps of times to enlist as a private, but he had lost both thumbs and a couple of front teeth, and the recruiting sergeant wouldn't pass him. However, as I say, everybody knows, now, what he *would* have been, and so they flock by the million to get a glimpse of him whenever they hear he is going to be anywhere. Cæsar, and Hannibal, and Alexander, and Napoleon are all on his staff, and ever so many more great generals; but the public hardly care to look at *them* when *he* is around. Boom! There goes another salute. The barkeeper's off quarantine now."

Sandy and I put on our things. Then we made a wish, and in a second we were at the reception-place. We stood on the edge of the ocean of space, and looked out over the dimness, but couldn't make out anything. Close by us was the Grand Stand—tier on tier of dim thrones rising up toward the zenith. From each side of it spread away the tiers of seats for the general public. They spread away for leagues and leagues—you couldn't see the ends. They were empty and still, and hadn't a cheerful look, but looked dreary, like a theater before anybody comes—gas turned down. Sandy says,—

"We'll sit down here and wait. We'll see the head of the procession come in sight away off yonder pretty soon, now."

Says I,—

"It's pretty lonesome, Sandy; I reckon there's a hitch somewheres. Nobody but just you and me—it ain't much of a display for the barkeeper."

"Don't you fret, it's all right. There'll be one more gun-fire—then you'll see."

In a little while we noticed a sort of a lightish flush, away off on the horizon.

"Head of the torchlight procession," says Sandy.

It spread, and got lighter and brighter; soon it had a strong glare like a locomotive headlight; it kept on getting brighter and brighter till it was like the sun peeping above the horizon-line at sea—the big red rays shot high up into the sky.

"Keep your eyes on the Grand Stand and the miles of seats—sharp!" says Sandy, "and listen for the gun-fire."

Just then it burst out, "Boom-boom-boom!" like a million thunder-storms in one, and made the whole heavens rock. Then there was a sudden and awful glare of light all about us, and in that very instant every one of the millions of seats was occupied, and as far as you could see, in both directions, was just a solid pack of people, and the place was all splendidly lit up! It was enough to take a body's breath away. Sandy says,—

"That is the way we do it here. No time fooled away; nobody straggling in after the curtain's up. Wishing is quicker work than traveling. A quarter of a second ago these folks were millions of miles from here. When they heard the last signal, all they had to do was to wish, and here they are."

The prodigious choir struck up,—

We long to hear thy voice,
To see thee face to face.

It was noble music, but the uneducated chipped in and spoilt it, just as the congregations used to do on earth.

The head of the procession begun to pass, now, and it was a wonderful sight. It swept along, thick and solid, five hundred thousand angels abreast, and every angel carrying a torch and singing—the whirring thunder of the wings made a body's head ache. You could follow the line of the procession back, and slanting upward into the sky, far away in a glittering snaky rope, till it was only a faint streak in the distance. The rush went on and on, for a long time, and at last, sure enough, along comes the barkeeper, and then everybody rose, and a cheer went up that made the heavens shake, I tell you! He was all smiles, and had his halo tilted over one ear in a cocky way, and was the most satisfied-looking saint I ever saw. While he marched up the steps of the Grand Stand, the choir struck up,—

The whole wide heaven groans,
And waits to hear that voice.

There were four gorgeous tents standing side by side in the place of honor, on a broad railed platform in the center of the Grand Stand, with a shining guard of honor round about them. The tents had been shut up all this time. As the barkeeper climbed along up, bowing and smiling to everybody, and at last got to the platform, these tents were jerked up aloft all of a sudden, and we saw four noble thrones of gold, all caked with jewels, and in the two middle ones sat old white-whiskered men, and in the two others a couple of the most glorious and gaudy giants, with platter halos and beautiful armor. All the millions went down on their knees, and stared, and looked glad, and burst out into a joyful kind of murmurs. They said,—

"Two archangels!—that is splendid. Who can the others be?"

The archangels gave the barkeeper a stiff little military bow; the two old men rose; one of them said, "Moses and Esau welcome thee!" and then all the four vanished, and the thrones were empty.

The barkeeper looked a little disappointed, for he was calculating to hug those old people, I judge; but it was the gladdest and proudest multitude you ever saw—because they had seen Moses and Esau, Everybody was saying, "Did you see them?—I did—Esau's side face was to me, but I saw Moses full in the face, just as plain as I see you this minute!"

The procession took up the barkeeper and moved on with him again, and the crowd broke up and scattered. As we went along home, Sandy said it was a great success, and the barkeeper would have a right to be proud of it forever. And he said *we* were in luck, too; said we might attend receptions for forty thousand years to come, and not have a chance to see a brace of such grand moguls as Moses and Esau. We found afterwards that we had come near seeing another patriarch, and likewise a genuine prophet besides, but at the last moment they sent regrets. Sandy said there would be a monument put up there, where Moses and Esau had stood, with the date and circumstances, and all about the whole business, and travelers would come for thousands of years and gawk at it, and climb over it, and scribble their names on it.

1907

A Fable

ONCE UPON a time an artist who had painted a small and very beautiful picture placed it so that he could see it in the mirror. He said, "This doubles the distance and softens it, and it is twice as lovely as it was before."

The animals out in the woods heard of this through the housecat, who was greatly admired by them because he was so learned, and so refined and civilized, and so polite and high-bred, and could tell them so much which they didn't know before, and were not certain about afterward. They were much excited about this new piece of gossip, and they asked questions, so as to get at a full understanding of it. They asked what a picture was, and the cat explained.

"It is a flat thing," he said; "wonderfully flat, marvelously flat, enchantingly flat and elegant. And, oh, so beautiful!"

That excited them almost to a frenzy, and they said they would give the world to see it. Then the bear asked:

"What is it that makes it so beautiful?"

"It is the looks of it," said the cat.

This filled them with admiration and uncertainty, and they were more excited than ever. Then the cow asked:

"What is a mirror?"

"It is a hole in the wall," said the cat. "You look in it, and there you see the picture, and it is so dainty and charming and ethereal and inspiring in its unimaginable beauty that your head turns round and round, and you almost swoon with ecstasy."

The ass had not said anything as yet; he now began to throw doubts. He said there had never been anything as beautiful as this before, and probably wasn't now. He said that when it took a whole basketful of sesquipedalian adjectives to whoop up a thing of beauty, it was time for suspicion.

It was easy to see that these doubts were having an effect upon the animals, so the cat went off offended. The subject was dropped for a couple of days, but in the meantime curiosity was taking a fresh start, and there was a revival of interest perceptible. Then the animals assailed the ass for spoiling what could possibly have been a pleasure to them, on a mere suspicion that the picture was not beautiful, without any evidence that such was the case. The ass was not troubled; he was calm, and said there was one way to find out who was in the right, himself or the cat: he would go and look in that hole, and come back and tell what he found there. The animals felt relieved and grateful, and asked him to go at once—which he did.

But he did not know where he ought to stand; and, so, through error, he stood between the picture and the mirror. The result was that the picture had no chance, and didn't show up. He returned home and said:

"The cat lied. There was nothing in that hole but an ass. There wasn't a sign of a flat thing visible. It was a handsome ass, and friendly, but just an ass, and nothing more."

The elephant asked:

"Did you see it good and clear? Were you close to it?"

"I saw it good and clear, O Hathi, King of Beasts. I was so close that I touched noses with it."

"This is very strange," said the elephant; "the cat was always truthful before—as far as we could make out. Let another witness try. Go, Baloo, look in the hole, and come and report."

So the bear went. When he came back, he said:

"Both the cat and the ass have lied; there was nothing in the hole but a bear."

Great was the surprise and puzzlement of the animals. Each was now anxious to make the test himself and get at the straight truth. The elephant sent them one at a time.

First, the cow. She found nothing in the hole but a cow.

The tiger found nothing in it but a tiger.

The lion found nothing in it but a lion.

The leopard found nothing in it but a leopard.

The camel found a camel, and nothing more.

The Hathi was wroth, and said he would have the truth, if he had to go and fetch it himself. When he returned, he abused his whole subjectry for liars, and was in an unappeasable fury with the moral and mental blindness of the cat. He said anybody but a near-sighted fool could see that there was nothing in the hole but an elephant.

MORAL, BY THE CAT

You can find in a text whatever you bring, if you will stand between it and the mirror of your imagination. You may not see your ears, but they will be there.

1909

Notes

"The Notorious Jumping Frog of Calaveras County"

1. **straddle-bug**: A type of long-legged beetle.
2. **fag end**: Slang for the last part of a race.
3. **fo'castle**: Refers to the section at the upper deck of a steamboat where the crew is housed.
4. **bully-rag**: Bullying.
5. **Andrew Jackson**: Twain believed Andrew Jackson (1767–1845), the seventh president of the United States, had been a disastrous president.
6. **Dan'l Webster**: Daniel Webster (1782–1852) was an American politician who became leader of the Whig party in 1836. The Whigs were a political party from roughly 1834 to 1856, and opposed Jackson's politics. Abraham Lincoln was a member of the party throughout most of this period.

"The Story of the Bad Little Boy"

1. **milksops**: Slang for timid or cowardly men or boys.
2. ***aqua fortis***: Literally, strong water, though also a term for nitric acid.

"A Day at Niagara"

1. **The noble Red Man . . . accoutrements**: Twain is commenting on the romantic portrayals of Native Americans in popular fiction, particularly in the work of James Fenimore Cooper, with novels such as *The Pioneers* (1823) and *The Last of the Mohicans* (1826).
2. **faix:** Faith.

"Journalism in Tennessee"

1. **Mush-and-milk journalism gives me the fan-tods**: Soft journalism will cause the chief editor to throw a fit.

"Science *vs.* Luck"

1. **seven-up; old sledge**: Card games similar to whist, also called "all fours." Points are scored in four ways: for the high trump, the low trump, the jack of trumps, and the game.

"Buck Fanshaw's Funeral"

1. **helpmeet**: A helpmate, or partner; in this case, a lover.
2. **"No Irish need apply"**: Refers to the discrimination against Irish immigrants and the signs that hung in shop and factory windows during the late nineteenth and early twentieth century: "Help Wanted—No Irish Need Apply."

"A True Story"

1. **"I wa'n't bawn in the mash . . . Blue Hen's chickens, I is!**: Aunt Rachel's mother was proud of who she was and she wanted her daughter to feel this same pride. She wasn't one to be made fun of because of the color of her skin or where she came from. Repeating this phrase helps Aunt Rachel calm herself in her own times of trouble as she recalls her mother's strength. Twain distinguished himself from other writers of this period by his use of humor and his masterful skill in portraying the common American speech.

"Luck"

1. **Crimean War**: The Crimean War (1854–1856), between Russia and an alliance of the Ottoman Empire, England, France, and Sardinia, resulted over the dispute concerning the holy places in Palestine.

"The Death Disk"

1. **Oliver Cromwell**: Cromwell (1599–1658) was the English general and statesman who led the parliamentary army in the English Civil War.

"A Horse's Tale"

1. **Buffalo Bill**: Nickname of William Frederick Cody (1846–1917), American showman famous for his Wild West Show.
2. **Army of the Frontier**: Civil War Union Army of the Frontier, as opposed to the Confederate Army of the Trans-Mississippi.

"Extract from Captain Stormfield's Visit to Heaven"

1. **Peters**: St. Peter, one of the Twelve Apostles who, according to Gospel, holds the keys to the kingdom of heaven. Originally Simon, he was the first to profess his faith that Jesus was the Son of God, and renamed Saint Peter.
2. **Charles Peace**: Charles Peace (1832–1879) was a notorious British burglar and murderer whose life and execution became the subject of several films and dozens of popular novels.
3. **Captain Kidd**: William Kidd (1645–1701) was a Scottish sea captain who became a famous pirate after he was hired by wealthy British merchants to attack pirate ships on the Indian Ocean. Kidd was later executed in London for his crimes. Legend has it Kidd buried a treasure somewhere along the Connecticut River.
4. **Homer**: Ancient Greek epic poet credited with authorship of the *Iliad* and *Odyssey* (circa 850 BC).
5. **Mahomet**: Muhammad, Arab prophet who founded Islam.
6. **Zoroaster**: Ancient Persian prophet.
7. **Langland**: William Langland (1332–c.1400), English poet.
8. **Chaucer:** Geoffrey Chaucer (1343–1400), English poet best known as the author of *The Canterbury Tales*.

INTERPRETIVE NOTES

Though the works contained in this volume belong to various genres and cover a wide variety of topics, many share common themes:

The Negative Influence of Religion. Twain was a religious skeptic and thought organized religion was a destructive force. From works such as "The Story of the Bad Little Boy" and "The Story of the Good Little Boy," satiric send-ups of the moralizing "Sunday-school" lessons he experienced in his youth, to the parody of "The Facts Concerning the Recent Carnival of Crime in Connecticut," in which the narrator goes on a killing spree after what is essentially a religious conversion, Twain's position on the merit of religious ideology and schooling become clear. Twain believed experience, not religious training or sheer belief, was man's only true path to moral enlightenment.

In "The Man That Corrupted Hadleyburg," Twain's retelling of the story of original sin, Hadleyburg, a town with a reputation of impeccable honesty, is a modern-day Eden in which the manipulations of "a stranger" (i.e., Satan) reveal the town's true nature of greed and corruption. It is interesting to note Twain's take on the role of Satan in the Eden myth. The stranger, Howard L. Stephenson, does not corrupt the town of Hadleyburg but, rather, exposes the corruption that already exists. Before the arrival of Stephenson, the citizens of Hadleyburg believe they are honest because they have a reputation for being honest. They are Baptists with good Christian values, but they have never had to make a real moral choice. Stephenson's manipulations change that forever, as evidenced in Richards' deathbed lament: "I was clean—artificially—like the rest; and like the rest I fell when temptation came" (p. 509). Cast out though better off, Twain suggests, for at the end of the story the citizens of Hadleyburg can no longer bask in an artifice of religious ideals. True honesty, in Twain's view, requires experience and moral vigilance. Ironically, it is Satan who puts the citizens of Hadleyburg on this path.

"Extracts from Adam's Diary," "Eve's Diary," and "Extract from Captain Stormfield's Visit to Heaven" are other examples of Twain's religious satire. Captain Stormfield's rich narrative is Twain at his comic best—the afterlife as adventure. Twain did not believe in heaven, but if he did, it would be inclusive, "trickling out thousands of Yanks and Mexicans and English and Arabs" (p. 752), and free from the bigotry he viewed Christian religion to be a source of here on earth.

Eastern vs. Western Values. As a frontier journalist in Nevada and California, Twain's accounts of his experiences in the mining camps and ghost towns of the West provided many easterners with their first glimpse of the new frontier. "The Notorious Jumping Frog of Calaveras County," the story that established Twain's reputation as a humorist, is an intricate narrative that ultimately juxtaposes the prevailing stereotypes of the time—easterners as civilized, educated, refined, though easily duped; westerners as uncivilized, poorly educated tricksters and schemers. Central to the story is the clash of cultures as the narrator Twain, an easterner, becomes subject to the "monotonous narrative" of Simon Wheeler, a westerner. It is clear from the beginning of the story that the narrator has not the slightest desire to know or understand Wheeler, and though he listens to the whole of Wheeler's account of Jim Smiley (a westerner who is ultimately duped by an easterner), he misses the point and the men part ways still strangers despite the time that has passed between them.

Though not as layered as "The Notorious Jumping Frog of Calaveras County," a tall tale illustrates opposing eastern and western sensibilities in "Jim Baker's Bluejay Yarn" as well. Twain relates the narrative of one Jim Baker, an isolated California miner so starved for conversation and companionship he begins to talk to animals, particularly blue jays. "There's more *to* a bluejay than any other creature. He has got more moods, and more different kinds of feelings than any other creature; and, mind you, whatever a bluejay feels, he can put into language" (p. 193). Blue jays may have a way with words, like westerners, though that does not mean they will always be understood, we learn, by an owl from Nova Scotia. Twain's ability to fuse both eastern and western sensibilities—to blend vernacular language with formal language—was the foundation of his unique humor.

Appearance vs. Reality. The theme of appearance and reality figures prominently throughout Twain's work. Mark Twain himself was, after all, a persona created by Samuel Langhorne Clemens. This device not only provided the writer with a narrative framework in which he was, in a sense, both author and audience, but also allowed him considerable control to create and upset a reader's expectations. People lie in Twain's stories. Hoaxes are perpetrated, identities are confused, and unrealistic expectations often end in disillusionment when met with the harsh realities of life.

The irony in "A Day at Niagara" provides a commentary on the unrealistic romantic depictions of Native Americans popularized in the fiction of James Fenimore Cooper and is a prime example of the author's use of his persona as a foil. Twain's narrator is so enchanted with Cooper's tales and legends of the "Red Man" that he cannot distinguish fantasy from reality—or, in this case, actual Native Americans from souvenir-hawking Irishmen in costume—and greets the "tribe" thusly: "Nobel Red Men, Braves, Grand Sachems, War Chiefs, Squaws, and High-Muck-a-Mucks, the paleface from the land of the setting sun greets you!" (p. 27). Not surprisingly, the encounter takes a violent turn and Twain's narrator is ultimately thrown into the falls, leaving him bewildered, disillusioned, and "lying in a very critical condition" at the end of the story.

"Cannibalism in the Cars" is another "firsthand account" in which Twain relates a gruesome tale told to him by a "benevolent-looking gentleman" he met in a way-station while headed out west. On one level, the stranger's tale is a commentary on the savagery of man and the depths to which he will sink when survival is at stake. Twain's narrator's revelation at the end of the story, however, suggests something quite different. Though Twain tells us early on of the man's political nature and that he "was perfectly familiar with the ins and outs of political life at the Capital" (p. 12), at the end of the story we learn that the man's tale is untrue, "the harmless vagaries of a madman" (p. 21), and that he was once a congressman. With these new details, Twain once again shifts our perception and reveals his ultimate purpose to be an inquiry into political motivation and ethics in government.

Instances of mistaken identity appear in "The Man That Corrupted Hadleyburg" and "The Invalid's Story." In the latter, misconceptions about a corpse prove fatal for the narrator when he succumbs to the fancies of his imagination over reason: ". . . imagination had done its work and my health was permanently shattered" (p. 237).

Human Greed and Hypocrisy. "The $30,000 Bequest" and "The Man That Corrupted Hadleyburg" perhaps best illustrate

Twain's view on the corruptive force of money. Twain was not against making money, but he wrote fervently about its destructive power and man's willingness to trade away his integrity for the almighty dollar. In "The $30,000 Bequest" Aleck and Sally spend years plotting and planning how they will spend (what we surmise) is an imaginary fortune. Consumed by dreams of their wealthy future, they become passive in the present. Their morals decay. Their family unravels. So upon the discovery that there is no inheritance, both future and present are literally lost and the couple goes insane. Sally's realization in the final chapter of "The $30,000 Bequest" makes Twain's opinion clear: "Vast wealth, acquired by sudden and unwholesome means, is a snare. It did us no good, transient were its feverish pleasures; yet for its sake we threw away our sweet and simple and happy life—let others take warning by us" (p. 685).

In "The Man That Corrupted Hadleyburg" Mr. and Mrs. Richards undergo a similar fate when they succumb to the temptations of wealth by "unwholesome means." One sin always leads to another, Twain cautions, and with it the weight of guilt. "But they were to learn, now, that a sin takes on new and real terrors when there seems a chance that it is going to be found out" (p. 506).

Sentimentality. In an 1876 letter to J. H. Burrough, Twain wrote, "There is one thing which I can't stand, and *won't* stand from many people. That is sham sentimentality—the kind a school-girl puts into her graduating composition; the sort that makes up the Original Poetry column of a country newspaper; the rot that deals in 'the happy days of yore,' the 'sweet yet melancholy past,' with its 'blighted hopes' and its 'vanished dreams'—and all that sort of drivel." Twain's attacks on sentimentality lasted throughout his career. Stories such as "The Esquimau Maiden's Romance," "The Story of the Good Little Boy," and "The Story of the Bad Little Boy" provide excellent examples in which Twain uses parody to mock sentimental conventions of popular fiction.

Critical Excerpts

Biographical Studies

Paine, Albert Bigelow. *Mark Twain, A Biography*. 3 vols. New York: Harper and Brothers, 1912.

Paine was Twain's authorized biographer. He even lived for a time with Twain and his family. This mammoth biographical work is the foundation for most later biographies of Twain.

> He [Twain] had been brought up in a town that turned out pilots; he had heard the talk of their trade. One at least of the Bowen boys was already on the river while Sam Clemens was still a boy in Hannibal, and had often been home to air his grandeur and dilate on the marvel of his work. That learning the river was no light task Sam Clemens very well knew. Nevertheless, as the little boat made its drowsy way down the river into lands that grew ever pleasanter with advancing spring, the old "permanent ambition" of boyhood stirred again, and the call of

the far-away Amazon, with its coca and its variegated zoology, grew faint.

De Voto, Bernard. *Mark Twain's America.* New York: Houghton Mifflin, 1932.

De Voto explores the roots of Twain's "tragic laughter" by examining how the social and physical landscape of nineteenth-century America shaped his many narratives.

> Criticism has said that he was incapable of ideas and all but anaesthetized against the intellectual ferment of the age: yet an idea is no less an idea because it is utilized for comedy, and whether you explore the descent of man, the rejection of progress or the advances of feminism or the development of the insanity plea or the coalescence of labor you will find it in that wide expanse.

Kaplan, Justin. *Mr. Clemens and Mark Twain: A Biography*. New York: Touchstone, 1966.

Kaplan's Pulitzer Prize–winning biography examines the strain between Twain's public and private lives. The book begins when Twain is in his thirties and working as a journalist in San Francisco.

> Diffidently and erratically, already past the age when others have chosen their vocation, he was beginning to choose his. For over forty years he had been a journalist in Nevada and California, with a brief assignment in the Sandwich Islands, and the pseudonym "Mark Twain" on its way to becoming an identity in itself, was already famous in the West. In 1865, on the advice of Artemus Ward, he had sent to New York a flawless story about the Calaveras mining camps.

Early Reviews and Interpretations

Turner, Matthew Freke. "Artemus Ward and the Humourists of America." *The New Quarterly Magazine* (April 1876).

Turner takes exception to Twain's satiric depiction of Christian ideals in his short stories and holds that Twain's "cleverness" pales next to popular humorist Charles Farrar Browne (1834–1867), who wrote under the name Artemus Ward.

> There is one sort of fun much employed by Mark Twain; against which I strongly protest. It is where he turns solemn or sacred subjects into ridicule. It may be a tempting resource to a professional jester, in search of a subject, to exercise his wits upon topics which only require to be treated with levity to make some light-brained people laugh; but it is quite unworthy of such a writer as Mark Twain. . . . At any rate, I counsel Mark Twain, if he is anxious for the suffrages of decent readers, in his own and this country, to leave profanity alone.

Henley, William Ernest. Review of *A Tramp Abroad*. *The Athenaeum* (April 1880).

In stark contrast to Turner's review, Henley comments on the "tenderness" in Twain's prose in this early review and points to the author as an important new voice in American literature.

> He has seen men and cities, has looked with a shrewd and liberal eye on many modes of life, and has always something apt and pointed to say of everything; finally, he shares with Walt Whitman the honour [sic] of being the most strictly American writer of what is called American literature. Of all, or almost all, the many poets, novelists, essayists, philosophers, historians, and such

> like notables (orators excepted) America has produced, the origins are plainly European. . . . Mark Twain is American pure and simple.

Archer, William. " 'The Man That Corrupted Hadleyburg'—A New Parable." *The Critic* (November 1900).

Archer's favorable review mentions the "adhesive quality" of "The Man That Corrupted Hadleyburg" and compares it to *Pilgrim's Progress* and *Candide* for its craft and "shrewd, penetrating" psychology.

> To return to "The Man That Corrupted Hadleyburg." I am not going to discount it by attempting to tell its story. Indeed, I could not if I would, even in six times the space that remains to me; for though it runs to only sixty pages, its construction is so ingeniously complex that it would take something like half that space to make even a comprehensible sketch-plan of its mechanism. A more tight-packed piece of narrative art it would be hard to conceive.

Critical Interpretations: 1940s and 1950s

Bellamy, Gladys Carmen. "The Microscope and the Dream." *Mark Twain as a Literary Artist.* Norman: University of Oklahoma Press, 1950.

In this essay, Bellamy explores the *The Mysterious Stranger* in terms of its autobiographical significance and holds that Twain's literary devices were, in essence, an attempt to "lend perspective, to lend aesthetic distance, to lend serenity; the very qualities Mark Twain needed most as a literary artist."

> He [Twain] was not a profound thinker. His reaction to life itself was emotional rather than intellectual, and his criticism of life followed the same pattern. Formal edu-

> cation, perhaps even a planned program of reading, might have aided him to bridge the gaps in his thinking, might have helped him to resolve his philosophical dilemma and thus to achieve philosophic unity in his work. But, on the other hand, formal education might have detracted from the buoyancy and freshness of his writing style. It is often the excellence of the writing itself—its vigor and vividness, its sincerity and emotional drive—which holds the reader's interest sufficiently to mask the weakness of ideas.

Lynn, Kenneth S. *Mark Twain and Southwestern Humor.* Boston: Little Brown, 1959.

Lynn traces the historical, social, and political influences on Twain's narrative technique in *Roughing It*.

> By substituting a victim's humor for a spectatorial humor, Twain transformed the comic treatment of the American frontier. Not only was his laughter more compassionate and humane, but the attitude of the narrator toward the West was psychologically more complex. . . .

Critical Interpretations: 1960s and 1970s

Rule, Henry B. "The Role of Satan in 'The Man That Corrupted Hadleyburg.' " *Studies in Short Fiction* (Fall 1969).

Rule's article explores Twain's use of Satan as a benefactor rather than corrupter in the story.

> Twain's characterization is derived from the Bible, which he had memorized as a boy during many weary Sabbaths. Many Biblical passages depict Satan as a servant of God whose functions are to test man's faith, punish his weakness and purge his flesh "that his spirit may be saved." Perhaps Satan's major service to man is to chasten his

pride. This is the role he employs to bring about the fortunate fall of the Eden in Hadleyburg. St. Paul himself was aware of Satan's usefulness as a means of humbling man's pride. . . . Perhaps this and similar passages in the Bible, in addition to the encouragement of his kind-hearted mother, inspired little Sam at the age of seven to rescue Satan from nineteen centuries of Christian defamation. Hadleyburg is the finest product of that long endeavor.

Geismar, Maxwell. *Mark Twain: An American Prophet.* Boston: Houghton Mifflin, 1970.

Geismar explores a number of Twain's short stories in terms of their social and historical context, as well as in relation to Samuel Clemens's personal life. In the following excerpt concerning "The $30,000 Bequest," Geismar compares the Fosters' downfall to Twain's own tenuous relationship with wealth.

> Clemens himself was expressing an artistic catharsis of his own earlier panic and frustration in the business world. If he had not suffered through the bankruptcy ordeal, he would not have understood, much less created such literature—in which a deeply personal experience was fused with a very pertinent kind of social criticism.

Gibson, William. *The Art of Mark Twain*. New York: Oxford University Press, 1976.

Gibson's study of Twain's lesser-known works is intensive. With sections on the developmental history of "Excerpts from Captain Stormfield's Visit to Heaven," and an in-depth analysis of the layers of meaning in "The Facts Concerning the Recent Carnival of Crime," the book provides an excellent resource for those wishing to learn more about his later short stories.

The Freudian dimension of the tale might be defined

fully by a practicing Freudian critic, which I am not. Nonetheless, anyone with an elementary awareness of psychoanalytical concepts can see that Twain anticipated Freud (who, we know, read the humorist with pleasure) in several striking ways, particularly in his chapter "The Anatomy of the Mental Personality" in *New Introductory Letter on Psycho-Analysis*. In his description of "the anatomy of the mental personality," for example, Freud occasionally uses effective metaphors, such as a cracked crystal for the complex relations of Germans, Magyars, and Slovaks, and the sustained metaphors of the geography, the exploration, and the anatomy of the psyche. Most vividly, he personifies superego, id, and external world as "harsh masters," and creates a genuine drama in which the ego, crying "Life is not easy," must make a go of life by reconciling the divergent and even incompatible demands of its three masters.

Critical Interpretations: 1980s and Beyond

"Kemper, Steven E. "Poe, Twain, and Limburger Cheese." *Mark Twain Journal* (Winter 1981–1982).

In this essay Kemper examines Twain's "The Invalid's Story" as a parody of Edgar Allen Poe's "The Descent into the Maelstrom."

Twain parodies the typical Poe character's perverse overexercise of imagination. Scores of Poe's characters accept as reality the distortion created by their excessive imaginations. In this way, Twain insists, absurdity defeats simple common sense. Thompson sticks his nose right in the cheese but does not even realize it. The narrator knows his friend is freshly dead and could not be decaying already, but his imagination betrays his common sense. To paraphrase an adage, they can't smell the Limburger for the cheese. As in Poe, unregulated imagination does them in, but Twain emphasizes the absurdity and humor of such excess, not its pathos and troubled genius.

Wright, Daniel L. "Flawed Communities and the Problem of Moral Choice in the Fiction of Mark Twain." *The Southern Literary Journal* (Fall 1991).

Wright's interesting study examines several of Twain's short stories in terms of setting, and points to examples of Twain's use of various towns to illustrate man's inherent desire to conform.

> In his fiction, Twain also cleverly uses the eyes of outsiders to offer new perspectives to expose the similar flaws of such "civilized" fictional communities as St. Petersburg, Dawson's Landing, and Eseldorf—types, all, of real communities. Twain also strives to expose similarly debilitated subgroups within these larger communities by looking within the larger society at such smaller groups as boy's gangs, aristocratic families, and mobs. By such exposure, Twain demonstrates that even modest familiarity with the patterns which govern group behavior will reveal the difficulty of an individual's achieving or maintaining moral integrity while a member of such a community, for the individual in each group is usually plied into conformity by a habit of unthinking acquiescence to the accepted code of the group and is trapped by a lack of courage to oppose this code when or if his conscience is aroused. Such communities are especially flawed, Twain suggests, because they nurture a moral apathy that anesthetizes the more acute and responsive individual conscience.

Questions for Discussion

"The Notorious Jumping Frog of Calaveras County," "Cannibalism in the Cars," "Jim Baker's Bluejay Yarn," "A True Story," and "A Day at Niagara" are examples of stories in which Twain, as narrator, introduces another character's story. What effect is Twain able to achieve with this technique of "framing" the story?

"The Man That Corrupted Hadleyburg" suggests that every man has his price. What events lead to the town's downfall? Do you agree with Twain that it only takes the right circumstance to show people are dishonest, and quite corruptible, at heart? How does Twain define "morality" in this and other stories?

How does Twain represent women in stories such as "Extracts from Adam's Diary," "A True Story," "Extract from Captain Stormfield's Visit to Heaven," and "The $30,000 Bequest"?

In "The Notorious Jumping Frog of Calaveras County," what differences in character and cultural background are apparent between the first narrator and Simon Wheeler? How do these differences affect your interpretation of the story? How do they affect the humor in the story?

How does Twain use religious imagery and biblical stories to comment on organized religion? From reading Mark Twain's short stories, would you consider him a spiritual person?

In "How to Tell a Story," Twain tells us the key to writing a good humorous story is "to string incongruities and absurdities together in a wandering and sometimes purposeless way, and seem innocently unaware that they are absurdities." Does he follow his own prescription in his stories? How does Twain employ this technique in narratives such as "A True Story"?

Suggestions for the Interested Reader

If you enjoyed *The Best Short Works of Mark Twain*, you might also be interested in the following:

Mark Twain Tonight (DVD, 1967). An amazing one-man performance by Hal Holbrook. You could swear you are sitting at one of Twain's lectures.

The Civil War: A Film by Ken Burns (DVD, 1990). A very watchable PBS miniseries on the Civil War.

The Complete Stories by Flannery O'Connor. This collection includes thirty-one stories by preeminent southern writer Flannery O'Connor (1925–1964). O'Connor, like Twain, was a master of dark humor and crackling irony. In literary terms, she did for the South of the mid-twentieth century what Twain did for the United States of the last half of the nineteenth century.

The Thurber Carnival by James Thurber. This is a magnificent collection of the best short work by humorist and cartoonist James Thurber (1894–1961), a worthy and talented follower in the tradition of Twain.